ORDINARY MAGIC

ORDINARY MAGIC

Ruth Porter

Photographs by the author

BAR NOTHING BOOKS
Montpelier, Vermont

Published in the United States by
Bar Nothing Books
100 State Street
Suite 351, Capitol Plaza, Box 3
Montpelier, Vermont 05602
802 223-7086
bnbooks@sover.net
SAN 256-615X

Grateful acknowledgment is made to
Autumn House Press and
Michael Simms, Executive Director
for generous permission to reprint
"Crossing Laurel Run" by Maxwell King
from *Joyful Noise, An Anthology of
American Spiritual Poetry*, edited by Robert Strong,
Copyright 2007, Reprinted by permission of
Autumn House Press

Design: Glenn Suokko, Inc.
Typeset in Adobe Jenson Pro
Special thanks to Annex Press
Printed in the United States

ISBN 978-0-9769422-3-8 (hardback)
ISBN 978-0-9769422-4-5 (softback)

FIRST EDITION

Library of Congress Control Number: 2009905399

Porter, Ruth King, 1940–
        Ordinary magic / Ruth Porter ; photographs by the
    author. — 1st ed.
        p. cm.
        LCCN 2009905399
        ISBN-13: 978-0-9769422-3-8
        ISBN-10: 0-9769422-3-2
        ISBN-13: 978-0-9769422-4-5
        ISBN-10: 0-9769422-4-0

        1. Vermont--Fiction. 2. Domestic fiction, American.
    I. Title.

PS3616.O786O73 2010   813'.6
                    QBI09-200052

Crossing Laurel Run
by Maxwell King

Climbing the arc
of the high-pasture hill
in six inches of new wet snow,
we track through a stubble
of the season's last cut of hay,
our boot prints puddling
with dark water.
Two old oaks are down
with ice in the branches;
as we cross Laurel Run
we hear a cracking and turn back
to see a towering poplar
fall dead with the weight.

In the evening,
together by the wood stove,
we sit in silence.
I stare at the page number
in my book; your needles
tick for a moment, then fall still.
I watch your face:
eyes closing, high cheeks
darkening with some thought
not shared with me.
I could tell you what I've lost;
that it is the same
as what you've lost.
And then we would fight again—
our struggle to move past
the truth, to find a way
to lend the greater weight to hope.

I put a hand on your arm;
you put a hand on my hand.
Isn't there something we might understand,
something we could know
in order to know what to say to each other?
You would say there is nothing to say.
For me, there is this,
perhaps only this:
the ice will come soon enough,
and we must try, until then,
to hold each other
in the incandescence of our own arc.

Chapter 1

Severance, Vermont   Friday, November 25, 1977

Just as George opened the front door, the phone rang. He stepped inside, shut the door, wiped his feet, dropped his briefcase on the chair by the telephone, and still he managed to answer it halfway through the third ring. As he picked up the receiver, he saw Laurie coming in from the kitchen. She stopped in the doorway when she saw him. He waved hello to her and said hello into the phone.

"George?"

"Speaking," he said. He almost added, "Who is this?" but he didn't. He knew he ought to know, and then, before she even had time to say the next sentence, he did know.

It was Ursela. She said, "I have something to tell."

"What?" he asked with a stab of fear in his gut. He knew it would be bad, and it was.

"Cal's been shot."

He said, "Oh my God. He's dead, isn't he?"

Laurie's hand went up to her mouth, and her eyes got big, but he had to hear more before he could tell her anything.

"I scared you too much. I'm sorry. He'll be all right."

"Where...."

"He's at the hospital."

"No, I mean, where was he shot?"

"In the foot."

"You don't mean it!" He almost laughed. Then he looked at Laurie's face and saw the terror mixed with disbelief, and he said, "Ursela, wait. I have to tell Laurie." He put his hand over the mouthpiece and said, "It's Cal. He's been shot in the foot, if you can believe it. I'll tell you more in just a minute."

Laurie nodded. Her hand was still over her mouth, but her eyes weren't quite so big.

"Ursela," he said. "Are you up there now? I'll come right up."

"I'm home again. Go see him, George. Tell him don't worry about chores."

"Okay, but wait. Before you go, tell me if you need any help out there."

"No, thank you. I'll be fine."

He might have argued with her, but just then Nora came around the corner. She stopped short when she saw them.

"Mom, what's the matter? You look awful."

George said goodbye and hung up. "It's all right," he said. "It's going to be all right."

"What's wrong, Dad? It's got to be pretty bad, or Mom wouldn't look so scared."

"Your Uncle Cal's been shot. That's what it is. But he's going to be all right. I've got to get up to the hospital to see him. You can't find out much from Ursela."

"I thought something happened to one of Lena's kids. You really scared me, Mom."

"I know," Laurie said. "That's what I thought too."

George didn't want to listen to a long, involved conversation. "I have to get going," he said to Laurie. "Will that mess up your dinner plans?"

Laurie had relaxed enough to think about dinner. "No. I haven't started anything. I didn't expect you this early. I just got home myself."

"Shall I come with you, Dad?"

"I guess not...unless you want to."

"Where were you, Nora? I couldn't find you when I got home."

"I was out on the sun porch, Mom. You should've called me."

"I did."

"I didn't hear you."

"Well, it doesn't matter."

George watched Nora standing at the foot of the stairs, leaning across the banister. Just then something in her expression made her look a lot like Laurie. He was so glad she was home again, at least until she decided what to do next. He was always forgetting how much he loved her. "Maybe you *should* come with me to the hospital. You probably want to get out if you've been in the house all day."

"Well, I...."

He didn't wait for her to finish. "The truth is, I'm worried about Ursela. She said she didn't need any help with her chores, but she's as bad as Cal. Neither one of them ever tells you what's *really* going on. I swear, I don't know how they deal with each other."

"But, George, if she says...."

"That's why I want to get up to the hospital to see Cal. He might think I ought to go out and give her a hand, and then I'd have to do that too. It could be a long night."

"I know what to do, Dad. I'll go out and see if I can help Aunt Ursela, while you go to the hospital."

"But, Nora, it's so far. It's already dark. And you don't know *anything* about farm work."

"If you don't want me to, Mom...."

Laurie was still standing in the doorway. They both watched her, waiting to hear what she would say. She folded her arms across her chest and leaned her shoulder against the doorpost. "It's fine with me," she said. "Only I don't see why your father feels so *obligated.*

They wouldn't do the same for us."

"Cal's my brother, Laurie. Of course I feel obligated."

"Well, Nora then. Why should *she* feel obligated, when all they've ever done...."

"Laurie!" he said, and she didn't say any more. He turned to Nora. "It'd be a big help to me if you felt like going out there. Your mom means you shouldn't feel like you have to."

"I'd like to, Dad."

"The back roads are going to be pretty muddy...it might snow... and hunting season always makes it worse."

"If you think I shouldn't...."

"Just be careful, honey. Don't be afraid to turn around if you get worried."

"Okay, Dad. I promise."

"Good girl." He stepped close to her and patted her shoulder. They were in this together. After all, they were both related to Cal. Laurie wasn't. He got out his ballpoint pen and took the notepad that sat beside the telephone. He picked up his briefcase to use as a desk, and put his foot up on the chair to support it.

Laurie said, "George, what are you doing?"

"Oh, I'm sorry," he said and quickly put his foot back on the floor. "I wasn't thinking."

She said, "I guess not." The sharp tone stung him for a second. He was sorry to have her catch him being a slob.

He sat down in the chair and balanced his briefcase on his knees. "I have to draw Nora a map of how to get out there." He looked at Nora. "In case you have forgotten."

She smiled at him. "Thanks, Dad. That's a good idea. I don't think I've been out there since high school."

He worked on the map, all the while wishing they didn't have to go. He pictured them all staying home together. They would have leftover turkey for supper, so Laurie wouldn't have to cook. He would make a fire in the fireplace, and they would sit around it and read and talk. They could talk about the old days. He loved it when Nora asked about when he was a child, growing up on the farm.

"You'd better try to get back as soon as you can, Nora. We might get some snow tonight. I heard it on the radio. Did you, George?"

"I thought it smelled like snow."

"Nora, take my car."

"Really, Mom?"

"I want you to. Yours isn't reliable...and you might need the front-wheel drive."

"If you're sure...."

"I'm sure."

George stood up. "Look, Nora. I want to show you this." He moved over so they were standing side by side. "You go up the hill out of West Severance—you remember how to get to West Severance?"

Nora nodded. She put a hand on the map to tilt it so she could see better. He looked down at her honey-colored hair and the curve of her cheek and thought again how much he loved her. She was a grown-up, a woman almost thirty, and in some ways a stranger. He didn't even know how much he knew about her life. He knew the superficial things—that at first she loved living in Boston and loved her job there, and that later, things changed. He didn't know why. And he didn't know how much pain it caused her. Did she go home to her apartment at night and cry? He had been to visit her. He knew what her apartment looked like. He could, and often did, picture her there, but it didn't give him any clues about how she felt. He could ask the obvious question—had she met anybody she cared about? But for that he would get a stock answer, a smile, a flip response, a few words that left him knowing as little as before.

"Do you see how to get there?"

"I think so. I think I'll remember it too."

"You take the road that goes up the hill out of West Severance. Bear Ridge. It's all dirt roads after that."

"I'll do fine, Dad."

"Okay, honey. We can compare notes later."

Now that he was actually ready to leave, he dreaded going. It wasn't six o'clock yet, but it was dark out. He'd had his overcoat on the whole time he was in the house, so he was sweaty. His clothes would turn clammy as soon as he got out in the cold. His glasses would steam up. But if he delayed, Nora would too, and he wanted her to get the trip over with and come home safely before the snow.

He handed her the map and set his briefcase down on the floor. "I'm off then," he said. "I'll see you both later. Wish me luck with cantankerous old Cal."

As he was closing the door, he heard Laurie telling Nora to wear winter boots, and Nora protesting. He thought about stopping by his office for a quick drink before he went to the hospital, but he decided he'd better not.

The car started the first time Nora tried it, and the heater blew warm. She could smell her mother's perfume. She backed down the driveway and out onto the street, even though they always told her not to go out backwards.

Going to Uncle Cal's gave her the perfect chance to get away so she could figure out what to do without them watching, saying she looked worried, trying to get her to talk about what was bothering her. All afternoon she had worried about how she was going to keep them from noticing. She had thought of saying she was going to the movies or over to visit Lena. She would never have thought of something like Uncle Cal's accident. And yet it gave her the perfect excuse to get away so she could decide what she should do. Because it wasn't something she could talk about, not to anyone, not even to Lena.

She hadn't been surprised. She knew before she went in to Planned Parenthood to get the results of the test. She had, in fact, been trying not to know it for a long time, and by the time she was on the old two-lane from Severance to West Severance, she knew that she didn't need to think it over, that she had known all along what she was going to do, that there was, in fact, only one thing to do, and that she had to hurry so she could get it done in the first trimester, when it was a simple operation.

She turned right at the blinking light in West Severance and headed up Bear Ridge Road. The woman at Planned Parenthood had told her about a place in Burlington where they did it for $250. Now that it was legal, it wasn't such a big deal anymore. She hadn't thought to ask if she would be able to drive herself home. But it didn't matter since she didn't want anyone else involved. Lena would be the logical person to ask, but she wasn't going to. She didn't want a big sister lecture on how she ought to be more careful. She didn't want any questions about who the father was and whether he knew about it. She wanted to do what she had to do and get it all settled as quickly as possible. It was her own private mistake, and she planned to keep it that way.

She came to the top of the hill and the turn off the pavement. She took a quick look at the map by the lights on the dashboard and set the map on her lap. The next turn would be a left. She hadn't seen much that looked familiar, but she hadn't been paying enough attention either. Aunt Ursela probably wouldn't know who she was after all these years. It was stupid of her to think of coming out to help. A fool's errand. She wished she had gone to Lena's after all.

It was a cloudy night. There were no stars and no moon. In town the sky looked black, but now, away from streetlights and house lights, it was gray and gave off enough light so that Nora could see the outlines of the fields and the darker shapes of trees and rocks. For a few minutes, a shadowy fox trotted beside her car and then turned off into some pine trees. It was so strange and so wild that after it was gone, she wondered if she had really seen it. The only thing that made her believe it was real was that she felt elated by the beauty of it and suddenly glad she had come.

At the last turn she stopped with her headlights on the mailbox so she could read the faded WILLARD written there. She turned onto Uncle Cal's road and started up the hill. She felt breathless, and her heart was beating faster than it should have been. It wasn't from fear. It was excitement. It had been a long time since she had come out to this place that had been such an important part of her father's life. For a while when she was in high school, it had been important to her too.

Part way up, the land flattened out, and there was the house ahead, a long, wooden shape at the end of the road. There were lights in the kitchen. The rest of the house was dark. It was hard to tell at night, but Nora thought it was still painted the same gray color. And there was the porch where they spent so much time on warm days. Things had to have changed inside, she knew that, but still she felt reassured.

There was an old pick-up truck and a big sedan parked in front. Nora stopped her car behind the truck. Before she could get out, two big black and white dogs jumped off the porch and came bouncing toward her, barking as they ran. Nora shut the car door and stood still, holding out her hands for them to smell. "You can't scare me," she said. "I like dogs. That's one of the things I missed about living in Boston."

A dog jumped up and put its front feet on her chest so it could sniff her face. "Get down," she told it. "Can't you tell I'm related to Uncle Cal?" The other dog was sniffing at her ankles. "I used to come here before either of you were around." One of the dogs lifted his leg to mark her tire.

She started toward the mudroom door, and the dogs got in line behind her. She opened the door a crack and tried to slide through without letting them in, but she made the mistake of looking into the hurt brown eyes of one of the dogs as she did so, and she felt too mean to leave them out after that. She opened the door wide. "It's your house," she said. "Come on. But only into the mudroom, until we ask."

She had to knock three times on the kitchen door before Aunt Ursela's round face appeared in the glass. She looked for a minute without recognition while Nora stood there, embarrassed. Then Aunt Ursela swung the door wide and said, "It's sweet little Nora, is it? What a surprise! And today of all days."

Nora came up the two steps, and Aunt Ursela grabbed her in a soft hug. Nora hugged her back shyly, feeling the rolls of flesh around her waist and thinking how she was exactly the same, only wider and grayer. She still smelled like biscuits. She was even wearing the same shapeless housedress and apron.

"I thought you were Conrad when I heard the dogs."

"Oh," Nora said, pulling back. "Is it all right if they come in? I didn't know any more...."

Aunt Ursela watched the dogs sniff at the wooden floor. "Look at them. There's still more blood. I've washed and washed...."

Nora couldn't help a small gasp. It was the first time she had thought about that part of Uncle Cal's accident.

"Come in, come in, Nora. Let me look at you. You're all grown up."

Nora stepped inside and shut the door. The kitchen smelled just the same, of strong soap, and underneath that, of old sour milk that no amount of washing could get rid of. "Is Uncle Cal going to be all right?"

"Oh dear, Nora, I hope so."

Nora hadn't ever seen Aunt Ursela worried or scared. She was always the one who fed everybody and made them all feel that everything would be fine. Seeing her upset made Nora wonder what she was doing here. She had her own problems to deal with. She hadn't even thought about how unfair it was that she would have to face this abortion alone.

"And even if he is all right, I don't know how we will manage the doctor's bills."

Nora's wish to run away passed. She wondered if she ought to say that her father could help with the bills. Instead, she asked what the doctor said about Uncle Cal's foot, but Aunt Ursela didn't know that either. They stood awkwardly in the doorway. Everything Nora thought of saying sounded stupid.

Finally Aunt Ursela said, "I can't think where Conrad is, and I'd better not wait any longer. I was goin to start early too, but then Roy Hughes came over to ask me some questions about Cal, and now it's late. I really have to get down to the barn. Cal always has chores done before this."

"That's why I came out tonight—to see if you needed help with the chores."

Aunt Ursela hugged her again. "I'm glad to see you, little Nora." She pushed her away so she could look at her. "But you'd get your good clothes dirty."

"I don't care."

"You don't have any boots."

"Oh. I'm sorry about that. I didn't even think about it. Mom told me to bring them. I thought she was talking about the snow."

Aunt Ursela got out the milk pail and fixed the little pot of warm water to wash off the cows. Then she came back to where Nora still stood by the kitchen door. "You can wait up here in the warm. I'll be back when I get done down there."

"No. I want to come with you."

"Nora, you haven't changed a bit. I'd hug you again if I had hands to do it with. Open up the door then. I'll find you some barn clothes."

They went out into the mudroom, and Aunt Ursela handed her a pair of rubber boots and watched while she sat down in the wicker chair and tried one on.

"Too big?"

Nora shook her foot, and the boot wobbled around. "Not too bad."

Aunt Ursela handed her a pair of thick green socks. "They'll fit with these."

"Thanks. Do you still knit all the time?"

"Somebody always needs somethin." She handed Nora a plaid wool shirt. "Put this over your jacket to keep it clean."

It was darker outside than it had been when Nora went into the house. Aunt Ursela was a small lump ahead of her, and the barn was a large one. The dogs went single file, leading the procession. The boots were stiff and made her clumsy. But the air was alive with the smell of earth and moss and dampness. "Do you think it's going to snow? Is it cold enough?"

"If Cal was here, he'd know. He always knows." Aunt Ursela

swung open the barn door and switched on the light.

When Nora stepped inside, she had to shut her eyes for a minute because of the brightness. She stood still, listening to the rustlings and stampings and chewings in the next room, and smelling the smell of dust and hay and manure that she remembered from long ago.

When the phone rang, Lena was upstairs reading the kitten book to Georgia. Jerry was downstairs. He was supposed to be changing Jimmy's diapers and getting him ready for bed, which was probably why he was so eager to answer the phone. Lena hoped it wasn't for her. Georgia hated it when they didn't get to finish the whole book. Lena tried to keep her mind on the kittens' difficulties, but she could hear Jerry downstairs talking. She hoped Jimmy wasn't getting into trouble.

She heard Jerry say, "Okay, I'll tell her." After a minute, which she hoped he spent checking on Jimmy, he shouted up the stairs to her. "Your mom said to tell you that your Uncle Cal got shot."

She said, "What?" and jumped up off Georgia's bed. She took a few steps toward the door before she turned back to hand the book to Georgia. "Look at the pictures. Mommy'll be right back."

Georgia started to protest, but she didn't wait to hear. She went down a few of the carpeted stairs in her socks. She'd left her shoes under Georgia's bed.

"Jerry, what did she say? Is he dead?" She was whispering so Georgia wouldn't hear.

Jerry was at the bottom of the stairs looking up at her. He had a dish towel in his hand. "No, it's not that bad. Your mom said he got it in the foot."

"In the foot?"

"Your mom said she thought maybe his gun went off accidentally or something, but they don't really have any details yet. Your dad's up at the hospital now."

"The hospital?"

"Well, sure. He had to go to the hospital. He's got to have a big hole in his foot."

"Shh, Jerry. Georgia...what's Jimmy doing anyhow?"

"I better go check. I left him in his high chair with some crackers." He started toward the kitchen. Over his shoulder he said, "Your mom said not to bother to call her. They won't know any more til later tonight."

"I'll call Nora then."

He was almost to the kitchen door. "Nora went out to see if your aunt needed help with the chores. Just wait a minute while I check on Jimmy. I'll call the newsroom and find out what they know. Maybe somebody's doing a story on it."

"Oh, Jerry. That makes it sound so...so big."

"I'll find out," he said, and then he started talking to Jimmy, and she went back upstairs to Georgia and the kitten book.

Sometimes she knew just how the kittens felt, alone in a dangerous world. Here was Uncle Cal with a hole in his foot, a terrible accident, waiting for anyone who went hunting. Dad used to hunt when he lived on the farm, and Jerry used to hunt before he got married. He still talked about it every year. One of these days, Jimmy was going to want to do it too. She ought to feel lucky that Uncle Cal was only shot in the foot. But she didn't feel lucky; she felt frightened. Dangers were closing in on her family, just like they were closing in on the kittens in the book.

After a few minutes, she could hear Jerry downstairs, talking on the phone. She read in a monotone, hurrying to the end. Georgia was so close to sleep that she didn't notice. She was too busy trying to hold her eyes open.

Lena knew she couldn't explain her feelings to anyone, not even Jerry. He would say she was being ridiculous, that she wanted to control everyone and everything. Jerry said that a lot lately. He was always telling her not to boss him around, that she reminded him of his mother. He used to love it when she watched out for him and worried about him. But these days he seemed to hate it. These days he always wanted her to leave him alone.

She knew they ought to spend more time together, but something always seemed to get in the way, either the kids or Jerry's job and the crazy hours he worked. She wished he would get a different job, but he got mad every time she suggested it. He loved being a reporter for the Sentinel, even though it meant he was gone most evenings covering some meeting or other. If he taught school or worked in an office, they could put the kids to bed and have some time together every night, instead of only once in a while.

She read the last words and shut the book. "There," she said. "The kittens all got safely home. Aren't you glad?"

Georgia's eyelids fluttered a little in her sleep.

She kissed Georgia's damp, rubbery cheek, smelling her baby smell. Then she arranged the covers and turned out the light, reluctant to leave now that she finally could.

She hadn't heard anything from Jerry and Jimmy for quite a while. She fished her shoes out from under Georgia's bed and hurried downstairs to see what they were doing.

They were both asleep on the couch, Jimmy lying in Jerry's arms. If she was very careful and very lucky, maybe she could get Jimmy into his bed without waking him up, and maybe after that she could get Jerry awake enough so he could tell her what he found out about Uncle Cal. Maybe they could even spend some time alone together for a change.

Cal's foot was throbbing so much he couldn't think. They told him it would feel better if it was elevated, and they stuck a bunch of pillows under it, but it didn't make any difference. All it did was force him to lie in one position. His bed was by the door, and the ward was full. People were talking, and a television was blaring, so when he heard a man's voice out in the hall saying his name, he wasn't sure he heard right. He didn't expect it to be George.

"How'd you know I was in here?" he asked when he saw George. He didn't bother to say hello. He didn't feel like socializing. He hurt too damn much.

"Ursela called."

"What'd she do that for?"

"I guess she thought I'd want to know," George said. He took off his overcoat and looked around for a place to put it down.

"Don't set that thing on my foot," Cal said.

George pulled the chair over to the bed and sat down and laid his overcoat across his lap. "I *do* want to know. How are you?"

"How do you think? If I was all right, I wouldn't be here, would I?"

George sighed.

Cal felt like saying that if you ask a dumb question, of course you're going to get a dumb answer, but he refrained. He didn't have the energy right then.

"Does it hurt?"

"It hurts like hell."

"Why don't you get them to give you something for the pain?"

"They already did. Or, at least, that's their story. I don't believe it. These damn nurses. If they can convince me I already took the medicine, then they get to keep it all for themselves."

George laughed.

Cal thought with bitterness that there was no sense in talking since no one ever took him seriously.

Then they were both silent, while George got more and more nervous, tapping one foot against the floor. Finally he said, "Ursela said to tell you not to worry about chores."

"I didn't. I figured the boys would come over."

"Nora went out to see if she needed a hand."

"Nora? The last I heard she was in Boston."

George was still tapping his foot. The hospital lights glinted off his glasses so that Cal couldn't see his eyes. "She came home a few days before Thanksgiving. I don't know what her plans are. She could be planning to stay."

Cal managed to smile at that, even though his foot was starting to throb in time to George's tapping. "The father's always the last to know."

George opened his mouth to reply, but he shut it again without saying anything. He just kept on tapping in time to the pain.

Cal shifted around on the pillows. He couldn't sit up because of his foot, and he was getting more and more uncomfortable. Neither one of them had any more to say.

George didn't look like someone who would be visiting the likes of him. He bet the other guys in the ward thought George was his lawyer. George sat there in his three-piece lawyer suit with his lawyer coat lying on his lap and his leather lawyer shoe tapping out the beat for the pain. They probably thought Cal was getting his lawyer to sue the guy who shot him. And, by God, he might, if he could just find out who did it.

After a while he said, "If I can catch up with the bastard who put me here, I'm goin to need your services."

"Nobody's told me what happened yet. Ursela didn't say anything."

Cal grinned, but his own smile felt to him like the leering grin a skull has on it. "Are you askin as my lawyer?"

"Oh, come off it, Cal. You think it wasn't an accident then."

"Hell no, it wasn't a accident. Did Ursela tell you it was?"

"She didn't say anything, except that you were up here, and I should come and see you. I don't know what she was thinking."

"God...Ursela. The more she says, the less you know."

"Cal?"

"What?"

"You didn't get into some kind of a shoot-out, did you?"

"Not yet, I didn't. But when I get out of here...."

"So it wasn't an accident then?"

"Well, hell no. Even if it was possible, which it ain't. You don't think I'd be stupid enough to do this to myself, do you?"

"I don't know anything about it, Cal. I wish you would just tell me what happened."

He started to answer snappishly, but he caught himself. It was the pain that made it so hard to think. He *did* want George to believe his version of events, even though he and George hadn't had much to say to each other in years. George had changed so much. Hell, he didn't even hunt any more. It was probably hopeless, but he would have to give it a try. He sighed. "All right. This is what happened. I was up in my tree stand—remember the ridge-line that goes almost straight north up the west side of the property?"

George nodded. "Of course. And the game trail below it. I used to hunt there too."

"I've got me a tree stand in a big maple near the top. It's a good spot. You can see all around. I was about to give up, so I sat down."

"So you were in your tree stand, and you lost your balance, and...."

"God damn it, George. Are you *tryin* to piss me off? I just told you I was sittin down."

George was laughing at him.

He had half a mind to tell George to get the hell out. He'd hardly seen him for years, and he didn't need him now. It was some woman idea that they ought to get along because they were brothers. The truth was they were just too different to have anything to do with each other.

"I'm sorry, Cal. I was teasing you. Go on telling me what happened."

"I don't see how you think I could shoot myself with my own rifle. It's ridiculous. That's what Ursela thinks too. What else did she say to you?"

"Nothing. Honestly. She said you'd been shot. I asked her where, and she said in the foot. That was it."

"Well, I don't know what the hell she thinks she's up to."

"Maybe she thought I'd want to see you." He was quiet for a minute, and then he said, "She was right too. I've missed you."

"God damn it, George! Do you want to hear what happened, or don't you?"

"Okay. Go on."

"So I was sittin there, and I heard a rustlin, and when I looked down at the trail, there was this big buck—you ain't never seen a rack like he had. The way he was hurryin, that some-bitch who shot me must've been right on his tail. I had a great shot, even sittin down like I was. That's why I put the stand there in the first place." Telling it made him see it all so clearly again that he stopped caring whether George believed him or not. He was back there in the woods with the leaves rustling and the buck panting a little as he ran uphill. "I didn't see him fall, but I *know* I hit him. You always know when you get off a good one. I had just taken my shot when, *bam*, he hit me in the foot and knocked me right out of the tree. Find the bastard with a trophy buck, and you'll find the guy who did it...and the motive too. As soon as they put my foot back together, I'm goin to get up there and look for evidence."

"It's going to be a while...."

"Like hell it is. I got down after it happened. I'll get back up when it's bandaged, or in a cast, or whatever the hell it is they're goin to do to it."

"Cal, did anyone from the police come to see you?"

"Well, yeah, one of them outpost troopers came in here. How'd you know?"

"They'd have to come about a gunshot."

"I don't think Ursela would of called the cops."

"No, someone in the emergency room called it in. They have to. What'd he ask you?"

"Pretty much what I told you. I think he asked the doctor some questions too."

"I'm sure he did. He would want to know some things about your injury."

"If he thinks I could of done this to myself, he's crazy."

"He might be able to establish that you didn't do it from the way the wound is."

"Well, I ain't holdin my breath. Those troopers can go around askin all the questions they want. This is my fight, and I'll take care of it."

"I hope you aren't planning to break the law, Cal."

"Not unless I have to, George. I'm just goin to do what the situation demands."

For a while he'd had a feeling that the guy in the next bed was trying to hear what he was saying. Now he turned around to see. The guy was lying there, looking straight at him with his watery, bloodshot eyes. His covers were tucked in tight around his neck. He had white stubble on his chin.

Cal was opening his mouth to ask him what the hell he was looking at when the old man said, "Pal, when you get ready to go after that bastard, you can count on me."

"Thanks. It's quite the story, ain't it? Shot me on my own land too."

"Probably was some god-damned out-of-stater," the old guy said.

"*And* took my deer."

"You got to fight. You ain't got a choice."

"That's the way I see it too," Cal said. He looked around at George, but George was just sitting there, like he hadn't heard any of it. He turned to the old guy again. "That's my brother, George. He's a lawyer. He don't believe in justice."

George said, "God damn it, Cal."

Cal smiled, trying to show that it was a joke, but he could feel the smile twist on his face, and he knew it didn't look real.

George stood up and started to put his coat on. "I don't believe in vigilante justice," he said.

Cal didn't want him to go. Once George left, he wouldn't have anything to think about except how much his foot hurt, and what they were going to do to it, and whether it was going to be all right. Suppose he couldn't ever walk again? He'd never get up in the woods. He'd never get to go hunting. He wouldn't be able to do anything but sit in a chair. He didn't know how to ask George to stay. There wasn't any reason for him to stay. Maybe the boys would come to see him later. Maybe Ursela would come. He knew she wouldn't. He looked up at George, standing there in his overcoat. "Thanks for stoppin by, George," he said.

"I'll be in to see you tomorrow, Cal. I'd like to know what the doctor says about your foot."

"So wouldn't I."

George started for the door, and then he turned back. "Do you think I ought to go out and help Ursela?"

Cal was going to say he'd get his good lawyer suit all full of shit and how would the jury like that? But he managed to stop himself in time. "She said she had it under control, didn't she?"

"Yes. She said not to worry."

"She would of called Conrad. Him and Paul can do what needs to be done."

"Okay. I'll see you tomorrow."

"All right, little brother."

And George walked out and left him alone with the throbbing. He looked around at the guy in the next bed to see if he might have something more to talk about, but he was asleep and snoring a little with his mouth open. His few teeth stood tilted like rotten fence posts. Cal wished he could drop off to sleep that way, like clicking a switch. But it was no use. His foot hurt too much. He would have to wait it out.

Chapter 2

Aunt Ursela was milking, squirting milk in rhythmic, staccato bursts against the side of the metal pail. Nora stood beside the cow and watched her aunt's hands pulling the teats, first one and then the other, as regular as pedaling a bicycle. It looked easy. Maybe she should ask Aunt Ursela to let her try.

Out of nowhere a man's voice right behind her said, "Well, if it isn't Nora, all grown up. It's been years since we've seen you out here."

Nora had heard nothing but the drum of the milk against the pail, paying attention only to the way the sound was changing as the bucket filled. She jumped and looked around.

Her cousin Conrad was standing there. "You scared me," she said, embarrassed that she had jumped.

"Sorry. I guess I was surprised to see you."

"I came out to see if Aunt Ursela was okay," she said, noticing how much he had changed. He was still tall and thin, but now, instead of being really grown-up, ahead of her on an exciting adventure, he looked middle-aged and tired. "You haven't changed at all, Conrad," she said.

"Gettin old, like everyone else."

"That's not true," she said emphatically, because it was true. Now he seemed closer to her parents' age than to hers. He was on the other side of the generation gap.

"My heifers was out again, Ma. That's why I'm so late. What's left to do?"

Aunt Ursela's forehead was resting against the cow's side. She turned her head without moving away from the cow and looked up at them. Her knitted cap slid sideways, almost covering one eye. "All of it. You know what to do better'n I do. I started with the milkin." She looked down at the bucket again.

"What can I do, Conrad? I really want to help. That's what I came out here for."

"Hang on. There's plenty for everybody. We'll get goin in just a minute. First I want to know if Dad's okay. What'd you hear?"

"Just that he was in the hospital, that he got shot in the foot."

Conrad nodded. "He's goin to be okay, ain't he, Ma?"

Aunt Ursela turned her head sideways to say, "I think so, but...."

"I mean, they can fix his foot...."

"It don't do no good to think about it tonight, Conrad. There's work to be done."

"Well, all right then," he said. He picked up his cap by the bill and settled it back on his head in the same place. "Let's see about chores and a job for Nora."

"I'd like to help," Nora said, conscious of how small a contribution she would be able to make. She could feel the restlessness all around her as the animals waited to be fed.

"Where's the skimmed milk for the pigs and the calves, Ma?"

"It's up at the house. I forgot it."

"I'll go get it."

"Don't bother, Conrad. We'll give 'em whole milk tonight. Paul can bring it down in the mornin."

"Okay. If you're sure." Conrad looked around the barn. "I guess Dad didn't clean out the manure this mornin. He was probably in too much of a hurry to get up in the woods." He thought for a minute, and a shadow passed over his face. "Too much of a hurry to get up there and get himself shot."

Nora didn't say anything.

After a little while, Conrad looked down at her. "The chickens could need feed and water. You might like to go in and see. And there's eggs to pick up. Dad keeps egg boxes right outside the door."

The chickens lived in a room partitioned off from the rest of the animals with boards and sheets of plastic. Nora stepped inside. It was warmer than the rest of the barn and dusty. For a moment she felt dizzy, remembering how she used to love coming out to the farm when she was in high school. She steadied herself on the doorpost and watched the chickens jump off their roosting bars to walk around the floor, scuffing up hay and dust and cocking their heads sideways to look at what had been uncovered.

Someday when she had her own place, she would have chickens. They didn't need much room. A backyard would do. Lena could have some now. But Lena wouldn't want them.

After a few minutes, Nora stood away from the doorframe. She didn't feel dizzy anymore. Conrad would be wondering why she was taking so long. The chickens' feed trough was half full. She picked up the metal container that let water out to them a little at a time. It was heavy. She didn't know how much was enough, but she decided they would be all right until morning.

She got some egg cartons from the stack outside the door and began to pick up the eggs carefully, one by one. There were almost three dozen of them. Some of them were still warm. When she couldn't find any more, she stepped out of the chicken house and closed the door carefully behind her.

As she tested the door to make sure she had shut it tight, she heard Aunt Ursela saying, "Well, you should of been here. That's all." She sounded cross.

Aunt Ursela was milking a different cow, and Conrad was standing in the gutter beside her. His hands were folded over the end of a long-handled shovel, and he was leaning his chin on them, so that the handle made a little stand for his head. He had a hurt look on his face. Behind him, the wheelbarrow was full of manure. When he saw Nora coming toward him carrying the eggs, he shut his mouth on what he had been going to say and smiled at Nora as though he was glad to see her, but his smile was weak and unconvincing.

Nora wished she wasn't interrupting their conversation, but there was nothing she could do except pretend she hadn't noticed anything. "Look at all the eggs I got," she said to fill up the uncomfortable silence. "I think they have enough food and water. What else can I do?"

Conrad stood there with his chin on his hands, leaning on the shovel. The sleeves of his jacket were frayed. Long threads hung down from his wrists like uneven fringe. There was a rip in the elbow on Nora's side and a dark patch on the bill of his cap from his dirty hand. Nora looked down, trying not to notice those things, which for some reason made her feel sad. There was a round hole in the toe of one of his boots too.

"Did you shut the door good?

"Yes."

"Remember when you left it open, and all the chickens got out?"

"What I remember is how mad Uncle Cal got."

"Hoppin mad. That's how mad Dad used to get. He'd just jump around and sputter when us kids did somethin dumb like that. He couldn't even get his words out, he'd be in such a fury." They both looked at Aunt Ursela then, but she wasn't listening.

"I used to love it out here when I was in high school. All of you were always doing interesting things. It wasn't that way at my house. It was boring there." She thought for a minute. "I'm afraid it still is."

"I guess everybody wants what they don't have."

"How's your little boy? He must be big. I remember how cute he was."

"Dwayne? He's seventeen now. All he thinks about is gettin his driver's license."

"Is he in high school?"

"At the vocational school. I want him to have a trade. Not like his old man. I'm still workin at the feed store after all these years." He smiled at her ruefully.

Aunt Ursela pushed the milking stool aside and stood up slowly with her hands on her back, as though she had to restack her vertebrae one by one. Then she leaned down again to pick up the full pail of milk. Conrad reached out to take it from her, but she pushed past him as though she hadn't seen his hand. She walked to the calf pen and looked in. "Did the calves get enough milk already, Conrad?"

"I believe so, Ma."

"I'll give this to the pigs then."

"Let me have the bucket. I'll do it. It's heavy."

"No. I want to." She struggled to raise the pail to the top of the pigpen fence. Nora and Conrad watched without helping, although Conrad took a few steps toward her before he stopped himself. The milk poured out of the bucket in a wide, white sheet. The pigs stood on their hind legs, propped against the fence, biting at the milk while it was still in the air. Aunt Ursela tilted the pail to stop the flow and lowered it so she could look inside. Then she poured more in another short burst and stopped to look again. She carried what was left to where the third cow was waiting.

She tucked her skirts carefully under her as she sat down on the low milking stool. Then she smiled at Nora, but when she looked at Conrad, she turned the smile off as completely as she had stopped the flow of milk into the pigs' trough. Behind her, the pigs snorted and splashed, fighting for the milk. "What's left to do?" she said to Conrad.

"I got the rest of this manure to take out, and when you're done with Star, we got to water 'em and get some hay and grain for 'em, and I guess that's about it."

Aunt Ursela didn't pay any attention to the hurt in his voice. "Let's get goin then," she said.

"I'll help with the manure, if there's another shovel I can use," Nora said.

"Look out in the old milk room where the big water tank is. Dad keeps his tools out there. You can set the eggs on top of the tank."

Nora found a shovel and brought it back to where Conrad was standing by the cows. The shovel was just like the one Conrad held except that it had tape wrapped around the middle of the handle.

"That one's broke," Conrad said. "Dad must've taped it back together."

"It's the only one I saw," Nora said. "I'll try it." She walked behind the cow Aunt Ursela had just finished milking. There was a mound of soft manure in the gutter behind the cow's back legs. She slid the shovel underneath the pile, trying not to get too close to the cow. It was too heavy for her to lift, and too heavy for the shovel. She could feel it give a little where the handle was broken and covered by tape. She slid half the pile off the shovel and looked around at Conrad.

He hadn't noticed. He was looking at his mother. "You just don't know, Ma. There was no way I could of come. I'm always caught in the middle."

"You don't have to do what Cheryl says every single minute."

"She's caught in the middle too. You ought to hear her mother some time."

"I'm glad I don't have to."

"Well, I'm here now."

"That's different. You have to do this."

Conrad sighed and shook his head a few times. He picked up a pile of manure and took it to the wheelbarrow.

By the time Aunt Ursela had finished, Nora and Conrad had picked up all the manure except what was underneath the cow Aunt Ursela was milking. They finished the last bit as she walked off with the pail and the milking stool.

Conrad handed Nora his shovel and pushed the wheelbarrow over to the side door near the pigpen. He set the wheelbarrow down while he opened the door, and then he disappeared outside pushing it.

Nora stood behind the cows, holding the shovels and looking at the open door, until Aunt Ursela came back.

"Put those away, Nora. Out where you found 'em."

"Okay." As she walked away, she saw Aunt Ursela letting the cows out of their stanchions. Each cow backed out at a stately pace. They all three headed for the door single file as Conrad came in with the empty wheelbarrow.

When Conrad went past his mother, he said, "I'll get their grain. You show Nora where the hay is, and she can throw it down to you. If you get three bales, there'll be some for mornin too."

Nora followed Aunt Ursela out to the hay bay. She climbed the ladder and dragged three bales to the edge of the loft. Down below she could see Aunt Ursela's head with her long braids coiled on top like a crown.

"Land 'em flat, Nora, so they don't break open."

"Okay."

Two of the bales landed the way they were supposed to, but the third stood on one corner before it flopped down. There used to be a swing out there made by Conrad and Paul. The stumps of the ropes were still hanging from the rafters. Nora remembered her cousins climbing to the loft and jumping off on the swing for a long ride across the open barn floor. Nora had only dared to do it a few times. It was tricky. If you didn't get the angles right, you would crash into the wall of the barn.

By the time Nora got down the ladder, Aunt Ursela was walking off with a bale in each hand. Nora picked up the last one by the strings and staggered along behind. It was heavy. She was glad Conrad didn't see how much harder it was for her than it was for Aunt Ursela.

When the chores were finished and they were leaving the animals, Nora looked back to see the three cows still held by the neck in their iron stanchions. Before she could stop herself, she said, "Do the poor cows have to stay like that all night? Don't you ever let them be free?" She was instantly sorry she had spoken. Conrad and Aunt Ursela smiled at each other, and Nora felt like a fool, betraying how little she knew.

The dogs appeared from nowhere as they were leaving the barn.

They all walked up to the house together. Nora was still smarting from their smiles. She had forgotten the eggs and then remembered them part way to the house. Conrad held them up to show her that he had them. They all laughed about that, and the tension eased a little.

It was warmer outside than it had been when they went into the barn. A few snowflakes were beginning to fall. They stopped near the door to the mudroom. Conrad handed Nora the eggs. He said, "I hate to think of Dad draggin himself out of the woods like he did."

Aunt Ursela said, "It's a wonder he got back at all."

"I'll try to get over here before dark tomorrow so I can get up there and find his deer rifle."

"You don't need to do that, Conrad. It's here."

"Dad dragged his rifle down too?"

"He must have."

"Well, I'll take it home and clean it then."

"I already checked. It looks fine."

Conrad laughed. "I should of known Dad would take better care of his gun than he did of himself. Ain't that just like him?"

"Come inside, Conrad, and have a piece of pie, if you already ate. I'm goin to fix somethin for me and Nora."

"Thanks, Ma, but I got to get home."

"Roy Hughes came out here."

"The sheriff?"

"Yup. He asked a lot of questions. He said the investigators would be out here tomorrow first thing to look at the scene."

"Police?"

"I guess so. He just said investigators. He wanted to know could they go up to the tree stand and look around."

"I would think they'd wait til Monday. Things always get a little crazy the last weekend of deer season."

"Roy said they'd of been here today if they hadn't run out of daylight. They want to take a look at the scene right away."

"What did you tell him?"

"Well, I didn't know what to say. I couldn't tell 'em not to come, could I? I mean, that would look funny. Cal ain't done nothin wrong, or at least, I don't know so."

"Did you tell 'em where to look?"

"Well, no. I thought you could tell me what to say, so I said I didn't know where they should go. There's a lot of woods."

"Ma, we don't know what happened up there. I think you're right. You'd better not get into it. Who knows whether Dad wants 'em pokin around or not. You better tell 'em they need to go to the hospital and talk to Dad. He can tell 'em how to get up there if he wants to, and he can put 'em off the scent if he wants to. You can ask Paul in the mornin, but I bet he'll say the same thing. See if he don't."

"Okay, Conrad."

"Paul said he'd be here in the mornin, and I'll be back tomorrow night. You don't need to go down to the barn at all if you don't want to."

Aunt Ursela nodded.

"I guess Dad'll have to stay in the hospital for a while."

She nodded again.

"Will you be okay, Ma?" He reached out, as though he was going to pat her on the shoulder, but his hand fluttered midway between them, and then he pulled it back.

"I'll be all right. Thank you," Aunt Ursela said. She didn't reach out to him, but her hands were full.

Nora followed her into the house. While Aunt Ursela was straining the milk and putting it away, Nora went into the bathroom. Everything there was just as she remembered it, the dark cupboards and wainscoting, the old-fashioned sink and toilet, the bathtub with its little legs. Nora pictured her mother shuddering at the potential for dust underneath that tub and the likelihood of greasy fingerprints on the wooden walls. She would be so horrified that she wouldn't even notice that in fact Aunt Ursela managed to keep it spotlessly clean.

Nora thought these things in a kind of frantic effort to change the subject so that she wouldn't have to notice how sick she felt.

It was ridiculous to be sick. She didn't mean to be pregnant, and she certainly didn't mean to have morning sickness when it wasn't even morning. She put up the seat of the toilet and stood in front of it indecisively, because there it was, the cold lump of it churning inside, until finally her stomach turned completely over, and she threw up. She knelt on the floor and hung on to the chipped and discolored bowl of the toilet, feeling surprised and appalled that her body was doing this to her. But it was all right. It was really all right, because she was going to fix it as soon as she could.

After a few minutes she stood up, trembling and so weak she had to hold on to the toilet to get to her feet. She was shaky and cold. She clung to the washbowl and looked at herself in the mirror. It was dim and crossed with dark lines. She looked like a ghost in it. She stood there, holding on to the washbowl and wondering how she was going to be able to face Aunt Ursela.

One of the best things about being home again was that she wasn't reminded of Adam so often. Especially here at Uncle Cal's, her former life seemed to have happened long ago and on another planet, which made it easier not to be sad about it. Once she got this last little leftover bit tended to, Adam would be out of her life, out of her thoughts, out of her body forever. And that would be a triumph over him. It was the only one she was ever likely to have, but she could have that much revenge at least.

She felt stronger. The whole thing was over as suddenly and unexpectedly as it had begun, and the thought of having to eat something, which had made her feel so queasy before, now sounded possible and almost nice.

She splashed water on her face and flushed the toilet and looked around the room to make sure she was leaving it neat. She didn't want Aunt Ursela to notice anything.

When Nora walked into the kitchen, her aunt was standing at the table. She had a pie balanced on one hand. With the other hand she was pushing dishes over to make room for the pie. Three of her china elves stood in the center of the table, which was already loaded with food.

Nora's stomach shivered a little. "I wish you hadn't gone to so much trouble," she said. "I'm really not hungry."

Aunt Ursela put down the pie and wiped her hands on her apron. "No trouble. Just cold food from yesterday." She looked at Nora with a smile, but the smile faded from her face. "What's the matter? You're so pale."

"Not a thing," Nora said emphatically. She pulled out a chair and sat down quickly, so that she would have a good reason to duck her head.

Aunt Ursela sat down across the table. "Poor Cal. I hope they feed him tonight."

"This looks good," Nora said, and then to cover whatever her stomach might decide to do, "I wish I was hungrier."

Aunt Ursela handed her a plate of cold turkey and sighed. "The food at the hospital is so bad. I don't know what Cal will do if he has to stay...."

"I bet he'll be home soon. I can't imagine Uncle Cal staying in bed for more than a day or two."

"And the bills. What will we do about the bills? I better ask down to the store. See if I can find some more houses to clean."

While Nora listened to Aunt Ursela, she had been taking small, careful bites of turkey, and now, to her surprise, she realized that she was quite hungry after all.

"And those little bones in his foot. How are they going to put all those little bones back together again?"

"You can't worry about that," said Nora, feeling for the first time since she got to the farm that she might be able to help a little. "They know how to do things like that. It's their job. This turkey is delicious. You should tell Mom how you cook it. It tastes much better than hers."

"It's not store-bought. That's why."

Nora could see that she was pleased. "I remember now. I'd forgotten how you always used to raise turkeys. Poor Uncle Cal. I'm sorry he has to miss this."

"I'm goin to make him up some food and take it in to him tomorrow. He ain't used to nobody's cookin but mine. He probably won't eat if I don't bring him somethin."

"I could take it in when I go tonight and bring it over to him tomorrow morning. I could put it in our refrigerator overnight." She paused. "It would be safe as long as Dad didn't get into it. But I could put a sign on it telling him not to."

Aunt Ursela actually laughed at that. "Thank you, but I'm goin in to see him soon as I get done with my work in the mornin."

Nora noticed with surprise that she was eating a lot—cold stuffing and cranberry sauce, Aunt Ursela's homemade bread and butter. Maybe as long as she didn't pay attention to what she was doing, it would be all right. "How did Uncle Cal's accident happen? Dad didn't really know any details."

"It wasn't a accident. He says somebody shot him on purpose and left him there."

"Really?"

"And how he ever got all the way back here with his foot like it was….and how he ever managed to keep his gun clean at the same time…." She took a deep breath. "You have to say that for Cal. He could be just about dead, but he'd still take good care of his gun." She looked at Nora's empty plate. "I see you're ready for some pie."

"Oh, I couldn't. I had too much already."

"You have to have a little piece. Just a taste. I'll be stingy." She slid a small piece of pumpkin pie onto Nora's plate before Nora could decide what to say in protest. "That's the other thing. Cal had his new winter boots on. They had to cut the one off him, and I think he minded that more'n the pain. He had this idea of how he could patch it, but, you know, it probably wouldn't of held."

Nora took tiny bites of the pie. She didn't want to empty her plate and have Aunt Ursela put more food on it. She couldn't trust her stomach to stay where it was supposed to.

"I tried to take off his boot before we went to the hospital, but it hurt him so much, I couldn't do it, and he got mad at me. He wanted me to just pull it off and never mind how much it hurt, but I couldn't. And then when we got to the hospital, they cut it off, even though he told them not to. I'm sure he thinks it's my fault."

Nora felt sorry for her. She remembered what it was like to make Uncle Cal mad.

"It was nice to see Conrad. I haven't seen him for ages."

"I can't say I have either."

"Oh. I thought...."

"Yup. He only lives a couple of miles on the other side of West Severance. But Cheryl works out in Severance. And the kids are always busy, busy. They get together with Cheryl's people on holidays. It ain't fair. I don't know when Elsie got a chance to see 'em last. But you can't say a word without you get your head taken off."

"Aunt Ursela, do you want me to stay for the night, so you won't be all alone?"

"Thank you, Nora, but you don't need to do that. I'll be fine here by myself."

"Are you sure? Because if you are, maybe I should help you clean up and then go. I've been watching out the window. It's snowing pretty hard now."

"Is it? I didn't even notice. Nora, you better get on home. It'll be easier if you go before it gets too deep, and I'll be fine. I don't need any help cleanin up."

"I'd like to help."

"No, honey, you get home before the snow is any deeper, and I thank you for comin out to see me."

"I'll try to get back to see you again soon. I'm planning to stay in Severance if I can."

"That'll be good for your folks. I wish Elsie would move back."

"How is Elsie?"

"She's all right. She works at that hospital down there to Randolph. She's okay. The twins are gettin big."

"Does she come up to visit you?"

"She don't get up that often. I wish she did. They were here the other day for Thanksgivin. They likely won't be back til Christmas."

"Maybe I'll get to see her then. Tell her I said hello, will you?"

"I will, and now you better get on home before the snow gets too deep. Thank you for the help."

"Okay, Aunt Ursela. I'll probably be back soon."

Chapter 3

Jerry came into the kitchen, rubbing his eyes and looking sleepy. His hair was sticking up in all directions. Lena thought how she liked it that way better than when it was combed and slicked down.

"I haven't even started the coffee yet," she said. "I was going to wake you up when it was ready. I just had to get Georgia and Jimmy going on their breakfasts."

Jerry kissed Georgia on top of the head.

Georgia said, "Sit down, Daddy."

Jimmy banged on the tray of his high chair with his spoon and said, "Dada."

Lena began to fill the coffee pot with water. At least she would get some coffee herself this way. She was glad Jerry was up, glad she didn't have to go upstairs to wake him, and still she couldn't help a twinge of irritation. If she had asked him to do something today, even if she'd asked him to do something fun, he would have slept until ten o'clock. But because his father wanted help with his firewood, Jerry woke himself up at seven in the morning. There wasn't any reason why that should annoy her, and yet it did.

She shut off the water and turned around with the pot in her hand. Jerry was sitting at the table beside Georgia. He was lighting a cigarette, even though they had both agreed that he should try not to smoke around the children. When he blew out the first puff of smoke, he blew it right on Jimmy.

Lena managed not to say anything by clamping her teeth together. She put the coffee into the basket, put on the lid, and plugged in the cord. Then she said, "Jerry, would it be all right with you if we didn't go with you to Williamstown? I want to go home and see what they know about Uncle Cal. And I want to spend some time with Nora."

"Sure thing."

"You mean you don't mind?"

"No, of course not. Why would I mind?"

Jimmy threw his spoon on the floor, and Georgia said she hated the way her cereal tasted and she wanted some potato chips. By the time they got both children back to their breakfasts, the coffee was ready. Lena poured them each a cup and put the cream and sugar on the table for herself.

She sat down beside Jimmy, but before she was even in the chair, Jerry blew smoke in her face. She pretended not to notice. She said, "Well, that's really good. I didn't want to spend the whole day trying to keep Georgia and Jimmy's hands out of your mother's knickknacks."

"No. You'd rather keep them away from your mother's knickknacks."

Fear stabbed at the base of Lena's stomach. All of a sudden, they were just about to get into a fight. She said, "I don't know what...." The words trailed off. She was stirring her coffee. She watched oily circles forming and reforming on the surface. She didn't look up. She didn't want to think about what was happening.

"You said you'd go with me. I don't want to spend my whole Saturday working on Dad's woodpile. And I went with you to your parents' on Thanksgiving."

Outside the windows, the light was white and still, reflected off the new snow. She would have to put the children in their snowsuits wherever they went. "Okay. We'll go with you," she said, still not looking at Jerry directly. And then, "I thought you said you didn't care."

"My mom and dad are expecting you," he said. When she looked at him, he turned away. "And anyway, it isn't fair."

"Jerry, I said we'd go." Her voice was hard.

Georgia and Jimmy were quiet, waiting for the storm they all knew was coming.

Then Jerry said, "Aw honey, it's all right. No sense in us all having to give up our Saturday. You go over and see Nora."

Georgia climbed down from her booster seat, and Jimmy banged on the tray of his high chair and then threw his spoon. Lena laughed, and then they were all laughing together. It was as though they had been frozen in place, waiting, and then the switch had been turned back on. "Thanks, Jerry," she said. "Maybe you'll get back early enough so we can all do something fun together."

Georgia climbed into Jerry's lap. "Let's make a snowman, Daddy. We can make it look like you, and we can put a cigarette in his mouth so everyone will know."

Jerry looked at Lena, and they both laughed, and Lena decided that she ought to wait for a better time to mention how he said he wouldn't smoke around the kids. After all, it wasn't like they didn't know he smoked.

As it turned out, it was lucky they didn't go with Jerry because it took so long to get Georgia and Jimmy dressed. If Jerry had waited for them to get ready, he wouldn't have gotten to Williamstown before noon. Lena had to round up all their winter clothes, a job she had been putting off for weeks. And when she had them both warmly dressed and heading out the door, Jimmy made a big poop in his diaper, much to Georgia's disgust, and Lena had to spend twenty more minutes getting Jimmy completely undressed and clean and then dressed again.

The living room clock was chiming eleven when she opened the door at Mom and Dad's. She sat Jimmy down on the carpet in the front hall so she could get Georgia out of her snowsuit and boots. No one answered when she called. Nora's car was in the driveway, but she could have gone somewhere with Mom. After Lena finished Georgia, she took off Jimmy's things and then her own jacket and boots. She piled all the clothes on the chair by the telephone, even though she felt guilty. She knew Mom would want her to hang everything up in the front hall closet.

She heard Georgia talking to someone on the sun porch, so she picked up Jimmy, who was trying to crawl upstairs, and went through the living room to find Nora sitting on the sun porch sofa with Georgia on her lap. They looked so sweet together that Lena stopped in the doorway. The white snow light was shining on their heads, which were bent toward each other. Nora's blonde hair was just a little lighter than Georgia's, which was going to be light brown someday, but which now still had a lot of red-gold in it. Nora was whispering, talking softly into Georgia's ear, and they were both smiling, unaware that she was watching.

Then Jimmy made a gurgling noise and squirmed to get down, and both their heads turned toward the doorway in surprise. Lena set Jimmy down on the floor and sat on the sofa beside them. "Where are Mom and Dad?"

"Mom's gone grocery shopping," Nora said. "I don't know about Dad."

"I'm glad you're here. You're the one I came over to see. How are you anyway?"

"Why are you sick, Aunt Nora?"

"I'm not sick," Nora said, and she smiled and kissed Georgia on top of her head.

"Why do you have to stay in your pajamas all day if you're not sick?"

"Georgia, get down and play with Jimmy so we can talk. Aunt Nora can stay in her pajamas if she wants to. She's a grown-up."

"I wasn't talking to you, Mommy."

Nora gave Georgia another kiss. "I'm not sick. I'm fine. I was just too lazy to get dressed." She set Georgia down on the floor.

Lena watched her sit back on the sofa and fold her bare feet up under herself. She looked tired and pale. Maybe it was living in a city that made her skin less clear than it used to be. "Are you really going to stay in Severance?"

"I hope so," Nora said, giving her a quick, questioning look. "If I can find a reasonable job, I'm going to stay."

"Nothing bad happened in Boston, did it?" Lena asked. She was watching Jimmy and Georgia to see if they were listening, but they weren't. They were happily occupied with the magazines on the coffee table.

"No. Of course not. I got sick of living there, that's all. You don't know what it's like. You've never lived in a city."

"I lived in Burlington when I was at UVM."

"Burlington doesn't count. You just don't understand."

"Please tell me then. I'd like to know." She was struggling to keep from feeling hurt.

"I can't. There's nothing to say. You just have to take my word for it, that's all."

"Well, I can be glad anyway. I mean I'm not glad it was awful, but I'm glad you're going to stay. It'll be great for me."

Nora smiled. Lena felt relieved. The conversation had gotten tense for some reason she didn't understand, but luckily now it was all right again.

Just then, Jimmy pushed a pile of magazines onto the floor, and Georgia told him he was a bad boy. That made him cry. Lena glanced at Nora and sighed and shrugged. She sat down on the floor beside Jimmy and pulled him onto her lap. She held him tight. He snuggled against her and put his thumb in his mouth. His eyes closed. She loved it when he was still like that. Then she looked up. Nora had a funny, needy and hurt expression on her face. She was leaning forward a little, watching them. It made Lena nervous. She asked about Uncle Cal to change the subject.

"He's in the hospital."

"I know that, but that's all I know. Is he going to be all right?"

"He got shot in the foot," Nora said. She was leaning back again.

"The rest of him's okay."

"Even in the foot could be serious. He's older than Dad."

"Dad went to visit him last night. I went out to see Aunt Ursela."

"That's what Jerry said. Did you go by yourself?"

"Sure."

"How did you even know the way?" She kissed Jimmy and stood him on his feet. "Okay, Jimmy. We're going to pick up. You have to help too."

Jimmy picked up a magazine by one corner and waddled over to the table. The magazine was so big that he kept stepping on it and almost falling down.

"Dad drew me a map," Nora said, "but I didn't need it. I knew the way from when I used to go out there when I was in high school. Remember that writing project I did my senior year? That's what started me going out there."

"I don't remember, but I don't remember what mine was either. It was probably something stupid."

"My class decided to make a booklet about old Vermonters and the old-fashioned ways that were starting to die out."

"Oh, that's right. I remember now."

"That was the best thing that happened to me while I was in school, one of the few times when school was really fun."

"We never did anything like that in my class."

"That's how I got to know Uncle Cal and Aunt Ursela and Conrad, Paul, and Elsie. I never would have otherwise."

"I wish I'd gotten to do something interesting like that."

Lena looked up at Nora from where she sat on the floor by the coffee table. With the snow light making a halo behind her head, she looked more like herself. They had such different lives.

"Remember how Dad used to call it 'the old home place'? I bet I've still got that booklet around here somewhere. My part was an article on Aunt Ursela making butter. There was picture of her with her electric butter churn. I gave her a copy of it. I wonder if she kept it."

Lena looked at Georgia being motherly, trying to make it easy for Jimmy to pick up the magazines, trying to give him a feeling of success. She could remember doing that for Nora. She used to dress herself and then Nora every morning. She felt a pang of love and fear for Georgia.

"I saw Conrad. He was out there last night. When I was in high school, he seemed so wonderful and grown-up. Now he's just old. He looks tired and worried. He was fighting with Aunt Ursela. They didn't say anything in front of me, but I could tell they were mad at each other."

"What did they say about Uncle Cal?"

"They didn't say much. Maybe Aunt Ursela left the hospital before the doctor saw him. I don't know."

Georgia and Jimmy had finished picking up the magazines. Lena had been helping them while she talked to Nora. As so often these days, her hands were in one place and her mind in another. Jimmy plopped himself down on her lap. She thought about checking to see if he was wet, but she decided not to. If he was, she would have to change him, and she didn't feel like it. She hugged him and buried her nose in his silky hair. He always smelled like cider.

Nora was watching her. "Did you like it when you were pregnant?"

"No, I hated it," Lena said with her nose still buried in Jimmy's hair. "That's a funny question. Why do you want to know?"

Nora looked out the window. Her voice seemed far away. "No reason. You and Jimmy looked so cozy, almost like one person."

"Sometimes it feels like that," Lena said. "But sometimes it feels like drowning, like I'm being pulled under water, and I can't get away." She had already said too much. She could tell Georgia was listening. She set Jimmy gently on the floor and stood up and stretched. She was thinking how Nora ought to get settled down so she could have a baby of her own. She would love to help Nora with that. Out loud she said, "The real question for now is, what are you going to do?"

"What do you mean?" Nora said, and her voice had an edge to it that was like a knife.

"I didn't mean anything," Lena said. "I don't know why you get mad. You're as bad as Jerry. I just wondered what you were going to do because I thought maybe I could help you." She had to try hard to keep her voice from trembling. She didn't want Nora or the children to see how close she was to tears. Georgia was watching, and her eyes were big.

Nora started to say something and then stopped. "I'm sorry. I hate it when people ask me that. Mom is always coming up with some new idea of what I ought to do. You know Mom. I haven't done anything since I got here."

"Mom's probably worried about you."

"What do you mean? Why?"

"No reason. I didn't mean anything."

"You and Mom both act like something's wrong with me. Everything's fine. Really. You just have to take my word for it."

"I'm glad of that."

"And I'm going to stay in Severance if I can find a job I like. I'm going to start calling my old friends too. Who's still around here anyway?"

"I don't know. I'm so tied down. I've lost touch with everybody. I did see Erika in the grocery story a while ago. Remember her? Erika Jourdan? She said something about Patsy. I can't remember where she said she was. Karen Holbrook is still in Severance, except her last name is Williams now. I see her once in a while."

"I never liked her much."

"She's okay. She has a baby about Jimmy's age. We get them together to play sometimes. His name is Jason."

Georgia looked up from the floor, where she and Jimmy were playing with Mom's drink coasters with the pictures of birds on them. Lena hoped Mom wouldn't mind. It gave her a few uninterrupted minutes to talk to Nora.

Georgia said, "When's Jason coming over?"

"I don't know. I was just telling Aunt Nora about him."

Nora said, "I saw Sandy Anderson in Boston last summer. She was married for a while, but they broke up."

"Why?"

Nora looked down at Georgia and Jimmy to make sure they weren't paying attention. Then she turned to Lena and said very softly, "He was seeing someone else."

"Oh God," Lena said, louder than she meant to. "I hate that."

"What's wrong, Mommy?" Georgia and Jimmy were both looking at her with big eyes.

"Nothing. Don't look so worried. It's fine. Really." Lena watched them until they went back to their game. Then she said, "I'm glad she left him. I can't understand how anyone could stay with somebody who treated them like that. I know what I would do if Jerry did that to me." She had one eye on the children. She spoke very quietly because she didn't want them to start asking questions. "I'd kick him out in a minute. I know I would. Even if it only happened one time."

"You don't know what you would do if it really happened."

"Yes, I do. I mean it. How could you trust someone after that?"

"Sometimes," Nora said with a pained expression on her face, "it doesn't mean very much." She started to say something more, but then she stopped and looked past Lena toward the door.

Lena turned around to see what she was looking at.

Dad was standing in the doorway. He was smiling.

"My two favorite women," he said.

"Don't say that, Dad. Mom has to come first."

"You worry too much, Lena. Mom's in her own special category, and she knows it. What's Jerry doing today?"

"He had to go over to visit his folks. He hasn't been out there for a while. We didn't see them on Thanksgiving. He told me to say hello to you and Mom."

Georgia walked a few steps toward Dad and stood looking at him. When he smiled at her, she said, "When Daddy comes home, we're going to make a snowman."

"Maybe," Lena said. "If he gets home in time. It might be too late."

Nora stood up. "I'm going to go get dressed. I'll be back in a few minutes." She patted Georgia on the head as she went past her.

Georgia started through the door right behind her. Over her shoulder she said, "I'm going with Aunt Nora. I can help her get dressed."

Lena smiled at Dad, and he smiled back. She loved the way he appreciated Georgia and Jimmy.

"If Aunt Nora wants you to leave her alone, you come back." Lena shouted after Georgia. "And be careful on the stairs."

"I know," Georgia called back. After a minute, they could hear her talking to Nora as she climbed the stairs.

Lena picked up Jimmy and hugged him and sat down on the sofa with him on her lap. "How do you think Nora is, Dad?"

"She's fine," he said. He was looking over her head out the window. "She's great. She's going to stay in Severance."

"I know," Lena said. "Dad, do you think....' And then she thought about it and stopped herself just in time, because he probably hadn't noticed how Nora looked. Maybe Nora wouldn't want him to notice. Maybe she got it wrong, and Nora was fine. Nora didn't look all right, and there were times when she seemed angry and far away. But it might be nothing. It might be because Georgia and Jimmy kept interrupting. Sometimes Lena was sure everyone was irritated by how short her attention span was, how childish she was getting because she hardly ever associated with grown-ups any more. Out loud she said, "Dad, what I meant to ask you was, how is Uncle Cal? Were you visiting him this morning? Nora didn't know."

Dad came over and sat down on the sofa. He held out his hand to Jimmy, but Jimmy acted as though he had never seen Dad before. "Shake hands with Granddad," Lena said, but Jimmy didn't move. He sat there like a little frog with his eyes bulging.

Dad reached into his pocket and pulled out his big, old-fashioned pocketknife with its mother-of-pearl handle. He held it out to Jimmy, and Jimmy snatched it without taking his eyes off Dad.

"You be nice, Jimmy, or I'll make you give that back," she said.

But Jimmy wasn't listening. He was turning the knife over and over in his hands, looking at it.

"I remember when you used to let me hold your knife. I remember how fascinated I was by all the different colors you could see when you turned it over in the light. I remember I thought we could take those pink and green places out and play with them, but I couldn't figure out how. Children think the craziest things."

She smiled at Dad, but he was watching Jimmy. He didn't say anything. Maybe he hadn't heard her either.

Then, after a long silence, he said, "Cal's going to be all right. The doctor came in this morning while I was there. He said Cal was a lucky man. It could have been so much worse. As it is, they are going to put it in a cast, and then he can go home."

"How...."

He looked at her then. His eyes were magnified by his glasses. Lena hoped her glasses did that for her eyes. "If you're going to ask me how it happened, don't even bother. Cal says someone shot him and took his deer."

"I still don't see how another hunter could have shot him in the foot."

"He says he was sitting in his tree stand, about to climb down, so I guess his foot could have been sticking out. That's the only way it makes sense. I guess it could have happened that way. Or it could have been an accident, but I wouldn't dare say so to Cal. I'll have to call Nick Simonetti on Monday."

"Who's that?"

"He's the state's attorney. The state troopers have been in to see Cal, and of course they've been out to the scene. Nick'll tell me what they think happened." He smiled at Jimmy and stroked his hair. "He looks like a Willard, doesn't he?"

"That's what Jerry's mom says. I hope he takes after you."

"Jerry's had some good stories lately."

"You mean his series on poverty? He's proud of those stories."

"He should be. It's about time we had some stories about what's happening to poor people in this state."

"Jerry's been traveling all over. He's been gone a lot."

"Well, it's been worth it. Don't you think so?"

"I guess. I haven't had a chance to read many of the stories yet. I'm going to, though. There just isn't time—the kids are around all day, and at night I'm so tired. But I'm going to make time."

"Do you want me to save them for you?"

"No thanks, Dad. Jerry brings them all home. He wants me to read them, and I will. I've got them all saved."

"I'd like to talk to you about them, to you and Jerry. What does Jerry think the state ought to do about it? It's worse than anybody thought. He does say that."

"I'm sure he'd love to talk to you about it. He's very involved."

"There was a story about Cal this morning."

"What did it say?"

"Nothing really. It was just a paragraph on the local page. It said he'd been shot in the foot and there was an investigation going on. That was all. But if Cal has his way, there may be more. Right now he's talking about gunning for the guy that shot him."

"I don't know whether to tell that to Jerry. He might want to go help."

"Cal acts like he's in a cowboy movie. I just hope his foot is bad enough to keep him immobilized for a long time."

"Can't you do something? You're a lawyer after all."

"Maybe I can. We'll see. I can ask some questions anyhow. The first thing is to find out what the troopers have got."

Nora came into the room carrying Georgia. Lena twisted the knife out of Jimmy's hands and handed it back to Dad quickly and secretively so that Georgia wouldn't notice and want her turn to hold it. Jimmy started to cry.

Georgia wiggled out of Nora's arms and came over to kiss Jimmy and to say how hungry she was. Lena stood up. It was time to get them home for some lunch and a nap. She could tell Nora and Dad were a little relieved that she was going to take them home before they got really whiny.

Later, on the way home, Georgia said that Aunt Nora really was sick, that when they went upstairs, Aunt Nora threw up in the toilet. Lena asked her several times, and she stuck by her story. For a minute Lena wondered whether Nora could be pregnant, but she dismissed the idea right away. If Nora had a boyfriend, she would be staying in Boston, or if she moved back to Vermont, he would be moving too. At the very least, Nora would have told them about him. No, it was too suspicious of her to think it. That's what Jerry would say.

Chapter 4

George was sitting at his desk in his office, trying to concentrate on what he was reading and not having much luck. This was one of those times when a cigarette would taste so good, when it would complete the moment, which was unfinished without it. But it was no use because he didn't have one. The only way to stop himself from cheating at moments like these was to not have any cigarettes around.

George could hear Annie moving around in the next room. He could tell she was walking toward his door by the way the floor creaked.

Then he saw her, or rather her head and shoulders, peeking around the partly open door. "Excuse me, Mr. Willard," she said.

"Open the door and come in, Annie. There's no one here but me."

"Oh no, Mr. Willard. I don't want to bother you when you're working. I just wondered if you were staying late."

"Yes, I thought I would. I'm behind. I've been up at the hospital when I should've been in the office."

"All right. If you stay, I will too." She was standing in the open doorway now, but still on her side of it, and she was smiling with pride.

"Thank you," he said, trying not to look dismayed. "But I won't need you. What I have to catch up on is reading."

"I have some things I should catch up on too." A flicker of doubt went across her face, and then she said, "Don't worry. You won't have to pay me extra."

"I'd be glad to pay you if I needed you, Annie, but I really don't."

"That's okay. I'll stay to keep you company."

"I'm sure your family will wonder where you are." It was his last hope. He took off his glasses and cleaned them and put them back on.

She stood in the doorway awkwardly. She was so thin that she looked like someone's stick-figure drawing. "No they won't. They probably won't even notice."

"Well, all right," he said, defeated. He couldn't picture himself ordering her to leave. "That's very nice of you. Wait until I finish this brief, and I'll take you out for something to eat."

"You don't have to do that, Mr. Willard."

"I'd like to. I was going to get myself some dinner anyway. Laurie and Nora have gone Christmas shopping in Burlington."

"Okay," she said, and a bright, childish smile spread across her face.

He watched her turn to leave. He always thought she was small and skinny because her legs and arms were like sticks. So he was always surprised to see that in the middle she was quite broad and square. He wished he'd asked her to close his door.

He waited a few minutes, and then he got up and closed it quietly. He looked up the state's attorney's telephone number and dialed it. The secretary said she'd have to see if Mr. Simonetti was with a client. Of course George knew that was a code. She'd have to go and see if Nick wanted to talk to him. And apparently he did, because he was on the line a minute later.

"George, how the hell are you? It's been a long time."

"I'm fine, Nick, and how are you?"

They exchanged pleasantries for a few minutes, and then Nick said, "So, what's on your mind, George?"

"Well," he said, hesitating. "You know that guy that got shot in the foot the other day?"

"Sure."

"He's my brother."

"Really? I should have put that together. Willard. Of course. I knew you came from out that way too."

"My brother—Cal's his name—says someone shot him on purpose and took his deer."

"That's what he told the troopers too."

"I was just wondering...."

"They're on the case, but they haven't found anything to speak of, not yet anyway. There was nothing at the scene. Of course the snow Friday night didn't help. They should've gotten there before the snow, but they were shorthanded because of the holiday. I think they found a couple of spent shells not too far away. They looked pretty fresh, but, hell, it's deer season."

"And that's it?"

"Over on the other side of the ridge, there was the site of a deer kill. They thought it was a big one. The guy dragged it out the other way, not through your brother's property."

"That's just what Cal said then."

"There's the question of intent, of course. Your brother seems to think he was shot on purpose. They haven't found anything that would indicate something like that, not yet they haven't. But they might. It's ongoing right now."

"You don't think it was an accident then?"

"Sure. It could have been. The guy might not have known he shot your brother. Anything's possible. It could've been a wild shot. Who knows? There's nothing definite yet."

"Then it doesn't look like he shot himself...by accidentally discharging his rifle when he was climbing down from his tree stand?"

"No. That's not likely. The trajectory of the bullet wouldn't support that theory."

"That's good to know."

"Of course we can't rule anything out yet, not this early in the investigation, but the placement of the entrance and exit wounds make that extremely improbable."

That was what he wanted to find out. He didn't know how he would say it to Cal, but it changed things. He thanked Nick and chatted for a couple of minutes so it would be easy to call him again. Then he tried to do some of the reading he needed to catch up on.

After about an hour, he couldn't concentrate anymore. He regretted staying late. If he had been quick enough when she asked him, he could have said he was going home, and then he would have had some time alone. He pictured himself sitting in the den in his favorite chair, with a drink on the floor within easy reach. He could have fixed a drink in his office with Annie there. He wasn't trying to keep his drinking a secret. It wasn't as though he had a problem. It wasn't something that affected anyone else. He just enjoyed it more when he was alone. And anyway, he was still struggling to give up smoking because Laurie wanted him to. Surely that was enough.

He lined the piles of papers up neatly with the edges of his desk and put all his pens in the drawer. Then he stood up, feeling stiff. He tried to stretch without being obvious about it. She was probably listening for the scrape of his chair on the floor when he pushed it back. She might knock on the door any minute.

"Annie," he said through the door. "Where shall we go for dinner? You choose."

She came into his room shyly. "The Severance Diner is fine, Mr. Willard."

"We could have a much nicer dinner than that."

"Oh, but it's fine. Really. They have good food there, and they're friendly too."

"If you say so," he said, wondering why he always got himself into the position of having to do what the other person wanted to do.

The diner was bright and filled with the clatter of dishes and voices, too bright and too loud after the dark winter quiet of the street. No one paid any attention to them, except for a waitress about Annie's age who said hello to her as they came in. They sat in a booth near the front, at George's insistence. He didn't want people to think he was hiding when they saw him with a young woman who wasn't his daughter. Severance was a small town, and people gossiped, even after the '60s and most of the '70s had changed attitudes and morals.

Annie wiggled out of her coat and let it fall behind her. George stood up again to take his off. He doubled it neatly and laid it on the seat and sat down beside it.

"I didn't even know you had a brother until he went to the hospital," she said with a pout.

"We're not close. We don't see each other very often, unless there's something wrong."

"Oh." She kept her eyes on his face, but she didn't say any more. She just sat there looking at him, as though she thought he was about to say something important, something she ought to try to understand.

"Our lives are so different. We don't have anything in common any more." He thought about it for a minute. "I don't know if we ever did. When we were kids, the Depression was going on, and we had to work all the time. We didn't have time for interests. We didn't have time for anything except work."

"How awful."

George was surprised. "I wasn't complaining," he said. "I was telling you how it was. It wasn't awful. We were all in it together, trying to survive. It was like that for everybody. People feel too sorry for themselves now. They don't know how to work." He spoke sharply, and then he saw her wide eyes, her babyish pout, and he was sorry. "I didn't mean you," he said. "You shouldn't pay any attention to what I said. I was a million miles away, thinking about what it was like when I was a child."

"That's okay," she said. She tried to smile, but he could see she was hurt.

Before he could think of how to apologize, the waitress was there to take their orders. George ordered a hamburger the way Annie did, because she said they were good, because she was eager and childish, and because he had hurt her feelings and didn't know what he should say to make it better.

He needn't have worried. By the time the waitress left them, Annie was cheerful again. She asked him if his brother was a lawyer also.

George almost laughed out loud at the thought of Cal as a lawyer, but he managed to be more careful of her feelings this time. He didn't even smile at the incongruous picture. "No," he said. "My brother Cal would hate it if anyone thought he was a lawyer....or a professional of any kind. I meant it when I said we don't have much in common."

"Oh," she said, looking down at the silverware and pushing the knife in line with the spoon and fork.

"It's a long story, and not very interesting."

"I don't mind," she said without looking up.

"All right, if you want to hear it."

"Yes, please."

"It's really the story of how I happened to become a lawyer myself. I mean, I'm the one who changed," he said, realizing for the first time, as he said the words, that maybe that was the way Cal saw it, that maybe Cal thought he, George, was the one who left them behind, the one who went away and never came back.

"I grew up on a farm in West Severance, one of those old sidehill farms where it was grow it, or make it, or do without— just me and Cal, who is four years older than I am, and our parents, of course. When the war came, Cal was already married with a baby. They needed people to stay on the farms to raise food for the troops, so they didn't draft Cal. I might have been able to get out of it too, but I didn't want to. I signed up as soon as I turned eighteen. That was right after Pearl Harbor. I suppose I might not have done it if I had known what it would be like. I was in the middle of it, mostly in France. The things I saw, the things that happened to my buddies, and I came through the whole war without a scratch. Sometimes I have a hard time understanding why I should have escaped when so many of my friends...didn't."

"Then I went home, back to the farm. And in some ways, that was even worse." He pictured it while he was telling it, and he had to take a deep breath and get a grip on himself to keep the tears from flowing into his eyes and maybe even overflowing onto his face. Luckily for him, their food came, so she wasn't paying much attention anymore, and he had a chance to think about the food to blunt the feeling of how alone he had been when he got back home to that vision of green safety and quiet he had carried with him through all the horrors he had seen in those alien places.

By the time he came home, Cal and Ursela were running the farm. They had three children by then, and the house was full. There wouldn't have been a place for him, even if he had been the same person who left, which of course he wasn't. He didn't belong there anymore.

He tried to tell them about what he had seen, what he had been through, how he had longed for them and held them in his heart through all of it. But they couldn't understand. How could they? Ma and Dad and Cal had never been out of Vermont. They couldn't imagine what it was like. He wouldn't have been able to either unless he had seen it for himself, seen how different things were in other places, even where there wasn't a war, and seen too how the whole world could be turned upside down by violence. Ursela had more of an idea of what he had been through than any of the others because she had lived in Germany until she was ten and her family immigrated to Vermont. The little boys, Conrad and Paul, were curious, but what they wanted to hear about were the guns and planes and tanks. They kept asking him if he had shot any Germans. He could have, but he didn't know. He hoped he hadn't, but how could he explain that to them?

The little boys were sleeping in the room that used to belong to him and Cal. When he came home, Ursela put them both to sleep in one bed so that he could have the other. But it didn't feel like home. Their clothes and toys were all over the place. He couldn't shine a light or smoke after they had gone to bed. He had nowhere of his own. He was a visitor, only there was no end to the visit, and no home to return to.

Annie was eating greedily, with her mouth partly open, and because he was slightly horrified by her manners, and embarrassed that he was horrified, and afraid she might notice, he tried to think of what he could say, and finally he settled on something lame about how good the hamburger was.

"I told you, didn't I?" she said, grinning and talking with her mouth full. "Oh, I know where the good places are. I used to waitress some before I got the job with you."

"That's interesting," he said, because it wasn't, and he felt guilty. But he was still half, or more than half, back in 1945 when he came home from the war, or rather when he found out, like the book says, that you can't go home again. "When I came home from the war, my brother was running the home place with his wife. Ma and Dad were still alive, but they weren't doing much of it. It was Cal's farm by then."

George knew he could have stayed on as a kind of hired man, if he hadn't been so lonely. But he craved the company of men who knew what he'd been through, who had similar experiences and stories to swap. He used to hitchhike into Severance and go drinking with his buddies. It was loneliness really, not the alcohol. They had nowhere else to meet except in bars. There were other guys who'd come home to find their places taken by people who stayed behind. His wasn't such a bad scene, not like what many other guys had to put up with. Still, there was a while there where he was drinking way too much. It was all a blur to him now.

"So I left," he said. "'How're you gonna keep 'em down on the farm after they've seen Paree?'"

Annie looked blank.

"That's an old song. You probably never heard it, did you?"

She shook her head.

"I wonder what's got into me tonight. I don't usually talk so much about myself. But who knows where I would be if I hadn't met Laurie. I was just drifting when we met. That was at a Grange Hall dance, but she was a town girl, from Severance. She took me in hand. After we got married, I went to UVM. There was this thing called the G.I. Bill. If you fought for your country, the government would pay for you to get an education. Laurie got a job and supported us. People act like this women's lib is something new, but Laurie didn't need any newfangled idea to tell her that's what she needed to do."

"I wish they had something like that for the people who went to Vietnam. My big brother would have liked to go to college when he got out of the army."

"He should have been able to. We should have been more committed to winning in Vietnam. When I was young, when the country went to war, everyone got behind the effort. No one stood on the sidelines helping the enemy by saying we should get out and go home."

"Yes, but...."

He held up his hand to silence her. "We don't need to get into it. My girls both think I'm wrong. It's over now anyway. I'm just sorry for the guys who had to go through such an experience without having their country behind them. That's all."

"Well, that's because we had no business getting into that war in the...."

"Annie," he said in what he hoped was a stern voice. "Don't. We don't want to argue about it. And besides, think of your brother." She started to say something, and he held up his hand again. "At least we can agree that there should have been a G.I. Bill after Vietnam. Now what would you like for dessert?"

Annie wanted chocolate cake, and the waitress brought it for her. Minutes later, George felt someone standing by the table. In the second before he looked up, he thought it was the waitress back again. But it wasn't. Old Fred Singleton stood there, looking down at them with his habitual air of stern disapproval. George started to stand up.

"Stay where you are, George. I'm just passing by."

George sank back onto the seat. "How are you, Mr. Singleton? I haven't seen you in quite a while."

"Getting by, George, getting by." He was looking down at Annie.

"I'd like you to meet my new secretary, Annie Cookson. Laurie has gone shopping in Burlington. This is Mr. Singleton, Annie. He's a lawyer too. He was a good friend of the man who helped me become a lawyer, the man I read law with when I got out of UVM." All the time George was thinking how glad he was that he had insisted they sit in the front. He hadn't seen Singleton for a long time, and here he was just when George was thinking about those long-gone days. It was as though he had conjured him up by thinking about him.

Annie smiled and went on eating with her mouth open.

"Well," Fred Singleton said. "Remember me to Laurie, George." And he walked off toward the door without looking back.

George said goodbye to Annie outside the diner and drove up to the hospital to see Cal. Visiting hours were in full swing. He could hear the party hum of many voices before he got to Cal's door. He hoped Cal didn't have visitors. It was difficult to talk to Cal's family and his neighbors. There were always awkward silences. Elsie was different, but Elsie wouldn't be here on a Monday night.

George stopped in the doorway. Cal was lying on his back with his eyes closed. He couldn't tell whether Cal was asleep or pretending to be. The old guy in the bed next to Cal's had a circle of people standing around him. In fact, everyone seemed to have visitors. George was glad he was there so Cal would have someone too, even if he would have preferred to be alone. After all the times George had been to the hospital to see him, he still didn't know if Cal wanted him to come.

He stepped closer to the bed and stood looking down at Cal's thin face, with its sharp blade of a nose. Cal opened one eye, looked at him for an instant, and shut his eye again. George was just about to say something, when Cal opened both his eyes and hitched himself up on his pillows.

"Jeezum crow, George," he said. "How long have you been standin there ready to pounce on me?"

"I just got here, and I wasn't going to pounce on you, as you put it. I was just trying to decide whether you were asleep or not."

"Well, that question's settled. I'm wide awake now."

"How're you feeling?"

"I've felt better." He hitched himself up a little higher. "Have a seat, unless somebody's gone off with my chair again."

"No, it's here," George said. "Right at the bottom of your bed." He carried it up near Cal's head and sat down. "What's the doctor say about your foot?"

"It's comin good. I'm goin home in a day or two. Maybe even tomorrow if I'm lucky."

"Tomorrow?"

"Don't sound so surprised. I can lay around at home as good as I can lay around here. Better maybe. I could get more rest with only one person to bother me, even if it is Ursela."

"What does the doctor actually say?"

"He won't say. But I'm workin on him, tryin to pin him down."

"You'd better leave it up to him, Cal. He knows what's best for you."

"Jeezum, George. Gimme a break. I wouldn't leave it up to him for a minute if I didn't have to."

George didn't say anything. He was just glad Cal thought he had no choice.

"If I had two feet, I'd discharge myself and walk home, but as it is...."

"I'm sorry, Cal. Maybe it will be tomorrow. Anyway, it's bound to be soon."

"You don't know how long a day can be in this hell-hole." He paused for a minute. George could see he was feeling sorry for himself. "And the nights are a lot worse than the days."

There was a long silence. George considered saying how nice it was for him to be able to come and visit Cal so easily, but he knew what Cal would say to that, and he didn't want to hear it.

"I asked Nick Simonetti about your case. He's the state's attorney."

"I don't know what that means, George. Does it have anythin to do with me?"

"If they catch the guy you say shot you, he's the one who'll prosecute."

"Why do you say it like that? I couldn't have shot my own foot with a rifle, so of course somebody shot me. What did he say about it?"

"They're still investigating, but they haven't found much of anything yet." He thought for a minute. "You know, that's strange, Cal, because you took a couple of shots out of your tree stand, didn't you?"

"Yeah."

"So why didn't they find the casings under the tree?"

"How would I know?" Cal said. He smiled a sly smile. "Maybe they wasn't lookin in the right spot."

"But you told them....Cal, oh my God! You didn't tell them wrong on purpose, did you?"

"Not exactly," Cal said, still smiling that shifty smile.

"What then?"

"I really didn't so much tell 'em wrong, as let 'em get the wrong idea stuck in their heads."

George didn't say anything. He tried not to look shocked.

"There's an old tree stand I built years ago. It's a couple hundred yards lower down. I just got the idea from their questions that they might think that was the one. That's all. It ain't a criminal offense to give poor directions, is it?"

"But why...? They're on your side, Cal."

"I don't know about sides, George. I want to get up there and look around and see what there is to see. Maybe I can find somethin that'll tell me who did this. I don't want a bunch of guys that don't know nothin about the woods trampin every place and messin it up."

"But it'll be a long time before you can...."

"We'll see about that."

"Now it makes sense. Nick said they found a couple of shell casings, but they weren't near where you told them to look. Cal, you'd better be careful."

"I was, George. And it sounds like they messed up my spot anyways. I should've told 'em more wrong than I did."

"They found where a big buck had been killed on the other side of the ridge."

"Damn! I knew it. That was my deer."

"The guy dragged it out to Scott Road. Nick didn't say, but I'm sure they've been checking weigh stations."

"Maybe he didn't get it tagged. He knew it wasn't his. He knew he done wrong."

"Maybe he didn't even know he shot you, Cal."

"At least you admit that much. At least you don't think I shot myself."

"The state police don't think so either, you'll be glad to know."

"That's progress. Now if I can just get out of here so I can find the guy."

George didn't say anything. He was hot with his coat on. He was trying to decide whether to take it off or to leave when Cal spoke.

"What's it like outside?"

"It was clear and cold today. We had a little snow on Friday night, and it's still on the ground."

"Snow?"

"Yeah, just a little. It'll be gone when you get out. It's supposed to warm up with maybe a little rain for the next few days. It was warmer tonight than it has been all day."

"I bet you can smell the water in the air."

"Probably. I didn't notice."

"You always can when it warms up like that."

"I'll try to notice when I leave."

"God, I wish I could walk out of here like you can."

It was so heartfelt a statement that George felt sorry. "You will,

Cal. You'll be walking again before you know it, and you'll forget all about this time."

"You don't know how important it is until you lose it. The thought of not being able to get up in the woods when I want to...."

"You'll be able to soon, Cal. Get a grip on yourself." It was frightening to see Cal's weakness exposed like that. Cal was always sharp and bitter and in control of himself.

"Right," he said. "I'll get over it." His voice was hard-edged again.

"That's more like it," George said, and then he stopped. He should have welcomed such a moment, a chance to hear how Cal was truly feeling, a chance to comfort him. The women's libbers thought men should be able to open up like that. But they didn't know how uncomfortable it was. And anyway, he wanted Cal to be himself. That was who he wanted to spend some time with. A Cal asking for sympathy and comfort wouldn't be Cal. It was repulsive to think of.

"I hope it warms up," Cal said. "I'm not ready for winter yet."

"It's here whether you're ready or not. It's almost Christmas. And remember that big storm on Opening Day."

"Yeah. But it didn't last, and anyway, we often have bare ground most of December."

"Laurie and Nora are up in Burlington Christmas shopping right now."

Then there was an uncomfortable silence. After a while, George said, "I hope they're home by this time." And then, when Cal still didn't say anything, "I guess I ought to be getting home myself. I'll be in to see you tomorrow."

"Okay. Make it early if you want to be sure to find me here."

"I will," George said. He carried the chair back to the foot of Cal's bed, said good-bye and left, feeling vaguely discontented with their conversation. He wished he was still smoking. A cigarette would be a comfort right now.

Chapter 5

It was twenty of ten when Nora parked just down the street from the Women's Health Collective in Burlington. Her appointment was for ten o'clock. She was early because she thought she would have trouble finding a place to park. She had left extra time for that, and then she found a parking place almost in front. That had to be a lucky sign, a good omen, a hint from the universe that she was doing what she ought to do.

She turned off the engine and sat looking at the building. It was made of wood and painted brown, old and shabby like all the other houses on Drew Street. Before the operation, she would have to have a consultation with a therapist. They wanted to be sure she knew what she was doing. *She* knew they would see that she had no choice. She had no job, no place of her own, and the baby had no father. It was an impossible situation.

The day was dark. There was rain, blown on an icy wind. It was just the right weather for what she was doing, a day of sad endings. The scraggly trees along the sidewalk were bare and black. Their last yellow leaves blew down the street, piling up in soggy corners.

The cold air was creeping into the car and surrounding her. It was time to go. She got out and stood there, holding on to the car and feeling dizzy and sick. That part would be over soon. No more sudden and unexpected throwing up. No more trying to hide it from everyone. When it was safely over, she could tell Lena about it. She wondered how Lena would react. Maybe, thinking of her own children, she would say that she shouldn't have done it. But, of course, by that time it would be too late.

Nora went up the steps. She was unsteady and had to hold onto the railing. For the first time, she was conscious of the baby as a person. They were going through this door together. She wasn't alone. She pushed the thought aside.

She gave her name to the receptionist, and while she was standing there waiting, she had this sudden sense of Adam standing by her side, waiting with her. It didn't mean anything, of course. He didn't even know. She hadn't dared to tell him. What if he had asked her if she was sure it was his? And anyway, by the time she first thought she might be pregnant, summer was over, and so were they. He was making up with his wife. He even let her see how happy he was about it. So it didn't mean anything. It was just one more way for her to hurt.

She went into the waiting room. The floor creaked. The chairs were kitchen chairs, and none of them matched. She sat down. When she looked up at the ceiling light, she could see dead flies on the bottom of the glass. She wondered where the bathroom was, hoping she wouldn't need to know. She didn't want to ask. Then everyone would know she was feeling sick. As long as she was sitting down, she wasn't wobbly. Maybe it would be all right.

The waiting room was empty except for a young couple who sat side by side, holding hands and staring straight ahead. They didn't look at her, and she tried not to look at them. She didn't want to see how worried they were. They were both frightened, that was what she noticed. He was as scared as she was, even though nothing was going to happen to him. He was thinking about what was going to happen to her. And that made her feel angry at Adam because he should have cared what happened to her and to their baby. He should have been there to support her, she thought, forgetting for a minute that she had never told him she was pregnant. But realizing that he didn't know didn't make her any less angry at him.

It was ten of ten by the clock over the reception desk. Nora picked up a magazine and flipped through it, but she didn't see it. She was too restless to read. All she could do was wait and think. Until this morning she had been doing pretty well at keeping Adam out of her thoughts. Now her anger faded into sadness. She had been trying not to let herself remember things. The way he looked when he wanted to kiss her, and then the clean, sharp smell of him when he came close. It made her feel weak and shaky. It had been hard to turn off thinking about him when he was all she had thought about all summer. She had given up everybody else, all her other friends. That was why she hadn't had any letters or phone calls since she had been home. Everyone had stopped trying to include her. It was altogether her fault. And still she couldn't help hoping one of her old friends would catch her up on all the news and maybe even tell her what was happening with Adam.

Last summer had been such a happy time for her. She had never felt that way about anybody else, and he seemed to feel that way about her too. He and his wife weren't getting along, so she took their two girls and went to stay at her parents' summer place on Nantucket. The idea was that he would come over on the weekends, and they could spend some time together and work it out. So at first Nora only saw him during the week, but then, later on, he would make an excuse to his wife, and they would spend the whole weekend together. It had seemed exciting and romantic. Nora had had boyfriends before, and sex too, but it hadn't ever been like that.

She looked back on it now with surprise. She could see that it couldn't have gone on like that indefinitely. It was feverish in its intensity. At least it was that way for her. Had he felt the way she did? Obviously not, or he wouldn't have ended it. *She* never would have ended it. Did he then not care about her? She didn't believe that was true—or she couldn't bear to believe that was true. Sometimes she wouldn't even think about it, and other times she beat herself with it, hurting herself as much as she could, telling herself that he never cared about her at all and that she was a fool, so stupid that she never saw how she was being tricked.

To give him his due, he never said he was going to leave his wife and daughters, and she never said it either, although it was there in her mind to dream about and to hope for. She could look back now and see how much of the whole thing was a fantasy in her head.

How much attention had she ever given to what Adam was really like? She didn't know that now, and she never would. What she could see was that it never would have worked. It was always a dalliance, a temporary fling, a summer romance destined to end after Labor Day when summer was over and real life began again.

Part of the hurt was that her dreams hadn't come true. They weren't even very worthy dreams, in the sense that they weren't built on anything real. They were built on a fairy tale that didn't have its roots in reality. She could see that there were lots of things about Adam that she very carefully did not look closely at, things she didn't or wouldn't have liked about him if she had been married to him. There was his selfishness for one thing. When she was with him, she was charmed by it as a boyish quality of intensely wanting what he wanted, but now, at a distance, she could see that his selfishness would be very hard to live with.

"Why think about him now?" she thought. "Why now, when I'm ending it, cutting the last connection to him?" Because she had been doing really well controlling her thoughts, not letting herself think about him, and now all these contradictory thoughts of him were overwhelming her, just when she was finally about to put him behind her for good. She loved him, even when he told her they had to end it because Amy and the girls were coming back from Nantucket and he had promised himself that he would try really hard to be a better husband and father. "See," Nora thought. "It was all about him. It was always all about him. Why would I, how *could* I have cared so much?"

Even when she was still in Boston, when she saw him often at work but couldn't talk to him or touch him because it was over, she could see that she was making up a fantasy Adam, different from the real one. And when she left, the one in her mind became different again, even though she tried not to think about him at all.

So here she was, almost free and clear, with him finally out of her life for good. You would have thought it would be the opposite— that he would fade away completely. But no, now that she should have been able to put him out of her mind, he rose up more vividly than ever. She couldn't help thinking about him while she waited. And she let herself, maybe because it was the end, maybe because she was scared to think about what they were going to do to her in a few minutes.

"It's the right thing to do—what I have to do for myself, and for everyone else too. It's the only solution. How awful it would be to have a baby in order to hold onto the memory of someone who isn't in your life any more." She had no second thoughts or confusion about it at all. It was lucky that it was over before she had any idea she might be pregnant because she might have been tempted to tell him, and it was so much better that he didn't know.

It had been wonderful to be with him, even to be in the same room with him at work, where they had to pretend they didn't know each other—like when he came into Mr. Blankenship's office, and he would call her Ms. Willard, and she could see the little teasing hint of a smile at the corners of his lips that made her want to kiss him even more because his lips were so wonderfully expressive. It wasn't possible to look at them and not immediately want to kiss them. And sometimes she would get quite flustered, sure Mr. Blankenship would notice something. But she couldn't tell if he ever did.

At five past ten a nurse came into the room and said, "Sarah?" The young woman stood up, and then her boyfriend stood up beside her, as though he were planning to go with her. The nurse shook her head at him, and he sat back down. Sarah followed the nurse hesitantly. In the doorway, she stopped and looked back at her boyfriend. She acted as though she were going to be executed.

As soon as she was out of sight, the boyfriend stood up and began to pace back and forth across the room, dragging his feet with a shuffling sound on the worn carpet. He walked as though he had no choice, as though he wasn't even aware that he was moving. His face was blank.

"At least she has someone to worry about her," Nora said to herself. "At least he's taking responsibility for what happened. He's probably helping her pay for it too. If I had a boyfriend like that, I might not be here at all." But she knew it wasn't true. She'd always known Adam was married. She'd always known it wouldn't last, even though she had allowed herself to fantasize about him divorcing his wife so he could marry her. She had believed in that moment, although now she couldn't imagine why she had. It was certainly nothing he did. She knew she had been foolish about the whole thing.

So when she got pregnant in that one last time when it was really already over, especially since she didn't even know she was pregnant until weeks afterward, she had set her lips in a tight line over the fact that it was her mistake, and she had taken the responsibility and the blame. She knew she had to fix this last piece of it alone. She had to lay it to rest, and then she could start over again. Maybe she had been in love with love, but she didn't know, and probably never would know, exactly how much she had cared for Adam and how much she had cared for her own fantasy about him. Luckily she wouldn't ever have to sort it out. After the abortion, there wouldn't be any reason to go back to it again. There wouldn't be any reason to have to tell anyone the embarrassing details, or to have to explain how she felt about him.

Nora remembered how they walked down the street together, laughing. But that wasn't him so much as how she felt when she was with him. She couldn't picture him to herself any more. She couldn't really see him. She was losing him. He was disappearing out of her life, and maybe there would never be anybody else she felt that way about. Maybe that whole part of her life was over forever. That's the way it was for Elsie.

Oh, she wished they'd hurry up and get it over with, and then

Adam would be gone, and she might be able to stop longing for him. She watched the boyfriend walking across the room, a small, underfed person with stringy, dark hair. He didn't look up from the floor in front of his feet, and he didn't notice her watching.

Nora hated to think of the look of fear on the woman's face. It was happening to her right now. She couldn't get away from them. She was trapped in some back room while they cut her baby away. What did they do with the baby after they took it out? Nora's hands were clammy, and there was a hard, undigested lump at the bottom of her stomach. She hoped she wasn't going to get sick before it was over. She hoped it wasn't going to hurt a lot. She would find out soon now, because it was going to be her turn any minute.

She looked at the clock for the hundredth time. It said twenty past, which meant she had been sitting on that hard chair in that ugly room for half an hour. No one had come in. There was no sign of the nurse. Maybe there was no one back there at all. But then what about Sarah? More likely something had gone wrong with her operation, and they were all busy trying to save her. Maybe she herself had had a premonition of what was going to happen to her and that was why she was so afraid. Nora wanted to get up and walk around. Perhaps she wouldn't have such crazy ideas if she could move around a little. But the boyfriend was still pacing back and forth. It would be ridiculous to have them both walking around the room, passing each other, perhaps bumping into each other. She had to stay in her seat and watch him moving mindlessly.

There was one spot on his track that made the same complaining squeak every time he walked over it. The noise was so regular that it was monotonous. Gradually it became more and more irritating, until Nora lost all sympathy for him and for his girlfriend.

She got up and went over to the receptionist. "Do you think I'm going to have to wait much longer?" she asked. "My appointment was for ten o'clock."

The receptionist looked up at her without quite meeting her eyes. "I think they got started late." She put her hands on her desk to push herself up out of the chair. "I'll go see what I can find out."

"No, that's okay," Nora said, sighing. "It's all right. I just wondered if you knew." And then, on impulse, she said, "I'm going outside. I'm not going anywhere. I'll be right outside the door when they're ready for me."

"But....," the woman said. She looked worried.

"It's all right," Nora said. "I need some fresh air. I'll be back in a minute."

"Don't go far then," the woman said. "Keep where you can see the door."

Nora nodded. She slowly zipped up her jacket right in front of the reception desk to give the woman a chance to change her mind, but the woman was busy with some papers and didn't look up when Nora opened the door.

The porch floor creaked as she walked across it. She meant to stay on the porch, but once she was on the other side of the door, she felt like going a little farther so that she was really outside.

It wasn't actually raining, but the air was damp, full of tiny drops of water. The skin of her face was wet before she had gone many steps away from the building. She took a deep breath, which smelled of water and damp earth and moss. It woke her up and made her feel alive again. She walked along the sidewalk toward her car. It felt wonderful to be out of that place. She wasn't dizzy or sick any more. She pretended not to notice what she was doing. This was the first really fun thing she had done for quite a while. She was in a conspiracy with herself. She felt like giggling.

She got in the car and turned on the motor and the heater and sat there while the car warmed up. She had to hurry. She was in a child's chase game. Any minute, they were going to come out the door in their white coats to get her. Everything about the whole morning had been ridiculous. She abandoned herself to the absurdity of it and drove away.

When she was on the highway, heading toward Severance with no one pursuing her, she began to consider what she had done. There was no way to explain it. She would never be able to go back there again. She would have to go to someone else and start the whole process over from the beginning. And suppose there was no one else in Burlington to go to? She would have to go back to Boston. That would be expensive, and it would take a long time.

She scolded herself with these reasonable and practical thoughts, but underneath, her real feelings were bubbling up. She wanted to laugh. She felt she had had a narrow escape. She would have to pay for it later, but right now she felt a great delight. She had eluded something nasty, something mean.

Chapter 6

Cal had been lying awake for hours, too nervous to sleep. It was the way he always felt the night before the opening day of deer season, but worse. When it was hunting season, there was a lot to do to get ready. And he had to leave long before dawn to be settled in his spot at first light. Here, in the hospital, all he could do was wait.

He heard the nurses changing shifts at six. More lights came on. The day shift made more noise. Daylight slid slowly into the room. Cal couldn't see much of the window from his bed by the door, but it looked like a cloudy, damp morning out there.

He knew it was going to seem like forever until he could get out of this damn place. He had tried yesterday to push Dr. McCormack into saying that he could go home today for sure, but all he could get out of the doctor was that he would give him a definite answer this morning. That wasn't enough to keep Cal from being so tense that he felt sick to his stomach. He couldn't remember when he had cared so much about anything, even hunting.

He tried to pass the time by listing all the reasons he hated being here. At the top of the list was having people around all the time. He couldn't ever get comfortable because he couldn't ever get away. There were patients in the other beds. Even at night, when he couldn't see them, he could hear them breathing and sometimes snoring. And if he managed to hobble into the bathroom without being seen, some busybody of a nurse was sure to knock on the door and start talking to him, if she didn't just barge right in. It was so hateful that several times, to his own horror and embarrassment, he had actually been close to tears.

People, people, people. That's what it was. People around all the time, watching you every minute, talking to you, so you couldn't even have any thoughts of your own without being interrupted. People watching to see if you might break some damn little rule that you didn't even know about until you had already broken it and been spotted. People, mostly nurses, but visitors too, his and other patients', fussing around, moving pillows, moving him, getting him things he didn't ask for and didn't want, saying they were trying to make him feel better, when they were actually making him feel much worse, although they never noticed that. He was out there in the middle of them all the time, no escape. And if he fell asleep with all that going on, someone was sure to come along and wake him up. It wasn't surprising that he was anxious to get out.

And he had to lie there and do nothing, until he thought he couldn't stay still another second. That part was even worse when people came to visit him, because then he had to pretend to listen while they said the same pointless things over and over, or else they asked him how it happened, and when he told them, if they bothered to listen at all, they didn't believe him.

Not that he had had that many visitors. Even though he didn't want people sitting by his bed and staring at him, forcing him to talk, he was still hurt that so few people had been to see him. Some of the neighbors had come by to satisfy their curiosity, and Ursela, of course. Elsie sent him flowers, like it was his funeral. His boys had only been to see him once each. He could understand Paul not coming in. Paul was always busy with his own affairs. But it wasn't like Conrad. Cal was actually worried about Conrad.

Biff came in the day after it happened. That was good. Biff heard about it when he went to pick up his mail and a sandwich at the store, and he came straight to the hospital without even changing his clothes, so that he left a trail of sawdust and the scent of pine all along the corridor to Cal's room. Cal heard all about Biff from the nurses later on. He was gratified to see how upset Biff was, although Biff didn't stay long and he didn't have much to say, except how thankful he was that it wasn't more serious. At that point, it seemed pretty serious to Cal, and he wasn't thankful at all. Still it was good to see Biff, good that he came straight from the woods and brought the smell of trees in with him.

George came in a lot. George impressed the other guys on the ward. Cal was ashamed by how much he wanted George to come in. He had seen more of George in the last week than he had in the last ten or fifteen years—since Ma died anyway, and that was in 1966. But, hell, he couldn't stay in bed to keep from losing touch with his brother. It was inevitable anyway. It wasn't like they could have a real conversation. George couldn't forget he was a damn lawyer. George couldn't even admit that someone shot at his own brother. He kept trying to get Cal to say he shot himself, when anyone could see that wasn't even possible. George was probably scared he'd have to take the case, and then he'd have to offer to do it for free, although you would think he would be eager to nail the bastard who shot his brother. George had changed. He had forgotten where he came from. He had moved up in the world, and he didn't have any more use for the ones he had left behind.

But George was his little brother, and he had to admit to himself that even though George had turned into an asshole, he liked it when George came to see him. Even when they didn't have anything to say to each other, it felt good to have him in the room. Part of Cal was embarrassed by that, and another part of him was proud of it in a way. Blood was thicker than water, although if you thought about it, that was a dumb statement, true, but dumb. He couldn't have told anybody about these feelings, not George, not Ursela, not even Conrad, who probably felt that way about Paul. But anyone he told would be sure to get the wrong idea. It was better to keep quiet.

Of course, much the worst part of being in the hospital was that he couldn't ever get outdoors. He couldn't even tell what the weather was like. It gave him a constant feeling of being disoriented, like he was dizzy and might fall over if he stood up too fast. The hospital was so insulated, so shut off from the outside. He hated being shut up like that. It made him feel like he couldn't breathe. Ever since the oil embargo, everyone had been insulating everything. He hadn't gotten sucked into the craze. There was never a moment in his own house when he didn't know what was going on outdoors—the weather just came in through the cracks. And he preferred it that way. It was a much more normal way to live. It was just one more in the long list of reasons why he had to get out of this place.

He lay on the bed, willing himself not to look at the clock, knowing it would depress him to see how long he had to wait before he could let himself hope. He was lying on his back with his eyes shut when he heard the nurse come in with his breakfast tray. He didn't bother to open his eyes. He could smell it, and he knew there wasn't any sense in looking at it, even for something to do to pass the time.

So he was taken by surprise when he heard the doctor say, "Well, Cal, are you just going to lie there and play dead, or are you going to sit up and eat your breakfast?"

"Jeez, Doc," Cal said, struggling to sit up without moving his foot any more than he had to. "I didn't know it was you."

"Cal, if you're not eating, we'd better...."

"I'm eatin. I'm eatin plenty, Dr. McCormack. Ursela brings me my meals."

"Every day?"

"Sure," Cal said. "She's a good cook, and it's what I'm used to."

Dr. McCormack laughed. "I guess that settles it. I'd better get you out of here to spare your poor wife the work."

"She's all right," Cal said. It annoyed him that the doctor thought he knew how he should treat his wife. It was Ursela's idea to bring him his meals. She wanted to do it. "She doesn't have to. She likes to cook."

"Well, if you want to stay with us longer, I could...."

"No, Doctor," Cal said quickly. "You know I want to go home." He almost choked up just saying the words. He had to look away for a minute. Buddy in the next bed was lying there with his eyes on Cal, taking in the conversation while he waited for them to bring his breakfast. Cal turned back to the doctor. "You said I could go today." He held his eyes steady on the doctor's face because he knew he was bluffing, and he didn't want the doctor to see that he knew it.

"Well, you can. You've been healing nicely."

Cal let out the breath he'd been holding. Gratefulness flooded through him, filling him up.

"It won't be so easy to stay quiet when you get home. Those bones aren't going to mend unless you give them a chance. Do you think you can stay off it?"

"Oh sure, Doc. You have my word." God knows he would have sworn on the Bible to get out of there.

"Have you got someone to come in and do your chores for you?"

"My boys have been takin care of things."

"And will they keep on?"

"Of course. They're good boys."

"Yes, I know. I remember when Conrad was in high school." He paused for a minute and looked at his watch. "Okay, then. I want to see you in my office in a couple of weeks."

"Thank you, Doctor," Cal said, trying to keep the emotion out of his voice and off his face. He felt like jumping out of bed, but he kept himself quiet. It was much easier to do now that he knew he was actually going to make it out of there.

He was so excited that he felt sick to his stomach. He thought of eating some of his breakfast, but it was so unappetizing that he thought he might heave it back up again. If a nurse caught him vomiting, she might get some harebrained notion about keeping him for an extra day. He drank a lot of water. Afterwards, he could feel the heavy pool of it lying in his gut, holding everything down. Most of the time he felt better, but every so often that water would slosh around and make him feel worse than ever.

He lay back on the pillows to think about getting dressed. Ursela would be along soon. He wanted to be ready to leave when she got here. It was good she hadn't been around when the doctor told him he had to stay off his foot. The doctor had practically said to stay in bed, and there wasn't any way he was going to do that. He just couldn't. He knew he was going to have to fight Ursela. He knew she would do her best to turn him into an invalid, but at least she wouldn't have the doctor's words to use for ammunition.

He had been lying in bed for days on end planning how he was going to make a support for his leg that would leave his hands free to work. He would use one of Conrad's old crutches that had been hanging up in the shed ever since Conrad broke his leg playing ice hockey in high school. The key would be holding it in place. He knew he was going to have to tinker around with where he put the straps. It wouldn't be right the first time. He was sure of that. Some of the straps would have to be adjustable so that he could wear more clothes when he was working outside. Luckily there was a lot of old horse harness hanging up in the tack room of the barn. He had all the leather straps he could use. He'd been thinking about it all week, and he had it figured out. Once he had a decent crutch, he could get back to work. He wouldn't be putting any weight on his foot, so it would be just as good as staying in bed, better really, if you thought of how beneficial it was to your circulation to get up and move around. He ought to remember that argument to use on Ursela when she tried to keep him in bed.

He needed to be able to carry his rifle up into the woods too, since he had promised himself two hunting days to make up for the two he missed. He wasn't going to take more than two—that wouldn't be right—but he wasn't going to settle for less either. The other business he had up there was to look for evidence at the scene of the crime, even though the cops had been all over all of it already and probably trampled on anything they didn't find. He wished he had had the nerve to send them to an entirely different place. It had happened too fast. He was in a lot of pain when they came in, and he was scared too. He didn't know if he was going to be able to get up there himself, and he wasn't thinking clearly.

It was almost certain to be a wasted effort, but still, he knew he had to try it. He had to see for himself, and soon too, before the snow came down to stay. Of course the shooter could have, and probably did, go back to the scene to look for any signs he might have left and to cover his trail. If Cal had been the guy, that's what he would have done, and right away too, especially after he heard—and he would have heard—that Cal was in the hospital, shot in the foot.

He wondered whether the guy got there and found the cops already on the scene. Saturday was still hunting season, so the guy would have had the perfect excuse. Cal wanted to find that shooter so bad. If he could just find him, he could squeeze it out of him. Let him keep the deer, for Chrissakes. It was only meat. If the guy would just admit what he'd done, Cal wouldn't even press charges. This wasn't a matter for the cops. It was a private fight.

It had been driving him crazy all week. It was torture to have to lie there knowing that every hour meant it would be that much harder to find anything. He had an awful lot to do, and it wasn't going to help to have to fight with Ursela every time he wanted to go outdoors.

He pushed himself off the bed and hopped over to the closet to get his clothes. By the time he got back to the bed with them, his good leg ached, and he was out of breath from the effort. He was already wearing his long underwear underneath the ridiculous hospital nightgown they insisted that he wear. The day after he got here, Ursela wanted to go out and buy him some pajamas, but he stopped her. No sense in throwing good money away on a special suit of clothes to wear in bed when long johns worked just as well. Even better, if you considered that he already had a head start on getting dressed. He worked himself back to the middle of the bed and put his foot on the pillows by lifting up his leg with his hands.

Beside him Buddy Longley was picking at his breakfast and watching. When he saw Cal looking at him, he said, "Well, I guess you'll be leavin."

"That's right," Cal said. "It's been good talkin to ya."

"Yeah. Same here."

"I got to get out there and see what I can turn up before the snow comes down."

"It'll be a while before you can do that."

"Christ. I hope not. I've laid around long enough. I got to catch up with that some-bitch before he gets fat eatin my deer meat."

"I wish I could give you a hand."

"I know you do, Buddy, and I appreciate it."

"I hope I'll get out myself before too long. Maybe I can give you a hand when I do."

"A guy can always use back-up. I think I'm dealin with somebody pretty hard-core here."

"I've been feelin a lot better in the last couple of days." He fed himself a spoonful of cereal with a hand that shook. "I ought to be able to get out of here soon if it keeps goin the way it has been."

"Has the doctor...."

"Naw. He won't say." He frowned for a minute as though he realized something, but the frown faded, and almost immediately he looked cheerful again. "He probably don't want to get my hopes up too soon. He must've seen I was comin along real good."

Cal thought, "The poor bastard. He don't even know he's terminal." But he didn't say anything. It wasn't his place to bring it up. By that time, he had his plaid shirt on and buttoned, and he had to stand up to put on his pants. That gave him a chance to turn his back on Buddy without saying anything one way or the other about his condition. Luckily his pants were baggy enough to go on over his cast. He buckled his belt and settled his suspenders into place and then lay back onto his pillows. He was light-headed. "It don't take long to lose your strength when you lay around like this," he said.

Buddy didn't reply. Cal sneaked a sideways look at him. He was eating his breakfast and making a lot of noise over it. He was such a skinny, little guy that he reminded Cal of a bird. "Of course, if I had to eat that slop...." he thought. It was pathetic. He'd never get his strength back that way.

After lying back on his pillows for a few minutes, he felt okay again, so he got his boot and sock out from under the bed and put them on. There wasn't much he could do about his other foot until he got home and was able to rig up some kind of boot that he could put on over the cast. He got out his handkerchief. It was dark blue and looked clean enough. He tied it around the end of the cast. It looked silly but not as bad as his naked toes sticking out.

He lay back down. It was uncomfortable with his booted foot hanging over the side of the bed, so he hoisted it up onto the covers. When Ursela came in a few minutes later, she gave him a look that said she didn't believe what she was seeing. She didn't even say hello.

"Ursela," he said patiently. "They got to wash all the beddin. It ain't makin 'em more work, you know. The doctor said I could leave any time."

She stood there holding the covered casserole dish with his breakfast in it. "You shouldn't put your dirty boot up on the bed."

"You didn't listen. They got to change it all anyways. I'm goin home."

She didn't act pleased at all. "What about your breakfast then?"

"God damn it, woman! That don't matter. I can eat it in the car." He almost asked her if she wanted him home, but he wasn't sure enough of the answer, so he didn't.

She looked distressed. "It's too hot, Cal," she said. "And I didn't bring a fork or a plate."

"All right!" he said, much too loud. "I'll eat it when I get home then. I'd rather eat it cold than stay here any longer. The doctor said I could go, and I'm goin." He stood up too fast and wobbled and had to grab the nightstand to steady himself. He tried to cover it up by opening the drawer to get out his comb and razor and toothbrush. He laid them on the top beside his glasses.

But Ursela had noticed how shaky he was. "Oh Cal," she said in her just-about-to-start-crying voice. "I have to put this down so I can help you." She still hadn't said she was glad he was getting out.

"I don't need any help," he said in a harsh voice. He hopped toward the closet, banging her shoulder with his arm as he went past her. "Sorry," he snapped, although he wasn't sorry. He felt like banging into her. He wanted to knock her into wanting him to come home.

He steadied himself on the closet door and tried to get a grip on his emotions. He didn't need to worry. The doctor told him to go. No one could stop him. He didn't have to be afraid.

Ursela was standing in the same spot, still holding the casserole. She hadn't moved except to turn around so she could watch him putting on his jacket. He managed it by leaning against the closet door. Then he had to hop past her again, back to the nightstand, so he could put his toothbrush and the rest of his things into his pockets.

Just that little bit of exertion tired him and made him feel light-headed again. He could have used a rest before he tried to leave, but he was too nervous and angry to sit still. "Good luck to you, Buddy," he said, because the poor old guy was watching every move he made. "Come on, woman. I can't wait around any longer."

"But, Cal, we got to tell them we're goin'."

"They know. The doctor said I could." He hopped to the door and held on to the frame. His leg already ached, and this was just the beginning. But it didn't matter, because he had to keep on. He started down the hall in what he hoped was the right direction. He hopped a few steps at a time, steadying himself by leaning against the wall. The fluorescent lights were pulsing in his head. He couldn't even see to the end of the corridor. He didn't know whether Ursela was behind him or not, but he couldn't look back. He pushed away from the wall and went on. The good leg was starting to get weak. It felt like it might fold up under him. He hadn't a hope of getting out of this damn place and yet he couldn't stop. Several nurses called out to him. He pretended not to hear.

Then he felt a hand on his shoulder, and a man's voice said, "Hold on there. You can't leave this way."

"What do you mean?" he said without turning his head. "You

just watch me." And he hopped a couple of hops that didn't get him anywhere before he stopped and leaned against the wall and looked around to see who he was talking to.

It was a young man, a hospital orderly with a soft, childish face. When Cal looked at him, he took his hand away from Cal's shoulder. "It's okay. You can leave," he said, "but you have to go in a wheelchair."

"I don't need a wheelchair." Here he was just barely able to handle this, and they were trying to make it harder. Ursela was standing there like a lump in her brown cloth coat with the covered dish in her hands. She wouldn't look at him. Right away he knew she was the one who had called for the attendant.

"It's hospital regulations, Mr. Willard. Everyone has to leave in a wheelchair. Stay right here while I get you one."

Cal didn't mean to wait, but he was too tired to try, and he knew he couldn't get away. In a few minutes he could see the orderly coming back with the wheelchair. He pushed it up behind Cal and gave him a nudge, and Cal sat down hard into the seat.

They started down the hall with Ursela following. They went so fast that Cal could feel a breeze on his face. He looked back at Ursela. She was getting farther and farther behind. Even though he hated to be beholden, he had to admit it was great to move so effortlessly and so fast. They were passing everyone. It sure beat struggling along on one leg.

They had to wait for Ursela at the elevator. She was out of breath, and her face was red. The young man took her covered dish and set it on Cal's lap without even asking. Cal wanted to say something on his own behalf, but everything he thought of sounded like he was trying to justify himself. He felt stupid sitting in a wheelchair with a covered dish on his lap. It was hot where it sat on his legs, and warm air rose toward his face.

While he was riding down in the elevator, Cal suddenly saw the reason everyone had to leave in a wheelchair. It was really very tricky of them. They had him. He couldn't leave without paying his bill. He was right too. The orderly wheeled him straight into the billing office from the elevator, while Ursela went to bring the car up to the front door. Cal had to sign papers saying he agreed with the charges, even though he was shocked by the size of the bill. He couldn't see that they had done very much except to pester him night and day and bring him food he couldn't eat. His foot probably would have healed all right without a cast. But he had no choice. That was their clever scheme. At least they didn't insist on having the money before he could leave. He had to consider himself lucky about that.

He was thinking about how he was going to pay the bill as he was being wheeled out the door, which was probably why it hit him so hard when he realized that he was out. He was free. He felt as though he had been shut in a coffin and someone had just opened the lid. The rain and the gray sky, the smell of dampness, the shine of the water on the pavement—it was all so beautiful that his heart tried to burst out of his chest. The feeling was so strong that for one stabbing second of fear he thought he might be having a heart attack. Then a flock of sparrows swirled around the light pole, giving their chinking cry, and he was back in the world. He thought he would never be annoyed by anything again.

But the drive home in the car made him tired, and the way Ursela was sitting forward, hunched over the wheel, started to irritate him. He was glad she was too busy to notice how the least little thing tired him out. He wished she didn't act like she was just about to do something stupid or dangerous, because it was stupid and dangerous to think like that.

When they drove up to the house, the dogs started barking, and Paul came out. He hurried over to Cal's door and opened it before Cal could do it himself. "How are you, Dad?"

Cal stood up, supporting himself on the car door. "I'm all right now that I'm out of that damned hell-hole." Paul was trying to grab him, and Ursela was hurrying around from her side of the car to help. Cal batted at their hands. "Leave me alone, Paul. I can do it."

"Let me help, Dad. You can't hop all the way to the house."

Cal shook off their hands and tried to get away. "God damn it," he said. "You're just like your mother. You want to turn me into a cripple." He swung around in time to see Paul giving Ursela a look that said they both knew they were dealing with a crazy man.

He hopped toward the mudroom door, but he didn't get very far before they caught up to him and took him under the arms, one on each side. He knew he needed them and that he had been unfair, but he didn't know how to say so. The best he could manage was to let them support him up the steps into the kitchen to the over-stuffed chair by the woodstove. They helped him out of his jacket and let him down gently.

"Thank you," he said, and then to cover his embarrassment, "Don't take that jacket away. I think I'm goin to need it."

Before Ursela had time to do more than draw in her breath to say she would build up the fires, Paul stopped her. "I did 'em, Ma. You got here sooner than I thought you would. It'll warm up in a minute. You just sit there, Dad, and take it easy."

Cal said all right because he had no choice. Ursela bustled out to the car to get the covered dish with his breakfast so she could get busy feeding him. Paul patted him on the shoulder and followed Ursela out the door. Cal didn't care. He'd rest until she got him his breakfast, and then he might feel strong enough to work on the crutch.

Chapter 7

It was a little after six when Conrad opened the back door and stepped inside. It was warm in the house, and it smelled like spaghetti. Conrad hoped that's what they were having for supper. He was really hungry. He cleared a corner of the bench and sat down to take off his boots. He had cleaned them off outside as well as he could, but they were still dirty. He had worn them to do Dad's chores at the home place and after that to do his own chores.

The rows of coat hooks were mostly empty, but Dwayne and Dorrie's stuff was scattered everywhere. Their jackets lay in a mound on the bench, and there were piles of boots and shoes and mittens and hats on the floor.

From the kitchen Cheryl said, "Is that you, Conrad?"

"Yes."

"You're late."

"I know. I couldn't help it." He went into the kitchen. Cheryl was setting the table. "I did Dad's chores, and then there were some other things he wanted me to do."

"How is he?"

"Okay. He can't do much, and that puts him in a bad mood."

"I guess it's good that he wants to try."

"Oh yeah. He even hobbled down to the barn, but he couldn't do anything when he got there." Conrad went to the stove and lifted the lid on the big pot. "Spaghetti?" he said. "It smells great. I'm hungry."

She smiled at him. "Get washed up then."

"Where are the kids?"

"They're supposed to be down in the basement doin homework. I hope they're not watchin TV."

"I don't hear any noise."

"They're too tricky for that. If they were watchin it, they'd have the sound way down. I'll call 'em."

No one said very much at dinner. Conrad kept going around and around in his mind over different ways of telling Cheryl about Walt's skidder. He didn't want her to say no before he even had a chance to explain the advantages of his plan to her.

Dwayne powered down two helpings of spaghetti while Dorrie was getting through the first half of hers.

"Come on, Dorrie. Ain't you done yet?"

"I will be in a minute. Go on."

"Okay. Hurry up, will you?"

Cheryl said, "Leave her alone, Dwayne. She's not finished with her dinner."

"I want her to hurry up."

Finally, Conrad said, "Have you done all your homework, Dwayne?"

"No, but almost."

"Well, go on down and do it. She'll be along."

"Okay, Dad, but I want to tell you...." He was looking at Dorrie while he spoke.

Conrad got impatient. He'd been dealing with people all day, and he'd had enough. "I don't want you to tell me anything, Dwayne. Go do your homework."

Dorrie said, "Ha, ha on you." She stuck her tongue out at

Dwayne.

Conrad turned around in time to see her. "You watch out too, Dorrie. We could give you both extra work."

"Sorry, Dad. I'll be good." She ate quickly and silently after that. In a few minutes she stood up and took her dishes to the sink and followed Dwayne to the basement.

After Dorrie was gone, Cheryl poured them each a cup of coffee and brought the ashtray over to the table.

"Why does your dad go down to the barn if he can't do any work? You'd think he'd stay up in the warm."

"Not Dad. He likes to be where the action is. Remember when I broke my leg when we were in high school?"

"Of course," Cheryl said through a cloud of smoke. "That was when I fell in love with you." She smiled at him.

"Dad took one of my old crutches and put straps on it. That way he can have his hands free."

"Does it work?"

"Not really. He spends more time foolin with it than he does on the chores. He's always tinkerin with it." Cheryl didn't say anything, so after a minute of silence, he said, "Walt Jackman came into the store today." He tried to sound casual. "He's really doin great cuttin firewood, and sometimes saw logs. He's goin to buy a new skidder."

"A new skidder? He *must* be doin good. Those things cost a fortune. There's a girl at work whose dad...."

"I don't mean new new. He's buyin a used one. It's just new compared to what he's got now."

"Walt's a nice guy. I'm glad he's doin well."

"Me too," Conrad said. "Are you done with your coffee? I'll help you with the dishes." He stood and picked up his plate and Cheryl's.

"You don't need to help."

"I want to. We can keep on talkin." He walked back to the table for more dishes.

Cheryl was up now too. She took the butter and milk to the refrigerator.

Conrad said, "Walt's sellin his old skidder for five thousand dollars."

Cheryl was bending over, pushing things around, trying to make room for the spaghetti sauce on one of the refrigerator's lower shelves.

"He would let me make monthly payments."

Cheryl stood up so fast she banged her head on the freezer compartment. "Ouch," she said, rubbing the place on her head. "That was dumb."

Conrad didn't know what to say next. Ever since Walt said he would take the money for the skidder in payments, he hadn't been able to think of anything else. He really might be able to swing it. But he couldn't do it without Cheryl.

He got more dishes and took them to the sink. She was filling the dishpan.

"How's your head?" he asked. It was lame. What he really wanted to ask was how she felt about him quitting his job. But he'd already seen her first reaction to that idea.

"It's okay. It wasn't anythin."

Conrad cleared the last things off the table. While he was there with his back to her, he said, "If I had that skidder, I could quit my job and go out on my own. Walt's doin so good. There's more business than he can handle, and it's only goin to get better with the oil crisis and all."

He looked at Cheryl's back. He couldn't tell if she'd heard what he said. He didn't know what he'd do if she said no. It wasn't that he had to do what she said, but he knew he couldn't do it without her support. He got a dish towel and stood beside her, drying the clean dishes. He didn't say anything. He was trying to wait to hear what she thought about it.

"That's an awful lot of money." She turned off the water and looked at him. "And if you didn't have a job...."

"But, Cheryl, it wouldn't be like that. I'd be gettin paid for the firewood and saw logs. And the more I worked, the more I'd get. Not like it is now."

He turned around to put a dry plate on the table, and there was Dwayne, standing in the doorway, his shaggy hair hanging down over his eyes the way it always did.

"Dad, I want to tell you somethin."

Conrad was irritated. "What is it, Dwayne? Have you finished your homework?"

"Well, not exactly, but...."

"Go down and finish your homework, and then we'll talk."

"But, Dad, this is important. Please listen." He looked over his shoulder. "It's about Dorrie. I might not get another chance. She thinks I'm in the bathroom."

Conrad sighed. "All right. What is it?" He saw that Cheryl had shut off the water and turned around to listen. "It's about Dorrie," he said to her.

"What about her?"

Dwayne said, "She's been skippin school."

"How many times?"

"I don't know, except for today. She did it before, a long time ago, and I said I wouldn't tell if she didn't do it any more, and it was okay. But she did it again today."

"How do you know?"

"She told me, and anyway, she wasn't on the school bus. She got home later. I bet Rudy gave her a ride home."

Cheryl sat down at the table. Then she jumped up to get her cigarettes and the ashtray and sat down again.

Conrad said, "Sit down, Dwayne. I'm goin to call Dorrie." He sighed. "We'd better get to the bottom of this right now."

"Oh no, Dad. She'll be mad at me for tellin on her."

Conrad looked at Cheryl, but she was lighting a cigarette and didn't notice. "I need one of those too," he said. He went over to the basement door and called to Dorrie, telling her to come upstairs, and then he sat down at the table beside Cheryl and took one of her cigarettes. "I left mine out in my jacket," he said. "You don't mind, do you?"

"Of course not," she said, pushing the matches toward him. "They all come out of the same carton anyway."

Conrad lit up and blew out a long stream of smoke. He was trying to cut down, but he really needed one right now. If only he and Cheryl could have kept on talking about whether or not to buy Walt's skidder. He would have to tell Walt something pretty soon, or he would sell the skidder to somebody else.

Dorrie came up the basement steps and stopped in the doorway. "Dwayne," she said, "I'll get you for this."

"Dad," Dwayne said. "See. I told you this would happen."

"Sit down here, Dorrie, and tell us whether you skipped school today or not. This doesn't have anythin to do with Dwayne."

"He said he wouldn't tell on me, and then he did."

"Dorrie," Cheryl said. "Stop tryin to get Dwayne in trouble. Did you skip school today?"

Dorrie wouldn't look at any of them. She looked down at the table where her hands lay folded in front of her. "Not the whole day."

"How much then?"

"I didn't leave til after lunch. All I missed was English and study hall and science."

"That's a lot."

"I was goin downstreet to buy Dwayne a Christmas present." She gave him a fierce look.

"Did you tell anybody at school you were leavin?"

"No, because they would have told me not to."

"Oh Doreen," Cheryl said. "What are we goin to do with you?"

"I don't know, Ma. Please don't be mad. I won't do it any more."

Conrad said, "You bet you won't, because we're groundin you til Christmas vacation."

"Don't do that, Dad. I'll be good."

"How'd you get home?"

"I went with Kim and Sandra, and they brought me home. Honestly, we didn't do anythin bad. We were lookin for Christmas presents. That's all."

It wasn't much of an offense. Conrad might have let her off if he hadn't been so sick of dealing with other people's problems. He said, "You're goin to come straight home from school on the bus every day. And you'd better be here, because we're goin to call and make sure you are."

"I'll be good, Dad."

"If you are, maybe we'll let you leave home on the weekends."

Dorrie burst into tears. She jumped up and ran to her bedroom and slammed the door so hard the whole house shook.

Cheryl said, "Oh, Conrad, maybe that's too much. After all...."

Dwayne was still sitting at the table. Conrad said, "Dwayne, go finish your schoolwork and get to bed."

"But it's early, Dad."

"I don't care. Get goin."

When Dwayne was safely out of hearing, Conrad said, "It's all right, Cheryl. We can ease up on her over the weekend."

"She was just Christmas shoppin. That's not bad."

"That's what *she* says. We don't know any more about it than that. She's gettin to the age where she could start doin some really dangerous things. We have to watch out."

"I know."

"And we can't ask Dwayne to spy for us. We have to call up and talk to her on the phone. Then we'll know she's here."

"Okay. I can do that."

"We'd both better do it, and at random times, so she can't try any tricks."

"Okay, but I think we're bein too tough on her. She hasn't done anythin bad."

"That's good. We'll catch her *before* she does anythin that could hurt her. Isn't that better?"

"I suppose so. Can I go and see if she's all right now?"

"Okay."

Later, when they were in their room getting ready for bed, Conrad said, "I wish we'd had a chance to talk about Walt's skidder."

Cheryl had just taken off her sweater. "Oh," she said. I forgot all about it." She sat down on the bed in her slip with the sweater in her hand.

She looked so lovely, so round and pink. Conrad wanted to sit down beside her and put his arms around her. But he still had on the clothes he'd worn all day in the feed store, and they were full of grain dust, so he didn't. He just stood there looking at her, wondering what to say.

"I was hopin we were goin to be able to get the money together to put a new roof on the house next summer." She sat there, folding her sweater and not looking at him. "At least the front half where it's so bad."

"I know, honey. I want to do that too."

She looked up at him then, and there were tears in her eyes.

Conrad just melted. "Oh honey. Let's forget about it. I don't mind workin at the feed store. It's okay." He sat down beside her and put his arms around her and kissed her round shoulder and her cheek. "And next summer we *will* be able to do the roof. Maybe we can even save enough to take a little trip some place."

She smiled at him and wiped her eyes.

"Where would you like to go?"

"I'm sorry, Conrad. I guess it's just Dorrie that has me so upset. I know you hate workin at the feed store."

"It ain't that. I've been there for so long, and nothin ever changes. It's a dead end, like it was for Dad. But I ain't complainin, because I've got you and the kids, and that's enough for anybody. Dry your eyes, and forget about it, and don't worry about Dorrie. Like you said, she didn't do anythin bad."

She kissed him then. He could feel the wetness of her tears on his face, and he thought how much he loved her. He also thought how he could take it a little farther, but he felt grubby from work, and it was late, and they were both tired.

Later on, when Conrad was almost asleep, she said, "Conrad? Are you awake?"

"Umm. I guess so."

"Well, listen then."

"Okay," he managed to say, although he could feel himself sliding back toward sleep.

She raised up on one elbow. He could feel her looking at him. "Let's do it, Conrad."

"What?"

"Let's buy Walt's skidder."

"Really?" He was awake now. He could just make out the curve of her face in the darkness.

"I mean it. We can swing it. I've been lyin here thinkin about it. We'll still have my benefits and my salary, and maybe if you do really good with it, like Walt's doin, we can even do the roof next summer."

"Oh honey," Conrad said. "You're the best. You've been stayin awake, thinkin how we could do this, because you knew I wanted to. That's so sweet." He put his arms around her, intending to pull her closer, but she resisted.

"Before you tell Walt anythin, you'll have to make sure John'll take you back if it doesn't work out."

"Oh sure. He'll do that."

"But you've got to ask him straight out, so you know you can count on it if the loggin doesn't work out."

"All right."

"If John says yes, I think we ought to do it."

"Oh honey, I love you," he said, as he was falling into sleep.

Chapter 8

Lena had just lifted Georgia out of the bathtub when Beebee started barking downstairs. Jimmy was sitting on the bathroom rug, wrapped up in a towel. He said, "Dada. Dada home."

She draped a towel around Georgia and went to the bathroom door and shouted, "We're up here, Jerry. I'm not done with the kids yet."

A minute later she looked up from putting on Jimmy's diapers to see Nora standing in the doorway. "Oh," she said. "You surprised me. I didn't know you were here. Is Jerry downstairs?"

"I didn't see him. What shall I do to help?"

Georgia said, "You don't need to dress *me*, Nora. I can do it myself."

"I'll watch you then. Show me how you do it."

Georgia dropped the towel and picked up her nightgown and began trying to figure out which was the part that went over her head. Nora stood watching.

"Jerry said he'd be back by six. I was planning to have them all ready for bed so you wouldn't have to do it."

"I don't mind. We'll have fun, won't we, Georgia?"

Georgia nodded. "You can go away, Mommy. Nora's here now." Her cheeks were pink from the hot bath, and her hair hung around her face in damp curls. Her nightgown was twisted under her arms so that her bottom half was bare.

Lena sat back on her heels and pulled Georgia down onto her lap. She hugged and kissed her and then stood her up again and straightened her nightgown. "You'll be a good girl for Aunt Nora, won't you?" she said.

By that time Jimmy, had squirmed to his feet and was trying to escape out of the bathroom. Nora caught him and held him.

"It's great having you home again, Nora. Do you really think you'll stay?"

Nora handed Jimmy down to her so she could finish dressing him. "Sure," she said, and then with an edge in her voice, "I don't see why not. It's my home too, remember?"

Georgia hugged her around the knees. "You could sleep over at our house, Nora. Grammy and Granddad wouldn't care."

Jimmy kept trying to wriggle away. Lena had to hold him down with one hand while she tried to put him into his pajamas. She said, "I wonder what could have happened to Jerry. You didn't see his car out front when you drove up, did you?"

"No. I'm sure he's not here. Where'd he go, anyway? I thought he had the day off."

"He was supposed to. There was something he had to do. A meeting? I can't remember what he said, but he promised to be back before six. What time is it now?"

"I didn't get here until six-thirty, so it's after that."

Lena helped Jimmy stand up. "There," she said. "You're all done. Let's go downstairs." She wanted to look out the front window to see for herself if Jerry's car was in the driveway. She really believed she would see it there. And at the same time, she didn't want Nora to notice that she didn't believe her, and she didn't want Nora to see that she was worried about Jerry and what he was doing. It was important to her that no one knew that, although she didn't know why.

"But, Mommy, I haven't brushed my teeth yet."

"That's okay. You can do it later. Maybe Aunt Nora will give you a snack before you go to bed." She scooped Jimmy up and started down the stairs carrying him. Georgia took Nora's hand, and they followed. They were too close behind for Lena to take a look out the window without being observed.

She set Jimmy down in the corner of the couch and went out to the kitchen to get him a cup of milk. Over her shoulder she told them that Georgia could stay up and see Jerry, but she was going to get Jimmy some milk and then put him to bed. She half expected to see Jerry in the kitchen, but of course he wasn't there.

By the time she got back to the living room with the milk, Nora was sitting on the couch with a big pile of Georgia's books on her lap, and Georgia and Jimmy were settling down, one on each side of her.

Lena picked Jimmy up, squirming and kicking. "Jimmy, wait. Jimmy, stop it. Listen to me." It made her even more anxious for Jerry to get home. Besides worrying what he was doing, besides wanting to spend some time with him, she really needed to get away for a little while. She sat down on the couch beside Nora. "Okay, Jimmy, you can listen to the story while you drink your milk, but after that you have to go to bed."

Nora started to read. Lena held the cup for Jimmy and wondered if it would get easier when Jimmy got a little older so that he and Georgia could play with each other. She thought back to when she and Nora were little. There were two years between them too, almost the same amount as between Georgia and Jimmy. The way she remembered it, she and Nora were always together. Mom said they fought all the time, but what Lena remembered was all the things they used to do together.

What was the matter with her anyway? Here she was sitting beside Nora and holding Jimmy in her arms. But she couldn't enjoy it because she was so anxious for Jerry to get home that she couldn't sit still. She wanted to spend the evening with him. She wanted to get some of the Christmas shopping done. It was funny that Jerry was so late. She was trying hard not to think that he might have had an accident. How could she take care of two children alone? Suppose he was seeing someone else? But she didn't even want to think such thoughts. It was unfair of her. He wouldn't think like that about her.

If he didn't get home soon, it would be too late to go. She couldn't take Georgia and Jimmy shopping for their own Christmas presents. Then there would be no surprises. She pictured herself walking through the toy department with Jerry. They would hold hands and laugh together and talk about the children.

Jimmy had finished his milk and was snuggled down in her arms, half asleep. Every so often she leaned down to bury her nose in his soft, wispy hair, to smell his baby smell, so different from Georgia's. She knew she ought to carry him up to bed. She kept putting it off because she was so comfortable, and because she loved holding him in her arms, even though there was another piece of her that wanted to be free of all the clinging and the snuggling for a while.

The door opened, and Jerry came in on a wave of cold air. Nora stopped reading and looked up. Georgia jumped toward Jerry, saying, "Daddy, Daddy," so loud that Jimmy shifted around and tried to sit up, but his eyes opened white, with his eyeballs still rolled up in his head, and he sank back against Lena, asleep again.

Nora looked at Jimmy's eyes, and then at Lena, and they both laughed.

"Pick me up, Daddy. Pick me up," Georgia was saying. She held onto Jerry's legs and jumped up and down.

"I thought you'd be in bed by this time, kitten," Jerry said as he lifted Georgia.

"No thanks to you, Jerry," was what Lena was thinking, but she said, "I told her she could wait up for you. Where were you, anyway?"

"I had this meeting. I couldn't help it."

Lena stood up with Jimmy limp in her arms. "He's finally asleep. I'll go put him down." She didn't want Nora to see how illogically angry she felt at Jerry, when she had been wishing for him to get there right up until the moment he arrived. Some new factor came into it the minute he walked through the door. It was a piece that she always forgot to take into account, something she always forgot to think about.

When she came back into the room a few minutes later, everyone was in exactly the same place. Jerry was talking to Georgia, who was still in his arms, and Nora was sitting on the couch watching them, with the book on her lap.

"It's after seven-thirty, Jerry. We've got to hurry if we're going to do anything before the stores close. You still want to go, don't you?" She tried unsuccessfully to keep the hard edge out of her voice. She was so angry at him that she knew they wouldn't have any fun, but staying home would be worse, and she had to get some Christmas shopping done.

Jerry looked surprised by her tone of voice, and that annoyed her even more. "Whatever you want to do," he said. "It *is* getting late."

"I want to go too. Can I, Daddy?"

"No, of course not, Georgia," Lena said crossly. "It's your bedtime. And anyway, we're going Christmas shopping for *you*."

"If it's for me, I should come too. Isn't that right, Daddy? Can't I come with you please?"

Jerry kissed her and set her down. "You heard your mom. She's the boss."

"Oh Daddy, please."

"Georgia, stop it." Lena looked at Nora. "Is it okay with you if we go? We could skip it."

"It's fine," Nora said. "Don't worry about Georgia. We'll have a good time. Come on, Georgia. Let's finish the book."

They left right away. Jerry hadn't taken his coat off, and Lena grabbed hers without even combing her hair or looking in the mirror. She was so angry at Jerry that she didn't care what she looked like. She had pictured the wonderful time they were going to have together, and he had spoiled the whole thing.

It was cold outside. Before she was off the porch, Lena was wishing she had stayed long enough to put on her boots and find a hat to wear. But she didn't want to go back inside because Nora would ask her what was wrong, and so much was wrong that she didn't want to be asked. At least the Christmas money was in her purse. She slung it over her shoulder and buttoned her coat. They walked in silent, single file to Jerry's car. He didn't even notice that she was mad. She opened the door. It was still warm inside, and it smelled like cigarettes, the way it always did. When Jerry turned on the ignition, the radio blasted out country music. Jerry turned it off quickly. "Sorry," he said. "I know you don't like that station."

"It's all right. I don't care." She could feel him looking at her, but she didn't turn her head. She stared straight through the windshield at the back of Nora's car.

"Lena, I know you're mad at me."

She shrugged, not looking around.

"Maybe we ought to talk about it?"

It sounded like a question. She didn't even shrug in reply.

He pulled the car out onto the street, but he didn't drive away. "Maybe we should skip this trip and spend the time talking instead. What do you think?"

"Oh come on, Jerry. We've wasted enough time already."

"Damn it! I don't even know where we're going."

"The Bargain Center, I guess, unless you have a better idea," she said without turning her head. "They have the biggest toy department."

Jerry stepped on the gas. "All right. We can go there. But you know what I think?" Now he was the one who wasn't looking around, and he didn't wait for her to answer either. "I think I ought to tell you where I was tonight."

Lena didn't say anything.

"I know you're mad because I was late getting home. Don't you want to know what I was doing?"

"No. I don't," she said quickly. "I don't want to hear some long excuse about how you couldn't help it, and it wasn't your fault." She was conscious of the fact that she was over-reacting. "This evening is already ruined, and we never spend any time together anymore. Telling me why you were late would just make the whole thing worse. And what's the matter with the telephone anyway? If you had called and told me you were going to be late, I wouldn't have been waiting and worrying and wondering all that time."

Jerry opened his mouth to say something and shut it again, and they were both quiet, thinking their own bitter thoughts until they got to the Bargain Center. Jerry parked the car and turned it off and looked at her. "Lena...."

Before he could say any more, she got out and slammed the door and started walking across the parking lot. After a few steps, she could hear him behind her hurrying to catch up.

They went through the big glass doors together and stood blinking under the fluorescent lights. Without saying anything, Lena started down an aisle toward the back, where the toys were, and Jerry followed, pushing a cart. Lena could hear it rattling behind her. She didn't look around, and she didn't wait for him to catch up. She knew she was being unfair, but she couldn't make herself act better.

When they got to the toy section, Lena heard Jerry turn down a different aisle, and she was instantly sorry she had been so unbending. She didn't know what she wanted, but she knew she didn't want him to go away. Still, she couldn't make herself follow him.

She was halfway down the next aisle, standing in front of the dolls, when Jerry called her to come see what he had found. She went reluctantly. She knew Georgia wanted a doll, and one or two of the ones on the shelf in front of her might do.

She said, "Okay," trying to keep the annoyance out of her voice.

When she got to Jerry, he held out a little bench with pegs in it. "Look at this. Jimmy will love it. He's always pounding on things."

"Yes. I guess he would." She took it out of Jerry's hand. "But it's so flimsy. Jimmy would break it in no time. Maybe we can find him one made out of wood, not plastic. One that would last better."

"I guess you're right." He hesitated. "I hate to put it back."

"We can always get it later if we can't find a better one. This one would be worse than nothing. Jimmy would love it, and then he would break it."

She went back to the dolls. After a minute, she could hear Jerry's empty cart coming down the aisle toward her. She couldn't remember which dolls had looked like they might do. "They're all so awful and cheap looking," she said when Jerry came up beside her.

"That's because they *are* cheap. But the kids won't care. Sometimes I think they like cheap things better."

"Well, I don't," she said crossly. Even when he was just on the other side of the aisle, Lena could fantasize about how she would like to spend some time with him, but as soon as he was there beside her, everything he did rubbed her the wrong way.

"Come on, honey. Pick one out. There must be one that Georgia would like. We could get that much done, anyhow."

"No. I don't think so. We'll have to go somewhere else, and it's too late tonight."

"What's down the other aisles? Maybe there are better toys somewhere else."

"I guess we ought to look, but I don't think we'll find anything."

They walked down the other aisles without seeing anything to stop for. Nothing seemed right. They left the store at eight-thirty without buying a thing. Jerry hadn't had any dinner because of his meeting. He wanted to stop, but Lena said she didn't think it would be fair to Nora. The real reason was that she didn't want to sit across the table from him, watching him eat. She was still too angry, even though she wasn't sure she could say what it was about.

Nora was in the kitchen when they got home. "Hi," she said. "Where are the packages?"

"We didn't find a thing. It was a complete waste of time. Plus Jerry never had any supper. How was Georgia?"

Nora was putting cream in her cup of coffee. "She was fine as soon as you left. I knew she would be. It sounds like we had a better time than you did."

"We shouldn't have even bothered. It was too late to start. You know? Sometimes it's hard to change gears."

"I know. It's hard for me too."

"Really? I always think you do that kind of thing so much better than I do." She looked down at Nora sitting at the kitchen table and felt like hugging her. It was so nice to have her company. She didn't say it because she didn't want Nora to think anything was wrong. *She* was the one who helped Nora. Nora might not like it the other way around. And Nora didn't look very strong right now. She looked tired, and her skin was gray under the harsh light from the overhead lamp.

Lena wasn't going to say anything, but before she could stop herself, she said, "Nora, are you okay? I noticed that you hardly ate any Thanksgiving dinner." She didn't say that Georgia told her that Nora threw up, because she didn't want to involve Georgia. "Are you feeling sick?"

"No, not at all. Do you think Mom noticed anything?"

"I don't know. Probably not. She was busy with her dinner, making sure everything was cooked just right." Before Lena had finished the sentence, a new idea had popped into her head, and she knew. Nora had cancer and was dying. The idea was so sudden and painful that her eyes filled up with tears, and she had to turn away quickly so Nora wouldn't suspect that she knew.

Just then Jerry came into the room. He didn't even say hello to Nora. He opened the refrigerator and said, "What's there to eat?" over his shoulder.

"Will a sandwich be enough?" Lena asked, trying to keep the hostility out of her voice.

Jerry sat down at the table and lit a cigarette. "That would be fine," he said. "Don't worry about me. I'll get it in a few minutes."

Lena pretended not to hear. She got out the bread and sandwich meat and cheese.

Jerry blew smoke right into Nora's face, but Nora pretended not to notice. "Did Georgia give you a hard time?"

"No. We had fun. I read to her, and then she told me a story. She was so cute. I hope I didn't keep her up too late. She hasn't been in bed very long."

Jerry said, "She's already sound asleep. They both are."

Nora looked over at Lena to see if she heard what Jerry said, and Lena kept her head bent over the sandwich she was making as though she hadn't heard anything. Easy to feel like kissing them in their sleep when you haven't been struggling with them all day long.

After Nora left, Jerry sat at the table, smoking and ignoring his sandwich.

Lena felt a perverse need to be a dutiful wife and sit with him even though she wanted to go to bed. Finally she said, "Aren't you going to eat, after all?"

Jerry slowly and carefully stubbed out his cigarette and then looked at her. "I'm sorry, honey. I know you're mad at me because I kept you waiting."

"I'm not mad. I think you're an asshole, but I'm not mad."

"We can do it again."

"It's not like you have all that many free nights, Jerry."

"I can't help that. It's my job. But it wouldn't have to be at night. We could go any morning."

"And take the kids with us?"

"We could ask Nora again."

"We can't just use Nora like a servant. She won't let me give her any money, so it isn't like she's a babysitter. It's a favor, and besides I don't think Nora's okay. I think she's sick or something. I'm really worried about her."

"She looked all right to me."

There were several things Lena could think of to say to that, but she had already gotten away with calling him an asshole, and she didn't want to push her luck, so she snapped her jaws together tight and said nothing.

Jerry picked up his sandwich and started to eat. The sound of his chewing was loud in the quiet room. Lena sat across from him, but she didn't look up. She was thinking about Nora.

After what seemed like a long time, Jerry said, "Honey, there's something we have to talk about."

"Oh, what?" she said without really listening to what he said.

"Lena, I have to talk to you about something serious."

"Oh God. It's late. Can't it wait?"

"Well, I....I mean...." He looked surprised.

"It's about money, isn't it?" she asked, sure she was right, and sure she could understand much better in the morning.

Jerry was looking down at his plate, pushing crumbs of bread around with his finger. "No," he said. "It's not about money, but it can wait...for a while, anyway. We do have to talk though."

Lena felt a twinge of fear at that. She wished she could see his eyes. If it wasn't about money, what was it about? She almost asked and then thought the better of it. She wasn't sure she wanted to know. She could hear the clock ticking. She could even hear Jerry's finger sliding across the plate.

"Aren't you worried about Nora, Jerry?"

"No. Why?"

"I just wondered if that was what you thought we ought to talk about?"

"About Nora?"

"I thought you might have noticed that she's not all right."

"I haven't noticed anything."

"But, Jerry, don't you think it's funny that she came back home all of a sudden? I mean, she's young and single. She used to love living in Boston. Why would she quit her job and come back to Severance?"

"Maybe she stopped liking it."

"Oh Jerry, come on." He refused to see what was so obvious. She could feel herself getting angry again. She swallowed it down.

"I don't see why people can't change their minds."

"Well, they can, but this is different. She's pale, and she looks awful, and she comes home for no reason. I know what that means."

"Did you ask her?"

"I can't. It's too awful."

He looked up at her, waiting for more.

"She has cancer, and she has come home to die." She spoke precisely, trying to control the emotion in her voice.

All Jerry could say was, "What?"

"It's the only thing that makes any sense." She stood and picked up Jerry's plate and carried it to the sink. She had to move around, had to do something. "You see why I can't ask her," she said with her back to him. She could feel the tears pooling behind her eyes. "She probably already knows it can't be operated on. Or maybe she doesn't want to go through all the torture cancer patients have to go through and then end up dying anyway. She's probably decided she doesn't want an operation." The tears were beginning to overflow. She turned around to look at Jerry. "That would be just like Nora. How could I ask her and make her have to tell me all that?"

"Aw, honey," Jerry said. He came over to where she stood by the sink and put his arms around her. "I bet it isn't true. You don't *know* anything. Have you asked your mom and dad?"

"I can't. How could I? I mean, I *know* there's something wrong. I mean, tonight all I did was say it was great to have her home, and she kind of snapped at me, so I didn't dare ask her any more....oh Jerry, I'm so scared." Right then she couldn't even remember why she had been angry at him. She was just glad he was there, holding her.

"It's okay, baby. It's going to be okay."

"I don't think so. There's something wrong. How can it be all right?"

Jerry didn't say anything. He just hugged her.

"I don't believe Mom and Dad will be able to handle it if Nora dies."

"Maybe you're just making the whole thing up, honey. Nora looked fine to me."

"Call it woman's intuition," she said in a muffled voice with her face still pressed against Jerry's chest. "I know something is wrong, and it must be something bad or she would tell me."

Jerry hugged her tighter and kissed her on top of the head. She stopped crying because it felt so safe in his arms. Of course, that didn't mean Nora was all right, but maybe she should try to put it out of her mind until she knew something definite, until Nora herself told her what was wrong. The only thing she could really do was to keep giving Nora good chances to talk, so she could tell her if she wanted to.

Jerry held her tight against him and said, "Come on, honey. Let's go to bed." Then he pushed her away so he could see her face and laughed and said, "It's getting late," and they both laughed, because they both knew they weren't going to bed to sleep but to make love, and it had been several weeks since they both wanted to at the same time.

They went around the downstairs, turning off all the lights. Lena let her mind pass quickly over how she had felt earlier. She didn't dare look too closely at how angry she had been at Jerry. She didn't want those feelings to come back now to spoil their lovemaking, and she didn't want to think about how scared she had been when he said they had to talk. She wasn't sure how much she had been afraid for herself and how much was because she was afraid for Nora.

They went up the stairs holding hands. Nearly at the top she stumbled and caught herself. She said, "Jerry...." and then put her hand over her mouth. They both stood still, not even breathing, and for a minute or so they heard nothing, and it seemed as though they were going to get away with it. Then there was a fretful, sleepy, little moan, and then the crying started, cross and only half awake.

"Who's that?"

"It's Georgia," she said. "I'll have to go. Maybe she won't really wake up if I hurry."

"They were both asleep when I looked at them a little while ago." He squeezed her hand before he let go of it. "Don't be long."

"I'll try." They were both whispering. "Don't you go to sleep before I get there."

"I won't."

She ducked into the bathroom ahead of Jerry and got a glass of water for Georgia, but Georgia was too close to sleep to drink it. She whimpered and reached up to hold onto Lena without even opening her eyes. She almost spilled the water into her bed. She must have had a bad dream. Lena tried patting her back and telling her it was all right, but it was no use. She lay down beside Georgia and wrapped her arms around her, and after a while Georgia got calm enough to be quiet, even though she still breathed in great, quivering sighs for a while.

Some time later, Lena woke up herself. Georgia was so soundly asleep that she didn't even shift around when Lena pulled her arm out from underneath her. Lena brushed her teeth and put in her diaphragm, but when she got to the bedroom, Jerry was asleep with the light on. He was snoring. She tried to wake him up, but she didn't try very hard because she felt too sleepy herself. She got into bed and turned out the light, and Jerry turned over and wrapped his arms around her in his sleep, and in some ways that was even better than if she had been able to wake him up.

Chapter 9

After Nora left, George and Laurie stayed at the dinner table, even though they were finished eating. It was peaceful. George sat there thinking how nice it was that they could be together without feeling the need to talk.

But Laurie was restless. She kept fiddling with the silverware. Then she said, "Nora didn't eat much."

"No? I didn't notice."

"Oh, George, when do you ever notice?"

"What's that supposed to mean?" He had a sinking feeling that he was about to hear something he didn't want to know.

"You're so buried in your work. You *never* see what's going on right in front of you."

That was the argument she always pulled out, the unanswerable one, because how could he justify himself when she was talking about something he didn't see? He stood and picked up his plate and the bowl of peas and started toward the kitchen. If he said a word, it would make the fight even more likely to blow up. He sighed. It was probably inevitable, no matter what he did.

Laurie came through the swinging door before it had a chance to stop moving. George pretended not to notice. He was busy trying to make room in the refrigerator for the bowl of leftover peas.

Laurie set her dishes by the sink and turned to watch him. By that time he had found a place for the peas and had no more excuse for keeping his head in the refrigerator. He had to stand back and close the door.

"I'm sorry I said that, George. But have you really not noticed a thing?"

"About Nora?"

"Yes, of course. Do you think she got fired from her job?"

"Laurie, for heaven's sake." He was shocked. "Why?"

"I don't know. I guess it's not very likely. I just know there's something going on. I'm trying to figure out what it could be. Has she said anything to you?"

"Only that she was glad to be home again. And I didn't ask for specifics. *I'm* glad she's back too. I don't want her to think about leaving again."

"That's another thing. She said she was going to find a job in Severance, but I don't think she's really trying. She didn't go out of the house at all today."

George said, "I'm going to get some more dishes. I'll be right back."

Laurie turned to the sink and started to rinse off a plate. "Oh, damn," she said. "The dishwasher's full."

George didn't wait to hear more. When he came back with another load of dirty dishes, Laurie was taking the clean ones out of the dishwasher and stacking them up on the kitchen table.

George went over to the sink and put some soap and water on the dishrag.

Laurie turned to watch. "What are you doing?"

"Just trying to get this spot off my pants before it sets up. They're clean except for this." He didn't say it had been bothering him since he dropped a forkful of potatoes in his lap at dinner.

"Is it greasy?"

"Not too bad. I think I can get it."

Laurie acted as though he was a slob, but he had always hated having spots on his clothes, even when he was a child. He and Cal were very different that way.

He rinsed the soap off and dried the place as well as he could with the dish towel. Then he picked up a stack of plates and took it to the dining room hutch. It gave him a chance to think for a few more minutes. He didn't know whether he was worried about Nora or not, but he had noticed that he was treating her very carefully. When he saw that, he'd told himself that it was because he had forgotten how much he loved her, how precious she was to him.

The hutch was an antique, made of dark, wide boards, irregular, like the floor of an old house. The dishes sat in rows behind small panes of wavy, uneven glass. He and Laurie bought the hutch a few years after they got married, when Nora was a baby. They paid $700 for it back then. It was much more than they could afford, but Laurie had to have it. At the time it had shocked him. It seemed almost like a sickness to want something so much. Because he didn't want anyone to know how he felt, he had managed to get the money together. And now that so many years had gone by, and it was still something that was important to her, he was glad he had managed to buy it for her, even though he was no closer to understanding why she cared.

He put the salt and pepper shakers back with the silver sugar bowl on the lazy Susan in the center of the dining room table. As he went through the swinging door, bringing another load of dirty dishes to the sink, he realized that he hadn't thought about Nora.

"This is the last of the dishes," he said.

"Good. Bring them over. I'm almost done with these."

George set the dirty dishes by the sink and went to the table for another stack of clean ones. "I'm sure Nora would have told us if there had been any trouble with her job," he said over his shoulder, as he picked up the dishes. Then he left the room without giving Laurie a chance to reply. Nora seemed fine to him, didn't she? He remembered that Lena had asked him about Nora last week. Had she and Laurie been talking to each other? Or had they both noticed something that he had missed? He hated to think he would miss something important. He preferred to think that Laurie was giving him a bad time about not paying attention because she wanted someone other than herself to blame when she got in a bad mood. Thinking that, he could believe that Nora was fine.

When he got back to the kitchen, Laurie was scrubbing the counter by the sink.

"I thought you were almost finished," he said.

Laurie turned to look at him, but her hand was still on the sponge on the counter. "She had an upset stomach just the other day, and she's put on weight, and her skin looks blotchy." It all came out in a rush. "Do you think she's pregnant?"

"Oh no, of course not. What a thing to think."

"And her clothes are terrible. Everything she wears is so baggy and shapeless." She turned back to the counter. "I knew that's what you'd say," she said, scrubbing hard. The words came out strained by her clenched jaw. Her brown hair swung across her face with the movement of her head. He couldn't see her expression.

He wanted to say, "Why did you ask me then?" But it would only escalate the impending fight. He kept getting drawn back to the edge of it. "How could she be?" he asked instead. "I mean, she doesn't even have a boyfriend."

"How should *I* know? She hasn't told me a thing." She ran some water on the sponge and squeezed it out and wiped the counter with hard, angry strokes. "Nobody tells me anything. All I know is that something's not right." She turned out the light over the sink and looked at him, twisting her mouth into an ugly, hurt smile. "It would be awful. She'd have to get an abortion. What would everyone think?"

"You don't need to worry about that. It's not like it used to be when we...I mean, nobody thinks much about...I mean, since the '60s nobody cares if a girl gets pregnant when she isn't married."

Laurie's smile twisted even more as she listened to him. It was painful to look at. "Come on," George said, "Let's go sit in the den."

"All right." But she said it wearily, as though she was only coming as a favor to him.

They went a few steps together toward the swinging door, and then Laurie put her hand on his arm and stopped him. "I do," she said.

"You do what?" he asked, thinking she looked old, or maybe tired.

"I care if Nora's pregnant when she isn't married."

He held the door open for her. Part of him was thinking, "Tired. It's because she's tired, and worried too." And another voice inside his head was saying, "Women. They are a complete mystery to me and always will be, even though for years I've lived with three that I love. But you can love something without understanding it." Out loud, as he walked down the hall behind her, he said, "But, Laurie, that's what *we* did."

She turned around in the doorway to the den. There were tears in her eyes. "Oh, *how* can you say that? It wasn't the same at all."

"I'm sorry, honey. All I meant was that you got pregnant too, before we...."

"But we *loved* each other. You make it sound dirty. You make it sound like it was all my fault." He started to put his arms around her, but she pulled away and went to where she always sat, at the far end of the cream-colored couch. "Besides," she said, wiping her eyes with her hands and wiping her hands on her skirt. "No one knew about us. Why, Mom doesn't suspect to this day."

George sat down in the red leather armchair. It was the only dark piece of furniture in the room. Laurie was always threatening to get rid of it because the seat sagged and the leather was ripped and scarred. But the sags conformed to his shape and were his own, and the fact that Laurie wanted to throw it away made him appreciate it even more.

"Shall I turn on the TV?"

"Not for me, thanks," he said. "I haven't finished today's paper yet."

"Well, I won't then. I don't want it for myself." Her hand reached out toward her book, which was lying open and face down on the seat beside her. The careless way she treated books was something that grated on him, although he could never have told her. He unfolded the paper and began to read.

He had only read a few paragraphs when Laurie sighed, flopped her book down, and stood up.

"Where are you going?"

"Honestly, George, how can you read in the dark? You'll ruin your eyes, if you haven't already." She walked over to his chair and switched on the light that stood beside him.

"Oh, thanks," he said. "I could have done that. You didn't need to get up."

"It's because you grew up without electricity. You think it's normal to read in the dark."

George hated it when she explained why he was the way he was. And how did she know anyway? Maybe his eyes didn't need as much light as hers did. Maybe his years without electricity had taught him how to use his eyes better than she could. But he didn't want to get into a long discussion, so he said, "Thanks. That's much better."

A few minutes later, he felt her looking at him again. She sighed. He carefully didn't look up, hoping she would go back to her book. But then she sighed a second time. He lowered the paper and looked at her. "What's the matter?" he asked, trying to sound sympathetic.

"It's nothing," Laurie said. "Or not much anyway."

"Something's bothering you."

"Well...yes." She thought a minute. "Yes it is. But I wasn't going to say anything because I knew you wouldn't like it."

"If something's bothering you, Laurie, I'd like to know. Maybe I could help you with it." And all the time he was thinking that he was crazy to get into it, that every time he opened his mouth, he got in deeper.

For a minute Laurie didn't say anything. She kicked off her shoes and folded her legs under her, so she was sitting on her feet. Then she smoothed back her hair and folded her hands in her lap, and all the time, George could feel his hands on the newspaper. He longed to be reading it.

"All right, if you really want to know, it's about Cal."

"Cal?" he said in surprise. He had thought of some things that might be bothering her, but he hadn't thought of Cal.

"Yes," she said. "We haven't heard anything since he left the hospital."

"True."

"And the only reason we knew anything then was because you were so nice about going up to visit him."

"You don't need to let that bother you, honey. Cal's always been that way." He lifted his paper slightly, thinking he had answered her worry, hinting that they could both go back to reading now.

"That's the whole point. Don't you see? Over and over you let Cal take advantage of you, and you never learn."

"What you're saying is that I'm stupid," he said, and he rattled the paper and raised it up in front of his face. At least he could pretend to read. There was a story by Jerry on the front page.

But she was determined to get into a fight, no matter what he did. "You don't have to get defensive about it. That's why I wasn't going to say anything. I knew that was the way you would take it."

"What do you mean by that?" he asked, while the real question was why he always let himself be drawn into it.

"See. You're not willing to listen to what I say. You just…."

"I'm listening. I've been listening right along. I heard you call me stupid. What else do you want me to listen to?"

"Oh George. I wasn't talking about you. I was talking about Cal. But you didn't want to hear it."

"Yes I did," he said, lowering the paper again, trying to act convincingly unemotional. He stood up. He usually didn't drink at home, unless they had friends over or something, but he felt the need of it tonight. It would help him keep calm and out of the fight. "Just wait. I'll be right back. I'm going to get myself a drink." He didn't ask her if she wanted one too.

He hurried out of the room, put some Scotch in a glass, and took it to the lavatory to add some water. He decided to skip getting any ice. It was better not to call attention to his drink with the sound of clinking ice cubes. But it really didn't matter, because she was going to be mad about something, maybe about everything. Nothing he did or didn't do would make any difference. Looked at in that light, it was probably a good time to have a drink in front of her.

He walked back into the den and sat down. Laurie was reading, or pretending to. She didn't look up, but she sighed.

"I'm sorry for the interruption, Laurie. Now, tell me what you were going to say about Cal."

She looked at him then, just as he was putting the drink to his lips.

"Please," he said. "I'm sorry it's troubling you. Maybe I can do something."

"You could stop drinking, George. That would be a big help." Her voice was cold.

"What?"

"You heard what I said."

"I thought you wanted to talk about Cal."

"Well, there's that too, but this is more important, and anyway, it all fits together."

George deliberately took another drink, watching Laurie's face over the rim of the glass as he did so. He could feel the soothing, all the way down inside of him. He took a slow breath and set the drink on the floor by the leg of his chair. "Don't let's start on that, Laurie. It isn't a problem for you, or for Nora, or for Lena, and it certainly isn't a problem for me, so why shouldn't I have a drink once in a while? It's not hurting anybody."

"George...."

"Stop right now, Laurie. I don't want to hear it." He felt he was being quite authoritative and that he was in the right. She was doing everything she could to make a fight. But the drink comforted him, and with it he was able to keep control. "Now, what were you saying about Cal?"

"It's just that Cal always treats you badly. Again and again you do something nice for him, but he's never grateful."

"I don't know about that. And anyway, all I did was stop up to the hospital a few times. He'd have done the same for me."

"I don't think so. The truth is you give and Cal takes. There. I've said it. It has been that way your whole life."

He sighed. "You don't know that, Laurie."

"I can guess. I can put two and two together from what I've seen. Look at what happened when your mother died. You let Cal take everything. You *gave* it to him."

"There wasn't much of anything."

"There was your parents' farm. You gave him the whole thing."

"It wasn't worth much—and only half was mine to give. Eighty acres of hillside fields and a house and barn that were falling down."

"People are always coming up here from New York and New Jersey, and that's just exactly what they're looking for."

"That's true now, but it wasn't then. Ma died before all those down-country people started coming up here. It wasn't worth much back then."

"See, George, that's just like you. If you hadn't been in such a hurry to give it away, you would have owned it when it got valuable."

Now it was George's turn to sigh. "I don't see what you think I ought to have done. Should I have forced my own brother to sell the family farm—the farm he'd lived on his entire life? *You* didn't want to live there. We could have built a house at the top of the ridge, but you didn't want to live so far out. Remember?"

"I wanted the girls to grow up in town." She picked at her skirt. "You did too. Have you forgotten that?"

"No. I haven't forgotten. I *have* wondered if we did the right thing. They had lots of friends and activities, but I think they missed a piece of their heritage."

"I'm not saying it was wrong to give Cal your share of the farm." She was careful not to look at him. "All I meant to say is that Cal is so ungrateful. You've done a lot for him. You'd think he would treat you better than he does. You're the one who ought to be angry, and yet, he always acts like we did something to him."

"Laurie...."

"Oh, I don't want to talk about it. I won't say any more. I'm sorry. Everything's been rubbing me the wrong way. It's because I'm so worried about Nora."

"What does Lena say?"

"About Cal?"

"No, of course not. About what's wrong with Nora. I'd like to know. Does Lena think Nora is...not all right?"

"I couldn't say. I haven't talked to her about it. I didn't want to worry her until I knew something definite. She has her own children to think about."

"I would think Nora would talk to her before she talked to anyone," he said, picturing them together and thinking how just a few years ago, "Nora and Lena" seemed like one word, how when you found one, you found the other.

"Maybe she has," Laurie said. "But I've been trying to talk to you about Cal, and you're avoiding that."

"No, I'm not. It's just that I've heard it all before. It's not exactly breaking news."

"Honestly, George. I don't know why I even bother...yes, I do too. I see you making the same mistakes over and over. So I *have* to try to say something."

"Supposing she is pregnant. What would be so bad about that...if she wants a baby, that is?" Then he started to smile, remembering. "I've never been sorry, have you? It's what we did."

She wouldn't look at him, and she wouldn't smile. "It's not the same thing at all, George. I think it's mean of you to think so. It would be humiliating if she were pregnant. Everyone would know. She would just have to have an abortion. Thank God they're legal now."

"That's like wishing Georgia or Jimmy didn't exist."

"Oh, it's no use," Laurie said, and she picked up her book. "I can't talk to you about anything." She began to read.

George raised his paper tentatively, ready to put it down when she began to speak again. But she didn't, and a little while later when Nora came in, she found them both reading.

"You two look cozy."

"Yes...well." George looked around at Nora standing in the doorway. "Come sit with us," he said.

"Just for a second. I want to get to bed." She sat down between them. "Are you okay, Mom?"

"Sure. Why wouldn't I be?" She was trying to sound cheerful, but she looked unhappy. "How is everyone over at Lena's?"

"All right. I read to Georgia. Lena and Jerry went Christmas shopping."

"How was that?"

"Not great, I guess. They didn't buy anything. I forgot to ask them where they went."

George said, "There's a good story by Jerry on the front page. I'm done with it if you'd like to read it."

"Thanks, Dad. I'm tired tonight. I'll read it tomorrow."

"It's part of his series on poverty in Vermont.

"Take your jacket off, Nora."

"I've got to go to bed, Mom. I'm really tired."

She stood up and went to each of them in turn, kissing them lightly on top of the head. Then she left. After a minute, they could hear her going very slowly up the stairs. They looked at each other, but neither of them said anything.

Chapter 10

When he and Paul came out of the barn into the early morning light, Cal could feel the storm coming. He thought he could smell snow in the air too. Ever since he came home from the hospital, he had been hoping to get up to the top of the ridge to his tree stand to see if he could find something that would give him a clue about who shot him. Today might be his last chance.

Paul opened the mudroom door and held it for him. "There you go, Dad," he said. Cal hoisted himself up the steps and into the house. Paul came in behind him and kicked his barn boots off in the corner. "I'll take the milk in to Ma," he said apologetically. Cal saw with surprise that his helplessness embarrassed Paul as much as it embarrassed him.

When Cal finally got his boot off and hobbled up the steps and opened the door into the kitchen, he heard Paul telling Ursela he didn't have time to stay for breakfast.

Paul went by him in the doorway. "Bye, Dad," he said. "See you tomorrow."

Cal knew he ought to say thank you, but he could feel Ursela listening to see if he would. She was pouring the fresh milk through the strainer, but she paused the flow of it so she could hear better. He slapped Paul roughly on the shoulder with the hand that wasn't on the crutch. "Okay," he said. Ursela wasn't watching, only listening. He was sure of it when Paul went down the steps, and she began the flow of milk again.

There was no pleasing Ursela these days. Everything he did was wrong, and if she didn't actually say so, he could feel her watching, hoping to see him doing something she didn't like. There wasn't any use in trying to say something to her because she would just deny it. Cal's own private opinion was that she had really enjoyed herself when he was in the hospital and she was running the place by herself, and now she was sorry to have him back. Well, she had no choice about that. The farm was his. He limped over to the table and sat down.

"I was just about to tell you to hurry up, Cal," she said. "Breakfast's been ready for a while."

"I can't help it. I've only got one damn leg to get around on."

In answer, Ursela set the plate of bacon down harder than she should have. He looked up at her, but she was already turning back to the stove. The kitchen was so hot that there were beads of sweat across her forehead. "I hope you're hungry. I cooked enough eggs for Paul."

"I'll do."

"Here's six, then. There's more in the pan." She put the plate down in front of him.

He knew he was being an asshole, but he couldn't say thank you. "Ain't you havin any?"

"Of course." She sat down with her plate and then jumped up to get the salt and pepper from the back of the stove. A few minutes later she was up again to get their coffee.

Uncle Herbie's Trading Post was on the radio. "Did you hear the weather?" Cal said.

"I missed it. They'll have it again at eight."

"It don't matter. They'll just say there's a big snowstorm comin, and we know that much already."

"They might tell us when."

"I bet it's late afternoon before it gets goin good. They'd be likely to get that wrong anyhow."

Ursela had made fresh biscuits. They were in a bowl, covered with a white cloth to keep them hot. Cal took three. He put a slab of butter on each one and then closed it up again so the butter would get a good chance to melt.

They ate in silence. After a while, Ursela pushed herself up out of her chair to put a few sticks of wood on the fire. When she came back to her seat, she said, "I guess I'll go downstreet for groceries before the storm."

He could feel her eyes on his face, but he didn't say anything, and he didn't look up from his plate.

"Do you want to come?"

"No. I guess not." He tried to sound undecided. He didn't want her to know that he was delighted. It was good luck for him that she was going away. With this snowstorm coming, today might be his last chance to get up in the woods to look for clues. It would be a lot easier to get up there without her giving him a hard time about it.

She actually looked a little relieved when he said he didn't want to come with her. "I thought I'd stop in at Ma's if you didn't mind."

"That's okay," he said, thinking it was getting better and better. She might stay all day at her mother's.

"It might mean I'd be gone a long time." The way she said it, it was almost a question.

"No problem," he said, as indifferently as he could manage.

"Do you think the snow'll hold off?"

"I expect so."

"Well, look, Cal. You can call over to Ma's if you need me to come home."

"I know." That started him thinking, because if he could call her, she could call him. "I might be out in the shop."

"Cal, you ain't supposed to do nothin. You know that."

"I was out there yesterday, and the day before too."

"That don't make it right."

"Well, of course. I know. Ain't you told me often enough?"

"So what are you goin out there for?" She sounded as though she couldn't believe she had to tell him again.

"I thought I'd build a fire and sit by it, same as I would in here. If I don't get the phone, you'll know that's where I am."

"You're supposed to keep your leg up...."

"Jesus, Ursela, I guess I can figure that out without help from you."

"Well, if you're goin to swear, I'll change my clothes and get ready to leave. I can do up the dishes when you finish."

He sat at the table for a few minutes after she left the room. He chuckled a little, telling himself that if swearing would cause her to leave him alone, then he guessed he could do more of it.

Finally he got up and went out to the mudroom. He put his hunting boot on. As soon as his foot got better, that single boot wouldn't be any use any more. It still made him mad the way they didn't even try to save the other one, just cut it off and threw it away. They didn't care how much it cost, or that it was almost new, or that with all these hospital bills, he didn't know when he would be able to afford another good pair of boots.

He had to go back into the kitchen for matches and paper. Ursela was at the sink, doing up the breakfast things. She had on her pink dress. It was tight over her wide hips, but it looked nice. He thought about putting his arms around her, but he didn't want her to think he was conceding anything. When they were young, he couldn't stop looking at her, and he couldn't keep his hands off her, but that was long ago. He hardly ever felt that way any more. "I'll be out back then," he said. "Goodbye."

She didn't answer or turn around, so he wasn't sure she heard him, but he left anyway. She knew where to find him.

She came out later to say she was leaving, but by that time, he had the fire going, and the shed was starting to warm up. He was sitting by the stove with his leg propped up on a log. He wanted her to *see* him doing nothing. A few minutes after she left, he heard the car going down the road. He was glad he hadn't gotten around to patching the tailpipe. It was handy to have the car so loud. He knew he was in the clear.

He went on whittling the stick he was working on. He shaved one end of it down to a sharp point, tested it a few times with his finger, and then threw it into the woodbox and stood up, leaning on his crutch. The other crutch was standing in the corner behind some boards. It wasn't hidden, but it wasn't out in plain sight either. Cal had added three harness straps to it. He hoped they would steady it enough so that both his hands could be free. It worked fine on the cement floor of the shop, and he was eager to try it outside.

He hobbled over to it and strapped it on, one strap over his shoulder, one around his waist, and the third just above his knee. It would have been steadier if he could have put it below his knee, but he had to be able to hold his foot up when the ground was unlevel, and that meant he had to be able to bend his knee. He stumped around the shop, trying it out. It might just do. He threw a couple of chunks of wood on the fire and dampered it down. Then he put on his jacket and hat. He already had two plastic bags in his pocket in case he found anything he wanted to bring home undisturbed, anything that might be a clue.

He thought about taking his gun, but he decided not to. He owed himself two and a half days of hunting for the days he missed, and he was going to take them. He had thought it all through while he lay in the hospital. He was due three days minus the four hours he had hunted Friday morning before he got shot, and that was the amount he meant to make up, no more, but no less either. But not today. Today was for gathering evidence.

Cal picked up his work gloves and stumped outside. It was a gloomy day, with a hard wind rattling the bare branches of the trees behind the house. Winter was shaking her bony fingers at him. He could already smell the snow.

He started up the back pasture. The dogs appeared from nowhere and ran ahead. It was heavy work. He was awkward and unbalanced. The tip of the crutch sank into the earth, even hardened with cold as it was. And he was so damn weak. He had to stop every five or six steps to catch his breath. He was embarrassed by his frailty, even though there was no one to see him. By the time he got to the top of the field, he was so weak that his legs were trembling. He'd have sat right down on the cold ground if he could have maneuvered the crutch out of the way without undoing all the straps. As it was, he stood leaning heavily on it while he looked down at the gray house and beyond it, at the fields and woods and road getting grayer with distance under the gray sky. It gave him strength to think how much he loved the place. Anybody who wanted to get him off it was going to have to shoot a lot straighter. It was his land, and he belonged on it. Of course it was his in part because George gave him his share, but George never cared about it the way he did. George was just acknowledging that when he gave him his half.

Standing still in the wind made him cold. He turned around. Up the hill, the dogs were sniffing under the trees. They looked completely absorbed, but he knew they would notice that he was going back to the house. They would stay with him, even though they didn't want to. It was obvious that he didn't have enough strength to get to the top of the hill unless he took all day to do it, and he didn't have all day. He started slowly down. He was all clenched up inside. At every step, he jabbed his crutch too deeply into the ground so that he had to pull it out again. He was furious, but he had no one to blame but himself and his feebleness. He had figured all the angles, except that his own damn body would go back on him. He'd never thought of that.

Part way down the slope, it came to him that if he could rig up some way to press down the brake pedals without using his foot, he could drive the tractor up to the tree stand. He ought to be able to make something he could use. Just thinking about it made him feel better. By God, he wasn't going to quit that easy.

He was in the shop, nailing a crosspiece onto the end of an old maul handle when he heard a woman's voice outside. At first he thought Ursela must have come home early, and he felt a flash of rage. He was trying to do something simple. All he wanted was to get up to the top of the ridge before the snow came down to stay, but something blocked his every move. It was like trying to walk through deep mud. He had to fight for every step.

The dogs started to bark outside the shop door. They barked the way they would at a stranger. He waited silently, hoping whoever it was would go away. It had to be some woman friend of Ursela's.

There was a knock on the door of the shop. "It's open," he said curtly.

The door opened a little way, and a young woman with short blonde hair looked in. All Cal could see around the door was her head and one hand. He had no idea who she was.

"Uncle Cal," she said, as though she had heard what he was thinking. "It's Nora. Can I come in?"

"Yes, come in. I thought you were in Boston," he said stupidly, because while he was saying the words, he remembered that George had told him different.

"I've moved back home." She went over to the stove and held her hands out over it. "It's cold out."

The dogs came in when she did. They settled themselves on the floor near the stove and looked at Cal in triumph.

After a little while, Nora said, "Where's Aunt Ursela? I looked for her in the house."

"She's gone downstreet. She'll be gone all day. She went over to visit her mother. They get jabberin to each other in German, and they don't know how to stop." He was hoping she would get the hint that there wasn't any sense in waiting for her.

But she didn't. She said, "How are you feeling? Mom and Dad were wondering."

"I'm all right. I can't get around worth a damn, but I feel all right."

"Does it hurt a lot?"

"What?"

"Does your foot hurt a lot?"

"It's okay."

Then there was nothing more to say. He waited, hoping she would get uncomfortable enough to leave, but she seemed content to stand by the stove, holding her hands out to the warmth. He turned around and put the last nails into the maul handle.

"What's that for, Uncle Cal?"

"It's a crutch."

"Oh, I see." But of course, she didn't. That was plain from her expression.

He sighed. "Come on outside, and I'll show you what it's for. I don't know if it'll work." He stepped past her, self-conscious about his crutch, and opened the door. He whistled to the dogs. "Come on," he said. "You can't stay here. I want you out."

Blackie jumped up and went out the door. He turned around, ready to come in again, while Peg was still getting to her feet and stretching. Her arthritis bothered her when she lay on the cement floor. She wanted to leave when Nora did, not before, and not after.

Finally, they were all outside, and Cal could close the door. The tractor was behind the house where he'd left it when he brought down the last load of wood, the day before the opening day of deer hunting. He didn't even know if it would start. He stumped awkwardly over to it with Nora and the dogs trailing behind. He was more surprised than anyone when the engine roared to life after only a few cranks. He had been so sure that that was the next difficulty he was going to have to deal with.

Now he had to get himself up into the seat with Nora watching. Ever since he'd been shot, it had been one humiliation after another. If he ever got a chance to get the guy that did it, it would make some amends for what he'd had to put up with. Nothing could pay back altogether, of course.

He set his brake crutch on the seat and tried to figure out how to get himself hoisted into the seat with only one foot to stand on. He made several attempts to pull himself up by holding on to the steering wheel, but his feet got all tangled up, or rather, the good foot had to be two places at once, and the bad foot was in the way.

"Maybe I could push you up there, Uncle Cal. Do you want me to try?"

"Oh no," he said, thinking that he should have waited until she left, so he wouldn't have to make a fool of himself. He wasn't going to get up in the woods anyway. There were too many obstacles.

They stood beside the tractor listening to the roughness of the engine. And that was when the best idea of all came to him. He wasn't even thinking about it. He was wondering if he ought to give up the whole idea of getting up to the top of the hill. Maybe he ought to just give up fighting it and take off the carburetor. He'd been meaning to clean those jets all summer. He could stay in the shop in the warm, and it wouldn't matter what Nora did, and when Ursela came home, she'd find him beside the stove with his leg propped up, just like he was supposed to be.

But almost without thinking about what he was saying, he asked Nora if she could drive a shift car.

"Yes," she said cheerfully. "I like them better. I think you have more control."

"Well then," he said, trying to sound like it wasn't a big deal. "Why don't you drive the tractor for me?"

"Me?" she said. "I couldn't do that. I've never driven a tractor before."

"Okay. I just thought you might could do it. But it don't matter."

He was reaching up to shut off the gas when she said, "Maybe...if you could show me...I mean, I could try."

His hand stopped pushing the gas lever and rested there, waiting. He tried not to look at her directly.

"If you think I could do it, Uncle Cal....I mean, I don't even know if it's hard or what."

"It ain't hard. It ain't that different from a shift car, easier maybe, when you get used to it."

She smiled at him. She was a good girl, and he liked the way she smiled. She had on a pretty, puffy dark-blue jacket and sneakers and no hat. He thought of trying to get her some different clothes so she didn't get all greasy and dirty, but it seemed too personal to talk about. And anyway, he was afraid she might change her mind. What the hell, young people never wore enough clothes, and she looked strong.

"So, Uncle Cal, tell me what to do."

"All right then." He pushed down the gas lever, and the engine roared. He looked at her. She was smiling with excitement. "This is how you set on the gas, see?" He cut it way back. "You don't do it with your foot. Okay?"

She nodded. "Let me try it." She gave it a lot of gas and then cut it back, and then she nodded again. "What else?"

They were standing one on each side of the tractor now. "Look down there at them two pedals. That's the brakes, and you have to put 'em both on at once, or else you get into trouble. Okay? I mean there's sometimes when you don't, but you don't need to know about them times. You just mash 'em both down if you need to. All right? But you probably won't need 'em at all, not on the way up, anyhow. We'll put you in a real low gear, so if you want to stop, it'll be plenty to cut back on the gas." She was beginning to look worried. He didn't want to say any more. "Why don't you try it out, Nora? Get the hang of it. You'll see how easy it is."

"Okay," she said. She looked doubtful. "Is that the gear shift?" She pointed to it.

"That's a little different too," he said quickly. There was a diagram of the gears on the knob of the shift lever. He touched the 2. "Just put it in second. You won't need to worry about shiftin."

"Uncle Cal? Is it going to be pulling this little wagon? Maybe we could take that off?"

"No, we can't. That's where I'm goin to ride."

"Oh." She was changing her mind. Add this to the list of false starts. He didn't say anything. He just reached for the throttle. Might as well quit wasting gas.

She gave her head a little shake like a dog coming out of the water.

"All right, Uncle Cal. Let's go. I just hope I don't hurt you, or the tractor, or something." She put one hand on the steering wheel and the other on the tractor seat and pulled herself easily up. Cal had just time to step aside.

"That's the way," he said. "You're a good girl. You just try it out."

She was looking down at him. "You tell me when to start."

"Wait til I get on the wagon." He stumped to the open back of it as quickly as he could and tried to put his bad leg up on the bed, but he couldn't get it there. The crutch kept him from being able to bend. He stuck his gloves in his pocket and took off his jacket, so he could unbuckle all the straps. He tried to hurry as much as he could. He could feel her turn on the seat to watch him. He finally got the damn thing off and his jacket back on. He threw the crutch into the front of the wagon and hoisted his bad leg up onto the bed, so that he was sitting sideways with his good leg dangling over the back, but so he could look forward to see what she was doing. Maybe he was actually going to get up the hill after all.

She was watching him intently. Her mouth was set in a tight line. It reminded him of the expression George used to get on his face when they were kids splitting firewood. "All right," he said. "Let's go." He made a waving motion with his hand in case she couldn't hear him over the noise of the engine.

The dogs must have heard him, because they came around the house, Blackie first, prancing and wagging his tail, and Peg, slow but still eager.

He thought of shutting them up so they wouldn't follow. He didn't want them to trample any evidence. But it meant getting out of the wagon and putting the crutch back on, and that was only the beginning. He would have to catch them too. He decided to skip it and hope they wouldn't get in the way. The cops had probably trampled everything anyway.

Nora turned around and spent a long time getting it into gear. At first the tractor lurched forward, and he thought it would stall, but then she settled down to it, and it smoothed out. He was just about to congratulate himself when she turned around to look at him with fear in her face, and he realized she didn't know where they were going. "It's easy," he shouted. "You just follow the road straight up."

She was biting her lower lip. She nodded, looked forward, and then back at him again.

"It turns down there by those trees and goes up to the top of the hill," he shouted.

She nodded again and smiled without letting loose her bottom lip. She made the turn all right and kept steadily on, not even looking back any more, except when they hit the steep part and he had to shout to her to give it more gas. He watched her back hunched over the wheel with her blonde hair flapping as she bounced up and down on the tractor seat.

Blackie ran off to the side, zigzagging through the woods, but keeping abreast of the tractor, while Peg trotted along the road behind the wagon.

The sky was gray behind the bare trees. The cold air smelled of exhaust. Cal was excited, impatient to get to the top, and a little annoyed that they were going so slowly. He had to remind himself that he was pretty lucky to be going at all, considering the difficulties. And he had to say she was a game one. He hadn't really thought she would try it.

They chugged along until they got almost up to the tree stand. Cal shouted, "Whoa," and then, "Brake, brake." And she tramped down on the brakes without the clutch, and the engine quit.

She turned around and said, "Oh, I'm sorry, Uncle Cal. It stalled. What should I do?"

"Nothin," he said, in a voice that was too loud for the quiet. "We're here."

"What? Where is here?"

"This is where he shot me. I came up here to look for evidence. I got to find out who done this." He stood on the good leg. Then he steadied himself against the wagon bed and reached in for his crutch.

Nora was still on the tractor, turned in the seat so she could look at him. "What are you looking for?"

"If I knew that, I wouldn't have had to come, would I?"

Nora didn't say anything, but she looked hurt, and he saw that she had caught her bottom lip with her top teeth again.

He had been too gruff. "If I knew what was up here waitin for me to find it, I could've sent Conrad or Paul to pick it up."

"I know, Uncle Cal, but I want to help you, and I don't know what to look for."

He knew he ought to say he was sorry for being so short. He even wanted to say something, only he didn't know how. All he could manage was, "Look for anythin suspicious."

"What would that be?"

"How would I know? You got to look around and see what you can see," he said, and then, when she just sat there biting her lip, "You'll know it when you find somethin."

He decided not to bother with the straps on his crutch. He was shy about doing all the buckles with her sitting there watching, and he probably wasn't going to need to have both hands free anyway. He stuck the crutch under his arm and stumped over to the big maple where he had his tree stand.

Nora climbed off the tractor and came over. "What's here, Uncle Cal?"

"Did you push the throttle in when it stalled?"

"You mean the stick that's like stepping on the gas?"

"Yes, and the key. Did you shut it off?"

"Oh, I'm sorry," she said. "I can't believe I forgot. It's lucky you told me." She shut off the tractor and came back and stood in front of him with a puzzled look on her face.

After a minute, he pointed to the boards he had nailed across two branches to make a platform.

"Oh," she said, looking up, "Is that where you...."

They both looked down at the ground, but there was nothing to see. The dead leaves there were the same as the ones under all the other maple trees.

"If your gun went off accidentally, wouldn't there be a kind of dug-out place? A bullet would do that, wouldn't it?"

"God damn it!" Cal said. "Why does everybody think I did this to myself?" There wasn't any end to how stupid people could be. And just when you least expected it too. "I don't even think it's possible. But that don't stop people from makin fools of themselves with harebrained ideas. Your dad sent you out here to see what you could find out, didn't he?"

"Oh no, Uncle Cal, of course not," she said. At first he believed her, but then her face changed a little. She looked away, and he wasn't so sure. "They wanted to know how you and Aunt Ursela were, if your foot was healing and all." She looked distressed. "Not what you think."

He wanted to believe her. He liked her spunk, and anyway, he was sick of the whole damn mess. He had thought about getting up here for so long and overcome so many obstacles to make it, that it was a disappointment to see that the whole thing had been a waste of time. There wasn't going to be anything to find. "God damn it!" he said. "Don't you see why I have to find that goddamned shooter? No one is ever goin to believe me unless I can find some proof."

"I believe you, Uncle Cal, and I'm sure Dad…."

"Jesus," he said, before he stopped himself. George wasn't ever going to believe someone shot him. It would mean a lot of law work, and there was nothing in it for him if he did it. George would want to believe it was an accident even if he saw the guy pull the trigger. "It don't matter who believes me and who don't," he said to her. "What I want is some proof. But I can see there ain't a thing here to find. That shooter might of come back and covered up his tracks. That's what I would of done. And then the state troopers came up and tramped all over the place. Who knows what *they* took away with them." He turned away so she wouldn't see the anger and disappointment on his face.

"Uncle Cal," she said. "Tell me how to help you, please. I want to. I mean it."

"All right. Okay. Let me think a minute." Because he was beginning to see that there wasn't any sense in standing up there, the very place he had fought so hard to get to, feeling sorry for himself because his evidence wasn't right under the tree with a ribbon tied around it. He needed to take a good look around, and he wasn't going to get another chance before spring by the look of this snow. He knew he wasn't going to be able to get down the steep bank so he could check out the game trail and maybe see if he could figure out where the shooter stood. But Nora could. Maybe she didn't know much about the woods or about hunting either. Maybe she wasn't good at looking, but she was all he had to work with, and she'd have to do.

Chapter 11

Nora waited for what Uncle Cal was going to say, trying not to think about how cold she was. Any minute, her teeth would start chattering, and he would notice. The icy wind blew little snowflakes through the black branches and made them clatter together with a hollow sound. Nora wondered whether Aunt Ursela was at home. She thought about how warm it would be in the kitchen. She pictured Aunt Ursela baking. The whole house would smell like cookies.

Uncle Cal's voice brought her back. "Okay, Nora, here's what you can do. You can check out that game trail." He pointed over the steep bank at the woods below. "I can't get down there with my foot like it is. I'll look around up here."

For a minute, while she thought about Aunt Ursela, she hadn't been cold. She shivered and tried to wrench her mind around to where she was. She looked down the bank at the bare trees and the leaves on the ground under them. She didn't see a trail. "But, Uncle Cal, how will I know where to go when I get down there?"

"You'll know. The trail's plain. Unless the state troopers have messed it up too bad. The animals use it. Look around it for anythin you can see. Look for anythin that don't belong."

"Okay, if it will help," she said, because she was sorry to see him upset and disappointed. She started down awkwardly, slipping on the leaves, conscious of Uncle Cal behind her, watching. She hoped he wasn't going to stand there the whole time. She wasn't at all sure she was going to recognize the trail, let alone anything unusual near it. But at least it warmed her up to be moving. On the way up the hill she had been too excited to notice the cold. She had been focused on the surprising fact that she, Nora Willard, was actually driving a tractor up into the woods, and it wasn't even that hard.

The bank was steep, and the ground was lumpy. Big rocks stuck up in places. Between the rocks, there were patches of slippery, wet leaves. Nora had to catch hold of trees to keep her balance.

When she got to the bottom, she walked a little way and turned around to ask Uncle Cal if she had gone far enough. He wasn't there. She couldn't even see the dogs. She felt a stab of fear to think she was all alone, but right away she realized that he couldn't leave without her, so he had to be up there near the tree with his tree stand, which she could see plainly from where she stood. She looked around, trying to figure out where she was supposed to be, and when she looked down at the ground, there was a candy-bar wrapper right at her feet. It was nestled in the leaves. If she hadn't stopped where she did, she would never have seen it. She reached down and picked it up. It was brown and green, the wrapper of a Milky Way. It was just what Uncle Cal was looking for, something that didn't belong there. Nora studied the surroundings, trying to fix her position so that she could point it out to him when she got back up there. A little group of short, bushy evergreen trees stood right beside her. She could use them for a marker. She started back toward the steep bank.

She was halfway to the top and out of breath from trying to hurry, when she tripped over a branch and would have fallen if she hadn't caught herself with her hands against the icy hillside.

When she looked up, Uncle Cal was there above her with an

exasperated expression on his face. "You didn't stay down there very long, did you?" he said.

He meant she hadn't stayed long enough, that she hadn't really tried. He thought she was giving up. That was because he thought she was coming back empty-handed.

She started to answer and then decided to wait until she got to the top. She scrambled the rest of the way up the bank and stopped beside him, hurrying to get her breath so she could tell him, and at the same time, trying not to let him see that the climb was hard for her. She pulled the candy-bar wrapper from her pocket and held it out to him. "Look, " she said.

He looked at the paper and then at her. He didn't say anything.

"I found it down there, Uncle Cal. It's what you said to look for—something that wasn't supposed to be there."

He took it out of her hand and stood silent, looking down at it and then out over the bank at the woods below. He was frowning.

"What do you think, Uncle Cal? Maybe it belonged to the man who shot you."

"Yes," he said. "Maybe it did. Can you remember where you found it?"

"I think so. I particularly tried to notice so I could show you."

"Good girl," he said. "That's the spirit."

She felt proud, and then right away she was scared she wouldn't be able to spot the place from up above. For a minute everything looked so different that she knew she couldn't recognize where she had been. But then she settled into looking, and in a minute she could almost make out where she went down the bank, and then she could see the little clump of evergreens. She pointed them out to him and told him how the candy wrapper was right on the other side of them, stuck down in the leaves.

"Well," he said, staring out there where she pointed. "It could have been his."

"Shall I go down there, so you can see exactly?"

"Yes, you do that. That would be good." And he patted her on the back.

So then she would have done a lot more than that for him. She hurried down the hill again and over to the little clump of trees and found the place where she had picked up the candy wrapper. She stepped right onto that spot and looked back up the hill at him. She was looking over the clump of evergreen bushes.

"This is where I found it, Uncle Cal."

"Stay right where you are, girl," he shouted back. Above the edge of the hill, she could see his head moving by jerks over to the tree where he had his tree stand. He stood at the base of it and looked down at her. They could see each other plainly. There was nothing in between them.

"Well," he called to her. "Look around. There just might be somethin else."

So then she was excited. She wanted to help even more. She wanted to do all she could. She got down on her hands and knees and stirred the leaves, trying to see to the bottom of them, trying to be systematic. What she hoped for most of all was that she would find a bullet, only she wasn't exactly sure what it would look like. But as she dug around, she began to suspect that there wasn't anything more to find. Her hands were so cold that they wouldn't move from their clawlike shape. When she couldn't stand it any longer, she stood up and shouted to him that she hadn't found anything else.

She was afraid he was going to tell her to look harder, but he didn't. He said to come on back, and when she got up the bank and could put her frozen hands into her pockets, he said, "You done good. That's the place the shooter had to of stood to get me."

"I'm sorry I didn't find any more."

"Maybe there wasn't anythin to find. We know the cops was up here. And maybe he was up here before that."

"What, Uncle Cal?"

"I would of come back to make sure I didn't leave nothin at the scene, you know." He thought for a minute. "Maybe that candy paper was somethin everybody missed, bein as how it was down in the leaves and brown and green like it was. He'd of been in a hurry too. He'd of been worried about the snow comin down so he wouldn't get another chance."

"I wish we could figure out who he was."

"He wouldn't want to take a chance on me findin out. There ain't but two people in the world that knows what happened."

Nora nodded.

He looked at her thoughtfully, and then he said, "No, there's three, because you know now. You seen the place too."

Nora nodded again.

"But you only got my say-so about how it happened."

"I believe you, Uncle Cal."

"I appreciate it. But it ain't hard evidence, is it?"

"No, I guess not."

"Well, it's all we're goin to get. And it's somethin. We know there was a guy over there behind them softwoods where it ain't likely anybody would of been, if he hadn't of been up to no good."

"That's evidence, isn't it?"

"It's all we've got, and right now we better see about gettin back home while we still can. I drug myself down from here once, but I don't want to do it twice. Let's go."

"Okay."

Nora followed him as he stumped along on his crutch, holding his hurt foot a little way off the ground. All the loose straps wriggled around him like snakes. When he got to the tractor, he made a few adjustments, and the engine roared.

"Okay, girl," he said. "Climb up."

Nora pulled herself up into the seat, realizing suddenly that she was going to have to turn the tractor around. She looked down at Uncle Cal. He seemed small and frail beside the big wheel of the tractor. "I don't know how to back up when it's pulling a wagon," she said softly.

He said, "What?" and then before she had a chance to repeat what she had said, he went on. "Oh, I know what you're thinkin. But it don't matter. It ain't hard, and anyway, you've got to. Just do what I tell you, and you can start by puttin in the clutch."

She did what he said. She almost knew she couldn't do it, but she also knew he was right, that she had to.

He put it in reverse and then stood aside and watched while she turned wrong. He shouted to her to stop and put it in first and told her to pull forward and try again. That happened three times. She was feeling desperate by the time the wagon went the right way, and she got the whole thing turned around so that it was ready to go down the hill. The dogs seemed to know that they were really leaving, because they appeared out of the woods and stood waiting by the side of the road.

Uncle Cal put it in second gear and told her solemnly not to step on the clutch and only to step on both brakes at once and lightly. He set the gas and told her it was all right to turn it down but not up. She wondered why he was so serious about it all, but she didn't let herself think about it much because she was starting to get cold again, and she wanted to get down there in a hurry. She didn't even want to know if she was scared, because the one thing she was sure of, without even having to think about it, was that she would never have the nerve to tell Uncle Cal that she was too afraid to do it.

At first it went fine. It was steep, but they chugged along slowly. Uncle Cal had told her specifically not to give it any more gas, so all she needed to do was steer, and that left her plenty of time to think. For the past few days she had been telling herself that she was crazy to have given up her job to come home. And to what? To Severance, where everyone else had a place and something to do, while she had nothing and needed so much.

But riding down the hill under the bare trees on land that had belonged to Willards for generations, Nora saw that the crazy move was not leaving Boston—it was walking out of the abortion clinic. Being pregnant was what limited her options and made her need so much. Being pregnant was what made it necessary for her to be a grown-up with a secure job and a home of her own. Being pregnant was what she had to do something about.

So Nora wasn't really paying that much attention when there was a click, and the tractor started going faster, much faster. She didn't know what she had done, or what she ought to do. She could hear Uncle Cal shouting, but she couldn't make out what he was saying, and she didn't dare take her eyes off the road to turn around and look at him. All she could do was steer and try to keep the panic from rising.

It seemed to go on for a long time, but it couldn't have. Whatever she did wrong, she hadn't done it until they were almost down the hill. When the ground leveled out, the tractor went more and more slowly until it rolled to a stop just inside the woods not far from the house.

Nora turned around to look at Uncle Cal. She was trembling. She didn't know what he was going to say. To her surprise, he shouted to her to put it in second gear and drive it around behind the house to his shop, and although she was afraid and confused, she did it. When she looked back to see what he would say, he held up a finger, meaning she should stay where she was and wait for him. She sat there trying not to look impatient, while Uncle Cal climbed stiffly off the wagon, picked up his crutch, and hobbled slowly over the where she sat on the tractor seat with the cold creeping so deep inside that she felt it in her bones.

He wanted her to back up again, and she did it, and then at last she could get down and find out exactly how weak and trembling her legs were and that they would hold her up even though they felt as though they wouldn't. The two dogs crowded up against her, almost knocking her over, wanting to be noticed.

"I think I'll go inside and see if Aunt Ursela is there."

"She's not. Her car ain't there. She's gone to her mother's. She always stays over all day."

"Well, I think I'll go home then, Uncle Cal."

"Okay, girl," he said. He looked relieved, as though he had been afraid he was going to have to invite her inside.

"Tell Aunt Ursela I said hello."

"I'll do that."

"And I'll tell Dad that your foot is getting better."

"You do that," he said. He turned off the tractor and went to the door of his shop.

Nora said goodbye and went around the house to her car. As soon as she started the engine, she turned the heater on as hard as it would go. It blew out ice-cold air, but she couldn't bring herself to turn it off until it warmed up, even though the cold wind made her even colder. She didn't want to miss that first second when the air turned warm. Now in the car, with the possibility of warmth, she was colder than ever, shaking all over with it. Her teeth were even clattering together.

She turned on the windshield wipers to clear off the snow. There wasn't much snow yet, but it was beginning to come down harder. She needed to get home before the roads got bad. It was lucky Aunt Ursela wasn't there.

Driving into town and finally beginning to thaw out, Nora thought about how she had driven a tractor and how scared she had been on the last part of the hill when the tractor had gone so fast. She had been so cold and in such a hurry to leave that she hadn't even asked Uncle Cal what happened, what she had done wrong. She thought about how she had been afraid, and how the weirdest thing was that she was afraid for the baby. She was planning to kill it, and she was afraid it would get hurt. It was so ridiculous that it was funny. She wished she could share the joke, but there was no one she could tell.

Chapter 12

It was a beautiful winter day. It had snowed all night, and it was still snowing a little. Even through the window Lena could feel how soft and white and quiet it was outside. The snowplow hadn't been by since early in the morning, and there were hardly any cars.

Lena was in the kitchen with the children. Jerry was still asleep. She didn't know what time he'd come home, and he hadn't left a note saying when to wake him up. She decided she would send Georgia up at ten-thirty. They should be finished making the bread by then if Jimmy kept on being good.

Jimmy was in his high chair playing with bits of cheese and banana and occasionally dropping a chunk onto the floor where Beebee was waiting. Sometimes she would snap at a piece of banana by mistake in her eagerness not to miss any cheese. Jimmy looked past Lena waving a piece of banana and smiling and saying, "Hey." Lena pinched off a small piece of the dough she was kneading and put it on the tray of his high chair for him to play with.

That got Georgia's attention. She was working on a small piece of dough on the table beside Jimmy. She had been working hard, but of course she wanted to know what Jimmy was getting. Lena was facing both of them across the table, but not really paying attention to them. She was coming down as hard as she could on the lump of floured dough with both her arms stiff and her hands in fists. Every time she leaned her weight on the dough, the table creaked. She was listening to the rhythmic creaking and trying not to think about sex in front of the children, in case it might not be good for them.

"Mommy, why won't you look?" Georgia said. "It's Aunt Nora."

When she said it, Lena remembered that she'd said it several times. "Aunt Nora?" She looked at Georgia, but Georgia was smiling and pointing a doughy little hand at something behind her. "What about Aunt Nora?" she said, already turning around, and there was Nora with snow on her hat, looking in the kitchen window, laughing and making faces at the children.

Lena said, "Come in the house," and held up her flour-covered hands so Nora could see why she didn't open the door.

"I tried to," Nora said, still laughing and looking in the window, her eyes shielded with her mittened hands, "It's locked."

"Oh, wait then," Lena said, realizing that she couldn't remember unlocking the door when she got up in the morning. She rubbed her hands together to get off the biggest scraps of dough. By then Jimmy was standing up in his high chair, ready to jump, so she went around to his side of the table and lifted him out of his chair, and then she went to the door with him riding on her hip. She was glad to think of Nora watching them through the window. She pictured how they had looked cozy and happy together while Nora watched. There were times she wouldn't want Nora to see, times when the kids had tantrums, times when she couldn't stand it anymore and got angry at them. She hated herself then. She wouldn't want Nora to see them like that.

When she opened the door, Nora came in stamping the snow off her feet, bringing with her a rush of pure, icy air. She looked so healthy and fresh that Lena saw right away that she had been silly to think anything was wrong. She wished she hadn't told Jerry her fears.

Nora took off her mittens and hat and jacket and dropped them in a pile in the corner by the door.

"Here, Nora, give me those. You're as bad as the kids."

Nora held out her arms to Jimmy, who leaned toward her, eager to go. "I'm not going to be here very long. It's not worth the trouble of hanging it all up. It's too nice out."

"Look at Jimmy. He wants you to hold him. I'll make you some coffee as soon as I finish the bread."

Nora sat down at the end of the table and kicked off her boots. Then she rearranged Jimmy on her lap and kissed him on top of the head.

Lena wanted to tell her how happy she was to see her looking so great, how scared she had been that something was wrong, how she had thought that Nora might have cancer and have come home to die. But now, with the sunlight reflecting on the snow, and the calm, white light filling the kitchen like a bowl, her fears seemed impossibly silly and unrealistic.

Nora said, "It's not cold out. We could take the kids for a walk. We could build a snowman."

Lena was kneading the bread. She could feel Georgia's eyes on her face, trying to read there what her answer was going to be. "All right," she said. "Just let me get the bread ready to rise, and I'll have an hour before I have to do anything else." She thought she would let Jerry sleep. He hadn't asked her to wake him up. "I'll be through in a minute." When she said it, she could feel Georgia relax.

Nora was nuzzling Jimmy on the top of the head, burrowing her nose in his hair. "Okay," she said, looking up. "I have something to tell you anyway."

"Is it bad?"

"No. It's good. I've been dying to tell you."

"Do you want to tell me this in front of the kids?" And she knew she asked because she was playing for time, afraid of what she was going to hear. Maybe it was hearing Nora say she was dying that scared her, even though Nora said it was good.

"Sure," Nora said. "They'll love it. I went out to see Uncle Cal yesterday. Mom and Dad hadn't heard from him since he went home, and they were wondering how he was. Anyway, you're not going to believe what I did."

"Well, tell me."

"Guess." She laughed and tickled Jimmy, and he wiggled around on her lap.

"I can't. You've got to tell me."

"Okay, here it is. I drove Uncle Cal's tractor all the way to the top of the hill in the woods behind his house."

"Really?"

"Yes. It's true." She tickled Jimmy again. "Do you believe it, Jimmy? I almost don't myself."

"But why? Where was Uncle Cal?"

Georgia was looking back and forth from Nora to Lena, and her eyes were round. Jimmy had stopped giggling and was sitting still to listen.

"Uncle Cal was there the whole time. This is how it happened. When I got out there, Uncle Cal was trying to drive the tractor himself. He had even built himself some little gadget so he wouldn't have to use his foot on the brakes. You know how he always invents things. But he couldn't get himself up onto the seat of the tractor with only one foot."

"He's not supposed to do stuff like that. He's only been home from the hospital for a few days. What did Aunt Ursela say?"

"She wasn't there."

"Well, but how...."

"Lena. God. I couldn't wait to tell you because I thought you'd think it was so great, and here you are talking like Mom. Georgia, Jimmy, don't you think it's great? Wouldn't you like to see Aunt Nora driving a tractor? It was pulling a wagon too. I drove it all the way to the top of the hill and down again with Uncle Cal riding in the back."

"Uncle Cal went too?"

"Sure. That was the whole point. He wanted to look at the place where he got shot before it got covered with snow. He wanted to check out the scene of the crime."

"Mom thinks it was an accident. She thinks he did it to himself."

"I know, but Mom doesn't like him. You should have heard them last night."

"Who? "

"Mom and Dad. I tried to tell them about it, but all Mom could think about was that I might have been in danger, and she wouldn't listen to anything I said."

"Were you scared? I would have been terrified."

Nora thought for a minute. "No," she said. "At first it was easy and amazing. I was loving it too much to be scared. I guess I couldn't believe I was actually doing it. And Uncle Cal made me go slow, so we were just bouncing along up the hill under the trees, and all I had to do was steer. But coming down...."

"Oh, Nora, now we come to the bad part."

"No. It wasn't bad. I went really slow coming down too. Uncle Cal made me. There was just one place....well, there was this sound like a click, and I guess I must have done it, only I don't remember touching anything, but suddenly it started going faster and faster, and Uncle Cal was shouting, and I couldn't understand what he said, and I couldn't remember what I was supposed to do with the brakes, how they were different than car brakes. But it only lasted for a couple of minutes, and then we were off the hill, and it stopped itself. I was scared then, but it didn't last long."

Lena picked up the bread dough and put it in the bowl. Then she reached across the table for the little piece of dough that Georgia had been working on. She was planning to tell Georgia that she was putting the baby piece of dough in with its mother, but Georgia was watching Nora and didn't seem to care. "Mom was right about it being dangerous."

"Mom didn't even know that part of it. She and Dad started arguing about whether Uncle Cal would get me to do something if it was dangerous—Dad said he wouldn't—and they never listened to me at all. You know how they are when they get going on each other. I kept thinking I could tiptoe out of the room, and they wouldn't even know I was gone."

Lena started to laugh then, and both children looked at her with big eyes, which made her laugh even harder, and pretty soon Nora was laughing too. "I keep thinking of their faces if they suddenly noticed that you weren't there any more. Sometimes I think we're the grown-ups and they're the children."

"I know. I think so too. Are you all done with the bread?"

"I just have to cover it." She got out a plastic bag and laid it over the dough and put a dish towel on top of that. "I've been worried about you since you got home," she said without looking at Nora. "I've been scared you might be sick."

"Really? I love it that you're worrying about me. Mom and Dad...."

Lena looked at her then, afraid again. There *was* something wrong then, wasn't there?

Nora looked to see if Georgia was watching, but Georgia was looking at her own hands, picking off bits of bread dough. Nora looked at Lena over Jimmy's head and silently mouthed the words, "I'm pregnant."

"What? How...."

"No one knows."

"I don't understand," Lena said stupidly.

"I wasn't even going to tell you, but I feel so lonely. I guess I'm really glad you saw something was wrong."

"Oh, baby," Lena said, feeling a great wave of sympathy and love and relief. "I thought you had cancer. I'm so glad it's this."

Georgia looked up. "What is it? What have you got? Can I have some too?"

That made them both laugh again, and Lena hugged Nora right around Jimmy. "It's something nice, Georgia. We're all happy."

"Okay," Jimmy said. "Outside."

"Can we go now, Mommy?"

"Yes. Sure. No. Wait a minute. Let's go in the playroom for a little while because I want to talk to Aunt Nora. And we'll go out soon."

"Let's go now, Mommy. You can talk to Nora later. Please. Come on, Jimmy. Let's go."

"Georgia. Be good. We'll go soon, but if you're not good, we won't go at all. Don't say any more."

Georgia must have heard the edge in her voice, because she said she would be good.

Lena wiped off their faces and hands, and they all went into the playroom with Nora carrying Jimmy on her hip. Lena dumped out the toy box, and Nora set Jimmy down in the middle of the spilled toys. Jimmy picked up a little plastic cow, and Georgia sat down beside him and took it away. Lena grabbed it and gave it back before Jimmy had time to react with anger or tears. She dug through the toys and found a plastic horse for Georgia. "Be nice," she said automatically. "We'll be right back."

As soon as she and Nora were around the corner, she said, "Now tell. What are you going to do? Are you glad? I was so scared you were going to die."

"I don't know what I'm going to do," Nora said. She looked unhappy.

"But, Nora, are you glad about this?"

"No. I guess not. It's not like with you. I mean I didn't want...."

Lena peeked in at the children. They were both sitting in the pile of toys. Georgia was bending toward Jimmy in a motherly way, telling him something. "I wish you were glad about it. I'm so happy to know there's nothing wrong with you. I really convinced myself that you had cancer and that you came home to die."

"You always make up a story, and then you believe it. I remember when...."

"Yes, but those were games. When I think about how close I came to asking Mom if she had noticed how sick you looked—I mean, that could have been serious."

"Oh God."

"Have you told her anything?"

"No, and I'm hoping I won't have to. She's looked at me funny a couple of times, but...."

"You'll have to tell her sooner or later."

"Maybe not. It depends on what I decide to do."

They were standing in the middle of the living room. Lena thought of suggesting they sit down, but she knew that as soon as they got comfortable, the kids would be sure to start to fight with each other or else to come out and interrupt their conversation. Then she realized what Nora had said. "You mean an abortion?"

Nora nodded.

Before she knew what she was going to say, she said, "But that would be awful." It just burst out. She didn't mean to say it, and Nora looked so miserable that she wanted to take her in her arms and comfort her, the way she would do with Georgia if Georgia got hurt.

She wanted to, but she didn't because she wasn't sure Nora would like it if she did. Nora looked as though she might cry any minute.

"I'm sorry. I didn't mean to say that. It just came out. I guess I was thinking about Georgia and Jimmy."

Nora shrugged, trying to act like she didn't mind. "I know," she said. "I've been thinking about them all the time. But I don't know what else to do. I don't have any of the things I need, no job, no place to live...."

"What about the...." She didn't know what to call him.

But Nora knew. "He's not involved," she said, and her voice had a new, harsh edge to it.

"That's not realistic."

"I can't help it."

"But tell me...."

"I'll tell you about it someday, but I can't now. All I can say now is that he doesn't know, and he's never going to know."

"But, Nora...."

Nora shook her head. "I was desperately in love with him, but he was married. I don't have any choice about this."

She looked so hurt that Lena hugged her. She didn't think about it. She just did it. She was patting Nora on the back and saying it was going to be all right when she heard a little voice behind her saying, "How did Aunt Nora hurt herself?"

Lena turned around. Georgia was standing in the doorway, her face tight with worry. "It's okay, sweetie. She'll be fine." Behind Georgia, Jimmy was looking on solemnly.

Nora gave her hair a shake and brushed her hand across her eyes and smiled. "I'm better, kids. See. Your mom made me feel better." She grabbed Lena's hand and squeezed it. "You did too. I'm glad I told you."

Lena's heart was bursting with love and worry. She didn't just want to help Nora feel better. She wanted to do something real, something significant, something that would make everybody happy. She looked around quickly to make sue the kids had gone back to their toys. "But when are you going to do something about it?"

"I don't know. I was there. At the clinic. It was all set up. And I walked out."

"But…."

"I can't explain it. I didn't even get my money back. Wasn't that dumb?"

"Oh sweetie. I'll help you. I'm just glad you're not sick with cancer or something horrible like that."

Then Nora hugged her. "Thanks. I'm glad I told you. I wish you could help. The hard part is knowing what to do."

"I know. I'm just thinking of what Mom would say."

"Mom cares too much about what the neighbors think."

"I know."

"She always has, and it's not good. Look at you and Jerry."

"What do you mean?" Lena asked with a sudden stab of fear. Did Nora know something about Jerry that she didn't know?

"Don't look so worried," Nora said. "I know you guys would have gotten married anyway. But remember how you had to hurry up because Mom flipped out at the idea of you living together?"

"Oh yeah. I'd forgotten that."

"That's all I meant."

"I guess you're right. I mean, when you think what Mom would say, I guess you have to do it."

"I've got to make up my mind soon too, because I'm pretty far along."

"How far exactly?"

"It's still the first trimester, but just barely. It gets more complicated after that."

"How did it get so late?"

"I don't know. It just happened. I kept thinking all fall that I would be home so soon, and I kept having to stay for one reason or another."

"But why didn't you do one of those tests with a kit from the drugstore?"

"I should have. I kept thinking those tests were wrong a lot and that I was going to be home any day. I wanted to go to Planned Parenthood and find out for sure. But maybe it was just that I didn't want to know until I was back home and safe."

Just then Jerry came down the stairs, looking sleepy and disheveled. He had on blue jeans and his old gray sweatshirt. "Don't let her force you to do it, Nora, whatever it is."

Lena said, "Stop it, Jerry. You don't know anything about it."

Jerry walked through the living room, rumpling his hair with both hands. His feet were bare. "Where are the kids?"

But they had heard his voice and were already rushing through the door toward his legs. Georgia said, "Daddy, Daddy, pick me up."

Jimmy held onto his father's trouser leg to steady himself while he looked up hopefully.

"Okay, little man, you first," Jerry said, bending over to pick Jimmy up. "Come on, Georgia. Daddy has two arms." He picked her up too and walked into the kitchen with them both.

Lena smiled at Nora, glad she was seeing Jerry at his best. Nora was smiling too, but it was such a sad smile that Lena couldn't bear it. "No," she said. "You can't do it, Nora. I mean, look at Georgia and Jimmy. I mean...."

Then suddenly Nora was crying hard. "What are you telling me to do? I don't know what you're telling me. Now I'm all mixed up.

You said you were going to help me, but I'm more confused than ever."

Before Lena could say or do anything, Jerry stuck his head through the door to say, "Where's the coffee, honey?"

"I forgot it. We were talking and….I'll be right there."

Nora had turned around, hiding her face when Jerry appeared in the doorway. Now she said, "Go on. I'll be out in a minute. I'm sorry I got so upset."

"I know. I'm sorry too."

"I'm going to wash my face. I don't want Jerry to see...or the kids. I'll be out in a minute. You go make him his coffee."

"Okay." Lena went into the kitchen, but her mind stayed back with Nora, wishing she knew what the answer was. She was absolutely on Nora's side in this. And at the same time she wondered how she would feel if there were a child who was a half sister or brother to Georgia and Jimmy somewhere in the world and she didn't know it.

Jerry was sitting at the kitchen table, and the kids were underneath it. Jerry looked up as she came in. "Where's Nora?" he said.

He looked so soft and tousled from sleep, and Lena was feeling so full of love, that without answering him, she went over and hugged him and tried to sit down on his lap. She thought he would hug her back, but he didn't.

He pushed her away and said, "Come on, Lena. You haven't even started the coffee yet."

Lena stepped back, trying not to show how hurt she was because Georgia was peering up at her from the shadows under the table.

She picked up the coffee pot and went to the sink. Out the window, the sun was clear and bright, but the time for taking a walk in the snowy morning had disappeared. Now it would be time to punch down the bread, and then Jimmy would need changing, and they'd both need lunch and naps.

When she turned around with the coffee pot, Jerry was smoking a cigarette.

"I thought you said you wouldn't do that in front of the kids."

Jerry took another long pull on his cigarette and blew smoke toward her. "I don't know what you want me to do. It's freezing outside, or hadn't you noticed?"

"I know, but…." She plugged in the coffee pot and turned around to punch down the bread, so she wouldn't have to look at him.

"I live here too, remember. Sometimes you get like…."

He stopped because Nora walked into the room. She was smiling. No one said anything. Each one of them was trying to act as though nothing was wrong. The children had been playing house under the table, but now they both peeked out to see why it was so quiet.

Georgia scrambled out between the chairs. "It's time for our snowman. Aunt Nora's putting on her jacket."

Jimmy crawled out behind her and carefully stood himself up, holding on to a chair.

Nora said, "I don't know, kids." She looked at Lena.

"I don't think we have time any more, sweetie."

"But, Mommy…."

"We have to put the bread in the pans. Aren't you going to help me?"

"You said we were going to make a snowman. We've been waiting."

"I want to talk to Daddy. I don't get very many chances to talk to Daddy."

Nora was standing by the door with her jacket and hat on. "I can take them out to play in the yard. I don't have to be home for a while."

"Oh please, oh please," Georgia said.

"All right, if you'll come in when Nora says to."

Georgia was nodding her head intensely, and Jimmy was looking solemnly at everyone in turn, waiting for Georgia to work out the deal.

"Nora, don't you want to stay and have some coffee? We could talk."

"No. It's beautiful out. More talking wouldn't do any good, and I'm sick of it anyway."

Later, after the children were finally in their snowsuits and had gone outdoors with Nora, Lena got herself a cup of coffee and sat down across the table from Jerry. He didn't look up. She watched him reading the newspaper, tapping his fingers while he held his cigarette.

Then she saw what he was using for an ashtray. "Jerry, that's one of Grandma Willard's china bowls. You can't use that." She scooped it out from under his hand and took it to the sink to wash it.

That stopped Jerry from reading. He looked up. "Where's the ashtray?" he said. His voice sounded as though he was being careful.

But, as Lena thought bitterly, if he was really trying not to get in a fight, he wouldn't have pushed her away when she hugged him. Out loud she said, "The ashtray's in the cupboard where it always is. I washed it last night."

Jerry sighed and sat there waiting.

Out the window over the sink, Lena could see Nora and Georgia rolling a snowball for the bottom of the snowman, while Jimmy waddled along behind them trying to help. The children's snowsuits were bright patches of red and blue in the sunlight. "I was wrong about Nora. She isn't sick."

"Bring me the ashtray, will you, Lena?"

She did it with a very bad grace, setting the ashtray down hard in front of him. It was a heavy square of glass, and it made a thud when she put it down.

Jerry sighed again, tapping off the ash of his cigarette and turning the page of the paper, which was spread open on the table.

"Jerry, did you hear what I said about Nora?"

"I told you she was fine. I said you were making it up about the cancer, didn't I?"

Lena got out the bread pans and began to rub the inside of one with a lump of butter. "I wasn't making it up. I knew something was wrong." She finished the first pan and started on the second. She was hoping Jerry would ask her what was wrong, but he didn't. She knew Nora didn't want her to tell, even though Nora hadn't actually said so. But Nora didn't know what it was like to be married. Nora didn't know about the closeness and sharing everything.

Then Lena thought about how that closeness wasn't there for her and Jerry right now and how that was probably because of the children, because she and Jerry hardly ever got a chance to talk to each other any more.

Jerry looked up at her. "Well, are you going to tell me about it, or aren't you?"

"I was trying to decide. I mean, I want to tell you, but Nora might not like it."

"That's okay. Don't bother. I don't care."

"Don't say that. You know I'm dying to tell you." She took a quick look outside to where Nora and the children were busy putting the head on the snowman. "She's pregnant," she said.

"I thought that might be it."

"She's been having morning sickness. That's why I was right. She *is* sick."

"She's going to keep it then."

"No, she's not. She can't. I don't know what she's going to do. I'm going to help her if I can." She gave him a stern look. "But, Jerry, if you say a word to anybody, I'll kill you."

"I won't," he said. "You know I won't. I don't have time for gossip anyway."

"I wouldn't call it gossip."

"What is it then?"

"I don't know."

"Listen, Lena, you and I have really got to talk about some stuff, and I can't seem to make that happen."

"What do you mean by 'some stuff'?"

"Stuff about us. We really have to."

"Oh," Lena said with a sinking feeling. "Can't it wait? I have to get this bread in the pans, and then the kids will be in again."

"I guess it'll have to."

"There'll be more time to talk when Christmas is over."

"I guess so," he said, but he didn't sound as though he meant it.

"I'll make some time then," Lena said. "Right now I want to concentrate on Nora and on Christmas."

"This is about you and me, Lena. You always have time for Nora or your mom or the kids, but you never have time for us."

"That's not true. I hate it when you say things like that."

"Okay. I'm going to shave. It's getting late."

So when Nora and the children came in laughing and stamping the snow off their boots, Lena was alone in the kitchen, kneading the bread. Nora looked a little surprised that Jerry wasn't there, but she didn't say anything about him, so Lena didn't have to either. Nora helped her get the children undressed, and then she left to walk home.

Chapter 13

Conrad left his jacket in the mudroom and went up the steps into the kitchen. He hadn't taken his boots off because he wanted to get going as soon as he could.

"I wiped my feet real good, Ma," he said. And then, "How're you doin, Dad?"

"I've been better."

Conrad held his hands out over the fire. He had forgotten his gloves, and his hands were freezing.

Ma was at the sink. She turned off the water and came over to the woodstove. "Is everythin all right, Conrad? Do you want a cup of coffee?"

"Yes it is, and yes I do. I want to talk to you and Dad."

"I knew somethin was up with you comin over in the middle of the day like this."

"It ain't anythin bad. I'd tell you right off if it was." He was hoping to make it quick. He knew she wasn't going to like it.

"Okay, then. Hold on while I get your coffee." She bustled over to the stove.

Conrad brought a kitchen chair over near Dad's and sat down. "Does it still hurt a lot, Dad?"

"Not so much anymore. It itches though. That drives me crazy."

"That means it's healin."

"I wish to hell it'd hurry up then."

Conrad didn't say anything.

"Don't make a big production out of it, Ursela. Just get the boy his coffee."

After a few minutes, she came over to where they were sitting, carrying the coffee in one hand and a plate of cookies in the other.

"I put you in some milk and sugar."

"Thanks, Ma."

"Want some tea, Cal?"

"No. Come on and sit down, or we'll never find out what this is about."

So she sat down in her chair and picked up her knitting.

Conrad was silent, sipping his coffee. Then he said, "Walt Jackman wants me to buy his skidder. He's gettin a new one."

Silence again, except for the click of the knitting needles.

"He wants five thousand dollars, and I told him I'd do it."

"Five thousand dollars! That's a lot of money."

"That shows how much *you* know about it, Ursela."

"It'll make money for me, Ma. The price of firewood's goin through the roof with all this oil embargo stuff."

"You got a job now."

"I'm goin to quit. I already told John. I'll be all done at New Year's."

"But you've got responsibilities, Conrad."

"I know. You don't have to tell *me* that."

"I think it's wrong. You'll be throwin away a good job."

He knew the conversation was going to go like this. "It's not a good job. It's a dead end. I've been there too long already."

"Your dad worked at that feed store for years. He didn't think it was so bad."

"Well, why'd he quit then?"

She paused her needles with a sharp intake of breath.

Dad said, "I saw somethin better to do. That's why I quit."

"You didn't like it either, did you, Dad?" Conrad could remember the arguments from when Dad quit. He knew they would be the same, and they were.

"I hated it. I couldn't wait to get outa there. I don't blame you for wantin to quit."

"Wantin to and doin it are two different things. He's got a family to support."

"Leave the boy alone, Ursela. He knows more about it 'n you do. I can't believe he stood it as long as he did."

"Thanks, Dad."

She got to her feet stiffly. Her feelings were hurt. "I guess I better get them dishes done up." She walked over to the sink, limping a little.

Conrad watched her until she got to the sink and turned the water on. Then he said, "I'm goin over to the landin where Walt has the skidder. You want to ride with me?"

"I might. You goin over to take a look?"

"I already looked. I'm goin over there to get it."

"How're you plannin to do that?"

"Well, Dad. I was hopin to use your low-boy trailer. It ain't broke, is it?"

"Not that I know of. I ain't used it in a while."

"Well then, what about it?"

"Look here. You're goin to need it a lot. Why don't you buy it from me?"

"I can't do it, Dad. I'd really like to, but I'm flat out. We had to borrow some money from Cheryl's mom as it is. I could give you some rent for it when I use it."

"All right, and what happens if it gets broke?"

"I'll pay to get it fixed, if I can't fix it myself. How about it?"

"I suppose that might work out. What're you goin to pull it with? That old beater of a cattle truck?"

"It ain't like I got a choice."

Just then Ma turned off the water and looked around. "What does Cheryl say about it, Conrad?"

"She wants me to. She knows how unhappy I am at the feed store. I could stay there for the rest of my life, and it wouldn't be any different."

"At least the money would be comin in."

"Cheryl's got a good job. You know that. You got security when you work for the state. We have it all figured out. It ain't a stupid thing to do, Ma."

"Nobody never got rich loggin and tryin to pay for a skidder."

"It's better'n what I'm doin now, and Cheryl says so too."

"Well, I hope you're right, and I'm wrong."

"You'll see, Ma."

"I hope so."

Dad said, "I'm goin over there with Conrad to pick it up."

"Cal, you can't. What about your foot?"

"I don't need my foot to ride in Conrad's truck. I can't sit around by the woodstove for the rest of my life."

"But, Cal...."

"I want to see what happens to my low-boy when Conrad loads that skidder on it and tries to pull it with his piece-of-shit truck."

"You heard what Dr. McCormack said."

"Conrad, go out and hitch the low-boy on. I'll be there in a couple of minutes. You got to learn to do that alone anyhow, and it ain't hard."

"Okay, Dad."

"I'll be back in time for chores, Ursela."

She didn't say anything. She just sighed.

Conrad went over to her and patted her broad, soft shoulder.

She jumped and turned around. "Oh, I didn't know you were still here."

"Don't worry, Ma," he said. He wasn't sure what he meant her not to worry about, but he didn't want to say more because he had to get going if he was going to have time to move the skidder.

She grunted a little and went back to washing the dishes.

Out in the mudroom, Dad was sitting in a chair, putting a plastic bag over his foot.

Conrad put on his own jacket and pulled his hat out of the pocket. "Take your time, Dad. It's goin to take a while to get your low-boy hitched on."

"It goes on easy. You'll see."

"Is it up in back?"

"Last time I looked."

"All right. I'll see you in a minute."

Conrad drove the big truck around the house to the east line of the back field, where Dad kept most of his old machines. It always looked the same, and it was always a little different. Conrad didn't look back there unless he needed something, sometimes a part off one of the junks, sometimes a functional machine.

The low-boy was about halfway up the field, just above a couple of junk balers. He backed up to it and got out of his truck to take a look. It was a simple hitch. In a few minutes he had it on his truck and held in place by a short length of chain.

He drove around to the front of the house again and stopped. Dad must have been waiting, because he came right out. Conrad rolled down the window and said, "You ready to go, Dad?"

"Did you get it hitched all right?"

"I think so. The brakes work, don't they?"

"Last time I looked."

"Get in then. I'll be ready in a minute. I got one more thing to do."

He got out and climbed into the back of the truck. He had forgotten to switch the hose to the other can of gas he was using instead of a gas tank. When he looked up, he saw Dad looking through the back window. Conrad was pleased. He thought Dad would be impressed. It was a slick arrangement.

But when he got back into the cab, Dad said, "What the hell were you doin back there?"

"My gas tank has a leak, so I'm bypassin it. No big deal. It works slick."

"God damn it, Conrad."

"Take it easy, Dad. You do things the same way." He started to back up, and then he stopped. "Can I take some of your chains? We might could need 'em."

"Look in my shop, hangin on the wall behind the door. If there ain't any good ones there, they'll be in the wagon behind the tractor. I ain't seen 'em since my foot got hurt."

So Conrad left the truck idling and went back to the shop. There were a lot of chains hanging on the wall. He picked out a couple that had decent hooks on both ends and slung them over his shoulder. They were so cold they stung his hands. He wished again for his gloves as he walked back to the truck with the chains clanking and dragging behind. He threw them into the back and opened the door to the cab.

Before he even had a chance to climb in, Dad said, "I been sittin here thinkin, Conrad. You ain't ready to go out on your own—an old truck, a second-hand skidder, and I don't even know what you got for a saw."

"It's old too, Dad. That's what I got. But I figure it might be now or never. I got to do with what I got. You still want to come with me?"

"I'm ready."

"Okay. Let's go."

When they were driving down the hill, Dad said, "You might could pick up a gas tank at the salvage yard. It wouldn't be that big a deal to put in."

"That's easy to say. But you run your machinery this way."

"When I ain't got a choice."

"If a guy had enough time and enough money, he wouldn't have to run this crap, but who has time or money?"

"Nobody I know, that's for sure." Then there was a short silence while they both thought about it. "I suppose George don't have any problems. When somethin breaks, he probably goes right out and buys himself a new one."

"Must be nice."

The sky was low and gray. The wind was blowing small flakes of snow across the road in front of the truck.

"You didn't pick a very good day for this trip. It looks like it could snow all day. It might could amount to somethin."

"I didn't have much choice. Today's my only day off all week. I need to get the skidder out of Walt's way so I can work on it."

"What's the matter with it?"

"Nothin much, mostly maintenance. I want time to go over it before I start tryin to use it."

"Where's Dwayne?"

"In school. He said he wanted to come with us, but Dwayne'd go to hell to get out of school."

"I remember the feelin."

"His grades ain't that good. It ain't goin to help to send him to the vocational school if he don't do the work and try to learn a trade."

Dad didn't say anything. They both knew how much Conrad wanted Dwayne to be an electrician, but Dwayne wasn't interested.

"He's good with engines. Maybe he'll give you a hand with your skidder."

"Not Dwayne. If it won't go over sixty, he ain't interested."

"That's the way kids are these days. He'll grow out of it."

"I wish he'd hurry up."

They rode on in silence for a while.

"Where's this skidder at, anyhow?"

"It ain't that much farther. We don't have to go all the way to Hardwick. We'll be takin a dirt road here in a minute. Walt's workin in a big woodlot over here."

"He must be doin all right if he can afford a new skidder."

"Well, it ain't new new. It's a step up for him is what it is. But it shows there's money in it, with oil prices goin the way they are."

"Don't forget gas prices are doin the same thing."

"I know. I may not make it. I may have to go back to the feed store. But I need to try it anyhow."

Dad gave a snort when he heard that. Still, he wanted Conrad to succeed, and Conrad knew it. Dad always got furious when he was worried. He was afraid for him. That's what made him so angry. Conrad looked over at his father's flinty profile, with his nose like the beak of a hawk and his mouth a thin line, a slit that could have been cut by a knife. Some ways he was hard to love, but Conrad loved him.

"Do you think I can get the skidder on your trailer all right, Dad?"

"I don't know. What'd Walt carry it on?"

"He has a trailer, but it's bigger'n yours."

"You might have to borrow his, if it won't fit on mine."

"Yeah. That's right. I could do that. I'm worried about it bein too wide."

"We'll find out when we get there. How much farther is it anyways?"

"We're almost there."

"Okay. So it'll keep."

"You're right, Dad." He looked around at him, grinning.

"You're damn right I am," Dad said, grinning back. "I just wish everybody would admit it."

Soon after that, Conrad turned off the pavement onto the dirt road. The snow was starting to stick. The road was white with it. No one had been along in a while. There weren't any tracks on the road.

"Here we are," Conrad said. He turned into the field. The skidder was parked beside a pile of logs.

"Kinda beat up, ain't it?"

"Well, yeah. That's why Walt got another one. If I luck out, I'll be able to do the same thing." Conrad pulled the truck up beside the skidder and shut it off. "You can stay right here, Dad. If you get cold, just switch the motor on again, so you'll have the heater. I'll leave it outa gear."

But Dad was already opening his door. "Nope," he said. "I want to take a good look at this thing. You might could be makin a mistake here."

"Walt's my friend, Dad."

"Yeah, well, friends are nice, but it don't hurt to keep your eyes open. Besides, I need to stretch my legs....the good one anyhow." He slid out of the truck awkwardly, bracing himself with the crutch.

By the time he got over to the skidder, Conrad was up in the driver's seat, turning the key, trying to get it to start.

Dad looked up at him. "It ain't nothin but scrap metal if it won't start."

Just then the big diesel engine turned over and started to fire. It was so loud that it wasn't possible to say anything. Conrad could feel the thud of the engine inside his chest. He looked down at Dad. He could see the same excitement and pleasure that he was feeling reflected on Dad's face. There wasn't anything like the roar of a big engine to make you feel powerful. Far below, he watched Dad as he hobbled over to the low-boy to put the tracks down. Conrad smiled at him to thank him.

Then he needed to concentrate on lining the skidder up with the tracks.

Dad was watching, but he could only make hand signals. There wasn't any sense in shouting because the sound of the diesel engine was bouncing off the trees and filling the clearing with pounding noise.

The first time Conrad started up the ramp, he didn't have the skidder lined up straight enough, and he had to back it down and come at it again. But he saw it as soon as Dad did, so he didn't need any help.

The next try Conrad got the skidder on the low-boy. It didn't take long to chain it down. It was hanging off on every side, but it was on. They got back into the truck.

"I just hope we don't meet somethin that hangs out as far as we do."

"We ain't got far to go. I'm goin to leave it at George Carleton's."

"George Carleton's?"

"Yeah. He wants some log lengths for next year. It ain't much, but it's a start. When people come into the store askin who does loggin,

John's goin to send 'em to me."

They bumped along over the snowy road in silence for a while. Then Dad said, "Next thing you know, Paul's goin to want to get himself a business."

"Maybe. I think Paul's pretty happy where he is."

"What's he think about what you're doin?"

"He hasn't said much—you know Paul."

"He could stand to take life more seriously," Dad said, and then, "He could stand to get a haircut."

"Paul got the looks in the family. That's for sure."

"His hair's too long."

"That's the new style, Dad."

"Well, it looks like he ain't got the money for a haircut."

"I didn't mean to leave Elsie out. I was thinkin about Paul and me. I didn't mean nothin about Elsie's looks."

"Elsie gets too many haircuts. Why does she want to do that to herself?"

"Poor old Elsie. I wish she'd get over Mike's death. It ain't goin to bring him back."

Dad said, "Elsie used to have beautiful hair." He stopped.

Conrad suspected he was thinking about Ma. Her hair must have been beautiful like that when she and Dad met. But Conrad could never have said anything to Dad about it. He didn't even like to *think* about it in front of Dad. He could never have said anything personal about Cheryl either. Those were things people didn't say to anyone. You wouldn't even say something like that to your wife.

There was a loud bang, and something shook the truck. "What the hell was that?" Conrad said.

The banging and shaking continued. "You'd better check it out. Take a look at that hitch."

Conrad slowed to a stop. "I can't get off the road, but we ain't seen anybody yet. Maybe it'll be okay." He got out of the truck and went to see. In a few minutes, he came back. "The low-boy's jumped off the hitch. It's ridin on the chain. I'm goin to have to unload the skidder to get it back on."

"Conrad. Listen to me. Back that skidder up just enough for the lowboy to get light on the front end. You don't need to take it all the way off. You didn't get the chain on the hitch tight enough. That's what's wrong."

"But, Dad, I tightened it up as much as I could. It would of been okay if I hadn't hit that bump too hard."

"You're always goin to hit bumps in the road, for God's sakes. Do it the way I say to. I've done it before. It's a hell of a lot quicker than unloadin."

"Okay. I'll try."

"And be sure to shorten up on that chain."

Conrad didn't answer. He went back and took the chains loose and climbed onto the skidder. She fired right up on the first crank. He already loved that pounding feeling. This was going to be really fun. He should have done it years ago.

When he thought he had backed up enough, he got down to take a look at the hitch, but it was still putting so much weight on the chain that he couldn't move it. He got on the skidder again and went back another foot. This time he could feel what Dad meant when he said the front end got light. He put the hitch back together and tightened the chain like Dad said to do. Then he pulled the skidder forward and chained it down and got back in his truck. It was warm inside the cab. His hands started to ache, thawing out.

"I'm sure glad you came along, Dad. I wouldn't of thought to do that."

"It works good, don't it?"

"Slick. Thanks."

It didn't take long to get to George Carleton's place, and the lowboy stayed on the hitch, even on the steep uphill grade at the end. They came out near the top into Carleton's dooryard.

Conrad drove slowly past the house. "He said he'd open up the fence so I could use the pasture behind his house for a landin."

"It's open. Keep goin. You can drive right in. Old George is okay. When he says he'll do somethin, he does it. I don't have anythin bad to say about George Carleton."

Conrad nodded in agreement. He parked the truck in the field. Dad got out with him to help with the chains.

When the skidder was unloaded, Conrad started to get back in the truck.

"Wait just a minute. What're you goin to do with my low-boy?"

"I was plannin to take it back to your place, Dad."

"Well, look. Why don't you leave it here? You'll be all done before long and movin on to the next job."

"I hope so."

"There ain't no sense wearin it out draggin it back and forth over the roads."

"Okay. Thanks, Dad. If you need it, I can bring it to you."

They both got into the truck. Conrad backed the trailer up beside the skidder and then got out and unhitched it.

This time when he started to get back into the driver's seat, Dad said, "Hold on here. Where's my chains?"

"They're still sittin on the low-boy."

"I don't mean you to leave 'em here to get lost and frozen."

"I know. I'm sorry. I just forgot. I'll get 'em right now."

He threw the chains in the back of the truck, and they started for home.

"It must be gettin on towards four o'clock."

"We can start your chores as soon as we get there," Conrad said. And then, "What's happenin about the guy that shot you? It's been a while. Have the cops found anybody yet?"

"Hell, no. I don't suppose they're even lookin. If I want that guy, I'm goin to have to track him down myself."

"What would you do if you found him, Dad? You ain't plannin to shoot him, are you?"

"I'd like to."

"But you don't want to go to jail, do you? I mean, you'd get caught for sure."

"That's just the way the government operates. Of course they'd catch the man who was only tryin to retaliate—somethin any normal person would do. And they never would have no time to go after the guy who started it all in the first place. It's just what you'd expect."

"Supposin you're right. Where does it get you? You can't take any revenge or you'll end up in jail. So what do you want to find him for?"

"For one thing, then maybe people like George would believe me. George thinks I shot myself—as if it was even possible."

"How do you know he does?"

"I can tell by the way he looks at me. He got it in his head in the beginning. Maybe it was somethin your Ma said to him on the phone. There's no talkin to either of 'em."

"Well, look, Dad, I've heard some rumors at the store. It ain't nothin you could act on, but just so you know."

"What're you talkin about?"

"Only that I heard about this guy who shot a trophy buck and put it in his freezer kind of fast, more fast than you would think someone would do, especially with a buck he ought to be proud of. But it might be just a rumor."

"What's the guy's name?"

"I don't know."

"Why didn't you find out?"

"To tell you the truth, Dad, I didn't want to know any more."

"That's the dumbest thing I've ever heard you say. How does that make any sense?"

"It might not make sense to you, but it does to me."

"So who told you about this guy? Is it anybody I know?"

"You can't trick me like that, Dad. I know what your plan is. I ain't that dumb."

"Okay, Conrad. Just find out that guy's name and tell me, will you?"

"If you promise not to shoot him." Before Dad could say a word, Conrad went on. "If you promise you won't even talk to him."

"For Chrissakes."

"I'll get you his name if you promise."

"How would I even know if it was the guy I was lookin for if I didn't talk to him at least? Use your head."

"I don't care, Dad. I don't want to help you put yourself in jail."

"It ain't my fault if the cops ain't got any sense. Why should I be punished for it?"

"I don't know, Dad. I just know I don't want to help you get in trouble."

"Well, Conrad, you ain't the only one with ears. I can find out from somebody else, you know."

"I can't do nothin about that. It just won't be me, that's all."

"That's pigheaded."

"Maybe it runs in the family, Dad." Then in case he had said too much, Conrad said, "Hey, thanks for goin with me today, and thanks for the advice."

"I wish I could say the same."

"Maybe someday you will."

"I wouldn't hold my breath if I was you."

By that time, they were pulling up in front of the house. "Let's go in and get warm, and then we can do your chores. Okay?"

"Okay."

"I'll put your chains away when we come out again."

"Don't forget."

They left it like that.

Chapter 14

Even before George got out the kindling and the newspaper, he could see himself sitting on the white couch with his book while the fire blazed up in the fireplace beside him. He was giving himself three days off work as a Christmas present. As usual, he had too much work, and he was behind in some of it, but he was planning to take the time off anyway. He hadn't told Laurie. If she knew, she would think up all kinds of things that he had to do right away. For the next hour or so, with Nora and Laurie gone to make some last minute deliveries of Christmas gifts, he would have the house to himself. He thought of it as a kind of grand opening to his three days off, and he planned to make the most of it by really enjoying his solitude.

He moved the screen and opened the damper and began laying the fire. He had never been able to convince Laurie that they needed a woodbox beside the fireplace. She didn't want to mess up her plushy beige carpet. George had to go out to the back porch to get a couple of small logs. Since there was no one to see, he set them down on the carpet, feeling a guilty pleasure in the rebellious act.

When he lit the fire, it flared up into a bright blaze. He replaced the screen and went to the den for his book, George Aiken's *Senate Diary*, which he had been reading off and on all fall. He brought it back to the couch and sat down, looking around the room with satisfaction. Maybe he wouldn't say so to her, but he could admit to himself that Laurie was right. Even though it was inconvenient not to have the wood stacked beside the fire, it was good to have the room neat and clean. They could relax there with their friends or with a book. In the beginning, he thought it was a mistake to have beige carpet and white upholstery, but Laurie was right about that too. There weren't many windows, but even on this dark winter afternoon, the room gathered and held light.

George was feeling satisfied with everything, until he noticed that the fire was almost out. He sighed and put down his still-unopened book and knelt down on the hearth. He pushed the sticks of kindling around a little, hoping they would catch, afraid of losing the fire completely. He began to wish he had never thought of having a fire. His precious time alone was dribbling away. Nothing he tried made the fire catch hold and flare into life. He felt more and more irritated. Finally he stood and set the screen back in place. It wasn't the fire he had imagined, but it might keep limping along. It might even get stronger when the chimney warmed up.

He sat down and picked up his book once more. His hands were dirty. He held them up to his nose. He could smell the sour, smoked smell of a fire that won't burn. He was uncomfortable touching the white pages of the book. It felt disrespectful to Senator Aiken, and he admired Aiken. He went into the lavatory and washed his hands and face and combed his hair. His face in the mirror still looked fairly young—youngish, anyway. Not like Cal's. *He* looked ten years older than George, rather than the three years older he actually was. But George knew he took much better care of himself than

Cal did, and of course it showed.

When he went back to the living room, he thought the fire was a little stronger. He went to the sideboard and fixed himself a modest-sized drink of Scotch and water. He decided to skip the ice and walked to the couch sipping the drink. He sat down and picked up his book, but before he even had a chance to find his place, he heard a woman's voice outside. He set the drink on the floor beside the couch, not really concealed but not in plain view either. He was regretting the end of his time alone and trying to muster a little Christmas spirit to greet Laurie and Nora with when he heard a knock on the front door. He set his book down and went to the door reluctantly, wondering who it could be.

It was Elsie. It had been so long since he had seen her, that he might not have known who she was, if Cal hadn't been standing at the bottom of the porch steps, scowling and leaning on a cane.

Elsie said, "Merry Christmas, Uncle George. Can we come in?"

Before George had a chance to say a word, Cal cut in. "We don't need to go in, Elsie. We're not stayin."

George said, "Merry Christmas, Cal. Come warm up by the fire. I'm so glad to see you." And he was aware even as he said the words and knew they were true, that there was a teasing element to his invitation, that part of him wanted Cal to come in just because he knew Cal didn't want to, and because what Cal had just said to Elsie had been painful to hear.

Elsie smiled her shy, boyish smile. "Come on, Dad. Do you want a hand with the steps?"

"I don't need any help," Cal said irritably. He started up the steps, leaning on his cane and wincing each time he put his foot down. George and Elsie watched.

"This has got to be your doing, Elsie. How did you ever manage to get him to come?"

"Oh," Elsie said airily. "We get along. I can handle him. Can't I, Dad?"

George looked at Cal laboring up onto the porch. He could almost see the cartoon bubble coming out of Cal's head with the words, "Bah! Humbug!" written inside. He tried not to smile.

When Cal made it onto the porch, George said, "This is an honor. I can't remember the last time you graced my house with your presence."

"Damn it, George. Don't make fun. It ain't decent."

"Come inside anyway. I haven't seen Elsie for years. Come on." He opened the door wide and stepped aside to let them by.

"We've got chores," Cal said, but he limped into the hall. He had a boot on his left foot. On his right was an open-backed leather bedroom slipper. George recognized it as one that used to belong to their father. "We just came to bring you some things from Ursela. Give him the bag, Elsie."

"What's this?" George said, as she handed him the grocery bag. There was a clink of glass as he took it. While they were still on the porch, he had noticed the bag in her hand and had been dreading this moment. He was embarrassed. He opened the bag and looked in, feigning surprise. There were two canning jars inside, a quart jar and a smaller one, each with a red ribbon tied around its neck.

"Ma sent you some of her famous dill pickles and some homemade raspberry jam."

George said thank you, wishing he could cover his awkwardness with a present for them. He hadn't even thought of Christmas gifts for Cal and his family. And all the while he could hear Laurie's voice finding fault, because whatever Cal and Ursela did was wrong in her eyes. "I'll put these under the Christmas tree. Come and sit down by the fire."

Elsie looked at Cal and gave a tiny shrug that George pretended not to see. He carried the jars over to where the tree stood in the corner of the living room and set them down with the other gifts. He could hear Cal stumping into the room behind him, and he cringed, knowing Cal was taking note of how Laurie had spray-painted the tree silver and hung it with tinsel and blue lights. George could imagine what Cal would say about it on the way home. There was no way for him to tell Cal that it was Laurie's doing, not his. There was no way to say anything without being disloyal.

When George stood up and turned around, Cal was leaning on his cane in the doorway, and Elsie was just sitting down on the couch. She took off her knitted cap and ran her hand through her hair, which was cropped as short as a soldier's.

"Take off your jacket, Elsie. And, Cal, come in and sit down."

Cal limped into the room.

Elsie turned to smile at him. "Sit down, Dad. We won't stay long."

Cal limped over to the big, overstuffed chair and stood with his hand on the back of it. "There's not much point in sittin down when we ain't goin to stay."

George sat down beside Elsie.

Cal said, "I know what you're thinkin, George, so don't bother sayin it." He lowered himself slowly into the chair. "Here I am, but not for long, and it'll probably take the both of you to pry me up and out of here. This is just the kind of chair I have trouble with."

George couldn't have said why he laughed. "You're a hard man to get along with Cal, and I'm still glad to see you. I must be crazy." All those years when he was out of touch with Cal, he would have said that their lives had taken them in such different directions that they had nothing in common, that they were strangers to each other and always would be. And here he was, feeling a closeness and a love for Cal based on exactly nothing, except that they had the same mother and father. It didn't make any sense, and it couldn't be denied. "What do you think about him, Elsie? How's the old rascal doing?"

Elsie looked at George and then at her father, smiling shyly.

George thought about how Elsie's smile was the only thing about herself that she hadn't succeeded in making masculine after Mike died. She didn't see it, so she probably didn't know how gentle and sweet and womanly her smile was.

"Dad's foot is healing just fine. But his disposition is as bad as it ever was. Right, Dad?"

Cal banged his cane on the floor, one quick staccato stomp for emphasis. "Elsie," he said. "You might...."

But Elsie stood up without paying any attention to what Cal was saying. "Uncle George, could I just poke at your fire a little bit?"

George said, "Sure. Why not? But I don't think it'll do any good."

Elsie moved the screen and knelt down on the hearth. George thought she looked around and noticed his drink, but she didn't say anything and neither did he.

Cal was watching with interest. He said, "You could die of the cold in front of that fire."

George felt like saying, "Don't worry, Cal. We have central heating here." But he knew it would antagonize Cal, so he refrained.

Elsie gave one push to the pile of sticks, and the fire blazed up immediately. She stood and silently replaced the screen.

"Thank you," George said. "And I really mean it. I spent a long time fiddling around with that fire, and I didn't get anywhere. I don't know how you did it."

Elsie shrugged. "That's what comes of growing up with a woodstove, I guess."

"But I grew up with one too."

Elsie laughed. "I forgot that."

Cal said, "You gave all that up when you turned yourself into a city slicker."

"Now, Dad," Elsie said. "Don't pay any attention to him, Uncle George. He needs to learn some manners." She looked over at Cal. "It wouldn't hurt you to learn some city manners. Look how nice Uncle George looks. You could stand to learn some about city clothes too. I wish Uncle George could teach you how to dress."

George didn't say anything. He tried to look like he hadn't heard anything, but inwardly he was cringing. He could feel Cal flinching clear across the room. He had been feeling uncomfortable about his clothes ever since Cal and Elsie arrived. He knew his casual wool slacks were more expensive than any clothes Cal had ever had.

"I don't need George to tell me what to wear. I might wear a red sweater if it was huntin season. I know how. Who says I'd want to dress like that? Who says I want to go around lookin like a Christmas ornament? What's it open season on, George? The neighborhood cats?"

George said, "Where are your boys today, Elsie?"

"They stayed with Ma. They were going to help her cook for the big Christmas dinner."

"How old are they now?"

"Eleven last July. It doesn't seem possible, does it?"

George said, "When are you going to teach them to hunt, Cal?"

Elsie looked thoughtful. "We've talked about it," she said. "Maybe next fall. Right, Dad?"

"I don't know," Cal said. "We might could do a little target practice this afternoon. If I take 'em out in the woods both at once, they'll probably end up shootin each other...or me."

"I'm glad I had girls," George said.

"That's what I wanted to ask you about, Uncle George. Dad said Nora was back home."

George nodded.

"Is she planning to stay in Vermont?"

"I hope so."

"I'd love to see her. I guess the last time I saw her was not too long after I got married, when she was working on that school writing project. I always liked Nora a lot."

"She always liked you too."

"What's she doing with herself?"

"If I tried to tell you, I'd probably get it wrong, but she and Laurie should get home any minute, and she can tell you herself."

"It all seems so long ago. So much has happened since those days." Elsie sighed. Then she gave her head a quick little shake and said, "I'll tell you some family news, Uncle George. Conrad's going to go out on his own. Did Dad tell you?"

"No, he didn't. What'll he do?"

"He bought a log skidder. He's going into the logging business. He's been at that feed store ever since high school, you know."

"We can't stay, Elsie." Cal was pulling himself up out of the chair. "We ought not to of stayed this long."

George and Elsie jumped up and then stood watching as Cal slowly raised himself onto his feet.

"Don't rush off, Cal. They should be home any minute."

Cal was up now, reaching for his cane. "It don't make no difference, George. We've been here too long already. Elsie'll have to finish talkin another time."

Elsie was zipping her jacket. "All right, Dad," she said. "You win." She looked up at George. "Tell Nora I hope to see her soon. We have to go down to Randolph tomorrow. I have to work. But we're planning to come up again in the middle of the week. She glanced at Cal. "If Dad gives the boys some shooting lessons, I know we'll be back. Tell Nora I'd love to see her."

"I'll do that, " George said. He walked beside Elsie to the door while Cal clumped along ahead of them.

"So don't forget, Uncle George, if you need some firewood, or if you run into anybody who has a woodlot that needs cutting...."

"Elsie, come on. We have to get out of here." Cal threw the words over his shoulder as he struggled with the porch steps. He didn't even say goodbye.

Still, George had to admit to himself that he was relieved that he hadn't been able to convince them to wait for Laurie and Nora. If they didn't come back for a long time, he would be stuck trying to think of things to say, trying to calm Cal, while pretending not to notice that he was using up the last scraps of his time alone.

As it turned out, Laurie and Nora arrived only a few minutes after Cal and Elsie drove away in Elsie's little car. They both came in and sat down near the fire.

"This is great, Dad. You look so comfortable. I wish I had stayed and kept you company."

"I wish you had too. Cal was here, and Elsie was with him. She really wanted to see you too, only you know Cal. He couldn't stay. The whole time he was here, he was trying to get away."

Laurie said, "What'd he come for then?" She looked over at Nora with a sour look on her face.

"They brought us some pickles and some jam made by Ursela,

and you can be sure it's good if Ursela made it."

"All right," Laurie said. "Don't get so defensive."

"How was Elsie, Dad? How did she look?"

"She said she was fine. I guess she looked fine. But, I don't know, there's something so sad about Elsie. I'm glad she's not my child. I don't know how Ursela can stand it. It's like her life is over."

"Maybe Ursela doesn't see it that way, George. And maybe it's just your imagination anyway."

"No, it's not. She's a young woman. She's only a few years older than Nora, and yet somehow her life is over."

"How do you know that? She didn't say so, did she? You said she looked fine."

"No, she didn't say so. This is what I mean. Why doesn't she find someone else? I mean I know she loved Mike, and it's sad he got killed in Vietnam, but other women have been widowed. Life goes on. Elsie looks fine, but her hair is still all chopped off shorter than most men wear it these days. And her clothes are men's clothes too. I mean she hasn't gotten over it."

"But, Dad, how could she get over it? He was the only person she ever cared about, and he's dead. I don't see how that's something to *get over*."

"I don't mean to sound indifferent. It's just that it makes me sad to see she has given up all that part of her life so young. It won't bring Mike back. Mike's dying was a waste, and this is a waste too. I was noticing today what a sweet, feminine smile she has. I was thinking she doesn't know that, or she probably would have tried to get rid of that too."

Laurie said, "Didn't Mike go to Vietnam with his two best friends?"

"I think so. Do you remember, Nora?"

"I didn't have too much to do with Elsie then. She was married, and I was at UVM, and she was a hawk, of course, when Mike enlisted, but yes, I think they all three went in together."

George said, "Brad and Pete. She named the twins for them, didn't she?"

Laurie said, "I wonder what happened to them. I wonder whether they help her at all."

"I don't know. Anyway, I hope you see her, Nora. She seemed to want to get back in touch with you. Poor Elsie. I feel sorry for her."

Laurie shifted impatiently in her seat. "You feel sorry for everyone, George. She doesn't *have* to act as though her life is over. She *chooses* to do that. You can't feel sorry for someone who does what they want to do."

"I think you can, Mom. It *is* sad. I mean, I think it was foolish of Mike to go to Vietnam, but I think it's awfully sad that he died, that Elsie has to live the rest of her life without him, that his little boys have to grow up without ever knowing their father. You can feel sorry about all of that and still think they made some wrong choices. Anyway, I wish I'd seen her. I had a present for Uncle Cal too."

Laurie looked surprised and tried to hide her interest. She couldn't seem to like anything about his family, although once in a while George could see that she tried. But what interested him most of all was what Nora said. He wanted to hear more. Here was a person he didn't know. But before he could think how to continue the conversation, Laurie started talking about dinner, and the moment was lost.

Chapter 15

It wasn't even four-thirty in the afternoon, but it was already beginning to get dark outside. It was extra early today because of the storm. Cal was sitting by the kitchen stove, feeling sleepy and stupid, the way he always felt when he had to sit around the house, talking and eating, when he couldn't get away by himself to do anything.

At least Christmas was over for another year. When you added Conrad and Paul and their wives and kids to Elsie and her twins, the house was way overloaded. So many people underfoot made Cal feel hemmed in. He got to feeling like he would do almost anything to escape. He could almost understand how an animal caught in a leghold trap would be willing to gnaw its own leg off to get free.

Ursela was in her glory, of course, cooking and waiting on everybody and getting so many compliments that it would be weeks before she'd be back to normal. Cal couldn't see the kitchen sink from where he was sitting, but he knew she was there because he could hear the clatter she made as she washed the dishes from the Christmas dinner. Everyone had hurried away early without even helping to clear up when they saw how hard it was snowing.

Conrad and Paul talked about the weather report on the radio. The weatherman said there was going to be eight to twelve inches of new snow. That convinced Elsie she needed to leave early before the roads got bad. Cal couldn't have given precise numbers, but he knew what it was going to do. He could have told them yesterday that it was going to be a heavy snow and that it was going to start in the middle of the day and keep on all night. All the signs said so. Even the chickadees were moving around less than usual. But nobody asked him, so he didn't say anything. Nobody believed what you said unless you could throw around some numbers.

He shouldn't feel annoyed by that because Christmas was over, and he was glad. He needed to get up and start doing something. That would make him feel more like himself again. He'd been sitting around all day, thinking of all the things he ought to do, all the things he wanted to do. And yesterday he'd had to go to town with Elsie to buy a present for Ursela. Elsie had insisted on that, and then she wanted to stop at George's house, which made the trip even longer. It was worse than usual because he had been trapped by his hurt foot for a month, and only in the last few days had he been able to get along without a crutch, although he still needed a cane. There were so many things he could be doing right now, too many. His mind flipped from one to the next.

"You want me to come help you clear up the dishes?" he said to Ursela.

"What's that?"

He heard her turn off the water.

"I couldn't hear what you wanted."

He had to say it over again, louder this time. "I don't want nothin. I said did you need some help cleanin up. That was all it was."

"There's not much left to do."

He heard her turn on the water again. Did she resent it because he'd offered to help her? There was no telling about women.

After a couple of dishes, he heard her turn off the water again. "Do you want me to bring you a piece of apple pie?"

"No," he said. "I'm goin out to my shop. I'm hopin this day won't be a total waste of time."

She didn't answer, and after a short pause, he could hear the water running and the clatter of dishes again, so he knew the conversation was over.

He would have to go out and make a fire and give the place a chance to warm up a bit before he could do anything. It was so late that by the time he really got going on anything, it would be time to quit and go to bed. It almost wasn't worth it. It wouldn't be worth it except that he had been sitting around for too long and felt ready to explode with pent-up energy.

He got his cane and put on his jacket and hat and went out without his boots. There was a path to his shop and only an inch of new snow so far. It was a soft and quiet evening. The snow was falling steadily out of a black sky. They were small flakes, and there wasn't much wind, so they were coming straight down. The only sound was the soft hissing as they landed. Already, just a few steps past the light from the mudroom door, Cal felt more at peace than he had for days.

He went around back and pushed open the shop door. He loved the loud, complaining creak of the door. It was a greeting. It meant he was home, more home than he was in the house, even though he had lived there all his life.

He built a small fire in his stove, and when he was sure it was going to go, he went back into the house for his barn clothes. Conrad and Paul had lugged water for the pigs and chickens and thrown down enough hay for Cal to feed out tonight, so Conrad wouldn't have to come back again. They had dried off Star a month early, so the milking was a little easier. Maybe it wouldn't be too long before he didn't need the boys twice a day, but it was going to be a while before he could clean the barn without help.

He fed the chickens and then the pigs. He had forgotten to bring down the garbage from the Christmas dinner. The pigs were going to like that, but they'd have to wait until tomorrow. He would give them all the milk so he didn't have to carry it up to the house. He milked the two cows and turned all three of them out to get a drink of water while he struggled over to the pigpen, carrying the second pail of milk. He fed out the hay and grain to the cows and brought them back inside. Then he turned out the lights and stood there for a minute listening to the sounds of chewing and rustling as the animals settled down for the night.

Just before he got to the house, he thought he saw headlights coming up the road. He hurried into the mudroom before whoever it was came around the final turn. It had to be a turnaround since it was too soon for the plow truck. He didn't think any more about it, even though it was odd that anyone would be out driving around Christmas night in a snowstorm. But then you never could predict what people would decide to do.

A few minutes later while he was taking off his barn boot and the plastic bag he put over his injured foot to keep it out of the manure, he heard a knock on the mudroom door and saw Nora looking through the glass at him.

He said, "Come in," and stood up to open the door for her, trying to disguise the way he startled when he saw her face through the glass of the door. By the time he got there, she was already inside.

"Merry Christmas, Uncle Cal. It really looks like Christmas outside, doesn't it?"

"You could say that," he said, while he tried to decide how to ask her what she was doing out here at night and in a snowstorm. "Come on in the kitchen by the fire," he said, stumping over to the steps, leaning on his cane. "You go first. I'm slow gettin up steps these days." He hoped Ursela was in the kitchen. She would find out what this was about.

But the kitchen was empty. Cal pushed Ursela's easy chair up a little closer to the stove and told Nora to sit down. She looked at her wet shoes and said, "Oh, look. I'm getting your floor all wet. I'll be right back."

As soon as Nora left the room, Cal shouted for Ursela. She had to be somewhere nearby. She had the television turned on.

The second time he called her name, she came around the corner.

"What's the matter now?" she said.

"We got company. Nora's here."

"Nora?"

"Yes, Nora. You heard me."

Just then Nora came up the steps into the room.

"Nora. What a surprise!"

"I came out to say merry Christmas," Nora said, looking from Ursela to Cal and back to Ursela again. "That's all right, isn't it?"

"There's nothin wrong, is there, Nora? Is somethin wrong at home?"

"Oh no. Is that what you thought? No, everything's fine. I was hoping I'd get to see Elsie and her boys."

Ursela said, "They left early. They wanted to get home before the roads got bad."

The three of them stood awkwardly near the two chairs, while the television blabbed away in the middle of everything, and Ursela kept looking around at it.

"Turn that thing off, Ursela," Cal said finally. "And bring up another chair here, so we can sit down."

She did it without saying anything, but her hand lingered on the knob of the television. He could see she didn't want to shut it off. She liked to sit by the thing in the evening, no matter what was on. It was lucky she didn't care, since they only got the one channel, and even up as high as they were, that one was all fuzzy and snowy. Cal couldn't see the point of it himself.

Ursela came back with one of the kitchen chairs. She put it down near the other two and sat down on it. "Sit, Nora," she said, waving at the easy chair she usually sat in herself.

Cal lifted the lid on the stove to see if it needed any wood. It was burning brightly, and he decided not to bother. He hoped his fire out back didn't need anything. He probably wouldn't get out there at all now with Nora here. He hobbled over to his chair and lowered himself into it, conscious that both Ursela and Nora were watching. When he was down, he said, "Okay, you can stop watchin. I ain't goin to fall over."

Ursela looked annoyed. And, of course, he'd said it to annoy her.

Nora thought it was funny. He caught her smile. She had some grit, that girl.

"I was hoping Elsie would still be here. I missed her yesterday too. Dad said you were over at our house with her."

"Yup."

"I wish I'd been there. Is she doing okay?"

Ursela reached over to pat Nora's hand, which was lying on the arm of the chair. "She was sorry she missed you too. I'm glad she didn't know you were comin today because she probably would of stayed to see you."

Cal could see Nora was getting the wrong idea. He wouldn't have cared if he hadn't liked her so well. "You oughtn't to say things like that, Ursela. She's got to think you don't want her here."

"No, I...."

But Ursela broke in. "She knows that's not so." She patted Nora's hand again. "She knows it's only because of the storm."

No one said anything for a minute, and when Cal looked at Ursela's face, he could see those big, heavy wheels turning in her brain. Ursela was slow to take on a new idea. But once it got there, it dug in deep, and there wasn't any way to dislodge it, a fact that often made him grit his teeth.

Ursela looked worried. "You shouldn't stay, honey. The roads are goin to get bad tonight."

"It's okay, Aunt Ursela. I don't have far to go."

"This is supposed to be a big storm. Maybe as much as a foot of snow tonight."

"I'll be fine."

"But, honey...."

"You can't tell her what to do like you do your own kids, Ursela. She's goin to think you don't want her here."

"Oh no I wouldn't, Uncle Cal. I *like* it when Aunt Ursela treats me like one of her children."

She smiled at Ursela who sat there full of herself. She was so sure Nora was on her side. And it wasn't that Cal meant to put her down. It was just that she could be so exasperating the way she always tried to mother everyone and everything that came her way.

"I've got a Christmas present for you, Uncle Cal," Nora said, standing up. "I'll get it. I left it in the mudroom when I took off my jacket and sneakers."

Cal heaved himself up to his feet and got a chunk of wood out of the woodbox. It was something to do until Nora got back, so he wouldn't have to see Ursela looking satisfied. He wondered why Nora would be giving him a present. It made him a little nervous. He dropped the stick of wood on the fire, sending a plume of sparks toward the ceiling. When he put the stove lid back and turned around, Nora was sitting in her chair with the package on her lap. It was done up in red and green paper. She held it out to him.

Cal was embarrassed, but he had no choice. He took the package and hobbled back to his seat, lowered himself into it, and put the package on his knees, careful not to look in Ursela's direction. He knew he ought to say something, but he couldn't.

"Well, go on, Uncle Cal. Aren't you going to open it?"

"Oh yeah," he said. "Thank you." He ripped open the paper. Inside was a box of Milky Way candy bars. For a second he didn't get it and sat there blankly.

"It's really a joke," Nora said.

"Right," Cal said. "It's a good one. Thank you. I appreciate it." And then, because he remembered the trip with Nora to the top of the hill to look for evidence, and because he didn't want to have to explain the joke to Ursela, he went on quickly, "Did your mother and father have a nice Christmas?"

"Wait a minute. Wait a minute," Ursela said. "Somebody needs to tell me this funny joke. I don't understand it."

"I'll explain it to you later, Ursela," Cal said in a last attempt to avoid what he knew was coming.

But there was no stopping Nora. "When Uncle Cal and I went up in the woods with the tractor and wagon looking for clues, we found a candy-bar wrapper. Uncle Cal thought maybe the man who shot him dropped it there. That's all." She looked from Ursela to

Cal and back to Ursela again with a puzzled expression on her face. "It was a Milky Way. That's all. I guess it isn't very funny."

Cal could have said something cutting and sarcastic, but not to Nora. He never felt like speaking to Nora that way. Instead, he said, "It's nice. It was a good joke. Thank you, Nora." He held out the box. "Here. Would either of you like a candy bar?"

Neither of them paid any attention. Nora looked worried, and he could tell that Ursela was just about to say something.

"I'll explain everythin later, Ursela." He could see her trying to figure it out, and he was still hoping that he wouldn't have to explain the whole thing. He definitely didn't want Nora to explain it to her. "She didn't know about the candy wrapper," he said to Nora. "I forgot to tell her."

Nora smiled at Ursela. "You weren't home the day I came out and poor Uncle Cal was trying to get on the tractor so he could go up in the woods to see if he could figure out who shot him."

"Really?" Ursela said, looking back and forth from one to the other of them.

"Yes," Nora went on, and Cal could see he was in for it. He told himself that Ursela didn't have any right to tell him what to do. But at the same time he knew that nothing would stop her from trying to run his life and keep him a cripple. She'd love it if he was helpless.

Nora was just opening her mouth to say more, to fill in all the details of that afternoon in the woods, to give Ursela a little extra ammunition. But before she had a chance to say anything, there was a knock on the mudroom door, a knock so loud that it rattled the glass.

The dogs both leaped to their feet and started to bark.

Cal jumped too. "What the hell?" he said. "It's gettin to be like New York City around this place."

Then the door opened, and someone said, "Can I come in?"

Ursela was starting to get to her feet.

"It's Biff," Cal said. "I wonder what *he* wants."

Ursela went out into the mudroom. Cal and Nora sat in their

seats listening to Biff talking as he took off his jacket.

Biff came up the steps behind Ursela. Before he was even in the room, he said, "Merry Christmas, Cal. I can't stay but a minute because my team's...." When he saw Nora, he stopped. "I didn't know you had company. I thought that car was Conrad over to do the chores." He looked at Nora, looked away, and then back at her again. It was clear that he liked what he saw. "Excuse me for intruding," he said. "I won't stay."

But Ursela had gone for another kitchen chair, which she set down beside Nora. "Sit down long enough to get warm, Biff. Would you like some pie?"

"I was hoping you'd ask me that," he said, and then he looked around at the others. "But nobody else is having any."

"That don't make no difference," Cal said. "Get him a piece, Ursela."

"Apple, pumpkin, or mincemeat?"

"How could I choose when it's your pie, Ursela? You decide for me, will you?"

"I'll give you a little piece of each one," she said. "Nora, let me get you some pie too."

"Thank you, Aunt Ursela, but I just couldn't."

Biff was still standing beside his chair. He said, "So, your name is Nora. Let me introduce myself." He held out his hand. "Clifton Barker, but everyone calls me Biff."

Nora looked up and smiled as she took his hand, and that was when Cal had had enough. "Sit down, Biff, and stop actin like you're a politician or somethin. Nora's my niece, my brother's girl."

"I didn't know you had a brother." He let go of Nora's hand reluctantly.

"Well, I do. A lawyer." He shrugged. "He's gone to town. We don't see much of him out here. He's forgotten where he came from."

"No he hasn't, Uncle Cal. He talks about you all the time."

"Talk is cheap."

Now it was Nora's turn to shrug.

"So, Biff, what brings you over here tonight anyhow?"

"It was partly the thought of Ursela's pie, but mostly I needed to give Queenie and Duchess a little exercise." He sat down. "I left them in the barn all day today. They were crazy to get out."

Cal could see Nora looking curious, but he didn't see why he should be the one to explain to her what Biff was talking about. There was already more interest on Nora and Biff's faces than he felt comfortable about.

Ursela came back with a plate of pie. "Tell me which one is the best," she said, smiling at Biff when she handed him the plate.

Cal thought that Biff had more of a way with women than he would have thought. Maybe he just hadn't noticed when it was only Ursela.

No one said anything. The click of Biff's fork on the china plate was uncomfortably loud. Cal wished he could go out to his shop to check on his fire, but it was hard to stand up, and worse with everyone watching.

Finally Ursela said, "Have you met Cal's niece, Biff?"

Biff nodded with his mouth full of pie.

Just as Cal knew she would, Ursela went on. Cal could see she was trying to stir something up. "Nora moved back here from Boston about a month ago."

"Oh," Biff said between mouthfuls. "You're from Boston originally?"

"No, I'm from here. I had a job in Boston for a while, that's all. I didn't like it."

"So you decided to come back to Vermont. Did you come back alone?"

Cal had to restrain himself to keep from saying, "She's not married, Biff. Did you see any rings on her fingers?" He almost groaned at the obviousness of it, but he stopped himself from that too.

Ursela sat there with a little smile on her face, pleased at the awful turn the conversation had taken. "Biff is a logger," she said to Nora. "He works with horses."

"Oh," Nora said. It was clear she hadn't any idea what that meant.

"They're right outside now. That's why I can't stay."

"Would you like some more pie?"

"I'd love some, Ursela," Biff said, standing up and handing her the empty plate. It was funny that Cal hadn't ever noticed before how good Biff was at saying what Ursela wanted to hear. "But I can't. I have to get out there before the horses cool down." He looked at Nora. "Would you like to see them? I hitched them to the corner post of the porch. If Ursela would turn on the porch light, you could probably see them from the window."

Nora and Ursela got up and went into the other part of the kitchen to turn on the light and look out the window.

Biff stayed by the stove with Cal. He said, "I overheard some guy in the auto parts store the other day. He was bragging about the big buck he took down, and he shut up in a funny way when he saw I was listening."

"Who was he?"

"I don't know. He was a mean-looking little guy, weaselly. I've seen him around, but I don't know his name. You might know him. I'll ask Tim the next time I go in there."

"I'd appreciate it."

"From the way he was acting, I got an idea he might be the shooter. How's your foot, anyway?"

"Oh, I guess it's comin, but it's slow. I'm gettin sick of bein a cripple. I can't even do my own chores."

"It could've been worse, Cal. That little weasel looked like a guy that wouldn't mind taking you down altogether if he thought he could get away with it."

Nora and Ursela had been looking out the window and exclaiming over the horses. Now they came back into the room.

"They're beautiful. What are their names?"

"Queenie and Duchess."

"They're both girls?"

"Mares. They're sisters."

"I'd love to see them up close some time. I'd love to pat them."

Nora and Ursela were standing with Biff and at a little distance from Cal, who was still sitting in his chair. If he had been closer, he might have tried to interfere. As it was, he just listened with misgivings when he heard Biff say, "Would you like a sleigh ride? I'm just giving them a run because they wanted to get out. I'm not going far. You could come."

"Oh," Nora said. "I don't know. I have to get home pretty soon."

"All right. Some other time then."

And that would have been the end of it if Ursela hadn't jumped in. "Nora, call home and tell them you're goin to stay over with us, and then you could go for a ride."

"Well, I...I don't know."

"You shouldn't be drivin home in this snowstorm, anyhow."

"Well, I...I could," Nora said. "It would be fun." Her eyes were shining. She looked very pretty. "Would you mind waiting while I call home?" she said to Biff.

"No, I'd be glad to."

The telephone was in the corner of the kitchen, so they could all hear what she said. It was clear to Cal that Nora's parents didn't know she had planned to come out to West Severance in a snowstorm.

After a short conversation, Nora said goodbye and turned around. "Okay, it's all right with them if I stay over. Thank you, Aunt Ursela." Then a shadow crossed her face, and she said, "Oh, but I can't go after all. I don't even have a hat or a warm jacket. I wasn't planning on being outside."

"That's nothin," Ursela said. "I'll get you a hat and a jacket and mittens too, and I'll get a blanket to throw over your legs. Go on now and put on your shoes."

Biff was heading into the mudroom, but he turned back to tell Ursela that he had a lap robe in the sleigh, so she could forget about the blanket. Cal sat in his chair, watching the whole farce. They had all forgotten about him.

Ursela bustled out into the mudroom after them to get things for Nora to wear. Why did women always want to be matchmaking when anyone could see that it would be disaster for everyone?

After a few minutes, Biff stuck his head around the corner. "I'll see you, Cal. Merry Christmas. I'll find out the name of that guy if I can."

"Thanks, Biff," Cal said. He had been so busy thinking of Ursela and her foolish matchmaking that he had almost forgotten what Biff had told him. It could turn into something.

Ursela hurried through the room. "I'll be right back," she said over her shoulder. "I want to watch them out the window."

Cal didn't say anything.

In a few minutes, she was back. "They looked so romantic," she said. "He tucked the blanket in all around her."

"Christ, woman. What are you up to?"

"Nothin. It's nice to see young people havin a good time. That's all."

"You'll be sorry. It won't turn out like you think it will."

"I ain't thinkin about how it'll turn out."

"Nora's a good girl. Gettin married ain't such a great thing to do."

Ursela said, "I don't think Nora even has a boyfriend, and all the others are settled and have families already."

"Maybe Nora is different. And what about Elsie? She don't have nobody, and she's doin just fine. You should stay out of it. Nora would get herself a boyfriend if she wanted one."

"I'm not doin nothin," Ursela said. She went over to the television and switched it on.

"Do you think George would like his daughter to be goin out with a horse logger?"

"I don't know what George would like. What's the harm in a sleigh ride? And anyway, since when did you start carin about what George would like?"

"I don't. I was just sayin he might object."

"Anyhow, I think Nora might be pregnant."

That was it. There was no talking to someone who didn't make sense. Cal stood up slowly, stiff from sitting. He went out of the room without looking at her or saying anything to her. He got his jacket and went out the back door to his shop.

The shop was warm, although the fire was almost out. He decided not to build it up. There was enough warmth in the stove to last until bedtime. He had been planning to organize his tools and clear stuff off his workbench, but he didn't feel like it anymore. He started to put the tools and scraps of wood away, but he soon ran out of patience and sat down by the fire. And after a while of sitting there thinking bitter thoughts about everyone, he got up and poked the fire, knocking apart the last few coals. He shut the dampers and left. There was nothing to salvage out of the day. He might as well go to bed.

Ursela wasn't in the kitchen, but the television was still on, so he knew she wasn't far off.

When he shouted for her, she appeared in the doorway. "I was just upstairs fixin Elsie's bed. I'm goin to put Nora in Elsie's room. What do you want?"

"Nothin. I just wondered where you were. I'm goin to bed."

"All right. I'll wait up for Nora. Besides, it's early."

"I don't care. I'm tired. My foot aches."

He saw her open her mouth to say something, and then he saw her think the better of it and shut her mouth again. He thought of things he could say to her about her meddlesome ways, but he knew she wouldn't listen. At least all this matchmaking had made her forget what Nora told her about how he went up in the woods looking for clues and how he talked Nora into driving him up there. And nobody knew the worst part—that they had freewheeled part of the way down the hill when the tractor kicked out of gear. He had known it could happen, that it was even likely to happen, but he had said nothing to Nora. And he didn't say anything to Nora afterward either, so she still thought she had done something wrong. And that was the way he was going to leave it too, since no one else knew how foolhardy he had been, letting Nora drive down the hill relying completely on the gears when it often kicked out like that.

Ursela would remember tomorrow and crawl him for the part she knew about, but he didn't have to deal with it tonight.

Ursela had moved into the room so that she could see the television set while she waited to see if he was going to say any more. But what was there to say?

"I'm goin to bed," he said, stumping toward the door.

"Okay," Ursela said without taking her eyes off the TV. She had moved her chair up close and was sitting down before he got to the door. She didn't even look in his direction. That was enough. Even though it was only a little after seven o'clock, he was all done, and glad to be done, with such a useless day.

Chapter 16

As soon as she stepped through the door, she could smell the horses. In the light from the front porch, they looked gigantic. They made Uncle Cal's cows seem quite ordinary. Nora hadn't ever been so close to something so big without even a fence in between. Biff was right behind her, and she didn't want him to know she was afraid, so she tried not to hesitate. She walked slowly but, she hoped, steadily forward, with her hand stretched toward them.

Right away they shook their heads, making their harness jingle, and she stopped in confusion. When she looked around, there was no one behind her, only the partly opened door. The voices inside seemed far away. "You're going to do this, Nora," she said to herself. "It's perfectly safe. Think of them as very big dogs."

She started forward again and was almost close enough to touch their noses when suddenly they both surged toward her, pulling at their lines.

Nora jumped back into what felt like a solid wall. For a second she was trapped and near panic.

But hands were on her shoulders, and Biff's voice was right by her ear. "Whoa there, Nora. Don't be afraid. They're just glad to see me."

"I didn't...I wasn't...I mean, I don't want to get in the way. I'm sorry I bumped into you like that."

"Step up and pat Queenie. She's the one on your left. She's very friendly."

"Oh," Nora said. "I hope she'll like me." She was conscious of Biff behind her, broad and solid, cutting off her retreat. Queenie's feet were so huge that where she had stepped around in the snow, there were circles the size of plates. The sharp animal smell of her filled the air. When Nora reached out her hand, Queenie pulled her nose up and away. Nora looked around at Biff. She wanted him to notice that she had done her part.

Biff stepped up and grabbed Queenie's harness. He jiggled her head a little while he spoke to her. "It's okay, girl. She's a friend." To Nora, he said, "Stroke her on the nose, but take your mitten off."

Nora did it. So there she was, almost underneath this huge creature, without a fence or anything in between them.

Queenie bobbed her head up and down, but she couldn't pull away with Biff's hand on her.

"Does she like this? Her nose is unbelievably soft."

"She does like it. And she'll like you too, when she gets to know you."

Nora didn't know how to respond to that, so she said, "Can I pat the other one too? "

"Yes, pat her too, and then we'd better go. I don't want them to get too cold standing here waiting."

Nora took off her other mitten and slowly raised her hand up to the huge nose. Maybe it was because she had seen her sister accept Nora's hand, or maybe it was because Nora knew, or felt as though she knew, more about horses this second time, but the horse didn't pull her head away.

"Look," Nora said. "She's letting me."

"That's a good girl," Biff said, but it wasn't clear whether he meant Duchess or Nora. "Okay," he said. "We should go. Climb in."

When she was sitting down in the sleigh, Biff tucked a blanket around her legs. "I'll be right back," he said. "I'm going to unhitch."

In a minute he sat down beside her, picked up the reins and made a clicking sound, and the horses began to move. Right away they were out of the circle of light, going down the road fast, with the snow swirling at them out of the sky, which wasn't black but a soft, luminous rose-gray, like a cloud. Nora had never seen the sky like that before. The sharp smell of the horses blew back toward them, along with the snow thrown up by their prancing, high-stepping feet. Nora could hear the slap of their feet on the road, the jingle and creak of their harness, and the hiss of the sleigh runners as they cut through the snow.

After they had ridden in silence for a while, Biff said, "Well, what do you think?"

Nora was in a trance—the soft, white world, the falling snow, the hiss of the sleigh runners, the beat of the horses' hooves on the road, the ringing of the harness and the smell of leather and horse sweat and manure—she had been picked up out of her own life and dropped magically into someone else's. "I think I've been turned into a character in a movie," she said out loud. To herself, she said, "This is the most romantic thing that has ever happened to me."

Biff was sitting forward with the reins held loosely in his hands. He was smiling. There was snow on his mustache.

Nora said, "Is this the way you always get around?"

He laughed. "No, of course not. I have a truck."

"Oh."

"Most of the time, they ride too. I have to trailer them to wherever we are cutting wood."

They were going along the road to West Severance now. There were no cars. There weren't even any tire tracks. The road lay untouched in front of them. The four of them were the sole proprietors of the bright, white night.

"Sometimes, when it's not too cold, we stay at the job. I put up a fence for the horses, and we spend the night in the woods. That's the best."

Nora tried to picture it, but she didn't know what horses looked like when they slept. She didn't even know if they lay down. She looked at Biff's profile, dark against the snowy landscape. She liked the way he looked. "A cowboy-poet with a sensitive mouth," she said to herself and was immediately embarrassed, afraid he might see into her head and know what she was thinking.

He turned toward her. "I'll take you to the place I logged last summer. I camped up there a lot. It's a beautiful spot. If you would like to...it's not far." It was almost a question.

"I'd love to," Nora said and meant it. "I don't think I could ever get too tired or cold. I don't ever want to go back to the ordinary world."

"You can see all of West Severance from up there."

"It won't be too far for the horses, will it?"

"Oh no. We were going there anyway. They love it up there."

Nora laughed. "How do you know that?"

"I always know. Look at them. They have already figured out that that's where I'm taking you. See how they pick up their feet and move right along?"

Nora laughed again. Everything made her feel like laughing. It was true. The horses were stepping along faster. The sound of jingling harness was louder. The snow was blowing back against Nora's face. Her cheeks were wet with it. Everything had picked up the excitement.

"They're just like people. They have places they like and other places they don't like. Maybe they're even more that way than people because they notice more than people do."

"When Uncle Cal was in the hospital, I came out to see if Aunt Ursela needed help. I was driving by here, and I saw a fox. It trotted along beside my car. It was so beautiful that it made me happy." She said the last sentence nervously, sure he wouldn't understand what she meant. But when she looked at him, he was nodding and smiling, and she felt an unexpected delight to see that he understood.

He didn't say anything, and after a minute of silence, she was ashamed of her thoughts. What difference did it make whether he understood her? *She* wasn't free, even if he was. That was something she didn't know. She hadn't dared to look at his left hand to see whether he was wearing a wedding ring. She had been afraid Aunt Ursela would catch her at it. She couldn't think of anything like that until after the abortion. She wanted to look at Biff again, but she didn't dare. He was so nice to his horses. He would be a good father. But not to this baby. This baby had no one to take care of it. Even its mother wanted to get rid of it. She was glad Biff couldn't see her face then because she suddenly felt ashamed and sad and confused.

When she noticed again, they were turning off the road into the woods. They were on a narrow road now, a white band under dark trees. They were going steeply uphill. The air smelled like Christmas under the evergreen trees. The sleigh runners hissed as they cut through the new, wet snow. Nora looked at Biff, but there wasn't enough light under the trees to see more than the outline of his face, and she was too shy to ask any questions.

They came out of the woods into the open, and the ground flattened out. Biff shouted "Whoa," and the horses stopped. He looped the reins over the curved front of the sleigh and climbed down. He went up to each of the horses and patted her and told her she was a good girl, and then he came around to Nora's side of the sleigh and held out his hand to help her down. He said, "Come with me. I want to show you something."

"What?" Nora said, as she took his hand. It was the second time they had touched. She climbed down, trying not to show how stiff she was.

"You wait," he said. "You'll see."

They walked across the snowy clearing side by side. The snow was over the tops of Nora's sneakers. She hadn't worn boots because she was sure she was going to be in the car or the house. She tried to step lightly, but she could feel the wetness seeping in around her ankles. Near them, the black stalks of weeds stuck up though the snow, but the far side of the clearing was blank and white.

When they got to the other side of the open space, Nora could see they were on a high plateau, which ended just in front of where they stood. Far below was a tiny town. There were lights in the windows and a white church spire. It was a toy village in a souvenir paperweight, the kind where you turn the globe upside down and shake it to make it snow.

"That's West Severance," Biff said. They stood there looking at it for a long time. Then Biff looked down at her. "I'm sorry," he said. "Why didn't you tell me you were freezing?"

"I'm not though," Nora said. "Anyway, it's beautiful here."

"You're shivering. You don't even have boots on. I ought to have noticed. Come on. We need to get back in the sleigh."

"I'm really not cold at all," Nora said, but even as she said the words, she realized how cold she was. It was nice of him to try to take care of her. She had an odd twinge of worry for the baby, and then she was afraid that he might somehow read her mind and know what she was thinking about. She was surprised that he hadn't put his arm around her when they were looking at West Severance far below. She was glad though. It would have spoiled it. She liked him even better than before.

When they were both in the sleigh again, Nora said, "The horses could have walked away while we were over there looking at the view. They weren't tied to anything."

"They know not to do that."

"You had them tied at Uncle Cal's."

"Yes, but this is where I had a log landing. They used to stand here every day, over and over, waiting for me to unhitch a log. They expect to stand here, and so they do." He spread the blanket over her lap and leaned across her to tuck it in around her. "I hope this will make a difference. You really ought to have boots on."

When he leaned across her, he smelled of evergreen trees, like Christmas. "I wasn't planning on being outside. I didn't think I would need boots. I just came out to see how Uncle Cal was and to bring him a Christmas present."

Biff picked up the reins and clucked to the horses, and they started up with a little jerk, turning to go back down the road they had come up.

"Your uncle's been good to me."

"Really?"

"When I was building my cabin, he loaned me his tools. I couldn't have done it without them."

They were passing under the trees now, first bare trunks, black and wet, with white snow outlining the branches. Then they came to evergreens. There was only a thin layer of snow underneath them, and it was dark.

"He sold me the land to build it on too."

"Uncle Cal?"

"He's lived on this land his whole life."

"I know. My dad grew up here too. My grandparents bought it when they got married."

"Cal told me that, and that they paid $2,000 for the whole place."

"I don't know about that. I wonder if Dad knows that Uncle Cal sold some of it."

"Probably. He must."

"No, because, you see, Dad gave Uncle Cal his share. He did it when Grandma died. And anyway, Uncle Cal and my dad don't have a lot to say to each other. I guess they're too different."

They were turning onto Bear Ridge Road now. Their tracks from before were the only ones on the road. The horses went faster, their heads bobbing up and down in time with their steps. It was warm under the blanket.

"Sometimes I wish my dad had kept his share. I always forget how beautiful it is out here."

"I wonder why he didn't."

"It was my mom. I remember them arguing about it after Grandma died. Dad wanted to build a house on the land, but Mom didn't want to live way out on a dirt road. She would've hated it. Dad could see it wasn't ever going to be any use to him to hold on to it, and Uncle Cal couldn't afford to buy him out. I guess he could've just kept his half and not done anything with it. I wonder why he didn't do that....but anyway, he didn't, so he probably doesn't know anything about it."

The horses turned up the road to Uncle Cal's. Biff said, "I guess you don't get out to visit your uncle and aunt that often, do you?"

"I haven't been out here in years, not since I was in high school, but that's going to change now that I'm living in Severance again. I lived in Boston for five years, but I got awfully sick of it after a while. I finally decided it wasn't worth it anymore."

"I know what you mean. I grew up in California."

"I really hope I can stay in Vermont. Of course, maybe I won't be able to find a job, or my parents will kick me out or something."

"I'm sure that won't happen."

Nora laughed and said, "You never know." But it wasn't altogether funny. There were reasons he couldn't know about.

They were almost to the house, and both of them were quiet. Nora was hoping and fearing that he would say something about seeing her again.

The horses had slowed to a walk. Biff noticed.

"They don't want to go to Cal's again. They thought we were going home."

"I thought they were sad because the journey was almost over."

"That's not the way they think about things."

"I could go on forever. It's such a beautiful night."

But all Biff said was, "Whoa," as they pulled up to Uncle Cal's door. And under the circumstances, that was a good thing, even though Nora felt disappointed. She got out from under the blanket and out of the sleigh, hesitating a little, waiting for him to speak. But he didn't say anything. "Thank you," she said. "I've had a wonderful time. I've never done anything like that before."

"I'm glad. Please tell your aunt and uncle I said good night and merry Christmas." And he clucked to the horses.

They started up, turning to go back down the way they came, and Nora was left standing on the steps, watching, thinking how a few minutes ago she had been part of it, and now they were gone. Then she turned and went into the house without knocking.

In the mudroom she took off her jacket and the hat and mittens Aunt Ursela had given her, and then she went up the steps into the kitchen. No one was in the room. She could hear Aunt Ursela and Uncle Cal talking somewhere upstairs. Uncle Cal sounded crosser than usual. Maybe he didn't want her to stay for the night. She hoped that wasn't what he was angry about; she hoped it had nothing at all to do with her, but there was nothing she could do about it anyway. There was too much snow, and the road wasn't even plowed.

She sat down in a chair by the woodstove and took off her wet shoes. Her socks stuck to her feet, and when she got them off, her skin was waxy and yellow-white, with the weave of the socks pressed into it. She rubbed each foot in turn and held it out to the fire. After a few minutes, the blood started coming back. There were splotchy patches of pink skin mixed with the yellow-white patches, and the soles of her feet felt prickly, as though someone was sticking pins into them.

Aunt Ursela came into the room. "Ah, Nora," she said. "I didn't know you were back. Where's Biff?"

"He said to tell you and Uncle Cal goodbye. I think his horses wanted to go home."

"That's too bad. I was goin to make cocoa. I thought you could sit by the fire and get to know each other."

"That would've been nice, but I guess he was in a hurry."

"What's wrong with your feet?"

"They're okay. My shoes and socks got wet."

"Oh Nora. You didn't even have boots. How did you get so wet? Your feet must be freezin."

Nora couldn't quite manage to say his name out loud. "He wanted to show me a place where you could look down at West Severance. It was beautiful there." She was surprised at how intently Aunt Ursela was looking at her.

"I can see you had a very good time. He's not married. He hasn't got anybody, not even a girlfriend."

Nora looked down at the foot she had been massaging. She could feel the blood rising up in her face.

Aunt Ursela came a few steps closer and patted Nora on the shoulder. "He's a very nice boy," she said. "Can I get you somethin to eat?"

"No, thank you. I'm fine."

"Well, I'm goin to bed then. I fixed Elsie's bed up clean for you. You haven't forgotten which was Elsie's room, have you?"

"Not unless it's changed. It used to be at the top of the back stairs, didn't it?"

"That's the one. I put some extra blankets in there for you. I think you'll be warm enough. Do you want somethin to sleep in?"

"I don't need it. I'll be fine. Thank you for everything, Aunt Ursela." And she stood up and put her arms around Aunt Ursela's soft, wide middle. "Tell Uncle Cal I said good night." She was in a hurry to get off by herself so that she could think over every detail of the wonderful and strange adventure she had just had.

Chapter 17

This was to be Lena's real Christmas present to Jerry, much more than the new socks or the book on journalism. And it was all coming together the way she planned. It was only seven-thirty, but Georgia and Jimmy were already asleep, worn out by the family visits and the new toys.

She had been plotting the details of her plan for weeks. She knew Jerry thought he might get a carton of cigarettes as a Christmas present, so he'd let his supply run low. It was an easy matter to hide his last pack so he would need to go out to the store.

Since the only place open on Christmas night was the supermarket on the other side of Severance, and since it was snowing pretty hard, Lena knew she would have at least a half an hour to get ready. It had been so long since she and Jerry had had a romantic evening together. They hadn't even made love for a long time, and she knew she was to blame. She was always so tired by the end of the day that the only thing she wanted to do was go to sleep. It wasn't that she didn't think about sex, but what she almost always thought when she got into bed was that tomorrow night would be better than tonight, when she was so tired. She reproached herself for that. It wasn't fair to Jerry. That was why she was going to make everything perfect tonight.

She put on her new green dress and some earrings. She took her glasses off and put in her contact lenses. It had been a long time since she had taken much trouble with her looks. Now that her eyes were showing, they looked pale and uninteresting. She got out her eyeliner and tried to make them look more dramatic. She remembered that she used to have some green eye shadow, but when she found it at the back of the drawer in the bathroom cabinet, it was too dried out to use. She brushed her hair and peeked in at each child and then went downstairs.

By the time Jerry came to the door, she had cleaned up the living room. The toys were all piled under the Christmas tree. She had turned out the lights and lit candles on the table and laid out the bottle of champagne she bought weeks ago. When she heard the click of the door latch, she threw herself down on the couch.

Jerry came in. He said, "Hey, what....?" And then he saw her sitting in the semi-darkness. "What are you doing?"

The way he said it made her nervous. Her heart was beating fast. It was only Jerry, so that didn't make any sense, except that it was her surprise, and she wanted it to be a success. "Jerry, come sit down here beside me," she said. "It's been forever since we've had an evening together. The kids are really tired. I know they won't wake up, and I bought us some champagne."

Jerry hung up his coat, but then he just stood there in the doorway. There wasn't enough light to see his face.

"Please come sit down. I'll open the champagne. It's going to be like it was before the kids were born."

"Okay," Jerry said, but he just kept standing there.

"What's the matter?"

"Nothing."

"Something is."

"Well, I don't know. It doesn't seem like good timing. I'm tired. I'm really tired. And anyway, you never asked *me*, Lena. You didn't bother to find out if I *wanted* to spend this evening this way. I mean, I don't even get a say in it, do I?"

"It's a Christmas present, at least I thought it was. And it was a surprise. If I asked you, it wouldn't have been a surprise."

"You act like of course this is what I want, but you never thought of asking me. You just assumed…."

"I can't believe it, Jerry. I've been planning this for weeks. I thought you would be so pleased. You always say…."

"Lena. I've been saying for weeks, no, even longer maybe, that we had to talk, but you couldn't even find any time for that. You always put it off."

"So, okay. Let's talk. I got everything done so we could spend some time together, so let's talk if that's what you want to do."

"Well…yeah…but…."

"What? Is something wrong? And please come over here. I can't even see your face."

"I do have something I need to talk about," he said without coming any closer. "*We* need to talk about, I mean."

Lena's heart felt heavy. She had to restrain herself. If she'd said anything, it would have been something bossy.

"But it isn't something big. I want you to be sure of that from the beginning. I'm afraid if I tell you, you'll get the wrong idea. You have to promise not to think it matters before I tell you."

"How can I promise what I'm going to think about it before I even know what it is?"

"See, that's just what I mean. You're going to get mad and make it into a big deal, and it isn't anything."

Lena got up and walked across the room to where Jerry was standing. She needed to see his face, and she couldn't ask him again to come to her. She felt self-conscious about her new dress, about having made an effort to look pretty. She didn't know which would be worse—if he noticed, or if he didn't. She looked up at him and said, "You've got to tell me now. I'm starting to get really scared."

He wouldn't look at her. He looked past her, over her head. "How do you think I feel? This isn't the way I thought this conversation would happen."

"It isn't the way I thought this night was going to go either. I thought it was going to be like it used to be before the kids. Now I find out you have somebody else."

They were both stunned by her words, Lena as much as Jerry. She had no idea that that's what she was thinking until she heard what she said. And she was stunned all over again when he didn't deny it.

"Lena, you don't understand."

"Oh my God. Then it's true. I don't believe it. How could you?"

Jerry took her hand and led her over to the couch. He said, "Sit down, Lena," as though she were sick and he was taking care of her. He stood there looking down at her.

She sat there, numb, waiting for what was coming.

"First of all, there isn't anybody else. You are the only one. You've got to believe that."

"Oh, this is so awful. I wish it wasn't happening. I can hear it. I know you're just about to say, 'I love you, but….' I can hear it in your voice."

"You've got it all wrong. See, I knew this was going to happen."

"You mean, I got it wrong and there isn't somebody else?"

Jerry started pacing back and forth across the room, walking past where she sat stiffly and formally on the couch. "No. What I mean is that it doesn't mean anything. It doesn't have anything to do with love." His back was to her when he said this.

"What doesn't have anything to do with love?" Everything was getting muddled with pain.

"Well, sometimes sex is just an expression of friendship. It doesn't necessarily have anything to do with a serious relationship."

"Who says, Jerry? And now I know it's true. That doesn't even sound like you talking."

Jerry stopped pacing and turned to face her. "God damn it. That's why I can't tell you anything. You always get the wrong idea. See. That's what you're doing right now. And I already told you that you were getting the wrong idea."

Lena looked at him for a long time in the dim light. She had been planning for and looking forward to a romantic night of love, but now she saw that she didn't want romance or even sex from him, that she hated him and found him physically repulsive. What could she have been thinking?

She sighed. "Look, Jerry, just tell me. It's simple. Either you're sleeping with somebody besides me, or you aren't. Which is it?"

"Well, a couple of times...but...."

"Oh great! I knew it." She felt a clear, cold rage. The confusion was gone. "Why did you try to lie about it?"

"I never tried to lie about it, Lena. I've been trying to tell you for ages. You're always too busy to talk. You knew there was something we had to talk about. I couldn't force you to listen, could I?"

"I didn't know it was anything like this."

"That's because you weren't paying any attention to me, to what I said." He started pacing again. "And you aren't now, either, because I've been trying to tell you that it isn't anything, and you won't listen."

Lena kicked off her shoes and put her feet up on the couch. She pulled her skirts over them to keep them warm. She wished she hadn't wasted her only pair of stockings without any holes or runs. But she couldn't leave the conversation now to go and take them off. "It might not be anything to you, Jerry, but it's something to me." She could see the whole thing plainly now. "You've broken our marriage vows. Maybe we don't even have a marriage anymore."

Jerry stopped in his tracks and stood in the middle of the floor, flapping arms helplessly. "Oh honey," he said, and he sounded like he was about to cry. "Don't say that. You don't mean that. I couldn't live without you and the kids."

She wanted to say, "Then what did you wreck our marriage for?" But she didn't. She didn't say anything.

Jerry sat down on the edge of the couch. "I've been stupid. Please give me another chance. I promise I won't let you down. I need you."

She was sitting with her feet on the couch and her knees up so that her folded legs made a wall between them. "This isn't about you, Jerry. I have feelings too. What about my feelings?"

He reached toward her as though he was going to take her hand, and she pulled back, hunkered down behind the bulwark of her knees. "Don't," she said.

He pulled his hand away as though he had touched something hot.

It pleased her to see the hurt on his face. "I don't know if I want you to touch me," she said.

He looked horrified.

"You never thought of that, did you, Jerry. It would only make me think of how you touched her. Who is she, anyway? Aren't you going to tell me?"

"I don't know. Do you think I should? Don't you think it'll make things worse?"

"I don't see how things *could* get worse," Lena said, taking a bitter satisfaction from the fact that he was asking her what to do.

"Oh honey. Don't say that. Won't you at least let me put my arms around you?"

"And then I'll think how you did that to her, won't I?"

"But it was different. I already told you that."

"Look, Jerry, I could torture myself picturing you touching her, and I don't want to do that to myself. You keep saying it was different, but how different can sex be? I mean, you had to touch her, didn't you?"

"Suppose I tell you who it is, and then it's even worse because you can picture her too. See what I mean?"

"Okay, so now I know it's somebody I know."

"I'll tell you if you really want me to, if you really think I ought to."

Lena rested her chin on her knees, looking at him over them. "If it was the other way around, if it was me cheating on you...."

"Don't talk like that. It's too awful."

"Well, but just think about it. What if it was that way, would you want to know?"

"I don't know. If it was somebody I knew, I guess I would go out and find the guy and kill him, so maybe it wouldn't be so good for me to know. I think it would just make everything that much worse."

"I don't care. I don't think I'm going to go out and kill anybody, and if I do, Jerry, I think it would be more likely to be you than some woman I don't even know very well probably. Anyway, I want to know, so I think you'd better tell me."

"All right, Lena. But don't say I didn't warn you."

"I won't. Now tell. I want to know everything, and then I guess I'll know how bad it is. Maybe I'll even know what I'm going to do about it." She started to get up. "I'm going to blow out these candles and put on some lights so I can see you."

"No, don't. I don't think I could tell you with the lights on. I probably wouldn't have even gotten this far."

"Oh Jerry, I can't understand that."

"I know," he said, and he looked so mournful that Lena actually felt sorry for him for a minute. Then he went on. "And I don't think you are going to understand the rest of it either."

Then she wasn't sympathetic any more, because she hated it when someone said she couldn't understand something. It was a wall that left her out. She wanted to think she could understand everything.

Jerry threw himself back into the far corner of the couch. He looked down at his hands. He picked at the palm of one hand with the other.

Lena thought he was never going to begin, and then he said it.

"It was Bobbi Langdon, but it only happened because she teased me into it. That's the part you aren't going to understand. I mean, it was more like recreation or something, and it doesn't mean anything. Sex doesn't have to be....important. I mean, it can be just something you do with a friend if you feel like it. That's the way a man feels about it. And Bobbi is a women's-lib person, so she thinks like that too. It's different with you because you are more old-fashioned. Besides, it didn't mean anything." It was as though he was talking as fast as he could to use up all the air space so he wouldn't have to hear what she thought about it. Finally he had to stop for breath.

"If it didn't matter, then why did you do it?"

"Oh my God. That's exactly what I mean. You just can't understand, can you?"

"Jerry, stop trying to blame it on me. If I don't understand, it's because you're not making sense." She was looking at him, trying to see what was in his face, but he was concentrating on his hands and looking away from her. "And it's Bobbi? That *really* doesn't make any sense. That's the one who rides the motorcycle all the time and wears all black, isn't it? I wouldn't have thought she was your type at all. She isn't even pretty."

"Pretty doesn't have anything to do with it."

"I wish I knew what did. I guess I really don't understand it. I mean, Bobbi Langdon?"

"It's different for you. Besides being a woman, you're home here with the kids. You don't necessarily notice that everything is changing, especially people's ideas about sex. I mean the sexual revolution has been around for a long time now, and it's kind of out-of-date to think of being faithful to one person for your entire life. I mean, I didn't want to be a *joke*. And Bobbi used to tease me about it all the time at work."

"Why didn't you tell me?"

"I don't know, Lena. I can't tell you everything, and besides it was embarrassing. She made fun of me, and us. And when she found out that we were together all through UVM and didn't go out with anyone but each other...and when she found out I hadn't ever slept with anyone but you, she really mocked me."

"But why did you tell her?"

"I wish I hadn't now. But we spent a lot of time together. Remember when we were doing that series on the welfare system back in October?"

"I remember the series."

"We had to be together all the time, and we went all over the state, and once we had to stay overnight in Brattleboro. Remember?"

"Now I don't even want to remember."

"You asked me, Lena. I wasn't going to tell you all the details because it just isn't that important. But you wanted me to."

"I know."

"So can I stop now?"

"You've told me all of it, haven't you?" You went to a motel in Brattleboro with her when I thought you were working. You probably even called us up to say goodnight to Georgia and Jimmy while you were sitting there in the motel room with her. It's disgusting."

"We shared a room because it was a lot cheaper, and so it just kind of happened. It wasn't a big deal, and it was even less of one after it happened."

"So that was the only time?"

"Almost."

"Jerry, what could you possibly mean? If there was ever a question with a yes or no answer, that was it."

Jerry got up and started to walk around the room again. "I'm not going to answer any more questions then. I've been trying to be nice about this, and I'm really sorry it ever happened at all, and I've been doing it all your way, just like we always do, and I'm sick of it. I'm really, really sorry, and I don't want to talk about it any more."

"So you slept with her other times too."

"I didn't say that."

"Well, it's true, isn't it? Maybe you still are for all I know. If you weren't, you wouldn't be getting so mad about it."

"No, it's over, Lena, I promise. Why do you think I wanted to talk to you about it? If it wasn't over, I would want to keep it a secret, wouldn't I?"

That's when Lena started to cry. The whole thing seemed so awful and hopeless. She sat there in her new dress, the first time in ages that she'd taken the trouble to look pretty, and she felt as though everything was crashing down around her.

Jerry came over and leaned down to put his arms around her. "Please don't cry. I'm so sorry I made you cry. I love you."

But Lena twitched her shoulders away from his hands. "Don't, Jerry," she said. "I don't think I want you to touch me. I have to think about what to do about all this."

Jerry pulled back. "But, Lena, you wouldn't...."

"I don't know. I have to think, and I can't. I feel sore all over like someone was kicking me or punching me, and I have to think."

"We could open the champagne...."

"And drink a toast to the end of our marriage?"

"Don't talk like that, Lena. Maybe things won't look so bad in the morning?"

"That's easy for you to say, but I don't care. I'm going to bed. You can lock the doors and turn out the lights."

She stood up and reached down for her shoes. She felt stiff and bruised. She went slowly upstairs without looking back at Jerry, carrying her shoes. She would probably ruin her stockings walking on them, but she was too sore to care.

Upstairs, she dropped her shoes in the hall and went into Jimmy's room. He was sleeping on his side, all curled up. The blanket was mostly off, so she reached over the side of the crib and tucked it in around him. He sighed and shifted a little in his sleep. He felt so warm that it almost made her cry. She couldn't kiss him without letting down the side of the crib, which might wake him up. She brushed his hair back from his forehead and whispered, "I love you," instead.

Georgia was sleeping on her back with her arms flung wide, the way she always did. Her silky hair was fanned out around her head. Lena kissed her soft, rubbery cheek. Tonight the feel of her skin and the smell of her, the sight of her sleeping so innocently, dreaming some sweet child's version of life, tonight Georgia's presence was so right when everything was so wrong that it hurt almost more than thinking of what Jerry did.

She went into their room and took off her clothes and dumped them on a chair, even though it was her new dress, and put on her nightgown and got under the covers on her side of the bed. She had thought about going to sleep in the guest room, but it would have meant putting sheets on the bed, and she didn't want to bother. So she curled up and pulled the covers over her head, and when Jerry came in some time later, she said, "Just stay on your side of the bed, okay?"

Jerry said, "Aw, Lena, don't. Do you want me to go somewhere else?"

She didn't answer, and after a while, she felt the covers rise up and his side of the bed tilt down as he got in. And a while after that, he began to snore. She lay there, knowing that this was certainly the end and that the snoring just proved it.

Chapter 18

It was a beautiful winter day, crisp and bright, with the sunlight reflecting off the fresh snow. Nora parked in front of the house. Uncle Cal's pickup and Aunt Ursela's old sedan were in the driveway. Behind the truck was a beaten-up little red car, Elsie's, of course.

When Nora opened the door of her car, she heard a loud noise that could have been a gunshot. She got out, and as she closed the door, she heard the noise again. It sounded nearby, but she didn't see anyone. Even the dogs weren't around. Before she got to the house, she heard another shot, if that's what it was.

She hadn't even knocked when Elsie saw her through the glass of the door and opened it. "Nora! I don't believe it. It's been years."

Nora walked up the steps, and they hugged. "I know. I can't even remember how long it's been."

"Too long anyway," Elsie said, laughing. "Here's Nora, Ma."

Aunt Ursela came over and hugged her too. "Nora was here a few days ago. It was Christmas night. I told you about it."

Elsie smiled.

Nora could tell she had heard all about Biff and the sleigh ride. She willed herself not to blush. "When I drove up, I thought I heard gunshots," she said.

"You were right. Dad's up in back with the boys. Target practice. It's all they think about."

Aunt Ursela said, "Sit down, Nora. Would you like some coffee?"

"If it's not a lot of trouble."

"It's not. I always have a pot goin when Elsie's here."

Elsie grinned at her. "I'll get it, Ma. I want to get some for myself anyhow."

Aunt Ursela brought a pitcher of cream, a plate of cookies, and the sugar bowl over to the table near the woodstove. Elsie carried two mugs of coffee and some spoons. They all sat down.

"Don't you want some coffee, Ma?"

But Aunt Ursela shook her head and picked up her knitting.

"I always forget how wonderful your cream is," Nora said, trying to pour some into her coffee mug.

"It's too thick," Elsie said. "You have to use a spoon."

There were more gunshots. For the first time, Nora noticed the dogs lying behind Uncle Cal's chair. "I was surprised the dogs weren't outside to greet me when I drove up."

"They have to stay in when the boys are shooting, and they probably would anyway. They hate guns."

"Uncle Cal's up in back too? How did he get up there?"

"Oh, those boys. They shoveled him a path and took a lawn chair up for him to sit in. They even lugged a bale of hay all the way to the top of the field through the snow so they would have something to shoot at. They wouldn't take no for an answer, would they, Ma?"

Aunt Ursela smiled into her knitting. "I believe your dad is just as bad. You'd think he wouldn't want to get anywhere near a gun after what happened. They're all just alike, I guess."

Elsie nodded.

Nora thought about her own father. As far as she knew, he didn't even own a gun.

"Brad 'n Pete are terrible. It's all they think about. They are always studying gun catalogues and arguing about what kind they're going to buy when they get old enough. They talk endlessly about which features are the most important. They drive me crazy with it. One of these days, I'm going to give in and let them buy something, and then watch out!" She was laughing again. "Now, Nora, tell us your news before they get done shooting and come in here and make it impossible to talk."

Nora felt a moment of panic. What did she mean? Could Elsie possibly know that she was pregnant? Suppose there were some telltale signs that she knew because she was a nurse. But that was impossible. She couldn't know.

"There's not much to tell," Nora said cautiously. "At first, it was exciting to be in Boston, but then I got to hate it. I missed my family, especially Lena's little kids. Every time I came home, they were bigger."

Elsie nodded. "They grow so fast, don't they? Wait til you see my two. They're enormous. Aren't they, Ma?"

"I wish Elsie would move back closer to us. Talk her into it, Nora."

"Now Ma, you know I can't....I've got a good job, and the boys like their school." She looked at Nora, making a face at her mother's idea. "We couldn't afford it anyway. And you couldn't help with Dad laid up like he is."

Nora said, "I'm staying with Mom and Dad now, and I have some savings, but I still don't have a job...."

"Conrad's going to quit his."

"Conrad? Why? I saw him not long ago. It was the day your dad got hurt."

"He's goin out on his own. He bought a skidder. He's goin into the loggin business."

Aunt Ursela looked up from her knitting. "He's makin a bad mistake."

"Now Ma. You don't know."

"I do too. He's got responsibilities."

"Dad did almost the same thing, and he had three children, not two."

"That's the reason I know what I'm talkin about. We've been scramblin to get enough ever since, and we don't have a mortgage to pay like Conrad does."

"They'll be okay, Ma. Cheryl's got a good job."

"I just don't think they'll make it, and I know what I'm talkin about."

"I've always wondered how *you* did it, Elsie. How did you manage to take care of your boys all by yourself?"

"Oh, Ma and Dad get the credit for that. When Mike died, I was living here with them. I was very pregnant, and I didn't have any job skills." She ran her hand through her close-cropped hair and smiled her sweet, sad smile. "I could have stayed with Ma and Dad forever, and they wouldn't have said a word. Would you, Ma?"

Aunt Ursela knitted for a minute, and then she looked up at Elsie. A smile curved across her wide face. "I love havin you and the boys to do for." She paused to take a stitch. "And your dad does too, even though he wouldn't never say so."

"Thanks, Ma. I know it." She took a sip of her coffee and then got up to stand in front of the woodstove with her back to it. "You know, I got married right out of high school. I didn't have any job skills. I don't know what we were thinking. Well, I guess we weren't thinking. We were young. We were planning our future. We didn't know Mike wouldn't have a future. *I* didn't, anyway."

She turned around and picked up the lid of the stove and poked at the fire. Sparks swirled up toward the ceiling. She got a stick of wood out of the woodbox and angled it in through the lid. Then she put in a second stick and closed the lid and turned around.

"When I was in the hospital, I heard that there was a shortage of nurses. I didn't pay any attention then. I was thinking about the babies and how Mike was gone and wouldn't ever get to see them. But later I remembered it. I had a job as a nurse's aide at the hospital here, but it wasn't long before I saw that I was going to need some training and that I wanted to be a real nurse, not an aide.

"They have a program in Randolph. I don't even remember how we got the money together, but everyone helped. I had to drive down there every day. Paul and Conrad kept my old car on the road." She stopped and thought. "Most of the time, anyway. Ma and Mike's mom took care of the babies." She sighed and came back to her seat. "I don't know how I got going on all that. It's ancient history. It was a pretty rough time."

Aunt Ursela reached out and patted Elsie's hand that lay between them on the table. "You worked like a demon to get that trainin. I think it helped you to be so busy, too busy to think about Mike."

"Yeah," Elsie said. "I've thought that too." She looked up at Nora, smiling. In her mannish clothes and chopped-off hair, she made Nora feel weak and feminine and frivolous. "You're different, Nora. You've got an education. And I had babies to take care of. You have a much better chance than I did."

She wasn't talking about Nora being pregnant, because she didn't know about that, and anyway, Nora wasn't planning on having the baby, so she wouldn't have to take care of it. But she could. For the first time, she realized that she could. It wouldn't be impossible. It wouldn't even be as hard as what Elsie did. Nora hadn't ever thought of that before.

Elsie said, "I know what you're thinking, Nora. You are thinking that I had Ma. That's how I did it, and that's true. She spoiled me rotten, didn't you, Ma?"

Aunt Ursela looked up. "I know everybody has hard luck, but it does seem like you got more than your share."

"Anybody could say that, Ma," Elsie said quietly.

Just then the dogs got up and went to the door, wagging their tails. They could hear the voices of the boys and Uncle Cal in the mudroom. Then the boys burst into the room, both talking at once. They came over to the table and stopped, one on each side of their mother, still talking about guns and shots and bulls-eyes.

Nora saw them looking around, at her, at Aunt Ursela, at the coffee things, until both of them saw the plate of cookies.

"I'm hungry, Ma," one of them said.

"We both are," the other one said.

"All right. You can each have one. But you have to eat them at the table and then you have to go away so the grown-ups can talk."

Each boy reached out and took a cookie, and then they went around the table in opposite directions to the empty chair on the other side, where they sat down together.

Nora watched them. They were so big, no longer little and cute and manageable, like Georgia and Jimmy.

Elsie smiled proudly. "This is my cousin, Nora," she said to them.

They both mumbled through full mouths. In a minute the cookies were gone, and they were heading toward the door.

"Hold on here, boys," Uncle Cal said. He was coming up the steps into the kitchen when they opened the door to go out. "You haven't cleaned the rifle yet. You have to do that before you're done."

"We know, Gramps. We were comin out to find you."

Uncle Cal hobbled over to his chair by the woodstove with the rifle in his free hand. He sank into the seat with a sigh, and then he looked over at the table and saw Nora. He even smiled a tight little smile and said hello to her.

Nora asked how he was feeling.

"I'd be all right if it wasn't for Elsie's little devils. Brad, go out in the mudroom and get the gun oil and the other stuff. Pete, you spread a couple of newspapers on the floor right here beside me. You'll have the women after you if you make a mess in here."

Elsie swung around in her chair. "Now, Dad. Don't try to scare them, cause you can't do it."

Brad came in with the gun-cleaning things, and the two boys sat on the floor at Uncle Cal's feet while he showed them what to do. Each boy had to try each part of the operation. Then they went to put the gun away. They carried it together.

When they came back, Uncle Cal said, "Okay, boys. Now you got to pick up this stuff here. Did you bring down that bale of hay?"

"No, Gramps. We want to leave it up there."

"We're goin to be here tomorrow. Remember?"

"I don't know if we'll do any more tomorrow. I'll probably be too tired to get up in back by then."

"Aw, Gramps."

"He's just kidding."

"We'll bring it down before we go."

"We promise, Gramps."

They hovered around Uncle Cal until Elsie chased them away.

Nora didn't stay much longer. It was nice to see Elsie. After all those years and all that had happened to her, Nora liked her as much as ever. But there really wasn't much they had to say to each other.

In the car going home, Nora allowed herself to play with the idea of not having an abortion, of keeping the baby. Both Lena and Elsie had something that was very satisfying. It was there in their faces. They weren't alone the way she was alone. It was a tempting thought, but it seemed too complicated to consider seriously.

Chapter 19

When George looked at the clock, he couldn't believe it was right. It said five of eleven. He had no idea where all that time had gone. He hadn't even got much work done. He thought about calling Laurie and decided against it. She was sure to be asleep. She probably wouldn't be worried even if she were awake. He had done this before, not often, but once in a while.

He straightened up the piles of books and papers on his desk. Things were so different with Corrine gone. He used to joke that she knew more about him than he knew about himself. She took care of everything. Annie probably didn't have it in her to be that kind of secretary, and even if she did, it would take her years to get there. He still hadn't gotten over Corrine leaving. He didn't even understand why she had to.

Outside the window, high in the sky, there was a soft light from the moon behind the clouds. It was quiet, the way only a winter night can be quiet, a kind of muffled stillness composed of the snow and the cold and the lateness of the hour.

He rinsed out his drink glass and put the bottle of whiskey away in the safe. Then he got his coat and hat, turned out the lights, and shut and locked the office door. He did it all slowly and methodically because he was suddenly very tired.

He could hear his footsteps echoing ahead and behind him as he walked down the shadowy passage. Partway down the stairs something happened. He wasn't even sure how. His foot caught on the stair above, and he tripped. He fumbled at the railing, but he wasn't able to stop his fall. He tumbled all the rest of the way down and ended on his back at the bottom. He was so surprised that he lay there for a minute without moving. Old age, with its faltering sense of balance, snuck up on a person, arriving when he wasn't thinking about it.

He stood up slowly and carefully. Everything seemed to be working. His shoulder hurt, and there were places on his legs that felt as though they had been bruised, but overall he was okay. He rearranged his clothes, trying to straighten himself up. No one was around. No one saw him fall. He was lucky it was so late. He felt in his pocket for his car keys, congratulating himself on his presence of mind in checking for them before he got all the way to his car.

He was glad when he got there and could sit down. The fall had made him unsteady on his feet. He started the car and drove very slowly. He knew he wasn't driving at his best, and he needed to be careful. But, of course, he didn't have far to go.

He was still downtown when there was a bump and a loud bang, and the car stopped suddenly. The sound and the concussion catapulted him back in time, back into battle, into the blood and the mud. He saw the familiar faces, saw the pain and the hope and the fear reflected there. They were so young. All of them wanted so passionately to live, and so few of them had. He felt again the awful guilt at the unfairness of it.

Someone tapped on the window right beside his face. It woke him up. He was confused at first. He didn't know why he was there, or how long he had been there. The person at the window was a policeman. He was looking in. It took George a while to resurface into the present. Then he put the window down. He thought he said, "What can I do for you, Officer?" But maybe he just thought it and didn't say it aloud. He couldn't tell. He was still confused.

When the window was open, the policeman asked to see his driver's license. George had to get his wallet out of his back pocket. That took a while. He smiled at the policeman, but the man didn't smile back. George saw now that his car had gotten itself up on the curb and bumped into the stop sign, pushing it over at an odd angle.

When he handed the policeman his license, the officer looked at it with no expression. He wrote the numbers down on his notepad and handed the license back. Then he asked George to step out of the car.

"You don't have to bother with this, Officer. I can explain everything."

"Step out of the car, please, sir." This time his voice had an edge to it.

So George got out and stood beside his car, a little shaky because of the fall. He was made to walk in a straight line with his arms out wide and to reach above his head to touch his two index fingers together. He wasn't sure, but he thought he did it all right. He tried to tell about the fall, but the man wouldn't let him explain. He just said politely, and a little sorrowfully, that he wanted George to get into the back seat of the police cruiser because he wanted him to come to the police station.

It was beginning to dawn on George that the man thought he was drunk. In the cruiser, George tried again to explain, but the officer held up his hand for silence. It was an awkward situation because he had had something to drink. He wasn't even sure how much, although he was sure it wasn't enough to make him drunk.

At the station, he felt very self-conscious, afraid that he wasn't walking straight enough. He was befuddled by all the bright lights. When he got to the desk, he saw that they were actually going to charge him and maybe even lock him up. It was all a terrible mistake, but no one would believe that. And once word got out that he, a respectable lawyer, had been locked up for drunken driving, his reputation would be ruined. Everyone would believe the worst.

They wanted to give him a breath test. He pulled himself together and asked if he could make a phone call. He knew they had to let him. He had been the lawyer that got the phone calls often enough. At first he was stalling for time. He held the phone in his hand and tried to think who to call. And then he knew. He asked the man behind the desk to look up Nick Simonetti's home number.

The phone rang for what seemed like a long time. George had almost decided Nick wasn't home, when a sleepy voice said, "What is it?"

"Nick, this is George Willard."

"What?"

"It's George Willard. I'm at the police station."

"Oh sorry. I can't wake up. Who are you there for?"

"Well, actually, it's me."

"You? Oh, okay. I get it. So who was the officer who brought you in?'

"I don't know. It was a young guy. I didn't know him."

"Go find out his name. I'll hold on."

So George put the receiver down on the desk and went over to where the officer was standing, just far enough away so he didn't seem to be listening. George found out his name and came back to the phone.

"Nick, it's James Everett."

"Okay. That's good. They haven't charged you yet, have they?"

"No. I told them I wanted to call you."

"That's good too. Look, tell them I'll be there as soon as I can, and you just sit down and wait til I get there."

"I don't think you have to do that, Nick. It's probably okay."

"George. Do what I say. I'll see you in a few minutes."

George went over to James Everett and told him that Nick would be there in few minutes. Everett nodded his head and didn't say anything. George sat down on one of the hard wooden chairs facing the desk.

It was then that he noticed the clock for the first time. It said almost two-thirty. That explained some things, like why he felt so tired, but it raised other questions, most notably, what could have happened to all those hours?

The next thing he knew, Nick Simonetti was standing in front of him. He must have fallen asleep in the chair, even though it was unlike him. He stood up.

"Nick, I'm glad to see you, but I'm sorry to bring you out like this. I didn't realize how late it was."

Nick held up his hand for silence. "Stay right there, George. I'm going to talk to these guys. I'll be right back."

George was clear enough to realize that Nick didn't want him there. *He* had been in the same position with clients before. He sat down again, but he was still confused. The night had gotten away from him. He knew everyone would think he was drunk, and he had to admit it was possible, although he didn't really believe it. He was always very careful about how much he drank. Maybe he was coming down with something. He tried not to watch Nick and Everett in a huddle with the man behind the desk. He didn't want them to think he was worried about the outcome.

After what looked like an earnest discussion, Nick came back. "Okay, George. We can go now."

"But what....?"

"I'm going to drive you home. We can talk on the way. Let's get going. We don't want to give them a chance to change their minds."

"Okay." He stood up too fast and had to grab Nick's arm to keep from sitting down again. They went down the hall arm in arm.

Outside, in the cold night air, George's head felt clearer. Maybe his catnap in the chair at the police station had helped also. He knew he shouldn't say, although he thought it was true, that he would be able to drive himself home. He was wondering about his own car as they reached Nick's, and as though Nick could read his thoughts, he said that he had made a deal with Everett. He was going to get George's car towed to Brad's Sunoco where George would have to pay the towing charges to get it back. "But he isn't going to charge you. Not this time, anyway."

"Thanks to you, Nick. I really appreciate it."

"Next time will be different."

"Of course. But there isn't going to be a next time."

"I'm glad to hear you say that."

"Because it was the fall, you see. I took a spill on the stairs coming out of my office, and it made me shaky and unsteady on my feet. And that's not likely to happen again."

"George, I think you were drunk."

"Oh no, Nick. It was the fall. I hadn't had much of anything to drink."

"How much?"

"I don't know exactly. I was working late in my office, but it couldn't have been much, because I never.... My driveway is the next one on the left. Thanks for everything, Nick."

Nick pulled into the driveway and stopped the car. George had his hand on the door handle when Nick said, "Wait a minute. I'd like to talk for a few more minutes, if you don't mind."

"Whatever you say. I thought you might be in a hurry to get back home. I'm sorry I woke you up."

"Actually, this is a good opportunity, and one I've been hoping for. Let me say it right out, as your friend. For quite a while I have suspected that you had a drinking problem."

"Me? Why me?"

"I don't know that I'm right about this, but I've seen the signs."

"Really?"

"I don't know, of course, but I'm usually pretty good at guessing. I wasn't surprised when you called me tonight, and the reason is that I've been there myself. That's how I know the signs so well."

"You?"

"You didn't know I had a drinking problem, did you?"

"I almost can't believe it."

"I've been sober for nearly eleven years now. Life is good, better than it ever was when I was drinking."

"I didn't know anything about this. I never heard anything from anybody. How did you keep people from finding out?"

"I don't know that I did. It was a long time ago."

They were both quiet for a minute. George was thinking that if no one knew about Nick, maybe no one would hear about him. It sounded as though Nick had had a real problem with alcohol, not like his own. He was about to ask Nick what had made him think he had a problem, or, and this was really almost the same question, why he thought George had a problem.

But before George had a chance to ask his question, Nick said, "I couldn't have done it without AA. No one can do it alone."

"You're in AA?"

"Oh yes. I have been all along. I still go to at least one meeting a week."

"I had no idea," George said.

"Well, listen, George. Think about it. There are lots of meetings to choose from when you are ready to join us. It has made an enormous difference in my life. It could do the same for you. The thing about alcoholism is that it's going to get worse, and that might mean more incidents like tonight."

George put his hand on the door handle again. He didn't want to look like he wanted out of there, but he did. "Thanks a lot, Nick. I really appreciate what you did for me tonight, and taking the time to talk and all this. I'm really grateful. I don't know that I need AA or anything else, because I don't know that I have a problem, but I really appreciate your wanting to talk to me like this, and thank you for bringing me home."

He got out of the car and walked up to the door. He could hear Nick backing out onto the street behind him. Laurie had left the door unlocked. He let himself into the dark hall, took off his coat and hat and started up the stairs. He must have been looking down, because he was about halfway before he happened to glance up. Laurie was standing in the shadows at the top. It startled him so much that he had to grab the banister to keep from toppling down the stairs a second time. What a night it had been, and it wasn't over yet.

"Oh Laurie," he said when he had righted himself. "You scared me. Is everything all right?"

"No, George, I don't think it is."

"What's wrong?"

"I think you had better tell me." Her voice was wide-awake and harsh.

"You mean because it's so late?"

"Well, that's certainly part of it. Why *are* you so late? Why didn't you call? There are other things too. Where's your car? I saw a strange car in the driveway."

"I can explain."

"I think you'd better. And most of all, I want to know where you've been all night. It's nearly morning."

By this time, they were standing together at the top of the stairs. George said, "I'm sorry I woke you up. Have you been awake long?" He was hoping to move the conversation into the bedroom so he could sit down. He still didn't feel really steady on his feet.

"A while. I woke up at twelve-thirty, and you weren't here. I couldn't go back to sleep after that. Where were you?"

George took a few steps toward the bedroom, but she didn't move, so he stopped. He couldn't afford to make the situation worse. "I was working late in my office...."

"Oh come on, George. You don't expect me to believe that, do you?"

"Laurie, I'm trying to tell you. That's just the beginning."

"Go on." She sounded disgusted.

He didn't look her in the face because he knew what her expression would be. "I'm trying to tell you what happened. It's the truth too."

"Okay. I'm listening."

"Could we go into the bedroom and sit down? I'm awfully tired."

"You're not the only one," she said in an irritated voice. "But you're right. We don't want to wake Nora up."

They went into their room and shut the door. Laurie got into her bed and turned on the lamp beside her. George sat on his bed, facing her. He reached down to take off his shoes, feeling drained by the events of the night. He longed for sleep, but it wasn't going to be possible until Laurie was satisfied somehow. He snuck a look at her. She was wide-awake, already scornful of the explanation she was going to hear.

"I didn't leave my office until around eleven," George said, still bent over his shoes. "I hadn't realized how late it was getting. I almost called, but I thought I would wake you up, and I thought I would be home in just a few minutes." He propped up his pillows and sat back on the bed with his sock feet on the coverlet.

He waited to see whether Laurie was going to say something, but she was silent, so he continued. "When I was going down the stairs, I caught my foot on something and fell. It was quite a bad fall, but I think I'm all right, except that I have felt unsteady and wobbly ever since."

He paused again. He really expected her to say something this time, but she didn't. Wasn't she worried about him?

The next part was a bit tricky to explain. He said, "I think I must have been hurt worse than I thought, because when I was driving, I think I passed out or something. Luckily I was going very slowly, and the car bumped into a stop sign and stopped. A policeman came along after I had been there for a while. He took me to the station, where I called Nick Simonetti, and he brought me home."

She still didn't say anything. He thought she might have fallen asleep, but he looked around at her and saw she was sitting up and staring straight ahead.

"That's the whole story, Laurie, and it's all true. Honestly."

She turned out the light suddenly. He could hear the covers moving as she lay down.

He said, "Don't you believe me?"

She didn't say anything. He waited. He was going to ask her if she was angry at him, and he was going to get up so that he could take his clothes off, but he fell asleep before he could do either.

Chapter 20

Biff drove up a little after seven. Cal and Ursela were sitting by the woodstove. Ursela had one of her shows on the TV with the sound up too loud as usual, so even the dogs didn't hear anything until Biff knocked on the door.

Ursela said, "Now what on earth could that be about?"

"It's Biff," Cal said, and he called to Biff to come on in.

Biff stuck his head in the door to say hello to Ursela. He was always extra polite to her. In fact he made kind of a production of it, which Cal thought was foolish. Then Biff said, "Are you ready, Cal?"

"Just as soon as I get my jacket I will be." He stood up and started for the door.

Ursela wanted to know where they were going of course, so Cal said, "We're goin to see a guy Biff knows."

Then she wanted to know if they were going to be late, and Cal said it wasn't exactly a social visit, and it probably wouldn't take long.

By that time he was in the mudroom with his outdoor clothes

partly on. He could see Biff in the doorway gearing up for a detailed explanation. He headed for the door, still putting on his jacket. "Come on, Biff. We can talk about it later."

Outside, as they got into the truck, he said, "It's better if we tell her about it when it's over, and she can't mess up our plans."

The night was clear and full of icy stars. "No snow tonight," Cal said. "I wonder why this Jason LaRue character wouldn't come to my place. He don't have any problem gettin here in huntin season."

"I think he's scared. I think he feels like he'll be safer if he's on his own territory."

"Well, that right there shows he's guilty."

"He could be just scared."

"Think about it. If he wasn't guilty, he wouldn't have anythin to be scared of, would he?"

"I don't know if it always works that way, Cal. Things can get complicated sometimes."

"That may be true sometimes, but there ain't nothin complicated about this situation. I mean, think about it, man. Somebody shot me out of my own tree, and if this guy did it, he's goin to pay. If he didn't do it, he ain't got nothin to worry about."

"I hope you're right."

"Well, hell, you know I am. Don't go gettin all lawyerly like my brother George."

"I won't. I'm here to back you up. You know that."

"I know you are, Biff. Good. And don't worry. The situation is simple. Either the guy did it, or he didn't, and we can probably tell just by lookin at him."

"I hope so."

They were driving on the dirt road that ran along the ridge west of West Severance. "I haven't been up here in a long time," Cal said. "All these places are new. Where do all these people come from? They ought to of just stayed where they were."

"Some of them probably came from California, like I did."

"Hey, I didn't mean you. You know that. You're a good neighbor."

"Thanks, Cal." He slowed down to look at a mailbox. "Jason LaRue lives along here somewhere. He said the name on the mailbox is Wilson. It's not that one. Maybe it's the next place."

They drove in silence, watching for the next opening. The headlights shone on a solid wall of trees on both sides of the road. "George and I hunted up here a few times with some of our buddies from high school. I graduated high school, did you know that? Not that it ever did me much good, but not that many did in them days, back before the war. Ma and Dad made us both finish. And George went on to bigger things. I got married. That's what I did with my education."

The next opening in the trees had a mailbox that said Wilson on it. Biff turned into the drive. It was short. There was a trailer at the end of the driveway, and a large old sedan was parked beside it. They got out of the truck. It was very dark under the trees, with no outside light to help them see their way to the door.

"He knows we're comin, don't he?"

"Yeah. I called him from your place a few days ago."

"Right. I forgot."

When they got to the door, Biff knocked, and before he even put his hand down, the door jerked open. The guy standing there was small and weaselly-looking, a young guy, with stringy blonde hair and a blonde mustache. He was wearing a T-shirt and blue jeans. He stood there and looked at them and didn't say anything.

Biff said, "Are you Jason LaRue?"

"What if I am?"

"This is Cal Willard, the man I told you about. I'm Biff Barker." He held out his hand, but the guy didn't move. He just looked at Biff's outstretched hand, until Biff pulled it back again and put it in his pocket. "Can we come in? You are Jason LaRue, aren't you?"

"I guess so," the guy said. Then he laughed nervously and said, "I mean, yes, I am, and I guess you can come in." As he stepped back into the room, he looked over his shoulder. Two scruffy little boys in pajamas were standing in the doorway opposite. Their mouths were open, and their noses were running. "You kids get outa here.

I already told you once. Now beat it," he said, and the little boys disappeared. Then he turned to Biff. "So what's all this about?"

Biff looked over at Cal, and then he said, "We wanted to talk to you about a little incident that happened back in deer season. That's all. We just want to know if you know anything about it."

"You mean when Old Man Willard here got shot?"

"That's me you're talkin about," Cal said, taking a limping step toward him.

"I figured," he said, looking down at Cal's bandaged foot. "All I know about it is what I read in the Sentinel. Same as everybody else."

Biff said, "You were hunting on Willard's property the day it happened."

"Maybe I was, and maybe I wasn't. Anyhow, so what? It ain't posted. I been over there a lot."

Cal was feeling more and more irritated by the guy and his smart-aleck attitude. But he could see that Biff was trying to keep things calm.

Biff said, "On that particular day, which was the day after Thanksgiving, were you hunting?"

"Sure. I always take time off around Thanksgiving, unless I get my deer real early. One year I was...."

Biff interrupted. "You got a big deer this year, didn't you?"

"That's my deer he got, God damn it."

"Wait a minute, Cal. Let's hear what he has to say."

Cal watched the guy's hands clenched into fists. He was tense all over, he was so ready for a fight, and Cal just hoped he would start something, because he, Cal, was just itching to get his hands on the little creep.

"Yeah," Jason LaRue said. "I got a big one this year, a six-pointer." He looked hard at Cal. "But he was mine. I tracked him all day that day."

Biff said, "What day was that?"

"The day you said."

`"The day after Thanksgiving?"

"Yeah."

"See," Cal said. "See. I told you so."

Biff waved his hand to shut him up. And Cal had to admit that Biff was smart and that he was doing a good job with the situation. He sounded like a lawyer, and he never lost his cool. "Where'd you shoot him?"

"It went right in through his ribs and came up through his heart—a great shot."

Cal started to say that if you looked at the trajectory, but he'd hardly gotten a word out before Biff cut him off. And anyway, no one saw the deer right after he'd been shot except for Jason LaRue, and you couldn't expect a straight answer out of him.

Biff said, "No, I meant to ask where you were hunting when you shot the deer."

"Look, I don't have to answer no more questions. What the hell *is* this? And in my own house too." Then he looked around and saw the little boys in the doorway, watching again. He ran at them, flapping his arms. "I'm goin to take my belt to you kids." The little boys disappeared, and he turned back to Cal. "If you don't want nobody on your land, you oughta post it. It ain't my problem. There's plenty of other places to hunt."

Biff said, "Hey, Jason, listen. Could we sit down? I think we ought to talk about this in a friendly way. Cal here wants to figure out what happened to him, and we were hoping you might be able to help him out. Just a friendly little conversation."

Jason looked at Biff, and then at Cal, and back at Biff again. "Well, I don't know…." he said.

"After all, you owe him a favor. You've had the privilege of hunting on his land."

"Well…oh hell, just sit down."

Biff sat down on the saggy couch, and Jason faced him in an easy chair. Cal couldn't quite bring himself to get comfortable, so he clumped over to a stiff, wooden chair near the couch.

They all three sat there looking at each other, until Biff said, "Well, maybe if you don't mind, Jason, you could tell us how you got your buck this year."

"I don't have to tell you nothin. The only reason you're in here now is cause I said you could come in, and then you want to sit down, and now you want...."

"God damn it, Biff," Cal said. "This ain't gettin us nowhere. The guy shot me. That's obvious, or he wouldn't be actin this way."

"I did not, you old bastard," Jason said, starting to push himself up out of his seat.

Cal started up too, as quickly as he could with his bad foot, but Biff was right there with his hands out, calming them down. "Wait a minute," he said. "Jason, you tell us your story, and then we'll know you didn't do it. See? And you, Cal, you sit back down and listen."

Cal said, "What the hell for?"

"I don't know, man," Jason said, running his hand through his stringy hair and looking at Cal. "You think he's goin to believe me, whatever I say?"

"Try me," Cal said. "What've you got to lose?"

Jason looked at Cal for a minute, and then, to Cal's surprise, he started right in telling it, hardly pausing for breath. "I had found that big buck a few days before, see. I knew where he liked to hang out. So that morning I got up there real early, and I jumped him just at daylight, not far outside the village." He looked at Biff when he paused, but he carefully didn't turn in Cal's direction. "Right outside of West Severance. I guess it wasn't long before he figured out that somebody was behind him because he started headin for the high ground. I didn't lose him, but he was backtrackin and windin all over the place. I couldn't get close enough for a good shot, but I was worryin the whole time that somebody else was goin to spot him, or maybe that I'd drive him right by some other guy who would take him away from me." He looked only at Biff again. "You know what I'm sayin?"

Biff nodded. "I understand. What happened next?"

Cal tried to look like he wasn't involved in what he was hearing, like none of this had anything to do with him. He looked around the room. The furniture was all brown and tan and beat-up, just like the carpet. It was hot, and the air smelled of fried food.

Jason's eyes flicked across Cal and then went back to Biff. "It was late in the mornin when he went onto Willard's. There's that ravine up the west side of Willard's land. It ain't exactly a ravine, but it's flat, with steep banks on both sides and a small stream goin through it. It leads up to the top of the hill, and the land is high on both sides all the way to the top. There's a game trail that goes up there, and my buck got on that. I think he was gettin tired and lookin for a easy up, because you'd have thought he would of had more sense than to get out in the open like that. And makin as much noise as he was too.

"And then, just before he got to the top there, where it kinda opens out, damned if he didn't slow down and look back to see if I was still there, and I see right then, that was my chance. I had the gun up and all ready to fire when I heard a shot...."

Cal jumped to his feet. "That was me! That was me!" He was so excited that he was jumping up and down. He could feel the flimsy floor of the trailer giving under him and the throbbing in his bad foot. "I shot that deer. My shot went home. You can tell when you get off a solid one." He stopped. Biff and Jason LaRue were staring at him like he'd lost his mind. He sat back down. "That was mine," he said.

"I don't know what you're talkin about," Jason LaRue said. "I heard a gunshot, and then I took my shot, and I saw I hit him. I followed him until he dropped, and I field-dressed him and took him home. I was on your property, but I never saw you at all."

Cal's voice was shaking. "I shot that deer. You shot *me*. You were standin there all ready to fire, and you heard my shot. You probably turned in the direction the sound came from, and then you pulled the trigger. And that was just when I was gettin ready to come down out of my tree stand."

Jason LaRue just sat there looking at him. Cal couldn't tell whether he thought Cal was crazy, or whether that look on his face meant he was finally getting it into his dim brain that it didn't happen the way he thought it did.

Cal said, "You thought you shot at that deer. I don't say you don't believe it. But what you really did was to shoot at me. You must have swung around towards me when you heard my shot, and so what you actually did was you shot *me*—in the foot. And then you left me right there and went on down the trail after my deer."

Cal could see that hit home. Behind LaRue his two little kids with their dirty faces and their runny noses were standing in the doorway again, watching their father with their mouths open. This time he didn't have to say anything. As soon as he looked at them, they were gone.

He turned back to Cal. "That's not the way it was. I don't care what you say. I remember it just as plain as plain."

"Well, I remember too. I had enough days lyin on my back in the hospital to get it pretty solid in my mind."

"You mean you had plenty of time to fix yourself up a story. Did they find the bullet?"

"No. It went right through. It's up there in the woods somewheres. It's up there though. It's your bullet, and it has my blood on it."

"Says you."

"You're damn right that's what I say."

"Look, I think you shot your own self in the foot, and you don't want anybody to know, so you drag me into it and make up this big story about how I shot you."

"You was there, wasn't you? We both agree on that. You was there below the buck, and I was there on the ridge above it."

"This is true. But the rest could be either way. It's my word against yours, and there ain't any witnesses. So we ain't goin to solve it, not ever."

"We'll see about that," Cal said, and then, "Come on, Biff. Let's get the hell out of here."

When they were back in Biff's truck, Cal said, "Well that's the guy all right. He's guilty as hell."

"I think so too, but you can't prove it."

"All you got to do is take one look at the guy, and you know he did it."

"That's not proof. It's just his word against your word. He's right about that."

"It happened on my land. That ought to count for somethin."

"The law doesn't work that way."

"That's what's the matter with it. It ought to go after the guilty. That's what it ought to do."

"You're right about that."

"I guess I'll have to get my brother George into this. Maybe he'll know how to go after this LaRue bastard. He's a lawyer, you know."

"Oh yeah. You told me before. Nora's father."

"That's right." Cal sneaked a look at Biff, but he couldn't tell anything in the dark truck with Biff watching the road ahead. Cal knew Biff had invited Nora to his cabin. Ursela said so. But he wasn't about to say anything about it. That would make him sound like one of Ursela's old biddy friends. He liked Biff, and he liked Nora, but he hoped it wouldn't work out for them. He didn't want Ursela getting into the matchmaking business. If it didn't work out, she wouldn't get any ideas.

There was another reason too. He'd never gotten around to telling George that he had sold some land. If Nora and Biff got married, the land would come back to the family, but George would find out he had sold it.

The silence had dragged on so long that Biff looked around to see what was going on.

"Yup," Cal said, as though he had been thinking about it all this time, "I'm goin to have to get George in on this."

Biff said, "I wish we had asked him if the cops questioned him. I meant to ask, but I forgot."

"He wouldn't of told you the truth anyhow. George might be able to find that out. Maybe the cops got a look at the deer while it was hangin."

"No. They couldn't have. That was what first made me suspicious of this guy. They said he put that deer in his freezer right away. He didn't hang it at all. They said he claimed he always did it that way."

"That right there ought to convict him. A guy that don't even hang it for a while so the neighbors can see. It ain't natural."

When they got back to Cal's, Biff wouldn't come in. He told Cal to be sure and tell Ursela he said hello, and he left.

Cal went into the kitchen where Ursela was watching another one of her TV shows with the volume all the way up. The dogs looked surprised when they saw him. They hadn't even heard Biff's truck.

Ursela didn't say hello. She started right in asking him where he had been.

"I went to see a guy about somethin."

"At night?"

"It ain't even nine o'clock. What's the big deal?"

"Who all went with you?"

"Just Biff. He carried me there. You saw him when we left."

"Who'd you go to see? Ain't you goin to tell me that?"

"No."

"It's got somethin to do with your accident then. I knew it."

"God damn it, woman. It wasn't a accident. Can't you get that through your head?"

"See. I knew it."

"I'm goin to bed," Cal said, and he stomped out of the room in disgust.

When Ursela got into the bed about an hour later, he was still awake. She said goodnight. The springs creaked, and Cal felt the bed sink as she got in on her side. She shifted her weight toward him, but he pretended to be asleep. He groaned a little, as though the noise and her moving in the bed was bothering him, and after that she was quiet.

Chapter 21

Nora was only five minutes late when she pulled off the dirt road into Biff Barker's short driveway and parked beside his pick-up. He had said to come at eleven-thirty, and the clock in her car said eleven-forty, but it could easily be wrong by five minutes. It was still within the boundaries of being on time. She turned the car off and took out the keys and sat there for a minute, looking out the window. There was no house, only trees going steeply up a hill in front of the car, and off to the side where the ground was flatter and more open, there was a small, unpainted barn, so new that the boards were still yellow. Nora could see Biff's two big horses peeping around the barn as though they were spying on her, so she knew she had come to the right place. Then Biff himself came out the open door with a large tan dog walking on each side of him.

Nora got out of the car, feeling shy, trying not to look as awkward as she felt. In her embarrassment, she said, "That's not your house, is it?" gesturing toward the barn.

He was smiling, but when she asked her rude question, a shadow slid across his face, a flicker of doubt in his smile.

"I'm sorry. That wasn't a very nice thing to say, was it?"

"That's my barn."

"I saw the horses."

His smile got a little more real, and he nodded. The two dogs stopped beside him. They were dignified and polite, but they were curious too. They stretched their noses forward, reaching toward her, and because they were so tall, their big muzzles were pointing right at her belly and the secret baby.

She would have liked to step back, but the car was there behind her. She laughed a little nervously and said, "All your animals are so large."

"This one is Wolf," Biff said as he laid a hand on a huge head. "And this guy," patting the head on the other side, "this one with the black muzzle is Bear. They are big, aren't they?" he said with satisfaction.

"I'm not scared of dogs. I like them." She held her hands out, palms up, and each dog courteously sniffed a hand. "That's one of the things I hated about Boston. The dogs you did see seemed so out of place and uncomfortable."

"I kept you out in the cold last time, and I intend to treat you better today. Come on up to my cabin."

"But where is it?" Nora said, looking around and exaggerating her confusion.

"It's up the hill a ways, not far."

"I wore boots like you said to."

"Good. The trail's not too bad, but I thought we'd come down later and see the horses. You'll need them then."

They started up the hill into the woods. The trail was a steep path bounded by untrampled snow that rose up on both sides. Nora followed Biff. The dogs were already far ahead, but they came flying back down again, one chasing the other. They ran out around Biff, but Nora stepped off the trail to give them room and sank into snow almost to her knees.

"Oh," she gasped. "I had no idea it was so deep."

"You already need snowshoes," Biff said. He stopped to wait for her.

Nora struggled back onto the trail and brushed off her blue jeans and the tops of her boots. They were leather and neither very warm nor waterproof. "I guess I'll know better next time," she said laughing. "I seem to be learning a lot of new things from you."

Right away she was sorry she had said so much, but when she looked, she saw he was walking up the trail again and hadn't heard anything. She was relieved, even though he looked wonderful in his cowboy hat under the snowy trees, the kind of man of the outdoors that made Adam seem silly and inconsequential at last.

She stood there for a minute, and then she had to hurry to catch up. The path was steep and smooth. Biff had scattered ashes along it to keep it from being so slippery. At first the sun flashed down through the bare branches, but then they came to a grove of pine trees where only tiny patches of light reached the ground, and the air was colder.

When Nora stopped to get her breath, she looked up, and there it was, as though it had just materialized that instant, a low log house with smoke threading up from its chimney into the large, dark trees that surrounded it. There it was, like magic in the heart of the woods with the two proud dogs standing on the deck in front waiting to greet them.

Nora stopped where she was. "Oh, I feel like Hansel and Gretel. I can't believe it. I didn't think your house would be like this."

"Come on," Biff said. "I'll show it to you."

"And did you really build it?"

"Sure."

"All by yourself?"

"Mostly. Come on."

On the deck, out of the wind, the sun was warm. Chickadees darted in and out of the pine trees, visiting bird feeders made from milk cartons and singing their "dzee-dzee-dzee" song.

Biff opened the cabin door. "Come inside. I need to check our dinner."

Nora followed slowly, under the spell of all the things there were to notice. She stepped through the door into a wall of warm air like a blanket. Biff's cabin had one room with sloping ceilings and big windows on each side. It was dark and shadowy after the bright sunlight. Nora shut the door and stood there getting used to the dim light.

In the middle of the room was an old-fashioned black-and-silver cookstove. Biff was looking in the oven. Without straightening up, he said, "Sit down. I have to check on our potatoes and build up the fire, and then I can show you around."

Nora sat down on the bench that was beside the door. "I'll take off my boots, so I don't get your floor dirty. You should hear my mom if anyone walks around the house with their boots on."

Biff took a pot out of the oven and set it down on top of the stove, and then he turned around. "Don't take your boots off if you want to see the bathroom. It isn't in here."

"Oh," Nora said, pulling her boot back on and standing up. "I would like to know where it is. Yes."

"Go down the steps off the deck and around the side of the cabin and follow the path. It isn't far."

"Okay."

"And I'll start our steaks. How do you want yours?"

"Rare, please," Nora said, thinking that was the right way to want steak cooked. But as she was leaving, she thought how she had to be able to eat it in front of him, and she said, "But not very rare, just in-between."

Nora stepped outside into the sharp, cold air and followed the path around the side of the cabin. The eaves of the roof came almost to the ground, and in that protected space on the wall of the house, Biff had hung up his tools. She thought her mom would like the way everything was so neat. She had been trying to keep her bedroom in order, ever since she moved back in with her parents, but somehow she never got it organized in a way that pleased her mother. She almost didn't want to admit that what Mom really wanted was to see no evidence that Nora was living in that room. She wanted it to look the way it did before Nora moved back. But Nora didn't like to think about that, and anyway, she was going to move out as soon as she could.

The outhouse was just inside the trees behind the cabin. She opened the door nervously, but it was as orderly and simple in there as everything else on Biff's place. There was a bucket of wood shavings on the floor and toilet paper on a holder made from the branch of a tree. Nora remembered the outhouse that used to be at Uncle Cal's before they got indoor plumbing. That was when she was five or six. She remembered how it was one of the arguments her mother always used on her dad about why she didn't want to go out to visit his relatives in the country. Lena used to have plenty to say about how disgusting and unsanitary it was. But Lena always took Mom's side of the argument, while she took Dad's, and she still couldn't see what all the fuss was about. You could certainly build your own place much more easily if you didn't have to deal with the complications of plumbing. She never knew what Cal and Ursela and their kids did about taking a bath. She was too little to wonder about it, and by the time she was in high school and was out there a lot, they had running water.

Nora left the outhouse door open a little way for light while she struggled through the many layers of her clothes. The toilet seat was so cold that it burned when she sat on it. She replaced all the layers of clothes and sprinkled some wood shavings down the hole, wondering whether Biff had cleaned his place up for her visit, or if it was always so orderly. Either way was intimidating.

Outside, the trunks of the pines were pink where the sun shone on them. Nora could feel their aliveness, how they shimmered with pleasure in the sun, and the day, and the simple joy of being there. And, of course, that made her think of the baby, destined so soon not to be. She wished she hadn't thought of it. It spoiled everything. Biff was so nice to her, calling her up to invite her to his house, remembering to tell her to wear boots, cooking dinner for her. He acted gallant in an old-fashioned way. Still, she didn't think it would work to tell him about the baby. After the abortion, when it was part of the past, maybe it would be different. But for now, since there were confusing sexual issues that she didn't even know how to sort out, it seemed easier not to deal with any of it. It wasn't Biff's baby, and it wasn't his problem, and it was too sad to think about. She gave herself a light slap on the face to remind herself that she needed to keep her thoughts under control.

Wolf and Bear were waiting for her on the deck. She opened the door without knocking—she didn't know whether to knock or not—and said, "Shall I let the dogs in?" to cover her own uncertainty.

Biff was at the stove with his back to the door. There was a delicious smell of cooking meat. "Leave them out," Biff said. "They take up so much room."

So Nora patted each big dog on the head and said, "Sorry, guys," and slipped inside to the warmth and the food, thinking how those were the essential ingredients of a home and telling herself she must remember that for the time when she could get a place of her own. She sat down on the bench by the door and took off her boots. "You'd better look out," she said. "It smells so good that I think I could eat everything and leave none for you."

Biff laughed. "I hope there's plenty," he said. "Ursela often sells me meat from her freezer, but when she heard it was for you, she made me take some extra, and she gave me some potatoes and peas from their last year's garden to go with the steak."

"That was nice of her." She put her boots under the stove, where several pairs of his boots were already. She pushed her jacket to the end of the bench and sat down again. Biff had set two places at the table with an odd collection of mismatched dishes.

"I hope I'm cooking these peas right." He turned around to her, holding the pot. "What do you think? Do they look right? I never cooked peas before."

Nora looked into the pot. "They look fine. Some people cook them too much."

"I didn't do that, did I?"

"No. They look just right."

"Okay. Then everything's ready." He poured the peas into a bowl.

"You can go and sit down at the other end of the table, and I'll bring the food."

"Okay. This is great."

"Ursela said just what you said about not cooking the peas too much."

"It feels funny that they know I'm over here."

"I don't know if Cal does. There's the butter for your potatoes. I got that from Ursela too."

"I'd better stop over there when I leave and say hello. I was out there a few days ago to see my cousin Elsie. This meat is delicious, by the way."

"Thanks. It helps when you start from something really good."

"Do you buy all your food from them?"

"I don't think they'd want me to do that. But they always have milk and eggs for sale, and butter. You probably remember that from when you used to visit them."

"Oh yeah, they had a refrigerator in the mudroom, and neighbors used to come up and take what they wanted and leave the money in a basket that Aunt Ursela kept out there. Conrad and Paul and Elsie sometimes joked about taking the money and blaming it on the customers, but I don't believe any of them ever did."

"They still have the same system."

"That was a long time ago."

"Well, I guess it works."

They both ate in silence for a few minutes, and then Nora said, "How did you meet them? You're not from around here, are you? I think I would have seen you around if you had grown up here."

"You're right. I'm not. I came here from California. But you don't want to hear such a long story."

"Yes I do. I'm sure I do." She looked around the cabin, with its neat bunks built into one corner and the pegs for clothes and the sloping ceiling and the books and the bright snow outside the windows. She waved her hand to take it all in and said, "To come from California and to end up with this. I'd love to hear about it. It must be an interesting story."

"Well, I don't know about that, but I'll tell you if you want to hear it. I think you ought to stop me when you get bored."

"Okay. I will."

"I came here with my best friend Andy, because of the free land. We drove across the country in an old station wagon with our girlfriends and all our stuff. We were planning to homestead."

"What free land?"

"Earth People's Park. You could stake out a claim, and it was yours as long as you lived on it. We stayed there for the summer, but we didn't have a good enough place for the winter. We had to leave when it started to get really cold. We had built a cabin, but it was really rough—not like this one."

"So that was how you learned to build like this."

He looked around the room thoughtfully. "I guess so. I sure learned what not to do anyway."

"I mean, because this place is amazing."

"It's a lot better than the one we built in Norton. And there's only one person here, which makes a lot of difference."

"Where is Andy...where are the others now?" She would have liked to ask if the girlfriend was still in the picture, but she didn't know him well enough for that.

"He's still around. He's working for a hardware store in Severance. I see him every once in a while. We always used to call him AC because his name is Andy Carpenter. He's got two kids now and a house in town. He dropped back into a regular life."

"But you didn't."

"No. Well, it was different for me. AC's girlfriend got pregnant, so they decided to get married. By that time, my girlfriend had already gotten homesick and gone back to California. She was AC's sister Bonnie. Was, I mean, she still is, but anyway, that left just the three of us in an apartment in Severance, and it wasn't very big, so when they got married, I had to move out."

"Where did you go?"

"I rented a room in a house in West Severance, but it was awful. I couldn't have any visitors, and I didn't have any friends at all. The guys I worked with at the granite sheds weren't very friendly because I was a hippie. I was really lonely, and that was when I met Cal."

"Really? I would think Uncle Cal might be against hippies too."

"He was nice to me when he didn't have any reason to be. I know what you mean about the way he talks, and I don't want to say that's just talk, because I don't want to put him down, but you have to look at what he does, not at what he says."

"Do you think he's okay? I mean is his foot healing? It seems awful slow."

"It was deep. It takes a long time for something that deep to heal. The bullet went all the way through, didn't it?"

"Oooooh, I think so. I don't like to even think about it."

Biff didn't say anything.

After a silence, Nora said, "My mom thinks he shot himself."

"Really?"

"An accident, you know? That he was climbing down from his tree stand, and his gun went off." She looked at Biff's face, trying to read there what he really thought, but she didn't know him well enough to decipher anything. Finally she said, "What do you think?"

He looked down at his empty plate. "At first I kind of wondered…. Oh say, would you like some more of anything?"

"I couldn't, but it was so good. I ate an awful lot."

"I should've got some cookies or a pie from Ursela. She always has stuff like that. I even meant to. I just forgot."

"Did you mean that at first you thought Uncle Cal might've shot himself?"

"No. I never actually thought that, but I wondered how it could've happened, and then I was in the auto parts store, and I heard this guy talking and…."

"You mean you might've found a guy who would actually admit it?"

"I don't know about that. All I know is that I found out this guy's name and where he lived, and I told Cal. We went over to his place and talked to him."

"Wow. When?"

"Just a couple of days ago."

"What happened?"

"Nothing really. The guy was very nervous. Cal thought it was because he was guilty, but I don't know. Cal can be intimidating."

"I know."

"The guy was smart enough not to say anything incriminating, so it ended in a draw. My guess is if he did shoot Cal, it was an accident. He might not have even known he did it. Cal thinks he did it on purpose to get the deer."

"Let me know what happens. I'm really curious about it. My dad, my mom, Uncle Cal, everyone says something different. It's hard to know.... Did Uncle Cal tell you I went up in the woods with him to look for clues? That was not too long after it happened."

"He didn't tell me. Did you find anything?"

"Only a candy bar wrapper down below the ridge where the person could've been standing."

"Well, that's something."

"That's what Uncle Cal said. He said the shooter would've been able to shoot from that very spot. Suppose he was waiting for Uncle Cal there?"

"I don't think it was anything like that. They both wanted the same deer. That's what it was about."

"I drove Uncle Cal's tractor when we went up there. I just came along when he needed somebody to drive him up to the top of the hill. It was right after he got home from the hospital. He couldn't have walked all that way."

"I didn't know you could drive a tractor."

"That's because I really can't. Uncle Cal told me what to do, and I did it. I think I was too scared of him to say no, but I was lucky. I did something wrong coming down, and we started to roll faster and faster. I couldn't do anything but steer because Uncle Cal told me not to touch the brakes. I don't even know what I did. It was scary."

"I know what happened. That old tractor of Cal's is always jumping out of gear, and then you just freewheel. I don't know why he didn't warn you."

"Really?"

"I bet he thought you wouldn't drive it for him if he told you it might jump out of gear. That would be just like Cal."

"I thought it was my fault. He didn't say it wasn't."

"No, and isn't that just like Cal too? I'm sure that's what happened. It sounds like you handled it okay."

"Well, I couldn't do anything but steer, and at the bottom it slowed down. Oh yes, now I remember. Uncle Cal told me to put it in gear so we could drive the rest of the way."

"That's what happened."

"It's funny. All this time I was sure I did something wrong. Do you really think Uncle Cal would do that—let me drive the tractor down when he knew it might pop out of gear like that?"

"Yes, I do, because that was the only way he could get up there, and he really wanted to look around. I know that. I offered to go up and look for him, and I'm sure his boys did too, but that's not Cal's way. He had to see for himself."

"That's the kind of thing that drives my mom crazy about Uncle Cal. Phew." Nora stopped herself before she said how hot it was in the cabin. She didn't want to take off the baggy sweater that hid how she was spreading out in the middle. No matter how hot she was, she didn't want Biff to think she might be pregnant. Even thinking about it in his presence made her uneasy.

"Let's talk about you, Nora. What made you move back, and what are you going to do now you're here?"

"Oh my God," Nora said to herself. "It's almost like he's reading my mind. Does he think I'm going to keep this baby?" She looked at him, wondering if he could really know, and how she could find out, and if he did know, should she tell him anything about it?

"I'm sorry. I must've said something I shouldn't have said. You look like you've seen a ghost."

"No, it's okay. Really."

"Please forget I asked."

"No, it's fine, really. I don't have any secrets. Really I don't. I had a good job working for an advertising agency. I was making a lot of money and I had a chance to move up to an even more interesting job, and I was so unhappy. I was lonely, and I hated the city, and I missed Vermont, so I quit. I don't think it was a very smart move. My mom thinks it was an awful thing to do. I can't tell what my dad thinks because he never says anything about it." She shrugged. "That's it. That's the whole story. I guess I'm starting over."

"I think that's terrific. You're following your heart, and that's just what you ought to do. Don't let it get you down if your parents don't understand. My parents don't understand what I'm doing either. It's because they grew up in the Depression. All they think about is security."

So maybe she could have told him about the baby. Maybe he would have been sympathetic about that part too. But it was too late now. "I hope you're right. I feel awful right now, like it was a really stupid idea. I have only found menial and boring jobs, and I haven't kept any of them for more than a few days. My mom thinks that's awful too. And the worst part is that I haven't even got a place of my own."

Biff stood up. "It'll come, Nora. Give it time to happen." He went over to the shelves by the door and got a big metal dishpan and brought it back to the table.

"I *could* get a place. I mean, I have some money saved, but I'm trying to be careful." Did he think she was saying she wanted to move into his cabin? Is that why he jumped up to do the dishes? She wondered if she ought to tell him that wasn't what she meant, but she wasn't sure how to say it. So she stood up and started trying to help him put the dishes in the dishpan, until she noticed that whenever she put a dish in, he took it out again. She said, "I'll set them here, and you can put them where you want them."

"Thanks," he said. "I have a system."

"I see that," she said, laughing. "I think you have a system for everything." She waved her hand at the orderly room. "It looks like you've got it all figured out a certain way. Do you always keep it this neat, or did you clean up because I was coming?"

He didn't look up from stacking the dishes in the pan, but he smiled. "I think it's always pretty neat. It comes from when AC and the girls and I all lived in a tent together. With that many people, if you don't keep things in order, it doesn't take long before you have complete chaos. I guess it's a habit I got into then."

Nora noticed that he didn't say whether he cleaned up because she was coming, but she couldn't ask the question again. Instead she said, "I guess you have a system for washing dishes without a sink, don't you?"

"It's pretty simple. I wash in this pan and rinse in another one, but I thought we would leave these and go down to see the horses."

"Don't you want help cleaning up first?"

"No. Let's not. I want to show you my horses. This job'll keep." He carried the dishpan over to the stove and dipped enough hot water out of the reservoir on the side of the stove to cover the dishes and pushed the pan back onto the warm corner of the stove. "There. They can soak."

When they opened the door, the dogs were both standing right there, wagging their tails hopefully.

Nora said, "They know we're going some place."

"They always know. I don't know how they do it."

The dogs pranced and jumped and ran ahead along the trail. Nora started down behind Biff, but she turned off to go to the outhouse, telling him she would catch up farther along.

Biff was already in the barn when she got there. He was just opening the big doors at the far end of the hall. It was dark inside after the bright, white snowlight. Biff was a black silhouette, and in the open doorway, the two huge horses stood in the bright light. The black of the door made a frame, and the horses stood as still as a painting inside it. Nora gasped at the beauty of it.

Biff looked around. "I'm going to put them in so we can brush them. Just stay there for a minute." He walked up to one of the horses and took her by the halter, clucking to her. She took a step forward, and her enormous hoof made a heavy, ringing sound that echoed down the hall.

Nora stood in the shadows, watching while Biff and the first horse disappeared into a stall. She was alone with the second horse, who stood in the open doorway. Nora half expected her to bolt into the barn, and she tried to figure out which way to run. But the horse stayed where she was, only shifting a little from foot to foot with her impatience to come inside.

Biff came out and shut the stall door on the first horse.

"Do they always do what you say? It's amazing."

Biff led the second one into the barn. "Well...yes...mostly," he said. "Not always, but mostly." He shut the second horse into her stall. "I'm going to leave the big doors open so we'll have some light. "I've been thinking of putting electricity in down here. It would be handy. I could have a freezer."

The horses were both looking over their stall doors, watching Biff. "They are hoping for some grain, but they're not sure what's going to happen, because it's early."

"Are you going to give them some?"

"Yes, and then we can brush them." He unlocked a padlock on a door at the end of the hall.

"What's that for?"

"I keep their grain and harness in here, and I leave a lot of my tools down here, chain saws and stuff. That's why I lock it up. It's too far away from my house, too tempting for anyone driving by."

Nora stood in the doorway and watched while he scooped grain out of a garbage can into matching buckets. Behind her she could hear the horses stepping around in their stalls and bumping against their doors in their excitement.

Biff hung a bucket in each stall, and then the only sound was of big teeth crunching and chewing. He said, "No, they're not always good by any means. They both have their moods. Queenie is worse than Duchess, but they're both women, so of course they're temperamental." He gave Nora a teasing look.

And she rose to the bait. "Oh come on, Biff, you shouldn't say that."

"No. It's true. A lot of teamsters have geldings because they're steadier."

"I don't know what gelding means, but you can't compare...."

"But you can, at least with horses you can. That's just what I'm saying, because a lot of guys say they wouldn't have mares because they're so unpredictable. I mean, I was really teasing you, Nora, but you can't help noticing that's what people say about human women too."

"Why don't you have geldings then, whatever they are?"

"They're males that have been...ah...fixed, you know?"

"Oh."

"But I might have, if I had been choosing. These were for sale, and they were all trained, and the price was right. I guess I didn't know what I was getting into, and now....well, now it's personal—we work together. We understand each other. I couldn't part with them." He left Nora standing in the hall looking at the big blonde heads buried in their buckets. Every so often one would pull out with a mouthful to chew, scattering grain in all directions.

Biff came back and handed her a heavy oval brush. "Who do you want to groom?"

"I don't know. Whichever one you think I should. I can't remember which one is which."

"This is Duchess right here. Let's do her first. She stands better." He opened the door to the stall and stepped inside. "Come on. They'll be done with their grain soon, and then they won't stand so still."

Nora just stood there. "But Biff," she said. "Can't we brush them from out here?"

"No, you can't. How could you reach? Come on."

"But their feet.... I'm afraid she'll step on me."

"Come on. I promise that won't happen. Come close and see how sweet she is."

Nora walked into the stall slowly. "Well, all right, but you promised."

"Don't be scared. She'll know if you are, and she'll think you know something she doesn't, that there's some danger that you know about."

"Well, that's exactly the way I feel in here. She's enormous."

"Yes, but she doesn't know anyone would be scared of her. She would think that was ridiculous. Come over here by her shoulder and pat her."

Slowly, trying to pretend she wasn't afraid, Nora walked up to the huge shoulder, and the horse turned her head slowly, thoughtfully, toward Nora to see what she would do. She stroked the huge shoulder and said, "Nice girl, nice girl." Then she laughed and said, "It sounds like I'm talking to a cat." She stroked the big soft shoulder some more. "She *is* nice. I remember that smell from when we used to go to the fair."

"Scratch her behind the ear. She likes that."

"Like a dog." She reached up and scratched behind Duchess's ear, and Duchess tilted her head down and leaned against Nora's scratching hand. "Look. She likes it."

Biff smiled.

They stayed in Duchess's stall for a while. Nora got brave enough to duck under Duchess's head, so she could stand on the other side and scratch the other ear. Then they went into Queenie's stall, and Nora scratched both of her ears. When they came out, Nora smelled like a horse and was proud of it. "I hope I still smell this way when I get home. My dad'll love it. They used horses for everything when he was growing up."

They stood in the open doorway. The two dogs had come back tired from wherever they were and had flopped down in the sun right outside the barn door. They were panting a little.

"Thank you for showing the horses to me. And thank you for making me go in with them. It was fun when I got used to it. I'd like to see them pulling logs out of the woods someday."

"Maybe we can do that. I'll call you sometime when I'm at Cal's or else in town."

"Okay."

"Would you like to come back up to the cabin for a while? I was planning to make us some cocoa."

"Oh thanks, but I ought to go over and see Uncle Cal and Aunt Ursela while I'm out here, since they know I was visiting you. I've had a very fun day."

She walked to the car, feeling him watching, feeling awkward, that there was something missing, something that should have been said and hadn't been, although she was glad he hadn't tried to kiss her or touch her, since she wasn't in a position yet to feel comfortable about that. Maybe soon. It was a reason to get going on the abortion, besides the obvious reason that she was running out of time. And then, when she had done that, she could let herself picture a romantic evening at Biff's cabin.

Chapter 22

When Conrad got out of the truck, he could feel the thaw in the air. The sun was already shining through the trees, and the chickadees were whistling their spring song. He took a look around. He'd only been at the new job site for a few days, just long enough to clear a small landing by the road and to start up into the woodlot. He had walked it with the owner, a guy John found for him. The guy had had a forester mark the trees to cut. The woodlot covered more than a hundred acres. It was beautiful, but a lot of it was steep. Conrad had never done such a big job. He was lucky to get it. Other guys had been looking at it too. He just hoped he could handle it.

He carried his saw to the tailgate and sharpened it while he smoked a cigarette and decided what he was going to do. He planned to make his skid roads as he worked his way up into the woods. He knew some guys got the roads laid out first, but this way he might be able to get a few loads done sooner and get some money coming in.

He ground out the cigarette in the mud. The saw was ready. He walked a little way up into the woods, set the saw on the ground, and started cranking on it, but he couldn't get it to fire. There was nothing. He cranked until his arm got tired, and then he wondered if he might have flooded it, even though he didn't smell gas.

He sat down on the stump of a tree he'd cut yesterday and took out his cigarettes again, just for something to ease his mind. The saw had been acting strange for the last few days. He kept hoping it would straighten itself out. He sat and looked at it while he smoked, and then he tried it again, but it still wouldn't start.

He sat back down on the stump. This was a waste of a beautiful day. It was already above freezing. The snow was melting. Everywhere there was the sound of dripping water and the smell of wet earth. It might even get to fifty degrees if the sun stayed out.

Conrad jumped up and grabbed the saw and started for the truck. Maybe Albert Gregoire could get it going. It might be something simple, although Conrad was pretty sure it wasn't. He knew the compression wasn't what it should be, and he didn't even want to think about what that could mean. It had only been three weeks since Albert had gone over the whole saw. It couldn't be good that he had to take it back so soon. Still, he had to. It was better than sitting in the woods looking at the damn thing.

Until this trouble with the saw, everything had been going well. He had been nervous when he began, but the last few weeks had given him confidence. George Carleton paid him and even gave him a bonus.

Conrad didn't know what he would do if Albert wasn't in his shop. But it didn't matter anyway, because there wasn't anything he *could* do without a saw, and there was only one way to find out whether Albert was there. He opened the window of the truck. It was like spring outside. The sun shone brightly on the snow. He had to squint to see where he was going.

He could tell he was getting in shape. At first, he had been so tired when he got home that he would just collapse wherever he was. Once he fell asleep in the shower. No one knew about that one. But once he fell asleep at the dinner table. They all noticed when he dropped his fork onto his plate and slumped down. When he looked up at the sound the fork made, Dorrie and Dwayne were staring at him with their mouths open, and Cheryl was carefully not looking his way.

Since then he had gotten stronger, even though his back hurt and his muscles were sore and kinked up when he got home at night. Sometimes Cheryl would rub his back with Bengay. That was the best. He would think he was too tired to stay awake another minute, even while Cheryl was rubbing his back, but he would wake up, and it would evolve into making love. Conrad grinned to himself just thinking about it. It was as good as it was when they first got married.

He pulled up beside Albert's house to the little garage that he used for a shop. Conrad couldn't tell whether there was a light on inside, but the door was open. That was a good sign. Albert wouldn't go very far and leave it open. Conrad got his saw out of the truck. Above the door and above the big garage doors were rows of deer antlers nailed to the wall. The building badly needed a coat of paint, but it would be impossible to paint around all those antlers. No wonder Albert didn't do it.

Inside it was warm. Conrad could smell smoke from the woodstove. The light was dim after the bright sunlight. He set the saw down on the counter. "Albert, are you back there?" he shouted. "Come take a look at this damn thing, will you? I can't get it to do nothin."

There was a clank of metal in the back, and Albert came around the end of the shelves, wiping his hands on a greasy rag. "Hello, Conrad. Nice weather, ain't it?"

"It would be if I could get some work done, but I can't do nothin with my saw."

Albert looked down at the saw on the counter in front of him. "It ain't been that long since I went over this saw. What's the trouble?"

Conrad sighed. "The damn thing won't start," he said.

"Well, let me take a look. We won't know nothin until I do. How's your dad, anyways?"

"He's gettin along. He still needs a cane, but his foot is pretty much healed."

"That's good."

Conrad watched in silence while Albert checked to see if there was fuel in the tank. He set the saw on the floor and pulled on the rope a few times. He looked for a spark, and then he put the saw back on the counter. Conrad wanted to ask him what he thought, but he was afraid of what he would hear.

"I guess your dad's lucky. It could of been a lot worse. It ain't been that long to be already healed."

"He still needs to get his strength back. But you know Dad. He ain't goin to sit around, no matter what anybody says."

Albert's head was still bent over the saw. "You just don't know who's goin to be out there with a gun these days. I worry about my boys when they go to deer camp."

"Yeah, I know."

Albert looked up. The light from the open door glinted off his glasses. He didn't say anything. He just looked at Conrad.

"What's wrong with it?"

"What ain't wrong with it is the question."

Conrad's heart sank. "I was hopin it would be somethin simple and you could get me goin again today."

"I'm sorry. I know you're just startin out on your business, but this saw is flat worn out."

"Ain't there some kind of a cobble job you could do on it?"

"I can replace the crank seals and put a new piston ring into it. I should've done that back in December when you brought it in, but I was tryin to keep your costs down for you."

"I appreciate it, Albert. It ain't your fault."

"It might could be time for a new saw, Conrad. What do you think about that?"

"I can't, Albert. I wish I could, but I'm out straight as it is. I ain't got enough money comin in, and now with the saw out of commission...I'm in one of them binds."

Albert had the spark plug out now. Conrad thought about how much he hated that old saw. He didn't know what else to say. He really didn't know what else to do.

After a few minutes, Albert looked up. "I'll put it to the front of the line, Conrad. I ought to be able to get it back to you tomorrow. It's goin to run you about sixty bucks. It's mostly labor."

"That's okay."

"But that ain't goin to solve your problems. This saw has had it. You're goin to need a new saw, Conrad."

"It don't do no good to say that. It ain't goin to happen."

"I'd tell you to borrow your dad's, but that one wouldn't last any time, the way you're usin it. What's Paul got these days?"

"The last I knew about it, Paul was borrowin mine."

"You'll just have to get yourself another saw, Conrad. You know that, don't you? There ain't any way you can keep this thing goin. I mean, I can get it goin, but I can't keep it goin. It's too worn. It's too old. It ain't up to workin all day every day like you need it to do."

"I know. I been afraid of that. I've known it for a while, I guess."

"It's just too old. It's been used too hard."

Conrad sighed and took out his cigarettes. He offered one to Albert and took one himself and lit both of them. Neither of them said anything. Conrad was thinking how hopeless it was to even think about a new saw. It didn't matter how much he needed one. There was no way he could manage it. He didn't know what Albert was thinking. It was probably, "Why doesn't this dumb shit get out of my shop and let me get back to work."

So he was surprised when Albert said, "Okay, Conrad. I wouldn't do this for very many people—I couldn't afford to—but you're a good man, and your dad has always been a good friend. I have a new Pioneer back there. It's a big one, a forty-one. It's a beauty. You're goin to love it."

"I'm sure I would, Albert."

"You won't believe how fast it is, especially when you compare it to this old thing."

"Albert, you're makin me feel real bad. I already told you I ain't got the money. I couldn't even buy a cheap saw, never mind a Pioneer."

"Hey, who said anythin about money? I know you're good for it."

"But I don't know when...."

"Look, Conrad, the saw's worth $300, maybe $310 or $320 after our governor takes his cut. When you get paid for one of your jobs in the next few months, you can pay me. I ain't goin to worry about it."

"It could be late spring before...."

"I told you it was okay. I hate to see a nice young guy bust himself for nothin. There ain't no way you can make it without a decent saw. This Pioneer is one of the best on the market. You got a chance with that."

"Can I try it out?"

"Oh sure, because I know once you try it, you ain't goin to give it up. Meantime, I'll do what I can with this thing so you'll have it for backup." He went into the back of his shop and brought out the big saw. He pushed Conrad's old one aside and set the new saw down on the counter in front of Conrad. It was big and shiny and clean. Conrad was a little scared of it. It looked so powerful.

As though he could see what Conrad was thinking, Albert said, "It's safer too. It's got this new chain brake, so it can't kick back on you."

That settled it for Conrad. He already wanted the new saw badly, and the chain brake gave him something to use to convince Cheryl that he needed to spend another big chunk of money that he didn't even have.

"Start her up. Listen how she sounds. She's a real high performance machine."

Conrad set the saw carefully down on the cement floor and pulled the starter cord. The engine started immediately.

"It's so quiet," he said to Albert.

"Take it to your woodlot and give it a good try out. You're goin to love it."

"Okay. I will," Conrad said. He shut off the saw and picked it up. "And thank you, Albert. I really appreciate it."

Albert waved him out the door. "I know, and I know you're good for it too. Tell your dad I said hello."

Conrad set the new saw on the seat of the truck beside him and drove off. Part of him was thinking there was no way the saw could be as good as Albert said it was. It didn't sound that strong. But if that was the case, he could bring it back, and he wouldn't have to say anything to Cheryl.

He looked at the saw sitting on the seat beside him. Of course, then he would be in the bind he was in before. So the other half of him was excited, hoping it was going to be the way Albert said. He didn't know what to wish for. Every time he looked over at the saw, he could see it sitting there, shiny and new, proud of itself.

"All right," he said out loud. "You're goin to have to prove yourself here in a minute. Don't look so smart-aleck. You might not be able to make it."

The saw just sat there.

"I'm warnin you. I can take you back to Albert if you can't cut it." He paused, listening to his own words. "Hey, that was a joke."

But nobody heard it because he was talking to himself. He'd always heard that only crazy people talked to themselves. He wondered if he was okay. Maybe it was bad for him to spend all his days alone in the woods. But then he remembered the endless conversations with customers, always about the same things, like the weather, and he was glad to be where he was, with only himself to talk to. "So what if I am crazy?" he said out loud, just to confirm it.

When he got to the woodlot, he put the saw on the tailgate of his truck and checked the gas and oil. Albert had filled everything up. Conrad was ready to try it out. He carried the saw over to where he had been cutting yesterday and set it on the ground and started it up.

"All right," he said to the saw. "Let's see if you're as smart as Albert thinks you are."

He carried the saw over to the tree he planned to cut next. It was purring quietly. It sank its teeth into the tree without even changing its sound very much.

Conrad cut a wedge out of the tree on the side he wanted the tree to fall on. He kicked the wedge aside and went around the tree to start the main cut. The saw bit deep into the tree. "You are amazin," Conrad said. "Albert was tellin the truth."

For the rest of the day, Conrad only stopped long enough to eat his lunch. He sat on a stump with his sandwiches and thermos of coffee while he ate and had a quick cigarette, and the whole time he was looking at the saw, which he had set on another stump.

In the afternoon, he had to stop to sharpen it, but that didn't take very long. He was amazed at how much he was able to do. Around four-thirty, the light was starting to fail, and Conrad decided he'd had enough. He walked down to the truck and then looked back up the hill at all the trees he'd dropped. He'd really done a good day's work.

He was tired, but he felt great. He loaded the gas and oil cans in the back and put the saw gently into the passenger seat. When he got home, he took everything out of the truck and put it on the floor right inside the door of the barn. Then he went on into the main room to check on the heifers. He walked down the aisle between their pens. They all had hay and water, but their pens were filthy. Conrad got out the wheelbarrow and the manure fork and cleaned all six of the pens. He wheeled the load out the back door and dumped it, and then he put fresh bedding hay in all the pens.

He patted all the heifers, but he stayed a little longer by his favorite. She was smaller than the others and almost all black, even though she was a Holstein. She stretched her head out over the bars of her pen so that he could scratch her neck. He called her Honey, even though he didn't like to name them. They didn't stay with him very long before they went back to the farms they came from. He knew some of them wouldn't be treated well, and since there was nothing he could do about it, he didn't like to think about it.

He could see that the chickens' pen could use some cleaning too, but he decided to skip that. He was so pleased with the warm weather and the new saw and the way he had gotten so much work done that he wasn't even angry at Dwayne or Dorrie, whichever one it was who hadn't done the chores the right way.

Conrad took off his outdoor clothes in the mudroom and went into the kitchen. Cheryl was standing by the stove.

"Where's Dwayne?" he said.

"He's down in the basement. I hope he's doin his homework. Why?"

"I have to talk to him about the chores. That's all." He went to the stairs and called, "Dwayne. Come up here."

Dwayne started up the stairs, already making his excuses. "I know what you're mad about, Dad, but it wasn't me. Today was Dorrie's turn to do the barn chores. I had to do the dishes, and I did 'em all too. You can ask Ma if I didn't."

By that time Dwayne was standing in front of him. "Okay, son," he said. "Go on back down. Tell Dorrie to come up. And tell her I ain't mad. I just want to talk to her. Okay?"

By the time Conrad finished, Dwayne was halfway down the stairs again. Conrad stood at the top, waiting. He could hear Dwayne and Dorrie talking to each other down below. He was just about to give up and go into the kitchen to see Cheryl, when Dorrie came slowly up the stairs.

"Hello, Dad. Did you have a good day?"

"Yes, Dorrie, but...."

"I'm glad. So didn't I." She smiled at him. "It was so nice outside. And I did the barn chores, Dad. I gave them all food and water. Didn't you see that?"

"Yes, but, Dorrie, you didn't clean the pens."

"I did, Dad. I really did."

"But they were dirty."

"I can't help it, Dad. That must of happened after I cleaned them."

"Dorrie," he said, but it was no use. Dorrie could out argue anyone. "All right then," he said, defeated. It wasn't worth pursuing.

Dorrie clattered back down the stairs, and Conrad went to the bedroom to clean up before dinner.

Later on, after dinner was over and the kids had gone back to their schoolwork, or Conrad and Cheryl hoped they had gone back to their schoolwork, Conrad said, "I've got to tell you what happened today."

"Nothing bad, I hope."

"No, it's good, or I think so, anyway."

"Oh dear. It sounds like it might not be."

"You can decide when I tell you. When I got to the landin this mornin, my old saw wouldn't start. I tried everythin, and then I took it to Albert Gregoire. He looked at it and said it was flat worn out."

"So what did you do?"

She was leaning a little forward across the table, looking at him with all her attention. And he was coming to the tricky part, because he knew she wasn't going to like him adding on this new debt. "I was leaving Albert's, and I didn't know what I was goin to do, when he called me back to take a look at a new P41 he had."

"Oh Conrad, how much did you spend? And where did you get the money from anyways? If you wrote a check, it'll probably bounce."

"Don't worry, honey. I didn't do that. Albert said I couldn't make it without a new saw, and I told him there wasn't any way I could find the money for one."

"I know you got a new saw. I can tell."

"Albert told me to take the saw and try it out and see if I liked it. He said he knew I was good for it, and I could pay him when I got some ahead."

"How much?"

"A lot, but this saw is amazin. You wouldn't believe how much I got down today."

"$200?"

"A little more than that."

$250?"

"More...."

"Conrad...."

"Well, about $300, but I don't have to pay him until I've got it. It's my chance to make a go of it, probably my only chance. This saw is so good, it might could even pay for itself."

267

"That's a awful lot of money, and we'll have to pay it back sometime."

"I know, honey, and I'll take it back if you say you want me to, but what can I do? The old one's completely shot."

Cheryl didn't say a word. She just sat there looking down at the table and her empty coffee cup.

Conrad said, "This saw has a new chain-brake feature, so that when the saw kicks back on you, like if you hit somethin when you was sawin, it would stop automatically, instead of cuttin you. My old one don't have that. That's how guys get hurt—when the saw kicks back on 'em. It's a real good thing to have, especially when you're workin alone." He saw that what he said made a difference.

She smiled at him then. "I guess we'll make it. It was nice of Albert to do that for you."

"Don't worry, Cheryl. It'll come out all right."

"I hope so," she said, and she got up to take the dishes to the sink.

Chapter 23

George set the drink on his desk and sat down and put his sock feet up, savoring the peace and quiet, even more than the anticipation of the whiskey. Wasn't it a good sign that he wasn't desperate for that first sip? If he had a drinking problem, like Nick said, surely he would take a sip before he sat down. He watched beads of water making trails in the condensation on the outside of the glass. He was glad he had finally put a small refrigerator in his office so he could have ice. He had thought about it for a long time before he did it because he knew he would have to explain it to Laurie sooner or later, and he couldn't really explain it. All his reasons were lame, except that he wanted ice for his drink, and he couldn't tell her that.

Of course, if he did decide to stop drinking completely, the refrigerator would turn out to be a waste, but that might be some time off. In the days that had passed since "the incident", as he called it to himself, he had tried to drink nothing at all. He had thought he would just stop, but it turned out to be much more difficult than he thought it would be. He was surprised at how important a drink was in the ordinary course of the day. He was surprised at the size of the hole there was without it. He had concluded that stopping suddenly didn't make any sense. It probably wasn't even good for you to do it that way. It made more sense to cut back little by little, giving your body time to adjust.

He knew Laurie would object to his going out in a snowstorm, so tonight he had forestalled the objection by saying he was going to walk to his office. It was a beautiful night, warmer than it had been all day. There was no wind, and the large flakes fell softly, straight down. In the quiet, George could hear all the little wet patterings as they landed. It was a ten-minute walk down the hill to Main Street, but he didn't see a single person out walking, and no cars went by. He had the whole soft, luminous night to himself. He sat at his desk, thinking about the peacefulness of the winter evening.

He loved being alone. It was only in the quiet that he could concentrate. At home the television was on, or else there was music, and Laurie moving restlessly, sometimes angrily, around the room. When he had a drink alone, he could pay attention to it. He could savor it. And then he thought, "No, that's not quite the truth. It's because Laurie doesn't understand. She thinks there's something wrong with taking a drink at all, unless you're at a party and you just do it to be polite because everyone else is." Then George remembered the knowing smile on the clerk's face yesterday when he went into the liquor store to get a new bottle of Scotch. He had thought the clerk was pleased with himself for knowing what George wanted, setting the bottle on the counter before either of them said anything. But now George wondered if he hadn't meant something else by his smile.

That was why he preferred to be alone. He didn't want people giving him conspiratorial smiles, and he didn't want people worrying about him. This was a private pleasure. It didn't hurt anyone. It wasn't anyone else's business if it was something important to him. And he didn't want anyone to know how important it was. People always got the wrong idea when you let them in on the private parts of your life.

"Or...." and the thought stunned him, so that he had to take a long, delicious drink before he could let it come into his consciousness in words, "maybe they would get the right idea. Maybe that's what I'm afraid of. Maybe the right idea is that I do have a drinking problem."

He sat sipping his drink and chewing over that idea. When the drink was gone, he made up his mind not to have another but to go home instead. He was pleased with himself for making such a choice. He went into the bathroom, where he rinsed the glass and washed out his mouth with Listerine, the way he always did. But now it was as though the scales had fallen off his eyes. He watched himself and wondered what it meant.

His life had narrowed down. He didn't see nearly as many people as he used to. He knew that. He'd known it for a long time now, even though he hadn't wanted to. He hadn't thought he was lonely, or isolated, or missing anything. He hadn't thought anything was wrong. But when Cal and Nora both came back into his life last fall, he saw that he had been missing something important. Still, he was positive there couldn't be any real connection between his loneliness and an occasional drink. How could there be? It didn't make sense.

Or did it? He put the bottle of whiskey back in the safe where he always put it. He had never thought that was odd before, but now he was watching himself, and he couldn't believe he hadn't noticed how secretive he was. A person wasn't secretive if he didn't have anything to hide.

George thought of himself as a disciplined person. Everyone always said he was. And it was true that it took a lot of work and a lot of discipline to put himself through college and read law until he could pass the bar, while he was supporting a wife and two children. But it still made him uncomfortable when he heard people talk about how hard he worked, about how much time he spent in his office. He knew they thought he had to force himself to go to work, when in actual fact, he spent so much time in his office because he loved being alone with his books and his law studies. He was always learning something new.

And besides, he could have a couple of drinks without anyone making a fuss about it. At least that was true before he started questioning it himself. He was thinking these things while he put on his coat and boots and while he turned out the lights and locked the door.

Outside it was still snowing. There was a soft, muffled glow around each streetlight, and when a car went by, its tires hissed on the wet pavement. The clock in the tower over City Hall said five past eight. In front of the Unitarian Church, a golden rectangle of light shone through the glass doors of the lobby onto the snowy walk. There were fresh footprints in the snow.

George walked up the steps and into the lobby without thinking what he was doing. As he opened the door, he told himself that he might as well see what was going on. He wouldn't have been tempted to stop if he had been driving, but it was early. Laurie wasn't expecting him, and he wasn't in a hurry to get home.

Right inside the door was a chalkboard announcing an AA meeting downstairs in the auditorium at eight o'clock. "This is ridiculous," George said out loud to the empty lobby. "I don't believe it." It was such a coincidence that it seemed fake. He could hear voices coming up the stairs. Feeling manipulated by forces that he didn't even want to put a name to, he started slowly down the steps—slowly, because he hadn't made up his mind yet. A lot of him thought he ought to turn around while he still could.

But then he heard a man say, "Hi. I'm Dave, and I'm an alcoholic." George forgot about himself for just a minute, intrigued by the man and what he had said. And in that minute, he arrived at the doorway, and it was too late to turn back.

The room was big and bare, filled with the bright, harsh light of fluorescents. There were rows of mostly empty, folding chairs, facing the podium where Dave was standing. Dave was somewhere in his early thirties, probably not much older than Nora. He was wearing blue jeans and a sweater. When he turned his head, George saw that he wore his brown hair long and in a ponytail.

How could this man have anything to say to him? He was just turning to leave when an old man came over to him, holding out a mug of coffee. George took it, and the old man gestured to a card table by the door, where coffee things were laid out. He was smiling.

"Thank you," George said, keeping his voice just above a whisper.

The old man nodded.

They stood in the doorway together for a minute, listening to the speaker, and then George said, "Do you know if they allow people to sit in on these meetings?"

The old man scratched the stubble on his jaw and frowned, but he didn't speak.

"See," George said in explanation. "I'm not an alcoholic, but I thought it would be interesting to see a meeting. Is that allowed?"

"Oh, I get you," the old man said softly, looking at the ceiling, instead of at George. "Sure. Most of the guys here are in the same place. Sure, it's okay. Go get yourself a seat and enjoy."

George thanked him and took a sip of the coffee to show he wanted it, which he didn't, and walked as quietly as he could to a seat on the center aisle, behind a broad man made even wider by his puffy winter jacket.

George tried to focus on the speaker, but it was hard to concentrate. The floor was dirty, and the chairs were hard. Almost everyone in the room was smoking, which made George want a cigarette even more than usual. He wished he had some cigarettes with him. Laurie was certain to smell the smoke on his clothes, and it would be a lot simpler to say he'd had a cigarette than to say he had been to an AA meeting, where everyone was smoking. He was already conscious that he was the only man in the room in a suit. He knew everyone else had noticed too. Even though he kept his overcoat on, it was clear that he was wearing a suit underneath it. The night of the incident Nick said something about "when you are ready to join us." George remembered that. But now, sitting here, he didn't see anyone like himself, or Nick. He felt like an outsider, alone and out of place. He wasn't going to come back, but if he did, he knew he would have to dress differently.

The man behind the podium continued with his story, and George became more sure that none of this had anything to do with him. He thought about the beauty of the winter night. He wished he were outside in the quiet of it, smelling the ice in the air, walking up the hill toward home. He told himself that if it wasn't for the old man, who would notice, and the cup of burned coffee in his hand, which he couldn't manage to drink, he would have left already.

Dave was saying, "But then two years ago, I got a job on the Sentinel sports desk." George paid more attention. This was somebody Jerry worked with. Maybe they were friends. "I had sent them some photos and written a few things for them as a stringer, but this was a full-time job, and I really didn't want to blow it. I could see I wouldn't get anywhere in the job, and maybe I wouldn't even be able to keep it, if I didn't curb my drinking. I thought I could cut back, but that turned out to be hard. In fact, I couldn't do it." George didn't want to hear any more, but he still had the problem of how to get out of there. He didn't want to listen, but he kept listening. "I can't drink in moderation. I know that now. It's all or nothing for me, and I really didn't want to lose that job. Almost everyone in the newsroom drank quite a bit." That made George wonder about Jerry. "No one else noticed how drinking was getting more and more of a hold on me, but then, there was no one close to me. My family was far away. My friends saw me when I wanted them to. I chose the time and place. I kept things to myself. I had always been a private kind of a guy. So I didn't think too much of it. I mean, I didn't immediately tie it to my drinking. I didn't see that what I was doing was hiding from myself and from anyone who knew me well enough to say anything. I didn't want to hear it. I didn't want to know I had a problem. I made up all kinds of stories whose purpose was to explain my behavior in other ways. I was quite creative."

The big man in front of George laughed at that line. He laughed sympathetically, as though he knew because he had done the same thing himself. George stood up, and without even planning it, he walked out, setting his still-full coffee cup down on the table by the door as he passed it.

The snowy night was even more wonderful than he had imagined. He felt delighted with his escape and pleased with himself for managing to pull it off so cleverly. That feeling evaporated right away. No one cared whether he was there or not. No one, that is, except himself, and he wasn't sure about his own feelings. Why had he gone in the first place? Why did he hate it so much when he got there? He walked slowly, thinking about how he didn't know how he felt and how maybe he didn't want the answers to those questions.

The bare trees were black against the soft, pale sky, and even blacker where the streetlights shone on them. The fresh snow was two or three inches deep on the sidewalks, but it was too wet to be slippery. George was glad for his boots. He had put them on mostly for Laurie's benefit, but if he had worn his shoes, they would have been wet clear through by this time. The snow was puffy, like a comforter around each house, with yellow squares lying on it from the lighted windows.

Supposing he was an alcoholic and he didn't want to admit it and that was why he hated the meeting so much? But there was no one there who was like him. Of course he felt alien and out of place. And everything was dirty and shabby and poor. He had fought so hard to get away from just such conditions. It was too depressing. He wouldn't go back. It wouldn't make any sense to go back. The advantage of that was that he wouldn't have to try to explain it to Laurie. And at the same time that he was thinking that he wouldn't go back, another part of him was knowing that he *would* go back, because somehow, much as he hated to think so, he knew he belonged there in that dingy basement with those shabby men. He hated it, and it felt like home.

He wished it wasn't so confusing. He didn't know whether he was glad to get out of there because he was running away from the fact that he was an alcoholic and needed help, or whether he was glad to get away because he didn't want a connection with those people and their grim lives. He wished there was some test he could take that would give him the answer....without letting anyone else know, of course. Some time later on, he knew he would need to think about what he had heard tonight and how it applied to him, but he didn't want to think about it now.

He solved the problem temporarily by walking very fast, concentrating on the length of his stride, feeling the stretch in his legs. Every so often he would stop, and, like a child, he would look around to see his tracks in the snow, picturing how someone would come along and see his footprints and think he must have been a giant to have such a long stride.

He arrived at his front door, exhilarated and out of breath. He let himself in and stamped the snow off on the mat. He could hear the television going in the den.

"Is that you, George?"

"Yes," he said, taking off his coat and shaking the snow from it.

"I thought it might be Nora."

"Where did she go?"

"What? I can't hear you."

"Never mind."

"What?" But she didn't come out in the hall.

George put his coat and hat and gloves in the hall closet and left his boots on the drying rack by the door. He took his shoes to the hall chair and sat down to put them on. He hated the fact that he couldn't put his shoes on without sitting down anymore. He was always glad when no one saw him.

In the den, Laurie was sitting under the lamp with her book open on her lap, but she was watching television.

"Where is Nora?" he asked again.

"I don't know," Laurie answered, without looking around. "You are both always going off no matter how bad it is out."

"Did she drive?"

"You're home kind of early," she said, still not looking at him.

"Yes...well...it's a pretty night. I'm glad I walked."

"Is it still snowing?"

"Yes, but the roads aren't bad. It's warm out, and the snow is wet."

She looked around at him then. "Aren't you going to sit down? Come and watch this show with me." Before he could say anything, she went on. "She said she was only going over to Lena's. That's what she said. Who knows whether it's the truth or not."

George sat down on the couch beside Laurie and patted her on the shoulder. ""She'll be careful. Don't forget she's been on her own for a long time now. And isn't it great to have her back with us again?"

Laurie sighed. "It's easy for you. You don't worry about her the way I do."

He patted her shoulder again. "Now, Laurie, don't get yourself all worked up. She's fine. She's a good girl."

Laurie sighed. "That's just because you haven't taken a good look at her. Something's going on. I know it. She doesn't look fine to me."

"She looks just the same. Believe me. You worry too much."

"Oh George. You wouldn't notice if she grew another head."

"You always say I don't notice things, Laurie, but it isn't so. Maybe I just see different things than you do."

"Well, take a good look at her when she comes home and *then* tell me how you think she is. That's all I ask."

"Okay. I can do that."

"Okay, then. Now can I watch the show? It's almost over."

"Sure." He patted her again and stood up. "I'm going to read the paper."

"Umm," she said, already involved in her program.

Chapter 24

Lena's head was stuffed up, and her eyes ached from crying. What she really wanted was to be alone to lie down in the dark and maybe cry some more, or at least to be able to think about doing it without interruption. Jerry had been gone for two days now. He hadn't even called today to see how the kids were. She didn't know where he was. If he wasn't at work, she wouldn't be able to get in touch with him, even if something terrible happened. It was awful, and no one knew, not even Georgia and Jimmy.

But of course, they did know. That was why they had been so impossible all day, crying and needy and mean to each other. It took forever to get them to settle down for the night. Nora had come in when they were both crying, trying by any means to put off bedtime. Nora had helped get them settled. She had been so sweet and cheerful about it that she made Lena feel even worse for wishing to be alone.

She kissed Georgia for the last time and looked in at Jimmy. He was sprawled out in the warm red suit like a snowsuit that she put on him at night because he wouldn't stay under the covers. She held her breath so she could hear his. It was soft and regular. She left the room and tiptoed down the stairs, trying to avoid the creaky places. When she got to the living room, she put her finger on her lips and motioned to Nora to follow her into the kitchen. She closed the door and said, "God, I didn't think we'd ever get them settled. They've been awful all day."

"They weren't so bad."

"They're always glad to see you. Sit down. Do you want a cup of coffee?"

"No thanks. I'm too full. Mom cooked a big dinner. I wish she'd let me help her once in a while."

Lena sat down across the table from Nora. The only light that was on was the one over the sink behind her. The kitchen was full of shadows. In the soft light, her eyes didn't ache so much. "I can't imagine Mom letting anyone else be in control of her kitchen, even one of us."

"But she's so busy, and I can't seem to find a reasonable job, or at least I haven't yet. I could help her."

Snow was falling. In the quiet spaces between the talking, Lena could hear little ticking sounds as snowflakes hit the windowpanes. She said, "Mom always has to do it all. You can't change that."

Georgia and Jimmy had left their drawings and their crayons spread across the end of the table. Both Lena and Nora began to put crayons into the box while they talked. It was easier to look at the crayons than at Nora. Lena was afraid Nora would notice that she had been crying.

"After I get the abortion, I think I'll have better luck finding a job. And there's Biff too. He's the one who took me for a sleigh ride on Christmas night. Remember? I told you about it, about his big horses and how it was like being in a movie."

Lena nodded, only half listening.

"I went to his house the other day. He lives in a little cabin in the woods out past Uncle Cal and Aunt...."

Lena was paying attention now, wondering with apprehension what Nora was going to tell her next.

279

"Don't look so shocked," Nora said. "I haven't gone to bed with him or anything."

"God, Nora. I mean, how old is he?"

"I don't know. That's a weird question. How could I ask him something like that?"

"Well, I mean, I thought he was as old as Uncle Cal."

"No, of course not. They're friends, but they're not the same age. Biff's in his thirties. I mean, it's okay, or it will be after the abortion. Then I'll be free."

"I don't think so."

Now it was Nora's turn to look shocked. "What do you mean?"

Lena got up and turned on the radio and sat back down again. "Just in case the kids get up," she said.

"Since when have you been listening to country music?"

"It's Jerry's station. Well, I guess I like it okay, but I turned it on so the kids wouldn't hear us."

"So what do you mean I won't be free even after I get the abortion?"

"That's not what I meant. It's just I don't think you're going to get this abortion."

"How can you say that? I've meant to do it all along."

"Well, why haven't you then? You've had plenty of time."

Nora started picking up the crayons again. She put them in the box slowly, one by one. The soft light shone gold on her bent head.

Lena thought how much she loved her. On the radio, Hank Williams was singing an old song of love and loss. It reminded her of Jerry, and she didn't want to think about Jerry.

After a while, Nora looked up. "That's the strange part," she said. "I don't know why I haven't done it yet. I keep asking myself that very question." She stared at Lena for a minute. "And I never have an answer."

"You want this baby. That's what I think."

Nora sighed. "It's true. You're right. I look at Georgia and Jimmy, and I think how much I love them, and I think how lucky you are to have them, and then I think how I could have one too, and then

I get all confused, because it doesn't make any sense. I don't have a husband, or a job, or a home." She sighed again. "And it's not like I have anything against abortion. I *believe* in it. I believe in a woman's right to choose and in women's liberation and all that stuff."

"But, Nora, this isn't about movements. It's about your life, yours and your baby's. It's not theoretical. It's personal."

"Can you imagine what Mom would say?"

"I can't imagine why she hasn't said something already. You're starting to show. You're starting to get that walk. And anyhow, it's almost too late. You must be five months along."

"Maybe.... I don't know for sure. I haven't been to the doctor."

"You've got to go, you know."

"I will." She paused. "I'll have to go if you're right, but all this time I've been thinking.... Oh, it's crazy. What a way to decide something so important. I can't believe I'm doing this."

"Nora, don't. You're doing fine. You've known all along what you were going to do. You just never told yourself what you knew."

Nora looked up at her then. Her eyes had lights in them, and her cheeks were flushed. She looked beautiful. "Do you really think so?" she said. But then a shadow passed over her face, and she looked down at her hands. "It's crazy. What would Mom say? She'd probably kick me out. Send me to a home for unwed mothers in Kansas or something."

"She can't do that. You're a grown-up. But you do have to tell her about it."

"How am I going to do that? I can't. It's why I planned to get an abortion in the first place. But then I look at Georgia and Jimmy, and I change my mind. Mom will not be all right with this."

"That doesn't matter. You have to tell her. She's going to start noticing any time now. I can't believe she hasn't already."

"Lena, what if you told her? Would you do that? She might not get so mad at you."

"Well, I can't. You have to."

"What do you think Dad will say? I don't think he has noticed anything yet, but then Dad never notices us."

"I don't know about Dad. He's very old-fashioned, but still, he doesn't care what people think. I think it might be okay telling Dad."

"Mom's the problem."

"Mom thinks too much about what people say. But it's not Mom's body, and it's not Mom's life. It's yours."

Nora jumped up and came around the table to hug Lena. "Oh, I love you. You saw it before I did. And you know how you get that slightly creepy feeling when someone says something to you that you know is a lie? I've been getting that feeling about my own thoughts, and I didn't even realize it until just now. When you said I knew all along, I guess I saw that that was why I came home, only I just couldn't admit it to myself."

"You were the one who figured it out for yourself by walking out of the abortion clinic that day."

"Do you really think so?" She stood by Lena looking down at her. "I've been so mad at myself for making such a muddled-up mess."

"Don't, Nora. You chose what you were going to do, and you did it all by yourself. No one even knew about it."

"And you don't think I'm doing this just so I won't have to spend money on an abortion?"

Lena laughed. "That's ridiculous." Then she stopped all of a sudden because she saw that she was thinking about Nora's problem, helping her figure out how to break the news to Mom and Dad, when she had a difficult announcement of her own to make. They weren't going to like it when they heard Jerry was gone. She was going to have to tell them, and sooner rather than later, but not right away. She could wait until they got over the shock of Nora's news. Nora should go first.

"What's wrong?" Nora said. "Why do you look so worried? You think it's a mistake to have this baby, don't you?"

"No, I don't. I was just thinking about telling Mom and Dad. That's all. You have to do it yourself, but I'll help you all I can." She sat there, trying to picture how it would happen. "Mom will call me up and want to know if you told me, and she'll want to know what I think about it, and of course I'll tell her how great I think it is, and how it isn't like it used to be. People don't think it's so shameful the way they did when Mom was young."

"I hope she'll listen," Nora said. She went around the table and sat back down. "But I don't know...."

"Look. Tell Dad first. Go to his office. Just show up there when he's about to leave—maybe after Annie's already gone. Ask him to help you tell Mom."

"Okay. I'm not scared to tell Dad. You don't think he'll want me to get an abortion, do you?"

"No. I don't. He's too...not countrified exactly, but too old-fashioned or something. I think he'll help you with Mom."

"Oh Lena, I love you so much," Nora said, and she snatched up Lena's hand and pulled it toward her, leaning across the table to kiss her fingers. "You always help. You always know how to make me feel better."

That made the tears flood into Lena's eyes, glad and sad at the same time. She could help Nora, but she couldn't make her own situation better. She pulled one of Jerry's handkerchiefs out of her pocket and blew her nose, dabbing at her eyes. "I have an awful cold," she said.

"I thought your voice sounded funny."

"It's been this way for days. It doesn't seem to be getting better."

"Mom would say you ought to go to the doctor."

"I will if it doesn't get better."

"Mom would say you should go right now."

"But you're not Mom."

"Lena, do you think Dad has a drinking problem?"

"What made you say that?" Lena asked, surprised.

"I was thinking how Mom is always on somebody's case about something, and it's usually Dad's, and it's usually about how much he drinks. You don't think he drinks too much, do you?"

Lena didn't know what to say. It was a subject she was hoping to keep to herself. Nora was watching her and waiting, so finally she said, "I don't know. I mean, I never see him at night." She felt that it was a poor answer.

Nora said, "I guess Mom's just complaining, like she always does. I know he drinks a lot, but why shouldn't he, if he wants to? Mom always wants everybody to be different than they are. I think she should keep quiet."

"Well, actually, Nora, I think she might be right. I wasn't going to say anything about this." Now she was speaking in a rush, eager to get it over with. "It could be just a rumor, but Jerry heard that Dad was drunk one night. He was downtown, and he ran into a stop sign and passed out. They had to take him to the police station."

"Really?"

"One of his friends came down and got him out."

"Does Mom know?"

"I only know what Jerry told me. I didn't say anything to Mom. You're the only person I've told."

"How long ago did this happen?"

"Two or three weeks ago, I think."

"I don't believe it. I was there, at home. I would have known if something like that had happened."

"Don't be so sure, Nora. If it happened, it's bad."

"He never drinks too much at home."

"No, he goes to his office. Why do you think he goes there at night so often? And Mom is at home alone, wondering if he's all right." That thought brought her close to tears because it was so like her own situation. She blew her nose. "This damn cold," she said from behind her handkerchief.

But Nora wasn't watching her face. She was thinking about Dad. "It's true about how much time he spends in his office at night. I guess I've been surprised by that. I thought he must have some unusually big cases right now or something. You might be right. Poor Dad."

That was when the kitchen door opened, and Georgia was standing in the doorway in her nightgown. She said, "I called you and called you, Mommy, and you didn't even come."

"I didn't hear you, Georgia. And anyway, why aren't you asleep?"

"But I was asleep, and when I woke up, there was something bad under my bed that was trying to get me. I needed you to look under my bed, but you didn't even come."

"Georgia," Lena said. She didn't know what to do. Georgia looked so sweet with her hair all mixed up from sleep, and the light from the next room making a halo around her. She looked like a little tousled angel, and Lena longed to have her in her arms. She came very close to telling her to come over and sit on her lap. But that would make it almost impossible to get her to go back to bed again. And she also wanted to be through with the children for the day. She needed some time for herself. So she said sternly, even though she felt full of love, "I'll come upstairs, and we'll look under your bed, but you've got to stay up there and go to sleep, okay?"

"But why can't I stay down here with you and Nora?"

"You can't, that's all. It's bedtime." She stood up. "You can give Nora a hug and kiss, and then we have to go."

Georgia went over to Nora and kissed her and then leaned into her lap and said, "Why don't you tell Mommy to let me stay?"

Nora just laughed and told her she had to do what her mother said.

Georgia gave up and followed Lena upstairs. They looked under the bed, and then Georgia got under the covers, and Lena tucked her in. She was angry that Georgia had tried to get Nora's help against her. She no longer felt like holding Georgia in her arms. She gave her a quick, perfunctory kiss. Georgia must have known because she didn't protest, even though she looked wide-awake.

On her way back to the kitchen, Lena stopped off in the bathroom. She happened to see herself in the mirror, and she hated how old and tired she looked. Her glasses were awful, and her hair was mouse-colored. "No wonder Jerry left," she said bitterly, even though she knew her looks had nothing to do with it. But Nora looked so pretty, and it made her feel even uglier, and that was a kind of jealousy that made her dislike herself even more. She sighed and smacked the light switch hard to turn off the light. She didn't want to start crying again. She thought wretchedly how unfair everything was, and now her hand hurt too.

On the way down the stairs, she thought about the baby. Would it be like Georgia or Jimmy? It could be quite different if it took after its father. She wondered why she hadn't given that any thought before.

She shut the kitchen door quietly and stood for a second in the passage. The room was narrow there, with glass-fronted dish cabinets built into the walls on each side. When she and Jerry looked at the house before they bought it, those cabinets were what made her want to live there. They were her favorite thing about the house then, and now, filled with her own dishes, she loved them even more. She wondered if she would have to move now that Jerry was gone. That idea made her angry at Jerry. How could he be so unfair? How could he throw away everything they had made together?

She turned off the radio in case Georgia called again and sat down, ready to hear more of Nora's confidences and determined not to tell any of her own.

Nora said, "Did she go to sleep? She looked so sweet in her nightgown. I hope this baby is a girl."

"She's still awake. She'll probably come down again. You just wait, Nora. You never get done with them."

"I was sitting here waiting for you and thinking about really having a baby of my own, and then I remembered Biff. What am I going to do about Biff?"

"I don't know," Lena said, trying not to let the irritation show in her voice. "Why do you have to do anything?"

"Maybe I don't. But Lena, you should see his house. It's the cutest little cabin in the woods, so cozy and private, and he built it all himself. You have to leave your car by the road and walk through the snowy woods to get to it. It would be wonderful to live there."

"It would be hard."

"Oh no, it's so beautiful."

"But suppose you had to do it every day? Suppose you had to walk all that way trying to carry the groceries and a baby?" She started picking up the crayons again.

"Oh Lena, you make it sound so ordinary. I just wish you could see it, that's all." She stopped for a minute. "But now you probably won't ever get a chance to. That's what I was thinking about when you were putting Georgia to bed."

"I think you might be in love with the house, not the man. Have you told him about the baby?"

"No. How could I? I mean, I don't know him very well. And I thought I could get away with not having to tell him."

"Well, now you'll have to tell him something, won't you?"

"I guess so. What a reason for wanting an abortion. I know it's dumb." She thought for a minute. "I guess I could just not ever see him again, and then I wouldn't have to tell. But no, that won't work because he's a friend of Uncle Cal's, so he's bound to find out about the baby, some time."

"That makes it hard. But, wait a minute, have you...I mean...."

"Of course not. You mean have I gone to bed with him? I already told you no. There hasn't been anything like that. He hasn't even touched me. How could I give him a chance until I had already had the abortion? But now...."

"You do have to tell him, and soon too."

"I know. I don't want to. That would be an awful reason to have an abortion, wouldn't it? So you didn't have to tell. I bet lots of people do that, actually."

"Well, how much can you want the baby if that is enough of a reason? I've been thinking you really wanted this child, but if you don't...."

"I do though, Lena. I really do. It's just that there are so many confusing aspects to it—what Mom will think, what Biff will think, how I'm going to take care of it all by myself."

"You shouldn't think about any of that. Just decide whether you want it or not. If you really do, the rest will work out."

"That's easy for you to say. You're so much luckier than I am. You have a house and a husband and...."

"I'm not as lucky as you think." She swept the rest of the crayons into a pile and dumped the pile into the box.

"You seem lucky to me. You have everything you...."

"That's just because you don't know. I haven't told anybody what's really going on. But never mind that. I want to ask you something entirely different. What about the father of this baby?"

"It hasn't got anything to do with him, and it isn't ever going to. I'm not going to tell him. I don't think he'd even care."

"Don't get upset, Nora. That's not what I meant."

"What then?"

"I've been wondering about the father of this baby. What does he look like? Can I see a picture of him?"

Nora's face instantly got stiff. Her lips narrowed into a tight line. "See. That's why I can't have this baby. I'm through with him." She paused. "Forever."

"I don't care about *him*. I was thinking about what this baby was going to look like."

"Well, you don't have to worry. He was good-looking. Too good-looking. That was part of my problem."

"But don't you have a picture?"

"No."

"So I could see for myself."

"Lena. I'm not going to show you a picture of him, okay?"

"But...."

"You're just going to have to wait. If I decide to have this baby, then you will see what it looks like when it's born."

"Well...."

"Listen, I did have pictures of him, but I ripped them up and burned the scraps. I don't want any part of him left in my life. That's my problem, see?"

Lena nodded. She felt like crying again. "Okay. But I want to ask you one more thing, so don't get mad, okay?" She took a deep breath and went on. "Suppose this baby takes after him. It could, you know. Will that be all right?"

"I guess it'll have to be. I mean, I don't have a choice about that, do I?" She stood up and walked over to the window and stood with her back to Lena, looking out. "The snow is so quiet. It puts a hush over everything." She turned around, and Lena could see the hurt on her face. "I really don't want to think about him. That part of my life is over. That was another reason I was going to have this abortion. But even if I have this baby, I'm not going to tell him. You can't change my mind about that."

"I'm sorry, Nora. *You* are the one I was thinking about. Suppose it takes after its father. Would that be okay? What would that be like, for you, is what I mean." She almost said how often she saw Jerry in Georgia and Jimmy, but she didn't want to make things harder, and she didn't dare to think how that was going to be for her now with Jerry gone. How would Nora feel when she saw him before her again in the looks and actions of her child? She couldn't say more than she had already. "Was he smart?"

Nora sat down heavily. "Enough," she said. "I don't want to think about him. It hurts too much." Her lip trembled a little. "What did you mean when you said you hadn't told anybody what was going on?"

"Just that."

"But what is it? Is something wrong? I won't tell anybody. I promise."

"Jerry's leaving us," Lena said. She didn't mean to tell. It just came out.

"What?"

"Jerry's gone."

"Where? What do you mean?"

"You know what I mean. He left us."

"Jerry? I don't believe it."

"Well, it's true."

"That doesn't make any sense. I mean, sometimes I've wondered why you wanted to stay with him. But I've never wondered why *he* stayed with *you*. He was amazingly lucky to get you."

"Thanks, but I guess he didn't think so."

"Did it just happen? I was over here a few days ago, and everything seemed okay then."

"Well, it hasn't been all right for a long time, but I thought we were getting somewhere. I guess we just stopped talking. I mean we stopped telling each other the truth. That's what I can see now. I knew we weren't getting along that great, but I thought time would straighten it out. We've been together for so long, if you count the time in college. I guess I had this crazy idea that Jerry needed me as much as I needed him. I thought he always would, but I was wrong, wasn't I?" She tried a tiny smile, but her lips were quivering. "He left a couple of days ago. I don't even know where he is when he's not at work." She began to cry again. She didn't even try to hide it.

"Oh Lena. What are you going to do?"

"That's just it. I don't know. It's all too new. I mean I knew something was going on. Jerry even told me about it, about her, but he made it sound like something that just happened, and I was even beginning to think I could get past it in my mind and maybe even forgive him, and we could be okay again. I hadn't said that to Jerry, but I had been thinking it. And then, before we could really talk about it, he came home and said he was moving out."

"How can I help? Shall I stay over with you?"

"No. I've got to learn how to be alone and not be scared, and anyway Mom and Dad might wonder. I don't want them to know. First you should break your news to them, and then when they've had some time to get used to it, I'll tell them mine. Okay? Until then, be really careful not to let them find out. That'll give me a little while to figure out how to tell them."

Nora started giggling.

"What's so funny? It isn't a joke, you know."

"No, Lena, I know it's not funny, but here all the time I've been thinking that I was the bad one who caused Mom and Dad so much worry—remember when I went out to California, and Mom got in such a panic?"

Lena nodded.

"So here I was, thinking you did everything just right, and I was the family fuckup, and I'm really glad you're down here with me in the mud."

"Thanks a lot," Lena said, but she was smiling too. "It's nice to have you back in Severance."

"I was thinking the same thing. I was thinking how impossible it would be for me to decide to have this baby if I was in Boston. I'm scared, but I'm resolved too. I don't know how I'll be able to manage, but I know I will, and you are right. I can see now that it was what I meant to do all along. You've helped me so much, and you've given me such good advice. I wish I could do that for you."

Lena smiled weakly. "I wish you could too. But I don't think anyone can do anything."

"You're right. I've got to tell Mom and Dad. But you do too."

"I've been doing everything I could to keep them from finding out."

"But Lena, you'll have to tell them some time, and the longer you wait, the harder it's going to be to explain."

"I know. I know. I can't do it, though."

"You know it's silly of us. Here we are worrying about what we're going to say to Mom and Dad, and we don't need to. I mean, we're both grown-ups, after all."

Lena's smile felt more real this time. "I know you're right because that's what I said to you before. But somehow I don't feel very grown-up right now. I'm scared to be without Jerry. I don't know if I can do it all by myself." She was crying again now. "I'm scared at night, and it's lonely taking care of the kids all by myself. I don't know how I'll manage all of it."

Nora came around to Lena's side of the table and put her arms around her. "Oh Lena, I love you. I'm scared too, but I'll help you. You always help me so much. We'll manage. We've got to. I'm so glad I have a sister like you."

For the first time in days, Lena felt comforted. It was odd to be the one who was being taken care of. She was used to being the strong one. But she felt better about things than she had since Jerry told her he was leaving. She was glad she'd told Nora, although she had meant to keep it secret. But it felt good to have Nora on her side.

Chapter 25

The thermometer outside the door said fifteen below when Cal went into the mudroom. It must have been close to freezing in there, even with the woodstove on the other side of the wall in the kitchen. But the fire was out. He could hear Ursela banging around, trying to get it started. He was still warm from being in bed. He hurried into his barn clothes before the warmth could escape. He should have brought his clothes into the kitchen last night, even though Ursela complained that they made the kitchen smell like a barn.

He pulled his overalls over his pants and put on two pairs of thick socks, working them on carefully over his bandaged foot. He had cut a slit in an old rubber barn boot so he could get it on over his bandage. It pleased him that he hadn't wasted anything, because the boot already had a leak and was no good even before he slit it. He slid a plastic bag over his sock foot before he put the boot on. It kept his foot clean for a while, until the plastic gave out. He put on a heavy flannel shirt and then his jacket, which was torn and had no buttons on it because he kept forgetting to ask Ursela to mend it for him. He couldn't see why she didn't notice. He resented having to ask her to fix it for him. He stuck his light woolen cap in his pocket to wear in the barn and put on the rabbit-fur hat with earflaps that Elsie gave him for Christmas. He put his gloves in his pockets and pulled on mittens.

Ursela was shouting through the closed door that he had forgotten his cane. He hated the way she didn't even bother to come over to the door and open it so she could talk in an ordinary voice. He shouted back that he didn't want the damn cane. She didn't answer. He was going to look in to see if she had heard him, but he thought, "What the hell. Why bother?" So he picked up the milk pail and the washpot for the cow's teats and opened the door.

Outside, it was absolutely still. The sky was rose-colored along the edge of the horizon, and pale, ice green above. The air was clear, pure, filled with liquid light. The weather last week had been so different. Then the light was thick and warm. Everywhere water was dripping, and things were thawing. The ground was wet and soft. Now, with every step, the snow crunched sharply. When he got past the corner of the house, he could see the moon, low in the west, about to set. Dad always called the full moon of February the Full Wolf Moon. Dad knew the names of all the full moons. Some of them were beautiful—the Strawberry Moon, the Flower Moon. He thought of the world, warm and green, full of flowers and fruit. It seemed impossible. But wasn't that the way with so many things? If they didn't happen over and over, you would never believe they could happen at all.

The moonlight lay cold and old across the snow. The shadows of the bare branches were a black tangle on his path. By the time he got to the barn door, he could feel the sharp, icy air all the way down his windpipe into his lungs. The Farmer's Almanac said there would be a spell of arctic air in early February that would last about a week. Of course it would come around the full moon. It was always colder around the time of the full moon.

He stepped inside and shut the door and stood for a minute without turning on the light. This was always one of his favorite moments. The air was warm after the cold outside. It smelled of hay and dust and manure and was full of soft, sleepy rustlings and stompings and chewings. Even though his foot wasn't completely healed and he was slow and clumsy, he was glad to be doing his chores alone. The barn was his again. When Conrad and Paul were helping him, he had to live with their schedules. It was a constant annoyance to him the way the chores weren't done on time.

Cal flipped the light switch, and the rooster began to crow. He took off his outside clothes and changed hats and checked the water in the tank. He had insulated it and built a lid over it, but even so, there was some ice built up around the sides of the tank and a thin layer on the surface of the water. A tank heater would solve the problem, but electricity was expensive.

He walked into the main part of the barn and took a quick look around to make sure everything was all right. Then he got out the milking stool and sat down under Daisy. He always milked her first. She was the leader, and she expected it. Star and Sue expected it too. They were born within weeks of each other three years ago. He'd named them Lena and Nora, until Ursela told him he couldn't. He didn't see why not. What harm was there in it? Those girls hadn't been out to the farm in years. George hadn't come out for even longer, and Laurie had probably never stepped inside any barn. Then he remembered that Nora had been out a couple of times since he'd been shot, and she'd been in the barn too. But Ursela was still wrong. Nora wouldn't have minded if he had named a heifer after her. She wasn't that kind.

Daisy's side was caked with manure. When he got up to get the cats' milk bowl, he picked up a handful of hay and tried to scrub off the worst of it, but it was dried into the short hair on her flank. He washed his hands in the disinfectant, got the cats' dish and the pail and sat back down. He wiped off Daisy's milk bag, squirted a little from each teat for the cats, and then he began. Right away he was in the rhythm of it, swaying a little in time to the clenching of his hands, hypnotized by the sound of the milk ringing against the wall of the pail, drifting in the warm, cow-scented air. He was half asleep and not thinking. He finished the first side, and then he finished the second and went back to the first to get the last few drops. His hands knew what to do without him telling them.

He stood up slowly, feeling the ache in his back. It took a while before he could straighten all the way up. He slapped Daisy on the flank by way of thanks and moved on to Sue. "Damn George anyway," he thought when he was back in the rhythm of milking again. "What'd he think I was, some kind of country girl he could sweet-talk?" George was up there at the hospital every day when he didn't really need the help, but now here he was in a situation where George could be useful, and where was George? Nowhere to be seen, that's where. He didn't know what to do about this LaRue character. He needed some law advice, and George was a lawyer. Anybody would think George would be falling all over himself trying to help. Well, anybody would be wrong. He finished Sue and straightened up. He was thinking more than he ought to about old George because when he slapped Sue to tell her he was done, she jumped so far, she almost kicked the pail.

The two sows were watching, standing on their hind legs, with their front hooves wedged between the boards of their pens so they could see over the top. When Cal stood up, they began to get excited, snorting and grunting, telling him to hurry. It hadn't taken them any time to figure out that they were going to get whole milk right from the cow and not have to wait for it to go through the cream separator any more. He hated to waste the cream that way, but there was nothing he could do about it. He couldn't carry all the whole milk up to the house and bring down all the skimmed milk with his foot the way it was. Ursela just had to give up selling butter for a while, even though they could use the money. But until his foot was really healed, he could only lug enough for the house and for their best customers.

He poured a stream of milk into each pig trough, saving only enough back to feed the calves. It was a job he hated. There was no good way to get the milk where it was supposed to be, because the pigs couldn't wait for it to get there. They had to try to bite the streaming milk while it was still in the air. It was all over in a few tumultuous minutes. They should realize that if they could wait, they would get more, because it wouldn't be splashed and wasted. But if they realized that, they wouldn't be pigs.

When he finished milking Star, he took the half-full pail out into the old milk room, set it down by the door, and covered it with the clean board that he always used. He put on his jacket and mittens and fur hat and picked up the maul and went out the back door into the cold to open up the trough where the cows got their water.

On the south side of the barn, the land sloped down steeply. The water line ran under the barn from the milk room to the south side, where it surfaced as the land sloped and formed a small brook that ran off down the hill. Cal had dug out under the end of the pipe and partly sunk an old bathtub there to make a pool where the cows could drink. He had put an extension on the pipe so that it went to the bottom of the tub before it ended. That kept cold air from blowing up the pipe and freezing it.

He stood for a minute looking down at the trough. There was no way to know how deep the ice was from the smooth surface, and he was reluctant to begin. Swinging the maul took a toll on his back. It was never very good, even at its best, and it was terrible now because of all the time he had had to spend sitting around and doing nothing.

He started by chopping a deep ditch in the ice all around the edges, being careful to leave several inches along the walls of the tub. That much at least was solid ice all the way down. Besides if his aim was off and he hit the wall of the tub, it could shatter. In this cold, everything got brittle and fragile.

After he had gone all the way around the circle, he tried a spot in the center. He hit and hit again. Four or five inches down, it was still ice. He began to get worried. Maybe this time it had frozen all the way down. He hit the same spot even harder. A geyser of water shot up, catching him full in the face. He dropped the maul and stood gasping, feeling the water running across his bare skin, so sharply cold that it burned. He took off his mittens and opened his jacket to get to the flannel shirt. He used the tail of the shirt to dry his face carefully. Any wetness would turn to ice and freeze his skin.

He stood there dabbing at his face, while his fingers got numb. That water must have been under a lot of pressure. The cold was seeping in through his clothes as he stood there. He had to start chopping again. The water was still pouring up out of the hole across the top of the ice, so he had to chop through it, and every blow splashed all over him and instantly turned to ice when it hit. He worked on the center, making the hole larger, and gradually there was less water splashing. The maul was so heavy that it was killing his back. He knelt down. Working that way, he couldn't swing as hard, but he didn't have to bend his back so much either. The hole got bigger, until all he had to do was even it off back to the layer of solid ice. He felt heroic, alone against an unfriendly universe. It was unfair that he, an old man, had to struggle like this alone with no help from anyone. It didn't matter that he was the one who told Conrad and Paul he didn't need them anymore. They could have realized that with the temperature at fifteen below, he was going to be having a hard time. And then, finishing off the job, he thought triumphantly that he didn't need them, that he didn't need anyone. He stood up slowly. Now it was his knees that he had trouble straightening.

He hobbled to the door of the barn and opened it. Every motion made a whispering, crackling sound as the ice moved on his frozen clothes. He shut the door and considered. He would thaw out in the animal warmth, but then everything would be wet. He could go up to the house and change, but that would take a while and make him late for breakfast. Better to work fast and get it done.

He opened the stanchions one by one and let the cows loose. When they were all free and bunched by the door, he opened it and herded them out so they could get some water. Then he got the fork and the wheelbarrow and began to clean. If he wanted George's help, he was going to have to ask for it. That much was obvious. He was sure Jason LaRue was the guy who shot him, even though Biff wasn't positive. But Biff had no idea what to do next, now they had found him. Biff would probably like to drop the subject, but he was damned if he'd do that, not when he knew the guy was guilty. All he needed was some lawyer advice about what to do next. Was that so difficult to give?

By now he had his jacket and hat off, and he didn't bother with them when he pushed the wheelbarrow out the door and dumped it over the edge of the slope onto the pile. Star was drinking, and the other two were pushing in, trying to get a turn. Cal was sure they'd had at least one drink already. Star was always last.

He hurried back inside. After he'd spread some sawdust for the cows, he parked the wheelbarrow by the pigpens and climbed over the fence. He worked as fast as he could with the pigs snuffling around his legs. "By God," he said out loud, "I might just as well go downstreet to George's office like any other customer and see will he sell me his wares. I got to do somethin. I know that."

He climbed out of the pigpen with the sow nipping at his heels. He was trying to hurry and to spare his foot at the same time. After he'd given the cows their hay and grain, he opened the door, and they came in eagerly, each to her own stanchion. He fastened them in, grained the pigs, and dumped the wheelbarrow. The water trough was way down from the cows' drinking. He dipped some water for the pigs and checked on the chickens, taking pleasure in the way he'd stopped all the drafts with plastic, so their corner of the barn was the warmest of all.

Then he was finished, except for his favorite calf. He didn't take any time with her, the way he often liked to do. The dampness was seeping through his clothes, and he was uncomfortable and anxious to get up to the house. So he threw in a forkful of hay for bedding and left her looking over the edge of her pen. "I'll pet you tonight, darlin," he said as he went into the milk room. He put on his outside clothes and left the barn, carrying the pail of milk.

The sun was up. Light lay across the snow in shafts of pale yellow. It was the first tender sign that spring, and with it color, would come back into the black and white, frozen world. But at minus fifteen, it had a way to go. Before he got halfway to the house, his clothes were stiff and hard again. He hurried as much as his foot would allow.

In the mudroom he undressed, and when he went into the kitchen, he hung his overalls and jacket over the edge of the woodbox.

Ursela turned around with the spatula in her hand. "What happened to you, then?"

"Nothin. My clothes won't dry out in the cold."

"Well, wash up. It's ready."

He was going to say something sharp, but he decided not to. The wall of warm air that met him when he opened the door between the mudroom and the kitchen had melted the angry words right off his tongue. The room smelled of coffee and bacon. He only said, "I left the milk out in the cool," as he went into the bathroom to wash his hands and face.

When he got back to the kitchen, Ursela had served their plates. He sat down at the table across from her. The biscuits were covered with a cloth. Steam was rising from the opening in it. The radio was on. "What did he say the temperature was last night?"

"I missed it."

"It was 15 below when I went out to the barn."

"Did the water freeze?"

"It had ice on it, but it's runnin."

"That's okay, then."

They ate in silence, concentrating on the food and on Uncle Herbie's Trading Post on the radio.

After a while, Ursela said, "I'd like to know how Conrad's gettin along in this cold."

"Probably shiverin while he works."

"He might stay out of the woods til it warms up a little."

"He might if he don't care about makin it. He'll be back in the feed store before long if he quits every time he gets cold."

"I know, Cal. I know. I'm the one who thought he ought to stay where he was. Remember? I didn't think he ought to of gone out and bought that new saw neither."

"He didn't have no choice about that."

"He didn't need to buy such a expensive one. He could of got one a lot cheaper 'n he did."

"And it would of crapped out on him next week or the week after, just like his old one done. So he'd have lost another workday and have had to get another saw. No, he didn't have no choice."

Ursela stood up. "Do you want some more eggs?"

"No. I'm good."

"Are you sure? There's more in the pan, already cooked."

"You eat 'em. I'm done."

Ursela put the eggs on her plate and sat down again. "So here's Conrad, no money comin in and payments he's got to make on a skidder, and now on a saw. How does that make any kind of sense?"

"Damn it, woman. How many times do I have to tell you? He ain't makin payments on that saw. Albert told him he'd wait for the money."

"Well, he still owes it, don't he?"

"Yes, but...."

"He owes it. Until he gets it paid off, his money ain't goin to be his own. It don't matter whether Albert's nice about it or not."

"God damn it."

"Don't swear at me, Cal. I know what I'm sayin. That's one of the reasons he has to keep on in this cold. He's so far behind. I just hate to think of him out there all day with the cold like it is, and you actin like you ain't even worried about him."

"Of course I'm worried, but I ain't worried about him gettin cold. There's lots worse that can happen. He ain't used to that kind of work, and he ain't that young. Plus he's all alone. He could get hurt, or killed. What about that?"

"Oh, Cal."

"See what I mean?"

But she didn't say anything. Instead, she jumped up and started taking dishes to the sink. Cal sat there wondering. Had she really not realized that what Conrad was doing was dangerous? He started to say something and changed his mind. He sat listening to Uncle Herbie while Ursela clattered the dishes in the sink.

After a while, she came over to the table for some more dishes to wash. "I'm goin to be gone most of the day, Cal. I got that new cleanin job to start, and I don't know how long it'll take me."

"What new job?"

"It's down in the village. Gladys Parker told her about me. I put some cold dinner for you in the refrigerator."

"Be sure she pays you. We need it."

"I know, Cal. That's why I put the word out that I wanted more jobs. Will you be all right? You don't need to go downstreet, do you?"

"I got some business, but it can wait til I can drive myself."

"What do you need in there?"

"I want to go see George, if you must know."

Ursela was back at the sink by this time, but the mention of George caused her to shut off the water and turn around. "What for?"

"Well, he's my brother, for one thing."

Ursela opened her mouth to say something, but he didn't give her a chance.

"I want to see can I hire his law services."

"Oh, Cal, I thought you were all done fussin over who shot at you."

"Well, I ain't."

"But the police...."

"Ain't done nothin, and they ain't goin to. If I want somethin done, I'm goin to have to do it myself. I've known that right along."

"I don't see what you can do, Cal. It's a police matter."

"You don't know nothin about it, Ursela. It's my business, not yours."

"I'm just afraid you're goin to get in trouble."

"You leave that up to me. If I have my way, I ain't goin to be in trouble, but somebody else is."

"Oh, Cal."

She turned back to the sink, and he got up and left the room. He really didn't want to talk about it.

Chapter 26

The stairs were wide and bare. The dusty gray wood creaked with every footstep, and the sounds rattled away down the long hall. Nora thought it was surprising that Dad ever got any clients when they saw where his office was. It was upstairs in an old brick building on Merchants Row, the same office he had had all the time Nora was growing up, but she hadn't been there that often, because she always felt that he wanted to keep his work life separate from his family. She was sure about that, although she couldn't remember anyone ever saying it in so many words.

Nora was nervous, although she kept telling herself she was being silly. But she didn't know what Dad would say when he found out. He might think she was wrong to have this baby. She *knew* that's what Mom would think. What would she do if they were both against her? When she was at Lena's, she believed she wanted the baby, and she believed she was strong enough to do it too, but she would be much more alone if both Mom and Dad were against it.

When she was almost to the door, it opened suddenly, and Annie came bursting out, all bundled up with a scarf wrapped around her mouth and nose. "Nora, hi," she said in a muffled voice. "Your father's in his office. You don't need me to stay, do you?"

"Not at all," Nora said, trying to seem calm, and at the same time, trying not to show how glad she was to have timed it so Annie wouldn't be there.

She went inside. The inner door was closed. She knocked and said, "Dad? Can I come in?"

"Is that you, Nora? What a surprise. Just a minute. I'll get the door." There was the sound of a drawer closing and then his footsteps coming toward the door. How odd it was that she knew so little about him, her own father.

There was a click as he unlocked the door, and then he stood there smiling in an embarrassed way. "Annie," he said. "She sometimes... well, that's why." He shrugged. It really didn't explain anything. "It's a nice surprise to see you, Nora."

"I need to talk to you, Dad," she said, trying to keep the shakiness out of her voice.

His eyes went over her face slowly, and then he stepped back. "Oh, honey. Sure. Come in. Sit down."

Nora nodded, feeling miserable. This could be a mistake. She sat down in the client's chair, but she couldn't make herself lean back. There wasn't any reason to be afraid to tell him. He loved her, and he was always gentle.

He sat down behind his desk and waited, watching her with a serious expression.

"Dad, I'm pregnant."

"What?" he said, and then, before she could say it again, he said, "I don't mean that. I heard you. I was just so....surprised. Are you sure?"

"Yes, positive. It's starting to show even. I thought you or Mom might have suspected."

"I don't think so. Well, a long time ago Mom said something, but she hasn't said anything since. I thought she decided she was mistaken, and I haven't...."

"What did Mom say?"

"I think she said she wondered if you could be pregnant, that you didn't look very well."

"Mom said that?"

"I thought she was just worried. But, anyway, that was a long time ago. I think it was before Christmas. What does she say now?"

"She doesn't know yet. I wanted to tell you first. I wanted to know what you think." She didn't complete her thought because she didn't say that she wanted to know what he thought when he didn't feel he had to agree with what Mom said about it.

"Ahh...I don't know. I didn't expect...."

"No, I know you didn't know this was coming, but you know now. What do you think I ought to do?" She knew she shouldn't pin him down, but she wanted to know what he thought. She needed to know. It was almost dinnertime, and she was going to go home and tell Mom, and she was going to do it tonight. She had promised herself that she would, and she needed to know what he thought first, if he would help her or not.

"Get married?"

"No, Dad."

"What does the father say?"

"He doesn't know, and he's not going to. He doesn't have any say in this."

"But...."

"He's already married."

"Oh, I see." He picked up a pencil and started turning it over and over again in his fingers, watching his fingers as they worked. "I guess then you ought to have an abortion."

"It's kind of late for that."

"Surely you aren't that far along."

"Well, no, I guess not. But it turns into a more complicated operation after three months. Besides, it doesn't matter because I've decided not to."

"I don't think you should hurry into such a decision. It's legal, and it's safe these days. I can help you."

Nora leaned back in the chair. "Thank you, Dad. I was hoping you would help me, but in a different way." She didn't feel scared any more. "I was hoping you would help me convince Mom that this was a good thing."

"I don't know, Nora. I'd like to help you, but...."

"I know, Dad. I can't ask you now that I see how you feel."

"Why don't you wait a few days? This is so sudden. Why don't you think about it for a few days before you tell your mother?"

"I'm going to tell her tonight. It's sudden for you, but I've been thinking about it for a long time, and I'm not going to change my mind."

"We didn't even know you were seeing someone. It all comes as such a surprise."

"I'm sorry."

"I wish you had told us about this boyfriend. I worried a lot about you being lonely in Boston. The boyfriend was in Boston, right?"

"That's right." She sighed. "If I'd told you about him, Dad, I would have had to tell you he was married, and I didn't want to tell you that." She paused. He looked so distressed sitting there, fiddling with the pencil. "I didn't want to lie to you about it. It was all stupid, and I'm glad it's over."

"But, Nora, it won't be over if you don't get an abortion. It's just beginning. But if you get an abortion, it will be really over. That's another reason to consider it."

Nora sighed again. "Dad, I wish this was different. Somehow I thought you would think it was okay for me to have this baby, even though I was pretty sure Mom would think it was a mistake. I hoped you would help me convince Mom that it was a good idea."

"Well, I can't do that, not with a good conscience. Why won't you wait for a while before you tell her? I don't know, of course, but I think you're probably right, that she'll think it's a mistake to do this. If you wait awhile, maybe you'll change your mind and you won't have to tell her at all, or at least, what you tell her can be different. See?"

"No, I can't do that. I've waited and waited and not understood why I did what I did, and now finally I see it was because I really wanted to have this baby, even though I know it doesn't make a lot of sense, and I know it will be hard. But I've decided, and I'm really glad to have it settled. It's time it was settled. So I need to tell Mom. I'm going to do it tonight."

"All right." It was his turn to sigh. "If that's what you have to do. Tell me this, do you want me there when you tell her?"

"Oh...I don't know. I had pictured it so differently."

"I'm sorry, Nora. I just can't feel all right about you putting your-self in such a difficult place when there's an easy solution. I mean, it's not the way it used to be when abortion was illegal. It used to be so dangerous. I probably would have said something different then."

"I know, Dad."

"I mean, how are you going to take care of this baby? You haven't even got a job, and if you did, who would take care of the baby? You can't expect your mother to take that on, and you can't expect Lena to do it either."

"I know, Dad."

"You've got to think about these things, Nora."

"I have been thinking about them, Dad. I know it isn't going to be easy, but I think I can do it. Other people have done it."

"They usually have help from the father, child-support payments at least."

"Dad, I know."

"I'm sorry. I'm not saying anything you want to hear, am I?"

"No, you're not, because I've already decided, so all you're doing is making me more scared."

"I'm sorry. I'm worried about you, and I'm worried about what Mom's going to say."

"So am I."

"I don't know whether to be there when you tell her or not."

"Well, maybe we should just wait and see how it works out."

"I can't help thinking you are making a big mistake. You are young. You have your life before you."

"I'm almost thirty."

"That's young. It's a mistake to make things so hard for yourself when you're just starting out. I hate to see it."

"It'll work out. When you see this baby, how maybe it's a little bit like Georgia and Jimmy, then you'll be glad I didn't listen to you."

"I hope so, but I don't know."

"Try not to worry." She stood up. "I'll see you at home."

"Don't you want a ride?"

"Thanks, but I have my car here. I'll see you at home."

She went around the desk and kissed him lightly on top of the head. She felt strong and brave, as though she had to do it right for his sake so he wouldn't have to worry.

But out in the dark, creaky hallway, her bravery disappeared like a balloon with its air let out. She sagged suddenly under the weight of the loneliness. It was just what she had been afraid of, although she hadn't really believed it would be like this. She had been so confident that he would be on her side.

It was cold and dark outside. She thought about how good it would be to stop at Lena's and tell her all about it and how wrong they'd been. Lena would comfort her. But then she thought that, no, this was her problem. Lena had worries of her own. She'd call her later, after she'd talked to Mom. She was going to have to learn to stand on her own. And who could tell. Dad had surprised her. Maybe Mom would too.

Chapter 27

George was glad he was hungry because everything he thought of saying as they sat at the dinner table seemed to lead inevitably back to Nora and what she'd told him. Luckily, Laurie's beef stew was delicious. She would be sure to think the reason he wasn't talking was that he was too busy eating. He couldn't remember whether he'd had any lunch. He'd probably forgotten to stop for it, which would explain why he was so hungry tonight. It might also explain his headache, although that could have been caused by worry about Nora.

There was no sound in the room but the clink of silverware on the china plates. After a little while, Laurie said, "I can't tell whether it's because my stew is so good or because it's so bad. Doesn't anyone have anything to say?"

"It's good, Mom. I don't know how you had time to cook something so delicious when you were gone all day."

"Oh, that's easy. I just put everything in the crockpot this morning, and it cooked itself. Do you want some more, George?"

"Yes, please." He passed his plate to Nora, who held it out for

Laurie to fill. "How was your day, Laurie?"

"It was okay. What about you?"

"Very quiet. I can't think of anything interesting that happened." But of course he was thinking about Nora and what she had told him. He couldn't help glancing at her as he said nothing interesting had happened, but she was looking down at her food and appeared not to have heard.

Laurie said, "I suppose the reason my day was so nice was that Rose took a sick day. I really think it's easier to do her work than it is to run around after her, trying to fix all the things she does wrong."

"Why don't you tell Mr. Earle about her, Mom?"

"You don't understand, Nora. He wouldn't do anything, and she'd probably find out, and then she'd be mad at me on top of everything else. She already doesn't like me."

"But if she's not doing her job…."

"Try telling her that. She thinks she knows more than anyone else in the office, and she's only been there for a year."

George didn't say anything, but he was glad Laurie was talking. It kept her from noticing how quiet he was.

After dinner, they all three carried the dishes into the kitchen. Laurie said, "You two go on. I'll clean up. I need the exercise."

George rubbed his forehead, where the headache was still lurking. "If you're really sure, Laurie, I guess I'll go read the paper."

"Yes, I am. You do that."

"I'll stay and help you, Mom."

"You don't need to, Nora. I'm fine."

"No, but I want to." She looked at George, and her mouth twitched into a small, nervous smile.

He shrugged, hoping to convey by that ambiguous gesture that he would stay if she wanted him to, or that she could wait for some other time to make her confession. He couldn't do more with Laurie right there, so he left, feeling cowardly but glad to get away. He stopped in the hall and stood there, massaging his forehead and trying to decide whether to get some aspirin. He told himself his headache wasn't bad enough, although he knew he thought that partly because he didn't want to go all the way upstairs to the medicine cabinet.

When Laurie came into the den later, he was comfortably settled in his favorite chair, reading the Sentinel. The headache had receded into the background.

Laurie said, "It's almost time for Love Boat." She switched on the television and sat down on the far end of the couch. "You're going to watch it with me, aren't you, George?"

"I guess so," he said. One look at her face showed him that Nora hadn't said anything yet. "Listen, I want to read you this."

"Okay," she said, but she looked distractedly at the television commercial that preceded her show. "If it isn't too long…."

George was just about to read a news story that was connected to the poverty series Jerry did in the fall, when Nora came into the room looking grim and nervous. She sat down between them on the end of the couch nearest to George. The theme music for Love Boat was playing.

George wanted to tell Nora she was choosing the wrong time for her confession, but he didn't know how to say anything without Laurie noticing. So he just sat there, worrying.

Nora looked at the television and then popped to her feet again. She went to the television and turned around to look at Laurie. "Can I turn this off? There's something I need to talk to you about."

"Oh, Nora. Now? Can't it wait until later?"

George felt sorry for Laurie then. It was her favorite program.

"It's important, Mom." Nora's lips were set into a thin line.

George felt sorry for her too. He looked down at his newspaper, which he still held open, ready to read.

"All right," Laurie said wistfully. "Turn it off then." She sighed. She seemed weary, but she was probably frightened by Nora's nervousness without even realizing it.

The click of the television was loud in the quiet room. They were all tense. George could feel his headache blossoming across his forehead again. He folded the paper and dropped it onto the floor beside his chair, aware as he let it fall how much it annoyed Laurie when he did that.

Nora sat down again between them, but she didn't say anything.

"What is it, Nora, that's so important it won't wait?"

Nora looked at Laurie, and then she looked at George, and then she popped up out of her seat again and went to stand with her back to the now-silent television set. "I'm sorry," she said. "I want to look at both of you at once."

"For goodness' sake, Nora. What *is* this about? Can't you sit down? You're making me nervous."

"I'm sorry, Mom. I know you wanted to watch Love Boat. But I need to do this." She got a chair from the other end of the room, a straight-backed chair that no one ever sat in. She put it down in front of the television set and sat down on it. "This won't take long, Mom."

Laurie sighed. "I wish I knew what was going on."

George's head was pounding. So far Nora hadn't told anything, and still it was going badly. Laurie was already alienated and annoyed. George couldn't think of anything to say that wouldn't make the whole thing worse.

Nora's eyes flicked across his face and away. She took a deep breath and said, "Mom, I'm pregnant."

"Oh, Nora, no. It can't be."

"Mom, I think it is."

"Oh my God. This is awful."

George and Nora looked at each other. She had certainly been right about how Laurie would react. And now that he saw Laurie's reaction, he was less sure of his own. Laurie seemed to think it was the worst thing that could happen. That was a little overboard, especially since she didn't even know what Nora meant to do about it.

Laurie broke the short silence. "Wait a minute. There's no sense in getting all upset. The first thing is to get a test, so you know."

"I have gotten a test, several of them, in fact, and I do know. The tests were all positive."

"Maybe they were wrong."

Nora stood up. "I don't think so. Look, Mom." She pulled the cloth of her sweatshirt tight across her stomach so they could see how pregnant she was.

Laurie gave a low moan.

Nora tried to smile. "I'm surprised that you haven't noticed already."

"Thank God abortion is legal now. It would be terrible if it was still illegal. What would we do? It was so dangerous then, and still people did it. Nowadays it's a simple procedure. You can have it and then go home."

"Mom, you need to let *me* tell *you* what I'm going to do. So can you be quiet and listen?"

"I'm just trying to help, Nora."

"Mom, please. I want to tell you the whole story. Try to understand."

"Go on, Nora. I'm listening. Stop telling me to, and start telling me what you want me to hear."

"When I came home at Thanksgiving, I was pretty sure I was pregnant."

"Thanksgiving? That was ages ago."

Nora nodded. "I got a test, and when it came back positive, I made myself an appointment at the Women's Health Collective in Burlington. I went up there for an abortion, and I waited for a long time, and finally I left and came home."

"I wish you'd told me. I would have gone with you. If I had been there, they would have given you the abortion. I would have made sure they gave you one."

"You don't understand. I didn't leave because they wouldn't do the operation. I left because...well, I'm not really sure why I left. I've been trying to figure it out ever since, but I didn't leave because they wouldn't give me an abortion. I was scheduled for one."

"I just wish I'd been with you, that's all."

"Thanks, Mom. But I think I'm glad you weren't there. I think that's why I didn't tell you. You know, I could have gone back. I could have made myself another appointment, and I didn't. For a long time I didn't know why I didn't go back, and I beat myself up for not going back, and I didn't tell you and Dad about any of it either. Now I'm beginning to see that it's because I want this baby."

"Oh no, Nora. You can't be serious." She put her hand up to her mouth in a gesture of alarm.

"I think I am. I know I am. I didn't think it would turn out this way, but I don't see what else to do now. When I went to Burlington, I had no idea of any of this. I had it all planned. I had an appointment, and I went up there and sat in their horrible, dingy waiting room, and I had to sit there for a long, long time. It seemed like hours. After a while, I thought I would step out onto their porch to get some fresh air, and when I went out there, I just kept on walking, and I didn't go back. I didn't plan it. I just did it. And I even thought if they were too mad at me, I could go somewhere else and have it done."

Laurie nodded.

The more clear Nora and Laurie thought it was, the more confused George seemed to get. Ever since last fall, when Nora came home and Cal got hurt, George had had this idea of how much he had missed both of them, missed everyone he loved, really, by being too withdrawn. When he came home from the war, and there really wasn't any space for him on the farm anymore, he had crafted himself a new life, a town life, and he hadn't looked back, until last fall anyway. And when he and Laurie disagreed about the girls, he had stood aside there too, thinking that he had to, that Laurie was always so positive she was right, that it was better not to fight with her about it. And now he was confused, confused about what Nora was doing, about what he thought about it, and even confused about whether it was possible to have more to do with either Cal or Nora.

He couldn't help thinking how Laurie would react if he told her that he had been to an AA meeting. The confidentiality they offered people wouldn't be near enough for Laurie. George knew she thought everyone in the family ought to keep things secret, no matter what the cost, because when one of them did something that could cause talk, it hurt all the rest. She had said as much. She would say George ought not to go to any AA meetings. Someone they knew might see him at one. She would say he shouldn't drink too much either. Someone might see him buying the liquor. He ought to just stop without making such a production of it. He knew that was what she would say, which was the reason he hadn't told her. Maybe Nora would have kept quiet too, if she had been able to.

"George," Laurie said. "What are you thinking about? I've asked you three times now what we ought to do."

"I'm sorry. I was thinking."

"I hope you were thinking about what we ought to do about this."

"I don't know that *we* ought to do anything. Nora's a grown-up, after all."

Laurie started to say something, but George stopped her.

"Wait a minute. You asked me what I thought. Now you have to listen."

"Everyone's always telling me to listen," Laurie said bitterly. "And no one ever listens to what *I* want to say."

"Okay, Laurie, just a minute here. I agree with you that Nora might be making a bad mistake. She's young and just starting out, and she's proposing to saddle herself with quite a burden. I hate to see it."

Nora said, "Dad, I want to...."

"Just a minute, Nora. I'm not done yet. Laurie, we don't want to convince Nora to have an abortion, no matter how much we believe she ought to do it. Think about it. Suppose she was sorry later. She would blame us for taking the life of her baby. We don't want that, whatever happens."

"I know she's going to be sorry later if she *doesn't* have an abortion."

"You can't know that. Only Nora can know that, and she has decided something different."

"Mom, every time I thought about making another appointment,

I would see Georgia and Jimmy in my mind, and then I couldn't do it, even though I kept telling myself I was going to. It's so strange because it's not like I think abortions are wrong or anything. It's just that something stops me."

"You're making a big mistake, Nora. I know I'm right. I don't see how you can think you are going to be able to take care of a baby all by yourself."

"Elsie did it, and that was twins. And I don't think Uncle Cal and Aunt Ursela helped her much."

"Elsie's different. And she probably has a widow's pension because her husband died in combat. You won't have anything."

"I know it, Mom, and I'm scared, but I'm still going to have this baby."

"Oh, Nora. You're so stubborn. Some day you are going to say you wish you'd listened to me."

"I hope not, Mom."

They were so intent on each other that neither of them noticed George massaging his forehead. In a minute he planned to go upstairs for aspirin.

Laurie seemed to have forgotten all about her television program. "All right, Nora, if you are determined not to solve this the simplest way, then you've got to tell the father. He has a right to know. I would want to know if I was him. Think what it would be like to have your own child walking around and not to know it."

"You can't make me feel sorry for him. Don't even try. And please don't take his side."

"But maybe he would want to marry you and make this baby legitimate."

"He can't. He's already married."

"Maybe he would want to get a divorce, so he could marry you."

"Oh, Mom, you just don't get it, do you? There was never a question of marriage. I always knew that sooner or later, I would be the one he would give up."

Laurie said, "He would probably want you to have the abortion then."

"Yes, I suppose he would. That's one of the many, many reasons why I'm not going to tell him."

"I don't think you're being fair. This child will be his as much as it will be yours."

Nora sighed. "I'm probably not being fair, and I know I'm doing things in a muddled-up, confused way. I don't seem to be able to do it differently though. I have to do it my way, even if everyone thinks it's wrong. I'm not going to tell him. I'm definite about that."

George could see the hurt twisting her mouth into a grimace. She was close to tears. He wished he was upstairs already, getting the aspirin. He hated to make it worse for her by witnessing her pain.

Her lips were trembling when she went on. "He doesn't care about me anymore. I don't think he ever did, actually. I fooled myself into thinking that because I cared for him, he had to feel that way about me. I'm kind of ashamed of that now." She smiled at Laurie, a rueful smile, an attempt to be brave that was the most painful part of all.

But Laurie was still determined, still sure she knew what Nora should do. She said, "Oh honey, I'm so sorry, but that's even more reason to have this abortion. I think I'll call up Lena and ask her to talk to you about it."

Nora stood up. "Call her if you want to. I don't mind. But she's the one who convinced me in the first place."

"What? Lena?"

"She said she thought I meant to have this baby all along, and that's why I walked away from the clinic last fall."

"But...."

Nora went over and kissed her mother on top of the head. "I'm going to bed, Mom. I can't even think straight any more. If you don't want me to live here now that you know, I'll be glad to leave."

Laurie didn't say anything. Nora kissed George on the cheek. "Goodnight, Dad," she said and left the room.

Behind him he could hear her feet on the stairs. He turned around in his chair and said, "I love you, Nora."

She didn't answer. He didn't even know whether she heard him.

But Laurie heard. "Why did you say that, George? You've hardly said anything all night. I don't know whose side you're on, even."

"I don't see why it has to be sides."

"Oh my God. Listen to you. And you've *got* to think she's making a mistake."

"Well, I do, but I'm not as sure about it as you are. It isn't all that different from what happened to us, after all."

"It's completely different! I don't know how you can say that. We were in love. We were planning to get married anyway. She's all alone."

"I feel the same way you do, Laurie. I hate to see her tie herself down to something so difficult at her age."

"I wish you'd told her so then. Most of the time I didn't even know whether you were listening."

"I was. I was thinking about how hypocritical it was of us to be talking her into having an abortion when we decided not to for ourselves."

"You can't compare those two, George. It's just ridiculous. It was against the law then, and horribly dangerous."

"Would you be urging her to get an abortion if it was still illegal? Because the other arguments still apply."

Laurie looked startled by the question. She thought about it, frowning down at her hands, which clasped each other in her lap. Finally, she looked up at George. "I don't know how to answer that," she said. "I would be awful scared for her, but I might. Like you say, the other reasons are still there. And what in the world am I going to say to my mother?"

"As little as possible is what I would recommend."

"Oh George. You're so unfair. She thinks a lot of Nora, but she won't understand this at all. No one will. It's going to ruin Nora's reputation if she decides to keep this baby. What will we tell people?"

"Now that's the way things really are different. I don't think people pay much attention to that kind of thing in this day of women's lib. There are lots of unmarried mothers around. That part has changed a lot since we were young."

"I don't know if you're right."

"I guess we'll find out, won't we?" He stood up and reached down to pick up his paper off the floor. He'd forgotten about his headache while he argued with Laurie, but when he bent over, it came pounding back.

"Oh George, honestly. The things you say. I wish I could talk to Lena about this, but it's too late to call her tonight. I'll have to wait until the morning. I hope I'll have time. I can't call her from work. I wouldn't want to talk about this where people could hear me."

George took a few steps toward the door. "I think I'll go up, Laurie. I'm tired."

"Don't run away, George. I hardly know what you think about this business."

"I hardly know myself. I'm confused, and my head aches. I'd like to sleep on it. Could we talk in the morning?"

"You know we won't. We'll both be in a hurry."

"We could try to make time. I just don't have much to say about it now. I'm too tired."

Laurie sighed. "All right. Go on. I'll be up in a while."

"Good night," George said. He started up the stairs, looking forward to the aspirin he was going to take.

Chapter 28

In the fraction of a second before it happened, Conrad had just time to think, "I'm goin to cut myself with this saw." He was limbing up the tree he'd felled, moving along the trunk, taking off branches one by one, and working faster than he should have been. There was a lot of debris around where the tree had fallen—dead branches, bushes, uneven ground, and rocks. It was hard to get a steady and solid place to stand, and he was hurrying. He wanted to bring out this last log before he stopped for the day.

It happened so fast. One minute he was limbing, and the next minute he was looking down at his own chewed thigh through the hole in his pant leg. While he watched, the red began to spill over the white, as the blood began to pour out. The saw was still idling in his hands. He shut it off and set it down on the ground, thinking that he needed to move quickly, but he felt slow and confused, and he wasn't sure what to do. The funny thing was that it didn't hurt. It stung a little, but the feeling wasn't nearly bad enough for what he had done. He looked down at his leg and quickly looked away. He didn't need to see it. What he needed was to decide what to do while he still had some time left.

He was almost at the top of the woodlot. It was a long way down to his truck. If he passed out up here in the woods, they probably wouldn't even find him until tomorrow, and who knows if he would be alive by then. No, it was clear. He needed to get down to his truck. Then he could find something to make a tourniquet out of. If he could stop the bleeding, or at least slow it down, he might be able to get himself to the hospital. He might not be able to do it, but he ought to try.

He looked down at his saw. He knew he should leave it right where it was, but he couldn't let it get ruined. It was such a good saw. And he hadn't even begun to pay for it. He picked it up and started for the skidder. He had decided, without really thinking about it, that his chances of getting to his truck were better if he drove down the hill, than they would be if he tried to walk. A pool of blood had already melted the snow around his foot, and when he took a step toward the skidder, it ran faster down his leg. He tried not to put much weight on that leg as he limped over to the skidder. His pant leg was soaked, but the blood was coming so fast that it didn't have time to get cold.

He put the saw behind the seat and climbed in, and the skidder started right up. That was a bit of luck when he needed it. He put it in a low gear and started down, willing himself to stay alert. Of course, if he blacked out and crashed the skidder and killed himself, his worries would be over. It would be so much easier just to close his eyes and give up.

But then he saw Cheryl so clearly that it was as though she was there, right in front of him, looking in through the windshield. He could hear her speaking as plain as anything. "Conrad, don't leave me." He felt a rush of love for her so strong that it woke him up again. He held onto the steering wheel as tightly as he could and rode that skidder down to the landing.

When he stopped and shut it off, he felt victorious. He had made it. He had been fixed on that moment all the way down the hill. But as he climbed out of the skidder, he saw that he wasn't in the clear.

He was still alone, and no one would miss him for hours. True, the landing was beside the road, and if he collapsed, someone might happen along and see him lying there and come to help, but that wasn't very likely. He needed to try to get to the hospital.

His leg had started bleeding harder since he stood up. He reached behind the seat of the skidder and got the saw. He meant to leave it where it was, but without thinking, he picked it up and limped with it over to his pickup. In the back end, he found an old shirt he had been using as a rag. He rolled it up and put it around the top of his leg and got a short stick, which he stuck under the rag. By twisting the stick, he could tighten the rag. He tightened down until he could hear the rag rip a little, and then he stopped. It slowed the bleeding, but it didn't stop it.

He put the saw on the seat and climbed into the pickup beside it. He felt dizzy and weak. Everything was out of focus. The rag around his leg was uncomfortable. It hurt more than the place where the saw got him. He felt strangely out of it, like he was watching the whole thing happening to someone else and didn't care about it that much.

He got the truck in gear and out on the road. He knew he ought to be going as fast as he could, but he kept finding himself going slower and slower, until the speedometer said twenty miles per hour or even less, and he would have to force himself to step on the gas. When he came out onto the main road, he felt a little better. If he was weaving or driving erratically, someone would probably notice and maybe even tell the state troopers.

He thought about pulling off the road to take a short rest before he went on. It was so hard to concentrate and so hard to keep sitting up, watching the road. If he slept for a couple of minutes, maybe he would get a little strength back. He had just about decided that that was what he was going to do, when Cheryl's face was there before him again. She was so real and solid that he couldn't even see the road, and he was about to point that out to her when she said how much she loved him and how she wanted him to keep going and not stop until he got to the emergency room. Then she started to fade out like one of those scenes at the end of a movie, and while she was getting more and more transparent, she was smiling at him with love, and he knew he had to do what she said to do, no matter how hard it was to keep going.

And he did too. It got easier when he wasn't trying to decide whether to stop or not. He could concentrate all his attention on staying on the road. He knew he was driving badly. When he made the left turn into the hospital, a woman in a car coming the other way gave him an angry look. But he didn't care. He didn't run into her car or into anything else, and he had made it all the way to the hospital.

He coasted to a stop in the parking lot. He was beginning to feel sick to his stomach. He shut off the truck and opened his door to get some air. He thought he would sit there until his head cleared enough so that he could find a parking space. He shut his eyes.

When he opened them again, he was looking at a white ceiling. He was lying on his back on a bed. They must have carried him inside. The ceiling was spinning. He shut his eyes again, but that made it worse. He opened them and looked down at himself. Two nurses were bent over his leg, talking to each other so quietly that he couldn't hear what they said. He didn't care anyway. It was their problem now. If he hadn't felt so dizzy and sick, that idea would have made him smile. His leg was beginning to throb.

One of the nurses glanced around and saw him looking at her. "He's awake," she said to the other one, and then she came up beside his head. She still had a pair of bloody scissors in her hand. She was young and pretty, with dark hair. He thought, "Well, I guess I ain't dyin if I can notice stuff like that. Cheryl would kill me, but she might feel like it anyways after this." Out loud he said, "How bad is it?"

The other one answered him. "We don't know yet. We're trying to clean it up a bit so the doctor can take a look. You're going to need a lot of stitches. We can see that much."

Conrad tried a small smile to show her that he could handle anything they were going to do.

The pretty one said, "Do you feel all right? You're not going to pass out again, are you?"

"I don't think so," he said, but he didn't know he was going to pass out the first time either.

"You've lost a lot of blood," she said. Then she went back to work on his leg.

Conrad lay there wondering whether he ought to ask her to call Cheryl, but he didn't have any idea what time it was. He didn't know whether she would be at work or at home. If some stranger called her, it would scare her much worse than if he did it himself. She wouldn't be expecting him home until after dark, so she wouldn't be worried about him yet. It made sense to wait until he knew how bad it was, and anyway, he couldn't get to a telephone.

He looked around the room. He was in a bed by the door. There were three other beds in the room. The one diagonally across from his had a curtain drawn around it. He assumed there was someone in there. The other two beds were empty. There was no clock, and there weren't any windows. But it didn't matter what time it was since he couldn't get to a phone until they had finished with his leg, and he'd already decided not to get someone else to call.

Conrad lay there looking out into the hall. There was almost always someone going by. It helped to keep his mind off his leg, which throbbed all the time now. Sometimes there was a sharp pain also, a pain that made him jump. He didn't say it, but he thought the nurses must be poking too deep. He just lay there quietly, trying not to jump.

Then, there was Dr. McCormack standing in the doorway, looking in. "I heard you were here, Conrad," he said. I thought I'd better come down and see why." He walked over to the bed and looked at him.

"Hello, Dr. McCormack."

"What did you do to yourself?"

"I don't know. I guess my saw slipped. It happened so fast."

Dr. McCormack nodded. "It always does, doesn't it?"

"How bad is it?"

Dr. McCormack patted him on the shoulder and smiled a little and said, "I'll try to find out. Just a minute." He moved down to where the nurses were working.

Conrad didn't want to act too interested, so he looked out the door into the hall. Dr. McCormack was talking quietly to the nurses. His back was turned toward Conrad. When he opened his eyes again a few minutes later, the doctor was looking down at him.

"Okay, Conrad. You're going to be fine once we put your leg back together, but it's going to take a lot of stitches, and I want to do it myself."

Conrad nodded. He was glad to put himself in the doctor's hands.

"You're a lucky guy. You didn't hit the bone. You just chewed up your thigh muscles in pretty good shape."

Conrad nodded again.

"I have a few patients to see, and then I'll be back. Meanwhile, these girls will get you all cleaned up and ready. Okay?"

Conrad said, "Good, Doc. I'll be waitin."

The doctor smiled. "I'm glad you've still got your sense of humor. I'll be back in a little while, and we'll get you fixed up." He started toward the door and then came back. "Does your wife know you're here?"

"Not yet. I was goin to call her when I knew how bad it was."

"We need to let her know. You're going to want a ride home."

"I got my truck here. I drove myself."

"I know you did. That's what they told me. I don't know how you did it in the shape you were in. Anyhow, you're going to need a ride home. Do you want me to call her?" He reached inside his suit coat and brought out a little leather notebook and a silver pen. "What's your number?"

"I don't even know what time it is," Conrad said.

The doctor looked at his watch. "It's five-twenty right now."

"She'll just be gettin home then. Yes, would you call her, Doc? She'll be startin to wonder where I'm at."

"Glad to. What's your number?"

Conrad told him.

"Okay, I'll call her." He put the notebook and the silver pen back into the breast pocket of his expensive jacket. "I'll be back soon." He went out quickly.

Conrad lay there drifting in and out for he didn't know how long. Sometimes the nurses were there, bending over his thigh, and sometimes he was alone. The lights were bright, and the room was cold, and everything but the throbbing of his leg was a little strange and out of focus.

Then Dr. McCormack was back again. He smiled at Conrad and took off his beautiful jacket. A nurse was standing beside him ready to take it carefully and hang it up. Dr. McCormack rolled up the sleeves of his crisp white shirt. "How's your dad doing?" he said to Conrad.

"All right. He's slow, but he can get around. He's back to doin his own chores."

"You Willards. You don't stay down for long, do you?"

Conrad tried a small smile. "I hope you're right." He was thinking about himself.

"Your dad's a good man. I've known him for a long time." He went to the sink and washed his hands and came back to Conrad's bed holding them out to dry. "Your wife said to tell you she'd come right in and for you not to worry about it."

"Thank you, Doc."

"Okay. Well, we'd better get going here, so we don't keep her waiting. You may feel something, but it should be just a prick once in a while. I had them give you a lot of Novocaine."

"That's all right. You do whatever you need to do."

"Good man. I will."

After that, the doctor was bent over his leg, working on it. The only time he said anything was to ask the nurses for something he needed, and one of them would hurry off to fetch whatever it was. Conrad lay there in a fog, trying not to think about anything. He wondered if Cheryl was out in the waiting room. He wondered whether she brought the kids with her. He wondered how long it was going to be before he could get back to work. He would have to call the owner up and tell him there was going to be a delay. The guy wasn't going to like it. He was in a hurry for the job to be over. But it couldn't be helped. Sometimes, especially when he felt a stab of pain in his thigh, he wondered how much longer Dr. McCormack was going to have to work on him.

Then, when he had given up thinking it would ever happen, Dr. McCormack sat back and looked around. "Well, I guess we got you back together again. One hundred and twenty-two stitches. That's what it took." He peeled off the bloody rubber gloves he was wearing. "The nurses will bandage it for you and tell you what to do to take care of it. I've got to leave." He went over to the sink and washed his hands and walked to Conrad's side, drying them with paper towels.

"Thank you, Dr. McCormack. I really appreciate it."

"It should come along fine. Tell your dad I said hello."

"I will."

"I have to get going. I'm already late. My wife's not going to like it."

One of the nurses held up the doctor's jacket. He slipped his arms in and gave a quick wave and was gone.

A few minutes later, Cheryl was standing by his bed. Her face was pale and streaked with tears. "The doctor said I could come and see you," she said, breathlessly. "Oh Conrad, are you all right?"

Conrad thought he smiled at her, but he wasn't sure. Everything was a little confused. "Sure, honey," he said. "They fixed it. Dr. McCormack did. I'm fine."

"He said he put in one hundred and twenty-two stitches."

Conrad nodded. "Where are Dwayne and Dorrie?"

"They're here. They're out in the waiting room. They wanted to come."

"Good. Dwayne can drive my truck home if I ride with him."

"Do you want to do that? We could get it tomorrow."

"No. Let's do it now."

Later, after his leg was bandaged, they put him in a wheelchair, and Cheryl pushed him out into the waiting room. Dwayne and Dorrie were sitting sprawled out on the chairs. Conrad saw them before they saw him. When they did, they both jumped up and came over to his wheelchair.

Dwayne said, "Oh Dad, are you all right?"

Dorrie started to cry.

"Don't cry Dorrie. It's goin to be all right," Conrad said, but he was touched by how their teenaged indifference to grown-ups had melted away to show how much they cared. Conrad could feel the tears pooling up in his own eyes, but that was because he was weak from loss of blood.

Cheryl pushed the wheelchair right up to the passenger-side door of the truck. "Now, Conrad, are you sure you want to do this tonight?"

"Yes, I am. Dwayne, do you have your learner's permit on you?"

"Yeah, Dad."

"Good boy. I want you to drive my truck. Okay? I'll ride with you."

"Okay, Dad."

So Conrad stood up. He was shaky, but he managed to push the saw out of the way and hoist himself into the truck.

Dwayne walked around the truck and opened the driver's door. He looked inside and started to shout. "Oh God! Dad, Ma....oh no!"

Conrad could hear Cheryl's voice from quite far away asking Dwayne what was wrong.

"Come over here, Ma. I don't know what to do."

"What *is* it, Dwayne?" Cheryl was saying impatiently as she came over to his side. Then, when she looked in the truck, she said, "Oh my God!" and burst into tears.

Conrad looked around at them standing in the open door of the truck, "What's the matter?"

"Oh, oh, oh, there's so much blood. It looks as though someone got murdered here," Cheryl said, crying even harder.

"It ain't that bad," Conrad said. "I'm still here."

She looked at him, trying to smile through her tears.

"But I need to get home."

She wiped her eyes and gave a little shake of her head. "I'm sorry, Conrad. Dwayne, you stay right there." She hurried off. In a few minutes she was back with the blanket she carried in her car. She spread it over the bloody seat. "There, Dwayne," she said. "Get in, and be careful going home. We'll be right behind you. Are you all right, Conrad?"

He nodded and smiled at her.

"Good. Let's get goin then." She was all business now.

On the drive, Conrad tried to watch the road, to tell Dwayne what to do, but he felt so detached from everything that he kept finding himself not paying attention, just sitting there half asleep.

Once he said, "How're you doin, Dwayne?"

And Dwayne said, "I'm okay, Dad. Don't worry about my drivin."

"I don't, Dwayne. You're a good driver."

That was all they said to each other until they got home. Then Cheryl and Dorrie helped him into the house. Nobody had noticed until then that his leg below the bandage was bare down to his boot, and his boot was a mess. The cold air stung his bare skin. He couldn't have made it into the house without Cheryl and Dorrie supporting him, one on each side.

Cheryl pushed the clutter of clothes off the mudroom bench. They lowered him onto it while they took off his boots. Cheryl sent Dorrie running after towels to put under the bloody one. Dwayne came in to help too, and between all of them, they managed to get him cleaned up and undressed enough and into bed.

Some time later, Cheryl brought him some pills for the pain. "Conrad, I don't even know what happened."

"I don't either. It happened so fast. One minute I was limbin a log, and the next minute my leg was bleedin." He swallowed the pills and handed her back the glass.

"It's that new saw, Conrad. It's too dangerous."

"Naw, honey, it was just a accident. It could've happened with the old one too. It might've been worse with the old one."

"You could get your job back." Her voice trailed off.

"I couldn't walk around the feed store like this."

"No, but I mean when you get strong again."

"When I get my strength back, I'm goin to finish the woodlot like I said I would."

"I know. I know you've got to do that, but I mean after...."

"I don't know about after. I may have to go back to the feed store. This thing is goin to put me way behind." He caught at her hand. "But we ain't goin to decide it tonight. Come on to bed."

She bent over and kissed him, but it was a motherly kiss, and he supposed that was all he was good for anyhow.

"I'll be back soon, Conrad. Go to sleep."

"I'll be waitin for you," he said, but he fell asleep. When he woke up sometime later with his leg throbbing, she was asleep beside him.

Chapter 29

After breakfast, Cal felt like doing something for a change. His foot was hardly bothering him anymore, and he didn't have to think about it much. He put his barn boots and jacket and hat on and went back to the woodshed, where he had the stove wood cut and stacked. Some of it still needed to be split.

He had to hunt around for the splitting maul. He hadn't used it since before his accident. It was a beautiful day, warmer than yesterday but still clear and cold. The late February sunlight was as transparent as spring water. The world was moving toward spring. You could see it in the light. The trees knew. They already had a faint red haze around their tops.

Cal picked out a likely looking chunk of wood and stood it on end in the snow behind the shed. It looked like a piece that was ready to crack apart. He settled his feet wide and raised the maul up behind his head, and then he came down with everything he had, and the maul went straight through and buried itself in the snow between the fallen halves of the log. He threw the pieces onto the stack and picked out another likely chunk.

Chickadees flew past on their way to the bird feeder, singing the clear, two-note whistle that was their comment on the beautiful day.

Cal worked slowly but smoothly for a while, glad he was able to split wood again, feeling the power when he brought the maul down straight through the wood to the ground, feeling the satisfaction when the chunks of wood popped apart. And then, as was bound to happen, he hit a bad one. He would have put it back on the pile, but he was afraid Ursela might notice all the ineffectual and shallow cuts in the end, evidence that he wasn't able to cut it.

He reversed the piece of wood, knocking the snow off the bottom end and settling the top into the hollow made by the logs that he'd already split. He thought if he put everything into the blow, it would be enough. It seemed important to beat that particular chunk of wood. He slammed and slammed at the end of it, but all he did was chew it up. The maul never sank in, never kept going until it came out the other end. It never even made a deep opening he could work on. He began to get angry. He hoped the anger would give his strike more force, but it didn't. It just made him think of Jason LaRue, and how he couldn't get anywhere with that situation either, although he ought to be able to. He knew the little bastard was the one who shot him, and yet he couldn't do a thing about it.

Finally, he gave up and stood the maul in the corner of the wood-shed. He ought to go to town and turn the whole thing over to George. He had been planning to do that anyway. George could handle it. And what was the sense of having a lawyer in your family if you didn't make use of his services?

He picked up an armful of split stovewood and put the unsplit chunk on top. He dumped the whole pile into the woodbox. Ursela wasn't in the kitchen, so he took the opportunity to load the piece he couldn't split into the stove. That was a satisfying conclusion to a problem. Now if he could deal with Jason LaRue as successfully….

He went into the bedroom and put on clean clothes to wear to town. When he came back into the kitchen, Ursela was mopping the floor. She told him not to come in because the floor was wet.

"How am I supposed to get through?"

She stopped mopping and leaned on the handle. "You could wait until it dries." She wasn't even smiling.

"God damn it, woman. I can't stand here and watch the floor dry. Are you crazy? I have things to do."

"Well, okay, then. Come across. I'll go over it."

So Cal walked through the kitchen, and Ursela came along behind him, mopping up his footprints. Over his shoulder he said, "I'm takin the car."

"Where're you goin?"

"I got to go into town to see somebody."

By this time, he was out in the mudroom getting his jacket. He couldn't hear what she said and had to go back into the kitchen and ask her what it was.

"I just wondered how you would get there. Do you want me to drive you in?"

"No I don't. I can manage. My foot's okay."

"Will you be back for dinner?"

"I plan to be."

"Good. Because I was thinkin I would go over to Conrad's this afternoon to see does he need anythin."

"I'll be back in plenty of time."

"All right then." And she went back to her mopping.

Cal was going to ask her if she needed him to stop for anything while he was in town, but she hadn't asked. He decided not to mention it. If he didn't know of anything, he wouldn't have to stop, and he might not feel like it later. His foot could start to throb, and that would make it hard enough just to drive back home. He certainly didn't want to have to come home and tell her he wasn't able to do her errands.

It was a long time since he had been able to drive—more than two months—and he wasn't sure his foot would be able to take it, even though the car was automatic and had power brakes. It was a gas-guzzling sedan, the kind you could get cheap since no one wanted big cars any more, not since the oil crisis drove up the price of gas. He could feel a kind of ache in the bones of his foot when he stepped down on the pedal, but it wasn't too bad, and he could use his left foot on the brake.

He had meant to use the trip to town to figure out what he was going to say to George, but he found he needed to concentrate on his driving. All he had time to think about was how Jason LaRue had messed up his life, cost him a whole lot of money in doctor bills, taken his deer meat, and wasn't even sorry.

"Revenge," Cal said to himself. "That's what I want." Only he wouldn't say that to George. Compensation. That's what he'd call it. That's what lawyers were good at getting. He didn't care what he had to call it, as long as Jason LaRue had to pay one way or another.

A car turned right in front of him. Cal had to jam on the brakes so fast that he forgot and used his hurt foot. That sure made it worse. He laid on the horn to let the guy know how stupid he'd been. After that, Cal decided he had better concentrate on driving. There were too many fools on the road anymore. Besides, if you could get shot out of your own tree, you weren't safe anywhere.

Cal hadn't gone to George's office since Ma died, when they had to sort out who would get the farm. He thought he remembered which door it was, and the wide steps looked familiar. On the wall inside the door was a list of the people who had offices in the building. George's name was there. So he was right. He started up the stairs slowly, leaning on the railing to take the weight off his foot. Stairs were always bad. When he got to the door with George's name on it, he knocked, and a girl said to come in.

He was in a kind of outside office with a young girl sitting at a desk. He didn't remember that part. Maybe it was a new addition. The girl was a scrawny little thing. She looked like she didn't want to be disturbed in what she was doing, so he didn't say anything to her. He just walked past her to the door of George's office, trying not to show his limp.

She kept watching him the whole way. If she had been a heifer calf, she would have been one of the ones they used to send to the sale. "A poor doer," they'd have called her. When he put his hand on George's door, she said, "What are you doing?" like it was her business to know.

"I'm going in to see George."

"You can't."

"I don't see why not. He's my brother."

"Well, you'll have to wait. He has a client in there with him."

Now Cal could hear voices from behind the door. He pulled his hand back.

The girl was still looking at him. After a minute she said, more kindly, "They're almost done. You could have a seat over there."

But Cal couldn't give her the satisfaction, even though it would have been better for his foot. Instead, he walked back and forth across the office, trying to make up his mind whether to stay and wait for his turn to speak to George, or whether to say to hell with him and leave. He would have left without hesitation if he hadn't been angrier at Jason LaRue than he was at the way George's hired girl was treating him.

He had just about decided to leave anyway, when the door opened and an old woman came out, buttoning a coat with a fancy fur collar. She had a matching fur hat on her head. She was so busy saying thank you to George that she never saw Cal at all and almost bumped into him.

George was right behind her. George saw him. Cal saw his eyes widen with surprise when he saw him, but he didn't say anything. He was too busy smiling at the old biddy and trying to hurry her out the door.

As soon as she was gone, George turned around and said, "Cal, what are you doing here?"

The girl interrupted. "He wouldn't tell me his name, Mr. Willard. He just said he was your brother." She obviously didn't believe it.

Cal ignored her. "I came to see you, George. Apparently, that's not allowed."

"I'm really glad you did. But...." He hesitated. "Nothing's wrong, is it? I mean...."

"You mean did I come here with some news that's so bad I had to come in person? No, nothing like that."

"I'm glad of that," George said. "Let's go downstreet and get some coffee or maybe some lunch. What do you say?"

"No, George. This here is business—private business." He looked around at the girl who was sitting there with her mouth a little bit open, listening to every word. "I want to go into your office, like a regular customer, and close the door." He gave the girl another look.

She got the message that time. She snapped her mouth shut and pretended to get interested in the papers on her desk.

"Sure, Cal, just let me check." He leaned on the corner of the desk. "Annie, what's next? Do I have anything scheduled?"

She gave a great show of importance, shuffling through her papers. "Not until two o'clock, when you're supposed to see Mr. Welch."

"Okay, then. Good." He pushed himself up to standing and started for his office. "Come on in, Cal."

Cal followed him and shut the office door behind them. The girl had her back to the door and pretended not to notice, but he knew she was glad he was gone.

"Have a seat, Cal," George said. He was already sitting down behind his desk. "How's your foot? I see you don't need a cane any more."

"It's not right yet, if it's ever goin to be. It still hurts a lot."

"I expect you're too cantankerous to kill." He was smiling. "What's on your mind?"

"I can be killed just like anybody else, George. That's why I need protection. So far I ain't gettin any—not from the law anyhow." He hated it when George made him into a joke.

"All right. Is that what this visit is about? That business last fall?"

"That's what I need some help with, if you'd like to give it."

"I will if I can. I hope you know that. You do know that, don't you?"

Cal looked around the room before he answered. Except for all the books, it wasn't that fancy. He had to admit that George didn't put on airs in his office the way he did in his house, and that probably wasn't George, but Laurie. Finally he said, "I hope you'll help me."

"Of course I will, but you'll have to fill me in on the details. What's going on?"

"I found the guy who shot me, or a friend of mine did. He's a good guy. Your Nora knows him."

"Nora knows the man who shot you?"

"No, of course not. She knows the guy who helped me find the shooter. We went to his house."

"That could've been dangerous."

"It should of been dangerous to him, but it wasn't."

"Did you talk to him? Did he let you inside?"

"Both. Not that it did any good."

"What did you think it would accomplish?"

"I don't know." He almost said it was a stupid question, but he managed to stop himself in time. "I guess I thought when he knew we had him, that it was obvious he was the one who did it, that he might admit it." He sighed. "I guess that was sorta dumb of me. He didn't admit a thing. He was just a smart-ass kid. He said it was my word against his and that we didn't have no proof."

"I think he's right about that."

"God damn it, George! Don't start takin his side. I want you to go after this guy. He's guilty. I want you to nail him."

"I don't know, Cal."

"What do you mean you don't know? I'll pay you your goin rate, if that's what's botherin you."

"It's not that. Surely you know it's not that. How do you know the guy you found is the right guy?"

"God damn it, George. You sound like him."

"What's his name, anyway?"

"Jason LaRue, the little creep."

"What does he say about it?"

"The thing is, he just about admits the whole thing. He followed that buck up the trail, the big game trail where I set up my tree stand. He said so. The buck stopped right near the top. That's where I shot him. This LaRue character even says he heard my shot, but he says *I* missed, and *he* shot and hit him. That's bullshit." He wasn't telling it right. He wanted to make it simple and clear so that George would see it the way it was, but he couldn't seem to get his thoughts arranged so he could tell it that way.

He started in again. "Listen, George. This is how it happened. He heard my shot and swung around while he was pullin the trigger, and he was pointin the gun in my direction, just as I started down out of my tree stand. It's so obvious. That's how come the bullet went through my foot. It's normal to swing around like that when you hear a shot, and if you already have your finger on the trigger…. why, hell, I wouldn't even hold it against him if he'd just admit it." He thought for a minute. "And give me back my deer meat, if there's any left."

"But, Cal…."

"But if he won't he's got to pay. That's where you come in."

"I don't know, Cal. It still sounds like you don't have much of a case. It's your word against his."

"It happened on my land! That ought to count for something."

"It doesn't work that way."

"Well, it ought to." He shook his head in disgust. "And you wonder why people want to take the law into their own hands."

"You don't have any evidence, Cal."

"That's what drives me crazy! There's all kinds of evidence. We were both there. A bullet went through my foot, and the little bastard stole my deer. What more evidence do you need?"

"But that's just hearsay. That doesn't count. Where's the bullet? Do you have it?"

"It went all the way through. It's up there in the woods some place. It's his bullet, and it's got my blood on it."

"Well, if you had that…."

"Get serious, George. You're the one that went off to be a soldier. I'm the one who stayed home and didn't see nothin. You're the one who ought to know better. How're you goin to find a bullet in fifty acres of woods? You couldn't do it even if it wasn't under three feet of snow. No one'll ever see *that* bullet again."

"What about the one that went into the deer?"

"My bullet? I guess you have to figure Jason LaRue is responsible for makin that one disappear."

"I don't know then, Cal. I don't see how you've got anything. Even the deer is gone."

"I've got the guy that did it. That's what I've got. I found him all by myself without any help from the law. Now I don't see why the law won't step up and do its job."

"If you could get him to talk…."

"God damn it! That's just what I mean. If I could get him to admit it, then I wouldn't care about the rest."

"I don't see how it would do any good if I came out to talk to him. Do you think I could get him to admit it?"

"No. Why would he? I don't think you could scare him into it. I thought you could do something without him admittin it. You want all the work done for you."

"I don't think I could take this case in good conscience, Cal. All I can recommend is what I would tell any client of mine, and that is, if you don't like my advice, you ought to find yourself another lawyer."

"Jesus, Mary, Joseph!" Cal said. He realized how sure he had been that George would be willing to help him. When he said he wouldn't, it was a sharp blow. "Blood is supposed to be thicker than water, George, but I swear to God, I think yours is thinner."

"I can't help what you think, Cal. I'm really sorry. I wish I could help you, but I don't see how I can. Not now. Not this way."

"Nora wasn't so damn particular. She came up in the woods to help me look for evidence."

"Nora did? My Nora?"

"That's what I said."

"I never heard that. When was it?"

"Last fall. Just before the snow came down to stay. A little bit before Christmas, I guess it was. She drove the tractor up to the top of the hill with me in the wagon, and she helped me look for evidence." Cal liked the complete surprise and envy obvious on George's face, surprise and envy that Cal could know things about Nora her own father didn't know. Cal remembered how coolly she had acted when the tractor jumped out of gear and started free-wheeling down the hill. "She's all right, that girl of yours. She has a lot of grit to her."

"And she drove the tractor? I didn't even know she knew how."

"I don't think she did, but she was willin to give it a try. That's what I meant about her havin a lot of grit." That was a lot for him to say. He wondered if George knew that.

"Well," George said. "That's really interesting. Did you find anything up there?"

"Not much. Nora found a candy wrapper. It could of been where LaRue was standin. He must have been right about there to of hit me the way he did. But a candy wrapper don't really tell you anythin."

"You know, Cal, I think the thing to do is to wait until the snow goes and then go up there and see what evidence you can find. I could go with you, if you wanted me to."

"There ain't goin to be nothin there in the spring that wasn't there in the fall. Less, probably."

"After the leaves have been all matted down by the snow, maybe something would show up that you couldn't see under the leaves in the fall."

"Maybe. But we don't need evidence. We already know who's guilty."

"We need proof."

"The proof's right there on his weaselly little face."

"That's not what I mean by proof. I mean some physical fact. Something that shows what happened, the way it would if we found Jason LaRue's bullet up there under the tree where you got shot."

Cal stood up. "Not much chance of that. And what do you mean 'we'?"

"I mean just that. I'd still like to help you, even though I can't take it as a case, not now anyway. But I still feel bad about that, and I'd still like to help."

"Sure, George." He took a few steps toward the door. "I guess I won't take up any more of your time. If you could send me the bill...."

"Knock it off, Cal. You know I won't charge you. Hell, I wouldn't charge anyone if I didn't take the case. And I hope you know I'd be glad to take it, if I could see any way to go with it."

He could see George wanted him to say it was okay, that he understood. But he was still too angry at George for disappointing him. All he could say was, "Don't get up. I'll let myself out."

George stood up as Cal opened the door. "I've still got some time, Cal. Want to go out and get some lunch?"

"No thanks. Ursela'll have my dinner waitin. I'll see you." He went out and shut the door without looking back. He didn't say anything to the girl. He just stomped past her desk and out the door, trying not to limp, with her watching him the whole way.

His footsteps were loud and uneven in the dark hall. Going down the stairs was always worse than going up. He made sure no one was around, and then he went down one step at a time, like a little child, putting a lot of his weight on the handrail.

He could see that he had believed all winter that George was going to help him. Now he could see that he would have to take his own private revenge on Jason LaRue. He was glad he said what he did about George's blood being thinner than water.

Chapter 30

It was Nora who answered the phone. Lena said, "I'm so glad it's you. I was afraid it would be Mom."

"She's doing the dishes. But you can't hide from her indefinitely."

"I know, but I can't deal with it tonight. I have other stuff to worry about."

"What's up?"

"I want to ask you for a favor, but I don't want you to do it if you don't want to."

"Ask me. It'll probably be fine. I'm not doing anything. Mom wouldn't even let me help with the dishes. She's still mad at me."

"She'll get over it."

"I don't think so, but tell me what you need. I can't talk about it now, anyway."

"It's this. Jerry wants me to meet him some place so we can talk. I was wondering if you could stay with the kids for a while."

"I'd be glad to. I'm not doing anything tonight, but do you think it's a good idea to see Jerry?"

"I think I have to. There are so many things we have to sort out. I guess I'll be glad to get some things clear. I don't mind seeing him some place, but he wanted to come to our house so he could see the kids. That's the part I don't want to happen. They miss him so much. They're always talking about him. I know it would break their hearts, especially Georgia's, if they saw him, and then he left again. I don't want them to know he's in town."

"You'll have to tell them some time."

"I know, but not now. I don't even know what to say to myself right now. It's too soon. So, can you come?"

"Sure. I'll be over in a few minutes."

"Thanks, Nora. That's great. I'll call Jerry and tell him."

Lena was able to leave on time because Georgia and Jimmy wanted Nora to read to them. She was glad to leave, glad to be alone. She was too nervous to pay attention to the kids. Her heart was beating fast, and her stomach felt as though the bottom had dropped out of it. She didn't want the kids to notice. It was nice the way they were both so crazy about Nora. She was going to be a good mother, and Georgia was going to love having a baby cousin. They needed to be told about it. But if they asked about the baby's father, she wouldn't know what to say. Tonight, when Georgia wanted to know where she was going, she said she was going to visit her friend, Katy Rayburn. She could see that Jimmy was listening intently. They believed what she told them. She hated to lie to them, but how could she explain to them that Jerry was nearby, and they couldn't see him, and he wasn't coming home? That would hurt them too much. She had to protect them from that.

She and Jerry had arranged to meet in the parking lot of the Sentinel. She was a few minutes early, but he was already standing in the doorway, having a cigarette and watching for her. She tried to notice how she felt when she first saw him—was she glad or sorry? But she was too nervous to pay attention to herself, and she didn't know whether she wanted to be glad or sorry to see him. She decided she was just scared.

Jerry opened the car door. Cigarette smoke swirled in with the cold air. More than anything, that smell reminded her of Jerry.

"Hi, Lena," he said. "It's great to see you." He climbed into the seat beside her.

Lena didn't know how to respond. "Do you want me to drive, Jerry? If you do, you'd better tell me where we're going."

"Huh?" he said. Even in the dim light, she could see that she'd hurt him.

"I'm sorry. I might as well drive. I don't mind." That was all she could manage.

"Okay. I don't care where we go, just someplace we can talk. The only place I really want to go is home."

"I can't help that, Jerry. I can't do that to Georgia and Jimmy. They're too upset about it all anyway."

"Don't they want to see me?"

"Well, sure. That's the point. It would be too awful for them to see you and then to have you leave again."

"But Lena, I don't want to leave again."

"Listen, Jerry, we can't just sit here with the car running." Her voice sounded cross in spite of her effort to keep the anger out of it. "Where shall we go?"

"We could go to the café in West Severance. No one we know would see us there."

"I don't care whether we see anyone we know, but I want to go someplace dark, because I know I'm going to cry."

"Aw honey, don't say that."

"Why not, since it's true?"

"I don't know. I thought you'd be glad."

"I don't see why. This whole thing seems pretty awful to me."

"Let's go to the Steak House then. It's dark there. Are you hungry? I am."

"No, I'm not, and that would be expensive, too expensive. We haven't paid any of the bills since you left, and they're all due, and there isn't much money left in the checking account either."

"Okay, but I've still got to eat. We can talk about money too. Let's go there."

When they got to the Steak House, Lena asked for the corner booth. It was very dark. Off in the corner like that, she wouldn't have to worry about anyone seeing her cry. She slid into the booth, and Jerry slid in beside her.

She waited until the hostess walked away, and then she said, "Don't. Please move. I don't want you to sit so close."

"But I've missed you so much."

"I don't care. You have to move."

"I want to be near you. Can't I stay here?"

"Jerry, you're not being fair."

"But I love you."

"You've got a funny way of showing it. You said you wanted to talk, and I want to too. We need to figure out a lot of stuff. We've got a lot of problems. You're not making it any easier."

"Okay. You win." He sighed and got out of the booth and slid in on the other side. He sat there looking at her, until she had to look down at her hands on the table.

After a few minutes of silence, she took off her jacket, leaving it behind her on the seat.

"Do you want me to hang up your coat?" He took off his own. He didn't have a hat or gloves, even though it was a cold night.

"No thanks. It's fine. What did you want to talk about? I have a few things of my own to say."

"I want to come home, Lena. I miss you and the kids. It was stupid, and it's over, and I want things to be back like they were before."

"That's so mean. I don't believe it."

Jerry looked as though she'd thrown something at him. He leaned forward across the table. "What are you talking about? Don't you want me to come back? I thought you'd be glad. I don't get it. This isn't the way I pictured it. I thought you would be glad. I thought you would want me to come home."

"Stop it, Jerry. You're going to make me cry, and the waitress is coming this way. I really don't want her to see."

The waitress had menus for them, but Jerry ordered a sirloin steak without even looking to see how much it cost, and Lena, feeling that someone needed to be sensible and grown-up, said all she wanted was a glass of water.

As soon as the waitress was gone, Jerry leaned across the table again and looked at her intently. "Why don't you want me to come home? I know the kids miss me, even if you don't. You're the one who's breaking up our family."

Lena was desperately trying not to cry, but that was too much. She felt completely alone. No one could ever understand her painful confusion. She couldn't even make Nora see. Everyone would think it ought to be simply one way or the other—she ought to leave Jerry or take him back. Nora would say one thing, and Mom the other, and they would both miss the point. She was really crying hard now. She couldn't believe she had come to meet Jerry, when she knew she would cry, and she had forgotten to bring a handkerchief. She grabbed her napkin before Jerry could offer her his handkerchief. She definitely didn't want to take his.

"Why are you doing this, Jerry? You go out and have a fun time pretending you aren't married. You lie, and you cheat, and then you want to come home and act like nothing happened? And then you say it's my fault?" She could see that she was making him angry, and the worst of it was that it wasn't what she meant to say. It wasn't that she didn't want him to come back home. But she didn't want him to come back as though nothing had happened either. She wanted him to know what he had done to her and to know what it felt like to her, and she wanted him to be sorry. But she could see she was making it all worse.

Jerry was sitting there, staring at her, watching her cry. She hated the angry look on his face. He didn't say anything. He acted like a child who knew he had to take his punishment and then he would be forgiven and could go home and forget the whole thing. He looked like he was hunkered down to wait out the storm, worried, but not too worried, because he knew that eventually she would let him come home. And that was probably true too, and it was also probably true that everything would go back to the way it was before, only with one difference, because she didn't think she would ever trust him again, at least not the way she did before.

There was a long silence while she thought about how badly she had been treated. She hadn't really been seeing Jerry, even though she was looking at him.

Then for the first time, she saw the miserable look on his face. He said, "You *are* going to divorce me, aren't you, Lena?" He sounded hopeless, as though for the first time he realized what he had done.

"I don't know," she said. "I don't know what to do." Suddenly she was no longer angry. She saw that it was bad for him too. "Everyone tells me something different, and no one knows what's right for me." She almost said, "what's right for us," but she stopped herself in time, thinking bitterly that there might not be an "us" any more.

Jerry's steak came. He offered to give her some, but she said she wasn't hungry. It was a huge plate of expensive food. He began to eat heartily, and she was less sympathetic. She watched in silent disapproval.

Then he looked up. "Lena," he said, "I know I've made you unhappy, and the kids too. If it's better for you and for them, then you ought to divorce me."

"I don't know what's better for us. I'm so confused. I don't know what to do." Just then, looking at her across the table was the old Jerry, the person she had fallen in love with so long ago. "Thank you, Jerry. I'm glad you said that. It means you're thinking about us. I didn't know you were before."

Jerry put down his fork and leaned toward her across the table, looking into her eyes. "I've been horrible and selfish, and I've made you all unhappy. I never meant to. I'm so stupid."

"It has been awful."

"Don't cry anymore. I want to come home and make it up to all of you, starting right now."

Lena had been leaning forward toward Jerry too, but when he said that, she sat back a little. "We've all missed you, Jerry. You know how much the kids want you to come home."

"And you, Lena?"

"I've missed you a lot. I didn't even know how much until I saw you tonight. But...."

"I'm so scared when you say 'but' like that. Have I ruined everything?"

"No, Jerry, I want you to come home, at least right now I do." She thought for a minute, surprised by what she had heard herself say.

Jerry grabbed her hand and held it in both of his. "Thank you, thank you," he said. "You won't be sorry. I promise."

"But Jerry, not tonight. That's what I was going to say before."

"Why not, if you know...."

"Because I want to do it right. I want us to change things so this won't ever happen again."

"It won't. I promise it won't."

"That's not enough, Jerry. That's not changing anything. It wouldn't have happened unless something was wrong."

Jerry dropped her hand and began to eat again. "You're making it into too big a deal. She never meant anything to me."

"I'm not talking about her. I don't even want to *think* about her. I'm talking about you and me."

"But Lena, where am I going to go?"

"What?"

"I moved out. I told Bobbi it was over and I was going home to you. That you were the only one I ever cared about. All my stuff's in my car."

"It's too fast. It won't work." She looked at his face and felt unsure. A minute ago he had been so happy and hopeful, and now he looked as though he might cry, and her heart went out to him. But something stopped her. "I can't, Jerry. I have to think about it." Was she being mean, trying to extract punishment? "And I need to talk to the kids and get them ready for this."

"I thought they would just wake up and find me there, and things would be back like they used to be when they used to wake me up in the morning."

347

"I don't know. I'm just not sure. I have to think."

"If this is going to take a long time, I'll have to find a place to live, and that'll be expensive."

"I can't help it. I don't know how long it will be. All I know is that tonight would be too soon."

"Maybe you don't really want me to come back. Maybe you were just saying that."

"I have to think about it some. I thought we were going to talk about how to divide up the money and what we were going to do about the house payments, that kind of stuff. And it would be nice if we didn't have to figure all that out. I know it would be more expensive if you had a separate place. I've been worrying a lot about how I was going to have enough money for everything. Could you stay with your mom and dad for a while?"

"Oh God! I don't think so. They'd be furious at me. They don't know about any of this. They probably wouldn't let me stay if they found out."

"Jerry, you've got to tell them. I told my parents."

"You did? What did they say?"

"Not a lot. They were too surprised."

"I bet they really hate me. Your Mom never liked me anyhow."

"She thinks I ought to get you to come back home and try to forget any of it ever happened."

"She does? Your mom? That's great. I never thought your mother would be on my side."

"It won't happen that way, Jerry. And if you think it's a question of sides or a question of pretending it never happened so there won't be any gossip, then you might just as well stay away."

"Don't get mad. I didn't mean anything, and I don't know what you're talking about when you say that about gossip. I don't care what people say."

"I know. But my mother does. She cares too much. This is more important than what other people think about it."

"I know that, Lena. I know you're right. We'll do it however you say. We've got our kids to think about. I can probably stay with

Chuck or Tom Osborne for a few days."

"It might be longer than that."

"Do you think so?"

"I don't know, Jerry. I don't know what I'm doing, and I don't know anyone to ask. I've got to just do what feels right, I guess. Until I have a better plan, anyhow."

"I suppose so. How long do you think it should be before I see Georgia and Jimmy? I miss them an awful lot."

"They miss you too. They talk about you all the time."

"Well, don't you think...."

"I have to think about it some, Jerry. I thought we were going to talk about how to divide things up. I had no idea you wanted to come home. You could call me tomorrow, and we could decide what to do next."

"Okay...but this is the reason I haven't called up before, even though I have been wanting to—what do I do if Georgia answers the phone? What do I say to her?"

"Tell her you miss her and that you're coming home as soon as you can. That's true, isn't it?"

"Yes it is. The sooner, the better."

"Just don't tell her where you are. They think you're out of town, somewhere far away. And don't tell her why. They don't know that part either."

"I'm glad of that."

"I hate to lie to them, but I didn't know how to explain it."

"I'm really glad they don't know. I would feel funny if they did."

Lena sighed. She felt like saying he shouldn't do something that he didn't want anyone to know about, but she managed to keep quiet, and after all, she was the one who hadn't told Georgia and Jimmy, the one who had lied to them. Maybe things were always unfair and it was childish to expect anything else.

As they left the restaurant, Jerry took her hand. "Is this all right, Lena? You don't mind, do you?"

"No, I don't. It's nice."

"I can't wait to come home again. It wasn't any good at all being away from you."

"Maybe we can make it better than it used to be so this won't ever happen again."

"Oh, it won't. It was very stupid of me, but I know better now. I know what's important to me now."

"I hope so, Jerry, but I want to change some things just to make sure. That is, if I can figure it out."

When they got to the Sentinel parking lot, Lena hated to say goodbye. She came very close to telling him to come home after all, but when she got to the house and saw Nora's car, she was glad she hadn't changed her mind. It would have been hard to explain to Nora.

She opened the door quietly and walked in. Nora was curled up on the couch reading, and Beebee was curled on the floor at her feet. When she saw Lena standing in the doorway, she thumped her tail three times. It made a loud sound in the quiet room.

Nora looked up. "Oh, you're back. I can't wait to tell you what I just decided. I'm really happy about it."

"You ought to lock the door when you're here all by yourself at night, Nora. I always do. You just don't know."

"Okay, I will. But listen. You're not going to believe what a great idea I had."

"Tell me. I'm listening."

"Okay. It's this—I'm going to name the baby Phoenix."

"But what if it's a boy?"

"I'm still going to name it Phoenix. That'll work for a boy. Don't you love it?"

"It's different."

"That means you don't like it."

"No, it doesn't. I just have to think about it for a minute, that's all. It's kind of a hippie name."

"So?"

"Mom is going to hate it."

"Mom hates the whole thing already. I may have to move out because Mom is so upset."

"That would be awful. Don't turn it into a fight."

"Tell Mom that. She's the one who's turning it into a fight."

Lena hung up her jacket and took off her boots and sat down in Jerry's easy chair. "It takes two to make a fight. Mom used to say that when we were little. Remember?"

"I know. But I don't see what I can do about it. The only way not to fight with Mom would be to go out and get an abortion, and I've already made up my mind I'm not doing that. Besides, it's too late."

"Does Mom know it's too late?" Now that she was home, Lena realized how tired she was, and how much of an effort she had been making when she was with Jerry.

"I told her it was too late, but I don't think she was listening. She went off on this long rant about what was everyone going to think and how she and Dad had a really good reputation in town and what was this baby going to do to it."

"Mom can be unfair."

"I know. She's not being fair about this baby. She acts like I got pregnant just to be mean to her."

"She's worried about you."

"She acts like she's worried about herself. Are her friends going to think she's not a good mother because her daughter got pregnant without being married? She's not thinking about me."

"You're not being fair either. It's because you're mad at her. She is worried about you."

"If she was, she'd pay some attention to me. She'd listen to what I have to say about it. She doesn't. She wants me to listen to her."

"When you're not mad anymore, you'll see. Mom was great when I was having Jimmy, and afterward too. She took care of Georgia a lot so I could rest. Especially in the beginning when I was getting up at night with Jimmy. You wait. When the baby is here, she won't be arguing against it the way she is now."

"Maybe so. But right now she treats me like I haven't got any sense, like I haven't thought about what this will mean to me, or to the baby, or to the rest of the family. She makes me feel stupid and worthless."

"She'll find out better. *I* know better. *I* know how much you've thought about it." Lena looked around the room. She was so glad to be home. It would be even better when Jerry was here too. She wondered how the kids were.

"I mean, I know it was dumb to get pregnant. She's right about that. And what's she going to do when I tell her what the baby's name's going to be? She's going to flip out all over again."

"I can see naming it Phoenix if it's a girl, but…."

"It could be a boy's name too. Why not?"

"I don't know. It just doesn't seem like it somehow."

"You just have to get used to it. Then you'll like it. That's just what this baby seems like to me—a magic creature that was almost destroyed and then came back better than ever. You'll see. It's funny about this baby. It's not even here yet, and already it's taking over."

Neither of them said anything for a minute. Lena was thinking how tired she felt and how nice it was going to be to go to bed.

"Anyway," Nora said, "I know it's a girl. I wasn't going to say anything because I was afraid you'd say I was being ridiculous, but I'm so sure. I had this dream. I was carrying a little girl in my arms, and she looked up at me and smiled. She was about Jimmy's age, and she had curly hair." She looked past Lena across the room, as though she was seeing the dream there. "I don't know how I knew she was a girl, but I did. Oh yes, I remember. She was wearing a pink dress. That's kind of dumb, isn't it? That was how I knew she was a girl. It was summer in my dream, and I was walking over to your house holding her. And all the time I was thinking how much I loved her. Then I woke up, and I knew her name was going to be Phoenix."

Suddenly, Lena had to see the kids right away. She needed to know they were both all right. She needed to touch them and kiss them and rearrange their covers. It was a hunger that wouldn't wait. "I'll be right back. I'm just going to take a look at Georgia and Jimmy." She went up the stairs quietly in her sock feet and tiptoed into Georgia's room. Georgia was on her back with her hair fanned out across the pillow. Lena kissed her on the cheek and went to see Jimmy. He was all curled into a ball, with his covers thrown off as usual. Lena kissed him too and covered him up, thinking how different they smelled. She knew that even in complete darkness, she would be able to tell them apart. She went back down the stairs to Nora, thinking about her dream.

"You think I'm being silly, don't you, Lena? Tell me the truth. You don't think my dream has anything to do with this baby, do you? I shouldn't have told you. It's too dumb. It can't be true. I know that's what you're thinking, isn't it?"

"Not at all."

"Then why are you looking at me like that?"

"I don't know. I didn't even know I *was* looking at you. I was thinking about what you said, about your dream, and I was remembering, because I had some dreams when I was pregnant."

"You did? I didn't know that. Why didn't you say so before?"

"I never told anybody but Jerry because it's such a strange thing. I almost don't believe it actually happened. Maybe I made the whole thing up."

"I know. I feel that way too. But that's the way dreams are."

"You can't be sure you're not making it up."

"Well, actually, I guess you are making it up. You make the dream up, don't you?"

Lena laughed.

"But tell me what you dreamed. Tell me what you told Jerry."

"It really wasn't much. I dreamed I was sitting in the back seat of a car, holding a little baby in my arms and looking down at him. That's all. With Georgia, it wasn't even that much. I just saw her in my dreams, and when she was born, I recognized her. That's why I never told anybody. Because there wasn't anything to tell. It's just that when each one of them was born, I had this feeling that I already knew the baby because I'd seen it before."

Nora jumped up and ran to where Lena was sitting and hugged her clumsily and hard. "I'm so glad you told me. That's just what it feels like. I was scared to believe it before."

"Maybe that's another reason why I didn't tell anybody but Jerry. Maybe I was scared to believe it." She stood up, wondering how late it was.

"I'm really glad you told me," Nora said. She put her arms around her again. "I'm so lucky to have you for a big sister."

Lena hugged her and then pushed her away so she could look at her. "Don't believe it too much."

"But you did."

"I know, but supposing it was a coincidence."

"Two times?"

"I don't know, Nora. I'm just scared you will be so sure that you know who this baby is, and if it's a boy, then what? You could feel angry at it, or cheated, or something."

"I didn't think of that."

"Maybe that's why I didn't dare tell anybody my dreams, anybody but Jerry."

"Oh Lena, what about Jerry? I can't believe I forgot all about how you were going to see him. What happened?"

"Jerry wants to come home."

"Wow! I didn't know that."

"I didn't either. I thought we were going to talk about how to divide things up."

"Are you glad?"

"I don't know. I'm not sure how I feel about it. I have to think about it some. He wanted to come home tonight. He thought he was going to. All his stuff was in his car."

"You don't need Jerry. You've been telling me I can take care of this baby by myself. You can do it too. We could be two single mothers together."

"I don't know, Nora. This is Jerry we're talking about. And the kids miss him so much. I just don't know what I ought to do."

"What do you want to do?"

"I don't know that either."

"I wish I could help you. You've helped me so much."

"Maybe I'll know more in the morning. I'm too tired to think about it right now. And you have helped me. You took care of the kids so I could see him. Thanks for doing that."

"It was fun. They were good."

"I'm going to need to see Jerry some more times before this gets figured out. Will it be okay with you to do more babysitting?"

"I'd love to. You know that."

"I can't even give you any money for it until Jerry and I get things figured out. I'm almost out of money."

"I don't need any pay." Nora went to the closet and got her jacket and turned to smile at Lena. "Unless Mom suddenly decides to kick me out."

"She won't do that."

"I don't know. She's awfully upset." She opened the door. "I'll call you tomorrow," she said, and she left.

Lena stood woodenly where she was, half of her thinking about Nora and their conversation, while the other half of her tried to decide whether to brush her teeth or to drop into bed without doing anything to get ready. She didn't want to think about Jerry or Nora or Mom. She didn't even want to think about Georgia and Jimmy. She didn't want to think at all.

Chapter 31

By early afternoon the thermometer said thirty-five degrees. The sun seemed brighter than it had for a long time. The snow sparkled. When Nora stepped out on the porch, she could hear the birds in the trees around the feeder. It was too early to think of spring, but she got hopeful about it anyway. As she stood on the porch in air that was washed clean by the winter cold and full of birdsong, she felt restless, eager for it to be here now, spring and warm weather, when she could shed all the extra clothes, and spring, when Phoenix would come, and she wouldn't be so heavy, laboring under the load of her belly. She felt more like doing something than she had in quite a while.

She had been doing less and less lately. There was no point in looking for a job anymore, since it was getting obvious, even through her baggy clothes, that she would need to leave it soon. And since Mom was so mad at her, Nora didn't feel like doing any of the things she had been doing around the house, little fix-up projects to surprise her. Mom was never pleased these days. She just sighed, or else tried once again to convince Nora she was making a mistake. Nora had never even dared to ask her if she wanted to feel the baby when it kicked. A few days ago Nora tried to tell her that she was starting to get excited about the baby, starting to get eager for the time when she would actually see it and hold it. But Mom didn't want to hear it. She cut Nora off, telling her not to be ridiculous, that she didn't know what she was saying. Nora retreated with hurt feelings, planning to talk to Lena about what it felt like when you were pregnant and getting close to the end and starting to look forward to the day when the baby would be here. She knew it was going to be hard. But that wasn't all it was going to be.

The thing to do was to drive out to see Uncle Cal and Aunt Ursela. It was a beautiful day for a drive, and she hadn't been out there for a while. She needed to tell them about the baby anyway, now that it was all settled.

She thought about leaving Mom and Dad a note saying where she had gone, but she decided not to. She'd be back long before either of them got home, so there wasn't any sense in bothering. She got in the car and rolled down the windows in the front seat, and then she turned on the heat. She had plenty of gas, so she went out College Street and then down Elm and over a small cross street she didn't know the name of, all residential streets, with houses getting progressively poorer and shabbier, until she picked up the two-lane to West Severance on the edge of town.

There the houses thinned out, and the snow banks got bigger. The snow glittered off the fields, making her wish she'd thought to bring sunglasses. Aunt Ursela would like it about the baby, although she might think Phoenix was too hippie a name. Aunt Ursela loved all babies, and she loved to take care of living creatures of every kind. It would be harder to explain to Uncle Cal, but still, he liked her. Maybe he would try to understand.

In West Severance, the houses got close together again. The West Severance general store was on the corner where she turned onto Bear Ridge. That was one thing that hadn't changed since she was in high school. The paved roads were bare, and in some places even dry, but Bear Ridge was rutted, with icy patches under the sand.

The snow banks hung over the road on both sides.

Nora parked in front of Cal and Ursela's big sedan. The dogs came out to bark at her. She went into the mudroom and knocked on the kitchen door. Aunt Ursela said to come in.

She was sitting by the woodstove knitting a red sock. The television was on. She looked up from her knitting and said, "Oh good. It's Nora. This is a surprise." She jumped up and went to the television, still holding her knitting as though she was about to make the next stitch. "Sit down there by the fire, Nora, and get warm."

"Okay. The house smells delicious. Is it bread?"

"It's in the oven. You can have some in a little while." She turned off the television and went back to her seat, still holding her knitting ready to work, and as soon as she sat down, her fingers began to move, smooth and fast.

"I don't want to interrupt your television program."

"It's fine. I don't care. It was just company while I made this sock."

"How are you and Uncle Cal?"

"Fine. Cal still limps, but his foot is almost healed."

"That's good."

"Did you hear about Conrad's accident?"

"No, I didn't. Is he all right?"

"He will be. It's always somethin, ain't it?"

"What happened?"

"He cut himself with his chain saw a couple, three weeks ago. One hundred and twenty-two stitches it took."

"Where was it?"

"On his leg right above his knee. He's lucky. He got himself to the hospital in time."

"I'm glad he's going to be all right."

"Me too."

"Where's Uncle Cal?"

"He's out back somewheres. In his workshop, I guess. How are you?"

"Good. Everybody's fine at home."

"That's good."

"It's a beautiful day outside. It seems like spring."

"We got a lot more winter to get through yet."

"It's already March."

Aunt Ursela laughed and kept on knitting. Her needles clicked in the silence.

Nora watched. "I wish I could knit," she said, thinking of baby clothes.

"It's easy. I could show you some time."

"I'd like that. I'm sorry about Conrad. How's Elsie doing?"

"Fine. We got a letter from her the other day. She was goin to come up when the twins were on their winter break, but her car broke down, and she couldn't make it."

"How old are the twins?"

"They'll be eleven in July. It don't seem possible, does it?"

"No, it doesn't. Elsie's only a few years older than I am."

"But Elsie got started young. She always knew what she wanted. There wasn't any stoppin Elsie when she knew what she wanted."

"I've been thinking about Elsie a lot lately. I wish she lived closer."

"So don't I."

"Why doesn't she move back closer to all of you?"

"She likes workin at the hospital down there, I guess, and the boys have their friends."

"I remember how she was when I was in high school. She was so pretty. That was when she was first married to Mike."

"She's still quite young, even now, I mean."

"I know."

"And she acts like her life is over. She never wears nothin but a man's white shirt and a man's pants. It's no use talkin about it. It's just lucky she has to go to work. At least she looks like a woman when she's in her nurse's uniform. You can't tell Elsie nothin."

Nora tried to think of something to say, but she couldn't think of anything.

"She's still young. She could marry again. Mike might want her to do that—someone to help with the boys. But no, not Elsie. She says she's had her romance and that part was over when Mike died. It's no good talkin to her. She won't listen."

"Maybe she's happy, Aunt Ursela. Maybe that's what she wants to do—be a nurse and take care of her boys. She doesn't have to do it that way. Maybe she wants to."

Aunt Ursela didn't say anything. She might not have heard. She stood up and set her knitting down carefully on the chair and went into the kitchen. Nora could hear her open the oven door. She could hear the clatter of the bread pans and the hollow sound of Aunt Ursela tapping on the bottom of the loaves to see if they were done.

When she came back to her seat, she said, "The bread's done, if you would like a piece. I'll give you a loaf to take home to your folks too."

"Thank you. I'd like some after a while. I thought I would go out and say hello to Uncle Cal first."

Aunt Ursela picked up her knitting and sat down, and immediately her fingers began to move again. "I think he's out in his shop. That's where he said he was goin."

"Okay. I'll be back soon."

In the mudroom, Nora picked up her jacket and boots where she had dropped them on the way in. The mudroom wasn't heated, and they were stiff with cold. She had come out without a hat or mittens again. She always forgot.

She knocked on the door of the shop, but there was no answer. The door creaked as she pushed it open. Uncle Cal wasn't there. After the bright spring day outside, the workshop was dark and cold. It smelled of old oil and sawdust and was cluttered with tools and broken things waiting to be fixed, but it didn't look as though Uncle Cal had been there recently.

Nora shut the door and stood wondering what to do. She could try the barn, or she could go back inside. She was trying to decide, when she heard the sound of banging, metal on metal. It sounded far away, but Nora began to walk in the direction it was coming from, around the back of the house and down the road into the woods. The road had been plowed, and there were fresh tractor tracks to follow.

The tractor was sitting in front of the old sugarhouse. Its engine was running. At intervals, there would be a burst of banging from inside the building.

Nora thought she was moving silently, but before she got close, the two dogs appeared from somewhere to sniff around her legs. She stopped in the open doorway. Uncle Cal was sorting through his sap buckets, banging them apart. He was bent over a stack of buckets with his back to the door. He loosened one at a time with a bang and set it gently onto the new stack. Nora said hello, but he didn't hear her. She was standing there watching him when he picked up the loosened buckets and turned around with the stack in his arms.

That was when he saw her. He was so surprised that he let the stacked buckets slip through his arms. They fell to the floor with a loud crash that echoed around the walls.

"Jesus, Nora. Why didn't you say somethin?"

"I did, Uncle Cal."

"Now I'll have to loosen up them buckets all over again. They're jammed good now."

"I'm sorry. I didn't mean to scare you."

"Talk louder, girl. I can't hear you."

"I'm sorry." Shouted like that, it didn't sound apologetic.

"Well, there's no need to shout at me." He stood up the jammed buckets and reached for his hammer.

There was no light in the sugarhouse except what came through the open door. Farther away from the light Nora could see only dark shapes and shadows. It was cold in the doorway. In front of her was the stale air that had been shut up inside since last spring, and behind her was the pounding engine and the smell of exhaust. Uncle Cal worked calmly in the middle of it all.

When he finished knocking apart the stack of buckets he had dropped, he picked them up and carried them out to the wagon behind the tractor. Nora stepped out of the way and then followed him to the back of the wagon, where she watched him settle the new stack of buckets beside the ones that were already there.

When he straightened up, she took advantage of its being a little quieter out there. "Can I help you? I'd like to."

Uncle Cal looked at her doubtfully. "I've only got the one hammer," he said. "I suppose you could load 'em as I get 'em apart." That was all he said. He went back into the sugarhouse, and Nora followed him and stood watching in the doorway as before.

But when he finished the next stack, he set it gently down in front of Nora's feet and went back into the shadowy interior for more.

Nora looked down at the stacked buckets. They looked heavy. She looked at Uncle Cal bending to work on the new stack. She was either going to have to lift those buckets up and carry them over the icy, rutted road to the back of the wagon, or she was going to have to tell him that she wasn't supposed to lift anything heavy because she was pregnant, and she couldn't help him, even though she had said that she would. And she would have to shout over the roar of the tractor engine. She thought about taking half the stack at a time. Then she looked at Uncle Cal bent over his syrup buckets and banging away with his hammer, and she decided she would just take a chance and hope she wouldn't regret it later.

She tried to lift the way you were supposed to. How ironic if she did something to hurt the baby after making up her mind that she wanted it after all. She picked up the stack of buckets, and, staggering a little, she carried them over the ruts in the road to the back of the wagon. She went slowly, trying to be careful. When she got back to the sugarhouse door, there was another stack waiting for her.

They must have done about a hundred buckets that way. Nora thought they did ten stacks of ten each, but she wasn't sure because she kept losing count. After what she thought must be at least a hundred buckets loaded into the wagon since she began to help, and only Uncle Cal knew how many before that, he said they had enough.

He stepped out of the sugarhouse and climbed up into the seat of the tractor. He was slow, but he seemed to be able to do it now. His foot must be healed. Nora thought about saying something, but she decided not to.

Uncle Cal leaned down. "I'll meet you back at the house, unless you want to ride on the wagon."

Nora shook her head.

"Close the sugarhouse door, will you?" The tractor moved off slowly, making even more noise than before. The dogs came hurrying around the side of the building. They started after the tractor and then turned back to stay with Nora. Slowly, it became quieter. Nora stood there as the sunshine and birdsong and the smell of the pine trees poured back into the vacuum left by the receding noise. She felt all right. She had gotten away with it, unless something happened later on. But she wasn't pleased with herself.

Now that Uncle Cal was gone, she couldn't understand why she had carried all those heavy buckets just because he said she could help. Why hadn't she simply said they were too heavy? She ought to be able to say no. She was sure she could. But just to be safe, she decided to go into the house because he might be planning to unload those buckets too, and she might feel compelled to help even without being asked.

Instead of knocking, Nora opened the door a little way and peeked in. Aunt Ursela was sitting in the same place, knitting as before. The only change was that the sock was noticeably longer. "Can I come in?"

Aunt Ursela jumped, and the ball of yarn dropped to the floor and rolled under the chair.

"I'm sorry. I scared you."

"Just foolishness. Come in."

Nora opened the door wide and stepped inside into warm air that smelled of fresh bread. It was thick and soft after the icy air of outdoors. It was like stepping into a hot shower.

"Go cut yourself some bread, honey. The butter's out there on the table. You know where everythin is."

"Thank you. I will. Your sock is a lot bigger than it was when I left."

"Yes, well, it don't take long to knit a sock after you've made as many as I have."

Nora got some bread and butter for herself. She put it on a small plate and sat down with Aunt Ursela by the woodstove. It felt wonderfully safe and cozy after being outside. "Uncle Cal's getting out his sap buckets."

"Oh, that's what he's doin."

"His foot seems completely healed."

"It's gettin there. It hurts him a lot at night, but I guess it'll be all right in time."

"That's good. I mean, there are so many little bones in your foot. It could've...I don't know what. It could've been a lot worse, couldn't it?"

"You could say that."

Nora sat there, eating her bread. It was getting close to four o'clock, time to be leaving, and she still hadn't told either of them about the baby.

She had just about decided she was going to come back another day to tell them, when Uncle Cal stuck his head in the door. "There you are, Nora," he said, "I thought maybe you decided to stay up there at the sugarhouse."

"Don't hold the door open, Cal. Do you want some fresh bread?"

Uncle Cal looked around the room. "I suppose I could do with some. I'll clean off my boots." He shut the door.

Aunt Ursela gave a little sigh and stood up. She put her knitting carefully down on her chair. With a groan, she reached underneath the chair for the ball of yarn and put it with the knitting. Then she went heavily into the kitchen to fix Uncle Cal a plate.

He came in and stood by the woodstove, waiting to be served. He didn't offer to help.

Aunt Ursela came back and handed him the plate. "There you go, Cal. Do you want a cup of tea to go with it?"

"I don't guess so. I'm goin back out in a minute."

Aunt Ursela sat back down and began to knit again, and for a few minutes no one said anything.

Nora sat there thinking how this was her chance. It wasn't often that they were both in the same room. She was nervous, so she burst into the silence without giving herself a chance to think about it. "I've got something to tell you both. Some news to tell you. I'm going to have a baby."

Silence. There was no response at all. The words dropped like stones into a still pool of water. They were there, and then they were gone. There wasn't even a ripple. After a little while, she said, as though she had been asked, "In about two months."

After another long silence, Uncle Cal said, "Well, that is news, Nora. I thought myself that you were puttin on a little weight."

"You did?"

"I didn't think much about it, but I thought so. Yes."

"Why didn't you tell me, Cal?" Aunt Ursela said crossly. "I wouldn't have sent her out on a sleigh ride with Biff if I had of known."

"You don't listen when I tell you things anyhow, Ursela, so why would I bother?"

"But, Aunt Ursela, I didn't know about the baby then either, not for sure anyway, and I had a wonderful time on the sleigh ride. I'm so glad I got to do that."

"I didn't even know you had a sweetheart, let alone this. You should of brought him out to meet us."

This wasn't going the way Nora thought it would. She had been so sure Aunt Ursela would be pleased. "I couldn't bring him out to meet you...for lots of reasons...but mostly because he's not my sweetheart any more."

Then there was another silence worse than the one before. Nora tried to smile at Aunt Ursela, but she was looking at her sock. "But I'm going to have the baby anyway." More curdled silence. This was getting as bad as telling Mom and Dad. The older generation, no matter who they were, just couldn't seem to comprehend new ways of doing things.

Aunt Ursela looked up from her sock just long enough to say, "All by yourself?"

"It's what I want to do."

Aunt Ursela said, "Oh goodness."

Nora tried a small tentative smile on Uncle Cal.

"Does Biff know?" he said.

"I'm going to go by his place today and tell him."

Uncle Cal was nodding. "That's okay then." But he was looking at Ursela, not Nora. "Young people have to do things their own way."

"My Lord, Cal, you sound just like when you're talkin about Elsie—whatever she wants to do, you can find a reason why it's a good idea. But look at Elsie. She's not happy. She acts like she's waitin for Mike to come back. These young people, they think they know everythin, but they don't know as much as they think they do. Elsie's had a awful hard time over the years, even though she had Mike's pension and help from his friends. And here's Nora settin out to do the same thing."

"If someone wants to do somethin, it shouldn't stop 'em if it's hard. They ought to do it anyway. Elsie would have had those boys even if she'd known Mike would be killed. There wasn't any stoppin Elsie, and Nora is quite a bit like her. She'll have to find a way to make it work, just like Elsie has."

"I think I can make it all right, Uncle Cal."

"The trouble with you, Ursela, you get a idea stuck in your head, and you can't let it go." He took his empty plate to the sink and came back. "You'll do fine, Nora. Don't let anybody tell you different." As he went out the door, he said, "I'll be out back, Ursela."

The door shut, and they sat there in the silence that wasn't cozy any more. After a little while, Nora took her empty plate to the sink. When she came back, she stopped by the door. "I'd better get going, Aunt Ursela. I was going to stop off and see Biff on my way home.

Aunt Ursela made a sniff or a snort, some kind of noise, and looked up from her knitting, still holding her hands in position to begin again. "Tell your parents we said hello."

"Yes, I will. I'll be back soon."

"You do that."

She didn't mention the loaf of bread, so Nora didn't either. "Tell Uncle Cal I said goodbye."

The smell of ice was in the air again, and the sunlight was fading into evening. The dogs came around the side of the house to sniff her legs, reading there what she had been doing in the house. She patted each long, intelligent head and got into the car.

It would be dark soon. The sun wasn't blindingly bright on the snow any more. If she hadn't said that she was going to Biff's today to tell him, she would have gone straight home. It was funny that it took about ten minutes to drive to Biff's, since his land was a piece cut out of the Willard farm. Biff showed her on a map how the only roads made a wide circle. Maybe his truck wouldn't be there, and she would have to come back another day. But what would she do if his truck was there and he wasn't in his barn? She had never been to his house without being invited. She pictured herself walking up that trail through the shadowy, almost-dark forest. It was an aspect of living in a cabin in the woods that she had never considered before.

And what about coming back? It would be completely dark then. He might walk her to her car, although after she told him what she was going to tell him, he might not. His truck was there. She pulled in beside it and sat there looking at the barn, thinking how she would peek in the door to see if he was there.

Just then the door opened, and he came out with his two big dogs walking one on each side of him. He was smiling.

Nora got out of the car and stood by the open door. He was so pleased to see her that it made her shy. "I was visiting Uncle Cal and Ursela, so I thought I would come over." She shut the door of her car.

"I just got home," he said. "But it won't take me long to get a fire going, and I can come back down later to feed the horses." He patted the head of one of his dogs.

"I can't stay," Nora said, thinking of the dark trail and the wild animals watching as she walked by. "I just stopped to say hello. Can I please help you feed your horses? Is that what you were doing?"

"Oh sure," he said. "If that's what you want." He looked disappointed.

"You'll have to tell me what to do," she said.

They went into the barn. "There isn't much. The horses are getting a drink of water. I'll bring 'em in, and we'll give 'em some hay and grain, and that's it."

When Biff shut the door, it was dark in the barn. The only light came from the open door at the other end, a bright square with the two golden horses standing in it.

Biff walked up to the first horse and caught her by the halter and spoke to her. She moved forward, setting her huge foot down with a hollow ringing sound on the wooden floor, so powerful that Nora pressed herself back against the wall to be safely out of the way. The horse walked out of the light into her stall, and Biff shut the half-door behind her.

"That must be Queenie," Nora said.

Biff looked around at her with such a pleased expression that she felt like a phony.

"I saw the sign over her door," she said, embarrassed, waving her hand toward the board with Queenie's name painted on it.

Duchess stood obediently in the doorway until it was her turn. When they were both in, Biff said, "I have to turn on the lights so I can get the grain."

With the snap of the switch, everything jumped into hard-cornered visibility. "It's so bright, it hurts," Nora said. "I was just thinking how beautiful the horses looked, coming through the door from the brightness into the shadows."

"They hate it too. They can't stop blinking when the light goes on."

"It was like a painting when they were standing in the doorway."

"Sometimes I'm glad I don't have electricity in my house," Biff said. He went to get the grain for the horses.

The horses stood waiting for him, looking down the hall toward the door they knew he would come through any minute. Their ears pricked forward and moved slightly to pick up every sound of what he was doing.

It was pleasant being with him in his barn. It made Nora forget for the moment that it was getting late, that she had to get home because Mom and Dad didn't know where she was, and it had put out of her mind why she had come to see Biff in the first place.

But when he came through the door with a dish of grain, Nora was suddenly in a hurry to get it over with. As he walked past her, she said, "Biff, I came over today to tell you I'm going to have a baby." The words came out in a rush.

Biff kept walking past her so that she was actually speaking to his back. When he got to Queenie's stall, he fumbled trying to open the half-door, and the dish of grain fell to the floor.

"Oh, I'm sorry," Nora said, jumping forward. "I didn't mean to blurt it out like that. Let me help."

Biff squatted down and started to push the pile of grain into the dish. Queenie was reaching her head out as far as she could, trying to help in her own way, and probably wondering why humans did things so strangely.

Biff pushed the grain into a pile. "It's not your fault. It just slipped out of my hand when I was opening the door."

Nora knelt down beside him. "But I shouldn't have told you that way. It was too abrupt." She scooped up a double handful of grain from the pile and put it back into the dish. She couldn't see his face.

"It's really fine. I can do it. You don't need to."

"But I want to." Up close he smelled like trees, a smell so strong it dominated the smell of horses.

"It hasn't got anything to do with you. There. That's plenty. There's too much dirt mixed in with the rest." He stood up, and holding the grain dish in one hand, he reached out the other to help her up.

"Thanks," she said. He still wasn't looking at her.

He opened the door and gave Queenie her grain and then went back to get the grain for Duchess. "I'm glad you told me your news," he said, as he walked away. "I wish you every happiness."

"Happiness doesn't have anything to do with it," she said, watching him giving grain to Duchess. "I'm not thinking about happiness. I've gotten myself into a mess, and I'm trying to get out."

"Just a minute," he said. "I have to go up in the loft and throw down a bale of hay."

When he came back, he broke the bale open between the two horse stalls, and as he did, and still without looking at her, he said, "You don't have to have a baby just because you get pregnant."

"I know."

"Unless you're a Catholic or something."

"I would've told you before, but I thought I was going to do that.... get an abortion, I mean."

"You weren't obligated to tell me."

"I came out today to tell Uncle Cal and Aunt Ursela. She was cross about it. It really surprised me. I thought Uncle Cal would be the one who would think it was wrong to have a baby when you were all alone. But Uncle Cal was nice about it. Aunt Ursela was the one who thought it was awful."

"Cal is quite a guy. He can always surprise you."

"Did you ever meet Elsie?"

"No."

"She's their daughter. She got married right after high school, and then her husband and his two best friends went to Vietnam. I used to think Elsie was the luckiest person in the world. It was Elsie and the three of them, Mike—that was her husband—and Brad and Pete. They did everything together. Elsie always looked like she was having so much fun. But Mike got killed in Vietnam, and Elsie was pregnant. I don't even know if Mike knew before he died."

"That's sad."

"I know. And then Elsie had twin boys. She named them Brad and Pete. They're about ten now. Elsie's a nurse in Randolph. She cut her hair really short, and she always wears men's clothes, and she's raising those boys all by herself. But I think if she can do it, I can, and that's pretty much what Uncle Cal said."

Biff was shaking the dust out of the hay and putting loose armfuls into the horses' hay feeders. Without stopping work, he said, "What did you mean when you said you'd gotten yourself in a mess?"

"It's a mess to have a baby without a husband, or even a boyfriend, or a job, or a place to live, isn't it? It seems like it to me."

"That sounds kind of old-fashioned. What about women's lib? What about all this talk about not needing men?"

"Don't make fun of me."

"I'm not. I thought women didn't need men these days. I thought that was the new way of doing things."

"I don't know what you mean. That doesn't have anything to do with me." After all these months of sorting out what she wanted to do about this baby, now, when she was finally sure that she wanted it and was going to have it, the news seemed to upset everyone else. "I wasn't ever particularly a women's-lib person."

"Here you are talking about having a baby, and you don't say anything about the father. You didn't get pregnant all by yourself, did you?" He smiled to show that he meant what he said as a joke, but it wasn't a joke.

"My situation is a lot more ordinary and old-fashioned than that," Nora said, pretending to look in at Duchess so Biff wouldn't see how close she was to tears. "Maybe I'll tell you about it some time."

"The father has rights too."

"You don't know anything about it, and I have to be getting home. My parents will be wondering where I went."

"Thanks for stopping by," Biff said, still handing out the hay.

Nora had to walk around him. She concentrated on where she put her feet so that she wouldn't step on the hay, and she forced herself to go slowly, although she wanted to get out of there as fast as she could. She didn't say goodbye, and neither did he.

Later on, when she thought about the conversation, she couldn't remember why it got so angry. It seemed to be all right, and then all of a sudden, it wasn't. At least she had done it. She wouldn't have to go back. She never even got to tell him the baby's name. She wondered whether he would have liked it. But it didn't matter now.

Chapter 32

George got out of the car and slammed the door. Two big collie dogs came running up from the woods road. They were barking. He hadn't been out to the old home place in years—he didn't even know how many. It felt strange to be here. The dogs were unfamiliar, but the house looked pretty much the same. There was a large cattle truck parked off to the side. If he went inside, he'd have to sit down and visit with Ursela, but if he backtracked the dogs' trail, he'd probably find Cal. The dogs had almost certainly been with Cal when he drove up, and it was Cal he wanted to see.

He walked down the woods road under the bare trees. The snow was still deep, but Cal had plowed. There were lots of tracks on the road, Cal and the dogs going both ways. There were horse tracks too, large ones, and that surprised him until he remembered the cattle truck. He didn't think Cal had horses.

The dogs walked beside him, assuming he knew where he was going, and he hadn't gone very far before he did. He should have known all along. Of course Cal would be in the sugarhouse.

The door was open, but Cal had his back to it. George didn't say anything for a minute. The sweet steam and the sound of the boiling sap brought back so many memories. For a few minutes he was a child again, and that was Dad, standing tall and thin and a little hunched, rowing with the skimming spoon in the bubbling pan.

Cal skimmed off some foam and threw a big spoonful into a bucket under the arch, and as he did, he saw George standing in the doorway. "What the hell?" he said. "How'd *you* get here?"

"I drove out. You're boiling already."

"The first. I'd like to make a little fancy. How come you're here? You ain't been out since Ma died."

"I came out to see you, to see how your foot is. Is it going to be okay to be sugaring?"

"Probably not. Standin on cement. Walkin a lot. It'll just have to take it."

"Suppose it keeps it from healing properly?"

"You sound like Ursela. I only put out three hundred taps, and I have a guy helpin me. That's the best I can do. I can't sit around for the rest of my life."

"I've been feeling bad since you came to see me in my office. I want to help you. I just don't think you have a case. Isn't there any way I can help you as a brother, not as a lawyer?"

Cal threw down another splat of foam. "For Chrissakes, George. A lawyer's what I need."

There wasn't any way to answer that. He watched Cal dip up some syrup from the take-off corner and study it as it dripped back into the pan. It was just the way Dad used to do it.

"The damn law says I ain't allowed to take care of Jason LaRue myself. Okay...if it feels that way about it." He held up the skimmer, dripping syrup, and looked at it again. "Then the law ought to do it for me. But does it? No. It wishy-washes around and ends up on Jason LaRue's side."

Cal put down the skimmer and opened the firebox door. The fire roared and flames curled out the top of the opening. Cal got the long poker and shifted the fire around some before he threw on new wood. "Everybody says the law is soft on criminals these days, but, by God, I never thought I would have to be the one to prove it."

"What can I tell you, Cal? If you don't have evidence, you don't have a case."

"If you got a guy that got hurt, and you got a guy that hurt him, I don't see what more you need. The rest is just lawyer games." Cal studied the syrup sheeting off the skimmer. "Okay," he said. "I guess it's time. Here goes." He put a bucket on the floor under the spout and fastened the flannel strainer over it with clothespins. Then he opened the spout.

George didn't say anything. He remembered how tense Dad used to get when he was taking off syrup. So many moments he had forgotten came pouring back into his mind as he watched.

Cal closed the spout and checked the sap level in both pans. "Dad would give it to me if he was here to see how I stoked the fire before I took off syrup. Remember how he used to have a fit about that?"

"I forgot that, I guess."

"He was sure we'd burn up the pans. I wouldn't have done it either, except we got talkin, and I forgot. I got away with it this time anyhow." He brought the bucket of new syrup over to the doorway and lifted the flannel. "What do you think? It might be fancy. There's half a gallon anyways." He set the bucket down on the bench in the corner.

George said, "This brings back things I haven't thought about for years. Mostly, I guess, it's Dad I'm thinking about, but Ma used to be down here too, didn't she?"

"We all worked our butts off at sugarin. I don't know why. There ain't that much money in it."

"I remember that. I remember how tired we got. Sometimes they'd let us skip school."

"Not very often. Besides, I thought you liked school. I was the one that hated it."

"I loved those days when we got to stay home."

Cal opened the firebox door and threw in a log and then straightened up to skim off some more foam. Clouds of steam rose around him. Something about the way he stood and moved around the arch was just like Dad, even though Cal was taller.

George said, "When you're down here boiling, does it make you think of when we were kids?"

Cal didn't say anything for a few minutes, moving the skimmer slowly around the pan. Then he said, "Mostly I think about when it was so hard, when Dad was startin to get sick and didn't want us to notice that he couldn't keep up the way he used to. I'd have to do extra and pretend I didn't."

"I didn't know that."

"You wasn't here, that's why. You went to the war, and you never came back."

"That's not so! I *did* come back. The only thing I wanted all those years *was* to come back. I always thought if I got killed, my ghost would come back. That's how homesick I was." He couldn't believe Cal had gotten it wrong all these years. He wished he could think of the right thing to say to make Cal understand how it was. "I spent the whole war thinking about home, how it was, what you all were doing, and what it would be like when I came home at last."

"But when you got back, we wasn't good enough for you no more."

"I don't see how you can *say* such a thing, Cal."

Cal threw a skimmerful of foam at the bucket. "Because it's true, that's why. You went overseas, and you saw the world, and after that, we wasn't good enough for you no more."

"You've got it all wrong, Cal. If you only knew how much I missed all of you, how I longed to be home again, how the vision of the farm in my mind was the only thing that kept me going all those awful years."

Cal threw down another glob of foam. "You never said nothin like that in your letters."

"How could I?"

"You sounded like you was havin quite the time over there."

"I didn't want Ma to know what it was really like. I didn't want to worry her."

"I think it hurt her some to think you liked it so much out there.

And when you got home, you didn't stay. You moved into town as quick as you could."

"When I got home, nobody needed me here any more. It was like the hole I left had filled in, and there wasn't any space for me any more."

Cal spoke so softly it was as though he was talking to himself. "I was so afraid you wouldn't come home. All those years, it was the only thing I wanted."

"Really, Cal? I wish I'd known that."

"Well, it wasn't something I could come out and *say*. Besides, there was so much work, and Dad wasn't well. I didn't have time to say nothin."

"I wish you had. Everybody was so busy, and I couldn't seem to get back into it. I just didn't fit anywhere. I think I was more homesick when I got home than I was in the war."

"You were the one who didn't want to talk. Every time I tried to find out about the war, you'd tell me I couldn't understand what it was like. You thought we were all too stupid, or too out of date, since you'd been out there and seen the world."

"You've got it wrong, Cal. No one had time to listen, and I didn't want to make a nuisance of myself, talking about stuff you didn't want to hear about. The only ones who had time to listen to my war stories were Conrad and Paul, and all they wanted to hear was what kind of gun I used and how many Germans I thought I'd killed."

Cal picked up a spoonful of syrup from the finishing corner and watched it drip back into the pan. He stood there for a minute, looking at the boiling sap and the shifting clouds of steam. Then he picked up another spoonful and watched it fall back into the bubbling pan. "The way I remember it, I tried to get you to talk about what it was like over there, and you said you couldn't tell me nothin because I couldn't understand what you were talkin about. You didn't *say* I was too dumb, but I think that's what you meant. I guess that's why you went off with Ken Earle and Joe Bisonette and those other guys from town."

"I was lonely. I felt like I didn't belong anywhere any more. Those guys had been through what I'd been through. They felt the same way. All I wanted was to come back home and fit in again."

Cal held up another skimmerful of syrup and let it sheet back into the pan. "Time to take off a little more, I guess." He put the bucket back under the arch and opened the spout to let the hot golden syrup out.

George stood in the doorway, remembering how it was when he came home, how it was just like it was right now, him standing and watching, wanting to help, wanting to be part of it, and not remembering what was needed. If he asked Cal what he could do, Cal would say, "Nothin," if he bothered to answer at all.

Cal watched the pan a minute and then lifted the flannel filter off one side of the bucket so he could inspect the new syrup. "Looks pretty good," he said. He poured the new syrup in with the other finished syrup. "I got to check the storage tank and see if I got enough sap left, and I got to get some wood in, George. Look out of the way."

George stepped out of the doorway so Cal could go out. He thought about following to help, but Cal hadn't asked him to. He didn't want to get dirty, and he didn't want Cal to mock him for trying not to get dirty. So he stood undecided, telling himself that someone needed to watch the boiling pans.

Cal made several trips, stacking the firewood beside the arch. Then he opened the firebox doors and rearranged the coals with the long poker. Sparks flew out, and the fire roared. He put in some wood and closed the doors. After he had picked up the skimming spoon and checked both pans, he said, "I guess you thought you went away to fight for your country, and for all of us, and when you finally got home again, you found that your own brother had robbed you of your share of the family farm." He said it shyly and without looking directly at George.

"What?" George said. It took him by surprise. "I never thought that. Did you think that was why I left? It was me. I didn't fit in anymore. I didn't know what needed to be done and what was coming next and how you were doing things. It seemed like I'd forgotten everything. I didn't belong anywhere. It was the worst time in my life, worse than combat. But it wasn't your fault. There wasn't anything either of us could have done about it. And it turned out all right in the end, didn't it?"

"I guess."

"But it wasn't you, Cal. I don't want you to think that. Did you ever talk to Ma and Dad about it? I wonder what they thought."

"No. I didn't. They were both proud of you because you fought for your country and because you got a education. Ma particularly used to talk about that—more than I liked to hear. You did so much with your life, and I did nothin with mine."

George was shocked. "I can't believe what I'm hearing. All these years—I never would have guessed we were so far apart. How could you think that?"

"You got to see the world. I never saw nothin. I ain't even been out of Vermont."

"But you've lived your life the way you wanted to, on your own terms, on your own land, familiar with everything about it, all its moods, all its seasons. I've been noticing lately how much I've given up, how much I lost by moving to town."

Cal skimmed over the boiling pan and threw down a skimmerful of dirty foam. "You wouldn't have to be a stranger out here. It ain't that long a trip."

"I know. I can't explain how I got so cut off. I've been hearing about you from Nora. She's been coming out here some since she moved back, hasn't she?"

"She was out the other day to tell us about the baby. I'd thought I noticed somethin recently."

"I didn't notice a thing, and I saw her every day."

"That's probably why. What do you think of her plans?"

"Plans? I didn't know she had any, but maybe that's because I wasn't paying enough attention."

"Havin this baby all by herself, no husband, nor nothin."

"I don't know what I think about that. She's determined to do it. Laurie is upset."

Cal said, "She's got sand in her craw. She's like Elsie."

"That's a good person to be like. Elsie hasn't had an easy time of it, but she does fine."

"Nora's tough-minded, like Elsie. Must be they get it from us."

George laughed.

Cal went into the corner of the sugarhouse behind the arch and came back with a pint bottle of Canadian Club whiskey. He unscrewed the cap and took a drink and held the bottle out to George.

George hesitated. He had decided not to drink anything any more, and to his surprise, it hadn't even been that difficult until now. Now he was being tested.

"If you can't drink without a glass, I might be able to find you somethin," Cal said, still holding out the bottle.

George took it then. "No, Cal, it's not that."

"You won't get any germs that way. The whiskey kills 'em."

George was holding the bottle in his hand, and there were all these reasons on both sides—first and at the top of the list, he wanted to. He knew just how it would taste and how it would feel—a hot flame that he could follow down into his stomach, making him come alive. Then there was Cal, and how it was a friendly gesture, a gesture of solidarity. He didn't want to insult Cal by turning it down.

"Give it back here then, if you don't want any. I'll drink your share."

"It's not that, Cal. I'm just surprised. I didn't know you drank."

Cal reached for the bottle and took another swig, exaggerating, actually saying, "Ahhh," when he lowered the bottle. "There's a lot you don't know. Do you want some, or don't you?"

"All right. Give it here."

"Don't do me no favors. If you don't want it, don't take it. You won't break my heart."

George snatched the bottle and took a big gulp and watched the hot ball of it all the way down. He wasn't immediately desperate for a second gulp. Did that mean he wasn't really an alcoholic?

Cal watched him. "The way I remember it," he said, "you used to be able to put away quite a bit of liquor. You were way ahead of me."

"I know," George said. "That's just the trouble. Recently I've been wondering about myself. Do you ever?"

"What?"

"Do you ever worry that it's got too much of a hold on you?"

"No, I don't. But I haven't had your opportunities. It takes money, and you got to get in to town, or at least into West Severance, to buy the stuff."

"You could've found a way, if you wanted to. Lots of people do."

Cal took the bottle and gulped another drink. "What's your point?" he said, wiping his mouth.

"Lately I've been wondering about myself. I haven't told anybody this, because I really couldn't, but I've been to a couple of AA meetings, and I've decided not to drink anymore at all."

Cal grinned at him and held out the bottle. He didn't say anything.

George took it from him. "You old devil, Cal. Don't you have any trouble with liquor at all?" He took another drink.

"My only trouble is how to get it, and where to hide it when I do."

"I know what you mean." He handed Cal the bottle. It wasn't a big bottle, and it was about half empty now. "I've been wondering lately about what I've been missing. You, for one thing."

"I've been right here the whole time. It ain't like I'm hard to find."

"I know. That's what I can't explain. And it's not what you said, that I thought I was better than you. It's not that at all. That's why I think I've got a problem. It might not be what anybody else would call a drinking problem, but it's getting in the way for me, and it just crept up on me, so I didn't notice. It wasn't until you were in the hospital and Nora decided to come back home that I saw how much time I had missed—how many years since I'd been out to the old place, or seen you, how little time I spent with Nora. That was when I saw that the center of my life was the time I spent alone in my office with my work....and with a drink. I don't know if I've got a drinking problem or not, but I can see that I don't want to do that anymore. So I've decided to quit while I still can."

Cal put the cap on the bottle and slid it into his back pocket. "Well, I admire that, George."

"I came out here today—and I'm really glad I did—to see if there was any way I could give you a hand, not as a lawyer, but as a brother."

"I doubt it. A lawyer's what I need."

"But now I see that I really came out to spend some time with you. This about helping you was just an excuse."

"I can always find work if you want it. You used to know how," Cal said. He opened the firebox doors and started to poke at the fire. "I hear 'em comin. Now we'll get goin again." Sparks billowed up, mixing with the clouds of steam.

George stepped back into the doorway, and as he did, something caught his eye up the woods road. Coming down the hill was a team of large workhorses, golden horses with white manes. They were stepping carefully, hunkered down a little, holding back the sap sled.

"What's this?" George said in surprise, although, of course, he knew.

Cal was loading a log into the fire. "That would be Biff. I told you about him. He's just in time too. I was about to have to let the fire go down for lack of sap."

Biff stopped the horses uphill of the sugarhouse and stepped off the sled. He nodded to George and looped the reins over the hame of the near horse. Then he set about connecting hoses from the gathering tank to the storage tank.

George watched the huge horses. They stood quietly, shifting their feet a little, but not enough to move the sled. They were sweaty across their chests under the harness, and they were breathing hard enough so that George could hear the sound of their breath over the sound of the boiling sap. After a few minutes, he could also hear the sap running into the storage tank.

George watched Biff as he walked over to join them. He wasn't a big man, but he was solid, with something of a cowboy about him.

"This here's my brother," Cal said, when he saw Biff in the door. "How'd you do?"

"Good," Biff said. "The tank's nearly full. It's still running a little on the south side."

"We can go on for a while then. It looks pretty good. There's a gallon finished." He pointed the skimmer at the bucket of syrup.

Biff had been looking at George standing beside him in the doorway. Now he took off his work glove and held out his hand. "Biff Barker," he said. "I'm a friend of your daughter's."

"Nora?" George said, but he knew it was Nora. He was wondering what the man meant by friend.

"Biff's the guy who found Jason LaRue for me," Cal said, skimming in the boiling sap. It was going hard again. There was so much steam that the pans had almost disappeared.

"What do you think Cal ought to do, Mr. Willard?"

"George," said George.

"Okay. What do you think?"

"I've been telling him he needs some evidence, but he doesn't like to hear it."

Biff nodded. "LaRue almost admitted it to us," he said. "But he knows enough not to say anything if the law comes around. He knows we don't have anything."

They both looked at Cal. It wasn't clear whether he was listening, but he scooped up a blob of dirty foam and threw it violently at the bucket. Parts of him disappeared into the shifting clouds of steam.

Biff said, "I'd better go check how it's running into the storage tank. It was nice to meet you."

"Same here," George said. He watched Cal rowing in the pan with the steam rolling up in clouds around him. It was getting late in the afternoon, and he was beginning to feel the damp and the chill. "I'd better be getting back into town, Cal," he said.

"Okay."

"I'm really glad I came out."

"Yup."

"It was good to see you."

"Yup."

"And to talk about things."

Cal threw down some foam and turned around to look at him. "I think so too, George. And I mean that." That was a lot for Cal to say, especially with Biff possibly within hearing distance.

George started down the woods road, and then he turned back. "Oh Cal," he said. "I can't believe I forgot to ask about Conrad. Nora told me about his accident. Is he all right?"

"He will be. I mean his leg will be. I don't know if he can recover from all the time he lost. He's just now gettin to where he can go back in the woods again. He ain't been able to work in a month, and of course the bills keep comin. I doubt he can recover from that."

"I wish I could do something."

Cal looked around at him. "You could make all his payments for him, George. That would help."

"I don't know...I don't think...."

"See," Cal said grinning. "That's what I mean. When you help somebody is when you give 'em what they need."

Later, on the drive home, George let himself wonder about Biff. He seemed unremarkable until you considered his horses. He wondered if Nora had told him about the baby. An interesting question, but one without an answer. He certainly couldn't ask Nora.

Chapter 33

It was mid-afternoon when Cal parked the car in the driveway and walked up to the back door. Paul's house wasn't much to look at, and it wasn't in good shape, but Cal always had to admire the location. From the dooryard you could see the whole of Severance lying in the valley below. It was a beautiful spot.

Paul opened the door. "Dad," he said, surprised. "What're you doin here?"

"I had to go to the feed store, so it wasn't much out of my way."

"Come in and sit down. I was just havin my mornin coffee. Want some?" He walked over to the stove in his sock feet.

Cal took off his hat and opened his jacket. "No thanks. I can't stay but a minute."

"Well, sit down, anyhow." Paul sat down at the kitchen table. He'd left his cigarette burning in the ashtray. He picked it up and took a long pull on it.

Cal sat down across from him and set his hat beside him on the flowery tablecloth. "You still workin the night shift then?"

Paul nodded. "Nine to five," he said, grinning. "I come home, do my chores, and go to bed. When I get up some time in the afternoon, I have the place to myself—like now. It suits me. Are you sugarin this year?"

"Tryin to."

"What about your foot then, Dad?"

"What about it? I can't sit around for the rest of my life. Biff Barker's helpin me. We've only had the one run so far. We made four gallons of fancy."

"That's good then."

"We were pleased. We've only got three hundred taps out."

Paul looked toward the window. "Nothin today, I guess."

"It's supposed to be warm and rainy for a couple of days. That's how come I'm in town. I was thinkin I might take my huntin day."

"What?"

"I meant to do it before I started sugarin, but I ran out of time."

Paul lit a new cigarette off the stump of the old one. "I don't know what you meant to do."

"I thought I might want to ask you to do my chores tomorrow mornin so I could go deer huntin."

"Now?"

"Well, I couldn't do it before with my foot the way it was."

"Are you goin to try to shoot a deer?"

"That's what you usually do when you go huntin."

"But that's against the law. Why don't you wait until fall since you've waited this long?"

"Because that would be *next year's* huntin season. It was last fall that I missed my days. I've been tellin myself right along that I was goin to make up for it."

Paul blew out a long plume of smoke. "Go up without a gun then."

"You smoke too much. You know that? You ought to cut back."

"If you didn't have a gun, you wouldn't be doin nothin illegal."

"God damn it! The law's all over me every time I turn around. It didn't used to be this way. I have to fight for my rights before they get me in a damn corner. The next thing you know, they'll be takin our guns away from us. What're you goin to say when they do that?"

"Whoa, Dad. Calm down."

"Why should I? It ain't right. Somebody's got to stand up for themselves."

Paul stubbed out his cigarette. Then he looked at Cal across the table. "Look, Dad, I'll be glad to do your chores for you, if you'll go without your gun. That's all. The meat wouldn't be any good this time of year anyhow."

"Forget about it. Just forget about it," Cal said. He stood and zipped up his jacket. "It's not worth it. Just drop it."

"Dad, I'd love to help you out. But...."

Cal picked up his hat off the table. The more he thought about it, the madder he got. "Damn it, Paul. I didn't ask you to help me. I said, 'I might want to ask you.' That's what I said. But I didn't ask you. I didn't, I haven't, and I won't." He opened the door and walked out, without another look at Paul and without saying goodbye.

Driving home, he wondered why he had even bothered to stop by Paul's. Tomorrow morning he would milk and feed the animals and then go. He would tell Ursela that he had to be up in the woods first thing. She would assume it was something to do with making syrup, so he probably wouldn't have to tell any lies about it. He could ask her to leave his breakfast, and he could come down later and eat it cold and clean the barn. He wouldn't need Paul at all.

The next morning when he stepped out of the barn, the day was just beginning. The light was soft and pearl-gray. It was going to be a day of water, of mist, of fog. Everything was dissolving. The rain was fine. As much water was going up as was coming down.

He had brought his hunting jacket and his rifle down to the barn, and he had made a special trip up to the house carrying the morning milking so he could leave for the woods from the barn. He didn't want Ursela to see him carrying his gun. But just as he stepped out the door and saw how everything was softening and melting, he remembered he didn't have his snowshoes. They were down at the sugarhouse, so he had to walk by the house carrying his gun after all. He went around the back where there were fewer windows. It was ridiculous to have to sneak around on his own place. If he hadn't talked to Paul, he wouldn't have felt that way. It was Paul's fault.

By the time he got to the sugarhouse, he could feel the wet seeping into his old boots, even though he had put plastic bread bags over his socks before he put his feet into the boots. He had waterproofed them with neatsfoot oil last night. But nothing worked. They were just too old. It still made him mad to remember how they had cut up his new boot at the hospital. So what if it had a bullet hole through it? The rest of it was good. He might could have patched those holes. To them it was nothing. They made lots of money. They could go out and buy new boots whenever they wanted. But he couldn't. What with all the doctor bills and being laid up for so long, it was going to be a long time before he could afford a new pair of boots.

Cal picked up his snowshoes at the sugarhouse and strapped them on his back for when he got to the end of Biff's road. It was a good road, much better than the one he had made himself last year with his tractor. He had hired Herman Jones to help out. Herman worked cheap, but you never knew whether he would show up or not, or if he would be sober enough to work when he did. And he always wanted to be paid in cash at the end of the day. It was a lot better working with Biff. A man could count on Biff. He was a hard worker. He took his horses up the hill before there was a sap run to get them used to the work and to bust out the roads. They spent several days at it. Biff didn't want money either. He was happy to work on shares.

Cal walked up the road into that other world, which was always right there, only most of the time he was too busy to remember it. His rifle was in his hand, and it felt just right. It was ridiculous to think of hunting without it. That would be a walk in the woods, not the same thing at all. Paul didn't know what he was talking about.

The air was soft. There was no wind. Everything was still. The only sound was the ticking made by drops of water falling from the wet black branches. The nearby tree trunks were black, but farther away, they got paler and paler, until they disappeared in the mist. There was water everywhere. It smelled sharp and clean. Underneath the smell of melting, faintly, Cal could smell the earth, waiting to begin a new season.

All this time Cal had been going steadily uphill. The farther he went, the more his anger fell away behind him. The things that seemed important back in his other life didn't matter here. He was getting pretty close to the top. There were some tracks on the road, but they were so spread out by the melting that it was impossible to tell what had made them. He decided to leave the road and work his way east along the top of the ridge. He propped his gun against a tree and unstrapped his snowshoes.

While he was kneeling down fastening the straps of the second snowshoe, something caused him to look up. There was a steep bank on the east side of the road. Standing on top of it, looking down at him where he knelt, was an enormous buck, the largest Cal had ever seen. Even though his horns hadn't started to grow yet, Cal had no doubt from his manner that he was a buck. The morning light coming from behind, outlined him as he stood proudly, looking down at Cal below. He was like a picture in a book, the king of the forest.

They stayed that way for a long time, looking directly at each other. Cal could feel the cold and the wet seeping through the knee of his pants, but he couldn't move. The buck was outlined by a thin line of light. He was the king of the forest. He was almost too big to be true.

After an eternity, Cal remembered his rifle behind him, leaning against the tree. He didn't move. He just thought the thought. But it was enough. The buck stamped his foot two times. Then he snorted, blowing air out through his nostrils. He wheeled around and was gone. There was nothing at the top of the bank but the black trunks of the bare trees.

Cal finished buckling his snowshoe and stood up, stiffly and slowly, as though he was waking from a dream. He couldn't be sure that what he had seen was real. He looked at the bank. It was steep, really too steep for snowshoes. But going around would be slower, and there was always the danger of losing the trail. So he went straight up, pulling himself along with his free hand, putting his feet in their snowshoes wherever he could between the rocks and the brush.

There was a trail. The buck was that real, at least. His footprints were there, sunk deep into the soft snow. There was a long mark where one hoof had dragged the snow a little when he wheeled around. After that, he went straight uphill. His tracks were deep, and his stride was long. Cal wished he had a tape measure to see just how long.

The buck began to seem more real than he had been even when he was standing right there at the top of the bank. Cal started to think he might be being given meat to replace what had been stolen from him last fall. The buck had come through the winter well, without losing too much weight. Cal had particularly noticed that. But he felt funny thinking the buck was meant for him, as though it was something he wasn't supposed to think, as though the thought could jinx him. He tried to put it out of his mind.

He tried to think about nothing but the trail. For a while it was plain. The buck went straight to the top of the ridge. Then he turned east on the old logging road that ran along the top. He wasn't sprinting but going fast and steady. To Cal it looked as though the buck knew he was being followed, because he was moving along so purposefully. Before he got to the end of Cal's land, he left the road and went north down the other side of the ridge.

It was open at the top, and the tracks were easy to follow. The air was full of mist and the sound of water dripping from the trees. There were several little flocks of chickadees calling to each other, and once Cal thought he heard a woodpecker. And then the track vanished. Cal was going through a brushy patch, and the tracks were plain, and then there was nothing. At first Cal thought he had probably not been paying enough attention. He had to watch where he put his feet so as not to snag his snowshoes in the brush. So he backtracked a little and looked more carefully. The trail was narrow, and he had had to put his own track on top of the buck's in a few places, but there was enough left to follow, and he could see the track was there, and then it wasn't. He searched the bushes carefully in widening circles, but there was nothing.

He looked around at the black trunks of trees disappearing in the mist, at the soft snow and the dripping branches with a few oak and beech leaves, pale and brown, still hanging on. The woods seemed empty now in a way it hadn't before he saw the buck. He stood still wondering what to do. It was spooky the way the trail vanished. If the buck was the ghost of last fall's deer, then of course he would be walking up the trail where he had been shot. Human ghosts always walked the place where they had been killed, so it made sense that animal ghosts would do the same.

Cal went west along the ridge until he came to his tree stand, all the while looking around at the woods, which seemed too empty. He scrambled down the bank to the game trail below. He realized afterward that he had been sure he would find the clear, fresh prints of the big buck. But he didn't. There were tracks on the trail, but only old ones, melting and indistinct. If the buck was alive, how could he disappear? If he was a ghost, why wasn't he walking where he was supposed to be? Cal stood still, unable to decide what to do, and then he started walking along the trail, going downhill for lack of a better plan.

The farther downhill he went, the thicker the fog became, until, near the brook, Cal couldn't see the ground at all. The trunks of the trees disappeared into the thick white mist that rose up from the ground and pooled in the low places. Cal began to know that he wasn't going to find the buck again, but he was soothed by the beauty and soft quiet of the woods this dripping morning until he didn't care. The brook was roaring with spring run-off. There were places where the ice was almost gone. Cal walked along beside it. Near where it crossed the road it went through a swampy meadow. There he came upon a piece of open ground where the snow had melted away. It was at the roots of a large pine tree where the ground sloped off to the south. The roots of the old tree gripped the ground. The grass was yellow and dead between the roots, and there were twigs and leaves and pine needles tangled in it, colors other than black and white. It was the first bare ground Cal had seen since before Christmas. It was beautiful.

It happened to him the same way every year. The first time he saw the bare ground after the long, white winter, it seemed so lovely that he couldn't stop looking at it, a patch of dirt with a few leaves and sticks and maybe some dead grass or a few green shoots. Later on it would be everywhere, and it would mean nothing. But for now, for this first moment, it stunned him, as it always did. And as always, he remembered the picture in his high school geography book of Christopher Columbus kneeling down to kiss the earth, a thing that seemed very queer all year except for this one moment when the earth appeared again from under the snow after months of being buried. At that one moment, the picture of Columbus made sense. It was what Cal felt like doing himself.

He followed the brook down to the road and clambered over the snowbank. But when he bent down to unfasten his snowshoes, he remembered his rifle. He couldn't walk down the road carrying it, not this time of year, not in the daylight. Anyone could come by and see him. He could get into serious trouble and maybe lose his hunting license, even though he wasn't doing anything wrong. And Jason LaRue didn't get into any trouble at all when he committed a crime. The unfairness of it made Cal seethe inside. He couldn't stand the stupidity of it. He climbed over the snowbank and went back up his trail.

At first he was furious. But as he walked through the woods, the anger dripped away like the melting snow, until finally he was left with a new understanding. He began to see that he would be there in the woods come November, and the big buck would be there too. What happened last November belonged to last year. A new year was beginning now. It didn't make sense to carry over the old grievance. If he could have turned it over to the law, it would have been different, but the law was too stupid. The law got it wrong. He had to drop the whole thing because it was last year's business. Of course, if he was out hunting and he came up on Jason LaRue on his land, he couldn't say what he would do. But he could afford to wait until the right moment was handed to him, and maybe it would be. He walked up the trail, grinning at the thought. Anything could happen, if he was willing to wait for the right moment.

He came out of the woods onto Biff's road just above the sugarhouse. He took off his snowshoes and knocked the snow out of the webbing and hung them up in the sugarhouse again. It had been good when George came out—like old times. He was still old George, even if they didn't have much in common, even if they lived such different lives. He guessed blood was thicker than water, in spite of what he'd said to George that time. Maybe George would get so he came out regularly. Maybe he'd even go hunting again. He used to love it. Maybe he'd tell George about the big buck he saw this morning.

By this time, he was back at the house. He stood his gun in the corner so he could clean and oil it later. He had thought about leaving it in the sugarhouse. It would be convenient. A lot of guys did. But he decided not to. The damp and the steam wouldn't be good for it. He took off his boots and jacket and went into the kitchen. Ursela wasn't there, so he didn't have to explain anything. He could smell breakfast, and he was hungry.

Chapter 34

They were both sitting on the kitchen floor putting on the kids' snowsuits. Lena was dressing Jimmy, and Jerry was trying to help Georgia. Both children were limp and sleepy, just waking up from their naps. Lena loved times like these, when they were warm and soft and half-asleep. But truthfully, she loved everything and everybody right now.

She looked at Jerry, sitting on the floor with Georgia on his lap. Jerry's long arms wrapped round Georgia. They were both concentrating on getting Georgia's foot into the leg of her snowsuit. Jerry looked up and saw her watching and smiled at her. She smiled back, and he made a little kissing motion in the air.

A few minutes later, Jerry set Georgia gently on the floor and stood up. "See how much you can do before I get back, Georgia," he said, and he left the room.

Lena assumed he was going to the bathroom, but as soon as he was in the next room, he said, "Lena, would you please come in here." His voice was stern.

Lena set Jimmy off her lap. Only his legs were in his snowsuit.

The top half pooled around him on the floor. She hurried into the living room, wondering what could be wrong.

As the door swung shut behind her, Jerry grabbed her and kissed her. At first, she was too surprised to do anything. She could feel the whole, long length of him pressed against her, and it was so nice that she put her arms around him and began to kiss him back.

After a minute, the craziness of it hit her. She pushed him away, trying to catch her breath. "Jerry, what are you doing? What's wrong? Why did you call me?"

"Nothing's wrong," he said, pulling her toward him again.

"Don't. Are you crazy?" But she was laughing. "Is this what you called me out here for?"

"It's your fault. I couldn't help it." He tried to pull her close again. "You shouldn't have smiled at me that way."

Lena gave him a quick peck on the cheek and twisted away before he had time to hold her there. "Georgia's going to come out here any second to see what we're doing. And if we don't get them ready, I'll be late picking up Nora."

Jerry reached for her again, and she grabbed his hand. "Come with us. Please. You've never been to Uncle Cal's."

"I don't know. What'll Nora say?"

"She won't say anything. She's going to find out that you're back sooner or later."

"But she might make some snide comments in front of the kids."

"She won't. Please come."

"Well, okay. Because I want to be with you."

"If she says anything, I'll tell her to shut up."

The kitchen door swung open. Georgia stood there in her snowsuit. "Don't tell me to shut up, Mommy. That's a bad word."

Lena and Jerry both laughed. Lena scooped Georgia up and kissed her. "I wasn't talking about you. I wouldn't tell you to shut up. What's Jimmy doing?"

"He's in the kitchen."

"I know that." Lena pushed the door open and went into the kitchen carrying Georgia and kissing her as she walked.

"What were you and Daddy doing?"

"Don't you like it that Daddy came home?"

"I don't like it when you act like little kids. You're grown-ups."

That was when Lena saw Jimmy. He was sitting by Beebee's water bowl in a pool of spilled water, slapping his hands on the floor. Splashes of water flew in all directions.

Lena said, "Jimmy," and he looked up smiling, and made another big splash for her to see. She set Georgia on her feet and pushed past Jerry to get a bath towel. When she got back to the kitchen, Jerry had picked up Jimmy and was carrying him, dripping, toward the sink.

"Wait, Jerry. Bring him here." She spread the towel on the table, and Jerry set Jimmy down on it. "Is his snowsuit wet clear through? I don't know what to put on him, if it is."

"We could put it in the dryer."

"I'd have to call Nora and tell her we were going to be late."

They folded the bath towel around Jimmy, patting him dry. He sat still. He liked being the center of attention. Georgia watched over the edge of the table.

Jerry put his hand down the leg of the snowsuit. "Feel in here. It's not wet inside. Let's just dry him off. He'll be all right."

"I guess we'd better. We're already late."

It was slow. Jimmy needed dry socks, and so did Georgia. She had taken a few steps into the pool of water on the floor. Finally, they were all ready. Jerry had the car warmed up, and Lena had put the bath towel on the wet place on the floor, since she didn't have time to mop it up. They were only ten minutes late when they got to Mom and Dad's, pretty good, considering all that had happened.

"Shall I honk the horn for Nora?"

"You don't need to. She'll be watching." Lena climbed out of the car and got into the back, holding Jimmy in her arms. She settled him down on her lap. Georgia was already in back, standing up to look over the seat.

Nora came out the door. Jerry said, "My God, she's huge. I didn't realize she was so far along."

"You haven't been around much lately. You've missed a lot of things." As soon as she spoke, she was sorry. When Jerry looked around at her, she could see the hurt on his face. He opened his mouth to say something, but just then Nora opened the car door.

"Hi, everybody. I was watching, but I didn't recognize the car until Lena got out." She sat down heavily in the front seat. "I didn't know you were coming home from your travels, Jerry."

Jerry was putting the car in gear. He didn't say anything, but Lena could feel him stiffen. She wished she hadn't said what she had said. She knew he was thinking that they were ganging up on him.

Georgia said, "Daddy had to go away for a long time, but he came back home."

Nora turned around in her seat so she could see Lena's face. "That's great," she said.

Lena managed to avoid Nora's eyes by fussing over Georgia's hat.

Suddenly Jimmy said, "Nah-wa," quite loud. That made everyone laugh and eased the tension. Jimmy was so pleased with himself that he clapped his mittened hands together and smiled at everybody.

Outside the car, the sun was bright, sparkling on the melting snow. There was water everywhere, and the excitement of spring.

Nora looked at Jerry. "Did you have a good trip?"

"Come on, Nora. Don't be mean."

Nora laughed. "I'm sorry. I couldn't resist."

After a minute Jerry said, "I didn't know you were so far along. How much longer before the baby comes?"

"I'm not as close as I look. I seemed to get big all of a sudden. I don't know why."

Lena leaned forward. "That's because you aren't trying to keep it a secret any more. Before that, you were kind of holding it in."

"Well, maybe. I don't know. But to answer your question, it's due around the tenth of May, but I'm hoping it'll be earlier. Were either of yours early, Lena?"

"Georgia was late. I thought she'd never come. Jimmy was a little early, but I can't remember how much."

"I hope this baby will be like Jimmy." Nora turned around and smiled at Jimmy.

Georgia stood behind the seat. She watched Nora. "Are you going to have a boy baby?"

That made everyone laugh again. Lena had to explain that no one knew, that it was going to be a surprise.

Nora said, "I didn't recognize your car, Jerry. I was expecting Lena's old station wagon. Have you got any other trips planned?"

"Cut it out, Nora. You don't understand."

"What don't I understand?"

"I'm really glad to be back. I'm not leaving again." He looked around at Lena and smiled. She smiled back, even though she felt shy in front of Nora. "No more trips," Jerry said. "Ever."

"Well, that's a good plan. Don't you think so, Lena?"

But they were in West Severance now, and Jerry needed directions to Uncle Cal's. Lena was glad to change the subject. No more comments from Nora for a few minutes at least.

Georgia wanted to know when they were going to get there, and Nora told her how she used to say the same thing when she was little and came out here with Granddad. "This is where Granddad used to live when he was a little boy."

"Why doesn't he live here now?"

"Because he married Grammy and moved to town to be a law-yer."

Lena was only half listening. Outside the window, the landscape was strange and familiar at the same time, like in a dream. "I don't think I've been out here since I was about ten."

Nora said, "I came out all the time when I was a teenager, when I was working on that Foxfire project in high school."

"You used to come out before that with Dad. I never wanted to. I didn't like it. I always wanted to stay in town with Mom."

"Mom never liked any of Dad's family. She still doesn't. They're too country."

"I think Mom was always afraid Dad would want to move out of town."

"I *know* he wanted to. I always hoped we'd do it—build a house on some of the family land."

"Nora, that's crazy. Mom would have hated it. Can you imagine her living in the country?"

"No, I can't. But I can picture myself doing it. I've always wanted to live out here."

By this time they were driving up Uncle Cal's road. Jerry said, "Is that the place up ahead? It looks kind of run-down."

Nora said, "They don't have much money. They live a hardscrabble sort of life."

"I guess it has been even harder since Uncle Cal hurt his foot."

Nora looked around at her. "Don't say that in front of him. He'd have a fit."

"What am I supposed to say then? Since he got shot in the foot? Is that better?"

"Yeah. I mean Uncle Cal would think so. He's sure everybody in the family thinks he did it to himself. Have you ever been out here, Jerry?"

"No, but I have relatives in Williamstown that live like this. They milk a few cows and raise their own food and manage to scrape by."

"Uncle Cal buys and sells and trades stuff too. When he can, I guess."

"Everybody has relatives up in the hills like this. You only see them at the Tunbridge Fair." Jerry stopped the car behind a big sedan. "Is this all right?"

Nora said, "That old gas hog is Aunt Ursela's. Just leave enough room so she can get out."

Beside the car was a pickup, and a little farther off there was a big cattle truck.

"Oh," Nora said, "Biff's here too." She turned away to open the door, but Lena thought she could see that she was blushing.

Georgia said, "I want to go to the fair."

Lena was opening her door. "We'll go when summer comes. Right now we're here to see Uncle Cal make maple syrup. Isn't that going to be fun?"

Jerry was getting out too. He said, "Who's Biff?"

"He's a neighbor of Uncle Cal's. He has horses. They must be here today too. You'll see."

Georgia was out of the car and pulling on Jerry's arm. "Let's go, Daddy. I want to see the horses."

"Which way should we go, Nora?"

"Let's go straight to the sugarhouse. We can say hello to Aunt Ursela later." She looked at Lena. "You look different." She looked again. "No, you don't. But you look really pretty today."

Lena started to say she was wearing her contact lenses for a change, when Jerry came around to their side of the car with Georgia hanging on his arm. "I'm back. That's what's different."

"Don't be so conceited, Jerry," Nora said. But Jerry and Lena couldn't help smiling at each other, a private smile that promised more later.

Jerry took Jimmy in his arms, and Nora went ahead, holding Georgia by the hand. The sun was bright on the snow. There was the sound of water dripping everywhere as they started down the road under the trees.

It felt just right to be walking beside Jerry. Every few steps their arms and shoulders touched. Lena knew Jerry was thinking about her the way she was about him. For a second she felt a twinge of fear. Maybe someday Jerry would leave again. Still, everything was so wonderful with him back. She didn't want to spoil what they had now by worrying about the future.

Up ahead under the tunnel of bare branches, Nora and Georgia had stopped and were looking at the ground.

"I was showing Georgia the horse tracks. Look there," Nora said as they came up.

"They must be huge," Jerry said. "That footprint is as big as a dinner plate. What kind of horses are they?"

"I don't know the name," Nora said. "But they are big. You'll see."

The road turned and went up the hill, and there was the sugarhouse above them on the hillside. It was a low building of gray, weathered wood. Clouds of steam were coming out of every opening.

"What's that?" Georgia said. "Is it a witch's house?"

They went up the hill in a tight group and stopped in the open doorway. Uncle Cal was in there, with his back to the door. It was dark in the sugarhouse after the bright sunshine. Steam boiled up out of the large pans. Uncle Cal rowed through it with a big spoon. Every once in a while he would hold the spoon up and look at it intently, while the drips fell back into the pan. Sometimes the fire flared up, throwing red light onto the dark walls.

Georgia stood very still, holding Nora's hand. When she looked over and saw Lena watching her, she said, "What's that old man doing in there?"

Uncle Cal must have heard her, because he swung around, surprised to see them all standing there, although he tried not to show it.

"We came out to watch you make syrup, Uncle Cal. Is that okay?" Nora said.

"You should of come sooner. We're all done with the good stuff. This batch is goin to be dark."

"We don't care. We want the kids to see how you do it. They've never seen it before."

"Well, this is how." He scooped up a skimmerful of dirty foam and threw it into a bucket under the arch.

"These are Lena's kids. Georgia and Jimmy. Did you ever meet Jerry, Lena's husband? He's right here, holding the baby."

Uncle Cal nodded in Jerry's direction. "We met. At your wedding."

Lena remembered Uncle Cal and Aunt Ursela at the wedding, how they had stayed in a tight group with their children and grandchildren, how none of them had had anything to do with anyone else, except for Elsie. Elsie was comfortable moving back and forth between the groups of people, but all the rest of them looked stiff and shy and awkward. Mom could have made them feel more at home, but she was probably glad they looked so out of place.

Uncle Cal opened the door of the firebox and stirred the fire. Sparks swirled up with the steam.

Georgia said, "Oh. Look at the fireflies."

Uncle Cal laughed and threw on more wood. Then he went back into the dark corner behind the smokestack and came out with a small pan. He looked into the pan. He blew into it. Then he wiped it out with his sleeve. They all watched silently. Even Nora didn't ask him what he was doing. Apparently, the pan still wasn't clean enough because he took a coffee mug from the back of the arch and dipped up a cupful of sap from the corner of the pan where the new sap ran in. He used the warm sap to rinse out the little pan, dumping the dirty sap into the bucket where he threw the skimmings of foam. He did all this without looking up once to see if they were watching. He shook out the last few drops by waving the pan back and forth. Then he handed it to Nora.

"What's this for?"

"It's for snow. Get it away from the trail where it's clean and pack it down until the pan's full."

"Well, okay," Nora said. "But why?"

"You'll see." He picked up the skimming spoon and began again to take off the dirty foam.

Nora said, "Come on, Georgia. Let's go get some snow for Uncle Cal. We're going to need your mittens."

Lena wanted to go too, but at first she was too shy of Uncle Cal to move. Then, when she could hear Georgia and Nora outside, she wanted to be with them so much that she turned around and bolted after them without even looking at Jerry or Jimmy.

They were just across the road. Georgia was plowing straight into the snow with the pan in her hand. Nora was behind her, awkward and unbalanced with her long coat trailing. Lena felt sorry for her and thought how she must have looked like that right at the end too. She remembered how she hadn't cared what she looked like. She just wanted it to hurry up.

She went over to Nora. "I can't believe the way you talk to Uncle

Cal. You're so brave."

Nora smiled. "He's nice. I like him."

"Aren't you scared? He always seems like he's going to bite your head off."

Nora said, "Watch out! He might hear you."

Lena swung around toward the sugarhouse. But then she saw Nora was teasing her, and she began to laugh.

They were both giggling when Georgia came back with the pan of snow. "What's so funny?"

Lena said, "Nothing," and then they looked at each other and started to laugh all over again.

"What *is* it?" Georgia said.

"It really isn't anything, sweetie," Lena said. "Let me see your pan of snow. Do you think that's what Uncle Cal wants?" She held the pan out so Nora could see.

"He said to pack it tight. Let's put some more in the corners, Georgia."

They pushed more snow into the corners. Nora carried the pan in to Uncle Cal. Lena and Georgia stepped into the doorway to see what he would do.

"Oh," Lena whispered. "He's making sugar-on-snow. I don't know why I didn't know that all along. You always hear about it."

Uncle Cal dipped his skimming spoon into the front corner of the boiling pan and dripped the hot syrup over the snow. He looked at it and then dipped more syrup. "There," he said. "Eat that."

Nora said, "How?" She looked down at the pan in her hands.

Lena was so curious, she forgot to be shy. She pushed past Georgia. The syrup in the pan was spread over the snow. "Do you eat the snow too?" she said. But at the same time she was reaching into the pan. The syrup lifted off the snow in a sheet, like soft wax. "It's chewy," she said. She pulled off a little piece and stuffed it in Georgia's mouth.

Jimmy said, "Me," so she fed a little piece to Jimmy too. Jerry's lips looked so inviting that she gave the rest to him. She turned around, feeling a little shy again, embarrassed that she'd taken it all to feed her family, but Uncle Cal and Nora didn't notice. Uncle Cal was dripping more syrup onto the pan of snow, while Nora watched. This time Nora and Lena got to eat it. They offered it to Uncle Cal.

"No. I don't want any. I get enough sweets just by standing here. It's for you."

They went around and around, putting little balls of the syrup into their own and the children's mouths, with Lena feeding Jerry too. Each bite was like a spoonful of syrup, except that it was cold and chewy.

Lena told herself it probably wasn't bad for you because she worried a little about giving the children so much, and yet, she wanted more herself.

They had to keep going outside to fill up with fresh snow. Lena had just stepped out the door with the pan in her hand when she heard a jingling sound and looked up the road to see two gigantic golden horses coming toward her. They weren't going very fast. Rather, they walked with a kind of staccato prance, kicking up a spray of snow with each step. Lena ran back inside and snatched Jimmy out of Jerry's arms. They were both surprised, but she didn't have time to say anything. She just handed Jerry the empty pan and took Jimmy outside to see the horses. She was so afraid he would miss them.

She stood on the edge of the road and held Jimmy up, even though he was scared and kept trying to burrow closer into her shoulder. "Look, Jimmy. See the big horses pulling that big tank. And there's a cowboy driving them. See?"

By the time they stopped in front of the sugarhouse, Jerry was beside her with Georgia in his arms, and Nora was peeking out the door. The horses stood where they were, blowing through their huge nostrils and making the harness jingle by shaking their heads. The man got off the sled and began to connect a hose from the tank to the sugarhouse. He nodded his head at them, but he didn't introduce himself. Of course, Lena knew who it was. She could see why Nora had been so infatuated at Christmas, when she went riding in the sleigh with him. He was like a character from a movie.

He finished connecting the hoses, and Nora came out to introduce him. Lena thought she must be embarrassed for him to see her so big. But she offered him some sugar on snow, and he took it. Behind them in the sugarhouse, Uncle Cal was taking off syrup. He called out to Biff that it was Grade B at the best and probably their last run of the year.

Lena stepped up close to the horses, and Jimmy stretched out a tentative hand, but when the closest horse swung her head around toward him, he pulled back quickly.

Georgia said she wanted a ride. Biff said she could sit on Queenie's back, but when Jerry started to lift her up, she changed her mind. Lena was glad, although she didn't say so. Anything could happen with such enormous creatures. If Georgia had said yes, she would have had to say no.

Later on, in the car going home, Jerry said, "I could tell Biff thought I was lucky to have a family. He practically said so."

"He seems nice," Lena said. "It's too bad it didn't work out."

Jerry said, "You mean because of the baby? He said, 'It won't be long now,' to Nora. That doesn't sound like he's bothered by the fact that she's going to have a baby."

"Stop matchmaking, you two. Jerry, you are even worse than Lena. It's one thing to make a friendly statement. It's another to sign on to be a father. And I'm not sure I want to share this baby with anyone."

Jerry looked around at Lena and smiled. "You don't know how nice it is," he said.

"I don't know how I'll feel when the baby is actually here, but that's the way I feel now. It's still more than three weeks away. A lot can happen in three weeks. Look at you two, after all."

There was a silence. Then Nora said, "What did Mom and Dad say about Jerry coming home?"

Lena considered trying to change the subject, but then she said quietly, "Mom and Dad didn't know he'd gone away."

"Lena," Nora said. "I thought you told them."

"Well, I was going to. But somehow I never seemed to get the right chance. Now I won't have to, so it's lucky really."

"Aren't you afraid they'll find out and be mad because you didn't tell them?"

"I don't know. I guess I'd rather just wait and see what happens. All that's over, and I'm glad."

"Well, I won't tell. You know that."

"I know."

After they got the kids to bed, they came downstairs together holding hands and sat on the couch. Lena rested her head on his shoulder. Jerry said, "Why did I want to leave all this? I must have been insane. If I ever do something like that again, just kick me really hard."

"I can't stop you. I tried to stop you this time, but it was no use."

"I think I've changed. I know what I almost lost."

"I hope so."

"I think I just wanted to be like everyone else—free love, no restrictions, all that stuff. But it wasn't so great. I know that now."

For answer, Lena burrowed a little closer beside him.

"So just don't ever let me do anything so dumb again."

"I won't."

They were both quiet. Lena was thinking about how nice it was going to be to go to bed with Jerry. Sex, of course, but more than that, just having him there to lock the doors and turn out the lights. It had been grim when she was alone. The safety of the house and of Georgia and Jimmy had all depended on her. If something bad had happened, it would have been all her fault.

Jerry said, "Tell me what you're thinking right now."

"I was thinking about how nice it was going to be to go to bed."

"Me too. Let's go now."

"But, Jerry, I was also thinking about how I had to do everything when you were gone."

"I know, baby. I said I was sorry about that." He stood up and reached down to take her hand. "Come on."

"Wait a minute, Jerry. I just want to say this. It was fun for you.

I was the one who had the hard part. I was the one who had all the work and the worry of the house and the kids."

"I kept my job, didn't I? I mean you make it sound like I was completely irresponsible."

"You didn't give me much money though. That was another worry."

"I know it was bad for you. You've told me enough times. I told you I was sorry. What more do you want?"

"Nothing." She started to stand up, and then she stopped. "But...."

"Lena, don't do this. I said I was sorry. I said it wasn't going to happen again. I don't know what else I can do. Tell me what you want me to do."

She stood up beside him then so she could look into his eyes. "This is what scares me. It wasn't awful for you, so what's going to keep you from doing it again?"

"Because I won't ever want to, that's why. Because I want to be right here, with you." He put his arm around her. "Now come on. Don't worry about things that won't ever happen. It's like being scared of ghosts."

"I know," she said, but she still wasn't sure. There was something that made her uncomfortable. Not often, but once in a while, it came across her mind like a shadow. But maybe Jerry was right. Maybe it was nothing. "All right," she said. "I won't worry about it any more. I know things are different now."

They went up the stairs with their arms around each other, walking awkwardly and giggling about it. When they got to the top, Lena pulled away to go check on the children, but Jerry stopped her. He wanted her to come to bed right away. He promised he would get up afterward and check on the kids.

But after they made love, Jerry fell asleep. When Lena came back into the room after kissing Georgia and Jimmy and pulling up their covers, she stopped in the doorway to look at Jerry. He was lying on his back, snoring a little. The covers were all crooked, and his chest was bare. Lena straightened everything and covered him. Then she kissed him on the forehead, the way she had Georgia and Jimmy, before she went around to her side of the bed. She got in and turned out the light, feeling more at peace than she had in a long time.

Chapter 35

The bucket was stuck on the hook under the tap. Cal could see what was wrong. The tap was bent, and so was the rim of the bucket above the hole for the hook. Biff had had to empty this bucket at least once a day when the sap was running. He hadn't said anything about having trouble taking any buckets down. But then Biff was a resourceful guy. He would have handled it himself without mentioning it.

Cal jerked the bucket, twisting it at the same time, and it came off the hook fast, so fast that it splattered him in the face with yellow sap. It smelled like rotten vegetables. He sighed and set the bucket on the ground. He pulled his handkerchief out of his back pocket and shook it open. It wasn't very clean or very dry, but it was better than his face. He patted his face dry and balled up the handkerchief and stuck it into his pocket again. The sun was shining. It seemed warm, but the wetness on his bare skin stung like ice.

Cal pulled the tap out with the claw end of his hammer and dropped it into the pocket of his work pants. Then he picked up the bucket. He poured out the rest of the yellow bud sap and a drowned moth and moved on to the next tree. He was hoping to get all the buckets down and stacked by the road today. Then he could pick them up with the tractor and woods wagon when it dried out enough to drive up the hill without tearing up the road.

He stacked ten buckets together, put the lids into the top bucket, and carried them out to the road. He had to wipe his face again. This time it was sweat. He was badly out of shape from being laid up all winter. That was something else he could chalk up to Jason LaRue. He got his watch out of his pocket. It was ten-thirty. He was working near the top of the hill. It wasn't far from his tree stand. It was a good idea to go look around the scene of the crime. He started up the road, puzzling over why he hadn't thought to go look before. Maybe he was going senile. Last fall when he couldn't walk, he was frantic to get up here and look around, and now, when he could do it, he didn't even remember. But that's always the way it goes. Anyway, it was a good thing he thought of it, because this was the best chance he would ever have, with the snow almost gone, and the woods still open and bare.

He walked around his hunting tree and kicked through the leaves and bushes on the northeast side, where the bullet would have gone after it left his foot. He got choked up remembering the suddenness of it and the pain, and that blew his anger into a blaze again, but it didn't last. He decided to check down below the ridge since he was there. He wasn't sure what he would do if he found anything, although he would like to have proof he could show to George. Some way he couldn't explain, he knew it was over. He went down the steep bank, sliding and catching himself on saplings, to the deer trail at the bottom.

The earth was coming out from under the snow, all fresh and wet and new. There were so many colors—the rusts and browns of last year's leaves, the black tree trunks, and the timid yellow-green of new growth. Everything was in color again after being black and white for a long time.

He kicked around in the leaves, went to the spot where Nora found the candy paper and looked up at his tree stand. There was a perfect line of sight to where he had been sitting. He ought to be grateful that he only got it in the foot. He knew he was right. This is where Jason LaRue was standing when he, Cal, shot the deer, and Jason LaRue shot *him*. Maybe some day he would bring George to this spot to show him how it was, some day when they were out hunting together like they used to do. There was a time when they always went out for deer together. George used to get more excited about deer season than he did. He'd love to get old George out in the woods again.

Cal worked his way up the bank. His foot wasn't entirely healed because walking up the steep slope hurt quite a lot. He started down the road. He had this idea that he would go into town and see George at his office and tell him how things had changed, how George didn't have to worry anymore about him going out gunning for Jason LaRue. He thought George would be pleased to hear that.

He went by the stacked buckets and down the road past the sugarhouse to where his pickup was parked by the house. He tossed the hammer into the pile of tools and oilcans and broken parts on the floor of the passenger side and started for town.

When he was about halfway in to Severance, he realized he hadn't even bothered to clean up. He almost turned back, but then he thought, "What the hell. George used to know what work clothes looked like, and I'm not goin to see anybody else but George and that skinny little know-it-all who guards George's door." It wouldn't hurt her to see that some of the family knew how to work hard enough to get dirty.

But as luck would have it, when he got to George's office, the front desk was empty, and the door to George's inside room was open. George was sitting at his desk, reading some papers. Cal stood in the doorway and watched.

All of a sudden, George looked up. "Cal! I don't believe it. I was thinking about you, and you appeared. It's like I conjured you up."

"Well, you didn't," Cal said, leaning against the doorframe. "I can get around on my own."

"I know, I know," George said. He stood up. "You just surprised me, that's all. I'm glad to see you. What're you doing in town this time of day?"

"I came in to see you."

"I'm glad, really glad. Is everything okay? Nothing's wrong, is it?" By this time George had crossed the room and laid a hand on Cal's shoulder.

"No. Everythin's fine. I just wanted to talk to you, is all." He was glad George wanted to see him, and he didn't mean to be gruff. It just came out that way.

"Well, come sit down then. I want to hear what it is. It's lucky I don't have a client here." They started across the room toward George's desk. Then George said, "No. Hold on. It's not legal business, is it?"

"No. It ain't."

"Then let's not sit here like it is. Let's go get some lunch. I'll treat you."

"No, I don't think so." Even more than before, Cal was aware of his stained work pants and broken boots, of how he had three torn plaid shirts on top of each other instead of a jacket.

"But, Cal, it's only eleven-thirty. You haven't had lunch already, have you?"

"I ain't dressed for it, George. Can't you see that? I probably even stink."

"You look fine, Cal. Where we're going, you'll fit right in."

"I don't want you to have to change where you eat because I'm not fit for polite company."

"I'm not. I never feel comfortable in those fancy places. I'm going to take you to the diner where I go every day, and you'll fit right in, believe me. It's all working guys. That's what I like about it. So what're we waiting for?"

"Ursela always gets my dinner at twelve. I didn't tell her I was comin to town."

"You'd better call her then." George reached across his desk and pulled the phone close. "You just got here, and we haven't even had a chance to talk. You couldn't get home in time. That settles it. I'm treating you to lunch. And you know what you smell like? You smell like the woods, like pine trees. It makes me homesick."

Cal gave up his resistance then and dialed the phone.

Ursela answered, "Ja?" the way she always did.

Cal said, "I'm in town, and I won't be back for dinner."

"I already started cookin."

"I can't help it. You got to eat anyhow."

"I wish you'd told me sooner."

"Well, I couldn't. I just found out myself. I'll see you later." And he hung up. He was feeling hemmed in by George on one side and Ursela on the other. He should have stayed up in the woods. He wished he was back there now. He didn't remember why he wanted to talk to George in the first place.

George had been in his shirtsleeves, but while Cal was on the phone he had gone around his desk and picked up his suit jacket from the back of his chair. He put it on by the door.

Cal was glad he didn't get out his lawyer's overcoat. The suit jacket was bad enough.

George locked the outer door of his office, and they started down the dim, creaky hall. Cal could feel the bulge in his pants made by the maple-syrup taps. He was conscious of them jangling together every time he took a step.

His pickup was parked on the street, so when they stepped outside, Cal said, "I got to stop by my truck a minute," and he unloaded his pockets onto the floor of the pickup. While he was standing there, he thought of the cans of syrup behind the seat that he was taking to the store in West Severance to sell. If he wasn't already annoyed with George, he could have given him some. He had some change for the parking meter, but that was all he had. He hated not to pay his own way, but this lunch would have to be George's treat. And, hell, it ought to be. *He* wouldn't waste money on eating out when he had perfectly good food at home.

Just down the street was a plate-glass window with Green Mountain Lunch written across it in fancy writing. George turned in, and

Cal followed him, feeling gloomy. He was glad when George sat down at one of the booths near the front. It was true that the few people they passed were dressed in work clothes. George seemed more out of place than he did.

After a few minutes a heavy, motherly waitress came over. "How're you doin, George? You're in early today." She set two menus down on the table.

"We don't need those, Terry. We want T-bones. Cook mine like you always do." George looked at him. "You want a steak, don't you, Cal? That's what I want to treat you to. You like it rare?"

Cal nodded. At least he wouldn't have to try to read the menu without his reading glasses. He wasn't sure how much he could see without them.

George said, "Good." He looked at the waitress. "Terry, this is my brother, Cal."

"Pleased to meet you," she said. She stuck out her hand for Cal to shake. "Your brother's a good customer—a good tipper," she said, and she winked. She looked from one to the other of them, and then she said, "You guys don't look all that much alike."

"Cal's older than I am."

"Only by four years," Cal said.

Terry laughed. "All right. I'll get your steaks started."

After she left, neither of them said anything. Cal was still wishing he'd stayed in the woods, taking down buckets. He knew he had come to town to tell George not to worry about him going after the guy that shot him, but somehow, now that he was here with George, he couldn't remember why it had seemed important to tell him right away. There George sat in his lawyer suit, buying steaks without even worrying about how much they were going to cost. Cal was overwhelmed by the great divide between them.

George didn't seem to notice. He leaned across the table, smiling at Cal. "I'm really glad to see you. What's on your mind?" He didn't make any small talk about the weather or whether it was a good sugaring year. He plunged ahead right to the point, as though his time was money, which, of course, it was.

Maybe George had lost his country manners, but Cal told himself that that didn't mean he had to lose his own. "It looks like spring's really here, don't it?

George nodded. "It's a beautiful day today. You must be all done sugaring."

"I been takin down buckets all week."

"How'd you do?"

"We done pretty good this year, considerin we only had three hundred taps out. We made eighty-five gallons. Of course I had to give Biff a share, but still, I got some to sell. I won't make my taxes, but I might get close."

"That's great, Cal. I'm glad. I know you've had a tough winter, not being able to get around because of your foot and all."

Cal shrugged it off. "It's always somethin, ain't it?"

"I know, but this was a tough one."

"Yeah. Well. I was pissed off for a long time there, especially when I found out who did it, but I guess I got over it."

"What are you saying?"

"Just what I said, George. I ain't gunnin for Jason LaRue no more. It's over."

"Cal, that's...."

"Hold on, George. I ain't sayin what would happen if I came on the little bastard up in my woods, and nobody wasn't around. There might just be a accident. I'm not sure I could help that." His lips twisted into a grin, but George didn't smile back, although he should have been able to see the humor of it.

"But I don't think he's dumb enough to hunt on my place again. And it won't happen if he don't come lookin for trouble." Now that he'd said it, it didn't seem like much to have come all the way to town for.

"Cal, that's good news. I've been worried you'd do something foolish."

"There wouldn't be nothin new there, George."

George laughed then. "Good old Cal. But you know what I mean. How's your foot anyway?"

"Oh...it don't hurt that much any more. I guess I'll live."

"I meant to get out to see you again before you got done sugaring."

"Well you didn't make it."

"That always happens to me. I guess it'll have to be next year."

"You wouldn't have to wait that long. I'm there all year round." That was a lot for him to say, and he was embarrassed after he'd said it.

"I know, Cal. Things are going to be different from now on."

"Nora and Lena were out last week."

"They were?"

"The last day we boiled. The syrup was pretty low grade by then, but we made some sugar-on-snow. The kids liked it."

George started to say something, but just then the waitress came over with their steaks. She put down the two big plates of food and coffee for George, and she brought Cal tea when he asked her for it.

They both concentrated on their food. Neither of them spoke. That's the way it always was at dinnertime at home. People paid attention to eating and not to talking.

After a while, George said, "How's the steak, Cal?"

"Not too bad. It's actually better than I thought it would be, considerin I didn't raise it myself."

"They know somebody local who raises beef for them. That's why I like it here. You don't have to give up everything when you move to town."

"I always thought you thought it was the other way around."

"I gave up a lot to move into town. I've never been glad about that."

Cal didn't know what to say. He'd always thought George looked down on the way they lived when he was a child.

After a while, George said, "I wish I'd known Nora and Lena were planning a trip to the farm. I'd have come with them."

"They said they wanted the kids to see a sugar operation."

"Did they like it?"

"They liked the sugar-on-snow pretty good. The horses too, I think."

There was another silence. Cal thought about the day George came out to see him in the sugarhouse and how they talked in a way they'd never done before. Cal said things he'd never said out loud to anyone.

George said, "I've been thinking about that day in the sugarhouse, the day I came out to see you. I've been thinking about some of the stuff you said."

"Me too."

"When I came home from the war, I only knew how it was for me. I never thought about how it was for you." He paused, listening to what he had just said. "No, that's not right. I did think about it, but I got it all wrong. I thought I was in your way. I was slowing down the work, and I didn't fit in anymore. There wasn't any room for me. I never thought you might be thinking I didn't want to be there."

"We weren't good enough for you after you'd been out and seen the world."

"All I wanted was to come home again."

"Well, it didn't seem like it, George, and you didn't say so neither."

"I know. None of us said what we were really thinking, did we?"

"How can you? People would think you was crazy if they knew what was goin on in your head most times."

"I don't know, Cal. I'm glad you told me what you were thinking. I'm glad I know it. I feel like I know you better."

Cal shrugged. He was very hot, but he couldn't take off his outside shirts because they were all ripped up. He didn't want to call attention to them. He didn't like the way the conversation was going, although he had to admit that it was his own fault. He was the one who'd hustled into town to tell George what was on his mind. And he wasn't even sure George had noticed what he said about not going out for vengeance any more. He tried again. "I hope I ain't gettin feebleminded, but I just ain't angry no more. My foot is healed. I got through the winter. I guess it's over. You don't think

I'm goin senile, or maybe gettin old-timer's disease or somethin, do you?" He was mostly joking, but not altogether.

"No, Cal, of course I don't. I think you've finally come to your senses."

"Now, wait just a minute here, George. It ain't right that that little bastard could come on my land and shoot me and leave me there while he took my deer. There ain't *nothin* sensible about that."

"That's not what I'm talking about. You can't do anything about that. That's already done. But you do have a choice about what you do about it. See?"

"It's pretty bad when you don't have a choice about gettin shot on your own land!"

George was laughing. At first that made Cal madder, but then he started to laugh too. It was like it was when they were little kids. Sometimes all they would have to do is look at each other to start laughing, and they couldn't have even said what they were laughing about.

Chapter 36

They were talking about Cal's accident, or whatever it was, when George started to laugh, and to his surprise, Cal began to laugh too. George couldn't have said what was so funny, and maybe Cal couldn't have either. It used to happen when they were little, and Dad would ask them what they were laughing about, but they couldn't tell him. It was everything and nothing in particular.

"Cal, I didn't mean...."

"It's okay, George. Forget it. I can't stay pissed off for the rest of my life. That's what I came in to town to tell you. I got over it, even though it ain't fair."

"I'm really glad, Cal."

"That's all I come in here to say, so we can talk about somethin else now, if you'd care to."

"I don't know," George said. "We don't have to talk about anything in particular. I'm just glad to see you."

"Well," Cal said. "Maybe I ought to of brought a little sip of whiskey in here with me. I wouldn't want you to get too dry."

"Come on, Cal. I haven't had a single drink since that day out in the sugarhouse. I haven't missed it that much either. That probably means I don't really have a drinking problem. If I'm okay without it, I mean. What do you think?"

"I wouldn't know."

"I haven't even been tempted."

Cal got a mischievous look in his eye when he heard that. "Maybe you ain't been keepin the right company, George. The way I recall it, you wasn't too hard to convince."

"Nobody could convince me but you," George said. "But the thing is that I almost always used to drink by myself."

"I was just foolin, George."

"I know, but I'm not. That's the thing that worries me. You always hear people say how bad it is to drink alone."

"Well, that's true. Think of the ones that really got it bad. Take old Herman Jones who works for me once in a while. He's always drinkin alone, and he's always drunk too."

"But, Cal, I'm not like that."

"I didn't say you were. You were talkin about was it bad to drink alone, and I would say yes, it could be."

"Well, I don't know what to think about it. I never let it get out of control. It's mostly for company."

"I don't get that exactly."

"I'm not sure I do either, to tell the truth, but it has been in my life since I left home, and it feels like I could give it up now I have you to talk to."

"That don't make sense."

"I'm not saying it does. I'm just telling you what it feels like. Sometimes what they say at those meetings makes sense, but mostly I feel like I don't belong there at all, and I always think they're going to find it out pretty soon and tell me to get out."

"I hate people like that."

"It's good to talk to you, Cal. It makes such a difference."

"I don't see why. I can't tell you nothin."

"I don't know why either, but I'm really glad you came in today."

"It must be gettin kinda late," Cal said, looking around.

It was true. The place was filling up with the lunch crowd, and they had been finished for quite a while. George looked toward the back of the room. Terry was there, but she didn't see him, or that was what he thought. But he must have been wrong, because a few minutes later she was standing by the table.

"Can I get you boys anythin?"

"You must have eyes in the back of your head, Terry."

"Of course," she said. "It's part of the equipment. Now what can I get you?"

"Just the check, thanks, unless you want something else, Cal."

"No. It was good. But I ought to get back to work. I don't usually run off a job like this in the middle of the day."

After Terry left the check and went away, George said, "I'm really glad you came in. You're the only one I can talk to. You're the only one who doesn't try to tell me what I ought to do. Maybe Nora wouldn't if I asked her. I don't think I could talk to Lena. When I try to have a conversation with Laurie about it, she gets so angry. I can't be sure whether I have a drinking problem or not."

"Well, I wouldn't say you did have, George."

"Really? That would be good. But wait a minute. Even if I don't have a problem, I don't like what it has done to my life."

"It looks to me like you're doin okay. You got a family, a big house. You work for yourself. You've even got a hired girl." He smiled that mischievous smile again. "Although she ain't much of a one. She's pretty puny. She's what Dad used to call a 'poor doer.'"

George laughed. "She's okay. She's strong enough to pick up the phone. I can just hear Dad saying that. And you're right. I can't complain. It's just that I've spent too much time by myself and not with the people who are important to me. Seeing you has made me realize that. If I don't drink, I'll have more time for you and Nora and...."

"How is Nora anyways? She was big enough when she was out to my place last week."

"It won't be much longer. I don't know exactly. I think a week or two, maybe."

"She's not gettin married then?"

"Not that I know of. But I remember one time you said that the father's the last to know. So maybe I just haven't heard yet."

"She'll have a hard time raisin it by herself."

"Elsie does okay, and she had twins."

"She gets a little somethin from the govermint. "

"Well, it brought Nora back to Severance anyway. I think Laurie will come around when she gets a look at the baby."

Cal nodded.

George said, "Let's go, shall we?" He felt like talking to Cal about himself but not about Laurie and Nora. That was something different.

They stood up together. George stopped by the counter to pay the bill. Then he took a few dollars back to the table for Terry. Cal was waiting for him outside. They started down the street side by side. Cal said, "Thanks," gruffly, looking down at his feet.

The sun was bright. Everything was melting. There was water everywhere. Still looking down, Cal said, "You should come out huntin like we used to do."

"I'd like that." They stopped at Cal's truck. "But I don't have a gun. I haven't owned one since I moved to town."

"Your old deer rifle is in the closet out to the farm, like it always was."

"It is? After all these years?"

"Well, nothin couldn't happen to it in the closet. It's still yours. I clean it every once in a while."

"I forgot all about it."

"Conrad and Paul used it a few times when they were little, before they had guns of their own. But they took good care of it. We didn't think you'd mind."

"No. Of course not."

"Elsie's twins have been after me lately to let 'em try it out. I'll have to do somethin one of these days, I suppose."

"It's all right by me, and I will come out and go hunting with you some time."

"I'd like that, George. Let's do it this year. We ain't gettin any younger."

"Okay. Let's."

"I'd like to show you where the little bastard was standin when he nailed me."

"Well, Cal...."

"Hold on. I told you it was over, and it is. I just want you to see it, that's all. When you stand there and look up at my tree, it's obvious. I want you to see that."

"Okay. I will then. This year. For sure."

Cal opened the passenger-side door of his pickup and fished around behind the seat.

George stood watching, not knowing whether he was supposed to wait, or whether it was already goodbye.

Before he could make up his mind, Cal came out of the truck with a gallon tin of maple syrup. He pushed it into George's hands. "Here," he said. "Take it."

"I can't, Cal. It's too much."

"No it ain't. I want you to."

"At least let me pay for it, then."

"You paid for lunch."

"Yeah, but...."

"Forget it, George. Just come out huntin with me."

"I will. But I'll be out to see you long before that."

"Good. So long then." He went around and got into the truck.

"Hey, Cal, thanks a lot for the syrup."

Cal waved and drove away.

George went into his building, up the echoing staircase and down the hall. His footsteps were loud in the empty hallway. His eyes had trouble adjusting from the bright spring sun to the gloom of the corridor.

Annie was back at her desk. She looked up expectantly. She obviously wanted to hear where he had been, but he didn't feel like talking. He checked the calendar. No one was scheduled to come in for another hour.

He went into his office and shut the door. He was really glad Cal had come to see him. But now that he was gone, there was an empty place. He missed him. It was strange, especially since they had gone for years without even talking to each other on the telephone. He wondered if Cal felt the same way about him. He'd never admit it if he did. And he had to say about himself that he wouldn't tell Cal he missed him either. He remembered how Cal had said that people would think you were crazy if they knew what you were thinking.

He could admit it to himself though. And here was a moment when he would have comforted himself, filled in the hole with a drink. If he had a drink, he might not have had to admit to himself that he wished Cal were still there. But he wasn't going to go back to that old way, at least he hoped he wasn't.

He thought about how Cal had come in to tell him he had given up the idea of vengeance. Poor Cal. That was a hard thing to come to. If only he could help. Cal had asked him for help, but he hadn't given him any. He knew Cal had had a rough winter, although he didn't know any of the details. But he knew Cal cobbled together a living however he could, buying and selling and trading to supplement his farming operation. He must have had to cut back a lot because of his hurt foot. He must have thought at first that if he could find out who shot him, he could get some money out of it, although if he had done some kind of cowboy shoot-out, it wouldn't have helped, even if he hadn't gotten caught and jailed for taking the law into his own hands. A dead shooter wouldn't have helped.

George was walking back and forth in front of his desk, having this conversation with himself. He set the can of syrup down and went around the desk and sat down and looked at it, and that was when it came to him. Cal must have outstanding hospital bills. George was pretty sure he didn't have insurance, and even if he did, it probably didn't cover all the hospital bills. So that was something he could do. The only question was whether to tell Cal or not. He thought about sending Cal the paid-up bill through the mail without saying he was the one who paid it, but he decided that wasn't a good idea. Cal would figure it out. It would make an uncomfortable place between them, like deeding the farm over to Cal had done, even though anything else would have been ridiculous. He couldn't sell Ma and Dad's place, especially not when Cal was keeping it going. And Laurie hated the thought of moving out of town. He knew he'd done the right thing giving Cal the place, and this would be right too. It made him feel good to think about it. He'd pay off Cal's hospital bills and not say anything about it. Maybe Cal would think the hospital had made a mistake. But *he* would know he'd been able to help. He sat at his desk, warming himself with the idea for a long time before he got to work.

Chapter 37

There it was again. Conrad knew it was really happening because it had happened before, but it was so strange that he knew no one would believe him if he tried to tell them about it. Ever since his accident, when he started up his saw and held it out in front of him, not even close to the place where he had cut himself, his leg would get crawly and jumpy, like it was afraid of the saw and was trying to get away from the danger. It was as though his leg had its own separate ideas about things. He could just hear how loud Paul would laugh if he tried to describe for him what his leg was doing, and if he tried to tell Cheryl, she would get all worried and motherly, like she thought there was something wrong with him. He couldn't tell anybody, even though he wished he could. Because weird as it was, he knew it was true. It had happened too many times, and usually when he wasn't even thinking about it.

He shut off the saw and sat down on a tree stump to have a cigarette. He had a couple days of work here, so there wasn't any sense in pushing to see how much he could do. The sky was blue, and there was a little breeze softly touching his face. The air was full of the sweet scents of earth and water and of plants beginning to grow. It was spring and a preview of beautiful days to come. Conrad felt grateful just to be alive. Two blue butterflies, like chips out of the spring sky, danced past him. He had been meaning to make some phone calls in order to get the next job lined up, but for some reason he hadn't done it yet. He didn't know where he was going after this job was finished.

He watched the smoke curling and twirling up from his cigarette, feeling happy to be exactly where he was, sitting on a stump in the spring woods. But gradually he began to feel that he wasn't alone. He got self-conscious, watching himself, as he felt he was being watched. He knew it was ridiculous, and still, he turned slowly around. On the other side of the clearing, at the edge of the trees, stood a tiny fawn, only a week or two old. He was standing absolutely still and unafraid and studying Conrad solemnly, with wide serious eyes.

Neither of them moved for what seemed like a long time, while Conrad's cigarette burned dangerously close to his fingers. He dropped it and moved his foot slightly to step it out, and when he looked up again, the spot under the trees was empty. The fawn was gone.

Conrad sat there, listening to the birds and the trickling of the runoff water, hoping foolishly that the fawn would come back, and thinking that he had known all along that there wasn't any sense in lining up another job because he was going to have to go back to the feed store. He was too far behind in his payments. First the accident, and then, just when his leg was strong enough to go back to work, mud season when he could only work on really cold days or risk turning his roads into mud holes. When the ground dried out enough so that he was able to get back to work full time, he was too far behind to catch up.

He stood and set his saw on the stump and took out his file and began to sharpen it while he thought over what he was going to do. Now that he knew he was going to leave this work, everything about it seemed painfully beautiful. The regular rasp of the file on the teeth of the saw turned into a song. The sweet breezes touched his cheek, as though trying to comfort him.

He thought he could stay where he was forever, but even while he thought that, he was also thinking that there wasn't much work time left in the afternoon. He decided to bring down the tops of the three trees he had cut. Then, if he had any of the afternoon left, he could buck them up at the landing.

He smoked another cigarette while he finished sharpening the saw, and then he carried it over to where the first top was lying. That was when he saw the patches of broad green leaves poking through the carpet of dead ones. The wild leeks were up. He looked around. There were patches everywhere, although he was almost sure there were none a few days ago when he had been standing in that exact spot.

He put down the saw and went and got his peavey. The sharp point might work almost as well as a shovel. He poked with the peavey around a patch of leeks, and then he was able to pull most of them out of the rocky ground without breaking them off. He made several piles as he dug. When he had a nice mess of them, he took off one of his shirts and wrapped them in it and stuck them behind the seat of the skidder to take home to Cheryl.

After that, he got busy. He trimmed the tops, and then he started the skidder. He loved that first loud crack of the engine as it came to life, shattering the silence. He thought about the skidder while he was chaining the tops and dragging them into position on the road so that he could drag them all down at once. He decided that when he finished this job, he would truck the skidder back to his house. He could go over it at night when he was all done at the feed store. It was a great chance to get it in good shape. Maybe he could even get Dwayne to help him.

Getting the tops dragged out to the road and lined up so he could hitch onto them all at once was a lot of work. He had to climb in and out of the skidder, adjusting all the chains until he got them right, but finally he was ready.

He put the skidder in a low gear and started her down the hill.

The tops made a wide load, sweeping down the road. They rolled and twisted some, bumping each other, but the chains held. Conrad loved bouncing along in the clatter of the engine and the clanging of the chains. He sat high above the ground, with a cigarette in the corner of his mouth. He felt like the king of the forest, guiding the slow procession down the hill. He was really going to miss this work.

When he got to the landing, he pulled the tops as close to the pile of firewood as he could get, and then he spent an hour sawing up the limbs into stove-length wood. About five o'clock, he called it quits for the day and started for home. On the way he stopped at Sanders General Store and bought a half-gallon of ice cream, the kind with strawberry and chocolate and vanilla, because everyone in the family liked something different.

After dinner, when he and Cheryl were sitting at the table with their coffee and cigarettes, Conrad said, "I bought some ice cream on the way home."

"You did? I didn't know that."

"You weren't in the kitchen when I got home. I put it in the freezer."

"I saw the leeks."

"They're up all over the woods."

"I don't know what to do with them."

"When Elsie and Paul and I were kids, we used to dig them for Ma. She'd make leek soup. It was delicious. I wonder if she still does. I should take her some leeks."

"You could ask her how she does it. I'd like to know."

"Okay. I will. But right now I'm goin to get the ice cream. I've got somethin I want to tell everybody."

Cheryl got out the bowls and spoons while he called downstairs to Dwayne and Dorrie. They came without argument when they heard about the ice cream.

"Hey Dad, can I have all three kinds? I'm really hungry."

"Dwayne, you just finished supper. You can't be hungry."

"Well, I am, Ma. It's all this homework I have to do."

Conrad piled up spoonfuls of ice cream in a mound of different colors. "There, Dwayne, that's all I can get in your bowl."

"Thanks, Dad." He took the bowl and sat down and began to eat.

Conrad looked at Dorrie.

"Just strawberry," she said.

Cheryl wanted a very small bit of chocolate. Conrad gave himself a lot of vanilla and less chocolate to even off what was left over. He sat down with his bowl and took a few bites before he said anything. He could feel Cheryl looking at him.

"What's the occasion, Dad?"

"I have a kind of announcement to make, and I want to thank everybody too."

Cheryl was taking tiny bites of her ice cream to make it last.

"This is what it is," Conrad said. "I'm goin to go back to work at the feed store, and I wanted you all to know."

"What?"

"Why?"

"Oh Dad. You don't want to do that."

"I can answer everybody at once. You're right, Dorrie. I don't want to, but I need to. I'm too far behind. Too many things got in the way. We need some steady money comin in every week for a while."

"When I get out for summer vacation, I'll get a job, Dad. I can help you."

"Me too," Dorrie said.

"Thanks, kids. That's really nice of you. It won't be forever, just for a while, until I get caught up. I haven't talked to John yet, but if he wants me to, I could start next week. I'll be done with Nathan's woodlot by then."

Cheryl said, "Oh Conrad, I'm sorry. I've been thinkin we had to do somethin different, only I didn't want it to be this."

"It's okay, Cheryl. I'll bring the skidder over here and get it in good shape. I can work on it nights when I'm done at the feed store. Maybe you'll help me some, Dwayne."

"Huh? Oh sure, if I can."

"I want to help too, Dad."

"Thanks, Dorrie. I'm hopin I can get some small woodlots to do in the evenin when the days are long. Maybe I can make enough money that way to get caught up, and then I could try it again. It might of worked if I had the skidder and the saw paid for before I started." He looked around at their faces and thought about how they really wanted him to be happy. He thought about how much he loved them. And he thought about how none of it mattered as long as they were together and all right. "Or maybe 'it's always somethin,' as they say, and I'll have to stay at the feed store." He looked around at them again. They were all three looking at him with love and worry. His heart swelled. "But that ain't so bad, as long as I've got all of you on my side."

Later on, when they went to bed, Cheryl was really sweet to him. "I know you loved bein out there on your own, Conrad, and I hoped you could keep on with it, even though I was scared for you."

"Tomorrow I'll call John, and I'll have to go by Ma and Dad's and tell 'em. Ma'll be pleased. She didn't want me to try it. She thought I couldn't make it."

"I wish she'd been wrong."

"This ain't goin to be forever. I'll get another chance." He kissed her and turned over. He lay there for a while thinking about his chances, and then he fell asleep.

Chapter 38

It was only a small feeling of discomfort, so small that it was hard to place exactly. Nora was sure she had had such a feeling before. It seemed so familiar. It wasn't at all alarming. Still, it had been strong enough to wake her up, and she was tired too. She turned on the bedside light and looked at the clock. It was only one o'clock, a long time until morning. The thing to do was to go back to sleep again now that the feeling was gone. It couldn't mean that the baby was coming, because it wasn't due for more than two weeks. This must be one of those pains that she seemed to have so many of these days, Braxton Hicks contractions, or something. Everyone said there were lots of them near the end.

Nora turned out the light and tried to find a comfortable position. There really wasn't a good way to lie down anymore. She couldn't lie on her stomach because then she would be lying on top of her baby.

Lying on her back with the full weight of her belly on top of her wasn't much better. It had to be one side or the other, with the great lump of her swollen stomach beside her, pinning her down.

She lay in the bed, trying to practice the breathing exercises. She had had to learn them from a book and from what Lena could remember. She wished now that she had gone to some natural childbirth classes. She could have asked Dr. Hamlin where to find them, although it was hard to ask him about anything. He disapproved of having a baby without a husband, and he thought it was terribly reckless of her to wait until she was five months' pregnant before she came to see him. Even so, she wished she had been more assertive on her visits to his office. If she had been, she might know what was going on now.

Some time later she was awake again. The feeling was back, the same but different. It could be what was supposed to happen next, or it could mean that something was wrong. How could she know which it was, since she hadn't ever done this before? Suppose something was wrong? Suppose the baby was dead? The horror she felt showed her how far she had come from the days when she thought she would have an abortion. Now the baby was real, already a part of her life. She knew she shouldn't think of it as a girl, but she was so sure. She already knew her. She already loved her. She knew they were going to be friends.

There was another pain like the one that had woken her up. She turned on the light. It was a little after two o'clock. She couldn't wake up Mom or Dad. The only thing to do was to go to sleep again. She lay still under the covers, trying not to think, but her heart was pounding.

After a while she got up and went to the bathroom. The hall was very still and empty in the dim light. She stood there for a minute listening hard, hoping to hear Mom or Dad. But there was no sound from their room, so she went slowly back to her bed.

Lena said that after you had a baby, your life wasn't your own anymore. But maybe it didn't have to be that way. She hoped it would be different for her. She lay there thinking about things and getting sleepy. But then there was another pain. It snapped her back into reality. She was like a fish on a line that a fisherman was playing with. She could swim along, thinking she was free. But when she got to the end of the line, she would feel that jerk of pain and know she had been fooling herself. She was hooked. There was no way out.

Some time later she was wide-awake again. When the pain let up, she went to the bathroom. Another pain hit on the way back, and she scurried into bed and tried to breathe until it was over. If the pains stayed that close together, she would have to tell someone. When the baby was really coming, you were supposed to time the pains and to time how long it was between pains. But was it really coming? It wasn't supposed to for two more weeks. If it wasn't coming, something must be wrong. She could call Lena and ask her. Lena would know. Lena would help her. But then she remembered that Jerry was back home. If she called, she would wake Jerry up. She decided not to.

If she could just get to sleep again, it might be morning when she woke up, and the pain might be gone, and she could go on the way she had been, even if it could only be for a short time. It had to happen, and soon. There was no way around that.

When she woke up again, it was twenty minutes until three. The pain was so real this time that she was scared. Something was definitely happening. She decided to tell Lena and Mom at three o'clock.

She turned the light off, but a few minutes later, she turned it back on. She thought it might be three o'clock, but it was only two forty-five. She turned the light off. When she turned it on the next time, only two more minutes had passed.' And the next time, even though she resisted for as long as she could, it was only four minutes closer to three. She told herself she couldn't get up until it was three o'clock, but she couldn't stay there any longer.

She got up, put on her bathrobe, and started down the stairs. She had already decided she would call Lena first, and from the downstairs phone, so it wouldn't wake up Mom and Dad. A pain overtook her on the stairs, and she had to stop and bend over, holding onto the banister until it passed. Lena was going to ask her how close together the pains were, and she didn't know. She didn't even know if they were regular.

The phone rang seven times. Nora was about to give up. In fact, she was starting to put down the receiver when she heard Lena say hello.

"Oh Lena, I'm so glad you answered."

"Nora? What time is it?"

"I'm sorry. It's three o'clock. I guess you were asleep."

"Well, of course."

"I'm sorry."

"What is it?"

"I don't know. Maybe it's nothing, but something's happening. I mean, I don't think it could be the baby coming, but I wanted to ask you about it."

"About what?"

"Well, I keep getting these pains like cramps in my stomach. They keep waking me up and...."

"Oh my God, Nora. Maybe...."

"But there are lots of contractions and stuff at the end, aren't there? I mean, how do you know...."

"How strong are they?"

"They keep waking me up and...."

"What does Mom say?"

"I haven't told her yet. I wanted to ask you first."

"I think you'd better wake her up."

"Do you? You think there's something wrong then."

"I don't know. I can't tell over the phone."

"Do you think maybe the baby isn't all right?"

"I don't know. Talk to Mom, and then call me back and tell me what she says."

"Okay. Do you think I should wake her up right away?"

"Yes."

"I hope she won't get mad."

"She won't. Do it now and then call me back. I'm going back to bed until you call."

"Lena?"

"What?"

"If something's wrong and I have to go to the hospital, will you come? You said you'd stay with me."

"I will. Don't worry. Just go tell Mom."

Nora hung up the phone and stood there looking at it. Did Lena think something was wrong? She went up the stairs slowly, pulling herself along by the banister. She went down the hall and stood at Mom and Dad's door with her hand raised, listening. There was no sound, not even Dad snoring.

She lowered her hand. She wasn't sure what to do. She decided to go back to her bed and think about whether or not to wake them up. She went slowly down the hall to her own room and sat down on the edge of the bed. What if Lena knew something was wrong and wanted Mom to be the one to tell her? The possibility of that grew in Nora's mind. She looked around the shadowy room. For the last few days she had felt more like her old self. She had had much more energy. She had worked hard to get the room ready for Phoenix. She got the old crib out of the attic and scrubbed it down and set it up beside her bed. Everything was ready now, but maybe she had done too much too fast. The feeling that something was wrong got stronger. That had to be why Lena told her to wake up Mom. Lena must know something she didn't want to tell.

Nora got up then and went down the hall to their bedroom door. She almost knocked, but she stopped herself. Suppose there was something wrong with the baby? Suppose Mom was glad? After all, Mom didn't want her to have this baby, so how could she help being glad? "But," Nora thought wearily, "I couldn't bear to see that in her face. It would make me not like her, and I don't want to not like her."

She went back to her room and began to get dressed. She had to go slowly, and once she had to sit down on the side of the bed and wait for a pain to go by. She didn't tell herself what she was doing, and she tried not to think about it, but she knew. Her mind was made up. She would go to the hospital and find out what was wrong, and if she was lucky, they would give her something to fix it, and she might even get home in time to go back to bed for a couple of hours.

She went down the stairs as quietly as she could, carrying her shoes. She sat down on the chair by the telephone to put them on. Should she call Lena? There wasn't anything new to tell her. She decided to leave a note instead. She wrote it on the telephone message pad.

> Dear Mom and Dad,
> I woke up in the night with the feeling that
> something might be wrong. I didn't want to
> bother you in case it was nothing. I've gone
> to the hospital to be on the safe side. I hope
> I will be back soon.
> Love,
> Nora

She put the notepad down on the kitchen table and went back through the dark house to get her coat. It wouldn't close in front over her stomach, but it was better than nothing. Outside it was dark and cold. There was a sharp smell of ice in the air, and the ground was hard with frost. She had to scrape a layer of it off the windshield. She got into the cold car and maneuvered out of the driveway around the other cars. She didn't know what she would do if a pain hit while she was driving, but when it happened, it wasn't too bad. She was able to keep driving right through it.

She parked in the emergency-room parking lot. Just inside the door, she had to stop a minute and support herself against the wall. This time it wasn't a pain. It was the bright lights, and the wide-awake people moving around and talking. It was too much, after the dark and the quiet and the aloneness of home. The woman behind the desk was staring at her, so she pulled herself together and went to sign herself in.

"What's the matter, hon? Is the baby coming?"

"I don't know. I don't think it could be labor pains. I'm not due for more than two weeks. I mean I know it *could* be early, but I just went to Dr. Hamlin, and he didn't think it would be this soon. Maybe it's not anything, but I keep getting these contractions."

"Dr. Hamlin's your doctor then? Did you call him?"

"No. I didn't want to wake him up in the middle of the night when it might not be important. I was hoping someone here could tell me if everything is okay. Unless it isn't," she finished lamely.

"All right. You have a chair over there, hon. Someone will call you in just a minute."

Nora sat down. Something must be wrong. She watched the woman behind the desk in case she knew and was going to tell somebody about it. She was freezing cold and damp with sweat.

The clock stayed still for several minutes and a bad pain and then moved forward with a jerk. After about ten minutes, although it felt much longer, Nora heard her name. She stood up. A man in a white jacket beckoned to her. She followed him through a swinging door behind the admitting desk and down a hall to an examining room where he handed her a hospital gown and told her he would be back soon. He went out and closed the door.

Of course. Why hadn't she remembered she would have to get undressed and be examined? She should have called Dr. Hamlin. He might have answered her questions over the telephone.

But it was too late now. She was freezing cold, and her stomach was so big that the hospital gown wouldn't meet in the back. She put her coat on again, even though *it* didn't meet in the front. She felt very alone, weary, and close to tears.

When the man came in again, she was sitting on the end of the table, wishing she had left her socks on but too tired and hopeless to get up and get them.

She saw he was only about her age. "Are you a doctor?"

He looked up from the chart he was reading and smiled. His glasses glinted in the fluorescent light. "That's right. What seems to be the trouble?"

But when she started to tell him how she was getting contractions, he cut her short. "I know that. It says that right here on your chart. I wondered if there was anything more, like your waters breaking or something. A reason why you thought it was time...." He looked at her, waiting for her to explain herself.

"But I *don't* know," she said, almost in tears. "I just got these pains that kept waking me up, and I thought you would know it was all right, like maybe it always happens a few weeks before the end, and then I could go back home again and not worry about it."

She looked at him, standing there with the chart in his hand and the light flashing off his glasses. "It's not fair. You're supposed to know," she said. "You're the doctor."

"Well, okay. Don't worry. Of course, I'll know. As soon as I examine you, I'll know. Now you need to be a good girl and lie down so I can see what's going on."

Nora sighed and lay back on the table with her feet up the way he said to, hoping she wouldn't get a pain while he was examining her. She had had one just before he came in, so maybe it would be all right. His hands were cold. She tried not to pay attention to what he was doing.

He pulled down the hospital gown and took a step back. "Well, congratulations. Your baby's on its way."

She looked at him in confusion. "It must be a mistake."

"You are four centimeters dilated already."

"But it's not due for two more weeks."

"Aren't you lucky? It has decided to surprise you and get here ahead of schedule."

"But...."

"You just stay right there. We'll have someone from obstetrics come down and get you."

"I wasn't planning on staying. I didn't bring anything with me."

"Well, plans change," he said. "I'll go out to the waiting room and tell your husband."

"No, don't. I don't have...nobody's out there. I drove myself."

"Okay, then," he said as he left the room. The door shut with a click.

And there she was. She didn't feel tired or hopeless any more. She was suddenly wide-awake. She was terrified. She had made such a mess of the whole thing from the very beginning, and now, she was about to have the baby, and no one even knew she was at the hospital. Why hadn't she called Lena back before she left? It seemed unbelievably stupid that she hadn't. But, of course, the answer was that she didn't think her labor was beginning. She thought something was wrong.

She had been crying a little while she thought these thoughts. Now she scolded herself. She was in for it, and that was that. She wiped her face on the skirt of the hospital gown. She hadn't even brought a handkerchief with her, but at least she didn't have to let any of these hospital people see her crying.

A few minutes later something bumped into the door, and a nurse came in pushing a wheelchair. "Come on, Mrs. Willard," she said. "I'm going to take you upstairs."

"I don't need that thing. I can walk."

"No, you can't. Get in."

"But, really. It's silly. I'd rather walk."

"That's against the rules. You have to go in a wheelchair. Get in."

Nora climbed slowly off the table into the chair, and the nurse put her clothes down on her lap and wheeled her to the elevator and from there to a room with a bed in it.

Other nurses shaved her and gave her an enema and put her into bed, all the time making cheerful conversation. But Nora was lost in a fog of fear and aloneness so complete that she didn't even pay attention to the pains that came and went.

Even when the bed got soaking wet, she just lay there. She didn't tell anyone.

The next time one of the nurses threw back the covers to check on her, she was surprised. "Nora, why didn't you tell us your waters broke?"

"I didn't know," Nora said. "I thought...." She could feel the embarrassment on her face. She had thought that there was no sense in saying anything, that it was just one more degradation, one more thing she had done wrong.

After that, the pains got stronger. She had to concentrate on her breathing while they were going on, and in between, she had to remind herself to relax.

Some unknown amount of time later, Nora looked up, and there was Lena, standing in the doorway.

"Lena. Is that really you?"

"How are you, Nora?"

"Oh God. I don't know. They say I'm having the baby right now. How did you find me?"

"Mom called when she got up and found your note. Why didn't you call me back? Why didn't you wake up Mom?"

"I don't know. I guess it was kind of dumb not to."

Just then she had to stop for a pain. It was a bad one, and it rolled over her before she could control it with her breathing. When it was over, Lena had her coat off and was standing beside her. She pushed Nora's sweaty hair back and stroked her forehead.

It was wonderful not to be alone any more. "I'm so glad you found me," she said.

"Mom's going to come as soon as she can. She had to go to work for a while and arrange something, but she's going to get here as soon as she can."

Nora reached out from under the covers and took Lena's hand. "I want Mom to come, but *you* are the one I was counting on. What did you do about Georgia and Jimmy?"

"Jerry got up to take care of them. He doesn't have to go anywhere until sometime this afternoon. We can worry about that later. Maybe the baby will be here by then." She gave Nora's hand a squeeze and smiled down at her. "They said everything was going the way it was supposed to."

"What time is it? I don't even know."

"It's a little before eight. There's plenty of time."

"It seems like I've been here forever."

"Mom wants me to call her up every hour to tell her how you are doing."

Just then they were interrupted by a nurse who came to check the baby's vital signs.

After she left, Nora said, "They do that a lot."

"That's good. You want them to know everything's still okay."

"What did you tell the kids?"

"I didn't. I didn't want...." She stopped speaking and looked at Nora.

"Go ahead and say it. You didn't want to get Georgia's hopes up until the baby is actually here, in case something happens to it when it's being born." She stopped for a minute, looking into Lena's face. "Or something might happen to me, but she would have to know about that sooner or later."

"Nora. Nothing's going to happen to you or to the baby. You heard the nurse say the baby was fine. That wasn't why I didn't tell her what was happening. I was in a hurry. I wanted to get here. I didn't want to get into a long conversation with her. You know she would have had a million questions. She always does."

Nora nodded and managed a small smile.

"I have been meaning to tell her more about the baby. I was just waiting until it was closer. I thought it was still a couple of weeks away."

"I did too. I guess you can't choose. At least it will be nice to have it over with. I'm awfully tired of lumbering around. I just wish my back didn't hurt so much."

"I remember that. Mine did too. Jerry rubbed my back for me. I'll go get some lotion from the nurses, and I'll rub yours for you. I remember it helped a lot."

"At first those nurses called me Mrs. Willard, but I saw one of them look at my hand, and after that, all of them started calling me Nora."

"You don't care what they call you."

"No, but I think that will happen more when I have a baby."

"It's simple. Just wear a ring. That'll fix it. I'll be right back."

When Lena came back, she rubbed Nora's lower back where it was cramped and aching. It felt wonderful. When the pains came, Lena helped her with the breathing, and afterward, she gave her chips of ice to suck on.

Nora asked her if she had had to take pain medicine when she was in labor.

"They gave me something with Georgia. I don't remember the name of it, but I think it was only a tranquilizer. It didn't seem to make much difference, and I think it helped mostly because I was scared."

"I'm scared right now, although it was worse before you got here."

"When I had Jimmy, I remembered that it didn't make much difference, and I kept telling myself I might take something, but I was going to wait a little while longer, and I ended up not needing it. Do you want me to go get the nurse to bring you something? I will, if you want me to."

"Maybe in a minute. It helps to know you didn't have to take anything."

"But everybody's different. I'll get you something anytime you say."

"Thanks, Lena. Just stay here with me."

The doctor came and went. Everything came and went. Nora felt cold and irritable. At one point she pictured how Adam was there when his wife gave birth and how it was just the two of them witnessing the precious moment together. But then she thought, "Wait a minute. Adam's child wasn't that old—was she four or five last summer?" It wasn't that long after the so-called precious moment that he was out getting another woman pregnant, which was pretty bad even if it was the first time he had been unfaithful to his wife, and Nora was pretty sure it wasn't. She reached out for Lena's hand again and held it and squeezed it and said, "I'm sorry I'm being so hard to get along with. I don't mean to be. I'm scared about what's going to happen next, I guess."

"It's okay. You're doing fine. Everybody gets irritable. It's part of it. I remember Jerry rubbing my back, and I thought, 'If he doesn't stop, I'm going to scream.' And he was just trying to be nice."

"That's the way I feel. It felt so great at first, but lately...I don't know. Something's changed.

"You are doing fine. It won't be too much longer now. That's the way you start to feel when it gets close."

"What did the doctor say? I'm six centimeters now, and I have to get to ten? Is that right? I can't remember."

"I think so, but he'll be back. Don't worry about the numbers. Your body knows what to do."

"I'm so glad you are my sister," Nora said, but before she had even finished the sentence, she was riding up the mountain of another pain, and she had to give it her full attention.

It went on like that for a while. Once or twice Nora almost fell asleep between pains, even though they were getting closer together and starting to hurt a lot more. But she had begun to get used to the whole round, lulled by it. Even though it hurt, she knew what to expect. It was predictable—Lena and the nurses, the room, even being cramped and shaky and cold. And the pains—for a few minutes there would be nothing but her and the pain, and then she would roll down the other side of it to the room, and Lena, and the nurses, and, once in a while, the doctor.

But her legs began to ache, and then they started shaking, and they shook so hard that Lena had to stand at her feet, holding her by the ankles, trying to hold them still. Her back hurt. Her pelvis hurt. She couldn't see how this was all going to end. It was going on too long, and nobody seemed to do anything. Even Lena wasn't helping.

Nora decided that no one was going to help her. She needed medication after all. She wasn't able to do any more without it. She decided that after the next pain, she would tell them to give her something. She was even planning what to say, when she heard the doctor say, "All right, Nora. You're a good girl. It's time to go."

And she was terrified all over again. "What do you mean? What's wrong?" she managed in a small voice.

"Nothing's wrong. You're a good girl, and you're doing everything just right. It's time to move on to the next stage. You don't want to stay here, do you? You don't want to do all this work for nothing. You want to see your baby, don't you?"

Things were already happening. The nurses were bustling around. Even Lena looked ready to move on. Only she, with fear bubbling through her, was hoping to stay where she was. But she didn't have a choice. Things were being done to her, quite beyond any choice she had in the matter. A nurse pushed a bed on wheels right up beside her, and one nurse got at her head and the other at her feet, and they began to lift her. Even Lena seemed ready to help.

Just then a pain, bigger than any that had gone before, started to roll over her. She tried to breathe, and one of the nurses said, "Wait. She's getting a pain. Go ahead, honey. Breathe into it. We'll wait for you."

When the pain had rolled on by, and she was left limp in its wake, they picked her up and slid her across to the new bed and wheeled her out into the hall, where the light was so bright it hurt her eyes. Her rolling bed passed someone on another rolling bed, and for a second, the Woody Allen humor of it broke through her fear.

They rolled her into another room and transferred her again. This time the bed, or table, was higher, and they put her feet in stirrups, spreading her legs wide apart. They put a sheet over her, but left the bottom part of her bare and exposed. She didn't care. She was long past modesty.

The room was stark, with harsh hospital lights. The doctor was there, smiling in a fatherly way.

She was made of ice. Things were going to happen, were already happening—everything was still the way it had always been, and it was just about to change, and she didn't know how. Then she got a bad pain, and she was so worried about it all that she forgot to do the breathing, which made it worse, until Lena reminded her and coached her through it.

She hated having her feet up in the air. To her surprise, she minded that more than being so exposed. But everything was queerly distorted by the pains, so that everything was unreal and not what anyone would expect. The pains were so close together that there was almost no time between them to rest and get ready for the next one. It seemed unfair that when they got stronger, they would also get closer together.

Still, she was even beginning to get used to that and was managing to do her breathing the way Lena wanted her to—panting mostly in the middle of the pain—when something new happened. She could feel all the bottom half of her pushing. It didn't hurt, and it didn't stop the pain. The two things were both going on at the same time. She didn't know whether it was supposed to be that way or not. Of course, she knew you had to push the baby out right at the end, but she didn't know if that was what she was doing. No one said anything about it, so she didn't either. She realized that she had almost forgotten about the baby. Up until this point, it had all seemed to be about her, and so much was happening to her that she hadn't had time to think about the baby at all.

And now, with almost a shock, she remembered what this was all about. With the next pain, the need to push was even stronger, and this time the doctor and the nurse both said to, and everybody got excited and enthusiastic. The whole atmosphere in the room changed. Lena was smiling and squeezing her hand. The doctor said he could see the top of the baby's head. And Mom was there too, standing beside Lena and smiling with love.

There was a moment of rejoicing, and then, when another pain started to roll over her and she began to push, the doctor told her not to, and she was thrown into confusion. "I can't help it. I can't stop it. It's pushing me."

But she tried to hold it back with everything she had, and the doctor said she was a good girl and doing fine. No one explained why she was supposed to hold it back when it wanted so much to be born. It didn't make any sense when it was all so close to being over. Still, she did what she was told, even though she resented it.

And then something hurt in a stinging kind of way. "People don't have any idea how many different kinds of pain they can feel all at once," she thought, and the doctor said the head was out.

Nora started to raise herself up to look, but she was too weak to sit up far enough, and no one helped her because they were all looking at the baby. Then she felt another push come over her, and this time it wasn't so strong, and she felt something wet and slithery, and everyone cheered, and the doctor held the baby up, sitting on his hand and still attached to Nora by the cord.

The baby was purplish-red, and she was crying. The doctor said, "It's a girl," but Nora already knew it was Phoenix, and in spite of the blood, she was beautiful.

Then there were more pains, and she had to push again until the afterbirth came out. But nothing mattered any more because it was all over, and it had turned out just right.

They covered her up and wheeled her into another room, one with a window, where the sun came streaming in. It was the middle of the day. Lena and Mom left to call Dad and Jerry, and Nora felt happy and hungry and wonderful. She lay there in the room, with spring sunlight coming through the window. She was tired and hungry, but happier than she could have imagined. It was as though, not just Phoenix, but the whole world had been born, fresh and bright and new. She lay there waiting for what was going to happen next, knowing that whatever it was, it would have Phoenix in it.

Ruth King Porter was born in New York City. She grew up in a small town in Ohio and graduated from St. John's College in Annapolis, MD. She and her husband, Bill Porter, came to Vermont in 1964 when Bill got a job on the *Rutland Herald*. In 1973 they moved to a farm in Adamant near Montpelier, where they have lived ever since. Porter raised their four children and most of their food and farm animals. She collaborated with her aunt, Bertha Frothingham, to edit a book of Maxwell Perkins' personal letters, *Father To Daughter*. Porter has also written a one-man show about Perkins and has written and published one previous novel, *The Simple Life*.

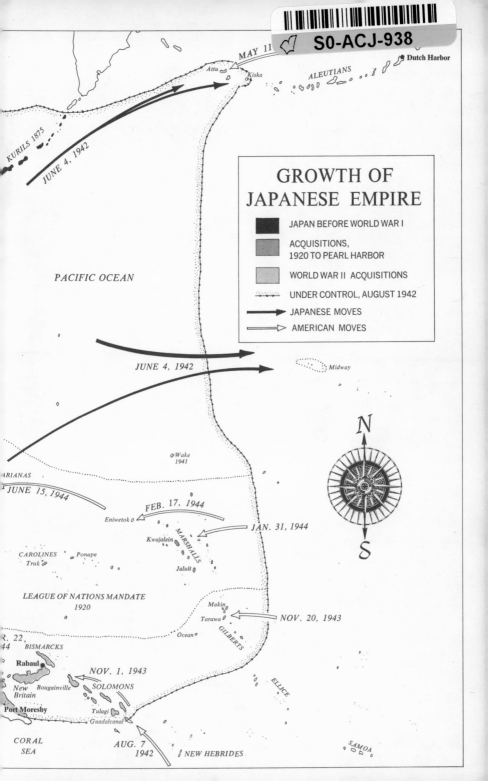

MAY 11

Attu   Kiska   ALEUTIANS   • Dutch Harbor

KURILS 1875

JUNE 4, 1942

PACIFIC OCEAN

GROWTH OF JAPANESE EMPIRE

JAPAN BEFORE WORLD WAR I

ACQUISITIONS, 1920 TO PEARL HARBOR

WORLD WAR II ACQUISITIONS

UNDER CONTROL, AUGUST 1942

JAPANESE MOVES

AMERICAN MOVES

JUNE 4, 1942

Midway

N

S

Wake 1941

ARIANAS

JUNE 15, 1944

FEB. 17, 1944

Eniwetok

JAN. 31, 1944

Kwajalein   MARSHALLS

CAROLINES   Ponape
Truk

Jaluit

LEAGUE OF NATIONS MANDATE 1920

Makin

Tarawa   GILBERTS

NOV. 20, 1943

Ocean

R. 22,
44   BISMARCKS

Rabaul

NOV. 1, 1943

New   Bougainville   SOLOMONS
Britain

ELLICE

Port Moresby

Tulagi

Guadalcanal

CORAL SEA

AUG. 7
1942   NEW HEBRIDES

SAMOA

JAPAN'S
IMPERIAL
CONSPIRACY

VOLUME II

JAPAN'S
IMPERIAL
CONSPIRACY

❧❦

BY DAVID BERGAMINI

VOLUME II

William Morrow and Company, Inc., New York

Photo Credits:
REGENT HIROHITO: *Underwood & Underwood*. THE WEIGHT
OF TRADITION: Sadako, Hirohito, wife in coronation robes, *Underwood & Underwood*. TRIP ABROAD: Yamagato, Hirohito & Prince
of Wales, Asaka on mountain, in car, *Underwood & Underwood*; Higashikuni, *United Press International*. HELPFUL KINSMEN: Kanin,
Kaya & wife, *United Press International*; Fushimi, Yamashina, Kuni
& wife, Takamatsu, *Underwood & Underwood*; Chichibu, Mikasa, *Pix,
Inc.* FAVORITE ADVISORS: Sugiyama, Yamamoto, *Underwood &
Underwood*; Suzuki Tei-ichi, Kido, Tojo, *Carl Mydans, LIFE Magazine © Time Inc.*; Konoye as Hitler, Konoye's body, *Wide World
Photos*. LOYAL OPPOSITION: Araki, *Foto Notori from Black Star*;
Ugaki, *Domon-ken from Black Star*; Honjo, *Hara Shobo*; Saionji &
Harada, *Iwanami Shoten*. VILLAINS AND VICTIMS: Inukai, *Underwood & Underwood*. JAPANESE AGGRESSION: Siege gun, *Underwood & Underwood*; three commanders, *United Press International*;
killing prisoners, *Carl Mydans, LIFE Magazine © Time Inc.* TRIUMPH AND DEFEAT: Hirohito on horseback, in railway car, *Wide
World Photos*. SARTOR RESARTUS: *Wide World Photos*.

19

PURGES OF 1935

THE ARMY GROWS DESPERATE

Neutralization of north China marked a chapter's end in the imperial program. Autonomous and under Japanese influence, the region would offer as much buffer zone against the West as Hirohito's great-grandfather Komei and his advisors had ever envisaged when they sought means of preserving Japan's security in the nineteenth century. North China could be used as a staging area for the Japanese Army to go north, or south, or even west into Mongolia and Tibet. For the majority of Japanese Army officers it was enough. To some of them it seemed more than enough—an overextension of Japanese capabilities which would only lead to disillusion, demoralization, and greed. Old-fashioned samurai were well aware that base, profit-conscious merchants—the traditional scum of the nation in samurai eyes—would exploit the area and see it as a steppingstone to the rice and oil fields of the East Indies.

A few days after the signing of the Ho-Umezu Pact in June 1935, Colonel Ishiwara Kanji, the zealous religious fanatic who had drafted the military planning for the conquest of Manchuria before 1931, submitted a hurried memo to Hirohito and the General Staff in which he stated categorically: "There is only one course for us: to consolidate and perfect our gains. If we do a fine job of reconstruction even only in Manchukuo, then the rest of China will follow us as a matter of course."

The time to attack Russia which staff planners had long calculated as optimum—namely, 1936—was fast approaching and no preparations were being made for it. The Strike-North Faction cast about for new forms of pressure to apply which might be more effective than organ-theory agitation. Two of the young antifascists who had been arrested after the Military Academy Plot and then released in late February 1935 circulated a pamphlet, which they had completed on May 11, entitled, "A Written Opinion on Purging the Army." In it they accused by name a number of Crows and Reliables, who were known to be close to the Emperor, of having officiated over such outrageously illegal activities as the March and October Plots of 1931.

In a more general way the authors held that factional strife could never be stilled until the Army was given a strong, upright, imperial leadership under popular, trustworthy figures. Count Terauchi's proposed policy of "purification" by straightforward discipline and outright dismissal of all troublemakers might be a cure but would effectively kill the patient and rid the officer corps of its best men. The other policy of constant manipulations and plots pursued by the ruling Control Clique would lead nowhere except to more vicious manipulations and plots. The members of the Control Faction—of Suzuki Tei-ichi's 1927 Study Group, of the Baden-Baden Reliables, and of the Three Crows—were all too deep in guilt and blackmail to supply honest leadership. Mazaki and Araki of the Strike-North Faction, by contrast, had played no part in plots, said the authors, except to prevent their fulfillment. It followed, then, that if respect for discipline and regulations was to be brought back to the Army, only Mazaki and Araki could set an honest example for younger officers and lead a genuinely sincere reform movement.

It was the first time that such revelations had been made in writing, and by June 1935 a privately printed edition of the pamphlet was being read avidly by everyone who could lay hands on a copy. The pamphlet seemed particularly timely because of the impending struggle in the Army over the August repostings. The rumor had reached the grapevine that War Minister Hayashi had promised to force out his friend Mazaki from the inspector generalship of education and rid the Army brass of its last tarnish of Strike-Northists.

The supporters of Araki and Mazaki sent out letters to all their sympathizers in the officer corps appealing for help in the forthcoming power struggle. By late June, on the basis of response to these letters, it was widely rumored that the Strike-North Faction would be able to call out at least a thousand officers in open insurrection if Mazaki's dismissal were forced through. A slim majority of the old-line generals who sat on the Supreme War Council advised Hirohito, Army Chief of Staff Prince Kanin, and War Minister Hayashi that such gross insubordination should be disregarded and the purge carried out as planned. At the end of June, Hayashi and Prince Kanin flew to Manchuria to explain the purge to the proconsuls of the Kwantung Army and remind them of their oaths of fealty to the Emperor. The two returned to Tokyo reassured that most of the men in the field could still be counted on to obey orders.

THE FIRING OF MAZAKI

On July 10 War Minister Hayashi called on Inspector General of Military Education Mazaki in his office on the edge of the palace woods and handed him the list of the August repostings. Almost all remaining Strike-North partisans in the bureaucracy were to be sent to the reserve or transferred to field commands. Mazaki himself was to be replaced as inspector general and moved up to the honorary position of supreme war councillor. Mazaki looked up from the list and stared at Hayashi accusingly.

Hayashi quickly said: "His Imperial Highness Prince Kanin wanted to have you removed from active service altogether, but I reported to His Highness that this would be impossible. However, if you cannot agree to this personnel shift, I must ask you for the sake of discipline in the Army to resign your commission."

"Very well," replied Mazaki, "if you publicly require it, I will resign. But personnel shifts are customarily approved by a joint meeting of all of the three chiefs [war minister, inspector general of military education, and chief of the Army General Staff]. If you should be allowed to force through this decision alone, you would damage the office of inspector general. Therefore I cannot give my consent on a purely personal basis; it must be done officially."

In demanding a full-dress confrontation with War Minister Hayashi and Chief of Staff Prince Kanin, Mazaki was requiring, in effect, that Prince Kanin, as the elder of the imperial family, take public responsibility for the decision to purge the Strike-North Faction from the Army. Implied in acceptance of this responsibility would be the larger one of having decided on the Strike South —of having done so, in secret, without consulting the councils of the other great families of Japan, the collective feudal leadership which still underlay the structure of the modern government.

The autocratic Prince Kanin accepted the challenge and the next day, July 11, told War Minister Hayashi to go ahead and schedule a conference of the three chiefs for the twelfth. When Hayashi phoned Mazaki with the news, Mazaki begged for a postponement. War Minister Hayashi refused it.

"All right," said Mazaki, "I shall come but I cannot prepare for a conference I know nothing about. I will merely be there without speaking."[1]

On the following morning when the conference of the three chiefs convened, Mazaki went straight to the attack. "Since I have not had time to study what these repostings are all about," he announced, "I would like to move for a recess."

The last surviving brother of Prince Asahiko—of Emperor Komei's chief counselor at Perry's coming eighty-two years earlier —nodded his head almost imperceptibly. At sixty-nine Prince Kanin was still one of the most handsome men in Japan. Now he stood up deliberately, ramrod straight, his mustache bristling, his luxuriant eyebrows slightly raised, and his square-cut, almost Occidental features set in cold hauteur. "How long do you need to prepare?" he asked.

[1] That afternoon, by no coincidence, retired Major General Eto Genkuro, who had helped to lead the attack on organ theorist Professor Minobe in the House of Peers, presented a formal petition at the palace asking that the Emperor declare himself an absolute sovereign rather than an organ of the government. On the advice of Privy Seal Secretary Kido, Hirohito decided to thank Major General Eto and promise him that the petition would be formally filed with the papers of the lord privy seal for the future reference of the Throne.

"Please give me three or four days," begged Mazaki, jumping to his feet.

"I have my own convenience to consider," stated Kanin, "so we will set the fifteenth as the date." He nodded again and Mazaki and War Minister Hayashi instantly backed from the office, bowing waist deep.

Mazaki drove directly to the home of retired War Minister Araki across the street from Meiji Shrine on the other side of the palace. After hearing his report on the meeting, Araki accompanied him back to the General Staff offices, beneath the southwest walls of the palace, and sought an immediate private audience with Chief of Staff Prince Kanin. Once admitted to Kanin's presence, Araki proceeded to deliver one of the casual, articulate monologues for which he was famous in his dealings with the monosyllabic members of the imperial family. War Minister Hayashi, he suggested, had made too much of an issue out of the August repostings and his attitude was considered by many of his colleagues to be "off the beaten track."

Araki continued somewhat threateningly: "If Mazaki's transfer is mandatory, I will persuade him to accept it, but I beg of Your Highness not to involve yourself directly, for that will only enlarge the strife and injure your cause."

"Then how," inquired Prince Kanin, "would you have me act at the three chiefs' conference?"

"Why, simply instruct Hayashi and Mazaki to confer together earnestly and bring you a plan for the repostings which they both agree upon."

"You think it sensible to try to achieve results through the consultation of only two men?" mused Kanin. "Well, all right, I will think about it."

In the ensuing three-day quest for compromise, War Minister Hayashi demonstrated repeatedly that he was pliable and that it was Prince Kanin who was adamant. Kanin would make only two concessions. He had wanted to put Lieutenant General Koiso, the March Plotter, in charge of Army Air Force headquarters and make Lieutenant General Tatekawa of the Literary Chrysanthemum vice chief of staff. At the urging of Araki, he finally agreed to postpone these moves and to leave Tatekawa and Koiso, who were his old cavalry cronies, in field commands.

Concerning the two most controversial transfers on the list, however, Prince Kanin remained absolutely inflexible. Mazaki, who pretended to greater righteousness than the Emperor, must go to the Supreme War Council, and former Secret Police Commandant Hata Shinji, who had been supplying Mazaki with information to use in making accusations, must resign his commission and retire to civilian life. It was rare for a member of the imperial family to show such personal animosity. In an effort to excuse Prince Kanin and so shield the Throne, War Minister Hayashi spread the report that it was really First Crow Nagata and other subordinates in the War Ministry who had insisted on Mazaki's dismissal.

At noon on July 15, an hour before the fateful three chiefs' conference was to commence, Araki made a final, unavailing attempt to break the deadlock. He called on War Minister Hayashi and warned him that it was unpatriotic to embroil a member of the imperial family in a matter of discipline for which Hayashi alone as war minister should be accountable; that historically any minister of the Emperor who sought to hide behind the Throne was automatically condemned by the Japanese people.

At one o'clock, after a hasty bowl of Japanese noodles, it was a worried War Minister Hayashi who convoked the three chiefs' conference. The Strike-North Inspector General of Military Education Mazaki once again leapt to the offensive. "Behind this conference," he declared, "I can see only impure motives." He drew from his uniform a document and laid it on the table. War Minister Hayashi and Prince Kanin saw at a glance that it was the "novel" which First Crow Nagata had drawn up for the government of Japan in the event that the March Plot had succeeded in 1931.

"This present plot, too," continued Mazaki, "has been created by the men of the March incident. It is the Control Clique which has destroyed discipline and caused unrest in the Army. Our pledge to the gods to purge the Army of vicious elements must be accomplished. And the first item on the agenda is to get rid of the Control Faction."

Prince Kanin's handsome face flushed and he interrupted: "Are you presuming to interfere in the duties of the war minister?"

"I have no place to hide," muttered Mazaki. "I may be a man of no ability but I am the duly invested inspector general of military education for the Emperor of Japan. I feel that the work of re-building the Imperial Army is of utmost importance and I also feel small when I find myself opposed by the words of Prince Kanin." Headlong, with words tumbling, Mazaki delivered his prepared thoughts on the realities of emotion in the ranks, of the institution of inspector generalship which he represented, and of the alien, unworthy motives which he saw behind this suicidal South-Striking purge of the Emperor's best samurai.

When Mazaki's outburst was over and he had spent his last blunt sentiment, Prince Kanin quietly declared: "I understand the inspector general's thoughts, but right now the Army is looking forward to the inspector general's resignation. You would prefer not to resign. Violence may come out of this meeting, but if so, the war minister is empowered to deal with it."

Once again Chief of Staff Prince Kanin arose and nodded, and Hayashi and Mazaki backed from the room, bowing.

RIPPLES AND THEIR CONTROL

War Minister Hayashi waited at the curb until the mortified Mazaki had driven away. A few moments later Prince Kanin emerged from General Staff Headquarters, all spit and polish in full dress, and climbed into the staff car which War Minister Hayashi had waiting. The two drove together with police escort to the Summer Palace at Hayama on the shore. Hirohito had arranged forehandedly not to be absent that afternoon on the imperial biological yacht. When the pair arrived at three o'clock, Hirohito saw Prince Kanin briefly in private, after which the chief of staff retired to a nearby inn. War Minister Hayashi meanwhile was held in conversation by Chief Aide-de-Camp Honjo and his assistants.

"I sensed that the situation was out of the ordinary and an emergency," noted Honjo in his diary. "So I had Aide Ishida listen to what War Minister Hayashi planned to report to the Throne. For myself I phoned Personnel Bureau Chief Imai and learned that the issue was indeed Inspector General of Education Mazaki, and that Field Marshal Prince Kanin had already committed himself to a stand. Therefore, after taking deep and sour consideration within myself, I officially reported to the Emperor the purpose of War Minister Hayashi's visit."

Emerging from Hirohito's presence, Honjo learned that now Mazaki, too, had arrived at the Summer Palace and was being entertained by one of the aides in a separate anteroom. Honjo went to greet him and learned that he wished to present a written protest to the Throne. Honjo returned to the Emperor and asked him if he would see Mazaki before War Minister Hayashi. Hirohito replied with a firm negative. And so at five o'clock Honjo reluctantly ushered War Minister Hayashi into the Imperial Presence. Honjo himself drank a whisky with Mazaki, advised him that his cause was hopeless, and sent him back to Tokyo with his protest still in his pocket.

In his tiny summer study, overlooking his beloved Sagami Bay, the well-briefed Hirohito was meanwhile putting War Minister Hayashi through an inquisition to make sure that what had happened would not be considered the responsibility of the Throne.

"As far as the main issue is concerned, the control of the Army," said Hirohito, "I am concerned that this appointment [of Mazaki to the Supreme War Council] may create a circular ripple. Do you accept responsibility for seeing that it will not spread?" Hayashi acknowledged that he would.

"And will you see to it that this does not affect the established regulations and process of law in regard to conferences of the three army chiefs?" Again Hayashi promised that he would.

"And War Minister Hayashi, if you find that men opposed to the principles of the inspector general of military education, such as Koiso, Tatekawa, and Nagata, have dealt unfairly with him, are you prepared to punish them in their turn?"

In view of the role played in the ouster by Prince Kanin, it was an unfair question, but the bland Hayashi scarcely blinked. "If I investigate," he said, "and find any unfairness I will deal with it severely."

Emerging much compromised from the Imperial Presence, War Minister Hayashi was cornered by Chief Aide-de-Camp Honjo and plied for a full report on the audience. He told Honjo of the Emperor's concern about causing circular waves but neglected to mention the Emperor's requirement that any unfairness must be punished.

After a restless, thoughtful night Honjo arose early the next morning and before breakfast called on three retired generals, three former aides of the Emperor, for advice. At 9:30 A.M. he begged audience with Hirohito and told him that he feared grave repercussions; that the imperial family had assumed an unprecedented amount of open responsibility; that it would be well for Field Marshal Prince Kanin and Field Marshal Prince Nashimoto[2] to take a conciliatory attitude toward the Strike-North Faction and do all they could "to smooth things over." Hirohito said that he felt it was too late for that but agreed to invite the two field marshals for lunch.

Hirohito went on to itemize in detail his personal grievances against the ousted Mazaki. He was constantly stirring up debate and criticism. He "acted against my will during the Jehol operation" of 1933 and had to be sent to the front to repair his error.[3] "I expected him to tender his resignation but he did not." Mazaki "has never shown much common sense." For instance, he recently sent an Army position paper to civilian advisor Count Makino, the lord privy seal, when everyone in the palace knew that it was utterly forbidden to mix civil and military business. "For some time now we have grappled with the need to take a firm stand toward China, yet it is said that Mazaki and Araki have recently tried to force War Minister Hayashi into adopting their views on the matter." Finally, "War Minister Hayashi says that the Military Academy Incident of last October was a plot engineered by Mazaki." In regard to this last accusation Honjo noted parenthetically in his diary: "Possibly Mazaki did mean to cause an incident which would be difficult to settle by court-martial but he surely did not mean the Military Academy Cadets' Incident in earnest."

That noon, while Hirohito was lunching in strict privacy with the two field marshals, Prince Kanin and Prince Nashimoto, the principal topic of conversation in other rooms of the palace was Major General Nagata, the first of the Three Crows of Baden-Baden. As chief of the Military Affairs Bureau, Nagata had concurred in the purge of Mazaki. Yet it was his written March Plot

[2] Nashimoto, the hostage imprisoned by MacArthur in 1945–46, was then the second oldest member of the imperial family.

[3] In which officers of Mazaki's Strike-North Faction had violated Hirohito's pledge to Chiang Kai-shek by breaching the Great Wall and penetrating China proper.

plan in the hands of Mazaki and Araki which now compromised the Throne. It was said that he had carelessly left the document lying about the War Ministry in a strongbox. There it had been found in 1932 and passed upward through channels to the then War Minister Araki, who had kept it. As if this were not reprehensible enough, Nagata had recently come out with two position papers, both of which hued closely to opinions held by Mazaki: that there would be no peace and stability in the Far East without Sino-Japanese friendship and that there could be no discipline within the Japanese Army unless a stop were put to the "unjust" practice of using the Army for political purposes. In short Nagata had become a liability, and Araki and Mazaki must be discredited.

After lunch Prince Kanin and Prince Nashimoto left the Summer Palace to return to Tokyo; Chief Aide-de-Camp Honjo was warned by the cigar-smoking grand chamberlain, Suzuki Kantaro, that it displeased the Emperor to hear excuses made in defense of ousted Mazaki; and Hirohito himself returned to duty by performing the ceremony of investiture for a new, more obedient inspector general of military education.

ARAKI'S REVELATIONS

Later that afternoon—July 16, 1935—a certain Lieutenant Colonel Aizawa Saburo called on First Crow Major General Nagata at the War Ministry and advised him to resign his post. Nagata knew the man as a master of *kendo*, the Japanese art of fencing, who had taught swordsmanship years ago at the military academy. Nagata also knew him to be a familiar of Hirohito's uncle, Prince Higashikuni, and of Prince Higashikuni's general factotum, retired Lieutenant Colonel Yasuda Tetsunosuke who had arranged the Prayer Meeting Plot. Back in the teens of the century when Prince Higashikuni had been the captain of a company, Yasuda had been one of his lieutenants and swordsman Aizawa one of his second lieutenants. Now, as Nagata knew, Aizawa was attached to the command of the 41st Regiment in Fukuyama on the Inland Sea some twelve hours away by train. How was it that he was here in Nagata's office full of indignation about Mazaki's dismissal? The dismissal had been announced on the radio only that morning less than ten hours ago.

As such thoughts flashed through First Crow Nagata's quick, filing-cabinet mind, swordsman Aizawa came to the end of his indignant tirade. Nagata thanked him for his interest in the nation's welfare and explained to him that Mazaki had been dismissed for the sake of discipline in the Army as a whole. Nagata added that he personally had no plans for resigning at present, and with that, pleading business, he saw Aizawa to the door in the comradely brusque manner for which he was renowned. As soon as he was alone, he called for Aizawa's dossier. It confirmed his recollections. Without more ado Nagata put through orders for Aizawa's transfer to the Japanese Territorial Army in Taiwan.

On July 18, before Aizawa received his new orders, the Supreme War Council met to put its stamp of approval on the August repostings already decided. Prince Kanin wisely sheathed the imperial power which he had brandished so autocratically at the three chiefs' conference three days earlier and did not attend. In his absence Araki and Mazaki put on a performance which confirmed the darkest fears at Court. Mazaki the day before had announced to all his friends who would listen that his dismissal had been "an intrusion on the supreme command" and had sought legal advice of the horse-faced Baron Hiranuma, president of the influential conservative National Foundation Society. Now, at the Supreme War Council, Mazaki and Araki turned a routine meeting into "four hours of anger," which, as one participant remarked, was "a rare thing to see in a group of old men."

The minutes of the meeting have not been preserved but according to the secret police sleuth assigned to inform himself on the proceedings, War Minister Hayashi opened with a monotone report on the sequence of events which had led up to Mazaki's resignation. Then four other generals, including Mazaki himself, stood up in turn to announce that they had no comment. Finally the articulate chieftain of the Strike-North Faction, former War Minister Araki, arose to his feet, beetled his brows at War Minister Hayashi, and said:

"When I left the war ministership what I asked was that you, Hayashi, and you, Mazaki, should get along, and reorganize and re-equip the army. I never suspected your integrity," he said, glaring at Hayashi, "but I never dreamed either that the friendship between Hayashi and Mazaki could be so weak. What hap-

pened? It must have been some major castastrophe to break the
bond between you two."

Hayashi disregarded the sarcasm and stared unblinking back at
Araki. "I am not aware that there has been any break in our friendship," he said.

"Oh," said Araki, "then you and Mazaki agree. No change in
your friendship. What beautiful control of the Army! I can't
understand this word 'control.' What does it mean?"

Hayashi responded by trying to sniffle in the sleeve of the
dragon. "Actually," he said, "someone did say that Mazaki was disturbing the Army and so I was obliged to do what I did."

"This other fellow, was he inside the Army or outside?"

"Inside."

"On active duty?"

"Not exactly."

"How many of him were there?"

Hayashi then muttered the names of three retired generals who
were known as cronies of Prince Kanin and also of Araki himself.
Two of them were classmates of Mazaki and Araki.

"These men," said Araki, "are excellent people but they are all
on the reserve list and remote from present conditions in the
Army. They have no right to opinions on personnel matters. If it
is true that these outsiders helped you to make your decision, it is
indeed an outrage. By and large, the whole proceeding strikes me
as rash and hasty. Any responsible war minister would have discussed matters at a conference of the three chiefs of the Army,
not taken precipitous action on the basis of outside advice. But
aren't there any other men involved?"

"No, only these three came to me," said Hayashi miserably.

"Just three outsiders? What were you doing as war minister
to let yourself be pushed around by three outsiders? I put it to you
that you made this decision yourself. And I ask you now, will you
change your mind when ten more powerful men come out on
the other side of the question?"

Hayashi did not answer. Having made it apparent that Hayashi
was too weak to serve as a responsible shield for the Throne, Araki
took advantage of the dramatic silence to lay three items in evidence on the table: First Crow Nagata's incriminating "novel,"

one of the March Plot smoke bombs, and a certificate written by the officers of the Chiba Infantry School attesting to the authenticity and purpose of the bomb.[4]

"These proofs," thundered Araki in the shocked silence of the Supreme War Council, "need no explanation here. Let us only consider for a moment whether this March Plot was wrong or right. Or is it possible that one of the anti-plotters like Mazaki was right? What on earth happened in these personnel shifts? Do you gentlemen think by such shifts we can control young officers who have already been led to ignore their superiors? I cannot permit the war minister to behave in such a double-dealing fashion. I feel ashamed of having recommended him."

General Watanabe Jotaro, the new inspector general of military education, was the first to find his tongue: "It is you who have upbraided us with these proofs of the ancient March Plot. Why have you had them so long in your own keeping? It is an insult—one I would like you to explain."

Araki said: "Now that it is too late, why add further to the blood-stained confusion? Such papers are never public papers. These, in particular, were discovered by accident in the belongings of a certain bureaucrat. Suppose these proofs were to be seen by all. What would happen? To keep them from the prying eyes of potential conspirators I have kept them personally as my private responsibility. I once considered burning them but slander is so popular nowadays and a man's name is so easily changed from white to black overnight that I just thought I might need them some time."

The meeting was effectively over though there was more argument. General Watanabe, the new inspector general, sought to establish the fact that Nagata's "novel" was a private plan written years ago in an excess of youth.

Araki replied: "Nagata was the chief of the Military Affairs Section in the War Ministry when he wrote this plan. He left it among his official papers. His superiors never asked him to explain it. It demonstrates a pure and utter corruption of discipline."

[4] The bombs had been kept in storerooms at the infantry school until 1933 when a fire had called attention to their presence. Araki, as war minister at the time, had been shown one of the bombs which had survived the fire and had kept it. He had ordered the rest to be destroyed.

War Minister Hayashi promised that he would make it his own responsibility to "discipline Nagata." The meeting broke up after a bootless but lengthy argument as to whether Araki had any right to possess the papers he had produced and as to whether they were public or private papers.

Little sickly General Matsui Iwane, later branded the Butcher of Nanking, professed after the meeting that he was completely astonished by Araki's revelations. After pondering them for a few days, he requested—in a voluntary gesture almost without precedent—that he be retired from active service and put on the reserve list. At a meeting of the Eleven Club on July 26, Hirohito's inner circle of Big Brotherly advisors resolved that Matsui's resignation was "most regrettable." Awakening to the fact that plots and murders of the previous years had been planned at the highest levels of government, Matsui felt that he personally must do something to save China. In his retirement he went directly to Peking and spent the rest of the fall there, in a private capacity, attempting to set up a native Chinese equivalent of the Greater East Asia Society which he had helped to found in Japan in 1933. The Chinese with whom he talked were understandably suspicious. As one of them later put it, "We thought Matsui's slogan 'Asia for the Asiatics' sounded like 'Asia for the Japanese.'"

On July 20, two days after the dramatic confrontation in the Supreme War Council, the ousted Mazaki came to the Summer Palace in Hayama to relinquish formally his staff of office. Beforehand Chief Aide-de-Camp Honjo begged the Emperor to be gracious with him and to accord him the customary words: "Thank you for your pains." Hirohito objected that once before when he had given such words to a military man dismissed in disgrace the fellow had gone about Tokyo citing the conventional courtesy as evidence that the Emperor had been on his side all along and had approved of the official stand he had taken.

"Mazaki," answered Honjo hotly, "may not be able to bend his principles but he is a faithful vassal and not such a man as would exploit the Emperor's words for his own private face."

A few minutes later, on his way to the audience chamber, Mazaki asked Honjo if it would be all right for him, when he saw the Emperor, to explain briefly the position he had taken. Honjo strictly enjoined him against doing anything so rash and irregular. And so Mazaki was given the bleak imperial thanks and retired permanently from the Emperor's presence. Chamberlains who witnessed his withdrawal described his open honest face as "smudged by tears."

NAGATA'S MURDER

News of the stormy session at the Supreme War Council, though censored from the newspapers, spread widely by word of mouth. With it traveled rumors that Araki was contemplating hara-kiri as a final protest and that the overwrought Mazaki elements might attack the War Ministry and burn it to the ground. In such an atmosphere, Lieutenant Colonel Aizawa, the fencing master who had warned First Crow Nagata to resign, received notification of his reposting to Taiwan. He at once traveled to Osaka, 300 miles away, and was received in audience by his old company commander, the Emperor's fork-tongued uncle, Prince Higashikuni.

What was said is unknown, but Higashikuni later volunteered the following account to Saionji's Secretary-Spy Harada: "Aizawa is an even simpler fellow than [my factotum] Yasuda. . . . When I was resting in Osaka after the recent maneuvers, Aizawa asked to see me. I at first declined, being exhausted, but when he said he was going to Taiwan I did see him. Apparently he really intended to go to Taiwan at that point and only got violent ideas after he went back up to Tokyo. Mazaki at that time was speaking slander of Nagata . . . and possibly he spoke in the same vein to Aizawa."

After talking to Higashikuni, instead of going on toward Hiroshima and Fukuyama, where his division was stationed—instead, that is, of going to pack for his transfer to Taiwan—Aizawa traveled in the other direction to Tokyo. There he did see Mazaki. According to Mazaki's own story, a story which the secret police failed to break down when they interrogated Mazaki for more than a year in 1936 and 1937, he advised Aizawa to obey orders and avoid violence. He added in jest, "If you want to kill anyone, take a stab at General Ugaki who began all this mess with the March Plot in 1931."

No longer sure of the resolve which had brought him to Tokyo, Aizawa went next to see Prince Asaka, Higashikuni's brother, who would later superintend at the rape of Nanking. According to the humorous story which Prince Asaka afterward told his best friends: "Aizawa said to me, 'I would like you to introduce me to General Ugaki,' and it appeared that if I had arranged the introduction, he would have assassinated Ugaki."

Prince Asaka declined to give the introduction. Instead, he did better. He went to the palace and told the chamberlain in charge of ceremonials that it was a matter of some urgency that he see the Emperor in private without attracting public attention. This was difficult because the Emperor was away at the Summer Palace in Hayama and no one could pay him a call without the journey being noticed. Therefore, Prince Asaka requested that when the Emperor came up to Tokyo on July 29 to attend the annual service for his grandfather at Meiji Shrine, Prince Asaka alone be allowed to serve as the member of the imperial family detailed to welcome him at the Tokyo railroad station. Somehow young Prince Kitashirakawa, twenty-four, failed to be informed of the arrangement and went to the station to ask his revered cousin a petty favor. Prince Asaka at once called the lord privy seal's secretary, Marquis Kido, and told him to make absolutely sure that, when Hirohito returned to Hayama, Asaka and the Emperor would have a few moments of complete privacy together. Kido promised to do what he could and found that the Emperor himself had already issued the necessary instructions. Imperial Household Minister Yuasa had cross-checked with the Emperor to be certain that the imperial wishes had not been misunderstood. Now Yuasa was "taking thought for the effect upon public opinion and doing his best to arrange matters." Kido was at pains to set forth in full in his diary his own part in these transactions and noted gravely at the end of his entry, "If the Emperor has already given the order it must be done as specified according to the unquestionable holy will."

When Hirohito returned to Hayama, Prince Asaka saw him off and all was settled. On August 5 War Minister Hayashi sent the vice war minister to plead with First Crow Nagata to accept a leave of absence and go on a trip abroad. Nagata steadfastly refused.

Having served for fourteen years as Hirohito's principal imple-
ment within the Army, having engineered the fall of the Choshu
clan in the 1920's, having recruited all the young faithfuls who
had participated in the plots to take Manchuria and suppress industrial and political dissent at home, he perhaps did not believe
what was about to happen to him. Or perhaps he had reached
a point in life where he felt required to stand on principle. Or perhaps he genuinely believed that the sacrifice of his life would help
the imperial cause which he had so long served.

In any event Prince Higashikuni's former subordinate, Lieutenant Colonel Aizawa Saburo, arrived at the War Ministry on
the morning of August 12, 1935, resolved to murder First Crow
Nagata. At the reception desk he gave the name of Major General
Yamaoka Shigeatsu whom he had known as an instructor at the
Staff College when he himself had been a fencing master at the
military academy. He was duly ushered into the office of Yamaoka
who was now director of the War Ministry's Equipment and
Supplies Bureau. Yamaoka was one of the Eleven Reliables chosen
at Baden-Baden. He had sided with the Strike-North group during
the faction fight but would survive the rebellion ahead and continue to hold field commands until his retirement in 1939. He
was known to fellow officers as a religious fanatic who worshipped
the ghosts in old samurai swords. He had a personal collection
of over one hundred historic blades and was responsible for the
regulation that all members of the Japanese officer corps should
own a sword and wear it at all public ceremonies. When the
overwrought Aizawa appeared in his presence, Yamaoka calmly
chatted with him and then, eschewing the telephone, sent a messenger boy to the Bureau of Military Affairs to make sure that its
director, First Crow Nagata, was in. When the messenger returned
with an affirmative answer, Yamaoka gave Aizawa directions as
to how to find his way.

Moments later Aizawa rushed through the outlying offices of
the sprawling Military Affairs Bureau, the largest in the Army, and
burst in on Nagata unannounced. Nagata was closeted with the
commandant of the Tokyo secret police.

"What is it?" he barked, without looking up.

Aizawa drew his sword with an audible swish. The secret police commandant gasped. Nagata sprang up, dodged a blow, and dashed for the door. Aizawa slashed at him and striped his back with blood. The secret police commandant tried to intervene and was pinked in the shoulder. Nagata, on his knees, struggled to open the door. Aizawa finished him off with a clean stroke that ran him through from back to front.

Leaving Nagata to die some minutes later, Aizawa ran to the office of Nemoto Hiroshi, a member of the 1927 Suzuki Study Group who was now in charge of the Army's Press Relations Squad.

"*Ah soka yattanai!*" ("So you really did do it!") exclaimed Nemoto.

Aizawa's finger was bleeding. He was sent under escort to the infirmary to have it bound up. On the way he crossed paths with Nagata's stretcher, which dripped blood. "I then remembered," he later testified in court, "that I had failed to kill Nagata with one blow and as a fencing master I felt deeply ashamed."

Having received first aid for his finger, Aizawa announced that he must return at once to his regiment in Fukuyama in order to pack his gear for the trip to Taiwan. He was, as Prince Higashikuni said, a simple fellow. He had committed a holy murder. He had been encouraged by the Emperor's two uncles. Prince Asaka had gone to see the Emperor in private to make sure that it would be all right. To Aizawa's "surprise," however, as he later testified, the secret police took him into custody and held him for trial.

When the secretary to the lord privy seal, Big Brother Marquis Kido, heard the news of First Crow Nagata's assassination, he failed in his diary to express his customary regrets. When Hirohito was informed of the murder by Chief Aide-de-Camp Honjo, he said, "It is extremely regrettable that such an incident has occurred in the Army. Please investigate and report the full details to me. Do you think it will be all right if I take my ordinary daily swim today?"

Honjo replied, "I, Shigeru, think this is an inexcusable incident but I do not think there will be any special succession of breaking waves as a result of it. And I will take pains to see that there are none. As for the honorable daily exercise, please go ahead with it."

PERIOD OF MOURNING

Nagata, once first among the Three Crows, had been murdered because he had allowed the evidence implicating the Emperor and his circle in the March Plot to come into the hands of the Strike-North Faction. He had also given indication that he parted with the Emperor over plans for war with China. Like most thoughtful Japanese he had considered friendship with China a prerequisite to the Pax Japonica which had been the national aspiration.

Nevertheless there was a certain meaningless malice about the sacrifice of Nagata. And it troubled members of the imperial circle who knew how deeply Hirohito was involved. Old Prince Saionji, when he heard Secretary-Spy Harada's report of the affair on August 16, muttered, "I thought that Japan could avoid it, but if these things happen often, perhaps Japan after all will have to take the course [of overthrowing monarchs] followed by France, Germany, and Russia." Harada noted that Saionji sighed "as if talking to himself."

For the next seven months all three Court diaries are eloquently gloomy. Chief Aide-de-Camp Honjo felt that the Emperor "mistrusts my attitude in regard to the recent imperial family incident." Saionji's Secretary Harada found himself increasingly out of things, and talking mostly to Foreign Office people. Kido became, if possible, more circumspect than usual in his jottings. Hardly anyone, in the Army or out of it, believed that Mazaki had engineered the killing of First Crow Nagata. Colonel Niimi of the secret police, who had been with Nagata when he died, was transferred to Kyoto; and Major General Yamaoka Shigeatsu, who had told Aizawa how to find Nagata's office, was reposted to a field command. War Minister Hayashi, who had stayed at home "with a cold" on the sultry August morning of Nagata's murder, was widely criticized: first for having foisted the responsibility of Mazaki's ouster on to Nagata's shoulders, then for having done nothing to protect Nagata. People called Hayashi "a silly man riding a good horse," "a fool in bed with a beautiful woman."

At Nagata's funeral there were two masters of ceremonies, one representing the Strike-North Faction, the other—Third Crow

Okamura Yasuji—representing the Strike-South Faction. The walls at the wake were banked with flowers from the palace. Chief of the Army General Staff Prince Kanin sent a message of condolence which called Nagata "a man of surpassing genius [who] . . . always took the lead both in Japan and foreign lands."

One of the mourners was Nagata's best friend, Major General Tojo Hideki, the later World War II prime minister. Ever since Baden-Baden he had served Nagata with a respectful devotion that amounted, in the eyes of his fellow officers, almost to servility. As soon as Nagata died Tojo had been granted leave from his command of the 24th Infantry Brigade in the southern island of Kyushu so that he could come to Tokyo for the obsequies. Now he stayed in Tokyo for a month settling Nagata's affairs and conferring with Field Marshal Prince Nashimoto, a friend of his late father, Lieutenant General Tojo Hidenori. Thereafter, until his own hanging in 1948, Tojo sent Nagata's widow a small but regular monthly allowance which he said came from his own pocket. At that time he made $1500 a year and had a wife and seven children.

When Tojo returned to duty in September he was entrusted with the extremely lucrative post of commandant of the Kwantung Army's secret police. Six months later when rebellion broke out in Tokyo, his secret police displayed uncanny efficiency in picking up all Kwantung Army sympathizers of the rebels and clapping them into preventive custody. From that time onward his career was meteoric: chief of staff, Kwantung Army, 1937; vice war minister, 1938; war minister 1940; prime minister and executive dictator in 1941. Throughout this rise he would be shown special marks of confidence by the Throne. And finally, during the war, he would be closer to Hirohito than anyone else except Big Brother Marquis Kido.

Under pressures generated by the Nagata murder, War Minister Hayashi on September 3, 1935, "saved the Cabinet" by resigning. The Cabinet itself was made to survive because its dissolution would have meant a general election, and a general election, unless carefully prepared, would almost certainly strengthen opposition to present policies. In War Minister Hayashi's place Hirohito was obliged to accept girl spy Eastern Jewel's adoptive kinsman, General Kawashima Yoshiyuki, a much compromised nonentity who stood politically in Erehwon.

Hirohito took an instant dislike to the new war minister but resolved to make the best of a bad situation. He took pains to have Kawashima carefully instructed from the outset: "The Army must be the Emperor's Army and all must unite and exert their efforts to make it a magnificent one. The Emperor personally wishes to supervise all diplomatic and military affairs so please inform him prior to making decisions on all matters."

Hirohito now found that one concession led to another. On September 16, news of the Prayer Meeting Plot of 1933 was finally allowed to be published in the newspaper. Prince Higashikuni's name, however, was not mentioned, and the trials of the guilty were to be postponed for another two years. On September 18 Professor Minobe, under great inducements, resigned from the House of Peers. In return, the various legal cases against him were dropped. On October 1, the Okada Cabinet, in a much negotiated statement designed to "clarify the national policy," promised "to stamp out the organ theory," to investigate the ideas and books of all professors, and to ban all injurious ones. On October 21 it was spread on the bureaucratic grapevine, and attested by Privy Seal Secretary Kido to be a matter of fact, that Prince Higashikuni was still paying his factotum, Lieutenant Colonel Yasuda, $86 a month for his help in past plots.

"SPIRIT OF POSITIVE FORCE"

By making concessions Hirohito was buying time while trying to consolidate Japan's new position south of the Great Wall. China's compliance with the terms of the Ho-Umezu Pact remained purely formal, superficial, and unhelpful. The Chinese smiled, as requested, at Japanese troops but made polite excuses not to assist them in any other way. Japanese plans for autonomous regions throughout north China were foundering for lack of influential Chinese who would serve as puppets.

On September 20, 1935, Foreign Minister Hirota—the only civilian to be hanged as a war criminal by the Allies in 1948—enunciated to Chiang Kai-shek "three principles of Japanese foreign policy": Nanking must help control anti-Japanese movements in

north China, she must sign a cultural agreement with Manchukuo and Japan, and she must join Japan in fighting the Bolshevik
menace in north China. In a fourth "principle," which Foreign
Minister Hirota transmitted verbally and in secret, Chiang Kai-
shek was informed that "centralization of power in China in the
city of Nanking is neither necessary nor desirable." It was almost
an exact repetition of the statement which Hirohito had approved
as secret Japanese policy a year earlier.

In his "principles" Foreign Minister Hirota was making a last
effort to realize Hirohito's desire that north China be made an
independent puppet state without resort to arms. The "principles"
were made explicit to Chiang Kai-shek because it was becoming
apparent that, without his co-operation, pressure alone would never
make north China independent. As Third Crow Major General
Okamura had just informed Prince Kanin: "It is predictable that
Chiang Kai-shek will persist in his negative attitude until he is
driven to the wall. . . . For the time being Japan must maintain
a policy based on the spirit of positive force."

In due course Chiang Kai-shek rejected Hirota's "principles" and
Emperor Hirohito accepted the need for positive force. On October 1, 1935, Finance Minister Takahashi sent word to Saionji, who
was celebrating his eighty-sixth birthday: "Several days ago the
foreign minister came to me and explained our plans in north
China. Now it seems that preparations for war are being made
in secret."

The preparations were spurred on two days later when Mussolini set a precedent and created a distraction by invading Ethiopia. Japan's underworld leader, "Darkside Emperor" Toyama,
promptly called a mass meeting to express sympathy for the fellow "colored people" of Ethiopia. The police used the meeting
as an excuse for a final crackdown on Toyama's Black Dragon
Society and on its affiliated lower-class religious sect, Omoto-kyo.
Thereafter the society held no more mass meetings and its once
powerful mafia-style leadership dwindled to a few score superan-
nuated rabble-rousers who maintained the society's dread name on
the door of a dusty one-room walk-up office on the periphery of
Tokyo's downtown business district.

World sympathy for the Ethiopians and failure of the Italians
to achieve a blitzkrieg conquest caused the Japanese General Staff
to refine its plans for China. On October 25, the chief of staff of

the Kwantung Army, a Strike-South lieutenant general named Nishio Toshizo, cabled the vice minister of war, another Strike-South lieutenant general, Furusho Mikio, advising him that propaganda must be carefully supervised and centralized in the planned war with China. "It must be made clear," he explained, "that when we do send our military forces to China some time in the future, we do it for the purpose of punishing the Chinese military clique and not the Chinese people at large."

The two princely chiefs of staff dealt sternly with Strike-North partisans who were still in a position to hamper the war preparations. In November Admiral Kato Kanji, the leader of the Navy's Strike-North Faction and a onetime friend of Navy Chief of Staff Prince Fushimi, was retired from active service. Remaining Strike-North admirals and generals were assigned watchdogs from the loyal ranks of Prince Kanin's Control Clique. In both Army and Navy a drastic reshuffle of the top brass was planned for December in order to remove Strike-North advocates from their last positions of power.

TENSION AT COURT

Prophets and supporters of the Strike-North policy were now faced by a loss of face. The "Crisis of 1936" was about to pass in peace. Chamberlains at Court waited tensely for the last day of 1935. The published plans of the Military Academy Plot of the year before made it abundantly clear that young dissidents might try to kill all the statesmen around the Throne. Kido, Harada, Makino, and the rest had been assigned plainclothes guards since First Crow Nagata's murder. But no one felt much reassured when, on October 30, an angry young man looked up organ theorist Minobe's name in the telephone directory and was narrowly apprehended at Minobe's door as he sought to break in with intent to kill.

Lord Privy Seal Makino, receiving anonymous letters and hearing constant gossip to the effect that he was "the originator of all past incidents," grew haggard with insomnia. His long-time cohort in the palace, Privy Council President Ikki, complained of intestinal bleeding. Even Chief of Staff Prince Kanin, a member of the Emperor's family, was not immune from attack. Prince Higashikuni, up to Tokyo on a visit from his command in Osaka,

told Secretary-Spy Harada on October 18, 1935, that there was
agitation in the ranks for Prince Kanin to resign because of "his
lack of sympathy for Mazaki and Araki." It was a "strange" idea,
said Higashikuni with indignation, because "princes never express
their sympathies." Harada nodded and then observed sanctimo-
niously that, of course, the impartiality of princes "should not extend to the distinction between right and wrong."

On November 27, 1935, Lord Privy Seal Count Makino begged
leave of the Throne to go into retirement. Privy Council President Ikki followed suit a few hours later. Both pleaded neuralgia,
decrepitude, and general ill health. Hirohito was loath to break
in new senior advisors and said that he would need time to consider their requests. For once old Prime-Minister-Maker Saionji,
when consulted, was pleased to agree with the Emperor. "Ikki
and Makino," he said, "are still capable of discharging their duties
as assistants to the Throne. I am eighty-six, with a bad memory
and bad eyes. It would be more natural to allow me to resign
first."[5]

Nevertheless on December 11, Lord Privy Seal Makino submitted his formal resignation verbally to the Throne. Hirohito,
expressing regret, promised to find a replacement for him as soon
as possible. Hirohito wished to make former Prime Minister Saito
the next lord privy seal but found that many chamberlains feared
Saito would be controversial because it was Saito's cabinet, in
1933, which had first endorsed the decision to try for a Strike
South. On December 20, while chamberlains were still endeavor-
ing to change Hirohito's mind, Count Makino forced the issue by
submitting his resignation in writing. Hirohito accepted it and
duly appointed Saito to take his place.

Privy Council President Ikki was persuaded to remain in office.
Hirohito personally recommended a new type of therapeutic belt
which he had read about as remedy for Ikki's sagging guts. At
the same time, as a sop to the Strike-North Faction, Hirohito
made General Araki a baron; as a prop for the Throne, he brought
back martinet General Terauchi from his preparations in Taiwan
to stand by close to the Throne in the troubled months ahead.

---

[5] Ikki was then sixty-eight and would live to be seventy-eight; Makino was
seventy-three and would live to be eighty-seven.

20

FEBRUARY MUTINY

(1936)

TEASING A SHOWDOWN

The venal old loyalists on the steps of the Throne had good reason to worry about their health. In effect, Hirohito had set them up as targets and was encouraging a group of would-be assassins to start shooting. The silent three-year struggle with the Strike-North Faction had gone on long enough. It was time for a confrontation. Hirohito and his kinsmen had decided that only an outright rebellion would shame the nation and provide justification for a thoroughgoing purge of disaffection. By the same token Generals Araki and Mazaki of the Strike-North Faction, along with many samurai of the old school, felt that a mutiny in the ranks, if large and protracted enough, would win popular support and force Hirohito to reflect.

The chosen assassin-dupes for the coming confrontation were the young antifascistic captains and lieutenants of the National Principle Group who had started the Military Academy Incident of the year before. They qualified as sacrificial moderators in the feud because, though nominally aligned with the Strike-North Faction, they were not really interested in any strategic concept abroad but only in reform and frankness at home.

The young men of the National Principle Group began meeting at bars and cheap geisha houses to consider the possibility of insurrection in November 1935. Their ringleaders were two former Army comrades, Muranaka and Isobe, who had written the seditious pamphlet in May which had called attention to First Crow Nagata's involvement in the 1931 March Plot. Their pamphlet had been pointed out to Chief of Staff Prince Kanin during his struggle in July to fire General Mazaki. It had angered him. On July 30 he had sent War Minister Hayashi on a special trip to the Summer Palace in Hayama to ask Hirohito to approve the expulsion of the two pamphleteers from the Army. To retire men from active to reserve status was not an uncommon form of punishment for Army dissidents but to expel them from the Army altogether was most unusual. Former messmates gave the two disgruntled new civilians much sympathy.

Emperor Hirohito's brother Prince Chichibu personally kept abreast of the plans of the National Principle Group through four of its members who had been his classmates in military academy. These four he regularly invited up to his villa for chats. And these four, when they later faced firing squads, protested in vain that Prince Chichibu had encouraged them. One of them left his family a note lamenting: "Prince Chichibu told me, 'When the coup d'etat comes, I want you to head a company and invite me to see you off as you march from your barracks.'" Another left a bundle of poems, written in prison, which the secret police impounded and turned over to Chichibu's equerry. Having gone through them, Prince Chichibu returned most of them to the young man's family. The bereaved parents felt greatly honored that Princess Chichibu had selected several of them with her own hand and had had them beautifully mounted and framed.

Prince Higashikuni and Prince Asaka, the Emperor's two uncles, also talked frequently with the young plotters and sympathized with their complaints. The rebels' greatest encouragement, however, came from Major General Tiger Yamashita who had charge of the palace effort to infiltrate the Strike-North movement with spies. Yamashita made a practice of meeting the young rebels at bars and having a drink with them. He introduced them to Third Crow Major General Okamura, who was now chief of Intelligence in the General Staff, and also to Colonel Nemoto of the War Ministry Press Relations Squad, who had grunted congratulations at swordsman Aizawa after the murder of First Crow Nagata. Tiger Yamashita and his companions all reported their observations to Chief of Staff Prince Kanin.

The young men of the National Principle Group were flattered by all the attention they were receiving from intimates of the Throne but knew enough to be wary. Their friends warned them against being exploited and told them, jokingly, that they were "natural leftists trying to dress on the right." The young men sent a deputation to the home of former War Minister Araki, the leader of the Strike-North Faction. Araki smiled at them encouragingly but carefully avoided saying anything by which he would commit himself. They went back to Major General Tiger Yamashita, the spy of the Strike-South Faction, and were advised by him "not to act without careful preparation." They set Christmas Day 1935, when Western military attachés would be out wassailing, as their tentative deadline for revolution.

On December 20 they sent an embassy to the second ranking leader of the Strike North, General Mazaki. He told them that they were fools to consider rebellion and doubly fools to consult him about their plans when they knew he was already discredited and under constant police surveillance. They accosted a third Strike-North general and got even more explicit advice: "The gods, the Emperor, and the good earth are all against you. The members of the Control Clique [Strike-South Faction] are just waiting for a half-prepared outbreak to give them an opportunity for a house cleaning."[1]

On December 22 Tiger Yamashita, the infiltrator from the ranks of the Strike-Southists, agreed to meet the young idealists at the Honored Parlor Restaurant in northern Tokyo. He did not keep the appointment, and when the conspirators had waited in vain for him all evening, they agreed to give up their plan for an outbreak on Christmas Day. On their way home a group of them

[1] The speaker was Lieutenant General Yanagawa Heisuke, who had been vice war minister under Strike-North leader Araki. He was known to Hirohito as a moderate of the Strike-North Faction and a close friend of the ubiquitous Colonel Suzuki. At this moment he was on his way to Taiwan to replace martinet Terauchi as commander-in-chief of Japan's territorial army there. Later, in 1937, he would clear himself of Strike-North guilt in Hirohito's eyes by devising the Hangchow Bay landing which enabled the Japanese Army to take Nanking.

stopped at a police station and voluntarily swore out a complete report on their own activities.

Still at large, the conspirators, on Christmas Eve, stopped for a few consoling thimbles of saké at the home of the ideologist of the Strike-North Faction, the tough old radical writer Kita Ikki, who had first split the Emperor's cabal in 1922 by refusing to participate in Hirohito's palace indoctrination center, the University Lodging House. Schooled by years of experience with the secret police, Kita advised the young men to be patient and await their opportunity. In the meantime he proposed that they participate in a small public rally to protest the appointment of former Prime Minister Saito as lord privy seal. He convinced the young officers that Saito had taken bribes in connection with the Teikoku Rayon Company stock swindle of 1934. The protest meeting was duly held on December 30, 1935, and was duly broken up by the police. Several of the young officers were taken into custody but all were released a few days later to ripen their plans.

At year's end Big Brother Marquis Kido, secretary to the lord privy seal, leafed into his diary the police report on the conspirators' latest insurrection plan: 1st Infantry, 1st Company, to take the home minister's residence; 3d Infantry, 3d Company, to kill the prime minister; 1st Infantry, 2d Company, to hunt down Lord Privy Seal Saito—and so on. Except for a few details it was substantially the Military Academy Plan of 1934 and also the plan that would be executed two months later. By the time that fateful New Year of 1936 had arrived, the chamberlains in the palace knew it almost by heart.

If any complacent courtiers retained a doubt as to the depth of disenchantment in the ranks of the Army, it was dispelled a few days later in January, when an entire company of Japanese infantry, together with their commissioned and noncommissioned officers, crossed the border from Manchukuo into Russia and surrendered to the Red Army. The officers hoped to create an incident which would redirect policy toward the Strike North. The men were simply glad to escape the Manchukuoan hell of torture and murder in which they were obliged to officiate. No body of Japanese soldiers had ever defected before to a foreign power, and everyone in authority realized that only desperation could have driven them to it now.

THE TALKING GODDESS

To prepare for the ill-conceived insurrection in the offing, Hirohito's double-dealing uncle, Prince Higashikuni, devised an ingenious religious fraud to blackmail and gag aristocrats who had criticized Hirohito most outspokenly in the past. On November 22, 1935, Prince Higashikuni had invited a religious confidence man, the ventriloquist, Ohara Tatsuo, alias Ohara Ryukai or Dragon-Sea, to a room in the old unused private quarters of Emperor Meiji in the southern extremities of the palace's gardens. There he gave Dragon-Sea a set of ceremonial imperial robes and other tokens of imperial favor including a pair of Hirohito's gloves and a cigarette case embossed with the chrysanthemum crest. To these props Dragon-Sea added a statue of the goddess of mercy which could talk—at least he could make her seem to talk—and thereupon he set himself up in business as an oracle in the little temple of Iribune in the Tokyo suburb of Shiina.

By Higashikuni's introduction Dragon-Sea acquired the patronage of former chief Court Lady Shimazu Haruko, who had been eased out of the palace in 1933 for her involvement in the Red Scandal and the concubine controversy. Lady Shimazu loved nothing better than an uplifting, shiver-filled seance. So did many of her best friends, and she was ideally well connected. As a cousin of Empress Nagako's mother and an intimate of Hirohito's own mother, the Empress Dowager, she was on fervent spiritual terms with almost every kindly body in the elder generation of the aristocracy—almost everyone who took a high-toned moralistic approach to matters of state. In addition to counts and countesses, the circle of her acquaintance included retired admirals, retired generals, leaders of veterans' organizations, and anti-organ theorists by the score. One of her dearest friends was Shinto priest Hata Shinji, the former commandant of the Tokyo secret police who had supplied damaging material against the Strike-South Faction during the struggle before Mazaki's ouster.

By mid-January Lady Shimazu was bringing her friends by droves to hear the ventriloquistic prophecies of Dragon-Sea's statue and to attend spiritualistic manifestations and materializations. Outside the walls of Dragon-Sea's fashionable little temple, trustworthy police agents stood nightly guard to take notes on attendance. In later police reports aged Admiral Yamamoto Eisuke figured prominently as a regular participant in the "services." He was one of the first choices for prime minister in the cabinet which the young insurgents of the National Principle Group hoped to bring to power. Many other prominent members of Tokyo's high society, particularly wives, also attended. All were thereby induced to hold their peace in the months ahead.

At the seances the congregations of aristocrats heard a combination of filth and philosophy which was provided Dragon-Sea by Prince Higashikuni. The gossip amused them and compromised them. According to former Court Lady Shimazu Haruko's confession, preserved in police files after she had been committed to a sanatorium in December 1936, spirits of people alive and dead appeared before the audiences and traded in all sorts of blasphemous gossip about the imperial family:

The dead spirit of Namba Daisaku [Hirohito's 1923 assassin, who missed] appeared with the living spirit of Prince Chichibu [Hirohito's brother]. Chichibu's spirit says that Namba steals the virginity of his fiancee.[2]

Prince Takamatsu [Hirohito's second brother] appears in spirit and says that his real mother, Lady Blank Blank, was one of Emperor Taisho's serving girls. . . .

The chamberlain [General Nogi] appeared who served the crown prince [Hirohito] and then committed hara-kiri. His ghost, dressed like an imperial prince himself, said, "I was defeated for saying that Prince Chichibu should be the one proclaimed Crown Prince. . . ."

The ghost of Emperor Taisho's chamberlain appears and says that he has been a lover of the Empress Dowager [Hirohito's mother]. . . .

Questions were put by the Kujos [the Empress Dowager's brother and sister-in-law]. . . .

Prince Chichibu's living ghost appears and speaks of his affair with Princess Noriko [Ito Noriko, who had been implicated in the Red Scandal at the Peers' School]. . . .

There is a front face and a back face to every mirror. On our front face it is inscribed officially that if we worship the gods they will pro-

[2] There may be a confusion of brothers here. Empress Nagako's brother, Asaakira, in 1924, broke off his engagement with a girl because it was discovered that she was having an affair with a kinsman of the Namba clan.

tect us. On the back face we believe that the Imperial Purpose will ultimately make itself clear and light the road toward restoration of the Throne. The back face is pregnant with such meanings and the front face is kept to convince ordinary men so that they may someday see around to the back. Faithful souls can approach the back of the mirror only gradually. And even beyond the back of the mirror there are further stages of enlightenment such as *himarogi* and so on which bring full revelation. Only men of the highest consciousness can attain them and it is very rare. . . .

On July 17 there will be a meeting of all the spirits of the world. It will be the first meeting of the Five Lights. . . . The honorable soul of the Emperor Meiji will not attend, being temporarily detained by the work of the Empress Dowager.[3] Then the way to clarification of the national structure and to restoration will be revealed—the way to divine government and to the world of a just god.

The work of the Five Lights is to decide on a regent and select an assistant for the time of minority of the crown prince [Akihito, who is still crown prince in 1970]. In the world of spirits the crown prince possesses the soul of Emperor Meiji and at the same time has a great-ness of his own self. This has been revealed to us. Therefore Prince Chichibu [Hirohito's brother] will withdraw in favor of Prince Taka-matsu [Hirohito's second brother], and Takamatsu will become the assistant and regent. The Emperor himself will die after fifteen years [1951]. . . . The Emperor has a karma [inherited guilt] to expiate and so cannot realize revelation and restoration. He cannot escape an early death. We have to achieve enlightenment and a supreme offering to the gods of our own soil in order to restore our gods and clarify the national structure. It is like opening up the rocks that they may speak but we have the key to do it. . . . The Five Lights will become ten, twenty, forty lights. . . . We must have faith and expand.

Wild words they were as Lady Shimazu recalled them to the police. But even the smut was enough, wild though it might be, to convict anyone of lèse majesté who listened to it without pro-test. The mysticism was worse, for it showed a definite longing to be rid of Hirohito and it imputed to him a fatal guilt for the many murders done during his reign.

[3] The Empress Dowager was then involved in petty palace intrigues against her son Hirohito. The identity of the Five Lights is mysterious. According to one well-educated Japanese guess, the first four may have been noted loyalists who died for the Throne in centuries past and the fifth may have been the re-cently sacrificed martyr, First Crow Nagata.

FINAL INCITEMENTS

On January 27, 1936, Prince Higashikuni sprang another trapdoor in his Pandora's box of blackmail when the police released some 500 sturdy sword arms who had been jailed on suspicion of complicity in the 1933 Prayer Meeting Plot. Under the supervision of Higashikuni's faithful factotum, retired Lieutenant Colonel Yasuda, the paroled convicts opened a headquarters and remained ready at hand as a riot squad—"all picked men"—who could be thrown into the breach if the forthcoming rebellion in any way misfired. Higashikuni's man Yasuda kept the prince informed of their doings by messages delivered by courier to the bodyguard at the gates of Higashikuni's villa.[4] In the event, the riot squad never had to be used but the men in it won freedom from prosecution by their stand-by service.

On January 28, 1936, the court-martial proceedings began against First Crow Nagata's killer, Prince Higashikuni's former second lieutenant, Aizawa. They were held in the most emotionally flammable surroundings possible: the barracks of the 1st Division. It was this division, one of the two stationed in Tokyo, which contained most of the young officers of the antifascist National Principle Group. It was this division which, on the papers of past plot plans, was expected to supply a majority of the forces for any rebellion. Court-martial defendant Aizawa had served as a captain and major in the division from 1926 to 1931, and the men of the division had just been notified in December that they were all to be transferred imminently to garrison duty in Manchuria. The 1st Division had never before been sent overseas except for action in time of war.

The advocate assigned to defend assassin Aizawa was Lieutenant Colonel Mitsui Sakichi, the young man who had forced his way into the home of the Mitsui cartel magnate two years earlier and who for several months had been working closely with the Strike-South Faction's spy in Strike-North ranks, Major General

[4] The chief of Higashikuni's bodyguard was Captain Kiyoura Sueo, the eighth son of former Prime Minister Kiyoura whom Hirohito had recalled from oblivion to lead the government during the Choshu purge of 1924.

Tiger Yamashita. In 1937, Mitsui would be given three years' suspended sentence for his part in the 1936 rebellion. In 1942, during the war, he would be elected to the Diet.

At Aizawa's trial Mitsui played to packed houses. "If an error is made at this trial," he orated, "it will have serious consequences. . . . If the court fails to understand the spirit which guided Aizawa, a second and even a third Aizawa will arise. . . . A large majority of the junior officers are determined to purge the Army of outside influence, and the nation sincerely desires that the Army will prove itself to be the Army of the Emperor."

Assassin Aizawa himself was put on the stand and cross-questioned sympathetically. He breathed not a word of his meetings with Prince Higashikuni and Prince Asaka. He testified, however, that on his first journey to Tokyo, when he warned Nagata instead of killing him, "I could not sleep on the train and in the morning I heard a voice, as if from on high, telling me not to act too rashly. . . . Only later did I come to realize that Nagata was the headquarters of all the evil. If he would not resign there was only one thing to do. I determined to make myself a demon and finish his life with one stroke. . . . When on the Emperor's authority the inspector general of military education was transferred to the honorable post of a Supreme War Councillor, it seemed to me like converting the Imperial Army into a private concern."

Big Brother Kido, secretary to the lord privy seal, kept close track of the proceedings at the Aizawa trial and worried about them. On February 2, after careful research, however, he decided that everything would be all right. He compared defense lawyer Lieutenant Colonel Mitsui with Colonel Ishiwara Kanji, who had planned the conquest of Manchuria, and with Colonel Hashimoto Kingoro, the firebrand who would later sink the U.S. gunboat *Panay*. All three felt the need for domestic reform and sympathized with the National Principle Group. "But when it comes to the point," Kido concluded, "they will all present a united front to outsiders."

While the Aizawa trial was in progress, the Diet was dissolved and the nation was treated to its first election campaign since

1932. The Strike-North group in the Army sided with the Constitutionalists on a platform of traditional samurai bravado. The Anti-Constitutionalists, Hirohito's Control Clique, and the Army Purification Movement backed incumbent Prime Minister Okada. Although fascistically inclined themselves, they campaigned under the slogan, "What shall it be, parliamentary government or fascism?" The people responded to the slogan by giving them a landslide victory: 205 Diet seats to 174 for the Constitutionalists. It was a clear triumph for Hirohito's public sentiments, and a rebuff to the fascist ideas he toyed with privately.

COURAGE AT STICKING POINT

During January the dissident young officers of the National Principle Group had paid calls on Prince Chichibu, on War Minister Kawashima, and on General Mazaki of the Strike-North Faction. They found everyone of importance friendly but evasive, not willing to support them nor yet to discourage them. General Mazaki, for instance, offered to lend them money but added, "If anything happens, don't say I gave it to you."

On the evening of January 28, the conspirators met with a sympathetic company commander, Captain Yamaguchi Ichitaro, who was the son-in-law of General Honjo, Hirohito's chief aide-de-camp. On February 10 they met again with Yamaguchi in the staff room of the 1st Regiment, 1st Division, where he was duty officer. There for the first time they discussed plans for a rebellion in concrete operational terms. The next day they sent a deputation to the home of the Strike-North ideologist, Kita Ikki, to see his disciple and servant, Nishida Chikara. Like themselves, Nishida was a friend and former classmate of Prince Chichibu. It was he who had first mimeographed and distributed intellectual Ikki's radical writings for Prince Chichibu in 1921. Now Nishida welcomed the rebels and promised to muster popular backing for them.

On February 15 the reluctant rebels finally revisited Major General Tiger Yamashita, their watchdog from the palace. The next morning the young officers took steps to see that they would have access to weapons from their divisional arsenal. Three days later Captain Ando Teruzo, the ringleader of the conspiracy who was closest to General Yamashita, threw a fresh crimp into the planning by admitting frankly at a cell meeting, "Now that it is decided, I do not dare to do it."[5]

The best that the other conspirators could agree to, after Ando's admission, was a tentative zero hour "about the middle of next week." On the following day, February 19, another meeting of the conspirators was heartened to hear that kindred spirits at the military school in Toyohashi down the coast had agreed to join in their plans by assassinating the venerable Prince Saionji.

On February 21, Isobe and Muranaka, the two pamphleteers who had been drummed out of the Army the year before, sought reassurance by meeting again with Chief Aide-de-Camp Honjo's son-in-law Yamaguchi. As duty officer of the 1st Regiment Yamaguchi promised that no one in the regiment who did not join the rebellion would ever receive orders to suppress it. That evening duty officer Yamaguchi invited to his home mimeographer Nishida, the number-two ideologist of the Strike-North Faction, and advised him to tell his master, old revolutionary Kita, that Plot Day had been set tentatively for February 26.

The next morning, P-day minus four, the young officers met, admitted to one another that they were frightened, and adjourned after writing the first draft of a manifesto which they meant to post on walls and broadcast over the radio when and if they ever captured the center of Tokyo.

On February 23, P-day minus three, they took out a supply of 2,000 rounds of ammunition from their division's arsenal and recruited several new captains and lieutenants. The plan to assassinate Prince Saionji sat ill with some of the more politically sophisticated backers of the plot. And that same day, February 23, Chief Aide-de-Camp Honjo's son-in-law Yamaguchi consulted the discredited Strike-North General Mazaki about it. On Mazaki's advice Yamaguchi went on to see a professional information peddler, Kamegawa Tetsuya, who had been acting as go-between

---

[5] At Yamashita's order, after the assassination of Prime Minister Inukai in 1932, Ando had, for several days, given refuge in his personal quarters to the Tokyo University student, Yotsumoto Yoshitaka, who had served as messenger boy between the Blood Brotherhood and Lord Privy Seal Count Makino.

to bring financial support to the plotters from a branch of the Constitutionalist Party.[6]

The next morning, February 24, P-day minus two, informer Kamegawa visited the civilian lawyer for the defense at the Aizawa trial, told him of the entire conspiracy, and begged his aid in persuading old Prince Saionji to recommend ousted General Mazaki as the next prime minister. The lawyer, a friend of Saionji named Usawa Fusa-aki, promised to do what he could and then warned Saionji that he was about to be assassinated.[7] The warning arrived in Okitsu through a typically complex chain of intermediaries including Saionji's steward, a Dietman named Tsugumo Kunitoshi, and Saionji's sometime private secretary, the industrialist Nakagawa Kojuro.

Saionji had no doubt as to the importance of the warning and acted on it without delay. He arranged to have what Secretary-Spy Harada called "an infallible line of liaison" kept open between Okitsu and the palace in Tokyo. He gave instructions to his servants to answer the phone naturally, as if they knew nothing and as if their aged master were still peacefully in residence. Then he had himself secretly carried away in a sedan chair over the hills behind his home. On the other side he was picked up on a deserted stretch of road by an official car which whisked him away to the well-guarded mansion of the governor of Shizuoka prefecture.

Meanwhile, on P-day minus two, Captain Nonaka, who was the senior officer of the plotters and the closest of them to Prince Chichibu, took the draft manifesto to the home of Strike-North ideologist Kita Ikki and asked his help in polishing it. Kita obliged by adding to the blunt sentiments of the soldiers much fiery rhetoric and difficult Chinese syntax to produce a contemporary classic—one which would be read aloud a few days later to Emperor Hirohito. After its composition Captain Nonaka sat down

[6] Specifically from Kuhara Fusanosuke, the founder of the Hitachi industrial empire. He was an ardent apostle of American-style capitalism resting on common stock and a broad basis of ownership of capital goods.

[7] At a clandestine court-martial in the home of the minister of justice a year later, the secret police sought to press charges against Defense Counsel Usawa as an accomplice in the plot. Usawa's timely warning to Saionji then saved him from prison, for after several hearings, when it became apparent that Usawa could not be tried without implicating Saionji, the proceedings against him were dropped.

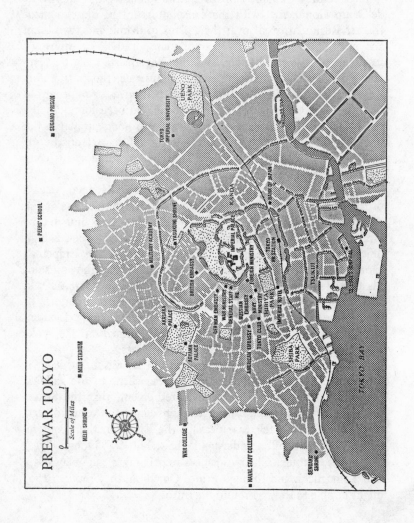

PREWAR TOKYO

Scale of Miles

MEIJI SHRINE ●

SUGAMO PRISON ■

PEERS' SCHOOL ■

MEIJI STADIUM ■

WAR COLLEGE ■

NAVAL STAFF COLLEGE ■

SENGAKU SHRINE ■

UENO PARK

TOKYO IMPERIAL UNIVERSITY

KANDA

YASUKUNI SHRINE ●

MILITARY ACADEMY ●

BRITISH EMBASSY ●

AKASAKA PALACE ●

ADAMA PALACE

GERMAN EMBASSY ●

WAR MINISTRY ●

GENERAL STAFF ●

RUSSIAN EMBASSY ●

NAVY MINISTRY ●

FOREIGN MINISTRY

IMPERIAL PALACE

TOKYO RR STATION

BANK OF JAPAN

TSUKIJI

ST. LUKE'S HOSPITAL

AMERICAN EMBASSY ●

TOKYO CLUB ●

IMPERIAL HOTEL

HIBIYA PARK

SHIBA PARK

TOKYO BAY

in Kita's parlor with Kita's henchman Nishida and made a fair copy on a scroll of fine rice paper for presentation to the Throne.

That evening Captain Yamaguchi, the son-in-law of Chief Aide-de-Camp Honjo, met with the conspirators in the duty room of the 1st Regiment, went over their plans in detail, and gave them 200 mimeographed copies of police maps of the war minister's residence, the War Ministry, and the Headquarters of the General Staff. The next morning, P-day minus one, the conspirators were delighted by a letter from one of their wives saying that old plotter Makino, the former lord privy seal, had been found finally, living quietly at a rural inn in Yugawara two hours away. On the basis of this intelligence one of the young officers set out by car to Yugawara to be ready to strike at the same time as his comrades in Tokyo.

That same morning, P-day minus one, ousted General Mazaki of the Strike North was called as a witness for the defense at the Aizawa trial. He refused to answer questions put to him in Aizawa's behalf on the grounds that anyone who had been a high official in the palace might not divulge, without the Emperor's express permission, matters which he had learned in the course of his official duties. After fifty taciturn minutes in court Mazaki also refused to answer the questions of newspaper reporters. In the afternoon Aizawa's military counsel for the defense, Lieutenant Colonel Mitsui Sakichi, delivered his summation. He spoke eloquently but brought out no facts, only feelings.

In the 1st Division barracks where the trial was being held, it was apparent to all that Aizawa would go silent to the gallows, that Mazaki would remain mute in retirement, that the Strike-South Faction had won. Out of religious hope, the young officers of the 1st Division felt that perhaps the Emperor, their contemporary, did not fully understand the realities. Through Tiger Yamashita, through Chief Aide-de-Camp Honjo's son-in-law Captain Yamaguchi, and through Prince Chichibu, they thought they might be able to show Hirohito the truth.

BLOODSHED AT LAST

After more than three months of high-level encouragement, the rebels were finally committed, in all good face, to make their move. All that evening the nineteen lieutenants and captains who were already parties to the conspiracy sounded out fellow officers of the 1st and 3d Regiments. Prince Chichibu had been a member of the 3d Regiment from 1922 until August 1935, but his name, which they used freely, won over only two new converts, both of them second lieutenants. The best that the conspirators could exact from most of their colleagues was a pledge not to interfere.

At 2:00 A.M. on February 26, without any pretense of secrecy, reveille was bugled in the 1st and 3d Regiment barracks in Azabu some twenty blocks from the palace. For the next hour the sleepy soldiers were treated to harangues from the conspirators and also to some words of warning from anti-conspirators. Nevertheless the soldiers responded with some enthusiasm and by about 3:30 A.M. 1,359 of them, together with 91 noncommissioned officers, had elected to follow the two captains, eight lieutenants, and eleven second lieutenants who were already committed. By 4:00 A.M. kits were packed and the insurgents began to move out. They left behind some 8,500 men in the barracks and in nearby officer quarters a number of sedulously snoring majors and colonels. They also left behind Chief Aide-de-Camp Honjo's son-in-law Captain Yamaguchi to make sure that the pledge of non-interference was kept.

Outside in the bitter February morning the rebels were joined by the 7th company of the 3d Regiment of the elite Imperial Guards Division, barracked within the holy precincts of the palace. Unlike the others, these men did not know that they were rebelling. Their leader, Chichibu's friend Lieutenant Nakahashi Motoaki, had told them that they were marching to a religious ceremony at Emperor Meiji's Shrine. Thirteen trucks were waiting to transport the advance guard. Three medical trainees were on hand to care for the wounded in case anyone got hurt.

Tokyo lay blanketed in snow. The flakes were still falling. The boots of the men crunched softly up the dark empty streets. It was less than a mile and a half march from their bunks to the walls of the palace. By 4:30 the scouts of the silent columns had taken up watch outside all the main nerve centers of bureaucratic Tokyo short of the forbidding walls of the palace itself: the Diet, the War Ministry, the General Staff offices, Police Headquarters, the Land Survey office, the Home Ministry, the Overseas Ministry, and even the Navy Ministry and Staff offices. Within the cordon of rebel pickets lay the residences of Prince Kanin, Prince Taka-matsu, the lord privy seal, the war minister, the vice war minister, the foreign minister, the vice foreign minister, the home minister, and the prime minister.

Before 5:00 A.M. the rebels had occupied their primary objec-tives. At the Sanno Hotel, which they intended to make their field headquarters, they roused guests from their beds—including two or three Westerners—and courteously manned the hotel switchboard to find fresh accommodations for them in inns and hotels elsewhere in the city. At the war minister's official residence they apprised War Minister Kawashima of their presence, and then, because he pleaded a bad cold and a need to sleep, left him undisturbed until 7:00 A.M. when he rose to parley with them. At Metropolitan Police Headquarters they simply mixed with the sergeants on night duty and doubled the guard outside.

In the offices of the General Staff lights were burning because Colonel Ishiwara Kanji, the strategist of the Manchuria campaign, now chief of the Operations Section of the General Staff, had received belated warning of the rising and was in conference with some of his staff. At about 5:00 A.M. Colonel Ishiwara stormed from his office, shot a rebel guard on duty outside, and screeched away in his official car to see what he could do. He could do noth-ing; he was too late.

The death squads had already gone out to be ready at the stroke of five to kill "the evil men about the Throne." At 5:05 the first squad struck. A hundred soldiers under the command of Chichibu's friend Lieutenant Nakahashi Motoaki of the Imperial Guards Division surrounded the home of the unkempt, bushy-bearded Santa Claus of Japanese finance, the brilliant, heterodox econo-mist, Finance Minister Takahashi Korekiyo, eighty-one years old. After wounding the policeman on guard outside, Lieutenant Nakahashi burst into the house, ran to the old finance minister's bedroom, ripped the covers from him and cried *"Tenchu!"* ("Heav-en's punishment!") When Takahashi opened his eyes, Nakahashi shot him thrice and then for good measure stabbed him twice. He died instantly.

At the same moment a second squad of 200 soldiers, a lieutenant, and three second lieutenants surrounded the home of the new lord privy seal and former prime minister, Admiral Viscount Saito Makoto, seventy-seven. The suave, good-natured old courtier was sleeping heavily after a late night at the American Embassy where he had viewed a private showing of the Jeanette MacDonald-Nelson Eddy movie *Naughty Marietta* with Ambassador and Mrs. Grew.

Hearing the young officers running into the house, Viscountess Saito rose from her husband's side in time to slam the bedroom door in their faces. "Please wait a moment," she cried.

By the time the young officers had forced the door, Admiral Saito had awakened and was standing behind his wife in his sleeping kimono. Three officers shot him almost simultaneously. Viscountess Saito fell on the body and clung to it tenaciously, weeping. Unable to drag her off, the young officers thrust in their weapons underneath her and pumped more bullets hysterically into the corpse. They later testified that they wanted to cut the old man's throat as well but could not because the woman was in the way.

In all forty-seven bullets were lodged in the admiral's body and his wife was wounded in both arms and a shoulder. On the way out the murderers paused at the front door to give three lusty "Banzai!" for the Emperor.

A third company of assassins under the command of Tiger Yamashita's minion, Captain Ando Teruzo, had attacked the home of Grand Chamberlain Admiral Suzuki Kantaro. They had been delayed for ten minutes by a skirmish at the gate in which they had wounded the policeman on guard. Grand Chamberlain Suzuki, too, had been at the Grews the night before. Ando found him in bed with the baroness and tarried to discuss national policy with him. The grand chamberlain was no mean juggler with words and he regaled Captain Ando for almost ten minutes.

Finally at 5:10 A.M., according to the official story, Ando invoked cloture with his pistol and fired three bullets into the sixty-eight-year-old chamberlain. "I can still feel a pulse," he announced to Baroness Suzuki, who stood by. "I shall dispatch him finally with my sword."

The baroness, with Spartan presence of mind, responded, "If you consider that necessary, let me do it." And so Ando "felt ashamed" and retired from the room.

For the next two days, while his comrades patrolled in the snow, Ando whiled away his hours in a nearby restaurant, the Koraku. Then, when the rebellion had collapsed, he made an unsuccessful attempt to commit suicide. Apparently he had made a deal with his wily old victim. Grand Chamberlain Suzuki was off the critical list four days later and lived to be Japan's last World War II prime minister.

Suzuki made a virtue of his "embarrassing" survival, as he called it, by a story which he loved to tell thereafter. It seems that one of the bullets fired into him lodged in a most tender part and the surgeon who treated him wrote a riddling, mock-heroic stanza celebrating his deft extraction of "the leaden ball from the honorable golden one."

While Grand Chamberlain Suzuki lay in agony, a fourth death squad of 300 men and five officers went for the third Strike-South admiral of the night, Prime Minister Okada Keisuke. His official residence was that same architectural monstrosity—a parody of Frank Lloyd Wright's Imperial Hotel—in which Prime Minister Inukai had been shot by the airmen of the Misty Lagoon four years before. Despite the earlier tragedy and the manifold warnings on the grapevine, there were only four policemen on guard. The attacking troops shot all four of them, and the five officers began a systematic search of the maze of rooms and corridors in the residence.

The seventy-three-year-old prime minister had spent the previous evening with his mistress, a famous geisha, and was in no mood to save himself. "It's all up," he said miserably. "Why get all excited?"

His maids and his brother-in-law secretary, Colonel Matsuo Denzo, however, dragged him from his bed and hurried him out of his own suite into the servants' quarters. Hearing the approaching footfalls of a search party, they shoved Okada unceremoniously into one of the toilets there and told him to draw the wooden cleat which would lock it from the inside. Then Colonel Matsuo, in a signal act of heroism, ran out into a courtyard nearby shouting, "Long live the Emperor." He fell instantly in a hail of machine-gun bullets, his face disfigured almost beyond recognition.

The soldiers who had shot him carried his corpse back to Okada's bedroom and laid it out. They compared the face with photographs and decided, with the help of prompting from the maids, that they had killed the prime minister.

In the morning secret-police officers infiltrated the area along the wall of the palace occupied by the rebel troops and fraternized with the soldiers. In the course of their investigations they learned from the maids at the prime minister's residence that Admiral Okada was still alive. Okada's son-in-law and another of his secretaries were called in through the rebel lines to perform obsequies over the corpse of Matsuo, the prime minister's stand-in. The now all-too-sober Okada was moved to a closet where he would be more comfortable. His mourners won the sympathies and relaxed the surveillance of the rebel guards.

On the following morning his surviving secretary, Fukuda Ko, brought a score of elderly secret-police pallbearers in frock coats to the Prime Ministry, together with a flu mask and horn-rimmed glasses. Disguised in these, the hungry, weary Okada joined the mourners at the coffin of his brother-in-law. As the bier was borne from the house, one of the aged pallbearers imported by the secret police fell to the ground in a mock heart attack and was carried off on a stretcher. In the confusion the shaken Prime Minister Okada was bundled into a car and escaped.

The killings in Tokyo were well co-ordinated with more attacks in the provinces. During the night of the rising, groups of soldiers, reservists, and cadet officers converging on Okitsu to assassinate aged Prince Saionji were met and dispersed by police. At Yugawara hot springs, where former Lord Privy Seal Makino was hiding at an inn with his twenty-year-old granddaughter Kazuko, the child of postwar Prime Minister Yoshida Shigeru, no precautions had been taken. At 5:40 A.M. a group of rebels who had set out on their mission at midnight arrived at the inn, set up a machine gun before the entrance, hailed the innkeeper, and demanded Makino. A moment later Makino's bodyguard appeared, blazing away with a gun. He wounded the leader of the squad, Captain Kono Hisashi, but was himself riddled with

machine-gun bullets. The spray of lead tore through the fragile
façade of the Japanese inn and wounded Makino's nurse and one
of his servants.

During the brief battle old plotter Makino and his granddaughter, together with other guests and members of the staff,
stole out the back of the inn and climbed the hillside behind it.
The wounded Captain Kono, who subsequently died under arrest,
ordered his men to set fire to the place. While the building blazed,
the soldiers trained their machine gun on the figures which could
be seen scuttling away up the slope.

According to the story told later by Makino and oft repeated
in after years by Makino's prime ministerial son-in-law, Yoshida
Shigeru, the former lord privy seal reached a point on the hillside
at which he found his breath too short and the ascent too precipitous for him to go farther. He slumped to a squat and faced
the would-be executioners below. His granddaughter Kazuko
stepped in front of him and spread her kimono to shield him.
Both felt that they were picked out by the flames and would surely
die. They could see the soldiers all too vividly against the bright
background of the fire, but the soldiers could see little of them
against the dark hillside.

The machine gunners did not shoot, and forty minutes after
the attack had started Makino was safely away in the hills. As
firemen arrived to hose down the blaze, the young rebels packed
up their machine gun and started back for the provincial garrisons
from which they had come.

Back in Tokyo, having gained their primary objectives, the
rebel troops went on to secondary ones. At 6:00 A.M. a part of
the same bloodthirsty group which had pumped forty-seven bullets into Lord Privy Seal Saito jumped from a truck outside the
home of General Watanabe Jotaro, who had taken Mazaki's place
the previous summer as inspector general of military education.
One of the young officers blew the lock on the front door with
machine-gun fire and then he and his comrades poured into the
house. Mrs. Watanabe confronted them at the end of the entry-
way and demanded the name of their unit. They threw her aside
and dashed into the living quarters where General Watanabe
stood waiting for them. Before he could bark out the order "Halt!"

he had taken his first bullet and then went down in a fusillade. A second lieutenant completed the attack by cutting the throat of the corpse with his samurai sword.

A HAND OF POKER

The violence was over. The rebels went on to occupy the offices of the five major newspapers later that morning and to wreck the presses at one of them, the conservative *Asahi*, but there were to be no more killings. In a fashion that astonished Western residents, the drama of the insurrection suddenly turned cerebral, and while it was being played out the 1,483 mutineers[8] were left in undisputed occupation of the heart of Tokyo. For three full days the rebels held the nerve centers of the Japanese Empire, and Hirohito engaged all officials dissatisfied with his rule in a silent test of strength. Personally, almost singlehandedly, he fought and won three major political battles. He refused, until the rebels had surrendered, to make any concessions as to the policy or personnel of the next government. He insisted that the Army take full public responsibility not only for the suppressing of the rebels but also for their rising, and that it do so, moreover, on its own authority, without invoking Hirohito's personal power as god-king. Finally he took a firm hand with the elders of his own Court and family and overruled a substantial bloc of them who rose in dissent.

When the rebellion had been suppressed, Hirohito's courtiers spread an account of events in the palace during those three days which their own diaries expose as false.[9] By so doing they meant to protect the Throne against reaction in case the coming gamble of war should turn out badly. Thus they suggested that Hirohito was forced by the rebellion to seek employment for his soldiers' idle hands and to consent in the preparations for war against China. The true situation is aptly illustrated by Chief Aide-de-Camp Honjo's diary. On February 25, the day before the rebellion, Honjo notes that the Emperor approved an enlargement

[8] 1359 soldiers, 91 noncoms, 21 officers, 3 medical corps trainees, 8 civilians, and one reservist.

[9] Until recently historians have had to accept it for lack of documentary evidence.

of the command structure for the Tientsin garrison army in north China to put it on a war footing. He asked Honjo to see that the enlargement be made in such a way as "not to excite foreign suspicion" and "not to make control inconvenient as was the case when we reorganized the Kwantung Army" [before the conquest of Manchuria].

"The problem," Hirohito had explained to Honjo, "is not what we do but world reaction to what we do."

21

SUPPRESSION

(1936)

RISING TO A REBEL DAWN

The record of Hirohito's great victory over the mutineers and
their sympathizers commences a few minutes before the first of
the early morning killings. At 5:00 A.M. Chief Aide-de-Camp Honjo
was shaken awake in his home in northwestern Tokyo by a second
lieutenant from the 1st Regiment who brought a note from his
son-in-law Captain Yamaguchi informing him that 500 officers
and men of the regiment had already left their barracks as insurgents and that more were going out every minute. Honjo was on
his feet instantly ordering the second lieutenant to go back to son-
in-law Yamaguchi and have him stop the rebellion and call the
men back.

"It is too late," said the second lieutenant.

"Do your best," commanded Honjo. Turning to the phone he
called the commander-in-chief of the secret police and the aide-
de-camp on night duty a few steps from the imperial bedchamber
in the palace. Both men were calm and noncommittal. Honjo
summoned a car and set out for the palace. On the way he encountered almost a company of soldiers near the British Embassy
just west of the palace. He deduced from their uniforms that they
were not Imperial Guardsmen of the elite Konoye Division and
that therefore they must be rebels from his son-in-law's 1st Division. He did not stop his car to parley with them.

Arriving at the Inner Palace at 6:00 A.M., Honjo learned that Hirohito was already up and at work at his desk. When he was received in audience a few minutes later, the Emperor said to him, "Make this incident end quickly and so turn calamity into good fortune." Then Hirohito added accusingly, "Only you, Chief Aide-de-Camp, worried beforehand that there might be such an outbreak."

Thinking of his son-in-law, Honjo said, "The young officers only mean to find a place for their sense of righteousness as individuals in the all-encompassing righteousness of the Emperor. They wish a little fresh air for their ideas to bloom in."

Marquis Kido Koichi, the secretary to the lord privy seal—secretary until two months ago of Count Makino and until fifteen minutes ago of Admiral Viscount Saito—was awakened at 5:20 A.M. by a phone call from the palace which told him of the attack on Saito. Kido at once "sensed an incident of great magnitude." He called Metropolitan Police Headquarters and found that no one there, being surrounded by rebels, could speak without constraint. So he called the official car pool and asked for immediate transportation to the palace. While waiting for it, he phoned Prince Konoye and Saionji's Secretary-Spy Harada to give them the news. When his driver arrived, he shrewdly directed the man to take a long way around the area which he imagined would be occupied by the rebels.

At six o'clock Kido was at his desk in the Imperial Household Ministry within the outer precincts of the holy palace walls. He made numerous phone calls to evaluate the situation including one, at 6:40, to Prince Saionji's residence in Okitsu. The maids there assured him that the venerable old man and the rest of his household were soundly asleep in bed. Kido has never revealed whether or not he knew that Saionji was really asleep miles away in the home of the governor of Shizuoka. In his dairy Kido wrote only: "I felt greatly relieved."

After making his phone calls and becoming as knowledgeable as he could, Kido waited at the Household Ministry for Saionji's Secretary-Spy Harada. On foot, with his Imperial Household pass in his hand ready to show to any rebel who stopped him, Harada arrived shortly before 7:00 A.M. and was given instructions by

Kido. After receiving them, instead of going to one of the north gates of the palace and proceeding to Okitsu to be with Saionji as duty demanded, Harada returned to his home in rebel territory and spent the next two days doing phone business as usual from a hideout in the house of a neighbor. Though he may not have known it, he was on the "shoot-at-sight" list of the rebel officers as "that meddlesome little baron." In going back to his neighborhood he played the part of heroic intelligence agent. He kept in constant telephonic touch with Kido and ventured out in the evening to observe the rebel camp.

After issuing instructions to Harada, Kido walked across the palace park and through the inner wall to Hirohito's own residence and offices. He found the aides-de-camp, Imperial Household Minister Yuasa, and Vice Grand Chamberlain Hirohata already in attendance outside Hirohito's study. They gave him more up-to-date intelligence than he had been able to elicit from his own informants on the phone: the grand chamberlain, the prime minister, and the finance minister had all been attacked, along with the lord privy seal. Like other trusted minions of the Throne, Kido was not to leave the palace for a week. He was given a temporary cubicle down the corridor from Hirohito's study in the Imperial Library. He bunked down on open stretches of matting floor in the rooms of chamberlains. He was on call to the Emperor twenty-four hours a day.

REBEL TERMS

Also at 7:00 A.M. that February 26—that *ni-ni-roku* or 2–26 as it is called by Japanese—War Minister Kwashima condescended at length to come down from his bedroom and parley with the rebel officers who occupied the ground floor of his residence. They gave him the original of the manifesto, of which they had plastered copies on all the walls of the occupied area, and demanded that he present it to the Emperor. They also stipulated that the government must announce a full restoration of the Emperor to power; that the Army must rid itself of factionalism; that the "arch traitors" of previous plots, including Generals Minami, Koiso, Tatekawa, and Ugaki, must be arrested; that some other officers of Hirohito's original cabal must be dismissed from the service; that General Araki must be made commander of the Kwantung Army in order to "coerce Russia"; and finally that the war minister should consult with Strike-North leader Mazaki before stating their demands to the Emperor. They recommended that he talk also to Lieutenant General Furusho Mikio, the vice minister of war, an aviation expert whom the Emperor trusted, and to Major General Tiger Yamashita who was—unknown to them— a palace undercover agent. War Minister Kawashima listened gravely to their requests and promised to do what he could.

At 8:00 A.M. Prince Fushimi, the chief of the Naval General Staff, arrived at the palace and went straight into Hirohito's presence. Units of the fleet, he reported, were being brought around from Yokosuka Naval Base into Tokyo Bay and could be ready, at a word from the Emperor, to shell the rebel positions. At the same time, he felt, it would be advisable to form a new Cabinet quickly and to compromise a little with the rebels. Since some of the rebels were close friends of Prince Chichibu, it would be wrong to deal with them too severely. Did not the Emperor agree?

Hirohito, who had had many disagreements in the past with Fushimi and knew that he was disposed to argument, replied only: "I asked for your report on the situation in the Navy. As to my opinions in regard to the present incident, I have given them already to Imperial Household Minister Yuasa."

"Have I your permission, Sire, to ask them then of Yuasa?"

"I would like to reserve judgment on that petition," snapped Hirohito, and waved Prince Fushimi from the room. Full of indignation Fushimi went directly to Big Brother Kido, the president of the Bureau of Peerage and Heraldry, and ordered him to circulate an account of the spat to all princes of the blood.

At 9:00 A.M. War Minister Kawashima, fresh from his parley with the rebels, arrived at the palace and was given audience by the Emperor. He produced the rebels' manifesto scroll and solemnly read it in the Imperial Presence.[1]

---

[1] I quote at length from the original. Its deep and alien feelings defy summary. And the only previously available translation, which may be found in one form or another in half a dozen textbooks of modern Japanese history, is an independent composition prepared in 1936 by a Japanese interpreter for the Tokyo office of *The New York Times*. It includes some ideas from the original but rearranges them and smothers all their fire and brimstone.

A Prospectus for Direct Action to Protect the Essence of
the Nation

After humble reflection as children of the land of the gods we submit these grievances to the one eternal god, the Emperor, under whose
high command we serve. The essence of our country consists first in
accomplishing the evolutionary formation of a single nation that is
one body and then in comprehending the entire earth under our roof.
The superior excellence and dignity of our national essence has grown
systematically, and by careful nurture, from the founding of the nation by Emperor Jimmu, to the transformation of society by the Meiji
Restoration. Now once again we are reaching the autumn of an epoch
in which we confront many outside lands and must make visible progress toward a new enlightenment.

Despite the critical period ahead of us, gangs of effeminate sadists
spring up in our midst like toadstools; we indulge our selfish desires
and interests; we allow superficial formalism to arrogate the absolute
sanctity of the Throne; we obstruct the creative evolution of all the
people, causing them to groan in anguish and misery. Increasingly
Japan is pursued by foreign troubles, and riding at the mercy of the
waves, becomes the butt of foreign ridicule. The elder statesmen, the
leaders of Army factions, the bureaucrats, the political parties, and so
on have all contributed as leaders to this destruction of the national
essence. . . . The March Incident and the special interests of false
scholars, false Communists, treasonable religious groups and the like
are all woven together in a dark plot which, though unrealized, has set
a most conspicuously bad example. The crimes are smeared so gory
across the heavens that we have reached a juncture at which bloodshed
is a mere figure of speech to express indignation. The pioneering self-
sacrifice of the Blood Brothers . . . ; the volcanic spouting of the
5–15 Incident; the flashing out of Colonel Aizawa's sword—truly these
men had reasons for what they did, reasons which have made them
weep.

How many times must lifeblood water the earth to produce a bit
of introspection and penitence even now at this late hour? As of old
we continue to play for time and look the other way out of private
greed and status seeking. Russia, China, England, and the United
States are within a hair's breadth, at this present outbreak, of ensnar-
ing our land of the gods and of destroying our culture, our bequest
from the ancestors. Is this not clear? Is there not light in fire?

Indeed there is, and grave uneasiness at home and abroad. The
false counsels of false vassals sap the national essence, shade the divine radiance of the Throne, and retard the Restoration. . . . At this

moment when the First Division has just heard its imperial order of dispatch overseas . . . we cannot help but look back on conditions at home. . . . In so far as we can, we and our kindred spirits must make it our responsibility to crumble the inner doors and strike off the heads of the treacherous army traitors in the palace. Though mere retainers, we now take a positive road as if we were the trusted lieutenants of the Throne. Even if our actions cost us our lives and our honor, vacillation now has no meaning for us.

We here who share the same grief and the same aspirations take this opportunity to rise as one man. To make the traitors perish, to make the supreme righteousness righteous, to protect the national essence and make it manifest, we dedicate our own true hearts as children of the sacred land, thereby giving our livers and brains to be consumed in the fire.

We humbly pray the sun goddess and the ancestors, riding on spirit wings, to lend us their dark assistance and second sight in our undertaking.

Eleventh year of Showa, second month, twenty-sixth day.

Hirohito listened in silence to the manifesto. Behind its impassioned words and its brave show of martial spirit, he could see a complete repudiation of all his warlike policies. In their veiled, belly-talking fashion, the rebels were begging him to shrink from the danger of further foreign entanglements and devote his energies to domestic reform and the preservation of Japan's traditional homespun virtues.

"Whatever their excuses," said Hirohito icily, "I am displeased. They have put a blot on the nation. I call on you, War Minister, to suppress them quickly."

Kawashima sought to find some small token of conciliation to give the men who occupied his home. But Hirohito forbade him to convey to them any message of sympathy and understanding from the Throne—merely that the Throne had been informed of their intentions.

FIRST DAY OF SIEGE

As soon as War Minister Kawashima had withdrawn to think over his predicament, Hirohito began to interview, one by one, all the generals who sat on the Supreme War Council. Confident that they would not be molested en route by their own Army's insurgents and eager to show their loyalty and give their advice to the Throne, they had all come to the palace early in the morning when Cabinet ministers and admirals were still conspicuous by their absence. Hirohito impressed on them one point: the Army must take the responsibility for suppressing "these violent rioters." If it did not, he would call in the Navy or go down to the barricades himself.

While the Emperor was personally reminding the elders of the Army of their duty, the six young rebel officers in command at War Minister Kawashima's residence waited for a reply to their demands and held court for a steady stream of senior officers who came to remonstrate with them or wish them well. Indeed, though it seems incredible, business at the residence, and at the nearby War Ministry and General Staff offices, went on much as usual despite the rebel pickets who stood guard at the doors.

The incongruity of the situation was demonstrated at 10 A.M. when Major Katakura Tadashi, the nephew of the Manchurian Incident's War Minister General Minami, came to Kawashima's residence on a routine staff errand. Major Katakura had helped to expose the Military Academy Plot in 1934 and had thereby betrayed most of the young men who were now insurgents. Not surprisingly, one of them, the pamphleteer Isobe who had been dishonorably discharged, greeted Katakura with a bullet in the head. Unfortunately for later Allied war prisoners in Burma, whom he worked and killed in 1944, it was only a flesh wound and Katakura recovered. Many of his fellow officers felt that he had received no more than he deserved, and the coming and going of callers at the war minister's residence continued unabated.

At noon, when the last Supreme War Councillor had emerged from the Imperial Presence, War Minister Kawashima dispatched Major General Tiger Yamashita to go from the aides' office in the palace out to the rebels and give them their answer. It was in brief: "The Emperor has been told your intentions; the war minister recognizes the sincerity of your motives; the Supreme War Council has met and decided to uphold the national prestige."

The message could not have had a more fateful ring. The bloodstained young rebels could sense in it the Emperor's icy attitude toward them. They were lost. If they were to die in vain, they

promised Tiger Yamashita that they would do so on their barricades fighting to the last man.

Yamashita phoned the palace. He was told to keep talking and
was promised reinforcements. Shortly afterwards he was joined
at the negotiating table by the ubiquitous Colonel Suzuki Tei-
ichi, who was known to be close to the Emperor, and by the commander of the 1st Regiment, Colonel Kofuji Satoshi, who could
be held responsible for the young officers as members of his command.

While the negotiators slogged on through a mire of patriotic
metaphysics, Hirohito convoked the highest consultative bodies
of the land and spent the afternoon with them. In one palace
room the Privy Council sat in the Imperial Presence; in another
met those members of the Cabinet who had finally dared to come
to the palace; in a third conferred the Supreme War Council, including Strike-North leaders Araki and Mazaki. The Cabinet had
been asked by the Emperor to see to continuance of civil government in the absence of Prime Minister Okada who still hid
in a closet at his residence. The Supreme War Councillors had
been asked by the Emperor to suppress the incident as quickly
as possible with a minimum of bloodshed.

It was a long afternoon. The Emperor was unwilling to appoint
a new prime minister because any change in the government might
be construed as a step toward reform and a victory for the rebels.[2]
Nor was he willing to ease the task of the War Councillors by
even a token gesture of conciliation. When the rebels had returned to their barracks he would resume constructive government.
Until then he took the position that he would sign nothing and
would preside over the realm as a displeased Presence and nothing more.

The Cabinet finally chose Home Minister Goto Fumio as their
de facto administrator. And the Supreme War Council finally
agreed to issue the rebels "a persuasion paper" and "an order."
The persuasion paper stated in brief: "You wished to attract the
Emperor's attention and you have succeeded; your sincere desire

2 It may be assumed that the secret police had informed Hirohito early that
afternoon that Prime Minister Okada was still alive. Not until the following
afternoon, however, when Okada had been safely smuggled out of rebel territory, was the news of his survival given to the courtiers around Hirohito.

to see the essence of the nation realized has been noted." The orders stated in brief: "In accordance with the National Defense Plan of fiscal 1935, you are to take up your prearranged positions for the defense of Tokyo alongside the other units of your division."

The Privy Council, meanwhile, which sat in the Imperial Presence, debated whether it would be better to make the rebels disband by sending them a direct order from the Emperor or to declare martial law and leave the responsibility for suppression to the Army. Hirohito, as was required in order to preserve an appearance of free debate, listened attentively but said nothing. He caused the second course of action to be taken, however, by a simple expedient: every twenty or thirty minutes he would have Chief Aide-de-Camp Honjo summoned and would say to him, as if asking for news, "Has the Army succeeded in suppressing the crazy violent rioters yet?" The Privy Council finally agreed to recommend that the reluctant Army should impose martial law.

At 3:00 in the afternoon 1st Division soldiers took up defensive positions according to the contingency plans of fiscal 1935 and were not joined by their rebellious comrades. At 5:00, after half a day of empty talk, Tiger Yamashita returned to the Palace to report. Three of the rebel officers tried to follow him into the holy precincts and had to be stopped by the Palace Guard.

After hearing Yamashita's disappointing news, Imperial Household Minister Yuasa relayed a request from Hirohito that all trusty vassals sleep in the palace that night and that martial law, as decided earlier by the War Council, be imposed on Tokyo from midnight onwards. War Minister Kawashima promised to comply but doubted that martial law would be effective. He asked Household Minister Yuasa if he might submit to the Throne a list of names which the Army would like to see in the next Cabinet. Yuasa rejected the request angrily and called it an attempted infringement of imperial rights. War Minister Kawashima "looked surprised" and went to see about setting up a martial law headquarters. Navy Minister Osumi was granted audience at 6:30 and implored the Emperor to ease the nation's tension by appointing a provisional Cabinet and a prime minister pro tem.

The Emperor refused. "If the Army had wished to avoid this confrontation," he said, "it might have given me a gently worded reproof." That evening the five rebel officers in the war minister's residence parleyed with no less than seven full generals, including Hayashi, Mazaki, Araki, and Terauchi. The dazzling display of brass failed to break the deadlock. The rebels repeated their earlier demands and added further that they must not be called traitors.

That evening the Cabinet resigned—not once but twice. The first time, at 9 o'clock, de facto Prime Minister Goto submitted a cabinet resignation *en bloc*. It was a routine gesture expected of a cabinet after a national disaster, and the Emperor routinely dismissed it. "Retain your posts with sincerity," he said, "until peace and order have been restored."

This was not enough, however. The ministers withdrew and returned to the anteroom where they had been in debate all afternoon. Intimidated by the assassinations that morning and to some extent sympathetic with War Minister Kawashima, they resolved to submit individual written resignations. They did so at 1:00 A.M. Hirohito had no choice but to accept them, but he ordered each minister to "remain in charge of political affairs until the realization of a new Cabinet." He was obviously put out. It had been an exhausting day.

Even members of Hirohito's own family felt that he was taking a dangerously uncompromising position. Prince Fushimi and Prince Asaka had asked for a meeting of the Imperial Family Council, and Hirohito's brother Chichibu, who sided with them, had been summoned from the country to attend it. The Lord Privy Seal's Secretary Kido had spent the evening feeling out the positions of Prince Asaka and Prince Higashikuni and had reported reassuringly of their loyalty.

But Hirohito was in no mood for reassurances. Still wearing the rumpled Army uniform that he had put on early that morning, he sat down shortly before 2:00 A.M. to read the resignation papers submitted by the Cabinet. At 2:00 he phoned Chief Aide-de-Camp Honjo, rousing him from bed: "War Minister Kawashima has submitted a resignation which is identical to all the others. Does he think that his responsibility is identical? With such a mentality he is not fit to be war minister."

"I suppose," sighed Honjo to his diary when the Emperor had hung up, "that he passed through the honorable latticed door [to bed] sometime after that."

THE SECOND DAY

When dawn came on February 27, P-day plus one, the snow had ceased but it was still cloudy. Martial law had been officially proclaimed at 2:50 that morning. At 5:00 A.M. Chief Aide-de-Camp Honjo was roused bleary-eyed from his makeshift pallet in the palace by a personal visit from Prince Fushimi. Fushimi reported to Honjo that young Army officers had called at the Fushimi villa during the night to ask him to take the post of lord privy seal as a means of settling the incident. He had, of course, refused to commit himself. At 7:00 A.M. the Emperor's uncle Prince Asaka called on the Emperor's brother Prince Takamatsu at the Naval Staff College to seek his support in urging Hirohito to appoint a new cabinet as soon as possible. Takamatsu declined.

In the palace the chamberlains' common room looked like a refugee camp. Elderly Cabinet ministers, generals, princes, and marquises sat about in their sleeping kimonos eating rice, drinking tea, and exchanging short guttural comments after an uncomfortable night. Just outside the palace gates, the rebel sentries still paced up and down on the snow. Service on the Center line of the subway was suspended, and commuters on their way to the business district and docks in southern Tokyo had to change many times in order to circle the stricken area around the palace. Hirohito slept late. After his usual hearty breakfast of oatmeal and eggs he did not reach his desk until some time between eight and nine o'clock.

When Chief Aide-de-Camp Honjo went to pay his good morning greetings to the Emperor, he was met with a barrage of gruff high spirits: "If the rioting mobsters do not begin soon to respect the orders of the Army high command, I can see that I will have to go down in person to the barricades."

Honjo replied: "The officers of the direct action group called out the Emperor's troops arbitrarily without orders. In so doing they intruded on Your Majesty's right of supreme command. Naturally this is impermissible but the spirit in which they acted deserves some consideration. They were moved entirely by patriotic convictions and thought they were acting on behalf of the nation. In their psychology there is no room to think of exerting pressure on you, Sire, or of abusing your prerogatives."

A little later Hirohito called Honjo and said: "They killed my right-hand elder vassals. Those crazy violent officers may not be excused in any way—not even in terms of their psychological motivation. To fell my most trusted vassals is a way of trying to strangle me with a silken cord and smother my own head in soft cotton."

"There is no question," admitted Honjo, "that it is the blackest possible crime to have killed and wounded the elder vassals. But though these young officers are confused and do not understand, they believe that they acted for the sake of the nation. That was their idea."

Honjo noted in his diary, "I repeated this to the Emperor in several different ways."

Hirohito shook his head and said, "Can't you admit, Chief Aide-de-Camp, that their action stemmed simply from their own passions and selfish ambitions?"

Having no adequate rejoinder to make, Honjo wrote in his diary: "On this day also the Emperor was very agitated by the fact that the Army's efforts to suppress the action group are not getting anywhere. He told me, 'I, *Chin*, would like to take command of the Konoye Guards and crush the insurgents personally.' "[3]

All day long the nation was held in suspense. In the course of it the stubborn Emperor called Honjo no less than thirteen times to ask him if the Army had acted yet. War Minister Kawashima and most of the other full generals busied themselves with the logistics of establishing a martial law headquarters in the secret police building a few blocks north of the palace perimeter. At 10:30 A.M. the Konoye Imperial Guards took up positions facing the northwestern edge of the rebel lines—and then sat tight. Loyal units of the 1st Division did the same along the southwestern and southeastern edges. Along the northeast edge ran the massive wall of the palace. During the afternoon the rebels broke into the Peers' Club, searched everyone they found there, and held an assortment of some sixteen marquises, counts, viscounts, and barons at pistol point until evening.

[3] *Chin* is the old imperial "we" used by Chinese emperors. Its ideograph represents the moon speaking into the ears of heaven.

Saionji's Secretary-Spy Harada passed through the rebel lines, talked to some of the detained peers, and was stopped on his way home by a rebel officer who recognized him. The officer later testified, "If he had not shown fear or if he had attempted to lie to me or run away, I would have killed him. But he spoke to me in such a small voice that I let him go with a warning."

During the afternoon lull, everyone was waiting for the arrival in Tokyo of Prince Chichibu, Hirohito's brother, the personal friend of the rebel leaders. Chichibu was expected to confront Hirohito that night at the scheduled meeting of the Imperial Family Council. Privy Seal Secretary Kido spent most of the day in conference with Prince Asaka and Prince Higashikuni discussing "remedial measures." It was rumored that the rebels or the Army meant to kidnap Prince Chichibu, and so at 5:17 P.M. when his train drew in to Ueno Station, he was met by a chamberlain and a strong police escort. Driven at full speed, sirens blaring, his cavalcade negotiated some four miles of city streets to arrive at the Inner Palace thirteen minutes later. He was ushered at once into the Imperial Presence and went on to dine with the Emperor in private.

At about 7:00 P.M. the royal brothers joined other princes of the blood in the Imperial Family Council Chamber.[4] According to chamberlains' gossip, voices were modulated and the atmosphere was urbane. Hirohito questioned each of the princes in turn and heard short prepared speeches that touched on a variety of topics including China, long-range military planning, and domestic reform. The main concern, however, was that the spirit of rebellion

---

[4] According to the Imperial House Law "the members of the imperial family shall be under the control of the Emperor" and the family council "shall be composed of the male members of the imperial family who have reached the age of majority." In addition the Emperor was expected to require the presence of an outside witness, specifically the privy seal, household minister, minister of justice, or president of the Supreme Court. In 1936 there were sixteen princes eligible to sit on the family council, six of the higher rank called *Shinno* and ten of the lower rank called O. The six *Shinno* were Hirohito's three brothers plus three princes of the less immediate family who had been created *Shinno* by Imperial election: Prince Kanin, the Army chief of staff; Prince Fushimi, the Navy chief of staff; and the fascistic Prince Kaya who had visited Hitler in 1934. The princes who took part in the February 27 meeting of the Council were brother Chichibu, brother Takamatsu, and cousin Fushimi, all *Shinno*; and uncle Higashikuni, uncle Asaka, cousin Nashimoto, and Prince Kanin's son, Haruhito, all O.

might spread to the provinces unless a new Cabinet was appointed promptly and a compromise worked out with the Army. Hirohito thanked his kinsmen, promised to think over their ideas, and at 8:30 the meeting adjourned on a note of noncommittal anticlimax. Prince Chichibu went on to a half-hour conference with Big Brother Kido.

Only two concrete results emerged from the family conference. Army Chief of Staff Prince Kanin, who was indisposed at his villa in Odawara on the shore, was asked to come to Tokyo and stand behind Hirohito "even if it is inconvenient." Kanin obeyed the next day but was given no reason to meet with his monarch for a week. Also that night Prince Chichibu penned a personal note to his friend Captain Nonaka, the highest-ranking rebel officer, asking him as a favor to withdraw his troops. Nonaka responded, after a day's thought, by putting a pistol in his mouth and pulling the trigger. Chamberlains were relieved to see that the princes of the blood, embarrassed though they might be by their many friendships and commitments in the ranks of junior officers, nevertheless chose to stand by Hirohito when it came to a confrontation. Chichibu left the palace that night at 9:10 P.M., accompanied once again by an army of police.

The next morning Hirohito sent his own impressions of the council meeting to Big Brother Kido, the president of the Bureau of Heraldry and Peerage, for inscription in the palace rolls: "Prince Takamatsu [my brother] is the best. Prince Chichibu [my brother] has improved greatly since the time of the 5–15 Incident. Prince Nashimoto was moved to tears when he asked my pardon [for this rebellion]. I appreciate him greatly. Haruhito [Prince Kanin's son] is fine. Prince Asaka talks of the individual's sense of righteousness and of its place in the over-all righteousness of the Throne, but being under radical influence, he is not blameless. As for Prince Higashikuni, he is showing good sense."

Hirohito, as family disciplinarian, had just been required to read police dossiers on Prince Higashikuni's recent blackmail plots and religious humbuggeries. The Emperor evaluated his kinsmen in terms of loyalty and disloyalty rather than by ordinary Japanese moral standards. At the quiet family conference he had proved himself above influence even by his own kinsmen.

Shortly after the council adjourned, Generals Mazaki, Abe, and

Nishi called at the war minister's residence and told the five young rebel officers in command of the ground floor there that they must give up hope and submit to the Imperial Will. If they did not, Strike-North leader Mazaki promised that he personally would lead the detachments sent to destroy them. Weary and heartsore the young men agreed to capitulate. At 11:30 P.M. the three generals reported back to the palace, and orders were issued to the sentries of the Imperial Guard and 1st Divisions to be generous that night toward common soldiers who sought to escape from the rebel-occupied area.

All was not over, however. The rebels, throughout their sad outing, had maintained radio contact with the radical Strike-North ideologist Kita Ikki in his hideout in the Tokyo suburbs. Heretofore in his long career as a professional revolutionary, Kita had always avoided overt participation in coup d'etat plots. Now, however, he realized that he was deeply implicated and would probably be executed if the rebellion failed. For the last two days he had stood by his radio transmitter encouraging the rebels at every turn, advising them on political subtleties and relaying to them heartening prophecies from his wife who had some reputation as a woman of occult powers.

After the generals had left the war minister's residence that night of February 27, P-day plus one, Kita about midnight talked to two of the rebel officers and told them that they should not yet give up: the pressure on the palace was mounting; if they lacked wind for the long run they would find themselves put to death summarily without a hearing. Kita added that his wife had dreamed an apocalypse in which the young officers ruled triumphant in a Japanese paradise where there were no poor. The rebels listened and agreed.

THE THIRD DAY

February 28, P-day plus two, was once again cloudy. Chief Aide-de-Camp Honjo was informed of the rebels' change of heart at 7 A.M. It meant that the rebels would have to be destroyed. It meant that Honjo's son-in-law Captain Yamaguchi Ichitaro would have to go to prison for giving aid to men who were now, clearly, traitors. It meant that Honjo himself after his long and loyal career was disgraced. Men who knew him said later that he aged sixteen years that day.

At about eleven in the morning Yamaguchi, the son-in-law, went to martial law headquarters and pleaded eloquently for almost an hour against issuance of orders to use force against the rebels. Generals and colonels listened to him in complete sympathy and said nothing. Finally a little before noon the martial law chief of staff, Colonel Ishiwara Kanji—that brilliant religious zealot who had planned the Manchuria campaign and had ever since preached peace with China—arose from one end of the long staff table and said, "We shall attack as soon as possible." He walked from the room and gave the couriers outside written orders to deliver.

The 1st and Konoye Divisions grouped for attack and planes revved up to bomb the rebel barricades. The rebel officers were told by radio, "Surrender or be attacked." The rebels replied that they would "not obey orders formulated by organ theorists who perverted imperial intentions."

At this point a "hold" was sent to the waiting attack forces because Prince Chichibu's message was being delivered to Captain Nonaka, and Tiger Yamashita had one last idea for a compromise. After a parley at the barricades, Yamashita came to the palace aide-de-camp office at one in the afternoon, accompanied by War Minister Kawashima. He gave Chief Aide-de-Camp Honjo a pledge from the rebel officers that they would all commit hara-kiri provided that a chamberlain would come out from the walls to witness their act with all due ceremony and report it to the Throne. Honjo reported the proposal at once to Hirohito.

Hirohito said, "If they wish to commit suicide let them do it at their own pleasure. To send an imperial witness to such men is altogether unthinkable."

Honjo muttered miserably that the 1st Division, in which his son-in-law was the duty officer, was loath to go into action against former messmates.

A nasal edge came into Hirohito's voice. "If the chief of the 1st Division," he said, "does not think he can act effectively, he does not understand his own responsibility."

Honjo noted, "I have never seen such severity and anger in the Emperor before."

Army leaders were stunned by Hirohito's rejection of the suicide proposal. Desperate and incredulous, son-in-law Yamaguchi phoned Honjo begging him to talk to the Emperor again. Honjo explained to him repeatedly that the Emperor had already expressed his will beyond any ambiguity and that there was nothing more to be said. When the son-in-law persisted, Honjo sadly hung up on him.

At 3 P.M. the droll Vice Chief of Staff Sugiyama—whose face was said to be as "noncommittal as a toilet door"—requested audience to make Hirohito a further explanation. There had been a misunderstanding, he said. The rebels did not expect an imperial witness at their suicides. They had merely hoped that a chamberlain might take a look at their bodies afterward and report to the Throne whether or not they had carried out their rites of disembowelment in a correct fashion. Hirohito dismissed the new face-saving formula with rekindled anger. When so informed, one of the rebel officers lamented, "But even airplane accidents are reported to the Throne."

Vice Chief of Staff Sugiyama returned to Hirohito and for almost an hour used all his jester wiles in an effort to make Hirohito more lenient. Finally he lay down in a doorway and told the Emperor to trample on him. The Emperor merely stepped over him and went to await developments in another room. Finally at 4:30 P.M. Sugiyama and the commander of the martial law force,[5] Lieutenant General Kashii Kohei, reported to the Emperor that it was too late in the day for an attack but promised him religiously that one would be launched first thing in the morning. Hirohito dismissed them curtly, summoned Chief Aide-de-Camp Honjo, and accused the Army leadership of gross insubordination.

"There is a rumor," said Hirohito, "that the Army belongs to the Emperor. There is another rumor that the Army is intentionally stalling in order to increase the significance of the incident."

"In the last few hours," replied Honjo, "people have been saying that in the present situation the Army is being evasive about following the Imperial Will in an intentional attempt to establish a military government. This sort of comment is extremely insult-

---

[5] No less than 23,491 men and 350 officers had been mustered to deal with the 1,483 mutineers.

ing to the Army of the Emperor and ignores the Army's honest
effort to resolve the incident quickly and peacefully." Honjo later
wrote in his diary:

Thus I appealed to the Emperor, saying that the public atmosphere
of misunderstanding directed against the Army was cruel and hard for
the men to bear. At that moment, without controlling my emotions,
I wept and could not speak. The Emperor walked from the room
without saying a word.

After a while, he called me and said: "You, Chief Aide-de-Camp,
appealed to me on the grounds that unjust criticisms are being leveled
against the Army and you did so with tears. But I say to you that if
this incident is not resolved quickly an uneasy situation will follow.
Three days have passed and the seat of government has not yet been
recovered. Foreign exchange has almost stopped and soon there may
be a run on the banks. Unrest is spreading outside the capital and
there is a danger of rebellion. The loyal elements of the First Division might even join their comrades who killed my hands and feet
and did the most brutal things to old men. I therefore permit you,
Chief Aide-de-Camp, to deliver your own dissenting comments and
feelings officially to the Supreme War Council, and then I require
you to bring this situation to an immediate resolution."

Honjo was supposed to take official responsibility for all the
Emperor's opinions regarding military matters. In the past when
the two men had differed, Hirohito had either coaxed the old
general into line or compromised a little himself. Now Hirohito
had specifically released Honjo from responsibility and asked him
to go on record, officially, as dissenting. In one and the same
breath Hirohito was saying that he had great respect for Honjo
and that he would no longer require Honjo's services as a confidant.

Accordingly [wrote Honjo in his diary] I requested of the War
Council that it send a representative to my office to speak to me.
General Araki [the Strike-North leader] came and I delivered to him
on the one hand my own sentiments and on the other the Imperial
Will. General Araki said, "I suppose that ever since the imperial order
was issued there has been no way except the exercise of military
force."

The two generals, Araki fifty-nine and Honjo sixty, stared at one another bleakly. They had graduated together from the military academy in 1898 and had worked together in a dozen different assignments for the General Staff since then. They both knew that Hirohito had often chosen in the past between the opinions of disagreeing advisors. They both knew that Hirohito had sometimes gone out of his way to find an advisor who would propose the course of action which he personally wished to follow. But Hirohito had never before ignored the advice of all his military councillors. Now the thirty-five-year-old god-king had emerged from the chrysanthemum curtain and was taking full autocratic responsibility. As the two elderly generals bowed curtly to one another, they bowed also to the Imperial Will. Thereafter all elders of the Japanese Army would behave as if they had no responsibility of their own but merely followed orders. It was a historic moment, and the two generals acknowledged it, in parting, by nothing more than a slight raising of the eyebrows.

The supreme military councillors made one last effort to prevent Hirohito from putting the Throne in a dangerously exposed position. At 7:30 P.M. a delegation of them, including former War Minister General Araki, former War Minister General Hayashi, and Vice Chief of Staff Lieutenant General Sugiyama, met Prince Kanin as he arrived by train from Odawara and tried to persuade him to change Hirohito's mind. Prince Kanin refused to interfere and drove on to his villa. The delegation of Army elders proceeded to martial law headquarters, convoked a meeting of the staff there, explained the situation, and gave it as a united opinion that "we must at all costs avoid an armed clash that will destroy Army morale."

Chief of staff of the martial law forces, Colonel Ishiwara Kanji, planner of the Manchurian campaign, had seen his orders held up since noon. Never known for his tact, he now rose, stared at General Araki, the spokesman of the delegation, and said: "This is a violation of the supreme command. Please state your name and rank, sir."

"You know perfectly well that I am General Araki. And I know that you are trying to insult a superior officer. I would advise you to hold your tongue."

"I cannot," said Ishiwara. "It is absolutely impermissible for soldiers to use the arms of the Throne against the Throne. That would be beyond common sense and has nothing to do with Army morale. You call yourself a general but I cannot believe anyone so silly can be a general in Japan."

For this devout outburst Ishiwara remained in the Army after the great purge of the months ahead. He was to be known in later years as "the last of the Strike-Northists." When he had stamped out of the staff room, Araki and the other generals had no way to prevent the attack planned for the morning. But they did persuade Martial Law Commander Kashii to do his utmost to persuade the rebels by means short of force. All night long sound trucks and radios along the rebel periphery repeated the refrain, "Surrender or be destroyed." Bombers flew over and dropped pamphlets promising forgiveness to noncoms and privates. Advertising balloons went up at dawn begging the troops to surrender for the sake of their wives and children.

Also that night Chief Aide-de-Camp Honjo's son-in-law Captain Yamaguchi was arrested by the secret police and held on suspicion of high treason.

HIROHITO'S SETTLEMENT

At eight-thirty on the morning of February 29, P-day plus three, units of the 1st Division moved through undefended segments of the rebel perimeter and began to evacuate civilians from the prospective battlefield. The rebels gradually drew back into the main buildings which they had occupied. At 9:00 Martial Law Commander Kashii went on the air to announce to the nation, "The young officers have finally come to the point of being considered rebels." At ten, as troops and barbed wire closed in on them, rebel enlisted men in twos and threes began to drift across the snow-covered lawns and parking lots around their strong points and give themselves up. At noon Prince Chichibu's intimate, Captain Nonaka, killed himself. By a little after two all the troops had surrendered and their officers were in secret-police custody.

Hirohito remained stubbornly suspicious until the last. When it was first apparent, at eight-thirty that morning, that the Army had given in, Privy Seal Secretary Kido advised him "to soothe people by appointing a new Cabinet." Hirohito replied that he would "wait until pacification is complete." Then when it was complete, he was all impatience. At two o'clock he had the conventional request to Prince Saionji—that he come up to Tokyo and recommend a prime minister—transmitted to Okitsu by telephone instead of the customary imperial messenger. Pleading lumbago, Saionji asked for a little time to prepare for the journey. At four o'clock Hirohito had him called again and told that Cabinet formation was urgent and that he must come as quickly as possible.

While Saionji collected himself a day passed, March 1. It was a Sunday, and for once on Sunday official Tokyo enjoyed not only the weekly official Western-style day off but a day of genuine exhaustion and rest. Hirohito was the exception. He was up early in Army uniform and remained at his desk until late in the evening. It was a regimen which he would insist on for weeks to come. He gave up his daily hour of exercise and paid no attention even when a delegation of his chief vassals came to him on March 18 and begged him to take better care of his honorable body. He knew well the military dictum that victory can be deceptive unless it is pursued inexorably to the last surrender of the last foot soldier.

On March 2, when the venerable Saionji did arrive in Tokyo, arrangements had been made by Hirohito's Big Brothers which would enable their leader, Prince Konoye, to refuse power in the manner of Julius Caesar—first the crown of prime minister, then the crown of lord privy seal. It was an elaborate gesture staged to prepare the way for a Konoye prime ministership when the war began with China. Konoye had never served in any public office but was known merely as a leader in the aristocratic House of Peers. The people needed exposure to the idea that he was prime ministerial timber. And though the docile people might accept him now, he did not wish to be in charge at a time when the Army was about to be ruthlessly purged. It would have made his leadership over the Army difficult in time of war.

Saionji made an attempt to expose the insincerity of Konoye's candidacy. When he found the Konoye name pushed at him from every direction by well-primed politicians, he spoke to Konoye and found him unwilling. When Konoye's modesty was admired in the newspapers, Saionji went ahead, over Konoye's objections, and insisted on proposing him officially to the Throne. Hirohito himself broke precedent by objecting that Konoye's health might not be good enough. Saionji declared that it was and repeated his recommendation. Hirohito had no choice, as a matter of protocol, but to summon Konoye on March 4 and ask him to form a Cabinet.

Emerging from his audience, Konoye confided to Lord Privy Seal Secretary Kido, "I am in real trouble." After a night's sleep Konoye returned to Saionji and begged for mercy. He brought with him a certificate from his doctor stating that his health would not be up to the responsibilities of office for at least another three months, that is, until the purge of the Army would be completed.

Saionji could then have ruined his young kinsman's career by announcing that, at a time of crisis, Konoye had refused to obey the imperial order to form a government. Instead, after long discussion, the old man softened. He let reporters know that he had a low opinion of political aspirants who could not sacrifice their health for the sake of the nation. Then, however, he returned to the Throne Room and announced that he was extremely embarrassed but would have to change his recommendation. This time he recommended a lesser member of Hirohito's middle-aged inner circle, Foreign Minister Hirota Koki.[6]

Hirota was commanded by Hirohito to form a Cabinet on March 5 but was not finally invested prime minister until March 9. In the four-day interim military and political circles made mutually insatiable demands on him as to both the policies and personnel of his Cabinet.[7] While Hirota's difficulties preempted headlines and left Japan without an official government, Hirohito quietly pushed through a number of stern disciplinary measures on his own.

On March 4 the Privy Council, sitting in Hirohito's presence, agreed to advise him to decree that the young officers of the rebellion be tried by court-martial in secret, that they be given no rights of appeal, and that their sentences be executed as swiftly

[6] A career diplomat, Hirota had started his career as a personal protégé of gang lord Toyama. He had made the acquaintance of Prince Konoye in 1921 and become one of Konoye's informants inside the Black Dragon Society.

[7] At Army insistence Count Makino's son-in-law Yoshida Shigeru, who would be prime minister five times between 1946 and 1954, was denied the powerful police portfolio of the home ministry.

as possible. On March 2 all full generals in the Army had offered to resign their commissions as a token of regret to the Throne for "the recent unforgivable incident." Now on March 6 Hirohito accepted the mass resignation as no mere gesture but a matter of earnest, effective April 23. Moreover, he saw fit to stipulate by name three exceptions to the general rule. General Terauchi, the leader of the Army Purification Movement, together with his cohorts General Nishi and General Ueda, would not resign. Terauchi would become war minister, Nishi inspector general of military education, and Ueda commander of the Kwantung Army.

When the cries of protest and the scurrying of feet in palace corridors had subsided, Chief Aide-de-Camp Honjo, waiting out a painful fortnight of face-saving delay before his own obligatory retirement, noted in his diary that the exceptions were "part of the Emperor's supreme right." In a similar vein on March 9, Hirohito ruled that the only members of the Supreme War Council and Army high command who did not need to submit their resignations were Field Marshal Prince Kanin, Lieutenant General Prince Asaka, and Lieutenant General Prince Higashikuni.

When the Hirota Cabinet finally established a workable milieu for itself and took office on March 9, Hirohito continued in uniform, at his desk from morn to midnight, giving his opponents an object lesson in non-organ imperatives. He changed his official signature on state documents from "Supreme Sovereign of the Great Land of Japan" to "Heavenly Emperor of the Great Land of Japan."[8] He considered abolishing the four regiments which had contributed men to the mutiny and then, in a gesture of magnanimity to the loyal majority, allowed them to keep their colors and remain a part of the armed services.

At the same time he approved tentatively a new draft plan for national defense which was drawn up in four parts by many different offices in the defense establishment: a financial section which "in accordance with the Constitution" might be shown to the Diet; an over-all policy and strategy section which might be reported to the Cabinet; a section on mobilization and manpower which might be revealed to the prime minister; and a section of detailed operational plans which might be seen in its entirety only

---

[8] It was a step he had been considering since late January.

by the Emperor and a handful of officers in the General Staff. One of its subsections, formulated that very month of March 1936, was a plan for night maneuvers near Peking which could be used—and would be used sixteen months later—to trigger the full-scale war with China.

The bulk of the new defense plan was devoted less to specific preparations against China than to an over-all buildup of national military strength. Japan had to be ready not only to win against the Chinese but also to discourage Western intervention. The Hirota Cabinet instituted a program of regimentation which was known, even at the time, as "the quasi-wartime economy." Military expenditures more than trebled in the next twelvemonth. Deficit financing, which had been held to a minimum by the late, clever Finance Minister Takahashi, murdered in the mutiny, now became the order of the day. Every aspect of economic life from factory norms to foreign exchange was made the thrall to cheap printing-press money and rigorous government control.

At the same time secret arrangements were made in minute detail for increasing the size of the Army from seventeen to twenty-four divisions. The seven new divisions were to be drawn from the reserve. So thoroughly were supplies, officers, and retraining facilities prepared for them in advance that when they were needed in the opening weeks of the war with China, they became fighting realities overnight. Thus, if we are to believe official records, the 114th Division was created in October 1937 and in less than a month was in China driving on Nanking.

While this dramatic 41 per cent increase was being planned in the over-all size of the Army, the angry Hirohito demanded a drastic purge of the men who would command it, a purge which would lead to a critical shortage of trained officers in the two years ahead. The need for the purge was undeniable, however, and was eloquently explained by Prince Kanin in a conversation with Saionji's Secretary-Spy Harada on March 3: "As we cannot get along without the cause of this latest outbreak—namely, our principle of keeping an excessively tight lid, no matter what, on our own stinking fish—we are forced to do a thorough job this time, even to the point of ruthlessness, in cleaning up the Army."

The unpopular task of carrying out the house cleaning was shouldered by the new war minister, the Purification Movement's

General Terauchi. Between March and August of 1936 he sent to pasture more than 2,000 of the 8,000-odd commissioned officers in the Army. The Strike-North contingent was almost wiped out and with it went the better half of the Army's strategic brain power. By way of compensation, the purge struck most heavily in the upper echelons and thereby cleared a way for the eventual promotion of fresh young talent.

To counter the resentment and the new politician-veteran coalitions which would inevitably spring up in the wake of the Throne's latest authoritarian measures, the Big Brothers of the Eleven Club devised a plan by which Hirohito could veto any Cabinet not of his choice and do so secretly without seeming to have played any part in the matter. Every Cabinet had to have a War and a Navy minister. The law, as revised in 1913, allowed these two posts to be filled from either the active or reserve lists of generals and admirals. As only active officers were bound by imperial orders, it was possible in theory for a prime ministerial candidate recommended by Saionji to fill a complete slate of Cabinet ministers without first obtaining the Emperor's approval. The Emperor, of course, could refuse to sanction such a Cabinet, but not gracefully, not without revealing his partisanship. And so in early May the Privy Council, sitting in the Imperial Presence, recommended to the Hirota Cabinet that the law be changed and that only officers on active service be eligible for the War and Navy ministerships. The Cabinet agreed to the change and Hirohito quickly signed it into law. Only when it was a fait accompli, on May 18, was it announced to press and public. Hirohito and his inner circle used it regularly thereafter to block the formation of undesirable cabinets or to topple cabinets which had served their purpose. That vague beast "The Army" was always held publicly responsible, and the fearful, reverent, taboo-stricken people politely ignored the reality—that Hirohito, since the mutiny, was in fact as well as name the Army's commander-in-chief.[9]

While such momentous changes were being made in the fabric

---

[9] No reserve officer had ever been made a service minister during the twenty-three years from 1913 to 1936 while such an appointment was legal. In 1944, however, when it was technically illegal, Hirohito would make a retired admiral Navy minister by simply calling the Navy Personnel Bureau and having the man's name—Yonai—reinstated on the active list.

of Japan, the protagonists of the February Mutiny quietly disappeared. Chief Aide-de-Camp Honjo was at first encouraged by
War Minister Terauchi to keep his post. "I too am in a position
of many troubles," he told Honjo on March 8, "so please do not
think of resigning."

But on March 16 Honjo wrote in his diary: "Terauchi came to
see me and told me the details of my son-in-law Yamaguchi's
guilt and said that he was sorry for me. . . . On that day Yamaguchi's family moved into my home. Their furniture was put in
the home of the elder Yamaguchi [a lieutenant general]. It is at
the request of the Yamaguchi family that my daughter and her
children have been sent to live in my house."

The next day, March 17, Honjo communicated his intention
to resign to the Emperor. "The Emperor asked me, 'To what extent
is your relative involved?'

"I said, 'It is not certain to what extent, but under present
conditions the first consideration is the cleansing of the Army and
I feel obligated to resign if only to set an example.'

"The Emperor replied, 'That may be right; I shall consider it
well.'"

By March 28, the resignation was accepted. Honjo received a
number of presents from the Emperor including money, art ob-
jects, and a pair of paperweights from the imperial desk. "I give
you those," Hirohito said, "because I have used them for a long
time." The Empress Dowager gave Honjo platinum cuff links,
fresh fish, and *omochi*—a type of holiday rice cake—which she had
prepared with her own hands. On April 22 Honjo was ordered
into the First Reserve with General Minami who had served
over him as war minister during the Manchurian Incident.

"I cannot help feeling a kind of sticky sentimentality," he wrote.

Other suspects were dealt with more harshly. The blunt, honest
number-two Strike-North leader, General Mazaki, was held by the
secret police for a year and a half. In the final weeks of 1936, still
stubbornly unrepentant, he went on a month-long hunger strike
at the end of which he refused even to drink water. Restored to
health by brute force of medicine in the hospital, he was finally
acquitted by a verdict which his friend General Araki, the articulate number-one Strike-North leader, later called "one of the
strangest legal documents in history." It cited all Mazaki's treas-

onable involvements in minute detail and then abruptly excul-
pated him in one brief declarative sentence. His pardon was widely
attributed to the efforts of Prince Konoye who wished to heal
the wounds of factionalism and unite the nation behind the war
effort.

Major General Tiger Yamashita, who had spied for the palace
in the ranks of the Strike-North Faction and who had served as
go-between in negotiating with the young rebels, found himself
reposted to the command of a brigade in Korea. For months he
worried that he had interpreted his instructions from the palace
too broadly, that he had gone too far in inciting the rebellion or
too far in attempting to mediate it. He sank into dejection and,
according to his wife, began to look about for civilian employment. Then, in December 1936, his palace contact, former Aide-
de-Camp Lieutenant General Kawagishi Bunzaburo, came to
Korea as his commanding officer. Kawagishi brought Yamashita
a personal note of encouragement and appreciation from Hirohito. After reading it, Yamashita took heart. He went on to rise
steadily in Hirohito's esteem until he conquered Malaya for the
Empire in 1942.

As for the young officers who had resorted to violence, they
were shot. Lieutenant Colonel Aizawa who had assassinated First
Crow Nagata returned after the mutiny to a court-martial which
was no longer open to the public. He was sentenced to death on
May 7 and executed on July 3. Nine days later thirteen of the
surviving nineteen officers who had led the mutiny followed him
to the firing squad. All had hoped for a chance in court to explain
their aspirations and grievances. Each had been given a single
hour before a panel of Army judiciary officers in a hearing that was
entirely secret.

At the moment of death most of them gave a last "banzai"
wishing the Emperor ten thousand years of life. Some of them
added a sardonic banzai for their disappointing friend Prince Chichibu. Several of them called out, "I leave my corpse to your discretion." One of them shouted, "I entreat those of the privileged
classes to reflect deeply." Another said quietly, "It seems that we
all cry ten thousand years for the Emperor on the steps of
Heaven, so I, too, repeat banzai for the Emperor and add a banzai
for my Imperial country."

Yet another sought to communicate a more difficult technical Army message: "In as much as the Japanese put absolute trust in their Imperial Army, their trust has been betrayed. Russia cannot be defeated in central Asia. That would bring Japan to destruction." The Strike-North group had wanted to attack Russia only at her eastern extremity, the Vladivostok region. After the occupation of China's main cities and agricultural valleys, Hirohito would attempt to strike at Russia in her soft underbelly, across the Mongolian deserts, in central Asia. The attempt would fail.

When it came time for the civilians of the February Mutiny to face their firing squad, Kita Ikki, the veteran ideologist of the Strike-North Faction, looked down the muzzles of the rifles and said, "Is it to be sitting or is this way all right?" When forced to squat, he shouted: "Hah! so the standing position of Jesus Christ and Sakura Sogo [a patriot crucified in 1645] is no longer allowed, eh?" His irony fell on deaf ears and his execution stirred little interest in the press, for it took place on August 19, 1937. By then the Japanese people shared his spirit of bitter cynical fatalism. By then they had allowed themselves to be marshaled and marched forward. By then they were at war with China and had been for the last month.

PART SIX

TRIUMVIR OF ASIA

22

NEUTRALIZING RUSSIA

(1936–1939)

DROWNING A RADIO

At seven o'clock on a May morning in 1936, two months after Hirohito's suppression of the Army Mutiny, Japanese commuters on the platform of the Shinjuku station in Tokyo eyed curiously two European hikers, bowed under what were obviously very heavy rucksacks. The commuters were all going toward downtown Tokyo. The two foreigners with their packs boarded a train in the opposite direction, out toward Mount Fuji. One of them was Max Klausen, a Red Army signal corps graduate, born to poverty on an island off the north German coast. His companion, Branko de Voukelitch, was a Yugoslavian photographic technician. Klausen had been in Japan only a few months and was ostensibly trying to set up a blueprint shop for copying the plans of architects and contractors. Voukelitch had operated for over two years in Japan as a correspondent for the French news agency Havas. Both men were Soviet agents. The weights in their rucksacks were transformers from a clandestine radio transmitter.

The two spies rode out into the glistening rice paddies of the countryside, changed to a trolley-car branch line, and completed the final leg of their journey by taxi over a dirt road to the resort hotel on Lake Yamanaka at the foot of Mount Fuji. The hotel servants who relieved them of their rucksacks remarked at once on the great loads they were carrying.

"We brought along half a dozen bottles of beer," explained Klausen hastily.

"We have plenty of beer here," said the hotel manager in injured tones.

As soon as possible that evening the two hikers hired one of the boats at the hotel waterfront and took their two rucksacks of beer out for a few hours of fishing and moon viewing. Away from the lights ashore, under the evening shadow of Japan's sacred volcano, they dropped the contents of their packs into the profound waters of the lake: three transformers, a knotted mass of copper wire, and a dozen gassy triodes. They breathed a relieved sigh of requiescat, for they had put to rest the last telltale remains of a bulky, badly engineered, Russian radio transmitter which had been smuggled into Japan two years earlier and had consistently failed to get out messages to Vladivostok.

In place of the scuttled transmitter one of the two hikers, the German, Max Klausen, had put together a more compact, more powerful, more easily dismantled sending set out of components bought in the already sophisticated hi-fi stores on Tokyo's shopping street, the Ginza. Over the new set, for the next five years, Klausen would transmit to Vladivostok the reports of one of the most successful intelligence operations in history, the Sorge Spy Ring.

The Sorge ring was successful not because it revealed Japanese secrets to the Kremlin but because it maintained a kind of liaison between the Kremlin and the Imperial Palace in Tokyo. Its reports helped to expose an anti-Stalinist "Strike-South faction" in the Soviet high command in Siberia—one which wished to attack fascist Japan and one which Stalin ruthlessly purged. Still more to the point, its reports repeatedly assured Stalin that the Strike-North activists in the Japanese Army would never be allowed to act. As a result Stalin left his long frontier with Japan lightly guarded, and Hirohito found it so much the easier to restrain his eager Strike-North myrmidons and use them elsewhere. In sum the Sorge ring helped to keep peace between Japan and Russia in the critical years, 1936–1941. The delicate understanding it established between Stalin and Hirohito enabled the one to prepare a defense against Germany and the other an attack upon the United States.

SORGE, THE MASTER SPY

Agents of most Western nations considered Tokyo the one information center in the world which, for reasons of language difficulty and native patriotism, could not be tapped. The "impossible" Soviet ring was founded in Tokyo by Richard Sorge, a middle-class German intellectual, with a Russian mother, who had conceived an idealistic hate for war while serving with the German Army on the western front in World War I. Brilliant as a journalist, beloved by all sorts of women, comrade to all sorts of men, Sorge was a spy's spy, so much the loner and double-dealer that not even his own superiors in the Fourth, or Intelligence, Bureau of the Red Army completely trusted him. Not until 1964, twenty years after his execution by the Japanese, was he acknowledged a Hero of the Soviet Union. During his hour of service in Japan, he hazarded his life for Russia and sent Moscow all his best information. But at the same time he also supplied information to German Intelligence and allowed himself to be used as a planting ground for information which Hirohito's intimates wished transmitted to Moscow.

Sorge had joined the Communist party in 1920, at the age of twenty-four, in Hamburg. He had gone to Moscow in 1924 and become a professional agent for the Comintern. Until 1928 he operated as such in Scandinavia. In 1929 he was reassigned to Red Army Intelligence and sent to Shanghai where he established himself as a specialist in Chinese agricultural problems for the German newspaper *Frankfurter Zeitung*. Between 1929 and 1932, in Shanghai, he made the acquaintance of two native-born Japanese who would later serve him as agents in Tokyo. Both of them were liaison men, closely associated with the Japanese Spy Service, who built their careers on the making of friends in leftist circles.

In June 1931 the questioning of a Malayan Communist by British police in Singapore led to the arrest of the paymaster of all Communist activities in Shanghai and the seizure of all his codes and account books. Thereafter the British, French, and Japanese police in Shanghai followed Sorge's trail closely. Sorge studiously refused to panic and remained in Shanghai writing his articles on

Chinese agriculture for nineteen more months. Then he returned to Moscow for rebriefing and reassignment.

Sorge personally suggested that he should operate next in Japan. On consideration, the brass of the Red Army accepted his proposal and gave him a single, specific mission: to try to warn Moscow in advance of any Japanese plans to invade Siberia. To prepare himself for this task, Sorge went home to Germany for a few months. He applied for membership in the Nazi party. He worked out free-lance contracts with fresh German newspapers. He begged letters of introduction from German notables to Japanese notables. Finally in September 1933 he arrived in Yokohama.

In his first year and a half in Japan, Sorge did little but make contacts and establish himself as a journalist. As was their wont with unknown Westerners, the Japanese police shadowed him closely but did nothing to check his activities. He drank heavily and wenched promiscuously with Japanese girls who duly reported to the police that he was a silent man and a good lover. He spoke no Japanese and associated mainly with other Europeans. He became a familiar figure talking to other Germans or other journalists at the bar in the Tokyo Club. He cultivated the staff of the German Embassy in Tokyo and made himself a valuable informant and good companion to the attachés there.

At the same time he was attempting slowly and secretly to acquire a ring of Japanese agents. Moscow naïvely sent him an Okinawan-born American Japanese from the Communist party in California to assist him as an intermediary. The Californian, an artist named Miyagi, was watched by the police as closely as Sorge himself. Nevertheless Miyagi arranged a number of secret meetings for Sorge with Japanese liberals and leftists. Most of them agreed to provide Sorge with information in order—so they understood— "to prevent a Russo-Japanese War." As a pacifist and an intellectual, Sorge astutely realized that in this common concern all the ideological slogans of East and West could be laid aside and that on this one objective the Kremlin could agree with many of the most patriotic Japanese. Sorge probably did not realize that one of the patriotic Japanese to whom his proposition appealed most was Emperor Hirohito or that the Japanese agents with whom he dealt were loyal to Hirohito.

Late in the summer of 1935 Sorge returned briefly to Moscow

to tell his chiefs that the Tokyo ring was ready to begin serious work and was only hampered by the incompetence of its radioman and the consequent difficulty of sending home reports. Moscow promptly recalled the radio operator previously assigned to Sorge and gave him an old Shanghai friend as a replacement. This was the hiker Max Klausen. He had been consigned to corrective proletarian labor in the Volga Republic because he refused to give up an anti-Communist White Russian mistress whom he had brought back with him from Shanghai. Sorge's admiration for Klausen's technical ability, however, carried enough weight to get the man restored to favor. Klausen's gratitude for the good turn rendered made him personally loyal to Sorge in a way that a doctrinaire Communist would have found impossible during the ideologically confusing years which followed.

In November 1935 when Sorge returned to Tokyo, Klausen followed him. On arrival Klausen set to work immediately building a radio transmitter of his own design, from locally available components, which he could assemble in ten minutes and take apart in five. During March 1936 he began to test it. In April he established contact with "Wiesbaden," the Russian station in Siberia set up to monitor his dispatches. In May he and the ring's photographic technician, Voukelitch, disposed of the old transmitter in Lake Yamanaka. Now the ring was ready to operate.

JAPAN'S LOYAL JUDAS

Three months after the drowning of the radio, the Russian spy ring gained a further sense of security on the banks of a second scenic body of water, this time the Merced River in California's Yosemite National Park. There, on August 15–29, 1936, the Institute of Pacific Relations, an organization backed by U.S. philanthropists, held a meeting of scholars to thrash out the questions at issue between China and Japan. The Japanese delegation to the meeting was chaperoned by the executive director of Japan's own shadowy spy service, retired Lieutenant General Banzai Rihachiro—the same man who had conferred with Hirohito just before the first of the three political assassinations of 1932.

Banzai shepherded a prepossessing flock of intellectuals who had been chosen to present Japan's most liberal face to the world.

One of them was the Prime-Minister-Maker's grandson, thirty-year-old Saionji Kinkazu, whom Hirohito's favorite Big Brother Marquis Kido had regularly consulted on all Communist problems since the 1933 Red scandal at the Peers' School. Saionji had with him a new friend and protégé, the thirty-five-year-old Ozaki Hotsumi who was the chief of the two Japanese "leftists" whom Sorge had cultivated since 1930. Ozaki was to be hanged as a traitor by the Tokyo secret police in 1944 but is remembered by knowledgeable Japanese aristocrats as one of the supreme patriots of his time.

Ozaki had been born—just a year after Hirohito, on May 1, 1901 —in a special compound of Strike-South-minded Japanese adventurers on the island of Taiwan. The compound had been organized by Emperor Taisho's prime minister, Katsura Taro, and by Big Brother Marquis Kido's father-in-law, the Meiji oligarch, General Kodama Gentaro. With such men as sponsors, Ozaki's father, an impecunious journalist, was able to send young Ozaki to the finest schools in the Empire. The boy attended a preparatory school in Taipei especially founded for twenty-six gifted children of the local Strike-South elite. He went on to the First Higher School in Tokyo, the best of the academies which placed young patriots at Tokyo Imperial University, Japan's Harvard.

Ozaki matriculated at the university at eighteen and began to specialize in German. Two of his best friends there were Ushiba Tomohiko, later a private secretary to Prince Konoye, and Matsumoto Shigeharu, also a future member of Konoye's "kitchen cabinet."[1] The three young men were all known as protégés of Prince Konoye's father, the founder of the Great Asia All-One-Culture Society.

At graduation Ozaki went on to a year of further training, in psychology and sociology, which was paid for by an old Taiwan friend, the influential doctor-administrator Goto Shimpei, who had recommended himself to Emperor Meiji in 1891 by poisoning a leading critic of the plans for the first war with China.

At twenty-five, after remaining as long as possible in the

[1] Today Matsumoto runs International House in Tokyo, a hostelry where young visiting scholars from abroad are accommodated and watched at minimal expense to all concerned. Ushiba was responsible during the war for putting in final form the "memorials" and "diaries" that Prince Konoye dictated for the Peace Faction as cover stories for the Emperor.

academic world, Ozaki put in two years learning the craft of journalist on Tokyo's big daily *Asahi*. He proved to be a tortuous writer and an unaggressive reporter, and so, after a brief tryout as an essayist on the *Asahi* magazine, he was sent overseas in 1928 to Shanghai. There he came into his own, not as a journalist but as a friend to Marxists of many nations. He began to read Marx himself and to learn the necessary dialectic jargon.

In 1929 Ozaki made friends with Agnes Smedley, an aggressive, mannish political malcontent from Missouri. She too was a journalist. She had taken upon herself the task of befriending the downtrodden of the Orient. For eight years in the 1920's she had been the common-law wife of an Indian revolutionary in Berlin. Now she took Ozaki into her cell of Asian nationalists and, according to her own boast, made him her lover.

In late 1930 Agnes Smedley introduced Ozaki to "an American sympathizer named Johnson," who was in reality Richard Sorge, Ozaki's later spy chief. Ozaki and "Johnson" took an immediate liking for one another and formed a masculine intellectual friendship which transcended and overrode both their personal ideologies. To judge from the sum total of evidence about these two suave, gregarious, close-mouthed men, Sorge believed in Russia as the fatherland of a world organization which would bring equality and peace to all people. Ozaki was more parochial but equally idealistic. He believed that Japan was the Messianic nation which would lead all Asia up out of its poverty and its servitude to Western exploitation. In Russia he saw only the best of many potential Western allies, and in communism he saw only a community creed of sharing which had been preached as an imperial ideal in Japan for centuries.

Neither Sorge nor Ozaki ever pried into the private life and thoughts of the other, yet the two were destined to die together fourteen years later, still loyal friends, in the chambers of the Tokyo Thought Police. For the first six years of the friendship, Ozaki knew Sorge only as "Johnson" and never tried to find out whether he took his orders from Russia's Red Army or from the guiding body of the international socialist movement, the Comintern. Sorge, in his turn, never asked why Ozaki was a socialist or whether he, too, took orders from some non-visionary agency of his own government.

In February 1932, when Soviet espionage in Shanghai was on the run, Ozaki was recalled by his newspaper, *Asahi*, to Japan. It was nineteen months later that Sorge arrived in Japan. In the spring of 1934 he sent his American-Okinawan intermediary to Ozaki and asked to meet him secretly in the deer park attached to one of the Buddhist temples in the old eighth century Japanese capital of Nara, twenty-five miles south of Kyoto. Ozaki kept the appointment and, in his own words, "readily agreed" to give Sorge whatever information was available to him as a reader of Japanese and a rising journalist. For the next two years the reports which Sorge smuggled out of Japan by courier through Shanghai were almost entirely based on Ozaki's journalistic insights. Because of Sorge's ability as a writer, the reports satisfied the Red Army's Bureau Four but they penetrated few veils of secrecy. The Sorge report on the 1936 Army Mutiny, as an instance, exhibited total ignorance of the factions, motives, and high-level palace participation which had been involved in the affair.

Ozaki could have written far more realistically about the mutiny, for his friend and former fellow leftist in Shanghai, Kawai Teikichi, a future member of the Sorge Spy Ring, had been in on its preparation. Kawai had gone on from Shanghai in 1932 to infiltrate Chinese Communist circles in Tientsin in north China in 1933. He lodged in Tientsin across the street from the Japanese Special Service Organ there, and it is difficult to tell from his results whether he was infiltrating Japanese circles for the Chinese Communists or Chinese Communist circles for the spy service. In 1935 he returned to Japan and lived in the home of Fujita Isamu, an operative of the Japanese spy service who had assisted in the 1928 murder of Chang Tso-lin, the 1931 March Plot, and the 1931 take-over of Mukden in Manchuria. Throughout 1935 Kawai served Fujita by making friends with the young idealistic domestic reformers who would participate in the Army Mutiny. Ozaki failed to communicate to Sorge any of this complicated background when Sorge filed his much applauded analysis of the Army Mutiny with Russian Intelligence, German Intelligence, and several European newspapers.

In 1936, after the February Mutiny, Ozaki's position in the inner world of Japan suddenly skyrocketed. Because of his old connections with the coterie of Prince Konoye's father and because of his knowledge of China and Chinese, he was recruited by a group of young men around Prince Konoye who hoped to rationalize and temper Hirohito's military ambitions in China. First, Ozaki was made a member of a China-study committee organized by his newspaper, *Asahi*; then he was sent to Yosemite with young Saionji and Lieutenant General Banzai of the spy service to present the merits of Japan's position in China to the world at large.

At Yosemite Ozaki delivered a well-reasoned defense of Japan's activities in China and thereby improved greatly his reputation among Japanese rightists. After the Yosemite meeting he was taken into the Eleven-Club circle of Hirohito's Big Brothers and at the same time, as a fully fledged agent, into Sorge's Spy Ring. In September 1936, at a tea party for the returning Yosemite delegation, held amid the Aztec Gothic of Frank Lloyd Wright's Imperial Hotel in Tokyo, Ozaki was officially introduced to "Johnson" and told that his old "American" friend was in reality a German named Sorge. Two months later Ozaki was recruited as one of the original members of the Showa Research Society, a body organized in advance to write position papers and slogans for Prince Konoye to use if, as anticipated, he should become the China-war prime minister in 1937.

Thereafter, as many writers have observed, Ozaki served as Soviet agent Sorge's chief source of high-level Japanese government information. For lack of access to the full texts of certain important diaries, however, Western scholars have failed to note that for the next three years, whenever a crisis threatened between Japan and the Soviet Union, Hirohito's favorite Big Brother Marquis Kido invariably consulted with Saionji Kinkazu. Saionji, in turn, transmitted his impressions to Ozaki and Ozaki to Sorge. Through this intelligence chain Hirohito repeatedly used the Sorge Spy Ring to allay the suspicions of the suspicious Joseph Stalin and keep Japan out of war with Russia.

INNER MONGOLIA

At the moment that Ozaki, the new link with Russia, was admitted into Hirohito's circle, the Japanese Kwantung Army in Manchuria made a tentative probe into Inner Mongolia along the southern borders of Siberia.

It was November 1936. Sleet collected on the wings of the observation plane and its movements, especially when it flew low,
seemed dangerously sluggish. Lieutenant Colonel Tanaka Takayoshi, the lover of Japan's girl spy, Eastern Jewel, hugged his
huge knees nervously in the skirts of his Chinese robe—his civilian
disguise—and peered out the cockpit window at the specks on the
snow-covered plain below. Tanaka watched the specks with humiliation. They were Mongol horsemen who had been under his
command since the start of the offensive nine days earlier on November 10. Now the offensive was over and the horsemen were
retreating to the east, back toward Japanese-controlled territory
on the edge of Manchukuo. Throughout the last week Tanaka had
directed their movements from the air, keeping in touch with
other Japanese spotter planes by radio and occasionally swooping
down to drop a bamboo cylinder of instructions.

Despite Japanese equipment and leadership, the Mongol rough-
riders had failed in their mission—failed to take Inner Mongolia
from China and make it once again an independent Tartar state.
At Pailingmiao, the Shrine of a Hundred Spirits, they had fought
and lost a week-long battle against the KMT forces of Chang
Hsueh-liang, the former Manchurian war lord. Colonel Tanaka
writhed inwardly because his orders forced him to fly back to
Mukden instead of sharing the hardships of his retreating men on
the ground. His fellow staff officers in the Kwantung Army would
make fun of him. Eastern Jewel would be disappointed, angry,
and scathing.[2] Worst of all, his face with the Mongols would now
be lost. Years of work would blow away into the steppes—and all
for lack of a few battalions of Japanese regulars to support the
brave but undisciplined Mongol cavalry.

The Mongol Prince Teh, a kinsman of Eastern Jewel, had first

[2] At this period Eastern Jewel's principal lover and main source of support
was a highly successful Osaka confidence man named Matsuo Masanao, alias
Ito Hanni. Through her introductions to Japanese Intelligence officers in
China, Matsuo had established himself as a liaison man, running guns and
carrying bribes from the Japanese Army to the dissident Canton faction of the
KMT. He worked directly for Major General Tojo and other leading Kwantung Army staff officers and had handled about $8 million (U.S.) worth of
Special Service funds. In kickbacks and commissions he had pocketed almost
$2 million for himself which Eastern Jewel had done her best to help him
spend. Now that Matsuo was falling under suspicion, however, she had returned to Manchuria in search of fresh patrons and pastures.

agreed to work with Tanaka in March 1933. Ever since then, at the Shrine of a Hundred Spirits, Prince Teh had headed a Mongol government secretly in league with Japan. Little by little it had won the allegiance of fifty-nine of Inner Mongolia's seventy-seven tribes or "banners." In January 1936 the Plot Section of the Kwantung Army—euphemistically translated as the Strategic Planning Section by most Western scholars—had detailed Tanaka to bring all Inner Mongolia, openly, into Prince Teh's fold. Hirohito and the Tokyo General Staff had approved the scheme on one condition: that it cost no more than a few million yen.

From Tokyo's vantage point an independent Mongolian nation, stretching across the north of China, would be moderately useful. It would cut the ancient caravan routes leading in to China from Russia and would help to isolate Chiang Kai-shek during Japan's planned war against the central KMT regime in Nanking. For Tanaka, who did not know the over-all war plan and had specialized in Mongol affairs since military academy, a "wedge between China and Russia" had become a premise for living. It would halt the spread of communism in China. It would facilitate a Strike North against Russia when the proper time came. And most important, it would rehabilitate the Mongols who Tanaka mystically believed to be a lost tribe of the Japanese nation itself.

In vain Tanaka had asked for more Tokyo support. When he had seen it was not forthcoming, he had undertaken to make do with contributions he could raise in Manchuria. The "Independent Volunteers' Squadron" of the Manchurian Aviation Company had provided him with thirteen light planes for air support. Manchukuoan Electric had fitted them out with two-way radios. The South Manchuria Railway Company had furnished 150 cars and trucks. The Kwantung Army had given the services of three fellow staff officers and $1.8 million in gold.

Now all was lost. Tanaka's plane dipped low so that he could drop his last cylinder of orders. Then he made for home. That night in Mukden he began a two-day drunken spree of protest against the stinginess of his superiors. He succeeded in making them offer the Mongol Prince Teh more money, on the strength of which one of Prince Teh's generals succeeded briefly in recapturing the Shrine of a Hundred Spirits. Thereafter all the Mongol horsemen made good their retreat through the snow. A few of them enlisted in one or another of Japan's puppet constabulary forces in Manchukuo. One group of them, on December 10, found constabulary duty so distasteful that they massacred the Japanese officers in charge of them and fled into the steppes. Most of the Mongols, however, followed Prince Teh when, on December 12, he forsook Japan and proclaimed his renewed loyalty to Chiang Kaishek.

THE GENERALISSIMO KIDNAPPED

On November 18, 1936, when the battle at the Shrine of a Hundred Spirits had first turned against Tanaka's cavalry rabble, Chiang Kai-shek himself had arrived by plane behind the front to inspect operations. Having lost Manchuria and the other northeastern provinces to Japan, Chiang was glad to associate himself with a Chinese victory over Japan. Since late in the spring of 1936, when his intelligence reports indicated that the Army mutiny in Tokyo had not in any way set back Japanese plans for the conquest of China, he had been busy fortifying the railroad lines which might be used by the Japanese in an attempt to move against him out of north China. At the same time he had announced his sixth bandit suppression campaign against the Communists of Mao Tse-tung in the northwest.

Not since 1925 had Chiang been so beleaguered by enemies. His power was secure only in central China along the valleys of the Yangtze River and its tributaries. Tibet, under the Dalai Lama, was virtually a fief now of British India. Outer Mongolia and the huge western province of Sinkiang had become economic dependencies of Russia. Manchuria and the Peking area were controlled by Japan. The Communist faction of Mao Tse-tung collected taxes in the northwest. In the southeast the perennially dissident generals of the KMT's Canton faction threatened rebellion. Sun Yat-sen's dream of a united China had lost its flush of youth, and Chiang, in Sun Yat-sen's mantle, was in danger of being regarded as just another war lord.

In going to the front, Chiang hoped to make sure of the allegiance of Chang Hsueh-liang and of his expatriate Manchurians. He had given Chang an important assignment in the sixth campaign against the Communists. But instead of attacking the Communists vigorously, Chang had entrenched his forces and diverted all the men he could spare to fight the Inner Mongolian battle on his extreme right flank. It was rumored in Nanking that Chang and the Communists had agreed to fight Japan first and settle their own differences later.

Chiang Kai-shek took with him on his inspection tour 200,000 words of important state papers, including his own diary for the years in which he had ruled the KMT. He needed the papers to persuade Chang Hsueh-liang that he had been acting in the best interests of China and buying valuable time by his repeated concessions to Japan. In return Chang, too, must show a statesmanly spirit and realize that alliance with the Communists might be more dangerous in the long run than temporary surrenders to the Japanese. Chang Hsueh-liang stubbornly refused to be persuaded, and he and Chiang negotiated for three weeks. Then on December 12, 1936, in an attempt either to coerce Chiang or to save Chiang's face before the inevitable settlement, Chang Hsueh-liang had his leader kidnapped.

It was five o'clock in the morning and Chiang Kai-shek was in his nightshirt. At the sound of shots he jumped from his pallet, ran to the rear of the temple in which he was camped, and scaled a ten-foot wall. Dropping to the other side he twisted his back and had to scramble painfully on hands and knees up the hillside beyond. Two white hares, he later recounted, guided him to a rocky overhang under which he could hide and rest. There, when it was almost noon, he confronted a group of the rebellious soldiers who were beating the bushes for him and courageously demanded that they either shoot him or provide him with a suitable escort back to his quarters. One of the dissidents, a battalion commander, respectfully offered his broad shoulders and carried Chiang in his nightshirt down the mountain piggyback. Chang Hsueh-liang and Chiang's own local bandit-suppression commissioner had him put to bed comfortably under guard, and negotiations were resumed.

That night in Shanghai Madame Chiang Kai-shek, her brother, her brother-in-law, and Chiang's Australian advisor W. H. Donald gave the news of Chiang's kidnapping as an exclusive to Hallett Abend of *The New York Times*. They thereby made sure that the story would first reach Japan from an authoritative Western source rather than from a suspect Chinese one. In China, where

news was always well controlled, it was an odd maneuver, savoring
more of publicity for an event which they had foreseen than of
concern for public knowledge about an uncertain situation which
had taken them by surprise.

Meanwhile in Sian, the town in the northwest where Chiang was
detained, Chang Hsueh-liang was beginning to read the 200,000
pages of state documents which Chiang demanded that he study
before they resume their conversations. In the next three days
Chang read, and Chiang Kai-shek stayed in bed, refusing to eat
and threatening, by suicide, to leave China without a leader.
Chang called in Chou En-lai, the later foreign minister of Communist China, to plead the cause of Mao Tse-tung. By the end of
the third day, Chiang Kai-shek had agreed "in principle" to present a united front of all patriotic Chinese factions against the
Japanese. Then for another ten days he remained in bed lecturing
eloquently on the republican principles of Sun Yat-sen and negotiating an elaborate save of face for himself in any future dealings
he might have with the Japanese.

Chiang's Australian secretary, W. H. Donald, flew into Sian, the
rebel stronghold, on December 14, 1936. Chiang's brother-in-law
T. V. Soong joined the negotiations four days later. And Madame
Chiang arrived in Sian to add her authority on December 21. While
his minions made secret promises, Chiang continued to lie abed,
saving face, daring his abductors to assassinate him, and maintaining, with stubborn courage and indignation, the rectitude of
all his past decisions of state.

On Christmas Day 1936, Chiang and his spokesmen were allowed to fly back to Nanking. With them went Chang Hsueh-liang
to surrender himself as a voluntary hostage to Chiang's brutal secret police. It was Chang's way of demonstrating to the Chinese
people the sincerity of his patriotism. And Chiang Kai-shek appreciated it. The police touched not a hair on the hostage's head
but simply put him under house arrest in one of the most comfortable mansions in Nanking. While he accustomed himself to a
life of leisure, his captor Chiang fulfilled the unspoken pledges
he had made during his own captivity. He called off the sixth
bandit-suppression campaign against the Communists and began
a succession of conferences at his country villa in the mountains
with all the generals and war lords who owed him allegiance. He

asked them one by one to stand by him in a long ordeal, a full-scale war with Japan—and to each of them he assigned commands and duties.

Chang Hsueh-liang remained under detention for the rest of his life. He never relapsed into the opium-smoking of his youth but instead cultivated the polite recreations of bridge, golf, books, fine food and wines, paintings, and handsome mistresses. In 1940 he was permitted a trip abroad and impressed all his fellow passengers on shipboard with his charming air of resignation and his excellence at the card table. After World War II, in 1949, he was brought to Taiwan under guard by Chiang Kai-shek, and there he remains a pampered prisoner at the age of seventy-two in 1970. He and his final mistress, Miss Chao, who is said to grow more seductive with each passing year, are still seen sometimes in Taipei attending the theater. At secret conclaves of the KMT leaders, it is reported that Chang still acts the part of a conscience for his eighty-three-year-old mentor, Generalissimo Chiang.

ALLIANCE WITH HITLER

On November 20, 1936, as Chiang Kai-shek began to negotiate the stiffening of backbone which his partisans required of him; as the Kwantung Army's gigantic Lieutenant Colonel Tanaka nursed his recent humiliation on the snowy wastes of Inner Mongolia; and as the new Soviet spy, Ozaki, was accustoming himself to the rarefied atmosphere of Konoye's inner circle, Hirohito at a Privy Council meeting approved Japan's first tentative alliance with Nazi Germany. The alliance was formalized five days later when Hitler's super-diplomat, Joachim von Ribbentrop, sat down at a table in Berlin with one of Hirohito's courtiers and signed a document known as the Anti-Comintern Pact. This instrument pledged Japan to act in concert with Germany in resisting the spread of communism. Secret protocols attached to it bound each nation to assist the other economically and diplomatically in the event that the other should make war on the Soviet Union.

Hitler and Ribbentrop had first begun to suggest such a pact to prominent Japanese visitors in 1933. The pact went against Hitler's early Aryan principles, as enunciated in *Mein Kampf*, but agreed well with his political objectives. At his direction the Ger-

man propaganda apparatus under Goebbels had begun in 1934 to
call the Japanese "the Prussians of the East." His Bureau of Race
Investigation had decided that German-Japanese marriages were
permissible because "the blood of Dai Nippon [Japan] contains
within itself virtues closely akin to the pure Nordic strain."
From Hitler's point of view the pact would help to neutralize
Russia when the time came for the *Wehrmacht* to overrun France
and the Low Countries. Hirohito's 1934 envoy to Berlin, Prince
Kaya, had come home pointing out that the pact would help to
neutralize Russia when the time came for the Japanese Army to
overrun China.

Throughout 1934 Japanese representatives in Berlin had remained coy and noncommittal to the German overtures. But in
the spring of 1935, when Hirohito decided on the war with China,
negotiations had begun in earnest. They were conducted for Japan in Berlin not by the Japanese ambassador there but by Major
General Oshima Hiroshi, the military attaché at the Japanese Embassy. Similarly in Tokyo they were conducted on behalf of Germany by Colonel Eugen Ott, the military attaché at Tokyo's
German Embassy. In the summer of 1936, when the pact was
finally ready for signing, Ott had returned home briefly to explain
all its unwritten ramifications personally to Hitler and Oshima
had done the same for Hirohito in Tokyo.

Ott had qualified for his mission in Hitler's eyes by useful
service on the personal staff of General Kurt Schleicher, the last
pre-Hitler chancellor of Germany. In Hirohito's eyes he was
recommended by understandings he had reached in 1933 as liaison
officer to Prince Higashikuni, Hirohito's uncle, at 5th Brigade
Headquarters in Nagoya.

Oshima, the principal Japanese negotiator of the pact, was also
an old friend of Prince Higashikuni, and he was sent to Berlin as
military attaché in March 1934, shortly after the conclusion of the
preliminary conversations between Higashikuni and Ott. It was
understood by Ribbentrop and Hitler that Oshima could speak for
the Emperor and for the chief of the Japanese Army General Staff,
Prince Kanin. And so he could. As an assistant attaché in Germany in 1921, at the age of thirty-five, Oshima had been privy to
all the plans of the Crows and Reliables of Hirohito's original cabal in the Army. He was not then designated as a recruit of the ca-

bal because he was already a member of the Big Brothers' Inner Circle. His father, General Oshima Kenichi, had studied with Prince Kanin in France in the 1880's, had gone along with Prince Kanin on a tour of the front during the Boer War in South Africa in 1899, had assisted as war minister in Prince Kanin's abortive Mukden coup of 1916, and finally had accompanied Kanin and the crown prince—to help "make arrangements"—during Hirohito's European tour of 1921.

SORGE'S FIRST EXCLUSIVE

At first the Japanese accepted the Anti-Comintern Pact without much comment. They had long needed an ally in Europe, and even having Nazi Germany for a friend seemed better than fighting the preventive war with Russia advocated by the Strike-North Faction. In the West, however, the pact was decried as a danger-ous fascist alliance, unfriendly to the democracies. France, the Netherlands, England, and the United States all released evidence to show that the pact contained secret military clauses in addition to the overt diplomatic ones acknowledged in its published text.

The Soviet Union, being the nation most directly threatened by the pact, had begun to spread rumors about the secret proto-cols more than a year before the pact was signed. Stalin, however, was less concerned by the protocols than other antifascist leaders because he knew what was in them. Germany and Japan had not committed themselves to assist one another militarily against the Soviet Union. In the event that either of the two contracting parties became involved in war with Russia, the other was simply pledged to provide diplomatic support and to "consult" with its ally on the joint military measures which might be taken. In short, neither Japan nor Germany had promised the other much of any-thing except friendly words.

Stalin knew this because Sorge had read the secret papers about the pact which had passed through the German Embassy in Tokyo and because Ozaki had kept abreast of the interpretation being placed upon them by men around Hirohito.

Eugen Ott, the German attaché in Tokyo, who had helped to negotiate the Anti-Comintern Pact, was one of Richard Sorge's prime contacts in Japan. When Sorge arrived in Tokyo in September 1933, he carried a letter to Ott from the chief editorial writer of *Tägliche Rundschau,* a liberal German newspaper. Sorge delivered his note of introduction in a visit to Nagoya where Ott had just concluded his preliminary conversations with the commander of the Nagoya Brigade, Hirohito's uncle Prince Higashikuni. Ott and Sorge had served in the same German division during World War I and soon became boon companions.

Through Ott, Sorge learned what few details of Kwantung Army strength in Manchuria the Japanese had divulged to the Germans in the course of the pact negotiations. In Sorge's opinion, which he swiftly conveyed to Moscow over Max Klausen's radio transmitter, the posture of the Kwantung Army constituted no threat to the Soviet Union and indicated no immediate intention of carrying out a Strike North. As a result, although Moscow made much propaganda out of the pact's secret protocols, the Red Army did not reinforce its garrisons in the Far East. Moreover, the day before the pact was made public, the Soviet government delivered Japan a calculated slap in the face by refusing to renew the Russo-Japanese treaty regulating quotas and privileges on the fishing banks off Siberia.

By his report on the Anti-Comintern Pact, Sorge proved to his superiors in Moscow that the two painstaking years he had spent in organizing his ring had not been wasted. His further reports, over the next five years, were to play an increasingly important part in enabling Russia and Japan to stand off from one another and prepare for their respective wars with Germany and the United States.

BLOCKING UGAKI

Although the Anti-Comintern Pact sailed smoothly, unopposed, through the Cabinet and the Emperor's Privy Council, it aroused noisy misgivings when the public realized what it meant to the West. The decrepit Saionji called it a fool's bargain which "will only result in Germany exploiting us." The leading Tokyo dailies joined Saionji editorially in pointing out that one untrustworthy ally had been bought at the cost of many true friends.

At Saionji's behest, the Constitutionalist party began sniping at the Cabinet from the floor of the Diet. One intrepid representative, the former speaker of the lower House, Hamada Kunimatsu, demanded that War Minister Terauchi—who was Hirohito's Army strong man of the moment—submit to a trial of courage. If the Diet voted that Terauchi was sincere, Representative Hamada promised to disembowel himself; on the other hand if the Diet voted that Representative Hamada was sincere, Terauchi would have to cut his belly. War Minister Terauchi declined to accept the challenge because the Constitutionalists had a majority in the Diet and would surely enjoy watching him commit hara-kiri. The next day, however, on January 22, 1937, Terauchi submitted his resignation in writing to Prime Minister Hirota. Hirota followed, late in the afternoon of Saturday, January 23, by offering the mass resignation of his Cabinet to Emperor Hirohito.

As always Hirohito insisted that old Saionji take the responsibility for recommending the next prime minister. When so informed by Lord Privy Seal Yuasa on the phone, Saionji asked to be excused, protesting that he was too frail to come to Tokyo to investigate the political situation properly before making a selection. Hirohito replied, through Lord Privy Seal Yuasa, that Saionji could do his research by telephone and then report his choice to an imperial envoy who would call on him in Okitsu.

"In that case, without further deliberation," said Saionji, "I warn you that I will recommend Ugaki."

General Ugaki was the bull-necked loyalist who had cleansed the Army of its Choshu leadership for Hirohito in 1925 and had then allowed himself to be duped and defamed by the March Plot of 1931. Since then, as governor general of Korea, he had made himself the leader of the many Army officers who took a moderate position between the Strike-North and Strike-South Factions. He had the support of the political parties and of the cartels. Most important, he was outspoken in his opposition to the planned war of aggression in China.

First on the phone and then in a face-to-face discussion the next day, Sunday, with Saionji in Okitsu, Lord Privy Seal Yuasa tried in vain to change the eighty-seven-year-old's mind. Returning discouraged to Tokyo that night, Yuasa went in directly to a two-hour audience with Hirohito. He persuaded Hirohito that, to avoid a public scene with Saionji, it would be best to let Ugaki try to form a Cabinet. At 10 P.M. Ugaki was phoned at the hot spring where he was waiting fifty miles outside of Tokyo and told to come to the palace immediately.

Ugaki had his limousine waiting and set off at once. Outside the entrance to the palace, the car was stopped by an unexpected roadblock set up by the secret police. As Ugaki blustered that the policemen were delaying a general on the Emperor's business, the barrier was opened and a figure stepped out of the night into the back seat and sat down beside Ugaki. It was Lieutenant General Nakajima Kesago, the chief of the secret police—the sadist who later that year would bring special oils from Peking to assist Prince Asaka in burning the bodies at Nanking.

Nakajima had been working closely with the palace on the maintenance of public peace since the February Mutiny the year before. Now he advised Ugaki to decline the mandate to form a Cabinet. A general like Ugaki, who had been involved in such previous Army plots as the March Incident, could not become prime minister, Nakajima said, without setting back seriously the program of Army discipline which had been imposed since the February Mutiny. General Ugaki thanked the sinister secret police chief for his advice and let him off at the next checkpoint, at the entrance to the Inner Palace enclosure. Then Ugaki drove on alone through the moonlit woods of the Fukiage Gardens. By the time he arrived at the Imperial Library he was doubly determined "to save Japan."

Hirohito admitted Ugaki to audience at 1:00 A.M.

"You may as well know," said the Emperor, "that Prime Minister Hirota has begged leave to resign, so I am asking you to form a Cabinet. I understand, however, that there is a movement against you in the Army. Do you think you can cope with it?"

"The situation is a complicated one," replied Ugaki with unusual modesty. "Please give me a few days, Sire, and I will see what I can do."

Hirohito nodded and dismissed him.

Two hours later, at 3:00 A.M., Marquis Kido, the first and favorite of the Big Brothers who had taken Hirohito in hand when

he was a little boy, received a phone call from one of Lord Privy
Seal Yuasa's protégés[3] telling him that the "right wing in the
Army" was prepared to block Ugaki's prime ministership.

After daybreak Marquis Kido went to the palace and conferred
with Lord Privy Seal Yuasa. Kido himself no longer had much of
an official position in the palace. As a part of the change in palace
window dressing after the February Mutiny, he had resigned
from the secretariat of the lord privy seal and retained only his
minor Court post as director of the Peerage and Heraldry Bureau.
Nevertheless, he now consulted at length with Privy Seal Yuasa,
with Yuasa's secretary,[4] and with one of Hirohito's military aides-
de-camp.[5] On returning home, Kido at once began cogitating
in his diary over the best man for the Emperor to appoint when
Ugaki failed to form a Cabinet.

While Kido and other courtiers were working against him,
Prime Minister-elect Ugaki set about routinely to form a Cabinet.
At four o'clock that Monday afternoon he called on outgoing
War Minister Terauchi and asked him politely to recommend a
successor to himself. Terauchi shook his head gravely and warned
Ugaki that officers willing and eligible to serve as war minister
might be difficult to find. An hour later, after consulting other
Army chiefs, Terauchi informed Ugaki that the three most appropriate candidates for the war ministership all declined the
honor. Ugaki responded angrily that in that case he would hunt
up his own war minister.

Late that night, at one o'clock, the vice minister of war called
an emergency meeting of his section chiefs and, in a ten-minute
briefing, advised them that Ugaki's search must be frustrated.

On Tuesday morning Ugaki took to the telephone. He knew
most of the 200-odd generals on the active list and had done favors
for many of them. Now, however, they squirmed evasively and

[3] Goto Fumio, a former home minister and leader of Strike-South colonials
in Taiwan. He would survive MacArthur's purge after World War II to return
to the Diet and become an elder statesman at Hirohito's Court in the 1960's.

[4] Matsudaira Yasumasa, who would succeed Kido as chief civilian advisor to
the Emperor in 1945 and would handle liaison for Hirohito with American
Prosecutor Keenan and with Keenan's star witness, the elephantine lover with
the elephantine memory, retired Major General Tanaka Takayoshi.

[5] Major General Nakajima Tetsuzo, who in some Japanese accounts has
been identified as the Nakajima who jumped into Ugaki's car the night before.

pleaded personal reasons for being unable to accept the war ministership.

In the afternoon, having consulted an authority on constitutional law, Ugaki tried a fresh approach. He himself was a general, and if reactivated from the reserve list to the active list would be eligible to take the portfolio of war minister in addition to that of prime minister. On inquiry he found that there were a number of other retired generals who would also be willing to take the war minister portfolio. By early the next morning, Wednesday he had queues of reserve officers waiting outside the doors of War Minister Terauchi and of Chief of Staff Prince Kanin, pleading their candidacies. Some of them were such obscure field commanders that chamberlains at Court were kept busy looking up their personnel records in case the Emperor should ask questions about them.

The Emperor had the power to order any officer on active service to take the war ministership. It was, however, a power which the Emperor had never exercised. On the other hand, the Emperor had frequently reactivated reservists to fill unpleasant commands during the conquest of Manchuria. Saionji had suggested to Ugaki that in the present crisis the Emperor could be called out into the open by being forced publicly to refuse to reactivate Ugaki or any of his cronies.

All that Wednesday morning Marquis Kido, Lord Privy Seal Yuasa, and other chamberlains consulted on what countermeasures to take against the ingenious new Saionji-Ugaki strategy. They decided finally to rely on a metaphysical argument. If the Emperor, they reasoned, should agree to see Ugaki a second time to consider his reactivation request, it would be tantamount to giving him a second order to form a Cabinet. In effect it would be asking the god to issue the same orders twice—a clear sacrilege. If a vassal failed to perform the Emperor's bidding, that was a fault in the vassal's virtue, but if, on failing, he tried to enlist imperial support for a second try, that would call in question the Emperor's potence and could not be permitted.

Ugaki arrived at the palace in the forenoon and was given this answer after being kept waiting for several hours. In vain he argued that he had the right of direct access to the Throne. Ancient precedents were adduced to show that he did not. Finally

Ugaki stamped from the outer ceremonial palace, threatening that he would never again wear the uniform of the Imperial Army. The next morning, Thursday, he formally tendered the resignation of his commission in the reserve.

On Friday, January 29, Hirohito called Ugaki to the palace to deliver his official report on the failure of his attempt to form a Cabinet. When Ugaki had finished reading and had begun stiffly to bow his way out of the Throne Room, Hirohito came forward, all solicitude, and apologized for having put Ugaki to so much trouble. The Throne, explained Hirohito, could never swim against the current of the times. Then he pressed back into Ugaki's hand his letter of resignation from the reserve and begged him to keep his salary and "to continue to do your utmost for the nation." Entrapped in the coils of patriotism and self-interest, Ugaki wavered for a few weeks and finally agreed to keep his commission and to accept the post of foreign minister in the Cabinet after next—a Cabinet which was to materialize three months later.

On that same Friday that Ugaki abandoned his attempt to form a government, a journalist, who was later tracked down and tortured and executed by the secret police, sent anonymous letters, beautifully penned and framed in black, to all the units which had been involved in the February Mutiny of 1936. He advised them that Prince Kanin, the senior member of the imperial family and chief of the Army General Staff, was the principal villain of the times and should be assassinated.

SAIONJI DROPS OUT

With the rejection of his protégé, the tragic old man Saionji—the knight in green armor of the restoration of 1868—gave up his futile, fifteen-year struggle to steer Hirohito from the shoals he saw ahead. After Ugaki's failure to form a Cabinet, Saionji was offered the alternative of nominating as prime minister either his old enemy, the far-right lawyer of the National Foundation Society, Baron Hiranuma, or General Hayashi, the former war minister who had eased the Strike-North Faction out of the Army bureaucracy before the 1936 mutiny. Muttering protests and dire predictions, Saionji allowed his name to be given to the choice of Hayashi.

Saionji reflected on this, his latest, capitulation for several days. He admitted to friends that he was approaching senility and that he spent most of his time living in the past. He complained that his secretary-spy, Harada, was constantly feeding him twisted or irrelevant information in order to distract him from concentrating on "the main trends of the time." Nevertheless he still had days of energy and complete lucidity in which he phoned old friends and understood completely the iron grip which Hirohito's middle-aged Big-Brother statists were taking on Japan. He felt personally responsible for them, for he had overseen their political educations. He also felt personally responsible for what they were doing. As long as he remained prime-minister-maker, the cartels and political parties of Japan would continue to look up to him as the leader of the young men at Court. And for the hundredth time he had just proved that he was not the leader. Perhaps if he resigned some other more forceful aristocrat of good sense would spring up in his place; perhaps his kinsman Prince Konoye and even Emperor Hirohito would begin to take their responsibilities more level-headedly.

Accordingly, in the week after Ugaki's humiliation, Saionji formally petitioned the Throne, asking that he be consulted no longer on changes of government. Hirohito refused to release him from his post of prime-minister-maker but allowed it to be inscribed officially on the Court rolls that Saionji would not have to come again to Tokyo for a Cabinet crisis. From now on the lord privy seal would relieve him of the duty of consulting with other elder statesmen on the nominee who should be recommended to the Throne as the next prime minister. In effect the lord privy seal would conduct all the business involved in the choice of a prime minister and simply inform Saionji of what he had done before carrying his advice to Hirohito.

Saionji welcomed this relief from responsibility and lived on for another three years and nine months as a sideline critic, sometimes crackling with sarcastic fire and sometimes remaining mute or ignorant.

The prospect of war with China dismayed the old man. What dismayed him still more was the prospect of direct involvement in enterprises which he considered rash and hazardous by members of the imperial family. On March 15, in an argument about

China policy with Secretary-Spy Harada, he learned that Prince Higashikuni was slated to command the Army Air Force when it would begin to bomb China and that Prince Asaka, the Emperor's other uncle, was expected later to lead the Japanese troops who would occupy the Chinese capital of Nanking.

"The devil you say!" piped the old man testily. "I tell you that this business of installing imperial family members in military posts is for the sake of making the Army act as the Emperor's army in the time of emergency. It is understood that the members of the imperial family are usually the Emperor's allies. Therefore it would seem that the main point in having allies in military posts is to persuade the military, as the Emperor's own army, to conduct operations even to the ends of the earth."

LAST WORDS OF THE PEOPLE

When Saionji had already given up, the Japanese people themselves made one last bootless effort to escape from going to war. Hirohito's courtiers realized that the pacifism of the masses needed some form of satisfaction and had shrewdly set up General Hayashi, the new prime minister, as a straw man of militarism for the people to destroy.

Misunderstanding something said to him by Hirohito at his investiture ceremony, Hayashi launched his regime by asking everyone "to honor the Emperor and the spirits of the forefathers and to realize the identity of government administration and religious ceremony." In other words, the people from now on should participate in government only by worshipping and Hirohito should officiate absolutely as high priest. Westernized liberals were quick to point out that Emperor Meiji had promised separation of church and state, and Hirohito hastily disassociated himself from Prime Minister Hayashi's sentiments.

On the floor of the Diet the antimilitary sniping which had toppled the previous Hirota Cabinet swelled to a chorus. Rumors of war planning against China was discussed in every corridor. On March 18, Hirohito's brother Prince Chichibu left Japan with a suite of fifteen of the great vassals to attend the coronation of George VI in London. He had a secret mission—of which nothing is known from Western documentation—to persuade George VI to renew an unwritten understanding as to Japan's privileged position in China which Hirohito felt that he had had with George VI's brother, the recently abdicated Edward VIII. On the eve of Prince Chichibu's departure, his equerry told friends that if the mission were not successful war with China could be expected in early July.[6]

On March 31, 1937, two weeks after Prince Chichibu's sailing, Hirohito finally dissolved the carping Diet and called for a general election. During the following month, while the politicians were out stumping, he made full use of his edict powers to find funds for fully manning the seven new Army divisions which he had created in skeletal form after the February Mutiny the year before.

When the masses convened at the polls at the end of April, they delivered a resounding vote of non-confidence in the militaristic, archaically devout Prime Minister Hayashi. Both of the major parties, the Constitutionalists and their traditional opponents, had asked for a vote for peace, and only the minority rightist party, the *Kokumin Domei* or People's League, had supported Hayashi. In the returns the Hayashi party won exactly eighteen seats in a House of 408.

A month later Hayashi resigned. He had served his purpose. The people had made their gesture. The seven new divisions were already established. Army men who wished to interfere in politics had been given a graphic demonstration of the Army's unpopularity and political incompetence. Now the way was clear to disregard the mandate of the voters and to appoint a popular civilian prince, a consummate politician, who could lead the people to war.

KONOYE

Prince Konoye, heir to the first of the five houses of the ancient Court family of Fujiwara, had been groomed as a national leader ever since his birth in October 1891. As a teen-ager he had been

[6] The equerry was Major General Honma Masaharu who would later be executed for his titular responsibility in the Bataan Death March. He was already well known and respected in Japan as "the linguist with the red nose" who had sat up all one night in 1932 translating into Japanese the Lytton Report on Manchuria.

the youngest of the aristocratic Big Brothers who attached themselves to the person of young Hirohito when he was still a toddler living in the foster care of Marquis Kido's father. Since 1921 Konoye had led Hirohito's forces in the House of Peers and had mediated for Hirohito with all sorts of troublemakers: with Konoye's kinsman, Saionji; with the tong of the Black Dragon; with the dissident Strike-Northists in Hirohito's Army cabal.

The tall, languid, elegant prince was a sybarite in private life, but in public he was a politician down to the tips of his gloved fingers. Hirohito's ambition to aggrandize Japan territorially and technologically before the eyes of the West interested Konoye hardly at all. He responded first to the challenge of domestic Japanese government and second to the challenge of leading the Buddhists of Asia. Systems of government—of people-manipulation and propaganda—fascinated him; deployment of military forces caught his fancy only sporadically as a tool of politics.

Since the 1935 imperial decision to prepare for war on China, Prince Konoye had begun to appreciate the gulf between his concerns and those of the Emperor. It mattered little to Konoye whether Japan fought Russia or the colonial democracies. Konoye wished only to unify Japan—to make it the most perfectly governed anthill in the community of nations. After the Army Mutiny of February 1936 he had lobbied tirelessly in the palace to prevent the number-two Strike-North leader, General Mazaki, from being harshly punished. In his fascination with the problem of creating a super-state, he dismissed Hirohito's territorial aspirations as narrow and irrelevant.

For these reasons Prince Konoye at first refused when emissaries from Court asked him to assume the prime ministership in 1937. Over a period of weeks, however, in the declining days of the Hayashi Cabinet, he made a deal with Hirohito: a free hand to reorganize the state domestically in exchange for giving his name to military consolidation of the Japanese position in China. Saionji encouraged Konoye to assume the responsibility, for Konoye was, after all, a Fujiwara and the old prime-minister-maker knew no other leader influential enough to obviate national disaster.

Prince Konoye submitted a list of Cabinet ministers to Hirohito and accepted Hirohito's command to form a Cabinet on

June 4, 1937. For the first time in twenty years Saionji had not
been consulted officially—only unofficially. The well-primed gentlemen of the press greeted Konoye with editorial enthusiasm,
comparing him with Prime Minister Okuma, "the professor,"
who had taken office in 1914 and had kept Japan from becoming
deeply embroiled in World War I. Konoye at once went on the
radio to announce an administration of national unification and
conciliation in which the military, the cartels, the bureaucrats,
and the political parties would all have a place. He looked forward,
he said, to the time when Imperial Japan would be governed by a
monolithic single party of patriots. He established a council of
advisors which included representatives of all dissident factions
and at the same time a fuel board to ration and control Japan's
most scarce military commodity: oil and gasoline.

MARCO POLO'S BRIDGE

On June 9, 1937, five days after the investiture of the Konoye
Cabinet, the porcine uncle of the Empress, Prince Nashimoto,
who would later be held as imperial-family hostage by MacArthur,
attended a banquet in his honor given by the brass of the Kwantung Army in the Manchukuoan capital of Long Spring Thaw.
Nashimoto had left Japan in late May when Prime Minister
Hayashi had announced his intention of resigning and had since
conducted a leisurely inspection tour of Japanese garrisons in
Korea and Manchuria. This particular Wednesday night he sat
beside the new chief of staff of the Kwantung Army, Lieutenant
General Tojo, Hirohito's future World War II shogun, and sa-
vored a succession of Chinese delicacies, including bird's nest
soup, Shansi dumplings, Peking duck, and Peking dancing girls.

In the midst of the banquet Tojo withdrew briefly to his office
to draft a telegram. He returned to table with it, showed it to
Prince Nashimoto, and consigned it to an aide for coding and
dispatch. It was addressed to the vice chief of the general staff
and the vice minister of war in Tokyo, both loyal opportunists.[7]
It told them in indirect Japanese fashion that the imperial family
had reached an understanding with the Strike-North officers in the

---

[7] Lieutenant Generals Imai Kiyoshi and Umezu Yoshijiro.

Kwantung Army. It promised that the Army would be given a chance to fight Russia after the ports and railheads of eastern China were in Japanese hands. Specifically the Tojo-Nashimoto cable stated:

FROM THE STANDPOINT OF OUR STRATEGIC PREPARATIONS AGAINST RUS-SIA, WHEN VIEWED AGAINST THE PRESENT STATE OF AFFAIRS IN CHINA, WE DEEM IT MOST IMPORTANT AND DESIRABLE, IN ORDER TO ELIMI-NATE THE THREAT IN OUR REAR, TO STRIKE A DIRECT BLOW AGAINST AND INTO THE NANKING REGIME—PROVIDED, OF COURSE, THAT IN OUR OPINION AT THE TIME WE HAVE SUFFICIENT ARMED STRENGTH FOR IT.

The next morning, when the saké cups had been cleared away, proconsul Tojo accompanied Prince Nashimoto in his plane back home to the nearest of the main Japanese islands, Kyushu. There, having worked out all the details of their agreement, the general and the prince parted, the one to fly back to his command in Manchuria, the other to fly on to report at the square mile of moat-girt palace in the center of downtown Tokyo.

Having secured the support of Tojo and the Kwantung Army, Hirohito pressed ahead with the final phase of war preparations. His uncle Prince Higashikuni flew to Taiwan to review the air units and some of the infantry units which had been trained for the invasion of central China. Prince Asaka, the other uncle, in-spected the 11th Division which was to be used for the attack on Shanghai. Prince Mikasa, Hirohito's youngest brother, flew home from London with a pessimistic progress report on Prince Chichi-bu's conversations with the new king of England, George VI. From the palace the twenty-one-year-old Mikasa proceeded to Yokosuka, the great naval base on Tokyo Bay, and told the officers there that the Emperor expected every man to do his duty.

On the last day of June 1937, the Army sought to attach a con-dition to its willingness to fight: namely, imperial approval for preparation of a foray across the Korean border into Russia in late 1938, fifteen months hence. Hirohito was ready to call a full-scale conference in the Imperial Presence with Army leaders in order to thrash out the question. Instead his courtiers arranged a meeting for him and for Chief of Staff Prince Kanin with War Minister Sugiyama. At the meeting Hirohito agreed to sanction staff studies of the possibilities in an aggressive probe of Russia but refused absolutely to make any promises. Two weeks later, at a social breakfast on July 13, Big Brother Marquis Kido dropped word of the Emperor's stand to Saionji Kinkazu, the imperial link with the Sorge Spy Ring.

War Minister Sugiyama was able to use the Emperor's small concession to quiet rebellious underlings, and on July 6 Hirohito received his final go-ahead from Prince Chichibu in London. Through a member of his suite, Chichibu reported the futility of his conversations with King George in a previously agreed-upon voice code: "Prince Higashikuni's problem with the lady in France has not yet been solved." Since Prince Higashikuni had left France more than ten years ago, it was a message that amused Japanese courtiers and successfully titillated and bemused its monitors in British Intelligence.

The next night, July 7, the war with China began on schedule at the Marco Polo Bridge. As described in Chapter 1, a Japanese soldier left his patrol briefly in order to urinate and his commander shelled a nearby Chinese garrison which was supposed to have abducted him. Local Chinese and Japanese diplomats quickly negotiated half a dozen settlements of the affair, but neither Hirohito nor Chiang would give the negotiators more than polite encouragement. Chiang secretly moved troops north and Hirohito had transports loaded with reinforcements in Japan. Chinese and Japanese soldiers picked quarrels in several fresh localities. Native constabulary in the autonomous regions founded by Japan two years earlier grew rebellious and in one town massacred 230 of their Japanese masters. Kwantung Army Chief of Staff Tojo, in the one combat experience of his career, led an expedition into Inner Mongolia and, after an efficient blitzkrieg, subjugated the areas which had eluded Japan's grasp the year before. The Japanese Tientsin garrison occupied Peking. With many protestations of peaceful intent, Prime Minister Prince Konoye dispatched three of the divisions of reinforcements lying at anchor in Japanese ports, and by the end of July they had landed and seized the key railheads throughout northeastern China.

PREVENTING PEACE

The Japanese Special Service Organ in Shanghai, the gateway to central China, at once staged a second incident. On August 9 a Japanese naval officer and a seaman tried to force their way into the Chinese military airport in Shanghai. They shot a Chinese guard who challenged them and were both shot in their turn. Within a week Hirohito had commanded the little tubercular general, Matsui, to lead an expeditionary force to central China and Prince Higashikuni to take charge of the Army Air Force in Taiwan and initiate a program of civilian bombing in Shanghai.

Two and a half months of street fighting followed, against Chiang Kai-shek's best divisions, and then the Japanese began their drive on Nanking. In December, Prince Asaka, the Emperor's limping uncle, relieved Matsui of command at the front and put Nanking to its month and a half of unspeakable torture.

During the genocidal debauch, that tall, tolerant, loose-jointed experimentalist, Prime Minister Prince Konoye, wrung his hands cynically. He told intimates that he did not approve of Hirohito's reliance on military force. He had tried first, he said, to restrict the war to north China, then to Shanghai in central China. Now the sinking of the U.S.S. *Panay* by one of his minions successfully deterred Hirohito from spreading the war at once down the coast to the environs of British Hong Kong in south China.

Konoye had expressed his unhappiness as early as October by threatening to resign the prime ministership. To stiffen his spine, Hirohito had put favorite Big Brother Marquis Kido into the Cabinet as minister of education in charge of propaganda. In November, when Hirohito took personal charge of the war by opening Imperial Headquarters, superior to the General Staff, on the very grounds of the palace, Prince Konoye had once more tried to resign—this time so sincerely that Education Minister Kido had warned him that his career would be over permanently if he bowed out now in a time of emergency.

Japan's allies, the Germans, did their utmost to mediate the war and find terms on which it could be settled. Ribbentrop pointed out from Berlin that miring down in the paddies of China

would emasculate Japan as a German ally against Russia, and
that the Third Reich was not in any way committed by the Anti-
Comintern Pact to help Japan fight Bolshevism south of the
Russian border. The German ambassador attached to Chiang Kai-
shek's refugee regime in Hankow communicated daily with the
German ambassador in Tokyo on new formulas for making peace.
Backed by Hirohito, however, the soft-spoken gentlemen of the
Japanese Foreign Ministry repeatedly increased the severity of
their demands on China. The much maligned "militarists" on
the Tokyo General Staff begged the civilian Cabinet to offer
realistic terms which Chiang might possibly accept, but Hirohito,
behind the scenes, remained obdurately hard of heart. No settlement would do short of complete Japanese mastery and the reduction of China to the status of a puppet dependency.

In late December when the rape of Nanking first began to look
as if it would fail to unseat Chiang Kai-shek, Hirohito took up a
suggestion, made earlier by Konoye, for threatening Chiang politically. Unless he would accept Japanese terms, Japan would no
longer recognize him as China's chief of state and would find a
rival to deal with in the KMT—one amenable to leading a puppet
government in China. The majority of officers in the Army General Staff opposed this new ultimatum as unrealistic and fought
it as they had earlier fought the preparations for the rape of Nanking. Chief of Staff Prince Kanin, the seventy-two-year-old elder
of the imperial family, interviewed each of his subordinates individually and suppressed their opposition. On January 16, 1938,
after a fortnight of hesitation, in a speech which he regretted for
the rest of his life, Prince Konoye announced and explained his
non-recognition policy to the people.

The sated Japanese troops in Nanking at once gave up their
weary efforts to raise new hackles of terror among the numbed
and starving survivors of the great rape. Chiang Kai-shek, in his
temporary capital upriver in Hankow, broadcast an appeal to all
Chinese to fight to the death. He ignored the Japanese ultimatum
and continued to rule free China. Hirohito was forced to acknowledge that the mass murders and rapes of Nanking had all gone
for nought. He excused himself by blaming War Minister Sugiyama Hajime, the Strike-South stalwart who always looked "as
blank as a bathroom door." Sugiyama, explained the playful

Hirohito, had assured him six months earlier that the Japanese
Army could "crush China in a month."

Although Hirohito is nowhere on record as saying so explicitly,
his actions make it plain that he did not want to end the war
with China. As long as the war lasted he had an excuse not to
honor his vague secret pledge to the Army to turn north against
Russia. Moreover, the Chinese hinterland provided an excellent
training ground for recruits. There eager young samurai could
learn to handle modern weapons with minimal casualties and at
minimal cost. There the troops could live off the land and maintain themselves as combat-ready veterans for the more demanding
campaigns against Western armies in the years ahead.

In effect the war with China kept the troublesome Army distracted but ready. The elite service, the Navy, had for fifteen years
received the bulk of appropriations earmarked for weapons' development. The Navy alone had the technological knowhow to
challenge the West. In the first eight months of the China War
it was the Navy's air force which provided the Army with dive
bombing at the front and with long-range strategic bombing of
China's inland cities. The Army's own air force was fit only for
transport duty and for short-haul dumpings of dynamite. Yet the
patrician technocrats of the Navy insisted that they needed
another four or five years to perfect their sophisticated seagoing
systems before launching a full-scale Strike South. Until then
Japan must only nibble at Southeast Asia and keep the Army from
wasting itself in futile expeditions against Siberia.

THE NANKING HANGOVER

When reports of the feckless incontinence of Nanking trickled
home along the grapevine from soldiers in the field, Japanese began referring sarcastically to Hirohito's "holy war"—so proclaimed
by propagandists—as the "unholy war." Education Minister Big
Brother Kido made a mighty effort, through carefully worded
editorials planted in the leading newspapers, to reassure the people that Nanking was an unfortunate accident. War Minister
Sugiyama imposed heavy penalties on returning veterans who
violated security by talking too freely about their combat experiences. Hirohito and Prince Kanin placated the General Staff by

showing renewed interest in contingency planning against Russia. General Araki, the popular Strike-North leader, was brought back from oblivion as education minister in charge of propaganda.[8] Big Brother Marquis Kido moved on to found a new ministry, Welfare. His mission was to correct the deplorable state of national health and physical fitness revealed in the draft call-ups of the previous autumn.

What to do with the conquests in China, that was the question pending. And Hirohito promised that he would give serious attention to the Soviet Union only when the gains in China had been consolidated. The Tientsin-Peking area in north China and the Shanghai-Nanking area in central China must be tied together by Japanese control of the north-south railroads connecting Tientsin with Shanghai and Peking with Chiang Kai-shek's new temporary capital of Hankow, up the Yangtze River from Nanking.

Athwart the north-south railroads, between the northern and southern areas of Japanese occupation, Chiang Kai-shek still had one of his best generals and armies. In February 1938, Hirohito directed his crack mobile division, the 5th, led by Lieutenant General Itagaki, the politician of the Itagaki-Ishiwara partnership which had conquered Manchuria in 1931, to drive down the Tientsin-Shanghai rail link. Itagaki's men teamed up with the 10th Division and drove two thirds of the way required of them. Then at Tai-er-chuang, or Dynastic-Child-Manor, in the first week of April 1938, the 10th Division marched into a Chinese ambush and was temporarily surrounded. Itagaki's mobile 5th came to the rescue with tanks and big railroad guns and succeeded barely in extricating their beleaguered comrades. Six thousand Japanese dead, however, littered the battlefield, and some thirty thousand Japanese casualties hobbled or were carried from it. Chinese journalists, long despondent, made much of the victory.

In mid-April Prince Higashikuni, the Emperor's uncle, and Viscount Machijiri, the Emperor's in-law and aide-de-camp who had

---

[8] Only a year earlier Araki had been calling Japan "a disagreeable society in which I cannot bear to live." He had vowed that if Mazaki, his lieutenant, was ever let out of prison, he and Mazaki would become mendicant Buddhist priests, traveling in rags and praying for the nation. Now Mazaki was indeed released from prison, and Araki, in return, had rejoined the Establishment.

accompanied Higashikuni to Paris in 1920, took personal charge as commander-in-chief and chief of staff of the Japanese 2d Army in north China which was detailed to avenge the defeat at Dynastic-Child-Manor. All of the ten Japanese divisions in north China converged on the Dynastic-Child-Manor area in May, hoping to surround and capture the shrewd Chinese general who had humiliated the forces of the Emperor.

In the last two weeks of May, however, the Chinese general—Li Tsungjen, a southerner who had backed Chang Hsueh-liang in his kidnapping of Chiang Kai-shek eighteen months earlier—skillfully retreated to the west, getting out not only his men but even his heavy artillery pieces from the closing Japanese pincer. When he had made good his escape his rear guard dynamited the levees which controlled the wayward second river of China, the Hwang Ho or Yellow. An entire flat province of dry river beds, where the Yellow River had formerly wandered in centuries gone by, was suddenly inundated in muddy water. Approximately 45,000 square miles of fertile farmland—an area as large and populous as New York State—was flooded. Tens of thousands of Chinese peasants perished. Japanese trucks, tanks, and field guns bogged down in mud. Chiang Kai-shek made relatives of the flood victims feel like patriots by announcing that China would go all out in her resistance to the Japanese and from now on would fight superior fire power with a "scorched earth" policy—a massive westward migration of peasants, moving like locusts and leaving nothing to eat behind them.

Despite flooded fields, Prince Higashikuni's men pressed on down the raised embankment of the railroad and joined up with comrades moving north from Shanghai. One of the two north-south railroads was secure. Prince Higashikuni asked leave to open the second one as well. The majority in the General Staff in Tokyo objected that the primary objectives of the war with China had been won. The principal cities and rail lines were in Japanese hands and it was time to stand pat and face back toward Russia. Hirohito's admirals, however, wanted to move on up the Yangtze River, 150 miles beyond Nanking, to the Anking airport which was within flying range of Hong Kong and the coveted harbors of the south China coast. Hirohito agreed with the Navy and ordered

the Army to proceed up the Yangtze first to Anking and then another 200 miles to Hankow which was the seat of Chiang's refugee government and also the terminus of the second of the north-
south railroads.

The advance on Hankow began in May 1938 and ended in October. Prince Higashikuni personally took command of four divisions which fought their way overland to the north and west of the
Yangtze in order to approach Hankow from the rear. Four more
divisions, under Lieutenant General Okamura Yasuji—the only
one of the Three Crows of Baden-Baden who remained alive and in
Hirohito's good graces—moved up the banks of the Yangtze to
attack Hankow frontally. Okamura took the strategic air base of
Anking on June 12, 1938, and pressed on upriver toward Hankow.
Chiang Kai-shek began to move the lower echelons of his bureaucracy still farther upriver to Chungking, above the easily defended
gorges of the Yangtze, more than 900 miles by air from the coast
and the Japanese ports of supply.

Above Anking Third Crow Okamura's men encountered the
boom and the forts of Matang, which had been designed for
Chiang Kai-shek by his German advisors three years earlier. They
were formidable obstacles. Okamura surmounted them by first
calling Tokyo and paying a bribe of over $100,000 (U.S.) to the
local Chinese commander. Chiang Kai-shek heard of the transac-
tion and shortly afterwards had the commander summarily executed.

It cost Chiang far more than $100,000 to repair the damage done
by the Japanese bribe. He desperately needed time to remove valuable men and materials from the rich valley of the middle Yangtze.
In an all-out effort he succeeded in raising and equipping provincial levies to fight a holding action around the sacred mountain
of Lushan, 80 miles above Anking. All summer Okamura's men
pounded a rubbery wall of resistance which sagged by day and
sprang back by night. Few of the Chinese peasants in the area
survived the months of village-burning battles except the children
who, on parents' orders, marched west alone in sad Pied-Piper
columns. Finally in September Okamura's men broke through the
Lushan impasse and moved ahead quickly up the next 120 miles
of Yangtze river bank to capture Hankow in October.

A SOVIET DEFECTOR

On June 11, 1938, when Okamura was still blasting his way into Anking, a Soviet general, G. S. Lyushkov, crossed the Russo-Manchurian border and gave himself up to the Kwantung Army. He described to Kwantung Army staff officers the disposition, organization, and armament of the twenty-five Soviet divisions in Siberia. He also stated that the Red soldiers in the Far East were demoralized by shoddy equipment and a growing difference of opinion with the Kremlin. The Russian commander in Siberia was General Vasili Blücher, a former advisor to Sun Yat-sen. He wanted Russia to give military assistance to China, particularly to the Chinese Communists, in an effort to stop "fascist" Japan. Stalin on the other hand felt that Russia could not afford to become entangled in the Sino-Japanese war while Hitler's power was growing menacingly in the West. Stalin's secret police chief, Lavrenti Beria, had infiltrated the Siberian command with agents and turned it against itself.

The staff officers of the Kwantung Army transmitted defector Lyushkov's intelligence to Tokyo. They reminded Chief of Staff Prince Kanin that the Army had been promised action against the Soviet Union as recompense for its unpleasant service in central China. They pointed out that if Lyushkov's intelligence was correct, now would be the ideal time for a full-scale Strike North, or at least for a limited probe of Red Army strengths and weaknesses.[9]

Chief of Staff Prince Kanin acknowledged the Kwantung Army's request but asked that defector Lyushkov be sent on to Tokyo for further questioning. It was possible that Lyushkov might be an agent for General Blücher, the Siberian commander, and might be enticing Japan to strike north in order to force

[9] In making their plea, the tacticians of the Kwantung Army counted heavily, but unrealistically, on the fact that two of their former representatives were now highly placed in Hirohito's councils. Lieutenant General Itagaki, the politician of the team which had led the Kwantung Army in its 1931 conquest of Manchuria, had been recalled from command of Japan's panzer division in north China to take the post of war minister in the Konoye Cabinet. At the same time, at the end of April 1938, Kwantung Army chief of staff, Lieutenant General Tojo, had gone home to serve under Itagaki as vice war minister.

Stalin into the Far Eastern conflict against his will. In Tokyo the interrogators of the Special Higher Police, who ordinarily dealt with "dangerous thoughts" only in the upper levels of domestic Japanese society, reported that they had insufficient knowledge of European affairs to make sure of Lyushkov's veracity. They asked that an expert be sent to help them from Himmler's Gestapo apparatus in Berlin. While the German intelligence agent was on his way, Hirohito and Prince Kanin ordered the Kwantung Army to wait in patience.

AN UNAUTHORIZED INCIDENT

The Kwantung Army obeyed Hirohito's wishes but the territorial army in Korea did not. Vice Chief of the Army General Staff Tada, who had opposed both the rape of Nanking and Konoye's non-recognition of Chiang Kai-shek, plotted with the commander of the 19th Division in Korea to start an incident on the Russian border. On July 3, 1938, three weeks after Lyushkov's defection, Soviet troops stationed at Lake Khasan, near the point where the borders of Siberia, Manchuria, and Korea all meet, observed two companies of Japanese troops taking up positions on the far side of the hill overlooking the lake. Three days later the Red soldiers noted with alarm that the Japanese were evacuating the civilian Manchu population from the area across the border.

The strip of land between the shores of Lake Khasan and the watershed to the west of it had previously been handled as Soviet territory in name and as an unfortified buffer zone in practice. The spot was beautiful and wild, but also important strategically, for it lay only 70-odd miles southwest of the Russian naval base of Vladivostok and only 15-odd miles northeast of the Japanese naval base of Rashin in Korea. On July 11, just a month after Lyushkov's defection, the Soviet forces at Lake Khasan moved into no man's land and began digging trenches on it.

On Wednesday, July 13, Korean Army H.Q. belatedly informed Tokyo officially of the Russian trench digging and asked permission to take countermeasures. The next day Vice Chief of Staff Tada warned the commander of the 19th Division at the front that he must improve liaison with Korean Army H.Q. in order to prevent it from sending any more cables which would excite the suspicions of the home authorities. At the moment, Tada pointed out, the Japanese government could only promise that the Foreign Ministry would protest strongly in Moscow.

On Friday, July 15, Vice War Minister Tojo scented Tada's plot and personally cabled the commander of the 19th Division:

RE RUSSIAN BORDER CROSSING OUR POLICY TO SETTLE BY DIPLOMATIC MEANS. IF RUSSIANS DO NOT ACCEPT OUR TERMS AND WITHDRAW, THEN AND THEN ONLY SHOULD WE CONSIDER PRUDENTLY THE POSSIBILITY OF PUSHING THEM BACK BY FORCE.

Tojo's word carried great weight. The day of his telegram, five Japanese secret policemen had crossed to the Soviet side of the border to take photographs of the fresh Russian foxholes on the hillside above the lake. The Russian border guards had shot and killed one of the photographers and captured his film. Yet for the next two weeks, the Japanese 19th Division fired not so much as a shot at the Russians. Instead it brought up all its strength, as quietly as possible, and entrenched itself on the Japanese side of the watershed.

HIROHITO'S ANGER

For five days, from the Friday of Tojo's cable until the Wednesday of July 20, Prime Minister Konoye and the members of his Cabinet could not find out what was happening. The officers on the Tokyo General Staff were not communicating with their opposite numbers in the War Ministry. Chief of the General Staff Prince Kanin was out of town at his summer villa and War Minister Itagaki deliberately sequestered himself. Vice War Minister Tojo used all his influence to get information and to summon Prince Kanin and War Minister Itagaki back to Tokyo.

Since the Lake Khasan incident had not been planned, Hirohito, at his summer villa, remained for several days entirely in the dark about it. Then on July 20, Prince Kanin and War Minister Itagaki returned to Tokyo. Tojo saw Itagaki. Kanin saw Itagaki. Kanin phoned the Emperor. Through his courtiers Hirohito immediately took steps to suppress the incident without unduly shaming the rebellious officers in the 19th Division and the General Staff.

The next day, July 21, Prince Kanin arranged that War Minister Itagaki be granted an audience by Hirohito at the seaside Summer Palace of Hayama at 11 A.M. sharp. Kanin met with Itagaki beforehand at his own villa down the coast to discuss all the background facets of the case. At about 10 A.M. a chamberlain called at Prince Kanin's villa to say that the Emperor hoped the audience would take place on time because he was eager to be out on the water for an afternoon excursion aboard his battered marine biological yacht. In the next hour War Minister Itagaki nervously suggested again and again to Prince Kanin that perhaps they should be starting for the palace. Prince Kanin kept asking Atagaki detailed questions about the men involved in the Lake Khasan incident with Russia. Finally at about 11 A.M., the scheduled time of the audience with Hirohito, Prince Kanin and Itagaki set out to drive to the palace. Itagaki was dismayed that it took a full hour. When he arrived in the Imperial Presence, an hour late, he was all nervousness.

"The foreign and Navy ministers," blurted Itagaki, "have both agreed to our use of force in the recent border incident with Russia."

"You!" exclaimed Hirohito. "You helped to bungle the Mukden incident in 1931 and the Marco Polo Bridge incident last year in China. You are undoubtedly one of the most stupid men in the entire world. From now on, unless it has orders from me, the Army is not to move so much as a single soldier."

Itagaki retired, covered with confusion. The next day he submitted his resignation and Hirohito refused it, apologizing for his impatience at being kept waiting and exhorting Itagaki to solve the unauthorized incident as quickly as possible.

Two days later, on July 23, Hirohito's favorite Big Brother, Marquis Kido, who was now minister of welfare in the Konoye Cabinet, met with young Saionji Kinkazu, for the first time in three months, to relate to him the Emperor's words with Itagaki. A day or two later, young Saionji's protégé, Ozaki, reported to Soviet spy Sorge that "Japan" had no intention of allowing the Lake Khasan incident to develop into a war. Even as an agent of the Soviet Union, Ozaki could not bring himself to say, "The Emperor has no intention . . ." Instead when Sorge pressed him to give solidity to his vague word, "Japan," Ozaki offered only theoretical arguments. He pointed out that the Japanese Army was fully engaged in its drive on Hankow and that the Kwantung Army had already detached several divisions to the south and was in no state to mount an attack on Russia.

THE MASTER SPY, DRUNK

Three months earlier, at the time of Marquis Kido's last meeting with young Saionji, the Japanese Foreign Ministry had just learned that Major General Eugen Ott, the German military attaché in Tokyo—the one who had negotiated the prior understandings for the Anti-Comintern Pact with Prince Higashikuni in 1933 and had made friends with Soviet spy Sorge in 1934— would be Germany's next ambassador to Japan. Ott did indeed become ambassador on April 28, 1938. He promptly elevated Sorge to an unofficial position as a consultant, with an office of his own, inside the German Embassy.

Sorge immediately ran a mission for Ott, and incidentally for himself. He delivered a packet of intelligence for Ott to a German agent in Manila and then another of his own to a Soviet agent in Hong Kong. On the evening of his return to Japan, in early May, he celebrated his infiltration of the German Embassy with a spree at his favorite Tokyo bar, *Das Rheingold*. When the bar closed at 2:00 A.M., he went on to drink an entire bottle of Scotch in a friend's room at the Imperial Hotel. Some time later, annoyed that his drinking companion would not ride on with him to further adventures on the back of his motorcycle, Sorge set off for home alone. He roared east down Hibiya Park and then north up Sotoboridori, or Outside the Moat Boulevard.

At the next intersection, with a growing sense of exhilaration and acceleration, he cornered left into the curving dirt road behind the Manchuria Railway Building and up the hill toward the American Embassy. Dirt, curve, and hillside were too much for his numbed navigational faculties, and his motorcycle skidded into the solid, whitewashed embassy wall. He knocked out his front teeth, broke his jaw, and scarred his cheeks for life. Through the good offices of the Japanese police, he saw Max Klausen, his radio operator, before being wheeled into surgery. Klausen barely managed to burglarize Sorge's home and remove from it all incriminating papers before its contents were catalogued and put under seal by an efficient representative of the German News Service.

General Lyushkov defected while Sorge was still recovering in Tokyo's most up-to-date hospital, St. Luke's (an institution of the U.S. Protestant Episcopal Church). German Ambassador Ott and his wife took care of Sorge in his convalescence and briefed him fully on the Lyushkov case as it developed. Throughout late June and early July Sorge was able to keep the Red Army's Fourth, or Intelligence, Bureau well informed on the case in so far as it was being revealed to the Germans. In the last week of July, Sorge relayed his intelligence from Ozaki, from Saionji, from Kido, and indirectly, at fourth hand, from Emperor Hirohito, that "Japan" would suppress the Lake Khasan incident short of war.

THE LAKE KHASAN MUTINY

Never would Sorge's credibility at the Kremlin be taxed more sorely. In flagrant disregard for Hirohito's wishes the Japanese troops at Lake Khasan caused the incident to escalate. On July 29, in the only known Army defiance of imperial orders on record, the 19th Division launched a full-scale attack on the Russian positions at Lake Khasan. All through the night Japanese artillery pounded away at the heights above the lake and the Russian border guards huddled in their holes. During the days which followed, the Japanese at first advanced a few hundred meters down the hillside and then were pushed back again by Soviet tanks and heavy aerial bombardment. Japanese flyers in Korea obeyed imperial orders and provided no air cover. They remained grounded even after August 8, when the Soviet Air Fleet began to bomb Korean bases behind the front lines.

The Foreign Ministry sought to save the Army's face by demanding concessions in its negotiations in Moscow. While the negotiations continued, the misguided men of the 19th Division suffered a terrible beating. Through the machinations of Vice War Minister Tojo, two of the division's four regimental commanders were replaced on August 1 by a pair of colonels who could be counted on to obey a cease-fire. One of them was Colonel Tanaka Taka-yoshi, girl-spy Eastern Jewel's huge lover, who would later become U.S. Prosecutor Keenan's star witness at the Tokyo war crimes trials. The other of them was Colonel Cho Isamu, Prince Asaka's former staff officer, who had promulgated the order to kill all prisoners just before the rape of Nanking, and who, in years to come, would be the last holdout in the caves of Okinawa. These two mad dogs of the Emperor won the confidence of their men by urging them to make suicide rushes against the Russian tanks. At one desperate juncture in the fighting they both took down their pants and stood exposed on a sandbag parapet to show the flagging captains and lieutenants of their command how loosely and courageously a Japanese officer should hang in the face of fire.

The battle raged on the scale of full war from July 29 to August 10. Japan's 19th Division suffered almost 10,000 casualties and the Russians fared not much better. But the Russians, aided by their tanks and planes, were advancing when the Foreign Ministry, on August 11, made a truce and agreed to return to the status quo ante.

The Japanese back-down vindicated Sorge's judgment and encouraged Stalin to adopt Sorge's view that war with Japan not only must be but could be avoided. In September 1938, a month after the cease-fire, Beria's secret police spirited away the Siberian commander, General Blücher, who had been a patron of defector Lyushkov and had wished to fight Japan. A month later, in October, Sorge borrowed from a German Embassy attaché the final report of the Himmler agent sent from Berlin to assist in the interrogation of Lyushkov. Early the next morning in his embassy office, from six o'clock to ten, when he was usually preparing a digest and interpretation of the day's Japanese news for Ambassador Ott, Sorge read the 100-odd pages of the report and, with his Leica, photographed most of them for transmission to Moscow. Siberian commander Blücher is reported to have died in Beria's dungeons a few months later.

THE VICTORIOUS STALEMATE

The Japanese Army was chagrined by its defeat at Lake Khasan and Hirohito made immediate concessions to save its face. In August, when the ink on the cease-fire was scarcely dry, he approved a General Staff proposal to plan a better staged, fully sanctioned workout against the Red Army, to take place the following year in the remote fastnesses of Mongolia. One aviation colonel was immediately given maps of the exact area in which the war would occur and instructed to devise air-to-ground communications suitable to the terrain and type of operations which might be expected there.

Seven weeks after the Lake Khasan cease-fire, on September 30, 1938, British Prime Minister Neville Chamberlain, wielding his much caricatured umbrella at the famous "peace-in-our-time" conference in Munich, conceded to Hitler the right to take back for Germany the German-speaking region of Czechoslovakia known as the Sudetenland. As Hitler's storm troopers poured into Czechoslovakia to realize Chamberlain's concession, Hirohito reimplemented the operational plan for the seizure of the south China coast which had been canceled after the sinking of the U.S.S. *Panay* a year earlier. On October 21, 1938, from a landing at the old pirate cove of Byas Bay, Japanese troops pushed into Canton, the principal city of south China.

Four days later, on October 25, 1938, the Japanese forces of the third of the Three Crows of Baden-Baden, Lieutenant General Okamura Yasuji, ended their six-month drive up the Yangtze River, past the sacred mountain of Lushan, and occupied Hankow, the principal city of central China. With Peking and Tientsin in the north, and Shanghai on the coast in the east, Canton and Hankow completed the roster of China's five most populous cities. All of them now lay in Japanese hands. Hirohito had no other ambitions in China except to keep open the railways between the five principal cities and make full use of the docks and harbors attached to them.

The Privy Council, Cabinet, and General Staff all agreed with Hirohito that from now on the war with China would be a holding operation. No offensives would be mounted except to gain limited tactical objectives or to serve as training maneuvers for green troops. Six new divisions, manned by 120,000 fresh recruits, had been created in April 1938 when this planned stalemate in China first received Hirohito's approval. Now the six new divisions were deployed for garrison duty in China. As the men in them gained experience, they would be transferred to other, more active commands in the years ahead. Until 1945, however, the China front would remain, in Japanese strategic thinking, only a schoolyard.

On December 16, 1938, Prime Minister Konoye founded an Asian Development Board to co-ordinate the economic exploitation of China. Having masterminded the looting of Nanking, the ubiquitous Suzuki Tei-ichi—now at last a major general—took charge of the Political Affairs Branch of the board.[10] He made it his economic mission to develop a native Chinese puppet government with enough influence to replace Chiang Kai-shek in the Japanese-occupied areas of China.

Two days later, on December 18, 1938, months of underground negotiation came to fruition when Wang Ching-wei, the vice chairman of the KMT party and a trusted lieutenant of Chiang Kai-shek, surreptitiously boarded a plane at the Chungking airport and flew to Hanoi in the north of French Indochina. From Hanoi he exchanged telegrams with Chiang, begging him to join Japan in the cause of Asia. At the same time he exchanged countless cables with Tokyo, asking assurance that he be given authority to govern in eastern China if he agreed to establish a regime there which would settle Sino-Japanese differences.

Wang's telegraphic communications were cut short a few weeks later when an assassin, variously reported to have been a Chinese secret agent and a hireling of the Japanese spy service, shot dead the man sleeping in Wang Ching-wei's bed. Frightened by the death of his bodyguard, Wang took to sea in a small coastal steamer made available to him by Japanese Army Intelligence. He was overhauled by a storm at sea, and having lost his way, was rescued from the gale by a large, conspicuously Japanese cruiser. Taken to Japanese-occupied Shanghai, he was housed and hidden first in one then another of three lavishly appointed, elaborately guarded villas. For fifteen months he continued to exchange communications with Chiang Kai-shek and then, in March 1940, he would agree to become the Japanese puppet in China.

[10] The presidency of the board was given to Yanagawa Heisuke, the retired Strike-North general who had rehabilitated himself by leading the flanking movement and breakthrough of the advance on Nanking.

On December 22, 1938,[11] Prime Minister Konoye, counting heavily on the arrival of Wang Ching-wei in Hanoi two days earlier, announced publicly that Japan sponsored a New Order in East Asia which would enable Asian peoples, under Japanese leadership, to realize their native aspirations and throw off the shackles of Western colonialism.

At the same time Konoye announced a New Structure politically for Japan. The people, he said, must unite monolithically behind the Emperor and co-operate in unselfish effort to wage a "holy war" of liberation for all Asian peoples. Konoye had in mind a plan for a single mass party which would rule Japan as effectively as the Communist party ruled Russia or the Nazi party ruled Germany. His announcement was received so coolly that he did not, in fact, launch the new mass party until October 1940, almost two years later.

The draft of the New Structure plan had been written for Konoye by Ozaki Hotsumi, the member of the Konoye brain trust who served as liaison link between young Saionji Kinkazu and Soviet spy Sorge. Sorge himself asked Ozaki what he thought he was doing in suggesting the plan, and Ozaki replied that he was looking forward to the time when Japan would become a socialist nation. He did not add that he meant a nation of communal share-and-share-alike, under the Emperor. Sorge would not have understood such a Japanese concept.

At the same tidying-up time in December 1938, Hirohito reposted two of his sharpest military thinkers: Major General Ishiwara Kanji, the religious zealot who had planned the conquest of Manchuria for him seven years ago, and Lieutenant General Tojo Hideki who had prevented the February Mutiny of 1936 from spreading into the ranks of the Kwantung Army. In the fall of 1938, Tojo had advocated a two-front army capable of waging war to the north or south as occasion might demand. Ishiwara had begged for a no-front army, trained to consolidate previous Japanese gains and to make peace with the natives in the occupied areas. When the dispute between the two men had crept onto the pages of the newspapers, Hirohito made a Solomon's decision by

[11] The occasion was a victory parade for Prince Higashikuni on his return from eight months of successful leadership of the 2d Army in the campaign to take Hankow.

pretending to fire both of them. He banished Ishiwara, the vice chief of staff of the Kwantung Army, to the command of a provincial arsenal. But he gave Tojo, the vice war minister, a challenging opportunity as head of the new office of Inspector General of Army Aviation. Tojo solaced and aggrandized himself by filling posts on no less than nineteen of the new boards and committees which had been founded as a part of Prime Minister Konoye's New Structure.

Just to list Tojo's memberships reveals how far Konoye had brought Japan along the road to totalitarianism. Tojo belonged to: the Japan-Manchukuo Economic Committee; the Central Air Defense Commission; the Manchukuoan Affairs Board; the Cabinet Information and Cabinet Planning Boards; the Scientific Council; the Central Price Committee; the Ship Control, Electric Power, City Planning, Home Industry, and Motor Car Manufacturing Committees; the Valuation Commission for Iron Manufacturers; the Disabled Soldiers' Protection Trust; the Naval Council; the Air Enterprises Investigation Committee; the National General Mobilization Committee; the Education Control Council; and the Liquefied Fuel Committee.

FIRST SPAT WITH HITLER

As soon as the old year's loose ends had been tied up, Prince Konoye greeted the new, on January 4, 1939, by resigning the prime ministership. He felt tired and hypochondriacal after his eighteen months at the helm, and he wanted to devote his full energies to negotiating the compromises, the reconciliations, and the outright purchases of loyalty which would enable him to form the single mass party he planned for the future.

Hirohito appointed in his place Baron Hiranuma, the long-faced lawyer-president of the staidly rightist National Foundation Society—the man who would act as Hirohito's spokesman and tormentor at the surrender deliberations in the Imperial Bunker six and a half years later. Being well known for his extreme anti-Bolshevism, Hiranuma might be able to quiet the resurgent Strike-North Faction which was disgruntled by Hirohito's continued postponement of the promised military probe into Russia. Moreover, if the probe had to be staged and should turn out unsuccessfully, Hiranuma could be easily saddled with the responsibility for instigating it.

Domestically Hiranuma made no changes in the programs and slogans announced by his predecessor. The "defense state" mobilized for "total war" continued to grow apace as cartel after cartel fell into cogwheel place in it. The New Structure for the bureaucracy continued to materialize committee by committee and board by board. Konoye in retirement continued his masterful management of the political world.

Under Hiranuma's aegis, the Navy pressed forward with preparations for the eventual Strike South by seizing two strategic bases in the South China Sea. On February 10, 1939, Prince Takamatsu, the Emperor's second brother, personally looked on from the bridge of a battleship while the Imperial Marines poured ashore onto the mud flats of Hainan, an island larger than Maryland and Delaware combined, lying off the southernmost point of the south China coast.[12] In the next three days Prince Takamatsu flew reconnaissance in a naval plane overhead while the conquest of the big island was completed.

A month later, in March 1939, the Japanese Navy quietly occupied the seven French-claimed but uninhabited Spratly Islands, strategically placed at a point in the South China Sea almost exactly equidistant from the Philippines, Indochina, and Borneo. Japan used the islands immediately as a base for seaplanes running cartographic missions down the ill-charted Borneo coast and carrying radios and technicians to spy rings in Mindanao and Vietnam. The existence of the islands had come to Hirohito's attention when one of his wife's in-laws had conducted an ornithological expedition there a few years earlier to study the island birds.

While Hirohito nibbled at Southeast Asia, Hitler swallowed the remaining Moravian and Bohemian scraps of Czechoslovakia. Then, in late March 1939, he paused briefly to survey the German position. He planned soon to turn west against France and England but first he had to secure his rear against Russia. He meant to

12 Hirohito, at a conference in the Imperial Presence three months earlier on November 30, 1938, had had the seizure of Hainan brought up and appended to his approval of the Army's plans for Wang Ching-wei's escape from Chungking.

seize half of Poland as a buffer zone against Russia and give the other half of Poland to Russia as a bribe. In return for the bribe, he hoped to negotiate a nonaggression pact with Stalin. Stalin, however, could not be trusted, and so, as further insurance against being nipped in the rear by the Russian bear, Hitler wished to commit Japan definitely to fight on the side of the Third Reich. Through Ribbentrop he pressed Japan to sign a tripartite pact with the Reich and Italy pledging all three nations to war if any of them should become involved in hostilities with Russia or the democracies of Western Europe.

Because of his prejudice against a Strike North, Hirohito had long refused Germany a promise of all-out military help even against Russia. As for promising to fight France and England as well, that, for the moment, was unthinkable. The Navy was not prepared to challenge Western naval supremacy in the Pacific until at least 1941, and preferably 1942. The naval development program which Hirohito had tenderly nurtured since 1922 still depended on Western imports of raw materials and machine tools. If Japan could once gain, even briefly, the naval edge in the Pacific, she might take the rubber of Malaya and the oil of Borneo and render herself independent of Western imports. Then and then only would she be ready to challenge the democracies to open warfare.

Hitler's demand for an immediate Berlin-Tokyo-Rome alliance of the fascist states against the rest of the world did not fit into the timetable which Japan, as an underdeveloped nation, had been patiently following for years. On the other hand, Hirohito had long stationed trusted emissaries in Berlin and was well informed on the might of the *Wehrmacht*. If, as seemed possible, Hitler would soon conquer the Netherlands and France, then Hitler would be a friend or enemy who could either give or refuse Japan the Dutch East Indies and French Indochina.

In a quandary as to whether to jeopardize the carefully worked out National Program by siding now with Hitler or to alienate Japan's potentially best friend by refusing to side with him, Hirohito squirmed in anguish. In early April 1939 he confided to Marquis Kido that the decision facing him was the most fateful of his reign. If he decided wrongly, he foresaw that he might someday find himself "left alone and stripped of my closest retainers and elder statesmen." He complained that he could not sleep, weighing the alternatives.

The Army pressed Hirohito to sign the pact with Hitler, and the Foreign Ministry advised him to protract negotiations with Hitler as long as possible. Navy Minister Yonai, one of those who would later sit with Hirohito in the bunker on the night of the decision to surrender, tipped the scales by stating flatly that the Navy, in its present state of development, could not hope to win in the Pacific even against the British fleet alone.

On Monday, April 24, 1939, Ribbentrop darkly hinted to Japanese Ambassador Lieutenant General Oshima in Berlin that if Japan could not reach a clear-cut decision as to which side she was on, Germany would be forced to improve her relations with the Soviet Union. That same evening, having consulted with his closest advisors, Hirohito made a final firm decision as to how far Japan was prepared to commit herself. He agreed to a full military alliance with Hitler—but on two provisos: that the clauses of the alliance directed against the democracies should be kept secret and that Japan's entry into World War II should not necessarily follow at once upon Germany's but should be made, in all good faith, as soon afterward as Japan's strength warranted.

On Tuesday, April 25, the five ministers of the Japanese Inner Cabinet met and approved Hirohito's decision. It was agreed by all that if Hitler would not accept the Emperor's provisos, the negotiations with Germany might have to be broken off and Japan might have to wait, perhaps even for decades, before being strong enough to act on her own. Wistfully, a Cabinet secretary observed that Germany, by her "loud talk," had caused the democracies to start rearming and so had spoiled everything.

Ott, the German ambassador in Tokyo, was informed of the Emperor's decision by Prince Higashikuni's former assistant of Parisian days, Lieutenant General Machijiri, now director of the powerful Military Affairs Bureau in the War Ministry. Knowing that Machijiri had been close to the Emperor for years as a palace aide-de-camp, Ambassador Ott, on Wednesday, April 26, nine days before he would be officially informed of the Emperor's stand by the Foreign Ministry, cabled his understanding of it to Berlin. At the same time he discussed the situation with his journalist-advisor, Soviet spy Sorge.

Hitler was enraged by Ott's news and rejected Hirohito's provisos out of hand. He ordered Ribbentrop to proceed at once with the conclusion of a nonaggression pact with Russia. Much talk continued to be exchanged between Tokyo and Berlin for another four months but the Führer scorned all Japanese attempts to hedge, and Hirohito stood firm by his decision not to join Hitler yet.

Reports of Hitler's anger and of Ribbentrop's negotiations with Russia filtered through to Tokyo, and Hirohito resolved to test Germany's trustworthiness. The Anti-Comintern Pact obligated Hitler to render Hirohito all means of assistance short of troops in the event that Japan became involved in hostilities with the Soviet Union. If Germany so much as swapped a stein of beer for a glass of vodka while such hostilities were in progress, it would constitute a monumental breach of faith. All those who advocated a German-Japanese alliance for the sake of promoting a Strike North would be eternally shamed and silenced. Accordingly, on or about the Russian holiday of May 1, Hirohito instructed old Chief of Staff Prince Kanin to activate the plans for a limited border war with Russia in Outer Mongolia. Ambassador Oshima in Berlin was advised to represent the incident to Ribbentrop as a pro-German act which would tie up Soviet troops in central Asia while the *Wehrmacht* was making sure of its half of Poland.

NOMONHAN (1)

On May 11, 1939, two hundred Bargut horsemen under the banner of an Inner Mongolian chieftain controlled by the Japanese, crossed the frontier into the Soviet protectorate of Outer Mongolia, at a point 500 miles northwest of Mukden, near the junction of the border lines of Manchukuo, Inner Mongolia, and Outer Mongolia. The Barguts were accompanied by patrols and advisors from the Japanese 23d Division, a unit of the Kwantung Army. The invaders rode some 15 miles into Soviet territory until they came to the scattered yurts and sheep pens of the village of Nomonhan, belonging to the Outer Mongolian Tsirik tribe. The villagers at once warned their kinsmen who manned a constabulary outpost for the Soviet government on the west bank of the Khalka River, some 5 miles farther into the hinterland beyond

Nomonhan. The next day the Tsirik troops from the log fort on the river sortied and drove the Barguts back to the border.

On May 14, the Inner Mongolian tribesmen reinvaded in force, backed by two companies of Japanese regulars. They swept the Tsiriks from the 20-mile strip between the border and the river and camped at nightfall just opposite the outpost of the Tsirik constabulary.

That night the Tsiriks alerted the local Russian advisor, Major Bykov. When Bykov drove up in his armored car to the fort the next morning he found it a shambles. It had just been bombed and strafed by five Japanese planes. Bykov at once phoned Ulan Bator, calling in the 6th Mongolian cavalry division and a detachment of Red Army regulars. By May 18, he had massed his forces on the west side of the river. The Barguts and Japanese on the east bank broke camp and vanished.

HITLER'S COLD SHOULDER

Hearing of the clash in central Asia, Hitler realized that Hirohito was brandishing the Anti-Comintern Pact at him and trying to shame him out of making a deal with Russia. Not one to be ashamed easily, Hitler saw a way of turning the Japanese move to his advantage. Stalin had responded warily to the German feelers for a nonaggression pact and was simultaneously talking with London about the possibility of an Anglo-Russian alliance. Only the threat of the Anti-Comintern Pact and of war on two fronts with Germany and Japan might persuade Stalin to refuse the British overtures.

Accordingly, Hitler had an icy message delivered to Japanese Ambassador Lieutenant General Oshima telling him that Japanese Army efforts to tie up Soviet forces in central Asia would be most welcome if indeed the Japanese Army was capable of tying up any Western troops anywhere. Hitler proceeded to salt this wound to samurai pride by turning toward Japan a calculated cold shoulder. On May 22, he ostentatiously signed a full military alliance with Mussolini and so cemented the much heralded Rome-Berlin Axis without benefit of Japanese inclusion. The next day he informed his fourteen most trusted generals and admirals that they must be ready for war with England before year's end and that they must not count too heavily on Russia remaining neutral because German relations with Japan had now become "cool and unreliable."

The subtle minds at Hirohito's Court were not taken in by these histrionics or disposed to ignore them either. If Japan helped to neutralize Russia by pursuing the probe into the Mongolian underbelly of Siberia, no harm would be done and Hitler would owe Japan a favor.

NOMONHAN (2)

On the night of May 22, when speeches about the new military alliance between Hitler and Mussolini were running on interminably at the Reich Chancellery in Berlin, Major Bykov, the local Russian commander in the Nomonhan area, moved a substantial force across the Khalka River to reconnoiter. It picked its way cautiously east through the night as far as the pastures of Nomonhan and there was suddenly set upon by Barguts and Japanese. After a desperate hand-to-hand tussle in the darkness, Bykov's force broke out of encirclement and escaped to the river bank.

On May 25 Bykov threw in all his forces in a counterattack and reoccupied Nomonhan. By May 27, having established over 10,-000 Mongolian constabulary on the east bank, plus two Russian machine-gun companies and a battery of 45-millimeter cannon, he moved his command post into one of the Nomonhan yurts.

The area seemed clear of Japanese and Bykov thought that the border incident was over. It was not. Hirohito had sent some of his most trusted minions to the fastnesses of Outer Mongolia to enlarge the incident and manipulate it delicately as an instrument of high state policy. At 3 A.M. on May 28 a regiment and a battalion of Japanese regulars, some 5,000 men assisted by a horde of Bargut horsemen, attacked the Russian encampment. The cautious Major Bykov had fortified his flanks by the book and was able to fall back gradually toward the river. He took a Japanese prisoner in the course of his retreat and learned that his assailants were commanded by Colonel Yamagata Tsuyuki and Lieutenant Colonel Azuma Otohiko.

At his testimony before the International Military Tribunal for the Far East, seven years later, Bykov did not indicate that he saw any special significance in these names. The fact was, however, that Yamagata and Azuma had been the last two aides-de-camp of Prince Asaka, Hirohito's limping uncle who had raped Nanking. Moreover, they had in their charge, as a lieutenant of artillery, Higashikuni Morihiro, the son of Prince Higashikuni and the intended of one of Hirohito's daughters.

The participation of a member of the imperial family under the tutelage of Prince Asaka's aides-de-camp persuaded the Strike-North elements in the Kwantung Army that Hirohito was finally fulfilling his vague promise that Japan would attack Russia when the proper opportunity arrived. Well-prepared staff plans emanating from Tokyo reassured even skeptics that the moment had come. The commander of the 23d Division and then the commander of the 6th Army, both veteran proponents of the Strike North, were soon committed wholeheartedly to the battle which had been started for the yurts of Nomonhan. Never would Japanese troops fight harder, against greater odds, for a more worthless piece of territory. Theoretically they had the Emperor's mandate to take Outer Mongolia and so control the Trans-Siberian Railway connecting Moscow with Vladivostok. In practice, however, Hirohito would commit only three divisions or about 60,000 men to the action and the battle would never progress beyond the 20-mile-deep strip of pastureland between the Outer Mongolian border and the Khalka River.

BELLY TALK WITH STALIN

While the 23d Division and then the rest of the 6th Army were being moved to the front in June of 1939, Hitler closeted himself with his generals at Berchtesgaden, planning the blitzkrieg of Poland. Stalin continued negotiations with both Ribbentrop and Great Britain's Neville Chamberlain. And in Tokyo Hirohito and the spy service made every effort to improve their channels of liaison with Stalin, the common unknown in the international equation.

On June 1, Ozaki Hotsumi, the Japanese patriot or traitor who belonged to Prince Konoye's brain trust and supplied Soviet spy Sorge with his best inside-Tokyo intelligence, took a new job as a direct advisor of the Japanese spy service. Since the fall of the Konoye Cabinet five months earlier, Ozaki had had no outlet for his talents except his non-too-competent journalism for *Asahi*. Now, through Konoye, he became a consultant of the research branch of the South Manchuria Railway, one of the oldest and most important clearinghouses of the spy service. It was run by Dr. Okawa Shumei, the multilingual scholar of Sanskrit and of the Koran, who had organized the Lodging House indoctrination center in the palace for Hirohito in 1922 and had gone to prison for Hirohito in 1934–35 for his managerial role in the 1932 assassinations.

On June 9, a week after Ozaki had begun work for Dr. Okawa, Big Brother Marquis Kido, now home minister in charge of police, met with his Red contact, Saionji Kinkazu, the grandson of the aged, impotent prime-minister-maker. Kido and Saionji talked alone for the first time since the outbreak of the Lake Khasan incident a year earlier. The next week Soviet spy Sorge filed a detailed intelligence report to Moscow, assuring Stalin that the Japanese buildup at Nomonhan portended no war but only a military exercise and a limited probe of Russian strength. Sorge was able to substantiate his assertions by giving evidence that new Japanese divisions were being shipped out, not battle-ready to Manchuria but green and ill-equipped for garrison duty in central China.

Stalin was understandably suspicious of the intelligence coming from Sorge in Tokyo, and in early July he appointed one of his most trustworthy and brilliant generals to command the Russian forces on the Mongolian frontier, opposite the continuing Japanese troop buildup. This was Lieutenant General Georgi Zhukov, a specialist in tanks and armor who would later become a field marshal and would share with Eisenhower in the laurels for the conquest of Germany. On reviewing the situation in the Nomonhan area, Zhukov asked the Kremlin for full support in repulsing what might well be an all-out Japanese attack. Stalin responded by giving Zhukov all the troops and equipment that could be spared and by suggesting to Hitler, on July 18, that after all Russia might be willing to conclude a nonaggression pact.

NOMONHAN (3)

On assuming his command, Lieutenant General Zhukov organized a classic of positional defense. He beat off half a dozen Japanese attempts to cross the Khalka River in the second and third weeks of July and began to build up gradually a reserve force behind his lines with which to take the offensive.

On July 19, in a night of fire, Zhukov's men withstood the best offensive which the Japanese forces in the area could muster. By July 24, Zhukov's first probing counterattacks had become so blistering that Lieutenant Higashikuni, the twenty-three-year-old son of Prince Higashikuni, decamped without orders from the field of battle. He waited in a town behind the lines for a reposting to a quieter theater. His new orders came through a week later and his equerry took full responsibility for having advised him to desert. His comrades in the field muttered over his exemption from normal discipline, but the story was suppressed by the censors and few of his tentmates lived to carry it home to Japan.[13] The commander of the 23d Division took the imperial desertion as an ill omen, but being committed fatalistically to the Strike-North concept, he only drove on his men so much the harder.

Soviet commander Zhukov knew precisely from Sorge's intelligence what forces the Japanese had committed to the war, and all through July and early August he methodically assembled behind his lines an absolute superiority over them—a superiority of three to two in manpower, two to one in planes and artillery, and four to one in armor.

HITLER'S TREACHERY

During Zhukov's preparations, Hitler and Stalin negotiated and, on August 19, 1939, agreed to sign their mutual Non-Aggression Pact. It pledged both Germany and Russia to refrain from making war on one another no matter what their respective commitments to other nations individually.

The next morning at 5:45 Zhukov launched his offensive. He had ready 500 tanks, 500 planes, 346 armored cars, and almost 80,000 men. He threw them all into the strip of territory 40 miles wide and 20 miles deep which the Japanese had occupied between

---

[13] Associated Press correspondent Relman Morin, who got wind of the story a few months later, was told by an Army Press Relations officer that the young prince had not really deserted but had been captured and held as a hostage by the Russians—which explained why Japan had been forced to make peace!

the Khalka River and the Mongolian-Manchurian border. Heavy flame-throwing Russian tanks led the way, spewing before them burning petroleum with a prodigality that the oil-poor Japanese could scarcely imagine. Never until the Pacific War would the samurai be given such a lesson in technology. And never at any time would they fight back more fanatically. It took Zhukov's tanks eleven days to roll the twenty miles to the border and 20,000 of the 60,000 Japanese defenders died in front of them. More than 50,000 of the 60,000 were counted afterward as wounded, dead, or missing in action.

Six years later, talking to Eisenhower's Chief of Staff Bedell Smith, Zhukov described the Russian triumph with low-keyed but callous braggadocio: "The Japanese are not good against armor. It took about ten days to beat them."

At the time of Zhukov's breakthrough, on August 23, Hitler summoned a meeting of his generals to explain his Non-Aggression Pact with Russia and his disregard for the Anti-Comintern Pact with Japan. "The [Japanese] Emperor," he shouted, "is a companion piece for the late czars of Russia. He is weak, cowardly, and irresolute and may be easily toppled by revolution. . . . Let us think of ourselves as masters and consider these people at best as lacquered half-monkeys, who need to feel the knout."

Hirohito did not hear these words until he read them in a book in 1957. Had he heard them at the time, it would have made little difference, for he had already determined through Nomonhan and Hitler's Non-Aggression Pact with Russia that he must exploit Hitler's strength if he could and must trust it never.

On August 31, after their ten-day offensive, the Russian tanks in central Asia drew up and stopped at the Manchurian border. Their guns were pointed east toward Tokyo. The Kwantung Army was rushing all its reserves to the front to contest their further advance. Zhukov paused, fearing a trap. And before morning he had received orders to release his heaviest armor and send it scurrying back toward the nearest railheads for express transportation west toward Poland.

On September 1, Hitler's *Wehrmacht* poured into western Poland to begin the rape of Warsaw. Bound by treaty and ashamed of the concessions made at Munich seventeen months earlier,

Great Britain and the nations of the British Commonwealth at once declared war on Germany. The Red Army began the next week to occupy eastern Poland. In a back street outside the Kremlin in Moscow, Soviet and Japanese foreign officers began serious negotiations for settlement of the Nomonhan incident.

THE HITLER-HIROHITO STANDOFF

News of the Soviet-German Non-Aggression Pact, turning the *Wehrmacht* loose on the democratic world, had reached Tokyo on August 22, 1939, the night before Zhukov's breakthrough at Nomonhan and Hitler's contemptuous speech about Japan to his generals. Big Brother Kido, the home minister, wrote in his diary: "However we consider the Anti-Comintern Pact and its attached secret protocols, we are startled that there has been this breach of faith." Prime Minister Hiranuma, who had lent qualified support to the strengthening of Japan's pact with Germany, considered the sudden turn in German diplomacy "intricate and baffling." He promptly tendered Hirohito his resignation and Hirohito accepted it.

Now, at last, the problems of many months had been solved. Hitler might be angry, but he owed Japan a favor and had implicitly set Japan free to abide by her own timetable in the Far East. Japan had suffered a great loss of face at Nomonhan, but the Strike-North Faction in the Army had suffered a decisive defeat at the hands of the Russians and had learned that promises of alliance made by Hitler were worth nothing.

Hirohito had sent the vice chief of staff, his former aide-de-camp, Lieutenant General Nakajima Tetsuzo, to the Nomonhan front on September 1 to bring about an end to hostilities. The officers of the Kwantung Army had begged to be allowed to mount one more counteroffensive on September 10 if only to save Japan's face. Nakajima had flown back to Japan, talked to the Emperor, flown again to Nomonhan, and suppressed the plans for the counteroffensive. Hirohito replaced the commander-in-chief of the Kwantung Army in Manchuria, and on September 16 the Russian and Japanese diplomats meeting in Moscow agreed to settle the war by a return to the border lines of the status quo ante.

Lieutenant General Komatsubara Michitaro, the Strike-North

commander of Japan's 23d Division, which had suffered 99 per cent casualties at Nomonhan, returned to Japan to die of an "abdominal ailment." Several officers of lesser rank blew their brains out or committed hara-kiri on the edge of the field of battle.

The Strike-North Faction which had troubled Hirohito since 1930 was dead at last. And for the next year Hirohito would be able to develop his private national plans in peace and quiet. The factories would hum with armament business. The quixotic liberals of Japan would continue to murmur, making it necessary to change the Cabinet occasionally. But the secret police would ably nullify all serious attempts at protest. And Prince Konoye, in retirement, would arrange to replace all previous political parties with a single mass party called the Imperial Rule Assistance Association. Germany in the meanwhile would march, and when the time was ripe Prince Konoye would resume office to lead Japan once again to war.

23

JOINING THE AXIS

(1940)

HURRIED BY HITLER

Between August 1939 and August 1940, patriotic Japanese almost forgot their favorite hobby of domestic political intrigue while they worked feverishly to prepare the country for World War II before Germany should fight and win it. Starts were made on over a thousand new military airplanes and over a million and a quarter tons of new or converted naval vessels. Twelve new divisions and a quarter of a million men were added to the Army.[1]

Domestic tabloids harped on what they considered the hypocrisy, self-interest, and overbearing of the Americans and British in their support of Chiang Kai-shek. But while the tabloids played upon inferiority feelings and old racial grievances, the official policy toward the United States, voiced by diplomats and English-language editorials, was conciliatory. The Army and Navy were stockpiling war commodities unavailable in Japan. Handsome prices were being paid U.S. businessmen for oil, scrap iron, and machine tools. U.S. Ambassador Grew was encouraged to make a speech "straight from the horse's mouth" about U.S. business grievances in China and was given to understand afterward that the speech had been privately applauded by men close to the Emperor.

---

[1] The 24th, 25th, and 32d through 41st divisions. This buildup has not been noted previously by Western historians.

The lawyer, Baron Hiranuma, had been succeeded as prime minister on August 30, 1939, by the "Army moderate" General Abe Nobuyuki. General Abe was, in fact, the least talented and most aristocratic of three officers who had played the part of "Crows" to Emperor Taisho.[2] In November 1939 Hirohito's Big Brothers saw that a Navy Cabinet would better please the United States and would better inspire the domestic armament effort. And so in January 1940, General Abe was succeeded by Admiral Yonai, the former Navy minister who had tipped the scales for Hirohito against accepting a premature alliance with Hitler.

Great events were afoot abroad which riveted Japanese attention. Stalin, after taking his proffered half of Poland, fought a war with Finland from November 1939 to March 1940 and won it without much dispatch or glory. Hitler, after securing his half of Poland, dug in for the winter behind his Siegfried line on the western border of Germany and kept the French waiting behind their Maginot line, just opposite, along the eastern border of France.

On March 25, 1940, one hundred members of the Diet, recruited by Prince Konoye but representing all parties, buried their difficulties and formed a League for Waging the Holy War. They agreed to support Prince Konoye, to collaborate with Germany and Italy, to rid Japan of laissez-faire, communism, liberalism, and utilitarianism, and to dedicate themselves to a New Order in East Asia.

The next month, April, Hitler conquered Denmark and Norway. In early May he ordered his panzers and paratroops to blitz Belgium and the Netherlands and so outflank the Maginot line.

LORD PRIVY SEAL KIDO

On May 8, 1940, the day that news of Hitler's order for the attack on the Low Countries arrived at the palace in Tokyo, Hirohito sent an emissary[3] to the first of his Big Brothers, the son of

[2] The other two were Araki, the Strike-North leader, and Honjo, Hirohito's former chief aide-de-camp.

[3] Matsudaira Yasumasa who would later succeed Kido as the Emperor's chief advisor, in November 1945.

his foster father, Marquis Kido Koichi. He asked Kido to take the post of chief civilian advisor to the Throne, that of lord privy seal. Kido had been out of public office for nine months advising Prince Konoye in behind-the-scene preparations for a new totalitarian state structure to be dominated by a single mass party, the Imperial Rule Assistance Association or I.R.A.A. Kido protested that he must first complete these political chores and that even then he could not consider the post in the palace until it had first been offered to Prince Konoye. Two days later he acknowledged to his diary that the way had been cleared for him and that he intended to give up his plans for becoming vice president of the new mass party.

During the next fortnight Kido exerted all his considerable powers of persuasion and blackmail to hurry Japan's politicians into line with the so-called New Structure. On May 26 he dined with Konoye and Count Arima of the imperial family to tell them that his arrangements were nearly complete. The three men agreed that the old political parties should be given a little time in which to save face before dissolving themselves and merging, and that the actual announcement of the New Structure should not be made until Prince Konoye became prime minister again. On this understanding Kido wound up his political mission three days later by securing the signatures of Japan's most important professional politicians on a contract which bound them all to cooperate in the New Structure and to dedicate themselves to "fulfillment of the national defense" and "an expansion in foreign affairs." The signatories further agreed that "politicians who do not join the new [I.R.A.A.] party shall not be cared for."

Marquis Kido turned over the finished plans for the New Structure to Prince Konoye at a last lunch on June 1, 1940. Then, from Konoye's Hate-China Villa in Yokohama, the dapper marquis drove straight to the palace where he was invested lord privy seal by Hirohito in a simple ceremony at 3 P.M.[4]

---

[4] The former Lord Privy Seal Yuasa, who had occupied the post since March 1936—and before that, since 1933, the post of imperial household minister—was at last allowed to retire and nurse the gastric ailments of which he had begun to complain in 1934.

THE FALL OF FRANCE

It was a critical month in which Kido, after years of apprentice-ship, finally took his public place at the Emperor's side. The German Army invaded France from the ill-defended Belgian border and swiftly threw back a hastily organized stopgap British expeditionary force to the beaches of Dunkirk. The remnants of the British rear guard evacuated the beaches on June 4. Mussolini declared war on the Allies on June 10 and invaded southern France. The government of the dismembered French nation, re-organized in defeat under Prince Kanin's old friend Maréchal Pétain, capitulated to the Axis on June 22.

The collapse of France and the Low Countries orphaned French Indochina and the Dutch East Indies, the richest colonies in Southeast Asia. It also sapped British power in the Far East by pulling back fleet units from Singapore to the defense of England's white cliffs. The pearls of Asia lay exposed on the half shell and Hirohito's councillors feared that if they were not grabbed quickly they would be appropriated either by Germany or the United States. If Japan offered to co-operate in the European struggle against Great Britain, a bargain could probably be worked out with Hitler. The United States, however, remained a great impon-derable. It might stir from its pacifist lethargy and block Japanese seizure of the Indies. As yet the Japanese Navy was still two to three years from acquiring the strength needed to challenge the United States.

Through his aides-de-camp Hirohito received and studied scores of position papers drawn up by young officers in the Army and Navy ministries. Some described Japan's position as a "fateful juncture" and some as "a moment of golden opportunity." Some dwelt on the impossibility of matching economic sinews with the United States. Others envisaged a Japanese Empire extending to Australia, to India, and even to a territory of Alaska which would include western Canada and the state of Washington.

In an anguish of indecision in the face of so many possibilities, Hirohito made a spur-of-the-moment progress to the tombs of his ancestors in the old Japanese heartland of Yamato. He was ac-companied by the new Lord Privy Seal Marquis Kido. According to the official chronology of the imperial house, invented during Emperor Meiji's reign, Japan's first emperor, Jimmu, had founded the Throne on February 11, 660 B.C. Therefore February 11, 1940, had been the 2600th birthday of the nation. Now Hirohito belatedly used the anniversary as an excuse to visit the old capital, Kyoto.

As the first stop on his pilgrimage, on June 10, he went to pray at the antique shrine of the sun goddess on the wooded slopes of Ise Peninsula overlooking the sea from which the imperial dynasty had come. There Kido stood by under the trees watching as Hirohito disappeared into a little hut of unvarnished white wood, the Holy of Holies, wherein reposed the fragments of the ancient sacred mirror in which every duly anointed emperor was supposed to be able to communicate with the mother of the Japanese race. Kido admitted to his diary: "My feelings were profoundly stirred and I wept. I prayed for the future fortune of the imperial family and reflected with awe on the importance of my new position. Before the imperial shrine of Japan, my mind widened and I felt large and fearless."

The heralded state visit of Hirohito to the tomb of Jimmu, the first emperor, which took place the next day, was perfunctory by comparison. At every intermission in the ceremonies, Kido was kept busy answering sotto-voce questions from the Emperor as to the significance of Italy's entry into the war.

The following day, June 12, after bathing at his Kyoto inn, Kido was honored to dine in privacy with the Emperor in the Kyoto Palace of the imperial forebears. He agreed with Hirohito that Hitler's overwhelming victory in Europe made it mandatory for Japan to take control of French and Dutch colonies in the Orient before they should fall into other hands.

That same day the foreign minister had signed a nonaggression pact with Thailand, the one other nation in the Orient besides Japan which could be considered its own master. Thailand had ceded large areas of Laos and Cambodia to French Indochina in 1893, 1904, and 1907. On the pretext of mediating Thailand's just claims for the return of these territories, Japan planned to introduce military observer teams into French Indochina and finally to take over the colony by a police action which could be represented to the United States as a temporary intervention. By befriending

Thailand in this manner, diplomatic brains in the Foreign Ministry hoped to win the trust of natives throughout Southeast Asia and so recruit them in movements to oust Western colonialism and replace it with Japanese colonialism.

At his private dinner with Marquis Kido in the dark and draughty paper-screened halls of the old Kyoto Palace, Hirohito acknowledged that Japan would soon need the discipline of Prince Konoye's contemplated one-party government if the nation was to take advantage of the Strike-South opportunities opened by the fall of France. On returning to Tokyo the next day, June 13, Kido set to work at once translating the Emperor's words into action. He advised the ministers of Admiral Yonai's Cabinet to stand ready to resign and make way for Konoye. He urged the vice minister of foreign affairs, Big Brother Tani Masayuki,[5] to press home negotiations with France, Great Britain, and the semiautonomous Dutch government of the East Indies. Tani embarked at once on conversations with Monsieur Charles Arsenne-Henry, the French ambassador in Tokyo.

The sudden "low" position of France enabled Tani to demand that Arsenne-Henry stop the flow of war supplies through Indochina into the "free China" of Chiang Kai-shek. By June 20 Arsenne-Henry and his Vichy masters had capitulated. They agreed to "recognize . . . Japanese . . . special requirements" and to let Japanese observers into Indochina to supervise the make-up of all trains running north from Hanoi. As a result, Chiang Kai-shek lost 80 per cent of his trade with the West. Another clause in the Franco-Japanese agreement forced the French settlement in Shanghai, on June 23, to turn over its defense sector to Japanese troops and to open the whole of the French Concession in Shanghai to Japanese police search and extradition.

The next day, June 24, an aide-de-camp reported to Hirohito that Chiang Kai-shek would soon meet with the Chinese puppet president, Wang Ching-wei, and with the Japanese vice chief of staff, to settle the China War before the Strike South should begin.

[5] Tani had run the China Desk in the Foreign Ministry from 1930 to 1933 during the conquest of Manchuria. Then Hirohito had been forced to rusticate him to Manchuria for three years in order to disassociate the Throne from his aggressive enthusiasm for leaving the League of Nations and prosecuting the Strike South.

The meeting eventually did take place, weeks later, with a trusted lieutenant standing in for Chiang, at the city of Changsha in the half-conquered lake country south of Hankow. Chiang, through his representative, refused to accept Japanese conditions for a "complete settlement of the China incident," but he did discuss, in great detail, a limited, unofficial truce with Japan in areas where there were no Chinese Communists. Though little known and almost entirely undocumented in the West, this unsigned truce was in reality observed rather strictly in the field until Japan's defeat five years later. The Japanese Army fought Mao Tsetung almost exclusively. Its probes into areas held by Chiang Kai-shek's forces were mostly arranged in advance with Chungking and amounted to little more than political gestures.

On yet another diplomatic front, the Foreign Ministry held talks with the British ambassador in Tokyo, Sir Robert Craigie. While they were in progress, the British and Australian governments inquired in Washington whether it might not be best to present Japan either with clear-cut concessions or challenges. The British Empire was ready on the one hand to join the United States in recognizing Japanese claims to China or on the other hand to assist the United States in an all-out trade embargo against Japan. U.S. oil and steel companies, however, were doing a land-office business with Japan and their lobbies in Washington argued ably against accepting either of the extreme alternatives recommended by the British. With considerable justice, President Roosevelt contended that he had no right to give away China for the Chinese and no mandate from Americans to provoke Japan to war. Appeasement of Japan would be craven and unjust; restraint of Japan would be politically unwarranted. Better to give Japan rope and let her prove to herself and the world that she was doing wrong. Then and only then would it be time to crush her back into her place.

Engaged in the Battle of Britain, England had no hope of protecting her interests in the Pacific except through the United States. On July 15, 1940, British Ambassador Craigie in Tokyo agreed to close for three months the Burma Road which brought Chiang Kai-shek supplies from the ports of India.

The fourth prong of the Japanese diplomatic offensive, against the Dutch East Indies, had seemed initially as if it should be the easiest to push home, but in the event it turned its point on a wall of stolid, stubborn Dutch charm. The Indonesian colony had announced its continuing loyalty to the Dutch queen who was an exile in London. In early July Vice Foreign Minister Tani demanded a renewal of defunct trade negotiations with the Dutch East Indies. The colonial government in Java complied by giving months of handsome entertainment to a high-powered trade delegation from Tokyo consisting of twenty-six oil and intelligence experts and the Japanese minister of commerce. In the end, however, the Dutchmen produced an abundance of sound technical reasons to show that they were unable to supply Japan with more aviation gasoline.

Throughout these predatory overtures to the French, Chinese, British, and Dutch, the war for air superiority known as the Battle of Britain continued to rage indecisively over southern England. As early as June 21, Prince Asaka, the Emperor's uncle and conquistador of Nanking, assured Hirohito that the British were losing and that, incidentally, Japan would do well to unify her Army and Navy air forces in emulation of the Luftwaffe. Hirohito shook his head and told his uncle that evidence as yet indicated no British defeat.

PRINCE KONOYE'S RETURN

On June 24, 1940, Prince Konoye resigned as president of Hirohito's Privy Council in order to devote himself full time to the final preparations for his second prime ministership. Four days later he showed Hirohito his provisional list of Cabinet ministers. Hirohito approved it in general but questioned whether the proposed war minister, Lieutenant General Tojo, had had enough combat experience to lead the Army in a time of anticipated warfare. In his years in Manchuria Tojo had secured a strong hold on the secret police and lately, by indefatigable membership on committees, had made himself the most powerful individual in the Army bureaucracy. Then again, in his current post as inspector general of military aviation, he had worked closely and well with the Emperor. Hirohito liked him and shared with him a concern for practicality and detail.

Lord Privy Seal Kido suggested that if the Emperor had any

doubts about Tojo's popularity with the field commanders, why not let Lieutenant General Anami—the man who had treated the young officers of the cabal to drinks on the night of Hirohito's accession to the Throne in 1926 and the man who would commit hara-kiri during the fake coup d'etat on the night of Japan's surrender in 1945—stay on in his present post of vice war minister as a foil and watchdog for Tojo? Anami was popular with field commanders and, having long served as a palace aide-de-camp, he could be trusted implicitly to act in the interests of the Throne. Hirohito accepted the suggestion appreciatively.

Eighteen days later, on July 16, 1940, the Yonai Cabinet tendered its resignation en bloc and the first of Japan's major political parties liquidated itself and waited, in a state of *nolo contendere* and suspended animation, for further orders. The last of the parties, the Anti-Constitutionalists, would follow suit a month later. In the meanwhile, on July 17, Lord Privy Seal Kido, after a perfunctory thirty-minute meeting with all Japan's living ex-prime ministers, recommended Konoye to the Throne as the next head of state. Lieutenant General Tojo learned that he was Konoye's choice as war minister the next day when he arrived back in Tokyo from an inspection of air bases in Manchuria.

On July 19, Tojo, Konoye, and Konoye's candidates for foreign and navy ministers met and agreed that they could all work together to "perfect a high-degree defense state." Three days later, on July 22, Hirohito accepted Konoye's slate and invested the neurasthenic Fujiwara prince once more prime minister. In the bitter opinion of old Prince Saionji, delivered months earlier when the subject had first come up, Konoye's reappointment was "like inviting a robber back to investigate his crime because no one else could be such an authority on it."

THE NEW ORDER

The languid Prince Konoye resumed office with two of the most energetic members of Hirohito's cabal at his back. One was Lieutenant General Tojo, former inspector general of aviation, former vice war minister, former Kwantung Army chief of staff, former Kwantung Army secret police chief, and before that, until the murder of First Crow Nagata in 1935, the Fourth Crow of

Baden-Baden who had fulfilled a score of difficult assignments in the bureaucracy as Nagata's factotum.

The other activist of Konoye's Cabinet was the foreign minister, Matsuoka Yosuke, a long-time hanger-on of the Big Brothers. He had attended the 1926 meeting in Hankow at which the Big Brothers' "China experts" had first formulated Japanese plans for using Chiang Kai-shek. Later, in 1932, he had negotiated settlement of the Fake War in Shanghai. In 1933 he had led Japan's delegation out of the League of Nations.

Matsuoka commanded the curiosity and respect of Hirohito's inner circle because he knew how to talk big and independent—like an American. Indeed, Matsuoka was as much American as he was Japanese. The son of an impoverished samurai of Choshu, he had been singled out as a potential talent at his coming-of-age ceremony in 1893 and had been sent the next year, at the age of fourteen, to live with an uncle who had emigrated to Portland, Oregon. Taken in by a mission school there he had lived up to all his early indications of precocity by graduating from high school and the University of Oregon, with a law degree, before his twenty-first birthday.

On becoming foreign minister, Matsuoka at once saw U.S. Ambassador Grew. He confessed to Grew that he was not an old-school diplomat but a blunt, honest sort of man. If war ever came between the United States and Japan while he remained in office, he hoped to see to it that both sides would know why. War, he said, "should not develop, as in so many other cases in history, through misunderstanding." Then he gave Grew an oral message to relay to President Roosevelt. In it he protested Japan's love for peace but asked the United States to give up its defense "of the status quo" and recognize the fact that "a New Order" was taking shape in the world.

That same day, July 26, 1940, the new Cabinet formally adopted its program, a document entitled "Main Principles of Fundamental Japanese National Policy," which had been drawn up by civilians under the direction of Prince Konoye. With considerable rhetoric and bombast, it declared Japan's intention "to capitalize on the inevitable trend in the development of world history" by "building a new order in Greater East Asia." For this purpose the Cabinet agreed to bring the China "incident" to a successful conclusion and to make Japan strong and self-sufficient in order to fulfill the national program. In the dialectic of the time this meant that Japan intended, one way or another, to gain control of the oil of the Indies. On the domestic front the Konoye government called for creation of a new form of government, economy, and culture in Japan. The people would be asked to give their complete devotion to the state, ridding themselves of all "selfish thoughts" and—in a phrase beloved by Hirohito—"cultivating a scientific spirit."

Hirohito took the Cabinet's decision as an approval for war and promptly that same afternoon activated a standing plan for removing the members of his family from positions of responsibility before the war should break out. He had the Army and Navy ministers informed that the two imperial princes, Kanin and Fushimi, who were chiefs of the Army and Navy General Staffs, might soon have to retire. War Minister Tojo replied that the Army would regret the loss of Prince Kanin as its leader but agreed that the Army could take a stand in the world more freely if its actions did not directly implicate the Throne. On the other hand Navy Minister Yoshida Zengo insisted that Navy Chief of Staff Prince Fushimi be left in office for at least nine more months as insurance against involvement in war before the Navy was ready for it. Hirohito listened to the Navy's point of view and for the moment suspended judgment on it.

The next day, July 27, the most important ministers of the Cabinet met with the chiefs of staff and some of the officers from palace Imperial Headquarters to ratify the program passed by the Cabinet and to discuss its military implementation. This was the first "liaison conference" between domestic policy makers and the field strategists of headquarters since the month after the rape of Nanking more than two years earlier. The officers from headquarters brought with them a plan entitled "Main Japanese Policy Principles for Coping with the Situation Which Has Developed in the World." It specified the measures which would be taken for cutting off Western aid to Chiang Kai-shek via Burma and Indochina. It called for stronger ties with Germany and renewed diplomatic efforts to neutralize Russia. And finally it committed all present to press for Japanese expansion into Southeast Asia and Indonesia.

"Positive arrangements," it declared, "will be undertaken in order to include the English, French, Dutch, and Portuguese islands of the Orient within the substance of the New Order." If possible the goals of the expansion were to be achieved by diplomacy and trade treaties; if possible the China incident was to be settled first before demands on the Dutch East Indies were made too stridently; if possible resort to force would only be made against Great Britain. But if necessary war with the United States would not be shunned and preparations for such a war must be completed by August 1941.

Navy representatives at the liaison conference refused to give their wholehearted backing to the outlined program. They insisted that every effort must be made to settle the China incident before any exploits farther afield and that war with the United States must be avoided at all costs.

In the next two days heated arguments about the respective Army and Navy positions almost tore the new Konoye government asunder. Army underlings accused Navy underlings of being frightened of war with the United States. Navy underlings accused Army underlings of stupidity in engaging the nation in actions like the China incident which could not be won. Civilian expansionists accused both services of being militarily incompetent and politically boastful. Prime Minister Konoye sought vainly to pour oil on the troubled waters. War Minister Tojo grew so impatient with the back-room bickering that he protested to Lord Privy Seal Kido that Konoye was a puppet for every faction and that unless Army-Navy and Court-bureaucracy relations could be improved, nothing would ever be accomplished.

The day after the conference ended, July 30, 1940, Hirohito personally analyzed the Cabinet's difficulties out loud and in so doing enforced, if not harmony, at least a truce. He ventured the opinion that Prince Konoye was trying to cut losses and shorten battle lines in China in order to release forces and divert public opinion in preparation for the nation's historic mission, the Strike South. The Navy, he said gently, wanted an absolute solution to the China incident before venturing farther. The Army, he said sternly, wanted an immediate entanglement in the south in order to cover up its failure in China. He added mildly that both points of view were ultimately based on a laudable sense of pride and a fear of failure. However, he concluded, the services must work together in co-operation with domestic politics and international diplomacy.

Bowing to Hirohito's wishes, the Cabinet smothered its internal differences and on August 1 subscribed to a vaguely worded declaration announcing that it was the "fundamental policy" of the new government to "found a Co-Prosperity Sphere in Greater East Asia." The adjective "greater" had a special significance which was missed by Western observers. It meant that Japan intended to embrace in her sphere not only China and the new Buddhism but also India and the old Buddhism. It meant, in short, that "co-prosperity" was to extend from Teheran to Honolulu and from Harbin to Port Moresby.

FRUGALITY AND HATE

"No nation," announced the epicurean Prince Konoye in a radio address on July 23, "ever became powerful by devoting itself to luxury and pleasure." And so, in the first weeks of the Konoye Cabinet, while the prime minister himself continued to take days off with professional male and female entertainers, the nation at large tasted the bitterness of police-state discipline and glimpsed the drabness of the toiling years ahead. At last the fun-loving populace, who had survived previous gestures at efficient totalitarianism with cynical jokes, was to march in clogs on a treadmill of overtime labor, keeping step with a steady blare of martial music.

Soon Ambassador Grew was noting in his journal, with astonishment and amusement, that concubines would no longer be allowed to have telephones. Soon Hirohito would make wives and geisha put away their bright kimonos by ordaining a new national dress, first for men, then for women, too: a dingy mustard-green schoolboy uniform of pants and high-collar jackets.

No Japanese was allowed to work for a foreigner except as a police spy. Indeed, no Japanese was allowed to work at all unless in dedicated service to the new total-war defense state. Many proprietors of small factories discovered overnight that they were producing "nonessential materials" and that they must return to operating lathes and drill presses for others as they had done when getting their starts in life a generation earlier. If they protested, they were beaten up by thugs.[6]

The gentlemen of the Japanese press, according to Prime-Minister-Maker Saionji, who was now in his ninety-first and last year of life, had begun to write "like drunkards." They spewed out adjectives in defense of Japan's "just cause" and buried news under mountains of mystical philosophizing in an attempt to beautify the underlying opportunism of Hirohito's national program. For the most part they played upon Japanese racial sensibilities in order to inspire hate of all white men except Germans and Italians.

THE COX CASE

As soon as France had fallen, on June 19, Japan's ambassador in Berlin[7] had told the German Foreign Office that Hirohito was ready to reconsider the Ribbentrop idea, turned down a year earlier, of joining Hitler and Mussolini in a firm tripartite military alliance. Flushed with victory, the Germans had replied with studied indifference. Possibly, they said, if Japan could offer Germany tangible advantages, such as supplies of raw materials, an agreement might be worked out. Japan, however, would have to abandon her traditional sympathies for that other island-nation, Great Britain. In particular the pro-British sentiments expressed by the English-language newspapers in Japan—most of which were edited by Englishmen—would have to be suppressed.

The moment Prince Konoye came to power, he and his Cabinet ministers agreed, on July 19, 1940, that they would satisfy the

---

[6] After the dissolution of the Black Dragon Society, underworld boss Toyama Mitsuru had, in 1936, made a truce with the Throne, negotiated by the Emperor's uncle Prince Higashikuni. As a result Toyama continued to rule the slums and the imperial entourage continued to use him for work considered too illegal for the police. Lord Privy Seal Kido, in late 1940 and early 1941, communicated regularly with Toyama through ex-convict Friar Inoue, the former leader of the Blood Brotherhood which had assassinated Baron Dan and financier Inoue in 1932.

[7] Kurusu Saburo, later one of the two special envoys sent to conduct smoke-screen negotiations in Washington while the Japanese fleet was stealing up on Pearl Harbor.

Germans by launching a campaign of vilification to turn Japanese against the British. Accordingly, on Saturday, July 27, while the Konoye government was still wrestling internally to reconcile Army and Navy fears of war, the secret police arrested fifteen British residents in the Tokyo area and accused them of being espionage agents. Most of them were typical British colonial businessmen of whom their own house servants could report nothing more damaging than a somewhat superior attitude of kindliness toward Japan. It was necessary to show, however, that they were polished spies and subtle double-dealers. The demonstration was difficult to stage but the accomplished Japanese secret police, drawing on years of experience in Manchuria, found a way.

On Monday, July 29, one of the fifteen British prisoners, a Reuters correspondent named Melville Cox, hurtled from an upper-story window of Tokyo secret police headquarters and crashed to his death on the pavements below. When attachés from the British Embassy were summoned to pick up his broken body, they counted no less than thirty-five needle punctures in his arms.

The other fourteen "spies" were released to be deported as personae non gratae. Some of them testified that they too had been given depressant and hallucinatory drugs. One of them recalled coming to his senses, between interrogations, before an open window through which he felt a powerful urge to jump. Out of a deeply suspicious animal shrewdness, he had resisted the urge. The British attachés who investigated Cox's case reached the conclusion that he had been similarly tempted and had succumbed.

The Japanese secret police produced a "suicide note" in Cox's own handwriting which they said he had written to his wife before his fall.

See Reuters re rents
See Cowley re deeds and insurance
See Hkg* re balance and shares in London
I know what is best
Always my only love
I have been quite well treated
but there is no doubt how matters are going.

* Hongkong Bank.

The note looked as if it had been written with more than one pen, one line at one interrogation, another at the next. Mrs. Cox was convinced that it expressed nothing which her husband might have wished to say. The British ambassador took her into the protection of his own home until he could get her out of the country, as quickly as possible, on a ship bound for England. The "suicide note" was advertised in the Japanese press as proof that Britain was spying on Japan and that Englishmen were enemies. The vast majority of Japanese were incensed.

THE BATTLE OF BRITAIN

Throughout August 1940, as U.S. Ambassador Grew noted in his diary, the new Konoye government concentrated on "building up the 'new structure' in Japan" and "marking time in foreign affairs while awaiting the result of the 'Battle of Britain.'" With less charity but greater accuracy, Grew could have said that Hirohito was waiting for an opportunity to throw Japan's weight into the war when it might tip the scales of history. Hirohito had much personal feeling, pro and con, for the British, but in his official capacity as Emperor he cared not who won the war in Europe as long as Japan could gain postwar influence which would enable her to achieve the national goal of domination over Asia. By mid-August it seemed clear that Japan's moment had arrived. Great Britain still staggered on the brink of defeat and the Germans had begun to admit that they needed help in delivering the conculsive shove.

On August 13, after weeks of coolness toward Japan, Ribbentrop sent his Far Eastern specialist, Heinrich Stahmer, to the Japanese Embassy in Berlin to say that Ribbentrop was ready to resume negotiations for strengthening the Japanese-German alliance. Foreign Minister Matsuoka responded by inviting Stahmer to Tokyo and by taking steps to create a pleasant atmosphere before Stahmer's arrival. On August 20 he asked and received the Emperor's permission to replace thirty-nine pro-Western diplomats abroad, including almost all chiefs of mission in North and South America. The purge was duly executed over the next three months, putting young men, close to the spy service, in charge of all key embassies and consulates.[8]

Also that day Matsuoka consummated weeks of secret negotiations by signing a new treaty with Vichy France on the future status of Indochina. After the arrival in Indochina of Japanese observers to prevent routing of war supplies through Hanoi to Chiang Kai-shek two months earlier, the Japanese had escalated their demands. Now they required that the French not only stop helping China but start helping Japan. They wanted air bases in northern Indochina from which to bomb the Burma Road and also staging areas and rights of transit which would enable Japanese armies to attack Chiang Kai-shek's southern flank across the Indochina border. Finally they even asked to station a few garrisons of "observers" in south Indochina within striking distance of British Malaya.

When Arsenne-Henry, on instructions from Vichy, gave in to these demands on August 20, he warned Matsuoka that the French colonials in Indochina might not feel bound by the arrangements made for them in Vichy and might, as a matter of pride, resist further Japanese encroachments. Matsuoka reported these possible complications back to the palace, and Hirohito promptly reassigned two trusted members of his Army cabal to the Indochina area to make a show of strength and stage a genuine battle with which to satisfy the French sense of military honor.[9]

As the move into Indochina was being mounted, Ribbentrop's Far Eastern expert Stahmer, on August 23, accepted Matsuoka's invitation and set out with plenipoteniary powers for Tokyo. The Battle of Britain was not going well. In dogfight after dogfight,

---

[8] For instance, the new ambassador to the Soviet Union, recommended by his years of diplomatic experience with geisha and bomb throwers, was retired Lieutenant General Tatekawa Yoshiji, the Peerless Pimp who had slept so soundly at the Literary Chrysanthemum on the night of the seizure of Mukden in 1931.

[9] Lieutenant General Tominaga Kyoji, chief of the all powerful Operations Department of the General Staff, stepped down to an advisory position in the command of the South China Army to mastermind the face-saving operation. Colonel Cho Isamu, the veteran intriguer who had helped rig the October Plot for the benefit of the League of Nations in 1931, who had issued the kill-all-prisoners order for Prince Asaka before the walls of Nanking, who had taken down his pants before the Russians at Lake Khassan, and who would eventually have himself decapitated at the mouth of a cave on Okinawa, was appointed by Hirohito to take command of the Army observer team in Hanoi.

the German fighter pilots had failed, even with numerical superiority, to clear the skies of southern England, or to inactivate the airstrips from which British night bombers were making devastating sorties against the invasion fleets which Hitler was trying to collect in the French channel ports. The Luftwaffe was planning to resort to the desperate measure of massive indiscriminate terror bombing.

On September 2, while Stahmer was still on the high seas, old Saionji heard of the plans for a military alliance with Hitler and guardedly observed: "By our present policies the Emperor's aura of sanctity will be made invisible and the assertion that His Majesty is wise and sagacious will become an untruth. . . . In the end, I believe, Great Britain will be victorious."

The next day Navy Minister Yoshida Zengo, a charter member of Hirohito's cabal, resigned in protest against the pact plan and the hastening of naval preparations which would inevitably follow from it. Hirohito replaced him with Admiral Oikawa Koshiro, a former imperial aide-de-camp whom he described as "easy to talk to."[10]

On September 4, Prince Konoye was received privately at the Imperial Library in the palace woods and submitted to Hirohito three "points of revision" which he said must be written in to the basic policy of the nation before his prime ministership could progress farther. First, the Emperor and his chief ministers must resolve to be willing to fight a war with the United States. Second, Japan must conclude a military alliance with Germany. Third, Japan and Germany must publish a joint statement announcing their intention to found a New Order in the world. Konoye told Hirohito that the war and foreign ministers had agreed to the three points on August 17 but that the Navy held out in opposition to them. With evident nervousness, Hirohito authorized Prince Konoye to bring the Navy into line if he could.

Three days later, on September 7, Luftwaffe commander Goering launched 625 of his bombers against London in the first of World War II's great fire raids. It was that night when flames engulfed miles of cockney slums that a charlady approached a

10 Oikawa would in turn resign from a position of trust, as Navy chief of staff, to protest Hirohito's studied deafness to U.S. peace feelers when kamikaze pilots were throwing their lives away in May 1945.

fireman who was battling with his hose and reportedly said: "Spare a few drops for my pot, luv, and I'll make you a nice cup of tea."

Japanese observers at the embassy in London remembered the wood-and-paper structures of their own capital and sent home to Tokyo thoughtful descriptions of the holocaust which they had witnessed. Having read their reports three days later, Hirohito suffered a moment of trepidation and doubt. He told Lord Privy Seal Kido that the German bombs had damaged the British Museum, endangering some of the manuscripts of Charles Darwin. Then he asked rhetorically whether Japan could not somehow use her influence with the Germans to mediate the European War and stop the headlong rush of world events. Kido made no reply. He knew that the Emperor was only indulging a mood, yearning wistfully for a return to Japan's old cautious war schedule and an escape from the pressure of opportunities offered by Hitler.

The previous morning, on September 9, Hirohito had already cast his lot. He had dropped in unexpectedly at a liaison conference of the Cabinet and General Staff in the Imperial Headquarters building on the palace grounds. There Foreign Minister Matsuoka was trying vainly to persuade the Navy's representatives to subscribe to alliance with Germany and to its implied accompaniment, war with the United States. The Navy was stubbornly contending that only disaster could result. Hirohito's arrival converted the proceedings into a Conference in the Imperial Presence. No record has been preserved of what words, if any, Hirohito uttered before the conferees. But the Navy representatives ceased to argue in broad terms against the pact with Germany and began, stiffly and professionally, to answer questions about their capabilities against the United States under optimum conditions at the end of a year's preparation. Hirohito seemed pleased by their answers. When the conference adjourned that afternoon no conclusions had been reached explicitly, but Prime Minister Konoye felt that the Navy, implicitly, had capitulated.

That evening of September 9, Foreign Minister Matsuoka welcomed Hitler's envoy Stahmer to Japan with a small reception in the lantern-lit garden of his residence—the setting which would later be remembered as the garden of atomic sunshine. Stahmer had arrived in Japan two days earlier and was eager to start doing business. Before the evening was over, he and Matsuoka, conversing in their common language, English, had agreed on the main purposes of the Tripartite Pact. Japan wanted a free hand in Southeast Asia. She should have it. Germany wanted pressure put upon the British fleet which still maintained naval supremacy in the Strait of Dover. Matsuoka undertook to supply it by having the Japanese Navy prepare to attack the British Far Eastern bastion of Singapore.

The next day, September 10, Matsuoka and Stahmer sat down together for a long day's haggle while they penned the original English draft of the pact which was to ally Nippon and the Reich militarily against the West. At every step in the talks Matsuoka cross-checked his concessions and reservations with the palace. Japanese and German texts of the pact were compared on September 11 and on September 12 the final text was ready for Hirohito's consideration.

On September 13, an unlucky Friday, Hirohito studied the text of the pact word by word for four and a half hours. He understood full well that he had a fateful decision to make which would almost certainly lead to war with the United States. He expected that many of even his closest advisors would be opposed to the pact. He knew, on reflection and meditation, that the institution of the Throne, representing his forefathers, must be cleansed in advance of responsibility for the pact. Nevertheless, when he had wrestled with all his misgivings, he approved the text of the alliance with one minor editorial change. He struck out five words, "openly or in concealed form," from a description of the kind of attack which might launch Japan's participation in World War II. They were too explicit, too suggestive of the actual event as it was envisaged by his naval planners.

Having approved the text of the pact with Hitler, Hirohito the next morning sought to allay the fears of the Navy by promising that Prince Fushimi, the chief of staff, would be allowed to remain in office, as requested, until at least April 1941. This was Hirohito's way of telling the Navy that the war would not break out immediately but that it would break out and that preparations for it must be hastened. At an unofficial liaison conference at Imperial Headquarters later that day, the Navy bowed to Hirohito's wishes and agreed to accept without protest the pact with Hitler and the accelerated national program.

For the benefit of the masses, the information officers of the Foreign Ministry had the newspapers whip up an outcry against the "Anglo-Saxon conspiracy" which was said to be strangling Japan's legitimate aspirations abroad. The pact decision happened to coincide with the arrival in Java of the trade-and-spy delegation which had been sent there in quest of aviation gasoline. The importance and righteousness of the oil mission filled the front pages. At the same time Japanese demands for bases throughout Indochina were masked by an agitation for reduction of Indochina's tariff barriers.

Finally, on that same Saturday of September 14, Hirohito requested that an official Conference in the Imperial Presence be convoked so that his ministers could second the pact decision and take responsibility for it. Hirohito warned Lord Privy Seal Kido to exclude from the conference all elder statesmen and former prime ministers who might cause time-consuming difficulties.

TRIPARTITE PACT

The historic Conference in the Imperial Presence, which allied Hirohito with Hitler and Mussolini, was duly held in the Paulonia Hall of the Outer Ceremonial Palace from three to six o'clock on the afternoon of Thursday, September 19. As always on such occasions the entire agenda had been carefully negotiated and rehearsed in advance so that every position—every agreement to take or refuse responsibility—would be clearly etched on the record. Hirohito sat motionless before a golden screen at one end of the audience chamber and said nothing. The other eleven participants sat at two long tables down the walls of the chamber and delivered their set speeches to one another back and forth across the Emperor's line of sight. The important policy statements were made by six of the participants.

On behalf of the Navy General Staff, Prince Fushimi inquired, "It is quite likely that a Japanese-American war will be a protracted one. What are the prospects for maintaining our national strength?"

In replying Prince Konoye, on behalf of the Cabinet, admitted that Japan depended heavily "on Britain and the United States for her principal war materials" but concluded that by stringent civilian rationing and careful use of stockpiles "we should be able, in the event of a war with the United States, to supply military needs and thus withstand a rather prolonged war."

After a detailed discussion of war materials and their procurement, Navy Chief of Staff Prince Fushimi observed: "In the end, we will need to get oil from the Dutch East Indies. There are two ways of getting it—by peaceful means and by the use of force. The Navy very much prefers peaceful means."

In regard to the provisions in the Tripartite Pact which might pledge Japan to make war on the United States if the United States made war on Germany, Prince Fushimi went on to say: "We must be able to determine independently when we should commence hostilities. What has been done about this?"

Foreign Minister Matsuoka replied: "The question of whether or not the United States has really entered the war will be decided by consultation among the three pact countries. . . . Since our government will make the final decision, it will be made independently."

Hara Yoshimichi, who had recently been appointed president of Hirohito's Privy Council of advisors, noted that the questions he had been asked to put by the Throne were already being voiced by Navy Chief of Staff Prince Fushimi. Then, as a professional politician of liberal but compromised views, he inserted a hesitant opinion on his own behalf: "I think it will be impossible to obtain oil from the Dutch East Indies by peaceful means. I would like to hear the government's views on this."

Foreign Minister Matsuoka replied: "Since Germany is now in control of the Netherlands, she can help us greatly in putting pressure on the Dutch East Indies. In international relations, it is often possible to work behind the scenes. . . . When Japan withdrew from the League of Nations some years ago, so many people wanted to sell us munitions that one had difficulty turning them down. If Japan would abandon all, or at least half, of China, it might be possible for the time being to shake hands with the United States, but still pressure on Japan would not cease—not in the foreseeable future."

The discussion returned to details of oil consumption and procurement. War Minister Tojo cut in impatiently: "In the end I think this question comes down to the matter of the Dutch East Indies. The liaison conference between the government and Imperial Headquarters held shortly after the formation of the present Cabinet . . . agreed that we should settle the China incident quickly and at the same time cope with the Southern Question, taking advantage of favorable opportunities. As for the Dutch East Indies, it was decided that we would try to obtain vital materials by diplomatic means, and that we might use force, depending on the circumstances."

Privy Council President Hara, on behalf of Japan's sane but silent cosmopolitan minority, asked several waspish but ineffectual questions about the degree of Japan's commitment if she signed the Tripartite Pact.

Foreign Minister Matsuoka stated simply: "The object of this pact is to prevent the United States from encircling us."

In conclusion Army Chief of Staff Prince Kanin, the elder of the imperial family, three days short of his seventy-fifth birthday, declared: "On the basis of our studies to date, the Army section of the Imperial Headquarters agrees with the government's proposal for a stronger Axis Pact with Germany and Italy. Furthermore, since the improvement of relations with the Soviet Union is extremely important both for the settlement of the China incident and for future defense policies, we would strongly urge that the government redouble its efforts in this area."

Summing up for the Navy, the other staff chief and imperial family elder, Prince Fushimi, said: "The Navy section of Imperial Headquarters agrees with the government's proposal that we conclude a military alliance with Germany and Italy. However, on this occasion we present the following desiderata: firstly, that every conceivable measure will be taken, even after the conclusion of this alliance, to avoid war with the United States; secondly, that the Strike South will be attempted in so far as possible by peaceful means, and that bootless friction with third parties will be avoided; and thirdly, that the guidance and control of speech and the press will be strengthened, that unrestrained discussion of the conclusion of this pact will not be permitted, and that harmful anti-British and anti-American statements and behavior will be restrained. Although it is recognized that the government and the Navy Supreme Command agree on the need to speed up the strengthening of naval power and preparedness, nevertheless we would ask the government now, in view of the great urgency of the time, to give us unstinting co-operation."

Finally Privy Council President Hara made a prepared statement on behalf of the Throne: "Even though a Japanese-American clash may be unavoidable in the end, I hope that sufficient care will be exercised to make sure that it will not come in the near future, and that there will be no miscalculations. I give my approval on this basis."

INDOCHINA

At the end of the conference in his presence, Hirohito arose with a stiff nod of approval and returned to the Inner Palace in his Mercedes limousine. Foreign Minister Matsuoka drove in the opposite direction to put in a full evening's work at his office. He at once cabled an ultimatum to Hanoi, the capital of French Indochina, giving the governor-general there three days to accede to the agreement which had been worked out between Matsuoka and the Vichy-French ambassador in Tokyo. The alternative, he implied, would be a full-scale Japanese invasion. Matsuoka spent the next several hours receiving the congratulations of cronies and approving messages of explanation to Japanese embassies in Western capitals.

At 3:00 P.M. on September 22, just seven hours short of the Japanese deadline, the French governor-general in Hanoi replied to Matsuoka's note, saying that he was obliged to accept the terms offered. He had tried to bargain. He had tried to hedge. He had even begged Vichy for help and guidance. Now, having found no other recourse, he capitulated.

That night, about eleven o'clock, Major General Tominaga Kyoji, the high-ranking emissary from the General Staff whom Hirohito had dispatched to the South China command for this purpose three weeks earlier, persuaded Japanese units to invade northern Indochina without official orders and in advance of the timetable agreed upon with the French. Colonial garrisons in the

Japanese line of march resisted and fought stoutly for three days. Then, when French military face had been saved and Tokyo had apologized for the impetuosity of its myrmidons, the occupation of northern Indochina was completed peacefully. Western newspapers said that the French had made a valiant stand. Japanese newspapers said that the soft French troops had proved no match for Japan's combat-tested veterans.

War Minister Tojo made a great disciplinary show after the unauthorized border crossing by recalling the commander of Japan's South China Army, Lieutenant General Ando Rikichi, and placing him on the inactive list. Hirohito at once reassigned the compliant general, secretly, to Strike-South preparations with the spy service in Taiwan. A year later, just before the attack on Pearl Harbor, Hirohito would reactivate Ando as the commander of the Japanese Army in Taiwan. The true instigators of the border crossing—Hirohito's emissaries—went on, unreprimanded, to delicate new assignments. Their ringleader, Major General Tominaga Kyoji, for instance, was put in charge of the Army Personnel Bureau in Tokyo to choose the commanders who would mount and lead the Strike South in the year ahead.[11]

The United States responded immediately to the Japanese move on Indochina by loaning $25 million to Chiang Kai-shek. The next day, September 26, President Roosevelt ordered a complete embargo on the sale of scrap iron and steel to nations outside the British Commonwealth and the Western Hemisphere.

On September 27, the Tripartite Pact was signed, with pomp and circumstance, in Hitler's presence at the Reich Chancellery in Berlin. By its first article Japan recognized "the leadership of Germany and Italy in the establishment of a new order in Europe." By its second article Germany and Italy extended the same recognition to Japan's predatory rights in Asia. Articles III–VI pledged the Axis partners, for a ten-year period, "to assist one another with all political, economic, and military means" if any one of them should be attacked by the United States. An addendum of secret protocols, on which Hirohito had insisted, left Japan free

[11] The other three principals were the outgoing chief of the Japanese observer team in Hanoi, Major General Nishihara Issaku; the incoming chief of the same mission, Colonel Kill-All-Prisoners Cho Isamu; and the South China Army's vice chief of staff, Colonel Sato Kenryo.

to decide for herself what would constitute such an American attack.

On the day that the pact was signed, *Asahi*, the largest of the Tokyo dailies, in which the imperial household owned stock, declared editorially: "It seems inevitable that a collision should occur between Japan, determined to establish a sphere of influence in East Asia, including the Southwest Pacific, and the United States, which is determined to meddle in affairs on the other side of a vast ocean by every means short of war."

During the weeks which followed, Japan's presence in Indochina was steadily strengthened. Hirohito confessed to Lord Privy Seal Kido that in his Indochina policy he felt a little as if he were looting a store during a fire. When Thailand, in mid-winter, pressed her claims on French-held areas in Laos and Cambodia, Japan interceded on Thailand's behalf. A lazy little border war was fought in which the most active participants were Japanese volunteers flying for the Thai air force and reinforced Japanese observer teams at the French rear, led by Hirohito's emissary to Hanoi, Colonel Kill-All-Prisoners Cho Isamu. The French colonial government again bowed to Japanese pressure and gave Thailand the territory she demanded. The ceded areas, covered with luxuriant rain forest, were then occupied quietly by Japanese troops and used for intensive training exercises in jungle warfare.

CLEARING THE DECKS

Realizing that the Tripartite Pact and the seizure of northern Indochina had committed Japan, almost certainly, to a premature and desperate war with the West, Hirohito's Court, in October 1940, activated its back-up plan for safeguarding the Throne in case the war should end in defeat. The first step was to withdraw the members of the imperial family from positions of responsibility; the second step was to create a cover story for them so that they would seem to have played no part in the events leading to war.

The withdrawal behind the chrysanthemum curtain was begun on October 3 when the seventy-five-year-old Prince Kanin, the last surviving brother of the prince who had counseled Hirohito's great-grandfather during the opening of Japan eighty years earlier, finally resigned his office of Army chief of staff. He was replaced by his minion, General Sugiyama Hajime, the man with "a face as noncommittal as a bathroom door." Although Kanin's retirement had first been suggested by Hirohito three months earlier, the wily old prince pretended that he was resigning in disgust at the recent unauthorized activities of his subordinates in Indochina. Speaking "confidentially," he told a Western correspondent, "not even I can any longer control the troops in the field."

Another member of the imperial family went further and actually sent word to U.S. Ambassador Grew that Hirohito had approved the Tripartite Pact out of fear of assassination by Army extremists.

Behind the scenes, a certain Captain Takagi Sokichi of the Navy began to consult regularly with Lord Privy Seal Kido and Secretary-Spy Harada. Captain Takagi had been assigned by Hirohito in 1939 to the Naval Staff College to study "postwar problems." He would remain at his task until 1946. Before the outbreak of war it would be he who would arrange to send naval listening teams to Europe to pick up and transmit any Western peace feelers to Japan. During the war it would be he who would organize the Navy's part in the Peace Faction which finally staged the reception for General MacArthur in 1945.

Secretary-Spy Harada made his contribution to the imperial cover story by producing a document now known as the Saionji-Harada Memoirs. He had been writing the memoirs for ten years as a part of his job of managing and distracting old Prince Saionji. In them he had regularly included all possible justifications for the Emperor's conduct and all possible gossip and ceremonial detail which might occupy Saionji's attention. Once a week he had taken the latest installment of the manuscript, neatly transcribed from dictation by Prince Konoye's sister-in-law, to Saionji for marginal comments and editing. Saionji had understood that the journal was being kept for Hirohito's perusal—to show the young Emperor the day-to-day complexities of politics. Harada was a good writer with a flair for color and personalities, and Saionji had enjoyed his role as editor. In Harada's pages the old man had often found it possible to look at trees and ignore the forest.

By October 1940, Harada's manuscript had grown to 10,000 pages, and now he showed it to Prince Takamatsu, Hirohito's favorite brother, a lieutenant commander attached to the Navy General Staff. Prince Takamatsu agreed that it would be a most valuable document in the event that the Emperor ever needed whitewashing. Arrangements were made to move the manuscript from the vaults of the Sumitomo Bank, where Harada held a nominal vice presidency, to the sanctity of Prince Takamatsu's villa, where Army secret policemen would not be tempted to destroy it in the interests of patriotism and the war effort.

These private preparations for the possibility of failure were made behind a façade of great public bustle and bluster. On October 8, the Japanese ambassador in Washington handed U.S. Secretary of State Cordell Hull a note warning that "future relations between Japan and the United States" would become "unpredictable" if Roosevelt persisted in curtailing U.S.-Japanese trade.

On October 12, Prime Minister Prince Konoye formally inaugurated his monolithic totalitarian party, the I.R.A.A. or Imperial Rule Assistance Association.

On October 16, sixteen million Americans registered for military duty under the new Selective Training and Service Act, the cornerstone for later U.S. war preparations. In the fortnight that followed, U.S. military representatives in Washington, London, and Java began conversations with their British and Dutch counterparts on joint defense planning for the Western colonies in Southeast Asia.

On October 17, Hirohito held a special ceremony at the Palace Shrine to invoke "the protection of the gods and a happy outcome to the treaty" with Germany.

On October 24, by Court arrangement, a delegation of Japanese naval officers traveled to Osaka, Japan's mercantile center, for a three-day conference with Japanese bankers. For the Navy's samurai to set foot in Osaka was a concession. In Osaka the traditional greeting was not "hello" or "good morning" but "are you making money?" True samurai so despised such materialism that during the three centuries of Tokugawa rule merchants had been ranked below artisans and farmers in the caste structure. Now, however, the aristocratic samurai needed help.

The naval delegation was led by Vice Admiral Yamamoto Iso-roku, commander-in-chief of the Combined Fleet, the suave oppor-tunist who had negotiated naval limitations in London in 1929 and 1934 and who would shortly devise and lead the attack on Pearl Harbor. Yamamoto told the bankers that unless the number of ships and aircraft in the fleet could be doubled in a year, he would be forced to retire to the Inland Sea and harass the enemy like a pirate while U.S. carrier planes were strafing Tokyo. The cunning elders of Japanese finance were pleased by Yamamoto's frank and unassuming approach and put their grizzled heads to-gether to fund a crash effort for completing the Japanese naval building program a year and a half ahead of schedule.

During the naval finance negotiations in Osaka, Hirohito suc-cumbed to worry and overwork and retired for two weeks with a severe case of flu. As soon as he had recovered, on November 9, he requested that a secret conference of staff chiefs and inspector generals be held in his presence two days later to review the prog-ress which had been made in military preparations.

The next day, November 10, Hirohito presided at an official celebration of the nation's "2600th birthday." He impressed all foreign ambassadors and correspondents by the clarity and force with which he delivered a set speech in favor of peace and science. He was introduced by his brother Lieutenant Commander Prince Takamatsu. Takamatsu's voice was broadcast on the radio as a sign to all Japanese that the decision to fight on the side of Ger-many had been approved by both the imperial family and the Navy.

DEATH OF SAIONJI

On November 12, 1940, when he had just turned ninety-one, and when all that he had lived for had just been thrown away, old Prince Saionji was reported at Court to be ill with a kidney inflammation. Secretary-Spy Harada hastened to the Sit-and-Fish Villa in Okitsu to have a few last words with the old man. "I told him," wrote Harada, "of the magnificence of the 2600th anniver-sary of the founding of the Empire and of Konoye's latest efforts to negotiate with Chiang Kai-shek."

"No matter what is done right from now on," murmured

Saionji, "I don't think Chiang Kai-shek will ever agree to what Japan says."

"The interview," wrote Harada, "was like that, and so I withdrew after five or six minutes."

Six days later Saionji delivered his last bon mot when he said to his doctor, "Never mind these details about the local parts of my body. Please endeavor more to see to the recovery of the strength of the whole body."

On November 24, weak but clearheaded to the last, the sad old man of Japanese liberalism finally expired, leaving the Throne without check or balance. Hirohito had sent fresh milk and flowers to his bedside during his sickness. Now, on November 25, Lord Privy Seal Kido went personally to Okitsu to express the imperial regrets.

At the obsequies Kido met, for the first time since the Nomonhan War in 1939, his former contact with the Sorge spy ring, Saionji Kinkazu, the grandson of the deceased. Kido had left young Saionji uninformed during the recent pact negotiations with Germany, and Soviet spy Sorge had had to rely for news entirely on his sources in the German Embassy. Kido's reason for neglecting his young protégé was not personal: Ribbentrop's pact negotiator, Stahmer, had simply brought word from Berlin that Sorge was finally suspected of being a Soviet agent.

A routine Gestapo security check in June 1940 had uncovered Sorge's early affiliations with the Communist party in Germany. The head of the Gestapo's foreign intelligence section, Walter Schellenberg, on reviewing the evidence, had decided that Sorge's dispatches to the Nazi Party Press Department were too valuable to dispense with as yet. And so instead of exposing Sorge, Schellenberg had sent a Gestapo colonel to Japan with the Stahmer Tripartite-Pact mission to keep an eye on Sorge. The Gestapo colonel, Josef Meisinger, was a dull-eyed robot who had made himself odious even in Berlin by his officious sadism at the rape of Warsaw in 1939. In Tokyo Meisinger quickly and clumsily revealed German suspicions about Sorge to colleagues in the Japanese secret police. The aristocrats around Hirohito learned of Meisinger's indiscretion and at once wrote off their links with the Sorge spy ring as too dangerous, politically, for further use.

Less than a week after Meisinger's arrival in Tokyo, Prime

Minister Prince Konoye had offered young Saionji Kinkazu the post of ambassador to Australia in an effort to get him out of harm's way. Young Saionji, however, had refused the appointment, saying that he did not wish to be expatriated at an exciting juncture in Japanese history. Konoye warned him that the nation was swinging toward the right and that Saionji, as a leftist, might find himself in a difficult position. Young Saionji hastily manufactured a camouflage for himself by becoming the leader of a rightist cell which included Mikami Taku, one of the young naval lieutenants, recently released from prison, who had led the deadly attack on Prime Minister Inoue in 1932.

Now, two months later, at Saionji's funeral in November 1940, Lord Privy Seal Kido adopted a noncommittal correctness in his dealings with the young Saionji heir. He would have further use for young Saionji in the months ahead, but for the moment he was turning his back on the ashes of old Saionji and on the muddled humane liberalism which they represented.

UNCANNY FORESIGHTS

On December 3, 1940, the day after Saionji's state funeral, Hirohito suffered one of his recurrent attacks of self-doubt and fear. Calling in Lord Privy Seal Kido, he complained that relations with the Soviet Union still gave no assurance of safety in the rear when Japan turned south. Negotiations for a new Russo-Japanese fishing treaty were going poorly. A special effort must be made to neutralize the colossus in the north. Kido was himself in a dark mood that day and struggled to find his usual words of comfort. In an astonishing display of long-range realism he admitted to the Emperor:

After this world war, the United States and the U.S.S.R. may unquestionably emerge unhurt when all other nations are devastated. I can imagine, therefore, that our country, which is placed between these two giants, may face great hardships. However, there is no need for despair. When these two lose the competition of other countries in their respective vicinities, they will grow careless and corrupt. We will simply have to sleep in the woodshed and eat bitter fruits for a few decades. Then when we have refurbished our manliness inside and out, we may still achieve a favorable result.

In so many words, Hirohito was reassured, in December 1940, that his purposed attack on the United States was a calculated gamble which could be recouped even if it lost. Kido's encouragement was bleak but still far more cheerful than the predictions of most of Japan's professional military strategists. For instance, Fleet Commander Yamamoto Isoroku, who would have to plan the attack on the United States, viewed the future with unrelieved fatalism. On October 14, he had dined with Secretary-Spy Harada, and staring gloomily into his saké cup, had conjured up a vision of apocalypse:

It is my opinion that in order to fight the United States we must be ready to challenge almost the entire world. . . . I shall exert myself to the utmost but I expect to die on the deck of my flagship, the battleship *Nagato*. In those evil days you will see Tokyo burnt to the ground at least three times. The result will be prolonged suffering for the people. And you and Konoye and the others, pitiful as it may be to contemplate, will probably be torn limb from limb by the masses. It is indeed a perplexing situation. We have come to such a pass that our fate is inescapable.

The national program had reached its point of benedictus and no return. The gods had spoken. Hirohito had committed himself. And well-informed Japanese like Vice Admiral Yamamoto might pray hopefully for miracles but realistically they could only prepare themselves proudly to do and die as samurai.

24

PASSIVE RESISTANCE

(1940–1941)

YAMAMOTO'S DUTY

Hirohito never reversed his decision of September 1940—to strike south even at the cost of war with the United States—but in the twelve months before Pearl Harbor he had to withstand constant pressure from those about him who still hoped for a national reprieve. Only Lord Privy Seal Kido and War Minister Tojo stood by him wholeheartedly and refused to question the Imperial Will. Surrounded by subtle, gentle opponents, Hirohito succeeded, nevertheless, in sponsoring and co-ordinating a secret war plan which surprised the world. It involved hundreds of thousands of men and millions of tons of valuable state property, yet neither its foreign nor domestic opponents appreciated its effectiveness until it was already well on its way to success. In realizing this astonishing feat, Hirohito made free use of the brains of officers in the Army and Navy—the only brains left in Japan which still dared to oppose the war openly and frankly.

One of the stoutest and most influential opponents of a war with the United States was its chief strategic expediter and implementer: Admiral Yamamoto Isoroku, the commander in chief of Japan's *Rengo Kantai* or Combined Fleet. Since his feats in negotiating increases in Japanese naval strength at the international disarmament conferences of 1930 and 1934, he had risen meteorically in his service. His flying protégés of the Misty Lagoon had proven themselves in the Navy's long-range bombing missions in China. His unorthodox weapons systems were now acknowledged to be the most efficient in the armed forces. He was the darling of every armchair strategist and the most popular commander in the fleet. No longer did he need imperial family patronage to find entertainment in the stews of Tsukiji. He now enjoyed the exclusive favors of Chrysanthemum Path, one of the seven most sought-after geisha in Tokyo.

Yamamoto had observed to his chief of staff after a successful exercise with torpedo bombers in May 1940 that a "crushing blow can be struck against an unsuspecting enemy fleet by mass torpedo attack." Detail by detail, throughout the summer of 1940, he privately worked out his daring plan for a surprise attack on Pearl Harbor—and nightly he brooded on the slips which could spill all his cup in a dark pool of blood and shame. He realized, as an experienced intelligence officer, that the Achilles' heel of his plan was security. How could he push such a gambling, controversial scheme through the wordy decision mill of Japan's family government without hints leaking out to the enemy through the innumerable middlemen and double agents who were part of the political system? How could he assemble an armada and move it two thirds of the way across the Pacific without alerting the U.S. radio picket ships which prowled the shores of Asia monitoring Japanese fleet messages?

Yamamoto answered the second question first. Throughout the summer of 1940 he taunted naval code experts with excoriating comments on the conventionality of the fleet's best communications disguises. As a result he was rewarded in October with a new Admirals' Code, a cryptographic system so complex and so novel in principle that Japanese signalmen had trouble using it and U.S. cryptanalysts failed to delve its mysteries until almost the end of World War II. Yamamoto began to use the new code for all top-secret fleet dispatches on November 1, 1940. The fact that it remained uncracked was to be one of the principal reasons for the success of Admiral Yamamoto's Pearl Harbor plan.

Yamamoto solved his other security problem by going directly to the summit of the Japanese pyramid. Late in November 1940, through his friend Prince Takamatsu, a commander in the Navy General Staff, he communicated the Pearl Harbor plan to Commander Takamatsu's brother, Emperor Hirohito. Hirohito was interested in it and after a few days' thought instructed Takamatsu to have it turned over for independent evaluation to a top-security circle of naval officers in the imperial cabal. On the advice of Takamatsu's close friend Rear Admiral Onishi Takajiro, who later conceived and commanded the kamikaze corps of suicide pilots, the study of Yamamoto's plan was turned over to one of the Navy's most brilliant flight officers, Commander Genda Minoru. Genda, during the first two weeks of February 1941, locked himself in his quarters on the aircraft carrier *Kaga*, at anchor in Ariake Bay on the southern island of Kyushu, and arrived at a minutely critical but favorable verdict. Agreeing with Yamamoto, he concluded—so he later wrote when he had become the commander of Japan's postwar American-equipped Self-Defense Air Force—"that the attack would be extremely hazardous but would have a reasonable chance of success."

On this assurance, while orthodox admirals wracked their brains for other, less desperate solutions to the problem of Japan's imperial ambition, Yamamoto went ahead and began training his most trustworthy fleet officers for the parts they would have to play in his scheme.[1] Late in the spring of 1941 he selected the harbor of Kagoshima, the old capital of the seagoing Satsuma clan, as the site for carrier-pilot exercises in dive bombing and low-level torpedo-dropping runs. Aside from its historic associations as the sixteenth century womb of the Japanese Navy, Kagoshima harbor was suitable because its topography closely resembled that of Pearl Harbor.

[1] The details of this previously untold story come from verbal sources, but the crucial point is recorded in the most unimpeachable of all primary sources, a memorandum written later that same year, in October, by Army Chief of Staff General Sugiyama: "In January 1941, in answer to Commander of Great Fleet Yamamoto, Emperor ordered Rear Admiral Onishi to research Hawaii attack."

It is an eloquent commentary on Japanese historical research that when this piece of primary documentary evidence—directly contradicting all the secondary accounts previously printed—was published (together with other memoranda by Sugiyama) in Japan in 1967, it appears that not a single Japanese much less Western newspaper carried an item on it.

UNIT 82

Yamamoto's dutiful war planning for the Navy was matched
in the Army by a research team, known as Unit 82, set up in
Taiwan. It came under the command of General Itagaki, the
Baden-Baden Reliable who had expedited the planning for the
conquest of Manchuria in 1929 and 1930. The real brains behind
the unit, however, were those of Lieutenant General Yamashita
Tomoyuki, the later "Tiger of Malaya." It was Yamashita in 1934
and 1935 who had led on the young officers of the National Principle Group to mount the February Mutiny and so discredit the
Strike-North Faction.

Before Tiger Yamashita could see his proposals for Unit 82
enacted, he was dispatched by Hirohito, in November 1940, to
make a first-hand study of the *Wehrmacht*'s preparations for the
invasion of England. In Yamashita's absence, an unsavory colonel
from Army Intelligence, Hayashi Yoshihide, was put in charge of
the unit.[2] Hayashi, however, was given as assistant Yamashita's
most trusted minion in the intrigues of 1934 and 1935, Tsuji
Masanobu, the former military academy instructor, now a lieutenant colonel. Tsuji had made a name for himself in dispatches
by his ruthlessly puritanic zeal as a field commander in China and
at Nomonhan. He was especially admired at Court for having
taken a torch one night in Shanghai and having personally burned
down forty Chinese brothels which he felt were sapping the fighting spirit of troops on their way to the front.

Tsuji joined Unit 82 on January 1, 1941 and was given charge
of the planning for what was expected to be the most difficult part
of the Strike South: the capture of Singapore. Junior officers were
assigned to study the subsidiary strikes against the Philippines
and the Dutch East Indies. The unit's first task was to cull and
collate the roomfuls of intelligence about Southeast Asia which
civilian agents of the spy service had been amassing in Taiwan

---

[2] Hayashi had masterminded the Nonni Bridge Incident which had served
as pretext for the Japanese invasion of northern Manchuria in November 1931.
Later in 1942 and 1943 he would make himself feared and hated as the director general of Japanese Military Administration in the Philippines.

since 1900, and more intensively since 1934 when Hirohito had first privately announced his decision to look south.

To open the doors for Tsuji and his colleagues in Taiwan and to show them around the archives, Emperor Hirohito delegated his mother's brother-in-law, Count Ohtani Kozui. Ohtani was the renegade abbot of Kyoto's *Nishi Hongan-ji*, or West Fundamental Temple of Buddha. In 1912 Count Ohtani had been discovered selling temple treasures and spending temple monies for his personal gratifications. He had resigned as chief abbot of his sect, which was and is one of the most popular and powerful in Japan, and had taken to missionary work, founding branch temples throughout China and Southeast Asia. In the mid-twenties he had been expelled from Java for nonpayment of the mortgage interest on a large temple property, a sacred mountain, which he had bought there. In some of the sultanates of Borneo and Malaya his missionary temples were closed as subversive organizations by the local rulers. He was, however, a good friend of the sultan of Johore, the wealthy potentate who owned the best rubber plantations in British Malaya. And in Japan he retained a position of great influence, at the center of the Strike-South circle at Court. After 1930 he divided his attention between Strike-South politicians in the Diet in Tokyo and Strike-South business colonials centered in Taiwan.

Under Count Ohtani's imperial tutelage, Lieutenant Colonel Tsuji and the other officers of Unit 82 were able to review all the geographic, ethnic, and political information on Southeast Asia stored by Japanese business and religious organizations in Taiwan. The young Army officers, trained in modern German techniques of blitzkrieg, found many gaps in the data which had been collected. In March Tsuji and his colleagues began to go along on overflights with Japanese commercial pilots and Japanese naval shore patrols to fill in the lacunae in the maps on hand. At the same time, at Tiger Yamashita's insistence, select shock troops were assembling on the island of Hainan and in the forests of northwestern Indochina for practice in techniques of jungle infiltration and for training in amphibious operations against reef-girt islands.

Yamamoto's Navy had meanwhile sent fresh spies to the Hawaiian Islands to watch with binoculars the comings and goings of ships through the entrance of Pearl Harbor. A monitor service was established for all radio messages in the Pearl Harbor area. The monitors got to know the call signals of the various ships in the U.S. Pacific fleet and the tastes of the various supply officers. After a few months of listening the monitors could tell which ships were in port by the orders for groceries delivered at various Pearl Harbor piers.

Farther to the east in Mexico, Japanese naval intelligence established a listening post in Baja California to keep track of U.S. Navy ship movements from West Coast ports and also an office in Mexico City to eavesdrop on the movements of the U.S. Atlantic fleet.

NATIONAL HALFHEARTEDNESS

Even while they presided over war preparations Admiral Yamamoto and his Army colleagues took every opportunity to plead with their political leaders "not to be dragged into war." Again and again Yamamoto recited a refrain which he had first delivered to Prime Minister Prince Konoye in August 1940: "In the first six to twelve months of a war with the United States and Great Britain I will run wild and win victory upon victory. But then, if the war continues after that, I have no expectation of success."

As the architect of the naval development program, Yamamoto was idolized in the ranks of the fleet and his views carried immense weight. His Army friend and counterpart, the strategic genius Lieutenant General Ishiwara Kanji, who had planned the conquest of Manchuria, agreed with Yamamoto and spread his gospel of caution to hundreds of junior officers in the Army.

By the end of January 1941 persistent failure to meet new, unrealistic ship and plane building schedules had persuaded many Japanese naval officers that haste was making waste and that the crash program inaugurated in September 1940 was actually retarding naval preparations. One of the few war plants which had met its norms was the mint which was printing paper money for use in the territories Japan hoped to conquer. There were pesos to spend in Manila, rupees to spend in Calcutta, pounds to spend in Brisbane, even dollars to spend in Honolulu—if and when enough ships could be built to transport the spenders. The worthless paper money became a joke in informed circles, and it was said that the crisp new bills "made ideal spills for lighting dream pipes."

Army procurement officers knew the difficulties of their opposite numbers in the Navy and helped to spread dissatisfaction with war planning to the Army rank and file. After years of steady growth, the Army was not budgeted in 1941 to add so much as a single new division. Before the war with China there had been seventeen divisions. Seven new ones had been mustered in 1937, ten in 1938, thirteen in 1939, and eleven in 1940. Now, on the eve of war, because of the taxing demands on the economy made by the Navy's crash program, the accumulated fifty-eight divisions, manned by over a million men, marked time in China with holding operations and elsewhere with training exercises.

In business and economic circles, too, the planning for war was meeting powerful opposition. The professional politicians of the Diet, brandishing their one weapon, the power to veto budget increases, cut appropriations for the new national mass party, the I.R.A.A., to which they were all supposed to belong, from 100 million yen (about $23 million) to a niggardly eight million yen (about $1.8 million). Prince Konoye persuaded Hirohito to have the Army bolster the sagging New Structure by instructing all reservists to join the I.R.A.A. Diet opposition persisted nonetheless, and Prime Minister Konoye was obliged to let the I.R.A.A. subside as "an educational and spiritual association" rather than a true totalitarian party. Count Arima, Hirohito's in-law, resigned as I.R.A.A. leader and his place was taken by the popular, retired General Yanagawa Heisuke, the one-time Strike-Northist who had redeemed himself in Hirohito's eyes by commanding the amphibious flanking operation which had made possible the drive on Nanking in 1937.

Bankers and industrialists fought Konoye's totalitarian structure by refusing to co-operate with the "New Bureaucrats" whom Kido had trained years earlier, from his desk in the Commerce Ministry, to take over the national economy and "rationalize" it for war. Since Hirohito and the Army and Navy were asking for a national budget amounting to two thirds of the national income —a budget of which 75 per cent would have to be met by deficit financing—the moneybags of the nation had their way. For a time it seemed that all war planning would have to be abandoned.

But the most talented member of Hirohito's cabal somehow negotiated a compromise. This was the ubiquitous Suzuki Tei-ichi, now
a lieutenant general. Since handling the looting of Nanking in
1937 he had had charge of the economic exploitation of China as
the acting director of the Prosperous Asia Institute or Asia Development Board. In April 1941, by agreement with the old men
of Japan's family cartels, he resigned his Army commission and
assumed command of the Cabinet Planning Board as a minister
of state in Konoye's government. In this capacity he undertook to
organize the Japanese economy by working within the framework
of the family alliances which had controlled high finance theretofore. So well did he succeed in his difficult post that he remained
at it, co-ordinating Japan's industrial war effort, until July 1944.

DIPLOMATIC OFFENSIVES

In early 1941, as second thoughts trickled down to the subordinate motor centers of Japan's military mind and as general dissatisfaction mounted with the perils and paucities foreseen in the
proposed war with the United States, Hirohito pressed for the
accomplishment of two diplomatic missions which had been
promised to him at the time of the Tripartite Pact decision:
negotiation of understandings with the Soviet Union and with
the United States. In his straightforward way Hirohito wanted the
Soviet Union to agree not to attack Japan from the rear when she
began to strike south in pursuit of the wealth of the Indies. In
return he was willing to relinquish Japanese oil and coal rights in
the upper, Russian half of the northern island of Sakhalin, lying
between Hokkaido and Kamchatka, and to promise Stalin that
Japan would not aid Germany in any future war against the
U.S.S.R.

The purpose of negotiating with the United States was more
subtle. Hirohito thought that the U.S. government, in view of its
probable commitment soon to join England in the war against
Hitler, might be willing to advise Chiang Kai-shek to cede Manchuria and adjacent provinces to Japan in return for Japanese
withdrawal from most of central and southern China. In addition,
to keep the samurai sword sheathed, the United States might
agree to special trade and oil exploitation rights for Japan in

Southeast Asia and the Indies. By consolidating and expanding such footholds, Japan might be able to gain the objectives of the Strike South without having to fight for them. If the United States stood on principle and refused to make the necessary concessions, a second function would be served by the Washington negotiations: they would gain time for the Navy and lull the Americans into a false sense of security while Yamamoto was preparing his attack plans. Most important, the negotiations, if skillfully reported in the Japanese press, would unite the nation behind the war effort, persuading pro-American Japanese that everything had been tried and that the United States still remained intractable.

Hirohito entrusted the American half of his diplomatic offensive to a sixty-four-year-old admiral, a genial six-foot tower of a man with a broad shoulder for responsibility, Nomura Kichisaburo. A Court emissary approached Nomura and asked him to accept the post of ambassador in Washington immediately after the Tripartite Pact decision in September 1940. At first, however, Nomura refused the appointment. He knew that he was being selected because, as a naval attaché in Washington during World War I, he had struck up a personal acquaintance with Franklin D. Roosevelt, then Assistant Secretary of the Navy. Nomura was pessimistic about exacting concessions from the United States, and he was aware that he might be used as a blind while Japan was training her guns. Throughout October 1940 he continued to refuse the Washington post, explaining candidly that he wanted no part in an "act which might disgrace the nation." Finally in November Hirohito summoned Nomura to a private audience and assured him that the U.S. negotiations would be carried out in a spirit of realistic sincerity. Then and only then did Nomura capitulate and agree to serve.

Hirohito assigned the Russian half of his diplomatic program to Foreign Minister Matsuoka Yosuke. Matsuoka could not be trusted to handle the American half because ever since coming to office in July he had shown a persistent inability to form a policy for dealing with America. Hirohito had commented on this inability many times but he was inclined to be tolerant of the foreign minister's peculiarities. After all Matsuoka was a Christian and had grown up in Seattle. Since 1926 he had served faithfully with Hirohito's Big Brothers in a multitude of assignments. He had shown great craft in negotiating the settlement of the Fake War in Shanghai in 1932. He had then predicted correctly that the West would take no reprisals if Japan walked out of the League of Nations over the Lytton Commission Report on Manchuria. A year later, in 1933, he had commanded much grudging Western admiration by his blunt and honest style in actually conducting the League withdrawal. Since then he had consistently pleased the Emperor with his straightforward cynicism and logic in regard to diplomacy.

In January 1941, when Nomura was packing his trunks to go to Washington, Hirohito pressed Foreign Minister Matsuoka to begin negotiating the desired pact of mutual non-aggression with Stalin. The Japanese ambassador in Moscow, Peerless Pimp Tatekawa Yoshiji, the retired lieutenant general who had slept out the seizure of Mukden with the geisha of the Literary Chrysanthemum in 1931, had been conducting preliminary conversations with Soviet Foreign Minister Molotov throughout the last quarter of 1940.

Japanese Foreign Minister Matsuoka insisted that, before Ambassador Tatekawa committed himself too deeply, Matsuoka should personally reconnoiter the European situation. Prime Minister Konoye, who had observed his foreign minister closely for fifteen years, at once warned Hirohito to look with suspicion on Matsuoka's proposed trip to Berlin. Konoye pointed out that throughout the mid-Thirties Matsuoka had shown signs of sympathy with the Strike-North Faction which advocated Russia as a safer opponent than the United States. Moreover Matsuoka, despite much threatening talk, did apparently harbor a feeling of obligation to the United States. It was known that, in 1933, without fanfare and out of his own pocket, he had erected a fine marble monument over the grave of the American woman in Seattle who had taken him in and raised him as a child. It was also known that he spoke mysteriously to American friends in Tokyo about his mission to prevent war between the United States and Japan. Finally, almost alone in Hirohito's entourage of intimates, he had remained on good terms with old Prince Saionji until his dying day.

Hirohito tended to dismiss the insinuations of Prince Konoye. After all, Matsuoka had negotiated the Tripartite Pact which gave Japan a semblance of claim to the Southeast Asia colonies of the nations which Germany had conquered in Europe. Also, Matsuoka had from the first upstaged Prime Minister Konoye and War Minister Tojo. He clearly had the fault of vanity. He loved the limelight and moved everywhere with a troupe of newsmen at his heels. Hirohito suspected that the shy and furtive Konoye was merely jealous of Matsuoka.

And so, in early 1941, Hirohito disregarded Konoye's doubts and gave Matsuoka leave to spend a month in Russia, Germany, and Italy, satisfying his stated need for first-hand knowledge of "world realities." In so doing, Hirohito made a mistake. He enabled Matsuoka to gain a position of importance in the eyes of the public and from that position to launch a six-month campaign of subversive procrastination against the imperial program.[3]

Matsuoka did not want Japan to sign a pact of neutrality with the U.S.S.R. because he hoped secretly that Japan would soon join Germany in war with the U.S.S.R. He knew from the reports of the Japanese Embassy in Berlin that, unless Ukrainian wheat and Caucasian oil were made available in desired quantities to the Reich's purchasing agents, Hitler might soon abrogate his non-aggression pact with Stalin and attack the Soviet Union. Matsuoka anticipated that Germany might win such a war quickly, in which case Japan would be unsafe from German aggression unless she held, as buffer zone, the eastern third of the Soviet Union. Then again Germany might bog down in Russia in a war that would last for decades. In that case Great Britain, supported by the United States, would ultimately win and Japan would be judged least harshly if she had attacked only communism. For the moment Matsuoka placed prime importance, for both personal and patriotic reasons, on the avoidance of war with the United States.

[3] The type of devious passive resistance in which Matsuoka was indulging was common in Japan at that time. U.S. Ambassador Grew reported several examples in the spring of 1941. In a translation of a speech by Hitler run in one of the English-language newspapers, for instance, a mischievous Japanese typesetter had changed "*Herrenvolk*, the master race," to "hairy horde, the monster ape."

MATSUOKA'S GRAND TOUR

On February 3, 1941, Prime Minister Konoye and the chiefs of
the Army and Navy met in liaison conference to consider Matsuoka's proposed trip to Berlin. They agreed that he was "voluble
and unconventional" and recommended that his powers and objectives be carefully explained to him before he set out. In particular they requested that Matsuoka make no promises to Hitler
about an immediate Japanese attack on Singapore.

Since the signing of the Tripartite Pact the German military
attachés in Tokyo had had a sand table set up at their embassy
to show Japanese visitors how easy it would be to take Singapore.
Naval members of Imperial Headquarters had witnessed the
table-top demonstrations and had returned tight-lipped to their
own charts of Japanese military capacity. Matsuoka had seen the
table-top maneuvers and had ever since taunted War Minister
Tojo with questions as to why Japan should not seize Singapore
at once. Tojo had responded by asking Foreign Minister Matsuoka why he had not yet forged the classic Eurasian alliance of
Germany, Russia, and Japan which geopoliticians had been saying for decades could someday dominate the earth.

As a result of the liaison conference of February 3, Hirohito
made his own personal study of recent diplomatic dispatches and
of Japan's foreign-policy posture. On February 7 he called in Lord
Privy Seal Kido and complained that the latest cables from Ambassador Kurusu Saburo in Berlin indicated a strong likelihood
that Germany would soon betray previous understandings with
Japan by attacking Russia. In such an eventuality, Hirohito asked,
was Japan obligated to give up the Strike South and assist Germany by a Strike North?

Kido did his best to soothe the Emperor by assuring him that
a German-Russian war would not break out immediately. Kido
acknowledged, however, that the Tripartite Pact with Germany
might create a serious problem if Japan, having already embarked
upon the Strike South, should be asked by Germany to "turn
around and go north again." Kido concluded that "we must therefore be extremely cautious in developing our Strike-South policy"
and that "we must use the opportunity of Matsuoka's impending

visit to Germany and Italy in order to get to the bottom of Hitler's and Mussolini's intentions."

Hirohito gave the problem several weeks' thought and then issued Foreign Minister Matsuoka strict instructions. In Italy and Germany he was to act purely in a private capacity and to find out as much as he could. In Moscow, however, he was to act officially and, if possible, conclude a neutrality pact with Stalin which would serve as an excuse for Japan not to join Germany in a war against Russia.

On March 3, the day Hirohito made clear to Matsuoka that these were his imperial wishes, Lord Privy Seal Kido met in another room of the palace with young Saionji Kinkazu, informing him that he was to accompany Matsuoka on his mission to Moscow and was to use all his left-wing connections to create a favorable atmosphere for talks between Matsuoka and Molotov, or between Matsuoka and Stalin. Saionji reported back to Ozaki, the Japanese agent who worked both with Soviet spy Sorge at the German Embassy and with Dr. Okawa of the spy service at the South Manchuria Railroad Research Institute. Ozaki duly briefed Sorge on the full background of Foreign Minister Matsuoka's trip abroad. Sorge then relayed his information to the Red Army's Fourth Bureau.

Sorge had always believed that the main purpose of his intelligence work in Tokyo was to prevent a Japanese attack on the Soviet Union. Now, in his radio dispatch to Siberia, he made it clear that Japan wished to strike south and needed only some assurance of Soviet neutrality in rear areas before doing so. The alternative, he stressed, might be Japanese participation in a German invasion of the Soviet Union.

After a parting audience with Hirohito on March 11,[4] Foreign Minister Matsuoka set out on March 12 with Saionji Kinkazu and other technicians to ride the long tracks of the Trans-Siberian Railway. He arrived in Moscow on March 15 and spent ten days there talking in a desultory way about the possibility of a Soviet-Japanese neutrality pact. Since he wanted Japan to fight Russia

[4] At which he proudly reported the conclusion of Japan's successful, self-interested mediation of the border dispute between Thailand and French Indochina. He made much of the fact that this was the first time that Japan had ever played the part of a Big-Power arbitrator.

as a preventive to the ills of fighting the United States, he did
not throw himself wholeheartedly into his task. With nothing
accomplished, he went on to Berlin, where he arrived on
March 26.

That night Hitler was preoccupied with an unforeseen political
coup in Yugoslavia which forced him to invade that country. He
postponed his state reception of Matsuoka until the next day,
March 27. He had already, three weeks earlier, written and circulated a memo to his officers explaining German objectives in
dealing with the Japanese foreign minister:

> It must be the aim of the collaboration based upon the Tripartite
> Pact to induce Japan as soon as possible to take active measures in
> the Far East. . . . Operation Barbarossa [the scheduled attack on
> Russia] will create most favorable political and military prerequisites.
> . . . The seizure of Singapore as the key British position in the Far
> East would mean a decisive success for the entire war conduct of the
> Three Powers. . . . The Japanese must not be given any intimation
> of the Barbarossa operation.

The state secretary of the German Foreign Office, Ernst Weizsacker, and the German naval commander in chief, Erich Raeder,
both disagreed with Hitler's desire to keep secrets from the Japanese and asked that Matsuoka be told about the planned invasion
of Russia.

On March 27, as soon as Hitler had delivered orders to deal
with the little problem of Yugoslavia, Matsuoka was given a
Wagnerian stage reception of black boots in goose step and of
dinner in full dress at the *Reichskanzlerei*. That night and for the
next week, Matsuoka remained closeted with the highest officials
of the Third Reich, spending the best part of four days with Ribbentrop and of four hours, on two occasions, with Hitler. He
learned that for the time being Hitler had definitely suspended
Operation Sea Lion, the invasion of England. Nevertheless, Ribbentrop pressed him to agree to an immediate Japanese attack
on British Malaya. Hitler told him that "never in the human imagination" had a nation been presented with such favorable opportunities. "The moment will never return. It is unique in history."
For once in his life Matsuoka listened and said little. "He sat there
inscrutably," wrote Ribbentrop's official secretary-translator, Dr.

Paul Schmidt, "in no way revealing how these curious remarks affected him."

As to Russia, Ribbentrop told Matsuoka that German-Soviet relations had become "correct but unfriendly." Hitler pointed out that the Reich had over 160 divisions massed on the Soviet frontier. Matsuoka and his aides had noticed the signs of preparations for war when they had passed through the Russian frontier the previous week. Ribbentrop admitted that a German war with Russia was "in the realm of possibilities" and assured Matsuoka that, if it broke out, the Reich would "crush the Soviet Union within a matter of months."

For his own part Matsuoka lied outrageously. He promised that he would work personally for a Japanese attack upon Singapore but would have to advocate such a move only "in hypothetical terms" for the moment because many influential "intellectuals" in Japan were still afraid of the Anglo-American partnership which had won the last world war. More forthrightly, Matsuoka revealed to the Germans that he was commissioned to seek an understanding with Russia which might free Japanese hands and make the contemplated attack on Singapore more attractive in terms of practical domestic politics. Ribbentrop warned him "not to get too close to Russia," assured him that Germany stood ready to attack Russia if Russia ever endangered Japan's rear, and finally agreed that a Russo-Japanese understanding would do no harm.

When Matsuoka had "sat inscrutably" for a week, eager to hear ever more and more of Ribbentrop's boastful persuasions, Ribbentrop's translator Dr. Schmidt noted that the proceedings were beginning to tax the "Gilbert-and-Sullivan" talents of the Third Reich's protocol officers. The dapper, energetic Matsuoka was a dwarf beside the sleek and bloated Ribbentrop. Cartoonists figured a shrewd sparrow beside a large pouter pigeon.

On April 1 Matsuoka sensed that his entertainment was growing wearisome to his hosts and gave them a brief respite by taking a two-day side-journey to Rome to talk with Mussolini. After enjoying Il Duce's most hospitable pomp he returned to Berlin for further soundings of German intentions. Hitler again granted him private audience and voluntarily committed himself to an assurance which Japan had not asked for: "If Japan gets into a conflict

with the United States, Germany on her part will take the necessary steps at once. . . . Germany will participate in case of a
conflict between Japan and America."

HUGGING THE BEAR

Matsuoka began his return to the East on April 6. Deceits were
buzzing in his ears but he traveled with a light heart for he had
revealed less truth than anybody else. Hitler demanded vehe-
mently that Japan play her part as an ally by attacking Singapore.
But Hitler was obviously planning a war soon with the Soviet Union
and would no doubt be satisfied if Japan waited a while and attacked Siberia instead. Hirohito favored the attack on Singapore
but was not yet ready for the concomitant of war with the United
States. He wanted Matsuoka to safeguard the Japanese rear in Manchuria by concluding a pact of mutual neutrality with Russia. If
necessary Matsuoka would have to obey his instructions. But later,
when the German-Soviet war broke out, he could tell Hirohito
that the totalitarian diplomats of the New Order regarded such
scraps of paper lightly. The Japanese Army General Staff had
wanted for decades to fight Russia. The *Wehrmacht*'s drive on
Moscow would provide the perfect opportunity. To spurn it
would be politically difficult for Hirohito. It looked as if, after all,
Matsuoka might be able to save Japan from war with the United
States and fulfill all his promises to friends in the West.

Arriving in Moscow on April 8, Matsuoka paid his first call not
on Foreign Commissar Molotov but on American Ambassador
Laurence Steinhardt. Over lunch he resumed with Steinhardt a
belly talk on the world situation which he had started fifteen days
earlier on his way to Berlin. In the course of these two conversations Matsuoka revealed much about his own motives. He wanted
Japan to avoid war with the United States, he said, because he
felt grateful for his boyhood years in Seattle. At the same time,
he warned, Japan might be obliged by the Tripartite Pact to fight
the United States if Roosevelt insisted on siding with Great Britain against Germany. Matsuoka made it clear that his friendly
feelings did not extend to the British and that he regarded them
as the despoilers and enslavers of the Orient. The sooner Hitler
conquered Great Britain, he said, the better. And he protested

that U.S. aid to Chiang Kai-shek and Churchill was prolonging war and misery on two continents.

In his outward-bound conversation with Steinhardt, Matsuoka had suggested that Japan was weary of war with China and might be willing to withdraw most of her forces from China if the United States would help by persuading Chiang Kai-shek to co-operate in saving the face of the Japanese Army. Matsuoka had added that U.S. leaders were naturally suspicious of him because of his action in leading Japan out of the League of Nations in 1933 but that they would find him a good friend if they would give him a chance. President Roosevelt, he said, was known as a shrewd poker player. Would he not gamble on Matsuoka's sincerity and assist him in the delicate task of handling anti-American elements in Tokyo? Finally Matsuoka stated that it was to the Soviet Union's advantage to encourage war between Japan and the United States.

Now, at his second meeting with Steinhardt, on April 8, Matsuoka was disappointed to learn that Steinhardt had cabled Washington the gist of his March twenty-fourth remarks but had not as yet received any response to the suggestion that Roosevelt should mediate the Sino-Japanese war. Matsuoka did not know that Steinhardt in his report home had discounted the possibility that the Japanese foreign minister could be sincere and had dwelt instead on his brash and boastful manners. So Matsuoka pressed ahead optimistically trying to persuade Steinhardt to plead his cause in Washington. He told Steinhardt that Hitler and Ribbentrop—he really meant Hirohito—were urging him to sign a neutrality pact with the Soviet Union and that he might have to comply. As yet, however, Foreign Commissar Molotov was asking Japanese concessions which Matsuoka thought he could represent at home as too high a price to pay.

Leaving Steinhardt to ruminate on these subtle considerations, Matsuoka went on, buoyantly, to see Foreign Commissar Molotov. Having piqued Molotov's curiosity by an apparent disinterest in advocating the proposed Soviet-Japanese pact, he at once left town for a sightseeing jaunt to the Hermitage art collection in Leningrad. Back in Moscow on April 12, after exerting his diplomatic charm as little as possible, he wired Tokyo that Molotov seemed unsympathetic and that the chance of concluding a pact with Russia was almost nil. The dour, pedantic Molotov that day would have been inclined to agree. Matsuoka had larded the conversations thus far with a liberal smear of insult and German propaganda. Molotov, however, did not know the full background as it was known to his master, Stalin.

Red Army Intelligence had received the cipher from Soviet spy Sorge in Tokyo explaining that the Konoye circle wanted the neutrality pact in order to free Japan to strike south. Young Saionji Kinkazu was in Moscow with Matsuoka, fully instructed by Lord Privy Seal Kido. He was telling all commissars to whom he had introductions that Japan wished to avoid joining in the German attack which well-informed Russians knew to be imminent. One justifying scrap of paper to weigh against the Tripartite Pact— that was all that Japan needed to remain on the sidelines.

From Lavrenti Beria's secret police apparatus and from the Red Army's Fourth Department, Stalin had access to the full particulars of the Saionji and Sorge representations. On the morning after Matsuoka's radiogram on the breakdown of negotiations, Stalin had a secretary phone Matsuoka and summon him at once to a private audience in the bed-sitting room where Stalin did most of his work.

Matsuoka took the offensive in the interview by lecturing Stalin on the meaning of the Japanese slogan *Hakko Ichiu*, Eight Corners Under One Canopy, which the first emperor, Jimmu, in the seventh century B.C. was supposed by mythologists to have proclaimed as the goal of the nation he was about to found. Matsuoka explained that the slogan did not mean that Japan hoped to conquer the earth but that Japan hoped to bring together all the peoples of the earth under one tent of mutual respect and comfort. Stalin fidgeted and listened impatiently for ten minutes and then interjected a single *da*, "Yes."

Then the conversation at once came down to business. Stalin urged that Japan sell him the southern Japanese half of Sakhalin, the island between Hokkaido and Kamchatka, which had been partitioned after the Russo-Japanese War of 1904–1905. Matsuoka replied that he was empowered to give away some Japanese coal and oil rights in the northern Russian half of Sakhalin but that the southern half of the island was now settled with Japanese and that Russia would be well advised to look for territorial expansion in the direction of Arabia and Iran rather than in islands near the Japanese homeland.

Stalin crinkled his mouth in a smile and said, "I agree." He pushed forward the proposed Japanese text of the Soviet-Japanese non-aggression pact and said, "Let's initial it." So they did and Matsuoka withdrew from the Kremlin greatly impressed and astonished.

The next day, April 14, less than forty-eight hours after his pessimistic cable home, an unexceptionable draft of the required pact lay before Matsuoka in his hotel suite, and Commissar Molotov was waiting to escort him to a celebration in the Kremlin. Stalin was again on hand and personally arranged the chairs for the speech making and vodka drinking which followed. When Matsuoka worried about missing his train home, Stalin called the commissar of transportation and told him to hold the Trans-Siberian express that night until whatever hour Matsuoka and his party might arrive at the station to board it.

At the end of the formal speeches, teetotaler Stalin raised a glass of red juice and boomed: "Banzai for the Emperor!"

In response Matsuoka raised his own glass and said: "The treaty has been made. I do not lie. If I lie, my head shall be yours. If you lie, rest assured that I will come for your head."

Stalin winced slightly and then said, with great seriousness, "My head is important to my country. So is yours to your country. Let's take care to keep both our heads on our shoulders."

Then Stalin toasted the Japanese delegation, taking special care to praise the contribution of its military members and of the Japanese ambassador, retired Lieutenant General "Peerless Pimp" Tatekawa.

"These military and naval men have concluded the neutrality pact from the standpoint of the general situation," replied Matsuoka mirthlessly, "but they are really always thinking of how to defeat the Soviet Union."

Stalin refused to be distracted by Matsuoka's surliness.

"The Japanese Army," he said, "is very strong. The United States may build a large navy but it will never have the spiritual strength of the Japanese Navy. Then again, I wish to remind all Japanese military men that Soviet Russia today is not the corrupt czarist imperial Russia which you once defeated."

After more toasts, Stalin said to Matsuoka, "You are an Asiatic and so am I."

Matsuoka raised his glass: "We're all Asiatics. Let's drink to Asiatics."

From the reception Stalin insisted on accompanying Matsuoka to the railroad station. On the platform he embraced the Japanese foreign minister and said, "The European problem can be solved naturally if Japan and the Soviet Union co-operate."

"Not only the European problem," echoed Matsuoka. "Even Asia can be solved."

"The whole world can be settled," said Stalin.

After enduring one final embrace, the diminutive Matsuoka boarded the waiting Trans-Siberian express and escaped from Stalin's hug.

KONOYE'S PEACE PLOT

On his way home from Moscow, Matsuoka dallied for five days of politicking in Manchukuo where he had spent the years 1935 to 1939 as president of the South Manchuria Railroad Company. There he explained his pact with Stalin to the leaders of the Kwantung Army and learned that he could still count on much Army support if he succeeded in turning Japan's war preparations from the south to the north. On April 20, when he was still in the Kwantung Leasehold port of Dairen, he received a telephone call from Prime Minister Prince Konoye, asking him to come home at once for an important conference.

In Matsuoka's absence, Konoye had secretly developed a plan of his own for starting the diversionary conversations in Washington which were called for as a part of the preparations for war. The previous fall two American Maryknoll Fathers had come to Tokyo to negotiate for the retention of Roman Catholic mission properties in Japan, Korea, and Manchuria which were in danger of government expropriation.[5] A few days before Christmas,

---

[5] The Konoye government, in a program reminiscent of 1601, was in proc-ess of de-emphasizing Christianity by organizing it into two denominations, one Catholic and one Protestant, both under the control of patriotic Japanese clerics.

The two Maryknoll Fathers were Bishop James Edward Walsh and Father James M. Drought. Father Drought appears to have been the most active of

1940, having had no luck in their mission, they were suddenly surprised by being allowed to see Foreign Minister Matsuoka in person. Matsuoka promised to do what he could for them if they would deliver a message for him to President Roosevelt. Matsuoka explained that he wanted to get in touch directly with the President, through a line that would be clear of tapping by the usual censors, code-breakers, and timid diplomatic officials, so that he and President Roosevelt could do something man to man about resolving the growing war tensions.

Word of Matsuoka's essay in private diplomacy leaked from his staff to Prime Minister Konoye. Konoye had the two Maryknoll Fathers summoned to his official residence and told that their efforts would be greatly enhanced if backed by the Army. The Fathers agreed and, to their surprise, were sent on to interviews with Rear Admiral Oka Takasumi, chief of the Naval Affairs Bureau in the Navy Ministry and Major General Muto Akira, chief of the Military Affairs Bureau in the War Ministry. These two veterans in Hirohito's cabal persuaded the Fathers that the military, in whom all real power in Japan was thought to reside, genuinely wanted to avoid war and had a concrete proposal to offer Roosevelt. Oka and Muto outlined the main points of the proposal and entrusted the working out of the final wording to the Fathers themselves and to a well-connected fixer and go-between of the financial world, Ikawa Tadao, who had been acting as their guide.

The salient points of the proposal were these: Japan would withdraw her troops from all but the northeastern corner of China in return for Chinese recognition of Manchukuo and a new Chinese government formed by merger of the Chiang Kai-shek and Wang Ching-wei regimes. The United States would help Japan procure oil, rubber, tin, and nickel in return for a promise that "Japanese activities in the southwestern Pacific area shall be carried on by peaceful means." The United States and Japan would act jointly to prevent the transfer of existing colonies in

the two. He died before the preparation of this book, but his part in the affair has been documented by Ladislas Farago, formerly of U.S. Naval Intelligence. Bishop Walsh was later imprisoned by the Chinese Communists and made headlines when he was released in 1970. His recollections differ in some slight details from Farago's account. For the most part Farago is followed here because his version fits best with Japanese sources.

the Far East from one European master to another, to guarantee the independence of the Philippines, and to persuade Great Britain to give up her Far Eastern "doorways" of Hong Kong and Singapore. Finally the United States would give "amicable consideration" to easing Japanese immigration to America and the southwestern Pacific area.

The two Maryknoll Fathers embarked for the United States on December 28, 1940, enthusiastic about the importance and realism of their mission. On arriving in San Francisco one of them telephoned a friend, financier Lewis Strauss, the later Atomic Energy Commission chairman, and asked him how best to proceed. Strauss provided an introduction to former President Hoover who was living in Palo Alto. Hoover suggested that the Fathers proceed at once to Washington and see Postmaster General Frank Walker, who was a Roman Catholic. On January 23, 1941, Postmaster Walker took the two peacemakers to the White House where they sat down in the Oval Study and explained the whole background of the Japanese proposal in a three-hour tête-à-tête with Roosevelt. The President was impressed by their story and by a memo which they left with him, stating in part:

> The Japanese government cannot admit, through official channels . . . that the Japanese would now welcome an opportunity to change their international, and modify their China, positions. . . . If the conservative authorities . . . can win, by diplomacy, a safe economic and international position, public opinion in Japan would restore the conservatives to complete control.

President Roosevelt welcomed the Japanese feeler. Like Prime Minister Konoye he felt that he needed time, politically as well as militarily, to prepare for entry into World War II. Over Secretary of State Cordell Hull's objections, he appointed Postmaster General Walker a "presidential agent," with a budget from the President's unvouchered funds, to run down the sincerity of the Japanese overture. Walker gave a go-ahead to the Maryknoll Fathers. On February 14, financier Ikawa, the guide who had led them through the bureaucratic labyrinths of Tokyo seven weeks earlier, arrived in San Francisco on the same ship with Admiral Nomura, Hirohito's new ambassador to Washington.

Ikawa, who had many friends on Wall Street and an American wife, quickly vouched for the authenticity of the proposal which the Fathers had brought home from Tokyo. To satisfy Postmaster General Walker that the proposal also had the backing of Japan's "militarists," Ikawa summoned from Tokyo Colonel Iwakuro Hideo, the chief of the Military Affairs Section of the War Ministry, a henchman of Military Affairs Bureau Chief Muto and a trusted subordinate of War Minister Tojo.[6] Colonel Iwakuro arrived in New York on March 21 and two weeks later, on April 5, a "draft understanding" which he and Ikawa had approved was submitted to President Roosevelt. The President was satisfied that it followed both the spirit and letter of the Fathers' original understanding and instructed Secretary of State Cordell Hull to present it to Ambassador Nomura as a basis for official U.S.-Japanese negotiations.

Hull's brilliant assistant on Oriental matters, Dr. Stanley Hornbeck, warned Postmaster General Walker: "Nothing that might be agreed upon between the American and the Japanese governments within the next few days or weeks will substantially alter the world situation in its material aspects. . . . The decision of Japanese leaders whether or not to move southward will be made in the light of the physical situation in Europe as they view it and the physical situation in the Pacific as they view it."

Nevertheless Hull presented the "draft proposal," as it was being called, to Ambassador Nomura for official transmission to Tokyo. Nomura cabled it on to Prime Minister Konoye on April 17, admitting knowledge of its background, stating its official U.S. government support, and asking for speedy action on it.

Konoye at once called the palace and explained all that had developed to Hirohito. The next morning Hirohito gave an audience to Ambassador Kurusu Saburo, the diplomat who had recently returned from Germany where he had signed the Tripartite Pact on behalf of Japan. Kurusu was to be sent later in the year to assist Ambassador Nomura in dragging out the nego-

---

[6] Iwakuro, after the ubiquitous Suzuki Tei-ichi, was the Army's leading economic wizard. He had been responsible for inviting the cartel of Ayukawa Gisuke, a U.S.-oriented believer in common stock and public ownership, to take over the muddled development of Manchukuo in 1936. After World War II Iwakuro would become the chief purchasing agent of U.S. arms for Japan's modern Self-Defense Forces.

tiations in Washington. After consulting Ambassador Kurusu, Hirohito summoned Prime Minister Konoye and told him to pursue the tack of the "draft proposal" as far as he wished but to remember that Japan must "keep faith with Hitler" and "must not jeopardize realization of the Greater East Asia Co-Prosperity Sphere."

The next day Konoye cleared the "draft proposal," as a basis for the U.S. negotiations, with the War and Navy ministers and with the two chiefs of staff, General Sugiyama and Admiral Nagano Osami.[7] It was then that Konoye phoned Matsuoka and asked him to cut short his triumphant progress through Manchuria and come home at once.

MATSUOKA'S STALL

Matsuoka deplaned at Tachikawa Air Base outside Tokyo on the morning of April 22. In his limousine, on the way to the palace to greet the Emperor, he was told by his vice minister about the Bishop Walsh negotiations in Washington. He pretended to be greatly put out that, during his magnificent accomplishments in Berlin and Moscow, others had usurped his office at home and begun making foreign policy without him. He knew that his government colleagues, as a matter of automatic Japanese etiquette, would defer to him if he seemed to feel that he had lost face. He had hoped to use the Bishop Walsh pipeline to draw Roosevelt into his private plan to embroil Japan in war with Russia. He was dismayed that his pipe had been uncovered and made into an official conduit. But now, as his future actions would show, he was resolved to subvert the Washington talks and break them off as quickly as possible. He saw that they were unrealistic. He knew that Hirohito and the Army and Navy would never concede enough to make possible a genuine settlement with the United States. He realized that formal diplomatic negotiations would be used by both sides to gain time for their own purposes. He could imagine that negotiations conducted in that spirit would only exacerbate ill will when they were broken off.

---

[7] Nagano had replaced Prince Fushimi as Navy chief of staff ten days earlier, thereby completing the imperial family's withdrawal from public posts of military responsibility. Prince Kanin had retired in favor of General Sugiyama as Army chief of staff the previous October.

When Matsuoka's limousine drew up in the palace at 7:30 P.M., he was received in audience immediately by Hirohito. He delivered a hurried report on his hobnobbing with the dictators of the world and gratefully accepted an invitation to take lunch with the Emperor four days later in order to reveal the full particulars. Then Matsuoka rushed on to the prime minister's official residence to attend a liaison conference with Konoye, the inner Cabinet, and the chiefs of staff.

At this conference Matsuoka gave an enthusiastic and boastful description of his dealings with Hitler and Stalin and then, when the negotiations with Roosevelt came up, dismissed them as just another feeler. Complaining of weariness after his long journeys, he excused himself at 11:00 P.M. and left his colleagues to deliberate alone on the Japanese response to the "draft proposal" forwarded by Ambassador Nomura. The military men stayed on with Prince Konoye for another eighty minutes and agreed to pursue the Washington negotiations "regardless of the foreign minister's attitude."

For the next ten days Matsuoka basked in attention, "recovered from fatigue," and refused to do anything about the note awaiting his reply from Ambassador Nomura. Finally on May 3 he dispatched an "interim reply," telling Nomura that the "draft proposal" was being studied and asking him to look into the possibility of concluding a full-scale neutrality pact with the United States which would obligate both countries to stay out of the war. When Chief of Staff Sugiyama pointed out to him that this posturing and procrastination would only succeed in making the United States distrustful of the negotiations, Matsuoka replied with an irrelevant taunt. If the Army had followed his advice and seized Singapore the previous autumn, he said, this whole difficult situation would never have come up.

On May 8 another liaison conference was called between Cabinet and Supreme Command to put pressure on Matsuoka and force him to authorize Ambassador Nomura to proceed with negotiations on the basis of the "draft proposal." Matsuoka continued to play for time. "It is my intention," he said, "to prevent the United States from entering the war, and to make her withdraw from China. So please don't rush me."

Navy Minister Oikawa replied that in his opinion the United

States did not want to enter the war; that she had everything to gain and nothing to lose by measures short of war; and that the time would never be riper than now for Japan to make a negotiated advance into Southeast Asia while the United States was preoccupied with helping Britain.

On the contrary, countered Matsuoka, the likelihood that the U.S. would not enter the war had recently decreased from 70 per cent to 60 per cent. His colleagues looked at one another in amusement at his American habit of bolstering arguments by quotation of exact but unfounded percentages. Then they listened seriously to his next statement.

"If the United States participates in the war, it will last a long time, and world civilization will be destroyed. If the war lasts ten years, Germany will fight the Soviet Union to secure war materials and food, and will then advance into Asia. What do you think would be the proper position of Japan at that time?"

The answer was implicit. Japan should side with the United States to secure Siberia and safeguard the western Pacific against German predation. No one at the liaison conference ventured to answer Matsuoka's question. As soon as the meeting had broken up, Matsuoka presented himself at the palace, asking for an audience. Hirohito had just returned to his desk in the Imperial Library after his usual light Japanese lunch of rice, fish, and vegetables. He summoned Lord Privy Seal Kido and kept Matsuoka waiting for forty minutes while he questioned Kido on "how to fathom Matsuoka and how to deal with him." Matsuoka was then admitted to Hirohito's presence at 2 P.M. and said, in the course of a long speech, "Unless we keep faith with Germany and Italy, I will have to resign."

Hirohito was only somewhat impressed by Matsuoka's protestations. After the audience, Lord Privy Seal Kido told Prime Minister Prince Konoye, who was waiting in an anteroom, "Matsuoka today has lost the imperial confidence."

The next day Prime Minister Konoye called a secret liaison conference between himself and the Army and Navy chiefs. Matsuoka was not invited or informed and the subject discussed was "how to deal with Matsuoka." Everyone present recognized that he had become a dangerous man, who could seriously disrupt the unity of the nation on the eve of war. The conclusion was reached, however, that Matsuoka must be given more rope before he could be eliminated.

By the following day, May 10, Hirohito himself was aware of the game Matsuoka was playing. To Konoye Hirohito complained: "Matsuoka says that an attack on Singapore will bring the United States into the war, and that that, in turn, will protract the world war and will force Germany, sooner or later, to invade the Soviet Union for war materials. Then Japan, he says, will have to denounce her neutrality pact with the Soviet Union and occupy Siberia as far as Irkutsk."

"It seems to me," concluded Hirohito, "that Matsuoka has been flighty ever since his return from Europe and that you should start considering a replacement for him."

MATSUOKA'S TREASON

If Hirohito had known the full extent of Matsuoka's "flightiness" he might have commanded the foreign minister to disembowel himself. On May 2 Dr. Heinrich Stahmer, the chief of Japanese-Reich relations in the German Foreign Ministry, had called Ambassador Oshima in Berlin to tell him, with icy hysteria: "It has been established that the U.S. government is reading Ambassador Nomura's coded messages." Oshima cabled this appalling news to Matsuoka on May 3. Matsuoka considered it for two days and then cabled Nomura in Washington: "It appears almost certain that the U.S. government is reading your code messages." At the same time Matsuoka urgently requested further particulars from Oshima.

In Berlin Oshima could learn only that his clearance for briefings on German preparations for war with Russia had been revoked, effective April 30, and that his earlier reports home on German war preparations had somehow got into the hands of the U.S. government which had made them available to the Soviet government. Since these reports had been sent to Tokyo and then relayed to Nomura in Washington in Japan's highest-security code, it was apparent that either the Americans could read the code or a high official in the Japanese Foreign Service was a traitor. Matsuoka at once ordered a complete security investigation of the Japanese Embassy in Washington, of Oshima's staff in

Berlin, and of his own Foreign Ministry Telegraphic Section in
Tokyo.

In Washington the U.S. Army's Signal Intelligence Service
and the U.S. Navy's Op-20-G, the two cryptanalytic units in
the intelligence sections of the armed services, ordered their
own outraged investigations. Decoded intercepts of the frenzied
Matsuoka-Oshima-Nomura exchange revealed that the U.S. ability to read Japan's top-secret messages was now, itself, an exposed
secret. This meant that one of the handful of U.S. officials cleared
to read *Magic*—as the decoded intercepts were called—had talked
too much. Worse, it meant that the Japanese would probably
change their codes—change them on the eve of war when there
might not be time to break any new codes.

U.S. cryptanalysis of Japanese government messages had begun in 1922 during the post-World War I Washington Naval Limitations Conference. It had continued more or less regularly ever
since, first in the State Department, then in the office of Naval
Intelligence, then in the offices of both Naval and Army Intelligence. In 1928 the original genius of this eavesdropping effort,
Herbert O. Yardley, had grown so disgruntled by lack of appreciation for his head-splitting efforts that he had turned traitor and
sold the secret of his work to the Japanese for $7,000.[8] As a result
the Japanese had learned early of American cryptanalytic inge-
nuity and had taken pains ever since to change and improve their
codes frequently.

In Yardley's day the Japanese codes had been manually con-
trived jumblings of the seventy possible syllables used in the
difficult Japanese language. Then in 1931 the Japanese had begun
to use mechanical encoding and decoding devices which jumbled
the syllables many more times and in many more ways than could
be readily worked out with pencil and paper. With the help of
mathematical analysis, call girls, fake power failures, and outright
safecracking, U.S. Naval Intelligence finally built its own replicas
of these first-generation Japanese coding machines in 1935, when
they had been in use for four years.

---

[8] Because of extenuating circumstances and the amount of undivulged information which Yardley still possessed, he was not tried for treason. Instead
he returned to U.S. government payrolls during World War II and was buried
with military honors at Arlington Cemetery in 1958.

Without realizing that their first machine, known to U.S. experts as the Red machine, had been compromised, Japanese cryptographers went on in 1937 from a mechanical coding device to one of the world's first electronic coding devices. Entirely Japanese in conception, it remained entirely baffling to U.S. cryptanalysts for twenty months of brainstorming. Then, in the twentieth month, August–September 1940, a young Army cryptologist, Harry Lawrence Clark, re-conceived the type of circuitry which the Japanese were using. The operatives of the Signal Intelligence Service built a generalized machine embodying Clark's principle, and by trial and error, plugging in its various possible interconnections on a sort of telephone switchboard, they finally managed to duplicate the actual circuits of the Japanese original. The U.S. Purple machine began to produce fully intelligible texts of Japanese cables and telegrams on September 25, 1940, the day before the signing of the Tripartite Pact in Berlin.

It was this monumental decipherment of Code Purple, the highest code of the Japanese government, that seemed suddenly wasted eight months later when Code-Purple messages from Matsuoka, Oshima, and Nomura revealed that the Japanese no longer had confidence in the code's security. Specially cleared agents of the F.B.I. investigated the offices of every one of the dozen or so U.S. statesmen who had access to translations of Purple messages. The investigation revealed that President Roosevelt's personal aides were sometimes lax and had left at least one copy of a decoded Japanese telegram crumpled up in an ordinary White House wastepaper basket.[9]

In the end, however, the F.B.I.'s investigators traced the security leak which had caused the damage not to the White House but to the State Department. In early April 1941, when Ambassador Oshima in Berlin had first started cabling sure warning to Tokyo of the German attack on Russia, one of his intercepted cables had been shown to Under Secretary of State Sumner Welles. Welles was not on the regular distribution list of officials who saw every

---

[9] As a consequence, from May to November 1941, F.D.R. was no longer allowed to handle *Magic* messages personally. Instead he was briefed on them by his naval aide, Captain John Beardall, who was permitted to read them, without taking notes, in the presence of a duly cleared pouch carrier at the Office of Naval Intelligence.

item circulated by *Magic* but on a subsidiary list of officials who
were given a glimpse of *Magic* messages when they were judged
to have "a need to know." As a result Welles did not appreciate
the full importance of *Magic* nor the years of intellectual labor
which had made *Magic* possible. His "need to know" was determined by a project he was working on: to bring the Soviet Union
out of the spell of Hitler's strength to the side of the Anglo-
American alliance. For this purpose he had shown a *Magic* translation of one of Ambassador Oshima's Purple-Code dispatches on
the forthcoming Russo-German war to the Soviet ambassador in
Washington, Constantin Oumansky. Oumansky had then confronted the German ambassador in Washington, Dr. Hans Thomsen, with it, and Thomsen had warned Ribbentrop in Berlin that
Japanese security was not secure.

While U.S. intelligence officers waited in misery for a completely new departure in Japanese coding techniques, Foreign
Minister Matsuoka and one of his old cronies from Manchuria,
the chief of the Telegraphic Section in the Foreign Ministry, conducted their investigation of everyone connected with the codes at
home and abroad. Originally Japanese naval officers had invented
the Purple Code and had built the Purple-Code machines with
Foreign Ministry funds. Now, however, the highest-security naval
communications were all being dispatched in the new Admirals'
Code, developed at the insistence of Yamamoto and sure to remain uncracked for many months to come. Army codes, too, were
not in question and Ambassador Oshima in Berlin was an Army
man, a lieutenant general. For these reasons Matsuoka and the
Telegraphic Section chief in the Foreign Ministry were able to
conclude their investigation with a whitewash.

On May 19, Matsuoka submitted a report on his investigation
to the Cabinet and to the palace stating that no traitors had been
uncovered, that the machine codes of both Red and Purple remained unbreakable, and that the security leaks alleged by the
Germans were the results of routine American cryptanalysis of
messages sent in the old-fashioned, paper-and-pencil, subsidiary
codes of Japan. These lesser codes would now be revised, but
Code Purple and Code Red would continue to be used and could
be considered fail-safe.

Matsuoka and a number of the clerks under him knew that Oshima's intelligence regarding German war with Russia had never been entrusted to one of the subsidiary pencil-and-paper codes. Yet Matsuoka succeeded ostensibly in persuading Hirohito and the Navy General Staff that Code Purple was still secure. For the remaining six months before Pearl Harbor, all top-secret Japanese diplomatic messages went on being sent in Code Purple and being read by U.S. intelligence officers in Army S.I.S. and Navy Op-20-G.

The American beneficiaries of Matsuoka's generosity could not at first believe their own good fortune. They warned that future Purple messages might all be intentional obfuscations and distractions. But as time wore on, they became convinced that Matsuoka had blundered and left unguarded the innermost citadels of Japanese deceit.

Perhaps Matsuoka meant to leave the United States with access to Japanese secrets or perhaps he wished to save the Foreign Ministry from disgrace at a time when it needed all its influence. Perhaps Admiral Yamamoto and others, sophisticated in intelligence work, knew of Matsuoka's whitewash and used it later to give U.S. eavesdroppers an unwarranted sense of complacency. Then, again, perhaps the naval liaison officers attached to the telegraphic section of the Foreign Ministry were bribed and blackmailed by Matsuoka's men to hold their tongues. In the lack of documentary evidence, it may be assumed that both Japanese and American intelligence experts acted with professional competence and tried to allow for all possibilities.

MATSUOKA'S MADNESS

Having hushed up the Code-Purple scandal at the Foreign Ministry in mid-May 1941, Matsuoka went on throughout late May and all of June to wage an extraordinary campaign of double talk within the councils of the Japanese government—a campaign which sounded patriotically belligerent and anti-American but which, at the same time, delayed Strike-South preparations and vitiated the negotiations in Washington. He had many silent allies in his efforts who joined him because they recognized that a desperate breakdown in faith threatened between the will of the people and the will of Hirohito, the people's god.

At noon on May 12 Matsuoka gave in after three weeks of urging from Prime Minister Konoye and the Army and Navy leaders and cabled Ambassador Nomura a revised version of the Maryknoll Fathers' "draft proposal" for improving U.S.-Japanese relations. U.S. Secretary of State Cordell Hull noticed at once that Matsuoka's revised draft omitted the previous Japanese pledge to use only peaceful, nonmilitary means in advancing Japan's position in the southwestern Pacific.

To make absolutely sure that the United States would not feel conciliatory, Matsuoka two days later called on Ambassador Grew and told him "that the 'manly, decent and reasonable' thing for the United States to do would be to declare war openly on Germany." Grew considered Matsuoka's harangue, though delivered off the cuff in an unofficial chat, "bellicose both in tone and substance." Lord Privy Seal Kido heard of Matsuoka's rudeness and promptly sent Grew a message begging him not to feel too put out. Prime Minister Konoye and Navy Minister Oikawa both let Grew know that they would prevent any hasty action by the foreign minister. At liaison conferences on May 12 and 15, Matsuoka's government colleagues did indeed question the soundness of his diplomatic technique. Matsuoka, however, insisted that he knew best how to handle Americans and how to make Roosevelt back down.

Nothing that happened in the following week tended to vindicate Matsuoka in his claims. Nomura reported pessimistically on U.S. reactions. Oshima cabled from Berlin that he had had to soothe Ribbentrop by telling him that the purpose of the Washington negotiations was to give "the pro-American groups among the Japanese people the impression that reconciliation between Japan and the United States is impossible." In Java the Dutch colonial government was so unintimidated by Matsuoka's big talk that the head of the Japanese negotiating team there reported deadlock and demanded that he be recalled to Japan so that he could spend his time in some more useful service.

Prime Minister Prince Konoye called a liaison conference of the Cabinet and General Staff chiefs on May 22 to talk over these negative results. Hirohito sent his thirty-six-year-old brother Prince Takamatsu to sit in on the proceedings as a member of the Navy General Staff.[10] Nothing daunted, Matsuoka put in one of his better performances, conjuring up bewildering geopolitical contingencies on almost every continent. Finally the level-headed Prince Takamatsu intervened personally in an effort to pin Matsuoka down:

MATSUOKA: I would like to discontinue negotiations with the Netherlands East Indies and recall Yoshizawa. I would also like to have the timing left up to me.

A CERTAIN PERSON [PRINCE TAKAMATSU]: I can well understand that the present attitude of the Netherlands East Indies brings us to the point of recalling Yoshizawa; but it is British and American support that allows the East Indies to assume this sort of stance. If we take this final step against the East Indies [of ceasing to negotiate], it means pushing forward with military operations for Malaya and even for the Philippines. It is therefore a grave decision, by which the nation will sink or swim, and such matters as scheduling and implementation must be given sufficient thought.

MATSUOKA: If we do not make up our minds, won't Germany, Britain, the United States, and the Soviet Union be united in the end and bring pressure to bear on Japan? It is possible that Germany and the Soviet Union may form an alliance and turn against Japan, and also possible that the United States may begin a war with Japan. I would like to know how the Army and Navy chiefs of staff intend to deal with such eventualities.

ARMY CHIEF OF STAFF SUGIYAMA: This is a serious matter. For the Malayan part of this decision alone, we must first lay a foundation in Thailand and French Indochina from which to mount our operations. I fully explained this point at one of the previous Liaison Conferences. The Foreign Minister has not yet done anything [about

---

[10] Army Chief of Staff Sugiyama, who took the only available minutes of the liaison conferences, complies with the imperial taboo by calling Prince Takamatsu simply *Bo*, a Certain Person. Gossip alone identifies *Bo* as the prince, and men in a position to know do not deny the identification. Moreover, at the eight important liaison conferences in which he took part—those of May 22 and 29, June 12, 16 and 25, August 16 and September 20 and 25 —*Bo* cut short generals and grilled ministers of state with an incisive authority unimaginable in anyone of lesser rank.

negotiating bases for us in Thailand and south Indochina], and I would like to be told why.

MATSUOKA: Before we proceed against Thailand and French Indochina, we must decide what to do about Britain and the United States. We cannot enter into negotiations without having our minds made up on this point. I will go ahead as soon as we have made up our minds.

NAVY MINISTER OIKAWA: What about Matsuoka's mind? Hasn't he gone queer in the head?[11]

And so it went for two hours. Leaving the Dutch East Indies question undecided, Matsuoka skipped on over the China problem and the German alliance problem. The other conferees did not hesitate to echo Oikawa's doubt about Matsuoka's sanity but they did hesitate to make the brilliant, famous foreign minister lose face by overruling him. Near the end of his performance Matsuoka gave a hint of the hope on which he was banking in his madness—the hope that Germany would soon suck Japan into a sensible, safe war with Russia. He introduced into the record a quote from one of the recent telegrams sent from Berlin by the Japanese ambassador there, Lieutenant General Oshima:

I [Oshima] said [to Ribbentrop] . . . in regard to the Japanese attitude in case of a war between Germany and the Soviet Union, I daresay the attitude of the Imperial Government will not be easily decided. Finally it will be up to the Emperor to decide.

LAST STRIKE-NORTH PLOT

Playing for time, refusing to facilitate the spurious negotiations with the United States, refusing also to start negotiations for Strike-South bases in Indochina and Thailand, Matsuoka weathered another liaison conference on May 29. He maintained plausibly that most Americans shared his own anti-British, anti-Chinese, anti-Communist bias and that they would soon force Roosevelt to accommodate himself to Japan's leadership position in Asia and need for *Lebensraum*. Home Minister Hiranuma, the long-faced lawyer of the conservative business community's Na-

11 *Matsuoka wa atama ga hen de wa nai ka?*

tional Foundation Society, sided with Matsuoka. Long a proponent of war with Russia, he was waiting, like Matsuoka, for the
outbreak of war between Germany and the Soviet Union. In vain
Prince Takamatsu sought to saddle Matsuoka with some responsibility for having originated the unfortunate conversations with
the United States.

"Didn't you get an American priest," he asked, "to start things
off?"

"No," said Matsuoka. "I did not. I know who did, but please do
not press me now to tell you who it was."

Prince Takamatsu fell silent, knowing that it had been Prime
Minister Prince Konoye.

Finally, on June 5, the long-awaited cable arrived from General
Oshima in Berlin saying that Hitler had officially informed him
that the Third Reich would soon open war on Russia. Oshima
advised Tokyo that, if an attack could not yet be mounted against
Great Britain in Singapore, it would be well to co-operate with
Hitler by striking at the Soviet rear in Siberia.

The next day, June 6, a brief liaison conference was held which
was so secret that Chief of Staff Sugiyama kept no notes on it.
Lord Privy Seal Kido's diary suggests that the Emperor may
have attended it personally for twenty-five minutes. According to
Hirohito's report to Kido later in the day, Matsuoka was insisting
that there was still a 60 per cent chance of a German-Russian
reconciliation but that until the outcome was clear all Japanese
negotiations and decisions should be postponed. Certainly the
Foreign Ministry should not now antagonize the United States
by asking the French colonial government of Indochina for bases
within striking distance of Singapore.

The next day, on June 7, at still another liaison conference,
Matsuoka greatly enlarged the areas for doubt by musing, "I wonder whether Hitler's intention to wage war is actually based on
his reported intentions to smash communism. I wonder if instead
he does not intend to attack [Russia] because the war is going to
last for twenty or thirty years."

"I think," added Chief of Staff Sugiyama, in a parenthesis in
the notes that he was taking, "that we will have to be alert to the
possibility of a reconciliation between Britain and Germany." In
short a Japanese move on Singapore was rapidly losing its most

attractive aspects. Germany might begin to prefer a Japanese move against Russia and Great Britain might feel free to send back adequate defense forces to Singapore. In the days that followed urgent messages went out from the officials of the War Ministry to the military aides at the embassies in Berlin and Rome asking for immediate warning of any signs of slackening in Anglo-German hostility.

In the impending Russo-German war, Matsuoka had at last found a good issue which brought him allies. The officers of the General Staff who had grown up with the mission of fighting a continental war against Russia began to smile at him during conferences and listen to his arguments. Even some members of the imperial family—notably Prince Higashikuni and Prince Fushimi—began to show sympathy for his views. If Hitler would only do what he promised this time, Hirohito might be induced to postpone his inherited crusade against the land of Perry and to capitalize on this golden opportunity by stealing through Russia's back door and seizing half the empire of the czars.

Hirohito and Prince Takamatsu, however, were not easily diverted. In the second week of June Hirohito read and approved a General Staff document entitled "Acceleration of the Policy Concerning the South." It called for immediate negotiations with the French in Indochina to allow Japanese troops to move into Saigon and the Mekong Delta and establish airfields and training centers. It resolved that French refusal would be countered by armed force and that in case of British, U.S., and Dutch intervention, Japan would "not refuse to risk a war with Britain and the United States." At a liaison conference on June 12, Matsuoka voiced innumerable objections both to the negotiations and to the posture of military threat envisaged in this plan. Finally that Certain Person, Prince Takamatsu, asked him, "Do you agree to using military force? Or do you disagree?"

"I do not disagree," said Matsuoka. But then he introduced a number of editorial quibbles which he wished to see embodied in the text of the accelerated program under consideration.

"How about the following arrangement?" cut in Prince Takamatsu. "Keep everything secret, adopt the present draft, and add the following clauses as understandings: first, we agree that we will finally execute the plan as it stands; second, since we will need time anyway to prepare troop movements, we will negotiate in two separate escalating stages; third, when the first-stage negotiations are complete, we will go on at once to the second-stage negotiations."

Matsuoka said that he agreed and was given time to consider matters of wording.

At the next liaison conference, on June 16, it quickly emerged that he had not agreed. He complained that previous agreements with Indochina would be invalidated by the new plan and that the Japanese presence in northern Indochina would become illegal. He warned that Japan would suffer reprisals and would probably lose her present supply of rubber, tin, and rice from the Dutch East Indies.

"If Vichy," he said, "does not agree to the occupation, it would be bad faith to force it on her. The previously signed treaty has not yet been ratified. Occupation by force is an act of bad faith. Japan is said internationally to lack integrity. I will fight for our international reputation, even if I have to fight all by myself."

Finally, Matsuoka, in so many words, threatened to expose the Emperor before the press. "Frankly," he said, "as the nation's foreign minister, I will have to report to the Emperor that this is an act of bad faith."

Chief of Staff Sugiyama tried politely to draw attention away from the threat by explaining the need to equip airfields in Indochina before the typhoon season in November. Navy Minister Oikawa chimed in with a remark to the effect that the Navy had never considered one of the possibilities raised by Matsuoka—that of an Anglo-Russian alliance—and would like time to investigate it.

Prince Takamatsu, however, was not to be put off. Looking blackly at Matsuoka, he said, "Can't you change your mind?"

"No," replied Matsuoka bravely, "I cannot."

Tojo intervened to emphasize the need for "finishing the job" in Indochina before the end of the year.

Matsuoka refused to budge from his threatening stance. "It is necessary, is it not," he said, "to make an official report to His Majesty about these preparations. . . . All this has happened because you didn't take Singapore last year as I suggested. When are we going to report officially on this matter to His Majesty? I would like you to give some thought as to how we may report to His Majesty."

"Thus," wrote Chief of Staff Sugiyama, "the meeting was adjourned so that the matter could be studied for two or three days."

HITLER'S INVASION OF RUSSIA

On June 21, after forty days of consideration, U.S. Secretary of State Cordell Hull gave Ambassador Nomura in Washington an American revision of the Japanese revision of the "draft proposal" for friendlier relations with the United States. What had once been a trenchant clarification of the two nations' mutual interests and disagreements had become, in the latest version, a pleasant but wordy expression of U.S. philosophy regarding treaties, trade, and the rule of free enterprise under law. Hull had, of course, been reading the uninterrupted flow of telegrams from Berlin to Tokyo and from Tokyo to Washington in the Purple Code which Matsuoka had kept in use after he knew it had been broken. As a result Hull indicated that—like Matsuoka—he did not expect his conversations with Nomura to succeed. Their function was only to gain time. To make sure of this point, he took another page from Matsuoka's book by accompanying his note with an Oral Statement. In it, pointing an insulting finger at the insulting Matsuoka, he said: "Some Japanese leaders in influential positions are definitely committed to . . . support of Nazi Germany. . . . So long as such leaders . . . seek to influence public opinion in Japan, . . . is it not illusory to expect . . . results along the desired lines?"

Hull dispatched this dishearteningly realistic missive to Tokyo at a time when he knew it would receive scant attention. A few hours later, as he and other well-informed statesmen had expected for several days, 160 divisions of highly mechanized German troops, protected overhead by the best squadrons of the *Luftwaffe*, poured into Russia. The world had never seen such a powerful army of invasion but no one in the chancelleries of the world was surprised. Japanese observers were particularly well informed on the war because they had been passing through the Russo-German frontier repeatedly in the preceding weeks, their binoculars focused, their cameras snapping. They had seen the flatcars of war materials and the crowds of uniforms on the German side and the placid farmlands on the Russian side. They knew that the Red Army High Command had brought back 150,000 of its best troops to European Russia from Siberia but they saw no signs of Russian fortifications between Warsaw and Moscow. Despite the lesson taught to Napoleon more than a century earlier, they did not appreciate Russia's reliance on sheer width of territory. They could not understand Stalin's confidence in the dependability of the Russian peasant at a time of sacrifice. They could not credit Stalin's ruthlessly realistic strategy of letting his land swallow Hitler's shiny host. They could only believe that the Third Reich would win in a matter of months.

As soon as the news of the German attack was fully confirmed, Japanese Foreign Minister Matsuoka called at the palace and asked Hirohito for an immediate Japanese invasion of Siberia. When Hirohito inquired what was to be done with the carefully prepared plans for the Strike South, Matsuoka recklessly spoke of fighting first Russia, then Great Britain, then the United States, and finally all three together. Hirohito ordered Prime Minister Prince Konoye and Lord Privy Seal Kido to investigate the foreign minister's "true intentions." On June 24, they reported back to the Throne that as far as they could tell, Matsuoka really did propose a two-front war on the north as well as the south. Hirohito postponed the liaison conference scheduled for that day so that he could review the military situation with the Army Chief of Staff Sugiyama. Matsuoka had gained in political strength from Hitler's move, and Hirohito needed to assure himself of the Army's determination to proceed according to plan.

He gave audience to Army Chief of Staff Sugiyama early on the afternoon of June 25. Sugiyama reiterated the arguments for the approved imperial policy of striking south. The ABCD powers— American, British, Chinese, and Dutch—said Sugiyama, were daily strengthening their "encirclement" of Japan. If the nation was to move forward toward the Co-Prosperity Sphere in Asia, Japan would have to secure bases at once in southern Indochina. Sugiyama emphasized the need for carrying out the occupation of southern Indochina by diplomacy if possible, but conceded that Japan should be ready to use force. Hirohito assented and asked specific questions about the dispatch of troops. How much would

it cost? Which divisions would be used? Where precisely would
the south Indochina bases and airstrips be built? At the end of
the briefing, Hirohito said, "I am greatly worried about international repercussions, but let it pass."

Army Chief of Staff Sugiyama left with Hirohito six detailed position papers: the first, an explanation of the strategic reasons for
securing bases in south Indochina; the second, a list of U.S. and
British preparations and provocations in 1941; the third, an intelligence assessment of ABCD military strength; the fourth, a
count of ABCD aircraft in the entire area of the southwestern
Pacific; the fifth, an evaluation of ABCD economic strategy for the
containment of Japan; the sixth, an evaluation of enemy political
strategy.

The postponed liaison conference was held later that afternoon.
The original purpose of the meeting had been to get Matsuoka's
approval of a revised version of the "Acceleration of the Policy
Concerning the South"—a version which left out the assertion
that Japan was ready to risk war with Great Britain and the
United States. Matsuoka gave an airy token acquiescence to the
Indochina acceleration plan in the opening minutes of the conference and then went on to fascinate all present by discussing the
implications of the Russo-German war. Navy Minister Oikawa
stated the Navy's firm opposition to a two-front war and then
begged Matsuoka: "In any case please don't talk so much about
the future."

Matsuoka said: "When Germany wins and disposes of the Soviet Union, we can't share in the spoils of victory without having
done something. We have either to shed blood or engage in diplomacy. It's best to shed blood. The question is what Japan should
want when the Soviet Union is disposed of. Germany is probably
wondering what Japan is going to do. Aren't we going to war when
the enemy forces in Siberia have gone westward? Shouldn't we at
least make a diversionary move? Whatever we do, I hope we will
hurry up and decide what it is."

The Certain Person, Prince Takamatsu, said, "Yes, but whatever we do, we must not do it prematurely."

Having adjourned on this inconclusive note, the conferees met
again the next day, and the day after, and again on June 28, June
30, and July 1. Throughout this almost continuous liaison con-

ference between the highest potentates of the Japanese state, Matsuoka filibustered and squirmed, made concessions and promptly retracted them.

On June 26 he ended the conference by saying, "I agree . . . but I won't put my agreement in writing."

On June 27 he protested: "I would like a decision to attack the Soviet Union. . . . You tell me to engage in diplomacy, but I don't think our negotiations with the United States will last much longer."

On June 28 he said: "To strike south is like playing with fire; and if we strike south we will probably go to war against Britain and the United States and the Soviet Union too. . . . I don't believe that now is the best time to enter the war, given the general situation. . . . The Navy has expressed the view that it is absolutely opposed to entering the war but it will not say so openly. . . . I would be pleased if our operations toward French Indochina were suspended."

On June 30, Matsuoka proposed a six-month postponement of the occupation of southern French Indochina. Navy Minister Oikawa whispered wistfully to Army Chief of Staff Sugiyama, "How about postponing it for six months?" The Navy's vice chief of staff echoed to the Army's vice chief of staff, Lieutenant General Tsukada Osamu, "Yes, let's think about postponing it for six months." However, Lieutenant General Tsukada—a charter member of the cabal, a life-long friend of Prince Asaka, and the chief of staff inserted under poor little General Matsui before the rape of Nanking—pointed out that the occupation of southern Indochina had already been sanctioned by the Emperor and "must be carried out."

Matsuoka made his last stand by predicting disaster in a Strike South and by challenging Chief of Staff Sugiyama to see any other outcome. Matsuoka concluded by saying, "If we occupy southern Indochina it will become difficult to secure oil, rubber, tin, and rice. Great men should be able to change their minds."

This implied slur on the greatness of the Emperor lost Matsuoka his staunchest supporter in the debate. The long-faced rightist lawyer Hiranuma, home minister and president of the conservative businessmen's National Foundation Society, responded coldly: "I, too, think we should go north. The question is whether we can. And in this we must follow the thinking of the military."

The leaders of the Army had already explained, on several occasions, that they could not mount an offensive ground war against Siberia as long as three quarters of the Army's available divisions were tied down in China. On behalf of the Navy, Chief of Staff Nagano now concurred. "If we get involved in the north," he said, "we will have to switch around all the preparations we are now making from south to north. This would take at least fifty days."

And so ended Matsuoka's desperate struggle to reverse imperial policy. Army, Navy, and right-wing politicians and businessmen had all supported him in his last-minute promotion of a Strike-North policy but none of them had been willing to go as far as he had in making noisy speeches and in laying down careers for principle.

At a meeting of the Supreme War Council later that night, the members of the imperial family went out of their way to inscribe in the record their own openmindedness toward the possibility of a Strike North. General Prince Asaka, the imperial uncle who had overseen the rape of Nanking, said, "It appears that we are sitting on the fence. Which is first, North or South? Personally, I think North might be best first."

Hirohito's other uncle, Prince Higashikuni, who was also a full general now, inquired archly, "What is the goal of going south?"

In replying, Army Chief of Staff Sugiyama chose his words carefully, for he knew that he was taking full responsibility for the decision which had been made. "There are," he said, "several possible timetables and methods for moving south, but for the purpose of survival and self-defense, we are thinking of going as far as the Netherlands East Indies—"

"From what the Navy tells me," interjected Prime Minister Prince Konoye, "we are not going all the way in one stroke. For the moment we will go as far as French Indochina. After that we will proceed step by step."

"Compared with the way Germany does things," laughed General Prince Asaka, "we are being pretty cautious, aren't we?"

"That's true," said Konoye, "but this is a matter of grave concern to our national fate. It is not hypothetical; it cannot be treated lightly."

The next day, July 1, 1941, Matsuoka surrendered as gracefully as he could. It was agreed at a liaison conference to proceed with the occupation of southern Indochina and with preparations for the Strike South. At the same time it was agreed that the Kwantung Army in Manchuria should be reinforced against the possible contingency of war with Russia. In regard to Manchuria, however, Army Vice Chief of Staff Tsukada said: "We are making preparations all right, but our intention is to get the minimum number of troops ready for action. We have no idea of preparing an unnecessarily large number of troops."

At the end of the conference, having surrendered unconditionally, Foreign Minister Matsuoka sought to maintain his future influence by declaring: "Things have turned out pretty well. That's because I listened to the opinions of all of you."

MATSUOKA'S OUSTER

On the day of Matsuoka's surrender, July 1, 1941, President Roosevelt in Washington sent a letter to Secretary of the Interior Harold Ickes, who was also petroleum administrator for national defense. He wished to persuade Ickes that the time had not yet come to force Japan into a corner by cutting off her oil supplies. "The Japs," wrote the President, "are having a real drag-down and knock-out fight among themselves and have been for the past week—trying to decide which way they are going to jump—attack Russia, attack the South Seas (thus throwing in their lot definitely with the Germans) or whether they will sit on the fence and be more friendly with us. No one knows what the decision will be but, as you know, it is terribly important for the control of the Atlantic for us to help keep peace in the Pacific. I simply have not got enough Navy to go round. . . ."

Unknown to the President, Hirohito had already opted to jump south and—at least to his own satisfaction—had settled the knockdown, dragout fight. That is, he had settled the fight in policy-making circles. In Army and Navy staff-officer circles it would rage on for another fortnight.

On July 2, the day after Roosevelt penned his letter, Hirohito and all his responsible ministers convened to approve the go-ahead into south Indochina and to reject the golden opportunity offered by a distracted Russia and an ill-defended Siberia. At this full-dress palace conference in the Imperial Presence, the conferees considered and adopted a long position paper entitled "Outline of National Policies in View of the Changing Situation." The key passages were only three:

Our Empire is determined to follow a program which will result in the establishment of the Greater East Asia Co-Prosperity Sphere. . . .

Preparations for war with Great Britain and the United States will be made. . . .

Our attitude in regard to the German-Soviet war will be based on the spirit of the Tripartite Pact. We will not enter the conflict for the time being. We will secretly strengthen our military preparedness against the Soviet Union. . . . If the German-Soviet war should develop to the advantage of our Empire, we will, by resorting to armed force settle the Northern Question.

Prime Minister Konoye, Army Chief of Staff Sugiyama, and Navy Chief of Staff Nagano all entered statements in favor of this program. Foreign Minister Matsuoka filed a lone dissent, pleading for a re-evaluation of national policy in light of the "new situation arising out of the outbreak of war between Germany and the Soviet Union." He predicted that Japan would never get what she wanted in the south by negotiating in Washington and would finally be forced into the dreadful alternative of war. In conclusion he stated glumly: "I believe that our Empire is confronted literally with a danger that has no precedent."

When Matsuoka had lapsed silent, his struggle was carried on by the cosmopolitan Hara Yoshimichi, once head of the Constitutionalist party and now president of Hirohito's Privy Council. Ordinarily at conferences in the Imperial Presence, the president of the Privy Council was supposed to ask questions on behalf of the Throne. Before this conference, however, Hirohito had requested a free debate and had positively ordered Privy Council President Hara to speak for himself. By letting everyone have his say, by allowing all objections to be officially set down in the palace records, Hirohito could release dissenters from responsibility and could get on with what had to be done.

"I do not think," stated Privy Council President Hara, "that the scheduled movement of our military forces into French Indochina is consistent with the assurances we gave last year to Indochina when we said that we would respect her territorial integrity."

Hirohito nodded and smiled.

"I believe all of you would agree," said Hara, "that the war between Germany and the Soviet Union really represents the chance of a lifetime for Japan. Since the Soviet Union is promoting communism all over the world, we will have to attack her sooner or later. Since we are still engaged in the China Incident, I see that we cannot attack the Soviet Union as freely as we would wish. Nevertheless, I believe that we should attack the Soviet Union when it seems opportune. . . . The Soviet Union is notorious for her habitual acts of betrayal. If we were to attack the Soviet Union, no one would regard it as treachery. . . . I would ask the government and the Supreme Command to attack the Soviet Union as soon as possible."

Hirohito, who had spent half his adult life fighting the Strike-North sentiments of the Army, nodded emphatically. Hara's objections were now inscribed in the palace rolls where they could be interpreted ambiguously as representing either Hara's private views or his official views on behalf of the Throne. Chief of Staff Sugiyama noted in his minutes: "The questions put by the President of the Privy Council Hara were relevant and pointed. The Emperor seemed to be extremely satisfied."

On emerging from the council, Hirohito returned to his desk in the Imperial Library to stamp his approval on a number of military orders for which the way had now been cleared. One was a call-up of the reserve so that it could man vacant military barracks in Japan and be ready to supply casualty replacements for the divisions of the standing army which would now be in the field. Another was a peculiar little order which created a new command in Manchuria, the Kwantung Special Maneuver, a Strike-South training exercise to which were reassigned most of the veteran troops of the Kwantung Army. A third was a posting of fifteen of the divisions left in Japan to Manchuria where they would bring up the strength of the Kwantung Army and Special Maneuver forces from 400,000 to 700,000 men. A fourth was an alert to units in Taiwan, Hainan, and South China to be prepared for new uniforms, new combat rations, and new amphibious landing manuals. A fifth was an authorization for the complete rebuilding of the Imperial Headquarters shed to the north of the Fukiage Gardens in the palace grounds. It was to be greatly enlarged and sheathed entirely in armor plate. Whereas formerly it had served as a handy private place for Cabinet ministers and staff chiefs to meet occasionally, it would now become a full-time liaison office with its own staff officers, maps, and records.

Having secured the acquiescence of his ministers in a formal decision to go South on July 2, Hirohito was chagrined to find that his nod, for once, had not settled the matter. The dispatch of troops to Manchuria worried the Sorge spy ring for a while—until Sorge's agents discovered that Army purchasing agents in Osaka were ordering mosquito nets instead of fur caps—but it failed to placate the field officers of the Army. All their lives long they had trained to fight and die if necessary in war against the Russians. Now they were called upon to mount a feint against the Soviet Union and at the same time, in the Kwantung Special Maneuver, to start practicing support operations for the Navy's Strike South.

It was more than most colonels could bear, and from July 2 to July 16, Japan's domestic atmosphere crackled with tension. Intelligent men of affairs encouraged the Army in its discontent because they knew that the alternative to attacking Russia would be a fearful and perhaps suicidal war with the United States. The murmuring against imperial policy reached such a pitch that the Home Ministry turned out all its police on twenty-four-hour alert and the Education Ministry closed all high schools and state universities.

During these two weeks of simmering revolution, Foreign Minister Matsuoka persisted in his devious efforts to sabotage the sham negotiations in Washington. U.S. Secretary of State Hull, he maintained, had personally attacked him in the American Oral Statement of June 21 and had, in effect, meddled in Japanese domestic affairs by trying to get him fired. Matsuoka made the most of this negative compliment and the press supported him in his lament. The right-wing forces of former Black Dragon lord Toyama held sympathy demonstrations in his behalf. Osaka businessmen raised the price of cotton for tropical khaki uniforms and lowered the price of wool for northern winter uniforms.

In the inner councils of state, however, Matsuoka was looked upon with increasingly hard eyes and listened to with increasingly deaf ears. At his final appearance before a liaison conference on July 12, Matsuoka gave voice to the last distracting insight which he would put forward as an American expert. "The American President," he stated, "is trying to head his country into the war. There is, however, one thread of hope, which is that the American people might not follow. . . . Japanese-American accord has been my cherished wish ever since I was very young."

War Minister Tojo said, "Even if there is no hope, I would like to persist to the very end. I know it is difficult, but it will be intolerable if we cannot establish the Greater East Asia Co-Prosperity Sphere and settle the China incident. . . ."

Navy Minister Oikawa said, "According to Navy reports, it appears that Secretary of State Hull and others are not prepared to provoke a Pacific war. Since Japan does not wish to engage in a Pacific war, isn't there some room for negotiation?"

Matsuoka countered, "Is there room? What will they accept?"

Oikawa suggested, "Something minor."

Matsuoka replied, "If we say we will not use force in the south, they will probably listen. Is there anything else they will accept?"

Oikawa said, "Won't they accept the security of the Pacific? The Open Door Policy in China?"

"Well," answered Matsuoka, after some further discussion, "I'll think about it." These were his last words in argument before his peers. On July 13 he took to his bed with a feigned illness and at first refused to read a revision of the revised revision of the Draft Proposal for friendly American-Japanese relations. A parade of Army and Navy visitors on July 14 persuaded him to promise to send the revision to Ambassador Nomura. That evening, however, when he felt more courageous, he withheld the new Japanese draft and cabled Nomura only the news that Hull's latest version was inacceptable to Japan.

On the following day, July 15, Matsuoka still kept to his sickbed and the rest of the Cabinet met without him. They decided to ask to resign in protest against his non-co-operation. That afternoon at three, Prince Konoye arrived at the Imperial Summer Palace in Hayama on the beach to discuss the situation. He found Hirohito somewhat hurt and suspicious. Hirohito had made Konoye swear when he had formed his second Cabinet in 1940 "to share joys and sorrows with the Throne all the way." It now appeared that the weak Konoye might be trying to drop his burden of prime ministerial responsibilities before seeing "his mission" through to the end.

"Why should the whole Cabinet resign?" demanded Hirohito. "Why not simply replace Matsuoka?"

Konoye explained that it would disturb the unity of the nation to be rude to Matsuoka and that it would be better to save Matsuoka from any semblance of disgrace by letting the entire Cabinet resign together. Then if necessary, said Konoye with a sigh, he would accept a fresh imperial mandate and would form a new Cabinet with a different foreign minister. After making absolutely sure that Konoye was sincere in his willingness to form a third Konoye Cabinet, Hirohito agreed to permit the second Konoye Cabinet to resign.

That evening, July 15, an imperial messenger called at Matsuoka's residence requesting him, since he was sick and could not attend Cabinet meetings, to lend his signature seal to Konoye so that it might be used to stamp urgent papers of state. As a loyal subject, Matsuoka had no choice but to comply. He knew, however, that his proxy would be used for a resignation of the whole cabinet and he took to the phone the next morning to muster his Army and business supporters. Konoye, at his phone, was equally busy assuring other Cabinet ministers that if they resigned they would be promptly reappointed to office.

In the afternoon, at 2 P.M. July 16, Hirohito took a moment out from the gathering Cabinet crisis to give audience to Lieutenant General Tiger Yamashita. Having suggested the Unit 82 Strike-South research group in Taiwan the previous fall, Yamashita had just returned from seven months of reconnaissance in Germany. He had submitted a report on his trip in which he warned that Japan's Army lagged far behind European armies and was woefully deficient in paratroops, medium tanks, and long-range bombers.

Yamashita had gone as far as the French coast and had seen at first hand the growing air superiority of the British Royal Air Force. He had schemed with his aides to pay an unscheduled inspection visit at a German radar factory and had come away with the knowledge that radar in the West was already a formidable tool of war while in Japan it still remained a crude toy of research. On the basis of such findings, Yamashita advised a two-year moratorium on all Japanese war plans and an all-out modernization of the Japanese Army. His recommendation was being used as a political weapon by junior members of the General Staff who wished to prevent Japan from committing herself to war in the south.

In the course of his audience with Hirohito, Yamashita redirected his thinking so that he derived new conclusions from his German field trip. On June 30 the General Staff had received a provisional Strike-South plan from Unit 82 in Taiwan. It revealed astonishing weaknesses in the British defenses for Malaya, grave inadequacies in the American position in the Philippines, and a negligible capacity for resistance in the Dutch East Indies. Presented with this assessment from his own minion, Lieutenant Colonel Tsuji of Unit 82, Yamashita was obliged to concede that the Japanese Army might be able to win victories in the south even if it could not vie with continental European arms in the north. He advised that the Army should not be used for offensive purposes at all if possible, but that if war was inevitable, employment in the south would be better than in the north.

Yamashita withdrew from the Imperial Presence to silence Strike-North proponents in the General Staff and to lead hesitant field officers toward the Strike South. Hirohito at once dispatched him to Manchuria to command the Kwantung Special Maneuver and four months later would put him in charge of the march on Singapore.

After talking to Yamashita, Hirohito accepted the resignation of the Cabinet *en bloc* and immediately issued the mandate to Prince Konoye to form a new Cabinet. The next afternoon, July 17, Konoye brought his proposed list of ministers to the Hayama villa and the following afternoon, July 18, Hirohito presided over the new Cabinet's ceremony of investiture. Foreign Minister Matsuoka was still on the phone. His portfolio of foreign affairs had been taken in the new Cabinet by Admiral Toyoda Soemu, a trusted member of the cabal who had attended Hirohito in 1921 in England. At the same time Baron Hiranuma, Matsuoka's chief ally in the final attempt to make Hirohito face north, was replaced as home minister by a nonentity, Tanabe Harumichi.

Gently as it had been expressed, Matsuoka's rejection by the Throne was pointed enough to lose the famous foreign minister his right-wing backing almost overnight. He retired to his small private home in the Mount Fuji foothills to contemplate in silence the sources of true political power. Five years later he was unearthed by Allied war criminal investigators, put in prison, and made to stand a few days' trial as the archvillain of Japanese diplomacy. In the month after the beginning of the International Military Tribunal he was excused from further appearances in the dock and released into the custody of doctors. Two months later, in the fall of 1946, he died of cancer. In his final days he said not a word about his one-man attempt to deceive Hirohito and redirect the imperial program by his big talk as an "American expert." He left behind him a family which had to live in Japan.

25

KONOYE'S LAST CHANCE

(1941)

THE OIL CRISIS

The same day, July 18, on which Hirohito invested the new
Japanese Cabinet, Roosevelt's American Cabinet met in Washington to approve an act of reprisal. The broken Purple Code, which
Matsuoka had saved from being scrapped, informed U.S. leaders
that Japan was about to occupy south Indochina and build bases
with which to threaten Singapore. The U.S. Cabinet therefore approved a proposal to freeze all Japanese assets in the United
States. All Japanese vessels in U.S. ports were to be prevented
from sailing. All Japanese balances in U.S. banks were to be impounded. All Japanese business transactions were to be suspended
in mid-air. The flow of oil, scrap iron, and machine tools from the
continental United States would cease forthwith.

Before these economic sanctions were announced, and before
Japanese troops began their move into south Indochina, the new
Japanese Cabinet at its second liaison conference, held in the refurbished Imperial Headquarters in the palace on July 24, heard
its new Foreign Minister Admiral Toyoda announce that the
American government would probably take exactly these measures
of reprisal which it had in fact already taken. "The United States,"
said Toyoda, "will adopt a policy of putting an embargo on vital
materials, freezing Japanese funds, prohibiting the purchase of
gold, detaining Japanese vessels, etc."

At the first liaison conference of the new Cabinet, on July 21, Navy Chief of Staff Nagano had explained that "in a war with the United States, there is now a chance of achieving victory. But the chance will diminish as time goes on. By the latter half of next year it will be difficult for us to cope with the United States. After that the situation will become progressively worse. The United States will probably drag things out until her defenses are built up and then will try to settle. As time goes by, therefore, the Empire will be put at a disadvantage. If we could settle matters without war, there would be nothing better. But if we conclude that conflict cannot ultimately be avoided, then I would like you to understand that time is not on our side. Furthermore, if we occupy the Philippines, it will be easier, from the standpoint of the Navy, to have prosecuted the war fully from the start."

As the Japanese fleet lived on oil, the Navy's need to fight—to fight now or not at all—would become compelling if the United States imposed an oil embargo. Everyone knew this, both in Tokyo and in Washington, yet the machinery of provocation and reprisal ground on remorselessly. Right on schedule Japanese Army tanks arrived in Saigon on July 24, and in the words of a contemporary press release "subjugated the city peacefully." The next evening F.D.R. duly announced the U.S. decision to freeze Japanese assets. Japan responded in kind and froze American assets. Japanese nationals in the United States were allowed to withdraw up to $500 a month from their frozen bank accounts. U.S. nationals in Japan were allowed to withdraw from theirs 500 yen a month—approximately one quarter as much.

The drawing of battle lines had a subtle effect on the feeling of the Japanese masses. They began to accept the inevitability of the war in store for them. The Tokyo stock exchange slumped to its lowest point since 1931. The Yokohama silk exchange shut down entirely. In their editorials the leading newspapers agreed that Japan had been challenged and would not back down. One tabloid called the U.S. reprisal an "insolent and outrageous challenge." *Nichi Nichi*, the third of the great dailies, said: "There is no greater misconception than to think that Japan will grow conciliatory because the United States strengthens her economic sanctions."

The acute Hirohito sensed the danger of fatalism among his

advisors even before its rigor mortis had begun to take hold on the masses. He had no intention of going to war if he could possibly get what he wanted for Japan by means short of war. On July 22, he warned Army Chief of Staff Sugiyama that he must not fall prey to war psychology and that use of armed force must be considered only as a last resort because "our national power is small and our economic resources are scarce."

Sugiyama noted in his daybook of memoranda: "This must be kept absolutely secret but to judge from His Imperial Majesty's questions today, he is obsessed by the hope of using nonmilitary means. Therefore, I will in future try to change his feelings. I think it will be necessary to guide him step by step."

On July 29 the Navy Chief of Staff Nagano Osami tried to impress on Hirohito the need for making a firm decision to declare war on Great Britain when it became necessary to seize Malaya. Hirohito evinced "extreme dissatisfaction" and warned Nagano against assuming "the inevitability of war with Great Britain and the United States." He instructed Nagano to confer with former Navy Chief of Staff Prince Fushimi, who was his patron. At the same time the Cabinet and staff chiefs were meeting in liaison conference to discuss the problems posed by the national morale.

The next day, July 30, Navy Chief of Staff Nagano reported back to the palace that he and Prince Fushimi were agreed that they would like to avoid war if possible. Assuming hypothetically the possibility of a war, Hirohito asked, "Is it certain that we will win?"

Nagano replied, "No, it is not certain that we will win."

Hirohito said, "Then I fear that our entry into the war might mean fighting in despair."

After the audience Lord Privy Seal Kido assured Hirohito that Nagano took too extreme a stance. Between an immediate decision for war, fraught with the possibility of disaster, and a decision to accept a steady diminution of national strength for lack of oil, there were, said Kido, still many alternatives. The diplomatic offensive might be pressed in Washington by a summit conference of Prime Minister Konoye and President Roosevelt. And if that failed, Japan could swallow her pride and adopt a ten-year plan "pinned on ultimate penetration of the South."

Hirohito realized that the Strike South could indeed be post-

poned for a few years and that it would be foolhardy to jeopardize seventy years of effort by striking prematurely. He therefore
asked Kido to determine whether, by waiting, Japan really could
improve her relative position. That is, before drafting a ten-year
plan for Japan, Kido should make a projection of normal U.S.
growth. Unless Japan could reasonably expect to surpass the
United States in absolute enlargement of her synthetic oil production, of her heavy industrial and machine tool capacity, and
of her merchant marine, ten years of crash effort would avail her
nothing.

Then Hirohito summoned Navy Minister Oikawa, his former
personal aide, and asked his views. Oikawa said that a majority of
naval officers were opposed to war with the West. The Emperor
nodded and Army Chief of Staff Sugiyama, who was standing by,
wrote in his notes: "I could not help thinking that we as a nation
have not yet come to a point at which we can reach a decision to
make war against England and America."

On July 28, the Netherlands East Indies had followed the
United States and Great Britain in cutting off all oil shipments
to Japan. On July 31 the U.S. oil embargo, announced earlier,
went into effect. After that date Japan's ability to fight against
superior odds could only ebb.

A CHOICE OF EVILS

During that last bleak week in July 1941, when all Japan realized that a decision must be made either to back down or to stake
everything on a desperate war with the West, an enterprising
Japanese reporter bulled his way into the villa of the discredited
former Foreign Minister Matsuoka, at the foot of Mount Fuji,
and extracted from him a statement. Waving a hand at the summit of the sacred volcano, Matsuoka confessed: "As viewed from
the top of the mountain, the international situation may present
a variety of different vistas."

Hirohito alone stood at the top of the mountain. He alone had
full access to Army planning, Navy planning, Foreign Ministry
planning, and the policy-making thoughts of all his intimate advisors. He fully understood the need to decide soon on war or
peace. He may have genuinely hoped that by negotiation and

threat he could wring a foothold in the East Indies from the British, Dutch, and Americans without having to fight for it. At the same time he was planning for the contingency of war, and in so doing he was preoccupied with considerations beyond the ken of his chiefs of staff.

He felt, for instance, that if the people were to support the war, they must first live with anxiety for a while and come to believe sincerely that the nation was being bled to death. As Prime Minister Konoye pointed out to Lord Privy Seal Kido on August 5, after an audience with the Emperor on the peace negotiations in Washington: "Suppose it turns out that Chamberlain was betrayed by Hitler. Still you cannot dismiss the fact that Chamberlain met many times with Hitler and so helped to prepare England for war."

On the other side of the equation Hirohito juggled military factors. If the Americans were to be taken by surprise and beaten, utmost security must shroud Japan's attack plans; they must be worked out and practiced down to the last detail; and Japanese officials—even the chiefs of staff—must be kept in ignorance of them until the last possible moment. Officials who had to deal with newsmen and ambassadors would stand a far better chance of lulling Western suspicions if they knew nothing of the attack plans than they would if they knew everything and tried to conceal their knowledge.

The available documents indicate that, in July and early August when Hirohito was pleading with his chiefs of staff to avoid if at all possible the use of military force, neither of the staff chiefs yet knew of the plan for Pearl Harbor. The fact that Hirohito had ordered the plan submitted to Vice Admiral Onishi in January, for an independent appraisal, first came to Navy Chief of Staff Nagano's attention in a memorandum headed "August 22, 1941," and this memorandum was not entered in the notebook of Army Chief of Staff Sugiyama—"the bathroom door"—until October 30, 1941.

"Keeping in mind," as he liked to say, "the whole situation," Hirohito in early August turned down a request from the commander of the truncated Kwantung Army in Manchuria for discretionary power in dealing with possible aggressive moves by the Red Army in Siberia. In the same week Hirohito encouraged

Prime Minister Konoye to arrange a peace meeting, if possible, with President Roosevelt in Hawaii; he asked Lord Privy Seal Kido to draw up a ten-year contingency plan for peaceful economic infiltration of the East Indies; and in another compartment of his security-conscious, protocol-observing existence, he reviewed the preparations which the Army and Navy were separately making for the possibility of war.

The Army plans were the first ones presented. Lieutenant Colonel Tsuji Masanobu, the brains of Unit 82 in Taiwan, outlined them to Hirohito's aides and to the officers of the Operations Department of the General Staff in a three-day briefing, July 24–26, 1941. Afterwards Chief of Staff Sugiyama congratulated Tsuji on a brilliant presentation and asked him, "What is your estimate of the rate at which the operations you have demonstrated can be carried out?"

"If we commence on Emperor Meiji day [November 3]," replied Tsuji, "we should be able to capture Manila by New Year, Singapore by National Foundation Day [February 11], Java by Army Commemoration Day [March 10], and Rangoon by the Emperor's birthday [April 19]."[1]

In support of Tsuji's plans Hirohito authorized massive troop movements to Manchuria in the first week of August 1941. There, the reinforcements gave the impression that Japan was about to strike at the Soviet Union. In reality, however, the reinforcements relieved the combat-tested veterans of the Kwantung Army from guard duty so that they could be trained for the Strike South. Starting in late July, General Yamashita, the Tiger, began two months of intensive exercises in which he selected and rehearsed the best units in the Japanese Army, some for the occupation of the Philippines, some for the campaign in Malaya, and some for the conquest of Java, Sumatra, and Borneo.

Soviet spy Sorge was radioed by his center in Siberia to turn all his attention to evaluating the intentions behind this latest build-up in Manchuria. Sorge responded at once with a message protesting that, as far as he could determine, no Japanese attack on Siberia was contemplated. He bolstered his contention at the

---

[1] In the event the attack would start more than a month late—on December 8—but the schedule would still be met. Manila would be captured January 2, Singapore February 15, Java March 10, and Rangoon March 8.

end of July by reporting that the Japanese Army was in process of requisitioning a million tons of merchant marine for transport to destinations which could hardly be continental. In early August he had Klausen radio the center that there was a "possibility of [Japanese] operations against the Dutch East Indies." On August 15, Sorge reported that his friends in the German Embassy in Tokyo had despaired of Japanese help against Russia. In late August, through his Ozaki-Saionji-Kido link to the Emperor, he learned that Hirohito had already decided against a Strike North at the conference in the Imperial Presence on July 2. Not until early October, however, could Sorge radio Moscow that Japan contemplated "no attack [on Russia] until the spring of next year at the earliest"; and that "there will be war with the United States this month or next month."

U.S. intelligence officers in Washington, working from afar with decoded intercepts of Japanese diplomatic messages, correctly assessed Hirohito's July 2 decision long before the Soviet ring in Tokyo. In memos GZ-1 and GZ-4, dated August 4 and 9, Lieutenant Commander Alwin D. Kramer of Naval Intelligence greatly impressed the men around Secretary of State Hull by extracting the following salient points from intercepts:

Japan will not go to war against the U.S.S.R. in the north.
She will intensify preparations for "the southward move."
She will immediately begin to "arm for all-out war against Britain and the United States to break the British-American encirclement."

In the second week of August, Hirohito commenced his review of the Navy's war planning. Combined Fleet commander Admiral Yamamoto had spent the spring and early summer of 1941 conducting exercises, in the guise of routine training, to make sure that his men and ships and planes were physically capable of the attack which he imagined for them. Off the Kyushu ports of Kagoshima, Kanoya, and Saiki and the Shikoku port of Sukumo, his dive-bomber and torpedo-plane pilots had proved their ability to follow maps and briefings and carry out difficult mock missions over unfamiliar mountainous terrains with a high degree of pinpoint success. Now in early August Yamamoto and a handful of his most trusted staff officers arrived in Tokyo to explain their military convictions to a select cadre of Hirohito's personal naval representatives.

Yamamoto still protested that war with the United States should be avoided if possible, but he insisted that if war was necessary he must first knock out the Pearl Harbor fleet or Japan would have no chance at all. Since his ideas were as yet known only to Hirohito, to Prince Takamatsu, and to a few fully reliable staff officers in the fleet, he gave his sales presentation not at the offices of the Navy General Staff but at the Naval Staff College, which was presided over by its dean, Rear Admiral Marquis Komatsu Teruhisa, the imperial family member who had run Hirohito's physical education program on the deck of the battleship *Katori* in 1921.

In the staff college Yamamoto's staff officers mingled with the students—the experienced fleet commanders and captains who were intent upon bettering themselves with instruction in the technical and strategic post-graduate aspects of modern naval warfare. Yamamoto worried that any serious-looking member of the college might walk by accident into one of his seminars and take out of it the rumor that Japan meant to attack Pearl Harbor. In the event, however, Yamamoto's table-top demonstration went off without interruption and convinced Marquis Komatsu and Prince Takamatsu that the Pearl Harbor plan was well thought out and had a real chance of success.

DEADLINE FOR WAR

Immediately after Yamamoto's table-top maneuvers, on August 16, Navy General Staff officers who had been present at the demonstration in the staff college presented to their opposite numbers in the Army General Staff and War Ministry a timetable of necessary political preparations for war. Their proposition was that the Cabinet, meeting in the presence of the Emperor early in September, should make up its mind to approve final preparations by the armed forces, starting in early October, unless the United States showed signs of giving in to Japanese demands earlier. The section chiefs of the War Ministry and Army General Staff agreed to the plan and began to circulate it for approval throughout the military bureaucracy. Although it had the backing of imperial henchmen like Marquis Komatsu, and was presumed to have the backing of Hirohito, it was considered only a position-paper project and was not shown to the chiefs of staff until late in the month, August 28.

Also on August 16, when the Navy's junior officers first broached this plan, Prince Takamatsu, as the "Someone" at liaison conferences, made a special request of the ministers present. "In the past," he said, "we have had cases in which secrets have been leaked out because they were discussed in the Cabinet. Therefore, except in matters of a grave political nature which must be submitted to the Cabinet, it is best if the full Cabinet should not be consulted."

Roosevelt and Churchill had just met in mid-Atlantic to sign their historic affirmation of democratic ideals, the Atlantic Charter. On August 17, as soon as Roosevelt had returned to Washington, Ambassador Nomura obtained a few minutes with him to beg that he meet personally with Prime Minister Konoye somewhere in the middle of the Pacific. F.D.R. at first seemed to respond favorably to the suggestion, but after consultation with the State Department he informed Ambassador Nomura that an American-Japanese summit conference would serve no purpose unless adequate spadework had been done in advance to make possible a meeting on level ground. By the end of August Konoye and Hirohito knew that the free-wheeling American President was not likely to be seduced even if the mid-Pacific conference could be arranged.

On September 2, Admiral Yamamoto and his staff officers gathered once more at Marquis Komatsu's staff college on the edge of the Shiragane imperial woods three and a half miles south of the main palace. This time the college was the rehearsal stage for all the naval operations required by the Army's Unit-82 Strike-South plan. Yamamoto's scheme was only a sideshow which might or might not be used on opening night. The main event was a demonstration of the Navy's tactical plans for supporting co-ordinated troop landings in Malaya, the Philippines, Wake, Guam, Borneo, and Java. Thirty-nine of Yamamoto's peers—the most gifted and technically-minded admirals, captains, and commanders in the Navy General Staff and Navy Ministry—had charge of the production. And until they were sure that the main event was feasible, they could not even consider diverting ships and planes for Yamamoto's hazardous enterprise. For six days Yamamoto watched and criticized their presentations, paring from their task forces all fatty margins of safety and gaining for his own ends a destroyer or tanker here and an air squadron or carrier there.

While Yamamoto fretted, the Army-Navy deadline for giving up negotiations and deciding on war was considered, on September 3, by a liaison conference. Navy Chief of Staff Nagano opened the debate by explaining: "We are growing weaker while the enemy is growing stronger. . . . When there is no hope for diplomacy and war cannot be avoided, we must be ready to make up our minds quickly." Seven hours later the conferees agreed that if the United States "does not meet our demands" by October 10 "we will then at once decide to commence hostilities against the United States, Britain, and the Netherlands."

When the conference closed at 6 P.M., the policy statement on which it had passed—"Essentials for Carrying out the Empire's Program"—was sent on for reference to the Imperial Library. Hirohito was expected to read it that evening or the next morning. Foreign Minister Toyoda and Prime Minister Konoye were both troubled by it because it seemed to emphasize the preparations for war more than the negotiations with Washington which were supposed to achieve Japan's goals without war. And so the next afternoon Foreign Minister Toyoda called at the Imperial Library to report on the deadlocked Washington negotiations and see how Hirohito was reacting. The Emperor had nothing special to say. On the following afternoon, September 5, therefore, Prime Minister Konoye called on Hirohito and pointed out to him that the first paragraph of the "Essentials" was devoted exclusively to military preparations and that diplomacy was relegated to the second paragraph. Hirohito agreed that this was a misplaced emphasis and promised to speak about it to the chiefs of staff on the morrow. Konoye begged him to summon the chiefs of staff at once and speak about it right away. Hirohito consulted with Lord Privy Seal Kido and decided to accede to Konoye's request.

The two chiefs of staff arrived out of breath at the library at 6 P.M. According to Army Chief of Staff Sugiyama's memorandum written immediately afterwards, Hirohito greeted them abruptly with an imperative:

"Do use diplomacy and peace as much as possible. Do not use diplomacy and war preparations as equals at the same time. Give diplomacy precedence."

The two staff chiefs stammered apologetic explanations of the order of paragraphs in the "Essentials" and Hirohito continued:

"Do you think the southern operations can be carried out as planned?"

Sugiyama gave a detailed defense of the Unit-82 proposals for operations in the Philippines and Malaya. The Emperor cut him short:

"There must be things which will not go according to plan. You say five months, but isn't it possible it can't all be done in five months?"

"Since both the Army and Navy have studied it several times," said Sugiyama stoutly, "it should be carried out almost exactly as planned."

Hirohito objected that amphibious operations were always fraught with unexpected difficulties and pointed out that in one mock landing exercise on the coasts of Kyushu recently the attacking force had theoretically lost half its men before they had reached the beach.

"That happened," said Sugiyama, "because our convoy started to move before the opposing air cover had been destroyed. I don't think the blunder will ever be repeated."

"Well then," asked Hirohito, "how about adverse weather?"

"That," replied Sugiyama, "is an obstacle which we must overcome."

"But you do think," said Hirohito, "that you can do what you plan? Remember that when you were war minister [in 1937] you said that Chiang Kai-shek would surrender immediately. But you still haven't made him do it."

In his memorandum Sugiyama then continued his narrative in indirect dialogue. "I took this opportunity," he wrote, "to elaborate and to explain to the Emperor the need to improve the outlook of the nation while it still has elasticity. Before all national power is spent, we must face obstacles in order to open up the national destiny."

According to a version of the same conversation written by Prince Konoye for the Peace Faction three years later, Sugiyama excused his mistaken forecast of prospects in China by admitting that he had underestimated the resilience and sheer size of the Chinese nation.[2]

Then, according to Konoye, Hirohito said acidly, "If you call the interior of China broad, isn't the Pacific Ocean even broader? How can you confidently say [this time that it will take only] three months?"[3]

According to Sugiyama's own account the Emperor merely said "in a loud voice":

"Are you absolutely sure this time that we can win?"

"I hesitate," replied Sugiyama, "to say I am absolutely sure, but I can say that there is a good possibility of winning. I cannot say that I am absolutely sure but I know that, for the price of a short-term peace of six months or a year, we cannot afford a long-term national catastrophe. We must think in terms of a lasting peace of twenty or fifty years."

"Oh, I see," said Hirohito, and once again he spoke "in a loud voice."

"We are not happy to wage this war," insisted Sugiyama. "We are thinking of war only in case all peaceful efforts fail."

Navy Chief of Staff Nagano interceded to remind the Emperor of the winter of 1614 when the first of the Tokugawa shoguns had invested the Osaka castle of the son of Hideyoshi, the great plebeian general who had invaded Korea in the 1580's and 1590's. Nagano pointed out that the shogun had finally taken the castle only by first making peace and persuading Hideyoshi's son to fill in the outer moats of the castle. Then by stealth the shogun had filled in the second line of moats as well and succeeded in crossing the third and final line to storm the walls and take the keep. Ac-

[2] The Konoye account of this scene is the only one which has previously been published in English. Despite the fact that it was written years after Sugiyama's account and written for a public relations purpose, I have introduced a portion of it here on the chance that Sugiyama, even in his private memoranda set down in the presence of the spirit ancestors, may have suppressed a part of Hirohito's wounding words to him.

[3] Sugiyama, as his memoranda state, had undoubtedly said "five months" rather than "three." The Unit-82 schedule did indeed call for five months: November 1941 to April 1942. But Konoye years later, recalling the breathtaking speed of Japan's actual advance, put "three months" into the Emperor's mouth by mistake.

cording to Nagano's analysis Japan should beware of a settlement with the United States which might fill her outer moat and should not be contented with one which failed to fill the outer moat of the enemy. "Hirohito listened with interest."

Finally Prime Minister Konoye said: "As both staff chiefs have acknowledged we shall try to use peaceful diplomatic means up to the end. I am in complete accord with the chiefs that after that and only after that will we go to war as specified."

The two military men bowed themselves from the room and Konoye thanked Hirohito for his support. Then Hirohito went to supper.

The next morning, from 10 A.M. to noon, September 6, Hirohito presided over a historic conference in the Imperial Presence which tied the next-to-last knot on Japan's neatly packed war bomb. As always at such conferences the important matters under consideration were circulated beforehand in written form, were read by all participants including Hirohito, but were alluded to rather than discussed. The speeches made were all set pieces, rehearsed beforehand and delivered out loud solely for the purpose of the record—for the assignment of responsibility on the sacred palace rolls.

At the beginning of the conference, all the Cabinet ministers and staff chiefs who were present emulated Hirohito as he sat at his little altar at one end of the room silently shuffling through the position papers before him to indicate that he found them familiar and all in order. One of the papers stated: "The purposes of war with the United States, Great Britain, and the Netherlands are to expel the influence of these three countries from East Asia, to establish a sphere for the self-defense and self-preservation of our Empire, and to build a New Order in Greater East Asia."

A second item stated: "A war with the United States and Great Britain will be long, and will become a war of endurance. It is very difficult to predict the termination of war, and it would be well-nigh impossible to expect the surrender of the United States. However, we cannot exclude the possibility that the war may end because of a great change in American public opinion, which may result from such factors as the remarkable success of our military operations in the south or the capitulation of Great Britain [to

Germany]. At any rate, we should be able to establish an invincible position: by building up a strategically advantageous position through the occupation of important areas in the south; by creating an economy that will be self-sufficient in the long run through the development of rich resources in the Southern Regions, as well as through the use of the economic power of the East Asian continent; and by linking Asia and Europe in destroying the Anglo-American coalition through our co-operation with Germany and Italy. Meanwhile, we may hope that we will be able to influence the trend of affairs and bring the war to an end."

A third of the position papers on the tables explained: "We must carry out military preparations as secretly as possible, conceal our intentions, and refrain from sending additional forces to southern French Indochina. . . . Diplomatic negotiations during this period should be conducted with a view toward facilitating the switch-over from political to military methods."

A fourth document under consideration concerned the "minimum conditions" and "maximum concessions" which Japan would accept from the United States as the price for peace. It stipulated that if "we promise not to use military force in the south, we must put China under the complete control of our Empire. To do that, it is absolutely essential to station the necessary forces there. . . . If they [the Americans] do not accede to the conditions that we propose, we must regard it as disclosing their true intention, which is to bring Japan to her knees."

In regard to the withdrawal of Japanese troops from China which the United States had persistently demanded as a prerequisite for serious negotiation of peace in the Far East, a codicil suggested: "We have no objection to affirming that we are in principle prepared to withdraw our troops [from China] following the settlement of the incident, except for those that are dispatched to carry out the purposes of the incident."

When these support papers had been leafed through and the imperial conference of September 6 opened, no one present pointed out the utter hopelessness and insincerity of Japan's negotiating position vis-à-vis the United States. Instead a parade of ministers took the floor one by one to take responsibility for advising simultaneous negotiations and war preparations until Oc-

tober 10, after which date war preparations should be finalized
and negotiations continued only in the hope of a miracle or as
a form of subterfuge. Prime Minister Prince Konoye, Navy Chief
of Staff Nagano, and Army Chief of Staff Sugiyama all spoke in
favor of the motion. Foreign Minister Admiral Toyoda gave a
straightforward, factual description of the entire course of the
Japanese-American negotiations theretofore. The ubiquitous Suzuki, now a retired lieutenant general in charge of the Cabinet Planning Board which ran the Japanese economy, described
the condition of the nation's strategic stockpiles and strongly
urged immediate acquisition of new sources of supply in the
Dutch East Indies.

Finally Privy Council President Hara arose. On this occasion
he had been enjoined strictly by Lord Privy Seal Kido to speak
only on behalf of the Throne and to make absolutely clear in the
record what Hirohito had said to the chiefs of staff the day before.
Accordingly, the Privy Council president said in part:

"I take it that starting now, we will prepare for war at the same
time that diplomatic measures are being used; that is, everywhere
we will try to break the deadlock through diplomacy, but if this
should fail, we will have to go to war. The draft seems to suggest
that the war comes first, and diplomacy second; but I interpret it
to mean that we will spare no efforts in diplomacy and we will
go to war only when we can find no other way."

When Hara had made his point on behalf of the Throne, Navy
Minister Oikawa hastened to reassure the Emperor that all present
understood his wishes and would respect them. Then Hara continued, "When the prime minister visits the United States in the
near future, he must be determined to improve relations by using
all conceivable diplomatic measures, even though we will be making preparations for war as a matter of policy. If the proposals
under consideration are given imperial assent, I ask all of you to
co-operate in promoting the aims of the prime minister's U.S.
visit."

Hara went on to ask Chief of Staff Sugiyama some technical
questions about Soviet diplomatic and military strength. Then
Hara said:

"I have been told that this war decision will be subject to careful deliberation and so I will not ask any further questions. I shall be satisfied if the diplomatic negotiations can be carried out under the conditions indicated in the attached papers, and so I give my complete consent to this proposal."

Since the conditions indicated in the attached papers were known to be completely inacceptable to the United States and had been inacceptable ever since Japan's invasion of China four years earlier, Hara's last statement on behalf of the Throne clearly settled the issue of war and peace. Hara went on to deliver a page of comment on the state of the nation's morale, asking everyone present to suppress dissidents and to encourage the people to pull as a team. Finally he concluded, "I would like to see courageous and drastic action taken, so that the decisions of the imperial conference can be carried out even if worse comes to worst."

Home Minister Tanabe Harumichi, who had succeeded Hiranuma at the time of Matsuoka's ouster from the Cabinet in July, proceeded to deliver a detailed explanation of the measures which would be taken by the police to keep the people in line. Then the decision to negotiate for five weeks while completing war planning—together with all the position papers which had been silently presented in its support—was unanimously recommended to the Throne.

Hirohito arose and, instead of nodding and making his exit as he usually did on such occasions, dramatically drew a slip of paper from his pocket and read a noncommittal little poem composed by Emperor Meiji, his grandfather, on the eve of the war with Russia four decades earlier:

> In as much as all
> the seas in all directions
> seem twins of one birth,
> how often must the winds and
> the waves clash in noisiness?

> *Yomo no umi*
> *mina harakara to*
> *omou yo ni,*
> *nando namikaze no*
> *tachisawaguramu.*

Having spoken in this dubious fashion on the side of the angels and philosophers, Hirohito withdrew, leaving his responsible vassals to contemplate, for a few silent moments of "awe and trepidation," the depth of his still waters. As events would soon show, he had just belly-talked Japan into war.

PRINCE KONOYE BOWS OUT

Prime Minister Konoye, immediately after the fateful conference in the Imperial Presence adjourned, had one of his secretaries phone the American Embassy and arrange a clandestine meeting for him with Ambassador Grew. The two men were driven to their tryst in specially provided unofficial cars, with plain license plates, which would not be noticed by reporters or policemen. They met at the home of Baron Ito Bunkichi, the adopted son of Prime Minister Ito Hirobumi who had died by assassin's bullet in Manchuria in 1909. All the servants in the house had been given the night off and Baron Ito's daughter personally served the conferees with food and drink. Konoye had with him his secretary, Ushiba Tomohiko, and Ambassador Grew his embassy counsellor, Eugene H. Dooman. The four men dined and talked together for three hours and, in Grew's words, "presented with entire frankness the fundamental views of our two countries."

In an effort to enlist Grew's help in arranging a Konoye-Roosevelt summit meeting, Konoye went to the length of assuring Grew that "we conclusively and wholeheartedly agree with the four principles enunciated by the secretary of state." These called on Japan to promise: "Respect for the territorial integrity and the sovereignty of each and all nations; support of the principle of non-interference in the internal affairs of other countries; support of the principle of equality, including equality of commercial opportunity; and non-disturbance of the status quo in the Pacific except as the status quo may be altered by peaceful means."

In his diary Grew continued:

Prince Konoye recognizes that the responsibility is his for the present regrettable state of relations between our two countries but, with appropriate modesty as to his personal capabilities, he likewise recognizes that only he can cause the desired rehabilitation to come about. In the event of failure on his part, no succeeding Prime Minister at least during his own lifetime, could achieve the results desired. . . . Prince Konoye told me that from the inception of the informal talks in Washington he had received the strongest concurrence from the responsible chiefs of both the Army and the Navy. Only today he had conferred with the Minister of War [Tojo], who had promised to send a full general to accompany the Prime Minister to the meeting with the President. . . . Prince Konoye repeatedly stressed the view that time is of the essence. . . . He could not guarantee to put into effect any such programme of settlement six months or a year from now. He does, however, guarantee that at the present time he can carry with him the Japanese people to the goal which he has selected. . . . He expressed the earnest hope that in view of the present internal situation in Japan the projected meeting with the President could be arranged with the least possible delay.

Konoye's desperate bid to involve Grew and Roosevelt in his own domestic political struggles continued for a month and ultimately came to naught. The State Department dissuaded Roosevelt from meeting with Konoye until the "Japanese government" could promise specific reforms in its international conduct. The position-paper writers and the responsible ministers of the Japanese government refused to let Konoye make the official assurances that were needed. Hirohito refrained from exercising his immense influence on Konoye's behalf.

The crux of the impasse was China. The United States insisted that Japan promise to withdraw her troops from China if and when a general Pacific settlement could be reached. Japan refused to make such a pledge except in the most vague and futuristic terms. On the other hand Japan insisted that she be given access once more to supplies of oil while the diplomatic settlement was being negotiated. The United States refused to comply unless Japan would make an equivalent gesture of solid, material good faith.

As the circular logic of the situation exhausted all the negotiators, both in Tokyo and in Washington, the Japanese Army and Navy were pressing forward with their war planning. At the Naval Staff College in southern Tokyo, the general table-top maneuvers neared an end on September 8 with a decision by the elder staff admirals, who acted as umpires, to let Yamamoto explain the strategic value of his Pearl Harbor plan and the tactical means by which he proposed to execute it. The admirals agreed that Yamamoto might hold a special top-secret map exercise from September 10 to September 12. He would be judged by twelve top-brass strategists in relation to his performance against five officers of an E-team (for England) and seven admirals, captains, and commanders of an A-team (for America).

That night, September 8, when Yamamoto had just won this chance to present his case, Marquis Komatsu, the dean of the staff college, held a banquet of celebration for members and intimates of the imperial family. Lord Privy Seal Kido attended with his mother, once a minor princess, now an old lady in her seventies.

The next morning, September 9, Yamamoto gave his over-all presentation to the umpires, explaining the forces he would need, the results he hoped to achieve, and finally the absolute strategic necessity for an early debilitating blow at the U.S. Pacific fleet. The umpires were impressed but reserved in their praise. If Yamamoto could demonstrate the technical feasibility of his plan in the "special maneuvers" scheduled for the next three days, the plan should certainly be incorporated, tentatively, in the over-all war strategy.

That afternoon, right after lunch, the two chiefs of staff reported on the progress of the war games to the Imperial Library. According to Army Chief of Staff Sugiyama, Hirohito greeted them buoyantly:

"Now I fully understand our operational plans. But what if there is pressure from the north while we are doing the south?"

"Once we start in the Southern Regions," replied Sugiyama, "we must look neither to left nor right until we have accomplished our purpose. We must concentrate on it to the exclusion of all else. I beg Your Majesty to assent to this proposition. If an incident occurs in the north, we can divert forces from China. We must not, however, stop our operations in the south half way."

"It pleases me to hear that," said Hirohito. "Diverting forces from China must be difficult for you."

Sugiyama replied that it would be difficult but not impossible.

The next day, September 10, Hirohito gave the staff chiefs permission for a full-scale national call-up of the reserve. "You may mobilize," he said, "but if the Konoye-Roosevelt talks should become successful, you will stop, correct?"

"Absolutely correct," replied Sugiyama.

Meanwhile, Yamamoto's map exercise had opened at the Naval Staff College. His forces, hypothetically, had rendezvoused, under complete radio silence, in the extreme north of Japan, the Kurile Islands, and begun a quiet voyage across the northern Pacific, far from trade routes. As they made their approach on paper to Hawaii, a yeoman stood by in the small crowded room where Yamamoto was playing his tactical game and calculated the fuel consumption of the various ships in the fleet on an abacus.[4] Despite the shrewdest moves which the opposing admirals in adjoining rooms could make on the basis of their knowledge of Yamamoto and of the false intelligence which the umpires thought fair for Yamamoto to throw in their direction, the Pearl Harbor fleet arrived unexpected at its destination and did great damage. In its retreat the umpires calculated that it might lose almost a third of its ships but that the loss which it had inflicted might be worth the price.

After this verdict, Yamamoto returned triumphant, on Saturday, September 13, to his Combined Fleet flagship, the *Nagato*. His staff officers spent a day going over the papers he had brought back from Tokyo and discussing the moves they must make next. Then, on the following day, Monday, September 15, Yamamoto and a few of his aides went ashore to reveal the Pearl Harbor plan for the first time to a representative of the Army.

At the headquarters of the Iwakuni Air Group, Yamamoto met with Count Terauchi Hisaichi, the general of the former Army Purification Movement who had reorganized civilian espionage for the Strike South in Taiwan in 1934; who had assisted the Court in overseeing arrangements in 1935 for the 1936 Army mutiny; who as war minister in 1936 and 1937 had carried out the Army's purge of the Strike-North Faction. Now, at sixty-two, Terauchi had been promised by Hirohito the post of Supreme Commander for the Southern Regions.[5] He and his protégé, Lieutenant General Tiger Yamashita—who had been specially flown in for the occasion from Manchuria—digested Admiral Yamamoto's plan and promised their support and co-operation in it. At the same time,

---

[4] The yeoman was later captured on Saipan where he gave American intelligence officers their first knowledge of the September 2–13 table-top maneuvers. He was interrogated by a friend of the author, Otis Cary, now a member of the faculty of Doshisha University in Kyoto and the administrator of Amherst House there.

[5] The Strike-South Faction's inclusive term for all the land between India and Australia.

they both agreed with Yamamoto that war would be a desperate gamble and should be avoided if at all possible.

A few days later, on September 21, Yamamoto and his staff began work on Order Number One, a comprehensive war plan so detailed that it would take an expert typesetter, cleared for top secrets, three days to set and print 300 copies of it. This was the order which, when stamped and signed by Hirohito, would launch World War II in the Pacific.

Unnerved by the speed with which war preparations were being pushed ahead and unwilling to take responsibility for them, Prime Minister Konoye began to think of ways of resigning. He had promised to share joys and sorrows with Hirohito to the end but he did not wish to go down in history as a complete fool and villain. He did not share Hirohito's interest and expertise in military matters and he could not believe that Japan's armed forces would have any success against the United States. On the other hand he understood diplomacy. Hirohito expected him to get what Japan wanted through negotiation and the threat of force, but Konoye felt that this would be impossible. Hirohito had inherited from his ancestors the sacred duty of cleansing Japanese soil of barbarians. Konoye had inherited from his ancestors a simpler mission: to guard the institution of the Throne and preserve it for posterity. He now began to think that he might be more effective in salvaging the institution of the Throne from the ruins of defeat than in saving Hirohito, personally, from the fate he seemed driven to pursue.

On September 18 four toughs jumped on the running board of Konoye's car as it was leaving his Kamakura villa and brandished daggers and pistols at him. The incident was kept out of the newspapers but widely publicized on the bureaucratic grapevine. It was even said, erroneously, that one of the thugs fired a bullet which missed Konoye's head by eighteen inches. The would-be assassins were arrested and kept in jail for a few months. All four of them belonged to a previously nonviolent faction of right-wing socialists who had long enjoyed Konoye's patronage. As a result the story was current at Court that Konoye had staged the attack himself in order to gain public sympathy and provide the first of several excuses for resigning the prime ministership. The alternative explanation had it that the war party was trying to intimidate him.

Two days after the attack, on September 20, Konoye attended a liaison conference of the Cabinet and General Staffs at which, under protest, he accepted October 15 as the final deadline for diplomacy with the United States. After that date negotiations might continue but mostly as a façade while war plans were being pursued in earnest. On September 26 Konoye told Lord Privy Seal Kido that the third Konoye Cabinet would have to resign unless the October 15 deadline could be further relaxed. Kido replied that Konoye was "behaving irresponsibly."

The next day, September 27, Konoye retired to his Kamakura villa for a rest and remained there until the first of the month, refusing to converse with anyone on public affairs.

Hirohito hardly noticed Konoye's unco-operative attitude, for he was immersed in the pros and cons of war. Thus, on September 29, he asked Lord Privy Seal Kido to investigate the amount of rubber the United States had stockpiled and to determine the quantity and quality of rubber which the United States could obtain from South America if Malayan and Indonesian sources were shut off. He was gratified to learn that the United States, under such circumstances, would have to depend almost entirely on synthetic rubber.

From October 1 to October 5 Hirohito was taken up with table-top maneuvers being held at the Army's War College. The exercises were to determine how long the Army would need to proceed "from Phase One of preparedness to Phase Two." Phase One called for some 400,000 troops to be mustered and ready near ports with adequate shipping in the heart of the Empire. Phase Two called for first-wave invasion forces to be waiting aboard transports on the southern frontiers of the Empire: Taiwan, Hainan, and Indochina. Hirohito had insisted earlier that Phase Two must be delayed as long as possible so as not to prejudice diplomatic negotiations. The Army had insisted that it would need three weeks to move from Phase One into Phase Two. The War College maneuvers demonstrated that the difficult and dangerous transition period could be abridged to two weeks.

The sulking Prime Minister Konoye finally returned from his tent to duty on October 1. The next day U.S. Secretary of State Hull, in an oral statement to Ambassador Nomura in Washington, reaffirmed the hard U.S. line that Japanese forces must withdraw from China as part of any lasting American-Japanese settlement in the Far East. A fortnight of frenzied political activity ensued in Tokyo. Influential Japanese pulled strings to get messages to the Emperor that war with the United States would be a disaster. Hirohito's closest advisors pinched themselves and told one another that they must be living through a bad dream. Navy Minister Oikawa suggested to Generals Tojo and Sugiyama that the Navy could not enter the war with any hope of success. Prime Minister Konoye alternately begged Ambassador Grew and Emperor Hirohito for help and comfort but was turned down by both. In Washington Ambassador Nomura began spending less time in secret negotiation with Secretary of State Hull—in a suite at the Wardman Park apartment hotel—and more time driving about the Virginia and Maryland countryside in sad meditation. Books have been filled with the comings and goings of that tragic fortnight, but nothing really happened, nothing changed.

Even Lord Privy Seal Kido had moments in which his dedication to the national program wavered. On October 9 he admitted to Prime Minister Konoye that the world situation was too complex for a clear-cut preference as to war or peace. Perhaps it would be best to live with U.S. economic sanctions, to be satisfied with a few of the provinces of China, and to ask the people to practice frugality and industry and build up the national strength for another ten years before seeking further expansion. If Konoye, he said, believed that this would be the best course for the nation, he should act on his own responsibility in favor of peace. If he had the conviction to pursue a policy of retrenchment, the Emperor, said Kido, could be persuaded to cancel the war decision of the imperial conference of September 6. Konoye promised to give the possibility serious thought.

The next day, October 10, Hirohito called in his cousin, former Navy Chief of Staff Prince Fushimi, and asked his opinion as to whether or not the Navy was prepared to fight. Fushimi replied that the Navy, despite pessimists like Navy Minister Oikawa, was not only ready to fight but to win. That same day Hirohito approved a combined Army-Navy command for operations in the Southern Regions and asked that the government reach a firm determination before the rapidly approaching deadline of October 15.

When the Cabinet met on October 12, War Minister Tojo expressed disgust with the continuing negotiations in Washington which were only wasting time and improving the relative position of the United States. Navy Minister Oikawa agreed that war was a possibility but asked that diplomacy be considered as an alternative. Moreover, said Oikawa, the decision should be made now for one or the other, for if diplomacy was continued much longer it would become a dishonorable smokescreen for war.

The next day, October 13, Hirohito indirectly admitted to Lord Privy Seal Kido that he saw no hope in further diplomacy. "The day after the war begins," he said, "we will have to issue an Imperial Declaration of War. Please see to it." He went on to disclaim all responsibility for the warlike sentiments of his people, observing that he had stressed his love for peace in the rescripts he had issued at the time of Japan's withdrawal from the League of Nations in 1933 and the signing of the Tripartite Pact in 1940. Finally, he asked Kido to make sure that lines of communication would be kept open for negotiating with the United States after war began. He suggested that a special envoy be sent to the Vatican so that the Pope could be used as a mediator.

On October 14, Prime Minister Konoye sent a last desperate message to President Roosevelt by the hand of Bishop Walsh, the Maryknoll Father who had first presented the basis for peace talks in Washington ten months earlier. He told Walsh to tell F.D.R. that unless a dramatic peace gesture was made immediately, the third Konoye Cabinet would have to resign and chances for a peaceful settlement would go aglimmering. Bishop Walsh accepted the assignment reluctantly for by now he was convinced that the United States was even less willing to patch up a peace settlement than Japan was. Nevertheless, as a matter of Christian duty, he accepted a place on a plane to Hong Kong, provided for him by Konoye, so that he could catch the next trans-Pacific Clipper.

As Bishop Walsh was embarking, Lord Privy Seal Kido and War Minister Tojo reached an agreement in the palace that the Konoye Cabinet must be replaced. Kido noted in his diary that

Tojo was willing to take the responsibility for a last postponement of military operations and a last try at diplomacy. Tojo reported as follows on the conversation to Chief of Staff Sugiyama:

KIDO: The next Cabinet will be difficult. The Army says we can fight on the strength of the September 6 decision in the Imperial Presence, but the Navy is worried. I think that is why Prime Minister Konoye can't make up his mind. He has to think as a politician.

TOJO: I asked the Navy Minister, "Has there been any change in the Navy's resolve since September 6? If there has been we will adjust plans accordingly." But he said, "No, there has been no change." . . . It seems to me that we have to stop trying to assign responsibility for the past and face up squarely to the question as to whether or not we can pursue the national program as decided.

To Sugiyama, Tojo added, "The Navy minister [Oikawa] won't say he has no confidence in victory but he continues, nevertheless, to talk that way. We can't make a decision because he won't commit himself. If the Navy can't make up its mind, we will have to look around for other solutions."

Sugiyama and Tojo agreed, after further chat, that one solution might be a new Cabinet with a new Navy minister.

By the next morning, October 15, everyone at Court was agreed that a Cabinet change seemed inevitable. Konoye reported that Tojo by now was so disgusted with procrastination that he would no longer talk to Konoye at Cabinet meetings. Hirohito was disappointed that Konoye should break his 1940 pledge "to share joys and sorrows with me to the very end." Nevertheless Hirohito approved the Cabinet change without demur, and all day Konoye's secretaries and the ubiquitous retired lieutenant general, Cabinet Planning Board Director Suzuki Tei-ichi, shuttled in and out of the palace as go-betweens in the quest for a suitable new government.

To accept the responsibility for the past and unify the Army and Navy for the future, War Minister Tojo and Prime Minister Konoye agreed on one point: that the best prime ministerial candidate would be Hirohito's scheming uncle, Prince Higashikuni, who had originally recruited Tojo and the rest of Hirohito's Army cabal in 1920. Lord Privy Seal Kido and other courtiers all

expressed horror at the thought of putting a member of the family
in front of the chrysanthemum curtain at a time when Japan
might enter a hazardous war with the United States. Hirohito
said that a Higashikuni Cabinet presented certain problems but
"might be all right."

After an afternoon and evening of scurrying conversations,
Konoye went late at night to Prince Higashikuni's villa to "feel
him out." Higashikuni asked for a few days to consider the proposal. While Konoye was absent from the palace, Hirohito and
Lord Privy Seal Kido interviewed War Minister Tojo and persuaded him to take the responsibility for forming the next Cabinet and for shouldering in it, simultaneously, the portfolios of
prime minister, war minister, and home minister.

The next afternoon Hirohito gave Tojo a private audience asking him if he would be willing to set aside the war decision of September 6 and take responsibility for holding the armed forces in
check while the final orders for war were postponed for another
month. Tojo noted that this additional time for negotiations
would be bought at the cost of a steady deterioration in Japanese
strength relative to U.S. strength, but he cheerfully acknowledged
that he felt strong enough politically to bear the responsibility.
A little over an hour later, at 5 P.M., Prince Konoye officially presented the mass resignation of his Cabinet.

The following day, October 17, Lord Privy Seal Kido solemnly
consulted seven of the living former prime ministers of Japan: the
Jushin or Elder Statesmen. The eighth, Baron Hiranuma, who had
supported Foreign Minister Matsuoka in his quixotic diversionary
schemes earlier that year, was conspicuously absent.[6] So were several others who might have been present if they had not been assassinated. Wakatsuki, the disgruntled dupe of the Manchurian
Incident, suggested that General Ugaki might make a good prime
minister. Hayashi, the dupe of the 1935 faction fight, sought to

[6] The seventy-five-year-old Hiranuma was recovering from a bullet which had
grazed his neck and nicked his jaw on August 14. Since the toughs who had
set upon him were some of Prince Higashikuni's Prayer-Meeting Plotters—
still out on bail because of Prince Higashikuni's influence with the police—
Hiranuma was understandably vexed. The fact that the Emperor had offered
him the services of one of the Court physicians and had sent him a basket of
fruit had failed to placate him. Since the accident, he had, however, given up
his outspoken criticism of the alliance with Germany.

settle responsibility on Prince Higashikuni. Then Lord Privy Seal Kido interrupted to propose Tojo. General Abe and diplomat Hirota both approved the choice. Admirals Okada and Yonai and the antediluvian Kiyoura all agreed to go along with it. Kido reported unanimity to the Emperor.

After confirming Tojo in his new triple responsibilities as prime, war, and home minister, Hirohito, about 6 P.M., called in outgoing Navy Minister Oikawa. From 1915 to 1922 Oikawa had been attached to Hirohito's person as naval adjutant and in 1921 he had gone along with Hirohito aboard the battleship *Katori* on the trip to Europe. In 1940 Oikawa had forced the Navy to accept the Tripartite Pact. Now Oikawa had taken more responsibility than he could, in conscience, bear. Hirohito gently told him that he would be replaced by Admiral Shimada Shigetaro who had also been close to Hirohito in the cabal in the early 1920's and who was a close personal friend of Tojo. It would be Shimada's responsibility, along with Tojo, to force the elder admirals of the Navy, against their better judgment, to embark on war with the United States. Hirohito thanked Oikawa for his long and painful service. Later, in 1944, as events turned out, he would make Oikawa the Navy chief of staff.

So it was that Tojo became prime minister of Japan and, in American eyes, the arch-villain of Japan's eighty years of planning for war with the West. On assuming office Tojo actually undertook to postpone the outbreak of war for a month, giving the eager myrmidons of the armed forces more time to ripen and rehearse their operations, giving the people more time to accept Japan's absolute rejection by the United States, and giving the diplomats one last impossible chance to negotiate Japan's inacceptable demands in Washington.

On October 18, Hirohito agreed to catapult Tojo, years ahead of normal schedule, from the rank of lieutenant general to that of full general. In the afternoon Hirohito and Kido went together to Yasukuni Shrine to worship the spirits of the dead warriors who had served the national program in the last century.

On October 20, in a routine conversation with Hirohito, Lord Privy Seal Kido took the opportunity to explain that he had suggested Tojo as prime minister in order to give Japan a moment's breathing space, for careful consideration, before leaping into a hasty war. Hirohito gazed at his favorite advisor and said, "You cannot catch a tiger cub unless you dare to enter the tiger's cave." It was the Japanese equivalent of "nothing ventured, nothing gained."

26

PEARL HARBOR

(1941)

SORGE'S ARREST

During the last two weeks of the Konoye Cabinet, the police arrested and imprisoned the members of the Soviet spy ring headed by Richard Sorge. At the time, German Gestapo observers ascribed the fall of Konoye to his embarrassingly close relations with Ozaki Hotsumi, the leading Japanese member of the ring. Western scholars, however, on review of the police files, have concluded that the arrests and the government turnover had little bearing on one another. Certainly, if Konoye was embarrassed, the "militarists" had nothing to do with it, for the arrests and interrogations of the spies were handled entirely by the civilian Thought Police of the Home Ministry. The military secret police were deeply chagrined that, in a matter of military security, they had not been able to strike first. The Thought Police, who had been watching the Sorge ring closely for over a year, were connected at a much higher level with state policy. They were probably directed to clean up the ring as a routine preparation for war at a time when the ring could serve state policy no further. Home Minister Tanabe Harumichi had served as the vice president and manipulator of puppet Henry Pu-yi's Privy Council in Manchukuo from 1932 to 1938.

The roundup of the ring began on September 29, 1941, when

the Thought Police took into custody Ito Tadasu.[1] After earlier arrests and interrogations as a subversive, Ito had been broken and made an informer for the police. They had then found him a job at the South Manchuria Railroad Research Institute, the spy-service center run by Dr. Okawa Shumei who had served as liaison man between palace and assassins during the terror of 1932. At the institute it was Ito's assignment to watch his fellow worker, the China expert Ozaki Hotsumi, who, as a member of the Sorge ring, had transmitted earlier messages from Lord Privy Seal Kido and young Saionji to Sorge for relay to the Soviet Union.

Now the Thought Police questioned informer Ito for eleven days before they felt that they had picked his brains clean. To the Thought Police, it seemed difficult to believe that Sorge could operate as he did within the German Embassy unless some larger conspiracy than his spy ring was involved. Finally, however, the interrogators were satisfied that Ito was concealing nothing and they moved on to their next arrest.

On September 11 they picked up Miyagi Yatoku, the Okinawa-born artist who had been sent to assist Sorge by the American Communist party in 1933. Miyagi alone in the Sorge ring behaved with unsophisticated heroics and refused to admit anything. In the first week of his interrogation he jumped or was pushed from an upstairs window of the Thought Police building, was caught by a tree, and only broke a leg.[2] He finally died in prison in August 1943.

Ozaki Hotsumi, the confidant of Prince Konoye and most valuable Japanese member of the ring, learned of Miyagi's arrest and waited stoically for his own. On October 14, he was supposed to eat dinner with Sorge at the Asia Restaurant in the South Manchuria Railroad Building. Leaving Sorge waiting in vain for him, he chose instead to spend a last evening with his wife and daughter. The next morning a single Thought Policeman came for him. He parleyed a moment with the man, made sure that his daugh-

[1] In English he has previously been known by an alternate reading of his name characters, Ito Ritsu.

[2] Being an American, Miyagi was suspected of being not only a Communist spy but also a U.S. spy. His continued existence, during the first year of anti-American war hysteria, greatly complicated negotiations for the rest of the Sorge spy ring and may have prevented the Thought Police from disposing of the ring as charitably as they might otherwise have done.

ter had left for school, and then without a further word to his wife left his home for the final three years of his life.

At the police station Ozaki authoritatively and successfully asked to see the chief prosecutor who would be assigned to his case by the Justice Ministry. The ordinary procedure of interrogation by detectives would not, he made clear, be required in his case because he was privy to state secrets for which detectives were not cleared and because he was already persuaded to tell the full truth. He was transferred at once to the detention section of Sugamo Prison where he began a three-year conversation with procurator Tamazawa Mitsusaburo who would present Japan's case against the Sorge ring in court. At the outset Ozaki revealed the names of all the agents in the ring and pleaded that both he and Sorge had been intermediaries in international negotiations rather than spies in the accepted sense. Months later, after countless interrogations, he would begin to confess that he was at fault in having always believed in a single socialist government for the entire world. Despite much time for thought and several written "changes of heart" he never succeeded in demonstrating a sincere rejection of his youthful idealisms. His interrogators all sympathized with him, but finally, after the fall of Tojo in 1944, when Peace Faction and kamikaze enthusiasts were delicately balanced on the scales of state, he was to be executed for the good and sufficient reason of political convenience.

After Ozaki's failure to keep his appointment and after learning that Miyagi, too, had disappeared, Richard Sorge spent two days waiting in fear. He admitted both to himself and to the other European members of his ring that the game was probably up. He drafted a halfhearted request to Moscow for reassignment, tried to book passage on a ship to Shanghai, and spent much time in bed, moping and dozing. Early in the evening of October 17, Max Klausen, the radio technician of the ring, called on him and found him finishing a case of saké with Branko de Voukelitch, the Yugoslavian photographic technician. Klausen was so depressed at the sight of Sorge lounging about fatalistically in his pajamas with a glass in his hand that he asked the news, contributed a fresh bottle of saké to the wake, and left it after ten minutes.

The next morning at 5 A.M. several Thought Policemen from the Home Ministry and an assistant procurator from the Justice Ministry waited outside Sorge's home for a German official car to go away from the curb out front. The head of the German News Agency was inside having a maddeningly mysterious conversation with Sorge which the police were never able to explain to their satisfaction. Sorge later insisted, throughout his interrogation, that the German had stopped by, at 5 A.M., simply to pick his brains on the recent change of Cabinet.

As soon as the German had left, the police presented themselves at Sorge's door and asked him to come with them for questioning in regard to his 1938 motorcycle accident. Sorge objected, as a foreign national, but was forced into a car and bundled off, still in his pajamas. The police noted that he had left behind him, open beside his bed, an arcane volume of sixteenth century Japanese poetry. That he might want to read it and understand it was set down in his favor.

Six days later, under severe and painful questioning, Sorge admitted that he was a Soviet agent and was handed over by the Thought Police to the assistant procurator from the Justice Ministry who had stood by at his arrest. This procurator, Yoshizawa Mitsusada, would become a familiar figure to American audiences at the 1951 Sorge hearings of the House Un-American Activities Committee. Alternately befriending Sorge and leaving him to the mercy of brutal guards, Yoshizawa would lead the broken spy question by question, revelation by revelation, process by due process through three years of examination, trial, judgment, and appeal. Finally Sorge would mount the gallows, forty-seven minutes after Ozaki Hotsumi, on the morning of November 7, 1944.

TOJO'S RESPONSIBILITY

In appointing Tojo simultaneously prime, war, and home minister, Hirohito gave him enough power to act as a shogun, a wartime dictator. Hirohito showed no uneasiness at delegating this immense power, for he was really delegating only responsibility and he trusted Tojo implicitly. Events would prove that his trust was not misplaced. Tojo and the Emperor had much in common: a quick appreciation of technical realities, a meticulous attention to detail, an impatience with too much indirection and belly talk, a charm which extended only to immediate personal relationships, and a blind pride in the righteousness of Japan's cause. Both men shared a conviction that "the Japanese race" had been persecuted by the white race. Both men had succeeded in cloistering themselves from the realities of Japan's own barbarous racism in dealing with fellow Asiatics.

In accepting the Emperor's mandate to be "shogun," Tojo promised to postpone war for a month, to discipline the noisy strategists who demanded war now or not at all, and to conduct a thorough, rational review of all the past policies and present exigencies which seemed to make war necessary. Hirohito does not appear, from his actions and comments, to have expected any change in policy from this review; rather, he seems to have wanted every argument and statistic, which had been working in his own mind, to be set forth sharply and clearly in black and white so that the fuzzy-minded politicians of his realm like Konoye would be made to see the need for war and so that posterity would understand his point of view. Accordingly, for a fortnight, from October 19 to November 1, shogun Tojo held the leaders of Japan in continual conference in order to make clear to them and their cohorts the rationale for the desperate gamble ahead.

At his first liaison conference of the Cabinet and General Staffs on October 23, 1941, Tojo expressed the Emperor's wishes firmly. Navy Chief of Staff Nagano said, "The Navy is consuming 400 tons of oil an hour. The situation is urgent. We want it decided one way or the other quickly." Army Chief of Staff Sugiyama said, "Things have already been delayed for a month. We can't devote four or five days to study. Hurry up and go ahead."

Tojo replied, "I well understand why the Supreme Command emphasizes the need to hurry. The government, however, would prefer to give the matter careful study and do it in a responsible way. There are now new ministers of the Navy, finance, and foreign affairs. I would like to have us decide whether the government can assume responsibility for the September 6 decision as it stands, or whether we must reconsider it from a new point of view. Does the Supreme Command have any objections?"

The two chiefs of staff both admitted that they could have no objections. For the next week, at daily liaison conferences, they watched Tojo parade experts, representing all factions in the Japanese state, and build up an irrefutable case for war. The presentations were long and complex. Little by little they brought out all the objections to war and contrasted them to the enormity of the retrenchment which Japan would have to make if she did not go to war while her oil and other stockpiles made war a feasible proposition. In the process the "experts" revealed a clear and bleak appreciation of the probable realities of the future.

The two chiefs of staff and their assistants argued convincingly with statistics that Japan could now seize Southeast Asia, with all its oil, rubber, tin, tungsten and rice, but that if she did not act now her ability to take the offensive would gradually wane until by mid-1942 U.S. defenses in the south would be too strong to breach. Thereafter Japan's military position would deteriorate progressively until a time would come only three or four years hence in which the United States could demand that Japan withdraw to her 1890 boundaries and she would have no rational alternative but to bow and comply.

The ubiquitous Suzuki, of the Cabinet Planning Board, backed the two chiefs of staff, but in the most pessimistic terms. If everything went perfectly and all norms could be met, Japan would just have enough steel, oil and ship producing capacity to tide herself over until the Dutch East Indies could be exploited and the Co-Prosperity Sphere could be made a self-sufficient economic bloc. Suzuki volunteered the information that accidents of weather or underestimates of the damage done by U.S. submarines could tip the scales and turn a slim margin of hope into a certainty of despair. Nevertheless, Suzuki insisted that this desperate gamble was preferable to the alternative of capitulation without a struggle. He predicted that Japan would lose little more by fighting and being defeated than by standing pat and being overpowered by economic pressure.

Finance Minister Kaya Okinori, a protégé of Prince Konoye, disagreed. He felt that the people might be willing to starve in order to meet military requirements but that, still, the military requirements would probably not be met. Runaway inflation might be prevented at home, but the conquered areas would have to be bled white. Japan might be able to take from Indonesia the war materials which she needed but would not be able to supply the manufactured goods which Indonesia now imported from Europe. Finally, Kaya refused to concede that the United States would necessarily take advantage of her strength in order to force Japan to her knees.

New Foreign Minister Togo Shigenori, the same who would later handle Japan's surrender notes in 1945, agreed with Kaya. He and Kaya failed to change the determination for war but they helped to lengthen Tojo's policy review until it became almost unbearable for the edgy military strategists participating in it. Finally, on October 30, a liaison conference adjourned with a firm pledge to sit again on November 1 and to remain sitting all day and all night, if necessary, until a conclusive recommendation could be made to the Emperor.

The next day, Friday October 31, Lord Privy Seal Kido met with Yoshida Shigeru, the postwar prime minister of Japan and son-in-law of Hirohito's former Lord Privy Seal Makino, and began conversations with him for the formation of the Peace Faction which would ultimately prepare for the contingency of Japan's surrender. Kido consummated his understanding with Yoshida at two further meetings on November 1 and 2.

Also on November 1 Admiral Yamamoto Isoroku and his staff gained Hirohito's editorial approval for their final draft of Order Number One, the comprehensive plan of Army and Navy operations which would be carried out in the months ahead. With Prince Takamatsu's blessing the top-secret plan went to a printer who would turn out three hundred numbered copies of it in the three days which followed.

THE CABINET CAPITULATES

Meanwhile, on November 1, shogun Tojo presided over the historic liaison conference which would decide on war. The conference of October 30 had adjourned noncommittally with an agreement to restrict future choice to one of three plans: 1) suspend war preparations and "sleep on logs and drink gall" for ten or twenty years while attempting to make Japan the industrial equal of the United States; 2) decide at once on war and forget

diplomacy; and 3) continue war preparations with a firm decision
to embark on war in early December while still conducting diplomatic negotiations "at a slow pace." Before the liaison conference
of November 1, between 7:30 and 8:30 in the morning, shogun
Tojo met for breakfast with Army Chief of Staff Sugiyama and
asked him to support plan number three. Sugiyama made no promises but nodded occasionally at Tojo as he ate his rice and sipped
his tea.

The liaison conference convened at the Imperial Headquarters
building just north of the Fukiage Gardens in the palace at 9 A.M.
It was to last for sixteen and a half hours, until 1:30 A.M. the
next morning. The reason for this wearisome argument was not
that anything new came up for discussion or even that there were
many points of disagreement. To be sure, Navy Chief of Staff
Nagano and Army Vice Chief of Staff Tsukada would both have
preferred to forget diplomacy altogether but they acquiesced without much struggle to the continuance of negotiations until the
last minute. Tsukada, in particular, wanted an early deadline of
November 13 put on the negotiations so that he would not have
to rescind operation orders after that date in case the United
States suddenly showed a willingness to compromise.

The training and mustering of some 400,000 men in the heart
of the Empire a thousand miles from the future fields of battle had
taxed both the logistic and the psychological resources of the
Army's officer corps. "I tell you," exclaimed Tsukada, "airplanes,
surface vessels, and submarines are soon going to start colliding
with one another." Navy Chief of Staff Nagano, however, observed wryly, "small collisions are incidents, not wars." Without
much argument, he and Tsukada agreed that war would be called
off if negotiations promised a settlement up to as late as midnight, November 30.

What protracted the proceedings for sixteen and a half hours
was the stubborn refusal of Foreign Minister Togo and Finance
Minister Kaya to make the recommendation to the Emperor unanimous. And what prompted their recalcitrance was their desire
not just to avert war but to avert a war commenced in a dishonorable fashion. Nothing in the record of what was said at the conference states clearly that Japan was deciding to deceive the

United States, but there was probably something to that effect in the position papers which were laid before the conferees because, early in the proceedings, Army Chief of Staff Sugiyama, in his minutes, recorded the following exchange.

[FINANCE MINISTER] KAYA: If there were hope of victory in the third year of the war, it would be all right to commence hostilities, but according to [Navy Chief of Staff] Nagano's explanation, this is not certain. Moreover, I would judge that the chances of the United States making war upon us are slight, so my conclusion must be that it would not be a good idea to declare war now.

[FOREIGN MINISTER] TOGO: I, too, cannot believe that the American fleet would come and attack us. I am not convinced that there is any need to start war now.

[NAVY CHIEF OF STAFF] NAGANO: There is a saying, "Don't rely on what may not happen." The future is uncertain; we can't take anything for granted. In three years enemy defenses in the south will be strong, and the number of enemy warships will also increase.

[FINANCE MINISTER] KAYA: Well, then, when can we go to war and win?

[NAVY CHIEF OF STAFF] NAGANO: Now! The time for war will not come later. . . .

KAYA and TOGO [*sic*]: Before we decide on this, we would like somehow to make a last attempt at diplomatic negotiations. This is a great turning point in the history of our country, which goes back 2,600 years; and on it hangs the fate of the nation. It's outrageous to ask us to resort to diplomatic trickery. We can't do it.

At 1:30 the next morning, Kaya and Togo still held out. The proposal to continue sincere negotiations up to midnight November 30 and then to start war a week later still had only majority support. The conferees adjourned with a vote to recommend the proposal to Hirohito even on this non-unanimous basis. Togo and Kaya, however, asked Prime Minister Tojo to give them until eleven o'clock in the morning before reporting their dissent officially to the Emperor. Finance Minister Kaya phoned the indefatigable Tojo shortly after daybreak to concede that he would add his vote to the majority. The bristling, correct Foreign Minister Togo held out to the dot of 11 A.M. and then, before perfecting the unanimity, succeeded in exacting from Tojo promises of support on two minor points which would give him some legitimate room to bargain in his dealings with the United States.

At 5 P.M. the tired Tojo reported the sweat-stained unanimity that had been exacted of the vassals to Emperor Hirohito. When Hirohito sought to go over the course of the debate in some detail, Tojo broke down and wept in the Imperial Presence. Much time, he said, had already been wasted in study. The deadline requested by the best strategists of the Army and Navy had already been missed by a month. The Supreme Command needed orders from the Emperor to begin the final training exercises for Army and Navy pilots who, being enlisted men, could not expect to prepare without orders. Finally Tojo begged Hirohito to call a conference in the Imperial Presence to formalize the war decision. Also, said Tojo, he hoped that the Emperor himself would support the decision.

Having seen many such protestations in his time Hirohito persisted in asking some questions.

"What ideas do you have," he said, "as to our justification for what we will do, so that we can uphold our honor?"

"We are still studying that matter," replied Tojo wearily, "and will report to you soon."

"I suggest," said Hirohito, "that we send a special envoy to the Pope so that we can use him as a mediator to save the situation if worse comes to worst."

Then the Emperor went on to ask several shrewd questions as to the reliability of Army-Navy estimates of iron and steel production and of shipping losses during the first year of war. Finally, he gave Tojo his approval for what had been transacted.

ORDER NUMBER ONE

The following day, November 3, Navy Chief of Staff Nagano received his bound, numbered copy of Admiral Yamamoto's Order Number One which incorporated the Pearl Harbor attack plan as a salient feature in a comprehensive blueprint for the whole

Strike South. Order Number One began with a preamble which attempted to give the justification for war which Hirohito wished to have explained:

Despite the fact that the Empire has always maintained a friendly attitude toward the United States, the United States has interfered in all the measures which we have taken out of self-preservation and self-defense for the protection of our interests in East Asia. Recently she has blocked our speedy settlement of the China Incident by aiding the government of Chiang Kai-shek and has even resorted to the final outrage of breaking off economic relations with us. . . .

After the preamble, Yamamoto quickly got to the main point: "The Japanese Empire will declare war on the United States, Great Britain, and the Netherlands. War will be declared on X-day. The order will become effective on Y-day." Yamamoto's order went on to prescribe in detail the units to be employed in the various operations and even the voice codes which would be used by his own Pearl Harbor forces. "The cherry blossoms are all in their glory," meaning warriors are about to fall, would signify, "There are no warships in Pearl Harbor; the American fleet has escaped." The message "Climb Mount Fuji" would mean "weather and other conditions suitable for attack." "Five hundred twenty is the depth of the moat at Honno Temple" (where the Great Musketeer Oda Nobunaga was betrayed and assassinated) would mean "Attack scheduled for 0520."

Some of the admirals who had attended the Yamamoto special maneuver in the Naval Staff College two months earlier still disapproved of the Pearl Harbor plan as a poor gamble tactically and as a mere gesture strategically—one which might temporarily knock out the U.S. Pacific fleet but one, also, which would affront the United States and make it difficult to negotiate a peace later when Japan had occupied the Philippines, Malaya, and the Dutch East Indies and could bargain from a position of strength.

Few in the Army knew of Yamamoto's plan. The over-all commander for Army operations in the south, General Count Terauchi, had been let in on it only six weeks previously. Army Chief of Staff Sugiyama, by the evidence of his own memoranda, had been informed of it a scant four days before. Shogun Tojo was probably still in the dark about it.[3] Civilians like Foreign Minister Togo simply knew that the Navy had a plan for "ambushing" the U.S. fleet. They assumed—and it was one of the assumptions on which they based their disapproval of war—that the "ambush" would take place only if the U.S. Navy was foolish enough to steam west in order to relieve the Philippines after it had been attacked. Only Hirohito, a few members of his family, the staff chiefs, and some of Yamamoto's own trusted naval colleagues yet knew of the Pearl Harbor plan.

As soon as Navy Chief of Staff Nagano received his copy of Order Number One on the morning of November 3, he took it to the palace. There he was joined by his opposite number, Army Chief of Staff Sugiyama, and together with Sugiyama he was ushered into the Imperial Presence. Hirohito had his own copy of Order Number One before him and began at once to ask questions about points which seemed unclear in it. The Western concession areas in China would be occupied *after* the attack began on Hong Kong, would they not? Sugiyama promised to look into the matter. The monsoon season, continued Hirohito, would adversely affect air operations over Malaya, would it not? Sugiyama gave the Emperor a sheaf of meteorological statistics and said:

"We had planned to overwhelm the enemy [in Malaya] by initial air attacks, but since it rains there now three or four times a day we will concentrate on surprise in the landing of troops. I think the Philippines will go all right. We are studying the two operations together and will decide appropriately."

Hirohito said, "Tojo is much concerned about rapid issuance of orders to the air forces."

Sugiyama answered, "The airmen and their support units are waiting in Dairen, Tsingtao, Shanghai, and other points, ready for take-off. We have studied all the disadvantages in delaying their flight orders and have found countermeasures. We now think that we can overcome all obstacles even if the imperial orders are not issued until after the final conference in the Imperial Presence. I, personally, think that this is the most proper way."

[3] Professor Robert J. C. Butow, who has made Tojo's various postwar statements one of his specialties, has written, "It would appear that Tojo did not learn of the navy's decision to adopt the [Pearl Harbor] plan until a day or two before the imperial conference of December 1."

"Yes," said Hirohito, "it's best to keep everything proper." Then, darting on, he said, "I suppose that from the point of view of national justification, it would be best to negotiate as soon as possible with Thailand [for permission to march across Thai territory into Malaya]. But from the point of view of military surprise, it might be better to postpone the Thai negotiations as long as possible. What do you think?"

"His Imperial Majesty," replied Sugiyama, "is absolutely correct. However, if we don't decide [how to continue the negotiations already in progress] we may betray our plans. Now as never before, the situation is urgent and we must be extremely cautious. I will study the matter, talk to the Foreign Ministry, and report to you again."

"What is the Navy's target date?" asked Hirohito.

Navy Chief of Staff Nagano, who had been standing silently by, replied briefly: "December 8 is the target date."

"Isn't that a Monday?" asked Hirohito.[4]

"We chose it," said Nagano, "because everyone will be tired after a holiday."

"Will the same date apply for all the other regions?" asked Hirohito.

"Well, since there is a great difference in distances [from our various mustering points]," replied Chief of Staff Sugiyama, "I doubt that we can co-ordinate all our attacks on precisely the same date."

Hirohito nodded. With his aides-de-camp he had pored over the charts of Southeast Asia for years. He knew well the distances involved and the difficulties of tides and winds and reefs. With his acquiescence, Navy Chief of Staff Nagano returned to the Naval Staff Headquarters on the edge of Hibiya Park just outside the palace gates. There Rear Admiral Kuroshima Kumahito, who had brought Nagano his copy of Order Number One from Yamamoto's flagship in the Inland Sea, was tensely waiting for him. "I just talked to Yamamoto on the phone," announced Kuro-

---

[4] Monday, December 8, Japanese time, or Sunday, December 7, U.S. time, was, of course, to be the date of Pearl Harbor. Previous American historians have reported that this date was chosen by Admiral Yamamoto himself in mid-November, and that Hirohito did not know of it or of the Pearl Harbor plan at all until December 2. General Sugiyama's memoranda, published in 1967, have set the record straight and made it credible.

shima. "He says that if you do not agree to his plan, he will have to resign from the service."

Nagano beamed, wrapped an arm around Kuroshima's shoulder, and said, "I fully understand how Yamamoto feels. If he has that much confidence in his scheme, he must be allowed to carry on with it. It has been approved."

Kuroshima had a plane standing by and flew immediately south to give Yamamoto the news. That night aboard the flagship *Nagato*, there was a solemn ceremonial drinking of saké. With the support of Hirohito, Prince Takamatsu, and Marquis Komatsu, Yamamoto and his men felt that they had given Japan a fighting chance.

THE WAR COUNCIL ASSENTS

Before affixing his seal of state to Yamamoto's Order Number One and converting it officially into a *Taimei* or Great Order, Hirohito summoned a meeting of the Supreme War Council to sit in his presence and approve on the following day, November 4. In addition to the Army and Navy ministers, the chiefs of staff, the commanders of the Kure and Yokosuka naval bases, two former Navy ministers, and a former commander at Kure, the meeting was attended by General Terauchi who was to command the Strike South, by General Doihara and Vice Admiral Shinozuka Yoshio of the spy service, and by Princes Kanin, Fushimi, Asaka, and Higashikuni. Hirohito sat silent at one end of the room while old Prince Kanin, just in front of him at a lower altar, presided and moderated. On the two tables running down the sides of the room, before the rest of the conferees, reposed copies of a single brief paper declaring the business of the meeting. It said:

To break open the present crisis, to fulfill the nation's inner life and self-defense, and to establish a New Order in Greater East Asia, the Empire, on this occasion, decides to make war on the United States, England, and Holland.

For this purpose the time to activate our military forces is set for early December.

Navy Chief of Staff Nagano opened the meeting by explaining that the purpose of going to war was to prevent Japan from being strangled by an alliance of the United States, Great Britain, and the Netherlands. "The Empire," he said, "is now facing the most critical situation of its entire history." Going on to describe the expectations of the Navy, he said: "If we start in early December with the strength we now possess, we have a very great chance of victory in phase one of the war. By phase one I mean the defeat of enemy forces in the Far East and the reduction of enemy strongholds throughout the southwestern Pacific. Our degree of success in this first phase may determine the outcome of the war." The recommendation to strike immediately, he continued, was based on careful study of three factors: "the present strength of our forces compared to the enemy's, the need to attack before being attacked, and meteorological considerations." He concluded his presentation with an oblique reference to the secret Pearl Harbor plan, which no one present, except the Emperor, knew much about, and with a plea for secrecy. "As mentioned above, the outcome of the war depends greatly on the outcome of phase one, and the outcome of phase one depends on the outcome of our surprise attack. We must conceal our war intentions at all costs."

Army Chief of Staff Sugiyama continued with a brief résumé of the forces on both sides which might be thrown into the battle. There were, he said, 60,000 to 70,000 men and 320 planes in Malaya; 42,000 men and 170 planes in the Philippines, 85,000 men and 300 planes in the Dutch East Indies, and 35,000 men and 60 planes in Burma. In addition, 300,000 men and about 200 planes in India, 250,000 men and about 300 planes in Australia, and 70,000 men and about 150 planes in New Zealand might be brought into play by the enemy as reinforcements. In practical terms he anticipated that Japan would have to contend with about 200,000 troops, 70 per cent of them "natives" who had the advantage of being "used to tropical climates" and the disadvantage of "inadequate training and a generally low fighting ability." However, some of the enemy planes, he cautioned, were "high-performance craft with relatively well-trained pilots."

Against the total 850,000-man strength of the enemy's front-line and reserve forces, Sugiyama pointed out that Japan could draw on 51 active divisions with "manpower of about 2 million soldiers." Against the roughly 200,000 men which the Army might realistically meet on the field, Sugiyama expected to use 11 Japanese divisions or about 220,000 men. He reported that "one division is already in Indochina, five are waiting and training in Japan and Taiwan, and five more will be transferred from the China theater. . . . They are all ready to move the moment the Emperor's Great Order is issued."

Sugiyama went on to explain that the enemy was increasing its air power at the rate of 10 per cent every two months and its ground strength at the rate of over 4,000 men a month, making it absolutely essential to attack soon. "The enemy forces, however, are scattered," he said. "Being able to attack with surprise and with our strength concentrated, we will be able to defeat the enemy units one at a time. Once we land successfully, we are quite sure we will win."

After Sugiyama's presentation the floor was thrown open for a perfunctory debate. Prince Asaka, the imperial uncle who had raped Nanking, set the tone by declaring impatiently: "This activation date of early December is about a month and a half later than the one decided upon during the time of the Konoye government. According to the explanation of the two chiefs of staff, it seemed then that the earlier we attacked the better. I fully agreed. What is the reason that early December has been chosen? Does it have something to do with these diplomatic negotiations?"

Prince Asaka was answered by his elder kinsman, the seventy-six-year-old former chief of staff, Prince Kanin: ". . . In international affairs it is necessary to co-ordinate military strategy with diplomatic strategy."

Prince Asaka next asked why the chiefs of staff were planning to fight a long war when it was apparent that only a short war—in view of national resources—would be advantageous. Prince Kanin, Navy Chief of Staff Nagano, and Prime Minister Tojo all responded to this question. In the course of their answers a number of pertinent observations were made. Prince Kanin saw only a 30 per cent chance of concluding a settlement with the United States but opined, also, that the United States was only bargaining at all because it had its own weaknesses: a navy divided between two oceans and a dependence upon Asiatic tin, rubber, and tungsten.

Navy Chief of Staff Nagano regretted that a short war seemed impossible, because he could promise that Japan would win a one- or two-year war but would face countless uncertainties in a three- or four-year war. The United States, he pointed out, was simply too big to be invaded, occupied, and defeated absolutely. Still, there was hope, he asserted, that Germany would conquer England and so make the United States receptive to a negotiated peace.

Prime Minister Tojo observed that he too would have liked to begin the war earlier but that diplomatic negotiations had gained time for military preparations. Army Chief of Staff Sugiyama reviewed the co-ordinated planning of the Navy and the 25th Army for the seizure of Malaya and expressed the conviction that military operations in the south would go according to plan.

The other imperial uncle, the devious Prince Higashikuni, then said: "It seems to me necessary to clarify our reasons for resort to force. What do you all think of explaining our justification and declaring the purpose of our holy war to the nation and the world? Then the people could set their minds on self-sacrifice at a time of national crisis."

Shogun Tojo replied: "I, too, think it imperative to clarify our national justification before we go to war. I am now studying the problem of a clear statement of our war purposes. As yet, however, I am not in a position to make such a clarifying statement in the presence of His Imperial Majesty."

Prince Higashikuni, disregarding Tojo's barbed words, plunged on blandly: "It goes without saying that we must anticipate a long war. Also, however, we must start thinking right now about concluding the war at an appropriate time. Indeed we must consider the possibility of using our commanding position under His Imperial Majesty to settle not only the differences between the United States and Japan but also those which disturb the world at large."

Tojo answered: "It is certainly desirable to end the war in a short period. We've studied the problem from many angles but as yet we have not come up with any really illuminating ideas. I regret that we have no means of controlling the life or death of the enemy. The possibility of a long war is 80 per cent. A short war is conceivable, however, under the following circumstances: destruction of most of the U.S. fleet—a distinct possibility, especially if the United States tries to retake the Philippines after we have occupied it; loss in America of the will to fight—a result which might follow a German declaration of war on the United States and German landings in England; control of England's lifeline—control, that is, of the shipping lanes which keep her from starving; finally, occupation and closing of the sources in the Far East of many of the military raw materials of the United States."

Later in the meeting, when pressed too far to accept all the responsibility for the war, the military members of the Supreme War Council who were not part of the imperial family began to protest a little. At one point Chief of Staff Sugiyama said: "Yes, when the monsoon blows [we may indeed encounter adverse meteorological conditions]. Our early studies showed clearly that it would have been best to finish our preparations in October and conduct our advance south now in November."

A few minutes later Field Marshal Prince Kanin asked that the meeting endorse unanimously the war decision. No one objected. Kanin turned to the Emperor and reported that the decision was recommended. Hirohito nodded, rose, and "withdrew into the Inner Palace."

When he had gone, the various members of the Supreme War Council individually approved for the record certain questions which they had submitted in writing to the General Staff before the meeting and which had been answered—also in writing, beforehand—by the responsible officers in the General Staff. These written questions and answers had been reviewed by the Emperor and were now formally entered as "source materials" on the palace rolls. Although not deemed worthy of live discussion at the conference, they included several surprisingly candid statements. They opened with a question by Prince Asaka requesting that the Army and Navy unify their command functions and co-operate thoroughly in the months ahead. The answer from the General Staffs was reassuring. After Asaka's questions, General Terauchi, the Supreme Commander for the Southern Regions was represented as asking, "Isn't there really any way to avoid a prolonged war?" The answer was, "There are no good ideas on that point but . . ." Again the hope was voiced that England would be occupied by Germany and the United States would grow tired of fighting.

Terauchi's next written question was: "What are the most

important points to remember in our administration of the occupied areas?"

The answer was: "First, secure raw materials; second, insure freedom of transport for war materials and personnel; third, in accomplishing these two objectives, we must not hesitate, as we did in China, to oppress the natives. On the other hand, we will not interfere in the details of government, as we did in China, but will make use of existing organizations and show respect for native customs."

A moment later the reading came to the questions of General Doihara, the aging espionage expert known as the "Lawrence of Manchuria." Doihara's second question was: "What is the official excuse for this war against America, Britain, and the Dutch?"

The answer was: "This is a clash between nations which have different world philosophies. The basic purpose of the war is to make the Americans do obeisance to us against their will—that and the establishment of the Co-Prosperity Sphere to make us self-sufficient. Before we achieve these ends we must be prepared for a long war. Our immediate short-term ends are to break out of encirclement, undermine the morale of Chiang Kai-shek, seize the raw materials of the south, expel the Anglo-Saxon race from Asia, make the Chinese and the peoples of the Southern Regions depend on us rather than on the United States and England, open a southern route for closer ties between Asia and continental Europe, and get a monopolistic corner on the rubber, tin, and other raw materials which the United States needs for military purposes."

Having considered such frank questions and answers and having taken responsibility for the war, the Supreme War Councillors adjourned without ever seeing Yamamoto's Order Number One on which they were implicitly passing.

THE FORMAL WAR DECISION

The next day Hirohito presented the same responsibility in still more disguised, security-conscious form to the assembled civilians of the Cabinet. Together with the most trustworthy bureaucrats, both civil and military, the Cabinet ministers met in full conclave for the conclusive conference in the Imperial Presence which fi-

nally passed upon the tactical plans that had been incubating for
months and the strategic plans which had been incubating for
decades. At these proceedings, on November 5, as a result of careful staging, all the right things were said to prepare the people
and the palace records for the hazardous gamble on which Hirohito and his family had embarked.

The written motion presented to the conferees for them to
pass was almost the same as the one laid before the Supreme War
Council the day before: hostilities against the United States, Great
Britain, and The Netherlands, beginning in early December. It
added: "Negotiations with the United States will be carried out
in accord with the attached document. . . . If negotiations with
the United States are successful by the beginning of December,
the use of force will be called off."

The attached document described two diplomatic offers which
would be made to the United States. The first, Proposal A, was
intended as an over-all long-range settlement of U.S.-Japanese differences. It promised:

Withdrawal . . . of the Japanese troops sent to China during the
China Incident; those in designated sections of North China and Inner Mongolia, and those on Hainan Island, will remain for a necessary
period of time after the establishment of peace between Japan and
China. The remainder of the troops will begin withdrawal simultaneously with the establishment of peace in accordance with arrangements to be made between Japan and China, and the withdrawal will
be completed within two years.
Note: In case the United States asks what the "necessary period of
time" will be, we will respond that we have in mind twenty-five
years. . . .
Japanese troops currently stationed in French Indochina will be
immediately withdrawn after the settlement of the China Incident or
the establishment of a just peace in the Far East. . . .
The Japanese government will recognize the application of the
principle of nondiscrimination in the entire Pacific region, including
China, if this principle is applied throughout the world. . . .
Regarding the interpretation and execution of the Tripartite Pact,
the Japanese government, as it has stated on previous occasions, will
act independently [without regard for Germany's interpretation]. . . .
Regarding the so-called Four Principles put forward by the United
States [respect for other nations' sovereignty, for the right of self-

determination, for their right to equal treatment, and in general for the status quo], we will make every effort to avoid their inclusion in official agreements between Japan and the United States—and this includes "understandings" and other communiques.

If this Proposal A failed to gain U.S. acceptance, Proposal B should be offered. This was to be a temporary settlement, a modus vivendi, based on a return to the position the previous June before Japan had occupied southern Indochina and the United States had frozen Japanese assets and interdicted Japan's oil supplies. As the price paid for it, in order to purchase time, both sides were to make promises:

Both Japan and the United States will pledge not to make an armed advance into Southeast Asia and the South Pacific area. . . .
The Japanese and American governments will co-operate with each other so that the procurement of necessary materials from the Dutch East Indies will be assured.

When everyone had had a chance to read the decision for war and the two diplomatic proposals by which war might still be averted, Hirohito entered the large ceremonial eastern audience chamber in the Outer Palace and the conference began. Foreign Minister Togo pleaded for help in laying Proposal A and Proposal B as sincerely as possible before the United States. The ubiquitous retired lieutenant general, Suzuki, who was president of the Planning Board, gave a summary of national strength and advocated war in case the United States should turn down the two diplomatic proposals. He spoke with a transparent optimism about increasing steel production, decreasing its civilian consumption and supplementing the merchant marine available for routine trade by the use of "presently idle sailing vessels provided with auxiliary engines."

"Since the probability of victory in the initial stages of the war is sufficiently high," he said, "I am convinced that we should take advantage of our assured victory and turn the heightened morale of the people, who are determined to overcome the national crisis even at the cost of their lives, toward production as well as toward [reduced] consumption. . . . This would be better than just sitting tight and waiting for the enemy to put pressure on us."

Finance Minister Kaya spoke next. He pointed out that the national budget had doubled since 1936 and that only the enforced contributions of the people through bond buying and high taxes had as yet saved the economy from runaway inflation. "The people," he said, "will continue to make every effort and endure sacrifices because they are the subjects of our Empire." He judged, therefore, that it would be possible to keep the country from financial collapse until the people began to die in large numbers from starvation. He warned, however, that "if we cannot supply the materials necessary to carry on military activities and maintain the people's livelihood, the national economy must collapse no matter how perfect the government's financial and monetary policy."

He further warned: "The areas in the south that are to become the object of military operations have been importing materials of all kinds in large quantities. If these areas are occupied by our forces, their imports will cease. Accordingly, to make their economies run smoothly, we will have to supply them with materials. However, since our country does not have sufficient surpluses for that purpose, we will not be able, for some time, to give much consideration to the living conditions of the people in these areas, and for a while we will have to pursue a policy of so-called exploitation."

Navy Chief of Staff Nagano followed with a reiteration of all the arguments for war made on the day before.

Then Foreign Minister Togo gave a résumé of the position in the talks in Washington:

The two parties have virtually agreed upon the matter of preventing the expansion of the war. On this question, what the United States wants is to exert military power against Germany as a right of self-defense, while Japan promises not to exert military force in the Pacific region.

With regard to peace between Japan and China: the two parties have not agreed upon the question of stationing and withdrawing troops. Japan must station troops in necessary places for a necessary period of time. . . . Nevertheless, the United States demands that we proclaim the withdrawal of all troops, but we cannot accept the demand. . . .

Both parties have agreed not to solve political problems in the Pacific region by military force. Concerning this, the withdrawal of troops from French Indochina is a problem we have not agreed on.

There was a discussion of the diplomatic impasse in which, at one point, Prime Minister General Tojo frankly stated, "We can expect an expansion of our country only by stationing troops [in China.]"

Finally Privy Council President Hara delivered a lengthy and carefully prepared statement on behalf of the Throne. It was a statement which Hirohito had personally requested and reviewed in advance and which still bore the imprint of his own turns of phrase and simplifying abstractions.

At the last Imperial Conference it was decided that we would go to war if the negotiations failed to lead to agreement. According to the briefings given today, the present American attitude is not just the same as the previous one, but is even more unreasonable. Therefore I regret very much that the negotiations have little prospect of success.

. . . We cannot let the present situation continue. If we miss the present opportunity to go to war, we will have to submit to American dictation. Therefore, I recognize that it is inevitable that we must decide to start a war against the United States. I will put my trust in what I have been told: namely, that things will go well in the early part of the war; and that although we will experience increasing difficulties as the war progresses, there is some prospect of success.

. . . I do not believe that the present situation would have developed out of the China Incident alone. We have come to where we are because of the war between Germany and Great Britain. What we should always keep in mind here is what would happen to relations between Germany and Great Britain and Germany and the United States—all of them being countries whose population belongs to the white race—if Japan should enter the war. Hitler has said that the Japanese are a second-class race, and Germany has not yet declared war against the United States. . . .

We must give serious consideration to race relations. . . . Don't let hatred of Japan become stronger than hatred of Hitler so that everybody will in name as well as fact gang up on Japan. . . .

[If we do not enter the war] two years from now we will have no petroleum for military use. Ships will stop moving. When I think about the strengthening of American defenses in the Southwest Pacific, the expansion of the American fleet, the unfinished China Incident, and so on, I see no end to difficulties. We can talk about austerity and suffering, but can our people endure such a life for a long time? . . . I fear, that if we sit tight, we may become a third-class nation after only two or three years. . . .

As to what our moral basis for going to war should be, there is some merit in making it clear that Great Britain and the United States represent a strong threat to Japan's self-preservation. Also, if we are fair in governing occupied areas, attitudes toward us would probably relax. America may be enraged for a while, but later she will come to understand. No matter what happens, I wish to be sure that the war does not become a racial war.

Do you have any other comments? If not, I will rule that the proposals have been approved in their original form.

No one said a word. Hirohito nodded his satisfaction and made his recessional. The war had been decided.

HIROHITO INCOGNITO

From that moment, until the Pearl Harbor attack a month and three days later, Hirohito worked night and day to review every detail of war planning. At the same time he impressed on his intimates the importance of gaining the full support of the people; of upholding a façade of propriety and due deliberation for the sake of posterity; and of deceiving the enemy.

As soon as the November 5 meeting had adjourned, Hirohito approved the dispatch of a special envoy to Washington to assist Ambassador Nomura. The envoy selected was Kurusu Saburo, a career diplomat who, as ambassador in Berlin in 1940, had consummated the Tripartite Pact with Hitler. His mission was a delicate one. He must suggest to President Roosevelt, without seeming to threaten him, that Japan was not bluffing this time in attaching a deadline to negotiations. Then, if the United States remained intractable and the deadline passed, he must overcome Ambassador Nomura's sense of honor in order to keep up the negotiations as a subterfuge. Finally, without endangering security, he must make everyone at the Japanese Embassy in Washington aware of the decision which had been reached in Tokyo.

A Pan American Clipper, on State Department instructions,

was kept waiting for forty-eight hours in Hong Kong so that Mr. Kurusu could board it. The new ambassador finally arrived in Washington November 16.

During Kurusu's eleven-day departure and journey, Hirohito repaired to his seaside villa in Hayama and there assumed incognito in order to assist personally at two final, three-day reviews of all war planning. So secret were these *gozen heigo*, these "soldier chess games in the Imperial Presence" as Chief of Staff Sugiyama called them, that not even the places at which they were held has ever been divulged. Some of them were probably conducted at sea aboard the flagship of the Pearl Harbor task force, the *Akagi*, and the rest at the Army base near Numazu about forty miles down the coast from Hayama by air, or about one hundred miles by sea.

The published record concerning these *gozen heigo* exemplifies the extreme circumspection of Japanese belly talk. Since late October Hirohito had been talking to his civilian chamberlains about the possibility of going down to Hayama for a brief "vacation." Since it was a bleak season of the year for such an outing, those who knew Hirohito's character assumed that he would be going to Hayama to disarm foreign observers by a show of unconcern before Japan's blitzkrieg.

Even with his military chiefs Hirohito disguised his reasons for wanting to attend the war games. It was his prerogative and his traditional duty to have a few private words with all generals and admirals when they left Japan on important missions. Now, when a great number of commanders were about to leave Japan all at once, a steady stream of military visitors calling at the palace might come to the attention of foreign observers and excite suspicion. Therefore Hirohito had asked the Army and Navy chiefs of staff to devise means by which he could hold his audiences with the commanders in secrecy. It was understood that in this fashion, under the pretext of a ceremonial farewell to his warriors, he could review all war plans without officially sanctioning any of them—without, that is, encumbering the Throne with responsibility for plans that might fail.

With these understandings and covers in mind, Hirohito called the two chiefs of staff into his presence immediately after the Imperial Conference on November 5.

"From the security standpoint," he asked, "when will we dispatch the commanders and the others to their posts in the field?"

"The Supreme Command," replied Sugiyama, "will talk over military plans for three days on the seventh, eighth, and ninth. After that the forces attached to their commands will have similar co-ordinating meetings. I do not think it advisable to dispatch the commanders too early to their posts lest our secret plans leak out."

The Emperor, noted Sugiyama, "seemed to understand well, made his decision at once, and asked several questions."

Hirohito left for Hayama at 10 A.M. November 7. At the seaside villa he was free of most of the protocol and security which beset him in the moats and walls of his Tokyo residence. His imperial marine biological yacht was recognized as a sacrosanct hideaway by both reporters and security police. It was equipped with ship-to-shore radiotelephone and running lights for night voyages.

Kido, who accompanied Hirohito to Hayama and took care of all state business for him during the "vacation," did not see his master from the morning of the seventh until the morning of the tenth. Then, after the general Army-Navy co-ordinating sessions, Hirohito appeared for a forty-five-minute chat with his chief advisor. He at once vanished again until the unit-co-ordinating studies had been completed on November 13. During this second disappearance, he is said to have been aboard the carrier *Akagi*, reviewing the co-ordination of the Pearl Harbor attack fleet.

On November 14, Hirohito resurfaced at Hayama to catch up on civilian developments and to receive briefings from Prime Minister Tojo, Foreign Minister Togo, and Finance Minister Kaya. On the fifteenth he returned to Tokyo.

As soon as he had "re-entered the palace gate" he gave audience to Army Chief of Staff Sugiyama. In his memoranda Sugiyama had eloquently filled the days of Hirohito's absence from Tokyo with eighty-three pages of compressed numerical tables on Japan's present and projected military-industrial strength in comparison with that of the enemy. Now, "on November 15, after the chess game with soldiers in the Imperial Presence," Sugiyama recorded Hirohito's afterthoughts.

"Where," asked the Emperor, "is the Strike-South commander going to set up his headquarters?"

"In Saigon," replied Sugiyama.

"Is there a possibility of our spoiling the Malayan rubber plantations?"

"I don't know," said Sugiyama. "There may be some damage. But since, except for the Kedah area, the roads are narrow, we think the best procedure is to advance in small units of a single regiment led by a few tanks. That way there should be little danger of damaging the rubber forests."

Hirohito nodded and asked Sugiyama for renewed assurance that military operations could be called off at any moment if the United States showed signs of agreeing to Japan's diplomatic demands. Sugiyama went so far as to swear that even if the enemy attacked Japan before Japan attacked the enemy, the Army and Navy had orders to contain the conflict as much as possible until the Emperor personally gave the word for war.

"I have explained to Terauchi and the other commanding officers," said Sugiyama, "that if diplomatic negotiations suddenly succeed through military backing, it will prove the strength of the military forces and make it possible for them to withdraw with honor."

FLEET DISPATCH

On November 7, the day of the Emperor's arrival in Hayama, Combined Fleet Commander Admiral Yamamoto had revealed to his most trusted staff officers that December 8 would be the day of attack. On November 10, after the first three co-ordinating days of the "war games in the Imperial Presence," Yamamoto had had Admiral Nagumo Chu-ichi, who would personally lead the Pearl Harbor attack force, order all the ship captains in his fleet to "complete battle preparations by November 20." That same day the first of twenty-seven of Japan's largest submarines —320-foot I-class boats with a cruising range of 12,000 miles at fourteen knots—slipped out of the fleet to thread its way between American reconnaissance areas and to take up a watch three weeks later outside the mouth of Pearl Harbor.

On November 11, having thoroughly committed himself and the Emperor to his Pearl Harbor plan, Admiral Yamamoto wrote to one of his mentors, a retired admiral and family friend, "I leave my family to your guidance. . . . What a strange position it is in which I find myself. I am having to lead in a decision diametrically opposed to my personal beliefs. And I have no choice but full speed ahead."

By November 14, most of the Pearl Harbor task force had gathered around Yamamoto's flagship in Saiki Bay, off the northeast corner of Kyushu, so that its captains could have a last word with the commander before they sailed. Admiral Nagumo Chuichi's flagship, the carrier *Akagi*, was still in the Tokyo area, at Yokosuka Naval Base, picking up the last of a consignment of special torpedoes which would be used for the attack on Hawaii. They were rigged for shallow running with wooden fins devised in September during trials at Kagoshima Bay. Ordinary torpedoes, it had been determined, would bury and waste themselves in the mud under Pearl Harbor's confined waters.

The other five carriers of the Pearl Harbor attack force now began detaching themselves one by one, and night by night, from Yamamoto's fleet to make their way around Japan to Hitokappu Bay, sometimes called Tankan Bay, a harbor of rendezvous in the northern extremities of the Empire, at Etorofu Island in the Kuriles. There, under the gaze of seals and walruses rubbing up their winter coats on the hard beaches, they were to load drums of oil which Yamamoto had received imperial sanction to cache months earlier in a shed beside a small concrete wharf. The drums would fill the tanks of the carriers and be stacked on their decks for the long dash across the north Pacific.

The last of the advance force of twenty-seven submarines, which were to gather as a wolf pack outside the mouth of Pearl Harbor two days before the attack, left the Inland Sea on November 18. They were accompanied by a tender and a cruiser which were to see them part way to their destination. Eight of them carried two-men "midget submarines" slung on their bellies. The midgets were detailed to slip through the boom and the nets at the mouth of Pearl Harbor and compound confusion by firing torpedoes and diverting fire when the crucial moment came. Their design and development had been sponsored since 1933 by Prince Fushimi of the imperial family. Their crews had been trained for one-way suicide missions but had not been allowed by Yamamoto to join the fleet until adequate provisions had been taken for their recovery by their mother submarines.

As the carriers and submarines involved in Yamamoto's grand design slipped from their anchorages, they kept radio silence— a silence which they would maintain until December 8. Yamamoto, from his flagship, would send them orders in the new Admirals' Code which U.S. cryptographers had not yet been able to decipher. Even if decoded, his messages contained the "voice code" signals —many obscure allusions to Japanese history—which had been agreed upon before the ships sailed. As a final security measure all the attack ships had new signal officers. The old ones, using their own recognizable touch on the radio-telegraph key, were ashore in Japan sending out call signals and bogus messages to one another as if they were still in their ships waiting for war in harbors off the southern Japanese coasts.

JAPAN'S WAR GOALS

Yamamoto's fleet would not sail from Hitokappu Bay until November 26. In the meantime, on November 16, special envoy Kurusu submitted his credentials in Washington and at once began to present Proposal A, Japan's final offer for an over-all settlement with the United States. When it was turned down out of hand, he proceeded to Proposal B for a modus vivendi and a return to the position prior to Japan's occupation of southern Indochina and America's freezing of assets. This proposal was formally tendered on November 20, turned down on November 22, and formally turned down in a U.S. counterproposal of general principles on November 26.

Except to a student of the period, the verbiage of the diplomatic notes might veil the reasons for the unyielding line taken by the U.S. government. They were succinctly stated in a memo to Secretary of State Hull from his advisor Joseph W. Ballantine on November 22: "You might say [to the Japanese] that in the minds of the American people the purposes underlying our aid to China are the same as the purposes underlying our aid to Great Britain and that the American people believe that there is a partnership between Hitler and Japan aimed at dividing the world between them."

Ballantine was correct in his assessment—up to a point. The position papers being written that month by junior members of the imperial cabal and duly forwarded to Hirohito's Office of Aides-de-Camp show that dividing the world with Hitler was the goal only of World War II. After that, there must eventually come another war in which Hitler and his half would be dealt with in their turn.

In World War II, it was planned that Japan would take most of India and everything east of India up to Central America and the Caribbean. "The future of Trinidad, British and Dutch Guiana, and British and French possessions in the Leeward Islands [however] is to be decided by agreement between Japan and Germany after the war." The rest of the Americas were to be handled according to their co-operativeness. "Mexico, in the event that she declares war on Japan, shall cede us her territory east of Longitude 95°30′ [Chiapas and Yucatan]. Should Peru join in the war against Japan, she shall cede territory north of Latitude 10° [half the country]. If Chile enters the war, she shall cede the nitre zone north of Latitude 24° [a populous seventh of the country]."

As for the United States, she would remain nominally independent after her surrender and would retain sovereignty east of the Rockies, but the Alaska Government-General of Japan's Co-Prosperity Sphere would "include Alberta, British Columbia, and the state of Washington." There would be other "governments-general" for southern India and the offshore African islands; for Hong Kong and the Philippines; for Oceania; for Melanesia; for Hawaii and the eastern Pacific; for Australia; for New Zealand and Antarctica. The East Indies, Burma, Malaya, Thailand, Cambodia and south Indochina, and Laos and north Indochina were each to be established ultimately as independent "kingdoms."

These were the objectives of World War II and some of them, it was recognized, might have to be deferred until after the war when they could be gained by further infiltrations and encroachments. Finally, however, would come World War III, the last war, the war with Germany, which was supposed to end in a single Japanese world state dedicated to the pursuit of the Japanese aesthetic of harmonious people and appreciation of nature. Ecologically the vision was perfect; practically it meant the elimination of all lower cultures which could not think in the politically sophisticated, technologically awkward terms of the Japanese.

A liaison conference of November 20 considered the "Essentials of Policy Regarding Administration of the Occupied Areas in the Southern Regions." In so doing, it approved this long-range vision, which was embodied in a bushel basket of supporting position papers. At the same time, specifically, it recommended to the Emperor a division of Army and Navy responsibilities in the areas which Japan expected to occupy immediately. Hirohito approved the recommendation six days later, on November 26. It was thus agreed that the Navy would administer Dutch Borneo and all the spoils of conquest to the east of it, and that the Army would administer British Borneo, Java, Sumatra, the Philippines, and everything to the west.

AMERICA STANDS PAT

On November 22 General Terauchi of the Strike-South forces paid his respects to Lord Privy Seal Kido before moving his headquarters from Tokyo to Taiwan, and Foreign Minister Togo gave Nomura and Kurusu in Washington an additional four days' leeway for bargaining. "There are reasons," he cabled, "beyond your ability to guess why we wanted to settle Japanese-American relations by the 25th [of November], but if, within the following three or four days, you can conclude your conversations with the Americans, if the signing [of some sort of agreement] can be completed by the 29th . . . we have decided that we can wait until that date. This time, however, we mean it. The deadline absolutely cannot be changed again. After that things are automatically going to happen. . . . For the present, this is for the information of you two ambassadors alone."

Foreign Minister Togo's warning that things would automatically happen if the United States did not agree to Proposal B before November 29 was monitored by U.S. military intelligence, decoded, translated, and handed to President Roosevelt within twenty-four hours of its dispatch. The mountain of evidence collected by the Roberts Commission and the Congressional Pearl Harbor hearings make it clear that the President and his chief advisors correctly understood the cable as a war ultimatum. They agreed, without dissent, to let Japan do her worst. For months they had been buying time by showing an interest in Japan's contention that she needed *Lebensraum* and deserved to have a privileged position in Asia. Now, although they knew that defenses in the Philippines were far from complete, they realized that Japan could not honestly be stalled much longer.

They encouraged Secretary of State Hull to draft a maddeningly moral statement of the position of the United States and to present it to Nomura and Kurusu as soon as possible. They fully expected that this statement might goad Japan into an attack on the United States. But according to Winston Churchill, who knew them all personally, they "regarded the actual form of the attack, or even its scale, as incomparably less important than the fact that the whole American nation would be united for its own safety in a righteous cause as never before."

On Tuesday, November 25, Roosevelt looked over Secretary of State Cordell Hull's draft of the rejection note to the Japanese and called a meeting of his inner Cabinet. In addition to Hull, those present included Secretary of War Henry L. Stimson, Secretary of the Navy Frank Knox, Army Chief of Staff General George C. Marshall, and Chief of Naval Operations Admiral Harold R. Stark. The six men had before them a memo from Colonel Rufus Bratton of Army G-2 predicting that war with Japan could be expected on or about Saturday, November 29. Everyone at the meeting knew that Colonel Bratton was one of the Army-Navy *Magic* group which routinely intercepted and rendered into English the highest-security diplomatic messages being sent out from Tokyo to Japanese ambassadors. No one present fully appreciated the unadvertised fact that the Japanese Navy had the Admirals' Code which had so far withstood all the efforts of the *Magic* group at decipherment.

Roosevelt opened the meeting by bringing up the approaching breakdown in negotiations with the Japanese. Hull added that the Japanese were "poised for attack." According to Stimson's diary, the President then said "that we were likely to be attacked perhaps (as soon as) next Monday, for the Japanese are notorious for making an attack without warning, and the question was what we should do. The question was how we should maneuver them into the position of firing the first shot without allowing too much danger to ourselves. It was a difficult proposition."

The President's inner Cabinet meeting broke up agreeing that Secretary of State Hull should indeed present his reassertion of general moral principles, turning down all Japanese proposals and rubbing Japanese sensibilities the wrong way. That afternoon War Secretary Stimson learned from intelligence sources in Shanghai that approximately 25,000 Japanese troops were embarking on thirty to fifty transports in the Yangtze River roadstead. The report indicated that they were bound for Indochina, Thailand, Burma, or the Philippines. Unknown to Washington, this was one of the eleven divisions selected for Japan's Strike South. Its conspicuous embarkation in Shanghai was intentional —a trial balloon to attract American attention during the sailing of Japan's other attack fleets. When Stimson called Roosevelt with the news, the President "fairly blew up—jumped into the air, so to speak" because he saw in it clear indication "of bad faith on the part of the Japanese" in their negotiations.

A few hours after Stimson got his intelligence from Shanghai —the evening of November 25 in Washington, the morning of November 26 in Tokyo—Hirohito learned that the Foreign Ministry momentarily expected an unfavorable U.S. note. Although it had not yet been presented, Kurusu and Nomura reported that the note would deny all Japanese requests and ultimatums and would, in essence, retract all the tentative U.S. proposals for a settlement which had been advanced since the previous April. Hirohito at once called in Lord Privy Seal Kido and said:

"Although it is with deep regret and anxiety, I am forced to admit that we have reached the point of no return. Before making our final irrevocable decision, however, I am wondering if we should not solicit the opinion of the Elder Statesmen [the ex-prime ministers of Japan] in one last wide-ranging discussion."

Kido agreed with the Emperor's suggestion because, as he pointed out, what was about to be done could "never be undone" if it turned out badly. Prime Minister Tojo, when consulted, objected strenuously that the Elder Statesmen should not be made to share in the responsibility for a decision in which they had taken no part. Overruling Tojo, Hirohito invited the Elder Statesmen to have lunch in the palace three days later, on November 29.

At about the hour that Hirohito was talking to Tojo the advance force of submarines, on their way to the mouth of Pearl Harbor, received a radio message in the Admirals' Code informing them that the Washington negotiations had passed the point of rupture. Still later in the day, at sundown in the Kuriles and before dawn in Washington, the Pearl Harbor fleet began to sail carrier by carrier from Hitokappu Bay. By the time that Hull had officially handed his note to Ambassador Nomura, at 5 P.M. Washington time, the fleet had vanished into the fogs of the north Pacific. Proceeding under radio silence, it steered a narrow course between the southern fringes of U.S. air reconnaissance from the Aleutians and the northern fringes of reconnaissance from Guam and Midway.

When he handed his note to Nomura and Kurusu, Secretary of State Hull was left in no doubt as to what the reaction of the Japanese government would be. As the two envoys wired to Tokyo that evening: "We were both dumbfounded. . . . We argued back furiously but Hull remained solid as a rock." Getting nowhere with Hull, they then asked to see the President. Hull made an appointment for them at the White House for two o'clock the following afternoon.

PEARL HARBOR PRECAUTIONS

The next morning, November 27, was the traditional American Thanksgiving Thursday. Secretary of State Hull called on the President early to inform him of the Japanese envoys' reactions to his note. Then Hull spoke on the phone with Secretary of War Stimson and told him, "I have washed my hands of it and it is now in the hands of you and Knox—the Army and the Navy." For the rest of the morning, guided by numerous telephone calls to and from the White House, the leaders of the Army and Navy were busy deciding what if any measures they should take. Two actions emerged from the phone conferences: all the aircraft carriers and half the Army airplanes were ordered out of Pearl Harbor and all the U.S. commanders in the Pacific were sent a war warning.

When Secretary of War Stimson telephoned the President to authorize the war warning, Roosevelt replied that he not only authorized but positively ordered Stimson to give "the final alert."

Stimson and Chief of Naval Operations Stark—"Betty" as he was always called by the President—promptly sent urgent messages to Panama, San Diego, Honolulu, and Manila. The stronger of the two, Stark's, said in part: "This dispatch is to be considered a war warning. . . . An aggressive move by Japan is expected within the next few days."

The warning went on to say that the move would probably be an "amphibious expedition against either the Philippines, Thai or Kra Peninsula [in Malaya], or possibly Borneo."

When the war warning arrived in Hawaii, Admiral Husband E. Kimmel and the Army commander there, Lieutenant General Walter C. Short, were already negotiating with one another as to how to comply with the instructions they had just received to send away all their aircraft carriers and half their Army airplanes. They finally agreed to activate a plan to send the planes and carriers on as reinforcements to Wake and Midway. The agreement was difficult to reach because it meant not only emasculating their commands but also putting Army planes under Navy jurisdiction. Nevertheless, Vice Admiral William F. Halsey was ordered to depart the next morning for Wake with the carrier *Enterprise*, three heavy cruisers, nine destroyers, twelve Marine Grumman Wildcat fighters, and some Army bombers from General Short's command. Vice Admiral J. H. Newton would depart for Midway with the carrier *Lexington*, three cruisers, five destroyers, and eighteen more of the Marine fighters on December 5. The third of Kimmel's aircraft carriers, the *Saratoga*, was in San Diego and could be left there for an overhaul.[5]

Admiral Kimmel later testified that he understood the Navy Department's "explicit suggestion" that he divest himself of all

[5] These dispatches of valuable fleet elements—first Halsey's with the most useful ships of the U.S. Pacific fleet, then Newton's with the next most useful ships—were both made just before weekends when it was most likely that the Japanese might try a surprise raid. As a further precaution the battleships remaining in Pearl Harbor were moored in pairs, with less valuable older ships to seaward, where they would be vulnerable to torpedo attack, and new valuable ships inboard where they would be shielded from torpedoes by land on one side and by additional layers of armor plate on the other, outward side.

Notwithstanding these shrewd safety measures, Admiral Kimmel, who had charge of Pearl Harbor, was later held responsible for the disaster which took place there. He was relieved of command along with Admiral Stark, the Chief of Naval Operations in Washington.

his fastest ships and his fleet air cover to mean that Hawaii was in no danger of attack. It was in this frame of mind, and in a negative spirit of caution, that he and General Short reacted to the war warning when it arrived in Hawaii later that day. On behalf of both of them, General Short at once wired Washington the full official extent of their response to the warning:

REPORT DEPARTMENT ALERTED TO PREVENT SABOTAGE. LIAISON WITH NAVY.

This meant that, after consultation with the Navy, General Short had ordered the lowest form of alert and preparedness for the forces under his command: a close lookout for signs of subversives and bombs in suitcases. Chief of Staff General Marshall, apparently in an absent moment, indicated that he had read General Short's report on the precautions taken by initialing the copy of it presented to him.

President Roosevelt's military advisors ordered the carriers and planes out of Pearl Harbor because these weapons were valuable and mobile. The war in Europe had conclusively demonstrated the importance of air power. Carriers, being defended by planes instead of big guns and heavy armor plate, could travel and maneuver almost twice as fast as most U.S. battleships at that time. Eight old, slow battleships and eight old cruisers were left in Pearl Harbor because little better use could be seen for them. They were already obsolescent weapons. They could neither escape nor defend themselves at sea.

Despite the precautions taken to save the carriers in the Pacific, and with them the best planes, cruisers, and destroyers, it appears from the record that no one in Washington really expected Pearl Harbor to be attacked. The Japanese Army was known to be moving transports down the China coast toward Malaya or the Philippines. It was already axiomatic, because of the careful publicity work of Hirohito's advisors, that the Japanese Army ruled supreme in Japan and had long ago encased official Tokyo thinking in a wooden suit of samurai armor. That the Army would allow the Navy to divert a strong force from the Strike-South operations and stage a daring raid on Pearl Harbor, four thousand miles off to one side, seemed highly improbable.

Not that a Pearl Harbor raid was thought to be unfeasible; on the contrary, Admiral Harry E. Yarnell had theoretically surprised and sunk the U.S. Pacific fleet with only two carriers during the U.S. naval maneuvers of 1932. As late as June 1940 the U.S. Army in Hawaii had been ordered: "Immediately alert complete defensive organization to deal with possible trans-Pacific raid." Still later, after the successful British torpedo plane attack on the Italian fleet at Taranto in November 1940, Navy Secretary Knox had advised War Secretary Stimson: "The success of the British . . . suggests that precautionary measures be taken immediately to protect Pearl Harbor against a surprise attack in the event of war between the United States and Japan." Stimson had responded by giving Pearl Harbor special priority in the allotment of anti-aircraft guns and of new radar equipment. Still later, in March 1941, Major General Frederick L. Martin, who commanded the Army air forces in Hawaii, supervised a study of the attack possibilities and concluded, as Yamamoto was doing at about the same time, that a carrier task force might best approach Pearl Harbor from the north and launch its planes for an attack at dawn.

All these studies and orders to take precautions were apparently made without conviction. They were contingency planning and nothing more. On January 27, 1941, Ambassador Grew had warned Washington of intelligence from the Peruvian Embassy in Tokyo that "in the event of trouble breaking out between the United States and Japan, the Japanese intend to make a surprise attack against Pearl Harbor with all their strength and employing all their equipment." U.S. Naval Intelligence forwarded Grew's note to Admiral Kimmel in Hawaii with the comment that "no move against Pearl Harbor appears imminent or planned for the foreseeable future."

U.S. naval strategists discounted the possibility of a Pearl Harbor attack for the same reason that a majority of the best Japanese naval strategists had opposed Yamamoto when he had presented his plan at table-top maneuvers in September 1941. The venture seemed to them then, and still appears to many of them even now, as a flamboyant gesture profiting Japan nothing. Tactically a few U.S. ships would be put out of commission for a while but strategically the Pearl Harbor base would remain undestroyed. And politically the United States would be galled at the very time when Japan wished to make a few quick seizures and then negotiate a truce. "It was," says one retired Japanese naval officer, "like sticking a spear into a sleeping hippopotamus while you were building a dam to take away half his pond."

Hirohito had known better than to think that U.S. leaders were genuinely asleep, and so he had intervened to force through Yamamoto's plan over the objections of most of the top brass in the Japanese Navy General Staff. Knowing nothing of Hirohito's power, the U.S. Office of Naval Operations had wrongly concluded, by majority vote, that a majority of their opposite numbers in Tokyo would have vetoed any plan to raid Pearl Harbor.

DIPLOMATIC DECEIT

That Thanksgiving Thursday, as soon as the orders that seemed necessary had been sent to Pearl Harbor and to the other U.S. command posts in the Pacific, President Roosevelt met on schedule, at 2 P.M., with the Japanese envoys in Washington, Nomura and Kurusu. Although he spoke with more charm and friendliness than Cordell Hull, Roosevelt backed his subordinate by refusing to hold out any hope of U.S. concessions.

That evening Kurusu was telephoned for a report on the conversation by an underling in the Foreign Ministry in Tokyo. The underling's name happened to be Yamamoto Kumaichi, but he was no relative of Admiral Yamamoto. It was already noon the next day in Tokyo and Yamamoto, wide awake, employed a previously agreed-upon voice code which the tired Kurusu found difficult to handle. U.S. naval monitors of the trans-Pacific cable chuckled at what they heard:

YAMAMOTO: How did the matrimonial question [the negotiations] get along today?

KURUSU: Oh, haven't you got our telegram yet? It was sent—let me see—at about six, no seven o'clock. Seven o'clock. About three hours ago. There wasn't much that was different from what Miss Umeko [Cordell Hull] intimated yesterday.

YAMAMOTO: Really? not much different?

KURUSU: No, not much. As before that southward matter, that south,

south, southward matter [the movement of the Japanese transports down the China coast], is having considerable effect. You know? southward matter?

YAMAMOTO: Ah so! the south matter? It's having an effect?

KURUSU: Yes, and at one time the matrimonial question seemed as if it would be settled. But well, of course, there are other matters involved too. However that was it; that was the monkey wrench. Details are included in the telegram which should arrive very shortly. . . . How do things look there? Does it seem as if a child might be born?

YAMAMOTO (in a very definite tone): Yes, the birth of the child seems imminent.

KURUSU: Oh it does? It does seem as if the birth is going to take place? (pause) In which direction? (pause, with confusion). I mean, is it to be a boy or a girl? [war or peace]

YAMAMOTO (after laughter and hesitation): It seems as if it will be a strong healthy boy.

KURUSU: Oh, it's to be a strong healthy boy?

YAMAMOTO: Yes. Did you make any statement [to the press] regarding your talk with Miss Kimiko [President Roosevelt] today?

KURUSU: No, nothing. Nothing except the mere fact that we met.

YAMAMOTO: Regarding the matter contained in the telegram of the other day [the sending of a personal peace plea from Roosevelt to Hirohito], no definite decision has yet been reached but please be advised that effecting it will be difficult. . . .

KURUSU: Well, I guess there's nothing more that can be done then.

YAMAMOTO: Well, yes. (pause) Then today.

KURUSU: Today?

YAMAMOTO: The matrimonial question, that is. The matter pertaining to arranging a marriage—don't break them off.

KURUSU: Not break them? You mean talks? (helpless pause) Oh, my! (pause with resigned laughter) Well, I'll do what I can. Please read carefully what Miss Kimiko [Roosevelt] had to say as contained in today's telegram. . . .

So it was that the Japanese envoys and their eavesdroppers in Washington learned that the response to Hull's note would be war, that a message to Hirohito would not help matters, and that from now on diplomatic negotiations must be continued only as a façade to conceal Japan's last-minute preparations.

Knowing of the Kurusu-Yamamoto conversation, President Roosevelt met with his War Cabinet—Hull, Stimson, Knox, Marshall, and Stark—at noon the next day, Friday, November 28. They discussed the likelihood of war that weekend without ever mentioning Pearl Harbor once. Roosevelt was still preoccupied with the possibility of sending—if only "for the record" now—a personal appeal to Emperor Hirohito. His advisors were more concerned—for the record—about Congress. They urged F.D.R. to deliver a message to the nation's legislators, warning them that war with Japan might break out at any moment.

As Stimson wrote in his diary, the President "had better send his letter to the Emperor separate as one thing and a secret thing, and then make his speech to the Congress as a separate and more understandable thing to the people of the United States. This was the final decision at that time, and the President asked Hull and Knox and myself to try to draft such papers."

Later that day the President and his advisors received intercepts of Japanese messages to consulates and embassies in South America ordering the destruction of all codes and secret papers.

On Saturday November 29 Secretary of State Hull told Kurusu and Nomura that he was willing to continue negotiations as long as Japan wished to negotiate. Privately he told friends that he was doing so, if not for the record, then at least "for the purpose of making a record."

Roosevelt retired for the weekend to await developments in his retreat at Warm Springs in the north Georgia hills where he had established a sanitorium for fellow polio victims. Nothing, however, happened. The Japanese division sailing down the China coast disembarked in Indochina and waited there for final orders. As General Marshall later described the anticlimax: "We entered into December without anything happening other than the continuation of these movements, which we could follow fairly well, down the China coast. . . ."

In Tokyo Hirohito was running, unhurried but with clockwork

precision, on the schedule which he had approved weeks earlier. At noon on Saturday, November 29, over Tojo's objections, he lunched with the ex-prime ministers of Japan and encouraged them to express their views at the formal Elder Statesmen's Conference which was to follow dessert. Eight former prime ministers were present, four military men and four civilians. Seven of them either objected that there was no need for war or maintained sullenly that they had been given insufficient information of late on which to base an opinion. Only one of the eight, the civilian diplomat Hirota, approved the war, and he did so, he said, because he felt that Japan could not better her negotiating position with the United States unless she demonstrated her readiness and ability to seize ground held by U.S. military forces. On behalf of the Throne, Lord Privy Seal Kido thanked them all for their opinions, indicated to them that war, regardless, was about to break out, and asked them all as patriots to help unify Japan in this time of unprecedented crisis.

As soon as the elder statesmen had left the palace, Prime Minister Tojo convened a liaison conference of Cabinet and Supreme Command. It was attended by no less than three "Unidentified Persons" who spoke with authority, as if they were members of the imperial family. They considered the value of continuing the negotiations in Washington and decided that considerations of secrecy and surprise far outweighed those of deceit and dishonor. As one of the unidentified persons stated, probably Prince Kanin: "I would like to see our diplomacy executed in such a way as to win us the war."

The next afternoon at 1:30 Lord Privy Seal Kido was called to the residence of Prince Takamatsu, the second of the Emperor's three brothers. In the presence of Prince Mikasa, the youngest of the brothers, Takamatsu told Kido that the officers of the Navy General Staff had agreed to appeal to the Emperor, saying that they had no confidence in the Navy's ability to win the war. Kido returned to the palace at 2:30 and after an hour's wait secured an audience with his master.

Hirohito, after hearing the message from Takamatsu, said, "As the Navy is having great trouble reaching unanimity of opinion, I feel as if I should avoid a U.S.–Japanese war, if that is at all possible, but just how, realistically, can I manage it?"

Kido replied: "I don't think it proper, even after long deliberation, for the Throne to take a step if there is still any shadow of doubt in the imperial mind. This is especially true on the present occasion because the decision is a unique one of great gravity. Accordingly I advise the Emperor to summon at once the Navy minister and the Navy chief of staff and ascertain what is the true feeling in the guts of the Navy. I also suggest that it would not do to alienate the prime minister at this juncture and that I would like the Emperor to consult with him also."

At 3:30 Prime Minister Tojo was received in audience by Hirohito, with Kido standing by. After that Navy Minister Shimada and Navy Chief of Staff Nagano conferred with the Emperor for about two hours. Kido waited restlessly outside the Imperial Study talking with the chief aide-de-camp at 4:00 and with the grand chamberlain at 6:00. Finally at 6:35 Kido was summoned into the Imperial Presence. Hirohito said:

"Instruct Prime Minister Tojo to proceed according to plan. The Navy minister and the Navy chief of staff have both given affirmative answers to my question regarding our war chances."

Kido wrote in his diary, "I immediately phoned the prime minister to inform him of the above: After stopping for supper with the Suos, I returned home about midnight."

This was the midnight of the deadline set earlier, after which war would become automatic and negotiations would become a sham.

A WEEK OF STRANGE QUIET

Fourteen hours later, at midnight Sunday, November 30, Washington time, the undecided Battle of Moscow continued to absorb Western attention and the critical weekend in Japanese-American relations seemed to be passing uneventfully into a new working week. Allied intelligence had observed that Axis nations seldom attacked except on weekends or holidays. There might yet be time for Christmas shopping. Perhaps, after all, Japan had been bluffing.

At that very moment, however—2 P.M., Monday, December 1, Tokyo time—Hirohito was bringing to order the conference in his Presence at which he would give the final go-ahead for war.

The conference was only a ceremony, but in the course of it several revealing statements were made. Foreign Minister Togo reviewed the unhappy eight months of negotiations with the United States. Navy Chief of Staff Nagano reaffirmed his pledge of the day before that the Navy had confidence. Prime Minister Tojo spoke at length on the morale of the nation.

"To stabilize the views held by the people," Tojo acknowledged, "it will be necessary to guide public opinion and at the same time to exercise rather strict controls over it."

Finance Minister Kaya delivered an exhaustive report on "Our Long-term Financial and Monetary Capacity." In it he promised that the government would underwrite the indebtedness of all banks, of all essential industries, and of all war-damage victims. He undertook to shore up the stock market by a policy of "unlimited buying on the part of the Japan Joint Securities Corporation."

Agriculture Minister Ino Tetsuya presented an equally detailed, equally visionary, and equally pessimistic report on the possibility of feeding the nation during a long war.

Finally, Privy Council President Hara stood up to speak on behalf of the Throne. He scolded the ubiquitous Suzuki of the Cabinet Planning Board for inadequate preparations against the contingency of enemy incendiary raids. Having registered the desire of the Throne for adequate fire-fighting equipment, he went on to explain in broad terms why Hirohito felt justified in deciding on war:

In negotiating with the United States, our Empire hoped to maintain peace by making one concession after another. But to our surprise, the American position from beginning to end was to say what Chiang Kai-shek wanted her to say, and to emphasize those ideals that she had stated in the past. The United States is being utterly conceited, obstinate, and disrespectful. It is regrettable indeed. We simply cannot tolerate such an attitude.

If we were to give in, we would surrender at a stroke not only our benefits from the Manchurian Incident but also our gains in the Sino-Japanese and Russo-Japanese wars [of 1895 and 1905]. This we cannot do. . . .

We cannot avoid a long-term war this time, but I believe that we must somehow get around it and bring about an early settlement. In order to do this, we will need to start thinking now about how to end the war. Our nation, governed by our magnificent national structure, is, from a spiritual point of view, certainly unsurpassed in all the world. But in the course of a long war . . . it is particularly important to pay attention to our psychological solidarity. . . . Be sure you make no mistakes in handling the inner turmoil of the people.

I believe that the proposal before us cannot be avoided in the light of present circumstances, and I put my trust in my officers and men whose loyalty is supreme. I urge you to make every effort to keep the people in a tranquil state of mind, in order to prosecute a long-term war.

In replying to the Throne, Prime Minister General Tojo said:

At this moment our Empire stands at the threshold of glory or oblivion. We tremble with fear in the Presence of His Majesty. We subjects are keenly aware of the great responsibilities we must assume from this point on. Now that His Majesty has reached a decision to commence hostilities, we must all strive to repay our obligations to him, bring the Government and the military ever closer together, resolve that the nation united will go on to victory, make an all-out effort to achieve our war aims, and set His Majesty's mind at ease. I now adjourn the meeting.

The bleak and hollow ring of these proceedings made no impression on Hirohito. According to Chief of Staff Sugiyama's minutes: "His Majesty nodded in agreement with the statements being made during today's conference, and displayed no signs of uneasiness. He seemed to be in excellent spirits, and we were all filled with awe."

Later in the day when Sugiyama reported to the Throne on the orders which had just been sent out to Saigon "concerning the responsibility of the forces in the Southern Regions," Hirohito said, "We couldn't have avoided this situation. I beg that the Army and Navy will co-operate."

Sugiyama expressed himself deeply moved by the Emperor's graciousness, and Hirohito asked, "Has there been any change in the disposition of U.S. forces?"

"Since my report to His Majesty this morning," replied Sugiyama, "we have heard that two troops of American Marines, each about 400 strong, have arrived [as reinforcements] in Manila."

Hirohito nodded and "seemed extremely satisfied."

That night all the ships of the Japanese Navy changed their call signals.

The next morning, Tuesday, December 2, Hirohito gave permission to Navy Chief of Staff Nagano to send out Great Navy Order Number 12 which told the various Japanese fleet commanders that the day of attack was December 8. This message, in Admirals' Code, was not deciphered by U.S. intelligence. Yamamoto relayed his own personal version of the message to the fleet steaming toward Pearl Harbor: "Climb Mount Niitaka 1208." Niitaka was the Empire's highest mountain.

That night, Tokyo time—Tuesday morning, Pearl Harbor time —Admiral Kimmel in Hawaii received a call from the Naval Intelligence officer in charge of monitoring Japanese fleet signals. He learned that analysis of Japanese ship movements had been confused by the change in call signals the previous day. The confusion was compounded by a shrewd suspicion on the part of the analysts that many of the signals coming in were phoney ones being sent by land-based operators. In conclusion, Naval Intelligence suspected that it had not heard a genuine signal from any Japanese aircraft carrier in the last week. The carriers, in effect, "were lost."

"Do you mean to say," asked Admiral Kimmel, incredulously, "that they could be rounding Diamond Head and you wouldn't know it?"

"I hope," replied Lieutenant Commander Edwin T. Layton, the intelligence officer, "they would be sighted before now."

On Wednesday, December 3, the Japanese Pearl Harbor fleet rendezvoused at 42 degrees north latitude, 170 degrees east longitude—a point in the empty north Pacific about 2,300 miles northwest of Pearl Harbor. There, in a light swell amidst fog, the carriers took on oil from the tankers which had accompanied them this far on their historic voyage. Then the tankers and their escort of short-range destroyers turned back toward Japan and left the fast light carriers to make their lightning run on Hawaii.

During the refueling, before the carriers started their dash, Hirohito confirmed their orders by giving an unprecedented secret and private audience to the commander of the Combined Fleet. Admiral Yamamoto had been left restless in home waters to co-ordinate the actions of all his scattered fleet elements. He now repeated to Hirohito his fears that Japan would be defeated in a long war. Hirohito repeated his reasons for believing the war justified and inevitable. Yamamoto promised, to the best of his ability, to fight like a man possessed. After the audience, by telephone, radio, and Admirals' Code, Yamamoto sent the carriers on their way.

Also that day, Japanese envoys in Berlin and Rome felt out the positions which would be taken by Japan's Axis partners in the event of an American-Japanese war. Ambassador Oshima in Berlin did not tell Ribbentrop what was about to happen but exacted from him a pledge that Germany would declare war on the United States as soon as Japan did and would not stop fighting until both Japan and Germany were satisfied with the peace terms. The Japanese ambassador in Rome, Horikiri Zenbei, was somewhat more straightforward, and Count Galeazzo Ciano, Mussolini's foreign secretary, noted in his diary that evening:

Sensational move by Japan. The ambassador asks for an audience with Il Duce and reads him a long statement on the progress of the negotiations with America, concluding with the assertion that they have reached a dead end. Then, invoking the appropriate clause in the Tripartite Pact, he asks that Italy declare war on America immediately after the outbreak of hostilities and proposes the signature of an agreement not to conclude a separate peace. The interpreter translating this request was trembling like a leaf. Il Duce gave fullest assurances, reserving the right to confer with Berlin before giving a reply. Il Duce was pleased with the communication and said: "We are now on the brink of the inter-continental war which I predicted as early as September 1939." What does this new event mean? In any case, it means that Roosevelt has succeeded in his maneuver. Since he could not enter the war immediately and directly, he has entered it indirectly by letting himself be attacked by Japan.[6]

[6] Ciano's catty but shrewd diary continues:

"December 4. Thursday. Berlin's reaction to the Japanese move is extremely cautious. Perhaps they will accept because they cannot get out of it, but the idea of provoking America's intervention pleases the Germans less and less. Mussolini, on the other hand, is pleased about it.

"December 5. Friday. A night interrupted by Ribbentrop's restlessness. After delaying two days, now he cannot wait a minute to answer the Japanese and at three in the morning he sent Mackensen to my house to submit a plan for a triple agreement relative to Japanese intervention and the pledge not to make a

By Thursday, December 4, the unannounced but de facto state of war between Japan and the United States was so clearly understood by both parties that Walter Foote, the American consul in Batavia, Java, found himself out in his backyard burning code books while his opposite number from Japan, who lived next door, was doing likewise with his secret papers just over the garden fence.

That night the Japanese Navy changed its fleet code, making the routine signals of its vessels not only scrambled but temporarily unintelligible. U.S. naval cryptographers interrupted their work on the unbroken Admirals' Code and succeeded in recovering the new fleet code in a matter of days—but not until after Pearl Harbor.

On Friday morning, December 5, Tokyo time, the Japanese task force of Tiger Yamashita and his long-time helper, Colonel Tsuji, cast anchor from Samah harbor, Hainan, and began their obvious advance against the beaches of Malaya. Later in the day, in Tokyo, Hirohito approved a Navy schedule for handing the final note to Cordell Hull. He understood that it would inform the United States of a rupture in diplomatic relations a scant half-hour before the appointed hour for the attack on Pearl Harbor.

Still later in terms of absolute time, the Friday morning papers in the United States headlined a Hearst exclusive: "Roosevelt War Plan." Isolationist military men, who have not yet been identified, had leaked from the office of the General Staff a number of authentic contingency planning papers for mobilizing the nation in the event of war. The political accusations and counter-accusations which followed helped to distract Americans for the next two days.

That night Washington time, the next morning, Saturday, December 6 in Tokyo, the Japanese General Staffs and Cabinet met in a liaison conference to assume formal responsibility for the timing of the final note which was to be served on the United States. Without much debate the conferees agreed that the note should be "dispatched at 4 A.M., Japanese time, on December 7"

---

separate peace. He wanted me to awaken the Duce, but I did not do so, and the latter was very glad I hadn't.

"December 8. Monday. A night telephone call from Ribbentrop; he is overjoyed about the Japanese attack on America. He is so happy about it that I am happy with him, though I am not too sure about the final advantages of what has happened. . . ."

—twenty-three and a half hours before the scheduled time of attack—and should be "handed to the President at 3 A.M. December 8, Japanese time": that is, at 1 P.M. December 7, Washington time, or at 7:30 A.M. December 7, Pearl Harbor time.

LAST DAY OF PEACE

As Saturday, December 6, dawned in Washington, the British high command in Singapore learned from aerial reconnaissance that two Japanese convoys had moved into the Gulf of Siam, off the southern tip of Cambodia, between Indochina and Malaya. They were moving at a leisurely pace westward as if to land troops on the eastern shore of the Kra Isthmus, the narrow point in the Malayan Peninsula where British territory abutted on Thailand. When Roosevelt heard this news between 10 and 11 A.M. that Saturday, it appeared that the Japanese would storm the Malayan beaches in about fourteen hours, or early on Sunday morning.

At noon, when Roosevelt was preparing to eat his modest lunch from a tray on his lap in the White House Oval Study where he worked, Naval Intelligence decoded a message from the Foreign Ministry in Tokyo advising envoys Nomura and Kurusu that the long-awaited reply to Hull's November 26 rejection of Japanese demands would be on the wires shortly. The reply to the rejection, said this "pilot message," would come in fourteen parts which must be presented to Secretary of State Hull at an hour which would be specified in later communications. Naval Intelligence realized that a declaration of Japanese hostility was in the offing and promptly informed the President.

Roosevelt gave the clerical help in the White House the afternoon off, so that they could have the last minutes of peace to themselves. For his own part he consulted privately with Secretary of State Hull, with Lord Halifax, the British ambassador, and with the Australian minister in Washington, Robert G. Casey. At the same time he rewrote the latest State Department version of the personal appeal which he had been agitating for ten days to send directly to the Emperor of Japan.

No records were kept of the activities in the White House that afternoon, but War Secretary Stimson noted in his diary that everyone was worried about the Japanese fleets converging on the Gulf of Siam. "That was what we were at work on our papers about. . . . The British were very excited. . . . Our effort this morning in drawing our papers was to see whether or not we should act together. . . . We all thought that we must fight if the British fought."

At 5:30 in the afternoon Roosevelt recalled his secretary, Miss Tully, from a cocktail party at the Mayflower Hotel and mixed a martini for himself and his old friend Vincent Astor who had dropped by at the White House to see if he could do anything to help. Miss Tully arrived breathless a few minutes later and took down the President's personal message to Hirohito.

It began with the words, "Almost a century ago the President of the United States addressed to the Emperor of Japan a message extending an offer of friendship. . . . That offer was accepted. . . ." Apparently Roosevelt did not fully realize that "that offer" had been accepted by Japan most reluctantly; that Hirohito's great-grandfather, Emperor Komei, had elected to be martyred, after thirteen years of domestic strife, rather than accept it. From this beginning Roosevelt went on to plead for justice and freedom from fear for all the peoples of Southeast Asia. He pledged that "there is absolutely no thought on the part of the United States of invading Indochina." After planting these prickers in Hirohito's pride, President Roosevelt drove them home with unction:

I address myself to Your Majesty at this moment in the fervent hope that Your Majesty may, as I am doing, give thought in this definite emergency to ways of dispelling the dark clouds. I am confident that both of us, for the sake of the peoples not only of our own countries but for the sake of humanity in neighboring territories have a sacred duty to restore traditional amity and prevent further death and destruction in the world.

Without fervor, without confidence, Roosevelt sent this missive on to Secretary of State Hull. "Dear Cordell," he memoed, "shoot this to Grew—I think can go in gray code—saves time—I don't mind if it gets picked up. F.D.R." Hull had some editorial reservations which were negotiated over the phone by dinner time. By 7:40 P.M. the White House had informed the Washington press corps of the President's dramatic gesture. At 8 P.M. Hull cabled

Ambassador Grew that a message from Roosevelt to Hirohito was on its way. At 9 P.M. the message was sent, triple priority.

While Roosevelt had been drafting and arranging to send his message to Hirohito, the particularly able lieutenant commander in the Office of Naval Intelligence, Alwin D. Kramer, had been supervising the decipherment of the first thirteen parts of the final fourteen-part Japanese rejection notice. The President's personal naval aide, Captain John R. Beardall, had gone off duty that afternoon leaving Kramer in direct contact with the President through a junior White House naval aide, Lieutenant Robert Lester Schulz. Now, at 9:30 P.M., half an hour after the President's message had been dispatched to Hirohito, Lieutenant Commander Kramer brought to the White House the first thirteen parts of the Japanese rejection notice. The fourteenth part, Kramer reported, had not yet been received and was apparently being saved as a final exclamation point to cap the epithets being hurled in the first thirteen parts.

Lieutenant Schulz at once delivered the thirteen intercepts from the pouch to the Oval Study where Roosevelt was waiting expectantly for them in the company of his favorite advisor, Harry Hopkins. Roosevelt spent ten minutes reading the 2500-word note, then handed it to Hopkins. Hopkins read it and handed it back to the President. As Roosevelt returned the top-secret document to Lieutenant Schulz for safe filing, he said in effect, "Harry, this means war." Hopkins agreed. Schulz stood at the door waiting to be dismissed while Hopkins and Roosevelt discussed the implications in some detail. Hopkins regretted "that since war was undoubtedly going to come at the convenience of the Japanese, it was too bad that we could not strike the first blow and prevent any sort of surprise."

"No, we can't do that," replied Roosevelt. "We are a democracy and a peaceful people." And then, raising his voice as Lieutenant Schulz later recalled, the President said, "But we do have a good record."

Roosevelt tried to call "Betty" Stark, Chief of Naval Operations, but found him out for the evening at the National Theatre. Rather than excite the theater audience by having Stark leave his box in the middle of the third act, Roosevelt told the White House operator to try the Stark residence in about half an hour by which time the admiral should have returned home. Then Roosevelt dismissed Lieutenant Schulz and the historical curtain fell on the scene in the White House Oval Study.

It was now the morning of Sunday, December 7, in Tokyo. The I-class submarines of the advance force had been waiting for more than a day outside Pearl Harbor watching the comings and goings of vessels through the harbor mouth. In the north the carriers of the task force were beginning to increase speed and veer south for their final approach. Admiral Nagumo, who commanded the flagship *Akagi*, was sitting in his wardroom listening to jazz and news reports from the local Hawaiian stations. He had run up the actual flag which Admiral Togo, Hirohito's former tutor, had flown at the battle of Tsushima straits, when he had crossed the T of the Russian fleet and sunk it in 1905.

At noon Tokyo censors intercepted the cable from President Roosevelt to Ambassador Grew, enclosing Roosevelt's personal message to Hirohito. While making inquiries, the censors held the cable and kept it from being presented to Grew. Through channels to Imperial Headquarters the censors determined that the cable would only be an inconvenience to the Emperor at this moment. Without anyone having to take much responsibility, the cable was at once packaged in all the permissible red tape of Japan's many police regulations and was unwrapped tape by tape so that it would not finally be presented to Ambassador Grew until late that evening. At 3 P.M. U.S. overseas broadcasts began to announce that the message had been sent, but Japanese police surveillance of shortwave radios was so efficient that few outside top palace and government circles heard the American broadcasts. At 5:30 P.M. the Pearl Harbor fleet turned full south and began its final dash at full speed, 26 knots. At 6:00 P.M. copies of Roosevelt's telegram were circulated by the censors to all officials who had reason to study its text.

At 6:15 P.M., when it was still 4:15 A.M. in Washington, Hirohito presided over a solemn feast. For security reasons it was held at Omiya Gosho, the palace of his mother, west of the main palace, on the estate where he had grown up. The Empress Dowager was not present. She had retired to a villa in the country, vowing with embarrassing frankness that she meant to get as far away as possible from the bombs which her son's policies would certainly bring on Japan. Lord Privy Seal Kido and other Big Brothers of the Emperor's aristocratic circle of intimates attended the party to toast the spirits of the commanders in the field and hear a prayer of supplication and benediction by Hirohito, the nation's high priest. The gathering broke up after less than two hours because Hirohito wished everyone to take a rest before the important events of the evening began after midnight.

A SUNDAY MORNING

While official Tokyo napped in preparation for the long night ahead, official Washington began to wake up to a tense Sunday morning. At 7 P.M. Tokyo time, 5 A.M. Washington time, the final fourteenth part of Japan's rejection notice started coming in to the skeleton staff on duty at the code machines in the Office of Naval Intelligence in Washington. The first thirteen parts had reviewed Japanese propaganda claims that the United States was an aggressive colonial interloper in the Orient, trying to strangle Japan in her normal growth processes. The fourteenth part announced that Japan was breaking off negotiations with the United States.

The alert Lieutenant Commander Kramer, who had distributed the first thirteen parts of the note to Roosevelt and his advisors late the night before, was back at his desk by 7:30 A.M. supervising the preparation of the fourteenth part. At the same time in the Japanese Embassy in Washington neither the last nor the first part of the note had yet been typed. There had been a final party the night before and Embassy staffers had gone to bed without realizing that the note must be ready for delivery by 1 P.M. the next day. Now an Embassy duty officer had just received the presentation instructions from Tokyo and was frantically telephoning his colleagues to summon them back to work. Not only must the note be ready by one, it must be typed by someone cleared for top secret. A muster of the officials who had the requisite clearance revealed that only one of them could type. While this individual struggled manfully, key by key, to prepare a fair copy for Nomura to hand Hull, Kramer's staff completed its own copy and Kramer delivered it to the White House and the Departments of State, War, and Navy by about 10 A.M.

Returning to his office, Kramer was now handed the American intercept of the presentation instructions. His eye fixed on the one o'clock deadline and he checked with his assistants to make sure that 1 P.M. would be dawn in Hawaii and two hours after midnight in Manila. Then, at 10:30 A.M., having phoned the news to Admiral Stark at Naval Operations, Kramer hurried over to the White House to deliver a copy of the presentation instructions to the President. Shortly afterward Ambassador Nomura underscored the importance of the one o'clock deadline by calling Secretary of State Hull and apologizing that, despite its being Sunday, he must see Hull at one that afternoon. Even without benefit of *Magic* intercepts, this unusual request, in the context of that crisis-conscious week, would have sufficed to make Hull and Roosevelt expect the worst.

Fully realizing, then, that Japan meant to start war on or about one o'clock, Roosevelt consulted his advisors and decided simply to wait. It was policy that the United States should not react until after Japan had struck. That was the way to keep an unblemished democratic record. What was more, the majority of the President's military advisors felt that Japan would gain only a small temporary advantage by striking first. There was a tendency on the part of U.S. admirals and generals to underestimate the fighting qualities of the Japanese soldier and the originality and daring of the Japanese strategist. Coincidentally many Japanese admirals and generals suffered from the same dangerous complacency in regard to American genius.

The White House switchboard had access to a direct line—the "scrambler phone"—which could put the President through in a minute to any one of the major U.S. command posts in the Pacific. If Roosevelt had realized that the Pearl Harbor base in Hawaii was on "third alert," looking out only for sabotage, it is inconceivable that he would not have picked up the phone and ordered all men to battle stations. Like every other fully informed leader, however, the President believed that the Japanese were moving against Malaya and that they lacked strength to strike in many directions at once.

Several of the President's advisors did suggest that a final warning be sent to commanders in the Pacific, but since a war warning had already gone out ten days earlier, no one considered such a message to be vitally important. At noon Chief of Staff General Marshall cabled Lieutenant General Short in Hawaii that Japan's envoys were going to break off negotiations at 1 P.M. Marshall's cable reached Short—by bicycle from the telegraph office—nine hours later, when the antiquated battleships of the U.S. Pacific fleet had already become graveyards.

During the busy morning of waiting in Washington, there was a last moment of doubt in Tokyo. About the time that Hirohito retired to nap, the Navy General Staff received a last intelligence broadcast from the Japanese consul in Honolulu. It reported that Pearl Harbor was full of battleships but contained not so much as one aircraft carrier. The Japanese naval planners knew that the U.S. Pacific fleet included at least six carriers. They did not know that three of them were currently on loan to the Atlantic fleet, or that the other three, as a precaution, were being kept out of Pearl Harbor as much as possible. The unknown whereabouts of the carriers represented a grave hazard to Admiral Nagumo's fleet; their absence from the target to be ambushed was a bitter disappointment.

When Admiral Yamamoto heard the news aboard his flagship in the Inland Sea, he considered the possibility of radioing Nagumo to conduct an air search for the missing carriers. On consideration, however, he decided to let Nagumo make his own decision. He dispatched to Nagumo only the following message: NO CARRIERS REPEAT NO CARRIERS IN PEARL HARBOR. Nagumo, when he received the message, flung it down with disgust on his chart table. He saw no option, however, but to proceed according to plan and try at least to sink the U.S. battleships.

At about this same moment—10:30 P.M. Tokyo, 8:30 A.M. Washington—Grew finally received Roosevelt's cable of appeal to Hirohito. For an hour and a half he struggled to make arrangements to deliver it. Finally at midnight he drove to the foreign minister's residence where he saw Togo fifteen minutes later. He demanded to see Hirohito personally. Togo replied that it would be impossible for the Emperor to entertain a foreign envoy at this hour of night but that he would undertake to disturb the Emperor and deliver the message if Grew wished to leave it. Grew handed Togo a copy of the message and drove home.

Ten minutes later, at 12:40 A.M., Togo telephoned Lord Privy Seal Kido at his official residence. Kido agreed that, for the sake of the record, the Emperor should certainly see Roosevelt's message at once. Moreover, Kido assured Togo that the Emperor would not mind at all being disturbed after midnight on this particular night. Kido promised to join Togo at the palace.

When Kido hung up and started leisurely to dress, it was 12:45. At that precise moment Japanese bluejackets in Shanghai began silently crossing over from the Japanese Concession into the downtown banking district of the International Settlement along the riverfront. British police observers did not attempt to contest this first conquest of the Pacific War but simply watched while the Japanese Marines seized customs sheds, set up road blocks, and trained field pieces on Western ships in the harbor. They took such swift control of the communications lines leading out of Shanghai that apparently no word of the take-over reached Western capitals for several hours.

At 1:30 A.M. Lord Privy Seal Kido drove from his official residence to the Imperial Library in the palace woods to assist Hirohito in the reception of the note from Roosevelt. At that moment on the deck of Admiral Nagumo's flagship, the aircraft carrier *Akagi*, some 230 miles north of Pearl Harbor, the first planes were preparing for take-off. It was 6 A.M. local time. The night was still black and the seas were wild. On the heaving flight deck, mechanics clung to the planes as they wheeled them from the lifts. Feet slipped on spray as the towering swell lapped over the ship's sides.

The pilot who was to lead the attack, Commander Fuchida Mitsuo, lurched toward his plane. As he came, he bound around his flight helmet a symbolic white headband such as samurai had always worn when they wished to indicate that they were dueling *à outrance*—fighting to the death. His plane, painted with red and yellow stripes, looked unearthly under the hooded blue lights on the flight deck. A 1,600-pound projectile was slung on the undercarriage—not an ordinary bomb but a fifteen-inch armor-piercing naval shell specially fitted with fins to make it fall true.

Fuchida and his crew climbed into their bomber, the *Akagi* swung around into the north wind, and the first of the Pearl Harbor raiders took to the air. In the next fifteen minutes another

182 planes—50 more bombers and dive-bombers, 89 torpedo planes, and 43 Zero fighters—would join Fuchida as he circled above the fleet. Then, with a dip of his wings, he would lead the way south.

Lord Privy Seal Kido found Hirohito in the study of his library in the palace woods listening to pops of static and incomprehensibly terse ejaculations which emanated from a high-powered short-wave set. At that moment, 1:40 A.M. in Tokyo, a Japanese task force was beginning to shell the dark, forested shores of Kota Bharu, the beachhead on the Kra Isthmus in northern Malaya where Japanese forces meant to land in order to start their overland drive on Singapore.

Knowing better than to disturb his master at such a moment, Kido silently took a seat. From time to time Hirohito gave a few words of commentary on the action in progress. From time to time the telephone jangled on Hirohito's desk and he received a confirmed bulletin from one of his aides-de-camp in the chart room of the Imperial Headquarters building a few hundred yards to the north of the library.

While Kido listened impassively in the Imperial Library in Tokyo, President Roosevelt in Washington was receiving his usual lunch on a tray in the Oval Study in the White House. His Scottish terrier, Fala, begged tidbits from the tray. His friend Harry Hopkins, in a V-necked sweater and slacks, lounged nearby on a couch commenting on the political scene.

At 2:05 A.M. Kido heard the actual short-wave transmissions from the assault boats of the Malayan invasion force as they hit the Kota Bharu beaches. In the next half hour the Japanese troops overran Anglo-Indian barbed wire entanglements and secured their foothold. Lieutenant General A. E. Percival, the British commander in Singapore, called in the news to the War Office in London. It was then 5:40 P.M. in England and 12:40 P.M. in Washington.

In the Imperial Library in Tokyo excitement had slackened enough so that Kido could explain to Hirohito that Foreign Minister Togo was waiting in an anteroom to discuss the message from President Roosevelt. Hirohito had Togo admitted, listened to him read the note from Roosevelt, voiced admiration for its sentiments, but regretted that it had come too late. Then Hirohito approved the wording of a rejection of the note which Togo had thoughtfully drafted in advance.

At 3 A.M., while Togo was in audience, Ambassador Nomura in Washington was supposed to be delivering the fourteen-part note to Hull which was meant to serve in lieu of a formal declaration of war. Instead, at that moment, 1 P.M. Washington time, Nomura was phoning the State Department to apologize about his staff's difficulties in decoding and typing the note. Would it be all right if he postponed his meeting with Hull until 1:45? Hull, since he already knew the contents of the note, nursed his wrath and declared that he was ready to wait as long as necessary until the representatives of Japan were prepared to show themselves.

At 3:15 A.M. Togo left the Imperial Library and hurried over to the Foreign Ministry to stand by at his own short-wave set. Kido lingered on in the company of Hirohito for another fifteen minutes—the fateful minutes that were to decide the opening round of the war.

TIGER, TIGER

Commander Fuchida of the Pearl Harbor attack squadron had sighted the coast of Oahu Island at about 3:05 A.M.—7:35 A.M. Hawaiian time, 1:05 P.M. Washington time. Flying at 9,000 feet, above broken clouds, Fuchida saw the white line of surf and the green mountains beyond through a "pink-stained morning mist." He was coming in with his planes on the north side of the island. Pearl Harbor and Honolulu lay on the south side. He therefore banked to his right and led his planes out to sea down the west side of the island so that his torpedo bombers could start their run on Pearl Harbor from the south—over water—low.

Running ahead of his pack, Fuchida rounded the southwestern corner of the island, Barbers Point, and surveyed the prospects. If his approach had been detected, there would be fighters in the air and his Zeros, which flew 5,000 feet above him, would have to fall upon them and win air superiority over the target area before the bombing could begin. He would then have to shoot off two smoke rockets—"two black dragons"—to indicate that total surprise had not been achieved.

Though Fuchida did not know it, total surprise should not have been achieved. A radar station, manned by two noncommissioned officers, had watched the approach of his air fleet for forty minutes. No one whom the two noncoms had been able to raise at headquarters by telephone would take the reported threat seriously. In another sector of communications and command, a Japanese midget submarine had been reported sighted, then shelled, depth-charged, and sunk by U.S. destroyer *Ward* outside the mouth of Pearl Harbor. But these reports, too, for the last hour, had gone unheeded.

Fuchida saw below him a scene so peaceful and unprepared that he could scarcely believe his eyes. "I have seen all German ships assembled in Kiel Harbor," he later wrote. "I have also seen the French battleships in Brest. And finally I have often seen our own warships in review before the Emperor, but never, even in deepest peace, have I seen ships anchored 500 to a thousand yards from one another. . . . Had these Americans never heard of Port Arthur [where the czar's Asiatic fleet was sunk in 1905]?"

At 7:40 A.M.—3:10 A.M. in Tokyo—Fuchida fired one black dragon. His dive-bombers responded by climbing toward an altitude of 12,000 feet. His torpedo bombers spiraled down to the level of the wave crests. His own plane with its accompaniment of horizontal bombers descended to 3,500 feet. But the Zeros far above had apparently failed to see his rocket. They were supposed to come down and support the bombers with strafing attacks. Once more Fuchida fired a single black smoke rocket. Now the fighters began tumbling. But so did the dive-bombers. The dive-bomber flight leader had misinterpreted the second rocket as meaning "incomplete surprise." After one black dragon he was supposed to follow the torpedo planes over the target. After two black dragons he was supposed to precede them in an effort to knock out anti-aircraft batteries.

Fuchida had a few split seconds in which to make a decision. The dive-bomber attacks would obscure targets for the torpedo bombers. The two types of planes might even collide. But the wing leaders were all veterans of the China War. The pilots had all learned by heart the topography of Pearl Harbor with a huge sand model constructed on the northern coast of Japan in October. Fuchida could count on his men to adapt themselves to the battle as it developed and keep in mind the objective of destroying the U.S. fleet. Breaking radio silence, he signaled *To-to-to,* "Attack, attack, attack." All his planes responded. It was 7:49 A.M.—3:19 in Tokyo.

Four minutes later all of Fuchida's 182 planes were converging on their targets from different angles and directions for their attack. On the Army runways of Wheeler and Hickam fields, the Marine runways at Ewa, the Navy runways on Ford Island, the Catalina flying-boat basin at Kaneohe, the planes were all parked neatly in compact clusters—a dream almost too good to be true. They had been placed this way so that they could be easily guarded from pedestrian saboteurs who might try to steal up on them and hurl bombs by hand.

In the harbor or on patrol at its mouth lay at least 90 vessels of the U.S. Pacific fleet: eight old battleships, an ex-battleship used as a target hulk, two modern heavy cruisers, six light cruisers, thirty destroyers, five submarines, nine minelayers, ten minesweepers, two repair ships, two cargo ships, three destroyer tenders, one submarine tender, one hospital ship, six seaplane tenders, two oilers, and two gunboats.[7] Not a puff of flak nor the glint of a rising wing tip suggested that any of them were aware of the death hurtling in on them.

So confident was Commander Fuchida of success that at that moment, 7:53 Hawaiian time, 3:23 A.M. Tokyo time, he sent out the radio message, *Tora, tora, tora,* "Tiger, tiger, tiger." It was a prearranged signal of triumph based on an old Chinese saying: a tiger may roam two thousand miles but he will always return home.

Through a freak of atmospherics, Fuchida's tiger-tiger signal was picked up directly in Tokyo. That Hirohito heard it person-

[7] *California, Pennsylvania, Maryland, Oklahoma, West Virginia, Arizona, Nevada,* and *Tennessee; Utah; San Francisco* and *New Orleans; Raleigh, Detroit, Phoenix, Honolulu, Helena,* and *St. Louis; Monaghan, Farragut, Dale, Alwyn, Henley, Patterson, Ralph Talbot, Coyngham, Reid, Tucker, Case, Selfridge, Blue, Allen, Chew, Cassin, Downes, Jarvis, Mugford, Bagley, Hull, Dewey, Worden, MacDonough, Phelps, Shaw, Cummings, Schley, McFarland,* and *Ward; Narwhal, Dolphin, Tautog, Cachalot,* and *Cuttlefish; Gamble, Montgomery, Breese, Ramsey, Preble, Tracy, Pruitt, Sicard,* and *Oglala; Grebe, Tern, Bobolink, Vireo, Turkey, Rail, Crossbill, Condor, Cockatoo,* and *Reedbird; Medusa* and *Vestal; Castor* and *Antares; Whitney, Dobbin* and *Rigel; Pelias; Solace; Curtiss, Tangier, Thornton, Avocet, Swan,* and *Harlburt; Neosho* and *Ramapa; Sacramento* and *Taney.*

ally on his own short-wave set is doubtful, but it was relayed to him in a matter of seconds by phone. Seven minutes after Fuchida had sent it, at 3:30 A.M., Hirohito dismissed Lord Privy Seal Kido so that he could return to his residence and catch a few hours of sleep before the busy ceremonials scheduled for the morrow. Hirohito showed the steel of his own nerves by retiring to do likewise.

Now, as the Emperor prepared for bed, America's nightmare, Pearl Harbor, played itself out in a chaos of smoke and fire. The first bombs and machine-gun bullets began splattering runways and decks at 3:25 A.M.—7:55 A.M. Hawaiian time. Japanese torpedo bombers ran in low from all directions on the eight battleships lined up along the eastern shore of Ford Island in the center of the harbor. Within five minutes four of the battlewagons had been pierced by one or more of the 1,000-pound explosive fishes. At the same time dive-bombers were swooping down to nest their eggs on decks, turrets, and bridges. The horizontal bombers, of which Fuchida's was one, dropped their armor-piercing shells with deadly accuracy. Some of them failed to explode but killed men literally by hitting them on the head. Some of them pierced too well and made their way right through the armored decks of the warships and out their hulls to bury themselves in the mud below. Still others blew up on the second or third decks of the battleships creating carnage in mess rooms, sick bays, and recreation areas.

Within the first twenty-five minutes of the attack, the 32,600-ton *Arizona,* commissioned in 1916, took a hit from a dive-bomber directly down her stack. The boilers blew up, touching off her forward magazine. With a great roar she broke in two and went down almost immediately, taking with her 1,104 lives.

The 29,000-ton *Oklahoma,* also commissioned in 1916, lost her trim from three torpedo hits and capsized before all the surviving members of her crew could climb topside to escape. Thirty-two of the captives were later released through holes cut with torches in her bottom plates.

When the eighteen-year-old, 31,800-ton *West Virginia* went down with one bomb and four torpedo hits, some of the men trapped in her compartments were not so lucky. The salvage crews who later raised her found a diary scrawled on a bulkhead by three men who had not died until sixteen days after her sinking.

On the 32,600-ton *California,* commissioned in 1921, fires reached the fuel tanks. She burned for three days before she finally foundered.

One of the battleships, the 29,000-ton *Nevada* commissioned in 1916, succeeded in getting up steam in an effort to escape. Japanese bombers at once converged on her and sought to sink her in the entrance of the harbor. Her skipper managed, however, with the help of two courageous tugboat crews, to beach her in sinking condition on a mud flat at one side of the harbor mouth.

Two of the most valuable battleships were protected from torpedoes and saved from being sunk because they had been moored on the landward side of *Oklahoma* and *West Virginia* which shielded them. The 31,500-ton *Maryland,* commissioned in 1921, sustained only bomb damage. The 32,600-ton *Tennessee,* commissioned in 1920, came off equally well but was so securely wedged between the sunken *West Virginia* and a concrete dock that she could not be towed away for repairs until more than a week later when the dock itself had been delicately dynamited.

One other big ship was sunk: the ex-battleship *Utah,* 21,825 tons, commissioned in 1911. Before the attack she was in process of being retired from the Navy and stripped of all fittings of any value. As a result she had lost part of her superstructure and was sheathed in planks and scaffolds. From the air she looked like a flattop. Delighted Japanese pilots squandered torpedoes on her with prodigal fury. It took them exactly eleven minutes of concerted attack to capsize and sink her. Fifty-eight members of her skeleton crew went down with her and their bones remain in their rusted steel casket to this day.

Of all the battleships, the fleet flagship *Pennsylvania*—33,100 tons, vintage 1916—came through with least damage. One reason was that she lay in dry dock, out of reach of torpedoes. Another reason was a gunner's mate who had been aboard the gunboat *Panay* in 1937. At the sight of the first Japanese plane he grabbed a sledge hammer, smashed the locks on the *Pennsylvania*'s magazine, and began, unauthorized, to pass out ammunition. His determination not to be caught again by the Japanese enabled the *Pennsylvania* to start putting up a withering defensive fire even before the Japanese pilots had cleared their first run. Dive-bombers tried to penetrate the barrage again and again but succeeded in striking the *Pennsylvania* only one glancing blow. Five days after the attack her repairs had been completed and she returned to service.

The frustrated pilots who could not get through to the *Pennsylvania* vented their rage on two destroyers in the dry dock in front of her. The *Downes* took a bomb in her torpedo magazine and blew up, bathing her neighbor *Cassin* in burning oil. Another destroyer, the *Shaw*, in floating dry dock, lost her entire bow.

Pieces of machinery from *Cassin* and *Downes* were later incorporated in new hulls so that these two destroyers would float again to taunt Japan and haunt her. The battleships *California*, *West Virginia*, and *Nevada* were all raised and completely rebuilt at great expense. Efforts to salvage *Oklahoma* only ended when she sank, under tow, on her way to a West Coast dockyard after the war was over. The Navy's determination to belie Japanese Pearl Harbor claims even extended to the sunken minelayer *Oglala*, which had been converted from an ancient Fall River steamer in 1917, but emerged from World War II as yare as a commodore's pinnace. Only *Arizona* and *Utah* remained unsalvaged and they were left where they sank as national shrines.[8]

At the same time that the ships were sinking in the harbor, the neatly parked airplanes were being destroyed on the runways ashore. Of the Marine Corps' eleven Wildcats, thirty-two scout bombers and six utility planes at Ewa, only two Wildcats and fourteen scout bombers could still be flown when the Japanese had left. Twenty-seven of the thirty-six Catalina flying boats at Kaneohe were demolished beyond repair. Six more were severely damaged. The remaining three were out on patrol and missed the action. Although no reliable statistics have ever been released on over-all air losses, at least 112 out of 148 good Navy combat planes were destroyed and 52 out of 129 serviceable Army fighters and bombers. Only 38 U.S. planes were able to get into the air and ten of these were shot down.

Almost all of this damage was done in the first twenty-five min-

[8] Other victims of the attack were the 1924 light cruiser *Raleigh*, heavy damage; the 1939 light cruiser *Helena*, heavy damage; the 1938 light cruiser *Honolulu*, moderate damage; repair ship *Vestal* and seaplane tender *Curtiss*, both moderate damage.

utes of the attack. After that the Zeros continued to spray burning decks and runways with machine-gun bullets but the bombers
had spent their loads. As they returned to their carriers, Commander Fuchida remained circling to observe the results of the
second attack wave. It flew in at 8:45: 78 more bombers, 54 more
torpedo planes, and 35 more Zeros. By now, however, the counter-
fire from the ships and shore batteries was well organized and
covered the harbor in an umbrella of flak. Twenty-seven destroyers,
five cruisers, and three battleships remained in fighting condition,
and even the beached *Nevada*, though technically sunk, was still
pouring shells into the sky. Of his first wave Fuchida had lost only
nine planes: one dive-bomber, three Zeros, and five torpedo planes.
The second wave, which attacked from 8:15 to 9:45, lost six Zeros
and 14 dive-bombers and accomplished almost nothing. Ships that
were already mortally wounded were finished off and hangars were
bombed at the various airstrips, but no important new targets
were attacked. The Submarine Base, the Naval Shipyard, the Naval Supply Center, and the fuel oil "tank farm" which held almost
as much petroleum as Japan's entire stockpile were all overlooked
through ignorance.

After watching the performance of the second wave, Fuchida,
shortly before 10 A.M., followed it home to the carriers of Nagumo's task force. He wanted to lead a third sortie to attack permanent installations. Nagumo overruled him. A third attack might
reveal the whereabouts of the fleet and jeopardize it. At the cost
of 29 planes and 55 men it had knocked out five battleships, three
destroyers, a minelayer, a possible aircraft carrier, and almost 200
of the enemy's planes. It had killed 2,008 U.S. sailors, 109 Marines,
218 soldiers, and 68 civilians—in all 2,403 Americans. Admiral
Nagumo saw no reason to risk such a record.[9] He turned his fleet
back into the fogs of the north Pacific and slipped away to make
an uneventful return voyage to Japan.

[9] The Japanese advance force of twenty submarines had not fared as well
as Nagumo's main fleet of six carriers. One of the I-class submarines was
bombed and sunk on December 10 and all five of the two-man midget submarines were lost without doing a trace of damage. One of them ran aground
on a reef and was captured together with its captain, Ensign Sakamaki Kazuo.
The other nine midget submariners are worshipped today at a special shrine in
the old naval academy at Etajima. Survivor Sakamaki lives on, undeified but
content, as a mechanic in Nagoya.

WAR

Three minutes after the first bomb fell at Pearl Harbor, Rear Admiral P. N. L. ("Pat") Bellinger got off an urgent all-points fleet signal: "From Cincpac to all ships Hawaii area: air raid on Pearl Harbor. This is no drill."

Unlike Army Chief of Staff Marshall's earlier message from Washington to Hawaii, Bellinger's signal crossed the gap to Washington almost instantaneously. The Office of Naval Operations at once transmitted it to Admiral Stark. "Betty" Stark called Navy Secretary Knox. Knox, after a moment of incredulity and argument—"They must mean the Philippines"—phoned the White House. President Roosevelt was eating an apple and sorting some new specimens for his stamp collection. He at once instructed Knox to obtain all possible details of the attack and to place the entire Navy on a war footing. When Roosevelt hung up, the brass ship's clock on his desk registered 1:47 P.M. or 8:17 A.M. Hawaiian time.

Eighteen minutes later Japanese Ambassador Nomura and Special Envoy Kurusu arrived at Secretary of State Hull's large, shabby, impersonal office to deliver notice of the rupture in Japanese-American relations.[10] Hull kept them waiting for fifteen

[10] The incompetence of the Foreign Ministry in failing to deliver the note on time later angered Hirohito greatly. In quest of justification he had Togo commission "A Study Concerning Hostilities on the Outbreak of War" from Tokyo's International Law Society. The lawyers submitted their findings on December 27, 1941. They began by saying: "Suppose that we declared war at 8:00 A.M. in Tokyo and what we wanted to assert with nominal time as the standard—that is, nominal as opposed to practical—is that we did not violate Hague Treaty Number Three." Then, concluded the lawyers, time zones could provide no defense, for though the attack on Pearl Harbor took place later in the day Washington or Hawaiian time than the hour of note delivery Tokyo time, still the attack on Malaya as per Malayan time preceded note delivery no matter what the frame of temporal reference.

The best that the lawyers could do was to find that the Hague Treaty was logically absurd. "It is not a violation of the treaty," they wrote, "to open hostilities in a far-off land only some 20 or 30 minutes after the delivery of the declaration of war to the diplomatic representative of the other country in one's own capital. Hence it is not impossible to say that the Hague Treaty Number Three is nothing but a bluff or simulacrum and that there is no need to respect such a childish treaty at the outbreak of a war in which the fate of a nation is at stake."

minutes, then gave them ample opportunity to study the American flag and secretarial standard behind him while he affixed his pince-nez and pretended to read the 2,500-word note. As he cast his eye down the paragraphs which he had already perused in *Magic* versions, he composed a little speech. Ten minutes later he looked up and delivered it, using his Tennessee mountain drawl to good advantage:

"In all my fifty years of public service, I have never seen a document that was more crowded with infamous falsehoods and distortions—infamous falsehoods and distortions on a scale so huge that I never imagined until today that any government on this planet was capable of uttering them."

Ambassador Nomura—a man whom Hull liked personally and affectionately called the "old codger"—opened his mouth to say something. Hull pointed a finger at the door and said, "Good day, gentlemen."

An hour and a half later, at 4 P.M. Washington time, 6 A.M. Tokyo time and 9 P.M. London time, Prime Minister Winston Churchill found himself closeted with Averell Harriman, a special envoy from Roosevelt, and with John G. Winant, the American ambassador at the Court of St. James's. Japanese troops had been advancing into British territory in Malaya for almost four hours. Churchill switched on the nine o'clock news and heard of the Pearl Harbor attack. At the urging of Harriman and Winant he promptly put through a call to Roosevelt and said, "This certainly simplifies things. God be with you."

At 7 A.M. Japanese time, some fifty minutes thereafter, Tokyo radio announced tersely that the Imperial Navy had opened hostilities on the United States with an attack on Hawaii. At the same moment Ambassador Grew was called by the Foreign Ministry to come at once to Togo's residence. At 7:30 Togo told Grew that the Emperor had rejected President Roosevelt's plea. Togo then handed Grew a copy of the fourteen-part note delivered in Washington. Grew went home to read it, to listen to the radio, and to await internment as an enemy national with diplomatic privileges. At 8:05 Japanese planes raided Guam, at 9:00 Hong Kong, and at 9:05 the northern part of the Philippines.

At 11:40, after several fanfares, the radio finally broadcast the Emperor's rescript proclaiming war. It ended with the words:

The hallowed spirits of Our Imperial Ancestors guarding Us from above, We rely upon the loyalty and courage of Our subjects in Our confident expectation that the task bequeathed by Our Forefathers will be carried forward, and that the source of evil will be speedily eradicated and an enduring peace immutably established in East Asia, preserving thereby the glory of Our Empire.

A day later Vice Admiral Halsey, returning to Hawaii with the carrier *Enterprise,* surveyed the damage at Pearl Harbor, and, as a barbarian, issued his blunt counter to Hirohito's high-priestly invocation of the shades. "Before we're through with them," said Halsey, "the Japanese language will be spoken only in hell."

Roosevelt that day delivered a special message to Congress and received an almost unanimous vote for war. Senator George Norris of Nebraska, who had voted against war in 1917, had now changed his mind. Only Representative Jeannette Rankin of Montana, who had also voted against war in 1917, still opted for isolationism. Never had the nation been more unified. More than a hundred thousand Americans were to die in the effort to subdue "Japanese militarism." And more than a million Japanese, who distrusted militarism but honored the Emperor, died to defend whatever it was that the Americans opposed. The two cultures clashed tragically, with a hate that fed on ignorance, but the clash enabled the United States to make war on Hitler.

PART SEVEN

ARMAGEDDON

27

THE STRIKE SOUTH

(1941–1942)

CONTROL OF THE AIR

When Hirohito's most intimate civilian advisor, Lord Privy Seal Marquis Kido, returned to the palace at 7:15 A.M. on the morning of December 8, he paused for a moment outside the private postern, by which he would enter the western half of the palace woods, and watched the dawn break. Afterward he wrote in his diary:

Turning up Miyake slope as I climbed the Akasaka approach [to the palace], I saw the brilliance of the sunrise, in a clap, over the [palace] buildings before me, and I worshipped. I was reminded that today is the day in which we have embarked upon a great war against the two powerful nations, America and England. Earlier this morning our naval air force launched a large-scale attack upon Hawaii. Knowing this and worrying about the success or failure of the attack, I bowed involuntarily to the sun and closed my eyes and prayed in silence. At 7:30 A.M. I met with the prime minister [Tojo] and with the two chiefs of staff [General Sugiyama and Admiral Nagano] and heard the good news of our tremendous success in the surprise attack on Hawaii. I felt deep gratitude for the assistance of the gods. I was received in audience by His Majesty from 11:40 to 12. I was struck to observe, if I may say so, that at this time when the nation has staked its future upon war, His Majesty seems completely self-assured and shows no trace of inner turmoil.

While Kido talked to the chiefs of staff at 7:30, dawn was just breaking farther west on the rocky little beach at Basco, the chief village on Batan Island, 140 miles north of Luzon, the principal and northernmost island of the Philippine archipelago. Five hundred Japanese soldiers sloshed ashore through the pearly surf and occupied the village without resistance. It was the beginning of the Japanese conquest of the Philippines.

An hour and a half later Japanese planes descended on the island of Hong Kong and destroyed its air force of three torpedo bombers and two Walrus amphibians. At the same time the regiments of Japan's 38th Division, stationed in Canton, crossed the border from China, the Sham Chun River, and began to fight their way east across the mainland dependencies of Hong Kong, the New Territories and Kowloon.

At about the same moment, in southern Thailand, Lieutenant General Tiger Yamashita opened his 25th Army Headquarters in a house in the town of Singora. He had come ashore with the second wave of his 5th Division less than half an hour earlier. Unexpected Thai police resistance had been swiftly silenced after an unopposed landing. With him he had most of the best division in the Japanese Army, the highly mobile, mechanized 5th which had had years of experience in China. It was assisted by the cream of Japan's tank corps, artillery battalions, and Army air squadrons. One of its four regiments had landed successfully at a second Thai town, Patani, some 20 miles down the coast to the south.

A third branch of Yamashita's army, the augmented 56th Regiment of the 23d Brigade, 18th Division, had landed 69 miles south in Malaya proper, at Kota Bharu. It was this landing on which Hirohito had eavesdropped over his palace short-wave set seven hours earlier. Fire from a prepared line of pillboxes in the trees just back of the beach had held down the attackers until daybreak, and British planes, flying in darkness, had sunk one and severely mauled another of the Japanese transports lying offshore. But shortly after first light a Japanese sapper had risen from the sand, stuffed himself into a gun port of one of the pillboxes, and while he was being shot to pieces enabled his comrades to lob in grenades, overwhelm the position, and attack the remaining pillboxes from the rear.

Yamashita's army was securely ashore at all three of its landing points. His main strength, the 5th Division, began immediately, while the day was yet young, to advance down the main highway of the peninsula connecting Thailand and Bangkok with Malaya and Singapore.

As Yamashita opened his drive that morning, fog hung over the Japanese air bases in Taiwan far away to the northeast. At both Army and Navy fields, pilots stood beside their planes waiting nervously for it to lift. The United States had thirty-five B-17 bombers or Flying Fortresses in the Philippines—a formidable striking force if it could attack the Japanese bases before Japanese bombers destroyed U.S. bases. About 7:30 A.M. Tokyo time, or about 6:30 A.M. Manila time, the Japanese Army pilots took off despite the fog and less than two hours later bombed Baguio, the summer seat of the Philippines' Commonwealth government. The raid severely damaged the golf greens around Baguio's Camp John Hay, demolished several outbuildings, and took nine lives. Lieutenant Colonel John Horan, the U.S. commander in Baguio, phoned in his losses to MacArthur's headquarters in Manila but somehow failed to get through to MacArthur's ear the fact that the Japanese were attacking the Philippines.

MacArthur had been awakened five hours earlier with the news of the raid on Pearl Harbor. He knew that Japan and the United States were at war, but he was pledged by both President Roosevelt and by Filipino political leaders to make absolutely sure that the Philippines would be included in Japan's theater of operations before he authorized counteraction.

Having retired from the U.S. Army in 1935 and taken a field marshal's rank in the Philippine Army, the sixty-one-year-old MacArthur had returned to active service only five months previously. In those months he had welcomed some 4,000 American and 82,000 Filipino green recruits into his command and had issued countless reassuring statements to the effect that the Philippines could be defended. Now at 5 A.M. and again at 7:15 and 10 when his air commander, Major General Lewis Brereton, urged him to authorize immediate take-off of all B-17's in the Philippines for a raid on the harbors and fields of Taiwan, MacArthur shook his head and said that such a raid must wait for clearer signs of Japanese intentions.

At his air headquarters Brereton kept his men on alert for defensive action. They had early models of radar and 107 good P-40 fighters with which to anticipate and jump enemy bombers. The most up-to-date planes in the Philippines, the B-17's, however, were difficult to protect. They could not stay in the air indefinitely and they could not perch, at least in Luzon, except on Clark Field, a wide-open plain of runways and flimsy hangars, some 50 miles north of Manila. The inadequate force of fighters on hand, none of which could hope to match a Japanese Zero in a dogfight, had to land periodically and refuel.

Despite MacArthur's six years in the Philippines, personnel were trained for peace, not war. Communications were dependent upon the Philippine telephone system and were undependable. Normal wartime safeguards and procedures were ill defined and inadequately rehearsed. The radar of Air Intelligence in Manila was new gear and easily misunderstood whenever a flock of pigeons flapped their wings in front of it.

All morning long fighters and bombers scrambled in response to false alarms. At 10 A.M., in Taiwan, the fog lifted and the Japanese naval air armada of forty-five Zero fighters and fifty-three Mitsubishi Betty bombers began to take off for their strike south against the U.S. air force in the Philippines. An hour later MacArthur decided that the best use for the ill-protected B-17's might be an attack after all, and he belatedly authorized Brereton to send them on a raid against the fields in Taiwan. At that moment the B-17's were flying defensive patterns in the sky, nursing fuel and staying out of harm's way. Brereton ordered them to land and fuel and arm themselves with bombs. They did so and most of the pilots seized the opportunity to go to the mess for lunch.

At about 12:30 the first Japanese Zeros arrived over Clark Field and began circling leisurely at 22,000 feet. Below them at 15,000 feet they saw a small patrol of U.S. P-40's on its way back to the nearby fighter field at Iba. One of the few Japanese air aces who survived the war remembered the scene as "ludicrous." For ten minutes he and his wing mates cruised, awaiting the arrival of the Betty bombers for which they were the scouts. Below him, parked on the runways, glistened sixty-odd aircraft, including twenty-one of the thirty-five B-17 Fortresses in which rested the entire offensive punch of U.S. forces in the Philippines. A communications breakdown had prevented the U.S. radar center in Manila from warning Clark Field of the vultures gathering overhead. At about 12:45 the Japanese air ace, Sakai Saburo, saw his bombers approaching from the north. They moved directly into their bombing runs.

The attack [wrote Sakai] was perfect. Long strings of bombs tumbled from the bays and dropped toward the targets the bombardiers had studied in detail for so long. Their accuracy was phenomenal—it was, in fact, the most accurate bombing I ever witnessed by our own planes throughout the war. The entire air base seemed to be rising into the air with the explosions. Pieces of airplanes, hangars, and other ground installations scattered wildly. Great fires erupted and smoke boiled upward.

The marksmanship of the high-level Japanese bombardiers was only matched by the performance of the Japanese fighter pilots who strafed Clark Field and shot down U.S. fighters which attempted to take off after the bombing was over. For an hour—a single hour, ten hours after the Pearl Harbor disaster—the Japanese planes continued to ravage the field. Other planes did the same at the two fighter bases in the area, Iba and Nichols Fields. When the raid was over, eighteen of the twenty-one B-17's in Luzon, fifty-three of the 107 U.S. fighters in Luzon, and twenty-five to thirty other U.S. aircraft had been destroyed. Fourteen of MacArthur's thirty-five B-17's escaped attack because they were based at Del Monte Field on the southern Philippine island of Mindanao, 600 miles farther south. These fourteen later plagued Sakai and his fellow Japanese airmen over the Netherlands East Indies. Forty-six days later, over Borneo, Sakai paid eloquent tribute to what the Japanese had accomplished and what MacArthur had lost at Clark Field:

Again. Dive, roll, concentrate on one bomber! This time I caught one! I saw the shells exploding, a series of red and black eruptions moving across the fuselage. Surely he would go down now! Chunks of metal—big chunks—exploded outward from the B-17 and flashed away in the slipstream. The waist and top guns were silent as the shells hammered home.

Nothing! No fire, no telltale sign of smoke trailing back. The B-17 continued on in formation.

For the eighteen B-17's destroyed on the ground at Clark Field that first day of the war, and for the seventy-eight other U.S. planes destroyed in the Clark Field area, the Japanese paid the price of not a single bomber and only seven Zeros. It seemed inconsiderable. On their return to Taiwan the Japanese pilots modestly claimed only forty-four kills and four probables. They were feasted that night as heroes. Yet the seven Zeros which they had lost represented value which neither they nor Americans could then appreciate. All seven downed Zeros had been piloted by flyers with years of experience in China. The Zero was a hot plane. It could dance mazurkas around U.S. fighters of heavier plate and firepower. But the Zero needed a thoroughly trained acrobat at its stick. And the seven Zero aces lost over Clark Field on December 8 began an attrition in trained men which Japan would ultimately come to realize as more important than patriotism.

Later that same afternoon, at 4 P.M. Singapore time, 5:30 P.M. Tokyo time, the Anglo-Indian troops in northern Malaya withdrew from Kota Bharu airfield. Japanese planes began using it immediately—first Navy Zero fighters and staff planes, then by morning Army Betty bombers. Theretofore all the Japanese planes had been flying at the limits of their range from fields in Indochina and strips on islands off the Indochina coast. Now they were ferried in to Kota Bharu via Thai airfields and could remain in the air for hours over the fighting lines before they had to return to their bases for fuel. By the dawn of the next day, December 9, they had captured air superiority over northern Malaya.

The first day of the war had ended with complete success for Hirohito. The American battleships had been sunk at Pearl Harbor. The long-range American bombers had been burned on the ground outside Manila. And the head of the roadway to the British bastion of Singapore had been occupied in force by the best troops in the Japanese Army. The foreign concessions in Shanghai had all peacefully capitulated. The nearest barbarian stronghold in the Far East, Hong Kong, almost 2,000 miles to the southwest and without hope of reinforcement, was under strong attack. It seemed that the cry of Emperor Komei, Hirohito's great-grandfather, was about to be answered. The barbarians had not yet been expelled from the Orient but all except Axis nationals would soon be prisoners.

Only a cloud the size of a man's hand marred that fine cold December evening in Tokyo: the British in northern Borneo, knowing themselves indefensible, had destroyed their runway at Lutong, demolished their refinery at Miri, and set a torch to their oil field at Seria. It was the first of many earth-scorching blazes which would damage the resources for which Japan had gone to war. Nevertheless Hirohito, after a long day of proclamations and meetings, retired well satisfied to his bedchamber behind the "grated gate" in his palace. Few of his footsore infantrymen slept more soundly than he did.

Early the next morning, December 9, as high priest at a special ceremony in the white-pebbled courtyard of the Palace Shrine, Hirohito reported the successful outbreak of the war to his ancestors. Throughout the Empire it was a day for prayer and rejoicing; for bowing to bad weather and contemplating the fall of rain; for digesting the victories of the day before and preparing more great deeds for the morrow.

At about 1 A.M., December 10, Tokyo time, 400 Japanese marines from a task force of nine transports landed on the beaches of the American island of Guam in the Mariana Islands, a Pan American Clipper stop about a third of the way east on the route between Manila and Hawaii. After three and a half hours of fighting, the 430 U.S. Marines and naval personnel on the island, together with 180 Guamanian Insular Guards, surrendered.

Shortly thereafter, as day lightened off the northern coast of Luzon in the Philippines, a picked force of about 4,000 men from the 2d Taiwan Regiment of the Japanese 48th Division waded ashore at Aparri, a town on the north coast which had an airstrip. The U.S. lieutenant who had charge of the 200 Filipino recruits in the town sensibly packed up his machine guns and withdrew at once into the hills toward the south.

At the same time, around the northwestern tip of Luzon, on the beaches of the town of Vigan which faced toward China, another detachment of the Japanese 48th Division landed unopposed to take a second airstrip in northern Luzon. Five of the formidable B-17's, the Flying Fortresses which had been in Mindanao two days earlier and had escaped the holocaust at Clark Field, were sent to bomb the Vigan task force. They serenely ignored anti-aircraft fire and fought off the attacks of Japanese fighter cover but were unable, due to the inexperience of their crews, to do much damage with their bombs. They left three transports burning and returned to their base.

CONTROL OF THE OCEAN

While Japan was taking control of the air and seizing strategic airfields, a tense game of cat and mouse was playing itself out along the coast of Malaya. The importance of the game was symbolic, for the winner might claim the long unchallenged title of Great Britain as Mistress of the Seven Seas. The latest-model British battleship, the 35,000-ton *Prince of Wales*, had sortied from Singapore on the evening of December 8 in a daring attempt to make a surprise raid on the Japanese transports landing troops in northern Malaya. She boasted a ninety-five-barrel battery of the most up-to-date machine cannon for use against hostile aircraft, plus thirty-two pom-pom muzzles and an assortment of standard anti-aircraft guns. All her armament firing together was said to be able to loft 60,000 projectiles a minute. Her 14-inch cannon could lob one-ton shells farther than the 18-inch guns of the biggest Japanese battleships. She was the pride of the British fleet.

Churchill and Roosevelt had signed the Atlantic Charter aboard the *Prince of Wales* the previous summer, and Churchill, over British Admiralty objections, had personally dispatched her to the Orient in November to quash Japanese belligerence. The new carrier *Indomitable* was to have accompanied her, but *Indomitable* had run aground on her shakedown cruise and Churchill had insisted that *Prince of Wales* go ahead into Far Eastern waters alone. He hoped that she would "exercise that kind of vague menace which capital ships of the highest quality whose whereabouts are unknown can impose on all hostile naval calculations." He envisaged her mission as that of an impregnable raider—of a presence that "appears and disappears, causing immediate reactions and perturbations on the other side." He told Stalin enthusiastically: she "can catch and kill any Japanese ship."

Sensing that they were to play knight errant, the crew of the *Prince of Wales* had irreverently dubbed her "Churchill's yacht." Despite the Battle of Britain, their beloved sixty-seven-year-old prime minister had learned to appreciate the sting of the airplane no better than had General MacArthur. Churchill had apparently forgotten the oldest and least romantic rule of chivalry: that the most heavily armored knight can be overthrown by grooms and bowmen if he does not have good grooms and bowmen of his own.

The men of the *Prince of Wales* were not downhearted, however, for in place of an aircraft carrier they had an escort of four destroyers and the formidable 32,000-ton battle cruiser *Repulse*. Though old in hull, *Repulse* had been completely rebuilt in the late 1930's and was now the equivalent of a pocket battleship. She boasted 15-inch guns, a speed of 29 knots, and an anti-aircraft battery hardly less fearsome than that of the *Prince of Wales* herself. Indeed, *Repulse* was 55 feet longer than *Prince of Wales*, slimmer and somewhat more maneuverable.

Hirohito and his naval brother, Prince Takamatsu, shared Churchill's romantic interest in the *Prince of Wales*. They, too, identified themselves with spectacular pieces of naval hardware and felt personally engaged in oceanic jousting. Ever since *Prince of Wales* had arrived in Singapore from Africa a week earlier, the young naval staff officers at Imperial Headquarters had wracked their brains for schemes either to lure her to sea or to destroy her at her berth within the heavily gunned Singapore harbor perimeter. When she took to sea of her own accord and was observed by Japanese spies in Singapore slipping out of the harbor into the cloudy gray twilight of December 8, Imperial Headquarters heard of her sailing almost immediately. The naval air aides in the palace were overjoyed. On Hirohito's authority they at once ordered an all-out effort to waylay and destroy the British dreadnoughts. A hundred of the best pilots in the Navy air force—the most gifted graduates of the Misty Lagoon Air Development Station—were told to stand by at airports in southern Indochina. All submarines were alerted in the lower half of the Gulf of Siam. Reconnaissance planes were sent out from Saigon to fly search patterns over the most probable avenues of approach which the *Prince of Wales* and *Repulse* might take toward the north Malayan beachheads.

Admiral Sir Thomas ("Tom Thumb") Phillips stood personally on the bridge of the *Prince of Wales*. He was the commander of all British naval forces in the Far East and had previously served as assistant chief of staff in the British Admiralty. Small, pugnacious, and brilliant, he had long played an unpopular role in the Admiralty as a champion of air power and a detractor of all capital ships except aircraft carriers. Now he found that the conservative fates had taken their revenge upon him by putting him in command of two beautiful capital ships which had no air support.

Tom Thumb Phillips had taken every precaution to slip out of Singapore unnoticed. He had succeeded in impressing even upon the overconfident, peace-minded public relations office of the British Navy in Singapore the need for secrecy about his foray. As a result half a dozen correspondents in Singapore had been offered a "four-to-five-day" blind press junket with no explanation except that it would be "exciting and important." Most of them—including the representatives of *The New York Times* and the Associated Press—naturally turned the offer down. O. D. Gallagher of the London *Daily Express*, however, sensed that it would involve the great new British battleship in the harbor and persuaded his American friend Cecil Brown of the Columbia Broadcasting System to gamble and come with him. The two correspondents promptly found themselves assigned, with misgivings, to a cramped and stuffy cabin on the battle cruiser *Repulse*.

Taking no chances on Singapore security, Admiral Phillips steamed at top speed due east toward Borneo throughout the night of December 8–9. By dawn he had reached the Anambas Islands which he rightly calculated would be beyond the range of the air search which Japanese staff officers would order if they had heard of his departure. December 9 dawned in accordance with meteorological predictions, for once. The sky was overcast and rain squalls could be seen both visually and by radar spotted all over the Gulf of Siam, offering welcome shelter from detection.

Having rounded the Anambas Islands, Phillips lunged north, directly toward the airfields in Indochina from which he knew that Japanese planes would be taking off to look for him. It was a well-considered plan. Japanese planes were looking for him, but closer to shore, on a more direct route between Singapore and the beachheads where the Japanese had landed.

After coming about into the teeth of the Japanese threat, Phillips had a message posted on all ships' bulletin boards telling the crews that "we are off to look for trouble." He explained that he intended "to carry out a sweep to the northward," to run up the coast under cover of bad weather, and then if not detected by sunset to turn shoreward and make an overnight dash toward the beachheads in southern Thailand where Tiger Yamashita was disembarking his main strength. "At dawn," he wrote, "we shall be to the seaward of Singora and Patani, where the Japanese landing is taking place. . . . I think it is most probable that only submarines and enemy aircraft are likely to be sighted."

A brave word, "only." It meant that Admiral Phillips expected to be intercepted by Japanese aircraft. To anyone who had read his unpopular arguments for many years previously, it meant that the *Prince of Wales* and the *Repulse* would almost certainly be sunk.

Nevertheless, until an hour before sunset on December 9, Admiral Phillips was confounded by good luck. Japanese air crews searched for him in vain to the west of his true course. At 2:10 P.M. a Japanese submarine compounded the confusion by reporting that it had sighted him less than 100 miles off the southern tip of Indochina. At that time he was, in fact, some 140 miles farther to the south and east. He had just changed direction slightly to bring himself still farther to the east, so that he was steering straight for Saigon.

Just after 5 P.M., about an hour before sunset, Phillips's luck ran out. The weather cleared and three Japanese reconnaissance planes on the horizon indicated to the admiral that he had been spotted. He was at that moment closer to the Japanese airfields in Indochina than were the beaches of Kota Bharu. He knew that his two great ships were in mortal danger. Before dark, while he could be sure that the reconnaissance planes were still watching, he turned west and began a high-speed feint straight toward the Japanese beachheads in Thailand which lay about eleven top-speed hours distant.

True to his expectations the Japanese reconnaissance planes had seen him, and on the fields near Saigon, Japanese naval bombers, armed for a dawn raid on Singapore, were hastily re-armed with torpedoes for an attack on capital ships. Four Japa-

nese reconnaissance planes took off at dusk in hopes of following
Phillips through the night, and forty-five minutes later eighteen
Japanese bombers and fifteen torpedo planes followed the re-
connaissance craft south to make a night attack.

Phillips meanwhile had conferred with some of his staff and
was scheming not only to deceive the Japanese but also to calm
the junior ratings on his own vessels. At 5:58 P.M. when it still
seemed to casual observers that he might be attacked at any moment, he knew from radar that no large flight of Japanese planes
was yet approaching and he stood down his tense gun crews from
first-degree to third-degree alert. At the same time he detached
his oldest destroyer, *Tenedos*, to retrace the course of the fleet
back to Singapore. Officially the *Tenedos* had engine trouble and
"needed oil." Actually the commander of the *Tenedos* was entrusted with the delicate role of decoy: he was to move away from
the main fleet and then start sending radio messages to Singapore
"as from Phillips." So well did he play his part that the antiquated
Tenedos succeeded in drawing the fire of a Japanese submarine
during the night and then the next morning of nine Japanese
bombers.[1]

Shortly after 8 P.M., when it was completely dark and he had
maintained his high-speed feint toward Thailand for more than
an hour, Phillips abruptly broke off the feint and doubled back
toward the southeast. The Japanese night reconnaissance and
bombing planes dispatched from Saigon looked for him in vain
along his projected course toward the Thai beaches and at about
midnight they returned disappointed to their bases. On the other
side of Phillips, some 50 miles to the east, the decoy *Tenedos* began breaking radio silence and quacking discreetly.

Phillips told his crews nothing of the dangerous game of blind-
man's buff and bluff that he was playing. At 9:05 P.M. he had his
captains announce to all hands that the fleet had been discovered,
that its mission must be aborted, and that he was running for

[1] The submarine squandered five torpedoes from a distance under the misapprehension that *Tenedos* was the much larger and therefore much closer
Prince of Wales. The air group spent their bombs on her out of sheer frustration because they had not been able to find the rest of the British fleet. Having
survived both attacks, the *Tenedos* would go on to assist in the evacuation of
Singapore and in the final naval holding actions in the Dutch East Indies, after
which she would retire to a well-deserved overhaul in Ceylon.

home. A little later, at about 12:45 A.M. on December 10, he again changed course. At that moment he was about 200 miles or less from the Japanese beachhead at Kota Bharu in Malaya. At that moment, fortuitously, his radio room received a message from Singapore stating that the Kota Bharu airfield had been in Japanese hands for more than twenty-four hours and had been in use by Japanese planes for at least twelve hours. Possibly this message came in response to a query broadcast by the decoy destroyer, *Tenedos*, a little earlier.

Hunted from the north, Phillips now knew that his pursuers had a resting and refueling point directly to the west. If he ran for Singapore at top speed, he might make port by noon the next day. He rightly feared that the Japanese naval air force, expecting him to do just that, would catch him short of the mark and sink him. If on the other hand he turned toward Kota Bharu at maximum speed, he might appear off the Japanese beachhead there with the sunrise at his back and shell the newly established Japanese shore positions for half an hour or more before the planes out looking for him converged to attack. For both these alternatives, he knew, his Japanese hunters must be fully prepared. And so, to make the most of the sacrifice of the two magnificent but unsuitable war machines at his disposal, he decided to take a third course which would extend the game and the gamble a little further and might even enable him to achieve what he was looking for as a raider: the element of surprise.

Phillips turned his ships slightly south and made for Kuantan, a harbor halfway up the Malayan coast between Singapore and Kota Bharu. At dawn, when he was about 60 miles offshore, he had his crews told that the Japanese were reportedly landing at Kuantan and that he was going in to shore with hope of shooting up a Japanese convoy of transports. Such a report of a rumor had, in fact, been sent to him during the night, along with many other pieces of confused intelligence, and it is possible though not likely that he believed it.

At 8 A.M. the *Prince of Wales* and the *Repulse* arrived off Kuantan, and Admiral Phillips sent the destroyer *Express* into the harbor to make sure that everything inside appeared as tranquil as it did outside. With the excuse that he had seen barges under tow to the north, he then turned in that direction to investigate. He crept up the Japanese coast apparently still hoping to sneak through and give his big guns to the battle being waged in the Kota Bharu area. By this time, however, more than a hundred Japanese planes were out looking for him, and the Kota Bharu airfield in front of him buzzed on his radar like a hornet's nest. He would have his best chance against the planes to the south which had been looking for him for hours and must be running short of fuel.

At 10 A.M., hearing that his decoy, *Tenedos*, was under attack by bombers to the southeast, Phillips gave up his sneak approach to Kota Bharu and moved out to sea where his ships would have maximum room to maneuver in the encounter which by now seemed inevitable. For forty-one hours he had played mouse. The moment had now come for him to run out his claws. On the basis of past fleet actions against aircraft, he could hope to hold off the Japanese planes until they were forced to return to their bases for fuel. Then he would have about seven hours before they returned —time enough to escape into the darkness of the next night. To harass him during those seven hours, the Japanese would have to divert planes urgently needed on the front in north Malaya. All such expectations—reasonable as they might be on the basis of past experience—were to be confounded in the next three hours by a single unforeseen circumstance: the Japanese pilots out hunting Phillips were better than any Western pilots previously encountered by the British fleet.

At 10:15 A.M. one of the 100-odd Japanese bombers spread out in search patterns over the lower half of the Gulf of Siam spotted Phillips's ships and at once notified the rest. In a moment twenty-seven Mitsubishi Betties armed for high-level bombing and sixty-one Betties armed for torpedo attack all turned their props toward the sighting point. They were piloted by the best airmen of the Misty Lagoon.

The first run on the British fleet was made at 11:17 A.M. by a nine-plane group which had won the Yamamoto Combined Fleet Prize for high-level precision bombing the year before. The nine prize winners selected the longer of the two capital ships below as their target and came in at an altitude of between 10,000 and 12,000 feet over the battle cruiser *Repulse*. Many of the men on the *Repulse* had seen the German and Italian efforts at high-level bombing of fleet units in the Mediterranean and were not concerned by the Japanese approach. Thousand-foot misses were customary in such cases and the anti-aircraft crews of the *Repulse* directed their fire at two low-flying Japanese planes which looked as if they might make a torpedo attack.

No Western bombardier—German, British, or Italian—had ever gone through the training and selection process of his prewar Japanese naval counterparts. At the Misty Lagoon Air Development Station the Japanese teaching technique of practice makes perfect, which is of great help in making the writing of Chinese characters an automatic hand-felt understanding rather than an intellectual exercise, had been carried to great lengths. At a time when bombsights were still in a crude state of development, the Combined Fleet Prize winners had developed an uncanny, split-second feel for co-ordinating hand, eye, wind, height, and speed.

Nine bombs from nine planes fell at least 10,000 feet toward the moving target of the *Repulse*, and the British crewmen below had time to watch them fall and to comment before they struck that they were falling remarkably true. All nine landed within 100 feet of the moving vessel, bathing her with spray and a moment of panic. Only one, however, landed directly on the decks of the vessel. It fell amidships on the catapult equipment which was designed to launch the *Repulse*'s four observation flying boats. The bomb disappeared through the struts of the catapult and exploded on the plates of the hangar deck below. There it destroyed the reconnaissance potential of the *Repulse*, started a distracting conflagration, and killed or disabled fifty of the ship's 1,309-man complement.

That first bomb augured truly of what was yet to come. British officers, who had been telling C.B.S. correspondent Cecil Brown only a few hours earlier that Japanese pilots were hampered by constitutionally faulty vision and by ineptly designed, inadequately serviced aircraft, now revised their estimates. Brown heard a gunner mutter, "Bloody good shooting for those blokes." The other correspondent, O. D. Gallagher of London's *Daily Express*, learned from officers with experience in the North Sea and Mediterranean that they had never seen such bombing either by the Luftwaffe or the R.A.F. The Japanese pilots themselves later said that they had never dropped a better bomb pattern even in practice.

While the crew of the *Repulse* fought flames and jettisoned debris, five torpedo planes from a second group of Japanese bombers attacked the *Prince of Wales*, launching five well-aimed, true-running torpedoes from five different directions. The officer at the helm succeeded in evading only three of them. One struck aft, disabling the battleship's rudders and reducing her speed from 30 to 15 knots. Another flooded her communications room, rendering her mute throughout the rest of the action and forcing Admiral Phillips to fall back on the slow, undependable sign language of heliograph, semaphore, and mast signals.

Listing and doomed to go around and around in a predictable circle—"an enchanted maiden in a waltz with death," as one poetic crewman later said—the pride of the British fleet had become an easy mark for any Japanese pilot who cared to test the marksmanship of her gunners. All her batteries of cannon and pompoms continued to blaze away, making her sinking a dangerous undertaking. The Japanese flight leader, Lieutenant Iki Haruki, with his own and three other planes' torpedoes unexpended, circled and studied the situation.

After fifteen minutes, at noon, when he had been joined by eighteen more planes, Lieutenant Iki launched a torpedo attack on the *Repulse*. Four minutes later the skipper of the *Repulse*, Captain William G. Tennant, proudly signaled his crippled flagship, the *Prince of Wales*, that *Repulse* was not yet seriously wounded and had successfully dodged the wakes of no less than nineteen torpedoes.

Lieutenant Iki called off his planes and again studied the situation. Twenty-four of the available sixty-one Japanese torpedo planes in the air had already spent their fish. Neither of the British dreadnoughts was yet sunk, although one was now an easy target. While Iki waited, the *Repulse* and the four destroyers drew in around the stricken *Prince of Wales*, making their curtain of defensive fire more dense but also giving the *Repulse* less room to maneuver.

At 12:20, after a sixteen-minute lull, Lieutenant Iki personally led fourteen torpedo bombers into the barrage to get the *Repulse*. Each of the fifteen planes attacked simultaneously from a different direction making it impossible for skipper Tennant to "comb the wakes" and twist his broadside away from the oncoming furlers of white water. According to Japanese accounts, no less than fourteen of the fifteen torpedoes found their mark. Captain Tennant dodged one of them, his twentieth, and then was hit by the rest. Five minutes after the attack started Tennant ordered abandon ship. Eight minutes later the ship sank. In those eight minutes, with a shocked, disbelieving calmness and order, 796 officers and men succeeded in jumping overboard and surviving in the oil-filmed waters. Another 513 ratings were carried under by the hull or drowned while waiting to be picked up by the attendant destroyers.

Captain Tennant himself was thrown into the water when *Repulse* capsized as she went under. He was sucked deep but bobbed to the surface and was rescued. One of the men in the control tower, at the top of the main mast, dived 170 feet and lived to swim away. A companion who followed him failed to clear the deck. Another companion plummeted into the ship's funnel. Twelve Royal Marines leapt for safety too far aft and were chopped up by the still turning propellors. Forty-two men from the engine room climbed up to the mouth of the dummy smokestack and were last seen trying vainly to cut their way through a wire screen which stoppered it.

When the *Repulse* went down, the score or more Japanese planes which remained armed turned their attention to the lame *Prince of Wales*. Five more torpedoes were driven into her and at least two bombs registered hits on her. She sank at 1:15 P.M., forty-two minutes after the *Repulse*. Because of the leisurely nature of her last minutes, only 327 of her complement of 1,612 failed to jump overboard and remain afloat until rescued.

Admiral Phillips chose not to be one of the survivors. He refused even to be manhandled to the rails and pushed. Fighting to the last, he pushed others and returned to the bridge to go down with his ship. For two days he had exercised the best half of the Japanese naval air force and had come within an hour, twice, of achieving surprise off the Japanese beachheads. On his own responsibility, deceiving even his fellow officers, he had made a supreme effort to make capital ships count for something in a world which had passed them by. Having failed, he wanted no part in

the inquest; he did not wish to serve as the scapegoat for the fol-
lies of senior admirals and politicians. He may have taken bitter
satisfaction in having proved, as he had often maintained in debate, that capital ships were no match for airplanes.

According to one of the two news correspondents who were
now sick with oil and clinging to flotsam in the water, one of the
Japanese planes dropped a message onto the screen destroyer,
H.M.S. *Vampire:* "We have completed our task; you may carry
on." It was the high-water mark of Japanese *noblesse oblige*, registered by one of the flower of Hirohito's Misty Lagoon air elite.
Only three of the Japanese pilots had been shot down by the two
great ships' vaunted anti-aircraft firepower but the like of those
pilots would never be seen again. They had carried the skill of
manual flying and fighting to a point of refinement which would
never be exceeded but which would shortly be superseded by electronic bombsights, radar, and computerized fire control.

The Japanese planes flew away without bombs or torpedoes
left for the destroyers and without even machine-gun bullets left
to strafe the survivors being picked up by the destroyers. A few
minutes later a belated flight of slow, American-made Buffaloes
from Singapore arrived to survey the wreckage and fly air cover
over the rescue operations.

The Japanese pilots, winging home to the northeast, radioed
news of their incredible victory ahead of them. It reached Hirohito at 3 P.M. Tokyo time, 1:30 P.M. Malaya time, exactly fifteen
minutes after the *Prince of Wales* had disappeared beneath the
sea. Lord Privy Seal Marquis Kido was talking to a diplomat when
the news was relayed to him by phone. Into the mouthpiece of
the phone, in his best approximation of a British accent, he
shouted, "Hup, hup, hooray!"

Japan had lost three planes and pilots. Great Britain had lost
two ships and 840 crewmen and officers. More important, the Allies, having lost control of the air on December 8, had now, on
December 10, lost all hope of keeping control of the sea in Southeast Asia. Allied land forces in the area could, from now on, expect that the Japanese would dispatch bombing raids and invasion
convoys at will. There would be no hope of protection from above
or of reinforcement from behind.

Churchill heard the news of the sinking of the *Prince of Wales* less than an hour after Hirohito heard it. It was then not yet 7 A.M. in London and the British prime minister was in bed opening his dispatch boxes. He later wrote: "In all the war, I never received a more direct shock. . . . As I turned over and over in bed the full horror of the news sank in upon me."

CONTROL OF THE LAND

After three days of war, the power of the Allies to retaliate by air had been smashed at Clark Field and by sea at Pearl and Kuantan Harbors. There remained, however, Allied land power, and on paper it looked impressive. In Malaya Lieutenant General A. E. Percival commanded 100,000 men: three Indian divisions, one British division, and one Australian division. During the course of the campaign his army would be reinforced by an additional 30,000 British and 7,000 Indian troops. His total force of 137,000 men would lack air support and tanks but would have plenty of trucks, armored cars, artillery, and ammunition.

In the Philippines MacArthur had about 112,500 men: 82,000 recently called-up Filipino reservists, 12,000 well-trained Filipino Scouts, 11,000 U.S. regulars, some 4,000 green U.S. reinforcements, and about 3,500 Marines and naval personnel.

In the Netherlands East Indies the Dutch fielded an inconsequential force of about 20,000 soldiers and 40,000 volunteers split up into a score of small garrisons sprinkled over a vast expanse of territory.

The Japanese were to destroy all these colonial armies in a matter of weeks: the "impregnable bastion of Singapore" in ten weeks, the Dutch power in thirteen weeks, and MacArthur's "Filamerican" army in twenty-one weeks. According to postwar Japanese accounts each of these triumphs was gained with a one-to-two inferiority in troops—a claim which may be doubted. Military textbooks all prescribed at least a two-to-one superiority for landings on hostile shores, and Japanese commanders knew their books.

Inconsistencies in the published Japanese record suggest that the units used in the Strike South were not at full strength but at double and even triple strength. For instance, at one point during the Malayan campaign the 114th Regiment in the 18th

Division—a unit which is claimed to have had a strength of 5,000 men—required no less than 550 trucks, loaded "to breaking point," to transport itself to the front. Anyone who has ever seen a Japanese truckful of soldiers must conclude that, at that moment, the 114th Regiment included from 11,000 to 16,500 men and that it was overstrength by a factor of two to three.

It profits not at this late date to play the military numbers game, but Japanese historians appear to have counted only front-line troops and to have ignored roughly equal numbers of men waiting in reserve or playing service roles in the rear. Without discredit to Japanese military prowess it may be said that, on all fronts, approximately one Japanese soldier was pitted against one Allied soldier in the early campaigns of the war and that the Japanese, despite the fact that they were landing on beaches and advancing into prepared positions, everywhere emerged victorious. They were veterans, the best troops in the Japanese Army, and they had air cover.

In Malaya, the first, largest, and most important of the encounters, three Japanese divisions—the 5th, 18th, and the 2d Imperial Guards, with a front-line strength of about 60,000 men—marched 600 miles down a two-lane road through the jungle and repeatedly threw back the combatants from a British force of 137,000 men. At the end of the road they crossed a mile-wide strait and captured Singapore, one of the half dozen major naval bases in the world.

The credit for this remarkable military achievement belongs largely to its planner, Lieutenant Colonel Tsuji Masanobu of Unit 82 which had worked out the Strike South on Taiwan the previous summer. Tsuji had pushed his plans through the roadblocks of other General Staff officers during his brief visit to Tokyo in August 1941. He was, as his fellow officers said, "a personage of great and mysterious influence." They compared his career with that of the ubiquitous Suzuki Tei-ichi who, as a retired lieutenant general, was now director of the Cabinet Planning Board and virtual dictator of the Japanese economy. Like Suzuki, Tsuji came of uncertain parentage; he had always exercised extraordinary authority over senior officers, possessed real ability, and was well connected at Court.

After graduation with highest honors from the military academy and then the staff college, Tsuji had become, in 1934, a tutor for the youngest and brightest of Hirohito's brothers, Prince Mikasa. Still barely twenty-six at the time of Pearl Harbor, Prince Mikasa had been consulted and had cast his lot with Hirohito in the final decision to go to war on November 30, 1941. On the night of August 14, 1945, Mikasa's closest friends and possibly Mikasa himself were to participate in the abortive but effective palace revolution which persuaded Allied intelligence officers that Hirohito had been an intimidated puppet of military strongmen.

Already in 1934, with Prince Mikasa's patronage, Captain Tsuji had recommended himself to Hirohito by his deft handling of the Military Academy Plot, the framing of Strike-North partisans which had smoothed the way for the strange face-saving rebellion of the Army in 1936 and for the capitulation of the Army to Hirohito's personal rule. Since that time, as a major and a lieutenant colonel, Tsuji had become an unpopular but effective missionary in the Japanese Army for Hirohito's gospel of Asia for the Asiatics. If anyone doubted his imperial mandate, he had only to show his credentials: a set of cuff links from Prince Mikasa, embossed with the fourteen-petal chrysanthemum of imperial princes, and a saké cup from Hirohito, embossed with the sixteen-petal chrysanthemum reserved for the Emperor himself.

Tsuji's plan for the conquest of Singapore was a good one, but it would not have succeeded without unusual co-operation from other Japanese Army commanders and from the Navy and the naval air force. Hirohito had made the co-operation possible by sending to the final Strike-South co-ordinating sessions in Saigon during November 1941 his eldest first cousin, the thirty-two-year-old Prince Takeda Tsuneyoshi.[2]

Through Prince Takeda and Prince Mikasa, and from Emperor

[2] Takeda was the son of Emperor Meiji's sixth daughter, Masako, and of Tsunehisa, one of the four young scions of the blood whom Emperor Meiji had selected as dinner companions during the last decade of his reign. Takeda's uncle was Prince Kitashirakawa who had died at the wheel of the powerful touring car in France in 1923. Kitashirakawa's son, Nagahisa, who was the same age as Takeda, had followed in his father's footsteps by crashing in a take-off from a Manchurian airfield while on a mission of the spy service in 1940. The three other surviving blood cousins of Hirohito were younger: Takahiko and Tadahiko, the boys of Prince Asaka, the Nanking rape commander, and Morihiro, the son of Hirohito's other uncle, the devious Prince Higashikuni.

Hirohito, Lieutenant Colonel Tsuji derived the power to borrow choice troops from other divisions and to make the five divisions assigned to the Malayan and Philippine campaigns stronger
than any Japanese divisions which had ever before taken the field.
For his own Malayan theater, in particular, Tsuji succeeded in recruiting most of the Japanese Army's tank forces, the best artillery, mortar and machine-gun units, and a host of auxiliaries including small-boat and jungle commandos, bicycle troops, all sorts
of bridge and railroad engineers, communication linesmen, and
field medics. When Tsuji had finished outfitting the Strike-South
forces, the other fifty-three Japanese divisions—sixteen left in
Japan, thirteen in Manchuria and Korea, nineteen in China, and
five in Indochina and Taiwan—had been stripped clean of offensive power. Their veterans and their ancillary units had both been
expropriated by the divisions at the front. Straw-stuffed scarecrow
units remained, fit only for marching police beats against guerrilla activity.[3] Disgruntled Strike-North partisans in the officer
corps bowed without protest to this raiding of their forces because they respected General Yamashita, the "Tiger," who had been
given charge of the Singapore campaign.

As well as armor and experts, the Japanese Strike-South forces
had a professional zeal which verged on fanaticism. Japan was
the underdog and every Japanese infantryman knew it. Before he
sailed he was issued a manual which bore the encouraging title,
Just Read This and the War Is Won. It concluded with realisms
which would have terrified any but toughened veterans:

When you encounter the enemy after landing, regard yourself as
an avenger come at last face to face with his father's murderer. The
discomforts of the long sea voyage and the rigors of the sweltering

[3] In Japan the 4th and 39th divisions were being held in reserve ready to
move anywhere at any time. The 7th, 19th, 20th, 52d, 53d, 54th, and old
Imperial Guards divisions were still in barracks. The 40th and 50th divisions
were in training. And the experienced 101st, 106th, 108th, 109th, and 114th
were on call-up status. In Manchuria and Korea remained the depleted 1st, 8th,
9th, 10th, 11th, 12th, 14th, 23d, 24th, 25th, 28th, 29th, and 57th divisions. In
China were the despoiled 3d, 6th, 13th, 15th, 17th, 22d, 26th, 27th, 32d,
34th, 35th, 36th, 37th 38th, 41st, 51st, 104th, 110th, and 116th divisions.
In Indochina and Taiwan the 2d, 21st, 33d, 55th, and 56th divisions stood
ready at full strength for assignments in the Dutch East Indies, Burma, and
Australasia.

march have been but months of watching and waiting for the moment when you may slay this enemy. Here before you is the man whose death will lighten your heart of its burden of brooding anger. If you fail to destroy him utterly you can never rest at peace. And the first blow is the vital blow.

Westerners—being very superior people, very effeminate, and very cowardly—have an intense dislike of fighting in the rain or the mist or at night. . . .

By jungle is meant dense forest in which a large variety of trees, grasses, and thorny plants are all closely entangled together. Such places are the haunts of dangerous animals, poisonous snakes, and harmful insects, and since this is extremely difficult terrain for the passage of troops, it will be necessary to form special operation units for the task.

This type of terrain is regarded by the weak-spirited Westerners as impenetrable, and for this reason—in order to outmaneuver them—we must from time to time force our way through it. With proper preparation and determination it can be done. Maintenance of direction and good supplies of water are the supremely important factors. . . .

You must demonstrate to the world the true worth of Japanese manhood. The implementation of the task of the Showa Restoration [the Reign of Hirohito], which is to realize His Imperial Majesty's desire for peace in the Far East, and to set Asia free, rests squarely on our shoulders.

> Corpses drifting swollen in the sea-depths,
> Corpses rotting in the mountain-grass—
> We shall die. By the side of our lord we shall die.
> We shall not look back.

The ancestor-haunted Japanese, who went into battle with this cheerless poetry burned on their minds, thought and fought like demons. They marched great distances with little food or sleep and then hurled themselves at surprised Allied entrenchments without regard for life. Though famished, groggy, and decimated, they attacked until they broke through. They took few prisoners in mopping up because they were encouraged to think that it would be a slur on the Emperor's virtue if they did not take more lives than they had lost.

Allied troops, by comparison—particularly the British in Malaya—fought under the misapprehension that they were innately superior. When they began to suffer more casualties than they inflicted, they were tormented by feelings of individual inadequacy and their group morale fell accordingly.

In the postmortem of later years Allied commanders were largely held responsible for this complacency. They underestimated the Japanese Army because it had failed to achieve any final victory over the ill-trained hordes of Chiang Kai-shek. They discounted the Japanese air forces and Navy because they thought that Japan during her war with China had had no money to build good planes and ships. They encouraged journalists to exude baseless optimism and noncoms to spread foolish tales about Japanese nearsightedness, imitativeness, and lack of individual initiative. As a result much genuinely sound staff planning was vitiated by troops who were not prepared psychologically for a hard fight.

MALAYA'S JITRA LINE

Colonel Tsuji personally accompanied the vanguard of General Yamashita's 5th Division forces when they crossed the Thai frontier and began their southward advance down the long paved road connecting Bangkok with Singapore. After minor skirmishes with Anglo-Indian companies which had been sent belatedly to fight a delaying action in southern Thailand, the Japanese advance units, about thirteen miles south of the border ran into the forward posts of the only prepared defense position in Malaya, the Jitra line.

With about 500 men and thirty light and medium tanks, Tsuji pushed ahead through the line. At 4 P.M. December 11, the third day of the war, he surprised the first Gurkha outpost while its men were away from their guns, taking shelter from the usual afternoon rainstorm under the rubber trees beside the road. The Japanese troops captured the guns and armored cars of the Gurkhas and pushed on south until a bridge blew up in front of them. Tsuji had his men wade the stream and fight defensively while the bridge was being repaired. Then his tanks rushed through both the Japanese and British infantry lines and succeeded in capturing the next bridge before it could be blown. Now the Jitra line, manned by more than 20,000 British and Indian troops, had been broken at its center, and all night long Allied troops from the flanks moved in to break off the point of the Japanese needle.

Tsuji's 500 men held their salient until, on the morning of December 12, they were relieved by an augmented regiment of some 10,000 men with more tanks.

That evening, after numerous telephone calls between the British front lines and the British command in Singapore 600 miles to the south, the Jitra line was abandoned; its minefields, entanglements and trenches, its caches of food and ammunition, and many of its guns, trucks, and armored cars were allowed to fall into Japanese hands. Half its defenders had been Indians who had never before seen a tank. All its armored cars were sturdy Rolls-Royce products left over from World War I. Nevertheless, there was no other prepared defense line to compare with it in the rest of Malaya. At rivers farther south, the Anglo-Indian-Australian forces would give a better account of themselves, but by then the Japanese infantrymen would be unbeatable. They would have lost their fear of the strange tropical surroundings and their awe of white soldiers. Their strength would have fattened on captured food, gasoline, trucks, and ammunition. Indian prisoners of war would have told all they knew about the positions ahead. And the triphammer sequence—advance, breakthrough, pursuit, consolidation—would have become routine.

Colonel Tsuji felt that at the Jitra line he had demonstrated the only tactics which would be needed throughout the campaign. Foot soldiers would ford rivers and infiltrate, enabling engineers to repair blown bridges; then tanks would lunge through and dash forward until stopped by another unbridged river. To keep pace with the tanks and to extend their salients even beyond the next river, the Japanese infantry would employ collapsible bicycles which they could carry on their backs across streams. By pedaling fast enough these bicycle troops could maintain a steady pressure on the rear of the retreating British troops and give them no time to regroup even when they had just left a blown bridge behind them. When disabled Japanese or British armor piled up at hard-fought road-blocks, impeding further advance, the bicycle troops would be at hand to heave the derelict armor off the road into the jungle. The concept of the bicycle troops was a pet of Hirohito himself. Japan was the world's leading manufacturer of inexpensive bicycles, and the thought of using them to chase Rolls-Royce machines appealed powerfully to the imperial imagination.

By a straightforward battering-ram approach, Tsuji believed that the Japanese Army could go all the way down the main road to Singapore. General Yamashita insisted that this main drive must be supplemented by flanking movements. Troops indoctrinated for jungle fighting must creep through swamps and turn British lines by passing through terrain considered impassable. "Small-boat parties" must compound the terror by running down the jungle-girt west coast of Malaya and creating pockets of infiltration deep behind the British lines.

Colonel Tsuji saw heavy losses in such adventures. General Yamashita refused to abandon any means which might keep the British off balance. Possibly Tsuji was right and lives could have been saved by leaving these peculiarly Japanese forms of blitzkrieg untried. General Yamashita had his way, however, and Prime Minister Churchill later gave much credit for the Japanese success in Malaya to the unnerving flanking movements, by boat and jungle, which made British forces pull back repeatedly, for fear of encirclement, from the hammering down the main road.

The minor tactical differences of opinion between Colonel Tsuji and his former patron, General Yamashita, grew into a major falling-out which would have important consequences of state. Yamashita first caused Tsuji to lose face before fellow staff officers by overriding him on the issue of the small-boat parties and outflanking movements down the west coast. Then Tsuji took the part of some Japanese troops who had committed unauthorized atrocities on the west coast island of Penang and was again overridden. Tsuji sulked and offered to resign. Yamashita refused to accept his resignation but failed to heal the breach.

Before the Malayan campaign was half over, Tsuji had begun a campaign of vilification against his commander which was jealously pursued in Tokyo by the politically-minded general, Prime Minister Tojo, and sympathetically represented at Court by Hirohito's brother, young Prince Mikasa who was Tsuji's patron and protégé. As a result, when Singapore fell, two months later, Hirohito would turn his back on his ablest general, would deny Yamashita a triumphal return to Tokyo, and would repost him directly back to his old command in Manchuria. Most important, Hirohito would turn a deaf ear to an audacious plan, advocated by Yamashita, which might have changed the course of the war. It was a plan for the immediate invasion of Australia.

WAKE

During the opening skirmishes of the battle for the Jitra line in Malaya, Allied forces won their only victory of the first month of the war. At dawn on December 11, a Japanese cruiser, six destroyers, and two transports hove to off the tiny two-and-a-half-square-mile coral atoll of Wake, an air Clipper stop about two thirds of the way from Manila to Hawaii. For forty minutes the Japanese ships shelled the atoll and then, having roused no answering fire, they moved in to land troops. When they were 4,500 yards from shore, Major James Devereux, who commanded the 450 U.S. Marines on the island, finally allowed his 5-inch gun crews to go into action.

Taken by surprise, the Japanese ships turned tail to get out of range. The Marines' four Wildcat fighter planes were wheeled from hiding places in the scrub which covered the island and managed to take off from the pockmarked coral airstrip which had been bombed repeatedly in the previous two days. As the Japanese task force retreated, the Marines' shore batteries sank one of the destroyers. The four Wildcats continued the attack beyond the range of the shore guns and sank a second destroyer. Most of the Japanese ships had been damaged and over 500 Japanese had been killed, with the loss of one U.S. Marine. The Japanese commander, Rear Admiral Kajioka Sadamichi, sailed back to his base on the Japanese mandated island of Kwajalein for refitting.

Kajioka would return twelve days later to complete his mission with six heavy cruisers, two aircraft carriers, fifty-four planes, and over 1,000 landing troops. Again the defenders of Wake would give a good account of themselves, killing over 800 Japanese and losing only forty-nine Marines, three sailors, and seventy civilians. At the end of a twelve-hour battle, however, 470 U.S. Marines, sailors, and airmen, together with 1,146 construction workers and other civilians attached to the air base, would become Japanese prisoners. A third of them would not live to be liberated.

HONG KONG

The retreat of Japan's fleet from its initial repulse at Wake was a unique movement. Everywhere else Japanese forces were advancing. Yamashita's tanks were capitalizing on their breakthrough of the Jitra line in Malaya and taking a heavy toll of ill-trained Anglo-Indian forces as they attempted to fall back upon a new defense position. In Thailand, on December 11, the support forces of the Malayan expedition reached an agreement with the Thai government, declared Bangkok secure, and moved on west into southern Burma to occupy a British aerodrome there, Victoria Point.

The next day, December 12, the U.S. Navy withdrew its remaining planes from the Philippines to Java, leaving the U.S. Army in the Philippines with a total cover of thirty-three Army fighters.

Allied commanders looked on askance and swore that Japan was violating every principle of offensive warfare by scattering her forces in all directions. In all directions, however, the Japanese buckshot continued to drill through. Small Japanese convoys were observed converging on British North Borneo. On December 15 and 16 they hit the beaches of Sarawak and Brunei and captured these two British protectorates almost immediately. In so doing they gained possession of wells which at that time produced more than one per cent of the world's petroleum. British demolition experts, however, had been busy for a week and had done their work conscientiously. The subterranean fires they had started would burn for a month, and when the pall of smoke had cleared, the wellheads would gush less richly.

Outside of Malaya, the main Japanese Army offensive in these days was aimed at the conquest of Hong Kong. The Japanese 229th and 230th regiments, 38th Division, with untold and unknown assistance from elements of the 18th, 51st, and 104th divisions, took five days to sweep down through the mainland dependencies of the British crown colony. On December 13 Major General C. M. Maltby completed the withdrawal of his forces to Hong Kong island, the showplace of colonialism, where some twenty-four square miles of handsome bungalows and gardens crowded up the slopes of a beautiful little mountain range encircled by a sunny blue sea.

For five days, December 13 to 18, General Maltby's 14,500 defenders—a quarter of them British troops, a quarter Canadian, a quarter Indian, and a quarter civilian, naval, and air volunteers—awaited the onslaught of the 20,000 to 30,000 Japanese soldiers gathering at embarkation points across the mile-wide waters of Kowloon Bay. All the while some of the best artillerymen in the Japanese Army rained shells upon Hong Kong's beaches and docks.

On December 18, under cover of dusk and the smoke of the great oil tanks which had been ignited by the Japanese shelling on the northeastern point of the island, some 10,000 Japanese troops from three regiments crossed the bay in barges and sampans and established themselves on a broad beachhead. They then surprised the British defenders by driving toward the least populous area of the island, the mountain peaks. For two days British forces waited to defend the valuable installations on the shore beside the Japanese beachhead while the Japanese troops stormed the difficult heights of the interior which were defended by small but well-entrenched groups of Canadian soldiers who had recently arrived from the plains of Manitoba.

The purpose of the strange Japanese tactic was quickly realized when the three invading regiments converged on the reservoir in the mountains which supplied the entire island with drinking water. Hirohito had taken a special interest in the reservoir during his visit to the island as crown prince in 1921 and had insisted upon being driven up off the beaten track of tourists to take a look at it. Now his men concentrated their first efforts on seizing it, and Major General Maltby, grasping the implications, committed all his reserves to the defense of the ridges and passes around the reservoir.

Several thousand of the best Allied and Japanese troops died around the reservoir in a five-day battle which the British ultimately lost. On December 23 the Japanese finally gained control of the chief pumping stations and reduced the main body of Hong Kong's defenders to the two-day supply of water which was left in the storage tanks in the city of Victoria.

While the reservoir was being defended and lost, Hirohito's

men made a lateral strike against the Hong Kong power station. It was defended by a group of wounded soldiers and a force of puffy-faced, middle-aged businessmen. These civilian volunteers were representative of the "colonialists" who had made Hong Kong a model colony and the most crowded enclave of peace, police, and opportunity in the Far East. True to the last to their "white man's burden," they defended the power station until they saw that their position was untenable. Then they sortied in a last brave gesture and were all killed. Many of them had learned to handle guns only in the week before. All of them could have remained noncombatants and could have chosen less certain death as civilian prisoners in a Japanese internment camp.

From December 23 to December 25, while other Japanese units were landing in force on Luzon, bombing Rangoon in Burma, and moving into Dutch Borneo, the Hong Kong attackers advanced steadily down from the captured reservoir in the mountains into the thirsty thoroughfares of Victoria, Hong Kong's chief city. Major General Maltby, at the insistence of the diehard civilian governor of the colony, Mark Young, had already rejected out of hand two Japanese recommendations of surrender, delivered under flag of truce.

On Christmas eve Japanese officers were instructed by their commander, Lieutenant General Sakai Takashi, to let the British know that if they did not surrender soon they would have to abandon hope of being taken prisoner at all. During Christmas morning lone survivors from overrun British outposts were released to bring this message to Maltby's attention and to tell how their comrades had all been killed. By afternoon Maltby could see that his forces were breaking up into pockets which the Japanese would be able to annihilate at leisure. Feeling that there was no use in fighting on when his men could no longer take a life for a life, Maltby got Governor Mark Young's approval to capitulate.

British troops and civilian volunteers in the western half of the island, who had been cut off and ignored after the Japanese seizure of the heights, refused to believe that the rest of the island had surrendered and continued fighting. They held a strong position at Fort Stanley, on a highly defensible peninsula at the southeastern corner of the island. Heavy bombardment from land and sea had failed to silence their batteries and their shells were inflicting high casualties on the Japanese. To hasten their surrender the Japanese, all through Christmas day and night, staged a gruesome display of escalating reprisal and terror. Early in the morning, the Japanese had captured St. Stephen's College outside the walls of Fort Stanley. On its premises they had found installed a field hospital. Obedient to General Sakai's orders they had begun their occupation of the hospital by bayoneting some sixty of the ninety-odd patients.

Later, when word of the surrender had been received and Fort Stanley still held out, they put four Chinese and seven British nurses in one room and about a hundred orderlies, doctors, and stretcher-bearers in another room. During the afternoon they took out the male captives, two or three at a time, and one by one, limb by limb, dismembered them. They chopped off fingers, sliced off ears, cut out tongues, and stabbed out eyes, before they killed. A few of the victims were allowed to escape to tell the Fort Stanley defenders what was happening. In the other room the nurses were made to scream. Beds of corpses were built for them on which they were tied down for raping.

At some time in the evening the four Chinese nurses and then the three youngest and prettiest of the English nurses were put to death by bayonet. About then negotiations with the defenders at Fort Stanley began to progress, and the last four elder British nurses were locked in a room and left alone. During the night Fort Stanley surrendered, and in the morning British prisoners were brought in to the hospital to clean up. They released the four surviving, gibbering nurses. They literally waded in blood as they gathered corpses for burial from the execution room. They carried away a hysterical British lieutenant who was the husband of one of the three British nurses who had been abused and then bayoneted. For the first Allied war captives, the years of imprisonment had begun.

LUZON

In the Philippines the main body of the Japanese invasion force, some 40,000 strong,[4] had begun landing from a convoy of seventy-

---

[4] My estimate. I saw the invasion fleet through field glasses from the mountains and have talked to Japanese generals about it. MacArthur, on the basis

three transports, plus auxiliary and escort vessels, on the beaches
of Lingayen Gulf, on the western shore of northern Luzon, on
December 22. They quickly joined up with the two detachments
of about 4,000 men each which had landed twelve days earlier
at Aparri and Vigan still farther north.[5] "Filamerican" troops
under the over-all command of U.S. Major General Jonathan M.
Wainwright, who had the responsibility for guarding the 500-mile-
long coasts of northern Luzon, offered light resistance at the
beaches and then fell back.

Wainwright used green Filipino reservists to contest the Japanese landings. He held a few thousand seasoned troops in reserve at important roadheads to the south of the Japanese
beachheads. It was his duty, as gracefully as possible, with a maximum show of force and a minimum loss of life, to abandon northern Luzon and fall back to the south.

For political reasons MacArthur had promised Filipinos that he
would defend all 115,000 square miles of the 2,000 islands in the
Philippine archipelago. In reality he had no intention of squander-
ing his little army of 26,500 trained fighters and 86,000 green recruits on any such impossible task. He had about 80,000 of his
men, including almost all his professionals, with him on the large
northern island of Luzon. There he intended to use them where
they would give the best account of themselves.

Since December 15 he had been moving stockpiles of ammunition and food into 400 square miles at the tip of Bataan, a small
peninsula which jutted south from the middle of the western
coast of Luzon and crooked its appendix across the northern half
of Manila Bay. On Bataan he would be able to wedge his green
troops between his experienced soldiers and fight a positional battle which would take the maximum toll of Japanese lives. Bataan
controlled the landward approaches to Corregidor, an island for-

---

of aerial reconnaissance, claimed that 80,000 Japanese came ashore. Japanese
commanders, in postwar prison interrogations, have claimed that only about
15,000 troops landed, those of the 16th Division's 20th Regiment and of the
48th Division's 47th and First Taiwan Regiments. I give other estimates in
what follows about the strength of other Japanese landings. Official Japanese
figures are noted in the footnotes.

[5] At Aparri a battalion and a half of the 2d Taiwan Regiment of the 48th
Division with a claimed strength of about 2,200 men; at Vigan the other,
"nuclear" half (i.e., including commanding officer and his staff) of the same
regiment with a claimed strength of approximately 3,000 men.

tress of concrete tunnels, artesian wells, and heavy guns which had been built at great expense to defend the entrance of Manila harbor.

The fall-back of General Wainwright's forces toward Bataan in the south left the northern half of Luzon undefended, including the summer capital of the Philippines, Baguio, which nestled in the pine-clad Benguet mountains some 30 miles east of the palmy shore where the Japanese had landed. The Japanese seized the approaches to the tortuous paved road which led up the mountainsides on December 23. That evening the U.S. commander in Baguio, Lieutenant Colonel Horan, drove his armored cars over a clay embankment to destroy them and began marching his men away into the hills to become a guerrilla chieftain.

On Christmas eve, American residents in Baguio anticipated by a few hours the fighting colonials of Hong Kong by establishing the Pacific War's first internment camp for Allied civilians. They gathered voluntarily at a local school in order to turn themselves over in a well-organized body, giving as little excuse as possible for rape or murder and retaining as much as possible of self-government. At the same time local Japanese fifth columnists took over Baguio's municipal government.

The advance troops of the Japanese Army, when they arrived in Baguio more than a day later, were presented with a peaceable, submissive city. They suspiciously wasted the opportunity, however, and proved the slogan "Asia for the Asiatics" to be propaganda. Within a week of their entry, the Baguio market place was empty; sentries stood at every street corner; the homes of the Hispano-Filamerican rich had all been sealed with Japanese-Army-property stickers and their furnishings removed to Japanese-Army bodegas; the native poor, who joined as scavengers in the looting, were being shot on sight. A semblance of good government would not be restored for a month. The substance—including adequate opportunities to earn and eat and hope for betterment—would not return until after the end of the war in 1946 and 1947.

The Japanese commander in the Philippines, Lieutenant General Honma Masaharu, climbed the ramp of one of his landing barges and came ashore at the Lingayen beachhead on the morning of December 24. As he did so, another 18,000-odd Japanese soldiers from twenty-four deep-sea freighters were landing east and south of Manila on the shores of Lamon Bay at the other side of Luzon.[6] They quickly joined up with about 8,000 more soldiers who had landed at the town of Legaspi, farther south on the same coast, on December 12.[7] In all, General Honma had at his disposal, converging on Manila, some 74,000 of the most brutal troops in the Empire.[8] Roughly 26,000 of them were advancing from the south. He had the other 48,000 with him as he advanced from the north. A further force of 12,000 to 15,000 retired veterans, the 65th Brigade, was on the high seas behind him, sent to provide reliable occupation troops for his rear.[9]

General Honma's landing at Lingayen Gulf and General Wainwright's quick withdrawal in the face of it compelled MacArthur to reveal to Filipino leaders his intention of standing to fight only in Bataan. His chief staff officers had all known that he could not fulfill his oft-reiterated public pledge to defend the whole island of Luzon, but no civilians had been let in on the staff secret and only sensibly discreet pessimists had guessed it. During the autumn of 1941, he had even gone so far as to discourage—"for the sake of Filipino morale"—the evacuation home to the United States of the wives and children of American civilians in the Philippines. The dissimulation was necessary because, without it, he would never have been able to bring over 80,000 Filipino reservists into his army in the final two months before the war broke out. The men called up hoped to defend their *barrios* or home villages. Had they known that they would serve hopelessly on Bataan, in order to gain time for a global U.S. strategy in which the Philippines counted for little, they would have thought twice before offering to sacrifice themselves.

MacArthur announced his decision to the president of the

---

[6] A battalion of the 33d Regiment of the 16th Division and all of the Division's 9th Regiment. Total claimed strength: 6,510 men.

[7] Two battalions of the 33d Regiment, 16th Division, with a claimed strength of 3,254.

[8] Honma's 16th Division was the force which had been left in Nanking after Christmas 1937 to carry out the last five disciplined weeks of the rape there. His 48th Division was the permanent garrison force on Taiwan; two of its three regiments were recruited from the old Strike-South community of Japanese colonists in Taiwan.

[9] The 122d, 141st, and 142d regiments looted from the 17th and other divisions in China, a claimed strength of 6,659 men which landed on December 28, 1941.

Commonwealth of the Philippines, Manuel Quezon, on the evening of December 23. By then most of the Filipino reservists were already organized in units, enjoying good pay, reliant upon their American officers, and indoctrinated with the belief that they could win. The Japanese landing at Lingayen Gulf was only twenty-four hours old. It had been expected for a fortnight and predicted in contingency planning for years, yet efforts to contain it had already been abandoned. Quezon felt deceived, for it was apparent to him that MacArthur had always secretly expected to fall back on Bataan. MacArthur himself was not as cordial as usual with his old crony, for an American policeman had been apprehended the week before trying to pass through the lines north of Lingayen with a message from Quezon to the colonel of the Japanese force which had landed on December 10 at Vigan.

Something like an abduction took place in the presidential Malacanan Palace that evening. Quezon agreed to become virtually a prisoner of MacArthur's staff officers and MacArthur made political promises in return. In later years, after the tubercular Quezon had died in a U.S. hospital, MacArthur honored the promises even to the extent of excusing from trial certain members of Quezon's staff who, in the meanwhile, had succumbed to Japanese blandishments and become quislings.

During the night of December 23–24, the most recent draft of Filipino inductees—a force of 9,000 men which MacArthur had hoped to add to his troop strength of 112,500—deserted in a body from their boot camp.

The next morning President Quezon met with his Cabinet ministers and, by his own account, "revealed the agreement with General MacArthur." As Quezon later explained it: "To avoid the destruction of the city and save the civilian population from the horrors of indiscriminate bombardment from Japanese planes and siege-guns, Manila was to be declared an open city."

Satisfied with the political cogency of this excuse, most of Quezon's Cabinet accompanied the president and a U.S. Marine guard of honor to Corregidor that afternoon. In the tunnels of the island fortress, at the tip of Bataan Peninsula, barely forty-eight hours after the Japanese had landed in strength on Luzon, the Philippine government established itself in refugee status, under

U.S. protection. It would soon go on to Washington where its exile would be extended for more than three years.

Having waited for the emergency to provide him with a propitious moment for the settlement of his difficult political problems, MacArthur now faced a still more difficult military problem. Some 80,000 dispersed and mostly ill-trained men had to be withdrawn into Bataan over a single two-lane paved road before 48,000 well-collected, highly mobile Japanese veterans could advance 120 miles to his northern flank and turn the retreat into a rout. Some of MacArthur's best units, fighting the other 26,000 Japanese invaders on the southeast coast, would have to drive more than 200 miles before they could reach the entrance to Bataan. What was worst, MacArthur, for fear of lowering Filipino morale, had stockpiled little food or ammunition in Bataan. These prerequisites for a defense had to be brought into the peninsula now, along with the great crowd of troops.

To carry off his fall-back on Bataan, MacArthur needed an act of Providence. Orderly withdrawal had always been difficult even for seasoned soldiers. In the twentieth century it had become more difficult because of the absolute dominance of mobile firepower which, in the tropics, could only travel on roads and railroads. Without air cover to protect his trucks and without broad thoroughfares to expedite their movements, MacArthur's withdrawal to Bataan was a desperate venture. After nine days, however, by January 1, 1942, most of MacArthur's men would be in Bataan, and after fourteen days, by January 6, even his brave and battered rear-guard units would pull back successfully into the Bataan perimeter, blowing their bridges behind them.

Some of the credit for this miracle belonged to the able officers and men who held off the Japanese during the retreat; the rest belonged to Lieutenant General Honma, MacArthur's opposite number. If MacArthur had faced a general of the caliber of Tiger Yamashita in Malaya, the withdrawal to Bataan might have turned into a disaster. Honma, however—"the linguist with the red nose" —had qualified for his command by seven years as a liaison and intelligence officer with the British Army, by six years as aide-de-camp to Hirohito's brother Prince Chichibu, and by sitting up all night in 1932 to give the Emperor a quick translation of the Lytton Report to the League of Nations. He had gained his only experience as a combat commander during the brief Japanese drive up the Yangtze against Hankow in the fall of 1938.

Honma had been put in charge of the Japanese expedition to the Philippines only after the plans for it had already been drawn up by the staff officers around Colonel Tsuji in Unit 82. Then, Chief of Staff Sugiyama had simply summoned Honma and handed him the plans as orders. Honma had demurred at this unusual treatment and had asked time for personal research and appraisal of the Philippine situation. "If you don't like your assignment," Sugiyama had barked, "we can give it to someone else." Honma had bowed quickly but stiffly and ever since that moment had followed his orders like an automaton.

The plans called for Honma to occupy Manila by mid-January. He went about his task without looking to left or to right. On his left guerrillas stole away to learn their trade in the mountains. On his right the "battling bastards of Bataan" cursed their drivers and kicked stragglers in noisy traffic jams which extended for a dozen miles on both sides of each of the two major bridges along the highway leading into Bataan.

Japanese pilots flew over the long lines of desperately impatient motorists and reported what they saw. But Honma ignored the scraps of firsthand intelligence which filtered up to him. He knew that MacArthur commanded only 20,000 to 30,000 properly trained troops, and he saw no great danger in letting such a small force dig in on Bataan. Even at its narrowest point, the peninsula was 14 miles wide and no 23,000 men could hold a 14-mile front against concentrated bombardment, determined bayonet charges, and amphibious outflanking movements. Given time to suffer the hunger and frustration of being besieged, the Americans would make easy marks. It was Honma's plan to occupy the uncontested streets of Manila and then turn at leisure to pluck the thorn from his side. As a former palace aide-de-camp, Honma should have known better. His error was to ruin his career and cost Japan at least 15,000 of her best troops.

MANILA

On December 27, when MacArthur began to feel that the retreat into Bataan might succeed, he made public his decision not to defend Manila and to declare it an open city. A few hours later, in Tokyo, Lord Privy Seal Marquis Kido, on behalf of the Emperor, interviewed Lieutenant General Tanaka Shizuichi, a former commandant of the secret police.[10] Out of the interview came an appointment for Tanaka as military governor and commander in chief of Japanese forces in the Philippines, effective as soon as General Honma should complete mopping-up operations there. As events turned out Tanaka would not be able to occupy his post until August 1942.

Hirohito took MacArthur's open-city declaration to mean that the campaign in the Philippines was nearing a successful conclusion. He urged Chief of Staff Sugiyama, therefore, to abbreviate the Strike-South timetable by six weeks and proceed at once with the invasion of the Dutch East Indies. According to the plans of the previous summer, the number of islands and sheer size of the Indies would require an expeditionary force of three augmented divisions of front-line troops, plus a corps of veterans for rear-area police and guard duty. The crack 2d Division from Sendai in northern Japan would be assisted by the 38th Division which had just taken Hong Kong, and by the 48th Division which Honma, supposedly, had no further use for in the Philippines.

Honma's staff officers, even in the strategy sessions months earlier, had protested that they must keep the 48th Division until after the reduction of the U.S. fortress of Corregidor. They were promised, instead, that they would not have to reduce Corregidor by assault but would be allowed to starve it into submission. Through an oversight Hirohito had not been informed of this understanding. If he had been, he would have disapproved it. An isolated Allied force, left in the rear of Japan's advance, might have no great military importance, but its continued resistance and its uncensored radio broadcasts would be of incalculable propaganda value to the enemy, affecting the attitude of conquered natives and the eagerness of the United States and Great Britain to accept Japanese peace terms.

[10] Tanaka had headed the secret police from August 1938 to August 1939 and again from September 1940 to October 1941. An Oxford graduate, with a fine Hindenburg mustache, he was a partisan of Konoye, a "moderate," a fence-sitter, an opportunist. He would re-emerge as the general of the Eastern Area Army who, at dawn on August 15, 1945, would enter the palace grounds to put down the gesture of revolt there against surrender.

When General Honma learned in late December that he was to give up the 48th Division even earlier than originally planned, he at once filed a protest with General Count Terauchi, the aged martinet of the Army Purification Movement, who presided in Saigon as the over-all field commander and arbiter of the various armies engaged in the Strike South. After making inquiries, Terauchi informed Honma that he would indeed have to give up the 48th Division but that perhaps, for the moment, the U.S. forces on Bataan could be considered part of the Corregidor defense forces and could be represented at Court as "a carp in a pond," unable to escape and easy to catch at any time, especially when hungry.

Terauchi sent this message to Honma verbally through the assistant chief of staff in Saigon, the commander of the 40th Division, Lieutenant General Aoki Sei-ichi. Aoki was used as messenger because he was flying to the Philippines anyway as Terauchi's representative at the official entry of Japanese forces into Manila—a victory parade scheduled for January 5. Hirohito also sent a representative to this ceremony: his cousin Prince Takeda, who had attended the final Strike-South co-ordinating conferences held in Saigon the previous November. Lieutenant General Aoki and Prince Takeda both arrived in Manila the day before the festivities, January 4. Aoki reported at once to General Honma. Prince Takeda conferred with a number of officers and learned the "real situation in the Philippines." That same night he communicated the results of his inquiries—by telephone or telegraph —to Hirohito.

The next morning, to the boom of guns and blare of trumpets, as General Honma, in full dress, was guiding his charger past the presidential Malacanan Palace of the Philippines, an aide discreetly handed him a telegram. It was signed Sugiyama, Chief of the Japanese Imperial General Staff. It curtly commanded him:

REPORT AT ONCE ON HOW YOU EXPECT TO PROCEED WITH THE BA-
TAAN OPERATION. THIS INFORMATION IS NEEDED IN ORDER TO REPLY TO
A QUERY PUT BY THE THRONE.

General Honma hurriedly pocketed the dispatch, but at a reception after the parade he closeted himself with Prince Takeda and learned the full extent of the bad news. In the opinion of the Emperor he had bungled the occupation of the Philippines. Corregidor might have been left to grow hungry and to be ridiculed as a "carp in a pond" if the main strength of U.S. forces in the Philippines had been destroyed first. As matters stood, however, Bataan could not be ignored, nor could the 48th Division be spared to help Honma repair his blunder.

Honma bowed silently to the Imperial Will but showed his resentment by assigning the vanguard for the attack on Bataan to the 65th Brigade under the command of Lieutenant General Nara Akira. Nara was a kinsman of former Chief Aide-de-Camp Nara Takeji, who had guided Hirohito in Army affairs from 1921 to 1933. The 12,000-odd men of Nara's 65th Brigade were middle-aged reservist veterans who had expected to play sedentary roles as rear-area occupation troops. They were eager, however, to prove themselves still worthy as front-line warriors, and Nara was happy to give them their opportunity, for he considered General Honma a timorous worrywart.

THE DEFENSE OF BATAAN

Starting with a night attack at 11 P.M. on January 11, 1942, Lieutenant General Nara flung his veterans against the forward U.S. position on Bataan, the Abucay line. After fourteen days of unremitting assault, he succeeded in forcing the Filamerican troops back ten miles to their second position, the Bagac-Orion line. There, in an all-out effort to break through, General Honma reinforced Nara with the 9th and 20th regiments of the brutal 16th Division which had raped Nanking. Almost half the men of the two fresh regiments were infiltrated by boat behind the U.S. lines and for the next week fought a desperate "battle of points and pockets" with the Filipino Scouts and U.S. pilots and Marines who backed up the Filamerican trenches. When the battle was over only one of the infiltrators had been captured; all the rest had died.

The Bagac-Orion line held firm, and on February 2 General Honma was forced to acknowledge that he had suffered a humiliating defeat. He committed his sixth and last regiment, the 16th Division's 33d, to cover the withdrawal of the rest of his men.

They stumbled back to rear-area field hospitals in appalling condition. Of one of the five regiments, the 20th, only 34 per cent of the men and none of the three battalion commanders still lived.

More than a third of all the combat troops under Honma's command had been killed in action[11] and two thirds of the remainder were incapacitated by sickness, wounds, or exhaustion. According to Honma's own postwar statement he had left "only 3,000 effectives."[12] The troops standing against him, including even the green Filipino recruits who were still learning how to fire a rifle, had made the most of their entrenchment and suffered far less grievously.

Having taken stock, General Honma felt forced to acknowledge his defeat in dispatches. A delegation of staff officers promptly descended upon him from Tokyo. It was led by Colonel Hattori Takushiro, the soft-spoken chief of the Operations Section, Operations Department, General Staff. It included a new chief of staff for Honma: Major General Wachi Takaji, a tough fanatic who had been chief of staff of the colonial Taiwan Army. The group met with General Honma on a sweltering afternoon, February 8, at his headquarters in San Fernando, 115 miles behind the battle line.

Operations Chief Hattori brought with him an official message from Imperial Headquarters, stamped with a palace seal which showed that Hirohito had read and approved its contents. It stated, in a sentence which burned itself on General Honma's vision: "The Emperor is acutely worried about Bataan." Honma cradled his head in his arms and wept. The visitors from Tokyo were embarrassed to see him so fatigued and emotional and they did their best in the weeks ahead to save his face. At the same time they effectively relieved him of his command, placed operations in the Philippines under the direct leadership of the Emperor, and relegated Honma to a titular capacity. They reported

[11] Officially 5,852 out of a total of 14,610. According to various unofficial sources, Honma also had—even after the 48th Division had been taken away from him—some 35,000 support troops. Used as replacements, these, too, had suffered heavy losses in the fighting, perhaps as many as 8,000 dead.

[12] Again he meant picked combat troops, for I know from personal observation that there were more than 3,000 able-bodied Japanese in Army uniforms in Baguio, 150 miles behind the front, strolling about the streets and buying bananas and papayas.

home that Honma acknowledged officially a need for reinforcements.

Colonel Hattori had brought with him from Tokyo a number of psychological warfare experts. It was through the efforts of these men that the "battling bastards of Bataan" first noticed that the Japanese command in the Philippines had taken a new tack. The Japanese psychologists were all surprised by the fact that the Filipino soldiers in Bataan, despite Japanese Pan-Asian propaganda, were standing and dying by their "colonialist American masters." On-the-spot inquiries revealed that the Filipinos in general were far more antagonistic to Japanese than to U.S. colonialism. As a result, efforts to woo Filipino soldiers away from their American officers were de-emphasized and a more basic psychological strategy was adopted. That is, the leaflets dropped on Bataan would no longer make ideological claims but would portray the simple joys of living: Philippine scenery, tables groaning with food, pretty girls in bed.

Before the next attack, Bataan must be softened up by privation and hunger. The Japanese knew from their own experience on Bataan that the jungle and the mosquitoes could take more lives than gunpowder. They knew, too, that the "battling bastards" had been living on half rations since New Year's Day. Time, therefore, would tell. In the phrase of the day, "an old carp in a large pond must be fished patiently."

For two months, February and March 1942, action on the Bataan front remained suspended while hunger and disease did their work. By March a thousand Filamericans a week were dropping out of the lines on sick call. By the end of March the U.S. field hospitals in southern Bataan contained 12,500 patients and could handle no more. In the meanwhile, Operations Chief Hattori had written a new plan of attack and was waiting for the troops who would execute it to be released from Japanese campaigns elsewhere.

MacArthur cabled home plea after plea for reinforcements, ammunition, or at least food. He could not believe that the Pacific fleet was now too weak to escort a few convoys through to the Philippines. He could not believe that Washington would dare to write off his entire force of 112,500 men. That was 6,000 men more than the number of U.S. servicemen who had died in the whole course of World War I. It seemed incredible to him that President Roosevelt could afford politically to begin World War II with such a loss—not while sending military aid across the Atlantic to England.

MacArthur had sworn publicly that the United States would defend the Philippines. He had buoyed up Filipino morale and loyalty with a flood of false promises. Now he found himself as utterly humiliated as General Honma. One of his former staff officers, Brigadier General Dwight D. Eisenhower, had the ear of Chief of Staff General George C. Marshall in Washington. Eisenhower, by his own account, had "studied dramatics under MacArthur for five years in Washington and four in the Philippines." He did not admire MacArthur's political methods of generalship and he took a cool East-Coast view of American commitments in Asia. The menace of the Swastika impressed him far more than that of the Rising Sun.

In the opening days of the war Eisenhower conducted a staff study for General Marshall, assessing over-all U.S. war objectives and priorities. In his report Eisenhower concluded that it was too late to help the men on Bataan and that, if Germany were to be defeated swiftly, no effective U.S. military pressure could be applied in Southeast Asia until at least 1943. The best that could be done immediately was to hold Australia. U.S. Navy staff officers concurred. They could send a few submarine loads of medical supplies to Bataan and Corregidor but no surface vessels: no convoys of troops, bullets, or food.

So it was that "the battling bastards of Bataan" were left to die. Only a sentimentalist, who saw the curses some of them later wrote against their native America on the walls of death cells in Japanese prisons, could question the logic of the decision made to sacrifice them. On the other hand it would be difficult for anyone to maintain that their lives might not have been sold more dearly on some other, better supplied defense line closer to Australia.

RETREAT FROM MALAYA

While the defenders of Bataan were winning the battle of bullets and beginning to lose the war against ill health and hunger, Hirohito's forces elsewhere gained steady ground by assault alone.

On January 23, a Japanese amphibious force landed at Balikpapan on the southeastern coast of Borneo and captured the last of Borneo's oil fields. As at Tarakan, Kuching, Lutong, Miri, and Seria in previous weeks, the wells were burning and the derricks had been dynamited. It would take months to put out the fires and start pumping oil again. With the taking of Balikpapan, however, the major ports of Borneo and Celebes were all in Japanese hands, and a huge wedge had been driven down the center of Indonesia, reaching more than half the way from the southern Philippines to Australia, and separating Java and Sumatra in the west from New Guinea in the east.

That same day, January 23, a force of Japanese marines backed by carriers from Admiral Nagumo's Pearl Harbor task force landed on the Pacific side of New Guinea, in Australian territory, and seized the strategic harbor of Rabaul at the eastern tip of the big Taiwan-sized island of New Britain. From Rabaul southeast stretched a dagger of islands—the Solomons, the New Hebrides, and New Zealand—through which all U.S. convoys to Australia would have to pass. Control of the air in the Rabaul area might make it possible to establish forward fields in the Solomons and New Hebrides and so isolate Australia. Indeed, only the lack of a long-range bomber like the Flying Fortress prevented Japan from cutting the sea-lanes to Australia immediately. The landing at Rabaul was contested by a handful of Australians, and soon Japanese workmen were busy extending the Rabaul airstrip. In the weeks ahead they were to make Rabaul such a fortress that U.S. offensives later bypassed it, leaving it behind, a starving enclave which marked the high-water of imperial fortunes.

On that same fateful day, January 23, British Lieutenant General Percival decided that he must abandon Malaya and retreat to the island of Singapore. Ever since Colonel Tsuji, his panzers, and his bicycle troops had pierced the Jitra line in northern Malaya six weeks earlier, withdrawal to new lines had become a dispiriting weekly routine for the British forces. In the course of the backward march, 20,000 of Percival's Indian troops, who had manned the front lines in northern Malaya, had been left behind in pockets and had surrendered. In southern Malaya Percival had shored up the lines by throwing in his Australian division.

The Australians had fought well. They had taken the offensive,

infiltrated, ambushed, and dispelled the growing notion that the
Japanese were peculiarly, demonically, at home in the jungle. In
the last ten days the Australians had inflicted heavier losses on
Yamashita's men than they had suffered earlier or would suffer
later. With another division as good as the Australians, Percival
might have held the line, for by now the Japanese attackers were
themselves hungry, footsore, and sick. But gaps in the Australian
position were plugged with Indian troops who had already been
chased south for 400 miles. The plugs broke and Percival had no
choice but to fall back on Singapore.

The Australian troops, for the most part, were disappointed,
because they were still fresh and had so far outfought the Japanese. Nevertheless they pulled back and with the help of English
and Scots companies succeeded in re-establishing a final line
across the southern tip of the Malayan peninsula. Some of the British companies had been used repeatedly to stiffen resistance up-
country; others were now brought up to the front for the first
time. Behind the new holding line, the spent Indian forces were
withdrawn across a stone causeway onto Singapore Island. The
Australians, fighting from rubber tree to rubber tree, followed.
The honor of bringing up the rear was accorded to the ninety
survivors of a battered Scots regiment, the Argylls, who backed
into Singapore at dawn on February 1 with their bagpipes inton-
ing "Highlan' Laddie" and "Jeannie with the Light Brown Hair."
At 8 A.M., the landward end of the massive 70-foot-wide stone
causeway connecting Singapore with Malaya was hurled into the
air by dynamite.

The British naval base was now supposed to be a self-sufficient
fortress. Only 300 feet of broken causeway and open water, however, separated it from the Malayan shore. Nothing but trenches
and barbed wire defended the beaches across from that shore, and
the big guns of the fortress, as Winston Churchill would later complain ruefully, were all pointed south, out to sea, in the opposite
direction to that from which the Japanese were attacking.

On the beleaguered island the British still had over 100,000
troops, including recently arrived reinforcements, and enough fuel
oil and ammunition to supply both the Japanese Army and Navy
for months. In addition the island was packed with native residents and refugees. Theoretically General Percival still had more

than enough power to beat back the Japanese invaders. In practice he would find his force of numbers an encumbrance.

General Yamashita, by comparison, still had only 60,000 troops in his front line and not enough heavy artillery and shells to subdue Singapore by bombardment. Unless he struck quickly, British morale might revive and remaining British strength begin to realize its potential. The brilliant Japanese campaign might turn into a costly, protracted positional battle.

Yamashita extracted a herculean effort from his engineering and logistics officers. Every capable soldier and every working gun left behind in the jungles was brought down the shell-pocked roads and over the half-blown, half-repaired bridges to the shore of the Johore Strait between Malaya and Singapore. Only four days after the British withdrawal across the causeway, Yamashita had assembled enough cannon and ammunition in the tip of Malaya to begin a softening-up bombardment. Necessary shells and even a few large-caliber railway guns were brought in over the quickly repaired tracks of the Bangkok-Singapore line. The Japanese naval air force, flying in close support from freshly captured airstrips only a dozen miles behind the new front, bombed and strafed Singapore without let or check.

General Yamashita personally directed the withering fire upon the streets of his objective from a glass-domed tower where he could see the effect of every explosion through his binoculars. The tower stood conspicuously on the northern side of the strait and might have been easily demolished by British gunners on the south side. The tower belonged, however, to the sultan of Johore. It was the private observatory attached to the sultan's palace. The sultan was one of the wealthiest men in the world. He dressed and spoke like an Englishman and had been most generous in helping British field hospitals in the weeks which had just passed. No British officer even considered the possibility of shelling his palace. No British officer knew that he was a close friend of Count Ohtani, Hirohito's mother's brother-in-law, or of Baron Tokugawa, the paymaster for Hirohito's lethal political plots in the early 1930's. General Yamashita and his staff made the exposed palace their headquarters at the insistence of Colonel Tsuji who had worked with Count Ohtani during the final planning for the Strike South on Taiwan the previous summer.

In effect, Yamashita had a third-hand invitation to use the palace from the sultan himself. The Japanese staff officers took care not to reveal their presence by lighting any fires in the palace stoves. Cold boiled rice was brought in to them from the rubber groves out back. There shell fragments flew and latex flowed, but on the palace lawns the British fire was conspicuously accurate in that it disturbed not so much as a divot.

Haunting the glass-domed observatory and subsisting on cold food, General Yamashita was able to know more about what was happening on the Malayan side of Singapore Island than his British opposite numbers at their headquarters on the seaward side. By telephone he and Tsuji directed Japanese gunfire not so much at British entrenchments as at the geometric lines of communications wire which connected them. By February 8 many British units were already isolated and many British officers and engineers were working desperately to maintain touch with General Percival's headquarters.

On the night of February 8, shortly after dark, Japanese troops in small boats began crossing Johore Strait. General Percival might have flooded the strait with burning oil, but he had not expected the Japanese attack so soon and his engineers were not ready. By dawn several thousand Japanese were ashore on the island, overrunning positions and taking prisoners.

Having landed, the Japanese troops drove through the Australian defense sector and made for Bukit Timah heights and the life-blood reservoirs of Singapore which Hirohito had inspected twenty years earlier. The story of Hong Kong was about to be repeated, but on a larger scale.

SINGAPORE'S AGONY

First light on February 9 discovered the men of the Japanese 5th and 18th divisions inching forward through Australian entanglements on the northwest coast of Singapore Island. In the armor-plated Imperial Headquarters shed on the north edge of the palace woods in Tokyo it was already 7:30 A.M., and sleep-deprived staff officers were anxiously preparing themselves to deliver the morning operations briefing to the Emperor. Information from the Singapore beachhead was fragmentary and confused.

To make matters worse Operations Section Chief Hattori, who ordinarily fielded the most difficult of the Emperor's questions, was away in the Philippines, conveying the imperial reprimand to General Honma and writing a new plan for the reduction of Bataan and Corregidor. Hirohito, who remembered every ridge and promontory along the north coast of Singapore from his circumnavigation of the island by yacht in 1921, was sure to be full of detailed queries. In addition he would be looking forward and asking whether the Army and Navy had yet written their position papers about the future.

On February 4, five days earlier, Hirohito had emphasized to a liaison conference between the government and high command that he wanted to follow the military success of the Strike South with a two-fold effort: militarily, to "expand the perimeter of Japanese occupation" and to "prepare for a long-term aggressive war of victory"; and diplomatically, to be ready for any Allied peace feelers which would make possible a quick peace settlement on Japanese terms. The staff officers in the headquarters shed were not united in their interpretation of the imperial wishes. The naval officers wanted to push on to an invasion of Australia. The Army officers preferred a quick peace but were ready to commit themselves to the conquest of Burma and the invasion of New Guinea.

As anticipated Hirohito called for his briefing early that morning and protracted it with question after question for many hours. In the course of the morning he approved the next day, February 10, as sailing date for Japan's Sumatra invasion fleet; he authorized the Army to proceed with the conquest of Burma and to start planning the conquest of New Guinea; he asked the Navy to pursue plans for the final destruction of the U.S. Pacific Fleet and the interdiction of U.S.-Australian supply routes.

When the staff officers' ordeal was at last over, in the post meridiem, Hirohito held Chief of Staff Sugiyama for a final tête-à-tête. Curiously enough, this private conversation was the only one in the entire day of which an official record has survived and been published. In it the ebullient Hirohito indulged in some ominous belly-talk by referring to a Chinese warlord named Yen Hsi-shan.

General Yen—who would ultimately die in Taiwan with the

title of "senior advisor" to Chiang Kai-shek—was known in the late 1920's and early 1930's as "the model governor of Shansi." He had graduated from military academy in Tokyo in 1909 and had long been considered by Japanese leaders as a protégé who might be used as a rival to Chiang Kai-shek. In 1928, when Chiang had first kicked at his Japanese traces, Hirohito's advisors had briefly contemplated abandoning Chiang and raising up Yen in his stead. It had been partly to impress Yen and give him time to reconsider his allegiances that Hirohito's troops had delayed the "northern march" of Chiang Kai-shek in 1928 by intervening from the Tsingtao Leasehold and massacring 7,000 KMT partisans in the town of Tsinan.

Yen, in 1928, had served the peaceful interests of his Shansi peasants by insisting on remaining neutral. He had again made much the same decision in the fall of 1937 when the Japanese Army entered Shansi. Mao Tse-tung's troops contested the entry and inflicted a temporary but bloody check to the Japanese forces at the battle of Ping-hsing-kuan Pass. After the battle, Yen refused to attack the retreating columns of Mao's army from the rear and persisted, once again, in maintaining his neutrality. In reprisal on November 7, 1937, elements of Japan's 5th Division, under the command of Captain Tsuji Masanobu—the same who was now the master planner of the Singapore campaign—massacred the inhabitants of Yen's home stronghold in the Shansi mountains. Yen, who was elsewhere with his troops, had then replied by affirming that the men of Shansi would stand with Chiang Kai-shek and the cause of China.

Ever since 1937 Japan had continued off and on to negotiate for Yen's support. A clerk in the offices of the General Staff kept a Yen file. At one time or another a dozen aspiring Japanese captains and majors in the Intelligence Department had proposed use of Yen for "settling the China Incident." The puppet governor of Japanese-occupied China, Wang Ching-wei, had written uncounted letters to Yen, asking him as an old school friend to reconsider his position—all to no avail.

By 1941 Japanese hopes for Yen had become a bad joke and his name, in World War II planning, had become a code word for certain acts of terror, butchery, and reprisal which were seen as possible necessities in the "pacification" of Southeast Asia. This new meaning had first attached itself to Yen's name in a General Staff discussion of the problem of the overseas Chinese. The expatriate Chinese merchants of Singapore, Manila, Batavia, and Surabaja had long contributed money and influence to Chiang Kai-shek's cause and it was foreseen that they would continue to play a subversive role in the conquered Co-Prosperity Sphere. An anonymous staff officer had suggested "the Yen Hsi-shan treatment" for them, and by extension Yen's name had come to cover all reprisals which were visualized in connection with the Strike South. It was inevitable that, here and there, an example would have to be made of Western colonials, so as to destroy their face in the eyes of the natives. It was inevitable, too, that the natives themselves might sometimes have to be intimidated.

Against this semantic background, on February 9, 1942, when Hirohito detained Chief of Staff Sugiyama after the exhausting morning briefing, the Emperor's in-camera remarks struck Sugiyama as particularly noteworthy.

"The Chungking government," said Hirohito, "seems to be weakening. Isn't it about time that Yen Hsi-shan came over to our side? What's happened to that operation since last time?"

Not for nothing was Chief of Staff Sugiyama called "the bathroom door." He was proud of his reputation for noncommittal belly-talk and now he chose his words carefully, punctuating them with grunts and expressive pauses.

"The Yen Hsi-shan operation," he said, "is a continuing and repeated thing. Looking back on its history, one sees that a Yen, in Chinese fashion, seeks to stretch time, look for fair weather, and gain the best possible terms from us. I'm afraid that, on the whole, such an operation may be too hastily planned from the beginning. That was why Yen could take advantage of us and give the impression that he had improved his position. From now on, however, since the over-all picture is expected to go on brightening for our side, the Yen side cannot be expected to initiate the moves. We are planning our handling of Yen Hsi-shan operations on that basis."[13]

---

[13] For lack of pronouns, singular-plural distinctions, and strong tenses, Sugiyama's Japanese was even more ambiguous than my English representation of it. I have tried to reproduce the flavor and sequence rather than a one-to-one word equivalence.

"I see," said the Emperor—and went on to ask about operations in Kyongju, a town in Korea where there had been a massacre in the Chinese quarter during the months leading up to the Manchurian Incident. Sugiyama made it clear that he followed what the Emperor was getting at by replying that the "Kyongju operation" was being taken care of by the Japanese Army stationed in south China. An eavesdropper might have thought he understood the conversation but would have detected nothing irregular in it. Sugiyama, however, interleafed an unusual note to himself in his memoranda: "Since His Majesty is quick to see ahead of things and ask questions in detail, I would like to be better prepared to give impromptu answers to questions about secondary developments."

The guarded but suggestive imperial question about Yen Hsi-shan operations disturbed Sugiyama, troubled staff officers in the field, and finally brought pain and horror to thousands of Chinese, Indians, Englishmen, Australians, Filipinos, and Americans. The Emperor's remarks reflected his dissatisfaction with the repulse on Bataan and implied that, to keep the war on schedule, he wished extreme measures to be taken. In early planning the Army had promised to take Singapore by *Kigensetsu*, National Foundation Day, February 11. It was important to Hirohito's pride as high priest to have something to offer his ancestors that day, but with *Kigensetsu* only two days away and with the Japanese troops moving forward by inches out of their Singapore beachhead it was unlikely that the British fortress would fall on time.

Sugiyama withdrew from the Imperial Presence to discuss the situation that evening with his aides. The next morning, February 10, he dispatched a staff officer by plane to Saigon to explain the Emperor's state of mind to General Count Terauchi, the over-all Strike-South commander. Terauchi consulted with General Yamashita by phone and then reported back to Tokyo that the Emperor could celebrate *Kigensetsu* by announcing to the gods the capture of Bukit Timah, the central high point of Singapore which overlooked and commanded one of the weak points in the island's defenses, spotted by Hirohito twenty years earlier: namely, its reservoirs. The next morning Hirohito duly went to the white-pebbled courtyard of the ancestors in the palace woods and formally announced to them that the capture of Singapore was assured.

A few hours earlier, only just on time, Japanese troops had consummated an all-night offensive by storming the rain-forested summit of Bukit Timah heights. Spotters swarmed up into the high trees to direct fire against British positions around the three Singapore reservoirs beyond. On the far side of the reservoirs wound the paths of the Botanical Gardens where Hirohito had walked twenty years before and where A. R. Wallace, eighty years before, had launched the theory of evolution.

During the day the Japanese forces occupied the western shores of the reservoirs, and General Yamashita had twenty-nine boxes of leaflets dropped on Singapore declaring that further resistance, no matter how heroic, would be useless. General Percival ordered a counterattack. Both he and Yamashita committed their best remaining troops to a desperate hand-to-hand combat which raged around the reservoirs for the next thirty-six hours. The reiterated shock of shell-burst and demolitions kept ears deaf and minds numb. Hot humid weather left uniforms limp and dark. Only the pungency of cordite and sweet rot of corpses masked the pervading sour smell of sweat. A pall of smoke from burning oil tanks hung between the island and the sky.

After dark on February 12, while the issue of the battle for the reservoirs still remained in doubt, Japanese divisional staff officers met with General Yamashita at his advanced headquarters a few hundred yards behind the lines. All had heard of the Emperor's impatience and all were exhausted by their efforts to give the Emperor better satisfaction. Some were wounded and some nodded and dozed in spite of themselves. The planner of the campaign, Colonel Tsuji, however, remained as demonically on edge as ever. He urged all to expend themselves utterly and hinted that he was relaying his exhortations directly from Prince Mikasa, Hirohito's brother. Tsuji later described in a book the situation as he then saw it:

Our Army was now deployed over the whole front and the strategic position seemed to reach a climax when we received a signal from General Headquarters. "On 15 February an officer attached to the Court of the Emperor will be dispatched to the battlefield. We can postpone the visit if the progress of your Army's operations makes it desirable to do so. We wish to hear your opinion."

There were some who said, "Let us welcome him," and others who argued, "We must postpone the visit of the Emperor's envoy for a little while"; and so opinions were divided into two camps.

Once previously during the China Incident I had been in a similar position when conducting military operations in Shansi together with the Itagaki group. During a bitterly contested battle for the reduction of Taiyuan Sheng, on 7 November, Shidei, the aide-de-camp to the Emperor, arrived on the battlefield. I immediately began to think of the reduction of the mountain stronghold of Yen Hsi-shan.

After a general discussion we unanimously resolved: "On the fifteenth day of February the enemy will positively surrender to the power of the august Emperor." We drafted these words as a telegram of welcome to the Emperor's envoy.

The next morning, February 13, Colonel Tsuji began a sixty-hour day of sleepless activity. At daylight a fresh note was dropped on General Percival's Fort Canning headquarters, couched in effusive, uncertain English, demanding surrender, promising leniency, threatening reprisals. In the afternoon, when Percival failed to respond, Tsuji made his shell-spattered way to the forward headquarters of the 18th Division, commanded by Lieutenant General Mudaguchi Renya, a loyal and sympathetic officer who as a colonel four years earlier had commanded the Japanese forces at Marco Polo Bridge and had touched off the war with China. The understanding General Mudaguchi put Tsuji in the hands of a dependable combat team which could take him beyond the front. A few hours later this team emerged from the trees behind the Alexandra Barracks Hospital, one of the two functioning medical units left in Singapore, and bayoneted to death 323 of the hospital personnel including 230 of the patients, many of them in their beds or on operating tables.

By the morning of February 14, Tsuji had seen to it that survivors of the Alexandra Barracks Hospital massacre were returning to British lines to explain what might happen to everyone in Singapore if General Percival did not surrender soon. Percival had over 100,000 fighting men and more than a million civilians under his charge. He got the message that afternoon, slept on it that night, attended an Anglican communion service early the next morning, Sunday, and then called a meeting of his unit commanders to discuss hopes and chances. Only five days earlier Percival had relayed to these same men a stern and inspiring Order of the Day:

It is certain that our troops on Singapore Island greatly outnumber any Japanese that have crossed the straits. We must defeat them. Our whole fighting reputation is at stake and the honour of the British Empire. The Americans have held out in the Bataan Peninsula against far greater odds, the Russians are turning back the picked strength of the Germans, the Chinese with almost complete lack of modern equipment have held the Japanese for 4½ years. It will be disgraceful if we yield our boasted fortress of Singapore to inferior enemy forces.

There must be no thought of sparing the troops or the civilian population. . . .

Since this order had been issued, the Japanese had continued to advance despite their numbers. General Percival's commanders now knew that neither they nor their men could match the uncanny performance of the canny veterans flung against them. In discipline, morale, initiative, co-ordination, weapons handling, and determination, Yamashita's picked troops had shown themselves superior. In a week all the defenders of Singapore, military and civilian, would die of thirst or bayonet wounds if they did not surrender now.

Fatigue, decimation, and shortage of ammunition might temporarily check the Japanese if the British forces could all resolve to die fighting, but experience had shown that badly mauled Japanese units always sprang back to life with an infusion of well-trained replacements. There were some Japanese units which had stormed position after position yet had remained at full strength, with unimpaired efficiency, throughout the whole 700-mile course of the Japanese advance from Thailand. By comparison, the quality of British units had steadily deteriorated. Another day or two of attrition would leave only the born fighters and survivors who could escape as individuals, fugitives, guerrillas, outlaws.

Percival's officers agreed to give up. That afternoon General Percival himself carried the white flag to the slope of Bukit Timah, where, in a Ford factory chosen by General Yamashita for the occasion, Great Britain surrendered her Far Eastern naval base. Percival in shirt and shorts and Yamashita in Kwantung Army tunic, leggings, and boots sat down at a table. Percival pleaded for conditions. Yamashita barked that there would be no conditions. Percival bowed his head and whispered the word unconditional. The oft-described scene came to an end at 7:50 P.M. Forty minutes later the guns stopped firing. Nature lovers noted that the silence was unearthly in its completeness. Singapore's rich bird fauna had flown the battleground and did not bring back so much as a twitter to the island until two dawns later. Historians have said that during the birds' absence the Western colonialism of Alexander, Richard the Lion-Hearted, Vasco da Gama, Columbus, Magellan, Tasman, Cooke, Raleigh, Clive, and Raffles found its quietus.

On Singapore and in Malaya, about 60,000 Japanese front-line troops took prisoner over 130,000 British troops: some 15,000 Australians, 35,000 Scots and Englishmen, 65,000 Indians, and 15,000 assorted local reservists, most of them Malays. The captives were herded into camps and prisons to endure more than three years of scornful abuse, brutality, slavery, and starvation. As soon as they were behind barbed wire the rest of the Yen Hsi-shan operation was carried out. The Japanese secret police screened the entire overseas Chinese population in Singapore and after a massive but cursory investigation, which lasted less than a month, selected between 5,000 and 7,000 undesirables to serve as an example for the rest. The most important of the hostages were killed by the secret police themselves through every graduated form of humiliation, terror, and torture known to man. The less important were turned over to Army execution squads for use in bayonet practice, sword demonstrations, or the amusement of the troops.

SWEET SMELL OF THE INDIES

As soon as the "Chinese Massacres" were well in hand in Singapore, Hirohito's favored staff officer, Colonel Tsuji, was to accompany a regiment of the 5th Division to the Philippines where he would carry on with the Yen Hsi-shan operation, this time against Americans. In the meanwhile, however, Tokyo and the Imperial Court were celebrating the capture of Singapore.

Lord Privy Seal Kido, who understood well the imperial temperament, had warned Hirohito as early as February 5, ten days before the fall of Singapore, not to fall prey to a mood of exultation. "The Great East Asia War," he said, "will not end this easily. In the final analysis there is only one road to peace and that is to fight the war so thoroughly that we include in it the process of reconstruction after the battles are over." The Emperor was impressed by Kido's caution and, according to Kido's diary, "leaked his heart on the matter to the Empress."

Five days later, on February 10, the eve of his National Foundation Day report to the ancestors, Hirohito had relayed his awakened doubts to Prime Minister Tojo:

I presume that you have given due consideration not to lose any opportunity for ending this conflict. It would be undesirable to prolong the war without purpose for that would only increase the suffering of commoners. I want you to keep this in mind and do everything possible for peace. I want you to take into account the present and future sensibilities of the Anglo-Americans, whom we cannot ignore. It will also be necessary for you to ascertain the Russo-German relationship and look forward to its outcome. At the same time we must not fail to obtain, to the fullest extent possible, the resources of the South. I fear that the quality of our troops will deteriorate if the war is prolonged.

The day Singapore finally fell, February 15, 1942, the cautious Kido was not summoned by the Emperor. Instead Prime Minister Tojo phoned during the evening to read Kido the telegram of victory from General Yamashita. The next morning, however, in a brief audience which lasted from 10:50 to 11, Hirohito informed Kido that, to end the war, Prime Minister Tojo was recommending an envoy to the Vatican. Hirohito explained the religious and other qualifications which such an envoy should have and asked Kido to find a man who would fit them. Kido promised to do his best and then "extended congratulations to the Emperor regarding the Singapore victory."

Hirohito, according to Kido's diary, was "very well pleased and said, 'You may think, Kido, that I harp on this tune, but I tell you again that it is my sincere belief that the excellent war results with which we are repeatedly favored, although they may seem to stem from divine providence, are really the results of our own providence and of the thorough research with which we did our planning.'"

Kido wept with gratitude at the compliment and bowed his way, snuffling theatrically, from the Imperial Presence.

The days which followed were stuffed with "excellent war re-sults"—enough to turn a lesser conqueror's head. Only long train-ing and sage advisors kept Hirohito's feet on the ground.

On February 7, Hirohito had watched newsreels showing the use of a recently formed paratroop corps in the invasion of the sparsely populated, little-defended Dutch island of Celebes. After seeing the film, he had approved the use of parachutists in large numbers for the capture of densely populated Sumatra. Now on February 16, the paratroopers had scored a success. Two days be-fore they had dropped in regimental strength behind Dutch lines near Palembang in southern Sumatra and now all Dutch and Brit-ish forces in Sumatra were evacuating the huge island and cross-ing the Sunda Strait to the central island and administrative center of the Dutch East Indies, Java. Sumatra was larger than California and twice as populous. It had been captured by 10,000 troops.

While the Army mopped up in Sumatra, the Navy extended to the north coast of Australia the wedge it had been driving through central Indonesia. On February 19, Marines landed almost unop-posed on the lovely, lazy tropic isle of Bali, off the east end of Java. Nearby, over the eastern Javanese city of Surabaja, twenty-three Zero aces of the Misty Lagoon were winning air superiority over the Dutch East Indies in a spectacular dogfight with about fifty P-40's, P-36's, and other outmoded Allied pursuit planes. Seven hundred miles farther east, other naval forces were establishing a beachhead on the Connecticut-and-Massachusetts-sized, half-Dutch, half-Portuguese island of Timor which lay only 300 miles off the Australian shore.

Also, on that same day, February 19, Admiral Nagumo's Pearl Harbor task force, standing off Timor, launched a devastating air strike on the northern Australian city of Darwin. Flying at the limit of their range, 189 of the crack bomb crews trained at the Misty Lagoon Air Station succeeded in sinking a U.S. destroyer, four U.S. transports, one British tanker, and four Australian freighters in Darwin harbor; in knocking out twenty-three Allied planes, ten of them beyond repair; and in demolishing several of Darwin's finest buildings, killing 238 Australians and wounding about 300 more. In exchange only five of the Japanese aces were lost. The other 184 crews returned from their mission, having posted a record for efficient use of gasoline and explosives.

In the fearful week which followed, Australians braced themselves for invasion. The Australian army was already committed in England, Africa, India, and the crumbling fortresses of the British Empire in the Far East. At home only 7,000 Australian regulars remained to fight—less than half the number which had just surrendered in Singapore. Man, woman, and child, the entire Australian population, dispersed over an area five sixths that of the United States, outnumbered the trained men of the Japanese Army by only five to one.

Admiral Yamamoto, the hero of Pearl Harbor, wanted to land an expeditionary force on the undefended north coast of Australia and at least terrorize the subcontinent with a division or two. General Yamashita, the hero of Singapore, seconded Yamamoto and offered to lead the invasion himself. Despite the vastness of Australian distances, he felt that it would be feasible to land a division almost immediately at Darwin and thrust hard and fast down the north-south railroad and road links toward Adelaide and Melbourne on the south coast. Later, he supposed, a second division could be put ashore on the east coast to leapfrog its way from port to port down toward Sydney. Tough as they might be, not even Australian civilians, he felt, would be any match for disciplined troops. Moreover, he thought that the clean, hygiene-conscious Japanese soldier would perform far better in the antiseptic wastes of Australia than in the septic jungles of Burma and New Guinea.

General Tojo, the prime minister, and most of the elders in the General Staff spoke against the Yamamoto-Yamashita plan. Admiral Nagumo's air raid on Darwin had been a successfully improvised spectacular, but full-scale invasion was another matter. The General Staff had no well-considered contingency plans for such an operation. In the Australian barrens, a Japanese force would have to depend entirely on supplies from the rear. The Japanese merchant fleet was already taxed to the utmost without taking on new assignments. Also, if the United States became alarmed and poured Flying Fortresses into Sydney, it would be difficult to maintain air superiority. On the Australian badlands Japanese columns would be fearfully vulnerable to long-range, high-level air attack.

On reviewing the arguments of both sides, Hirohito decided that the invasion of Australia could be postponed until after the conquest of Burma. In terms of global strategy and of dividing the world with Hitler, an advance toward India and the Middle East took precedence over the capture of the Australasian land's end.

Hirohito announced his decision with characteristic oblique-ness at a liaison conference in the Imperial Headquarters shed on February 23. He probably knew, through Japanese monitoring of Corregidor's radio traffic, that President Roosevelt, the day before, had directed MacArthur to leave Corregidor and assume command of Allied forces in Australia. He certainly knew that almost 20,000 British troops in Burma had just surrendered or been surrounded after the Battle of Sittang Bridge on the road to Rangoon. As he had done with increasing frequency of late, Hirohito attended the liaison conference impromptu, embarrassing his deputies and forcing them, without preparation, to deliberate in the Imperial Presence. Instead of listening to the discussion, however, as he sometimes did, he pointedly ignored the burning issue of an expedition to Australia and manifested his disinterest in it by asking two explicit questions about unimportant side issues.

His first question concerned relations with the neutral Portuguese in eastern Timor. It suggested that he wanted Portugal kept friendly so that she might act as a channel of mediation in Japan's efforts to seek a peace settlement. His second question had to do with the stabilization of currencies in Japan's rapidly multiplying conquered territories. It indicated a desire to consolidate gains already made before embarking on new conquests. The liaison conference responded by promising to find ways of staying on good terms with the Portuguese in Timor and of saving Filipinos, Malays, and Indonesians from runaway inflation.[14]

---

[14] The financial solution was curious and ingenious. It was resolved that the paper scrip of Japanese occupation currencies would be convertible into yen but that, henceforth, there would secretly be two kinds of paper yen with separate sets of serial numbers: one redeemable in precious metals and circulated only in Japan; the other worth nothing except as a promissory note against the future of the Japanese Empire.

After the liaison conference of February 23, Hirohito did not meet again with his ministers for twelve days. In those twelve days all the scattered Japanese landings in the islands off southeastern Asia were fused to form a single massive addition to the Empire. Japan's new perimeter reached to within easy flying range of Australia and except for the U.S. forces on Bataan and Corregidor, 1,600 miles behind the front lines, it contained only guerrilla pockets of resistance. The keystone to the vast addition was Java, the densely populous administrative center of Indonesia.

On February 25, Field Marshal Sir Archibald Wavell of Britain, who had been given charge of combined British, U.S., and Dutch forces in Indonesia, dissolved his command as hopeless and withdrew his headquarters to India. Most British and some U.S. forces proceeded to withdraw with him. The Dutch, who had contributed several of their ships and planes to the defense of Singapore, fought on, embittered and almost alone. On the sea they were allowed to keep command of the U.S. heavy cruiser *Houston*, the British heavy cruiser *Exeter*, the Australian light cruiser *Perth*, three British destroyers, and four old U.S. four-stack destroyers. These they combined with two light cruisers and two destroyers of their own in a fourteen-ship fleet for the defense of Java. Two Japanese invasion armadas, of forty-one and fifty-six transports, plus escort vessels, were approaching the island from the north across the Java Sea.

The Dutch admiral, Rear Admiral Karel Doorman, sallied out with his squadron to attack the smaller of the two Japanese fleets. He engaged it on February 27 and in a seven-hour action lost two of his cruisers, three of his destroyers, and his own life. Next day the remnants of his fleet tried to escape to Australia through the Lombok and Sunda Straits at the east and west ends of Java. Shadowed by Japanese aircraft and pursued by Japanese surface vessels, all three of the remaining Allied cruisers and two of the destroyers were ambushed and sunk. Only the U.S. quartet of antiquated four-stack destroyers succeeded in getting away. The ill-conceived Battle of the Java Sea, the largest fleet action since Jutland, was over. The Allies had sacrificed five cruisers, five destroyers, and about 3,000 lives. None of the Japanese warships had sustained more than minor damage, which could be repaired at sea.

Following the battle, elements of the Japanese 2d and 38th divisions landed in western Java, and elements of the 48th Division and 56th Brigade in eastern Java. They made short work of the 15,000 Allied regulars and 40,000-odd reservists and volunteers in the Java defense force. After a week of confused skirmishing, the Dutch governor general of the Indies, on March 8, agreed to capitulate to the Japanese 16th Army commander, Lieutenant General Imamura Hitoshi. The formal instrument of surrender was signed by the Dutch four days later.

Also on March 8 fell Rangoon, the capital of Burma. The last trainload of dispirited refugees pulled out toward Mandalay in the north even as the first Japanese soldiers were entering the city, unopposed from the south. Since Rangoon was the only port of any consequence in Burma, the 50,000-odd Anglo-Indians of the British Army there were now effectively cut off from help except from China. Chiang Kai-shek sent three divisions to their rescue, and over the next two and a half months, the "Burma Corps" fought its way backwards along jungle tracks and river banks to the Indian and Chinese frontiers. Thirteen thousand men of the British Army were lost along the way. The Japanese 15th Army, of two divisions and about 35,000 front-line fighters, lost 5,000 men.

On March 7, the day before the Dutch surrender and the fall of Rangoon, a liaison conference in Tokyo formally adopted a plan called "Basic Principles of Future Operations." This plan responded to Hirohito's feelings that the war must continue to be prosecuted aggressively but that Japan must not overextend herself or neglect the consolidation of the immense territories which she had already conquered. Specifically the plan called for further Army advances in the Burma theater, with a view to the possible conquest of India; further Army-Navy probes in the New Guinea-Solomons area, in order to cut Pacific supply lines and isolate Australia; and further action by Admiral Yamamoto against the U.S. fleet in the central Pacific.

During the morning of March 9, the day after the Dutch surrender and the fall of Rangoon, Hirohito realized that, for the last forty-eight hours, he had been neglecting his civilian advisors. He at once telephoned Lord Privy Seal Kido at his office in the Imperial Household Ministry in the Outer Palace and asked him to come on over to the Imperial Library in the palace woods for a chat. Kido hurried to respond and later wrote in his diary:

The Emperor was beaming like a child. "The fruits of war," he said, "are tumbling into our mouth almost too quickly. The enemy at Bandung on the Java front announced their surrender on the seventh and now our Army is negotiating for the surrender of all forces in the Netherlands East Indies. The enemy has surrendered at Surabaja and also, on the Burma front, has given up Rangoon." He was so pleased that I hardly knew how to give him a congratulatory answer.

Hirohito had a right to feel complacent. More than a month ahead of schedule his myrmidons had accomplished all that they had promised to accomplish and more than he had been sure they ever could accomplish. A month short of his forty-second birthday, he found the goals of his youth suddenly realized. It would take weeks of buoyant weariness and happiness before he set his feet again upon the ground and acknowledged that the ancestors still required more of him.

FALL OF BATAAN

On March 11, two days after Hirohito had expressed his military euphoria to Kido, General and Mrs. MacArthur, with their four-year-old son Arthur, boarded a PT boat under cover of darkness and escaped from the besieged enclave of Bataan and Corregidor.[15] Before embarking MacArthur had taken pains to tell all

[15] Hirohito that day added an odd footnote to history by having the liaison conference formulate an explicit policy for dealing with the large numbers of Jews who had been brought into the Empire with the acquisition of Singapore and Java. "With special exceptions," no Jews would be allowed to immigrate into the Empire in the future. Those already present would "be treated as nationals of the areas in which they reside, except that, due to their special racial characteristics, surveillance of their homes and businesses will be intensive and all pro-enemy activity on their part will be suppressed and eliminated." In other words, an Amsterdam Jew captured in Batavia would—despite his Dutch passport—be treated as an Indonesian rather than a Hollander. On the one hand he would be exempt from internment as an enemy national; on the other he could claim no protection under the rules of war. The object of the decision was "not to persecute the Jews" as that "would make propaganda for the United States" but to "select carefully those Jews who can be used for the Empire and give them appropriate treatment."

who remained behind that he went with reluctance, at presidential orders. "I shall return," he said—an assurance which was to become his slogan for the next three years.

The accommodations provided for MacArthur in his escape were not the safest available. He might have gone by submarine as did a group of Army nurses from Corregidor almost two months later. Some say that he chose the PT boat himself for theatrical reasons; others that there was someone in logistics who hoped he would perish en route. In any case the spray-soaked dash through enemy lines was a genuine adventure for a man of sixty-two. It lasted thirty-six hours and took MacArthur and his family 600 miles: from Luzon in the northern Philippines to Del Monte on Mindanao in the southern Philippines. Most of the way lay along enemy-controlled shores, over enemy-controlled seas, under enemy-controlled skies. The PT boat had to crash through squalls and fifteen-foot waves. It passed within sight of a Japanese cruiser. Its skipper had to navigate most of the way in the dark.

When MacArthur landed, exhausted, in Mindanao, he learned that he must wait a day for the four B-17 Flying Fortresses which had been sent for him from Australia. Only one of them arrived. Two of the others had turned back with engine trouble and the fourth had crashed into the ocean. The survivor, a battered veteran of three months of bombing missions, suffered from faulty brakes and inoperative turbosuperchargers. MacArthur refused to fly in it. He fired off angry messages to Washington and Sydney and waited for another two days while a more fitting fleet of three span-new B-17's were being flown up from Australia for him. In these on the night of March 16–17, he and his family and staff traversed the 1,400 miles of Japanese-controlled air to northern Australia.

Shortly after his arrival MacArthur asked for a press conference and told reporters:

I am glad indeed to be in immediate co-operation with the Australian soldier. I know him well from World War days and admire him greatly. . . . I have every confidence in the ultimate success of our joint cause, but success in modern war requires something more than courage and willingness to die. It requires careful preparation. This means furnishing sufficient troops and sufficient materiel to meet the known strength of the potential enemy. No general can make something from nothing. My success or failure will depend primarily upon the resources which our respective governments place at my disposal. My faith in them is complete. In any event I shall do my best. I shall keep the soldier's faith.

In this statement—one of the most clear and honest of his career—the chastened MacArthur apologized for past mistakes to the men he had left behind and promised them vengeance. Theirs, however, would be the hunger, humiliations, filth, fever, torture, and despair of imprisonment, and theirs the curses against MacArthur and Roosevelt which would be found scribbled on death-cell walls when Japanese concentration camps were liberated three years later.[16]

On March 10, a few hours before MacArthur began his personal anabasis from Corregidor, British Foreign Secretary Right Honorable Anthony Eden delivered a speech in the House of Commons revealing and protesting to all the world that Japan had committed abominable atrocities on a wide scale in Hong Kong. Eden was probably moved to speak by Chiang Kai-shek's secret service agents who were reporting to Chungking that Japanese rapine was continuing at Singapore. Five thousand Chinese had been executed there as examples. Women and children evacuated from Singapore in small boats at the last minute had been strafed by Japanese planes and torpedoed by Japanese naval launches and submarines. A shipful of wounded men accompanied by sixty-four Australian nursing sisters had been sunk off Banka Island on the Sumatra coast. The wounded men who managed to get ashore were almost all bayoneted on the beach. Twenty-two of the nurses with them, landing in a lifeboat, were waded out

---

16 As a sixteen-year-old, suffering from dengue fever and malnutrition, I spent the first week of February 1945, after the U.S. liberation of Manila, in one of those cells in old Bilibid Prison. It was a room about 12 by 20 feet, solidly walled on the short sides and open to the air through iron gratings on the long sides. It was then a hospital ward for American civilian internees who had passed their first thirty-six months of Japanese imprisonment outside Baguio in the mountains to the north. I shared the room with five other fellow internee patients. A year earlier it had been stuffed with fifty to a hundred veterans of Corregidor with bashed limbs, malaria, and dysentery. I long studied a graffito on the wall above me reviling Roosevelt and MacArthur in obscene terms. The author, I was told, had died in the cell of hunger, thirst, and a general septicemia.

into the surf and machine-gunned. A single survivor of the massacre, Sister Vivian Bullwinkel, was now in a prison camp in Sumatra.

On March 13, Lord Privy Seal Kido spoke to Hirohito about Eden's Hong Kong disclosures. Hirohito refrained from doing anything to prevent recurrences. It was the position of his uncles and some of his other Army advisors that the commission of atrocities fortified Japanese troops for the role they had to play and persuaded them that they must never surrender because, if they did, what they had done unto others would be done unto them.

On March 27, Chief of Staff General Sugiyama flew to Sumatra to "inspect the front" and unofficially to assess the prisoner-of-war situation there and in Singapore. Almost a quarter of a million civilian and military captives had fallen into Japanese hands. It was Sugiyama's mission to convey to all commanders Hirohito's feelings about prisoner treatment. To satisfy the outcry in the West and prevent Japan from seeming uncivilized, the prisoners must be put in regular camps and must be dealt with in an organized fashion. They must not, however, be pampered, any more than the common Japanese soldier. Nor must they, insofar as possible, become a financial burden upon the Empire. They must work for their board and lodging and must not be allowed to aid the Allied cause by escaping and becoming propagandists on Allied shortwave radio stations.

On April 3, Chief of Staff Sugiyama completed his inspection of the newly conquered Dutch East Indies and went on to the Philippines. There the time had come to fish out the carp in the pond and silence the subversive "Voice of Freedom" being broadcast every evening from transmitters on Bataan and Corregidor. The Filamerican defenders of the U.S. enclave in the heart of the Co-Prosperity Sphere had sat in foxholes for two months licking their wounds, subsisting on half rations and contracting malaria and bacillary dysentery.

While the U.S. forces had deteriorated, General Honma's command had been strengthened to make impossible any second miscalculation. His battered 16th Division and 65th Brigade had been restored to full strength in February with fresh replacement troops who were by now trained and integrated into the skeletal veteran units which had survived the January offensive. In addition some 15,000 men had been brought in from the crack 4th Division stationed at Osaka in Japan. The reserve force in Indochina had contributed about 11,000 men from the 21st Division. Colonel Tsuji, the planner of the Malayan campaign, had brought from Singapore an augmented regiment of his 5th Division veterans and another augmented regiment of volunteers from his 18th Division—in all about 20,000 troops of the highest quality.

In sum total Honma's 14th Army now numbered about 110,-000 of the best front-line troops, supported by enough artillery to blast a breach in the Maginot Line. U.S. Major General Edward King's Bataan command, by comparison, consisted of just over 70,000 gaunt, listless, fever-wracked, dysentery-ridden gun-bearers. Only a quarter of them had ever considered themselves soldiers and of these less than half were still classified as "effectives." Even in this small fraction of fractions on whom General King most relied, morale was low. The men felt that they had already held out longer than any other Allied troops in the Far East. They had been abandoned and adjudged expendable. They wanted food and rest and they yearned for decent capture and imprisonment.

April 3, the day that Chief of Staff Sugiyama arrived in Manila, was Good Friday 1942. It was that day that the overwhelming Japanese forces gathered in northern Bataan began their offensive. The "Good Friday attack" ran ahead of its timetable and over-achieved its objectives almost from the moment of its launching. The eastern half of the Filamerican line collapsed in the first twenty-four hours of fighting. A handful of relatively well-fed U.S. officers repeatedly halted routs and reformed lines by brandishing pistols. The men on the western half of the Filamerican line were ordered to make a counterattack on the Japanese flank. Only a few of the front-line troops even tried to obey the order. The rest felt themselves too weak from hunger and disease to drag themselves over the tops of their trenches.

On April 9, six days after the beginning of the Japanese offensive, Major General King was forced to acknowledge that the men on Bataan were no longer a fighting force and would soon be annihilated company by company. General Wainwright, whom MacArthur had left in over-all command on Corregidor, ordered him to go on fighting to the death. King could see no prospect of inflicting much damage on the enemy by sacrificing the 70,000 men under his command and so decided to disobey Wainwright's orders.

Under flag of truce King drove through the Japanese lines and sat down with General Honma's senior operations officer at a table set out in the open before the Lamao Experimental Farm Station. King asked that U.S. trucks, which were fueled and ready for the task, be allowed to move his men to the detention camps where the Japanese wished to imprison them.

"Surrender must be unconditional," said the interpreter.

"Will our troops be well treated?"

"We are not barbarians," snapped the interpreter.

On this slender reassurance, King handed over his pistol in token of Bataan's unconditional surrender.

THE DEATH MARCH

For the next twelve days the no-longer "battling bastards" were herded out of their foxholes and prodded forward, without benefit of transportation, toward the town of San Fernando, 60 miles away. Many of them staggered with weakness from the outset of the march. Before the march was over all of them staggered—all, that is, who still lived.

The word had gone out on the Japanese Army grapevine that General Wainwright, who still held out on Corregidor, must be shown what would happen to his men if he did not surrender quickly: that the Filipino people must be made to appreciate the toughness of their new masters and the utter humiliation of their old ones.

Some of the Japanese officers on Bataan protested that their men did not follow belly talk and suggestions and did not cause prisoners to die without explicit orders. Underlings of Colonel Tsuji telephoned several of these recalcitrant commanders and told them that the order to get rid of American prisoners stemmed from Imperial General H.Q. in the palace. A few commanders refused to be bullied by Colonel Tsuji's "influence" and insisted that they see the Emperor's order in writing. Tsuji never produced the written order, but the careers of officers who decided to ignore his directions did not prosper, and the career of Colonel Tsuji prospered exceedingly. Within the year he was back in the

General Staff in Tokyo, meeting frequently with Hirohito as one of his closest advisors on military operations.

The responsibility for the Death March was later taken by General Honma and he was executed for it by MacArthur. At the time of the Death March, however, Honma was virtually a captive himself—of the staff officers who had been sent in from Tokyo to assist him and to repair the blunder he had made initially in letting the Bataan forces entrench themselves. Knowledgeable former members of the Japanese General Staff place the entire responsibility for the Death March on these unwanted helpers: on "Tsuji and the China gang," on "staff officers from Imperial Headquarters," on "experts in Yen Hsi-shan operations."[17] After the war Hirohito's Army minions gave Honma the role of scapegoat and he accepted it because of his failure in Bataan before the Death March, not because of his titular authority during it. In effect, MacArthur, by an ironic twist which pleased his Japanese misinformants, had Honma sentenced to death for having been an inefficient enemy.

When the Death March began at Mariveles on the southern tip of Bataan, many Japanese officers who realized and opposed what was about to happen made a point of showing their disapproval in front of the common soldiers who were to be the executioners. Some of these dissident officers offered canteens of water and packs of cigarettes to marchers. Others stopped prisoners to ask if personal effects had been stolen from them, then slapped the faces of noncommissioned Japanese pilferers in order to re-

[17] Japanese officers tell no tales on one another but the membership of the "China gang" is well known from other sources and contexts. It consisted of General Staff intelligence officers who emerged from the plots of the early 1930's as protégés of Prince Higashikuni and Prince Asaka, and who went on to play important roles in the Marco Polo Bridge Incident and the rape of Nanking. Three of the most important of them involved in the Bataan Death March were: Major General Wachi Takaji, who in March 1942 was forced on Honma as his new chief of staff and who, in 1937, as chief of the Special Service Organ in Peking had arranged the Marco Polo Bridge Incident; Lieutenant General Mudaguchi Renya, who brought Honma his 18th Division reinforcements from Malaya, and who, in 1937, had commanded the Japanese regiment at Marco Polo Bridge; and finally "Kill-all-prisoners" Cho Isamu of the October Plot, the Nanking rape, the Lake Khasan Incident, and the 1945 last stand on Okinawa. In April 1942 Cho was a major general handling liaison between the headquarters of General Terauchi in Saigon and of General Honma in Manila.

turn to the prisoners their wedding bands and watches. Still other Japanese officers went to the length of seeking out and publicly embracing tottering Americans whom they had known before the war at U.S. colleges. None of the Westernized Japanese officers, including General Honma, however, tried to countermand the secret orders which had been spread by Colonel Tsuji and his fellow staff officers. The orders seemed to be backed by imperial authority brought to Manila by the hand of Chief of Staff Sugiyama on April 3.

The guards assigned to escort the U.S. prisoners over the 60-mile course of the Death March were hardened veterans of the 16th Division. Almost all of them had been wounded in the first attacks on Bataan in January and early February. Many of their sergeants had officiated under Prince Asaka and Nakajima Kesago at the rape of Nanking in December–January 1937–38.

The whole concept of the Death March was infused with peculiarly Japanese notions of excuse, justification, and legality. None of the U.S. prisoners were taken out forthrightly and butchered as the Chinese captives had been at Nanking. Instead the sick and weary who fell out of step, either to relieve themselves or to catch a moment's rest, were cuffed with a fist or rifle butt. Once dazed and down, they were shouted orders in Japanese to resume their place in line and if they did not respond immediately they were stabbed with bayonets or shot in the head for desertion and disobedience. To encourage desertion the marchers were given little food and no water and led past farmyards and wells. When they broke for clean water they were shot. When they lapped at the polluted waters of carabao wallows and privy overflows they were allowed to drink their fill. Most of those who succumbed to such temptations died a few days later of severe, untreated intestinal infections.

Japanese witnesses at the trial of General Honma after the war insisted—without justification—that the rigors of the Death March were no different from those endured routinely by any Japanese soldiers in boot camp.[18] Western witnesses protested that the

[18] As an unnoticed boy, taking care of the trash and garbage at the Japanese guard house of Camp Holmes Internment Camp in the Philippines during the war, I formed the impression that Japanese garrison life, except for Taiwanese and Koreans in work battalions, was no harder than garrison life in

prisoners of Bataan before they began their 60-mile march were already sick men. In rebuttal the Japanese witnesses said smugly that, yes, everyone had been surprised by the weakness and malnutrition of the American captives. The American prosecutors at the trial correctly maintained that Honma's officers had known the American troops would be starving and had counted on that factor to make the Death March effective.

From San Fernando, the terminus of the Death March, the men of Bataan were transported another 40 miles north by rail to Camp O'Donnell, a swampy field of huts and tents surrounded by barbed wire, where most of the survivors were to spend their first six months of imprisonment. On the train ride to O'Donnell each boxcar was packed with over a hundred men —as tightly as Tokyo subway cars in rush hour. The steel doors were closed and there was no ventilation system. Sick men suffocated and died in the stench. Strong men rode standing on the bodies of their dead comrades.

Of the 70,000 "battling bastards" who had surrendered on April 9, only 54,000 arrived in Japanese custody at Camp O'Donnell. Between 2,000 and 3,000 of the 12,000 Americans who surrendered are known to have died during the march, and about 8,000 of the 58,000 Filipinos. Another 6,000 Filipinos, more or less, are believed to have dropped out of the Death March columns and survived. Some were allowed to escape in return for bribes. Some melted into the crowds of spectators at Lubao and San Fernando near the end of the march. Some dropped into roadside paddies and cane fields, played dead, and were spirited away by the peasants. A handful of American airmen and officers did the same and lived to lead guerrilla bands of fellow drop-outs in the years ahead.

The full horror of the Death March was best appreciated by those who brought up the rear. They saw the results of deeds which Japanese had never done to Japanese, which Germans had never done so publicly to Jews, which Western troops had not experienced since Khartoum or the Black Hole of Calcutta. Corpses and faded purple intestines were draped by the yard on

---

the U.S. Army. The Japanese guards were better fed than their civilian counterparts at home and, through official Army brothels, better serviced sexually than their American counterparts in the field.

Filipino farm fences. Open-mouthed bodies lay in puddles along the roadside ditches. Beheaded torsos leaned against walls, squatting frozen in their last act of toilet.

News of the great reprisal spread quickly from the Filipino barrios in northern Bataan. In the last stretches of the march, the streets of Lubao and San Fernando soon became lined with Filipino women bearing food, water, herbals, and bandages which were passed to the marchers despite the sternest efforts of their guards. Behind the peasant women wealthy Filipinos from Manila stood looking for their sons. In shops and cantinas deals were made with Japanese captains and sergeants which saved the lives of some of the Philippines' most prominent scions. The same deals greatly strengthened Japan's puppet government in the Philippines during the three years ahead.

Through Chief of Staff Sugiyama and through daily reading of secret police reports, Hirohito was at least indirectly responsible for the Death March and aware of its magnitude.[19] Japanese attuned to such delicate matters point to certain episodic sidelights in the Court records which suggest that Hirohito, at the time of the march, was feeling no regrets. On the contrary he was busy preparing fresh brutalities for other occupied areas and silencing objections from softhearted women in his Court circle.

On April 5, Hirohito approved the appointment of a certain Korematsu Junichi as chief secretary and effective regent for the civil administrator of the entire eastern half of the Co-Prosperity Sphere. It was an incredible choice. Korematsu was a mobster from the slums, one of those who organized shape-up bosses and controlled Japanese coolie labor. Lord Privy Seal Kido knew the man well and had long used him as a personal go-between and informant in dealings with the ultranationalistic gangs of the underworld. Now Korematsu would dispense his rough-and-ready street justice over the extended exurban neighborhood of Celebes,

---

[19] If Hirohito did not issue secret orders for the Death March in advance, he should, at the least, have known of it in time to save most of its 10,000 victims. Even assuming that somehow, during the twelve days of the march, he shirked his reading chores and cut himself off from his usual sources of information, then he would still have to be held accountable, because a year later when the U.S. government allowed the Death March to be publicized throughout the world, Hirohito ordered no investigation, no courts-martial, and no punishment of the executioners.

New Guinea, the Bismarcks, the Marianas, the Carolines, the Marshalls, and the Gilbert Islands.

Under Korematsu's administration villages and sub-tribes of inarticulate or uninfluential island "cannibals" would disappear without trace. They would be replaced by Japanese colonists who, later in the war, held banquets at which were served, literally, the barbecued limbs of shot-down American fliers. Little is known of this dark chapter in Japanese oppression, and Korematsu, its chief architect, went down with a torpedoed ship on his way home for a palace briefing in 1945.

On April 17, as the Death March neared its conclusion, Lord Privy Seal Kido was summoned to the seaside villa in Numazu at which Hirohito's handsome fifty-seven-year-old mother, the Empress Dowager Sadako, had lived in self-imposed, disapproving exile since three days before Pearl Harbor. She subjected Kido to a two-and-a-half-hour grilling on "the steps which had led to the war and subsequent expressions of brute military strength." Afterward Kido joined Hirohito who was in the neighborhood attending a fleet exercise. Lord and vassal, they went mushroom-picking together on the grounds of the Hayama imperial villa. In the course of the botanical ramble, Kido reported at length and in privacy on his conversation with the Queen Mother. Having heard him out, Hirohito abruptly left the pathway, entered the underbrush, and with his own hand plucked up a specimen of *Siler divaricatum* (or *Ledebouriella seserioides Wolff* as it is now classified). The root of this little herb, related to parsley and carrots, and called *bofu*, was much prized by old peasant ladies as a cure for the rheums and stiffnesses of their old men. Hirohito ceremoniously presented his specimen of it to Kido and delivered a brief factual disquisition on the pharmaceutical folklore surrounding it. Kido listened, laughed, abandoned his recital of the fears and compunctions of Hirohito's mother, and turned the conversation into more manly channels.

WHAT DOOLITTLE DID

The next morning at dawn, April 18, 668 miles to the east of Tokyo, a small U.S. task force of two carriers and a cruiser was discovered by the Japanese picket boat *Nitto Maru No. 23*.

Twenty-nine minutes and 925 shells later, the *Nitto Maru* sank under the fire of the U.S. cruiser *Nashville*. Vice Admiral William Halsey, aboard the carrier *Enterprise*, advised his other carrier, *Hornet*, that Tokyo had almost certainly been alerted. A few minutes later Colonel James Doolittle of the U.S. Army led sixteen B-25's from the *Hornet's* deck to begin—from a launching point 150 miles farther out than planned—the first air raid on Tokyo.

Flying individually, each plane for itself, Doolittle's raiders came in over Japan at tree-level altitude shortly before noon. They crossed the coast at sixteen different points, dispersed over almost 200 miles of shoreline. Japanese defenses were not ready for them because staff officers had calculated that the two approaching U.S. carriers would not be able to launch a threat with standard-issue short-range Navy bombers for many hours yet. Ten of Doolittle's planes zeroed in on Tokyo minutes apart and from several directions in a diabolical random fashion which confused and terrified the most brilliant tacticians at Imperial General Headquarters. Doolittle's own plane, the first to arrive on target, flew directly over the Imperial Palace, which he had been told to spare, and dumped his 2,000 pounds of incendiary clusters in downtown Tokyo, in the Shinbashi station area. The other nine Tokyo raiders hit steel plants and oil refineries in north Tokyo and along the dockfront in south Tokyo. Some of the latecomers were hounded by Japanese fighters and jettisoned their bomb loads haphazardly in order to lighten ship, gain speed, and escape. They hit a middle school, a hospital, and several purely residential streets. By chance they also ignited a large, camouflaged oil-storage farm which burned black and heavy for many hours after the raid was over.

Three more of Doolittle's raiders struck factories and oil tanks in Yokohama; two hit the industrial town of Nagoya on the way to Kyoto; one struck Kobe on the Inland Sea and caused a remarkable amount of damage to the Kawasaki aircraft factory.

By one o'clock in the afternoon the raid was over. Fifty Japanese were dead, 252 wounded, and ninety factory buildings gutted. A fuel farm and six large gas tanks had been subtracted from Japan's most precious stockpile, her liquid fuel.

One of Doolittle's raiders, short on gas, turned north to Russia and landed near Vladivostok. After a three-hour feast of celebration and toast drinking with the staff of the local Russian commander, the plane's five-man crew was flown to central Russia where it was interned for over a year before being allowed, diplomatically, to escape into Iran.

Doolittle's other fifteen marauders made for Chuchow, a railway town in south central China, about 200 miles south of the Yangtze, in an area which the Japanese had never taken the trouble to occupy. All of the planes ran out of fuel short of their mark. Three of the crews crash-landed in the ocean south of Shanghai, a few yards from the shore; one pancaked on the still waters of a rice paddy; the other twelve, over mountainous terrain farther inland, set their planes on automatic pilot and bailed out. It was a rainy night. The planes crashed against mountain tops. The parachutists—except for one whose chute did not open—sprained ankles and cracked ribs against wet mountainsides all over the Chinese province of Chekiang. The men of one crew floated to earth just south of Japanese-held Nanchang and were taken captive immediately.

The crews of two of the planes which crash-landed in the surf off the shore both suffered debilitating injuries. One of them, due to the efforts of a single uninjured nineteen-year-old corporal, David J. Thatcher, was smuggled out of Japanese eastern China on stretchers by hardy peasants in the employ of Chiang Kai-shek's resistance fighters. Along the way, the pilot, Lieutenant Ted Lawson, had to have his gangrenous leg amputated, under Novocain, at a missionary infirmary in Lishui. The crew of the other plane which crash-landed was not so lucky. Two of its men had drowned, with severe internal injuries, on their way to the beach. The other three crewmen made contact with Chinese partisans but were shortly afterward betrayed by a double agent and captured by the Japanese.

In the end, five of Doolittle's eighty men were detained in the Soviet Union, three died in crash landings in China, sixty-four found their way to Chungking, the capital of unoccupied China, and eight suffered the terrors of Japanese vengeance.

The eight captured airmen were assembled in Nanking and Shanghai and after a day of gentle routine field interrogation were flown to Tokyo for torture by the secret police. Hirohito was consulted a week later, on April 28, as to his wishes in disposing of them. He refused to commit himself directly but through his intimate, Chief of Staff Sugiyama, he suggested that all eight of them be tried and executed for crimes against the civilian populace of Tokyo who had died in the raids.

For six months the newspapers controlled by the imperial family inveighed against the airmen and denounced them as mass murderers of school children and hospital patients. Prime Minister General Tojo, who knew the facts of the raid and also the facts of Prince Higashikuni's mass bombings of Chinese civilians in 1937, waged a one-man campaign of legal rectitude on behalf of the airmen. He pointed out that there was no statute on the books which made it a capital crime for an enemy flier to bomb Tokyo.

Finally in October Tojo succeeded in persuading Hirohito to commute the sentence of five of the prisoners to life and to execute only three of them. The condemned were flown back to Shanghai. One of them, Lieutenant Dean Hallmark, the pilot of Doolittle's plane number 6, was no longer sane enough to appreciate what was happening to him. On the afternoon of October 15 he and the pilot and gunner of plane number 16, Lieutenant William Farrow and Sergeant Harold Spatz, were taken to a cemetery outside Shanghai and shot. One of the remaining five captive Doolittle raiders died in solitary confinement in a Japanese prison in 1944; the other four lived to be liberated by American parachutists who dropped into the Peking area on August 20, 1945.

Hirohito's wrath against the American raiders was as nothing compared to his wrath against the Chinese peasants who had helped most of them escape. On April 20, two days after the Doolittle raid, he instructed the third and last of the Three Crows, General Okamura Yasuji, the senior commander in China, to prepare for a reprisal expedition against the Chinese province of Chekiang where Doolittle's pilots had found refuge. A few days later Hirohito stamped orders for a punitive sweep through Chekiang and adjoining areas south of the Yangtze "to destroy the air bases from which the enemy might conduct aerial raids on the Japanese Homeland."

Hirohito's orders were unusually specific on this occasion:

The captured areas will be occupied for a period estimated at approximately one month. Airfields, military installations, and important lines of communication will be totally destroyed.

Separate instructions will be issued in regard to matters pertaining to the moment of withdrawal. . . .

The commander in chief of the China Expeditionary Army will begin the operation as soon as possible. He will concentrate on the annihilation of the enemy and the destruction of key enemy air bases in the Chekiang area.

A hundred thousand Japanese troops were called from garrison duty to break the uneasy truce with Chiang Kai-shek. They began to descend on Chekiang only a fortnight after the last American plane had crashed. They continued to ravage the entire Pennsylvania-sized area of Chekiang and adjoining Kiangsi for three months. When they finally withdrew in mid-August 1942, they had killed 250,000 Chinese, most of them civilians. The villages at which the American fliers had been entertained on their way west to Chungking were reduced to cinder heaps, every man, woman, and babe in them put to the sword. In the whole of Japan's brutal eight-year war with China, the vengeance on Chekiang would go down unrivaled except by the ferocious march on Nanking in 1937.

It was not the damage caused by Doolittle or his sacrilege in violating the sacred air space of Japan which angered Hirohito. The raid was clearly a propaganda spectacular staged to hearten U.S. servicemen and civilians who were tired of defeats. It had cost more than it had gained and was not likely to be repeated. Moreover, it had reminded Japanese that their islands were vulnerable to air attack from the empty oceans toward the sunrise; it would help the government in getting the people to take air-raid drills and civilian defense seriously.

What most disturbed Hirohito was the answer implicit in the raid to the peace feelers which he had put out through Lisbon and Geneva after the fall of Singapore. He had offered then to halt Japan's advance at any moment and stop the massacre of hopelessly beleaguered Allied garrisons. Until the Doolittle raid, he had hoped that his diplomatic feelers might still elicit a response. Doolittle's incendiaries, however, clearly stated that the United States was not yet ready to settle, that the terms had not changed since the Hull-Nomura conversation of 1941, that Roosevelt still insisted on "self-determination" and "freedom of opportunity" throughout Asia before he would consider any Japanese claim to a "special position" there.

It would be a long war and the butchery in Chekiang, to prevent U.S. planes from flying off the airfields there, was but one of the preparations which Hirohito approved in an effort to increase Japan's staying power. First the Co-Prosperity Sphere would be "completed and perfected" by eliminating the last Western enclave in Asia: Corregidor. Then—so the plan stated—the Navy would advance into the Coral Sea between New Guinea and Australia in order to capture New Caledonia and cut U.S.-Australian shipping lanes. Finally an armada would be dispatched to occupy Midway Island on the way to Hawaii and force the remnants of the U.S. Pacific Fleet to fight a decisive last battle.

THE DEATH OF CORREGIDOR

All through April 1942 heavy Japanese artillery on the newly won peninsula of Bataan dueled with heavy American artillery on Corregidor, the island rock off the tip of the peninsula. The U.S. guns had been emplaced scientifically at great expense before the war. The rock was honeycombed with tunnels filled with ammunition and impervious to bombardment. At first the Corregidor guns had the best of the shoot-outs simply by virtue of caliber. But gradually the Japanese ability to look down and report hits from airplanes gave the mobile field pieces on Bataan an advantage. One by one the great 10-ton mortars of Corregidor were silenced by direct hits which first smashed the steel gun ports and finally stopped the U.S. muzzles with rubble. By May 3 only two of the big guns were still firing and the whole of Corregidor's "topside" looked like a newly excavated quarry. That day and the next the Japanese batteries redoubled their barrage in what was obviously intended as a final softening up.

Between 11 P.M. and midnight on May 5, some 600 Japanese out of an amphibious assault force of over 2,000 survived the two-mile crossing from Bataan and succeeded in digging in on Corregidor's blasted shingle. All through the night the 6,500-odd Filamerican defenders filed from their tunnels and attempted with rifles and bayonets to drive the invaders back into the bay. Honma poured all the men and assault craft he could muster into maintaining the beachhead. Despite his reinforcement by some 50,000 men six weeks earlier, he was desperately short of combat troops. Simply being in Bataan had given most of his men dysentery or malaria.

When the sun rose, General Wainwright had sent out from the tunnels his last infantrymen: the "4th Provisional Battalion," a pick-up team of trained paint scrapers and deck swabbers left in Manila harbor by merchant and naval vessels. They, too, had failed to dislodge the Japanese foothold. One more night or one more amphibious assault, Wainwright calculated, would leave Corregidor a disorganized, demoralized invitation to total butchery. And so at 10:15 A.M., as Honma was considering asking for more reinforcements, Wainwright radioed him for free passage through the lines under flag of truce.

In his first interview with General Honma, General Wainwright tried to capitulate in the name of Corregidor alone. He was, however, the titular commander of all U.S. troops in the Philippines: the 50,000 who still clung to life in Japanese prison camps, and the 20,000 who still marched free in Mindanao, Panay, Leyte, Samar, Mindoro, and North Luzon, as well as the 6,500 deafened, shell-shocked members of his personal command in Corregidor.

Honma gave Wainwright twelve hours to think over his offer and suggested that, if he did not strike the colors for all U.S. forces in the Philippines, those who were already in Japanese clutches might suffer dearly for it. When Wainwright returned from Honma's command post on Bataan, he found that, during the cease-fire, Japanese troops had swarmed ashore on Corregidor and occupied even the entrance to the central Malinta tunnel which housed the rock's hospital and kitchens.

After a sleepless night Wainwright had no choice but to order the U.S. troops in the southern islands of the Philippines to submit themselves, undefeated, to Japanese captivity. Since Wainwright commanded only 6,500 men and Major General William Sharp in Mindanao commanded more than twice that number, it was a difficult order to enforce. In what was, for the United States, the most humiliating moment of World War II, Wainwright on the next day, May 7, broadcast his decision from the Japanese radio station in Manila. MacArthur in Australia ordered Major General Sharp to pay no attention to the broadcast since it was obviously made under duress. Wainwright, however, followed up his radio speech by sending members of his staff to carry letters from him, under Japanese escort, to Sharp and his other subordinate commanders.

Sharp, for one, acknowledged that the American lives which the Japanese already held in their hands counted for more than anything which he and his men could accomplish militarily. He surrendered most of his scattered troops and forced his satellite commanders in other southern islands to do likewise. At the same time he encouraged those few Filamericans who knew the terrain and had the individualistic talents for it to take to guerrilla warfare. General Honma was satisfied. The men of Corregidor were moved to the starving, disease-ridden Japanese concentration camps without special reprisal. And those U.S. soldiers in the south and far north who were willing to sacrifice prisoner-of-war status for the precarious and totally unprivileged status of guerrilla-spy fought on. Some of them succeeded so well as irregulars that, in the mountains of Mindanao, they maintained throughout the war a prison camp in which the inmates were Japanese.

During the final bombardment of Corregidor and the days of General Wainwright's humiliation, Prince Higashikuni's twenty-five-year-old son, Morihiro, the classmate, companion, and near twin of Hirohito's Army brother, Prince Mikasa, represented the imperial family in a triumphant tour through the conquered southern areas. In Bali, on May 4, he gave audience to air and naval commanders who were supposed, in the weeks ahead, to occupy or isolate Australia. On May 8, he was in Manila to witness a bedraggled procession of U.S. troops from Corregidor being walked through the downtown streets on their way to concentration camp. Because of General Wainwright's co-operation, it was not a death but merely a humiliation march.

THE CORAL SEA

On that same day, May 8, Japan's scientifically planned and predictably successful Strike South suddenly jerked to a halt. It had been moving ahead of schedule because of a long run of good luck: the right rain and the right shine whenever needed and many a hole-in-one bomb drop. Now abruptly the laws of chance reasserted their arbitrary authority in one of the most impartially accident-ridden encounters which has ever changed the course of history. It was as if ships and planes were momentarily forgotten while Amaterasu the Sun Goddess squatted down with the Statue of Liberty to shoot crap.

This event, which has been charitably remembered as a battle, the Battle of the Coral Sea, took place in the amethystine, reef-girdled waters which separate eastern New Guinea, the Louisades, the Solomons, the New Hebrides, and New Caledonia from the northeastern coast of Australia. Nowhere on earth basks a balmier or more beautiful sea basin. There it was that the weirds went wild and improvised.

Scientific cryptanalysis gave the U.S. Navy an initial advantage by telling Rear Admiral Chester Nimitz, the post Pearl Harbor commander of the Pacific Fleet, that the Japanese were going to send an invasion force around the high mountainous barrier of New Guinea to seize Port Moresby. This was the main Australian base on the south shore of New Guinea and commanded the approaches to Australia's populous east coast. In his advance information, Nimitz saw a fine opportunity to lay an ambuscade. The carriers *Enterprise* and *Hornet*, however, were still on their way back to Pearl Harbor from launching Doolittle's raiders. Consequently Nimitz could arm his trap with only the heavy carrier *Lexington* and the medium carrier *Yorktown*. The Japanese Port Moresby task force included two heavy carriers, *Zuikaku* and *Shokaku*, and one light carrier, *Shoho*.

On route to the battleground the Japanese forces stopped off to land a garrison on the little island of Tulagi, just north of Guadalcanal in the Solomons. Nimitz's carrier commander, Rear Admiral Frank Jack Fletcher, revealed his presence prematurely by sending his carrier planes on May 4 to attack the Japanese beachhead on Tulagi. In three waves and 105 missions, his pilots expended twenty-two torpedoes, seventy-six 1,000-pound bombs, and over 80,000 rounds of machine-gun bullets and succeeded in forcing one Japanese destroyer to beach, in killing the skipper of another with a machine-gun bullet, and in sinking five seaplanes, four landing barges, and three minesweepers. "Disappointing," Admiral Nimitz later termed the results and urged more target practice for all hands.

Having given himself away, Admiral Fletcher first fled south, then turned abruptly west with hopes of intercepting the separate Japanese fleet of Port Moresby-bound troop transports which he calculated would be rounding the eastern tip of New Guinea at any moment. Japanese Admiral Inouye Shigeyoshi, with his main striking force of heavy carriers and superior planes and pilots, steamed south in hot pursuit of Fletcher. On the night of May 6, heading south, Inouye passed 60 miles from Fletcher, heading west. Both were desperately looking for one another but it was the closest they would ever come to seeing one another. At daylight on May 7, Inouye's search pilots sighted an eastward-sailing destroyer and a flattish-topped oiler, the *Neosho*, which had been detached from Fletcher's fleet after refueling the previous day. Mistaking them for a cruiser and a carrier, the Japanese reconnaissance pilots called in fifty-two bombers which administered a massive dose of overkill, sinking the destroyer and leaving oiler *Neosho* a derelict which had to be scuttled.

Meanwhile Admiral Fletcher had learned from his scout planes that two carriers and four heavy cruisers were steaming toward him from the northwest. In reality the only force which might have answered to this description was that of the ships which had passed in the night and were now in exactly the opposite direction. The squadron seen by Fletcher's scouts consisted of two elderly light cruisers and some gunboats which were tagging along as reinforcements for the escort of the Port Moresby invasion transports. Admiral Fletcher, however, could not afford to wait for confirmation of the scouting report, because he felt he must strike first or be stricken. Accordingly, he launched an all-out attack on the phantom force with ninety-three of his best planes and pilots.

Admiral Inouye at that moment was receiving accurate reports of Fletcher's position but regarded them with a wait-and-see attitude because some of his fliers already claimed to have sunk one U.S. carrier that morning—the oiler *Neosho*—and were now reporting another U.S. carrier force far to the west. This last was an eager Australian-led detachment of cruisers and destroyers which had steamed on ahead of Fletcher's main strength in order to look for the Port Moresby invasion transports.

Admiral Inouye decided to do nothing while waiting for clarification of the conflicting intelligence being passed along to him. He knew that the United States could not possibly have more than five carriers in the entire Pacific; that two of these had just accompanied the Doolittle raiders and could not yet have reached the New Guinea area without wings; and that, therefore, some of the four carriers being reported to him by his reconnaissance pilots must represent either misidentifications or a diabolical American plot.

While the prudent Inouye waited for enlightenment, the Statue of Liberty made a lucky throw. En route to target, Fletcher's hastily dispatched planes happened to notice off to starboard another covering force for the Port Moresby invasion, a hitherto unsuspected quantity, the Japanese light carrier *Shoho* steaming along independently with a light screen of cruisers and destroyers. The U.S. dive-bomber flight leader, Lieutenant Commander William L. Hamilton, knew a bird in hand when he saw one. He led in his ninety-two torpedo and dive-bombers to the attack and, despite indifferent marksmanship, succeeded in sinking *Shoho* in twenty-six minutes. Some 500 Japanese sailors and pilots went down with their ship. According to a few captured survivors, their vessel sank because the last of the attacking American planes, frustrated by *Shoho*'s obstinate buoyancy, crash-dived into her and blew her up with unexpected suddenness. According to U.S. records, only three of the American planes failed to return to their flight decks.

Later that same afternoon three of Fletcher's cruisers and five of his destroyers crossed the exit from the passage through the Louisades by which the Port Moresby invasion transports were supposed to enter the Coral Sea. Admiral Inouye at once instructed the invasion fleet to hang back and tread water while his carrier planes disposed of the threat. Forty-two Japanese bombers attacked in three waves but Rear Admiral John Crace, the Australian commander of the squadron, succeeded in dodging the bombs without a scratch. No sooner had the Japanese bombers disappeared over the horizon than Crace was set upon by U.S. land-based B-26's from Australia. By skillful maneuvering he succeeded in surviving this "friendly" attack also and lodged a protest which MacArthur's public relations officers succeeded in suppressing and disregarding.

As dusk fell on May 7, the *Lexington* and *Yorktown,* which were equipped with radar, and *Zuikaku* and *Shokaku,* which possessed superior search auxiliaries, had still failed to locate and hit one another directly. Admiral Fletcher decided to postpone future battle until morning, and Admiral Inouye sent out twenty-seven bombers and torpedo bombers to make, if possible, a night attack. In one of the few well-informed decisions of the battle, Fletcher learned of their approach from radar and sent up interceptors in time to jump them in the twilight. For the first time in World War II, the American pilots had the best of a dogfight and shot down nine planes for three losses. The surviving eighteen Japanese pilots became confused on their way home and six of them tried to land on the *Yorktown.* Communications officers aboard the American carrier did all they could to copy blinker signals and bring the Japanese pilots into range of the *Yorktown's* guns, but only one of the enemy planes could be blown out of the sky before the rest of them were spooked and ran away to look for friendlier decks. Eleven of the remaining seventeen ran out of fuel while still searching and "splashed" in the ocean.

The next morning at sunup, May 8, the two carrier fleets finally learned one another's position from their scout planes. *Lexington* and *Yorktown* promptly launched all their available aircraft to attack the Japanese fleet. Equally promptly *Zuikaku* and *Shokaku* launched all their available aircraft to attack the American fleet. Compared with earlier performances against Pearl Harbor or Tom Thumb Phillips, the Misty Lagoon bombardiers were distinctly below par. The *Yorktown* evaded their blows entirely except for a single bomb which penetrated four decks and killed sixty-four men below. The *Lexington* was hit by at least two torpedoes and two bombs but maintained full steam and 25 knots. An early list was corrected by counterflooding. It looked as if the "Old Lady," which still included in her crew a few veteran hands who had been with her ever since her commissioning in 1928, might yet survive. Then at thirteen minutes to one in the afternoon her smothered fires somehow met a seepage of high-octane gas, touching off a succession of fires and explosions which ultimately, more than seven hours later, sent her settling, fully trimmed and right side up, to the bottom. All but a few of her crew, who had been killed in the fight, swam away and were rescued.

While *Lexington* sank, her planes and *Yorktown*'s had caused Admiral Inouye to retire. *Zuikaku* had waited out the American attack under the cover of a tropical ocean cloud burst. *Shokaku*, caught in the open, had suffered as much deck damage as *Lexington* and had been counted sunk by U.S. planes. But below decks *Shokaku* was still sound. U.S. torpedoes at that time in the war were almost as difficult to work with as the lumbering, heavily armored flying machines which American pilots had to use as launching platforms. As Japanese Zero pilots could be sure of shooting down unmaneuverable U.S. fighters, so Japanese ship skippers could be sure of seeing the wakes of approaching U.S. torpedoes, of turning in time to avoid them or, if necessary, laying on steam and simply outrunning them.

So it was that *Lexington* sank after the battle from an explosion deep in her vitals while *Shokaku*, her decks mangled and smoking, sailed away from the action and returned to Japan for extensive repairs. *Zuikaku* went with her and had to wait in port for months before new pilots could be found to replace those whom she had lost.

Yorktown, the surviving U.S. carrier, also limped for home and for what should have been, under ordinary circumstances, months of refitting, liberty, and dry dock. Having recovered many orphans from the *Lexington*, however, she had aboard a full complement of fliers and planes. And it turned out, as a matter of necessity, that her repairs could be greatly abbreviated and that she could be sent to sea again after only a few days.

The tactical score for the Battle of the Coral Sea stood at one Japanese light carrier sunk and one U.S. heavy carrier sunk. The strategic score, from the Japanese point of view, was one invasion temporarily postponed. Hirohito was irked and impatient, but not concerned. He expected to resume the southeasterly advance in

July and drive it home to the shores of New Zealand. On May 26, eighteen days after Coral Sea, he asked his chief aide-de-camp, General Hasunuma Shigeru, to have someone look into the handling of a touchy diplomatic question: the sovereignty of New Caledonia. This Massachusetts-sized island north of New Zealand belonged to the French, but whether to De Gaulle or Pétain remained a moot point. Would Vichy or Berlin be offended when Japan annexed it?

From the U.S. point of view the stand-off at the Coral Sea represented a month or more of time in which U.S. manufacturers might yet make good their boast of technological pre-eminence. The reckoning was to come only a month later at Midway. The manufacturers were not ready for it and by all rights the United States might then have lost the war. But the Statue of Liberty was now throwing sevens.

MIDWAY

Two square miles of barren briny scrub were at issue. Midway's two islets, Sand and Eastern, together with an undeveloped, uninhabited rock named Kure a hundred miles to the west, lay all alone in the northwestern quadrant of the Pacific Ocean. Midway's airstrip, a third of the way on a direct line from Pearl Harbor to Tokyo, served as the salient point in the U.S. air-search-and-patrol triangle maintained between Midway, Pearl Harbor, and the Aleutians. Without Midway, U.S. intelligence would have no relay station through which to radio-eavesdrop on the Co-Prosperity Sphere and no early warning line of air reconnaissance with which to detect incoming Japanese invasion fleets.

On the battle for Midway's unprepossessing acres rode more than President Roosevelt and his chiefs of staff cared to admit at the time. Indeed, few battles since Thermopylae have been fought more desperately and for better reason. If the Japanese had won the battle they would have been in a position to carry out their plan for taking Hawaii in August 1942. They intended to go on to seize the Panama Canal and terrorize California, forcing the United States to abandon Australia, cancel plans for an expeditionary force to the European theater, and concentrate all resources on the defense of the U.S. West Coast. Under these conditions, Japanese strategists thought that the Anglo-American alliance would break down; that combined German-Japanese pressure would make American business interests turn against President Roosevelt; that perhaps the leading American families, assumed to be politically conservative, would bring the United States over to the Axis side. Fortunately for the inner peace of Washington, American strategists never had to evaluate, even contingently, the realism of these Japanese hopes. U.S. forces at Midway had incredibly good luck and made the most of it.

Admiral Yamamoto advanced on Midway with the most formidable fleet ever assembled up to that time: ten battleships, eight aircraft carriers, twenty-four cruisers, seventy destroyers, fifteen large I-boat submarines, eighteen tankers, and forty auxiliary vessels and transports—in all 185 vessels. His carriers, two heavy, three medium, and three light, together with his four small seaplane carriers, could put up 352 of the lethal Zero fighters, 105 dive-bombers, 162 torpedo bombers, fifty-six reconnaissance craft, and ten land bombers—a total of 685 airplanes.

Part of Yamamoto's forces were to open the battle with diversionary landings at Attu, Kiska, and Adak at the western end of the Aleutian Islands arc. These were expected to bring the U.S. Pacific Fleet out of Pearl Harbor and start it steaming north. Then Yamamoto's advance force—the heavy carriers of Admiral Nagumo—were to begin softening up Midway 1,500 miles to the south. Landings on Midway would follow from heavily escorted transports. The U.S. fleet would naturally turn west to counterattack. Admiral Nagumo's carriers would retreat. The U.S. fleet would pursue and find themselves ambushed by Yamamoto's main force lurking to the west of Midway. There, Yamamoto, on the bridge of his gigantic 64,000-ton flagship, the *Yamato*, would supervise personally while the immense long-range guns of his battleships blew the U.S. fleet out of the water.[20]

This was the imperial plan for the Battle of Midway. To frustrate it Admiral Nimitz, the over-all commander of the Pacific

[20] Most of the Japanese battleships weighed far more than they had been registered as weighing with the prewar naval limitations committee in Geneva. *Yamato*'s "special-type 16-inch guns" actually had a caliber of 18.1 inches and could carry 25 miles. Similarly the heavy Japanese carriers *Kaga* and *Akagi*, registered at 27,000 tons, actually weighed in at 36,000 tons, and the "light" 10,000-ton carriers *Hiryu* and *Soryu* really weighed over 17,000 tons.

fleet, could call upon exactly three aircraft carriers, no battleships, eight cruisers, fourteen destroyers, and twenty-five submarines. By any criterion—number of ships, tonnage, firepower, or carrier planes—he was outnumbered almost three to one. What was more, on the basis of past performance, Nimitz had no reason to think that his men or his machines would be any match, individually, for their Japanese counterparts. He had to fight, however, because Japanese seizure of Hawaii and of West Coast ports must be delayed until the superior manpower and industrial capacity of the United States began to make themselves felt. Two or three more unexpectedly brilliant Japanese victories would begin to sap American strength at its wellhead.

Nimitz had one major advantage over Yamamoto: he knew enemy intentions beforehand. U.S. Naval Intelligence had warned him even before the Battle of the Coral Sea that the Japanese were planning something big in the central Pacific in early June. Even without full access to Yamamoto's Admirals' Code, U.S. cryptographers had made enough sense out of monitored Japanese fleet messages to learn the gist of Yamamoto's plan and to know that it was directed against a point in the Pacific called AF for "American Forces." Nimitz's own analysts thought this point was Midway; analysts in Washington, who thought more globally, believed AF stood for Hawaii. Nimitz had the garrison on Midway send out a bogus radio message complaining that their water distillation plant had broken down. A few days later U.S. Navy monitors picked up a Japanese message informing Yamamoto that AF was short of fresh water.

On his own responsibility, Nimitz had already set in motion the U.S. plan for the Battle of Midway. It was simply to get into Midway as many men, guns, and airplanes as the islets would hold and to move as secretly as possible into Midway waters every available fighting ship.

On May 26, nine days before the battle, the U.S. carriers *Enterprise* and *Hornet* pulled into Pearl Harbor from a vain dash toward the action in the Coral Sea after their successful sneak approach on Tokyo with the Doolittle raiders. Their tired, liberty-hungry crews were set to work at once preparing the ships to sail again in less than forty-eight hours. The navigator of the *Enterprise*, Commander Richard Ruble, listened to the briefing for key officers on the forthcoming Midway mission, and said, "That man of ours in Tokyo is worth every cent we pay him."

The next day, May 27, the carrier *Yorktown* limped into Pearl Harbor from her drubbing nineteen days earlier in the Coral Sea. She had made the 4,500-mile voyage under her own steam but at ten knots attended by a swarm of fretfully solicitous destroyers. She leaked badly from near misses, and the one bomb which had hit her had penetrated four decks and touched off fuel and ammunition fires which had made a shambles of her interior. The Japanese counted her sunk. Admiral Nimitz gave his shipyard commanders three days to repair her. American welders and fitters moved aboard at once and wrought wonders which could not be matched at that time by any Japanese shipyard. Some of them worked on her without sleep for the next forty-eight hours. Some of them were still aboard her and returned ashore in tugs when she cleared Diamond Head on May 30 and hied herself after the *Enterprise* and *Hornet* which had left for Midway on May 28.

The sailing of the American carriers, with their screens of cruisers and destroyers, was entirely unknown to Admiral Yamamoto. In operational planning he had assigned the task of keeping watch on Pearl Harbor to his advance force of submarines, commanded by Big Brother Vice Admiral Marquis Komatsu Teruhisa, the cousin of the Empress who had presided at the Naval Staff College during the Pearl Harbor planning in 1941. Marquis Komatsu exercised his submarine command at Midway from Kwajalein in the Marshall Islands, 2,000 miles from the scene of action. His flagship was the *Katori*, a vessel registered as a light cruiser of 6,000 tons. She was the namesake of the battleship on which Marquis Komatsu and Hirohito had wrestled and played croquet during the crown prince's world tour in 1921.

Marquis Komatsu had great confidence in the Midway operation and a belief that the immense superiority of Japanese naval forces would inevitably tell in Japan's favor. He was preoccupied with planning the details of an envisaged raid on the Panama Canal after the battle. His submarines were supposed to take up their advance scouting stations outside Pearl Harbor and in two cordons between Pearl Harbor and Midway eight days before the battle. In the event none of them reached their stations until four days before the battle. During those four days of tardiness *Enter-*

prise, Hornet, and *Yorktown,* too, slipped through the Japanese early warning zone and took up a vigil in the cloudiest available stretches of ocean northeast of Midway.

Despite his preoccupation with future victories, the bookish Admiral Komatsu realized that his submarines had failed to provide any knowledge of the whereabouts of the U.S. fleet. His picket submarines had arrived on station too late to detect advance movements of the U.S. fleet, and his snooper submarines had encountered too many patrols in the Hawaiian area to launch scout planes for a look at the berths in Pearl Harbor itself. On or about June 3, Komatsu notified Admiral Yamamoto of his failure to make sure that the U.S. fleet was still in Pearl Harbor. Apparently, however, he did not call to Yamamoto's attention the late arrival of his picket submarines between Pearl Harbor and Midway. It was a serious lapse, but because of Komatsu's membership in the imperial family, Japanese historians in later years would allude to it only obliquely, and American historians, in their exhaustive postmortems, would follow the lead of the Japanese.[21]

When Admiral Yamamoto sailed out from Hashirajima anchorage off Hiroshima in the Inland Sea on May 27, he had ample evidence to know that Admiral Nimitz in Hawaii was expecting him. Yamamoto's radio monitors for several days had reported unusual message activity between U.S. ships and command posts. From his first day out of port his lookouts spotted the periscopes of U.S. submarines shadowing his great fleet. Nevertheless, he had no reason for concern. Now that his ships had sailed, it mattered not what U.S. admirals knew. Knowledge would do them no good unless they could act upon it, and they could not act upon it without moving their ships through the cordons of surveillance which Yamamoto believed to be strung across the northern Pacific by Marquis Komatsu's submarine wolf pack.

A week later, at dawn on June 3, Yamamoto's northern force

[21] Despite his blunder, Marquis Komatsu, who had been one of the Big Brothers of Hirohito's youth, remained in command of Japan's submarine fleet and rose to the rank of full admiral. After the war he was elected to the House of Councillors, the successor to the House of Peers. At this writing he is eighty-two years old and lives near former Lord Privy Seal Kido within an old man's stroll of the western postern of the palace. His daughter is married to Kido's son.

began operations by launching twenty-two bombers and twelve fighters for a raid on Dutch Harbor, the main U.S. base in the Aleutians. To the puzzlement of the attackers no U.S. planes were caught on the ground and the only targets were oil tanks and a radio shack. On their way back to their flight decks, the raiders spotted some U.S. destroyers offshore, but the weather closed in and for the next three days the northern force milled about in it waiting on events to the south.

By that evening the forces for the Battle of Midway were in position. Yamamoto's four advance carriers, under Admiral Nagumo, were steaming in on Midway through a front of bad weather from the northwest. Since the attack on Pearl Harbor, Nagumo's task force had fared proudly, raiding Darwin in February and sinking the British carrier *Hermes*, plus a cruiser and a destroyer, off Ceylon in April. Admiral Nimitz's three carriers, which as yet had no boastworthy record, were steaming about surreptitiously northeast of Midway, hiding in squalls and awaiting their chance. The Americans knew that the Japanese were in the vicinity; the Japanese thought that the Americans were at least 1,200 miles to the east beyond the Japanese submarine picket lines.

At 4:20 on the morning of June 4 Admiral Nagumo's carriers began to launch thirty-six bombers, thirty-six dive-bombers, and thirty-six Zeros for a strike against the airstrip and Marine garrison at Midway. Half an hour later when the planes had all reached their formations and were winging on their way, Nagumo had routine precautions taken against the unlikely possibility that there might be a U.S. fleet in the area. Reconnaissance planes took off belatedly to execute a lackadaisical search pattern over the surrounding ocean. Seventy-two of the bombers and thirty-six of the fighters remaining on board Nagumo's carriers were armed with suitable weapons for attack, if necessary, on hostile surface vessels.

On Midway the Marine garrison, which had been greatly reinforced with men and machines during the previous fortnight, knew from aerial reconnaissance that a convoy of Japanese troop transports was approaching from the southwest. The men had been told to assume that Japanese carriers were simultaneously descending from the northwest. And so at 5:53 A.M., when the incoming Japanese planes appeared as bogeys on a radar screen, U.S. pilots were ready and waiting. Fifteen B-17 Flying Fortresses had already taken off to bomb the convoy of transports to the southwest. They were redirected toward the carriers in the northwest. The other sixty-two pilots on Midway scrambled. Thirty-seven of them turned their bombers toward the carriers; twenty-five of them spiraled up for altitude so that their fighters—their obsolescent Buffaloes and their seven untried Wildcats, span-new from the production line—could fall upon the approaching Japanese planes.

The U.S. bombers passed their Japanese opposite numbers coming the other way and the pilots thumbed noses at one another without fighting. The twenty-five Marine fighters tangled with the thirty-six Japanese Zeroes. In a ten-minute dogfight two of the Zeroes and twenty-two of the new Marine F4F Wildcats and old F2A-3 Buffaloes had been put out of action. Ten of the U.S. crews and three of the planes survived but the men were bitter. "Any commander," reported one of them, "that orders pilots out for combat in an F2A-3 should consider the pilot as lost before leaving the ground."

Having disposed of Midway's fighter cover, the remaining 106 Japanese planes strafed and bombed every target on the ground which they could see. They destroyed the hospital and fuel tanks on Sand Island, demolished the powerhouse, mess hall, and PX on Eastern Island, ruptured the fuel lines to the airport gas pumps there, and pockmarked the runways. They were surprised at the amount of anti-aircraft fire they encountered, for they had been told that there were only a few hundred Americans on the islands when in fact the garrison had been built up to over 5,000. The American defenders were so well prepared with trenches and sandbag emplacements that only eleven of them were killed and few of their guns put out of action.

When the Japanese fliers had spent their bombs and bullets, they felt disappointed. They had caught no U.S. planes on the ground and it was obvious that they had not destroyed Midway's firepower. Four of the Japanese bombers had been shot down or were so badly mauled that they would splash on the way back to their flight decks. At 7 A.M. flight leader Lieutenant Tomonaga Joichi, the scion of a great Nagasaki textile family, turned for home and radioed Admiral Nagumo: "There is need for a second strike."

The fifty-two Midway-based U.S. bombers were now converging on Nagumo's carrier force. They had been indoctrinated in the previous week with a full understanding of the importance of their mission. Either they sank the Japanese carriers or the Battle of Midway and perhaps the war would be lost by the United States. It is commonly said that the concept of suicide pilots was invented by the fanatic, fatalistic Japanese. On the contrary it was first put into practice by American pilots at Midway.

From 7:05 to 10:20 on that morning of June 4, seventy-eight U.S. crews hurled themselves at low altitude against the Japanese carriers.[22] Few of them expected to survive. Most of them knew that, even if they did survive, they had not enough fuel to make it home. Forty-four out of the seventy-eight crews perished according to their expectations. Worst of all they did not manage in their dying to register a single hit on any of the Japanese ships. The apparent futility of their sacrifice, the inferiority of their weapons, and the superior professionalism of their antagonists frustrated them as they died, but by a stroke of luck their lives were not wasted. Their insistent, ill-co-ordinated attacks finally drove Admiral Nagumo to make a fatal error of judgment which cost Japan her hope of winning the war.

In brief detail what happened was this. At 7:05 A.M. six U.S. Avenger torpedo bombers bore in on the Japanese fleet. They launched their fish while trying to evade the bullets of Zeros which were on their tails. Their slow, ill-finned, ill-fused torpedoes were all dodged successfully by the helmsmen of the Japanese carriers. Only one of the six Avengers flew away from that bomb run. Next at 7:11 A.M. came four Army B-26 Marauders, also armed with torpedoes. The Zeros got one of them, the anti-aircraft guns got another, and the other two skipped away over the spume for home. Their torpedoes, adroitly avoided by the Japanese helmsmen, ran away toward the empty horizon. At 7:55 sixteen of the newest Marine dive-bombers descended on the Japanese fleet in a long, gentle glide attack, which was all that the flight com-

[22] The high-level bombing by fifteen B-17's from Midway is excluded from these figures as a tactically different species of attack.

mander felt his green pilots were capable of executing. Six of them were shot down by Zeroes, two more by flak. Two of the remaining eight planes survived and all eight of the crews. Again, there were no hits.

At 8:14 A.M. the fifteen B-17's from Midway dropped 127,500 pounds of bombs on the Japanese ships from 20,000 feet. None of the bombs killed anything but fish. The B-17 crews all survived because they were flying too high for the carriers' antiaircraft guns.

Three minutes later eleven antiquated Marine Vindicator dive-bombers, known irreverently by their crews as "Vibrators," arrived belatedly over the Japanese fleet and swooped down at the battleship *Haruna*. Nine of the crews came through the curtain of fire and fled. The *Haruna* steamed on unscathed.

For over an hour Admiral Nagumo and his ship captains had been fully occupied with excitement and maneuvering as they dealt with these five ineffective U.S. air raids. At 7:15, after the first two, Nagumo had been convinced that the Midway airfield would need a second drubbing, and had ordered the 108 planes of his second-wave force disarmed of torpedoes for fleet attack and rearmed with bombs for land-installation attack. Then at 7:28 A.M. a Japanese search plane had reported an enemy fleet of indefinite numbers and composition over the horizon to the northeast. Nagumo requested confirmation and clarification and while waiting for it, at 7:45, ordered his sailors to suspend rearming of the second-wave force and stand by.

Nagumo's staff officers realized belatedly that they had committed a tactical error in using planes from all four carriers for the first strike and in retaining half the planes of each carrier for the second strike. If, instead, they had dispatched all the planes from two carriers against Midway and retained all the planes from the other two carriers for action against surface vessels, they would now have been in a position to send out the planes of one reserve carrier against the reported American fleet, ready the planes of the other reserve carrier for a second strike at Midway, and keep the decks of the two empty carriers clear for the retrieval of the planes which had already been committed. As matters stood, the four carriers were all disconcerted by the various demands which might be made on them. They had to be ready to recover planes from Midway, to send out planes armed with bombs, and to send out planes armed with torpedoes. As a result the hangar-deck-to-flight-deck elevators were stuffed with contradictions and countermanded orders. Planes were being moved up. Planes were being moved down. And bombs and torpedoes were being stacked, exposed, on the flight decks.

The minutes from 7:55 to 8:35 were taken up with the third, fourth, and fifth Midway-based American air strikes. In the midst of them, at 8:20, the exasperatingly vague pilot of the Japanese search plane to the northeast reluctantly and incredulously reported that the U.S. fleet elements he was glimpsing through breaks in the clouds included "what appears to be a carrier." Nagumo at once ordered any and all stand-by planes which had been rearmed with bombs to be slung once again with torpedoes for fleet attack. He might then have begun to launch an air strike except that the returning planes from the raid on Midway were now circling and asking permission to land. For the next fifty minutes their reception fully occupied Nagumo's flight decks.

The U.S. carriers *Enterprise*, *Hornet*, and *Yorktown* had long ago received reports as to the approximate position of the Japanese carriers. Rear Admiral Fletcher of the battered, half-repaired *Yorktown* and Rear Admiral Raymond Spruance of the *Enterprise* and *Hornet* had also, however, their own delicate decision to ponder. In order to make the most of their secret existence and of their inferior numbers, planes and pilots, they had to achieve success with their first fly-off or their decks would never be in a condition to send off a second wave. All planes had to be committed once and for all on the first strike.

After consultation Fletcher, who was in over-all charge, agreed with Spruance that the *Hornet*'s and *Enterprise*'s planes should take off immediately to make the most of the element of surprise and that the *Yorktown* would hover in the rear and add to the enemy's discomfiture as soon as the exact location of the enemy was established and stabilized by the first attacks. Accordingly, between 7 and 8 A.M., while the Midway bombers were spending themselves against Nagumo's fleet, the *Enterprise* had launched thirty-three dive-bombers, fourteen torpedo planes, and ten fighters, and the *Hornet* had launched thirty-five dive-bombers, fifteen torpedo planes, and ten fighters. Since the range to target was at least 150 miles, the fighters would have almost no chance of returning unless they spent little gas in dogfighting. The torpedo planes would have a slightly better chance if they found their quarry at once and did not have to hunt for it. The dive-bombers would have the best chance and might reasonably be expected to return home unless the search for the Japanese fleet was a long one. As it turned out only the dive-bombers did not fly a one-way mission; survivors from the fighter and torpedo-plane groups, such few as there would be of them, were almost all going out to spend hours in the ocean swimming about in life jackets. The rest of them were going to their deaths.

The *Hornet*'s thirty-five dive-bombers and ten fighters flew to the reported position of the Japanese fleet, then flew a little farther, then turned south to search for the Japanese ships in the direction of Midway. The *Hornet*'s ten fighters ran out of gas and splashed near Midway where their crews were mostly rescued. The thirty-five dive-bombers landed on Midway, refueled, and remained a viable reserve force which finally returned to their ship after the battle was over.

The thirty-three dive-bombers from the *Enterprise* also proceeded to the reported position of Nagumo's carriers and, finding it vacant, turned north to search the waters away from Midway. They continued to search after most of their pilots had any hope of eking out the fuel left in their tanks for the return home.

Meanwhile the fifteen torpedo planes from the *Hornet* and the fourteen torpedo planes from the *Enterprise*, escorted by the ten *Enterprise* pursuit planes, succeeded in finding the Japanese fleet. Lieutenant Commander John C. Waldron, the flight leader of the *Hornet*'s torpedo planes, had had a brief conference with his skipper before taking off and had led his planes to the north of the anticipated Japanese position. He was loved by his men as an eccentric from South Dakota who boasted of his Sioux ancestry, prided himself on his instincts, and insisted that they all carry hunting knives for use in possible crash landings near Robinson-

Crusoe islands. He told his men that he had a hunch that the Japanese admiral would make a sudden change of direction to the north. Waldron's hunch, which may have been suggested to him by his skipper, proved correct. In case it did not, the fourteen torpedo planes from the *Enterprise* were flying off to his left, bisecting the angle between his flight and that of the two dive-bomber groups.

At 9:20 A.M., when Nagumo had just finished recovering his Midway raiders, Commander Waldron arrived overhead with his knife-girt crews from the *Hornet*. The directness of his flight from deck to target would have done credit to a honeybee on route to its hive. The night before Waldron had memoed his men: "If there is only one plane left to make a final run in, I want that man to go in and get a hit." Now Waldron's followers, in their lumbering Devastator torpedo bombers, clung to his tail through the Zeros and the flak. They last saw Waldron standing up through the blasted dome of his cockpit as his flaming plane disintegrated and spattered into the sea. All fifteen of the Devastators launched their torpedoes, missed with them, and were blown from the sky. A single one of the thirty crewmen, Ensign George Gay, the pilot of the fifteenth plane, survived to watch the rest of the battle from the ocean. There he alternately supported and concealed himself with a buoyant black cushion which he had retrieved from the flotsam of his plane.

No sooner had Waldron's men fallen than the group of fourteen torpedo bombers from the *Enterprise*, which had been following him off to the south, veered in to make their own suicide runs. Four of them launched short, banked away, and survived. The other ten dropped their torpedoes inside the flashing white cloud above Nagumo's ships. None of them came out of it and none of their torpedoes found a mark.

By the superb flying of his Zero pilots and the sharpshooting of his gunners, Nagumo had now survived the attacks of eighty-one U.S. planes in seven separate attacks. The last two attacks had been executed by twenty-nine planes which clearly came from U.S. carrier decks. Up to that moment Nagumo had received news of only one U.S. carrier in the area—obviously a small one or it could not have slipped through the submarine cordon outside of Pearl Harbor or escaped immediate and exact identification by his reconnaissance aircraft. Twenty-nine torpedo planes were about all the attack that might be feared from one small carrier.

After a few minutes of waiting, Admiral Nagumo made his fateful decision. He ordered his ready-armed torpedo planes brought up to his flight decks for take-off against the troublesome American fleet. He knew, of course, that any of his carriers, with planes and fuel lines exposed on their top decks, would be highly vulnerable to bombs from above. He had just repelled two flights of torpedo planes, which obviously came from the mysterious American carrier. There should also be dive-bombers from the carrier, arriving at approximately the same time as the torpedo planes, or slightly earlier. More than an hour earlier, he had, indeed, survived the attacks of two waves of dive-bombers. Had these come from Midway or from the carrier? It was anyone's guess whether he had already coped with the U.S. carrier's dive-bombers or whether they were still out looking for him. Nagumo decided to gamble on the probability that they no longer existed, had never existed, or had long since returned home without finding him.

At 10:15 A.M., the 108 planes of Nagumo's second strike were finally on deck, armed with torpedoes and ready for take-off. At that moment, in a most improbable development, twelve more U.S. carrier torpedo planes appeared above. It seemed incredible that any American commander would have sent out three waves of planes all armed with such ineffective weapons as the slow, untrue American torpedoes. Admiral Nagumo did not know it, but he was now under attack by the torpedo planes of the third American carrier, the late-launching *Yorktown*, which was supposed to have been sunk in the Coral Sea. His men coped with the attack as efficiently as they had coped with the torpedo planes of the *Hornet* and *Enterprise*. His tired Zero pilots splashed seven of the *Yorktown*'s planes; three more were knocked down by gunfire; two disappeared damaged, limping for home. Again Nagumo's skippers, by skillful steering, combed the white hairs of the torpedo wakes and let them pass.

The four Japanese carriers turned into the wind and prepared to launch the 108 planes of their second strike. The 108 planes of the first strike, which had bombed Midway, were below decks, waiting rearmed, by the elevators, to follow them out in an overwhelming blow against the U.S. fleet. At that moment the destiny of the United States hung by the slender thread of half an hour's launching time. If the Japanese second strike had taken off, all of the U.S. carriers would almost certainly have been sunk and the Japanese carriers would have been in a condition, once more, to survive.

Instead, at that moment, 10:22 A.M. June 4, the last available U.S. planes, the last hope of the U.S. fleet, happened to converge at once upon the Japanese carriers. The *Yorktown's* complement of seventeen dive-bombers came in from the southeast after a relatively businesslike flight from deck to target. Out of the southwest, however, came a miracle: the thirty-two dive-bombers of the *Enterprise* which had been wandering about the Pacific for more than three hours. The *Enterprise* pilots had abandoned their original "interception course" and turned to search north more than an hour earlier. They had long since gone beyond the halfway point in their gas supply, and their flight leader, Lieutenant Commander C. Wade McClusky, had accepted the probability that they were all on a one-way mission. McClusky had sighted a Japanese destroyer twenty-five minutes earlier which was returning from chasing down a reported U.S. submarine. Assuming that the destroyer was heading toward the rest of the Japanese fleet, McClusky had made a sharp turn and adopted the destroyer's course. Now he was rewarded by the sight of Nagumo's whole task force spread out below him.

Nagumo's Zero pilots were all at lower altitudes where they had just finished off the torpedo planes of the last American attack, which had begun only seven minutes earlier. Nagumo's sailors were absorbed by the maneuver of turning the carriers into the wind for launching planes. Nagumo's decks were piled high with flammables and explosives. Coming from opposite directions, Lieutenant Commander Maxwell Leslie's dive-bombers from *Yorktown* and McClusky's from *Enterprise* had achieved perfect surprise and now made the most of a perfect target.

McClusky and most of his pilots screamed down upon the 36,800-ton Japanese carrier *Kaga*. The rest ran the gauntlet of the 36,000-ton carrier *Akagi*. The seventeen *Yorktown* dive-bombers released over the 17,500-ton carrier *Soryu*.

Most of the planes emerged intact from the fire of the unprepared Japanese gunners. Fourteen of the thirty-two *Enterprise* dive-bomber crews even managed to nurse their planes and their fuel supplies home to the U.S. fleet. McClusky landed with five gallons left in his tanks. Some of his pilots came in dead stick. All but two of Leslie's *Yorktown* dive-bombers flew home.

The twenty U.S. dive-bomber crews which perished had sold their lives dearly. In six minutes they and the twenty-nine surviving crews had crippled a Japanese fleet which, in the previous three and a quarter hours, had repelled ninety-three[23] other American planes and destroyed forty-four of them without suffering a scratch.

Four U.S. bombs scored direct hits on the decks of *Kaga*, two on *Akagi*, and three on *Soryu*. All three flattops were at once turned into high-octane infernos. The Japanese carriers' damage control compared unfavorably with their gunnery. Their sailors were samurai, not smiths. And later that day, when fires had licked into magazines, when bulkheads were popping everywhere like firecrackers, when engine-room crews had been gassed, and when lists had increased to the capsize point, all three carriers were finally abandoned.

The undamaged 17,500-ton carrier *Hiryu* launched a tiny reprisal raid at five minutes after noon when it was apparent that the rest of the carriers were burning out of control and doomed. Only eighteen of *Hiryu*'s sixty-three planes, her dive-bombers, took part in the raid, yet they succeeded. They found the *Yorktown*, and the seven of them which penetrated *Yorktown*'s fighter cover scored three direct hits. Five of the *Hiryu*'s planes flew home and the *Yorktown* was left a pillar of fire. Skilled American mechanics, however, quenched the fires and made *Yorktown* outwardly battleworthy again in two hours. Then a second

[23] Fifteen high-level Flying Fortresses, none of which had been destroyed; thirty-seven torpedo and dive-bombers from Midway, twenty-three of which had been destroyed; and forty-one torpedo planes from the U.S. carriers, twenty-one of which had been destroyed.

pathetically small flight from the *Hiryu*—this time of only five planes—found her again and sunk two torpedoes into her ravaged guts. All five of the Japanese planes survived her gunfire and flew home. Again the mechanical geniuses of the American fleet kept *Yorktown* afloat. They had her under tow and might have brought her ghost back to Pearl Harbor again, if, the next day, she had not been finished off, once and for all, by two more torpedoes, this time from the Japanese submarine I-168.

In the aftermath of the battle, as both sides began to retreat, *Enterprise* pilots and orphaned *Yorktown* pilots hunted down the *Hiryu* and took their revenge. They left her so dead in the water that, at 5:10 A.M. on June 9, Admiral Nagumo ordered the destroyers attending her to sink her.

Before Coral Sea and Midway, Japan had had ten carriers, rated *in toto* at 215,100 tons.[24] After Midway she had left five carriers with a displacement of only 96,100 tons. She had lost 55 per cent of her striking power. During the remainder of the war her shipyards would launch another five carriers, displacing 142,800 tons. By then, however, these replacements for the vessels lost at Midway would seem hopelessly inadequate next to the carriers which were sliding by the dozen down U.S. ways.

Worse still for Japan was the loss of skilled pilots. Only six had perished in the dawn raid on Midway, only twelve in the defensive morning dogfights against U.S. raiders, only twenty-four in the attempts to find and then to sink the *Yorktown*. But in the pyres of the flight decks and in the ocean later were lost more than half the crew members of the 280-odd planes which went down, caged, in the hulks of the four sinking Japanese carriers. All the early morning flush had been taken from the mists of the Misty Lagoon. Japan had lost almost half her aces. Their years of experience, and of cool hand-eye co-ordination, gained over China, Luzon, Malaya, and Java would never be reproduced in the hectic Japanese manufacturing effort of the next three years.

---

24 There were also a half dozen Japanese merchant vessels rigged with flight decks. Such improvised carriers came to dominate the Japanese carrier fleet toward the end of the war. For lack of prestige, morale, and armament, none of them ever accomplished much.

With the carriers and the pilots Japan had lost all hope of fighting an aggressive war and winning it. There remained only a process of attrition and a hope that by stout defense the United States could be induced to pay a fair price for peace.

The six minutes of stubborn heroism and good luck which had finally enabled the United States, with its superior radio monitoring and code breaking and analysis, to win the Battle of Midway could not, at first, be believed by Admiral Yamamoto, in his 64,000-ton battleship to the rear. Until almost midnight of June 4, 1942, he continued to order countermeasures—even an artillery duel between his ships and the shore batteries on Midway. Shortly after midnight, however, when two of his carriers had sunk and two more were fit only to be scuttled, he gave up and called for a general retreat. Earlier in the afternoon one of his staff officers had asked: "How can we apologize to His Majesty for this defeat?" Yamamoto had replied, "Leave that to me. I am the only one who must apologize to His Majesty."

No one in the Navy General Staff screwed up courage enough to tell Hirohito of the Midway debacle until some time after 3 P.M. on June 5, when it was 6 P.M. June 4 Midway time.[25] In Tokyo terms, "Abandon ship" had been ordered on the heavy carrier *Kaga* at 1:40 P.M., and the medium carrier *Soryu* had sunk at 4:13 P.M. *Akagi* and *Hiryu* were both derelicts already and would have to be abandoned later that night. Hirohito had spent the early afternoon in routine scheduled audiences and had only begun to ask how the Battle of Midway was going about 3 P.M. Thereafter, for the next twenty hours, he remained incommunicado to all but naval staff officers.

Lord Privy Seal Marquis Kido was officially told of the Midway disaster the next afternoon, June 6, at 1 P.M., by a naval aide-de-camp. Kido did not see the Emperor that day or the next. Instead he passed his time with his brother, Wada Koroku, the nation's leading aeronautical engineer, and with other leaders of the aircraft industry who might suggest balms for the sudden painful wound which had been inflicted in Japan's air arm. Finally

---

[25] Tokyo's clocks ran three hours earlier by the sun than Midway's but by the calendar one day later.

at 10:40 A.M., June 8, Kido was summoned into the Imperial Presence. In his diary he wrote afterward:

We talked about the Midway battle. I had supposed that news of our terrible losses would have caused him untold anguish. However, his countenance showed no trace of change. He said that the setback received had been severe and regrettable, but that notwithstanding he had told Navy Chief of Staff Nagano to carry on and to make sure that naval morale did not deteriorate. He emphasized that he did not wish the future policy of the Navy to become inactive and passive. I was very much impressed by the courage displayed by His Majesty today and I was thankful that our country is blessed with such a good sovereign.

Hirohito had lost. Kido knew that he knew it. But, on Kido's advice, he would not admit it for another three years.

28

CRUMBLING EMPIRE

(1942–1944)

MIDWAY DISMAY

To adopt a sumo-wrestling image used by an admiral in a letter to Lord Privy Seal Kido after the Battle of Midway, Japan had fancied herself a fencer in beginning the war—a small, deft, light-footed samurai. Through the protection of the gods, she wielded a fairy foil, an Excalibur of gossamer and lightning which had been kept for her, imbedded in the rock of ages, ready to be pulled out at the moment of her destiny. The terrifying U.S. monster, brandishing a battle-ax, must be dodged and pinked and slashed until it sighed from loss of blood and sank to its sluggish knees. Hirohito had given modern shape to Japan's holy sword in his naval air arm and its fast, light Zero fighter plane. At the Battle of Midway, the sword had broken off at its hilt.

Outside of Hirohito and his top courtiers, almost no civilians in Japan were allowed to know the fearful news of what had happened at Midway. On June 9, the day after Hirohito emerged from complete despair and resumed contact with his advisors, he called from the shadows General Ando Kisaburo, a trusted sixty-two-year-old partisan of the Strike South who had been one of the early patrons of Prime Minister Tojo. Hirohito appointed Ando czar of propaganda, serving in the Cabinet as a minister without portfolio.

The next day, June 10, Tokyo radio broke its five-day silence on the subject to announce that Japan had won a great victory, sinking two American carriers at Midway and destroying 120 U.S. planes for the loss of one Japanese carrier and thirty-five planes. Previously the Japanese news media had ignored some setbacks in China but never before had they had to tell such an utterly outrageous lie. On the following morning, June 11, Hirohito asked Chief Aide-de-Camp Hasunuma whether it might not be well to reinforce popular acceptance of the false news by issuing an imperial rescript in praise of the Japanese commanders at Midway. Hasunuma consulted Lord Privy Seal Kido, and Kido, being less committed to war logic than Hirohito, saw the Emperor at once and persuaded him that the Throne was not yet so desperate as to make sacred rescripts into vehicles of propaganda.

Through the Navy General Staff Hirohito issued instructions that the wounded from Midway be brought back to Japan under tight security and impounded in tightly packed wards at Yokosuka Naval Hospital outside Yokohama. There they were to be held incommunicado until they could be healed, heartened, hushed, and reassigned.

Also on June 11, Kido received a visit from former Lord Privy Seal Count Makino's son-in-law Yoshida Shigeru. The versatile and accommodating Yoshida, who had led the first public political Strike-South movement as a trial balloon for Hirohito in the early 1930's and who would become for Hirohito the perennial prime minister of U.S.-dominated postwar Japan, was now charged with the difficult duty of organizing a Peace Faction for the possible political contingency of defeat. At a time when all but victorious thoughts were considered treasonable by the Thought Police, Yoshida's assignment was delicate and dangerous.

Even before Midway, Yoshida's Peace Faction had already established itself as a viable enterprise, subversive but countenanced. The initial task had been to enlist the services of Prince Konoye and of his right-wing partisans in the business community, in the rackets, and in the underworld of labor leaders. Here were the traditionalists and the practical patriots who could be relied upon to see future Japanese interests even through the purple filters of war propaganda.

The first difficulty had been in harnessing Prince Konoye himself. The Fujiwara prince felt keenly his failure in averting the

war and was bitter about the downfall of the third Konoye Cabinet. In the second week of December 1941, when other Japanese
were celebrating the Pearl Harbor victory, Konoye had gone about
Tokyo making himself unpopular with dire predictions as to the
future. Prime Minister Tojo, on December 17, asked Hirohito to
muzzle him. On December 16, Kido had already moved in that
direction by having a long heart-to-heart talk with Konoye. He
had impressed upon the former prime minister that Japan was
at war now, that the Emperor was deadly serious about prosecuting it, that loose pessimistic talk would not be condoned, and
that, if Konoye expected defeat for Japan, he must serve the
nation by preparing for it constructively.

Konoye took hard to his new role. Plotting peace quietly in
back rooms did not suit his talents. He was more at home under
the lights, leading mass rallies. Kido, however, held an ax over
his head: exposure as a spy for treasonable association with Saionji
Kinkazu, Ozaki Hotsumi, and Soviet agent Sorge who were now
under investigation or interrogation by the police. Prime Minister Tojo, who believed in seeing the war through, would be happy
to prosecute Konoye if given a nod to do so. Konoye bowed to
this argument, and a month later, on January 20, 1942, he met
again with Kido, secretly, in one of the detached garden pavilions
of the Kinsui Restaurant, where the rice at that time of year came
in a little cold but the talk could be entirely private. There he
reported to Kido on his first tentative efforts. He was in touch
with Prince Higashikuni and with Count Makino's son-in-law
Yoshida, also with Army and Navy staff officers who had been
handling the contingency planning for defeat since 1938, and he
was working on drafts of memoirs about his first, second, and
third prime ministerships which would help to absolve the Emperor of his responsibility if and when they ever fell into enemy
hands.

Meanwhile the ailing gossip Baron Harada, formerly secretary-
spy in the household of the late Prime-Minister-Maker Saionji,
was handling liaison with the police on the Sorge case. He reported to Kido on January 24, 1942, that Saionji Kinkazu, the
grandson of the Constitution-framing patriarch, was severely condemned by police investigators for his part in mediating with
the Soviet Union through Sorge during the years 1938–41. Kido

had the secret police take an opinion poll of the leaders of various Japanese tongs, factions, and interests. The poll found that, when informed of the particulars of the Sorge case, the leaders were almost unanimously indignant against the "upper-class intellectuals" who had brought Red spies to the very portals of the Throne Room. A retired admiral, speaking for a naval veterans' group, succinctly voiced the consensus: "I take it for granted that Konoye has been put in custody, and that the announcement is being withheld in view of its international repercussions."

With this poll in pocket to use in managing Konoye, Kido advised Hirohito that it would be all right to spare Konoye embarrassment in the Sorge scandal. Hirohito called in the home minister, Yuzawa Michio, on February 19, 1942, and discussed the Sorge case with him in detail. On March 17, Saionji Kinkazu, Konoye's former intimate and the Sorge ring's contact, was taken into custody. He was tactfully interrogated for two months and then given two years in prison, sentence suspended.

Kido had the Imperial Court evince an attitude of strictly correct, wait-and-see impartiality about the Saionji case. Viscount Musha-no-koji Kintomo, director of the Peerage and Heraldry Bureau, was deeply concerned that his close association with the young Saionji might trouble the Throne. After consulting Hirohito, Kido assured Musha-no-koji that there was no cause for alarm: Hirohito himself would protect the Court from guilt by association and would see to it that young Saionji was fairly treated. In public token of the fact that the Saionji case must not be judged too hastily, Kido himself ostentatiously undertook the ceremonial duty of go-between in arranging the fashionable wedding of Saionji Fujio, a grandnephew of the late prime-minister-maker, with Aikawa Haruko, the daughter of Aikawa Yoshisuke, who had brought common-stock financing to Japan in the 1920's and had managed the industrial development of Manchukuo for the Army in the 1930's.

The marriage of Fujio and Haruko was celebrated at Frank Lloyd Wright's Imperial Hotel on the afternoon of April 3, 1942. The guest list included enough titled courtiers and beribboned admirals and generals to impress upon even the most zealous military secret policeman that the Saionji name was not to be dragged in the mud lightly. At the same time it was noted that

Prince Konoye had begun to speak politely, almost meekly, of Prime Minister Tojo. This was because Kido had had a brutally frank conversation in private with Konoye before the wedding, on March 20, and had, in Kido's own words, "strongly and persistently impressed upon Konoye the need for prudence."

After the wedding, on April 12, the chastened Konoye, who despite his years as prime minister remained the youngest and most easily teased of Hirohito's Big Brothers, called on Kido and obediently "submitted for an opinion" a draft of a memoir on the course of the Japanese-American prewar peace negotiations. Kido curtly urged him to take it home and rewrite it; it did not yet go far enough as a document of state in exculpating the Emperor.

This was the background against which Peace Faction leader Yoshida Shigeru called on Kido at his room in the Outer Palace on June 11, 1942, six days after the Battle of Midway. Yoshida knew that all chance of winning the war had been lost and felt that the Peace Faction must take diplomatic action at once to salvage as much as possible of Japan's empire before attrition set in. He proposed to Kido that Prince Konoye be sent immediately to Europe—with himself, Yoshida, in attendance as guardian-secretary—and there make a serious effort to see Allied diplomats and work out the terms of a peace settlement.

Yoshida submitted his proposal in the form of a letter written on paper suitable for presentation to the Throne. In this remarkable document—previously untranslated—the sixty-three-year-old Yoshida showed scant respect for the fifty-year-old Konoye, acute solicitude for Hirohito's personal pride, and a total lack of appreciation for the swiftness of events in a world at war:

Mr. Konoye's primary purpose at the present pass is to do his utmost for the completion of the war and the establishment of a lasting peace. He might well take with him an ambassador or other emissary and a staff of Foreign Ministry experts. Under the guise of an inspection trip to Europe, he would travel west and on the way, whenever invited, he would talk to the heads of states and to various local leaders. He should proceed through the Soviet Union and other nations and on the way, in his informal capacity, should stop for a while in some such neutral state as Switzerland which is strategically situated between the belligerent camps. There he would be able to watch the development of political affairs and at the same time his suite would be able to induce influential men of various nations to approach him.

If Germany then seemed to be winning, U.S. and British representatives might come to him, looking for a way out. If otherwise, Germany might turn to him with similar purpose. His background leads me [Yoshida] to think that both the United States and Germany would consider him their ally. If I [Yoshida] take due advantage of that fact, I could become the vanguard leader of the peace.

If after several seasons in Europe, there does not seem to be any ray of hope, Konoye should start for home as if nothing had happened. On the other hand, if there is hope, I [Yoshida] will invite suitable cultural and military officials, scholars, and business leaders— always when possible men with good connections in Europe or America —to join us and help us prepare a draft of a peace treaty which may be submitted to His Majesty as an initial position paper. At the same time we shall try to enlighten the nation as to where our true interests lie. Once the time comes ripe for world peace, Konoye will thus be enabled, at the request of the imperial government, to attend the peace conference as a plenipotentiary, taking with him all the responsible members of his suite. I, as a member, will be in charge of the peace-making business at his plenipotentiary headquarters.

Not too surprisingly Kido pocketed Yoshida's letter and told the prime-minister-to-be of postwar Japan that, before he and Konoye could go on a peace junket to Europe, there was "much to be considered." No doubt Konoye and Yoshida might get better terms than Japan would be able to get if she fought on. But Kido, as a civilian, was not sure enough of his assessment of the military situation to be positive that this was so. And he knew that the people, after all the sacrifices they had made, the triumphs they had gained, and the propaganda they had swallowed, would never accept a realistic peace settlement now when they seemed to own all Asia. Hirohito himself had not yet given up the war. He might be persuaded personally that he had lost his gamble and that it would be best to give back the Indies, the Philippines, Malaya, and China in return for Manchuria and oil concessions in Borneo, but publicly the institution of the Throne could not afford to seem so cowardly and sell so short.

Konoye's proposed trip abroad might be of use later in the war if Japan's empire began to prove costly for the Americans to recapture. Now, after the Battle of Midway, it could only impress the West as an admission of weakness. It could serve no purpose which could not be served as well by the tentative informal conversations which were taking place and getting nowhere between Japanese and Allied spokesmen in Rome, Lisbon, Teheran, Bern, Buenos Aires, Madrid, Moscow, Stockholm, and Bangkok. Later in the war, perhaps, when the democracies began to appreciate the immense military strength of Russia and the Japanese people began to feel weariness, hunger, and fear, it might be possible to negotiate a peace acceptable politically to both sides.

Kido was bound by his oath of office to tell Hirohito of Yoshida's proposal. Being a loyal vassal he presumably performed his bounden duty, but if so, he did not record the particulars in his diary. Instead Japan maintained a greedy appearance before the world and let slip her last chance of negotiating an advantageous peace.

"WHAT CAN THESE SHIPS BE?"

Before sending any special plenipotentiaries abroad, Hirohito hoped to recoup the Midway disaster and regain a bargaining position for the various peace emissaries he had posted to neutral capitals. In this endeavor the Japanese Army undertook to do by land what the Navy, at the Battle of the Coral Sea, had failed to do by sea: break in the door of northeastern Australia.

On July 21, 1942, an augmented Japanese regiment of about 8,000 men landed at Buna on the northeast coast of the island of New Guinea. Without opposition they established a beachhead and began to move inland toward the 7,000-foot passes of the Owen Stanley Range which lay athwart the overland route to Port Moresby. Australian scouts watched their advance and MacArthur began hurriedly to organize forces which would contest their passage through the mountains.

Hirohito and his staff at Imperial Headquarters expected that the Army thrust across New Guinea would be the focus of war activity in the months ahead. The day after the New Guinea landing, however, on July 22, 1942, the U.S. 1st Marine Division set out from Wellington, New Zealand, to create an altogether different theater of war which the Tokyo General Staffs had not contemplated. The Marines held a dress rehearsal in the New Hebrides north of New Zealand and went on, on August 7, to land 11,000 strong on an island still farther north, in the nominally Japanese-occupied Solomon Islands. Their selected target was the second most southern island in the chain, one that they would make famous, a Delaware-sized mound of coral, rain forest, and inactive volcano: Guadalcanal.

Guadalcanal was held by 2,500 Japanese of whom 400 were soldiers and the rest laborers and engineers. They were at work building an advance airstrip there. They made no effort to contest the U.S. landing but sent off a plaintive radio message to the Japanese stronghold of Rabaul 650 miles to the north, asking, "What can these ships be?" Then when the ships began disgorging, they hurriedly abandoned their half-built airstrip and retreated into the jungles of the interior.

The Japanese lack of fight disappointed some Marines, but most found their hands full enough without having to contend with hostile enemy fire. The jungle alone prevented the men of the first wave from reaching the positions which they were supposed to occupy on their first night ashore. Behind them, the beaches were piled high with unsorted, unmoved supplies—a logistic nightmare. Beyond, in the surf, landing barges milled about in confusion, vying with one another for empty stretches of beach where more cargo could be dumped and left as quickly as possible.

Hirohito and Combined Fleet commander Admiral Yamamoto were both informed of the American landing promptly, and in less than four hours forty-five Japanese planes out of Rabaul were diverted from a raid on New Guinea to an attack on the nascent American beachhead. An Australian coast-watcher, left behind months earlier on the Japanese-held island of Bougainville, saw the Betties and Zeros pass overhead and gave forty-five minutes' warning of their coming on his jungle radio. As a result, several hundred American airmen from carriers *Saratoga*, *Wasp*, and *Enterprise* were ready and waiting over the U.S. beachhead when the Japanese planes came in. Avoiding the eighteen Zeros, they dived on the twenty-seven Betties and wrought such havoc that the Japanese bombardiers scored but one direct hit, on the destroyer *Mugford*.

Less than half the Betties survived and started for home. The Zeros stayed on, looking for revenge. The Grumman Wildcat pilots obliged with a dogfight—but cautiously. They held together in six-plane clusters and made the most of their superior numbers. Even so they lost several planes and splashed only one Zero. They took, however, something of greater importance to the morale of the Misty Lagoon virtuosos: the right eye of one of the greatest air aces of World War II, Sakai Saburo.

Sakai had been dogfighting since 1937 and had sixty planes to his credit, plus a score or more probables. He came up from the rear on the bellies of eight planes, in a group, which he thought to be Wildcats. Too late, as he closed with them, he realized that they were bigger than Wildcats, some of the new Avenger-class torpedo bombers. They looked like Wildcats from the rear and they had lured him in by feigning fear and tightening up their formation. Realizing that he had been trapped, he put his engine on overboost and tried to jump through them with his guns blazing. He hit two of them and was riddled by all sixteen of their tail guns. A burst shattered his windshield and caught him in the head.

Moments later Sakai regained consciousness in the full freshness of the slipstream which poured into his perforated cockpit. He did not know it at the time but his right eye had been destroyed and his left was lidded with dried blood from head wounds. Spitting on his scarf to wipe away the blindness, flying sometimes right-side up and then again repeatedly upside down, regaining consciousness again and again off on a tangent or just above the water, he somehow managed to fly a devious route home to Rabaul. Over the empty ocean and the occasional green islets, his moments of sober compass study and recollection served him miraculously. With the little vision left in his left eye he landed his plane that evening, empty of gas and two hours after the other stragglers of his flight had already come in. The best eye surgeon in Tokyo enabled him to keep the sight of his left eye, to become a flight instructor and test pilot, and even to go back into action in a Zero against the next generation of U.S. planes over Iwo Jima in 1944. Again he would survive and would emerge from the war credited with sixty-four Chinese, British,

Dutch, and U.S. combat aircraft, a record unexcelled by any other living ace of the war in the Pacific.[1]

THE SALVOS OF SAVO

During the hours of Sakai's flight home to Rabaul, Hirohito was considering the threat of the American landing on Guadalcanal. He was vacationing at the time in Nikko, the magnificent mausoleum city of the Tokugawas, some 75 miles north of Tokyo. As an expert geographer, he did not need to be told that Guadalcanal lay 650 miles south of the Japanese advance air base of Rabaul and over 780 miles north of the advance U.S. air base on Efate in the New Hebrides. How many American troops had come ashore was unclear to him, but evidently they planned to stay because they were reported to have laden the beaches with supplies and to have set up anti-aircraft guns. If left to their own devices they would complete the airstrip begun by Hirohito's own engineers and from this unsinkable platform would be in a position to seize control of both air and sea in the southern Solomons area.

There were two ways of countering the American threat: land men on Guadalcanal in an attempt to drive out the Americans, or try to neutralize the new American base by building in haste and in secret rival airfields on other islands of the southern Solomons like San Cristobal or Malaita. Since Japanese air routes to Rabaul were shorter than U.S. supply routes to New Zealand and the New Hebrides, even one Japanese airstrip in the southern Solomons would have an advantage over the field which the Americans were preparing.

Nevertheless, on the advice of his military aides, Hirohito decided to launch a counterinvasion of Guadalcanal. It was a questionable decision—if only because top Army generals, who would have to supply the troops for the effort, considered Guadalcanal a Navy problem and refused to appreciate its strategic importance. Adroit commanders of the dissident Strike-North group,

---

[1] Two other Japanese, who died, ran up higher scores: Nishizawa Hiroyoshi, 104, and Sugita Shoichi, eighty. In Europe, however, Sakai's mark was topped by two Finnish aces and over a score of Germans, led by the "Black Devil of the Ukraine," Erich Hartmann, who accounted for no less than 352 Allied planes. The top Allied ace, excluding Russians, was Richard Bong of the U.S. Air Force, with forty kills, all made in the Pacific Theater.

who were charged with the defense of Manchuria against the Russians, had only recently recovered the crack units which they had lent to the Strike South in 1941. To the best of their bureaucratic abilities they did not mean to lend again. General Yamashita had returned to their midst embittered, his plan for invading Australia vetoed. On his way back from Singapore to Mukden, he had not been given a victory parade in Tokyo. Indeed he had not been allowed to land in Japan at all, not even to see his family.

Because of the sulky attitude of General Yamashita and his partisans in the Kwantung Army, Chief of Staff Sugiyama planned to use only the troops available in the eastern part of the Empire to repel the American invaders. These, he assured Hirohito, would be more than sufficient. The 28th Regiment, formerly of the 17th Division but now in process of being built up to a division in its own right, was awaiting orders in Guam where it had gone for the aborted invasion of Midway. The 35th Brigade, 18th Division, could be detached from occupation forces in the Philippines and in the Palau Islands east of the Philippines. The 2d Division and, if necessary, most of the 38th Division could be spared from garrison duty in the East Indies. In all 60,000 well-trained troops could be thrown at the Americans without drawing at all from the continental forces in General Yamashita's sphere of influence. The problem would be to provide transports and naval escorts which could move the men for the counterinvasion to Guadalcanal.

The Rabaul commander, Vice Admiral Mikawa Gunichi, began immediately to test the difficulty of the transport problem. On the very night of the American landing, as soon as Hirohito had made his decision, Mikawa embarked all spare sailors and soldiers in Rabaul on six small transports and sent them on their way toward Guadalcanal. The next afternoon, August 8, U.S. submarine S-38 waylaid the little convoy and sank the largest of the transports with two well-placed torpedoes. More than 300 of the troops drowned and Mikawa recalled the other five transports to Rabaul.

That night the last of some 500 Japanese troops on two islets, Tulagi and Gavutu, off the north coast of Guadalcanal died fighting. They took with them more than 200 U.S. Marines. This small, violent action, in which no quarter was asked or given, put a seal of blood and pride on Hirohito's decision. The right to possess the 2,500 square miles of jungle on Guadalcanal would be contested bitterly for the next five and a half months.

A few hours later, at 1 A.M. August 9, Admiral Mikawa arrived in person off Guadalcanal with five heavy cruisers, two light cruisers, and a destroyer. His crews were in perfect prewar trim, unthinned by replacements and undaunted by the process of attrition which had already overtaken the crews and pilots of Japanese carriers. Mikawa's men had long specialized in night engagements and had trained for this moment for years: the first artillery duel between Japanese and U.S. surface fleets.

Mikawa surprised an equal force of U.S. cruisers and destroyers, equipped with radar, and sank it. In this Battle of Savo Island four Allied cruisers and a destroyer went to the bottom. Another cruiser and two destroyers were crippled and had to be sent home to dry dock. About 1,600 Allied sailors, most of them Americans, perished in the action—an action for which the exact casualties remain to this day officially untabulated in the U.S. Navy Department. Admiral Mikawa lost no ships and only fifty-eight men killed and fifty-three wounded. He later attributed his victory to the carelessness of U.S. commanders, the poor marksmanship of U.S. gunners, and the excellence of the Japanese oxygen-powered torpedo.

Despite his victory, or perhaps because of it, Admiral Mikawa returned to Rabaul without landing more than a few hundred troops as reinforcements for the tiny body of Japanese hiding in the Guadalcanal jungle.

Hirohito cut short his vacation at Nikko and on August 12 returned to Tokyo.

So began a routine of survival which became increasingly familiar and lethal to both sides. Every afternoon, a little before dusk, when U.S. planes had started home for their airstrip on Guadalcanal, a Japanese surface fleet—of destroyers usually—would break south from the area of Japanese Rabaul-based air superiority. At close to thirty knots, heading down "the Slot"—the channel between New Georgia and Santa Isabel islands—the Japanese raiders would arrive off Guadalcanal shortly after midnight. There they would have an hour to shell the U.S. airstrip, now named Henderson Field, and to land reinforcements on Cape Esperance at the Japanese end of the island. At about

1:30 A.M. they would turn and run for home, just in time to be taken under wing by Japanese early-morning patrols from Rabaul before being overtaken by planes launched at dawn from Henderson Field.

By day the tables would be turned. Holes in Henderson Field would be bulldozed over; damaged U.S. planes would be dragged from the underbrush, patched up, and put in the air with amazing celerity. Until the next sunset the U.S. dry-land air base would reassert unassailable authority over 100 miles of sea in every direction. Japanese ships would shun the area and marching Japanese soldiers on their end of Guadalcanal would prudently skirt clearings.

U.S. strategists sought repeatedly to break Japan's reign over the night. Theoretically, U.S. skippers had a great advantage because radar, which had not yet been installed in Japanese vessels, made it possible to "see in the dark" and take a bead on approaching Japanese vessels before their crews had been called to quarters. Vigilant Japanese crews, however, slept by their guns and responded instantly when fired upon. U.S. guns, as yet, were not powered by flashless explosives. Given one spurt of flame in the night, one target, and the Japanese gunners and torpedo men were always ready to demonstrate their expert marksmanship. As a result, the nightly "Tokyo Express" of Japanese destroyers repeatedly emerged from U.S. traps claiming correctly that they had ambushed their ambushers.

Japanese strategists, for their part, kept trying to break the U.S. hold over the daylight hours. Again and again large flights of Zeros and Betties seized control of the air over Guadalcanal for a few hours, shot up U.S. air facilities, and returned home after suffering heavy losses and achieving nothing permanent. The next morning there were always planes again to take off from Henderson Field and resist the next Japanese air raid.

Japan did not possess the thousands of planes flying in waves from Rabaul which would have been needed to keep uninterrupted daytime air superiority over Guadalcanal. Consequently U.S. pilots always had time to land and refuel between Japanese raids. In addition, since they fought near home, they could often bail out and survive after their planes had been technically shot down. A day or two later they would be back in action with a new plane or one put together from a dozen wrecks by Henderson Field's uncanny mechanics. As the days passed these U.S. advantages told heavily on the thinning ranks of the Misty Lagoon airmen. New Japanese pilots, arriving daily in Rabaul from accelerated flight courses, proved increasingly incompetent. The mighty Zero, when flown too often without adequate overhaul, proved increasingly treacherous. By the end of August Japanese pilots were flying mostly one-way missions and were saving these supremely patriotic efforts for occasions when they could do something valuable to further the objectives of the next night's Tokyo Express.

TOJO'S THIRD HAT

The deteriorating Guadalcanal situation made Hirohito edgy and precipitated a crisis in the Cabinet. Foreign Minister Togo persisted in looking upon the conquests of the Strike South as temporary acquisitions made solely for the purpose of striking a better bargain with the United States. Hirohito acknowledged that the territories Japan had seized might have to be given back if the war went wrong, but he refused to think of them as poker chips and nothing more. He had liberated them from Western colonialism. He had added their strength to the Empire. At the very least, they represented distances and battlegrounds which would cost the barbarian dear and keep him out of the homeland for many years.

Buffered by the conquered territories, Hirohito thought he could look forward to a long, slow war. After Midway he had ordered Japan's next generation of airplanes and other weapons to be ready for mass production by the end of 1944. He had encouraged Army commanders to build monuments to Japanese war dead in Singapore and Manila, to establish schools for teaching the Japanese language to the natives, and to select local leaders to head puppet governments—José Laurel in the Philippines, Sukarno in Indonesia, Ba Maw and U Nu in Burma.

Foreign Minister Togo refused to take seriously the Co-Prosperity Sphere and the New Order in East Asia. He assigned lowly Foreign Ministry clerks to handle relations with the various quisling governments. He kept all his skilled diplomats at work on the peace problem: on relations with Hitler and Mussolini, the possible victors, and on dealings with neutral nations, the possible mediators.

At the urging of the retired ubiquitous Lieutenant General Suzuki Tei-ichi, chief of the Cabinet Planning Board for wartime legislation, Hirohito had decided to create a Greater East Asia Ministry which would relieve Togo of responsibility for intramural Co-Prosperity Sphere diplomacy. Togo at first had acquiesced in the new ministry as a piece of unimportant imperial finery, but on second thought he had realized that he might be hampered in peace negotiations with the West unless he could speak knowledgeably for the native political leaders in the former Asiatic colonies of the West.

In particular Togo saw that he must keep the right to negotiate with Chiang Kai-shek. If all diplomacy in Asia came under the authority of the proposed new ministry, the only channel to Chiang would be through the puppet Chinese government of Wang Ching-wei. Wang would muddy the waters and prevent the making of the sort of realistic settlement with China which Togo saw as a necessary preliminary to peace with the West. China was beaten. Japan was in process of being beaten. Asia must salvage itself from the wreckage. Hirohito had agreed in principle that all Japanese troops should be withdrawn from China. On this pledge Togo had high hopes of constructing a mutually face-saving treaty with China. Without such a treaty, Togo saw no prospect of making a bargain with the United States. And without a free hand for himself, unrestricted by the proposed Greater East Asia Ministry, Togo feared that he would be unable to negotiate fruitfully with Chiang Kai-shek.

Togo felt fortified in his convictions after talking to Nomura, Kurusu, and other members of the former Japanese Embassy in Washington who returned to Yokohama on a diplomatic exchange ship on August 20, 1942. Lord Privy Seal Kido's daughter and his son-in-law, Tsuru Shigeto, a lawyer and member of the spy service, were also among those repatriated. The homecomers told of the incredible unity which had been wrought in the United States by Pearl Harbor and of the fearsome all-out mobilization of U.S. industry. Hirohito gave lunch to Nomura and Kurusu on August

21 and on August 25 received a briefing from repatriated Navy Captain Yokoyama Ichiro—also of the former Washington staff—who had had charge of Japanese espionage in the United States.

Also on August 25, Foreign Minister Togo came to the palace to speak against the proposed Greater East Asia Ministry and to urge Hirohito to pursue negotiations with Chiang Kai-shek as expeditiously and sincerely as possible. Hirohito listened non-committally, spoke irrelevantly of his chats with the repatriates from Washington, and obliquely reminded Togo of the Foreign Ministry's failure to declare war on time the previous December. The thorny Togo felt rebuked and left the palace looking even more stiffly correct than usual.

A week later, on September 1, the establishment of the Greater East Asia Ministry came formally before the Cabinet for a vote. Foreign Minister Togo refused to make the vote unanimous and insisted that, if the new ministry was established, he would have to resign. Prime Minister-War Minister Tojo reported to the palace that he, too, would have to resign unless Togo could be brought around. Hirohito asked why Togo could not simply be replaced with a different foreign minister. He was told that no qualified diplomat was willing to set himself up as an opponent of the upright Togo by stepping immediately into Togo's shoes. Hirohito suggested that, in that case, Prime Minister Tojo could hold the portfolio of foreign minister along with those of war and prime minister which he already held.

Tojo demurred. He had already taken responsibility for representing both military and civilian factions in the government. If he also undertook to represent both the war and peace factions in it, his political position would become untenably broad.

Hirohito was "surprised" by General Tojo's modesty and called in Navy Minister Shimada to do something quickly to find a way out of the impasse. Shimada went directly from the Throne Room to an hour and a half tête-à-tête with Prime Minister Tojo. At 5 P.M. September 1, when the conversation had been going on for an hour, Shimada phoned Lord Privy Seal Kido and asked that a further, more complete clarification of Tojo's position be made to the Throne. Twenty-five minutes later, when Hirohito had promised to understand all the fine points of Tojo's scruples, Tojo relented, agreed to fire Togo, and undertook to wear, for himself, all three hats of prime minister, war minister, and foreign minister.

Two weeks later, when the crusty Togo had retired and diplomatic passions had been calmed, a pair of minor members of the Eleven Club, Tani Masayuki and Aoki Kazuo, agreed respectively to shoulder the positions of foreign minister and Greater East Asia minister in the resuscitated Tojo Cabinet. In that interim, on September 7, Baron Hiranuma, the long-faced lawyer who was the leader of Japan's most respectable conservatives, saw the Emperor in private audience about the "Chungking Operation." The next day, September 8, a special envoy was dispatched to China, with Hirohito's instructions, to renew peace negotiations with Chiang Kai-shek. The negotiations would continue, off and on, at the same high, secret, official level throughout the rest of the war. They would accomplish nothing but exchange of ideas until Japan finally admitted defeat. Then, however, they would contribute to the Japanese Army's efficient turnover of eastern China to the forces of Chiang Kai-shek rather than to those of Mao Tse-tung.

SEESAW STRUGGLE OF SUPPLY

In Washington, too, the costly insolubles of the Guadalcanal situation caused much political anguish. Officially the U.S. government was committed to total support of Great Britain against Germany and minimal attention to the Japanese threat against Australia. President Roosevelt, however, had appointed Admiral Ernest J. King to over-all command of the two U.S. fleets, and King was well known to be far more interested in the Pacific than in the Atlantic. On taking office, he had single-handedly committed several important U.S. officials, one by one, to the Guadalcanal gamble. Now, with President Roosevelt's assistance, he was repeatedly finding new planes and ships which could be subtracted from the "crusade in Europe" and stuffed into the breaches being blown in Japan's stubborn defense of Guadalcanal.

For the sake of Guadalcanal's pestiferous swamps and solemn, empty forests, no less than seven major fleet engagements were fought and no less than four major Japanese land offensives were repulsed. Only after these actions could U.S. forces call the tiny

Guadalcanal beachhead their own and go on to occupy and investigate the other 2,400 square miles of the island.

The Savo Island engagement, first of several U.S. naval disasters, was followed, on August 18, by the landing on Guadalcanal of the Japanese augmented 28th Regiment, which had been standing by on Guam since the Midway rebuff. This regiment was led by Colonel Ikki Kiyonao (or Ichiki Kiyonao as he is usually but incorrectly called), a kinsman of Hirohito's pre-1933 Imperial Household Minister Ikki Kitokuro. Colonel Ikki led his men against U.S. positions in one of the first large banzai charges of the war. The well-entrenched Marines stood by their machine guns and repulsed the attack with dreadful slaughter, killing more than 800 Japanese and losing only fifty Marines.

Another naval battle ensued for the right to land more Japanese reinforcements on Guadalcanal. It is remembered as the Battle of the Eastern Solomons. It was an air engagement, fought on August 24–25 between Japanese and U.S. carrier pilots. It ended in a numerical victory for the United States. The 10,000-ton light carrier *Ryujo* and destroyer *Mutsuki* were lost by Japan, while the U.S. carrier *Enterprise* was forced to withdraw after three direct bomb hits and a heavy loss of life.

Despite the American victory, the Japanese were able to land on Guadalcanal most of the 35th Brigade, 18th Division, from the Philippines and Palau: another 10,000 or more men to add to the 8,000–9,000 survivors of Ikki's 28th Regiment. The newcomers were commanded by Major General Hyakutake Seikichi,[2] the younger brother of Hirohito's Grand Chamberlain Admiral Hyakutake Saburo.

While Hyakutake's men marched to their positions through the jungle, the Japanese Navy forced some late adjustments on the balance sheet left by the Battle of the Eastern Solomons. On August 28 Marine dive-bombers caught the Tokyo Express at sunset and lit a fire in *Asagiri* which blew the Japanese destroyer out of the water. During the breakfast hour on August 31, submarine

---

[2] Also known as Hyakutake Haruyoshi and Hyakutake Harukichi. He himself used Seikichi, the Chinese-ified form of his given name, for prewar *Who's Who* entries. His parents preferred Haruyoshi, the Japanese reading. Harukichi, found in previous English-language accounts, is a mixed reading coined by a SCAP interpreter.

I-26 torpedoed the U.S. aircraft carrier *Saratoga,* forcing her to withdraw from the theater of operations for over three months. On September 3 and 5 were sunk three old U.S. destroyers on transport duty, *Colhoun* by bombing, *Little* and *Gregory* by shellfire from the "Express."

Hyakutake's fresh troops mounted full-scale bayonet charges against Marine trenches on the nights of September 12 and 13. A recorded fifty-nine Marines and 708 Japanese died. On September 16 Hirohito personally informed Lord Privy Seal Kido that the Japanese counterattack had failed.

Hyakutake had his men withdraw and regroup by dint of long treks through the jungle. They lacked food. They lacked medicine. They found no farms to pillage. The barks and herbs of the rain forest provided bitter sustenance. By the time they had complied with orders, they had lost far more men to malaria and hunger than they had ever lost to bullets.

On September 14, during Hyakutake's retreat, the submarines of Big Brother Marquis Komatsu's wolf pack enjoyed a run of luck. They heavily damaged the U.S. battleship *North Carolina,* standing off Guadalcanal; fatally damaged the destroyer *O'Brien;* and sank on the spot the carrier *Wasp.* Only two U.S. carriers remained seaworthy in the Pacific: *Hornet* and *Enterprise.* Despite the U.S. defeat and while Tokyo celebrated it, American Admiral Fletcher, on September 18, ran an unexpected convoy up to Guadalcanal and succeeded in landing the whole of the U.S. 7th Marine Division and all its supplies before Japanese airmen at Rabaul were aware of what had happened.

For the first time the U.S. troops on Guadalcanal had adequate supplies of chewing gum, cigarettes, earth-moving equipment, and ammunition. Some of the supplies, to be sure, were not strictly essential. White shoe polish, for instance, soon glutted the Marines' barter market. On the other hand, some useless items possessed great morale-building potential, and a few days after the 7th Marines' landing every man jack on the island was issued, with breakfast, three condoms. The shouts of delight could be heard almost to Rabaul. Visionaries spoke of the day when nurses and W.A.C.'s would arrive on the island. Realists wrote letters home describing the new general-issue containers that would keep candy fresh in the swamps. On September 23, Marine commander

Brigadier General Alexander Vandegrift mounted his first serious offensive against Japanese positions on the east end of the island. He gave it up quickly when sixty-seven Marines were mowed down from well-placed, well-entrenched Japanese gun positions.

Ten days later, over Prime Minister Tojo's objections, Hirohito publicly upheld the sentence of death passed on three of the captured American fliers who had bombed Tokyo with Doolittle. He thereby impressed upon the Japanese masses that they were in a war to the death.

On the night of October 11–12, the U.S. fleet again ambushed the Tokyo Express, this time successfully. For U.S. destroyer *Duncan*, which was sunk, the Japanese skippers parted with heavy cruiser *Furutaka* and destroyers *Fubuki*, *Muragumo*, and *Natsugumo*, also sunk. At last U.S. surface vessels could claim a victory. It was marred only slightly by the fact that the Japanese ships before they sank had made a major supply drop to Hyakutake's troops on the island. This small Japanese accomplishment was immediately nullified, on October 13, when advance groups of the 164th Regiment of the U.S. Army began landing on the island. That night, however, two Japanese battleships came down the Slot with the usual Tokyo Express of destroyers and turned big guns on Henderson Field for seventy minutes. Thirty-four of the thirty-nine U.S. dive-bombers on the field and sixteen of the forty Wildcat fighters were destroyed beyond repair.

The Japanese naval sacrifice was followed by the largest offensive yet on the part of the gradually built up Japanese land forces. In addition to the remnants of Ikki's men and Hyakutake's men, most of the Japanese 2d Division from the East Indies was now stealing about through the jungle. The combined Japanese force of some 30,000 men was led by a new commander, Lieutenant General Maruyama Masao, a former military-academy classmate of Hirohito's two uncles and a late (1923) recruit of Hirohito's early spy ring in Europe. Being a fully professional soldier and not merely a nepotistic adjunct of the Imperial Court like Ikki and Hyakutake before him, Maruyama promised sure results. He marshaled his men for a three-pronged attack which was to be coordinated with a major Japanese fleet effort.

Due to breakdowns in communications and delays imposed by

the jungle, the big Japanese effort dissipated itself over a four-day period like a string of wet firecrackers. The tank attack took place a day early, on October 23, because the tank commander had failed to hear of a twenty-four-hour postponement. Nine tanks and 600 infantrymen perished as a result. On October 24 Maruyama's main effort piled 2,000 corpses before Marine entrenchments but failed, at bayonet point, to overrun them. Two nights later a Japanese regiment, which had been detained by the jungle, burst from the trees in one last banzai fizzle. More than 2,000 Japanese soldiers had been killed and had taken with them less than 200 of their well-entrenched Marine adversaries. In the words of a Marine commander, Maruyama's men had fallen prey to "impetuosity, arrogance, and tactical inflexibility."

During the land action on October 25, the U.S. and Japanese carrier fleets closed to within striking distance of one another in an effort—the Santa Cruz Islands battle—to provide air cover for the men ashore. The Japanese task force withdrew after carriers *Zuiho* and *Shokaku* and heavy cruiser *Chikuma* had been severely damaged and light cruiser *Yura* had been sunk. The U.S. force, however, had lost permanently the services of destroyer *Porter* and carrier *Hornet*. Only one U.S. carrier in the whole Pacific, the *Enterprise,* remained operative, and once again the redoubtable *Enterprise* had sustained much damage, including the loss of forty-four crewmen killed.

HUNGRY AND MAROONED

Hirohito bleakly admitted to Kido on October 27: "The second attack has failed. We will make another." Kido had spent the week encouraging the Peace Faction to perfect its undercover organization and to pursue its preparation of cover stories against the contingency of defeat. He had met with Konoye in Tokyo University Detached Hospital on October 21 and had arranged since then for a clandestine meeting of all important peace proponents early in November at which they could be briefed on the political problems of peace and assigned specific missions. On October 28, after acknowledging the failure of the "second attack," Hirohito gave his personal instructions to a new Japanese ambassador to Rome, Hidaka Shunrokuro, empowering him to assure the Vatican that Japanese armies were ready to withdraw from China and that Japanese claims to a privileged-nation status in Southeast Asia would be minimal if peace could be restored.

President Franklin D. Roosevelt, too, was nervous. As a nautical enthusiast and former Assistant Secretary of the Navy, he was alarmed by the disappearance of U.S. carriers from Guadalcanal waters and fearful lest the Marine heroes, on the eve of the 1942 Congressional elections, be cut off from air support. Minutes after the sinking of carrier *Hornet* at the Santa Cruz Islands Battle, he memoed the chiefs of staff "to make sure that every possible weapon gets into that area to hold Guadalcanal."

In response to Roosevelt's pressure, the Marines on October 30 mounted their second offensive against the Japanese end of Guadalcanal and were again repulsed after seventy-one Marines had been killed. The Japanese positions attacked were those of General Hyakutake's men. General Maruyama and General Ikki were both lost in the interior of the island, still retreating, starving, and trying to regroup after their disastrous repulse a week earlier.

During the Marines' election-eve attack, General Hyakutake wired urgently for relief on behalf of his debilitated forces. In the first week of November two battalions of the Japanese 38th Division from the East Indies—some 5,000 men—were duly landed by the Tokyo Express to be added to the hungry mouths already present.

On November 8, with the elections over, Vice Admiral William Halsey, U.S. Navy Commander South Pacific, called personally at Guadalcanal to take a firsthand look at the situation. He was regaled on his first night by a shelling from the Tokyo Express and a bombing from "Washing-Machine Charley," the one extraordinary Japanese night pilot who regularly marked Henderson Field for the offshore destroyers by dropping flares and a 250-pound bomb on it. After a night behind rotting sandbags, Halsey held a press conference in which he delivered a famous prescription for the winning of the war: "Kill Japs. Kill Japs. Keep on killing Japs."

The Japanese effort to supply Halsey with the most necessary ingredient for his formula—cannon fodder—reached its high point a week later when eleven Japanese transports carrying the remaining 17,000-odd men of the 38th Division set sail from Rabaul with suitable naval escort. There followed the naval Battle of Guadalcanal in which, once again, Japanese fleet units overcame U.S. radar advantages of foreknowledge and night vision with superior gunnery and ship management. The battle was rejoined on three successive evenings. When it was over the U.S. Navy had lost seven destroyers, plus three salvageable derelicts; two cruisers sunk and two heavily damaged; and one badly mauled battleship. The Japanese had lost only two battleships and two destroyers from the fleet but with them eleven transports and more than a tenth of the reinforcement troops of the 38th Division. Some of the surviving foot soldiers were dumped in the waters off Cape Esperance to make their way ashore and join the Japanese Guadalcanal expeditionary force; most were returned as salvage to Rabaul aboard Japanese destroyers.

The U.S. Navy had suffered another humiliating defeat, but the Japanese Navy had failed in its purpose of landing a fully equipped Japanese division on Guadalcanal. The United States already had two of its divisions on "the Canal," each equal in firepower and together equal in manpower to a Japanese division. The Japanese still had more than a division's worth of men on the island but not nearly enough ammunition, food, and medicine to make them able-bodied troops.

The news of the Navy's latest victorious failure reached Tokyo in the early morning hours of November 16. Prime Minister Tojo promptly called off a scheduled visit to Manila and points south. Hirohito ordered his former athletics director, Big Brother Admiral Komatsu, to devise means of using his wolf pack of submarines for supply purposes to keep the men on Guadalcanal from starving. Lord Privy Seal Kido belatedly digested news of the battle the next evening, November 17, while listening to orchestral extracts from *Götterdämmerung* at a farewell concert conducted by the great German maestro Felix Weingartner. Two days later, on the nineteenth, Hirohito asked Kido to make necessary arrangements for a state visit to be paid soon to the tombs of the imperial ancestors in Kyoto so that Hirohito could go to pray at the shrine of Amaterasu, the sun goddess, on Ise Peninsula.

Admiral Komatsu's submarine fleet experimented for several weeks with methods of using torpedo tubes to launch watertight drums of rice. While the tests were in progress, the 30,000 Japanese on Guadalcanal lived on root soups and ancient, mildewed packets of dried fish. By the end of November a minority of the front-line troops, manning the Japanese trenches, were fully ambulatory. The others waddled about on ankles plump with the fluids of beriberi. The destroyers of the Tokyo Express continued nightly to drop drums of supplies off Cape Esperance, but U.S. torpedo boats prevented the drops from being made close to shore and early morning U.S. strafing planes, plus fickle tides and currents, prevented many of the drums from ever being picked up by the hungry Japanese on the beaches.

By the end of the month, the Japanese had been goaded into piling the decks of the Tokyo Express with food containers and stuffing even some of the destroyers' torpedo tubes with rice and soya sauce. In the small hours of November 30 Halsey's men lay in wait for one of these supply runs with six destroyers and four heavy cruisers. Rear Admiral Tanaka Raizo—or as he was known to the Marines on 'Canal, "Tenacious Tanaka of the Tokyo Express"—had with him that night only eight destroyers of which six had been modified for transport duty and partially stripped of armament. Tanaka steamed unwarned into the American trap and emerged from the other side of it with all his sharpshooting gun crews blazing away at their best and luckiest. The fiasco which followed has never been fully explained, but some of the U.S. ships were certainly fired upon by one another as well as by the Japanese. Tanaka dropped no supplies that night, but his squadron expended all its torpedoes and returned to Bougainville with the loss of one destroyer. Behind him he left chaos. Heavy cruiser *Northampton* sank. Heavy cruiser *Minneapolis* had taken two Japanese torpedoes. Heavy cruiser *New Orleans* remained incredibly afloat and wallowed off for home under her own steam at five knots despite the loss of 120 feet of bow, more than a fifth of the ship. In the after engine room of heavy cruiser *Pensacola* a fire raged out of control for twelve hours. The bushwhackers had been whacked, and it was evident to U.S. captains that they had much to learn about the use of radar in night actions before they could depend on it.

Tanaka's brilliant victory did nothing to ease Hirohito's concern for the hunger of the 30,000-odd Japanese troops on Guadalcanal.

Somewhat tartly he ordered Big Brother Admiral Komatsu, whose carelessness had contributed so importantly to the defeat at Midway, to spare not his elite submarine corps in running the U.S. blockade. Over the grumbling of his skippers, Komatsu put eleven submarines on immediate Guadalcanal duty and a number more into dry dock for modification as underwater transports. By early January a score of I-boats had been fitted to carry "freight tubes." These were rafts, powered by two torpedoes and steered by a big rudder and a crewman in a loincloth. After the contraption was released from periscope depth, it bobbed to the surface and would carry two tons of food to a beach as much as two and a half miles away. By late January the underwater sleds and their valiant helmsmen were bringing ten ounces of rice a day to every one of the 30,000 famished defenders of Guadalcanal. In the supply operation, Admiral Komatsu, however, lost two of the veteran wolves of his pack: I–3 on December 9 and I–1 on January 29.

WAR'S FIRST BIRTHDAY

On the Guadalcanal beachhead, U.S. commanders waited for hunger and malaria to do their work in the Japanese ranks. The U.S. force now included elements of four Army divisions as well as of two Marine divisions. On December 7, the American anniversary of Pearl Harbor, Marine General Vandegrift turned over his command to the Army's Major General Alexander Patch and accompanied the sick and tired remnants of his 1st Marine Division to Australia for rest and rejuvenation. Less than two thirds of the men were still fit to sit in a trench. Many of them, on the happy day of embarkation, found themselves too weak to swarm up the cargo nets and had to be hauled aboard the transports in slings. No Marine was too weak, however, to mutter a last contented four-letter word at the sight of Guadalcanal dropping below the horizon.

Hirohito celebrated the end of the first year of war the next day, December 8, by exchanging empty telegrams of congratulations with Hitler and Mussolini. The Japanese carrier fleet had been lost at Midway. The rest of the aces of the Misty Lagoon had fallen one by one over Henderson Field. The Army's infantrymen had not been able to demonstrate their long-vaunted

spiritual superiority over the U.S. foot soldier. Only in the obsolescent art of surface fleet actions, which had brought Japan to
the fore as a military power in the days of Emperor Meiji, had
the hand of the samurai kept its cunning.

Hirohito's cup of misery was topped off to overflowing by his
mother, Empress Dowager Sadako. Three days before Pearl Harbor Sadako had withdrawn from Tokyo to her villa in Numazu
where she had sequestered herself with cronies of the late Prince
Saionji in visible demonstration of her antiwar sentiments. Hirohito had complained of her lack of patriotism; finally, on September 18, in a gesture of extraordinary humility and sincerity, he
had sent Empress Nagako personally to Numazu to remonstrate
with her. Unable to refuse Nagako's pleas, the lovely fifty-eight-
year-old queen mother had agreed to return to Tokyo on December 5 when she would have completed a full year of self-imposed
exile. She had kept her promise. Now, on December 8, she was
back in her Tokyo palace where she ceremonially belonged. But
Hirohito almost wished that he had let her stay in Numazu. He
understood that no sooner had she resumed residence than she
had begun telling her friends that she had come home to share
the suffering of the people of Tokyo in the months ahead.

On December 9, 1942, the first day of the second year of the
war, Hirohito arose with hearty gruffness to make a new start.
At 10:30, observing a quaint old Court custom, he bestowed articles of his apparel and other souvenirs on his most trusted courtiers and brusquely went on, at 10:35, to have an hour-long talk
with Lord Privy Seal Kido. Kido adjured him to do nothing rashly
logical, but to nurse the nation's resources, fight as long a war as
possible, and give his political advisors maximum opportunity to
salvage some sort of favorable settlement.

Hirohito went on to a liaison conference with the chiefs of staff
and principal Cabinet ministers at which was debated at length
and finally recommended to him for approval a most curious
act of state. From now on, it was resolved, the Emperor would
continue freely to attend liaison conferences as he had been doing
for the last fifteen months, but his attendance would no longer
convert the proceedings automatically into a Conference in the
Imperial Presence. Instead such meetings would now be officially
designated as Political-Military Liaison Conferences Which Hap-

pen To Take Place Before His Majesty.[3] The minutes of them would no longer have to be entered on the palace rolls. Observations made at them would no longer be officially binding reports to the Throne, on which a man staked his honor and his life, but simply thoughts and nothing more.

Prime Minister Tojo personally arose in the presence of Hirohito, who was present only unofficially, and promised to explain officially to Hirohito in the Throne Room the object of the resolution. It would enable Hirohito to communicate "frequently to his ministers his decisions regarding national imperial affairs and war guidance"; it would allow him to satisfy his need "to make sure of the decisive willingness of the members of the government and of the supreme command, as his duty-bound assistants, to carry out the war to its end"; and finally it would inaugurate the first of "frequent conferences with His Majesty undertaken without complex procedural arrangements and limitations."

Hirohito withdrew, nodding approvingly, to his Throne Room in the Outer Palace to receive Prime Minister Tojo's official report on the meeting which had just been held at Imperial Headquarters in the Imperial Palace. At last, in this moment of national emergency, Hirohito had been freed to exercise his authority openly without being held responsible, as a sacred institution, liable before the ancestors and the sun goddess, for every notion which tripped across his tongue. The mummery had ended and from now on appearances would have to be kept up only for the sake of the masses and of the Americans if they conquered.

Thirty-six hours later, at 7:50 A.M., Friday, December 11, 1942, Hirohito emerged in state from the *Niju-bashi* or Double-bridge Gate of the palace and with police sirens shrilling and tires screaming arrived at Tokyo station in time to pull out with his own chrysanthemum-emblazoned special train precisely at 8 A.M. The train stopped at Kyoto station at 4:10 P.M. Fifteen minutes later Hirohito stepped down from his Rolls-Royce in the palace grounds of his ancestors.[4]

[3] *Gozen ni Okeru Diahonei Seifu Renraku Kaigi.*

[4] In the interval he had nodded at dignitaries gathered to greet him in the station and had completed, at rush hour, through the narrow, crowded streets of the old capital, a drive for which modern "kamikaze" cabbies usually require fifteen minutes even in the early morning hours before sunup.

The next day, with equal dispatch and security, Hirohito traveled along the branch line from Kyoto south to Ise Peninsula and the shrine of the sun goddess, Amaterasu. From Ise station, in an amphitheater of wooded hills, his cavalcade drove to the holy Isuza River, through the great wooden π-shaped arch marking the entrance to the sacred precincts, and across the open park where pilgrims camped. He stopped at the "cleansing brook" for a traditional sip of water. On foot now, Hirohito and his retinue entered the forest of giant cryptomerias which surrounded the holy of holies. They paused at the fence, beyond which commoners could not go, then entered the hallowed enclosure of the shrine buildings. At the outer shrine belonging to the goddess of grain Hirohito officiated at a service for the continued fertility and prosperity of his people.

Then the Emperor of Japan left his worldly attendants behind him and went on alone, deeper into the forest, to the inner shrine of Amaterasu. It was a severely simple hut, preserving the architectural styles used by Hirohito's forebears when they still lived somewhere in southeastern Asia two thousand years earlier. It was built of unfinished ground cypress or *hinoki*, the tree of the sun, and thatched with bark of *hinoki*. The gable rafters from the interior crossed through lashings and protruded from the thatch in a pair of horns at either end of the roof. The eaves and doorposts were wrapped in ornaments of bright brass. White silk curtains stirred in the breeze before the entrance and on either side stood fresh branches of *sakaki*, the tree of the gods, *Cleyera ochnacea*, the Shinto equivalent of the mistletoe used by the ancient Druids of Britain.

Outside the inner shrine Hirohito was served a light midday repast by the chief priestess of Ise, a distant cousin. He was by now well versed in the Ise mysteries and no longer felt embarrassed by his high-priestly role in them. He had paid his first visit to the shrine a few days before leaving Japan in 1921 for his European tour. He had returned to it to report on his marriage in 1924, on his official enthronement in 1928, and again, on conquests, several times thereafter. He had now made his pilgrimage more often than any other Emperor before him, including even his devout grandfather, that deft master of the appropriate gesture, Emperor Meiji.

Hirohito munched the garnished rice slowly and gazed at the tall cryptomerias. Then he dismissed the priestess and passed alone into the holy of holies which housed the remains of Amaterasu's sacred mirror of wisdom. He spent almost an hour of prayer within while his retainers fidgeted in pious silence a stone's throw away at the outer shrine.

Kido wrote in his diary:

Since this was an unprecedented occasion, I did not dare to guess the depths of his feelings. It was enough to be one of his retainers and to assume the burden of honor in being able to attend him at such a momentous ceremony.

ADVANCING BACKWARD

Fortified by communion with the wellsprings of his race and his power, Hirohito returned to Tokyo the next day greatly relieved and ready at the same time to retrench and to fight on. During the next two weeks his grand chamberlain's brother, General Hyakutake, repulsed the third U.S. offensive on Guadalcanal with little difficulty. One entrenched Japanese veteran and five of the recently arrived U.S. Army G.I.'s died for every few feet of ground which changed hands. After suffering several hundred casualties, the G.I.'s withdrew. General Hyakutake, however, celebrated no triumph, for behind his lines men continued to die ignominiously of disease and malnutrition. Staff officers at palace headquarters clamored for a Japanese offensive, but Hyakutake advised that his men were too debilitated to mount one. In accordance with the sober realization he had reached at Ise, Hirohito decided to swallow his pride and the Army's and save as many men from the Guadalcanal debacle as possible.

The imperial decision to evacuate Guadalcanal was officially handed down by Hirohito at a meeting in the ironclad headquarters shed in the palace woods on the morning of December 31. After the meeting Hirohito said to Chief of Staff Sugiyama:

'Our withdrawal from Guadalcanal is regrettable. From now on the Army and Navy must co-operate better to accomplish our war objectives. I was thinking of issuing an imperial rescript of congratulations if we had taken Guadalcanal. What do you think of issuing one anyway? The men fought hard up to today, so I would like to issue such a rescript. When would be a suitable time?'

'At once would be best,' said Sugiyama thoughtfully. 'But the rescript cannot be issued publicly. It must be given to the commanders secretly.'

Hyakutake and the other Japanese commanders on Guadalcanal duly received the Emperor's words of praise a week later. Some of them murmured that they would have preferred an order to crawl forward and die fighting. Some of them journeyed to the front to see if they could not lead a banzai charge in which to end all the suffering. But the men in the trenches were too sick to move and their officers lacked enough lasting energy to organize them for any concerted action.

In a masterpiece of tact and deception a fresh battalion from the 38th Division in the East Indies was landed on Guadalcanal by the Tokyo Express on January 15 with the avowed purpose of spearheading a new Japanese offensive. Front-line Japanese troops were pried from their foxholes and heavily timbered rainforest bunkers with the reassuring promise that they were being redeployed for a final victorious battle. The Japanese fleet sortied in strength from its main base at Truk in the Carolines north of the Solomons and began to sail south.

Expecting suicidal attacks from both land and sea, U.S. commanders tightened their stomach muscles to preside over a great slaughter. Instead a small sea battle took place off Rennell Island to the south, and while it was being fought the Tokyo Express, from February 1 to February 7, 1943, evacuated from 1,000 to 3,000 Japanese from Guadalcanal every night. When the eight-day exodus had been completed at least 11,000 able-bodied Japanese soldiers had escaped; another 21,000 were found and counted as corpses by the U.S. forces; almost 10,000 more vanished from the books into the catch-all category of the missing.

Tokyo propagandists boasted of the evacuation as a great victory—a difficult tactical maneuver which they termed "an advance by turning." Japanese civilians were not deceived, however, and archly circulated many jokes about the virtues of "advancing backward." Nor were U.S. commanders unduly elated, for they had been cheated of living prey and left to destroy a charnel house.

Moreover the U.S. Navy had had the worst of its engagement with the Japanese decoy fleet in the waters off Rennell Island. After days of maneuvering, the Japanese vessels sailed home with only a few buckled plates while U.S. destroyers picked up crewmen from a sunken U.S. heavy cruiser, the *Chicago*.

In all, in the seven naval engagements associated with Guadalcanal—Savo Island, Eastern Solomons, Cape Esperance, Santa Cruz Islands, naval Battle of Guadalcanal, Tassafaronga, and Rennell Island—the U.S. Navy had lost eleven to six in destroyers, six to three in heavy ships of the line, and two to one in carriers. U.S. submarines and planes, however, had equalized the total by preying upon damaged Japanese war ships in their long, half-speed voyages back to base. In sum the U.S. fleet had lost to the sea two large carriers, six heavy cruisers, two light cruisers, fifteen destroyers, and one big passenger-liner transport, the S.S. *President Coolidge*. It had lost to the repair dock a large carrier, two battleships, three heavy cruisers, three light cruisers, and eight destroyers.

Admiral Yamamoto, by comparison, had lost a small carrier, two battleships, three heavy cruisers, one light cruiser, eleven destroyers, sixteen small and large troop transports, and five submarines.[5] None of his seriously damaged vessels had succeeded in returning to port, but he had on his hands two large carriers, four heavy cruisers, a light cruiser, and a destroyer which had sustained enough damage to merit a return to shipyards on the home islands.

Japan could claim a naval victory at Guadalcanal and even a small tactical plus for having successfully evacuated the island. On the ground and in the air, however, Japan had suffered disastrously. She had killed about 5,000 American sailors for a loss of

[5] This count of twenty-five U.S. to twenty-three Japanese fleet vessels differs from the oft-quoted twenty-four-to-twenty-four score given by naval historian Samuel Eliot Morison. To itemize, then, the Allies lost carriers *Wasp* and *Hornet*; heavy cruisers *Canberra, Vincennes, Quincy, Astoria, Northampton,* and *Chicago*; light cruisers *Atlanta* and *Juneau*; destroyers *Jarvis, Colhoun, Little, Gregory, O'Brien, Duncan, Meredith, Porter, Barton, Laffey, Cushing, Monssen, Walke, Preston,* and *Benham*. The Japanese Combined Fleet lost light carrier *Ryujo*; battleships *Hiei* and *Kirishima*; heavy cruisers *Kako, Furutaka,* and *Kinugasa*; light cruiser *Yura*; destroyers *Mutsuki, Asagiri, Akatsuki, Yudachi, Fubuki, Ayanami, Takanami, Teruzuki, Makigumo, Muragumo,* and *Natsugumo*; and submarines *I-123, I-172, I-15, I-3,* and *I-1*.

only about 3,000 Japanese sailors.[6] But she had lost about 2,000 Japanese airmen for a toll of less than 600 U.S. airmen. And in ground troops she had lost more than ten to one: more than 20,000 Japanese soldiers as against less than 2,000 U.S. Marines and Army G.I.'s. From the American point of view Guadalcanal had been a naval campaign and a naval debacle. From Hirohito's point of view it had been a great naval and aristocratic success, attended by appalling loss of life for the commoners of the Army and the expensively trained noncommissioned officers of the Misty Lagoon flight cadre.

NO WORK, NO FOOD

Never again after the desperate six-month campaign for Guadalcanal would Japanese and U.S. fighting men meet on equal terms. The Japanese would be gradually outnumbered on the sea and in the air until, in the final stages of the war, U.S. skippers regularly enjoyed a ten-to-one superiority in ships and U.S. pilots about a fifty-to-one superiority in planes. Through control of sea and air, U.S. ground commanders were able to choose battlefields where the numerical strength of the Japanese Army could not be called into play and where U.S. soldiers could be sure of an overwhelming advantage in firepower.

As a trained strategist, Hirohito could foresee these inexorable developments after the Battle of Midway and be certain of them after the vain banzai charges of Guadalcanal. Nevertheless he insisted that Japan fight on, and he continued so to insist while Japan's war dead mounted from less than 100,000 to more than a million.

Hirohito exacted this fearsome sacrifice of his people partly because he found it unbearable to see his life's vision shattered. He could not bring himself to admit failure in his mission of conquering, unifying, and "enlightening" Asia. He could not report to the gods that the pernicious Western creeds of cosmopolitanism and of individual conscience, soul, and salvation were still at

---

[6] These are my own totals of ship-by-ship estimates based on casualty reports or descriptions of ship damages. Official figures, as former Marine officer Samuel Griffith wryly observes in his *The Battle of Guadalcanal*, have never been "tabulated."

large on Japanese soil. Most important, however, Hirohito felt that he could fight on because his advisors advised him to.

Paradoxically, Lord Privy Seal Kido urged that the war must be continued on account of the people. If defeat came prematurely, he feared popular resentment against the Throne. After the 1905 war with Russia, mobs had rioted in the major cities to protest the paltry monetary and territorial gains which Emperor Meiji had accepted in exchange for the Japanese corpses piled outside Port Arthur and Mukden. This time there would be no gain at all for the men lost in China, Malaya, Luzon, Java, or the faraway exotic islands of the Pacific. The Japanese public must be carefully prepared for the bad bargain. In 1943, when any offal carter or radish farmer could look at a newspaper map and see the rays of the rising sun spreading across a third of the earth, no statesman could with impunity sign away the new conquests and restrict Japan again to her tiny home islands.

The people must lose their bloodstained booty by their own failures before they would accept the loss. And more subtly they must be committed to the enterprise of empire before they could agree to abandon it. The conquests had come so easily, and so few Japanese had participated in them, that a majority of the people had only an intellectual interest in them. If they were given away, the village schoolmasters would cry treason and the people would resent the blood spilled for nothing. But if each mile of foreign shore was fought for, the people would come to identify the distant coral strands with dead village boys. They would feel keenly each retreat and would begin to appreciate the glory of the empire which Hirohito had planned for them. Eventually the mothers of the land would cry, "Enough." Only then could come a time when it would be safe to give back the conquests.

Most subtly of all, there was the question of guilt sharing. A part of every Japanese wanted to dominate the earth and accept tribute from once-proud Chinese, Europeans, and Americans, but few Japanese had ever aspired to burn out Chinese eyes, to castrate Englishmen, or to eat the flesh of Americans. By issuing discreet orders which would induce large numbers of Japanese to participate literally in such bestialities, Hirohito's secret police experts planned to give the entire nation such a guilty conscience that it would never dare to make any one man—least of all Hirohito—

responsible for Japan's wrongdoing. Through sharing guilt the whole populace could be prepared to accept gratefully any peace which did not exact of it an eye-for-an-eye, tooth-for-a-tooth vengeance.

It was these darkly delicate considerations of people-control that led to the horrors of the Japanese concentration camps. No one scapegoat suffered in them. Hirohito's secret police and camp wardens dispensed death without prejudice as to race, religion, color, or sex. And they did so, fortunately, without benefit of scientific ovens and gas chambers. Nevertheless, for anyone who was not Jewish, the Japanese camps were more deadly than the German. Of 235,473 British and American troops captured by the soldiers of the Third Reich, 9,348—or 4 per cent—died in the Nazi camps. Of 95,134 British, Australian, American, Canadian, and New Zealand troops captured by the Japanese, 27,256—or 28.65 per cent—died in the Japanese camps.[7]

Civilians interned by the Japanese were issued the same rations as military prisoners but fared far better. Indeed, in some civilian camps the death rate ran lower than normal actuarial expectations for communities of like size in the United States. There were no overweight problems and no underexercise problems; no stimulants and few excitements. As residents in the Orient, the civilians knew the Japanese and local hygiene; they had native friends on the outside who got food to them; they had wives, children, and doctors interned with or near them, keeping up their standards of cleanliness, cheerfulness, and community feeling. They coped with the same captors, the same latent brutality and smouldering hate, but they were not despised by the Japanese for being soldiers who had surrendered. Nor were they used by the Japanese for slave labor.

Differences in worm's-eye view, as revealed in hundreds of books

[7] Of 21,726 captured Australians, 7,412 men or 34 per cent; of 21,580 captured U.S. soldiers and sailors, 7,107 or 33 per cent; of 121 captured New Zealanders, thirty-one or 26 per cent; of 50,016 captured Britishers, 12,433 or 25 per cent; of 1,691 captured Canadians, 273 or 16 per cent. The differences in death rates reflected partly a difference in Japanese feeling about the nationalities involved and partly cultural differences in the tractability and adaptability of the various national groups. Complete figures for captured Dutch and Indian troops are not available. Partial figures, however, suggest that the Dutch suffered about the same gross and percentage loss as the U.S. troops and the Indians about the same as the British troops.

published after the war by former captives of the Japanese, have persuaded many historians that Japanese brutality was unorganized, individual, haphazard. This was not the opinion of most of the writers of these books, nor is it borne out by available Japanese records. On the contrary, surviving directives of the Prisoner of War Information Bureau and Prisoner of War Management Section suggest that it was imperial policy, gradually, patiently, plausibly, and almost legally to exterminate the prisoners to the last man. Locally, Japanese camp commanders and guards construed instructions from Tokyo in order to be humane but never did they have to stretch their instructions in order to be brutal. Moreover, in every camp, whether a good one or a hellhole, each new set of instructions from Tokyo brought about at least a temporary increase in severity.

Japan's policy in regard to the political use and physical abuse of prisoners was enunciated by Hirohito at the very start of the war on December 24, 1941, sixteen days after Pearl Harbor. That morning, a Wednesday, at his usual weekly meeting with the Privy Council, sitting in plenary session, he pushed through an executive motion for the establishment of a Prisoner of War Information Bureau under the War Ministry. The motion was passed without comment or debate, and the "attached papers," of which copies lay before each privy councillor, became law of the land.

The attached papers were couched in judicious belly talk. They declared that the Privy Council, in 1912, had already ratified a convention of the Powers, agreed to at The Hague in 1907, calling upon governments at war to establish bureaus to deal with information and affairs pertaining to war prisoners. With this preamble, Hirohito's Privy Council agreed that Japan's prisoner-of-war bureau would report to the vice war minister, would be directed by Army officers below the rank of colonel and Navy officers below the rank of captain, and would be staffed by clerks of *heimin* or lower-class status. It would engage in research and information about prisoners of war. It would "make and revise a file card for every prisoner." It would "hold in trust and remit to families the belongings and testaments of dead prisoners." It would "handle the monetary affairs of prisoners" and "notification of the bereaved." It would assist enemy governments in telling next of kin about enemy nationals in Japanese hands. In effect the attached documents subscribed to by the Privy Council left little hope that prisoners taken by Japan would ever return to their homelands alive.

The Prisoner of War Information Bureau quickly became a thriving branch of the Tokyo bureaucracy, and the efficient secret police did indeed provide it with file cards on almost all Allied captives. Pilots taken on Bataan, missionaries captured in Baguio after a lifetime of work in China, businessmen who had fled Hong Kong only to be apprehended in Surabaja, prostitutes evacuated from Shanghai and caught on a ship in Manila harbor—all were astonished, when they were interrogated and screened, at the completeness of the dossiers which the Japanese had already compiled on them.

By April 1942, after the fall of Singapore, Rangoon, Java, and Bataan, the Prisoner of War Information Bureau and its subsidiary, the Prisoner of War Management Section, had almost 300,-000 charges, about a quarter of them Allied civilians and the rest white and native troops of the British, Dutch, and U.S. armed forces. No matter how it could be manipulated—squeezed out of natives, paid from frozen Allied assets, or reduced by murder—the budget for administering, guarding, and feeding these captives could not be calculated at less than about $10 million a year or $30 a man per annum. This was one six-hundredth of the national revenue and more than Hirohito's frugal economists, during Japan's great gamble, cared to spend.

On April 28, 1942, ten days after the Doolittle raid on Tokyo, Prime Minister Tojo, in his capacity as war minister, called a conference of his bureau chiefs in the War Ministry building outside the palace walls. Chief of Staff Sugiyama had just told him that it was the policy of Imperial General Headquarters to make an example of the captured Doolittle fliers by executing them. Tojo intended to fight against the executions, which he considered hypocritical and barbaric. But he wanted something to offer Hirohito in their place. After a brief discussion with his subordinates, he proposed that, in accordance with the imperial slogan of "no work, no food," the 300,000 war prisoners in the Empire should be made to earn their keep. The chief of the P.O.W. Information Bureau, Lieutenant General Uemura Seitaro, objected that, according to the Hague conventions, prisoners of war should not be required to perform labor useful to their captors. They might raise food and cut wood for their own maintenance but they were not supposed to have to sweat on the docks or in the war plants of the nation which held them. In addition, any work they did outside of their camps was supposed to be recompensed. Finally, their officers—the most highly educated P.O.W.'s—were specifically exempted from all work, even in their own maintenance.

Tojo dismissed the objections of P.O.W. Chief Uemura as impractical. The Foreign Ministry had already informed the West in January, through Buenos Aires, that Japan did not subscribe to the antique Hague conventions but would respect their humanitarian spirit. This meant, in Tojo's view, that the sooner all war prisoners were put to work, for their own support, the longer they would survive.

What seemed right to Tojo in the political circumstances in which he operated in Tokyo turned out to be only partly right for the scattered war prisoners who had been taken all over the new empire to the south. Ratified by the section chiefs at the War Ministry and duly approved by Hirohito at Imperial General Headquarters, the decision to use war prisoners as laborers spared the lives of many Americans who had been marked out for extinction and cost the lives of many other captives who had theretofore enjoyed tolerable conditions of imprisonment.

Up to that time Allied troops who had surrendered easily to Japan had not been treated too badly and Allied troops who had held out tenaciously against Japan had been treated abominably. The U.S. defenders of Guam, for instance, having bowed quickly to the inevitability of defeat, were now being adequately fed and housed at concentration camps in Japan and China to which they had been transported without mishap. On the other hand the U.S. defenders of Wake, who had repulsed one Japanese task force and taken heavy casualties before surrendering to another, had been starved, beaten, and decimated by ceremonial executions.

The contrasting treatment given to the Wake and Guam garrisons had been meted out on a much larger scale to the prisoners taken at Singapore and at Bataan. The Battling Bastards who had caused the Japanese such pain on Bataan had already suffered the horrors of the Death March. Now the 9,500-odd Americans and

44,500-odd Filipinos who had survived the march were continuing to die by the tumbrel at their detention point halfway between Manila and Lingayen Gulf, Camp O'Donnell. Here was a soggy potter's field, strewn with rotting palm-thatched barracks and pup tents, served with only a score of running-water faucets, subdivided by barbed-wire fences, and surrounded by stockades, searchlights, and machine guns. Here, before the end of 1942, 1,500 of the American and over 20,000 of the Filipino Death-March survivors would succumb to floggings, bayonetings, shootings, diphtheria, dengue fever, malaria, infected wounds, beriberi, scurvy, or simple starvation, debility and hopelessness.

Because of Tojo's decision 6,000 of the Americans at Camp O'Donnell would be moved out in June 1942 to join some 2,000 fresh American captives from Corregidor at the all-white Camp Cabanatuan in the more healthy foothills to the east. The diseased veterans of Camp O'Donnell brought with them a rich stew of intestinal parasites which killed 2,000 of the 8,000 inmates at the Cabanatuan Camp in the next three months. The remaining 6,000 plus fellow survivors at Camp O'Donnell and various camps in the southern islands of the Philippines—in all about 12,000 men—were hardy specimens. They had lived out of an original total of about 18,000 American military captives in the Philippines. Another 3,000 U.S. soldiers and sailors had been captured elsewhere in the Pacific and Orient. They had suffered a few hundred deaths in imprisonment. All told almost 15,000 American P.O.W.'s still remained alive in Japanese hands and of these over 14,000 would survive to be liberated three years later.

Tojo's excuse for them—"Let them eat as long as they work"—proved sufficient to save the lives of most of them. In the months ahead they made their way as miners in the Kyushu coal pits, stevedores on the Yokohama docks, yardmen in Osaka station, machinists in Kobe factories, trench diggers in Manchuria, railroad builders in Thailand, and even as script writers and announcers for Tokyo radio.

P.O.W. slave laborers, who received, depending on rank, a take-"home" pay of between three and thirty cents a day, began arriving in Japan about a month after Tojo had handed down his decision to call for them. On May 30, 1942, when the Combined Fleet had set out for Midway, Tojo personally inspected one of the first P.O.W. shipments at Zentsuji, in Shikoku, across the Inland Sea from the port of Osaka. It included both Americans from Bataan and Englishmen from Hong Kong and Singapore. Tojo told the Zentsuji camp commandant:

Prisoners of war must be placed under strict discipline insofar as that does not contravene the laws of humanity. It is necessary, however, not to be obsessed with mistaken humanitarian notions or swayed by personal feelings which may develop in time through long association with prisoners of war. The present situation in this country does not permit of anyone lying about idle while eating freely. Keeping these sentiments in mind, I hope that you will see to it that your war prisoners are gainfully employed.

On June 25, after the defeat at Midway, Tojo addressed a Tokyo conclave of all P.O.W. camp commandants from Taiwan, Korea, Manchuria, and Japan:

You are especially requested to take into account the characteristic viewpoint at your places of posting and so treat the prisoners of war entrusted to your charge as to make the local populace there appreciative of Japanese superior qualities and cognizant of the unique privilege and honor which they enjoy in being subjects during the reign of His Gracious Majesty.

On July 7 Tojo spoke to a similar gathering of concentration camp commandants from the Philippines and Southeast Asia. He exhorted them: "Insofar as you can, short of becoming inhuman yourselves, supervise your charges rigidly and permit no idleness."

On August 13, after the American landing on Guadalcanal, the Japanese secret police in Korea reported on a well-advertised parade of P.O.W.'s from Singapore who were landed at the Pusan docks and then marched through the Pusan city streets:

The arrival of 998 prisoners captured in Malaya had a great effect on the public at large—especially on the Koreans. About 120,000 Koreans and about 57,000 Japanese bystanders lined the streets of downtown Pusan to see the prisoners pass by. Many of the onlookers sneered at the bad manners and indifference displayed openly by the captured British troops and thought it quite natural that an army so lacking in national spirit should be defeated. They realized afresh the magnitude of the victory gained by the Imperial Army. . . . Worthy of special mention is the fact that the Koreans, when they saw the Korean guards accompanying the prisoners, realized that they are directly participating in the war for Great East Asia.

The secret police report went on to quote bystanders who had been asked for their impressions. One common Korean response was: "It's easy to see they lack patriotism by the way they go along whistling indifferently. They are absolutely slovenly." Another was: "When we saw their frail unsteady appearance, we thought 'No wonder they lost to the Japanese forces.'" The most common Japanese reaction quoted by the secret police was one of sober anxiety: "The appearance of the prisoners made me realize that we can never afford to be defeated." Or, as another Japanese said: "They have no shame, but some arrogance still, so they must be treated firmly. Also we must not lose the war."

The Japanese secret police did not have enough presentable Bataan captives to put in a parade. The fittest thousand P.O.W.'s from the Philippines would have wrung tears of pity from a meeting of the Black Dragon Society. Consequently the first American prisoners selected as laborers were brought in small groups to special convalescence camps in Japan proper and there given a few weeks' fattening up before being sent to work at rail yards, docks, and coal mines.

The "frail, whistling" British troops deemed fit for display in Korea had been lucky in their treatment up to now. So had their fellows who remained in Singapore. So had most of 20,000-odd Dutch troops taken on Java. It was on these Britishers and Hollanders that Tojo's "no-work-no-food" decision—favorable to U.S. P.O.W.'s—fell most heavily.

In Java the Dutch soldiers, on the battlefield or in the process of being recognized as prisoners, had been almost decimated. Thereafter, however, they had been assembled in camps where they were loosely guarded and allowed, for the most part, to fend and forage for themselves. On an island of easy agriculture, plentiful food, and a three-hundred-year tradition of Dutch rule, they managed well to keep up their health and good spirits. The 35,000-odd Britishers, 15,000-odd Australians, and 14,000-odd Anglo-Malay volunteers captured at Singapore had been more strictly but even less harshly used. General Yamashita, the Tiger of Malaya and level-headed student of the German *Wehrmacht*, had given them the run of the whole northeastern tip of Singapore Island, the Changi area, where the British Army had been quartered before the war. Here were airy three-story barracks built by the British, surrounded by lawns, tennis courts, and arbors of bougainvillea. The accommodations were more crowded than they had been before the war but far less crowded than the encampments from which the British troops had been fighting since Pearl Harbor. The official Japanese ration of a pound of dry rice, a tenth of a pound of meat, and a quarter of a pound of vegetables, dairy products, and condiments per man per day was more than enough to keep the prisoners in lean good health. When it failed to meet specifications due to the inefficiency or graft of a Japanese supply sergeant, its shortcomings could be repaired by black-market traffic with natives "outside the fence."

The relative comforts, however, of British P.O.W.'s began to deteriorate rapidly after Tojo had issued the executive order that prisoners must work to be fed. At first General Yamashita merely subtracted from the British camp area a few lawns and golf courses. Then he built fences around the immediate area of the barracks and installed guard garrisons and blockhouses. Finally, in July 1942, after his unsuccessful plea to Hirohito to let him lead an invasion of Australia, he was posted back to Manchuria.

His successor required all inmates of Changi to sign a statement: "I, the undersigned, hereby solemnly swear on my honour that I will not, under any circumstances, attempt to escape." British officers citing the Hague conventions, refused to order their men to sign. On September 2, 17,300 of the most high-spirited British and Australian prisoners were marched into the eight acres of prewar Selarang Barrack Square so that they could watch the execution—by Sikh firing squad—of four of their number who had escaped three and a half months earlier and had just been recaptured and brought back for punishment. After the execution, the 17,300 interested witnesses were held at attention waiting for their officers to tell them to sign the Japanese oath. They continued to stand under the tropic sun and moon for three days, surrounded by machine-gun emplacements. They had in their midst two water faucets and were allowed three times a day to stand at ease in order to eat rice handed in to them in pails. They were told they had been put on a third of their regular rations. On the third day their British officers advised them that they had "proved compulsion" and could sign the Japanese oath without any sense of responsibility. Even so the enormous phalanx of men took another day to disperse, and some two or three score men of hardened puritan principles remained standing and insisted upon being taken away for final breaking by the torturers of the Japanese secret police.

Thereafter the administration of British P.O.W.'s in Singapore began to approximate that of the newly reformed camps for military prisoners in the Philippines.

THE RAILROAD OF DEATH

Shortly after the first levies of Allied slave labor began to be exhibited in Korea, Hirohito approved in principle a General Staff plan for linking the rail systems of Thailand and Burma. A Japanese soldier could travel by train from Pusan in Korea to Mukden, Peking, Hankow, Canton, Saigon, and Bangkok. Forty miles beyond Bangkok, however, at the Thai town of Bampong, the overland transportation system ended against a wall of some of the thickest, most unhealthy jungle in the world. West of Bampong, swamps and ridges and gullies succeeded one another so closely that there was almost no pleasant forest land for over 200 miles. In the thickets, however, there were enough monkeys and human outcasts to support a rich fauna of malarial mosquitoes and other primate parasites. A single track led through the dense tangle. It had been cut by a British geological survey more than a decade earlier and subsequently abandoned by British and Indian forestry service men as being beyond upkeep.

On the other side of this wilderness, at the eastern Burmese frontier town of Thanbyuzayat, began the Anglo-Burmese rail system which extended to the western frontier of Burma. There gaped another two-hundred-mile gap which, when bridged, would lead to the Anglo-Indian rail system. Beyond the western camel towns of India lay another gap, Baluchistan, after which it was clear rolling, along well-laid lines, all the way to Calais and the English Channel.

Not for naught had the courtiers of Hirohito's great-grandfather, Emperor Komei, sacrificed their dignity to ride, with robes flowing, on the donkey-sized steam engine shown off by Commodore Perry at Uraga. Japan's domestic railroads rivaled the world's best, and all Japan's conquests up to 1941 had been posited and pushed forward on the rail lines of Manchuria and China. Other armies might march on their bellies; the Japanese Army glided like a snake—and went hungry between railroad stations.

After the capture of Rangoon in March 1942, the possibility of converting Japan's probe of Burma into a full-scale invasion of India began to seem attractive to Hirohito. In June the Navy's repulse at Midway, and the decision not to invade Australia, made the Army's presence in Burma positively indispensable. Nowhere else could the Army exert its numerical strength to Japan's advantage and put real pressure on the Allies. The sea-lanes between Singapore and Rangoon, however, were beset by Allied submarines. The overland portage along jungle trails between Bangkok and Rangoon was slow and expensive. If the divisions in Burma were to threaten India seriously, they would need at their back a supply route along railroad tracks. As soon, therefore, as the Americans took the amphibious offensive at Guadalcanal, Hirohito ordered an all-out effort to lay track along the abandoned Burma-Thai geological cut. Japanese engineers resurveyed it and estimated the earth which would have to be moved, and the embankments, trestles, and bridges which would have to be constructed.

Some 3,000 Australian P.O.W.'s from Singapore, recruited under the new slave-labor system, had spent the summer repairing airfields for Japan along the western coast of the Malayan Peninsula in the southern extremities of Burma. Now, in late September, they were disembarked from sweltering ship holds at Moulmein and Ye, the southernmost ports on the Burmese rail network. The first of them arrived at Thanbyuzayat, at the northern end of the unbuilt Burma-Thai railroad, a few days later on October 1, 1942. Most of them were young men, bronzed, lean and fit after months of hard work in the sun and of adequate feeding and foraging at the airfields where they had been employed. In a

few months they would all be either dead or walking caricatures
of death.

By November the Australians had been augmented by unhard-
ened Britishers from Changi in Singapore and by Hollanders
from Java who were already sick and starving after long sea voyages
under hot, tight bulkheads. Before the end of the year, almost
10,000 prisoners would be clearing jungle, heaping dirt by the
basketful on embankments, and chiseling through hillsides at the
Burmese end of the railroad. A like number of captives, mostly
British, would be at work in Thailand at the other end of the
envisaged line.

The workers in Thailand, if comparisons are possible, had the
harder lot. Theirs were the longest segments of line to build, the
highest hills, deepest gorges, and most pestiferous swamplands.
Both groups, however, suffered from much the same delusions and
heartbreaks. They had left Singapore under the impression that
they were going to "Shangri-la," an undisclosed location in a more
congenial climate to the north where their care would be supervised by representatives of the International Red Cross. Instead
they emerged hungry and heat-exhausted from packed holds and
cattle cars and found themselves put in the care of Korean menials
from work battalions—some of the most abused, ignorant, and
corrupt peasants who ever wore the uniform of an army.

Prodded on by these Korean guards, the cheated P.O.W.'s set
out at once on forced marches through the jungle. Some of them
walked 20 miles, some 150. At the end of their treks they found
that Shangri-la was an unimproved jungle clearing where Japanese soldiers had built a few sodden lean-tos out of saplings and
palm-leaf thatch. The camp sites were evenly spaced out along
the route of the projected railroad and chosen with an eye more
to geometric regularity than to geographic suitability. Many of
them happened to fall in swamp bottoms where swarmed malarial
mosquitoes even in dry season.

Armed only with axes, picks, and shovels, the prisoners began
work in the midst of the monsoon or wet season. Ditch as they
might, their camps turned quickly into morasses. From dawn to
dusk they cut and hauled trees, shoveled dirt, and picked at rock.
By night they washed and cooked and tried to live. They had little
to eat but sacks of the lowest grade of polished rice wherein the

most vitamin-rich content crawled in the form of weevils and maggots. Most of them were soon afflicted by the grotesquely bloated ankles and testicles of "wet beriberi" or by the flaking shins and falling dandruff of "dry beriberi." Their malnutrition was increased by dysentery and their despondency by almost universal diarrhea.

By November no one was healthy but no one who took a sane view of his own psychological condition cared to report himself sick. The sodden palm-thatched long houses known as "hospitals" flowed with such fecal stench and despair that a man indisposed could lie down and die of disgust in any one of them. Dedicated doctors and orderlies worked without sleep to do some good, but they had no medicines, and Japanese medical inspectors refused consistently to make any available. Boiled water, salt, and soda were the main drugs at hand and men who suffered from tropical ulcers, dysentery, and malaria needed at least one more important pharmaceutical: hope. This the doctors and orderlies could not dispense and they had to watch thousands of young men die of combinations of minor ailments, which could have been easily cured by food, rest, and sanitation.

The end of the 1942 rainy season in December brought a temporary improvement in rations and work conditions which lasted for about six weeks. Then in February 1943, after the Japanese withdrawal from Guadalcanal, Hirohito approved a speed-up in the construction schedule, requiring that the railroad be finished, not by December 1943 as orginally planned, but by August. All able-bodied Allied P.O.W.'s in Singapore, Sumatra, and Java were moved north to hasten the work. When 60,000 of them had been put in harness, the project still progressed too slowly and the Japanese marched in no less than 270,000 indentured Malays, Burmese, Thais, and Javanese. These hordes of native conscripts lacked discipline, leadership, medical personnel, interpreters, and the resourcefulness conferred by even elementary school education. As a result they suffered horribly and a third of them died.

Hirohito's call for haste lengthened the work shifts of P.O.W.'s from eight to twelve to sixteen hours. During the final frenetic months of railroad construction, the columns of sick white coolies were often driven from their camps at daybreak and not returned to them until 2 A.M. The night work was done by electric lights which glimmered dim and bright as the men who turned the handles of small manual generators wearied, collapsed, and were replaced in a never-ending nightmare cycle.

In the mornings when work parties had set out from camps, Japanese engineers regularly sent Korean guards into the hospital shacks to rout out additional laborers. At one of the larger camps men too weak to stand were forced to sit in rows and tug at ropes to help in log hauling. Men who collapsed were sometimes left to die and sometimes killed by thrashings with bamboo poles or lashings with wire whips. The malingerer who prolonged a squat in the bushes to take a brief nap or smoke a scavenged cigarette butt was commonly punished by being made to lift his eyes toward the sun and stand for an hour holding over his head a boulder or a bucket of earth. Those few men who attempted to escape either died quickly in the jungle or were triumphantly recaptured and publicly tortured to death as examples. Some were gibbeted; others simply tied to trees to die of thirst or ant bite.

In executing these abominations, the Japanese relied heavily upon their brutalized Korean menials and upon a handful of crazily violent noncommissioned officers. The regular Japanese troops in the area mostly averted their eyes or made sporadic efforts to ease the prisoners' lot. Japanese railroad engineers and doctors on the other hand—men who should have represented enlightened Japanese civilian opinion—actively encouraged the killing of the prisoners. Instead of demanding better equipment and food for their slaves, the engineers insisted on turning them out in numbers sufficient to meet work quotas. The doctors were still more knowingly inhuman in that they regularly certified sick men fit for work. Men dehydrated by dysentery they sent to sweat in the sun. Men dizzy with 104-degree fevers they sent to teeter atop high bridge trestles. Many lost their balance and fell to their deaths on the rocky bottoms of ravines far below.[8]

[8] The most cruel Japanese secret policemen were regularly those who had lived abroad, who nursed grievances for slights suffered in the West, and who felt a special need to prove their patriotism to fellow Japanese. Most doctors and engineers, having attended Western Universities, shared to some extent in this pariah outlook. In addition the doctors had no squeamishness about physical suffering or the sight of blood. Many of them assisted at tortures or per-

As it took a coldly intellectual Japanese or a miserably sadistic one to supervise the building of the railroad, so it took a coolly resourceful prisoner or a magnificently animal one to survive the conditions of the labor. Then in June of 1943 another protagonist entered the drama: *Vibrio comma*, a bacterium which took its toll impartially of strong or cunning prisoners and of cold or cruel Japanese. The epidemic of Asiatic cholera began in an encampment of impressed Tamil laborers from Burma and swiftly spread, like the plague it was, to Allied P.O.W. camps and Japanese guardhouses. All work on the railroad ceased. The Japanese donned face masks of white gauze and barred the gates of their blockhouses. The rank and file of P.O.W.'s withdrew in final despair to their mouldering huts. Many of the strongest of them, who had heretofore held off the amoebas and bacilli of dysentery and the plasmodia of malaria, were taken by convulsions and died in hours, grinning like wolves.

Only the P.O.W.'s own medical teams, traveling from camp to camp with the reassurance of knowledge and a few simple hints on the boiling of water and on the quarantine and care of the stricken, managed to prevent panic and wholesale death. The Japanese themselves were frightened into demanding air shipments of cholera serum from Japan. Nevertheless, before the epidemic had been brought under control, some British P.O.W. camps had been decimated and some of the Asiatic coolie camps had been entirely wiped out. Crews of Allied P.O.W.'s sent to clean up the Asiatic camps, which were the centers of infection, found tabloids of death which surpassed belief: rat-ravaged fields of corpses flooded with liquids from latrines which had burst their embankments. Fire and lime brought hygiene back to the jungle, but the stench and the horror never left the nostrils and minds of the clean-up details as long as the men in them lived.

After the great epidemic of June and July 1943, cholera never left the railroad of death. Later cholera outbreaks, however, were quickly suppressed with doses of Japanese serum and full Japanese co-operation. The pathetically proud Allied prisoners also co-operated more fully after the epidemic and completed the rail-

sonally wielded swords at beheadings. One of them, in western Burma in 1944, encountered an African in a group of British captives, tied him to a tree, and cut his heart out to demonstrate to orderlies that it was as red as any other.

road by November. Some of them were kept on after November, as maintenance crews, to rebuild and replace embankments which, a year earlier, they had purposely underpinned with rotten logs and adulterated with vegetable fill which they had known would cause cave-ins. Some of the maintenance crews even lived to become obsessed by their handiwork and to curse British planes which began bombing the rickety timber bridges late in the war.

Most of the jungle construction camps were abandoned early in 1944. Surviving P.O.W.'s were returned to Changi concentration camp in Singapore and the native laborers to scores of small villages in Burma, Thailand, and Malaya.

Not until after the war was a full reckoning made of the cost of the railroad. It had taken 331,000 men to build: 61,000 Allied P.O.W.'s and roughly 270,000 natives. Of these some 72,000 to 92,000 of the Asiatics—between 25 and 30 per cent—had died, having done less than half of the work. Of the 61,000 Allied P.O.W.'s 20.6 per cent or 12,568 had died: 6,318 Britishers, 2,815 Australians, 2,490 Hollanders, 356 Americans, and 589 whose nationalities were never determined. In laying down their lives they had constructed a 250-mile railroad which would have to be abandoned after the war and given back to the wilderness. They had built nine miles of bridges and moved 150 million cubic feet of earth, about as much as they would have moved if they had dug fifteen decent graves for each corpse they had left behind them. Together with the Asiatic laborers, they had left one dead body for every thirteen feet of completed track. If Japan had lifted a finger of her managerial genius, the idiotic waste of life could have been avoided and the railroad built more quickly, cheaply, and lastingly. As handled by Imperial Headquarters, the project had only one virtue: it was a way of killing prisoners that could be justified to Prime Minister Tojo and other responsible officials in the Tokyo government.

FELLING JAPAN'S ANGEL

While Hirohito's disappointments were being vented on Allied war prisoners, President Roosevelt took a small vengeance of his own: he sanctioned the assassination of Japan's great naval hero and air angel, Admiral Yamamoto Isoroku, the author of the sneak attack upon Pearl Harbor. The chance came for the assassination when Yamamoto's Navy signalmen, in a low-security code, five days in advance, broadcast to the whole Pacific area the itinerary of an inspection tour which Yamamoto planned to make of the front lines on April 18, 1943.

Since the previous April 18, when Doolittle had raided Tokyo, everything had gone badly for Yamamoto. As the caretaker of Japanese air power, he had taken personal responsibility for Doolittle's violation of sacred air space over the Imperial Palace. Because of the need for a counterstroke, he had hastened his plans for a decisive blow at the U.S. fleet and had lost the Battle of Midway. Again he had taken all the responsibility upon himself. Then, at Guadalcanal, his vaunted eagles of the Misty Lagoon had proved incapable of overcoming improved U.S. aerial tactics and superior numbers of U.S. planes. There were no longer words with which to express his regret to Hirohito. Since Guadalcanal nothing Yamamoto could think of had been able to check the run of American success.

In the final six weeks of 1942 the first U.S. fighter planes capable of dealing with the Zero had begun to arrive in the Southwest Pacific: Lockheed Lightnings. These P-38's could not "turn square corners" with the Zero in a dogfight, but they did not need to for they were far bigger, heavier, and faster. No longer did U.S. pilots have to attack only in groups for a single downward pass at diving speed. The Lightning could run away from a Zero in level flight, could turn at leisure, and come back with guns blazing.

The mighty Zero, over Singapore, had flown circles around the British Spitfire, had shot down seventeen out of twenty-seven veteran dogfighters of the Battle of Britain with the loss of only two Zeros. Earlier the Spitfires had demonstrated a similar superiority over the *Luftwaffe*'s best fighter, the Messerschmidt 109E. The Zero, then, could lay just claim to being the world's best fighter plane. Now, however, it had met its match. In the big twin-fuselage Lightning, the U.S. pilot no longer needed to fear individual man-to-man combat. Like the Zero, moreover, the Lightning had range. It could accompany bombers to a target 600 miles away and return with gas to spare.

Having spent his entire career as an apostle of air power and of technical excellence, Admiral Yamamoto needed only a glance at intelligence reports on the Lightning's capabilities to realize the fateful significance of the new American plane. Yamamoto knew that the next generation of Japanese fighter planes—the *Shidens* and *Raidens*, or Lightningbolts and Thunderclaps, planes which would make a limited appearance in 1945—were still on the drawing boards.

In 1941, in agreeing to lead the Navy prematurely against the United States, Yamamoto had pinned his hopes on the Zero and on his belief that Americans had no deep interest in Asia and would be eager to accept a negotiated peace with Japan. Now the Lightning nullified the Zero, and in mid-January 1943 President Roosevelt, meeting with British Prime Minister Churchill at Casablanca in North Africa, blasted Yamamoto's other hope.

"The elimination of German, Japanese and Italian war power," Roosevelt announced to reporters after the conference, "means the unconditional surrender of Germany, Italy and Japan."

Yamamoto knew that neither Hirohito nor Japan could surrender unconditionally. Hirohito could not do so because of sacred oaths to his ancestors; the Japanese people could not do so out of pride and out of fear of unconditional American vengeance.

In his despair, Yamamoto was called upon to regain air superiority for Japan over the battlefields in the Southwest Pacific where Japanese soldiers and Marines were dying. After the decision had been reached to evacuate Guadalcanal, the next concern was New Guinea. There U.S. and Australian troops had crossed the Owen Stanley Range from Port Moresby in late October 1942 and in December 1942 and January 1943 had pinched out the three Japanese beachheads of Gona, Buna, and Sanananda on the other side. The Australians had lost over 5,000 men in the action, the Americans over 2,500, and the Japanese about 12,000. At Buna, in particular, the Allied troops had inched forward—through kunai grass against coconut log blockhouses—in one of the most desperate struggles of the war. Had it not been for a dozen tanks floated around New Guinea from Port Moresby on rafts, the Japanese troops might have held out indefinitely.

The fall of Buna had distressed Hirohito. Expressing himself mildly so that no one in the General Staff would resign or commit suicide, he nevertheless reproved Chief of Staff Sugiyama in an audience on January 9:

Our men fought well but the loss of Buna is regrettable. I understand the enemy used twelve or more tanks. Don't we have any tanks in that area? Now I assume that we will send adequate reinforcements, will we not, to Lae [Japan's next stronghold on the north shore of New Guinea, about 150 miles northwest of Buna]?

In response to Hirohito's suggestion, on February 28, 1943, 6,912 Japanese troops in eight small transports, accompanied by eight destroyers, set out from Rabaul to reinforce the New Guinea enclaves. Yamamoto undertook to provide the convoy with air cover. But between March 2 and March 4, in the Battle of the Bismarck Sea, U.S. planes from Guadalcanal and New Guinea destroyed all of the convoy's transports, four of its eight destroyers, and 4,000 of its troops. Most of the men lost were left swimming in the water where they were systematically massacred by machine-gun fire from U.S. aircraft and torpedo boats.

At the Battle of the Bismarck Sea sixteen P-38 Lightnings engaged forty Zeros, kept them occupied at altitudes ranging from 10,000 to 30,000 feet, and swapped "kills" with them on an equal basis. Far below, U.S. bomber pilots were employing, to good effect, a new technique called skip-bombing, which made the most of their ability to score near misses. B-25's and A-20's roared in low over the wave tops, where the gunners on Japanese ships had the least chance of hitting them. The U.S. bombs were fused to explode five seconds after release when the drop-plane had got clear. It mattered not if the bombs fell in the water: they would still explode and, in sufficient quantities, they would eventually spring a ship's seams and literally shake her to death.

The fast, high-level interception work of the thundering P-38 Lightnings, coupled with the low-level skip-drops of the U.S. bombers, struck Yamamoto's aerial samurai, trained for machine-gun sharpshooting and precision bombing, as crude and unsporting. No one, however, could gainsay the effectiveness of the new American tactics. Long after the Zeros, their gas spent in vain pursuit of the evasive Lightnings, had returned to their bases, the skip-bombers hammered away at the Japanese fleet. When most of the fleet had foundered, the Battle of the Bismarck Sea had been won undeniably by the Americans.

Hirohito was quick now to find fault. He saw at once that, having been discovered by U.S. pilots, the convoy should have made for the nearest Japanese port, Madang, far up the New Guinea coast out of range of the U.S. planes. There it could have regrouped and doubled back at its leisure down the coast toward Lae—where its troops were needed. It could have moved stealthily at night, ship by ship, and creek mouth to creek mouth.

On March 3, even before the Battle of the Bismarck Sea had ended, Hirohito upbraided General Staff Chief Sugiyama for this stupid exhibition of inflexibility:

Why ever didn't you make a change in plans and land the troops at once on Madang? We have suffered what can only be described as a disaster. I hope we can learn a bitter lesson from it and make it a basis for more successful operations. Please act in future so as to relieve my anxiety. Strengthen our aerial forces where they will be needed. Prepare reinforcement routes through safe areas. Move step by step with careful deliberation. Proceed so that Lae and Salamaua won't turn into another Guadalcanal. After all, our withdrawal there was caused, was it not, by a certain laxity on the part of our forces on the island, a complacency from too many easy victories earlier? All right. So much for that. Now how are we going to make best use of the forces remaining to us?

Since the enemy is strong in the air [replied Sugiyama, abashed], we plan to reorganize our airfields around Madang, and our air defenses, and our transport routes, and we hope to follow His Imperial Majesty's guidance.

The Emperor's displeasure over the Battle of the Bismarck Sea was quickly communicated to Admiral Yamamoto at his great fleet base on Truk atoll in the Carolines. Without much hope he came to Rabaul personally on April 3, with some 300 of his best remaining Zero pilots, to see what he could do to regain Japan's initiative in the air. He proceeded to launch his aces in a series of 100-to-200-plane attacks against Guadalcanal and U.S. bases in New Guinea. By striking such massive blows he hoped to outnumber U.S. planes locally and so achieve a favorable kill-to-loss ratio. U.S. pilots, however, felt no shame in fighting briefly and running away to rear-area fields where the Zeros could not follow for lack of gas. When the raids were over, the U.S. planes returned to their bases, alive to fight again.

The Japanese pilots vented their spleen by shooting up ships and ground facilities in the target areas but failed to cause any damage that was commensurate with their own normal operational losses in such long-range flights. Another forty-two of Yamamoto's prized naval aviators perished in the raids from enemy fire and mechanical failures. They succeeded in sinking half a dozen Allied ships and in shooting down several dozen U.S. planes—twenty-five by U.S. count, 134 by Japanese—but they failed to take a toll which gave any promise of reversing the course of the war.

After the third of the four big air strikes—a 174-plane assault on General MacArthur's headquarters at Port Moresby—Yamamoto could already see that his new strategy had failed. On the afternoon of April 13, when the last stragglers from the raid could be accounted definitely lost, a message went out in an ordinary fleet code known to U.S. monitors as JN 25. It announced that Yamamoto intended to pay a visit to forward bases in the northern Solomons on April 18, the anniversary of the Doolittle raid. It gave his itinerary precisely: take-off from Rabaul 8 A.M.; arrival Shortland Island 10:40; departure Shortland 11:45; arrival Buin, Bougainville, for lunch, 1:10; departure Buin 6:00; return to Rabaul 7:40. The message was signed by Vice Admiral Samejima Tomoshige, the local air commander, Yamamoto's subordinate. Until five months earlier, Samejima had been Hirohito's chief naval aide-de-camp. He had been posted to Rabaul as an expression of Hirohito's concern for the course of the air war there.

As soon as Samejima's message had been broadcast, Yamamoto armed himself with two bottles of Johnny Walker Scotch and looked in uninvited on a gloomy party that was being held by a group of his flight officers. Not for them that night was the gaudy splendor of Rabaul's "Naval Consolation Unit," or brothel, staffed by 600 Japanese and Korean girls. The airmen were drinking in a spirit of chaste samurai masculinity to toast the departed souls of comrades who had perished in the recent raids. Yamamoto, who had a notoriously weak head for liquor, broke his usual rules of temperance and threw himself into the anesthetizing mood of the wake. Before long, waxing sentimental, he had penned a letter to all dead and living members of the naval academy class of 1904 which he forced his cupmates to sign.

The letter is not extant but something about Yamamoto's manner that night caused his fellow officers to express great concern, in the four days which followed, about their commander's proposed trip to forward bases. On April 17, the day before the trip, Yamamoto lunched with Lieutenant General Imamura Hitoshi, the conquistador of the Dutch East Indies and now the commander of the Rabaul Army Group. Imamura warned him of the dangers of U.S. air ambush and told him of a narrow escape which he had had himself over Bougainville. Yamamoto promised Imamura that he would fly south with an adequate escort of six Zeros. That afternoon Rear Admiral Joshima Takaji, one of Yamamoto's best friends, flew into Rabaul from Bougainville to plead that the inspection trip be canceled.

"When I saw that foolish message," he said, "I told my staff, 'This is madness.' It is an open invitation to the enemy."

Yamamoto smiled gratefully at his concerned friend but refused to change his plans.

In courting death, Admiral Yamamoto sought to end his career at its height before the decline which he saw as inevitable. Because of the indiscreet Fleet message of Hirohito's former naval aide-de-camp, he had, in effect, imperial sanction to secure for himself the most honorable place in the samurai's Valhalla, that of a battle casualty. Other high-ranking Japanese officers might have to take the painful second-best course open to a man of honor, hara-kiri; Yamamoto, with the Emperor's blessing, would die swiftly, if he could, by an enemy bullet.

Not being aware of these subtleties, President Roosevelt was glad to be of service and to help Yamamoto shuffle off his mortal coils. The itinerary of Yamamoto's front-line inspection was picked up by U.S. monitors at 5:55 P.M., April 13, 1943, local time, at two separate listening posts: Wahiawa on Oahu and Dutch Harbor in the Aleutians. Decoded transcripts of the message were in the hands of high-ranking members of the Office of Naval Intelligence in both Washington and Hawaii about five hours later. It was then 5 A.M. in Washington and 11 P.M. in Honolulu.

Admiral Nimitz in Honolulu was just going to bed and President Roosevelt in Washington was about to rise.

Roosevelt ordinarily read his pouches right after breakfast and should then have seen the decoded message about Admiral Yamamoto's trip. Whether he did or not is a moot point which several diligent researchers have failed to resolve. The ambush or assassination of an enemy leader is a delicate matter. It invites retaliation in kind. Few statesmen have ever been willing to authorize it because assassination is a relatively easy mission for the espionage service of a major nation to accomplish.

Captain Ellis Zacharias, the deputy director of the Office of Naval Intelligence, an officer with ready access to Roosevelt, showed himself in the days which followed a determined advocate of the Yamamoto assassination attempt. Six hours after Roosevelt's breakfast, at 8:02 A.M. Hawaiian time, when Pacific Fleet Commander Nimitz had finished his own breakfast, Zacharias's man in Hawaii, Commander Edwin Layton, kept an appointment to see Nimitz on a matter of great urgency. Ushered into the admiral's office, he laid down a copy of the intercept and said, "Our old friend Yamamoto."

Nimitz nodded, scanned the intercept, and replied, "Well, what do you say? Do we try to get him?"

"Assuming that we have planes able to intercept him," replied Layton.

"What would be gained by killing him?" asked Nimitz.

"He's the one Jap," said Layton, "who thinks in bold strategic terms. . . . Aside from the Emperor, probably no man in Japan is so important to civilian morale."

Nimitz nodded and asked two questions: were there any better, younger admirals who might replace Yamamoto as the commander of Japan's Combined Fleet; was there any effective retaliation Japan could take? Layton answered in the negative on both counts. Nimitz at once wrote an order to Admiral Halsey, in charge of Southwest Pacific, to determine whether or not his fliers might have a good chance of intercepting Yamamoto on his tour and shooting him down. That same evening, when Halsey's staff had queried the squadron leaders on Guadalcanal, Nimitz got a positive answer. It was relayed to Washington.

A few hours later when Washington awakened, Deputy Chief of Naval Intelligence Zacharias discovered that only one man in the U.S. Navy's high command, Frank Knox, the Secretary of the Navy, had any qualms about the assassination. Knox insisted on getting an opinion from the Navy advocate general as to the legality of the operation, from churchmen as to the Christianity of the operation, and from Air Force General Hap Arnold as to the feasibility of the operation. All his consultants agreed with President Roosevelt that the operation should be carried out. O.N.I. man Zacharias had his staff collect an in-basketful of precedents for international assassinations, kidnappings, and intimidations. Frank Knox gave in, and by the evening of April 15 the best fliers on Guadalcanal were busy preparing to satisfy Yamamoto's "immortal longings."

The go-ahead to Guadalcanal went out coded as Operation Vengeance with a top-secret security rating and a unique "presidential" priority rating. The air commander on Guadalcanal assigned a squadron of P-38 Lightnings to the task and ordered special long-range belly tanks for them from MacArthur's stores in New Guinea. A pinpoint interception was called for, at a distance of 450 miles from home base, and it would have to be flown at the lowest possible, most radar-avoiding, fuel-consuming altitude. The pilots would have to be warned to fly by the horizon and pay no heed to the sparkling waves just below them: otherwise they might become bemused by the splashing sunlight and trip themselves up on rushing walls of water.

It was an improbable mission, but every pilot on Guadalcanal who heard of it volunteered to go along. Only a select eighteen, under the command of Major John Mitchell, received invitations: fourteen of them to fly cover and four to execute the kill. One of the killer planes piled up in take-off. The other seventeen P-38 Lightnings flew north at an altitude of 30 feet by a devious route which kept them out of sight of all islands along the way.

The Lightning pilots climbed out of the west, up from the sea, on Bougainville at 9:33 A.M., exactly two minutes before Yamamoto was expected from the north. As the U.S. airmen stared at the peaks of the island rising out of a tenuous overcast, what had seemed optimistic in planning took on a wildly visionary hue.

Even if Yamamoto's planes arrived on schedule the chance of seeing them and gunning them down before they landed began to seem remote.

Then one of the pilots of the cover group, Captain Doug Canning, glimpsed a glint of sunlight on a wing tip against the dark mountains three miles away. He broke radio silence in a husky voice that was almost a whisper: "Bogeys eleven o'clock. High."

In the sudden confused melee which followed, the three killer Lightnings came out of dives at high speed to streak past startled Zero pilots and quickly overtake the two staff bombers. So brief was the encounter—less than five minutes—that the U.S. cover planes watched from above and never had a need to engage. At the first hint of danger, the two bombers dove for speed and made off in different directions just above the canopy of the rain forest. Both were the new model of Mitsubishi Betty stripped of armor and loaded with engines and gasoline for flights of up to 4,600 miles. So big were they and so well could they burn that their crews called them *kamaki*, flying cigars.

The killer Lightnings were on their tails immediately, followed by swarms of desperate but lagging Zero pilots. Admiral Yamamoto was killed almost instantly—sooner, perhaps, than he had expected—by a machine-gun bullet through the base of his skull. His plane, with its dozen or more passengers and crewmen, plummeted into the jungle and burned. There were no survivors. The other bomber was splashed in the ocean just off the coast. Three of its occupants miraculously survived: the pilot; Yamamoto's paymaster; and his chief of staff, Vice Admiral Ugaki Matome, the brother of General Ugaki who had purged the Army for Hirohito in the 1920's and then in the 1930's had been disgraced through the March Plot. Of Yamamoto's staff intimates, Ugaki alone remained to tell of the Fleet god's death.

The U.S. Lightning pilots flew back to Guadalcanal to wrangle over who had shot down what. They were reprimanded for talking too much and for endangering the U.S. code-breaking program. Then they were given medals, shipped home, and silenced. Only after the war, more than three years later, was their story finally given to the public. Even then full documentation of White House participation in the affair remained classified as it still does today. Because of a minor infraction of the international chivalric code, official Washington would keep a secret, keep it well, and keep it more or less indefinitely.

Unprodded by any press release from Washington, Tokyo withheld the news of Yamamoto's death for thirty-four days while soldiers cut their way through the jungle to his wrecked plane and positively identified his charred remains. No one doubted that he had died, however, and Hirohito was so informed immediately. Lord Privy Seal Kido heard the unnerving news from the Emperor's own lips the very morning after the ambush. He wrote in his diary, "I felt shock and bitter grief."

A party of reformed Bougainville headhunters, drafted for the purpose, bore Yamamoto's body to the Japanese base at Buin. There his limbs were ceremoniously cremated and carried in a small white box onto the battleship *Musashi* for transport back to Japan. When the *Musashi* steamed into Yokohama on May 21, Tokyo radio announced that Yamamoto had "met gallant death in a war plane." For the next two days naval officers from all over Japan trooped aboard *Musashi* to pay their last respects. On May 23 the ashes were moved ashore to a funeral train which was greeted at Tokyo railroad station by a crowd of thousands, including all Cabinet ministers and leading bureaucrats and palace officials.

For the next thirteen days rites were performed over the ashes at Yasukuni, the shrine for warriors outside the north gate of the palace. A packet of ashes was given to Yamamoto's wife for interment at his home town of Nagaoka on Honshu's northwest coast. Another packet was given to his mistress, the geisha Kawai Chioko, for her prayer shelf. A third packet was prepared for Yamamoto's official Tokyo funeral.

Since Emperor Meiji's restoration, the Throne had sanctioned only eleven state funerals, ten of them for noblemen and members of the imperial family. Only one had been accorded a commoner, Admiral Togo Heihachiro, the victor over the Russian fleet in 1905 and later the chief of Hirohito's faculty of tutors. Admiral Yamamoto's was to be the second state funeral for a commoner in Japanese history.

Beforehand Yamamoto's last minutes were thoroughly scrutinized to make sure that he was deserving of the honor. Investigators learned that just before boarding the plane for his final flight, the hero of Pearl Harbor had handed an aide a scroll of fine rice paper on which he had inscribed in his own bold calligraphy a copy of a poem written by Emperor Meiji forty years earlier. He asked that the scroll be given to Samejima, the admiral who had sent out the fateful broadcast of his itinerary, the admiral who, until the previous October, had been the Emperor's chief naval aide-de-camp. The copied poem said:

> Now has come the time
> For those of us who were born
> Here in warrior land—
> Now has come the time for us
> To make ourselves truly known.

Another poem, composed in Yamamoto's own words, was found in his cabin on the vast 64,000-ton battleship *Yamato*, where he had had his headquarters. It was a long, imperfect free-verse effort which had never been reduced to the discipline of a proper thirty-one syllable *tanka*:[9]

> So many are dead.
> I cannot face the Emperor.
> No words for the families.
> But I will drive deep
> Into the enemy camp.
> Wait, young dead soldiers.
> I will fight farewell
> And follow you soon.

Having passed muster, even in his poetic sentiments, commoner Yamamoto was duly accorded a state funeral with full honors on June 5, 1943. The date had meaning, for it was the anniversary of

[9] Yamamoto's screed was not shown at once to the Emperor lest it upset him. Instead it was entrusted for presentation to the Throne to Baron Harada, the former secretary-spy who had been attached to the late Prince Saionji. Harada kept it for over two months and then gave it to the Empress's steward, Marquis Hirohata Tadataka. Hirohata brought it to Lord Privy Seal Kido on August 18 and discussed with him whether or not the Emperor should see it. Kido noted only the subject of the discussion in his diary and did not mention what conclusion was reached. Presumably he voted for showing the scroll to Hirohito, otherwise he would have omitted the matter from his diary altogether.

the day on which Yamamoto had withdrawn defeated from Midway. Fifteen hundred official mourners and a throng estimated at a million gathered in or near Hibiya Park, south of the palace, to hear the funeral oration and accompany the small white box of ashes to its final resting place. Along the way naval bands played Yamamoto's own chosen Western anthem, the famous *marche funèbre* from Chopin's second piano sonata. The cortege wound its way through the crowded streets out to Tama River Funeral Park in western Tokyo and there, in a newly consecrated Yamamoto shrine, the nation's share of the ashes was buried beside the shrine to Admiral Togo, the other honored commoner who had become a Fleet god.

Hirohito was not allowed to attend funerals because they would make him unclean as national high priest and would force him to perform intricate ceremonies of ablution. However, Lord Privy Seal Kido attended Yamamoto's funeral on behalf of the Throne and reported feeling "a profound sense of nothingness." Hirohito promptly asked to pay a visit to the Fleet to improve naval morale. The next day, June 9, however, an accident took place in the magazine of the 38,900-ton battleship *Mutsu*, at anchor in Hiroshima harbor. The gigantic warship, larger than any yet sunk in combat, blew up and sank immediately. So few sailors remained aboard to perish in the catastrophe that the naval military police and civilian Special Higher Police investigated the incident as a possible example of espionage or Fleet protest. Nothing could be proved, however, and after a two-week delay, on June 24, Hirohito duly paid his visit to the Fleet and commiserated with wounded men brought back from the war front.

HOPE FISHING

Admirals might wait for decisive fleet engagements; generals might talk of tactical withdrawals; industrialists might explain temporary industrial bottlenecks; but many knowledgeable civilians called continuance of the war "fishing for hope." Sympathetic to Yamamoto's quick grab at immortality, but lonelier by the loss of one of his sturdiest vassals, Hirohito had to go on living and fighting. He had no advisor to compare with Yamamoto for long-range military thinking. The sixty-three-year-old Chief of Staff

Sugiyama was an agreeable pachyderm who could accept scoldings
and countermanded orders without taking offense. The fifty-eight-
year-old Prime Minister Tojo was a correct military politician
who could stand up to fellow officers, suppress civilian trouble-
making, and resist cartel bribes. The once ubiquitous Suzuki Tei-
ichi, now the staid fifty-four-year-old chief of the Cabinet Planning
Board, had specialized increasingly in economic matters and had
come to talk like a banker. Lord Privy Seal Kido, fifty-three, was
a civilian, adept in civilian arts such as image making, police work,
and espionage. Moreover Kido was now exerting much of his cold
and awesome hysteria, and his meticulous cunning, to advance
planning for peace.

In Yamashita, the Tiger of Malaya, Hirohito might have found
the type of popular military leader who could make the most of
Japan's dwindling opportunities. But the outspoken Yamashita,
who had frowned on the Yen Hsi-shan massacres and had urged
immediate invasion of Australia, was now in an I-told-you-so position. Hirohito left him in Manchuria.

Instead of Yamashita, Hirohito took into his private councils
Yamashita's former staff officer, the brilliant young zealot, Colonel
Tsuji Masanobu, who was eighteen months Hirohito's junior.[10]
After propagating the verbal orders for the Death March in the
Philippines, Tsuji had accompanied General Hyakutake Seikichi
to Guadalcanal where he had masterminded the last two abortive
Japanese attempts to throw the Marines back into the sea. Following the second failure, Tsuji had returned to Tokyo to admit
candidly his errors in judgment and to urge the evacuation of
Guadalcanal, which had turned out successfully. Long known to
Hirohito and ardently sponsored by Prince Mikasa, Hirohito's
youngest brother, Colonel Tsuji had impressed Hirohito by his
frankness. As 1943 wore on, however, Hirohito saw that Tsuji was
too young, fanatical, and provincial ever to replace Yamamoto as
an easy-going, informal stimulant in the processes of strategic decision making. In August 1943, without hard feeling, Hirohito
sent Tsuji back to China to play the role he loved best, that of
staff-officer intermediary between the palace and its Army proconsuls abroad.

[10] Some Japanese biographical dictionaries give Tsuji's birth year as 1903,
but according to his own account he was born on October 11, 1901.

In the early months of 1943, during the retreat from Guadal-canal and the northeastern coast of New Guinea, the desperation which had driven Yamamoto to invite death had oppressed Hiro-hito as well. Shortly after his January scolding of Staff Chief Sugiyama for having no tanks at Buna, Hirohito had tongue-lashed Prime Minister Tojo for lagging industrial efforts. Taking a page from the book of his predecessor, Prince Konoye, Tojo had retaliated by falling sick and indulging in absenteeism. Lord Privy Seal Kido had promptly begun a list of possible new prime min-isters and had, at the same time, written in his diary, "However, I respect Tojo."

Tojo's health quickly improved; he received kind words from the Throne; he agreed to stagger on with Japan's burden. He brought into the government, as his assistant, a new vice war min-ister, Lieutenant General Tominaga Kyoji, whom Hirohito had long recognized as an authentic Army expert on air power. At the same time Tojo invited into his Cabinet half a dozen industrialists to serve as ministers without portfolio and advise on war produc-tion.

While Tojo was encouraged to fortify his government for prose-cution of the war, Lord Privy Seal Kido went on making contin-gency preparations for the chance that Japan might have to surrender and be occupied by enemy troops. On February 4, 1943, at the home of his secretary and postwar successor, Matsudaira Yasumasa, Kido met secretly with former Prime Minister Konoye to review Peace Faction planning. They agreed to exploit to the fullest U.S. fears of communism and to promote the idea that the Japanese people, in the dark hours of defeat, might turn Com-munist if they were stripped of their god-emperor.

On March 18 Kido reassured Yoshida Shigeru, the postwar prime minister of Japan, that he was the real leader of the Peace Faction and that Prince Konoye, due to ill health and American distrust, could never be more than the faction's figurehead.

On April 7 Hirohito ordered Kido to have two diplomats of the imperial coterie change places: Ambassador Shigemitsu Mamoru to return from the Embassy in Nanking and take the portfolio of foreign minister; Foreign Minister Tani Masayuki to go to Nanking to handle relations with the Chinese puppet government there.[11]

---

[11] Much later, in 1956–57, Tani was made ambassador to Washington.

Shigemitsu had for some time been agitating for a quick peace with Chiang Kai-shek: a withdrawal of Japanese troops from China in return for a break in diplomatic relations between Chiang and the Anglo-American Alliance. Both Shigemitsu and Tani believed that such a peace could be made and that they had the necessary contacts with Chungking to negotiate it. The pipeline was to run through Sun Fo, the son of Sun Yat-sen and former lover of Japan's girl spy Eastern Jewel.[12] Sun Fo would communicate Japanese proposals to his mother, Madame Sun Yat-sen. She, being a Communist on the one hand and the sister-in-law of Chiang Kai-shek on the other, would then negotiate the necessary understandings with both Chiang and Mao Tse-tung, the two fighting leaders of China.

Hirohito invested Shigemitsu as foreign minister on April 23. At the same time Hirohito brought back into public office another Big Brother, Viscount Okabe Nagakage, whom he invested as education minister in charge of propaganda. Like Shigemitsu, Okabe had lost some favor with the Throne by inclining toward the Strike-North Faction in the early 1930's. Other sympathizers with the Fight-Russia group would ride in on the two men's coattails. By bringing them back into office Hirohito not only made a bid for the support of the disaffected Strike-North partisans on the domestic scene but also indicated to foreign analysts that Japan was again worried by the threat of communism and was re-enlisting the services of leading anti-Communists.

Two days after the Cabinet shuffle, on April 25, Lord Privy Seal Kido was told by Prince Konoye that contacts in Chungking reported favorably on prospects for an over-all peace settlement that would include the West as well as China. Madame Chiang Kai-shek, said Konoye's informants, had recently learned on a trip to Washington that "U.S. war leaders are surprised by the power of the Soviet Union and have decided, as a result, not to defeat Japan and Germany too utterly."

[12] Debauched and corpulent, Eastern Jewel was now a "soul broker" for the Chinese community in Peking. She brought to the attention of the Japanese secret police Chinese merchants who still possessed hidden gold, and when they were arrested, she arranged and took a percentage of the ransoms which they paid for their release. She needed the money because she now had to hire professional actors and sing-song girls to satisfy her various sexual appetites.

In early May Shigemitsu, the new foreign minister, pressed forward with his Chungking negotiations. On May 13 he reported to Kido that the greatest obstacle in the talks was a Chinese feeling that the Japanese military would override any agreement which could be drawn up and would remain in China fighting no matter what treaty was signed by the Foreign Ministry. Kido told Shigemitsu to tell Chiang Kai-shek that Japan would honor her diplomatic commitments and that, if necessary to control the Army, Hirohito was prepared to appoint an imperial prince as prime minister.

The next day, May 14, Kido asked for an audience with Captain Prince Takamatsu, Hirohito's brother in the offices of the Navy General Staff, and having explained to him what was afoot, asked for his and the Navy's fullest co-operation.

Prime Minister Tojo was quick to see the virtues of a peace offensive and to propose to Hirohito that it be broadened to cover not only China but also other occupied territories. Why not promise independence, at one time or another, to all the lands Japan had conquered? Why not promise to withdraw troops from them at an appropriate moment and leave them with their own duly constituted, independent, anticolonial governments? Why not call a conference of Greater East Asian puppet leaders later in 1943, in November, to make public and ratify these magnanimous Japanese goals? Hirohito broached Tojo's idea to Lord Privy Seal Kido on May 19. Kido agreed that it was an excellent suggestion which would fit well into other peace planning. So encouraged, Hirohito telephoned Kido a few minutes later to ask for his opinion on what to do with Hong Kong: leave it British, return it to China, or declare it an independent protectorate of Japan?

While participating in these peace arrangements, Hirohito had indirectly admitted that the war was lost but he had not neglected its prosecution. He had lunched or dined several times a week with industrialists in an effort to alleviate Japan's growing shortages of airplanes, transport ships, machine tools, alloys, petroleum products, and rice. Before anything could grow out of the understandings reached at these meetings, the American industrial monster struck again with a new invasion, this time to the north in Arctic waters.

ATTU

Admiral Yamamoto's hunger for death had communicated itself rapidly to all ranks in all theaters. Even the guards in concentration camps far behind the front lines had begun to talk of the impossibility of winning the war and the inevitability of dying. The numbing new fatalism first expressed itself in action on the desolate island of Attu in the Aleutians.

Attu had been occupied by Japanese troops as a consequence of the Midway debacle. Initially the advance on Attu had been meant as a feint to distract American forces from the main thrust of the Midway operation across the Pacific toward Hawaii. However, when Midway turned to disaster, Attu had been occupied by a few hundred Japanese troops, unresisted, in order to save face and report something successful to the Japanese home front. Attu was the closest to Japan of the islands which stretched across the North Pacific from Alaska. Less than a thousand miles separated Attu from the northernmost of Japan's own seasonally inhabited Kurile Islands which arced north from Hokkaido toward Siberia's Kamchatka Peninsula.

By May 1943, a few weeks after Yamamoto's death, the Attu garrison had grown to 2,630 men. A still larger number of Japanese troops had garrisoned little Kiska, 170 miles farther east toward the American mainland. To U.S. troops these distant Alaskan outposts meant little. Their bone-strewn seal beaches and mushy interiors of muskeg bottomland and tundra plateau were hardly worth fighting for. Their only inhabitants were Russian fur traders and a few hundred native Aleut Eskimos. They had no trees at all and no shrubs higher than a man's knee except for a solitary fir on Umnak, the advance listening post for Dutch Harbor off the Alaskan coast. This one conifer had been flown in, potted, from Seattle, 2,400 miles away. It had been surrounded by a wooden stockade and posted with a sign which declared it the "Umnak National Forest."

On May 11, 1943, defying fogs and the unpredictable Arctic island winds known as williwaws, an American fleet stood off Attu and began to put ashore 11,000 U.S. troops. The 2,630 Japanese defenders of the island, softened up by a naval barrage, knew what to expect and bottled themselves up in the most defensible valley on the island. Eighteen days later the cautious U.S. invaders reached the valley from both ends and began to move in on it. The Japanese were by now hungry and spent from waiting, and their commander, who had been informed by Tokyo that he could expect no reinforcements, called together his staff officers. He told them that it was time for the entire garrison to die. Only by dying could Japanese express the sincerity of their purposes to Americans and at the same time abide by their oaths as soldiers to the Emperor.

The result of this resolve made a deep impression upon the U.S. troops on the island. The last 1,000 of Attu's garrison sortied that night from the old Russian seal station of Chichagof in a banzai charge. They broke through U.S. night picket lines to annihilate an American field hospital and a quartermaster depot. Half of them were shot down in the attack. The other half, at least 500 men, pulled the pins from the grenades tucked into their belts and blew themselves up. Neither Hirohito nor the U.S. troops could understand their bootless sacrifice, for neither had ever known their depths of hunger and hopelessness. U.S. observers were appalled by the piteous waste of life and by the peculiar way in which the cuddled grenades could clean men of their brains and insides while leaving outer shells of bone and skin intact. No G.I. philosophers, however, shed tears for the suicides. Before dying the Japanese garrison had taken 1,800 U.S. casualties, including 600 dead.

Imperial Headquarters had lost radio contact with the Attu garrison on May 27, two days before the suicide charge. As a result, the first news of what had happened on the dark cold hillsides of the island reached Tokyo through American broadcasts. Most Japanese who heard the bulletins applauded the suicidal courage of the defenders. Even Lord Privy Seal Kido was impressed. He noted in his diary: "I sincerely bowed to Colonel Yamazaki Yasushiro and to his men. I felt a sad and limitless rage."

Hirohito, however, was displeased. Suicides might become necessary in the latter stages of the war to evoke American pity and guilt; they might become necessary in the mid-stages of the war to complete the people's sense of participation; but now, in Hirohito's view, was still the first stage of the war, and suicides were wasteful.

By June 6, 1943—the day after Yamamoto's state funeral—Hirohito had had a week in which to weigh the consequences of the Attu debacle. He had seen that Japan would now have to garrison and fortify her northern islands, the Kuriles. This effort would take ship tonnage that was already fully engaged in provisioning Japanese expeditionary forces elsewhere and in bringing back raw materials to Japanese factories. The improvident frugality which had been exercised in the arming and supplying of the Attu outpost would now exact a heavy price. Hirohito called Chief of Staff Sugiyama and complained:

It is regrettable that we have had to follow this kind of strategy. In future please look ahead before making troop commitments. . . . I wonder if the Army and Navy are really co-operating. . . . We have now suffered frequently from a break in communications, caused by the enemy, between ourselves and the front. Please keep that in mind in future operational planning.

The next day Prime Minister Tojo saw the Emperor and announced ominously to Lord Privy Seal Kido after the audience: "The war has reached a decisive stage. The attitude of Germany will bear watching. Over there, too, the situation has changed."

It had indeed changed. On May 12 the last German troops had been driven from North Africa, and now the Allies were preparing to invade Sicily. For Tojo, who had championed alliance with Germany and Italy, the German retreat was personally humiliating. As a matter of honesty and self-punishment in the presence of the Throne, he had warned Hirohito that Japan now fought alone and that Hitler, if possible, would make his own separate peace.

On June 8, the day after Tojo's confession, Hirohito completed his study of the Attu Island tragedy. To Chief of Staff Sugiyama he was now scathing:

You foresaw this contingency [of Attu being cut off] yet for a full week after the enemy landed on May 12 you took no remedial countermeasures. You apologize that the fog was heavy but you surely knew in advance about the fogs at that latitude. You must have foreseen fogs. Are you sure that the Army and Navy are really communi-

cating with one another frankly? It seems to me that one service makes
a brave boast and the other promises irresponsibly to back up that
boast. You must be sure that you can accomplish what you agree upon.
To make a fine agreement and break it is worse than to reach no
agreement at all. We will never achieve any success in this war unless
the Army and Navy can consider their conflicts honestly and frankly.

If fog inhibited our movements, it was surely a mistake to invest
ships and airplanes in that theater, for ships and airplanes consume
a lot of oil. If we go on fighting this way we will only make China
rejoice, confuse neutrals, dismay our allies, and weaken the Co-
Prosperity Sphere. Isn't there any way somehow, somewhere, of meeting U.S. force squarely and of destroying it?

The Army is doing fine in Burma. Maybe in its own element the
Army will not be defeated, but on the islands in the ocean the full
strength of the Army cannot be brought to bear. . . . You have said,
Sugiyama, that the Navy's ability to fight a decisive battle "covers"
us against disaster in this way, but I am afraid that this ability no
longer exists.

The bland and genial Sugiyama, usually so optimistic, had no
reply to make. As cheerfully as he could, he reminded the Emperor that a joint Army-Navy air strike was planned for the morrow
against the Flying Tigers, the American volunteer air corps in
China. The next day, June 9, Hirohito was pleased to be able to
commend Sugiyama upon the success of the raid. Sugiyama took
the opportunity to beg the Emperor for full support of the Army's
campaign to hold what was left of New Guinea. He gave it as his
opinion that New Guinea and other outposts which Japan held
in the southwestern Pacific, although they might seem remote,
represented the "last-ditch chance to defend the nation."

READINGS FROM TOLSTOY

In order to follow his master's thoughts, Lord Privy Seal Kido
found it necessary at this juncture of the war to read one of Hirohito's favorite books, *War and Peace*. He found in it "ideas of
great interest for current affairs." It was Tolstoy's thesis, in his
saga of Russia's struggle against Napoleon, that the war fever of a
people, when once aroused, must run its course; that a kind of
redemption by bloodshed must take place before a nation could

make a fresh start. Also, Tolstoy felt that it was sentimental hypocrisy to wage war by rules as if it were a game. To be of any cathartic value, war should be total and fought to the death. Tolstoy's ideas fitted well into the fanatic spiritualism of Japan and helped to explain to Kido why Japan must follow the course that she did.

Kido's excursion into Russian literature was prompted by a new American move in the Solomon Islands. Throughout early June 1943, aerial reconnaissance told of an invasion fleet gathering off Guadalcanal. Hirohito fretted because costly Japanese air strikes and submarine attacks failed even to hamper the U.S. buildup. On the night of June 20 an advance force for the U.S. thrust— two companies of the 4th Marine Raiders—landed unopposed at Segi Point on New Georgia, more than a third of the way from Guadalcanal to Rabaul, and there began to build an airstrip. For lack of air support Japanese ground forces in the area failed to dent the little enclave and the Marines in it methodically developed it as a reception center for much larger American landings ten days later.

Hirohito was dismayed by the brazen self-confidence of the American invaders and angered by lack of co-ordinated Army-Navy thinking on how to deal with them. The Navy General Staff improvised plans for strengthening fleet and air units in the area. The Army General Staff wrote recipes for reinforcement which smacked of the same stale tactics that had failed in the Guadalcanal campaign. Both chiefs of staff spoke evasively when Hirohito asked them if they could hold New Georgia. For someone who would speak frankly to him out of firsthand knowledge, Hirohito sent to Truk in the Carolines and summoned home his cousin, his one-time sparring partner, Admiral Marquis Komatsu of the submarine fleet. Arriving in Tokyo early on June 29, Komatsu confirmed Hirohito's worst fears: the Solomons could not be held.

Prime Minister Tojo was scheduled to set out the next day on a long-postponed inspection tour of the "Southern Areas." After a stormy morning of consultation at the ironclad Imperial Headquarters shed, Hirohito called Tojo and entrusted him with an imperial message to all commanders in the Solomons. It asked them to fight a tenacious holding action, giving and taking no quarter and selling their lives as dearly as possible.

Tojo sought to cheer up Hirohito with brave reassurances, but he only succeeded in making Hirohito blaze up in a rare exhibition of temper:

You keep saying the Imperial Army is indomitable but whenever the enemy lands, you lose the battle. You have never been able to repulse an enemy landing. If we do not find somewhere to stop them, where, I ask you, is this war going to end?

Tojo flew to Rabaul the next day, June 30. His arrival coincided with the main U.S. landings in New Georgia which put more than 10,000 troops ashore on five different beachheads. Tojo found most of the front-line commanders assembled to greet him. With some severity he told them that, due to the Italian-German collapse in North Africa, the Allies would soon have major forces to spare for offensives in the Pacific. Japan desperately needed to build up reserve strength in rear areas with which to stem the Allied onslaught. Consequently forward garrisons, for the time being, would have to live on their own resources without hope of reinforcement or supply. If they fought well, they would gain time for Japan to make up the losses of her recent bad-luck streak and marshal a counteroffensive.

Back in Tokyo every patrician was mobilized for the total war effort. Only by showing herself ready to fight with every sinew could Japan hope to keep a bargaining position at the peace table. Empress Nagako herself rolled bandages and helped to wrap comfort packages for the men at the front. Lord Privy Seal Kido, for his part, joined his engineer brother, Wada Koroku, in proselytizing indefatigably for complete devotion to the construction of airplanes. Even Hirohito's eldest brother, Prince Chichibu, who had often differed with the Throne, now set up his personal aide-de-camp at a suite in Tokyo's Sanno Hotel to co-ordinate all peace dealings with Chiang Kai-shek.

While Tojo was still in Rabaul explaining total war and the new policy of abandonment for the beleaguered garrisons in the Solomons, the Allies on July 10 staged an awesome exhibition of their might in the European theater. One hundred and sixty thousand Allied troops stormed ashore from 2,000 ships onto the beaches of Sicily. As in New Georgia the Axis defenders found themselves hopelessly outnumbered in every medium: land, sea, and air. A stage in the war that had seemed "decisive" a month earlier now seemed all too clearly decided.

On July 25 the King of Italy and the Italian Grand Council deposed Mussolini, put him in protective custody, and gave the rule of the Italian realm to Marshal Pietro Badoglio and a care-taker Cabinet which was charged with the delicate duty of sur-rendering. The next day Lord Privy Seal Kido warned Hirohito that one Axis partner would drop from the Tripartite Alliance at any moment and that the other, Germany, could no longer be trusted to help Japan. Soon Japan would fight alone. Kido told Hirohito, "We must prepare for the worst."

Three days later, on July 29, Kido received a visit from Major General Matsumoto Kenji, the personal aide-de-camp of Prince Higashikuni, Hirohito's devious uncle. The secret police, said Matsumoto, were beginning to look into the peace plots of Prince Konoye and Prince Higashikuni. In translation from belly talk this meant that the secret police, with the connivance of Peace-Faction leaders, had put Peace-Faction members under surveil-lance as subversives and had begun to compile dossiers on them which would tend to clear them of war guilt in American eyes.

During August, while the Allied army conquered Sicily, while Badoglio and southern Italy waited to surrender, and while Hitler studied what countermeasures to take in northern Italy, Hirohito assimilated statistics and understood what Kido meant by "pre-paring for the worst." U.S. submarines that month took a dreadful toll of Japanese shipping. Almost half the prewar merchant fleet —3,000,000 tons—had gone to the bottom since Pearl Harbor and, despite heroic efforts, Japanese shipyards had replaced only two thirds of the losses. In the air, too, Japan was losing more fighting and transport craft than her factories could produce.

On August 5 Chief of Staff Sugiyama submitted to Hirohito a detailed report on the hopeless situation facing the Lae and Salamaua garrisons on the north coast of New Guinea and the Munda-Kolombangara garrisons in northwestern New Georgia. Hirohito was so distressed by the report that he dropped his usual

mask of moderation and self-control and exchanged words with
Sugiyama that would have made a less hardened counselor resign.

HIROHITO: It's not good in any area. Can't we hit the U.S. forces hard
anywhere?
SUGIYAMA: No, in all areas it's only a matter of time. We're doing our
best at the front lines. I'm extremely sorry.
HIROHITO: You may well be. If we are forced to retreat gradually like
this, the uplift for our enemies, and the effect even on neutrals, will
be great. Where in the world are you going to dig in? Where do you
propose to fight a decisive battle? I don't think that we can afford to
keep being pushed back like this, bit by bit, do you?

Three days later, in another audience with Sugiyama, Hirohito
repeated his plaintive refrain again and again: "Can't we take the
offensive somewhere? . . . Isn't there any way to strengthen the
air force quickly? . . . Isn't there any possibility of slapping
the Americans one sharp blow?"

By way of answer Sugiyama submitted to Hirohito the preliminary findings of a top-secret study of counteroffensive possibilities
which had just been drawn up by the leading department chiefs
of the General Staff. The study began by comparing the two
threats confronting Japan: that of the British thrusting east out
of India and that of the Americans and Australians thrusting
north from Guadalcanal. Of the two, said the study, the American
threat demanded the more urgent attention. To check it would
require that strength for a major counteroffensive be built up in
some rear area like Taiwan or the Philippines. Transports, planes,
guns, supplies, and men would have to be held back and saved
up from current operational expenditures. The study demonstrated in cold figures that present military commitments left no
slack for such a buildup.

Suppose then that Japan reduced her commitments by pulling
back her legions into a smaller defense perimeter and cutting
civilian expense to subsistence level. The study examined what
could be gained by cutting off all imports of rice to Japan, by
sending no more supplies to Japanese forces in the Solomons
and in the Marshall Islands, and finally by abandoning to hunger
the forces in New Guinea, Rabaul, and the Caroline Islands. The

study concluded that all three of these drastic measures would have to be taken in order to prolong the war and that even then "we will not be able to accumulate enough strength in rear areas" or "to mount an adequate counterattack against the enemy."

By the end of Sugiyama's recital, the mask had fallen again over Hirohito's features. Mechanically he asked time to consider the study. Somewhat later by telephone, he instructed Sugiyama and then Navy Chief of Staff Nagano to have exhaustive, independent studies prepared of war prospects by the Operations and Intelligence departments of both the Army and Navy General Staffs. The operational studies—described earlier[13]—were completed by the end of the year and were both more bleak than Sugiyama's preliminary findings. The studies prepared by the Intelligence departments of the two services are not extant but are said to have prescribed subterfuges closely resembling the events, described in Chapter 2, which would actually take place in and around the palace at war's end a year and a half later.

While hungry Japanese soldiers continued to hurl themselves against the U.S. beachhead on New Georgia in the Solomons, Hirohito received ample confirmation of Staff Chief Sugiyama's chilling conclusions. On August 11, Vice Admiral Nomura Naokuni, a former chief of Naval Intelligence, returned by submarine from Germany, went straight to the palace, and told Hirohito that the condition of the Third Reich was parlous. On September 2 Foreign Minister Shigemitsu reported to the Throne a continuing lack of progress in peace negotiations with Chiang Kai-shek and with U.S. operatives in Europe.[14] Shigemitsu recommended, and Hirohito approved, the sending of a special envoy to the Japanese Embassy in Moscow to see what could be done to enlist Soviet help in negotiating a peace settlement. The scheme later foundered in bogs of bureaucratic Soviet disinterest.

On September 2 the Allies landed in Italy. On September 8 the Badoglio government surrendered in the name of the king. Ad-

[13] See Chapter 2, page 79.
[14] One of the latest Japanese peace feelers had been extended through a presumed U.S. agent in Sofia, Bulgaria. Such repeated Japanese overtures were either too subtly worded to excite American interest or U.S. documentation on them remains classified. Most of the files of the wartime Office of Strategic Services were taken over by the C.I.A. after the war and have not been opened to public inspection.

miral Carlo Bergamini, the commander in chief of the Italian
Navy, with eighty-five warships from the bases at La Spezia,
Taranto, and Trieste, attempted to dash south to Malta and give
himself up to the Allies. Along the way, however, he was overtaken by German dive-bombers and sent to the bottom in his
flagship, the *Roma*.

On September 9, Hirohito attended a liaison conference at
which it was decided to close Italian embassies, freeze Italian assets, and intern Italian nationals. On September 10 the Nazis
seized Rome, and a select cadre of German paratroopers began
briefing for a special mission. Two days later they dropped behind
Italian lines, extricated Mussolini from house arrest at one of his
villas, and brought him back to Rome to serve as a German
puppet.

Hirohito that day of September 10 approved in principle the
transfer of seventeen of the thirty-four under-strength divisions
left in China, Manchuria, and Korea to Taiwan and the Philippines. The Army opposed the decision because it left the
Continent inadequately defended against Russian and Chinese
Communist forces, and even against Chiang Kai-shek. Moreover,
U.S. submarines prowling the China Sea made the operation
hazardous. Hirohito, however, argued that, if U.S. submarines
made it dangerous now to ship 300,000 men across the China
Sea, they would make it doubly so when the men were needed to
repulse U.S. landings in the Philippines. Conversely, if Russia
threatened to attack, U.S. submarines might not be too zealous in
interfering with troop shipments in the opposite direction, from
the Philippines back to the mainland.

The Navy had asked that some of the troops from the Continent be sent beyond Taiwan out to forward posts in the Marshall
Islands. Hirohito, however, sided with the Army in this one particular. Already the garrisons in the Marshalls could not be adequately supplied with rice and bullets. It would be a waste and a
hardship for the Empire to send them more men. In justification
of his sentiments Hirohito gravely quoted a favorite proverb of his
father, Emperor Taisho: "Affection between father and son, fair-
ness between ruler and ruled."

During the last half of September 1943, Chiang Kai-shek rebuffed the peace proposals extended through Madame Sun Yat-sen

by saying that he did not trust the sincerity or authority of either
the Japanese Army or the Japanese Foreign Ministry. Anything
but direct dealings with Emperor Hirohito, he suggested, would
be a bootless conversational exercise. As a token of his readiness
for such dealings, Hirohito, on September 22, gave an unprecedented private audience to Wang Ching-wei, formerly a KMT
lieutenant of Chiang Kai-shek and now the puppet president of
Japanese-occupied China. Wang was unwell and would die of
cancer in a Japanese hospital fourteen months later. After explaining to him Japanese hopes for a peace settlement, Hirohito said,
"I pray for your health and that you may establish peace in the
Far East."

Afterward, to Kido, Hirohito shook his head and added with a
half puzzled, half mocking smile: "Wang kept asking, 'How can I
manifest and incorporate in my own vile body Your Majesty's
sacred virtues.' He spoke as if he thought he were a Japanese!"

Despite Hirohito's great condescension and show of favor,
Wang was unable to persuade Chiang Kai-shek to accept Japanese
peace terms. To break with Roosevelt and Churchill in exchange
for a Japanese troop withdrawal from China would have left
Chiang alone to cope with Mao Tse-tung and Stalin. Since he
feared his wartime ally Mao more than anyone else, Chiang opted
to be patient and to leave Japanese troops in eastern China as
long as possible.

On September 25 the ideologist of the Strike South, Doctor
Okawa Shumei, re-entered Court records after several years of
absence. Having masterminded the plots of 1931 and the assassinations of 1932 he had passed under a cloud of polite police surveillance until 1935. Then, officially released "from prison," he
had rejoined the spy service and had held a position of authority
in the South Manchuria Railroad Research Institute over Soviet
spy Sorge's Japanese accomplice, Ozaki Hotsumi. During the war,
while Ozaki languished in prison, Okawa had remained a top spy-
service operative and maintained close touch with his former chief
assassin, priest Inoue Nisho, who now lived in the home of Peace
Faction figurehead Prince Konoye. Because of his many services,
Dr. Okawa had only to speak in order to be heard. He now sent a
message to Lord Privy Seal Kido suggesting to him that the final
Prince Higashikuni Cabinet, projected for the end of the war,

should include as an advisor or minister without portfolio retired Lieutenant General Ishiwara Kanji, the blunt, irascible strategist who had engineered the conquest of Manchuria in 1931.

Kido dismissed Okawa's suggestion as "sincere but naïve." At the same time he noted in his diary that Okawa wanted the matter discussed with Count Makino, the eighty-two-year-old former lord privy seal who had masterminded Court liaison with all the plotters, assassins, and coup d'etat artists of the early 1930's. Kido had a healthy respect for his charming, nervous, soft-voiced predecessor and did not seek out his company. Perhaps he felt it enough that he met frequently with Makino's son-in-law, the projected postwar prime minister, Yoshida Shigeru. On this occasion, however, when Kido did not immediately consult with Makino, Makino finally came to Kido. The result was that Makino took an increasingly active part in Peace Faction planning, and Manchurian conquistador Ishiwara—"sincere but naïve" though the idea might seem—did in fact become an advisor to Japan's surrender Cabinet. In that capacity twenty-three months later, he would tour the country telling the people that his old rival Tojo was alone responsible for the mistake of having gone to war with the United States.

On October 5, ten days after the reappearance at Court of Strike-South apologist Okawa, Hirohito began to allow leading war-criminal suspects to retire from possibly incriminating public offices. The first to go was the ubiquitous retired general, Suzuki Tei-ichi. In relieving him of his onerous duties as Japan's war-production czar, Hirohito honored him with permanent ministerial rank at Court[15] and a full-time assignment to peace planning.

Meanwhile Hirohito's Army brother, Major Prince Mikasa, had been trying to find out why Chiang Kai-shek would not accept the favorable peace terms which Japan had offered through Madame Sun Yat-sen. Chiang's wartime ally, Mao Tse-tung, seemed to be to blame, but Mikasa could learn nothing for sure. He expressed his frustration to Kido on October 8 by observing contemptuously that China had hedged all her bets. She had a Wang Chiang-wei government to deal with Japan if Hirohito won the

---

[15] Without such rank he would have been ineligible under Court rules to see and advise the Emperor in private.

war, a Chiang Kai-shek government to deal with the United States if Roosevelt won the war, and a Mao Tse-tung government to deal with the Soviet Union if the real winner turned out to be Stalin. "There are three heads in China," said Mikasa, "but only one body. As yet the Yenan [Mao Tse-tung] government has not been fully appreciated."

In early October Japan's leading fascist publicist and pro-German fanatic, Nakano Seigo, heard of secret peace planning at Court and in the Cabinet and swiftly recruited a conspiratorial band of right-wing labor heelers and Army veterans to assassinate Prime Minister Tojo, Lord Privy Seal Kido, and others. The plot came to light when one of its least responsible recruits, a disabled veteran named Terai who made a living by showing his wounds to a dozen different sympathetic widows, abducted an aristocratic priestess from one of Tokyo's shrines and took her on a ten-day spree to the fleshpots of Atami. When the authorities caught up with Terai, he revealed the assassination attempt and the Thought Police moved in on fascist Nakano.

A few days later, on October 27, Nakano committed ritual suicide in prison. The story was put out on the grapevine that he had been ordered to do so by Tojo because he refused to divulge the names of certain imperial princes who were associated with his plot. No knowledgeable person believed this carefully leaked rumor. Hirohito alone could expect to be obeyed in ordering a man to commit suicide. And all adult princes of the realm were closely associated with Kido, one of Nakano's intended victims. Consequently the double-talk of the official rumor was reduced to a single inescapable conclusion: Nakano had threatened, in his enthusiasm for the war, to expose Court plotting for peace. When told in prison that the Emperor was displeased, he agreed to show Hirohito the sincerity of his aims by taking his own life.

END OF THE PUPPET SHOW

The Allied thrust up the Solomons continued. On November 1, U.S. troops landed unopposed on the northernmost island of the archipelago, Bougainville. In easy striking distance of Rabaul, they bulldozed an airstrip and held it well against numerous Japanese counterstrokes. Prince Mikasa and Lieutenant General

Anami—the former imperial aide-de-camp who was to commit suicide as war minister in 1945—flew south on November 4 to bolster the morale of the men in the field. Anami stayed on to take command of the faltering Japanese defense of western New Guinea.

The renewed American advance detracted somewhat from a proud moment in the life of Prime Minister Tojo when, on November 5, he presided over the convocation of a Greater East Asia Conference of all Japanese puppet leaders from the occupied territories. The meeting was held in the chilly auditorium of the Diet Building, just behind the prime minister's residence outside the south wall of the palace. Blue woolen cloths covered the U-shaped string of conference tables. At the head of the U, where braziers of hot coals filled the cloths with warmth, sat Tojo and the Japanese delegation. Down the legs of the U, where there were no braziers, sat the representatives of the conquered territories: on Tojo's right, Ba Maw of Burma, Prime Minister Chang Chung-hui of Manchukuo, and Wang Ching-wei of eastern China; on Tojo's left, Prince Wan Wai-thya-kon of Thailand, President José Laurel of the Philippines, and Chandra Bose, the ward of Black Dragon Toyama, who had been groomed for twenty-seven years in Tokyo and Berlin to become the leader of Japan's "government in exile" for India. Sukarno and other Indonesian leaders had not been invited to the conference because Japan needed the raw materials of their land and was not prepared to grant Indonesia independence.

To the other puppet leaders Tojo orated on a text of "Asia for Asiatics." He promised them all "self-determination" as soon as possible. Thailand would remain independent—with Japanese advisors. Burma would be turned loose in 1944 and the Philippines in late 1944 or early 1945. Mukden and Nanking would both have new liberalized treaties with Japan. Chandra Bose would rule India as soon as the Japanese Army could conquer it.

The puppet leaders professed to be greatly moved. "One billion Orientals, one billion people of Greater East Asia!" cried Laurel of the Philippines. Laurel had been entrusted by MacArthur's captive, the prewar Philippine president Quezon, with the task of dealing with the Japanese. Now he distrusted Japan even more than he distrusted America.

"All the nations of East Asia should love their own countries," declared China's noncommittal Wang Ching-wei, "and should love their neighbors and love East Asia."

"I have heard the voice of Asia calling to her children," mused Burma's Ba Maw, "but this time it is not in a dream."

"It is undeniable," said Tojo in his usual short, positive manner, "that the nations of Greater East Asia are bound by indissoluble ties of blood.[16] I therefore believe firmly that it is our common goal to secure stability in the Greater East Asian area and to create the new order on a basis of wealth and happiness for all."

Tojo was at least half sincere. Having given his life to Japan's imperial conspiracy; having permitted the murder of his patron, the first of the Three Crows, Nagata Tetsuzan, in 1935; having, in short, seen the dreams of his youth burn into the ash of old men's cigars, he was convinced that the one justification for all that Japan had done must be, historically, the liberation of Asia from Western colonialism. Most aged Japanese generals in post-war Japan would hold to this slender thread of self-excuse.

During the Greater East Asia Conference, Hirohito himself gave lunch in the palace to the delegates and spoke a few kind words to each of them. Then, after a last tea ceremony in the Shinjuku Palace gardens and a last banquet at Tojo's official residence, the puppets set out to return to the harsh realities of Japanese rule in their homelands: printing-press money which Japanese quartermasters gave for what they took; a spy-hostage system by which Japanese secret police controlled influential native families and institutions; levies of conscript labor for the roads, railroads, and fortifications demanded by Japanese tacticians; countless "rationalization schemes" devised by Japanese economists to make sure of crops and products useful to Japan; and finally the relentless cant and mass meetings exacted by Japanese propagandists.

On November 19, 1943, as soon as the Co-Prosperity Sphere bunting had been taken down, Lord Privy Seal Kido received a secret briefing at his official residence from Rear Admiral Takagi Sokichi, the strategist who had been called upon by Hirohito's di-

---

[16] This was roughly equivalent to saying that Birmingham Afro-Americans, Boston Brahmins, Hungarian Magyars, Spanish Basques, and Orange Irishmen were all blood kin to Romans because all professed to Christianity.

rective earlier in August to assess war prospects for the Navy. With a few well-chosen graphs and deductions, Takagi told Kido that Japan had no hope and would have to give back everything. His opposite number in the Army, Colonel Matsutani Makoto, he said, was even more pessimistic and feared that Japan might have to be decimated before the enemy wearied of killing and allowed Japan to survive at all as a nation.

Prince Higashikuni had a lunch to recruit noblemen for the Peace Faction the next day, November 20, at the Kasumigaseki imperial villa near the Diet Building. After dessert Kido drove out to Hongo, a sub-ward north of the palace, to meet Konoye at a private hospital where he was recovering from minor surgery. The Emperor was busy for the next three days with military concerns arising from the U.S. landings on Tarawa and Makin in the Gilbert Islands, on November 21. Kido did not confer with him on Rear Admiral Takagi's black assessment of prospects until November 24. Then, after a week of consultations, Hirohito appointed a panel of civilian economic experts, headed by the ubiquitous Suzuki Tei-ichi, retired head of the Cabinet Planning Board, to check Admiral Takagi's conclusions. The next day, December 3, Kido learned that negotiations between Wang Ching-wei and Chiang Kai-shek had broken down once and for all in personal recriminations between the two.

Hirohito celebrated the second anniversary of the war, in somber mood, by making a state pilgrimage to the tomb of Fleet god Yamamoto. Kido, for his part, visited the grave of the unheeded prime-minister-maker, Prince Saionji. Neither the advice nor the forgiveness of the dead, however, could go far toward relieving the fearful ordeal for Japan which loomed ahead.

By mid-December 1943, complete intelligence returns had come in from the Allied summit conferences of November: a meeting in Cairo of Roosevelt and Churchill with Chiang Kai-shek and then a meeting in Teheran with Stalin. The analysts reported that Chiang Kai-shek would never now jeopardize his alliance with Roosevelt for the sake of an early peace with Japan and that Stalin was prepared—notwithstanding the Russo-Japanese neutrality pact—to join in the spoiling of Japan as soon as Germany was laid low.

Three days before Christmas, Kido received one of his rare visits from Count Makino, the knowledgeable, eighty-two-year-old former lord privy seal. Makino asked Kido to see Count Kabayama Aisuke, a seventy-nine-year-old operative emeritus of the spy service who had news of interest to communicate. Kido obediently gave an hour of his busy day that very afternoon to Kabayama. The old count gave him an evaluation of U.S. public feeling based on the reports of Japanese students—Ambassador Bancroft Scholarship winners—who had just returned from New York on an exchange ship. According to the students, most Americans had little hostility toward Japan and little interest in the war in the Pacific. The Pacific war, said the students, was widely considered a private enterprise of "Roosevelt and his henchmen."

Kido thanked Count Kabayama for his intelligence and wrote in his diary, "We must be determined to have ready a secret plan for the conclusion of the war."

During the next two weeks Hirohito took advantage of the holiday season at year's end to make his own over-all appraisal of war prospects. He had the underlings of Imperial General Headquarters to lunch. He even read a letter from Saionji's old Black Dragon informant, Takuno Dempu. Finally, on January 4, 1944, he transmitted his conclusions briefly to Kido. On the one hand, for the sake of the nation's pride, he wished to prosecute the war fully. On the other hand, for the sake of the nation's survival, he wished to have a sound plan ready for defeat. Kido, writing in the first person, set down the gist of his understanding of the Emperor's feelings, in a memorandum attached to his diary entry for January 6, 1944. This memorandum, mentioned earlier in these pages, became the blueprint for postwar Japan.

Kido began by observing that, if Germany could somehow resume the initiative, prospects would brighten for Japan and the rest of the memorandum could be disregarded. If, however, Germany succumbed, Japan must not fall prey to undisciplined pacifists and traitors like Badoglio. There must be a planned approach to peace in which the government at all times remained responsive to imperial bidding. After the Tojo Cabinet fell, as fall it must when "its continuance becomes quite difficult,"[17] the

[17] This state of affairs did come to pass six months later, in July 1944.

next Cabinet should probably be instructed by the Emperor in advance as to the specific opinion-forming mission it was expected to fulfill along the way to peace. So too with the next Cabinet, if a next Cabinet should prove necessary.

In regard to the nation's pride of face, Kido pointed out: "It is clear in the imperial proclamation of war that the Greater East Asian conflict was aimed at breaking down what were called the 'siege lines' of American-British-Chinese-Dutch encirclement. For the time being, therefore, we can consider it as a satisfactory conclusion of the war if we have accomplished this objective."

As to peace terms, Kido concluded that "only considerable concessions on our part will be acceptable to the enemy"—self-determination for all Pacific nations with the possible exception of Manchuria.

Kido acknowledged that his assessment might seem to some "weak-kneed and conciliatory," but he went on to explain that he was surrendering not in spirit and not forever but only to the brute force of American technology. In a paraphrase of Hirohito's own lordly sentiments, he wrote:

Looking over the future trend of the world, I believe that we must preserve and cultivate our real power in the state for about one hundred years. Through our experience in the Sino-Japanese conflict, the Soviet-German war, and the development of aircraft, we have gained insight into the real strengths of the U.S.A. and U.S.S.R. We have also suffered a terrible attrition of our own national strength. Accordingly, assuming that these assessments are correct, we should avoid at all costs being isolated and attacked by the other nations of the world as a colored race. With this goal in mind, I believe that the best course for us is to retain the effective power in the state secretly and to cooperate with the Soviet Union and China. Those nations are essentially Oriental in their thinking. Through them we can maintain our stand against the Anglo-Saxon powers of the United States and Great Britain while we watch developments.

29

FALL OF THE HOMELAND

(1944–1945)

THINNING THE GARDEN

Not Tolstoy, not even Machiavelli, ever dreamed in their historical philosophies of an entire nation embracing agony with such eager and unnecessary self-sacrifice as that of the Japanese in the next eighteen months. One out of every seventy Japanese stoically threw away his life for Emperor Hirohito—and this after Hirohito had admitted to his closest advisor, Kido, that the war was lost.

Hirohito could have surrendered in January 1944. The police, to be sure, would have had to deal with some diehards, but if the military realities had been explained to the people at large they would certainly have accepted defeat. Indeed many of them would have welcomed it. By prolonging the slaughter for another year and a half, Hirohito gained no better terms from the Allies, but he did preserve the unity of his people: their sense of persecution, their commitment to being Japanese, and their feeling of participation in his own imperial dream.

No doubt in acting as he did Hirohito was moved partly by wishful thinking and by pride and fear of humiliation. The fragmentary documentation, however, which in this period records mostly imperial acts rather than imperial conversations, suggests that considerations of state overrode Hirohito's complex personal emotions. In the hour of crisis the Spencerian biologist and the national high priest took charge of the imperial personality, leaving even less scope than usual for the man.

If Hirohito had stopped the war in January 1944, initial acceptance of his decision might have given way later to grumbling. When death and rationing had ceased, and when the nation's huge war plant had been dismantled and taken away by the Allies for reparations, many would inevitably say that he had sold out too cheaply. Millions of unemployed factory workers might find time to look back critically over the last quarter century and perceive the imperial conspiracy. On the other hand if the war were fought out to the brink of national ruin, the same millions would be too busy, as bombed-out refugees scratching a living from the rubble, to think of anything but their own survival.

Then, too, if Japan surrendered in the pink of health and productivity, the Allies would be far more likely to take revenge than if she surrendered hungry, sick, and decimated. By having to kill defenseless Japanese, the white soldiers would be moved to feel pity or guilt. By seeing Japanese give their lives away, the Americans would be forced to wonder if, after all, Japan had not fought sincerely for a cause.

Also, the Allies needed to be given time to fall out with one another. The American-Russian partnership had been formed in a moment of desperation. It could be expected to flaw and crack as soon as victory began to cool war enthusiasms. If Japan could hold out for a year or two, either the Americans or the Russians would grow eager to enlist Japanese support against the other.

Finally, Hirohito, both for scientific and high-priestly reasons, believed firmly in the value of death. The population of crowded Japan needed to be thinned before it would fit back into the narrow confines of the home islands to which the Allies promised to restrict it. Better for the nation to be thinned by enemy bullets than by fratricidal competition for enough to eat.

The killing could ease the Japanese conscience. When it was over, no Japanese would need to feel any further debt to the outside world. Japan would have paid for her predations limb for limb and eye for eye. She would not need to say, "*Sumimasen,*" the conventional equivalent for "Sorry," which literally means, "We are not yet equal; I owe you something." By balancing the moral books with a program of death, Hirohito could hope to enable

Japan to start again after defeat with a renewed sense of pride and righteous resentment.

In letting die the myrmidons who had failed him, Hirohito meant no special malice. As archbishop of Japan's spiritualistic religion, he believed—apparently sincerely—that warriors cut down in battle were fortunate. The shades of most men, who died complacently like oxen in their stalls, tended to fade in the afterlife and were soon forgotten by the living, but the souls of unavenged heroes were strong and lived long. They were given a warm home at Tokyo's Yasukuni Shrine and there, in that Valhalla, they fed daily on the prayers, offerings, and admiration of pilgrims.

GILBERTS TO MARSHALLS

Hirohito had been moved to consider the dark subtleties of national death and rebirth primarily by the U.S. invasion of the Gilbert Islands in November 1943. Earlier Allied offensives in New Guinea and the Solomons had demonstrated U.S. material superiority, but Japanese forces had not been so outnumbered as to lack a fighting chance. In the Gilberts, however, U.S. strength was overwhelming; there was no contest. This U.S. ability to mount a crushing onslaught in mid-Pacific while also supporting MacArthur's endeavors in Australasia and Eisenhower's vast enterprises in Europe had first convinced Hirohito—at least in the bookkeeping compartment of his mind—that Japan must be ready to abandon her gains and minimize her losses.

The U.S. invasion fleet for the Gilberts included twice as many aircraft carriers as Japan had ever owned: eleven fast fleet carriers and eight escort carriers. In addition there were no less than twelve battleships, fourteen cruisers, and sixty-six destroyers. This armada landed 6,472 American soldiers on Makin, where there was an 800-man Japanese garrison, and 18,600 veteran Marines on Tarawa, where there was a Japanese garrison of 2,000 laborers and 2,500 soldiers. Behind the total U.S. assault force of 25,000 stood a reserve of 10,000 more front-line fighters and an auxiliary of 73,000 with 6,000 vehicles and 117,000 tons of cargo. Six days after the landings, the Gilberts were secure. A thousand U.S.

fighters had died and almost all the 5,300 Japanese-Korean defenders.

Seventeen Japanese and 129 Koreans had been taken prisoner. The Japanese were all unconscious or immobilized by wounds at the time of their capture. When they regained their senses they protested that they should have died and that they could never return to their families in Japan. On the other hand, having admitted themselves dead to their own society, they were eager to be helpful to their captors and to find, if possible, a new life.

The great steel press which Admiral Nimitz was using to crush Japan's scattered outposts clamped next upon the Marshall Islands. The 8,675 Japanese manning Kwajalein were assaulted by 41,000 U.S. troops on January 31, 1944, and a week later, with the sacrifice of 372 U.S. lives, all but 805 of the defenders had been buried and accounted for. Eleven days later 8,000 U.S. Marines and soldiers took on the 3,000-man Japanese garrison of Eniwetok. By February 22 the island was secure with a loss of 339 U.S. dead and 2,677 known Japanese dead. Sixty-four Japanese were taken prisoner.

AIR NAVY

When Eniwetok was given up for lost on February 21, the Tokyo daily *Mainichi* ran an unauthorized editorial voicing a suppressed popular sentiment: "WARS CANNOT BE WON WITH BAMBOO SPEARS." The Thought Police investigated but preferred no charges, for it turned out that *Mainichi*'s editors were not traitors but patriots supporting Hirohito's brother Prince Takamatsu in a campaign for increased aircraft production and improved use of aircraft.

The *Mainichi* indiscretion gave the public its only hint of a difference in strategic opinion which had been argued on the steps of the Throne for over a month. On January 24, when the U.S. fleet was just staging for its advance on the Marshalls, Prince Takamatsu petitioned Hirohito to adopt a new aerial strategy proposed by air enthusiasts in the Navy General Staff. The Army and Navy were bickering over their allotment of aircraft output. It would be better, said Takamatsu, if neither service got a share and if all new planes were given to a new service, an air force.

Alternatively the traditional Navy might be scrapped completely and replaced by an air force. The point was that scarce planes were being wasted by traditionalists in support of ineffectual conventional troop and fleet movements. Instead, if Japan was to survive, planes must be employed, in their own right, by men who understood their capabilities. They must be expended for one purpose only: to sink the aircraft carriers by which the United States was extending her air superiority into Japanese waters.

In the circles of senior fleet officers, observed Prince Takamatsu, the ideas of the late Admiral Yamamoto were only beginning to be accepted. Yamamoto had developed Japan's air power as an arm of the fleet. Now his ideas were already outmoded. As he himself would have been the first to perceive, the arm had outgrown the body. Fleets now needed airplanes for protection but airplanes did not need fleets except as floating gun batteries, around floating air fields, in offensive actions, far out to sea. In defensive actions, close to landing fields ashore, airplanes did not need fleets at all.

It had been the dying hope of Yamamoto to use Japan's 64,000-ton super-dreadnoughts, the *Yamato* and *Musashi*, in a "decisive" shootout with the smaller-gunned battleships of the U.S. fleet. Now this proposal, which Yamamoto had considered a desperate expedient even in 1943, had been seized upon by other senior admirals and made an article of fatalistic faith. Almost complacently they told their juniors: Wait until the American fleet comes to us; then we will meet it in a great surface action which will decide everything.

In the opinion of Prince Takamatsu's iconoclasts the traditionalists' "decisive battle" was a dream which would never be realized. Even if the surface fleets ever came within range of one another, aircraft would still deliver the telling blows. And at sea, from now on, U.S. airmen would always enjoy numerical superiority because their country was producing more aircraft carriers each month than Japan could build in a year.

Japan's only hope was to capitalize immediately on her unsinkable immobile aircraft carriers, the countless islands which crowded her half of the Pacific. If all the Navy's technical competence were immediately rechanneled into air operations and if all the money being spent on warships could be diverted to aircraft manufacture, it might be possible quickly to patrol Japan's island outposts with a highly mobile air fleet. Ten thousand planes—less than five months' factory output—would be enough to overwhelm all the planes which U.S. carriers could bring into Japanese waters. If such a force could be hurled from island airfields at the next U.S. invasion armada, a dozen or two U.S. carriers would be sunk. Carriers took longer to build than airframes. Japan would gain time to improve her defensive position.

Prince Takamatsu's proposals were too rational to dismiss and too radical to adopt—at least not without a major political upheaval. And so Hirohito promised only to study them. He had long believed in air power, but so he had in all naval technical innovations, over the sea, on it, or under it. To junk Japan's big ships would be to antagonize all senior saltwater skippers and many of the great vassal families to which they belonged. To allocate the cream of Japan's aircraft production to the new Air Navy would be to antagonize the more plebeian Army as well. At best the proposed air strategy would only buy time, for it was apparent that the United States could eventually build a bigger plane than the B-29, capable of striking the homeland from bases as far away as Australia or Hawaii. Then Japan's cities would be burned down without a U.S. task force ever entering Japanese waters. Nevertheless, after ten days of consideration in which he heard arguments on every side of the issue, Hirohito made up his mind that Takamatsu was right.

On February 2 Hirohito summoned Lord Privy Seal Kido and gave him a military briefing of unprecedented fullness. Then he asked Kido whether, in his opinion, the military advantages to be gained from an Air Navy would outweigh the disadvantages of a dictatorial imperial decision overriding the advice of both chiefs of staff. In listening to the Emperor's strategic disquisition, Kido had particularly noted that the proposed Air Navy would not assure Japan of victory. He, therefore, advised Hirohito that, at this juncture in national life, it would be most unwise to act in any fashion that might be construed as tyrannical. Hirohito nodded and somewhat curtly asked Kido to discuss the matter directly with Prince Takamatsu. This was Hirohito's method of telling Kido that he meant to have his way and that it was up to Kido to remove the political obstacles.

In his work with the Peace Faction, Kido was already having trouble enough finding postwar witnesses to excuse, disguise, or shoulder Hirohito's responsibility in the authoritarian decisions of the past. Now Kido was expected somehow to conceal another dictatorial act, a war decision unpalatable to all Hirohito's senior military advisors. It was a hopeless assignment but Kido, without murmuring, set about it as if it were a challenge. He found, to his relief, that he had an ally in the loyal prime minister, General Tojo. If worse came to worst, Tojo would take responsibility for advising Hirohito to dismiss the two chiefs of staff. It would be better, of course, if the two chiefs would change their views. And failing that, perhaps they could be induced, by promises, to resign quietly for reasons of health.

THE "CHUNGKING MANEUVER"

During the complex political process which ensued—an imbroglio which lasted for eighteen days and involved all the great lords of back-room Tokyo politics—Kido noted in his diary a single imperial diversion. On February 14 Prime Minister Tojo came to the palace to give Hirohito a progress report on the efforts of Colonel Tsuji Masanobu, the executioner of Singapore and Bataan, to negotiate peace or at least postwar understandings with Chiang Kai-shek.

According to Tsuji's latest communication he had made good contacts in Shanghai with the Chinese underground and with Chiang Kai-shek's secret police apparatus, the Blueshirts. Soon, during a "special inspection" of forward areas, he would meet with direct emissaries from Chiang Kai-shek. He had hopes that they would take him to Chungking so that he could talk face to face with General Tai Li, the commander of the Blueshirts, and with Generalissimo Chiang Kai-shek himself.

Hirohito was pleased with the news. His brother Prince Mikasa had made Tsuji's negotiations possible. During a visit to occupied China the previous November, Mikasa had suggested and authorized a two-week memorial celebration for Chiang Kai-shek's mother on the eightieth anniversary of her birth at Chiang's home town, Fenghwa, in occupied Chekiang province. Colonel Tsuji had overseen the festivities there and afterwards, through the Blueshirts, had sent Chiang Kai-shek a memorial album containing photographs of the affair and inscriptions conveying to Chiang the good wishes of Wang Ching-wei, Prince Mikasa, and Hirohito.

Although Hirohito had great hopes for this essay in personal diplomacy, Colonel Tsuji would fail in his "special inspection" trip to negotiate safe passage for himself to Chungking. Chiang Kai-shek's emissaries wanted further assurance that Tsuji could speak for Hirohito. As a result Tsuji would make arrangements for one of his best Blueshirt contacts, a double agent named Miao Pin, to go to Tokyo and engage in direct conversations with Hirohito's uncle Prince Higashikuni. The reciprocal arrangements for Tsuji to go to Chungking and deal with an intimate of Chiang Kai-shek were not realized. Instead, five months later, Hirohito would send Tsuji on a temporary assignment of greater urgency in Burma, one from which he would not finally escape to make his long postponed Chungking pilgrimage until the war was already over.

SACKING THE STAFF

Though lightened briefly by Tsuji's "Chungking maneuver," the gloom of the political crisis in Tokyo was deepening daily. Then, on February 17, 1944, a devastating U.S. carrier-based air raid on Truk Island in the Carolines, the Pearl Harbor of Japan's surface fleet, persuaded Hirohito that he could wait no longer for Kido and Prince Takamatsu to work out a smooth political settlement. Japan must have an Air Navy immediately.

On February 18, the day after the Truk raid, Hirohito summoned his blunt, broad-shouldered, many-hatted "shogun," General Tojo, and authorized him to request the resignations of both chiefs of staff: Navy Chief Nagano, who had taken responsibility for Pearl Harbor planning, and long-suffering, bland, "Bathroom Door" Sugiyama, who had stood close by Hirohito's side ever since the Army mutiny of February 1936. Neither Nagano nor Sugiyama thought to oppose Hirohito personally or even to disagree explicitly with his strategic thinking. That was not the Japanese way. Rather, both men felt bound by leadership promises which they had made to subordinates whose careers and livings would be adversely affected by Hirohito's decision.

Sugiyama, in particular, felt obliged to reject Tojo's request to resign.[1] He felt that a protest had to be inscribed in the record on behalf of the Army. Kido and Tojo had not been able to find a single suitably qualified and willing replacement for him. To enforce the Air Navy decision Hirohito would have to appoint Tojo, who was already prime minister and war minister, as chief of staff as well. This would be a clear violation of national custom. As Sugiyama told Tojo's go-between, the vice minister of war, on the afternoon of February 19:

I cannot accept this demand. Supreme military command and civilian government cannot be combined. Their separation is an ironclad tradition of our form of government. If the war minister and the Army chief of staff are one and the same person, political considerations will find their way into military decision making, and the entire system of discipline by which orders are accepted in the field may well break down.

That evening Tojo called a meeting of himself, Sugiyama, and the third of the Army's Big Three, the inspector general of military education, General Yamada Otozo. A quiet man who had long preoccupied himself with the administration of Hirohito's experimental germ warfare program, Yamada was present not to say anything but to vote with Tojo.

During the course of the meeting Sugiyama blamed Hitler's interference with staff matters for the "mistake made at Leningrad." Tojo shot back: "Hitler was originally a common soldier and I detest the thought of being associated with him. I am a Japanese general. All that I have done as prime minister, I have done with due consideration for military implications."

A tense debate followed, but in the end, when Sugiyama saw that Yamada sided with Tojo, he bowed to majority opinion. He added, however, that before resigning he would submit his protest for the record to Hirohito. He did so on the morning of

[1] Nagano simply awaited the outcome of the power struggle and then retired to private life. He returned to the headlines briefly in January 1947 when he died of a complex combination of infirmities during his trial as a Class A war-crime suspect by the Allied International Military Tribunal for the Far East.

February 21. Hirohito accepted the written protest gracefully, saying:

I too felt uneasy about the combining of political and military leadership but I talked the matter over with Tojo and he has promised to keep it in mind. That satisfies me. It is, as you say, an extraordinary breach with tradition, and for that reason I ask you to be discreet and co-operative about it so that we may have success with it for the war effort.

Sugiyama could say no more and the heroic Tojo bravely shouldered the triple responsibility for civil prime ministerial politics, for war ministerial bureaucratic management, and for General Staff planning of war strategy.

INDIA, THE LAST OFFENSIVE

On being invested executive dictator of Japan, Tojo's first act was to move all government meetings into the palace: those of the Cabinet and War Ministry as well as those of the General Staffs. Although studiously ignored and obscured after the war, the fact was that all these meetings were now open to informal attendance by Hirohito and that Hirohito often took advantage of Tojo's arrangements to attend. The Japanese press at the time acknowledged that the Emperor had imposed "direct imperial guidance."

Under the aegis of Tojo's long-time naval crony, Admiral Shimada, who was now Navy chief of staff as well as Navy minister, strenuous efforts were made to realize Prince Takamatsu's Air-Navy dream. Every promising naval recruit was tried out for flight training. Construction of hundreds of small airstrips began on scores of small islands. Naval aircraft production rose above 2,000 planes a month and goals were set at 50,000 airframes and engines in the fiscal year ahead. Rather than scrap the existing surface Navy, which still contained many valuable vessels and officers, Shimada and Tojo, at the end of February, moved it from its home anchorage in the Inland Sea to a roadstead in the Lingga Isles, off Sumatra, a hundred miles south of Singapore. The aim was to cut back the maintenance costs of the fleet while its remaining strength was being expended. At Lingga Roads it would have easy access to the Indonesian fuel oil it burned and would be in easy steaming distance of the anticipated battlegrounds off the Philippine Islands where its obsolescent ships were to be sacrificed.

Next Tojo ordered the Army to mount a counteroffensive at the one point where it was strong and the enemy was weak: the frontier between Burma and India. This frontier was guarded by a hundred-mile-wide corridor of trackless jungle and mountains. Since the collapse of British resistance in Burma two years earlier, various Allied commando units had made raids through it from India. Now Tojo ordered an army of 155,000 men—three Japanese divisions and one puppet Indian division recruited from the ranks of Singapore war prisoners by Chandra Bose and his Indian government in exile—to march through the terrain barrier from east to west and invade India. The Japanese columns dutifully set out on March 8, 1944. They had no proper means of supply and no hope of living off the wild, almost uninhabited countryside. Yet to the consternation of British Lieutenant General William Slim, who had charge of India's defense, they crossed the frontier and in a month had taken up positions in eastern India from which they threatened the important railheads of Imphal and Kohima.

Throughout late April and early May General Slim brought up to the front every available reserve. At one point the British garrison in Kohima was reduced to last-ditch defense of two hills. Then, however, attrition began to tell on the enfeebled, dispirited Japanese soldiers. They failed to press home their attacks. The monsoon season intervened. In the wet, an unprecedented breakdown in discipline took possession of the Japanese Army. It retreated despite orders from Tokyo to advance and despite the orders of its commanders on the scene to hold firm. In the Japanese withdrawal 65,000 died, a few hundred by British bullets, the rest by disease, hunger, suicide with grenades, drowning in rivers and quagmires, and finally by fratricidal strife and murder. When the remaining half of the expedition got back to the plowed fields of Burma in late June and early July of 1944, reports quickly filtered back to Japan that the samurai escutcheon had been smirched beyond cleaning and that the Army had lost its stomach.

To still the wagging tongues and to discourage the possibility of U.S. landings in loosely held areas along the south China coast, the Army in China, early in June, broke its truce with Chiang Kai-shek to mount a major thrust south from Hankow along the branch railroads to Canton and the borders of Indochina, Thailand, and eastern Burma. To resurrect Burma Army morale, Colonel Tsuji Masanobu, the great samurai apologist, the great believer in the Japanese Army's spiritual purity, the great executioner of death-march vengeance, was taken from his negotiations with Chungking and reposted to Rangoon. There he rallied the retreating remnants of Japan's India expedition and succeeded in making them once more an effective fighting force—adequate in the dark months ahead to fight a delaying action against a major British advance out of India.

DECISIVE BATTLE

Far to the south and west of India, Rabaul had been cut off in the early months of 1944 and 30,000 Navy plus 70,000 Army personnel had been abandoned there to survive as best they could beside their own sweet-potato patches. The 15,000 men remaining of the once crack 6th Division on Bougainville attempted an all-out offensive against the U.S. Marine "perimeter" from March 9 to March 17 and killed 263 Americans for a loss of 5,469 Japanese dead. The starving Japanese survivors retreated into the hills to become guerrilla farmers. In New Guinea, too, the Japanese retreated and starved. On May 27 MacArthur's leapfrogging advance up the New Guinea coast bypassed the last Japanese strongpoints at the northwestern tip of New Guinea and struck at the offshore island of Biak. The local Japanese commander withdrew into the caves at one end of the island and continued to resist for a month. When the caves of Biak had been incinerated, 460 U.S. servicemen had died and 10,000 Japanese. On the nearby island of Noemfoor another 1,714 Japanese and sixty-six U.S. troops were killed. The G.I.'s rescued on Noemfoor 403 emaciated survivors of a 3,000-man Indonesian coolie gang which had been transported thither as slaves to work on the fortifications.

The capture of Biak brought MacArthur's troops into easy reach of any number of lightly defended small islands in eastern

Indonesia which could be used as final stepping-stones for the reconquest of the Philippines. On June 15, however, nine days after the Normandy D-day in Europe, Admiral Nimitz's naval armada stole a march on MacArthur by advancing into the Mariana island chain and landing Marines on Saipan from which U.S. long-range bombers, the new B-29's, could raid Tokyo.

The very day of the Saipan landing, B-29's from bases deep in China gave a small demonstration of what lay in store by striking a glancing blow at factories in Kyushu, the southernmost of Japan's home islands. This raid marked the beginning of the bombing of Japan, and Hirohito was quick to realize that, if Saipan fell, bombing of Japan would become routine.

Nimitz employed no less than fourteen battleships, fourteen cruisers, twenty-six carriers, and eighty-two destroyers in the Marianas campaign. Hirohito sent out from the Philippines, to seek a "decisive battle," almost all the expendable remnants of the Japanese fleet: four battleships, nine carriers, seven cruisers, and thirty-four destroyers. In the Battle of the Philippine Sea on June 19–20, three out of five of Japan's heavy carriers were sunk and almost 400 of her 473 carrier planes were shot down. Nimitz lost about 100 of his 956 airplanes and none of his ships.

The "decisive battle," on which surface fleet commanders for several years had based their hopes and their assurances, had now been fought. It had come to an appallingly decisive end. The big guns of Japan's super-dreadnoughts had never been brought to bear. The issue, once again, had been settled at long range by air power. Prince Takamatsu's predictions had been borne out. But Prince Takamatsu's Air Navy, because of the sluggishness of the home front, was not yet a force in being. Hirohito was incensed that a substantial part of it—400 planes—had been lost in support of the no-longer-needed Japanese carriers. From now on planes would operate from the decks of carriers only in coastal waters whence they could, if necessary, find quick refuge on airfields ashore.

WANTED: A DIVINE WIND

After the Philippine Sea engagement had been broken off, one of Prince Takamatsu's partisans, Captain Jo Ei-ichiro, looked aft at the smouldering havoc on the flight deck of his light carrier *Chiyoda* and sat down in his cabin to pen a radiogram. Having been recurrently a naval aide-de-camp to His Majesty, and having been second man in naval intelligence at the Japanese Embassy in Washington during most of the 1930's, he expected that his missive would be given personal attention by Hirohito. He sent it to Vice Admiral Onishi Takijiro in the Ministry of Munitions, the friend of Prince Takamatsu who in January 1941 had arranged for the Throne of secret independent evaluation of Yamamoto's Pearl Harbor plan.

Captain Jo's radiogram reached Onishi on June 21 and was reported to Hirohito by Prince Takamatsu on June 22. It was couched in bluntly lucid terms such as few Japanese appreciated better than Hirohito:

NO LONGER CAN WE HOPE TO SINK THE NUMERICALLY SUPERIOR ENEMY AIRCRAFT CARRIERS BY CONVENTIONAL ATTACK METHODS. I URGE THE IMMEDIATE ORGANIZATION OF SPECIAL ATTACK UNITS TO CARRY OUT CRASH-DIVE TACTICS.

Hirohito, too, had digested the fearful lessons of the "decisive battle." Planes had been wasted in a conventional fleet operation. Tojo's naval partner, the Navy Minister and Navy Staff Chief Shimada, was to blame. He had promised to support the concept of the Air Navy and then, for the sake of old fleet friendships, had allowed planes to be thrown away in this asinine "decisive" debacle.

Prince Takamatsu found Hirohito determined that Shimada must soon be removed from the government and that, because of Shimada's stupidity and the great loss of planes in the Philippine Sea, the use of crash-dive tactics should indeed be given serious consideration.

The idea of the suicide pilot had been implicit in Prince Takamatsu's Air Navy proposals from the beginning. Staff studies conducted in 1943 had shown, incontrovertibly, that crash divers could sink more enemy shipping, per man lost, than could pilots using conventional bombing and torpedoing techniques.

From a popular propaganda viewpoint, the airplane was an ideal suicide vehicle. The pilot alone in his cockpit could be compared with the individual samurai swordsman who, in a thousand Japanese romances, cut a spectacular dying swathe through the ranks of his enemies. As yet no anti-aircraft batteries invented stood more than half a chance of exploding a plane hurtling down from the sky in a full-throttle dive. And with one well-aimed crash a plane could sink a vessel costing thousands of times its own worth. By comparison, the banzai charge of massed infantry took real courage and discipline. It offered no satisfaction to the samurai sense of individual heroism. It cost many lives. And because of the astonishing firepower of the enemy's bazookas, flamethrowers, and automatic rifles, it offered little hope of gain.

Japan's simple, functional, inexpensive aircraft, too, were admirably suited to throw-away use. Indeed, the quantity production methods of wartime had rendered many of them good for little else. Defective aircraft were pouring from the assembly lines and could not be relied upon to give service over a protracted period of time. Maintenance crews in combat areas were not up to correcting the flaws left by the factories. More planes were being lost in ordinary operational use or during ferrying flights to forward areas than were being downed in combat. Those which arrived intact at the front were expended cheaply by hastily trained pilots who lacked the skills to fight off enemy interception and to place bombs and torpedoes on target.

A one-way flight by a resolute patriot determined to crash into a major U.S. warship would multiply by at least a factor of ten the effectiveness of every plane which Japan could manufacture. The plane itself would have to be good enough only to get to the theater of operations and fly a single mission. The pilot would have to be good enough only to take off, follow a leader, and then steer straight toward a target. A single plane loaded with gasoline and a 500-pound bomb could wreak more mayhem by a crash dive onto the deck of a carrier than two well-placed torpedoes or a dozen conventionally delivered bombs.

Finally, Japan had the patriots who were willing to die. Western individualism—the Christian doctrine of soul and conscience, against which Hirohito had inveighed a decade earlier in his conversations with Chief Aide-de-Camp Honjo—did not permit U.S. pilots to expend themselves suicidally except in moments of combat stress such as they had experienced at Midway. Japanese youths, by comparison, had been brought up to believe in themselves as junior members in a national family. The survival of the family and of the elders of the family seemed infinitely more important to them than their own physical survival. In frugal, realistic Japan the rearing of a child was considered an investment in the future. While still in his twenties and thirties a man was held a debtor to the society which had fed, clothed, and educated him. He did not reach decision-making maturity until he passed the symbolic age of forty-one. If he died of natural causes before that age, his spirit would live on in the afterworld but would never attain much influence there for lack of achievements in life. If, however, he died in battle, his spirit would have accomplished something; it would be promoted one rank by the Emperor; it would be given a permanent abode at the warriors' ghostly rest home, Yasukuni Shrine.

Despite all these irrefutable reasons, Hirohito knew that his political advisors, including Kido and even General Tojo, were opposed to any regular, officially sponsored use of pilots for suicide missions. It was one thing to order a half-literate farm boy to charge to sure death in the heat of battle; another thing to keep a corps of semiskilled pilots on permanent suicide call, taking lessons in the most effective techniques of self-destruction. The morale of such a corps could be sustained only by religious fervor and formal imperial blessing. At a time when Hirohito's most sane and cosmopolitan advisors were all racking their brains for ways to refurbish the Emperor's public image after the war, the use of suicide pilots seemed lunacy unless it could absolutely guarantee victory. And that not even its staunchest proponents could promise.

In the educated classes there was also a feeling of embarrassment about combining the traditional Japanese code of the swordsman with the Western technology of the airplane. Well-traveled Japanese sensed that use of suicide pilots would shock Westerners, would be branded fanaticism, and would be remembered with suspicion long after other war passions had cooled.

In talking to Prince Takamatsu about Captain Jo's proposal at the Imperial Library in the palace woods on June 22, 1944, Hirohito alluded briefly to these pros and cons and pointed out that the public-relations side of the question needed much study. Taka-matsu was forearmed for this objection. Captain Jo's suggestion, he said, was not an isolated phenomenon. On June 19, three days earlier, Captain Okamura Motoharu of the 341st Air Group, during an inspection of the Tateyama base, on the peninsula due south of Tokyo, had presented a similar petition for "turning the tide of war" to Vice Admiral Fukudome Shigeru of the Second Air Fleet. Kukudome had shown the petition to the vice chief of the Navy General Staff, Vice Admiral Ito Sei-ichi, and Ito was now a proponent of the suicide-pilot idea. So were many of the pilots in the ranks, for they were sick and tired of suffering 50 per cent casualties in mission after mission without achieving results.

Hirohito admitted that, if the idea were presented as a popular ground swell coming up from the ranks, it might be possible to allay the fears of Kido, Tojo, and other advisors. Certainly some such *kamikaze*, divine wind, was needed if the enemy armadas were to be wrecked short of the sacred Japanese shore. For the moment, however, Hirohito would authorize Takamatsu only to pursue design studies for an easy-to-produce piloted bomb which would take maximum economical advantage of kamikaze talents if they were ever harnessed.

SAIPAN AND TOJO'S FALL

By the time Hirohito took this new responsibility on his sacerdotal conscience, the week-old U.S. invasion of the Marianas had put some 70,000 Americans ashore on the island of Saipan. Like the monster in some postwar Japanese science fiction film, the invaders had systematically destroyed the ingeniously prepared positions, traps, and strongpoints of the 30,000-man Japanese garrison.

Saipan was the first of Japan's prewar possessions to be attacked by the enemy. It was the largest of the islands which Japan had seized from Germany during World War I and held under League of Nations mandate. It was a beautiful place and Japan had colonized it heavily, studding its green hills with sawmills and sugarcane fields. In addition to the 30,000 soldiers on Saipan, there dwelled at least 25,000 civilians.

As the battle turned against the Saipan garrison, a question arose: how to instruct the civilian inhabitants. Previously, except for a few prostitutes and bureaucrats, no Japanese civilians had come within U.S. reach. Now an entire Japanese community, including many of low caste, who had emigrated for lack of opportunity at home, was about to fall prisoner. There was a danger that the civilians would be captured alive; that they would be surprised and pleased by U.S. treatment; that they would be used in U.S. propaganda broadcasts to subvert the fighting spirit of the rest of Japan. A Japanese civilian prisoner encampment was, indeed, erected behind Marine lines on June 23 and soon had more than a thousand inmates. It had electric lights which were left conspicuously blazing at night. Thrice daily its mess tents exhaled a sweet savor of cooking rice and meat and were queued by long lines of evidently happy, expectant Japanese.

Hirohito found the defection of the Japanese civilians on Saipan disturbing, and at the end of the month an imperial order went out encouraging civilians who were still at large to commit suicide.[2] The order did not demand suicide; it empowered the commander of Saipan to promise civilians who died there an equal spiritual status in the afterlife with that of soldiers perishing in combat. On June 30 the prime minister, war minister, and chief of staff, namely General Tojo, intercepted this order and delayed its sending. It went out anyway, the next day, after Tojo had brought it to the attention of Kido and other civilian advisors in the palace.

Five days later, on July 6, organized resistance on Saipan collapsed, and Admiral Nagumo, the former Pearl Harbor task force commander who had charge of naval forces on the island, squatted at the mouth of a cave, slit open his abdomen, and then had an aide standing behind him dispatch him with a bullet into the back of his head. That night the starving remnants of the main Japanese garrison on Saipan charged U.S. Marine lines. Those who

---

[2] Some apologists for Hirohito have asserted that this and other deadly orders issued at other times under the imperial imprimatur were all actually sent by someone at Imperial Headquarters who dared to abuse the seals with which Hirohito stamped state papers. The impious scofflaw has never been identified. Half the staff of the palace, beginning with Lord Privy Seal Kido, would have felt obliged to cut open their bellies if the sacred seals of the Throne had ever been misapplied.

failed to be killed by U.S. machine guns took their own lives with grenades, revolvers, mines, swords, knives, and sharp stones.

On July 8 the Marines moved unhindered through the stench of bodies toward the north tip of the island. There over 10,000 Japanese civilians were destroying themselves: dashing their babes against rocks, hurling their children and wives into the sea, jumping from the high cliffs. Before the Marines could stop the slaughter, on July 12, most of the civilians had accepted Hirohito's offer of a privileged place in ghosts' paradise. Marine veterans looked down into the surf, awash with the bodies of children, and turned away with troubled minds and queasy stomachs.

Over-all there fell on bloody Saipan some 15,000 Japanese civilians and about 30,000 Japanese soldiers and sailors. Even so, the Marines took their first major bag of prisoners: 921 Japanese troops and 10,258 civilians. Of 67,451 U.S. combat troops 3,426 died.

As soon as Saipan had been secured, the Marines, on July 21, invaded Guam. This was the largest of the Marianas—209 square miles as compared with Saipan's 70 square miles—and the one island of the archipelago which had belonged to the United States rather than to Japan before the war. Between July 21 and August 10, some 55,000 U.S. troops fought there against about 20,000 defenders. Some 10,000 Japanese were killed in the campaign and another 8,500, who hid in the hills, were killed in the year which followed. Only 1,435 U.S. troops died and only 1,250 Japanese were taken captive.

The third island of the Marianas, 40-square-mile Tinian, was invaded by 15,614 Marines on July 24. After three days of blistering pre-invasion pounding, in which the first use was made of napalm, a mixture of explosives and petroleum jellies, the 9,000 men of the Japanese garrison put up a ragged resistance. In a week 5,000 of them could be counted dead and the rest permanently missing. The Marines had lost 389 killed in action and had taken 252 prisoners. The Japanese airstrip was quickly improved to become the finest runway for long-range bombers in the Pacific. From it, a year later, would take off the *Enola Gay* with the bomb for Hiroshima.

During the slaughter on Guam and Tinian, Hirohito was forced by his nearest and dearest to give up the war, give up his direct participation in Cabinet and staff meetings, and inaugurate the

programed succession of de-escalations in war spirit which had
been planned by the Peace Faction. Hirohito was reluctant to accept this final turning point in his life but he bowed to it—after
a week of vacillation—under pressure rather than coercion. He
admitted to his closest advisors that he was beaten and had been
wrong; he did not abdicate his place as spiritual war leader.

The moment of Hirohito's resignation was probably July 7, the
day after the collapse of organized resistance on Saipan. That day
Prince Takamatsu asked Lord Privy Seal Kido to arrange more
athletic exercise for Hirohito and more clerical help for him. On
July 11, as the horrible suicide of Japanese civilians on Saipan
neared its end, the senior generals of the Army and admirals of
the Navy, including some of the Strike-North Faction which had
opposed Hirohito in the 1930's, met without fanfare at the Army
Club north of the palace walls and agreed quietly that the time
had come to bury factional differences, to draw in protectively
around the Throne, and to make a symbolic change in leadership
by ousting the war "shogun," General Tojo.

Accepting the verdict of his senior officers, Tojo immediately
tendered his resignation to the Throne. Hirohito at first rejected
it and encouraged Tojo to shore up his political position for a
while longer. Hirohito did not believe that Peace Faction planners
could really whitewash him and felt that it would be cowardly for
him even to let them try. He and Tojo might sometimes differ but
Tojo, he said, was still the strongest war leader in Japan. Tojo took
two days to consider the Emperor's request.

The planning to use suicide pilots disturbed Tojo; if only for
the quiet of his soul in the afterlife, he did not want to take responsibility for sending thousands of Japanese young men to certain death when he knew that their sacrifice could not win the
war. In addition Tojo owed loyalty to Admiral Shimada, his Navy
minister and Navy staff chief; Hirohito wished to make Shimada
the public scapegoat for the Marianas debacle. If Shimada were
jettisoned from the government it might be possible, thought
Hirohito's political advisor Kido, to leave Tojo in office. The main
complaint of the critics was the "part-time strategy" of war leaders
who had to run the civilian bureaucracy as well as the General
Staff offices. Since the U.S. island-hopping campaign made the
war mainly naval now, it would be enough for the moment to dis-

miss the part-time naval strategist and to leave General Tojo in office.

After discussing the situation with his patrons, with his partisans, and with Admiral Shimada, Tojo promised Hirohito on July 13 that he would make an effort to stagger on with the burden of government. During the next five days, however, in trying to give his Cabinet a face-lifting and fresh lease on life, he encountered so much hostility and vilification that he saw he had no sound basis of co-operation with which to work.

On July 18 Tojo submitted his resignation unequivocally to Hirohito, and two days later, Hirohito broke with tradition by investing two men at once with the prime ministerial responsibility. The wizened General Koiso Kuniaki, whose March Plot had paved the way for the invasion of Manchuria in 1931, was to head the partnership; he was to be assisted by the big, hearty Admiral Yonai Mitsumasa, as Navy minister and assistant prime minister. Since Yonai had been a full prime minister earlier, in the first half of 1940, he was no longer on the active list of naval commanders. He was, therefore, ineligible by law to serve as Navy minister. Hirohito solved this small difficulty by a stroke of his seal as commander in chief: he simply reinstated Yonai to the active list.

DESPERATE SHO

Early in August 1944, not long after the Koiso-Yonai partnership had removed Cabinet meetings once again to a discreet distance from the palace, Hirohito approved production of the Ohka missile, a 4,000-pound bomb, equipped with wooden wings, a cockpit for a pilot, elementary flight controls, and five small rockets which could propel it for a distance of 19 to 20 miles from its point of release by a "mother" bomber. Production models of the Ohka would not be ready for use until the very end of the kamikaze effort and then would give poor results. The building of them, however, involved civilian workers in the kamikaze program, making it all too clearly official.

The Ohka scheme dismayed those of Hirohito's advisors who had the care of his public image. They redoubled their efforts on behalf of the Peace Faction. At 2:23 P.M. on August 25, still a full year before the Americans would set foot in Japan, Lord Privy Seal

Kido emerged from an hour-long audience with the Emperor at the concrete library in the palace woods and drove to his official residence outside the palace walls. There he spent the last half of the afternoon, from 3 P.M., getting to know an officer he had asked to see who was reputed to have the most formidable memory in the Japanese Army. The officer was retired Major Tanaka Takayoshi and this was the first of several interviews with Kido which would ultimately launch Tanaka on his second career, that of star witness at the American war crimes trials: witness for the prosecution, witness for the defense, guide to U.S. prosecutor Keenan, informer, double agent, and patriot *par excellence*.

Meanwhile Allied strategists had been fiercely debating the course to follow in reaching Tokyo and ending the war. General MacArthur maintained that the United States was committed primarily to the lifting of Japan's yoke from the Philippines. To this political pledge, which MacArthur considered a matter of national and personal honor, the reduction of Japan should be considered secondary. Some British and Dutch statesmen went further, advocating step-by-step reconquest of all the islands in the South Pacific so that they could be put back under stable colonial administration before Japan fell, and before Allied war zeal fell from fever pitch, and before the inevitable postwar peace conference bickering began. The most narrowly efficient and technologically minded commanders in the U.S. Armed Forces, especially admirals, saw no valid military reason for shedding blood and spending bullets in the East Indies, Malaya, or the Philippines. They instead advocated the quickest possible seizure of Japan by the throat: landings on Taiwan and in friendly areas on the south China coast, or possibly landings in the Bonins and Ryukyus, followed by a direct assault on the home island of Kyushu.

A week after the investment of the Koiso-Yonai Cabinet in Tokyo, President Roosevelt paid a state visit to Hawaii and resolved these strategic issues in a meeting, on July 27, with MacArthur and Nimitz at the home of an old crony, Chris Holmes, on Kalaukau Avenue in the Waikiki suburb of Honolulu. MacArthur spoke eloquently of the political advantages to be gained by reconquering the Philippines before assaulting Japan. Roosevelt nodded his sympathy with MacArthur's arguments. Nimitz agreed, somewhat reluctantly, that he would as soon destroy the remnants of the Japanese fleet and naval air arm in Philippine waters as in the China Sea, the Bonin Trench, or the Okinawan Deep. And so was decided Final Strategy Japan. The chiefs of staff in Washington would continue to debate it for another ten weeks before it would be made official.

On September 15 MacArthur's Army forces advancing north from Australia and Nimitz's Navy forces sailing west from Pearl Harbor pinched in on the Philippines with co-ordinated landings at Morotai in the Molucca or Spice Islands, halfway between New Guinea and Mindanao, and at Peleliu in the Palau Islands off the eastern shores of the Philippines, two thirds of the way from Guam to Mindanao. At Morotai MacArthur's men quickly over-ran a garrison of 500 with the loss of only thirty-one dead. At Peleliu the Marines encountered a stout garrison of over 10,000. The desired airstrip and local air superiority were gained in a week but heavy fighting continued for two months.

Improving on the lessons learned in the caves of Biak, the Japanese commander on Peleliu, Colonel Nakagawa Kunio, assisted by an envoy from the palace Office of Aides-de-Camp, made best possible use of the hollows in the coral underlying the main ridge of Peleliu's hills. Drilling had interconnected the vacancies left by prehistoric marine organisms and cement had been added within their gossamer-gothic architecture. Neither shells nor bombs could pierce their galleries from above and Marines equipped with the most long-spurt flamethrowers had to move with extreme caution whenever they came to a turning in a tunnel.

Colonel Nakagawa and his imperial adviser, Major General Murai Kenjiro, held out in their well-stocked subterranean command center for seventy days and finally committed ritual suicide together on the night of November 24–25. Other Japanese, still deeper in the coral Hades, held out longer. Thirty Japanese from an inner cave burst out to kill a number of careless G.I. souvenir hunters in December. And the last five Japanese did not dig out from the labyrinth and surrender until February 1, 1945.

Assured by the landings on Morotai and Peleliu that the Philippines were, indeed, the next U.S. objective, Hirohito affixed his seal to a General Staff defense plan called SHO.[3] The name stood

---

[3] Hirohito had temporarily withdrawn from overt political activity, but he was still commander in chief.

for "victory" but the deliberations surrounding the inception of SHO reveal that it was considered a plan for one last glorious *Götterdämmerung* gesture before defeat. In effect it coolly prescribed the sacrifice—self-destruction was the term used by the planners—of almost 250,000 soldiers and 50,000 sailors. They were not expected to win any victories, unless "by a miracle," but they were expected to sell their lives dearly and so prove to the enemy Japan's will to resist—her "sincerity."

The most total SHO sacrifice was expected of the Navy. Its big ships were no longer of much value. They did not have oil with which to operate. They must not be captured by the enemy. It was the duty of their captains to shoot up the U.S. armada as much as possible and get sunk.

The Air Navy, on the other hand, was expected to preserve itself insofar as possible for defense of Japan's home shores. Most of it was still in training in Japan and would be kept there, uncommitted. The rest, about 2,000 planes which were already operating from bases in Taiwan and Luzon, would strike only if they could do so to advantage, by sinking U.S. carriers. If they could not do so with reasonable expectation of success, they were to exploit the fact that they were land based and had hundreds of safe fields to fly to. That is, they were to run away and live for the day when the Air Navy was ready for battle.

The Army's part in SHO was more conventional. The 250,000 soldiers who had been shipped to the Philippines early in the year were to fight to the death for every island, every mountain range, every hill and rill.

The long-range value of the suicidal SHO operation as a means of exacting improved surrender terms from the enemy escaped most Japanese Army officers. About September 20 a group of them who had been sympathetic to the Strike-North Faction in the 1930's conceived a political plot to overthrow the Koiso Cabinet and replace it with a more talented and realistic "war prosecution government" headed by General Yamashita, the Tiger of Malaya who had been exiled to Manchuria. Members of the conspiracy approached Prince Asaka and Prince Takeda asking for their support. Asaka and Takeda, through Hirohito, promptly reported to the lord privy seal. Kido was not about to have an unknown step thrown into his carefully programed staircase of governments leading down to surrender. At Kido's suggestion, Tiger Yamashita was recalled to Tokyo, given a week of briefings, and then reposted to an assignment which would fully occupy his genius: the command of the 250,000 fated soldiers in the Philippines. Yamashita obediently reported at Fort McKinley outside Manila on October 6. From a platform in a blacked-out hall that evening he explained to his assembled commanders: "I have been told by our Emperor that the crisis will first develop on this battlefield. This gives us all a heavy responsibility."[4]

On October 10, the growing monster of Admiral Halsey's fast carrier task force—nine heavy attack carriers, eight light attack carriers, six battleships, fourteen cruisers, and fifty-eight destroyers—forayed into Japan's home waters and launched air raids against Okinawa and the other islands of the Ryukyu chain connecting Kyushu with Taiwan. The raids caught few planes on the ground but smashed up many of the stopover fields needed by the Air Navy if it was to strike back in the Philippine area. The next day Halsey's planes temporarily decommissioned many of the landing fields in northern Luzon.

Finally, on October 12 and for three days thereafter, the 1,068 planes from the U.S. task force, supported by B-29's from China,[5] took on the thousand-odd planes which Japan had stationed in Taiwan. More than 500 of the Japanese planes—about a twentieth of the projected Air Navy, about a tenth of the Air Navy already in being—were destroyed either in the air or on the ground. In addition, on the third day of the strikes, the U.S. pilots uncovered and bombed some fifteen new airfields on Taiwan with which Air Navy officers had hoped to achieve a measure of surprise when the time came for full deployment of their forces. For these gains

---

[4] Three days later, on October 9, Hirohito dispatched a special envoy to Moscow—an inveterate critic of Matsuoka diplomacy, Morishima Goro—with a letter from Lord Privy Seal Kido to Ambassador Sato Naotake. The letter was meant for showing to Russian Foreign Ministry officials as evidence that Sato was empowered to seek Stalin's help as a mediator in ending the war. No detailed account of Morishima's mission or of Sato's dealings with Molotov has yet been released, but, as suggested in Chapter 2, the seed fell on ground frozen by the cold of a Russian diplomatic winter.

[5] The first 500 of the gleaming Superfortresses, each capable of carrying four tons of bombs for 3,500 miles, had begun to arrive at bases in China and the Pacific only that summer.

Halsey paid a modest price: less than 100 planes lost and two cruisers out of action but successfully towed away.

Having destroyed *in utero* the morale of the recently conceived Air Navy, the U.S. forces turned to their main task, the reconquest of a beachhead in the Philippines. There were 840 ships in the converging U.S. armadas, including forty-seven aircraft carriers, ten battleships, thirty-one cruisers, and 176 destroyers. About 1,600 planes based on the carriers were supplemented by an equal number of bombers and long-range fighters flying from China, Tinian, Morotai, and Peleliu.

The deft elimination of Japanese air power from Taiwan was recognized by the Tokyo General Staffs as a major disaster calling for desperate countermeasures—one of them being a complete withholding of the news from the Japanese public. For the sake of morale the Navy concealed the full extent of its losses from the Army, and the Army the full extent of its losses from the Navy. Only Hirohito and a few of the highest officers in the General Staffs were told the whole truth. Hirohito promptly issued a rescript congratulating his airmen on a great victory and commiserating with Taiwanese who had suffered from the U.S. raids. At the same time, privately, he overrode the last objections of his political advisors and ordered that the remaining planes of the Air Navy be used, as needed, for suicide attacks.

On October 17 Hirohito dispatched Vice Admiral Onishi Takijiro, Prince Takamatsu's go-between in Pearl Harbor and kamikaze planning, to take charge of the air remnants in the Philippines. On October 18 Hirohito gave his final approval to the naval part of operation SHO: the sacrifice of Japan's remaining oil-eating carriers and battleships. On October 19, having discovered that there were only some sixty planes in condition to fly left in the Philippines, air envoy Onishi drove out to the Air Command center at Mabalacat, north of Manila, and personally informed the flight leaders there of what was expected of them:

> In my opinion there is only one way of assuring that our meager strength will be effective to a maximum degree. That is to organize suicide attack units composed of Zero fighters armed with 250-kilogram bombs, with each plane to crash-dive into an enemy carrier. . . . What do you think?

Long silence greeted Onishi's words. Many Japanese flight leaders had long advocated *tai-atari* or body-crashing tactics. Frustrated pilots had often collided deliberately with Flying Fortresses in a last angry effort to destroy them. Only four days earlier, when the U.S. Leyte invasion armada had first been sighted steaming in from the east, Rear Admiral Arima Masafumi, a scion of the imperial family, had reportedly taken personal charge of a ninety-nine-plane attack group and had shown the way by crash-diving into a U.S. carrier. The assembled flight leaders had no way of knowing that, according to U.S. records, there had been no suicide attack on any U.S. ship that day or on any of the four days since. To them it seemed only that now, pursuant to Arima's example, Admiral Onishi had arrived from the Emperor, asking them to make good their boasts and give their lives.

At length one of the fliers said soberly, "The chances of scoring a hit will be much greater than by conventional bombing. It will probably take several days to repair the damage one of us can cause on a flight deck."

With this self-deprecating stoicism the *Kamikaze* Corps was officially formed, and in a few hours Admiral Onishi had recruited more willing suicide pilots than he could find room for in serviceable planes.

LEYTE AND LEYTE GULF

The next morning, sunup October 20, 1944, the 420 transports and 157 warships of MacArthur's assault force—about two thirds of all the 840 U.S. ships involved in the invasion—began putting ashore the first 145,000 men of the vast 200,000-man expeditionary force which was to recapture the island of Leyte in the central Philippines. The Japanese had only 20,000 men on the island, later to be reinforced by 50,000 more. A typhoon of naval fire swept inland from the beaches, curtaining a massive ship-to-shore movement of men in landing craft. By noon such a deep beachhead had been established that General MacArthur himself landed, with representatives of the Philippine government in exile. In an historic address to the Filipino peoples, he reinaugurated the Voice of Freedom broadcasts which had been suspended at the fall of Corregidor two and a half years earlier.

As the U.S. Army blasted inland, paving its way with Japanese corpses, the remnants of the Japanese Combined Fleet sortied to execute its part in the SHO plan, the battle for Leyte Gulf. This last and largest of history's naval surface engagements, involving 218 Allied warships with 143,668 crewmen and 64 Japanese ships with about 42,800 crewmen, was fought over a six-day period, October 23 to October 29. Its Japanese planners had little hope for it beforehand, but looked on it as a quick and glorious way to dispose of vessels and crews which would otherwise have to be deactivated for lack of fuel oil. They had admitted this frankly to Hirohito before he gave his final approval to the operation. The scene was a joint Army-Navy meeting in the ironclad Imperial Headquarters shed on October 18. There Rear Admiral Nakasawa Yu-u, Naval Operations Section chief, called the Philippines "a fitting place to die," and pleaded: "Give us of the Combined Fleet a chance to bloom as flowers of death. This is the Navy's earnest request."

Hirohito granted the request but restricted the Navy to a modest, practical, inglorious objective: to attack, if possible, the U.S. troop transports lying off the Leyte beaches. The Navy General Staff drew up a plan which divided the available Japanese ships into three forces, Northern, Center, and Southern, each of which was to approach Leyte Gulf from a different direction by a different passage.

Center Force, the mightiest Japanese fleet to seek action since Midway, consisted of two 64,000-ton super-dreadnoughts, *Yamato* and *Musashi*, plus three ordinary battleships, ten heavy cruisers, two light cruisers, and fifteen destroyers. It advanced from the west, making for San Bernardino Strait which opened, between the southern tip of Luzon and the island of Samar, on the waters to the north of the Leyte beachheads. Before he set forth from Lingga Roads the commander of Center Force, Vice Admiral Kurita Takeo, had to deal with the murmuring of officers who resented the senselessness of the sacrifice ahead. He called them together on the deck of his flagship, the heavy cruiser *Atago*, and told them:

It would be shameful to have the fleet remain intact while our nation perishes. I believe that Imperial Headquarters is giving us a glorious opportunity. You must remember that such things as miracles do happen. Who can say that we have no chance to turn the tide?

So hopeless was Kurita of any success except by miracles that in steaming toward the Philippines he did not even take the routine precaution of posting destroyers ahead of him as picket ships to guard against submarine attack. Consequently, at dawn on October 23, two boats of the U.S. wolf pack, *Dace* and *Darter*, welcomed him in Palawan Passage, just north of Borneo, with two workmanly spreads of torpedoes. In twenty minutes two of Kurita's heavy cruisers, his flagship the 13,400-ton *Atago* and her sister ship the *Maya*, both went to the bottom. Almost 2,000 sailors drowned. Another thousand survivors, including Kurita himself, were picked up by destroyers to continue their desperate foray. They had to leave behind *Takao*, a third 13,400-ton cruiser, which had taken a torpedo in her engine room.[6]

All that day the remaining twenty-nine vessels of Center Force plunged on toward Leyte, tracked intermittently by U.S. submarines and scout planes. At the same time Japanese air reinforcements were arriving at the airfields north of Manila. By the scheming of General Yamashita's faction in the General Staff, all 350 of the fresh planes were assigned to the Second Air Fleet of Vice Admiral Fukudome Shigeru rather than to the First Air Fleet of the kamikaze enthusiast, Vice Admiral Onishi. Fukudome was a sympathizer but not yet a convert of the kamikaze creed. That evening Onishi pleaded in vain with Fukudome to release some of the planes to him for use in suicide attacks. Onishi, in his entire First Air Fleet, had only thirteen planes which could fly. Fukudome, however, insisted that before he would give Onishi any planes he meant to mount one last massive conventional air attack on the U.S. fleet: a 250-plane raid scheduled for the next morning.

About 150 of Fukudome's planes, in three waves, did arrive suc-

[6] She was towed back to Borneo by destroyers. In efforts to get a second shot at her the U.S. submarine *Darter* ran aground on a reef and had to be evacuated and destroyed by her companion vessel *Dace*.

cessfully over Admiral Halsey's fast carrier task force during the following day. They were driven off with more than 50 per cent losses. One of them, however, diving alone, out of a cloud, planted a lucky bomb on the 11,000-ton light carrier *Princeton*, starting fires below which ultimately crept into fuel tanks and magazines. After most of *Princeton*'s crew had been taken off, her after half erupted in a series of spectacular explosions which bombarded nearby ships with massive pieces of debris. On cruiser *Birmingham*, which stood by alongside helping to fight the fires, the rain of fall-out, which included whole jeeps, took 200 lives, twice as many as were lost on *Princeton* herself. By late afternoon the last fire fighters were withdrawn from *Princeton*'s forward decks and U.S. escorts dispatched the blazing derelict with torpedoes.

During Fukudome's conventional air attack on Halsey, 259 of the 1,068 planes in Halsey's task force were off in the Sibuyan Sea on the other side of Leyte—the "backside" as it was called by the Americans—hammering away relentlessly at Kurita's oncoming Center Force. All day the U.S. pilots bombed, strafed, and torpedoed, inflicting some damage on every ship in the Japanese fleet. They gave special attention, however, to one of the two super-dreadnoughts, the 64,000-ton *Musashi*. No ship afloat could lay better claim to being unsinkable. Her huge hull was honeycombed with watertight compartments. By midafternoon it had successfully absorbed nine torpedoes and five bomb hits. Then at 3:20 P.M. the planes of three U.S. carriers came in on *Musashi* to deliver a death blow. In the course of the attack she took ten more torpedo and twelve more bomb hits. Her "special-caliber 16-inch guns"—a naval limitations euphemism for 18.1-inch guns—had never been fired in action. Now in desperation they were loaded with a type of grapeshot called *sanshiki-dan* which would scar the insides of their barrels. Not even thundering bursts of grapeshot, however, could deter the intent American pilots. One by one the great guns jammed and the torpedoes struck home. At 7:35 P.M. the leviathan *Musashi* stood on end and slid under. With her drowned 1,023 of her understrength 2,399-man crew. Survivors were picked up by Japanese destroyers and taken to Manila.

On *Musashi*'s sister dreadnought *Yamato*, Admiral Kurita had been vainly sending out pleas for land-based air support. At 4 P.M.

he decided that he must at least pretend to retreat. He radioed Imperial Headquarters:

. . . . CONCLUDE IT BEST TO RETIRE TEMPORARILY BEYOND RANGE OF HOSTILE PLANES UNTIL FRIENDLY AIR UNITS CAN ENABLE US TO RESUME ADVANCE.

So it was that U.S. pilots, when they broke off their attack late in the afternoon, reported to Halsey that Kurita was fleeing west with half his ships smoking. At 5:14 P.M., however, when the American planes had disappeared over the horizon, Kurita again reversed course and bent *Yamato* and her screen of damaged battleships and cruisers back toward San Bernardino Strait at the fair speed of 20 knots. An hour later, when he was already on his way, he received a message from headquarters which strongly confirmed his decision:

ALL FORCES WILL PROCEED FULL SPEED TO THE ATTACK AND TRUST IN DIVINE GUIDANCE.

As Kurita resumed his advance, Admiral Onishi in Manila was prevailing upon his fellow air fleet commander, Admiral Fukudome, to use the remaining Japanese planes in the Philippines for suicide missions. In the U.S. fleet standing off the eastern coast of Leyte, American commanders were hastily preparing receptions for the other two prongs of the Japanese attack: the Southern Force which Halsey's pilots had sighted at 9:18 that morning 250 miles to the southwest, and the Northern Force which task force fliers had belatedly discovered at 3:40 that afternoon 400 miles to the north.

The Southern Force was a small one of two battleships, a heavy cruiser, and four destroyers. It was obviously making for Surigao Strait, the southern entrance to Leyte Gulf, between Leyte and the northern tip of Mindanao. There, since noon, preparations had been underway to give it a robust welcome. In the strait it would run a gauntlet of U.S. motor torpedo boats and at the exit from the strait it would encounter the broadsides of six U.S. battleships, eight cruisers, and twenty-eight destroyers. Admiral Halsey had no fear that it would break through into Leyte Gulf, a confidence that was fully justified by the event. Between 11 P.M. and 5 A.M. the whole of Southern Force was blown out of the water except for one destroyer. A reinforcement squadron of three Japanese cruisers and four destroyers, which had come all the way from Japan rather than from Lingga Roads, arrived in Surigao Strait too late for the main action but in time to pick up some survivors. Nevertheless over 4,000 Japanese sailors perished.

Convinced that Center Force had been turned back and confident that Southern Force was being annihilated, Admiral Halsey, at 8:22 P.M. on October 24, steamed off through the night with his task force to attack Northern Force which lay off Cape Engaño on the northeast coast of Luzon. The appearance of Northern Force had surprised him and reports that it included a number of aircraft carriers excited him.

Northern Force had sortied from the supposedly abandoned Combined Fleet anchorage in Japan's own Inland Sea. U.S. submarine skippers had watched the exit from the Inland Sea, the Bungo Strait, throughout Halsey's earlier attacks on Taiwan. They had concluded, from seeing only a one-way scurrying of small vessels into the Inland Sea, that all major Japanese fleet units had, as described by Intelligence, left the Inland Sea months earlier for Lingga Roads. Accordingly they had given up their watch and returned to their proper business of sinking Japan-bound tankers and merchant vessels.

On October 20, two days after the withdrawal of the U.S. wolf pack, Northern Force had emerged from Bungo Straits undetected. Its commander, Vice Admiral Ozawa Jisaburo, was at first relieved and then positively embarrassed by the lack of attention given to him in his dash south. His was a decoy force of one heavy aircraft carrier, three light carriers, two modified battleships with small flight decks, three light cruisers, and eight destroyers. All were ships which had been half mothballed during the previous four months. They had lain at their berths, forbidden to expend fuel and obliged to give away their technicians, one by one, to the Manpower Resources Board. They were considered expendable because now Japan was defending home waters in reach of land airfields and had no further use for carriers.

In the forthcoming engagement, it was the explicit assignment of Admiral Ozawa's Northern Force to lure Admiral Halsey away from Leyte waters and to get sunk by Halsey while Admiral Kurita's Center Force was breaking through. Because of the nature of their mission, the Japanese carriers were manned by skeleton crews and carried less than half their complement of planes: altogether 108 aircraft of all types. The planes were not intended to take part in the battle. They were only aboard the carriers in order to hop a ride to the Philippines where they were being sent as reinforcements for the shattered air wings at Mabalacat.

Arriving undetected off Luzon, Northern Force commander Ozawa saw that he would have to call attention to himself. Early on October 24, therefore, when he dispatched his planes to their bases in the Philippines, he asked the pilots, en route, to strike a glancing blow at Halsey's task force. The scheme worked to perfection: the Japanese planes attacked Halsey from safe heights and distances and most of them succeeded in landing at their assigned fields in Luzon. Halsey's radar technicians noted the direction of attack; search planes were sent out; Ozawa was discovered; and now Halsey was speeding north with his fleet of flattops, leaving behind him an opening for Kurita's battered Center Force when it emerged from San Bernardino Strait.

At 5:40 A.M. on October 25, 1944, Halsey, with twelve of the sixteen fast carriers remaining to him since *Princeton*'s sinking the previous afternoon, had reached a point halfway up the eastern Luzon coast. There and then he began to launch his first air strike against Ozawa's Northern Force, 150 miles farther north, which was steaming a box pattern waiting to be sunk. Far to the south the few survivors of Southern Force were backing out of Surigao Strait aboard the reinforcement flotilla which had rescued them. Not so far to the south Admiral Kurita of Center Force had emerged from San Bernardino Strait shortly after midnight, and passing Halsey's rear guard going in the opposite direction, was heading down the east coast of Samar toward Leyte Gulf.

At that moment, in a shack beside a field outside Davao on the big southern Philippine Island of Mindanao, Japan's first six successful kamikaze pilots were receiving their final briefing. The place was one that inspired patriotism for here Japan had had a colony since the fourteenth century. Admiral Onishi had spread the kamikaze gospel widely in the last six days. Volunteers for suicide flights had come forward at every air base in the Philippines. Onishi himself had organized official Special Attack Units at Mabalacat on Luzon and at Cebu City on Cebu in the central islands. The Mindanao unit was unofficial but it had received authorization the evening before to commence operations. Onishi extended to it the same promise he had made to the units he had visited:

You are now all gods, without earthly desires. One thing you will want to know is that your own crash dive is not in vain. Regrettably, we will not be able to tell you the results. But I shall watch your efforts to the end and report your deeds to the Throne. You may all rest assured on that point. I ask you all to do your best.

Each of the six young pilots had volunteered for suicide duty because all the other pilots had. They had been selected because they were the least skillful and most expendable aviators at their base. They had accepted their selection because they were not outstandingly successful young men in other ways and felt themselves suitably unworthy, indebted, and deserving of their fate.

Each of them drank a little saké and then a cup of pure water. Each wound a ghostly white cloth around his forehead. This was the symbolic *hachimaki* worn by the samurai of old when they wished to show that they were entering battle resolved to die. Over their white sweat bands the fledgling crash divers pulled on their tight flight helmets. Then, as nonchalantly as they could, they swaggered to their planes and took off in the first light of dawn.

Out in Leyte Gulf the forces on which Halsey relied to guard his rear were going about routine business. The six battleships, eight cruisers, and twenty-eight destroyers which had destroyed the Southern Force at the exit of Surigao Strait were standing at ease, catching up on sleep and looking up ammunition ships from which to replenish their stores of armor-piercing shells. Farther north between the Leyte beachheads and Kurita's Center Force cruised three flotillas of light, slow escort carriers or "baby flattops." The southernmost of these forces, Taffy One, included four escort carriers with a complement of 118 planes. The northernmost, Taffy Two and Taffy Three, included fourteen escort carriers with a complement of 336 planes. Each baby flattop mounted a single 5-inch gun and carried a flight deck for about twenty-eight planes. Each was protected by the thinnest of armor plate. Three of them were converted 11,400-ton tankers; the rest were 7,800-ton items mass-produced by the Kaiser Corporation.

As dawn broke on October 25 all three of the Taffy escort carrier groups were launching workaday flights to provide cover for the fleet and support for the infantry ashore. Admiral Kurita's Center Force was assumed to be hundreds of miles away, a fleet of cripples wallowing their way home. However, at 6:40 A.M., Kurita's masthead lookouts spied Taffy Three on the horizon. Three minutes later a pilot from the escort carrier *Kadashan Bay*, on routine antisubmarine patrol, reported incredulously that he was flying over what looked like four Japanese battleships, eight cruisers, and any number of destroyers. A moment later bright flashes of antiaircraft fire persuaded him as well as the distant onlookers of Taffy Three that he was suffering no illusion.

Consternation reigned on both sides. Admiral Kurita assumed that he was encountering Halsey's fast carriers and that Ozawa's decoy mission had failed. Rear Admiral Clifton Sprague of Taffy Three realized that his little squadron of four 7,800-ton escort carriers, three destroyers, and four destroyer escorts was only 20 miles from the biggest guns in the Japanese fleet, the biggest guns afloat anywhere.

Admiral Sprague immediately launched or recalled all the 168 planes under his own command and urgently requested assistance from the 168 planes of Taffy Two and the 118 planes of Taffy One. He ordered his carriers to run away at full speed, which was 18 knots as compared to the 20 knots of which even the most battered of the Japanese vessels were still capable. He had his ships belch the thickest possible screen of smoke.

At 6:59 A.M., only twelve minutes after the sounding of general quarters, 14-inch and 18-inch shells from the Japanese cruisers and battleships began to splash in lurid geysers of orange and purple dye-marking beside the U.S. escort carriers. At first the Japanese aim seemed good. Several ships were straddled with shots and took violent evasive action, trying to hide themselves in the spray from explosions where the skippers knew the next salvo would not fall.

At 7:01 Admiral Sprague threw his code book and security regulations overboard and sent out a plain-language May Day to all U.S. units in hearing. At 7:06 he acknowledged that he had reached "the ultimate in desperate circumstances" and estimated that all his carriers would be sunk in five minutes. He ordered his three destroyers and four destroyer escorts to charge the Japanese array of three battleships, seven heavy cruisers, two light cruisers, and nineteen destroyers advancing against him.

In one of the proudest moments of U.S. naval history, Sprague's destroyers and destroyer escorts not only obeyed his order but seriously disturbed the Japanese formation. Destroyers exchanged broadsides at close range with battleships and destroyer escorts with heavy cruisers. By a combination of luck and good ship handling none of the U.S. small fry were immediately sunk in their desperate attack, and the fifty-odd torpedoes which they launched gave Sprague's carriers a moment's respite. Only one of the torpedoes made a sure hit—on the heavy cruiser *Kumano*—but the rest forced the Japanese ships into strenuous evasive turns which threw them into disarray. Kurita's flagship, the super-dreadnought *Yamato*, found herself chased by two spreads of torpedoes, port and starboard, which threatened to run up her stern garbage chutes. She succeeded, at full steam ahead, in outdistancing them, but by the time their propulsion was expended, she had removed herself so far from the running battle that she never succeeded thereafter in catching up with it.

During the wild melee of the U.S. destroyers' banzai charge, Admiral Sprague and his little thin-skinned carriers took refuge in a providential rain squall. He abruptly changed course in it and came out of it on the side where the Japanese fleet was not. He thereby gained more than fifteen minutes of time and opened the range between himself and the Japanese big guns by several miles. By 7:45 his own hundred-odd planes plus an equal number from Taffy Two were raining the Japanese fleet with torpedoes, bombs, and bullets. When they ran out of projectiles they landed for more on the decks of Taffy Two or on Tacloban Field ashore on Leyte. When concerted strikes were not yet near at hand, pilots without bullets kept Japanese gunners busy by weaving "dry runs" through the flak. "The air attacks," said one of the Japanese officers afterwards, "were almost incessant."

In this incredible battle, in which the Japanese surface vessels had more than a forty-to-one superiority in firepower, the U.S. planes made up the difference. During the first forty-five minutes of action they had created mayhem on the decks of all the Japanese ships and had crippled three of the seven Japanese heavy cruisers. The amazing American victory would have been still more devastating if all U.S. planes in the area could have come to the aid of Taffy Three. But at 7:40, Taffy One, the southernmost of the three U.S. escort carrier groups, was prevented from rendering any substantial assistance by the first blowing of the divine wind, the kamikaze.

The six pilots who had dedicated themselves to suicide at Davao air base two hours earlier bore in on Taffy One from the south after a 250-mile flight. At least two of them were exploded in mid-air as they dived on escort carriers *Suwanee* and *Petrof Bay*. A third broke through to carrier *Santee*, crashed on the flight deck, and penetrated it to blow a 15-by-30-foot hole in the hangar deck below. Sixteen of *Santee*'s crew had been killed and twenty-seven wounded. A gasoline fire roared beside a stack of 1,000-pound bombs. It was put out in eleven minutes and *Santee*'s crew began emergency repairs which would enable her once more, in a matter of hours, to receive aircraft. The three remaining fliers from Davao took notes on what had happened. One of them, about fifteen minutes later, dove out of a cloud on carrier *Suwannee*, tearing through her flight deck and exploding against her hangar deck with much carnage. The two last kamikaze pilots flew home to Davao to report that none of the crash divers had succeeded in sinking their targets.

Failure of the kamikaze-stricken Taffy One to send out her air strike enabled Kurita's fleet to close again on the fragile fleeing carriers of Taffy Three. In the desperate action which followed, the U.S. destroyers, having no more torpedoes, engaged the Japanese battleships and cruisers with machine-gun fire. Two of the three destroyers and one of the four destroyer escorts were sunk with a loss of more than half their heroic crewmen. Kurita's ships broke through to the escort carriers and should have sunk them all. But the Japanese marksmanship was poor. And aging Admiral Kurita, who had not slept for seventy-two hours and who still suffered from the swim he had taken the day before in the Sibuyan

Sea after the torpedoing of his first flagship, was issuing orders erratically and inconsequentially.

Kurita commanded the cream of the Japanese fleet, but it did not have the morale of 1941. Its officers knew and resented the fact that they had been sent on a silly suicide mission. They were more preoccupied with the state of their souls and the manner of their final gesture than they were with the conduct of the battle.

U.S. morale, by contrast, was superb. When the Japanese heavy cruisers closed with *Fanshaw Bay*, the Taffy Three flagship, between 8:30 and 9, Admiral Sprague directed the gunner of his single 5-inch cannon: "Open fire with the peashooter as soon as the range is clear." At about 8:50, when escort carrier *White Plains* drew abreast of heavy cruiser *Chokai*, the U.S. gunnery officer pleaded with his men, "Hold out a little longer, boys, we're sucking them into 40-millimeter range." The U.S. carriers were being hit and hit repeatedly, but by armor-piercing shells which passed right through them without exploding. *Fanshaw Bay* was punctured by four 8-inch shells and *Kalinin Bay* by thirteen. The escort carriers' handymen were scalded with steam from burst pipes and drenched with inrushing sea water, but in the elation of battle they somehow welded patches on hulls and stopped the holes.

At 9:07 one of Taffy Three's six baby flattops, *Gambier Bay*, took a hole too many and sank. Destroyer *Hoel* had sunk twelve minutes earlier. Destroyer *Johnston* and destroyer escort *Roberts* were in process of sinking. So were the Japanese heavy cruisers *Chokai*, *Chikuma*, and *Suzuya*. The lost Japanese ships totaled 34,400 tons; the lost U.S. ships 15,450 tons. At 9:11 Admiral Kurita ordered his vessels to break off action, regroup and survey losses. "Goddammit," shouted the signalman on *Fanshaw Bay* to Admiral Sprague, "they're getting away." Observed Admiral Sprague, with a sigh of relief in his report, "I had expected to be swimming by this time."

The dazed Admiral Kurita drew back and wandered about aimlessly in the Philippine Sea for the next nine hours while he argued with his staff officers. He was still convinced that he had encountered Halsey's task force. He contended that he had inflicted heavy damage on it and that he had made his gesture and was justified in retreating. Most of his staff officers knew better.

Under continued air harassment, however, they finally allowed Kurita to send the necessary radiograms to Tokyo and then to withdraw, that night, through San Bernardino Strait toward safer waters.

Taffy Three, as soon as Admiral Sprague could believe that the Japanese fleet was really retreating, sent half its planes in pursuit, sent the other half out to search for survivors of sunken U.S. ships, and then generally relaxed. While most hands were in their wardrooms, toasting one another in coffee, at 10:50 A.M., five more kamikaze flew in, this time from Admiral Onishi's original group of devotees at Mabalacat in Luzon. They approached over the wave crests, below radar range, then soared to 5,000 feet and dived. One missed the bridge of *Kitkun Bay*, tripped over the port catwalk, and tumbled exploding into the sea. Two others went for *Fanshaw Bay*, the Taffy Three flagship, and were blown up before they struck. Another pair started for *White Plains* but pulled up short, riddled with 40-millimeter bullets. One of them came on to explode near *White Plains*, causing eleven casualties. The other veered off to strike *St. Lo* unexpectedly amidships. Flaming debris ignited torpedoes and bombs stacked on the hangar deck. Seven quick explosions followed and at 11:25, thirty minutes later, *St. Lo* foundered. The Kamikaze Corps had made its first kill.

As *St. Lo* sank, Admiral Halsey off Luzon was sending out his third and most telling air strike of the day against Ozawa's Northern Force. By the time its 200 planes returned to their decks all four of Japan's decoy carriers, including the big 27,000-ton *Zuikaku* which had participated in the Pearl Harbor attack, were in sinking condition. By the end of the day all four had sunk. By the end of the Japanese withdrawal, two days later, a crippled heavy cruiser and two wounded light cruisers were finally dispatched by the far-ranging and tenacious U.S. airmen. Other derelicts of the battle were shadowed relentlessly and finally hunted down in various Philippine harbors within the next month: heavy cruiser *Nachi* on November 5, light cruiser *Kiso* on November 13, battleship *Kongo* on November 21, and heavy cruiser *Kumano* on November 25.

In all, including these after-actions, Japan lost by the Battle of Leyte Gulf four battleships, four attack carriers, eight heavy cruisers, five light cruisers, and seven destroyers. With the ships perished about 15,000 sailors. The U.S. Navy lost a light cruiser, two escort carriers, three destroyers, and less than 2,000 sailors. For a mind like Hirohito's, only one bright statistic emerged from the quixotic venture: nine Japanese kamikaze pilots and their planes had been spent in exchange for over 100 American lives lost, three U.S. escort carriers grievously hurt, and one sunk. A new hope shone on the edge of the dark clouds surrounding Japan. If means could be found to make every Japanese die as effectively as the kamikaze pilots, there would be no Americans left to take possession of Japan after the dying. This vain hope was to see several more hundreds of thousands of Japanese to their deaths.

After the two successful kamikaze attacks on U.S. ships in Leyte Gulf, Imperial Headquarters sent the new commander of the Special Attack Corps, Vice Admiral Onishi, a message of personal congratulations from Hirohito which Onishi was authorized to read to the kamikaze volunteers under his tutelage. Its wording had been carefully considered by Lord Privy Seal Kido and other palace advisors for some time:

When told of the special attack, His Majesty said, "Was it necessary to go to this extreme? The men certainly did a magnificent job."

At the front in the Philippines, Onishi added, "His Majesty's words suggest that His Majesty is greatly concerned. We must redouble our efforts to relieve His Majesty of this concern."

THE GREAT DYING

In subduing Leyte after the Battle of Leyte Gulf about 4,000 U.S. soldiers and sailors died in process of killing some 65,000 Japanese.

The immense U.S. expeditionary force went on in early 1945 to invade Luzon and the other islands of the Philippines. At the cost of 10,400 American lives, another 256,000 Japanese were destroyed.

Iwo Jima came next, a volcanic mountaintop protruding from the sea halfway between Guam and Honshu. It was needed as a way station for the escorts of B-29's flying against Tokyo. On Iwo between February 19 and March 27, 1945, about 21,000 Japanese and 6,812 Americans perished.

The capture of Iwo enabled fleets of 200 to 300 B-29's to range at will over Japan's home islands. On the night of March 9 the first massive incendiary raid on Tokyo burned to death 80,000. Over the next twenty weeks fire raids on five other major urban centers, plus return visits to Tokyo, and at length a systematic burning of fifty-eight secondary Japanese cities cut short an additional 150,000 civilian lives.

At the same time, from April 1 to June 22, 1945, U.S. forces conquered Japan's sixteenth century acquisition, the island of Okinawa, where Commodore Perry had put in on his way from Taiwan to Tokyo Bay in 1853. The Okinawa campaign killed 12,500 U.S. servicemen, 110,000 Japanese troops, and about 75,000 Okinawan civilians.

Then, at last, the war ended with the climactic slaughter of 140,000 at Hiroshima and Nagasaki.

Half this fearsome tragedy—the tentative, time-consuming efforts of the Japanese to achieve a war settlement and the hasty impatience of the Allies—has been recounted already in Chapter 2. The other half, the dying, has been described in moving detail by many writers but will never be done full justice, for death is personal and so many deaths cannot be personalized.

The cold, cold statistic is that, in all, 897,000 or one of every seventy-eight of the proud, emotional Japanese people died in those last nine months of the war. They died with animal ferocity and despair, buried in caves and trapped between infernos. They died full of hate and hungry craving: famished, thirsty, and febrile; broken, twisted, and maimed; soiled, suppurating, and loathsome to their own nostrils. Their American executioners—of whom 32,000 also died, and bravely—did only what the Japanese themselves seemed to demand before they would surrender.

Patriotically overwrought after fifteen years of indoctrination, prickly proud after four years of strutting Asian overlordship, genuinely fearful for the sacred homeland under American vengeance, few Japanese could contemplate defeat without writhing inwardly. At the same time few Japanese had accepted propaganda at face value; they were too literate and cynical, too close to the frugal, industrious struggle of Japanese life. Many knew at heart that their defiance of death for the sake of honor was a romantic posture, the stylized grimace of the samurai with his blade flashing in the moonlight.

If the Japanese masses had been told that the bulk of their Navy and a fifth of their Air Navy had been destroyed in the Leyte action, and that the United States had three times as many ships and planes in the Pacific as Japan had ever produced, popular sentiment in favor of surrender would have swelled mightily.[7] The masses were not told, however—neither by Hirohito on domestic radio nor by President Roosevelt in shortwave broadcasts.

As a nation predicated upon a moral code and a belief in self-government by indigenous peoples, the United States, after the capture of Saipan, should have mounted an all-out campaign to tell Japanese of U.S. war grievances, accomplishments, goals, and international commitments. At best such a campaign would have shortened the war; at the least it would have strengthened the U.S. position in postwar Asia. If U.S. planes had dropped leaflets and shortwave sets on Japan as well as bombs, and if the taped voices of Roosevelt and Churchill had been put on the air each night projecting the humanity of Allied convictions, Hirohito might have felt compelled by public opinion to accept defeat before the worst of the blood bath. Even if he had used the fall of Germany on May 7 as an excuse to capitulate, he would still have saved about half a million lives.

Unfortunately Roosevelt and Churchill were concerned mainly with American and European politics. Their constituents labored under profound ignorance and distrust of the Japanese masses. Psychological warfare experts were unsure of the best arguments to use in approaching the Japanese. Writer-translators who could

---

[7] After the war U.S. Strategic Bombing Survey teams conducted a poll to find out when the misinformed Japanese public began to realize that its side had lost. They discovered, as might be expected, that every reverse which could not be concealed from the people increased the number of pessimists. Two per cent of the population despaired of winning in June 1944 before the fall of Saipan, 10 per cent in December after the first heavy B-29 attacks, 19 per cent by March 1945 when the fire raids began, 46 per cent by June after the collapse of Germany, and 68 per cent by August when the atomic bombs fell. The will to fight descreased proportionately, and by the time of surrender 64 per cent of the people had reached a point at which they felt they were personally unable to go on with the war.

wield a mighty pen in Japanese were as scarce in the West as sumo wrestlers. An all-out information war had never been waged before. It would be expensive. It could not win as surely as killing. Consequently no leaflets were regularly dropped with the bombs on Japan until mid-May 1945. And warnings to evacuate specific cities, before they were burned out by massive incendiary attacks, did not begin to be issued until July 27, only ten days before Hiroshima.

So it was that Allied leaders did little to subvert the plans of the Peace Faction. The people of Japan were allowed to reach a state of political disinterest and preoccupation with survival, a state of mind beyond recrimination, before being told that their war sacrifices had been in vain. Hirohito did his utmost to keep them in hope—facing death optimistically—until he was personally ready to surrender. In the last months of the war he repeatedly abused his power of imperial rescript to announce victories in place of defeats. Even at the end, in his historic surrender broadcast of August 15, he personally added the phrase "not necessarily to our advantage" in describing recent war developments.

No one knew better than Hirohito that Japan was defeated; no one could explain why with more logic and candor; but no one clung more tenaciously to straws of unrealistic hope. The shame at having to admit to the ancestors, the people, and the enemy that he had committed Japan prematurely to war with the West was more than he could bear. He saw no alternative for himself in surrender but suicide or retirement in disgrace. He knew that Kido and Konoye had already discussed temples in which he might live in priestly penance after his abdication. And so, although he approved the stand-by measures of the Peace Faction for the sake of the Throne, he remained, for his own sake, addictively engrossed in every desperate effort to salvage some sense of accomplishment from his reign.

THE WILL TO KILL

The reckless do-or-die of Japan in her final throes at first frightened U.S. combat troops, then puzzled them, then disgusted them, and finally moved many to genuine compassion. The brute misery of the Japanese soldiers in their caves and the forlorn desperation of their banzai charges made it increasingly difficult to "Remember Pearl Harbor." And as Japanese prisoners began to be taken in large numbers, their co-operative, industrious, affable ways belied the other wartime maxim: "No good Jap but a dead one."

G.I. hatred for the Japanese probably crested and began to ebb in February 1945 during the battle for Manila. After the U.S. landings along Luzon's Lingayen Gulf, on January 9, MacArthur's troops moved on the Philippine capital cautiously, entering its northern suburbs on February 3. Yamashita had pulled back the bulk of his army into defensive positions in the mountains around Baguio. He had planned to give up the Manila area without a fight and so spare its million-odd Filipinos from the hardships of siege, bombardment, and street fighting.

Hirohito's Imperial General Headquarters had other ideas. At the last minute, over Yamashita's objections, Tokyo Headquarters sent into Manila a naval landing party of some 15,000 sailors and marines under Rear Admiral Iwabuchi Sanji, a former imperial aide-de-camp. Together with 4,000 to 5,000 soldiers, whom Yamashita had left in the city to demolish Army stores and munitions dumps, Iwabuchi and his men contested the city street by street, house by house, and sewer by sewer. A month later when the last sailor had been blasted from his hole, the finest sections of Manila had been turned to rubble.

Iwabuchi made his last stand in Intramuros, the old Spanish walled town in the south of the city. Having themselves decided to die, Iwabuchi's men showed no mercy to the Filipino civilians whom they had entrapped with them. They raped the women and machine-gunned the men. When the battle was done, 1,000 Americans had died, 16,000 Japanese, and 100,000 Filipinos.

The desperate Japanese tactics combined with another circumstance in Manila to feed G.I. hatred. In the northern outskirts, on their first two nights in the city, February 3 and February 4, the U.S. troops liberated some 5,000 Western internees and prisoners of war who had endured three or more years of Japanese captivity. The emaciated *libérés*, who weighed in at between eighty and a hundred and twenty pounds apiece, told chilling stories of starvation, medical negligence, beating, torture, and capital punishment for trivial offenses. Worse, the captured records of concentration camp commandants revealed that Japan had not intended any of these wretched prisoners to return alive into American hands. Only a last-minute dash into Manila by MacArthur's armored flying columns had prevented Japanese guards for complying, reluctantly, with orders from Tokyo to get rid of their charges.

The first discretionary hints to kill prisoners rather than let them fall into the propaganda-making hands of the enemy had been issued in stages by Imperial General Headquarters during the latter half of 1944. In Borneo Japanese commandants had obeyed instantly by instituting a series of death marches and impossible jungle construction details which killed all but six of 2,000 Australian prisoners of war there.

On Palawan, the most southwestern of the large islands of the Philippines, the local commandant decided to dispose of his P.O.W. work force on December 14, 1944, when lookouts reported a large U.S. convoy steaming past the Palawan coast. He ordered the 150 U.S. prisoners under his charge—men captured in the fall of the Philippines in 1942—to take cover in three air-raid shelters. Then, quickly, he had his own soldiers pour buckets of kerosene into the shelter entrances and throw in lighted torches. As burning prisoners came rushing out through the curtain of flame, they were swept with machine-gun fire and bayoneted. Nevertheless some broke through to leap off a fifty-foot bluff into the sea. While the Japanese soldiers were busy shooting at heads bobbing up in the surf a group of prisoners from one of the shelters broke out of an escape tunnel they had been digging which opened on the cliff face. They too dropped into the surf and hid in the rocks at the base of the cliff.

Japanese landing barges patrolled the edge of the bay hunting down the escapees until well after dark. Five, however, survived. At nine that night they swam the bay together and got away into the jungle. Days later they reached a guerrilla encampment where they were sheltered until U.S. forces reoccupied Palawan in March 1945, three months later. Then they led their liberators back to the bluff by the sea and directed the disinterment of the charred bones of their comrades.

Executions cheated the G.I.'s of only some of the prisoners they had hoped to liberate; many more had been spirited away to Japan. In late 1944, when Japanese troops and nurses were still

being brought to die in the Philippines, and when more than half
of Japanese shipping between the colonies and the home islands
was being sunk by U.S. submarines, Tokyo ordered all troop transports returning empty to Japan to take on as many P.O.W.'s as
possible. The prisoners might be of service as slave labor; their
presence in Japan, subject to Japan's pleasure, might count for
something in later peace bargaining.

The wasted transportees were huddled into the hulks so sick
and close that on some vessels a quarter of them died at sea in the
course of what should have been a three- or four-day voyage. Some
fell dizzily and drowned from outboard toilet scaffolds. Others
lay down in the excrement of the holds and expired of thirst and
hunger. On most of the vessels, at the first indication of U.S.
submarine attack, the hatches were battened down. If a torpedo
struck, the inmates were left to break out or go down as best they
might after Japanese crews had already abandoned ship. A surprising number of practiced survival experts did succeed in swimming away from such sinking prisons and in living to tell about
it.[8]

[8] I had a heartwarming encounter with one of these survivors on the night
of February 5, 1945. Old Bilibid Prison in Manila, where internees from Baguio
had been subsisting for the last two months, had been liberated the day before
and was now surrounded by fires spreading from demolished Japanese ammunition dumps. The U.S. Army was evacuating us all to the Ang Tibay Shoe Factory about two miles north beyond the flames. There were only enough trucks
for the sick and debilitated, and so I and another sixteen-year-old set off down
the burning street with our parcels of cherished belongings—our coconut-shell
dishes and spare loin cloths—slung between us on a carrying pole. Filipinos,
who were also fleeing from the fire, cheered us on with shouts of *"Mabuhay"*:
banzai, hurrah, victory. In the garish tumult, a half-filled U.S. Army truck
stopped to offer us a lift. It came from a separate compound in Old Bilibid
which had housed 800 military prisoners of war.

I sat down in the truck next to a shriveled Englishman, a London cockney.
He had worked on the Burma-Thai railroad. He had survived to be shipped out
of Singapore for Japan on a prison hulk. Coast-running up the western side of
the Borneo-Philippine archipelago, his ship had been torpedoed by a U.S. submarine off Mindoro. He had swum ashore and joined the Mindoro guerrillas,
been recaptured, and finally reduced to his present straits in Manila. Having
outlined all this, he began to chant for me his favorite poem, stanza after
stanza: Kipling's paean to the common soldier, "Tommy Atkins." The truck
lurched across yawning gaps in the pavement. The flames leapt high on both
sides of the street. Manila burned and my companion was wracked by dysentery. But he rose to heights of bitter eloquence and ecstasy as he drove home
to me: "It's 'Thank you, Mr. Atkins,' when the guns begin to roll."

U.S. publicists made much of the privations described by liberated U.S. prisoners. As a result, the War Ministry in Tokyo felt obliged to clarify previous hints and make sure that no more captives would be recovered by the enemy. The new instructions, couched in the least subtle belly talk possible, went out to prison camp commandants in a secret telegram under signature of Vice War Minister Shibayama Kaneshiro on March 17, 1945:

PRISONERS OF WAR MUST BE PREVENTED BY ALL MEANS AVAILABLE FROM FALLING INTO ENEMY HANDS.

THEY SHOULD EITHER BE RELOCATED AWAY FROM THE FRONT OR COLLECTED AT SUITABLE POINTS AND TIMES WITH AN EYE TO ENEMY AIR RAIDS, SHORE BOMBARDMENTS, ETC.

THEY SHOULD BE KEPT ALIVE TO THE LAST WHEREVER THEIR LABOR IS NEEDED.

IN DESPERATE CIRCUMSTANCES, WHEN THERE IS NO TIME TO MOVE THEM, THEY MAY, AS A LAST RESORT, BE SET FREE. THEN EMERGENCY MEASURES SHOULD BE CARRIED OUT AGAINST THOSE WITH AN ANTAGONISTIC ATTITUDE AND UTMOST PRECAUTIONS SHOULD BE TAKEN SO THAT NO HARM IS DONE TO THE PUBLIC.

IN EXECUTING EMERGENCY MEASURES CARE SHOULD BE HAD NOT TO PROVOKE ENEMY PROPAGANDA OR RETALIATION.

PRISONERS SHOULD BE FED AT THE END.

Perhaps this stipulation that every prisoner be given a last meal proved too difficult to fulfill; in any case, camp commandants generally disregarded the directive from Tokyo and in the final five months of the war killed far fewer than they might have of the Allied prisoners still in custody on bypassed islands and in Japan proper.

Among the foot soldiers, enthusiasm for killing and being killed was running out on both sides. At the beginning of the Luzon campaign, U.S. troops took almost no prisoners. By the end of March, they were taking prisoners in lots of a hundred. Ultimately over 50,000 starving Japanese soldiers would give themselves up in the Philippines and would be nursed back to health in U.S. pens and field hospitals.

Even Kamikaze Corps pilots began to suffer from loss of fighting spirit. Theirs was the highest morale in the Japanese armed services because they alone were taking more lives than they were

losing. Between the Battle of Leyte Gulf and the beginning of
the battle for Manila two months later they expended 378 suicide-
plane and 102 escort-plane crews but sank sixteen U.S. ships and
damaged eighty-seven more. In the process they lost about 600
men and killed about 2,000 U.S. sailors. U.S. skippers feared and
hated their wild attacks, but the kamikazes themselves knew that
they were not killing massively enough to change the course of
the war.

Kamikaze commanders agonized over mission assignments. By
the end of January 1945 new suicide pilots were being drawn
mainly from the ranks of bookish university boys, capable of learning the rudiments of flying in a few weeks but not of arousing
excessive sympathy in the minds of the veteran air officers who
had to send them to their deaths.

Sakai Saburo, the ace who had lost an eye over Guadalcanal in
1942, expressed the feeling of most professional Japanese fighters
toward suicide tactics when he was required to fly a one-way mission against Saipan early in the battle for Iwo Jima.

He resented the assignment from the start, calling it "a death
without meaning, without purpose." He later wrote:

I appreciated better than most the wisdom of relying upon my own
strength and my own skill to escape the death which in a dogfight was
never more than a split second away. I could count only upon myself
and my wingmen. . . . A samurai lives in such a way that he will
always be prepared to die. . . . However, . . . there is a great gulf
between deliberately taking one's life and entering battle with a willingness to accept all its risks. . . . Man lives with his head held high;
he can die in the same fashion. . . .

Acting on such sentiments Sakai led his two wingmen to within
50 miles of Saipan. He saw seven of the eight bombers and five of
the eight fighters accompanying him shot out of the air by U.S.
Hellcats. By superb flying he led his wingmen out of the ambush
and continued to search for the U.S. fleet. Then the weather
closed in and he turned back to Iwo, bringing both his wingmen
home with him.

Only two other pilots survived the flight. On alighting, Sakai
stumbled over one of them, lying in shame in the darkness beside

the runway. He picked the man off the ground and arm in arm with him marched to the office of their commander. There, with a mounting sense of anger, Sakai reported the total and predictable failure of the mission. No one said anything. He was reposted home to Japan to live out the war as a flight instructor.

FIRE BOMBING

The war-weary sense of perspective which had begun to touch the one-eyed Sakai after seven years of air combat in China and the Pacific was a novelty among airmen, for they seldom had to see the results of their handiwork at close range. It had not begun to affect Sakai's opposite numbers from the United States, who now, with the fall of Iwo Jima, were called on to deliver the final telling blows on Japan. Newly graduated from accelerated mass flight-training programs, they questioned no orders but killed innocently, on a scale which would horrify a generation of commentators.

The air massacre of Japan opened with the devastating March 9 fire raid on Tokyo. In the days which followed it, Allied moralists missed their supreme opportunity to uphold, elucidate, or repudiate the rules of civilized warfare which Western diplomats had written into the treaties and protocols of international law in previous decades.[9]

The March 9 attack was ordered by Major General Curtis LeMay on his own discretionary authority as B-29 commander in the Marianas. LeMay, however, had recently been appointed to his post as a result of President Roosevelt's dissatisfaction with previous failure of the B-29 program to hasten the end of the Pacific war. On the day before the March 9 raid, LeMay gave a verbal briefing to Major General Lauris Norstad, an emissary from Air Force commander General Hap Arnold's staff. Then LeMay wired General Arnold in Washington to prepare "for an outstanding show."

[9] Some of them later protested against the atomic bomb because it seemed new and fearful or because—to paraphrase Hilaire Belloc—it was a weapon which the United States had got and the Soviet Union had not. They would have stood on firmer ground, with less suspect political motives, if they had protested the equally lethal use earlier of the "conventional" incendiaries.

The raid marked a sudden change in U.S. bombing tactics. Previously the B-29's had struck at industrial targets from high altitude in an effort to cripple Japanese war plants by precision bombing with ordinary explosives. Incendiaries and anti-personnel bombs had been used only sparingly and experimentally. On March 9–10, however, under cover of midnight, the B-29's came in over Tokyo low, at from 5,000 to 8,000 feet, dropping exclusively incendiaries and on the densely populated poor districts in the southeastern sections of the city. In these wards the Japanese were caught unprepared. They had hardly begun to carry out the anti-incendiary programs which were underway in other urban areas: the tearing down of houses to create firebreaks and the evacuation of all non-essential women and children to the countryside. The weather, too, played its part, for Tokyo that night was a center of air turbulence. Strong shifting winds fanned the flames and drove them in first one direction and then another.

The B-29's started the raid by dropping two strings of incendiaries which marked the center of the sixteen-square-mile target area with a blazing cross. Succeeding waves of B-29's drew a circle around the cross and then filled in the dark quadrants. Through the target wound Tokyo's Sumida River, fed by hundreds of sewage canals which crosshatched the entire area. The flames leapt the canals, destroyed bridges and trapped hysterical mobs of refugees on burning islands. Discipline and etiquette broke down. Many of the weak were trampled; the strong survived briefly and then burned or suffocated. The wind fed the flames and the heat fed the wind. Thermal tornadoes known as fire storms or dragon tails howled back and forth through the fire fronts, leaping into the sky and touching down again on cool ground with blazing fingerprints. The rising drafts from the fires severely buffeted the B-29's more than a mile overhead and the smoke blackened their bright fuselages with soot.

When the fires had been put out four days later the Japanese government admitted an official toll of 78,650 dead—500 more than the official toll it would admit after Hiroshima five months later. As in the case of Hiroshima, the official count was determined in after years to be a conservative estimate. To this day no one knows for sure, but students of the available records generally conclude that the March 9 raid on Tokyo was more lethal than the atomic bombing of Hiroshima.

After the fire raid, a handful of U.S. divines rose in their pulpits to protest indiscriminate bombing of enemy civilians, but no one paid much attention. The United States, in numerous treaties regarding the conventions of war, was on record as condemning civilian bombing. The Roosevelt Administration, however, considered itself unbound by rules of war which the enemy had already flouted.[10] Both Germany and Japan, to the best of their capabilities, had indiscriminately bombed the civilians of Allied nations. Now, therefore, it was thought just for the enemy to reap the tares which it had sown. No distinction was made between the poor of Hamburg and Berlin, who had played some part in allowing Hitler to rise to power, and the poor of Tokyo who had simply inherited Hirohito, without passing upon him.

Emperor Hirohito was quick to appreciate the injustice which would be felt by the impoverished victims of the fire raid. Since mid-December 1944, after the first heavy conventional raids on Tokyo, he had been living, for the most part, in the complex of tunnels and shelters which had been constructed in 1942 under his prewar work place, the Imperial Library, *Obunko*. When the first B-29 pathfinders began dropping their incendiary sticks, shortly before midnight on March 9, he was still at duty in his underground command post, half napping and half waiting up for two important phone calls concerning expected developments. One would tell him about a final Japanese Army take-over from French puppets in Saigon, the other about the birth of his first grandchild, the offspring of Princess Shigeko and Prince Higashikuni's son Morihiro. After midnight both labors were successfully concluded and he would have retired except that he had begun to hear of the horrifying raid then in progress.

During the night, either by accident or invention, sparks from

10 On the other hand Roosevelt was careful to honor commitments from which he had not been released by enemy action. During the Iwo Jima campaign, when Japanese soldiers were taking many U.S. lives from hot, sulfurous tunnels dug into the slopes and inner craters of the volcanic cones there, a serious proposal was made by the U.S. General Staffs to resort to poison gas. The proposal reached President Roosevelt's desk and was returned marked: "All prior endorsements denied—Franklin D. Roosevelt, Commander-in-Chief."

fires in southeast Tokyo three miles away supposedly alighted in the Fukiage Gardens and were beaten out on the very porch of the Imperial Library. It was even said that a U.S. pilot had dropped a single incendiary within the sacrosanct palace enclosure. But LeMay had issued explicit instructions to all B-29 pilots to spare the Imperial Palace because "the Emperor of Japan is not at present a liability and may later become an asset." Earlier precision bombing by B-29's had been disappointingly imprecise but not to the extent of three-mile misses.

In the morning, on arising and coming to the surface, Hirohito surveyed from afar the damage to the Tokyo slums and asked to visit the devastated areas in person so that he could extend his condolences to the bereaved and homeless. Three days later, having given the matter judicious thought, Lord Privy Seal Kido opined that it would be most unwise, politically, for the Emperor to pay an ordinary state visit to the ruins, attended by the usual armies of policemen and prepared through the usual infiltration of the populace by secret police agents. If the visit was to be paid at all it must be arranged to look like an informal, spur-of-the-moment imperial whim. Hirohito insisted that, even on these difficult terms, he owed it to his people. And so, six days later, on March 18, after elaborate preparations, Hirohito walked informally, as if impromptu, through the burned-out shacks along the banks of the Sumida River and shook his head, with a sad countenance, at the heaps of ash and charred bodies still in evidence there.

The fire convinced the Japanese lower classes, as no propaganda ever could, that surrender was, indeed, out of the question and that Americans really were demons bent on exterminating all Japanese.[11] After the raid it took the atomic bomb to persuade them that anything could be worse than the imagined cruelty of U.S. occupation troops. Japanese who had traveled or associated with Westerners in prewar Japan knew better, but they were in a minority. Moreover, even they felt apprehensive. It was clear from plain-language transmissions of the U.S. fleet that racial

[11] According to the later U.S. Strategic Bombing Survey's poll, belief in victory at this point in the war fell off far more sharply than will to fight. In short, the Japanese masses took the fire raids stoically as meaning that they must die.

hostilities had deepened alarmingly since Pearl Harbor and that few Americans any longer looked upon "Japs" as human beings.

LAST BATTLE

Desperately the Foreign Ministry officers who had supported Hirohito in going to war looked toward Stalin as a sane, humane, neutral mediator. As peace feelers were vainly pursued in Moscow, the monster of the U.S. armada and expeditionary force clawed its way ashore on Okinawa and proceeded, with 183,000 soldiers, to exterminate the well dug-in 110,000 Japanese defenders.

Nine hundred and thirty kamikaze pilots hurled themselves to death against the U.S. invasion fleet, sinking ten destroyers, an escort carrier, and six lesser ships, and heavily damaging 198 vessels including twelve carriers, ten battleships, five cruisers, and 63 destroyers, and killing over 3,000 U.S. sailors.

On April 6, five days after the American landings on Okinawa, Japan's surviving 64,000-ton super-dreadnought, *Yamato*, which had once been Admiral Yamamoto's flagship, made a suicide sortie from the Inland Sea toward Okinawa. She was accompanied by other activated remnants of the Japanese fleet, including a cruiser and eight destroyers. She never had a chance—not even to train her vaunted 18.1-inch guns on a worthy target. She was shadowed from the start by U.S. submarines. And she went down short of her mark under U.S. air attack. With her sank her escort cruiser, four of her destroyers, and about 3,000 hands. Her crewmen perished to little purpose. They demonstrated discipline to "Great Orders," stamped by Hirohito. They kept their great floating coffin from ever falling into enemy hands.

On the night of June 21 when the last trench lines on the southern tip of Okinawa had been breached and the remaining defenders were waiting in caves to be killed, Lieutenant General Ushijima Mitsuru and his Chief of Staff Lieutenant General Cho Isamu held a last feast with other officers in their command cave. They drank up the last cases of Scotch whisky which they had carried with them in their retreat and then made ready to commit hara-kiri. Commander Ushijima, an old-fashioned samurai, told self-deprecating jokes in a soft voice and impressed all who heard him with his fatherly manner. Chief of Staff Cho, however, who had issued the "kill-all-prisoners" order for Prince Asaka outside of Nanking in 1937, had been living on whisky for several days and marred the final rites by "boisterous talk." Earlier he had issued an official suggestion to all Japanese civilians on Okinawa to kill themselves. Now he wrote last messages to friends in Japan. One of them, sent to Prince Asaka's villa for transmission to Hirohito, had a sober ring: "We fought as valiantly as we could with the best strategy, tactics, and technical aids available but our efforts counted for little against the material might of the enemy."

Cho and Ushijima had a white cloth spread at the mouth of their cave, and having nostalgically watched the set of the moon, knelt down upon it at 4:10 A.M. on June 22, to face north toward the palace and perform their final act of service. Commander Ushijima had calmly cut open his belly when nearby American troops, hearing sounds in the dark, flung grenades toward the cave entrance. The hard-drinking Chief of Staff Cho half rose as if to order another attack. His second, standing behind him to dispatch him in case his death throes proved too painful, promptly scythed downward with a drawn sword and cut off his head. So it was, according to Army gossip, that butcher Cho died: not by his own hand with honor, having first laid down his guts upon the ground, but by beheading, at the hands of another, like any common thief in Tokugawa times.

HEAD ABOVE SHAME

Japan was beaten as thoroughly as any nation had ever been beaten in history. The average intake of food for every citizen had fallen to less than 1,700 calories a day.[12] Most storage tanks for fuel oil and aviation gasoline had been pumped dry. All ships but a few wooden coastal vessels had ceased to ply even the Inland Sea. Ferries to smaller home islands were being sunk daily. Railroads were running on a catch-as-catch-can basis. The Continent

---

[12] Captives of the Japanese at that time enjoyed 800 to 1,300 calories a day. After the captives had been liberated, however, ordinary Japanese citizens remained on short rations for many months. They suffered little from acute forms of malnutrition like beriberi but they suffered greatly from hunger-aggravated diseases like tuberculosis.

was cut off. A million Japanese soldiers, from Seoul to Singapore, had no way of coming home to join in the final fight.

Sharpened staves of bamboo were handed out as spears to the villagers along likely invasion beaches in southern Japan. And then the U.S. B-29's proceeded to drop the sophisticated atomic bomb.

Hirohito had been expecting to negotiate a surrender in September or October after the loss of perhaps another million of his loyal subjects. The bomb, as he later told MacArthur, gave Japan an excuse to surrender earlier. That is, it forced Hirohito to "bear the unbearable" humiliation of surrender immediately. He realized, correctly,[18] that it would be only a matter of time until an atomic bomb was dropped on Tokyo. Then the entire imperial family would be wiped out and Japan, from Hirohito's point of view, would cease to exist.

Having accepted the irrefutable logic of the bomb, Hirohito acted on it with great decisiveness. As detailed earlier, he overrode the quibbles and vacillations of his chief vassals at the historic meeting in his air raid shelter at midnight on August 9, 1945. Again, on the morning of August 14, when his ministers had debated the Allied reply to Japan's surrender note for two days, he cut off their deliberations and ordered them to accept the U.S. terms without further ado.

In these his final acts as absolute god-king, Hirohito reportedly carried himself well, and for the most part, exuded a serenity and readiness to face death which inspired his retainers. At 9:15 on the morning of August 12, when the Allied reply to Japan's surrender note had just been received and studied by the Foreign Ministry, Lord Privy Seal Kido privately pointed out to Hirohito that the Americans insisted on an eventual form of government in Japan dictated by the will of the Japanese people. This insistence on democracy, said Kido, was the issue which most troubled the imperial advisors.

"If the people didn't want an emperor," said Hirohito with conviction, "all would be futile. I think I can trust the people."

---

[18] General Carl A. Spaatz, the commander of the U.S. Strategic Air Forces, had already urged strongly that the next atomic bomb be dropped on Tokyo. Two more of the bombs were on their way to Tinian ready for assembly and delivery in the next few weeks. If Hirohito had rejected the Hiroshima-Nagasaki ultimatums, his underground bunker would almost certainly have been crushed forthwith.

Kido found Hirohito's high-priestly self-confidence a little breathtaking. It turned out, however, to be justified. According to a careful polling of Japanese opinion by the U.S. Strategic Bombing Survey months later: "The Emperor largely escaped the criticism which was directed at other leaders, and retained the people's faith in him. It is probable that most Japanese would have passively faced death in a continuation of the hopeless struggle had the Emperor so ordered."

The sublime detachment of Hirohito was shared, to an extent, by other members of the family. On the afternoon of August 12, from 3 to 5:20 P.M., Hirohito had all the adult princes of the blood attend him in the Imperial Library. He asked their support in his decision to accept the Allied note received that morning. The corpulent, seventy-one-year-old Prince Nashimoto—patron of Tojo, go-between with the Kwantung Army before the China War, and since then lord custodian of national shrines and chief priest to the sun goddess at Ise—arose as senior prince and pledged Hirohito to full co-operation of all present. For the next two hours the princes talked over the roles assigned to them by the Peace Faction in the days ahead. No detailed record of their deliberations is extant but the central issue was clear and simple. Hirohito's Navy brother, Captain Takamatsu, who was one of those present, had stated it succinctly to a General Staff gathering nine months earlier: "How to be defeated gracefully."

That evening, as soon as the Imperial Family Council had adjourned, War Minister General Anami, who had been explicitly charged by Hirohito with the task of controlling the Army in defeat, was given an audience by Hirohito's Army brother, Lieutenant Colonel Mikasa. The two met in Mikasa's palace air-raid shelter which adjoined Hirohito's. Anami complained that the Army was being made to take all the blame for the war and pleaded with Prince Mikasa to intercede with his brother for a fairer distribution of war responsibility. With remarkable sangfroid, Mikasa refused. He pointed out that the Army bureaucracy had taken a leading role in advising the Throne since the Manchurian Incident in 1931. Not only had the generals advised but on occasion they had "acted not perfectly in accordance with imperial wishes."

Princess Mikasa, in the next room of the princely shelter, noticed that the prince and the war minister were speaking loudly to one another.[14] She had the impression that Anami was arguing against surrender plans and that Prince Mikasa was insisting upon them. Later that night, when Anami had left, a group of staff officers also called at the Mikasa bunker. One of them, noted the princess, had been a classmate of the prince in military academy. Again voices were raised and the prince took his guests up into the moonlit gardens so that they could talk without disturbing the family.

Two nights later it was a mysterious Lieutenant Colonel X, fitting the description of Prince Mikasa, who led a group of Mikasa's military academy classmates in the elaborate palace coup, previously described in detail, which was billed as an attempt to prevent Hirohito from surrendering. The commander of the palace guard was assassinated in the presence of Lieutenant Colonel X. War Minister Anami retired to his villa to commit suicide. Most of the young officers of the rebellion followed Anami's example except Lieutenant Colonel X, who vanished.

While the Army was taking responsibility for the war in this peculiar fashion, Hirohito, by his own account, lay awake in his bed in the Imperial Library, above ground, until the alarmed whispers of chamberlains in his anteroom told him that the abortive insurrection had been staged as planned. Then he rolled over and went to sleep. He had not needed to worry about the behavior of his people. Almost a million of them had died in the last year. Their deaths had been more painful to them than to him, but they remained his obedient children. Tomorrow noon, when his voice would go out on the radio, acknowledging to them the fact of defeat, they would weep loyally. They would sympathize with him in his humiliation. They would be grateful to him for his final mercy. Now, the next concern was the behavior of the conquerors.

In the morning, after the minions of Colonel X had withdrawn from the offices of Japan Broadcasting Company and Tokyo radio had gone back on the air to announce the impending imperial broadcast, Grand Chamberlain Admiral Fujita Hisanori reported

[14] Princess Mikasa Yuriko was the eldest daughter of Viscount Takagi Masanori. She was cousin to Big Brother Baron Takagi Yoshihiro and kin to Rear Admiral Takagi Sokichi who, since 1939, had had charge of contingency planning for defeat in the Navy General Staff.

at the Imperial Library for work as usual. He was called in for his first audience at 8:10 A.M. As he straightened up from his deep bow of morning felicitation, he first noticed how tired the Emperor looked, and then, in spite of himself, he smiled appreciatively. On the shelf for ornaments, recessed in the wall behind Hirohito's back, had stood for years the busts of Darwin and Napoleon; now Napoleon's had been quietly replaced by Abraham Lincoln's. The Emperor had spoken without saying a word.

EPILOGUE

NEW CLOTHES

TO SPOIL THE SPOILS

In the bright darkness of the flamethrowers and burning cities, in the dark darkness of the destroyed palaces and rifled archives were gestated not only a new Japan also a new Asia. The Far East of Western colonialism would never be the same comfortable place again. In the final months of the war Japanese commanders in China, Indochina, Malaya, and Indonesia worked around the clock trying to negotiate lasting understandings with local puppet political leaders. After the surrender, the younger princes of the imperial family were sent out to the legions overseas to make sure that they would surrender peacefully—Prince Kanin Haruhito, the son of the long-time chief of staff, to Singapore; Prince Asaka Takahiko, the son of the rape commander, to Nanking; and Prince Takeda Tsuneyoshi, Hirohito's principal wartime go-between with the legions, to Manchuria. As a result, before French, British, and Dutch troops returned to Indochina, Malaya, and Indonesia, sizable Japanese arsenals had been turned over to native patriots and many Japanese advisors had gone underground to assist local independence movements.

The Japanese advisors were not treated with much gratitude and many of them were subsequently betrayed to Allied justice. Throughout Southeast Asia, however, the Japanese arms handouts fortified native opposition to reimposition of Western colonial rule. Particularly in Malaya, Indonesia, and Indochina, bands of irregulars benefited from the Japanese largesse and figured prominently in guerrilla activity against the British, Dutch, and French during the first year after the war. Later these resistance movements became increasingly Communist-dominated. In Malaya the British fought the guerrillas to a standstill and managed a settlement on favorable terms. In Indonesia a former Japanese puppet, Sukarno, finally emerged triumphant over the Dutch and proceeded to make his country, which was naturally the richest in Asia, into one of the least solvent. In Indochina, where the Ho Chi Minh faction gained control of the independence movement, the little brush fire on which the Japanese had poured fuel grew into a major conflagration which burned for more than a quarter of a century.

The great Japanese proponent of these last-ditch, cheat-the-enemy tactics, which did little good for Japan or for Asia but which did severely embarrass the West, was Colonel Tsuji Masanobu. This angry young messiah of Asia for the Asiatics, who had worked during the war with credentials from Hirohito and Prince Mikasa and had directed the slaughter of thousands of English and Chinese captives on Singapore and of Americans on Bataan, now got himself to a Thai monastery outside Bangkok. Disguised in the saffron robes of a Buddhist priest, he sought to make his temple hideout the headquarters for underground movements throughout Southeast Asia. His lines of communication, however, were poor from the start. They were made worse when the British Army, which had just chased fleeing Japanese units across Burma, went on to occupy "neutral" Thailand. In October 1945, when British agents began to sniff the incense around Tsuji's monastic cell, Tsuji threw himself upon the mercy of Chiang Kai-shek's Blueshirt agents who were also operating in the Bangkok area. The Blueshirts smuggled him away to Indochina and thence to Chungking where he finally achieved his wartime ambition of talking to Chiang Kai-shek about the future of Asia.

As a calling card to Chiang, Tsuji reproduced, annotated, or translated a decade's worth of Japanese strategic planning against communism in Manchuria and north China. Out of gratitude Chiang Kai-shek released from prison a number of Japanese war criminal suspects and took on half a dozen of them to serve as advisors in his postwar struggle against Mao Tse-tung. The chief of them, who became for a while one of Chiang's intimates, was former General Okamura Yasuji, the third of the Three Crows of Baden-Baden, on whom Hirohito had first relied as a nucleus for conspiracy in the 1920's.[1]

Tsuji remained in China with Chiang Kai-shek until February 1948 when it became clear that Mao Tse-tung and his Communist armies would win the Chinese civil war. Then Chiang began to see less of his Japanese military advisors and his soldiers massacred many unrepatriated Japanese colonists on Taiwan. Taking these hints, Tsuji, in March, returned secretly to Japan. For the next four years he lived in a state of negotiated hiding, politely ignored by U.S. Allied Occupation forces, and supporting himself with books and articles about his checkered career. In 1952, as soon as the Occupation had ended, he was elected to the Diet where he made laws and continued to write books until 1961.

Then, at a time when Japanese news correspondents were first beginning to cover the war in Indochina and to look for exposés of Western military excesses, Dietman Tsuji visited Ho Chi Minh's capital of Hanoi as a feature writer for *Asahi*. While there he vanished. Ho's Viet Minh government could not explain his disappearance and never produced a body to show that he had died. Japanese veterans' associations, which had proved themselves diligent in bringing home ashes or bones of dead Japanese soldiers from islands in the Pacific, made no effort to recover Tsuji's remains.

Popular rumor in Japan has it that Tsuji did not die but continues his spectacular career in Hanoi. Some say he works there as an agent for the U.S. Central Intelligence Agency; others, that he is an assistant minister of propaganda, helping Japanese corre-

---

[1] Lieutenant General Nemoto Hiroshi, another veteran member of Hirohito's Army cabal, became a recruiting agent for Chiang on Taiwan. Still another, Lieutenant General Sumita Raishiro, was made assistant to his fellow Tokyo military academy graduate, the much abused governor of China's Shansi province, General Yen Hsishan. Some of those who fought for Chiang later went on to serve Emperor Haile Selassie in Ethiopia. They were led from 1953 to 1962 by former Lieutenant General Ikeda Sumihisa who, as Cabinet Planning Board member, had attended the historic surrender meeting in Hirohito's bunker on the night of August 9, 1945.

spondents turn out tales of U.S. atrocities; still others, that he remains a stalwart of the prewar Japanese spy service directing Pan-Asian, anti-Western movements in Southeast Asia.

VENGEANCE OF THE VICTORS

Before Japan's surrender, Allied troops killed thousands of Japanese soldiers who, with a little trouble and risk, might have been taken prisoner. In a few isolated areas of reconquest, the killings continued even after the surrender. One of the largest butcheries took place under the aegis of Australian commanders in British North Borneo. There, 6,000 Japanese soldiers who had surrendered were told to stack their arms at Pensiangan and march 150 miles to Beaufort for internment. The previous year these same troops had wiped out many native villages on the Borneo coast suspected of having traffic with U.S. submarines. Now, therefore, vengeful surviving tribesmen were turned loose on the disarmed Japanese columns to enjoy a headhunt in which all but a few hundred of the 6,000 Japanese perished. Some of the Australians who stood by were ashamed of their complicity in the crime and later exposed it for the death march it was.

The atrocities committed by Allied infantrymen on the surrender battlefields could be half excused as products of war passion. More outrageous acts of injustice took place thereafter in courts of law where thinkers should have had time to think. Out of ignorance and lack of appreciation for Japanese politics, MacArthur's war-crime prosecutors sedulously ignored leaders like Tsuji, Prince Mikasa, and Emperor Hirohito and zealously tried, defamed, and hanged military officers who knew no morality but obedience to orders.

Immediately the war had ended, many of the pathetic psychopaths and syphilitic madmen who had been used in the administration of Japan's prisoner-of-war program were tracked down by Allied military policemen, identified by former Allied captives of Japan, and given rough-and-ready justice. Some were beaten during interrogation. Some were identified by face alone and tried under names which were not their own. Some were summarily put to death after hearings lasting less than an hour. By their own private admission, however, none of them was murdered in his cell and none of them was executed without cause.[2] Few tears were shed for them even in Japan, for they had been misfits in their own tolerant familial society.

Altogether about 5,000 Japanese were arrested for the calculated reprisals of state and individual acts of brutality which had taken the lives of over half a million Asiatics and Westerns. Most of those apprehended had committed their crimes against Western nationals who represented less than a tenth of the victims. About 4,000 of the suspects were brought to trial before U.S., British, Australian, and Chinese military tribunals which sat in scattered courtrooms from Guam to Rangoon and from Timor to Tokyo. Of the 4,000 some 800 were acquitted, some 2,400 were sentenced to three years or more of imprisonment, and 809 were put to death.[3] In addition several thousand Japanese captured by Russian troops in Manchuria died in Siberian labor camps.

HANGING THE TIGER

Although there was some inhumanity in the Allied handling of lesser Japanese war criminals, it was not such as to excite much

[2] A committee of nine convicts in Tokyo's Sugamo Prison collected from fellow inmates all the complaints they could about Allied war-crime trial procedures throughout the Empire. They wrote up their findings in a mimeographed volume called *Senpan Saiban no Jisso*, The Real Facts of the War-Crime Trials. It makes pallid reading beside the affidavits of former Allied P.O.W.'s written at about the same time. In Hong Kong former Japanese secret policemen were struck with rulers, threatened with their own torture tools, knocked down in the course of unwanted boxing lessons, and forced as punishment for food riots to walk barefoot on broken glass. In Singapore former concentration camp guards grew thin on two meals a day, each of which had to be eaten in five minutes. In Tokyo a U.S. interrogator named Dyer, attended by a Nisei interpreter, sometimes brandished a gun and sometimes massaged throats threateningly in efforts to make suspects sign confessions. No Japanese claimed that he had been hung by the thumbs, or filled with water and jumped on, or touched with lighted cigarettes at penis tip, or kept awake with drugs while fine slices of flesh were being cut from his hams, delicately sautéed and eaten before his eyes. These were charges which could be made and authenticated only by liberated Allied prisoners of war—prisoners, moreover, who had simply fought the Japanese, not tormented them in concentration camps.

[3] This figure, which includes 802 minor and seven major war criminals, is the Japanese count. I have had no luck in attempts to declassify complete war-criminal statistics in Washington, and I am told that complete figures for war-criminal processes held by the Nationalist Government in China are not available in any case.

comment even in the Japanese vernacular press. What did arouse the censure and derision of Japan was the ignorance which the West displayed in its initial handling of so-called major war criminals.

The first "major" trials were held in Manila in late 1945 and early 1946. They began with the prosecution of General Yamashita. The Tiger of Malaya had drilled the Special Maneuver forces for the Strike South in Manchuria in 1941. He had bested General Percival in Malaya in 1942. He had embarrassed General MacArthur by his skillful defense of Luzon, with pitifully equipped forces, in 1945.[4] These achievements were still fresh in the minds of the Japanese public when, on October 29, 1945, General Yamashita was put on trial for his life as a war criminal. To many outside observers in the West as well as in Japan, it seemed that MacArthur was indulging in petty vengeance. In reality MacArthur was simply playing politics. The Philippines, he felt, were his constituency. On arriving in Tokyo, he had decided to spare Japan and rebuild it as a bulwark against communism. If he did not treat Japan harshly, his Filipino constituents would feel cheated, and so he picked on General Yamashita to serve as a scapegoat whose trial would distract Filipinos during the early months of the lenient Allied Occupation of Tokyo.

The Yamashita trial served its political purpose admirably. For over a month Filipino survivors of Japanese atrocities paraded themselves before five U.S. generals who sat in court-martial over Yamashita. Little girls pulled up their frocks to show the court their multiple bayonet wounds. Older girls testified to the circumstances of their rapes. No attempt was made by MacArthur's uniformed prosecutors to show that any of these brutalities had been ordered by Yamashita. On the contrary the trial brought out clearly that the orders authorizing latitude in discipline for such

---

[4] If MacArthur's tactics in the Philippines in 1941–42 had been brilliant, Yamashita's in 1944–45 had been inspired. On the same terrain, against similar odds, MacArthur had held out on Corregidor with a small fraction of his command for six months; Yamashita, with most of his starving troops, had held out in the Luzon mountains for eight months and had only surrendered when ordered to do so by Hirohito. Five thousand of Yamashita's soldiers had defended Corregidor, the island bastion at the mouth of Manila Bay, for eleven days in 1945 after the first landings on the island by U.S. forces. Four thousand of MacArthur's men had surrendered the same island in 1942 less than twelve hours after the first Japanese had set foot on it.

acts had emanated from Tokyo and that Yamashita, locally, had tried in vain to countermand the hints of Imperial General Headquarters. The trial definitely established that most of the atrocities of which the Filipinos complained had been committed by the aristocratic Naval Special Landing Force which had intervened belatedly to fight for Manila in direct contravention of General Yamashita's orders. All Japanese witnesses agreed that Yamashita, off in the hills, had no means even of communicating with the desperate sailors in Manila, much less of directing them.

During the Yamashita trial, half the Allied correspondents attached to MacArthur's suite were in Manila, away from Tokyo. In their absence MacArthur was having his first meetings with Hirohito and attempting, in the words of his political staff chief, Brigadier General Courtney Whitney, to "blackmail Japan" into acceptance of Occupation reforms. MacArthur paid for this arrangement by receiving a poor press at the trial in Manila.

The New York Times's Robert Trumbull wrote: "All precedents in law have been thrown out the window. . . . There are no regulations governing the American War Crimes Commission, except those it makes for itself, and it has made very few."

Newsweek described spectators as "scandalized by the break with Anglo-Saxon justice" and observed that "even third-hand hearsay is admitted as evidence."

Henry Keyes of London's *Daily Express* at one point reported: "Yamashita's trial continued today—but it isn't a trial. I doubt if it is even a hearing. Yesterday his name was mentioned once. Today it was not brought up at all."

No doubt, as a seasoned Japanese commander, Yamashita could have been faulted for moral turpitude on a number of counts—though perhaps not in a court of law. He had, after all, assisted Hirohito in betraying the Strike-North movement and in bringing about the February Mutiny in 1936 which had enabled Hirohito to insist upon a Strike South. In 1938–39 he had been chief of staff of the tough North China Army Group at a time when it had carried out more than one reprisal massacre of Chinese villages. In his 1940 trip to Germany, he had stolen radar secrets from Hitler. By training Strike-South forces in Manchuria in 1941, he had conspired with Hirohito in plans for aggressive war. During his term as commander in Malaya he had failed to check the secret police in their killing of 5,000 of Singapore's Chinese merchants.

The one offense for which Yamashita could not be faulted was inhumane treatment of Westerners. In the non-Asiatic, Junker-trained half of his mind—the half he used in dealing with the West—he was a stickler for correct war conduct. He had incurred the displeasure of Tsuji and Hirohito by disciplining officers of his command who permitted battlefield atrocities against British troops in the Malayan campaign of 1941–42. In December 1944 he had taken pains—and expended gasoline—to take all U.S. war prisoners and internees out of the mountainous areas of Luzon around Baguio where he planned to make his own last desperate stand. His restraining influence had helped to prevent commandants of prison camps in the Philippines from acting on suggestions from Tokyo Imperial Headquarters to kill all U.S. prisoners rather than let them be liberated.

Nevertheless, MacArthur, in his studied ignorance of Japanese history and his desire to please and exploit the Emperor, chose to prosecute Yamashita for crimes of which he was far more innocent than most Japanese commanders. What followed put a lasting stain on the American escutcheon and created an embarrassing precedent which would be remembered by American lawyers and jurists later after the My Lai incident during the Viet Nam war.[5]

As well as the rape of Manila, of which he was innocent, Yamashita was charged with the command responsibility for the incineration of 150 American P.O.W.'s on Palawan Island in December 1944 and for a series of reprisal massacres against Filipino villages in the province of Batangas in the early months of 1945. The facts were, as brought out in the trial, that Palawan was under command of the Tokyo-directed Air Navy at the time of the atrocity, and that the Batangas reprisal raids were also ordered from Tokyo rather than from Yamashita's command post in the

[5] In January 1971 Columbia University Professor Telford Taylor, a retired brigadier general who was U.S. chief counsel for the prosecution at the Nuremberg trials, was reported by *The New York Times* as saying that, under the rule of the case of General Yamashita, U.S. General William C. Westmoreland, former commander in Viet Nam, "could be found guilty" of war crimes. Yamashita's former defense attorney, A. Frank Reel, protested to the *Times:* "Under the Yamashita rule as set down by the United States Supreme Court, Westmoreland would be convicted."

mountains. In addition, even Filipino witnesses admitted that the Batangas villages had been centers of guerrilla activity. It was a recognized rule of civilized warfare that guerrillas had no rights. To the American mind, however, this rule did not justify the machine-gunning, burning, and bayoneting of women and small children, a crime against humanity which had indubitably been committed several thousand times in Batangas under Yamashita's nominal authority.

The Batangas massacres supplied the one instance of possible criminal negligence on Yamashita's part which might have justified singling him out as an example from the whole hardened corps of Japanese Army officers. When the time came, however, for Yamashita to speak in his own defense, he half closed his eyes under the bright lights of the courtroom and delivered himself with simple eloquence:

I did not hear at once of the events which took place nor did I have prior knowledge that they might take place. . . . I was under pressure night and day to plan, study and execute counterstrokes against superior American forces. . . . Nine days after my arrival in the Philippines I faced an overwhelming American tide moving on Leyte. . . . I was forced to confront superior U.S. forces with subordinates whom I did not know and with whose character and ability I was unfamiliar. As a result of the inefficiency of the Japanese army system, I could not unify my command; my duties were extremely complicated. The troops were scattered and Japanese communications were very poor. . . . I became gradually cut off from the situation and found myself out of touch. I believe under these conditions I did the best job I could have done. . . . I did not order [any] massacres. . . . I put forth my best efforts to control my troops. If this was not enough, then I agree that somehow I should have done more. Some men might have been able to do more. However, I feel I did my best.

Despite the evidence at hand, and despite Yamashita's maverick position in domestic Japanese politics—a position which could have been explained to the court by any reasonably articulate Tokyo ward heeler—Yamashita's judges decided that a military commander, even when uninformed and countermanded by higher authority, should still remain responsible for the acts of his troops. It was a blithely irresponsible postwar decision which would later cause much distress to U.S. Army lawyers. It meant in effect that every senior, from general up to president or prime minister, was responsible for the orders obeyed by every junior. It meant that legal responsibility for war crimes could be adjudged, by reductio ad absurdum, to anyone in a chain of command regardless of his character, motives, and state of knowledge.

Yamashita's sentence of death was handed down in Manila on December 7, 1945, the fourth anniversary of Pearl Harbor. Yamashita's able defense lawyers, who were all volunteers from the legal section of MacArthur's own U.S. Army, appealed the sentence up to the U.S. Supreme Court. In January 1946 the court chose to hear the appeal but after a month of study declined to overrule the military tribunal which had sat in Manila. By a vote of five-to-two the U.S. Supreme Court justices avowed that a military commander did indeed have criminal responsibility for the misdeeds of his underlings, no matter how extenuating the circumstances. Justices Harlan Stone, Hugo Black, Felix Frankfurter, William Douglas, and Harold Burton assented in this argument. Justices Frank Murphy and Wiley Rutledge dissented. Murphy who penned the thirty-two-page dissent, in which Rutledge concurred, wrote with a special authority because he had some knowledge of the Orient, having once been U.S. High Commissioner in the Philippines:

. . . Never before have we tried and convicted an enemy general for actions taken during hostilities or otherwise in the course of military operations or duty—much less have we condemned one for failing to take action. . . .

This petitioner was rushed to trial under an improper charge, given insufficient time to prepare an adequate defense, deprived of the benefits of some of the most elementary rules of evidence, and summarily sentenced to be hanged. In all this needless and unseemly haste there was no serious attempt to prove that he committed a recognized violation of the laws of war.

He was not charged with personally participating in acts of atrocity or with ordering or condoning their commission. Not even knowledge of the crimes was attributed to him. It was simply alleged that he unlawfully disregarded and failed to discharge his duty as commander to control the operations of the members of his command, permitting them to commit acts of atrocity. The recorded annals of warfare and the established principles of international law form not the slightest precedent for such a charge.

This indictment, in effect, permitted the Military Commission to make the crime whatever it willed, dependent upon its biased view as to the petitioner's duties and his disregard thereof. . . .

In our opinion such a procedure is unworthy of the traditions of our people or of the immense sacrifices they have made to advance the ideals of mankind. The high feelings of the moment will doubtless be satisfied but, in the sober afterglow, will come the realization of the boundless and dangerous implications of the procedure sanctioned today.

No one in a position of command in any army, from sergeant to general, can escape these implications. Indeed the fate of some future President of the United States and his Chiefs of Staff and military advisors may well have been sealed by this decision. . . .

That there were brutal atrocities inflicted upon the helpless Filipino people, to whom tyranny is no stranger, is undeniable. That just punishment should be meted out to all those responsible is also beyond dispute. But these factors do not justify the abandonment of our devotion to justice in dealing with a fallen enemy commander. . . .

Today the life of General Yamashita, a leader of enemy forces vanquished in the field of battle, is to be taken without regard to the due processes of law. There will be few to protest. But tomorrow the precedent here established can be turned against others.

A procession of judicial lynchings without due process of law may now follow. . . . A nation must not perish because, in its natural frenzy of the aftermath of war, it abandoned its central theme of the dignity of the human personality and due process of law.

When the text of Justice Murphy's dissent arrived in Tokyo in February, General MacArthur issued his own counterstatement on the Yamashita case:

I have reviewed the proceedings in vain search for some mitigating circumstances on his behalf. I can find none. . . . The soldier, be he friend or foe, is charged with the protection of the weak and unarmed. It is the very essence and reason for his being. When he violates this sacred trust, he not only profanes his entire cult but he threatens the very fabric of international society. . . . The transgressions . . . revealed by the trial are a blot upon the military profession, a stain upon civilization. . . . Particularly callous and purposeless was the sack of the ancient city of Manila, with its Christian population and countless historic shrines and monuments of culture and civilization which, with campaign conditions reversed, had previously been spared. . . .

No new or retroactive principles of law, either national or international, are involved. The case is founded upon basic fundamentals and practice as immutable and as standardized as the most natural and irrefragable of social codes. The proceedings were guided by that primary rationale of all judicial purposes—to ascertain the full truth, unshackled by any artificialities of narrow method or technical arbitrariness. The results are beyond challenge.

I approve the findings and sentence of the Commission and direct the Commanding General, Army Forces in the Western Pacific, to execute the judgment upon the defendant, stripped of uniform, decorations and other appurtenances signifying membership in the military profession.

The vehemence of MacArthur's assertions and the richness of his prose betrayed an ill-informed anxiety. However, his fears were needless. Yamashita's American lawyers appealed to the court of last resort, the White House, but the fledgling president, Harry Truman, declined to meddle in MacArthur's business. And so Yamashita was given a last meal of asparagus, bread, and beer. It was almost the tenth anniversary of the 1936 February Mutiny in which he had helped Hirohito to assert absolute power over the Japanese Army and point it south. After a brief nap, at 3:27 A.M. on February 23, 1946, General Yamashita climbed the scaffold of New Bilibid Prison, outside Manila. He bowed curtly north toward the far-away palace of the god-king. The trap sprang and he was hanged until he was dead.

CUTTING OFF THE NOSE

As soon as sentence had been passed on General Yamashita on December 7, 1945, the military court in Manila began proceedings against General Honma, the "linguist with the red nose" who had translated the first pirated copy of the Lytton Report on Manchuria in 1932. Honma was tried for having been over-all commander in the Philippines when the Bataan Death March took place in 1942. Somewhat guardedly Japanese witnesses at the trial brought out the true state of Honma's command during the Death March, revealing that it had been pre-empted by higher authority vested in staff officers from Tokyo and Singapore. The U.S. generals who sat as judges discounted this testimony as a weak excuse. From their own experience in the U.S. Army they could not imagine how colonels like Tsuji could usurp the command of a lieutenant general like Honma.

Honma's American defense lawyers themselves did not appreciate the intervention of imperial influence in Honma's command business. As a result, they relied in their presentation on an ill-informed argument that really was an excuse; an argument which they could substantiate only through the opinions of some Japanese journalists and civilian bureaucrats; an argument to the effect that no orders had been issued for the Death March and that it had developed as an unpremeditated act of passion on the part of vengeful Japanese soldiers. The five U.S. military judges could see only evasion and prevarication in such an argument, for they knew that the Death March had continued for a week, that verbal orders had been issued for it, and that at one point its stumbling columns had passed within a mile of General Honma's headquarters. And so, as rational men, they sentenced Honma to execution before a firing squad.

Honma's American lawyers exerted themselves to postpone execution of sentence for three months and to appeal the case, once again, to the U.S. Supreme Court. Honma's chief counsel, John H. Skeen, Jr., pleaded that it had been "a highly irregular trial, conducted in an atmosphere that left no doubt as to what the ultimate outcome would be." As before, however, the court decided to let the Manila verdict stand, and Associate Justice Frank Murphy saw fit again to file a powerful dissent. "This nation's very honor," he wrote, "as well as its hope for the future, is at stake. Either we conduct such a trial as this in the noble spirit and atmosphere of our Constitution or we abandon all pretense to justice, let the ages slip away, and descend to the level of revengeful blood purges."

Justice Murphy's persistent and eloquent objections stung Mac-Arthur. When Honma's lawyers appealed to him for clemency after the Supreme Court decision, MacArthur, on March 21, 1945, issued a lengthy explanation of his reasons for executing the verdict:

I am again confronted with the repugnant duty of passing final judgment on a former adversary in a major military campaign. The proceedings show the defendant lacked the basic firmness of character and moral fortitude essential to officers charged with the high command of military forces in the field. No nation can safely trust its martial honor to leaders who do not maintain the universal code which distinguishes between those things that are right and those things which are wrong.

[Here MacArthur interpolated a fine tribute to the fighting achievements of the Battling Bastards of Bataan. He continued:]

No trial could have been fairer than this one. . . . Insofar as was humanly possible the actual facts were fully presented to the commission. There were no artifices of technicality which might have precluded the introduction of full truth in favor of half-truth, or caused the slanting of half-truth to produce the effect of non-truth, thereby warping and confusing the tribunal into an insecure verdict. . . . Those who oppose such honest method can only be a minority who either advocate arbitrariness of process above factual realism, or who inherently shrink from the stern rigidity of capital punishment. . . .

If the defendant does not deserve his judicial fate, none in jurisdictional history ever did. There can be no greater, more heinous or more dangerous crime than the mass destruction, under guise of military authority or military necessity, of helpless men, incapable of further contribution to war effort. A failure of law process to punish such acts of criminal enormity would threaten the very fabric of world society. . . .

On final appeal President Truman again did not presume to stand in the way of MacArthur, and on April 3, 1946, General Honma fell before a U.S. firing squad. In his final letter to his children he exhorted them to look for the "right direction" in life rather than to follow the customary direction of bringing flowers to his grave. "Do not miss the right course," he wrote. "This is my very last letter."

Since "our forces were being demobilized in the Philippines," explained MacArthur later, "the remaining United States cases of this kind were tried by the International Tribunal in Tokyo."

TOKYO TRIAL DEFENDANTS

In the Manila trials MacArthur unwittingly rid Hirohito of two subjects who had differed with Imperial General Headquarters in 1942. Yamashita had insisted upon decent treatment of British war prisoners in Singapore and then had predicted dire results unless Japan followed up her initial triumphs with an invasion of Australia. It was Honma's sin that he had seen no need for haste in taking Bataan and then that he had pleaded for an enlightened and humane administration of the Philippines.[6] MacArthur, of course, knew only that Yamashita and Honma had caused the Supreme Commander Allied Powers (SCAP) much unfavorable publicity during the war and after it; and that the State Department wanted future trials of Class A Japanese war criminals to be conducted with more care. For the Tokyo trials of Japan's wartime government leaders, therefore, MacArthur spared neither time nor expense.

Since, by the custom of their society, Japanese leaders always solicited the advice of subordinates and sought out supporters who would be willing to share responsibility for decisions which might go wrong, it was no mean task for MacArthur's war-crime investigators to compile a roster of major war criminals. In Hirohito's retinue there were few foolhardy blusterers who could stand beside Hitler's gang in Germany and be called most blameworthy for leading Japan to war. Selection of Class A war criminals was made doubly difficult by the restriction that neither the Emperor, nor members of his family, nor anyone who would implicate them should be indicted. Finally, as pointed out in Chapter 3, defendants for the trials were selected only after much consultation and negotiation with the palace.

Given the peculiar circumstances, MacArthur's prosecutors performed as well as they could. They produced a list of defendants which included several of the commoners who had participated

[6] His efforts at leniency were regularly countermanded by Imperial General Headquarters. To cite an instance, he had Western missionaries in Baguio released from internment camp on January 29, 1942. A day later fresh orders arrived from Tokyo and all but a dozen of the 170-odd libérés were reinterned. I was fortunate in that my family was among those left at liberty, on a technicality, for eight months, as a gesture to save General Honma's face.

most actively in Hirohito's imperial conspiracy. It excluded all but two of a number of suggested candidates who had been at odds with the Throne. These two were little General Matsui, the scapegoat of the Nanking rape, and Matsuoka, the noisy American-bred diplomat who had put on a lonely wheeling-dealing show with Hitler in 1941 in a last vain attempt to make Hirohito consummate the plans of the Strike-North faction. The list even contained the name of one man, Dr. Okawa Shumei, the spy-propagandist, whom palace chamberlains were anxious to keep out of the witness box. It would have brought to court two more of the same sort except that Prince Konoye and Hirohito's former chief aide-de-camp, the Strike-North General Honjo, chose to disbar themselves on the eve of their arrests by committing suicide. The remaining defendants could be counted upon to keep the secrets of Japan's ruling inner circle.

In all, twenty-eight defendants were chosen for the Tokyo trials. The oldest of them was Baron Hiranuma, the seventy-nine-year-old lawyer for right-wing interests who had returned to Hirohito's side in the final agony of the bunker and the surrender. Hiranuma was a member of Emperor Meiji's generation and a crony of old Chief of Staff Prince Kanin who had reportedly died in hospital "of hemorrhoids" on May 21, 1945.

Ten of the twenty-eight defendants ranged in age from seventy-two down to sixty-four and belonged to the in-between generation of Emperor Taisho. They had been brought into the palace circle by Taisho's contemporaries, Field Marshal Prince Nashimoto and Fleet Admiral Prince Fushimi.[7] The remaining seventeen defend-

---

[7] The Taisho group included General Matsui and diplomat Matsuoka. Its other members were General Minami Jiro, seventy-two, the war minister at the time of the Manchurian Incident; General Araki Sadao, sixty-nine, the canny, compromising, golden-tongued leader of the Strike-North faction; Admiral Nagano Osami, sixty-nine, the Pearl Harbor chief of the Navy General Staff; former Prime Minister Hirota Koki, sixty-eight, the Black Dragon Society graduate who had headed the government for Hirohito after the 1936 mutiny; Field Marshal Hata Shunroku, sixty-seven, a stalwart of the Throne, who complained that he could not hear to answer questions because he had been the "Western Army" commander, headquartered in Hiroshima, when the bomb clapped over his air-raid shelter; General Koiso Kuniaki, sixty-six, the March Plotter and post-Tojo prime minister in 1944; General Umezuo Yoshijiro, sixty-four, the chief of the General Staff at the time of surrender; and finally Togo Shigenori, also sixty-four, who had been foreign minister both at the time of surrender and of declaration of war.

ants were all either members or satellites of Hirohito's own Big Brotherhood. They broke roughly into three groups: Army officers who were contemporaries and close associates of Hirohito's fifty-eight-year-old uncles, Prince Higashikuni and Prince Asaka;[8] bureaucrats who had gone to school with Hirohito's fifty-six-year-old foster brother Marquis Kido;[9] and political thugs and polemicists from the coterie of the late fifty-four-year-old Prince Konoye.[10]

The care which had gone into the selection of these defendants—these twenty-eight men who were to bear the whole guilt of Japan's pride, greed, and cruelty—was justified by their conduct in court. They lived in Sugamo Prison, wearing G.I. cast-off clothing and eating G.I. rations throughout the two and a half years of the trial. Their families on the outside were shunned by neighbors and suffered poverty, hunger, and cold. Nevertheless they went into court each day and submitted patiently to the alien intricacies of the quasi-judicial, quasi-political process which had been arranged for them. They hid the violence and arrogance which had characterized them in years gone by. They read books of philosophy and religion in their cells and listened attentively

[8] The military men included Tojo's Navy Minister Shimada Shigetaro, sixty-three; Baden-Baden Reliable Doihara Kenji, the "Lawrence of Manchuria," also sixty-three; sixty-two-year-old General Tojo, the self-proclaimed villain of the war, who as combined prime minister, war minister, and chief of staff had finally shouldered all the responsibility; Baden-Baden Reliable Itagaki Seishiro, conquistador of Manchuria, sixty-one; the Strike-South ideologist and former Army spy, Okawa Shumei, sixty; wartime ambassador to Berlin Lieutenant General Oshima Hiroshi, also sixty; Tojo's vice minister of war, Kimura Heitaro, fifty-eight; the Army's ubiquitous economics expert, Suzuki Tei-ichi, fifty-seven; one of Suzuki's henchmen, Muto Akira, who had ended the war as Yamashita's chief of staff in the Philippines, fifty-four; and finally Tojo's wartime Military Affairs Bureau chief, Sato Kenryo, only fifty.

[9] In addition to Kido himself the only men tried from this group were wartime Finance Minister Kaya Okinori, fifty-seven, and two fifty-eight-year-old diplomats: Shigemitsu Mamoru of the Peace and Strike-South factions, and Shiratori Toshio, a one-time Big Brother who had gone astray by espousing the cause of the Strike North.

[10] After Prince Konoye took poison, his contribution to the conspiracy was recognized by the indictment of just two of his men: Hoshino Naoki, the chief of his pre-war Cabinet Planning Board, fifty-four, and retired Colonel Hashimoto Kingoro, fifty-six, who had sunk the U.S.S. *Panay* and gone on to head the youth movement in Konoye's mass party, the Imperial Rule Assistance Association.

to the translated, fragmentary half-truths brought out against them.

The defeated Tojo, who had failed in his attempt to commit suicide at the time of his arrest, regained popular Japanese respect be setting his fellow defendants an example. He listened to every word of his accusers and caught American prosecution lawyers in a thousand ideological contradictions, political hypocrisies, and outright errors of fact. He did so with such spirit and back-biting wit that even chief prosecutor Keenan developed a grudging respect for him. He might be the bureaucratic accomplice in much rapine but he was undeniably a man of self-respect and presence of mind. When his patriotic burden as scapegoat became too heavy for his family to bear, he even had the freedom of spirit to suggest—as described in Chapter 3—that he had ordered no crimes without Hirohito's authorization. As soon as Hirohito saw to it that the Tojo family was better provided for, Tojo retracted his hint, resumed his difficult duty, and carried it on to the gallows.

Sturdy vassals though they might be, the twenty-eight defendants at the Tokyo trials caused palace chamberlains many restless nights. Diplomat Matsuoka and General Matsui, in particular, had no reason to feel beholden to the Throne. Fortunately Matsuoka, who professed Christianity, died of tuberculosis at the start of the trial, and the half-senile, inarticulate General Matsui never publicly wavered in his devout loyalty. Potentially more dangerous was the undisciplined, unprincipled intellectual Okawa Shumei, headmaster of the palace indoctrination school in the 1920's, geopolitical apologist for the Strike South, and go-between in a dozen plots and assassinations. Prime ministers and commanders of armies might be trusted to go to their deaths quietly, but Okawa, the scrivener, even with the best of intentions, might say more than he should.

So it was that Okawa, alone of the defendants, was helped to cop a plea. Whether American complicity or gullibility most figured in his escape from justice has not been established, but the extraordinary facts of his case are on record and have not been disputed. In May 1946, during the reading of the indictment at the beginning of the International Military Tribunal for the Far East, Okawa fixed a foolish smile on his face, unbuttoned his shirt, and gradually caught the tittering attention of the gallery by scratching his chest. When the shirt slipped off one shoulder, Chief Justice Webb ordered the sentries guarding the dock to see that the prisoner kept himself presentable. Okawa humbly promised to behave, but a few minutes later he began again to undress. An American M.P. was stationed behind him to restrain his arms and preserve decorum. He fell quiet for a few hours. Then, abruptly, when the M.P. had relaxed his vigilance, Okawa rolled up his copy of the charges made against him, leaned forward, and resoundingly slapped the shaven pate of Tojo who sat in front of him. Hauled from the courtroom, he told reporters:

Tojo is a fool. I'm for democracy. . . . America is not democracy. . . . She is Demo crazy [which in Japanese meant demonstration crazy]. . . . I am a doctor of law and medicine. I haven't eaten in seventy days. You see, I eat air. . . . I am the next emperor of Japan. . . . I killed Tojo. . . . I killed him to save the reputation of his respectable family.

It was Okawa's last day in court. For weeks thereafter he regaled American and Japanese doctors at Tokyo University Hospital with accounts of visitations he had from such as Emperor Meiji, Edward VII of England, and President Woodrow Wilson. Mohammed the Prophet, he said, was a particularly helpful familiar as he and Mohammed were collaborating on a new Japanese version of the Koran.

With coaching from Japanese doctors and some help from Japanese laboratory technicians, Okawa succeeded in persuading the American doctors who examined him that he was suffering from tertiary syphilis, or according to the official diagnosis, "psychosis with syphilitic meningoencephalitis (general paresis)." This was an irreversible condition leading usually to insane incompetence and swift death. After consultation with chief prosecutor Keenan, the American doctors allowed the court to be advised that Okawa could not "differentiate between right and wrong" and lacked "the ability to understand the nature of the proceedings against him." He was remanded to the care and comfort of a Japanese sanatorium. There he sat out the rest of the war crimes trials writing a 400-page "introduction to religion." When the judicial proceedings were over, he was released to die. Instead he promptly recovered, published several lucid books, and convinced all his friends that his syphilitic insanity had been a hoax. He finally did die of a stroke in December 1957 at the age of seventy-one.

TOKYO TRIAL RESULTS

Doctor Okawa was widely known to have been the rogue mediating between the palace and rightist thugs in all the plots which had intimidated the nation early in the 1930's. The misplaced medical mercy shown to him confirmed the automatic presumption of the Japanese public that the war crimes trials would dispense more politics and propaganda than justice. To members of Japan's web society it was incredible that precisely twenty-eight of all the hundreds of retainers who had served the Throne in the previous two decades could be singled out as the master criminals most responsible for Japan's misfortunes. The International Military Tribunal was accepted, therefore, as just one of the many ceremonies of American democracy—of *demo-kurushi* or demo-suffering, as it was called—which would have to be lived through.

As the trials continued, however, many Japanese who had never traveled abroad were impressed by the evidence produced of Japanese savagery overseas. Bitterness at the superficiality of Allied fact finding, the inappropriate political biases of Allied historical interpretation, and the manifest self-righteousness of Allied law began to be tempered by sober horror at what Japan had done. The realization grew in Japan that the nation was convalescing from a sickness of evil and that both Japan and the world at large were better off because of her defeat.

Soldiers and diplomats who had traveled in previous years through the Co-Prosperity Sphere, and who had recoiled at what they saw, made sure that the public acknowledged the national guilt. Indeed Foreign Minister Shigemitsu, reporting to the palace after hearing MacArthur speak at the surrender-signing ceremony aboard the U.S.S. *Missouri* on September 2, 1945, asked Hirohito to his face:

"Would it have been possible for us, if we had won, to embrace the vanquished with such magnanimity?"

Hirohito accepted the snide rebuke with a sigh and murmured, "Naturally it would have been different."

Throughout the trials recognition of the fact that the kamikaze spirit was one of death and that the chewing-gum spirit of the G.I. was one of life gradually seeped down into the Japanese mind. As the trials neared an end in 1948, a Japanese newspaperman, reporting the consensus he found on the streets of Tokyo, observed: "If Japan had won we would be using slave labor to build bigger pyramids than the pharaohs. Instead we are erecting new factories with American bulldozers."

Having apologized many times individually and collectively for the wrongs they had done, most Japanese buttonholed by newspapermen in 1948 expected a reciprocal understanding and mercy from the International Military Tribunal in its verdict. Earlier, at the start of the trials, when U.S. troops had just created a favorable impression by their forbearance, goodwill and high spirits, MacArthur could have proclaimed almost any public figure in Japan a war criminal and executed him out of hand, without being questioned. By 1948, however, the long historical exegesis of the trials had demonstrated beyond doubt what Japanese newspaper readers had always known: that Tojo and his colleagues in the dock were a sample of the war guilty and could only be punished as a symbolic sacrifice to the angry spirits of those whom Japan had wronged.

Accordingly, when the courtroom hearings ended and Doihara, Hirota, Itagaki, Kimura, Matsui, Muto, and Tojo were sentenced to hang, almost all Japanese pronounced the judgment *hidoi*, harsh.

During their final months in Sugamo Prison, all seven of the condemned men, in obedience to samurai custom, gave clippings of their hair and nails to prison-visiting kin. These relics were already enshrined and revered on family prayer shelves when—at a minute after midnight on the morning of December 23, 1948 —the trap opened under Tojo and he fell to his death. His and the six other bodies were cremated and secretly disposed of by U.S. prison wardens.

A Japanese lawyer who claimed to have had access to the funerary ovens brought scrapings of ash to General Matsui's family, saying that they were portions of the genuine remains of the hanged men. The lawyer's tiny boxes of gray dust were buried on the Matsui estate behind the bronzed goddess of mercy, sculptured partly out of Yangtze River mud, at the shrine of remorse, up on the hillside overlooking Atami and the sparkling waters of Sagami Bay where Hirohito pursued his marine biology. All the families of the deceased and thousands of other elder Japanese quickly accepted the relics as genuine and began to pay regular pilgrimages to the shrine with prayers that the mistakes of the war would never be repeated.

To most of the pilgrims the spirits on the hill were not martyrs but creditors. Japan and the Emperor, it was felt, owed them an apology. They had died to satisfy good American intentions. They should have been avenged but it was impossible to take revenge on good intentions. Nearest of kin were forced to admit to the war criminal shades that the zealous kamikaze spirit had been abandoned, that samurai ideals were dead, and that, for the time being, Japan must play the buffoon and lie low.

IMPERIAL CARETAKERS

Yoshida Shigeru, the former Peace Faction leader who had become the prime minister of occupied Japan, described his people's plight as "the comic helplessness of being Japanese." By this wry remark he meant only that, during his term of office, all native Japanese political activity had to be suspended and all talents devoted to circumventing or softening the reform directives, the "SCAPINS," which daily issued from MacArthur's headquarters to be "Potsdammed" through the Diet onto the nation's law books. Except for a year-long interregnum in 1947–48 of well-controlled lower-class Socialist government, which embarrassed MacArthur but failed to deter him from execution of his programs, Yoshida remained in charge of the "comic helplessness" from May 1946 to December 1954.

In common kamikaze frustration and guilt at being alive, the Japanese were politically unified in defeat as they had not been in victory. No factions of Army, Navy, and civilian bureaucrats were left to bicker with one another. All were hungry together. And so, despite the best ideological fertilizers which MacArthur could plow in, only one middle-of-the-furrow party would grow in Japan, and that was Yoshida's, the Liberal-Democratic Party. It made Japan a more perfect one-party state than Prince Konoye had ever been able to achieve through his gang-sponsored, secret-police-supported Imperial Rule Assistance Association. The Liberal-Democratic label, however, covered a multitude of sects and schisms. It included both the old Constitutionalist Party, the *Seiyukai*, and the *Seiyukai's* loyal opposition, the progressive, imperial anti-Constitutionalist *Minseito*.

Beneath its bland surface Yoshida's party was still fundamentally flawed by the same kind of disagreements which had divided the Strike-North and Strike-South groups in prewar Japan. In the warrior caste of the samurai, many were individualists and traditionalists who persisted in seeing modernization and collectivism as the main threats to Japan's heritage. They maintained the Strike-North position that the Russian ideology from across the western sea was the most subversive for Japan. The less specialized, less military-minded nobles of Court rank, above the samurai, continued to see the main danger toward the east in the land of Commodore Perry. It was there that people were controlled by financial rather than family status, by wages rather than religion, by the chance to earn ease rather than the opportunity to gain salvation through service to a lord. Individualism for the working classes was still anathema to Court nobles, and Russian communism continued to seem far less destructive of the Japanese social fabric of family allegiances than did the anti-socialism of American Protestants.

In the postwar era, as before the war, the scions of samurai outnumbered those of Court nobles. In 1954, when the Occupation had come to an end and the Korean War had restored economic health to Japan, political strife awakened within the Liberal-Democratic Party. The majority unseated Yoshida and replaced him with Hatoyama Ichiro, the Strike-North partisan of General Araki and Prince Saionji, who as education minister from 1931 to 1934 had led the attack upon Prince Konoye's professorial imperial apologists, the organ theorists.

Between December 10, 1954, and December 23, 1956, under constant attack from the scholars and publicists whom he had once offended, Hatoyama formed and dissolved three Cabinets.

He had the votes but not the influence to stay in office. As historians, since the Occupation, have not been able to draw upon subpoenaed diaries, the mechanics of Hatoyama's downfall remain hidden. Since his retirement, however, Japan has been ruled again by prime ministers possessing Hirohito's confidence: first by Kishi Nobusuke, the former minister of commerce in the wartime Tojo Cabinet, then by Ikeda Hayato, former finance minister in the Yoshida and Kishi Cabinets, then by Kishi's younger brother, Sato Eisaku.[11]

Sato and Kishi, who have dominated the ruling Liberal-Democratic Party since 1957, hail from the same south-Choshu area of fishing villages and belong to the same network of impecunious samurai families as did Emperor Meiji's great Constitutionalist prime minister, Ito Hirobumi. As Ito's heirs, they hark back to the Meiji era and command allegiances which antecede pro and anti Constitutionalist or Strike-North, Strike-South factionalism. Under their tutelage Japan has pursued the traditional foreign policy of Ito and the Constitutionalists: expansion abroad by peaceful means only—by economic opportunism, by cultural promotion, and by not so much as a ripple of military muscle.

FACTORY POWER

At the end of the war Japanese felt that American production of aircraft carriers and airplanes had overwhelmed the homeland despite the superior spiritual prowess of Japanese warriors. As a family they resolved that Japan would never go to war again without overwhelming material strength. The peaceful policies of Kishi and Sato have started Japan moving toward such strength —moving with a swiftness that is the wonder of the economists of other nations.

Japan has passed France, Great Britain, and West Germany to become, economically, the world's third most powerful state. In the lands and islands which Hirohito once hoped to dominate by force, Japanese trade reigns supreme. Filipinos, Indonesians, and even Australians depend on Japanese salesmen for most of

---

[11] Kishi was born a Sato and adopted by the Kishi family. His father, conversely, had been born a Kishi and adopted by the Sato family.

the manufactured goods they import and on Japanese buyers for most of the raw materials they export.

Japan has become a great factory. Pylons strut across her green hills. The concrete of superhighways lies heavy on her paddy lands. A belch of smoke, which darkens the poetic heart of the samurai, threatens to blot out the sacred sun. Opinions differ as to the outcome. Some Western economic analysts say that problems of pollution will ultimately halt Japan's growth. Others say that Prime Minister Sato and the board of what is anxiously called Japan Inc. have simply not yet dealt with pollution. Until 1965 the per-capita income of Japanese was held below $500 a year. Then, in the next five years, when there began to be a little room in Japan's factory building program to pay the builders, the per-capita income abruptly trebled to over $1,500 a year. If pollution has to be reduced, it may be that workers will temporarily go without raises again while money is being invested in smoke and waste control.

Barring any sudden breakdown in Japan's well-collected mercantile genius, Western economists agree that by 1980 the Japanese gross national product will exceed that of the Soviet Union and before the year 2000 that of the United States.

Neither the half-free American economy nor the rigidly planned Soviet economy has been able to match the Japanese growth rate except fitfully. Bureaucratic shortsightedness recurrently bogs down Soviet booms in bottlenecks and surpluses. U.S. spurts peak out in runaway opportunism, inflation, and technological unemployment. Japan, by comparison, has shown an uncanny ability, through a spirit of internal co-operation and cohesion, to damp out economic fluctuations. Japanese industrialists have regularly worked together for the sake of the nation while still competing for the sake of themselves. Japanese workers have regularly foregone spendthrift consumption in favor of saving and have worked long hours for fringe benefits rather than quick purchasing power.

Japan's astonishing economic growth in the 1950's and 1960's is no new or passing phenomenon. It is simply a resumption of Japan's equally astonishing development from 1867 to 1944. The American B-29's caused a temporary setback, costing a decade of hard work, but from the grand view of the economist, Japan, since she started from a state of medieval technology and monetary bankruptcy in 1867, has continued to increase her wealth more steadily and rapidly than any other power—and this despite her cramped area, dense population, and acute lack of natural resources.

The secret of Japan's achievement has been her stern, hierarchic family system of government, combining as it does many of the most galvanizing features of individualism as well as collectivism. Young Japanese have regularly shown great initiative, secure in the belief that parents will excuse and a supreme parent, the Emperor, will sanction their acts. Old Japanese, even the most rich and greedy, have conferred, compromised, and worked together like brothers. Simple methods, realistic goals, and a sense of mission—of "God with us"—continue to inspire even the hypermodern Japan of the 1970's. As a result its bullet trains run on time and its videotape recorders work smoothly. Its public libraries and sewage systems are few, but its exchequers overflow with the hardest currencies of international exchange and its supercities contain almost no slums.[12]

Prime Minister Sato personally presides over Japan's Supreme Trade Council on which the wizened, hard-eyed bankers and industrialists of Japan sit to agree upon annual national goals and division of world markets. The great cartels, which were officially broken up by MacArthur, continue to act as well-integrated units. The directors of the fragment companies of the Mitsui combine, for instance, all occupy the same building, consult with one another over private phone lines and across private corridors, and remain loyal to the dictates of the Mitsui family.

The Sato government holds all the big-business families together in a super-family. It grants them preferential credit, tax incentives, and insurance in all their overseas investments. Intercartel meetings of managers are held regularly, under government auspices, to agree upon price-fixing and sales propaganda in for-

[12] Broad areas of Tokyo, Osaka, and a few other large cities are covered with crowded shacks which appear to the casual tourist to be no better than slum dwellings. Nor are they except in one important psychological respect. Each shack has a tiny garden a yard or two square, and almost all the inmates of the shacks have bank or postal savings accounts. Almost none of the slum dwellers are on relief and few of them are even supported by relatives. Only in the 1960's did the municipal governments of Tokyo and Osaka begin to acknowledge that their shanty towns presented any social problem at all.

eign lands. Japan's growing foreign-aid program is carefully discussed with export division managers so that it will dovetail with over-all economic planning, creating long-term credits and raw-material processing capacity in areas abroad where Japanese traders see market potential. The Japanese government owns a profit-making corporation called JETRO which supplies overseas advertising to Japanese firms and sells them information about favorable foreign investment opportunities. Sato's Supreme Trade Council not only helps to set the annual goals of Japanese economic expansion but also advises on the means by which the cartels will be most willing to achieve the goals.

Since the war the great Japanese merchant families, who a century ago were just above untouchables in caste, have all been privileged to form ties of marriage with the Court nobility or with the imperial family itself. Today the men who sit on Sato's council consider themselves aristocrats. They have been let into the "inner circle" as they never were before the war. They are now part of the elite in the most nearly tribal society which has adapted to the upheavals of the last two thousand years. As such they have adopted the imperial mission which is to defend Japan's ghostly heritage from molestation by the outside world.

MacArthur hoped to change the religious mission of the Japanese upper classes by his benign occupation of Japan. But he elevated Yoshida and other leading enemies of the United States to high office and he persecuted the less well-born enemies of Russia, even putting the political leader of the Strike-North movement, General Araki, in prison as a war criminal. As Prime Minister Yoshida observed: "The Occupation was hampered by its lack of knowledge, and even more so perhaps by its generally happy ignorance of the amount of requisite knowledge it lacked."

THE SILENT EMPEROR

In developing his blind spot toward the Emperor, MacArthur accepted views handed down to him by Ambassador Grew and other prewar diplomats. He then refused to consider and, by suppressing evidence, prevented others from considering, the truth about the Emperor as it might have been revealed in captured documents. That a mere mortal could fill the role of god, leaving unsatisfied the need for a larger, omnipotent, omnipresent Being, exceeded the imagination of MacArthur and many other Christian thinkers.

MacArthur was shrewd in seeing Hirohito as an indispensable helpmate in reforming Japan. MacArthur was shortsighted in believing that Hirohito could be emasculated by forgiveness and forgetfulness. It did not hurt Hirohito to have underlings take the blame for him, for that was customary in Japan at any time. It did hurt MacArthur, however, to make light of Western science and justice by strapping blinders on the International Military Tribunal for the Far East.

Had MacArthur been wiser and stronger he might have insisted that the trial of minor war criminals—of concentration camp commandants and secret-police torturers—was enough, and that the punitive sentiments of politicians in Washington and Canberra should not be extended to policy-shaping members of Hirohito's retinue. Indeed, if he had been supremely wise and strong, he might have insisted that the roughly $9 million spent on trying Tojo and his colleagues be used instead for a nonpunitive inquiry into the mechanics of leadership which had led Japan to offend the world. Truth, in short, could have been pursued, could have been put on record, and could have provided the Japanese people with more reliable clues to self-government than any of the fragile American relationships with Japanese aristocrats which MacArthur left behind him.

Now that MacArthur has passed into history, events have left Hirohito still warmly enshrined in the hearts of his tribe. A majority of Japanese still feel the imperial taboo and speak of their ruler only with great diffidence. Some politicians are willing to comment snidely upon Hirohito in private, but they do so more to suggest their noble birth and cosmopolitan independence than because they feel any irreverence. Some plebeian Marxists make theoretical statements against the institution of the Throne but seldom dare to attack Hirohito personally except through veiled, technically inoffensive hints. For instance, one of the most scurrilous booklets of anti-imperial propaganda, which may be bought at left-wing bars in Tokyo, is a handsomely boxed pamphlet containing ninety-nine identical pictures of Hirohito, looking his coldest, most sneering, and least lovable. Not a word illuminates this protest except a title and a designation of publisher: "Portrait of our Imperial Parent; Imperial Household Ministry."[13]

Since the end of the war, Hirohito has said little and allowed his public image to be rewrought by competent professional image-makers. In the early days of the Occupation, Prince Higashikuni, the prime minister for the surrender, apologized to the nation for unsuccessful imperial family leadership. Hirohito followed the apology with a tour of provincial areas. It was widely reported that when one of MacArthur's aides had tried to shake his hand he bowed graciously and said, "Let's do it this way, in the Japanese style, without touching." On his tour, however, he adopted the new American style and shook hands vigorously with his native Japanese constituents. Those who made contact with the divine hand were awed; a few of them were startled into attempts at conversation. Hirohito became famous for the unvarying words of his noncommittal response: *Ah so desuka?* "Oh, is that so?"

The Japanese masses supposed that in his bows and hand-shakes Hirohito was wearing a hair shirt before the world and drinking gall. The symbol of Hirohito's humiliation came to be the famous photograph showing MacArthur in casual khaki stand-ing head and shoulders above the newly non-deified god-king in his seedy wartime morning clothes. Whether Hirohito felt his shame as keenly as others felt it for him may be doubted. In any case he endured it with good spirits and benefited by the fact that all Japanese felt sorry for him. Never before had he occupied such a warm place in the affection of his subjects.

Hirohito continued to do public penance throughout the seven years of the Occupation. In 1946 he was forced to dissolve the imperial family holding company and give most of his fortune back to the people. Throughout the war crimes trials, he read

[13] Supporters of the Throne are sensitive about Hirohito's appearance. In 1968 a cosmopolitan young Japanese publisher, the son of one of the diplomats who represented Hirohito at the signing of surrender on the battleship *Missouri* in 1945, read a part of the work in hand with a view to having it translated for the home market. He reached the description of the Emperor at the August 9, 1945, conference (in Chapter 2) and slapped the manuscript down in anger. "This book," he said, "will never be published in Japan. You cannot describe the Emperor so."

every word of testimony and legal wrangling and occasionally
asked his courtiers to insert corrections in the record through
Court-controlled witnesses. In 1947, after many unavailing eva-
sions, he was compelled to let his uncles and cousins be demoted
to the rank of commoners. In 1948, when sentence was about to
be passed on Tojo and the other major war criminals, he threatened again, as he had at the start of the trials, to abdicate. Mac-
Arthur made concessions in other matters but refused to interfere
with the judgment of the Allied jurists presiding on the tribunal.
Having gained a little leverage, Hirohito, after all, sent Mac-
Arthur a pledge that he would not abdicate.

Having made his gestures of penitence and resistance, Hirohito took a new suit into his wardrobe for the first time since
the war and settled down to live out the last three years of the
American Occupation in apparent preoccupation with his hobby
of marine biology. When the Occupation ended in 1952 he gradually and guardedly resumed a part in national affairs. How large
a part will not be known for a generation or more until publication of some of the relevant documents. A little is known already,
however.

Under the pretext of advising the Imperial Household Ministry,
retired prime ministers and other public figures have reconstituted
a near facsimile of the Privy Council which MacArthur abolished
in 1945. As a "symbol of state" Hirohito retains the duty of putting
his seal upon some 10,000 government documents annually. Since
1957 he has demanded, in exchange for discharge of this duty,
that he receive regular briefings, at least once a week, from the
prime minister. In the more than fourteen years of the Sato
brothers' stewardship of the nation, his "imperial questions" have
been seriously considered and respected.

PRIVY POCKETING

During his silence, Hirohito has been quietly gathering the
major ingredient of private power: money. At the end of the war
his family holdings stood at about three billion yen with an official value of less than a $100 million and a real value of $400 to
$500 million. A small fraction of the fortune was in greatly depre-

ciated bank deposits. About a tenth of it—a capital investment greater than that of any of the cartels except Mitsui[14]—was in damaged war factories. The bulk of it was in undepreciated land, gold, and jewels. SCAP succeeded in taking away about two thirds of this treasure and giving it to the Japanese government. Almost all the rest had been entrusted, during the closing months of the war, to loyal trustees. Acknowledging the impossibility of tracing all this buried wealth, SCAP made it illegal for the Emperor, in the years ahead, to accept gifts of any size.

Socialists in the Diet have periodically investigated the transactions of the Imperial Household Ministry in an effort to enforce the law, but adequate policing has not proved possible. It is estimated that the submerged imperial fortune, held in trust by loyal brokers, may now amount to considerably more than $1 billion.

In addition to his concealed assets, Hirohito has gradually amassed, by completely open means, a little gambling bankroll in the stock market, estimated to be from $40 to $50 million. Some of this money, which has grown quickly because of remarkable investment opportunities, represents repayment, through information, of some of the hidden imperial funds. The seed crystals from which it has grown, however, have been laid aside from the legal spending money allotted to Hirohito annually, by Diet vote, since 1947.

The Diet annually passes on three separate appropriations for the upkeep of the imperial family. The largest (some $12 million in 1970) goes to the upkeep of Hirohito's palaces and villas. A second (some $200,000 in 1970) goes to the support of the families of Hirohito's daughters and brothers, each of which receives a tax-free allowance of about $30,000 a year. The third appropriation goes into the privy purse of Hirohito and his son, Crown Prince Akihito, who reached the age of thirty-seven in December 1970. It, too, is tax free, but it represents almost pure profit because the imperial grounds and buildings, the imperial garages and marinas, the imperial tables and wardrobe, the imperial entertainments and protocols, and the imperial travel accounts are all cov-

[14] The eleven branches of the Mitsui family held 390 million yens' worth of capital goods; the two branches of the Iwasaki's, who ran Mitsubishi, held 175 millions; the Sumitomo's held 315 millions; and the Imperial Household Ministry somewhat more than 330 millions.

ered by the separate, principal appropriation in support of the imperial household.

This mad money of Hirohito was set at a niggardly $22,000 a year in 1947.[15] By the end of the Occupation in 1952, it had been raised to $83,000, by 1965 to $189,000, by 1968 to $233,000, and by 1971 to over $300,000. Since the imperial allowance is all tax free, accessible and as good as the national exchequer, it enables Hirohito to stand pat with the largest of the cartels or to dive with the fastest plungers. Assisted by more than a score of investment counselors—a part of the permanent palace staff of about two thousand menials, chamberlains, guards, and experts—Hirohito has invested in the stock market wisely. (It is said that his portfolio is a bit heavy in electronics and hotels.)

In addition to giving Hirohito an annual raise in allowance, the Diet has also appropriated to Hirohito's use a number of special building funds which have been augmented by tax-deductible contributions from loyal subjects. In 1959 the villa of the Crown Prince was rebuilt. In 1962 Hirohito's wartime living quarters, the Imperial Library in the Fukiage Gardens, were expanded, modernized, and refurnished. In 1963 construction began on a new ceremonial palace to take the place of Emperor Meiji's magnificent edifice which had burned down on the night of May 25, 1945.

Completed in 1967, the new palace cost over $36 million. It is a handsome, modern concrete building with traditional roofs of green copper. Its seven wings, containing no less than 243,000 square feet of floor space, include a banqueting hall which can accommodate 3,000 guests. Its architect, Yoshimura Junzo, who also designed the Japanese house in New York's Museum of Modern Art, withdrew from the project in 1965, two years before its completion. It was claimed that he had aesthetic differences with Hirohito's chamberlains about some of the furnishings. In fact, after his departure, the underground areas of the palace, which include a 120-car garage, were redivided and greatly im-

---

[15] Eight million yen with an official value of $160,000 and an actual value of about $22,000. It was one of the curiosities of the postwar Japanese economy that, as it recovered strength, MacArthur's experts gradually allowed the yen to seek its level on the market. As a result the yen was at first worth less and later more than its dollar quotation. I have used the factor of 360 to one for all post-1946 conversions.

proved with vaults and stairways which do not appear in his original plans.

The new palace was considered such a success that Prime Minister Sato set aside another $2 million in 1968, to build Hirohito a new summer villa, with advanced marine research and communications facilities, on the least polluted, westernmost shores of Suruga Bay, near Shimoda, 110 miles from Tokyo.

DEMORALIZED PRINCELINGS

While Hirohito has silently prospered, his many kinsmen, who strutted about the Empire on inspections during the war years, have adjusted poorly to enforced retirement. Their undignified comments, carouses, cupidities, promiscuities, and other assorted incompetences as private citizens have repeatedly embarrassed the Throne and titillated a generation of Japanese tabloid readers.

Kanin Haruhito, the disentitled son of Prince Kanin Kotohito, former Army chief of staff, managed a "tourist agency," an "iron works," and two "trading companies" during the hectic giveaway years between 1945 and 1949. All four ventures operated at a loss, and Kanin's wife grew weary of her husband's role as a SCAP-palace pander. In her dissatisfaction she developed an intimacy with one of Kanin's former Army subordinates, a Mr. Takahashi. As she was, in her own right, a daughter of the noble Ichijo family and the headmistress of a fashionable girls' school, her dalliance excited gossip. After a showdown with the directors of the school, she abruptly walked out on all her former life and, in partnership with Mr. Takahashi, opened a successful coffeehouse on the Ginza in downtown Tokyo.

Another child of the late Prince Kanin, his fifth daughter Hanako, was married to the third son of the former Prince Fushimi, chief of the Navy General Staff. The two had been brought together for the first time on their wedding day after a courtship entirely by photograph. In 1951, after three children and twenty-four years of marriage, he was running a chicken farm on a vestige of his former properties and she, at home, was eking out the family budget by giving lessons in American dancing at their former princely villa. The menage fell in ruins on the night of July 18 when he returned from the chicken farm to stumble in upon her in the villa cloakroom making love to one of Hirohito's chamberlains, a Mr. Toda. After the divorce, she and Mr. Toda, at Hirohito's insistence, got married.

One of the family scandals touched Hirohito closely. On a bleak February morning in 1966 the grandson of Tokugawa Iesato, husband of Hirohito's third daughter, Kazuko, was discovered gassed and naked in a frowsy Tokyo walkup flat. Beside him lay the body of the proprietress of a bar called the Isaribi. A leaky gas fire had made sordid tragedy and public shame of an assignation which might have been held secretly, romantically, and safely in any proper princely villa of prewar days.

Through such revelations the Japanese middle classes—a rigidly proper group compared with either the Japanese upper or lower classes—have developed a jaundiced view of the lesser members of the imperial family. This view has helped to hold the many demoted princes in their new plebeian place. Former Prince Higashikuni, as the most forward and froward villain of the clan, has repeatedly tested the public to find out if it has yet relented at all.

After resigning as prime minister, Higashikuni pooled assets with March-Plot financier Tokugawa Yoshichika, the wartime director of Japan's Southeast Asian espionage headquarters at the Singapore museum and botanical gardens. Together they started an antique business. They made a successful failure out of their venture by putting nice Japanese pieces into the hands of influential Occupationaires. Then, in 1947, they declared themselves bankrupt and Higashikuni went on to new enterprises, chief of which was a religious sect which he named Ultra-Modern Cosmopolitan Buddhism.

To serve as high priest in his new religion Higashikuni took back into partnership the spiritual confidence man, Ohara Ryukai. Fifteen years earlier Ohara had supplied Higashikuni with the talking statue of the goddess of mercy which had figured in the Prayer Meeting Plot and others leading up to the February Mutiny of 1936. During the war Ohara had been imprisoned for five months for $400,000 worth of accumulated fraud. Notwithstanding his past record, Ohara still made an imposing chief priest. Ultra-Modern Cosmopolitan Buddhism spread rapidly and enjoyed a

particular vogue in the spiritually starved ranks of retired servicemen.

In 1950 SCAP outlawed the "Higashikuni religion" as a subversive military organization. Its Blue-Cloud-Mountain-Dragon-
Sea Temple—a piece of property which had formerly belonged to
the Army's judge advocate—was auctioned off to the highest bid-
der as seized contraband. In 1952, as soon as the Occupation had
ended, the new owner of the property brought a complaint to
court saying that minions of Prince Higashikuni were trying to
terrorize him and had just burned down his house. Higashikuni
settled out of court with a promise to cease and desist. A decade
later, however, in 1962, he had the aplomb to bring a countersuit
of his own, claiming that the land in question had been given to
his family by Emperor Meiji and remained his by divine disposition. The case dragged on through the courts from June 1962 to
February 1964. A Solomon of a judge finally suggested that the
only way to decide the divine rights of the matter might be to call
Hirohito into court for expert testimony. Higashikuni promptly
dropped his claim.

SHADOWS BEHIND CURTAINS

Half emancipated by the Occupation, half shackled by tradition,
the sensitive, literate, emotional Japanese public has been sorely
tried and torn by the demands made on its feelings since the
war. It has repeatedly demonstrated its affectionate loyalty to the
Throne by oversubscribing palace reconstruction schemes. At the
same time it has repeatedly demonstrated its distrust of former
imperial princes and of former Japanese Army and Navy officers
if they speak too resurgently or militantly. With fear of the bad
old days is coupled a genuine regard for the American G.I. and
for the democratic institutions he brought to Japan. On the other
hand, with traditional loyalty to Shinto and the Throne is coupled
a doctrinaire belief that Japan must someday, somehow avenge
herself by besting the United States. This conviction varies in
emotional content from fierce hatred to unhappy fatalism but it
is widespread, and nothing that the most good-natured G.I.'s
might have done could ever have uprooted it.

Throughout the last twenty years most mass movements in Japan have been mobilized as instruments of policy for dealing with the United States. Demonstrations outside the U.S. Embassy in Tokyo have regularly featured a platoon of vociferous leftists accompanied by regiments of common folk who turn out because they enjoy demonstrating and because they respond to the hints of policemen, ward heelers or student leaders. Rioters may feel in need of expressing indignation, students may think they are genuinely radical, but in politically sophisticated Japan they are mustered by organizers who can usually be identified as the ambitious retainers of staid public figures—men who express official horror at the disorders after they have taken place.

In 1960 when the United States still needed bases in Japan for planes and short-range missiles, Japanese mobs rioted obstreperously against renewal of the U.S.-Japanese Mutual Security Treaty, forcing cancellation of a visit to Japan by President Eisenhower. Nine years later in 1969, when the security treaty came up again for renegotiation, high-spirited students looked forward to staging the biggest and best riots in Japanese history. Their leaders had been planning novel escapades of protest for a full three years beforehand. When the time came, however, Liberal-Democratic bosses had the word spread that circumstances had changed since 1960; that ICBM's made bases in Japan a matter of convenience rather than necessity for the United States; and that the Mutual Security Treaty was now more to Japanese than American advantage. A single nationwide demonstration was staged in March 1969 in which 100,000 people participated. Thereafter the United States agreed to consider seriously the return to Japan of Okinawa and the Liberal-Democratic leadership discouraged further mob scenes.

After cancellation of the anti-American riots and extension of the security treaty, students in October 1969 expressed their disappointment by demonstrating violently against universities. Relative to the tens of thousands of students and policemen engaged, few heads were broken. For the first time since 1945, however, police boxes were smashed and tramcars turned over not for American benefit by a people united in defeat but for domestic benefit by genuine dissidents. The students had only vague ideas as to why they were protesting or by what chain of command they had been encouraged to protest. They felt a resentment, however, against the apparent fact that democracy was a sham and commoners were once more being manipulated as pawns in policy struggles taking place behind the scenes.

Since at least the early 1960's the fundamental question at issue within the inner sancta of Japan's closed society has been whether, and if so how, Japan should try to dominate her neighbors. Aged Strike-North partisans in the Self-Defense Forces and in the Liberal-Democratic Party have pleaded as ever for candor, for forthright rearmament, for open declaration of limited, practical, foreign-policy goals. In particular they have asked that Japan reach a negotiated understanding with the West, enabling her to take over most U.S. responsibilities in Asia and to compete on equal terms with Communist China for pan-Asian leadership.

Discredited remnants of the Emperor's Strike-South Faction, including all members of the imperial family, have carefully avoided offering any ultimate alternative to the program suggested by the Strike-North partisans. Rather they have piously supported Prime Minister Sato in his policy of all-out peaceful economic development. Some of them have admitted privately that they see no reason on the one hand for alarming the United States by an excess of candor and on the other for relieving the United States prematurely of its costly military burdens in the Orient. If Japan can continue to infiltrate foreign markets and outstrip the United States in rate of economic growth, there will eventually come a time, they say, when Japan can confront the land of Perry and MacArthur on equal terms. Then it will not be necessary to seek a negotiated understanding with the West; Japan's pre-eminence in Asia will be an accomplished fact.

During the last decade Japan's high-level secret introspections have found public expression in several incidents which no Western observer can know for sure how to interpret. In general, however, it is the heirs to the Strike-North heritage who encourage popular unrest for they are the partisans of international frankness and public discussion. Prime Minister Sato is on the side of silence. Hirohito's imperial kinsmen support Sato but do not object to an occasional incident as means of gauging popular sentiment.

One of the earliest outbreaks connected with the great debate was the "Three Nothings Incident" of 1961. Mikami Taku, the paroled Misty Lagoon flight lieutenant who in 1932 had shot Prime Minister Inukai through the head, resolved twenty-nine years later that "direct action" was once again needed to bring Japan to her senses. He approached members of the Self-Defense Forces for co-operation in a coup d'etat. They reported him to the police. When he was arrested he insisted that he had meant no harm and had only wanted to bring to nothing three great evils—bribery, taxes, and unemployment. For his "three nothings" he was appropriately sentenced to three years of imprisonment.

In 1932, when he assassinated Prime Minister Inukai, it had been hard to tell whether Mikami, in his headstrong idealism, was most under the influence of ex-Navy pilot Prince Yamashina, the Emperor's kinsman at the Misty Lagoon, or of War Minister Araki, the Strike-North leader. In June 1961, when he went to prison for the second time, it was still impossible to be sure for whom he acted, for he was still close both to retired General Araki and to former Prince Higashikuni.

On February 26, 1965, shortly after he emerged from prison, Mikami participated in a rightist rally which again raised many eyebrows. The occasion was the twenty-ninth anniversary of the February Mutiny of 1936. Mikami was guest of honor at the unveiling of a public monument in memory of the rebels. Beside him on the speakers' platform sat Sagoya Tomeo, who had shot Prime Minister Hamaguchi in 1930, and Blood Brother Konuma Tadashi, who had shot financier Inoue Junnosuke in 1932. Sagoya now read his given name as Yoshiaki and Konuma his as Hiromitsu but all present knew perfectly well who both men were.

The principal speaker that day was none other than the eighty-seven-year-old former General Araki, still full of droll Shavian eloquence even after ten years in prison as a war criminal. Political connoisseurs took the strange get-together of aged assassins as a warning to Hirohito that Japanese idealism could no longer be used privily to intimidate but only publicly in frank and open discussion.

During the five years from 1965 to 1970 Prime Minister Sato's government undercut the outspoken Strike-North partisans by relaxing somewhat the stern thrift of Japan's economic revival and allowing some of the nation's earnings to be diverted from factory building to workers' wages. As a result taxable per-capita income and consumer spending both trebled. Almost every farmhouse gained its electric rice cooker and television antenna. Only idealistic students and samurai diehards could any longer complain of the direction in which the nation was heading.

In 1967, with little protest, an old national holiday was revived: February 11 or National Foundation Day. On this date, until disabused by MacArthur's men in 1948, Japanese had long celebrated Emperor Jimmu's mythical ascension to the Throne in 660 B.C. Now, on February 11, 1967, 100,000 pilgrims showed their approval of returning to old ways by journeying to the countryside outside Nara in the Kyoto area and paying homage at Emperor Jimmu's supposed tumulus.

LONE CRY OF ANGUISH

Nearly three more years of prosperity passed before the ill-conceived student riots of October 1969. These were directed very largely against the organ-theory academicians of the 1930's. When the public showed no sympathy for the rioters, it looked as if the old partisans of the Strike-North movement had fought and lost their last quixotic battle with the Japanese Establishment. One determined spirit, however, who had supported the students and shared their dissatisfactions, was not prepared to give up. Somehow nation and Emperor must be made to see the dangers of economic imperialism and to cherish the beauty of the old Japan. For months this solitary samurai considered the means of protest at his disposal and settled at last upon the traditional one, the ultimate gesture of sincerity, suicide. It was to be one of the most spectacular suicides in Japanese history.

The unlikely hero—or villain—in this act of self-destruction was none other than Japan's celebrated novelist Mishima Yukio. He was a man of good samurai family who had graduated during the war from Japan's most exclusive academy, the Peers' School. With sufferance, because of his manifest talent, he had gone on to become something of an eccentric. He furnished his house with the most ugly Western Victorian furniture. He was a homosexual. He kept a wife and two children. He had been repeatedly considered as a candidate by the Nobel Prize committee in Sweden. Since adolescence he had been haunted by memories of the kamikaze pilots of 1944–45 and by a sense of inadequacy in not having been one of them. According to his critics his writings apotheosized a life style of sex every night followed by suicide every morning.

A dramatist and actor as well as a novelist, Mishima was theatrical. Words on the printed page were never enough for him; as proof of conviction, he demanded of himself deeds also. Having reached manhood at a time when all Japanese youths seemed hungry and small compared to U.S. Occupation troops, he made a fetish of body-building and succeeded in changing his appearance from that of a pale intellectual grub to that of a magnificently muscled Japanese adonis. With money from movies he outfitted a selection of his fans as an army—the *Tate-no-kai*, or Shield Society. Their gold braid and fancy dress struck some Japanese as a calculated mockery of militarism, but their sincerity seemed genuine. They decried the pall of smoke and self-deception settling on Japan; they lamented the loss of old Japanese cultural values; they criticized Hirohito for having never explained to the people frankly where he had been going in the war, why he had rejected a fight to the death at the end of the war, and what he looked for now after the war.

Novelist Mishima played with his following of toy soldiers by day and wrote furiously by night. Between 1948 and 1968 he published twenty novels, thirty-three plays, and over a hundred articles and short stories. In all his works he plowed one furrow deep: the theme of death and the need to sacrifice one's life for a cause, either through aggressive violence or introspective suicide.

Mishima idolized the young officers of the February 1936 Mutiny, the idealistic dupes of the Strike-North-Strike-South confrontation who had thrown away their lives in a vain appeal to the imperial conscience. In 1969 his sympathy for the 1936 rebels involved him in a controversy with a literary scion of the imperial family. This was the second-rate novelist Arima Yorichika, a son of Count Arima who had figured in imperial-family infiltration of left-wing groups during the 1930's. Arima maintained that the 1936 rebels "far from being misguided but pure revolutionaries were out-and-out murderers."

In late 1969, during his dispute with Arima, Mishima impressed his friends as being unusually despondent. He was weary of passive intellectual attainments. He was forty-four. He suffered from the crisis of middle age. He was working on the final volume of his most ambitious piece of fiction yet, a tetralogy called *The Sea of Fertility*. It was a bitter misanthropic title referring to one of the ill-named maria on the barren face of the moon.

As Mishima neared the end of his opus, draining himself of words, he sought to sweeten his imagination by involving himself in the student rallies and riots of October 1969. When they came to naught, his gloom deepened. One day in February 1970, a high-school student who was a complete stranger to him came to his house and waited at his gate for three hours to ask him a single question: "Sir, when are you going to kill yourself?"

Mishima reacted to the student as if he were an imperial messenger of the sort which had bidden men commit suicide in the days of the Tokugawa shoguns. Shortly after the visitation, he broached to his intimates in the Shield Society his first tentative ideas for the melodramatic scheme which would answer the boy's question.

Under the extreme, lifelong pressure of Japan's feudalistic Mafia-style family society, many men have reached Mishima's state of spiritual exhaustion and have resolved on suicide as the only relief. Since Japanese are trained from childhood to be frugal and to be ambitious, every aspiring suicide always tries to gain a little immortality by making his death count for something. Mishima was no exception. He knew from his American literary friends how little Japanese political indirection was appreciated in the West. He knew from a leading Strike-North partisan, his friend Nakasone Yasuhiro, the director of Japan's Self-Defense Forces, that the struggle for a frank foreign policy had been fought in the inner circles of government and had been lost. He also knew, from his study of the rebels of the February 1936 Mutiny, that the most telling way to embarrass the Throne was to die, calling for open international expression of Japanese feelings and for responsible direct rule by the traditional master of indirection, the Emperor.

And so Mishima, realizing that he was one of the best-known Japanese outside Japan—one known, moreover, for his cosmopolitanism and love of Western books and furniture—decided to make an unmistakable international sacrifice of himself. With a troupe of his theatrical soldiers of the Shield Society, he gained admittance on November 25, 1970, to the Ichigaya Headquarters of Japan's Self-Defense Forces. This was a place full of memories: the site of the prewar military academy, of the 1945 General Staff Offices, and of the postwar International Military Tribunal for the Far East. In 1970 its inner compound was surrounded by a sprawling complex of barracks and barriers. Any ordinary Japanese would have needed more than one officially stamped pass to enter the inner compound, but Mishima reached it without difficulty. So did half a dozen of his uniformed followers and also two Japanese news photographers.

Mishima and his men marched into the office of a friend, General Mashita Kanetoshi, tied him to a chair, threatened his aides with swords, and demanded that the officer corps of the Self-Defense Forces be assembled to hear a speech by Mishima. Helpless before the swords of Mishima's troupe, the armed M.P.'s guarding the headquarters went scurrying off to announce a muster over the public address system. In minutes 1,200 men, many of them officers, had gathered below the balcony from which Mishima was to hold forth. As cameras clicked Mishima strode forward. He delivered a ten-minute exhortation, begging Japan to return to the ways of her ancestors, to wipe the industrial smog from her green hills, to make the Emperor directly responsible for rule, to renounce the hypocrisy of pacificism written into the drably phrased Constitution which MacArthur had forced on Japan, to give up financially irresponsible dependence upon a U.S. "nuclear umbrella," and to admit forthrightly that the Self-Defense Forces were the best Army, Navy, and Air Force in Asia.

Despite the considerable co-operation which Self-Defense Force leaders had extended to Mishima, they had failed to give him a microphone with which to make his final words heard. Some of the 1,200 men gathered to hear him shouted "*Baka*" and "*Bakaro*" at him—"You idiot, you peasant"—and drowned out the logic of his eloquence. Mishima cut short his address, stalked back inside from the balcony, and turned to the difficult part of his gesture, for which he had done the most intensive psychological self-preparation. He knelt and ripped open his belly with a knife. One of his gold-braided retainers hacked and hacked again at his neck with a sword. When Mishima had finally been decapitated, his headsman knelt in turn, cut his own belly and was decapitated by a second retainer.

Many Japanese remarked upon the extreme sincerity and traditionalism of Mishima's suicide. The gory rite of decapitation by a second had been seldom practiced since the eighteenth century. Most of the important twentieth century suicides had made sure that they would be seconded by men who were good pistol shots or who knew how to cut into the carotid artery from the back of the neck.

Mishima's friends and admirers in the West could hardly believe the sacrifice he had made of his great talent. In the shocked obituaries which they wrote for New York, Paris, and London newspapers, they sought to explain his action in purely personal terms, acknowledging that they had never understood his political compulsions. None ventured to examine the merits of the cause for which he had killed himself.

In Japan an editorialist of the imperial faction, Yamamoto Kenkichi, was quick to point out that the act of violence made a Roman candle of Mishima's career, leaving "one flash in the darkness and nothing else." Novelist Arima of the imperial family contented himself with private observations to the effect that the futility of Mishima's death exposed the theatrical trumpery of the 1936 February Mutiny.

After the event the men of the Self-Defense Forces who were interviewed by newsmen all expressed regret that they had booed Mishima and showed admiration for his courage in acting upon his convictions. To a man, however, they continued to disagree with him. The Emperor, they insisted, should not and could not be held responsible for Japan—not in 1971 any more than in 1945. The MacArthur Constitution, they said, was right in defining him as a "symbol of state" rather than a living god.

"The Emperor should be a symbol," declared one sergeant, "a pillar the people of Japan can rely on in their hearts. He should not be in politics himself, nor should he be used by those who are in politics."

Despite the devout naïveté and historical ignorance manifested by such remarks, Japanese editorialists agreed in conclusion that the men of the Self-Defense Forces had proved themselves true individualists, true citizen soldiers, true products of postwar democracy.

At Mishima's funeral—a tolerant Buddhist affair attended by
fashionable friends in maxis, minis, and bell-bottoms—one eulo-
gist tried to break through the all-pervasive complacency by
begging Hirohito "for even a single word [of comment on the
suicide] from the imperial family."

On the balcony, and in his essays and articles for several years
before mounting the balcony, Mishima had been asking Hirohito
to break silence and say something meaningful and religious
about the sacrifice of World War II. Hirohito had not responded
then and he did not respond now. Instead, on January 5, 1971,
forty days after Mishima's suicide, the Emperor appeared in public
to officiate at the award-giving in the annual poetry-writing contest. The theme of the year was the word *ie*, meaning house or
home or clan. Hirohito's own contribution to the contest was:

> Amid the cedars,
> I see a clump of houses,
> and then the cedars
> step out row after long row
> across the Tonami plain.[16]

Some Japanese opined that Hirohito, in this verse, had spoken out
for pollution control on behalf of more trees and less houses;
others insisted that he had spoken for continued breakneck economic development and for less trees and more houses. To all
obvious intents and purposes Hirohito spoke not at all. The bright
television lights seemed to bother him. He closed his eyes and
seemed to be sleeping.

THE FUTURE

In 1931, when Japan invaded Manchuria and began her march
toward Pearl Harbor, the United States did not have the military
strength in the Orient to say her nay. As a result some five million human beings would die. This suffering, and all the present
evils in Asia which stemmed from it, could probably have been
averted if the United States had known how to contain Japan.
The United States has since learned the lesson that deterrent
military strength is a prerequisite to the containment of other

[16] A sacred wilderness area near the north coast in western Honshu.

nations. On a worldwide basis, however, no strength can ever suffice unless it is applied with mechanical advantage. To threaten an entire nation is to insult a people and gain more enemies than can ever be defeated. Far wiser is it to keep force as a basis for polite private conversations with the key leaders of a possible opponent.

If U.S. Intelligence agencies, backed by military force and speaking through the State Department, could have discreetly threatened to expose the machinations of the Throne at any time before September 1931, the Pacific half of World War II could most likely have been postponed indefinitely. Without bloodshed a situation could thereby have been achieved for U.S. interests in Asia which would certainly have been no worse than that which was achieved through much bloodshed.

Again in the 1970's U.S. leaders had to give grave thought to Japanese-American relations. The septuagenarian Hirohito was a spent samurai, who could not be a war leader again after the shame of 1945. He had carried himself well under the humiliation of defeat, but as long as he reigned, Japan would persevere in the ways of peace. In the fall of 1971 he planned to round out his *Showa* era by paying a flying visit to Bonn, Brussels, Paris, and London. He was scheduled to set out on September 27, the fiftieth anniversary of his report to the gods after his history-shaping 1921 European tour. Thereafter, it was rumored, he would turn over most state business to his son, Crown Prince Akihito, who would be thirty-eight in December 1971.

As tutor to the crown prince during the Occupation, Elizabeth Gray Vining gave Akihito a favorable report card as a bright, charming, and sensitive young man. According to courtiers, however, Mrs. Vining may have taken an indulgent view of her charge and may have closed her eyes to some of the tough, cynical ways of thought which had been trained into him during the first thirteen years of his life before her coming to Japan. Nonetheless it has been attributed to Mrs. Vining's tutelage that Akihito later broke precedent with tradition by marrying a commoner of no Court rank, the daughter of a wealthy cartel owner, whom he met on a tennis court. On trips abroad to Europe and the Philippines, Akihito has impressed foreign observers by his polish and understanding of local problems.

Like Hirohito before him, Akihito has inherited a religious duty in which vengeance has a part. Like Hirohito, too, he can be relied upon to do conscientiously whatever he believes he should do. Only the Japanese people, who are individually moral, courageous, and literate, can be expected to redirect national policy if it threatens to lead Japan again toward excesses. At the moment the people are busy enjoying the recent betterment in their lives. They are apathetic to calls upon both their conscience and their patriotism. Nevertheless, within the ceremonial formulas of the democracy which MacArthur left them, they will be asked soon to take sides in the debate about the goals or vengeance which Japan should ultimately pursue.

In the past men like Saionji, Araki, Matsuoka, and Mishima, who hoped to influence national policy making, have sacrificed themselves in the traditional Japanese manner—by passionately polite hints. They have failed to do more than embarrass their aristocratic patrons. If the Throne is to be made a true symbol of state and servant of majority interests in Japan, criticism of it and of national policy may have to be expressed more explicitly in the future.

Many Japanese will try to dismiss from mind the ugly story told in this book, assuring themselves that it is a simplification. In a sense they will be right. Here the ideas of leaders have been put forward as the mainsprings of Japanese political action, whereas, in practice, Japanese tend to think of politics only in terms of personal ties between friends who have done favors for one another. If these pages have done scant justice to the complexities of allegiance and loyalty in Japan, perhaps they will stimulate Japanese historians to recount fully the personal relationships involved in the undoubted events of Hirohito's reign. Up to now Japanese explanations of the period have struck many Westerners as either allusively circumstantial or mystically broad.

To face reality, to earn the goodwill of neighboring peoples, and to make Asia a responsible fourth force which can stand apart from America, Russia, and Europe are hard tasks without glamor. They can be achieved only by exorcising the spell of the ancestors, by blowing away the heavy halo of taboo which encircles the Throne, and by shattering the devout silence which makes conspirators of all who enter service in the palace. Japanese know and dread the alternative, which is to dive back into the Pacific to grapple once again with Commodore Perry's leviathan.

GLOSSARY

Following is a descriptive list encapsulating or amplifying characters, events, groups, organizations, and geographical features mentioned in the text of *Japan's Imperial Conspiracy*. Offices and departments of the national government are described elsewhere, in the chart "Japan's Prewar Government" on pages 484–485. Relationships within the imperial family are delineated in the genealogical tables on pages 346–348. Names in capitals within the text are cross-references to other entries.

ANAMI KORECHIKA (1887–1945). Army officer, military academy classmate and protégé of Hirohito's uncles Prince HIGASHIKUNI and Prince ASAKA. From 1926 to 1933 he was Hirohito's favorite aide-de-camp. Thereafter, except for a brief term as vice war minister in 1939–40, he served mostly in the field, bringing morale to his men and first-hand knowledge back to Tokyo. In December 1944 he was recalled from his command in New Guinea and made war minister. He encouraged the attempted palace coup on the night of surrender, August 14, 1945, and then committed hara-kiri.

ANTI-COMINTERN PACT. Agreement between the Japanese and German governments, signed in Berlin on November 25, 1936, to act together against the spread of communism. Secret provisions of the pact bound each nation to assist the other economically and diplomatically if either waged war with Russia.

ANTI-CONSTITUTIONALIST PARTY (*Rikken Minseito*). Political party founded in 1927 by HAMAGUCHI OSACHI to offer organized, professionally managed opposition to the CONSTITUTIONALIST PARTY. Prince SAIONJI KINMOCHI recruited financial backing for it. After July 1940 the Anti-Constitutionalists, and the Constitutionalists as well, ceased to exist as parties and were replaced by the IMPERIAL RULE ASSISTANCE ASSOCIATION.

ARAKI SADAO (1877–1967). Army officer, protégé of Emperor Taisho, military academy classmate of HONJO SHIGERU and MAZAKI JINZABURO, and the most eloquent spokesman for the STRIKE-NORTH FACTION. An intelligence expert specializing in Russian affairs, he served in the St. Petersburg Embassy from 1909 to 1918, then with YONAI MITSUMASA in the Vladivostok Special Service Organ during Japan's Siberian Intervention. In 1925–26 during the purge of the CHOSHU leadership from the Army, he commanded the secret police. Fallow years followed in which he ran the Army's staff college, gathered a group of supporters in the officer corps, and spoke out increasingly against the policies of the STRIKE-SOUTH FACTION. In December 1931, after the seizure of Mukden, he came into power as war minister with the Constitutionalists. For the next five years he fought a shifting battle with Hirohito on national policy and finally retired in defeat after the FEBRUARY MUTINY in 1936. Araki returned to prominence briefly as minister of education during the 1939 NOMONHAN INCIDENT. After World War II he submitted quietly to prosecution as a war criminal. Emerging from "life imprisonment" in 1955, he soon returned to his old ways and began to agitate for the strengthening of Japanese military power to deal with Russian threats. Until his death at ninety he kept various caches of secret state documents from the 1930's as guarantees for his continued health and freedom from persecution.

ARMY PURIFICATION MOVEMENT (*Seigun-ha*). An organization in the Army officer corps promoted in 1934–35 by Lieutenant General Count TERAUCHI HISAICHI. Its followers advocated strict obedience to orders and nonintervention in politics.

ASA-AKIRA, Prince Kuni III (1901–   ). Son of KUNIYOSHI, brother of Empress Nagako, childhood playmate of Hirohito. He graduated from the naval academy in 1921 and in 1925 married his second cousin Tomoko, daughter of Admiral Prince FUSHIMI HIROYASU. In 1942, as a rear admiral, he commanded the air squadron which supported the occupation of Timor. Later in the war he supported Prince TAKAMATSU in promotion of the kamikaze corps. In postwar Japan he ran the Kuni Perfume Company and a marriage brokerage. Later, as conditions eased, he became a gentleman farmer known for his sheep dogs and his orchids.

ASAHIKO, Prince Kuni (1824–1891). Son of KUNIYE, nineteenth Prince FUSHIMI. He became chief counselor to Emperor KOMEI and leading proponent of expelling Western barbarians from the Orient. Empress Nagako is his granddaughter.

ASAKA YASUHIKO, Prince (1887–   ). Eighth son of ASAHIKO and uncle of Hirohito. A professional Army officer, he was commander at Nanking in 1937 during the massive reprisal massacre which took about 140,000 Chinese lives. In the postwar era he was known as one of Tokyo's best golfers.

ASIA DEVELOPMENT BOARD (*Koa-in*). Established by Prince Konoye, then prime minister, in December 1938 to co-ordinate the economic exploitation of China. Major General SUZUKI TEI-ICHI was head of the Political Affairs Branch of the board.

BANZAI RIHACHIRO. Retired lieutenant general, veteran of Japanese intelligence in China, former advisor to Yuan Shih-kai in Peking. In the 1930's he became director of the "CIVILIAN SPY SERVICE."

BIG BROTHERS (*Ani-bun*). A descriptive term used by courtiers to designate a group of energetic aristocrats who were considered to be like elder brothers by Hirohito. All were nine to fifteen years older than he was. All had come often to his foster home to play with him as a child. All were PEERS' SCHOOL classmates either of his uncle Prince HIGASHIKUNI, born in 1887, or of his foster parent's son, KIDO KOICHI, born in 1889, or of Prince KONOYE FUMIMARO, the highest ranking noble of the Court clan of Fujiwara, born in 1891. At first, in addition to Higashikuni, Kido, and Konoye, the most influential of the Big Brothers were FUSHIMI family scions: Prince ASAKA YASU-HIKO, Prince Kitashirakawa Naruhisa, and Marquis Komatsu Teruhisa. Some other Big Brothers, who remained important in Hirohito's counsels until the close of World War II, were the Army officer Marquis Inoue Saburo; the courtiers Count FUTARA YOSHINORI, Baron HARADA KUMAO, and Viscount Okabe Nagakage; also the diplomats Shigemitsu Mamoru and Tani Masayuki.

BLACK DRAGON SOCIETY (*Kokuryu-kai*). A Japanese patriotic tong professing a credo of Asia for the Asiatics. The powerful underworld boss TOYAMA MITSURU founded it in 1901 with the initial purpose of supporting Army Chief of Staff General YAMAGATA ARITOMO's position that Japan should control all of Manchuria up to the Amur or Black Dragon River, the boundary between Manchuria and Siberia. Black Dragon lord Toyama was a patron of Sun Yat-sen, who met with Chinese exiles in Black Dragon headquarters in Tokyo to found a revolutionary party—the Kuomintang or KMT of Chiang Kai-shek. The Black Dragon Society later supported the STRIKE-NORTH FACTION in the Army, and its influence dwindled as that faction was gradually eliminated in the 1930's.

BLOOD BROTHERHOOD (*Ketsumeidan*). Select group of apprentice spies trained for work in China as an adjunct of the EVERYDAY MEIJI BIOGRAPHICAL RESEARCH INSTITUTE in Oarai. Agents belonging to the brotherhood acted as assassins in the killing of Inoue Junnosuke and Baron Dan in 1932.

CABAL. See EMPEROR'S CABAL.

CABINET PLANNING BOARD (*Kikaku-in*). The central organization controlling Japanese economic mobilization for World War II. For his part as chief of the board, retired Lieutenant General SUZUKI TEI-ICHI was found guilty of war crimes in 1948 and sentenced to life imprisonment.

CHERRY SOCIETY (*Sakurakai*). An organization of Army junior officers, under the aegis of Army Intelligence chief General TATEKAWA YOSHIJI. It lobbied for conquest of Manchuria and larger military budgets in 1930. Some of its members were admitted to the EMPEROR'S CABAL.

CHICHIBU, Prince (1902–1953). First brother of Hirohito. Often at odds with the Emperor, he sympathized with the STRIKE-NORTH FACTION in the FEBRUARY MUTINY of 1936.

CHO ISAMU (1896–1945). Army fanatic, member of the CHERRY SOCIETY and of the EMPEROR'S CABAL. In 1931 he planned the OCTOBER PLOT. From August 1934 to July 1937 he was employed in drawing up plans for Japan's war with China. In December 1937 he was chief of staff for Prince ASAKA outside Nanking and issued a notorious order for the prince: "Kill all prisoners." In the spring of 1938 he commanded the 74th Regiment in the border war with Russia known as the Lake Khasan Incident. During training of Strike-South forces in the summer of 1941, he served as vice chief of staff to General YAMASHITA TOMOYUKI. On the eve of war he was assigned to the staff of General Count TERAUCHI HISAICHI in Saigon. Later in the war, July 1944, he became chief of staff of the 32d Army on Okinawa. There, in June 1945, having put up a good defense, he committed suicide rather than surrender.

CHOSHU. A large clan in the southwestern corner of the central island of Honshu, of which Mori was the leading family. When Emperor KOMEI enlisted Choshu support and advice in his struggle with the TOKUGAWA shogunate, clan leaders urged unification under the Emperor and a program of expansion on the Asiatic continent to create buffer zones between Japan and the West. Choshu samurai led by General YAMAGATA ARITOMO dominated Emperor Meiji's new Imperial Army and monopolized key posts until its reorganization in 1924. Disgruntled Choshu officers and retired officers supplied much of the backing for the STRIKE-NORTH FACTION during the 1930's.

"CIVILIAN SPY SERVICE." A paramilitary espionage organization which co-ordinated and supplemented the work of the Army and Navy Intelligence departments of the Tokyo General Staffs. Its directorate, which worked out of the Imperial Palace through the fronts of charitable and cultural organizations, was mostly staffed by retired military intelligence officers. Its agents worked in the diplomatic corps of the Foreign Ministry and the marketing staffs of cartels engaged in foreign trade. Its network blanketed Asia and extended into all the major cities of the West. Founded by Emperor Meiji's Imperial Household Minister Count TANAKA MITSUAKI, the spy service was directed throughout most of Hirohito's reign by retired Lieutenant General BANZAI RIHACHIRO.

CONSTITUTIONALIST PARTY (*Rikken Seiyukai*). First important political party in Japan, founded in 1900 by Prime Minister ITO HIROBUMI, who hoped to create a counterbalance to the autocratic power of Emperor Meiji and a basis for constitutional party government. Constitutionalists in general favored economic rather than military expansion. In the Diet which had the power to veto increases in budgets, they sought to curtail military appropriations. Later leaders of the

party were Prince SAIONJI KINMOCHI; Hara Takashi, prime minister
in 1918–21 (when he was assassinated); and retired General Count
Tanaka Gi-ichi, who attempted while prime minister in 1927–29 to
moderate young Emperor Hirohito's aspirations for China.

CONTROL CLIQUE (*Tosei-hai*). The minority of the EMPEROR'S
CABAL in the Army which remained loyal to him from 1930 to 1936
and supported him and the STRIKE-SOUTH FACTION in an anti-
Western policy of expansion into Southeast Asia and Indonesia. The
name Control Clique was meant to appeal to those who feared possible
lack of self-control in Hirohito's policies for Japan. The dissident half
of the Emperor's Cabal was the IMPERIAL WAY GROUP. Prominent
members of the Control Clique were SUZUKI TEI-ICHI, DOIHARA
KENJI, ITAGAKI SEISHIRO, TATEKAWA YOSHIJI, and KOISO KUNIAKI.

DOIHARA KENJI (1883–1948). Army officer, protégé of Prince KANIN,
one of the ELEVEN RELIABLES, known as the "Lawrence of Manchuria." Throughout most of the 1920's he was attached to the General Staff, running espionage errands to eastern Siberia and North
China. In March 1928 he was employed as a military advisor by
Manchurian warlord Chang Tso-lin. In August 1931 he took charge of
the Japanese Special Service Organ in Mukden, declaring himself
mayor of the city on the morning of September 19 after the outbreak
of the MANCHURIAN INCIDENT. He went on in November to become
Special Service Organ chief in Harbin where he prepared for Japanese seizure of that city also. Doihara had a large part in the administration of the new puppet state of MANCHUKUO until 1937, when he
abruptly began a second career as a respectable field officer, commanding the 14th Division and later the 5th Army in North China. In
October 1940, assuming a professorial role, he was appointed principal
of the military academy. In June 1941 he accepted the inspector generalship of military aviation. During the war he held successively three
imposing commands of armies in rear areas. Doihara's earlier activities
in Manchuria had not been forgotten, however. In 1948 he was convicted as a war criminal and hanged.

DOLLAR SWINDLE (*Doru-bai*). First element in the TRIPLE INTRIGUE
of 1931–32. It was a financial maneuver advocated by the Emperor's
close advisors among the BIG BROTHERS and the ELEVEN CLUB to win
support from certain Japanese bankers and cartelists by inviting them
to speculate in foreign currencies with advanced knowledge of the
government's intention to renounce the gold standard. The govern-

ment fulfilled its pledge in late 1931, to the great financial disadvantage of the banking and industrial interests.

EAST ASIA ALL-ONE CULTURE SOCIETY (*Toa Dobun-kai*). Movement begun in Japan and extended to China by Fujiwara Prince Konoye Atsumaro, father of the future prime minister, Prince Konoye Fumimaro, to promote Japan's mission as the leader of Asian culture and politics.

ELEVEN CLUB (*Juichi-kai*). A group of about twenty PEERS' SCHOOL graduates of like mind and like age who met more or less regularly with Marquis KIDO KOICHI on the eleventh evening of each month. Most of them were courtiers or aristocratic bureaucrats; a few were military officers or diplomats. They discussed imperial policies, plans, and plots under consideration by Hirohito or by his official advisors. In either modifying or activating policy, they were extremely influential. Marquis Kido started the club in 1922, on November 11—the eleventh day of the eleventh month of the eleventh year in the reign of Emperor Taisho. The club held its last recorded session on January 11, 1945.

ELEVEN RELIABLES (*Jushu na jinsai no juichinin*). Junior Army officers thought trustworthy enough to approach as possible recruits for the EMPEROR'S CABAL by the THREE CROWS. Most prominent of the Eleven Reliables came to be TOJO HIDEKI, DOIHARA KENJI, KOMOTO DAISAKU, ISOGAI RENSUKE, ITAGAKI SEISHIRO, WATARI HISAO, and YAMAOKA SHIGEATSU.

EMPEROR'S CABAL (*Showa Rikukaigun no Chushin*). An elite cadre of intelligence officers recruited in the 1920's to work in secret for Hirohito's programs within the Army and Navy. The leaders of the cabal, brought together by Hirohito's uncle, Big Brother Prince HIGASHIKUNI in October 1921, were the THREE CROWS—Majors NAGATA TETSUZAN, Obata Toshiro, and Okamura Yasuji. They promptly enlisted a group of fellow junior officers known as the ELEVEN RELIABLES. The cabal's immediate goals were to modernize the Army and displace the old-line CHOSHU leadership. Further recruits came into the cabal through the UNIVERSITY LODGING HOUSE, the SUZUKI STUDY GROUP, and the CHERRY SOCIETY. Around 1930 the cabal split into the IMPERIAL WAY GROUP, which supported the STRIKE-NORTH FACTION, and the CONTROL CLIQUE, which supported the STRIKE-SOUTH FACTION.

EVERYDAY MEIJI BIOGRAPHICAL RESEARCH INSTITUTE (*Joyo Meiji Kinenkan*). Front organization in Oarai, 50 miles northeast of Tokyo, for co-ordinating intelligence supplied by the various branches of the "CIVILIAN SPY SERVICE." Nearby were two affiliated academies which trained agents for espionage work. The institute was organized by a longtime Court official, Count TANAKA MITSUAKI, who had been household minister to Emperor Meiji. Ostensibly it was a museum where scholars labored to prepare an official biography of Meiji. The institute was closed down and its staff moved elsewhere in 1932 when people began to point out that it had been deeply involved in the assassination of Prime Minister Inukai during the MAY FIFTEENTH INCIDENT.

FAKE WAR (*Shanhai ni kensei undo*). Second act in the TRIPLE INTRIGUE of 1931–32, a diversionary attack on the Chinese half of Shanghai in January 1932. In return for stopping it before it involved the Western segments of the city, the Japanese government expected that the League of Nations would abandon all thought of imposing economic sanctions against Japan for aggression in Manchuria. Expectations were fulfilled and the Fake War was brought to an end in March 1932.

FEBRUARY MUTINY (*Niniroku Jiken*). Armed uprising in Tokyo, organized by officers of the Army's crack 1st Division, who hoped to persuade Hirohito to change his national policy. They sought domestic reform and a return to the traditional values of the samurai ethic. They were set on by members of the STRIKE-NORTH and STRIKE-SOUTH factions, both of which hoped that the mutiny could be used to further their own political ends. In the early hours of February 26, 1936, soldiers of the 1st and 3d regiments led by two captains and nineteen lieutenants marched out of their barracks to kill "the evil men about the Throne." Assassination squads murdered Finance Minister Takahashi Korekiyo, Lord Privy Seal Admiral Viscount Saito, and General Watanabe Jotaro, inspector general of military education; they failed in attempts to kill Prime Minister Okada Keisuke and Hirohito's Grand Chamberlain Admiral SUZUKI KANTARO. Rural accomplices also failed in out-of-town attempts to murder former Lord Privy Seal Count MAKINO NOBUAKI and Prince SAIONJI KINMOCHI. The rebels occupied the center of Tokyo for three days before surrendering. Hirohito refused to bow to any of their demands, and after their suppression he demanded the resignation of most of the generals in the Army. He made a notable exception of General Count Terauchi of the ARMY

PURIFICATION MOVEMENT, who became the next war minister. Two officer-leaders of the mutiny committed hara-kiri, thirteen others were executed by firing squad. In the months following, practically all officers of the Strike-North Faction were retired from the Army, and full-scale preparations were made to carry out Strike-South policies.

FUJIWARA. An imperial clan originating in the seventh century A.D. under the patronage of Emperor Tenji. Fujiwara princesses served as wives and concubines to emperors and Fujiwara princes acted as intimate advisors to the Throne for thirteen centuries. Two of the last of the Fujiwara princes were SAIONJI KINMOCHI (1849–1940) and KONOYE FUMIMARO (1891–1945).

FUSHIMI HIROYASU, Prince (1875–1947). Son of SADANARU, he was the twenty-second Prince Fushimi. He became an admiral and served Hirohito as chief of staff of the Navy from 1932 to 1941.

FUSHIMI, House of. A collateral branch of the imperial family, founded in the fourteenth century, which traditionally supplied husbands for the unwed daughters of emperors. Through the efforts of KUNIYE and ASAHIKO, its influence at Court increased greatly in the nineteenth century at a time when other imperial branch families were dying out for lack of male issue. Fushimi power reached its zenith in alliance with the SATSUMA clan and the Imperial Navy during the first half of the reign of Hirohito. A Fushimi princess, Nagako, daughter of Prince KUNIYOSHI, became Empress of Japan at her marriage to Hirohito in January 1924.

FUTARA YOSHINORI, Count (1886–   ). A member of Hirohito's boyhood BIG BROTHERS, later married to a cousin of the future Empress Nagako. He accompanied the Crown Prince on his European tour in 1921 and continued thereafter to serve as imperial public relations agent. He and SUZUKI KANTARO were largely responsible for creating the impression common in Western countries of Hirohito as a Westernized young liberal.

HAMAGUCHI OSACHI (1870–1931). Organized a new political party in 1927 to unite various factions opposed to the Constitutionalists. Shot by an assassin in November 1930, he was incapacitated and finally died in August 1931.

HARADA KUMAO, Baron (1888–1946). Prince SAIONJI KINMOCHI's political secretary, ELEVEN CLUB member, one of the BIG BROTHERS. His grandfather was Harada Kazumichi, an advisor of Emperor Meiji.

He attended Kyoto University with other Big Brothers, graduating with KIDO KOICHI in 1915. Following Hirohito to Europe, he stayed on there to help Prince HIGASHIKUNI with intelligence work. Returning home, he became Prime Minister Kato Taka-aki's secretary in 1924. From 1926 to 1940, while acting as liaison between Hirohito and Prince Saionji, he wrote a nine-volume, 3,000-page record of his political transactions known as the "Saionji-Harada Memoirs."

HIGASHIKUNI NARUHIKO, Prince (1887–   ). Ninth son of Prince ASAHIKO, uncle of Hirohito, Army officer, BIG BROTHER. He managed the formation of the EMPEROR'S CABAL in 1921 and went on to play a personal part in almost every one of the plots, intrigues, and incidents of the next twenty-five years. At the end of the war, having achieved the rank of field marshal, he took responsibility for all he had wrought by becoming prime minister in the first two humiliating months after Japan's surrender.

HONJO SHIGERU (1876–1945). Army officer, protégé of Emperor Taisho, military academy classmate of General ARAKI SADAO. A China expert, he served as military advisor to North China warlord Chang Tso-lin from 1921 to 1924. In August 1931 he was made commander of the KWANTUNG ARMY to carry out the well-considered plans of the EMPEROR'S CABAL for the seizure of Manchuria. He fulfilled his assignment well and was rewarded with the post of chief aide-de-camp to Hirohito in April 1933. For the next three years he sought gently to persuade Hirohito to give up STRIKE-SOUTH aspirations. He failed. His nephew participated in the FEBRUARY MUTINY. And in March 1936, with many marks of imperial regard, he was forced to resign his position in the palace. Throughout the next nine years, however, he was summoned and consulted privately by the Emperor as a loyal dissident. On November 20, 1945, informed that he was about to be arrested as a major war criminal and tried for his part in the MANCHURIAN INCIDENT, he committed ritual suicide. Revealing extracts from diaries he kept during his service as chief aide-de-camp were published in Tokyo in 1967.

HONMA MASAHARU (1887–1946). Army officer, protégé of Prince CHICHIBU for whom he served repeatedly as aide-de-camp between 1927 and 1937. Though considered too pro-British by many of his fellow officers, he was valued for his fluent English. In 1932 he read and summarized for Emperor Hirohito the LYTTON COMMISSION Report, a 400-page document, in twenty-four hours. Put in charge of the invasion of the Philippines in 1941, he was reproved by the Emperor for failure to prevent MacArthur's forces from digging in on Bataan. His command authority was promptly pre-empted by Colonel TSUJI MASANOBU and a group of staff officers who came from Tokyo with imperial orders. The disgraced Honma sulked in his tent, virtually shorn of authority; it was he, however, who was executed for the Bataan death march by the Allies in 1946.

HO-UMEZU PACT. Agreement between China and Japan concluded by Chinese General Ho and the commander of the Japanese garrison at Tientsin, Strike-South General Umezu Yoshijiro, in June 1935. It provided that Chiang's troops in the North China province of Hopei be withdrawn—in the face of Japanese preparations to attack—leaving the North China area open to Japanese penetration and exploitation.

IMPERIAL RULE ASSISTANCE ASSOCIATION (*Taisei Yokusan-kai*). The mass party organized by Prime Minister Prince Konoye in 1940 to replace all other political parties in Japan.

IMPERIAL WAY GROUP (*Kodo-ha*). The antagonists of the CONTROL CLIQUE and the majority party in the EMPEROR'S CABAL. They became disaffected with Hirohito's national strategy in the early 1930's and supported the STRIKE-NORTH FACTION in agitation for military preparations against Russia. Put down by Hirohito in the FEBRUARY MUTINY, leaders of the Imperial Way Group were retired from the Army in 1936, but followers continued to resist imperial policies through the war and into the half century following the war. Principal purged Imperial Way Group leaders were MAZAKI JINZABURO and one of the THREE CROWS, Obata Toshiro. Important unpurged sympathizers with the movement were ISHIWARA KANJI, YAMAMOTO ISOROKU, and YAMASHITA TOMOYUKI.

ISHIWARA KANJI (1889–1949). Army officer admired for his intellectual brilliance but cordially detested by most of his peers for his religious preaching, uncompromising frankness, and self-righteous sense of mission. Ishiwara headed his class at military academy and went on to staff college in 1915, only six years later. In the 1920's he served for four years as an instructor at the staff college and for three years as an attaché and intelligence agent in Berlin. He became a member of the SUZUKI STUDY GROUP and was accepted belatedly into the EMPEROR'S CABAL. In October 1928 he was attached to the staff of the KWANTUNG ARMY to draw up plans for the seizure of Manchuria. Assisted by the salesmanship of ITAGAKI SEISHIRO, he saw his proposals accepted, and in 1931–32 he executed the military half of them with awesome efficiency. From August 1935 to September 1937 he was employed, with many outspoken qualms, in supervising war planning for the conquest of central China. During the FEBRUARY MUTINY of 1936 he insisted upon strict obedience to Hirohito's orders in dealing with the young mutineers. Having refused to side with either the STRIKE-NORTH or STRIKE-SOUTH factions, he survived the purges which followed the mutiny, but in the first year of the war with China he saw his worst fears confirmed and made himself increasingly unpopular by his critical outbursts against imperial policy. After December 1938 he was relegated to garrison commands. Finally, in March 1941, he was retired to the reserve with the rank of lieutenant general. He returned briefly to prominence in 1945–46 by making speeches for the government in exculpation of the Throne and accusation of General Tojo. The effort broke his health. During the war crimes trials the International Military Tribunal sent a deputation to take testimony from him on his sickbed. Assorted debilities, exacerbated by wartime malnutrition, ended his life in 1949.

ISOGAI RENSUKE (1886–1967). Army officer, one of the ELEVEN RELIABLES. He conducted the preliminary negotiations for the HO-UMEZU PACT in 1935 and acted as governor general of Hong Kong during World War II. After the war he was tried and judged guilty of war crimes by the Chinese, but was pardoned by Chiang Kai-shek through the intercession of TSUJI MASANOBU.

ITAGAKI SEISHIRO (1885–1948). Army officer, one of the ELEVEN RELIABLES, a tough, engaging, back-slapping specialist in China intelligence work. In May 1929 he was posted to the KWANTUNG ARMY to assist ISHIWARA KANJI politically in planning the seizure of Manchuria. In 1932 he ordered the incitements for the FAKE WAR. From August 1932 to March 1937 he served on the KWANTUNG ARMY staff as chief advisor on Manchukuoan affairs. In this capacity he shared with DOIHARA KENJI the responsibility for sore aggression and exploitation of the new colony. In the first year of the war with China he commanded the 5th Division. As war minister from June 1938 to September 1939 he presided over two disastrous border wars with Russia, the Lake Khasan affair and the NOMONHAN INCIDENT. Thereafter he served as a commander of rear-area armies in China, Korea, and Malaya. After the war he was tried for war crimes in Manchuria and hanged beside Doihara.

ITO HIROBUMI (1841–1909). A Choshu samurai who became the leading spokesman of Japan during the reign of Emperor Meiji. He supervised the drafting of the Constitution of 1889. As a gradual opponent of the war policies of General YAMAGATA ARITOMO he tried to avert the Russo-Japanese War. While he was prime minister in 1900, he founded the CONSTITUTIONALIST PARTY. He was assassinated in Korea in 1909.

JIMMU. The legendary first Emperor of Japan, or of YAMATO, who according to tradition ascended the throne in 660 B.C. and according to archaeologists reigned in the first century A.D. All Japanese emperors are descended from him, though not all patrilineally or by primogeniture. Hirohito is accounted the one hundred and twenty-fourth of the line.

KANIN KOTOHITO, Prince (1865–1945). Adopted son of Emperor KOMEI, seventh son of KUNIYE. Having outlived the last of his brothers, he ranked from 1923 to 1945 as the senior member of the imperial family. At the same time being a professional Army officer, a graduate of French military academies, who had risen through the officer corps to the rank of field marshal, Prince Kanin became the gray eminence of Japan's military establishment. Always an activist, he presided over an attempt in 1916 to assassinate Chinese warlord Chang Tso-lin and occupy Manchuria. In 1921 he personally showed Hirohito the World War battlefields of France. In the 1920's his pro-tégés TATEKAWA YOSHIJI and KOISO KUNIAKE assisted their juniors, the THREE CROWS and the ELEVEN RELIABLES, in recruiting the EM-PEROR'S CABAL. In December 1931, during the conquest of Manchuria, Prince Kanin accepted the highest post in the Army, that of chief of staff. He retained it throughout the 1930's, while the war with China was undertaken, until October 1940. Thereafter, in his late seventies, he remained at Hirohito's side, manipulating Army elders, until his death on May 21, 1945.

KAYA TSUNENORI, Prince (1900–   ). Grandson of ASAHIKO, first cousin of Empress Nagako, husband of a niece of Empress Dowager SADAKO, and childhood playmate of Hirohito. In 1934 he and his wife paid a state visit to Hitler and returned admiring the Third Reich and supporting alliance with it. As a major general in 1943, he served on the faculty of the Army Staff College supervising war strategy. After the war he occupied sinecures in the Taisho and Nisshin Life Insurance companies.

KIDO KOICHI, Marquis (1888–   ). First of the BIG BROTHERS and founder of the ELEVEN CLUB. A diligent bureaucrat, he was responsible in the Ministry of Commerce and Industry for much of Japan's early industrial planning for war. In 1930 he became secretary to the lord privy seal and in 1940 lord privy seal. He remained Hirohito's closest civilian advisor throughout the war. In 1948 the International Military Tribunal sentenced him to life imprisonment; he was paroled in 1956. His diaries were published in Japan in 1966.

KITA IKKI (1882–1936). Political theorist whose major work, *The Fundamental Principles for the Reconstruction of the Nation*, provided many of the basic ideas of Japanese fascism, particularly those of the STRIKE-NORTH FACTION. After the FEBRUARY MUTINY he was executed for having written the manifesto of the mutineers.

KMT. Abbreviation for the Kuomintang, political party in China ultimately headed by Chiang Kai-shek.

KOISO KUNIAKE (1880–1950). Army officer, intelligence specialist, protégé of Prince KANIN, a senior member of the EMPEROR'S CABAL. As a General Staff emissary to Inner Mongolia in 1915–17 he arranged for the Mongol invasion of Manchuria which was co-ordinated with the 1916 Japanese attempt on the life of Chinese warlord Chang Tso-lin. In the early 1920's he was responsible for seeing that aviation intelligence gathered by Japanese attachés in Europe was fully utilized in the development of a Japanese Army air force. In 1931 he masterminded the MARCH PLOT. Vice war minister in 1932, commander in chief of the Korean Army in 1935, minister of colonization in the Cabinet in 1939 and 1940, governor general of Korea from 1942 to 1944, Koiso finally became prime minister in the desperate kamikaze months of July 1944 to April 1945. After the war he died in prison while serving a life sentence as a war criminal.

KOMEI, Emperor (1831–1867). The last Mikado of old Japan in whose reign, in 1853, U.S. Commodore Matthew Perry forced his way into Tokyo Bay at cannon point. In the last fourteen years of his life, Komei cast about vainly for vassals strong enough to expel the Western invaders, enforce Japan's traditional policy of seclusion from the world, and preserve the sanctity of Japanese shores—the religious trust handed down to him by his imperial ancestors. In the course of his stubborn efforts Komei endorsed a long-range imperial policy for Japan: to cast out the barbarians and conquer a buffer zone in neighboring lands which would keep them from ever intruding again. By insisting on this goal too early he demanded the impossible of his vassals. The martial samurai clan of CHOSHU which had first suggested the goal to him was humiliated by his insistence on immediate action. Leaders of the clan had him murdered, with the connivance of a sympathetic nobleman, Iwakura Tomomi. His fifteen-year-old son MEIJI was accepted as his successor.

KOMOTO DAISAKU (1893–1954). One of the ELEVEN RELIABLES in the Army officer corps. In 1928 he blew up a railroad car carrying Chang Tso-lin, the warlord of North China, and so launched Japanese aggression in the Manchurian area, climaxed by the MANCHURIAN INCIDENT. Having taken responsibility for the assassination of Chang, he enjoyed a comfortable life as a member of the board of directors of Japan's SOUTH MANCHURIAN RAILROAD. He died of natural causes in his villa outside Kobe in 1954.

KONOYE FUMIMARO, Prince (1891–1945). Highest ranking FUJIWARA prince, youngest of the BIG BROTHERS. As prime minister from 1937 to 1939, he assumed responsibility for the war with China; as prime minister again in 1940–41, he acquiesced in the Emperor's STRIKE-SOUTH plans, organized the IMPERIAL RULE ASSISTANCE ASSOCIATION, and prepared the way for totalitarian government. Resigning in favor of TOJO HIDEKI in October 1941, Prince Konoye acted as titular leader of the PEACE FACTION during the war. On the eve of his arrest, after the war, as a major war criminal, he took poison. His Princeton-educated son Fumitaka, or "Butch," was sentenced to twenty-five years at hard labor by a Moscow court for war crimes against the Russians in Manchuria; he died in 1956 at Ivanova prison camp in Siberia. Prince Konoye's brother Konoye Hidemaro conducts the Tokyo Symphony Orchestra.

KUNIYE, Prince (1802–1875). Nineteenth Prince FUSHIMI, he was the adopted son of Emperor Kokaku and the father of sixteen sons of his own. He was the progenitor of the entire modern imperial family except for the houses of Hirohito and his three brothers.
KUNIYOSHI, Prince Kuni II (1873–1929). Son of ASAHIKO, grandson of KUNIYE, father of Empress Nagako. He was an early advocate of air power and of germ warfare. One of his protégés was YAMAMOTO ISOROKU.

KURUSU SABURO (1888–1954). Career diplomat who negotiated the TRIPARTITE PACT and who was special envoy to Washington in November 1941 assigned to guide Ambassador NOMURA KICHISABURO in his negotiations with the U.S. State Department.

KWANTUNG ARMY (*Kanto-gun*). The portion of the Japanese Imperial Army stationed in Japan's KWANTUNG LEASEHOLD in Manchuria. Employed to protect Japanese interests on the Continent, it won a reputation as containing the toughest units in the Army. The success of Japan's invasion of Manchuria, begun with the MANCHURIAN INCIDENT, was largely the result of its effectiveness. At some points in their careers, most members of the EMPEROR'S CABAL served as staff officers with the Kwantung Army and came to be known, especially in the West, by the misleading euphemism of the "Kwantung Army gang."

KWANTUNG LEASEHOLD. Territory in southern part of Liaotung Peninsula, MANCHURIA, including ports of Dairen and Port Arthur. It was acquired by Japan after first Sino-Japanese War, 1895, and then relinquished under international pressure; China then leased the area to Russia. After the Russo-Japanese War it was occupied by Japan, and in 1915 Japan acquired a ninety-nine-year leasehold on it from China. It became the base for the KWANTUNG ARMY, the terminus for the SOUTH MANCHURIAN RAILROAD network, and the arsenal of Japanese strength on the Continent.

LYTTON COMMISSION. The League of Nations' Commission of Inquiry, headed by Lord Lytton of Great Britain, appointed to investigate the circumstances of Japan's invasion of MANCHURIA. The commission's conclusions, set forth in the Lytton Report, were that Japan's action was not in "self-defense" and that the subsequent state of MANCHUKUO did not result from any native independence movement. The report recommended that Manchuria be given an autonomous administration under Chinese sovereignty. The Lytton Report was adopted by the League over Japan's objection, in February 1933, and Japan's withdrawal from the League followed.

MACHIJIRI KAZUMOTO (1889–c. 1950). A well-connected Army officer, son of Count Mibu Motonaga who was a celebrated loyalist nobleman at the Court of Emperor Komei. He was the adopted son of Viscount Machijiri Kazuhiro, master of rituals at the Court of Hirohito, and brother of Count Mibu Motoyoshi who married the elder sister of Prince Higashikuni. Machijiri married Empress Nagako's first cousin Yukiko, the elder sister of Prince KAYA TSUNENORI. In 1919 Machijiri accompanied Prince HIGASHIKUNI to Europe where he helped to recruit the THREE CROWS and found the EMPEROR'S CABAL. Returning to Japan, he had command of artillery of the Imperial Guards in 1926 and became an aide-de-camp and liaison officer for Hirohito in 1930. He left the Emperor's side briefly after the FEBRUARY MU-TINY in order to carry out a purge of dissident junior officers in the War Ministry. He left it again in October 1937 to take charge of the influential Military Affairs Bureau in the War Ministry during the personnel manipulations which preceded the rape of Nanking. Other delicate assignments followed, some in the Army bureaucracy in Tokyo, others in command or staff posts with the armies in China. In the seven months before Pearl Harbor, Machijiri ran the Chemical Weapons Branch of the Army which handled both gasses and gunpowders. During the war, from 1942 to 1944, he commanded Japan's garrison army in French Indochina. He retired from military life in May 1945 and died a few years later.

MAKINO NOBUAKI, Count (1862–1949). A member of the SATSUMA nobility, he was a principal companion of Crown Prince Hirohito on his European tour in 1921; as lord privy seal from 1925 until the end of 1935, he was the Emperor's principal advisor, closely involved in the intrigues to eliminate adherents of the STRIKE-NORTH FACTION from the Army and the government hierarchy.

MANCHUKUO. Japanese name for the pseudo-independent state set up in February 1932 and eventually comprising the three provinces of Manchuria and the province of Jehol.

MANCHURIA. Region in northeast China, including the Liaotung Peninsula on which Japan's KWANTUNG LEASEHOLD was situated. In the seventeenth century it had been the homeland of the Manchu conquerors of China. After the MANCHURIAN INCIDENT in September 1931 the Kwantung Army took it piece by piece and made it a slave state of Japan, renamed Manchukuo.

MANCHURIAN INCIDENT (*Manshu Jiken*). Japanese designation for the seizure of Mukden, capital of Manchuria, on the night of September 18, 1931, by the KWANTUNG ARMY; pretext for the attack was an explosion on the railway. In reality the Japanese government, through assignments to various Army officers, notably ISHIWARA KANJI, had been planning the conquest of Manchuria for more than two years.

MARCH PLOT (*Sangatsu Jiken*). Scheme devised in the early months of 1931 by the Emperor's close supporters—principally Lord Privy Seal MAKINO NOBUAKI, his protégé Dr. OKAWA SHUMEI, and STRIKE-SOUTH FACTION officers in the War Ministry and Army General Staff

—to compromise the politically moderate General Ugaki Kazushige, war minister and potential leader of the CONSTITUTIONALIST PARTY. The plotters involved Ugaki in a weird plan to seize the Diet and declare himself military dictator; the plan was never intended to be effected, but it was sufficient to incriminate Ugaki as disloyal to the Emperor. He was removed as war minister and appointed to the politically harmless position of governor general of Korea. Intimidation of Army moderates around Ugaki opened the way for militants to proceed with plans for the conquest of Manchuria.

MATSUOKA YOSUKE (1880–1946). American-educated diplomat, foreign minister who negotiated non-aggression pacts with both Germany and Russia and whose indecision concerning policies and intentions toward the United States led to his replacement in July 1941.

MAY FIFTEENTH INCIDENT (*Go-ichi-go Jiken*). Japanese designation for the threatened coup d'etat which resulted in the assassination of Prime Minister Inukai on May 15, 1932. The assassination, promoted by the EMPEROR'S CABAL and by the ELEVEN CLUB because of Inukai's opposition to substantial budget increases for the military, was the final act in the so-called TRIPLE INTRIGUE; in effect, it ended government by political party in Japan.

MAZAKI JINZABURO (1876–1956). Army officer, protégé of Emperor Taisho, military academy classmate of ARAKI SADAO and HONJO SHIGERU. Noted for his loyalty and blunt honesty, he was put in charge of the 1st Regiment of the Imperial Guards in July 1921 during the delicate months of Crown Prince Hirohito's absence in Europe. He later became the leader of the IMPERIAL WAY GROUP in the EMPEROR'S CABAL. In 1931 he and his followers supported the war ministership of the urbane Strike-North leader Araki Sadao. Between 1932 and 1935, first as vice chief of staff, then as inspector general of military education, Mazaki feuded with Prince HIGASHI-KUNI and repeatedly criticized palace policy making. In the summer of 1935 Chief of Staff Prince KANIN openly required him to resign as inspector general. As a consequence the schism deepened in the Emperor's Cabal and finally had to be dealt with in the bloody confrontation of the FEBRUARY MUTINY. After the mutiny Mazaki was interrogated for months by the secret police, refused to admit any guilt, went on a hunger strike, and was finally acquitted. He withdrew from public life and spent most of his last twenty years puttering about his ancestral estate on the island of Kyushu.

MEIJI, Emperor (1852–1912). Son of Emperor KOMEI, he completed the overthrow of the TOKUGAWA shogunate and effected the restoration of direct rule by the imperial house. During his reign Shinto was established as the state religion, industrialization and foreign trade were entrusted to the ZAIBATSU, and the buildup of the Imperial Army and Navy was climaxed by victory in the Russo-Japanese War of 1904–05. Meiji was succeeded by his son Yoshihito, Emperor TAISHO.

MIKASA, Prince (1915–   ). Third brother of Hirohito, Army officer, patron of TSUJI MASANOBU. After matriculating at the military academy in 1934, he specialized in tanks and graduated in 1936. He remained attached to the tactical communications headquarters of the cavalry throughout most of the war years. In 1944, as an associate member of the PEACE FACTION, he accepted a desk in the Office of Military Education to work with other junior officers who had been his classmates. In August 1945 a group of his charges staged the abortive palace coup on the night of surrender. During the Occupation he went back to school and became an "anthropologist" specializing in the ancient tombs of Babylon, Egypt, and Japan. He became known as the nonconformist of the imperial family, fond of wearing sports jackets and given to open-minded discussion of republican and proletarian views.

MILITARY ACADEMY PLOT (*Shikan-gakko Jiken*). Plan for an armed uprising in Tokyo, intended to arouse the Emperor to "renovate the nation," devised in November 1934 by a group of cadets at the military academy with the backing of Army staff officers who were partisans of former War Minister ARAKI SADAO and the STRIKE-NORTH FACTION. The plot was disclosed to the War Ministry by STRIKE-SOUTH FACTION spies in the academy—notably TSUJI MASANOBU—and its cadet leaders were put under arrest. However, the plans of the plotters were to become the basis for the FEBRUARY MUTINY in 1936.

MISTY LAGOON AIR DEVELOPMENT STATION. Naval air force training station, established under the command of YAMAMOTO ISOROKU, on Kasumi-ga-Ura, the Misty Lagoon, 30 miles northeast of Tokyo. Its function was to train Navy pilots in torpedo-bombing techniques in preparation for aircraft-carrier operations. A group of Misty Lagoon fliers assassinated Prime Minister Inukai during the MAY FIFTEENTH INCIDENT.

NAGATA TETSUZAN (1883–1935). Army officer who assumed leader-ship of the EMPEROR's CABAL in the 1920's and came to be known as the first of the THREE CROWS. As a major general in 1932 he headed the Intelligence Department of the Army General Staff, then in 1934 became chief of the Military Affairs Bureau in the War Ministry. In 1935 he was assassinated because he was opposed to plans for war with China and because his part in the MARCH PLOT, exposed by Strike-North generals, had grown embarrassing to the Emperor.

NASHIMOTO MORIMASA, Prince (1874–1951). Fourth son of ASAHIKO and elder half-brother of Hirohito's two uncles Prince ASAKA and Prince HIGASHIKUNI. He graduated from military academy in 1896; studied and traveled—incognito, under the name of Nagai—in Europe 1903–04 and 1906–09; rose to the rank of colonel in 1910, general in 1923, and field marshal in 1932. In 1936, during the FEBRUARY MUTINY, he ingratiated himself with Hirohito by his unquestioning loyalty at a time when imperial family councils were divided. In May 1937, on a visit to Tojo in Manchuria, he secured a pledge of co-operation in the planned war with China from dissident Strike-North elements remaining in the KWANTUNG ARMY. He was rewarded in October 1937 by appointment to the remunerative sinecure of lord custodian of national shrines and chief priest of the sun goddess at Ise Shrine. Second to none in the spiritual realm and second only to Prince KANIN in the Army, he continued as one of Hirohito's closest family advisors until October 1945. Then he was arrested and held for six months as MacArthur's hostage during negotiation of changes in Japan's fundamental laws and institutions.

NATIONAL FOUNDATION SOCIETY (*Kokuhonsha*). Right-wing national-istic organization of businessmen and labor leaders, which sometimes applied brakes to imperial policy making in the 1930's. Its director, Baron Hiranuma Kiichiro, was prime minister during the NOMONHAN INCIDENT in 1939 and president of the Privy Council from March 1936 to January 1939 and again from April to August 1945.

NATIONAL PRINCIPLE GROUP (*Kokutai Genri-ha*). An organization of dissident Army junior officers concerned with the Army's role in pol-itics and the conflicts between the STRIKE-NORTH and STRIKE-SOUTH factions. The organizers were in sympathy with the officers involved in the MILITARY ACADEMY PLOT of November 1934 and were to be the leaders of the FEBRUARY MUTINY in 1936.

NATIVE-LAND-LOVING SOCIETY (*Aikyojuku*). Commune of philosophic farmers, followers of Tolstoyan doctrines, which maintained a co-operative located in the region between Oarai and Mito. Prince Konoye and Prince HIGASHIKUNI arranged an endowment for the society in 1930.

NOMONHAN INCIDENT. A major border conflict fought in Manchuria with the Soviet Union in 1939. Though hushed up at the time, it involved tens of thousands of troops and cost the Japanese Army thousands of lives. The Japanese troops who provoked it were soundly defeated. As a result the STRIKE-NORTH FACTION in Japan was discredited.

NOMURA KICHISABURO (1877–1964). Retired admiral, ambassador to the United States in 1941 who conducted the final Japanese negotiations with the State Department before the attack on Pearl Harbor.

OCTOBER PLOT (*Jugatsu Jiken*). Scheme promoted by the Emperor's BIG BROTHERS and their supporters in the Army, in October 1931, to create an impression at the League of Nations that the Japanese government was in danger of a coup d'etat by militarists. Certain young Army officers were encouraged to enlist in a synthetic plot, devised by Lieutenant Colonel Hashimoto Kingoro and Intelligence Major CHO ISAMU, to assassinate the prime minister and members of his Cabinet. The plotters were duly exposed (but merely placed under house arrest), and the government was able to announce its escape.

OHTANI KOZUI (1876–1948). Maternal uncle of Emperor Hirohito by marriage, an early supporter of the STRIKE-SOUTH FACTION, and Buddhist missionary in the East Indies and Malaya. His friendship with the sultan of Johore helped to make possible the swift capture of Singapore in February 1942.

OKAWA SHUMEI (1886–1957). Propagandist and ideologist for the STRIKE-SOUTH FACTION and one of the top operatives in the "CIVILIAN SPY SERVICE." He was a doctor of philosophy (Tokyo Imperial University) and a linguist proficient in English, French, German, Sanskrit, Arabic, and several other languages. He worked as an intelligence agent in China for the Army General Staff from 1911 to 1918. In the 1920's he was director of the UNIVERSITY LODGING HOUSE. A protégé of Count MAKINO NOBUAKI, he figured in the MARCH PLOT, the OCTOBER PLOT, the BLOOD BROTHERHOOD, and the MAY FIF-

TEENTH INCIDENT. As a defendant in the war crimes trials in Tokyo in 1946 he escaped sentence by feigning insanity.

OSHIMA HIROSHI (1886–   ). Chief negotiator with Hitler from 1934 to 1945; officially ambassador to Germany from 1938 to 1939 and again from 1940 to 1945.

PALACE SHRINE (*Kashikodokoro*). The trio of Shinto shrines on the grounds of the Imperial Palace where Emperor Hirohito worshipped his ancestors and did obeisance to replicas of the three sacred treasures of the imperial regalia: the mirror of the sun, the necklace of agriculture, and the sword of war. Remnants of the originals of the three treasures are housed in shrines in the provinces. The sword, enshrined on a piece of sacred ground in the city of Nagoya, was destroyed by a U.S. bomb in 1945.

PANAY INCIDENT. The sinking of the U.S. gunboat *Panay* in the Yangtze River, December 12, 1937, by Japanese artillery commanded by Colonel Hashimoto Kingoro during the campaign to capture Nanking. President Franklin Roosevelt and American Ambassador Joseph E. Grew protested vigorously, and the ensuing international crisis probably deterred Japan from its planned attack on Hong Kong. (Colonel Hashimoto of the OCTOBER PLOT, a protégé of the then Prime Minister KONOYE FUMIMARO, later became executive director of the IMPERIAL RULE ASSISTANCE ASSOCIATION.)

PEACE FACTION. A group of General Staff officers, diplomats, and politicians who in 1944 and 1945 drew up detailed plans for the contingency of defeat. Founded in 1939 by Navy Captain Takagi Sokichi and Army Colonel Matsutani Makoto in the General Staffs, the group was gradually expanded during the war under the titular leadership of Prince KONOYE FUMIMARO, the active leadership of YOSHIDA SHIGERU, and over-all supervision of KIDO KOICHI. Prince MIKASA and Prince TAKAMATSU discussed its activities regularly with Hirohito at a weekly gathering of the imperial family to watch newsreels in the palace. By the end of the war the Peace Faction's organization included leaders from all spheres of Japanese life, and its planning covered everything from demonstrations of protest at the surrender to planes held in readiness for the transportation of peace negotiators.

PEERS' SCHOOL (*Gakushuin*). Organized by Emperor Kokaku in 1821 (reorganized and named in 1877), to educate the sons of royalty and nobility for roles in government. The school provided Hirohito's formal education between the ages of eight and fourteen; its head-master was General Nogi Maresuke, commander of Japanese forces in the assault on Port Arthur in the Russo-Japanese War. After World War II the school was opened to gifted commoners, and Crown Prince Akihito studied there under the tutelage of an American, Elizabeth Gray Vining.

PRAYER MEETING PLOT *(Shimpeitai Jiken)*. Scheme to blackmail groups of the Emperor's political opponents devised by Lieutenant General Prince HIGASHIKUNI, prominent Big Brother and uncle of Hirohito, in the summer of 1933. The absurd plot—to assemble several thousand rightists in the guise of pilgrims at the Meiji Shrine in Tokyo for prayer and the Emperor's blessing, after which they would proceed to terrorize the capital with a series of political assassinations—was never intended to succeed; its purpose was to embarrass the sponsors enlisted for it by Prince HIGASHIKUNI, all of whom represented interests allied with the STRIKE-NORTH FACTION.

SADAKO, Empress Dowager (1885–1951). Wife of Emperor Taisho and mother of Emperor Hirohito. A strong and gracious woman, she disapproved of Hirohito's warlike policies and made her palace a salon for aristocrats who sought to keep him from going to war and later from continuing it.

SADANARU, Prince (1858–1923). Twenty-first Prince FUSHIMI, four-teenth son of KUNIYE. He was a French-educated apostle of Western-ized military organization for Japan and served as a field general in the 1894–95 war with China and in the Russo-Japanese War of 1904–05. He was lord privy seal from 1912 to 1915, an intimate advisor of Emperor Taisho and one of his group of SIX PRINCES.

SAIONJI KINMOCHI, Prince (1849–1940). One of the authors of the Constitution of 1889, a leader of the CONSTITUTIONALIST PARTY (later he helped finance the ANTI-CONSTITUTIONALIST PARTY), twice prime minister—finally the last Constitutional father *(genro)*. In 1921 he accepted the role of prime-minister-maker, official advisor to the Emperor on the appointment of Cabinets. Until his retirement in 1937 he represented to many Japanese the last liberal Westernizing influence in prewar Japan.

SATSUMA. A large clan in the island of Kyushu, of which Shimazu was the dominant family and Kagoshima the hereditary stronghold. A large proportion of officers of the Imperial Japanese Navy in the decades leading up to World War II were descendants of the old Satsuma clan, traditionally seamen-warriors.

Six Princes. Intimates and advisors of Emperor Taisho, including Sadanaru, twenty-first Prince Fushimi, and his brothers Prince Asahiko and Prince Kanin. They plotted the unsuccessful attempt to assassinate Chang Tso-lin, warlord of Manchuria, in 1916, favored the invasion of Siberia during World War I, and opposed the Choshu policies of Army Chief of Staff General Yamagata Aritomo.

Sorge Spy Ring. Masterminded by German intellectual Richard Sorge the ring provided liaison between the Russian and Japanese governments in the 1936–41 period and in effect helped to maintain peace between the two countries. One of Sorge's sources in Tokyo was Saionji Kinkazu, leftist grandson of Prince Saionji Kinmochi; another was Ozaki Hotsumi, Marxist intellectual and a protégé of Prince Konoye Atsumaro, father of Prince Konoye Fumimaro. Both men remained loyal to the Emperor while at the same time being in a position to assure the Kremlin that the Strike-North Faction would not wage war against Russia. Foreigner Sorge and commoner Ozaki were executed as spies in Tokyo in 1944 but aristocrat Saionji Kinkazu was spared; in the 1960's he was Japan's representative in Communist Peking.

South Manchurian Railroad (*Mantetsu*). A Japanese government corporation formed to build railroads on rights of way in Manchuria acquired in 1905 with the Kwantung Leasehold. Railroad police garrisons along the rights of way kept the lines of track open for the Kwantung Army so that Japanese influence in Manchuria, from 1905 to 1931, could never be denied. At all important junctions on the railroad a Kwantung Army military mission or Special Service Organ operated through local hirelings to keep a finger on local political pulses. Engineers of the railroad later facilitated Japanese Army movements by repairing or laying track across the China and through the Burmese and Sumatran jungles.

Southward Movement Society (*Nampo-kai*). A branch of the "Civilian Spy Service," utilizing Japanese commercial travelers and Japanese emigrants to Southeast Asia. It was set up in Taiwan in 1934, soon after Strike-South General Count Terauchi Hisaichi took command of Army forces there. Information about Malaya, the Dutch East Indies, and the Philippines supplied by the society's agents was used by Army staff officers in 1941 in planning the military campaigns which opened the war.

STRIKE-NORTH FACTION (*Hokushin-pa*). Proponents of the idea that Japan must devote all her military energies to preparing for an inevitable war with Communist Russia. A few of the Strike-North Faction, particularly the leaders of the IMPERIAL WAY GROUP in the Army, had a genuine ideological phobia against communism; many more, however, simply hoped that by turning Japanese belligerence against Russia, Japan could remain on friendly terms with the West. These pacifists in war paint included some of the noisiest CONSTITUTIONALIST PARTY politicians who spoke for a Strike North in the Diet.

STRIKE-SOUTH FACTION (*Nampo-ha*). The minority in the Japanese establishment which dared, under the leadership of Hirohito, to insist upon a national policy of expansion into the rich lands of Southeast Asia and Indonesia, thereby incurring the antagonism of the colonial Western powers, The Netherlands, France, Great Britain, and the United States. Historically the first advocates of a Strike South were the lords of the SATSUMA clan and their in-law allies at Court, the imperial branch family of FUSHIMI, with which Hirohito allied himself by his marriage to Empress Nagako in 1924. Satsuma-clan and Fushimi-family kinsmen dominated the Japanese Imperial Navy which carried out the Strike South in 1941 and 1942. In the Army the CONTROL CLIQUE in the EMPEROR'S CABAL fought for the Strike South against the IMPERIAL WAY GROUP. They were backed by industrialists who had foreign trade interests in Indonesia and the South Seas and by priests of the imperial family who believed that Emperor Jimmu, the progenitor of the imperial line, had come from the south. Most important, they were supported by Hirohito himself, who saw no profit for empire building except in the islands of the south where there were rubber, oil, and room for colonists.

SUGIYAMA HAJIME (1880–1945). Army officer, protégé of Prince KANIN, a senior member of the EMPEROR'S CABAL, nicknamed "Bathroom Door" for his noncommittal facial expression. In 1912 he drew up the first General Staff contingency plan for the capture of Singapore. In the 1920's he handled procurement for the fledgling Japanese Army air force. After assisting in the MARCH PLOT and MANCHURIAN INCIDENT, he rose to vice chief of staff in 1934 and war minister in 1937 during the first year of the war with China. In 1940 he followed

Prince Kanin as Army chief of staff, a post which he would continue to fill until February 1944. From July 1944 to April 1945 he was again war minister. After the surrender in August 1945 both he and his wife committed ritual suicide. A volume of his memoranda written during his term as wartime chief of staff was published in Tokyo in 1967.

SUZUKI KANTARO (1867–1948). Admiral, chief of the Navy General Staff 1925–29, and grand chamberlain to the Emperor 1929–36. Severely wounded in the FEBRUARY MUTINY, he remained an advisor to Hirohito but withdrew from public office. In April 1945, at the age of seventy-seven, he was summoned by Hirohito to be prime minister, and he smoothly operated the domestic political machinery during Japan's surrender.

SUZUKI STUDY GROUP (*Kenkyu-kai,* later *Mumei-kai* and *Isseki-kai*). Army officers under the direction of (then) Major SUZUKI TEI-ICHI who prepared position papers in 1927 urging that North China warlord Chang Tso-lin be disposed of and his province of Manchuria acquired by Japan. The group included ISHIWARA KANJI, several graduates of the UNIVERSITY LODGING HOUSE, and two of Hirohito's aides-de-camp, Viscount MACHIJIRI KAZUMOTO and ANAMI KORECHIKA.

SUZUKI TEI-ICHI (1888–   ). One of the most capable officers in the EMPEROR's CABAL, specialist in economics, and protégé of Marquis Inoue Saburo of the BIG BROTHERS. Having known Chiang Kai-shek at military academy in Tokyo in 1907–10, he was assigned from November 1920 to December 1926 to assist and observe Chiang during the latter's rise to power in the KMT. From 1927 to 1929 as a member of the operations section of the General Staff, he successfully urged preparations for Japanese seizure of MANCHURIA. By 1930 he was closely associated with Marquis KIDO KOICHI and the ELEVEN CLUB. From 1930 to 1933, first as an attaché in Peking, then as chief of the China Squad, Military Affairs Bureau, War Ministry, he planned the monopoly-granting system which was used for the economic exploitation of MANCHUKUO. After a brief stint as head of Army press relations, he was employed almost uninterruptedly from 1934 to 1941 in planning and executing the economic exploitation of China. From November 1937 to April 1938 he had charge of the organized sacking of Nanking. For the next three years he was the leading spirit in the ASIA DEVELOPMENT BOARD. In April 1941 he retired from the Army to become a minister of state in the second Konoye Cabinet and head of the CABINET PLANNING BOARD. In this capacity he mobilized and administered Japan's war economy until the fall of Prime Minister Tojo in July 1944. After the war the Allied Military Tribunal sentenced him to life imprisonment, from which he was released in 1956.

TAISHO, Emperor (1879–1926). Son of Emperor MEIJI, father of Emperor Hirohito. He was not a personal force during his reign; the policies of the period, including Japan's participation in World War I, were largely determined by his advisors, the SIX PRINCES. After 1921, when Taisho suffered a stroke and consequent mental incompetence, Hirohito acted as Regent.

TAKAMATSU, Prince (1905–   ). Second brother of Hirohito, professional naval officer. From 1935 to 1945 he had a desk in the Navy General Staff offices. His intimacy with Admiral YAMAMOTO ISOROKU was largely responsible for Japan's adoption of the Pearl Harbor attack plan. During the war he was closely associated with the development of an Air Navy and the final resort to kamikaze tactics. After the war he was active in the affairs of the Imperial Household Council and such cultural organizations as the Rebirth Society, the Sericulture Association, the Red Cross, the Maison Franco-Japonais, and the Japan Basketball Association.

TAKEDA TSUNEYOSHI, Prince (1909–   ). Grandson of Emperor Meiji and son of Meiji's sixth daughter, Masako, he was one of the ablest of Hirohito's generation in the imperial family. During World War II, as a major, later lieutenant colonel, he served as Hirohito's personal liaison officer to the Saigon-based staff of General Count TERAUCHI HISAICHI. After the war he escaped the financial pinch felt by some of his cousins and retired to his estate in Chiba, where he raised prize cattle and polo ponies.

TANAKA MEMORIAL. A report to the Throne by Prime Minister Tanaka Gi-ichi on the Far Eastern Conference of 1927, a meeting of Japanese Foreign Ministry officials and Army commanders from Korea and Manchuria to formulate policy for China and Manchuria. The actual text has been lost, but a Chinese version, widely circulated in translation in the West, presented the *Memorial* as Japan's blueprint for world conquest. Japanese sources, however, show that Tanaka's report was actually intended as a plea to the newly acceded Emperor Hirohito to pursue a policy of economic rather than military aggrandizement.

TANAKA MITSUAKI (1843–1939). As imperial household finance auditor, PEERS' SCHOOL director, assistant minister and then minister of the imperial household between 1891 and 1901, he became one of Emperor Meiji's closest confidants. During the last decade of Meiji's reign he established a single clearinghouse and co-ordinating directorship for Japan's proliferating autonomous espionage agencies. After Meiji's death, under guise of writing a definitive biography of Meiji, he moved most of the paper work of his "CIVILIAN SPY SERVICE" to a cover organization, the EVERYDAY MEIJI BIOGRAPHICAL RESEARCH INSTITUTE in Oarai, north of Tokyo. When the institute was closed following the MAY FIFTEENTH INCIDENT, he frequented the palace, took too proprietary an interest in Hirohito's sex life, and after his ninetieth birthday was eased out of Court circles with the excuse that he had become stone deaf.

TANGKU TRUCE. Agreement negotiated between Chiang Kai-shek's representatives and Major General Okamura Yasuji of the THREE CROWS in May 1933, following Japan's invasion of Jehol. The province was ceded to Japan and the area south of the Great Wall was declared a demilitarized zone.

TATEKAWA YOSHIJI (1880–1945). Army officer, master intriguer, protégé of Prince KANIN, and a senior member of the EMPEROR'S CABAL. He was commended by Emperor Meiji for conspicuous service as leader of a band of irregulars behind enemy lines during the 1904–05 war with Russia. After serving as an intelligence officer in Switzerland during World War I, he was appointed confidential secretary to War Minister Oshima Kenichi, the father of OSHIMA HIROSHI. During the purge of Choshu leadership from the Army in the mid-1920's, he handled the Europe-America desk in the General Staff. In 1928 he supervised the assassination of Chinese warlord Chang Tso-lin. In 1930 he sponsored the CHERRY SOCIETY. In September 1931, when he had become a lieutenant general, he carried secret imperial instructions to Mukden and closed his eyes approvingly when the MANCHURIAN INCIDENT broke out. In 1939, having retired from the Army, he was appointed ambassador to the Soviet Union and conducted the preliminary negotiations for the Soviet-Japanese Non-Aggression Pact. Returning to Japan in 1942, he assumed leadership of the youth corps of the IMPERIAL RULE ASSISTANCE ASSOCIATION. He died on the eve of his arrest as a war crimes suspect in September 1945.

TERAUCHI HISAICHI, Count (1879–1946). Son of Field Marshal Terauchi Masatake who was war minister throughout the last nine years of Emperor Meiji's reign and prime minister for Emperor Taisho from 1916 to 1918. Hisaichi, the son, overcame an undistinguished early start in the Army by coming out for an end to factionalism in the Army and an unquestioning obedience to imperial orders. He founded the ARMY PURIFICATION MOVEMENT and after the FEBRUARY MUTINY in 1936 he was appointed war minister to purge adherents of the IMPERIAL WAY GROUP and the STRIKE-NORTH FACTION from the Army officer corps. Still the martinet, he presided from Saigon as commander in chief of all Japanese armies in the Southwest Pacific area from 1941 to 1945. His uninspired leadership and harsh disciplinarian spirit was responsible in part for the failure of samurai chivalry during the war years. When the end of the war came he was too sick to attend surrender ceremonies or be arrested as a war criminal.

THREAT OF COUP D'ETAT. Third element in the TRIPLE INTRIGUE of 1931-32. Political activists and espionage agents of the BLOOD BROTHERHOOD and the NATIVE-LAND-LOVING SOCIETY along with a cadre of officer-pilots from the Navy's MISTY LAGOON AIR DEVELOPMENT STATION were recruited by the Emperor's inner circle of BIG BROTHERS and ELEVEN CLUB members to execute a series of political assassinations which were climaxed by the murder of Prime Minister Inukai in the MAY FIFTEENTH INCIDENT. The earlier OCTOBER PLOT had also been intended to give the impression of dangerous instability in Japan's internal affairs, but the Threat of Coup d'Etat was more convincing. It persuaded many foreign observers to be patient with Japan and many domestic onlookers to fear for their lives.

THREE CROWS. The first and foremost officers of the EMPEROR'S CABAL, recruited in Europe by Prince HIGASHIKUNI in 1921: NAGATA TETSUZAN, Obata Toshiro, and Okamura Yasuji, of whom Nagata was to be the most influential. All three were trained in military intelligence and were serving in Europe at Japanese embassies as attachés. Their immediate assignment was to formulate plans to mechanize the Imperial Army and to purge it of CHOSHU leadership. During their first meeting in Baden-Baden, Germany, in October 1921, the three officers chose the ELEVEN RELIABLES. Nagata was eventually assassinated; Obata broke with the cabal in the 1930's in disagreement with its objectives; Okamura went on to become an army commander in China, advisor later to Chiang Kai-shek, and after the war a leader in the organization of Japan's Self-Defense Forces.

TOGO HEIHACHIRO (1847-1934). Admiral in command of the Japanese fleet during the Russo-Japanese War, popular hero of the decisive victory of Tsu-shima Strait in 1905, and later chief of Crown Prince Hirohito's board of tutors. In the early 1930's he became estranged from Hirohito and a sympathizer with the STRIKE-NORTH FACTION. His son Togo Minoru rose to the rank of rear admiral in the war and afterward served as a night watchman at Yokosuka Naval Base, standing guard over U.S. submarines and destroyers.

TOGO SHIGENORI (1881–1950). Career diplomat, son of a SATSUMA clan samurai. He was second secretary in the Japanese Embassy in Berlin in 1920, counselor there in 1929, and ambassador in 1937–38. He was appointed foreign minister in the Cabinet of TOJO HIDEKI in October 1941 and was replaced in September 1942; he was foreign minister again in 1945, in the surrender Cabinet of SUZUKI KANTARO. He died in St. Luke's Hospital in Tokyo in 1950 while serving a twenty-year sentence as a war criminal. He and his German wife, whom he married in 1920, had one daughter; he adopted her husband, Togo Fumihiko, who became consul general in New York in 1967.

TOJO HIDEKI (1884–1948). Army officer and World War II prime minister. He was a protégé of Prince KANIN, who had studied and toured in Europe with Tojo's father, later a lieutenant general. Through the prince Tojo became one of the original members of the EMPEROR'S CABAL and was chosen as one of the ELEVEN RELIABLES. He graduated from the military academy with highest honors and won a place in the 3d Regiment of the Imperial Guards in 1908; in 1916 he became adjutant to War Minister Oshima Kenichi, father of OSHIMA HIROSHI. During the 1920's and early 1930's he rose steadily but inconspicuously as the protégé and shadow of NAGATA TETSUZAN. After Nagata was assassinated in 1935, Tojo was taken under wing by Prince NASHIMOTO and immediately appointed commander in chief of the secret police in Manchukuo. In March 1937 he was made chief of staff of the KWANTUNG ARMY. He became vice war minister in May 1938 and war minister in July 1940. He succeeded Prince KONOYE FUMIMARO as prime minister in October 1941 and took responsibility for leading Japan into war with the United States. After resigning as prime minister, war minister, and Army chief of staff in July 1944, he remained an active advisor to the Throne until the end of the war. Under Allied arrest and prosecution for more than three years, October 1945 to December 1948, he defended himself ably and went to his hanging bravely.

TOKUGAWA. Clan that provided the shoguns between 1603 and 1868, beginning with Tokugawa Ioyasu (1542–1616). The Tokugawa shogunate ended with the fifteen-year-old Emperor MEIJI announced restoration of direct rule by the imperial family and enforced it with the aid of the CHOSHU and SATSUMA clans by defeating the last shogun, Tokugawa Yoshinobu, Lord of Mito, in a battle near Kyoto. Thereafter the Emperor moved the capital of Japan from Kyoto to the old Tokugawa stronghold of Tokyo (Edo). Tokugawas continued to take part in Court life and political intrigue; Baron Tokugawa Yoshichika financed the MARCH PLOT in 1931 and directed espionage activities in Southeast Asia during World War II from Singapore.

TOYAMA MITSURU (1855–1944). Patron-founder of the BLACK DRAGON SOCIETY and leader of the underworld in Japan from about 1890 to about 1936. Discredited finally because of his insistence upon fighting Russia and avoiding war with the Western powers, he yet remained a hero of the Japanese masses and was consulted by Prince HIGASHIKUNI for political advice as late as 1940.

TRIPARTITE PACT. Agreement made by Japan, Germany, and Italy (signed September 27, 1940) in which the three powers pledged, for ten years, "to assist one another with all political, economic, and military means."
TRIPLE INTRIGUE (*Sanbo no sanbo*). Designation for the crucial events in Japanese politics in 1931–32: the DOLLAR SWINDLE, the FAKE WAR, and the THREAT OF COUP D'ETAT.

TSINGTAO LEASEHOLD. Enclave including the port city of Tsingtao on the south coast of Shantung Peninsula in northeastern China, leased to Germany in 1898. Japan took it from Germany in 1914, returned it to China in 1922, and reoccupied it from 1937 to 1945.

TSUJI MASANOBU (1901–1961 or later). Army fanatic recruited by the EMPEROR'S CABAL through the CHERRY SOCIETY in 1930; later mentor and protégé of Prince MIKASA. In 1934, during Mikasa's term at military academy, Tsuji was an instructor there and exposed the MILITARY ACADEMY PLOT. He went on to prove himself a tough, zealous, brilliant staff officer in Manchuria and North China. In November 1940 he was attached to the command of the Taiwan Army to draw up plans for the conquest of Malaya. In February 1942, on the staff of General YAMASHITA TOMOYUKI, he saw his plans come to fruition in the Japanese capture of Singapore. A month later, reposted as chief of the Operations Squad, General Staff, he was in the Philippines where he took part in the capture of Bataan and then supervised the Death March. Later the same year, in October, he was on Guadalcanal directing vain Japanese efforts to dislodge the U.S. Marines. In August 1943 he was reposted to China in charge of secret but unsuccessful peace negotiations with Chiang Kai-shek. In July 1944, after the collapse of Japan's invasion of India, he was sent south to shore up the morale of the Burma Area Army. At war's end he went underground in Bangkok and through contacts in the Chinese secret police was smuggled out to Chungking. There he assisted in staff planning for Chiang's war with the Communists. As soon as danger had passed that he would be tried for war crimes in Japan, he returned home, wrote bestsellers entitled *Underground Escape, Singapore, Nomonhan,* and *Guadalcanal,* and was elected to the Diet in 1952, 1954, and 1956. He mysteriously vanished in 1961 while visiting Hanoi.

TWENTY-ONE DEMANDS. The substance of a bold diplomatic note presented to the new Republic of China by Japanese Foreign Minister Kato Taka-aki in January 1915. China had no recourse but to accede to most of the demands until they could be renegotiated with arbitration by the Western powers at the peace conferences following World War I. In consequence China conceded to Japan the right to occupy the TSINGTAO LEASEHOLD, to build a railroad inland from Tsingtao to Tsinan, to occupy the KWANTUNG LEASEHOLD for an additional ninety-nine years, and to exercise control of Chinese iron mines as collateral for Japanese loans to China. A final group of demands caused such international stir that Japan withdrew them; they would have forced China to accept Japanese advisors in political, military, and economic affairs and to allow Japanese railroad building throughout central China. Twenty years later Chiang Kai-shek's refusal to grant a similar set of demands brought on the 1937–45 Sino-Japanese War.

UGAKI KAZUSHIGE (1869–1956). Army general who as war minister in 1924–25 carried out the plans devised by staff officers of the EMPEROR'S CABAL for reorganizing the Army. Later, taking a moderate position between the extremists of the STRIKE-NORTH and STRIKE-SOUTH factions, he acquired a large following in the Army officer corps and was courted by both political parties as a potential prime minister who might keep the Army from executing its planned seizure of Manchuria. Before he could realize his political ambitions, however, he was compromised by the MARCH PLOT in 1931. Consoled by the post of governor general of Korea from 1931 to 1936, he was rebuffed in a second attempt to become prime minister in 1937. In 1938 he served for four months as foreign minister in the first Konoye Cabinet. After the war Ugaki sat in the Upper House of the Diet from 1953 until his death.

UNIVERSITY LODGING HOUSE (*Daigaku-Ryo*). Cover name for the indoctrination center for junior Army officers established on the Imperial Palace grounds soon after Hirohito became Regent. The purpose of the Lodging House was to educate carefully chosen officers in ideology, strategy, and tactics for the expansion of the Japanese Empire into neighboring lands. Organization and curriculum were entrusted to Dr. OKAWA SHUMEI.

WATARI HISAO (1885–1939). Army officer, one of the ELEVEN RELIABLES, a specialist in Anglo-American intelligence. Assigned in 1932 as guide to the LYTTON COMMISSION, he made heroic but unavailing efforts to show the Commission only the bright side of Japanese rule in MANCHUKUO. He died, a major general, in China in 1939.

YAMAGATA ARITOMO, Count (1838–1922). Army general and leader of the CHOSHU clan. He was the principal architect of the Imperial Army as it was developed during Emperor Meiji's reign. His concepts of military strategy for Japan became the basis of policies pursued by the STRIKE-NORTH FACTION.

YAMAMOTO ISOROKU (1884–1943). Naval officer and protégé of Empress Nagako's father, Prince KUNIYOSHI. Trained in the Russo-Japanese War and later in the naval staff college, Harvard University, and the Japanese Embassy in Washington, he played a leading role in the development of the Japanese naval air force. In 1924 he took charge of the MISTY LAGOON AIR DEVELOPMENT STATION. In 1929–30 he attended the naval limitations negotiations in London. In late 1934 he led another delegation to London where he announced Japanese abrogation of the Naval Limitations Treaty. In 1936–39 he was Navy vice minister, and from 1939 on he was commander in chief of the Combined Fleet. In his last command he planned and executed the daring attack on Pearl Harbor. In April 1943 President Roosevelt had him ambushed and shot down by U.S. Army Air Force pilots while he was on an inspection flight in the Solomon Islands.

YAMAOKA SHIGEATSU (1884–   ). Army officer, one of the ELEVEN RELIABLES. A Shinto fanatic, with great faith in the spirits' inhabiting cold steel, he was responsible for the Japanese Army regulation that all officers must own swords. He was implicated in the murder of NAGATA TETSUZAN in 1935. He sympathized with the STRIKE-NORTH FACTION, became increasingly an embarrassment to his seniors, and was finally discharged from the Army in 1939.

YAMASHITA TOMOYUKI (1888–1946). Army general, the "Tiger of Malaya," who captured Singapore in February 1942. An intelligence specialist in German, he was brought into the EMPEROR'S CABAL through early acquaintance with TOJO HIDEKI and later membership in the SUZUKI STUDY GROUP. Before the FEBRUARY MUTINY he played a difficult part in leading on the rebels, for which Hirohito later sent him a secret commendation. Thereafter Yamashita became chief of staff in North China in 1938 and inspector general of Army aviation in 1940. In 1941 he led a delegation of officers to Germany to meet with Hitler and study *Wehrmacht* methods. Later that year he took charge of the training of the troops that were to be used in the invasions of Malaya, the Philippines, and Indonesia. After capturing Singapore he differed with Hirohito and was rusticated to command of the First Army Group in MANCHUKUO. In September 1944 he was posted to the Philippines, where he directed a brilliant defensive campaign against superior U.S. forces. In February 1946, after a trial much criticized by U.S. jurists, he was hanged as a war criminal.

YAMATO. The name for the early imperial realm in Japan which encompassed the fertile valleys from the harbor of modern Osaka inland to modern Kyoto.

YONAI MITSUMASA (1880–1948). Naval Intelligence officer specializing in Russian. He was chief of Special Service Organs in Vladivostok in 1918–19, the first year of Japan's Siberian intervention. Alternating between sea duty and intelligence posts, he rose to be Navy minister, 1937–39, and prime minister January–July 1940. Although opposed to the war with the United States, he returned to the Cabinet to serve as Navy minister and preside over the sinking of the Japanese fleet from July 1944 to December 1945. Thereafter he gave evidence at the war crimes trials in Tokyo. Because of his deceptively frank manner he was known to Japanese as "the goldfish minister" and "the lamp shining in daylight."

YOSHIDA SHIGERU (1878–1967). Diplomat and celebrated postwar prime minister of Japan. He was a member of the Takenouchi family, which was related by marriage to the imperial family through a daughter of Prince ASAHIKO, Yoshida grew up in Court circles and married a daughter of Count MAKINO NOBUAKI. He was first secretary in the Japanese Embassy in London in 1921 and was in Gibraltar to welcome Crown Prince Hirohito on his way to England. As consul general in Tientsin and later in Mukden in the 1920's, he played a leading part in formulating imperial policy regarding the Chinese revolution, Chiang Kai-shek, and Mao Tse-tung. In 1928 he tried to persuade the KWANTUNG ARMY to seize Manchuria. In 1933 he launched the first political agitation for a STRIKE-SOUTH policy. From 1936 to 1939 Yoshida was ambassador to Great Britain. Throughout the war he served in Japan as a member of the PEACE FACTION. Having been arrested by the secret police in 1945, he was deemed pure of war guilt by SCAP investigators. He then served as foreign minister from September 1945 until May 1947 and concurrently as prime minister from May 1946 to May 1947. He was appointed prime minister again in October 1948 and continued in office until December 1954. Historians generally credit him with Japan's successful accommodation to the Allied Occupation and the nation's subsequent resurgence as a first-class power.

ZAIBATSU. Any large Japanese family holding company, equivalent to a cartel in Western countries. The three great *zaibatsu* in twentieth century Japan have been Mitsui, belonging to the eleven branches of the Mitsui family; Mitsubishi, belonging to the Iwasakis; and Sumitomo, belonging to the Sumitomos. Together with the Imperial Household Ministry, which administers investments for the Throne, these three *zaibatsu* have controlled Japanese banking, heavy industry, and foreign trade both before and after World War II.

NOTES

In what follows I have not cited sources for personnel information or for conclusions drawn from knowing the employment and whereabouts of my characters at a given moment. I have collected this information little by little in my own card files. I have transcribed much of it from manuscript materials ("Notebooks" and "Personnel Records") lent to me by Hata Ikuhiko. Some I have filled in from casual references in the Japanese literature. The rest is available in the personnel records or lists of officeholders reproduced in the appendices of Harada's memoirs, of *Taiheiyo senso e no michi*, and of Hata's *Gun fuashizumu* and *Nichu senso*. A little personnel information may also be found in the annual *Daijin-mei jiten* [Dictionary of Illustrious Men] published by Heibon-sha; in *Who's Who in Japan*, published biennially from 1912 to 1944; and in IPS Document 1606.

The numbers at the beginning of Notes refer to page numbers in the text. Unnumbered notes following refer to material on the page as specified.

1. Rape of Nanking

There are no general accounts of this unchronicled but notorious episode in history. Except as specifically noted, my account follows Hata, *Nichu senso-shi*, 280–86, for military details; Timperley, *Japanese Terror in China*, and Hsu, *War Conduct of the Japanese*, for atrocity details; *Asahi* (both eds.) and the "Personnel Records" of Army, Navy, and Foreign Ministry officers compiled by Hata for comings and goings at the front. The Shimada and Usui volumes of *Gendai-shi shiryo* provide most of the extant Army documentation; Kido, *Nikki*, provides most of the insight into "the Center." I have chosen between minor textual differences in Timperley and Hsu by reference to papers at the National War Memorial in Canberra which appear to be mimeographed copies of original letters written by Western observers in Nanking during the rape. Many observers gave testimony and affidavits to the International Military Tribunal for the Far East (IMTFE).

I am indebted to Penelope Bergamini, Valle Fay, and Sharon Corsiglia for their assistance in the preparation of these citations.

From its "Proceedings" (microfilm, Yale Law School Library) I have consulted pp. 2624 ff., Minor S. Bates; pp. 4460 ff., George A. Fitch; pp. 3900 ff., John Magee; pp. 4470 ff., James McCallum; pp. 4450 ff., Lewis S. C. Smythe; and pp. 2527 ff., Robert O. Wilson. The notes of German observers John H. D. Rabe and General Alexander Ernst von Falkenhausen (Library of Congress microfilm WT5, pp. 4459–69) provided most useful and dispassionate corroboration of the Americans' accounts. In addition to specifically cited sources I have consulted: Ando, "Sense to kazoku"; Chamberlain; Hashimoto Kingoro, "Iwazumogana no shirushi" [A Record of Matters Better Left Unsaid], *Jinbutsu Orai*, March, 1966; Hata, "Higeki," in *Himerareta Showa-shi*; Imai Seiichi, "Misshitsu"; Ito Takeo; Nakano; *Taiheiyo senso e no michi*, 3; Harold S. Quigley, *Far Eastern War, 1937-1941* (Boston: World Peace Foundation, 1942); Yabe; and Yokoyama Taketsune, *Matsui Taisho den* [General Matsui's Story] (Tokyo: Kakko-sha, 1938).

6 A Japanese private . . . into the bushes to urinate: Morishima, 131.

7 Hirohito had directed his General Staff; see *Taiheiyo senso*, 8:214–16, also Chs. 17–19 of work in hand. All Japanese Army operation plans were drawn up in the offices of the General Staff and were personally approved by Hirohito. Then they were forwarded to commanders in the field with specific directions—also approved by Hirohito—defining the latitude for personal initiative which would be tolerated on the part of officers at the front; Gen. Seijima Ryuji, IMTFE "Proceedings," 8111 ff.

War with China part of the national program: see Chs. 5, 6.

By the 1920's, Hirohito had decided: my interpretation of the events recorded in Chs. 7–9.

Chiang ceased to co-operate before 1930; see Suzuki Tei-ichi in *Himerareta*, 20–25.

8 Matsui's visit to Emperor: *Asahi*, Aug. 16, 1937. Details of palace protocol from Honjo and Kido, *Nikki*; palace interior and grounds, Terry and Vining. I discussed Matsui's feelings and opinions with his relative, the priestess at Atami, and have drawn on accounts of his personality by Ito Kanejiro and Abend, *Life in China*.

10 A great honor for Matsui: Ito Kanejiro, 1:209, gives a circumspect but revealing discussion of Matsui's character.

Matsui's plots to prevent war: Harada, 6:62, and interview with former colonel in the secret police.

11 Matsui a devout Buddhist: Abend, *Life in China*, 268–85.

12 Matsui to Konoye: *Konoye Memoirs*, 320 (passage referred to here is in penciled notes or rough draft written by Konoye's secretary Ushiba Tomohiko, some years after 1937); see also Suda, 110 ff.

Chiang saved his best troops: he used over 400,000 men at Shanghai; Liu, 198.

13 Prince Higashikuni as head of Army Air Force: *Asahi*, Aug. 14, 1937; also June 9, 1937.

14 Five divisions: (the 9th, 13th, 101st, 3d, 11th); U.S. Army Forces Far East, *Japanese Monograph* No. 7, 12–14.

15 Grand Imperial Headquarters: Imai Sei-ichi, "Misshitsu," 78 ff.; Usui, *Gendai-shi*, 9:384; see also Crowley, 356–57.

Ishiwara and plans for Manchuria: see his entry in *Nihon jinbutsu-shi taikei* [Japan Biographical Outlines] (Tokyo: Asakura Shobo, 1960).

Toa Renmei: Fujimoto, 187.

Koa Domei, ibid.

16 Shimomura Sadamu and drive on Nanking: for his own version, see Usui, *Gendai-shi*, 9:379 ff.

Pledged themselves to Hirohito personally: see Ch. 7.

Two young officers: Col. Muto Akira and Lt. Col. Kimihira Masatake. They had been chiefs of Operations Section and Operations Squad in the Army General Staff; they now became vice chief of staff and assistant vice chief to Gen. Matsui. See Hata, *Nichu*, appendices.

Suzuki attached to 16th Div.: November 1, 1937, IMTFE "Proceedings," 2355; Hata, *Nichu*, 362, and *Gun fuashizumu*, 351. This was an odd posting, for the orders reproduced in Shimada, *Gendai-shi*, 8, show that the 16th Div. already had a Col. Nakasawa as its chief of staff. He was a former Army medical school instructor, *Rikugun jitsueki teinen meibo* Sept. 1929, 255. Nakasawa was described simply by retired Lt. Gen. Fujisawa Shigezo as "a torturer" (interview).

Suzuki one of Army men whom Hirohito relied on most: Kido, *Nikki*, and Harada, *passim*.

17 Testimony on Suzuki's trips to war front: Lt. Gen. Fujisawa Shigezo (interview) remembers seeing him in Shanghai; Suzuki himself implied to IMTFE that he never left Kyoto, "Proceed-

ings," 35172 ff. Repeated inquiries by me in Kyoto veterans' circles in 1965–66 failed to turn up anyone who remembered seeing Suzuki in Kyoto in 1937. For the staff of the Kyoto headquarters of the 16th Div. under Lt. Gen. Nakaoka Yataka, see Usui, *Gendai-shi*, 9:213.

Suzuki as intermediary: interview with retired major general, privileged source. See also Usui, *Gendai-shi*, 9:308.

Hirohito's rescript: IMTFE, "Judgment," ch. 5, part B, 700–701.

18 In late October a second flotilla: Hirohito's orders to Lt. Gen. Yanagawa dated Oct. 20, Usui, *Gendai-shi*, 9:213.

Half the men purged from the army: Matsui, interrogation March 8, 1946, IMTFE, "Proceedings," 3460.

19 Yanagawa quoted: letter dated Oct. 7, 1937. The Japanese text: *Kimi yasunze yo sudeni sugitari sanzu no kawa tenkoku no mon o hiraku mokusho no ma.*

Morning of November 5: this and two paragraphs following based on Hata, *Nichu*, pp. 282 ff., supplemented by Ito Kanejiro, 1:33, 38, 57–59; 2:110 ff.; and Moritaka, 5:41–43.

Yanagawa's *tanka*: Ito Kanejiro, 1:59: *Asagiri no/mada hare-yaranu/sono naka ni/kyujippun no/machi-tosakana./ /Okimi no/makase no manimani/yukumichi ni/kyo no nagame wa/tada namida nari.*

20 Advertising balloons: *Taiheiyo senso* 4:32; Moritaka, 5:42.

Provincial Chinese levies: Liu, 199.

6th Div.: a tough unit traditionally recruited from the lowest class of peasants in the Kyoto area; Hata, interview.

Lt. Gen. Tani "galloping off": Ito Kanejiro, 1:333.

British correspondent quoted: Timperley, 72. He was correspondent in China for the *Manchester Guardian*.

21 Nakajima a "hard man": Hata, *Nichu*, 286.

"An expert marksman": quotation from Ito Kanejiro, 106–7.

"Nakajima drank": Tanaka, interview.

"After we broke out of Shanghai": retired Lt. Gen. Fujisawa, interview.

22 Claim of 390,000: Hata, *Nichu*, 285.

Lines drawn on map: Usui, *Gendai-shi*, 9:387; Hata, *Nichu*, 283–84.

Emperor's order: relayed through Prince Kanin, Usui, *Gendai-shi*, 9:390.

Tada's disapproval of attack: Tada was backed by Col. Kawabe

Torashiro, chief of War Guidance Section of General Staff, who was on an inspection trip to the front, advising postponement of the attack in his telegraphic dispatches; Hata, *Nichu*, 284. Shimomura was backed by Muto Akira, Kimihira Masatake, and Matsui's chief of staff, Tsukada Osamu, later chief of staff for Gen. Terauchi in World War II; Hata, ibid., 283–84, 343; Horiba, 109 ff.; Usui, *Gendai-shi*, 9:380.

24 Shimomura and Tada: for Shimomura's account of his coaxing, as told here and on next page, Usui, *Gendai-shi*, 9:387 ff.

First cable to Matsui: Hata, *Nichu*, 343; see also Usui, *Gendai-shi*, 9:392.

Second cable: ibid.

25 Thrust across the Tai-Hu: see Operations Log of 9th Div., reproduced in Usui, *Gendai-shi*, 9:230 ff.

27 Japanese terms summarized: Jones, 60, n.4.

28 Chiang ends negotiations: J. T. C. Liu, "German Mediation in the Sino-Japanese War, 1937–38," *Far Eastern Quarterly*, Feb. 1949, 16; also Dirksen to Neurath, Dec. 7, 1937, in *Documents on German Foreign Policy, 1937–45*, series D, Vol. 1, 799 (Washington, Gov't Printing Office, 1949).

Chiang leaves Nanking, Dec. 7: Hollington K. Tong, *Dateline: China* (New York: Rockport Press, 1950), 31–48.

29 Prince Asaka's attitude "not good": Kido, *Nikki*, 468.

"To sparkle before the eyes of the Chinese": Nakayama Yasuto, testimony to IMTFE, "Proceedings," 21893; see also 33081 ff., 37238 ff., 32686 (Canberra) ff.

Matsui's commandments: ibid., 47171–73.

Asaka's arrival at the front: IMTFE Exhibit #2577 (Canberra), 4.

Nakajima wounded: *Asahi*, Dec. 8, 1937.

Nakajima's report to Prince Asaka: Tanaka, interview.

30 Orders issued from Asaka's headquarters: Tanaka, *Sabakareru* 44–45; see also Harada, 7:152; Ando, "Senso to kazoku," part 2, 86.

Hirohito described: Harada, 6:87–88.

31 Prince Konoye protests: Kido, *Nikki*, 602–03.

Konoye quoted: ibid.

32 Konoye quoted: Kido, *Nikki*, 608; see also Harada, 6:171, 175, for insight into Hirohito's state of mind.

Hirohito's orders to attack Canton: Usui, *Gendai-shi*, 9:222.

Sinking of the *Panay*: this and next three paragraphs based on

IMTFE "Proceedings," 3520–3552, also 21362–435, 3466 ff., 38181 ff.

34 That Roosevelt's message might presage a declaration of war: Butow, *Tojo*, 389, n.46.

Grew and *Panay* incident: Grew, *Ten Years*, 204–213.

35 Yamamoto accepts responsibility: Harada, 6:189; also 183 in which Yamamoto tells of meeting between Navy Minister Yonai and Prime Minister Konoye when Yonai went to dine with Hirohito on December 11, the day before the *Panay* was sunk.

30,000 troops embarked: retired Lt. Gen. Fujisawa, interview; Usui, *Gendai-shi*, 9:222.

Presumption that Konoye sent messenger to Hashimoto: see, e.g., Matsui's explanation of Hashimoto's motives in Abend, *Life in China*, 273.

Konoye's emissary mistakenly apprehended: retired Maj. Gen. Kajiura Ginjiro, interview; also Suda, 112.

Konoye quoted: Harada, 6:180.

Statement drafted by Hirohito's kinsman Machijiri: Horiba, 110; in observance of the imperial taboo, Horiba identifies Machijiri by office rather than by name. That Machijiri is meant, however, is clear from Hata, *Gun fuashizumu*, 357, and *Nichu*, 347. For Horiba's credentials, ibid., 365.

36 "Hate-China" Villa: a typical Japanese pun. The house was known as Tekigai-so or Outside Ogikubo Villa. *Tekigai* written with different characters, however, means "anger against enemies."

800,000 had fled upriver: Smythe et al, 4.

Rearguard of about 100,000: ibid., introduction, i.

Brick walls of Nanking: description of Nanking from J. Van Wie Bergamini, verbal.

Behavior of Chinese troops in Nanking: Rev. James McCallum's journal for Dec. 19, 1937, quoted in introduction to Smythe; IMTFE "Proceedings," 47174–175, 4470 ff.

37 Matsui's contribution of $3,000: equivalent to $10,000 Chinese. Hidaka Shunrokuro's testimony to IMTFE, "Proceedings," 21465; letter of Jan. 7, 1938, from Nanking Safety Zone Committee to Fukuda Tokuyasu of the Japanese Embassy in Nanking, Timperley, 193–94.

Twenty-two Westerners remaining in Nanking: count from Gen. Alexander von Falkenhausen memoranda, Jan. 15 and Feb. 10, 1938, to German Foreign Minister Baron von Neurath, via German Embassy in Hankow, found in German Foreign Office

file of memoranda and telegrams, Nov. 1936–March 1938, IPS
Document No. 4039, Library of Congress microfilm WT-5,
4462–69. Germans: John H. D. Rabe of the Siemans Co., Chris-
tian Kröger of Carlowitz & Co., Eduard Sperling of the Shanghai
Insurance Co., Rupert Hatz, R. Hempel, Auguste Gounan. Amer-
icans: university professors Minor Searle Bates, Charles Riggs, and
Lewis S. C. Smythe; J. V. Pickering of Standard Oil; physicians
C. S. Trimmer and Robert O. Wilson; Y.M.C.A. secretary
George A. Fitch; missionaries Rev. John Magee, Rev. Ernest H.
Forster, Rev. James McCallum, Rev. W. P. Mills, Rev. Hubert L.
Sone, Miss Minnie Vautrin, Mrs. Paul de Witt Twinem, Miss
Grace Bauer. An Englishman: P. H. Munroe-Faure of British
Asiatic Petroleum. Not included in Falkenhausen's count were
two Russians and three other unidentified Europeans. See also
Timperley, 25.

9th Div. on Dec. 9: Operations Log of 9th Div., Usui, *Gendai-
shi*, 9:230 ff.

Leaflets dropped from planes: Nakayama Yasuto, testimony
to IMTFE, "Proceedings," 21895 ff., 47173–175.

Prince Asaka described: *Asahi*, Feb. 24, 1938; date, ibid., Feb. 8,
1938.

39 Nanking noodles: *Asahi* (Tokyo ed.), Dec. 11, 1937.

Spotters in two blimps: Timperley, 24.

40 Y.M.C.A. secretary George Fitch quoted: ibid., 26.

Saké issued to sailors: Hashimoto Kingoro, testimony to
IMTFE, "Proceedings," 3532 ff.

41 Chinese soldiers mingling with refugees: Timperley, 27, 171.

Report written by Gen. Alexander von Falkenhausen: cited in
full in note on page 37.

Fitch quoted: Timperley, 26–27.

Matsui's parade route: Nakayama Yasuto, testimony to
IMTFE, "Proceedings," 21899–907; Okada Takashi, testimony,
ibid. (Canberra) 32738; Nakasawa Mitsuo testimony, ibid. (Canberra), 32623–627.

42 Buddhist chaplains' prayers: defense summation for Matsui,
IMTFE, "Proceedings," 47177–183.

Japanese troops returned as ordered: Nakayama, testimony,
ibid., 47174–175; Hidaka Shunrokuro, ibid., 21448–466.

A dozen Chinese women: extrapolation from Safety Zone Committee complaint no. 211, in Timperley, 162; complaint no. 178,
ibid., 158; McCallum's testimony to IMTFE, "Proceedings,"

4480 ff.; Bates's diary for Dec. 21, 1937, ibid., 2639 ff.; see also complaint no. 5, Hsu, 130, and Magee testimony, IMTFE "Proceedings," 3918 ff.

Drunk and disorderly on a bender: case no. 219, Timperley, 161, amplified by Magee testimony to IMTFE. "Proceedings," 3910 ff.

American missionary quoted: in a letter by Lewis S. C. Smythe, Dec. 15, 1937, Timperley, 19.

Three hundred civilians dead: Smythe et al, Table 4.

Western newsmen plan to leave: Hsu, 160, 162, 164–65.

43 Falkenhausen quoted: his report cited in full in note on page 37.

Nakajima's assignment from Prince Asaka: Hata, *Nichu*, 286.

Muto's "responsibility for billeting": Nakayama; testimony to IMTFE, "Proceedings," 21905–06, 21913–15.

Secret policemen supervising looting and standing guard while soldiers raped women: case nos. 81 and 94, Timperley, 147, 151; Smythe quoted, ibid., 19, 52, 56; also Fitch quoted, ibid., 37.

44 Muto's manpower: Usui, *Gendai-shi*, 9:214–15.

Water not turned on until Jan. 7: Falkenhausen, report cited in full in note on page 37; also Fitch quoted, Timperley, 24.

Magee's film circulated by America First organizations: Tong, 47.

45 Fitch quoted: Hsu, 163.

Men planted neck deep in earth: Tong, 48, confirmed and amplified at my request by Office of Information, Republic of China, Taiwan.

46 Smythe quoted: Timperley, 19.

Army storage shed containing two hundred pianos: Bates's testimony to IMTFE, "Proceedings," 2630 ff.

High officers, including Nakajima: Tanaka, interview.

48 Men "buried" in river clung to reeds for hours: see, e.g., affidavit of Chinese medical corpsman Captain Liang Ting-fang, IMTFE "Proceedings," 3370 ff.

49 Entombment of Sun Yat-sen: Jansen, 1–5.

Col. Hashimoto in Matsui's cavalcade: Abend, *Life in China*, 271.

50 Drunken laughter of soldiers at victory parade: *Showa no Kiroku* [The Showa Record], Nihon Hoso Kaisha [Japan Broadcasting Corp.] (Tokyo: NHK Sabisu Senta, Oct. 1965).

Muto's promise to consider accommodations in countryside:

IMTFE Exhibit No. 2577; Nakayama, testimony, IMTFE "Proceedings," 21899–907.

Matsui quoted (lines 33–38): Okada Takashi, testimony, IMTFE, ibid. (Canberra), 32738.

51 Matsui's press release quoted: ibid., 3510–11.

Memorial service at Nanking airport: ibid., 47183–87, 21901–07.

Matsui's poem: Ito Kanejiro, 1:212.

52 Matsui to his Buddhist confessor: Hanayama, 186.

Matsui quoted on China war: Okada Takashi, testimony, IMTFE "Proceedings" (Canberra), 32749 ff.

Prince Asaka's headquarters then 30 miles from Nanking: Iinuma Mamoru, testimony, ibid., 32655, 32673.

Matsui sent back to Shanghai: Nakayama Yasuto, testimony, ibid., 21907–916; Kazue Sakaibara, testimony, ibid., 32686; Okada Takashi, testimony, ibid., 32752.

53 One of Americans at Nanking quoted: Rev. John Magee, testimony, ibid., 3900 ff.

Thermit and strips of paper: John Rabe, Library of Congress microfilm WT 5, 4459–62.

54 Fitch cited: Timperley, 35.

Chinese soldiers in hiding, not 6,000 but 20,000: ibid., 27, 38; Hsu, 161, 171.

Muto quoted: testimony, IMTFE "Proceedings" (Canberra), 3552 ff.

114th, 6th, 9th divs. withdrawn: Nakasawa Mitsuo, testimony, ibid., 32623–627.

Prince Asaka in Nanking Dec. 25 to February 10: Iinuma Mamoru, testimony, ibid., 32673.

Matsui to Abend: Abend, *Life in China*, 270–73.

55 Matsui to Asaka's chief of staff: IMTFE Exhibit No. 2577; "Proceedings" (Canberra), 47187 ff.

Matsui to Japanese diplomat: Hidaka Shunrokuro; see his testimony, ibid., pp. 21448 ff.

"I considered that the discipline was excellent": Matsui, interrogation, March 8, 1946, ibid., 3459 ff.

Prince Kaya "talked earnestly to second lieutenants": *Asahi* (Osaka ed.), Jan. 20, 1938.

56 A third of the city destroyed by fire: Rabe, Library of Congress microfilm WT5, 4459–62.

57 Summary of economic distress: from findings reported in Smythe.

Nanking veterans' reports, War Ministry's suppression orders: IPS No. 625 Supplement, Library of Congress microfilm WT5, 641–43.

Nanking "the ten-year shame": Horiba, 109 ff.

Japanese spokesmen's claims at war crime trials re Nanking: defense summation for Matsui, IMTFE "Proceedings," 47187 ff.

58 Hirohito's "extreme satisfaction" expressed to Prince Kanin: *Asahi* (Tokyo ed.), Dec. 15, 1937.

Prince Kanin's telegram: ibid.

Hirohito presented silver vases to Matsui, Asaka, and Yanagawa: *Asahi* (Tokyo ed.), Feb. 27, 1938.

59 Three other members of imperial family: Prince Higashi-kuni, Prince Kaya, Prince Takeda II; see *Asahi*, March 8, 25, Apr. 4, May 31, June 20, Aug. 30, Oct. 28, Nov. 4, Dec. 22, 1938.

Matsui quoted: Hanayama, 186. On the night of his execution Matsui said: "I sincerely appreciate the infinite grace of the Throne. It happens that I have come to be sacrificed for the Nanking Incident" (ibid., 255).

61 Four million corpses: my own estimate including more than one million Japanese, two and a half million Chinese, and more than 100,000 Americans (in the Pacific theater).

2. A-Bomb

For this chapter, in addition to sources cited or listed in the bibliography, I have drawn for background on: Ronald William Clark, *The Birth of the Bomb* (New York: Horizon Press, 1961); *Hiroshima Plus 20*, by the editors of *The New York Times* (New York: Delacorte Press, 1965); and William Bradford Huie, *Hiroshima Pilot* (New York: G. P. Putnam's Sons, 1964).

63 HIROSHIMA: details of bombing mission, Amrine, 152–55, 176–79, 199–202; description of Hiroshima, John Hersey, *Hiroshima* (New York: Alfred A. Knopf, 1946); deaths, *Genshi bakudan saigai chosa hokoku-shi* [Collected A-Bomb Damage Investigation Reports] (Tokyo: Nihon Gakujutsu Shinkokai, 1953, 1961), 19 ff.

66 NAGASAKI: details of *Bock's Car* flight, Craig, 75–88, 90–97; description of Nagasaki and details of attack, Robert Trum-

bull, *Nine Who Survived Hiroshima and Nagasaki* (Rutland, Vt., and Tokyo: Charles E. Tuttle Co., 1957), Pt. 2, *passim*.

67 William L. Laurence quoted: Feis, *Japan Subdued*, 116, n.5.

69 N. 1: crewmen of the bomb plane deny it: see Craig, 85–86, description of flight over Kokura, based on his interviews with crew members.

Clear blue sky: Trumbull, *Nine Who Survived*, 111: Nagai Takashi, *We of Nagasaki* (New York: Duell, Sloan & Pearce, 1951), 102, 146; among accounts in Japanese, Gembaku Kokunai, *Hiroku daitoa senshi* (Tokyo: Fuji Shoen, 1953), 330, 340.

71 N. 2: bombardier's two-mile miss: telephone interview, Kermit Beehan; *Bock's Car*'s radio message to Tinian, quoted, Craig, 97.

74 Stimson to Truman, Apr. 25, 1945: Stimson's memorandum in his article, "The Decision to Use the Atomic Bomb," *Harper's* magazine, February 1947.

Truman in his memoirs: *Year of Decisions* (1955), quoted, Amrine, 53.

May 1, Grew met with Stimson and Forrestal, Forrestal quoted: Feis, *Japan Subdued*, 15.

Truman's statement of May 8: ibid., 16.

75 Truman wrote to his family: *Year of Decisions*, quoted, Amrine, 79.

Stalin to Hopkins, "give them the works": Robert Sherwood, *Roosevelt and Hopkins*, 903–4, quoted in Feis, *Japan Subdued*, 18.

75–78 Interim Committee: ibid., 30–40.

77 Scientists' answer: Amrine, 108.

Franck Committee: Feis, *Japan Subdued*, 40–44.

78 Edward Teller quoted: by William L. Laurence in N. Y. *Times* News Service dispatch, Aug. 1965.

79 Navy peace mission: see note on page 93.

Okamoto's mission: for a full account see Tatamiya, 115–42.

80 Navy and Army reports: Butow, *Japan's Decision*, 22, 26.

Kido conceded war was lost: Kido, *Nikki*, 1078–79.

82 "Peace Faction": That the Peace Faction's assignment was contingency planning for defeat is my own interpretation of the evidence. I explained it in 1966 to Koizumi Shinzo, the courtier who had charge of the education of Crown Prince Akihito, and he did not demur. To my mind the salient considerations are as follows: Col. Matsutani Makoto and Rear Adm. Takagi Sokichi

were assigned to work on contingency planning for defeat from 1940 onward (Hata, interview; also Butow, *Japan's Decision,* 20–22, 26–27, 38–40, 83 n.3). Takagi, in particular, maintained close liaison thereafter with civilian members of the Peace Faction (see, e.g., Harada, 8:316–18, 365–69, 379). The civilian Peace Faction leaders, Konoye and Yoshida, maintained close liaison with Hirohito's right hand, Lord Privy Seal Kido, and with Kido's secretary and successor, Matsudaira Yasumasa (Kido, *Nikki,* e.g., 945–47, 967–68, 1005, 1024–25, 1056–57, 1109–10). Princes Higashikuni, Kaya, Mikasa, and Takamatsu were all involved in Peace Faction schemes at one time or another during the war (see, e.g., Butow, *Japan's Decision,* 14 n.18; Coox, 8, 100, 126; Toland, *Rising Sun,* 824; Kido, *Nikki,* 1003–5, 1057–59). They met informally with Hirohito during the war years at weekly palace newsreel showings (Ando, "Senso to kazoku," Pt. 2, 89). Peace Faction members were responsible for creating the postwar illusions that Hirohito was a pawn of militarists and that the Peace Faction itself had to operate in a clandestine manner for fear of police persecution. The first illusion is belied by Chief Aide-de-Camp Honjo in his *Nikki* (see my notes to Chs. 17–21) and by Chief of Staff Sugiyama in his *Memo* (see my notes to Chs. 24–29). The second illusion is belied by such considerations as the following: As *naidaijin* and former *naimudaijin* (lord privy seal and former home minister), Kido Koichi had unsurpassed control of Japan's police apparatus. (In Japan proper, as the Sorge case demonstrated, the military secret police or *kempei* remained biddable colleagues of the metropolitan police and subordinates of the Thought Police or *tokko*.) The Peace Faction held receptions openly and on a lavish scale to recruit volunteers for special assignments (Kato Masuo, 15). By renting space in the Dai Ichi Building (testimony of Okada Keisuke. IMTFE "Proceedings," 29259–63), the Peace Faction shared quarters with local Army Area Headquarters which supervised discipline throughout the Tokyo area during the days before and after the surrender.

Former foreign minister to Kido: *Nikki,* 1206. The speaker was Togo Shigenori, who returned to the Cabinet as foreign minister in April 1945.

83 Mass arrest of Peace Faction members (the so-called Badoglio incident): my interpretation of the evidence. Yabe, 2:45 ff., demonstrates that only Kido could have supplied the information on which the police based their charges against Konoye

and Yoshida. The terms of the wartime relationship between Kido
and Konoye-Yoshida (Kido, *Nikki*, 933–1171 *passim*) make it inconceivable that Kido could have betrayed his friends out of animosity or indiscretion.

Konoye's "diary": published as *Konoye Nikki* (Tokyo: Kyodo
Tsushinsha, 1968).

84 "Memorial to the Throne," read to Hirohito: Kido, *Kankei
bunsho*, 495–98. Butow, *Japan's Decision*, 47–50, gives translation from which quotations here have been taken; see also his
note (54, on p. 47) on the Konoye text.

Hirohito's underground retreat: Imai Sei-ichi, "Misshitsu no
naka," 78 ff.

N. 3: Information from several interviews, but see Takeda,
Seiji-ka, 99.

85 THE GREAT BLUFF: this section based on Kido, *Nikki*, as
cited, and interviews with Koizumi Shinzo and another palace
official.

86 Hirohito would abdicate: Vining, *Crown Prince*, 170. Mrs.
Vining, as tutor to Crown Prince Akihito, was living in the palace
in the war-crimes trial period and was acquainted with the Emperor's inner circle.

86–87 Details of palace grounds and interior: ibid., *passim*.

87–88 "The American fleet," Hirohito said: discussion between Emperor and Kido based on *Nikki*, 1134.

88 "The situation is extremely grave": for the basis of Emper-
or's statement, see a joint Army-Navy Report on War Prospects,
Jan. 1945, reproduced in *Translations*, 1: No. 15.

89 He became a willing cog: see Kido, *Statements*, 2:175, "I
perceived that an important resolution was being formed in his
mind, and after that I exchanged opinions with the Emperor still
more intimately."

Kido's poem: *Nikki*, 1167.

Hirohito gave private audiences: The best known of the Emperor's interviews is that with Prince Konoye, and the most revealing account of it may be found in Hayashi, *Nihon shusen-shi*,
19 ff. For Kido's memoranda on seven of the audiences see his
Kankei bunsho, 492–510. I have assumed that in addition to those
seven audiences of state Hirohito also gave unofficial audiences
to some or all of the prominent Japanese who stopped by in Kido's
office during February and March (see Kido, *Nikki*, 1169–84
passim).

90–91 Hirohito's audience with Koiso: Kido, *Nikki*, 1180.

91 Koiso's resignation: for additional resignation reasons see Hayashi Shigeru et al, 2:45.

Kido spent the next two weeks: *Nikki*, 1181–94.

Hirohito accepted Kido's recommendation: ibid.

Hirohito quoted re Suzuki: Matsudaira Yasumasa, *Statements*, 2:418–24.

92 "A peace prime minister": In the officer corps, War Minister Anami was known to have been given the mission of ending the war; Maj. Gen. Nagai Yatsuji, *Statements*, 2:616.

Suzuki "given to understand": Butow, *Japan's Decision*, 67. See also Matsudaira, *Statements*, 2:418: "The Emperor told me after the war, 'I was aware of Suzuki's sentiments . . . and I was convinced that he understood my sentiments.'"

Grew asking for Japan to be reassured: Feis, *Japan Subdued*, 15–16.

93 Home minister, education minister consulted with Kido: *Nikki*, 1197.

On May 1, Hirohito warned Kido: ibid., 1198.

Kido went through family strong room: ibid., 1199.

Fujimura's dealings with O.S.S.: Fujimura, *Statements*, 1:135–58.

94 Pressure mounted on Navy General Staff: for one case of pressure see Hayashi Shigeru et al, 2:128–29.

Prince Takamatsu came to the palace: Kido, *Nikki*, 1201–2.

Prince Kanin's death: *Asahi*, May 22, 1945.

N. 6: O.S.S. dropped Fujimura: Brooks, 133.

95 Fire raid destroyed ministries, ignited Outer Palace roof: Kido, *Nikki*, 1203.

96 Cabinet resolved not to leave capital: Kido, *Nikki*, 1208–9.

Council in the Imperial Presence: Hasunuma Shigeru, *Statements*, 1:295–302; Matsudaira Yasumasa, ibid., 2:417–31.

97 Hirohito, "A concealed clause": Matsudaira Yasumasa, *Statements*, 2:425. In Matsudaira's further statement, note: "The Emperor consistently continued his efforts and scheming, but since most of this was behind the scenes and the matters handled were very minute, it would be difficult to explain them in detail here."

Kido drafted a written plan: *Nikki*, 1209; *Statements*, 2:171–84. Matsudaira Yasumasa, ibid., 2:418, says of Kido's plan: "Among my duties as secretary to the Lord Keeper of the Privy

Seal, the task of submitting intelligence reports to him was particularly important. Both he and I were of the impression that, since the military had started the war, they no doubt had some definite plan for ending it. Since such a plan would be top secret I assumed that the military had kept it even from the Lord Keeper of the Privy Seal. Moreover, the Emperor never discussed matters pertaining to the High Command with Kido."

98 Kido arranged meeting of Big Six . . . confirmed at meeting in Imperial Presence: Kido, *Nikki*, 1211–13.

Through intermediary: Hayashi Shigeru et al, 2:133–34.

99 On Independence Day: Feis, *Japan Subdued*, 46.

Fresh intelligence from Switzerland: Tatamiya, 119–29.

Kido summoned Prime Minister Suzuki: Kido, *Nikki*, 1215.

100 Suzuki Tei-ichi came to palace: ibid., 1216.

Hirohito's private audience with Konoye: ibid., 1216–17.

100–101 Togo-Sato cables: texts given here are based on U.S. Intelligence intercepts which were seen by government officials at Potsdam (texts in Butow, *Japan's Decision*, 130, citing *The Forrestal Diaries*, ed. Walter Millis); I believe the originals (Togo to Sato, No. 891; Sato to Togo, No. 1382; Togo to Sato, No. 893) repose in the Japanese Diet Library among *Gaimusho* (Foreign Ministry) papers collectively entitled *Teikoku no taibei seisaku kankei no ken* (Imperial Policy Vis-à-vis the United States). A fuller translation of Nos. 1382 and 893, made from *Magic* intercepts, may be found on National Archives Microfilm No. 8-5.1 CA, "Translations of Japanese Documents" (vol. 2, no. 9, "Japanese Foreign Ministry Radios exchanged between Togo and Sato from 12 July to 7 August 1945," Document No. 57938). In Sato to Togo where the version quoted reads "Japan is defeated . . . We must face that fact and act accordingly," the version supplied for Document No. 57938 by the Allied Translator and Interpreter Service has, "If it is correct to assume the war situation has taken an extremely unfavorable turn since [the Imperial Conference of June 8], the government must make a crucial decision."

101 Negotiations with Russia: see Togo Shigenori, *Statements*, 4:237–78; Togo, 294–308.

102 Efforts of Grew and others re a warning of atomic holocaust: Feis, *Japan Subdued*, 25–26.

103 "Baby born satisfactorily": reports and reactions to A-bomb detailed, ibid., 63 and note.

Churchill on July 22 to Stimson: Stimson diary for July 22, 1945, quoted, ibid., 75.

Churchill, "was never even an issue": *Second World War*, 6:553.

Eisenhower remembered later: quoted, Amrine, 169; see also Feis, *Japan Subdued*, 178, n. 1.

Stimson, "in the manner best calculated": quoted, ibid., 173. Operational order: quoted, ibid., 88.

104 Truman, "I casually mentioned to Stalin": *Year of Decisions*, 416; cited, ibid., 89–90.

Stalin four days later: ibid., 98.

Potsdam Declaration: text in U.S. Dept. of State, *Occupation of Japan: Policy and Progress*, 1946.

"to us . . . just something to be ignored": my translation from Obata, 7:327.

Broadcast on July 28: Zacharias, 421–22.

105 Togo cable, Aug. 2: *Translations*, 2: no. 9.

"The whole city . . .": Kawabe Torashiro, *Statements*, 2:98–100.

106 Hirohito and Kido met in Imperial Library: *Nikki*, 1222.

Japan's atomic research effort: Yanaga, *Since Perry*, 623.

Kido urged the Emperor: *Nikki*, 1222.

Hirohito to Togo, ". . . tell Prime Minister Suzuki . . .": ibid.

August 8 in Tokyo: for an account of events see "Fateful 8 August," *Translations*, 3: no. 1.

107 "blew Joey off the fence"; *N.Y. Times*, Aug. 9, 1945.

Sato's appointment with Molotov: Brooks, 172, based on Togo Shigenori, *Statements*, 4:285–89.

Lt. Marcus McDilda: his story told by Craig, 73–74.

108–116 Big Six meeting followed by council in the Imperial Presence (pages 111–16): Hasunuma Shigeru, *Statements*, 1:295–302; Hoshina Zenshiro, ibid., 1:480–86; Ikeda Sumihisa, ibid., 1:551–57; Kido, *Nikki*, 1223. See also Butow, *Japan's Decision*, 167–77.

109 "A cruel thing to say": Craig, 148.

110 Anami's career: Hata's "Personnel Records."

Expertise in *kendo*, personal habits: Brooks, 44–45.

111 Baron Hiranuma might be invited: see Miyazaki Shuichi, *Statements*, 2:543.

112 Kido assured Hirohito re Hiranuma: *Nikki*, 1222, 1223.

At 11:25 P.M.: ibid., 1223.

112–113 Hirohito unkempt and haggard-looking: my translation from Oya, *Ichiban nagai hi*, 24.

113 Secretary Sakomizu Hisatsune's uncanny feeling: This somewhat fanciful reconstruction is based on the evidence of the painting itself (see paragraph below, in text) and on a remark by Sakomizu (*Statements*, No. 61476) to the effect that he felt himself already in the spirit world. He redescribed the scene in the bunker often after the war to friends in Tokyo, and two of them, Tony Kase and a privileged source, told me that my version sounded right.

115 Hiranuma, "In accordance with . . .": Miyazaki Shuichi, *Statements*, 2:550.

117 Japan's note: text in Butow, *Japan's Decision*, Appendix D. Canberra cabled London: Australia, "Cablegrams, 1945–1946," No. 225 to London, Aug. 9, 1945.

Second cable: ibid., No. 1138 to Washington, Aug. 9, 1945.

118–119 Byrnes's Note: Butow, *Japan's Decision*, Appendix E.

120 At 5:30 that morning: account here follows that given in Brooks, 215–16, 218–19.

121 Foreign editor of Domei and Navy captain: Brooks, 216–17, also 228–29, based on interviews with editor Hasegawa Saiji.

"a menial belonging to . . .": Brooks, 216, has *reizoku* as the word used by the Domei editor to translate the crucial phrase in the Byrnes note ("the Emperor . . . shall be subject to"); he gives the English meaning as "subordinate to." The word *reizoku*, however, is a strong one, implying vassalage or even serfdom.

122 At 8:20 A.M. Army and Navy chiefs met: Hasunuma Shigeru, *Statements*, 1:295–302.

At 11:00 A.M. Togo at palace: Kido, *Nikki*, 1225; Togo, 324–25.

Anami, audience with Hirohito: Kido, *Nikki*, 1224.

Hiranuma received by Hirohito on Sunday: ibid., 1225.

123 Anami encouraged group to stage rebellion: Ida Masatake, *Statements*, 1:511.

Lt. col. of secret police, Tsukamoto Makoto: see his account in *Statements*, 4:413–17; see also Craig, 139–41.

125 Now did begin, in earnest, to plot coup d'etat: Tsukamoto Makoto, *Statements*, 4:413; Ida Masatake, *Statements*, 1:510–19.

126 Kido, "stricken with consternation": *Nikki*, 1225.

Council in the Imperial Presence, Aug. 14: ibid.

Hirohito's remarks as basis for imperial rescript: ibid.; also, Kido, IMTFE "Proceedings," 31191–94.

127 Anami told subordinates to abandon coup: Oya, *Longest Day*, 77; Takeshita Masahiko, *Statements*, 4:75.

Kido received visit from Prince Mikasa: Kido, *Nikki*, 1225.

Prince Konoye called on Kido: ibid.

Lt. Gen. Mori saw Emperor's chief aide-de-camp: The aide, Gen. Hasunuma Shigeru, gave account of events of Aug. 14 in *Statements*, 1:295–302; Oya, *Ichiban nagai hi*, 82, quotes Gen. Hasunuma, for which I have given my own translation.

128 Gen. Tojo's son-in-law, Tojo's visit to Anami: Oya, *Longest Day*, 156.

129 Difference of opinion between Anami and Yonai: ibid., 155–56.

Emperor's wishes communicated to Yonai: ibid., 165–66.

Emperor emended Anami's insertion: ibid., 166.

130–131 Arao remained to talk with Anami: Oya, *Ichiban nagai hi*, 102–3.

131–144 Reactivation of coup d'etat plans: narrative of officers' actions between 9:30 P.M. Aug. 14 and approx. 7:30 A.M. Aug. 15, including the suicide of War Minister Anami, based on: Ida Masataka, *Statements*, 1:510–19; Hayashi Saburo, ibid., 1:391–411; Takeshita Masahiko, ibid., 4:68–86; Oya, *Ichiban nagai hi*, 104–200 (and English version, *Japan's Longest Day*, 300–350); Brooks, 303–351; Craig, 181–201.

131 A fake coup: This interpretation—my own—of the evidence seems to me an inevitable consequence of the assumption that Japanese, and particularly Japanese in a position to know, behave logically in order to achieve practical ends. The opposite assumption, that Japanese leaders are irrational or that they put up with irrational behavior on the part of their subordinates, strikes me as difficult to reconcile with Japanese achievements. In this case, the behavior of all the participants in the coup achieved what most concerned them: the protection of the Emperor from American prosecution. No single piece of evidence in extenuation of the Emperor has been cited more frequently than his supposed helplessness in the face of the coup that night.

133 Togo reads lengthy postscript: text quoted, Togo, 336–37.

Anami to Togo: ibid., 335.

Anami to Suzuki: Sakonji Seizo, *Statements*, 3:191–98.

134 Recording session: Oya, *Ichiban nagai hi*, 120–21; *Longest Day*, 209–12.

138 A few minutes later Hatanaka shot Mori: Ida Masatake, *Statements*, 1:511, says shooting occurred at 2 A.M. I have followed Ida's chronology except in this particular; other sources indicate that the shot was fired earlier.

141 Chamberlain Tokugawa Yoshihiro: see his account in *Statements*, 4:295–300.

142 Anami's poem: *O-okimi no/fukaki megumi ni/abishi mi wa/i-i nokosubeki/kata koto mo nashi*; Oya, *Ichiban nagai hi*, 144.

144 Last days of Gen. Tanaka Shizichi: Tsukamoto Kiyoshi, *Statements*, 4:410–12.

145–146 Text of imperial rescript: U.S. Dept. of State, *Occupation of Japan: Policy and Progress*, 1946; also in USAFFE, "Japanese Monograph" No. 119, along with Hirohito's exhortations at the moment of defeat to the Army and Navy.

3. *Defeat*

150–151 Kido consulted only Hiranuma: Kido, *Nikki*, 1226–27.

151 Hiranuma's teeth: Oya, *Longest Day*, 320.

Higashikuni bargained with Hirohito: Ando, "Senso to kazoku," Pt. 1; Kido, *Nikki*, 1226–27.

155 "disposal of government goods": Army order no. 363, top secret, Aug. 17, 1945, IPS Document No. 539.

The $10-billion give-away and later Diet investigation: Gayn, 156, 496.

Ishiwara's anti-Tojo stumping: ibid., 67–68.

Tojo's consideration for menials: *Asahi*, Dec. 22, 1965.

155–156 Underground web of clubs and caches: Brines, 104; Gayn, 46, 88, 136, 154.

156 $2 billion sunk in Tokyo harbor: Singapore *Times*, Apr. 9, 10, 1946.

Time capsule on Kanawa: Alan S. Clifton, *Time of Fallen Blossoms* (London: Cassell & Co., 1950), 28–32.

Fears of U.S. vengeance: see, e.g., Hayashi Shigeru et al, 1:84; Imai Sei-ichi, "Kofuku to iu genjitsu," 74.

158 Secret police assigned to traffic beats: Kido, *Nikki*, 1228–29; Gayn, 51.

Sadist Brown and observer Tokugawa: Bush, *Circumstance*, 183, 256.

"flames of burning documents": Kodama, 173.

Destruction of destruction orders: IPS Document No. 539.

159 Empress Dowager's help enlisted: Koizumi, interview.

Refurbishing foreign embassies: see, e.g., Piggott, 367.

Perry's plaque restored: Imai Sei-ichi, "Kofuku," 75.

159–160 Konoye, Ban, and the R.A.A.: Sumimoto, 59; Gayn, 233–41.

160 Munitions factory turned into "Willow Run": Gayn, 212–16.

One-yen-a-year men: Sumimoto, 58; also Kido, *Nikki*, 1222, 1229–30.

Well-born lady translators: Sumimoto, 58; Gayn, 178–79; Wildes, 35.

161 Diehards quieted: Butow, *Japan's Decision*, 223, n. 28; Ando, "Senso to kazoku," Pt. 1, 87.

161–170 MISSION TO MANILA: except as cited, this section based on USAFFE "Japanese Monograph" No. 119, 15–17; Kawabe Torashiro, *Statements*, 2:91–97, 107–8; Matsumoto Shunichi, ibid., 2:444–50; Ohmae Toshikazu, ibid., 3:59; Okazaki Katsuo, ibid., 145–46; Craig, 237–49.

163 Kawabe reported to Hirohito: Kido, *Nikki*, 1228 (Aug. 21, 1945).

163–167 On differences in Allied thinking on postwar policy for Japan: Far Eastern Advisory Commission, A4–9, unlettered appendix; Australia, "Cablegrams 1945–1946"; Feis, *Japan Subdued*, 147–52 and *passim*; Wildes, 3, 71; Price, 2, 187 ff.

165 MacArthur, "something out of mythology": Lee, 178.

167 MacArthur disregarded suggestions: MacArthur, 283.

MacArthur's background: Gunther, 31–44.

MacArthur-Willoughby policy for Japan: Eichelberger, 260; MacArthur, 282; Wildes, 72.

168 MacArthur on the Japanese sickness: Frazier Hunt, *Untold Story of Douglas MacArthur* (New York: Devin-Adair, 1954), 338–39.

MacArthur's proposal to land at once in Tokyo: see Hunt, 395.

169 Sketch of Willoughby: Gunther, 72, 74, 75.

Willoughby's biases: Charles A. Willoughby, *Maneuver in War* (Harrisburg, Pa.: Military Service Publishing Co., 1939), 235.

"shatteringly simple formula": Willoughby and Chamberlain, 310.

Sketch of Whitney: Gunther, 71, 73.

"We blackmailed Japan": Claude Monnier. "Working Paper on Constitutional Revision in Japan, 1945–46" (Ph.D. dissertation, University of Geneva, April 1964), 16–17.

170 "United States Initial Post-Surrender Policy for Japan": text in Maki, 124–32; also Martin, 123–150.

171 Kamikazes asked to kill selves before Americans: Arisue Seizo, *Statements*, 1:69.

Early landing at Atsugi by daredevil: Morison, 14:359.

171–172 Reception at Atsugi, Shinagawa hospital: Kato Masuo, 256 ff.; Craig, 285 ff.; *N.Y. Times*, Sept. 2, 1945.

172 P.O.W.'s evacuated: ibid., Sept. 1, 7, 1945.

Second day of occupation: Willoughby and Chamberlain, 294.

Admirals trying to beat MacArthur ashore: Eichelberger, 263.

172–173 Churchill on MacArthur's personal landing at Atsugi: quoted, Willoughby and Chamberlain, 295.

173 MacArthur landed and motored to Yokohama: Craig, 292 ff.; Whitney, 215 ff.

Yokohama's only egg: Sheldon, 29.

U.S. reporters to Tokyo: Brines, 23, 26; Kato Masuo, 259.

174 Police reports shown to Hirohito: Kido, *Nikki*, 1230–31.

G.I. crime rate revealed therein: *Asahi Journal*, Jan. 30, 1966, 74.

174–175 Considerations of Hirohito: Kido, *Nikki*, 1229–30, supplemented by interviews with Koizumi and the most aristocratic of my privileged sources.

175 Hirohito's threats to abdicate: MacArthur, 288.

176 Hirohito loath to hand over war crime suspects: Kido, *Nikki*, 1230–31.

Kido advised against abdication: ibid.

Higashikuni called on MacArthur: Ando, "Senso to kazoku," Pt. 1; also Whitney, 247.

177 MacArthur waited for Hirohito overture: MacArthur, 287.

Occupation proceeded apace: Eichelberger, 264 ff.

Wainwright and Percival: Whitney, 216 ff.

Difficulty in finding Japanese to sign surrender: Imai Sei-ichi, "Kofuku," 74–75.

On the *Missouri*: Whitney, 217 ff. (an account written by Kase for Whitney, later included in his own *Journey to the "Missouri"*); also Shigemitsu, 374.

178 Shigemitsu began negotiations with MacArthur: ibid., 375–76; Willoughby and Chamberlain, 302.

Hirohito's address to the Diet: N.Y. *Times*, Sept. 4, 1945; Willoughby and Chamberlain, 301; MacArthur, 280.

Konoye to Kyoto: Sumimoto, 131, 185.

179 Official U.S. occupation of Tokyo: N.Y. *Times*, Sept. 6, 8, 11, 1945; Craig, 312–13.

180 Japanese atrocities: see, e.g., Lord Russell, 66, 77, 180–86; John B. Powell testimony, IMTFE "Proceedings," 3268 ff., 3277 ff.

Konoye and Shigemitsu suggested as criminals: N.Y. *Times*, Sept. 9, 1945.

182 Tojo's arrest: Butow, *Tojo*, 446–67; Craig, 315–17; N.Y. *Times*, Sept. 12, 13, 1945.

A 32-caliber Colt: some writers say a Colt .38. Its serial number was 535330.

183 "All the so-called war criminals . . .": Kido, *Nikki*, 1234.

184 Shimada's arrest: N.Y. *Times*, Sept. 13, 1945.

"Government . . . of nonmilitary elements . . . trembling under threats from the Black Dragon": ibid., Sept. 12, 1945.

184–185 Black Dragon: for history of the society see Byas, *Govt. by Assassination*, 193–202; also Jansen, 33–102 and *passim*; for list of its actual members, see Storry, *Double Patriots*, 312–13.

185 Two of the men mentioned had never belonged to society: Kato Genchi, Hashimoto Kingoro. A third already dead: Uchida Ryohei, A fourth, Tojo's victim: Nakano Seigo. Three others no longer members: Hirota Koki, Kikuchi Toyosaburo, Ogata Taketora.

Konoye visit to MacArthur, Sept. 13: Yabe, 2:581; Shigemitsu, 379; Kido, *Nikki*, 1234. Eichelberger quoted: N.Y. *Times*, Sept. 14, 1945.

186 Kido saw most suspects before their arrest: Kido, *Nikki*, 1227–35.

Baldwin on Emperor as junior partner: N.Y. *Times*, Sept. 14, 1945; Higashikuni quoted on forgetting Pearl Harbor and Hiroshima: ibid.

Eichelberger and MacArthur criticized: N.Y. *Times*, Sept. 17, 1945.

187 Suzuki's outrageous lie: quoted, ibid., Sept. 16, 1945.

Willoughby accepted idealized account of Emperor: Willoughby and Chamberlain, 291.

Shigemitsu replaced by Yoshida: see Higashikuni, *Watashi*, 169.

188 MacArthur moved to Embassy and Dai Ichi Bldg. in Tokyo: Whitney, 227–32; Gunther, 52.

Higashikuni's first press conference: *N.Y. Times*, Sept. 19, 1945.

189 Sen. Russell's wish to try the Emperor: Singapore *Times*, Sept. 20, 1945; *N.Y. Times*, Sept. 19, 1945.

Higashikuni's Sept. 20 call on MacArthur: Ando, "Senso to kazoku," Pt. 1, 87–88.

Sept. 25, Japanese allowed to use short-wave bands: Singapore *Times*, Sept. 25, 1945.

Hirohito met the press: Kido, *Kankei bunsho*, 512–14; *N.Y. Times*, Sept. 25, 1945.

190 Headlined the next day: that is, on the morning of Sept. 25 New York time, the night of Sept. 25 Tokyo time.

Palace disavowal of Kluckhohn's report: *N.Y. Times*, Sept. 29, 1945; Singapore *Times*, Sept. 27, 1945.

Hirohito rehearsed for meeting: Kido, *Nikki*, 1237.

191 Hirohito's meeting with MacArthur, 287–88.

192–193 Hirohito's conversation with MacArthur: a composite drawn from several of MacArthur's own accounts to interviewers. The most complete version is given in Far Eastern Commission, Australian Delegation, Interim Report, Feb. 11, 1946. I have also made use of an account of the meeting in the possession of Otis Cary and MacArthur's own *Reminiscences*, MacArthur's final remarks, asking for Hirohito's advice, are from Hirohito's own report immediately afterward to Kido (*Nikki*, 1237). See also Willoughby and Chamberlain, 327.

193 Japanese attempts to suppress Hirohito-MacArthur photograph: Wildes, 77.

Hirohito's glee: Kido, *Nikki*, 1237–38; 1243.

194–198 FIRST QUARREL: this section a synthesis drawn from Yabe, 581 ff.; Sumimoto, 132–33; Hayashi Masayoshi, 266 ff.; Kido, *Nikki*, 1239–40; Yoshida, 64–68; *N.Y. Times*, Oct. 7, 10–14, 18, Dec. 2, 1945; MacArthur, 305; interviews with Koizumi and Tanaka.

198 Occupation now manned by fresh recruits: *N.Y. Times*, Oct. 16, 1945.

MacArthur's disenchantment with all occupation armies: MacArthur, 282.

199 "widespread promiscuous relationship": Sheldon, 120.

Yoshiwara ruins off limits: Craig, 296.

199–200 G.I. encounter like an opium dream: verbal, from a

personal friend who was engaged at the time to his present wife. A very similar story is told by Sheldon, 42 ff.

201 Ando Akira and his Dai-an club: Wildes, 36; Sheldon, 145.

202 Entertainments and investment opportunities: Wildes, 35–36; Gayn, 178–79; Sumimoto, 304; Matsumoto, interview.

203–204 Burma-Thailand railway figures: Wakefield, 176.

Class A Criminals charged with "conspiracy," etc.: IMTFE "Indictment."

Matsudaira felt out supposed criminals: Koizumi and aristocrat (privileged source) have both confirmed this statement. Tanaka Takayoshi, in interviews and in "Kakute Tenno," "Oni kenji," and *Sabakareru rekishi*, has provided a wealth of circumstantial detail that supports the statement. See also Kido, *Nikki*, 1137, 1153 (Aug. 25, 1944, Nov. 16, 1944).

206 Nashimoto's menial chores: Sugamo, *Senpan*, see n. 2 on page 1345, Epilogue; Kurzman, 246.

206–207 Kido's last month of freedom: *Nikki*, 1238–57.

207 Trip to Ise: ibid.; also Kido, *Kankei bunsho*, 139–40. In the latter Kido thought it good that the elderly spectators sat instead of kneeling in the prewar fashion. "The ties of the imperial family are invisible," he wrote, "beyond all theories about the problem of war responsibility. People with oxcarts bowed. Just before the train entered the Tsu station in Mie-ken a widow held up a picture of her late Army officer husband. I watched her face and thought, 'She is a true Japanese.'"

"I heard the news with a calm heart": Kido, *Nikki*, 1255.

209 Konoye's suicide: Gayn, 30 ff.

210 Kido disinfected: Sugamo, *Senpan*, see n. 2 on page 1345. Epilogue.

"Now that the dead wood has been removed": courtier was Matsudaira Yasumasa, quoted by Cornelius Ryan in London *Daily Telegraph*, Dec. 20, 1945.

211 Vories mission: interviews with William P. Woodard, who had access to Vories's diary kept by his widow, Mrs. Hitotsuyanagi Meireiru; also with Roy Smith, who came to Japan at the same time as Vories and has since taught in Kobe; also Sumimoto, 131, 185.

212 Drafts of non-divinity proclamation: Far Eastern Commission, Australian Delegation, "Interim Report," Annex VII.

Shidehara's final revision: Sumimoto, 135–36.

212–213 Non-divinity proclaimed: Wakefield, 145; Holtom, 219.

213 Hirohito's poem of 1946: I am indebted to Kitagawa Hiroshi for the Japanese text; the translation is mine. See also Wakefield, 144; Brines, 98.

213–218 DICTATING DEMOCRACY: except as cited, this section based on Kido, *Nikki*, 1240–42; Kido, *Kankei bunsho*, 514–26; MacArthur, 300–1; *N.Y. Times*, Oct. 22, Nov. 2, 22, 1945.

214 MacArthur's requirements of new Constitution: Far Eastern Commission, Pacific Affairs Division, "Memorandum."

215 U.S. draft of Constitution forced through: ibid.; Whitney, 248 ff.; Gayn, 126–29.

217 Resignation of fifteen princes: *Straits Times*, Apr. 8, 1946. Wake in the palace: Fujishima, 61.

Imperial fortune liquidated: Wildes, 82; Gayn, 136.

Constitution promulgated: for a complete text and a comparison with the old Constitution, see Borton, Appendix IV.

218 Self-Defense Force: interviews with Tony Kase and Hata Ikuhiko. Officers in the Self-Defense Force in the 1960's include the sons of World War II Prime Minister Tojo; of conqueror and commander in Indonesia, Lt. Gen. Imamura Hitoshi; of Class A war crimes defendant and wartime Military Affairs Bureau chief, Sata Kenryo; of 1928 War Minister Shirakawa Yoshinori; and of wartime P.O.W. administrator, Hamada Hitoshi.

Hirohito at Hiroshima: Brines, 91.

219–220 Differing Allied views on choice and culpability of war crime defendants: Far Eastern Advisory Commission, WC 5–401; see also Australia, "Cablegrams, 1945–1946."

220 MacArthur quoted on distaste for trying vanquished: MacArthur, 318.

MacArthur's wish to limit indictment to Pearl Harbor: *N.Y. Times*, Nov. 25, 1945.

MacArthur asked to be relieved of responsibility for trials: MacArthur, 318.

221 Keenan's character: Butow, *Tojo*, 496: William J. Sebald with Russell Brines, *With MacArthur in Japan: A Personal History of the Occupation* (New York: W. W. Norton, 1965), 157.

Keenan's statements to press: *N.Y. Times*, Nov. 16, Dec. 1, 7, 8, 15, 1945; also Singapore *Times*, Dec. 14, 1945.

222 Keenan's staff: Far Eastern Commission, Australian Delegation, "Interim Report," Annex VII, Report on war crimes prosecution progress, Jan. 7, 1946.

223–224 MacArthur's defense of Emperor, visit of Far Eastern

Commission, and Australian members' report: Far Eastern Commission, Australian Delegation, "Interim Report," Annex I.

227 Agreement on use of evidence by Japanese defense lawyers: Sumimoto, 314.

228 Keenan's star witness and assistant: Tanaka Takayoshi, "Kakute Tenno," "Oni kenji," and interviews.

229 Description of courtroom: John Luter dispatch no. 291, May 11, 1946, to *Time* magazine.

Statistics of trial: Webb Collection, "IMTFE papers covering a series of applications . . . ," item (f).

230 Webb's work and character: see Webb Collection, "Inward and outward correspondence with SCAP, Feb. 1946 to Feb. 1948," *passim.*

Webb to Evatt: Webb Collection, "Miscellaneous Correspondence, 1946–1948," reproduced in memorandum of Sept. 15, 1948, to Maj. Gen. Myron C. Cramer.

231 Comyns Carr on possible suppression of minutes of Imperial Headquarters meetings: IMTFE "Proceedings," 21685; see also 21680–690 in Canberra copy.

Keenan's attempt, Sept. 25, 1946, to exonerate Hirohito: IMTFE "Proceedings," 29303 ff.

232 Kido's diary eight days before Pearl Harbor: *Nikki,* 927–31.

232–233 Keenan's press leak: *N.Y. Times,* Sept. 26, 1945.

Webb's press leak: *North China Daily News,* Sept. 27, 1945.

Tojo's brother arrested: *N.Y. Times,* Oct. 12, 1947.

233–234 Logan in direct examination of Tojo, Dec. 31, 1947: IMTFE "Proceedings," 36520.

Tanaka arbitrates: "Oni kenji"; interviews.

Kido promised the Tojo family betterment: my own conclusion, confirmed by a friend in Kyoto who made inquiries on my behalf of Mrs. Tojo whom he knew socially.

Keenan's entertainment in Atami: Tanaka, "Oni kenji"; "Kakute Tenno."

235 Webb to MacArthur on *Life* article: Webb Collection, "Inward and Outward Correspondence with SCAP."

Quote from Webb's second draft of judgment circulated Sept. 17, 1948: Webb Collection, "IMTFE papers," item (e), 271–74.

237 Justice Bernard quoted: IMTFE, "Separate and Dissenting Opinions," Dissenting Opinion of the Justice from France, 20–23.

Keenan, "the sentences are stupid": Tanaka, "Oni kenji," 278.

4. Imperial Heritage

In writing this chapter I have tried to provide a guide to the Japanese past and at the same time to fit my findings about 1920–1945 into the whole context of Japanese history. For this purpose I have used only materials already available in English, pointing up in them features which seem to me to have been neglected.

For the lives of the emperors I have relied upon Richard Ponsonby-Fane's *Imperial House of Japan*, 28–116, 229–91, 295–332, 369–405; on his *Sovereign and Subject*, 19–84, 93–248; on his *Studies in Shinto and Shrines*, 1–135; and on his *The Vicissitudes of Shinto*, 81–117.

For the wider history of shoguns and people I have depended mainly upon G. B. Sansom's authoritative three-volume *History of Japan*.

For the early prehistoric and semihistorical periods I have used Komatsu Isao's archeological summary, *The Japanese People*, and J. E. Kidder's *Japan Before Buddhism*.

I have found most useful the translated excerpts from early Japanese works included in *Sources of Japanese Tradition*, compiled by Tsunoda Ryusaku, Wm. Theodore de Bary, and Donald Keene.

Other general histories which I have consulted: Storry's *A History of Modern Japan*, Leonard's *Early Japan*, Natori's *Short History of Nippon*, and *A History of East Asian Civilization*, vol. 2, by Fairbank, Reischauer, and Craig.

On specific facets which interested or puzzled me, I found help in Ballou's *Shinto*, Bunce's *Religions in Japan*, Gouverneur Mosher's *Kyoto: A Contemporary Guide* (Rutland, Vt., and Tokyo: Charles E. Tuttle Co., 1964), and Takeyoshi Yosaburo, *The Story of the Wako: Japanese Pioneers in the Southern Regions*. A. L. Sadler's biography of Ieyasu was also useful, and so was Oliver Statler's *Japanese Inn*.

My account of the introduction of firearms into Japan, on pages 268 ff., is based almost entirely on Noel Perrin's "Giving Up the Gun" in the *New Yorker* magazine (November 20, 1965).

5. The Coming of Perry

For the most part this chapter is based on accessible English-language sources which I have not thought it necessary to cite in detail: principally, Sampson, vol. 3, Beasley, Barr, Reynolds, Perry, Heuskens, Preble, Yanaga's *Japan Since Perry*, and the books of Statler and Ponsonby-Fane. In Ponsonby-Fane I have drawn particularly on *The Imperial House of Japan*, 115–29, 281–91, 332–38, 405–17, dealing respectively with emperors, shoguns, imperial consorts, and imperial mausolea; on *Sovereign and Subject*, 248–52 (Tokugawa Mitsukuni), and 252–60 (Iwakura Tomomi); on *The Vicissitudes of Shinto*, 119–21 (the civil war), 248–50 (Shimazu Nariaki), 320–24 (Prince Kitashirakawa Yoshihisa); and on *Visiting Famous Shrines in Japan*, 380–90 (Shimazu Nariakira).

In addition I have absorbed points of view and atmosphere from George Akita, *Foundations of Constitutional Government in Modern Japan, 1868–1900* (Cambridge, Mass.: Harvard University Press, 1967); R. P. Dore, *Education in Tokugawa Japan* (Berkeley and Los Angeles: University of California Press, 1965); Richard Hildreth, *Japan As It Was and Is*, 2 vols. (Chicago: A. C. McClure & Co., 1906); Arthur May Knapp, *Feudal and Modern Japan* (Yokohama: Kelly & Walsh, Ltd., rev. ed., 1906); Joseph H. Longford, *The Evolution of New Japan* (Cambridge: Cambridge University Press, 1913); and Albert M. Craig, *Choshu in the Meiji Restoration*, Harvard Historical Monographs, XLVII (Cambridge, Mass.: Harvard University Press, 1967).

287 Discussion of the House of Fushimi: interviews with Koizumi Shinzo and a member of the Ohtani family, supplemented by reference to Japanese biographical dictionaries and the genealogical charts in the works of Ponsonby-Fane.

293 Prince Asahiko: here and in what follows my account of Asahiko's activities is taken from the brief biography of him written by his grandson, Empress Nagako's brother, Higashifushimi Kunihide.

308 Lord I-i's assassination: here I have supplemented the account in Barr with that in Okakura Kakuzo, *The Awakening of Japan* (1904. New York: Japan Society, Inc., reprint, 1921), 135–36.

322–323 The killing of Komei: Murofushi, 34 ff., supplemented by Koizumi interview and Ninagawa Arato, *Tenno* (Tokyo, 1952), 105.

327 Meiji's birthplace: I am indebted to Otis Cary for pointing out the cottage to me.

329 The crowds knelt in waves: On his own entry into Edo a decade earlier Heuskens, 141, wrote, "an officer shaking his paper fan sufficed to cause hundreds of persons to step back."

334 Meiji amassed fourth largest concentration of capital: Kuroda, 135. Young Saionji teasing Yamagata: Harada, 4:66–67.

338 Origins of the Diet: Fukuzawa Yukichi, "The History of the Japanese Parliament," *Transactions of the Asiatic Society of Japan*, Tokyo, 1914, 577 ff.

340–342 LORD HIGH ASSASSIN: Byas, *Govt. by Assassination*, 173–88.

343–344 Meiji's celibate headquarters in Hiroshima: Akimoto, 291–92.

6. *Hirohito's Boyhood*

353–354 EARLY BABY: These four opening paragraphs are based on an interview with a nobleman of one of the "five families." I repeated the story to Koizumi Shinzo, former chief tutor for Crown Prince Akihito, Hirohito's son. He sighed, acknowledged that he had heard the same gossip, and shrugged it off, saying, "In those days almost anything was possible." For documentary corroboration of the story, see n. 2, page 354 in text.

Since 1758 all emperors begot by mistresses: Ponsonby-Fane, *Imperial House*, 16, 21, 22.

Yoshito's wedding: Baroness d'Anetham, *Fourteen Years of Diplomatic Life in Japan* (London, 1912), entry of that date.

N. 2: see Piggott, 125; *Enthronement of the Emperor*, Futara, "The Life of the Emperor," 47; Fleisher, 21. Also note statement of Ponsonby-Fane, *Imperial House*, 337.

356–359 Hirohito's foster home: Tanaka Sogoro, *Tenno no kenkyu* [The Emperor's Studies] (Tokyo: Kawabe Shobo, 1951), 232–37; Koizumi, interviews.

359 Hirohito's first and last drink: Honjo, 254.

Kido Koichi's lineage: The most aristocratic of my sources gave me this story about Kido's mother. Support is lent to it by *Kido Nikki* in which Kido refers to his mother with unusual respect and to an elder relative of his mother as Chutaro-sama, a familiar given name coupled with a respectful *sama* suffix which Kido accords to no one else in his entire diary.

"Konoye? He was a nice man. When I was at Peers' School, I used to make him cry by teasing him, but I thought he was a very nice man." Higashikuni in interview by Matsumoto Seicho, *Bungei Shunju*, January 1968, 160 ff.

360 Sun Yat-sen in Japan: Jansen, 105–30.

360–367 FELLING GOLIATH: this section on the Russo-Japanese War, except as cited, based on Yanaga, *Since Perry*, 294–300; Hargreaves; and Thomas Cowen, *The Russo-Japanese War* (London: Edward Arnold, 1904).

361 Toyama's visit to Ito: Kuzu Yoshihisa, *Toa senkaku shishi kiden* [Stories and Biographies of East Asian Adventurers] (Tokyo: 1933–1936), 1:705, cited by Jansen, 109.

364 $65 million bribe: Post Wheeler and Hallie Erminie Rides, *Dome of Many-Colored Glass* (Garden City, N.Y.: Doubleday & Co., 1965), 306 ff.

365 Baltic Fleet lost at Tsushima Strait: Scherer, *Meiji Leaders*, 103.

366 Terms of Portsmouth Treaty unpopular in Japan: Yanaga, *Since Perry*, 311–17.

On rioting which made Katsura Cabinet resign: see Harrison, 187–89.

Only Hirohito's Big Brothers exulted in victory: based on interviews with Arthur W. Hummel and Roy Smith who were teaching in Japan at the time.

Yamagata warned war too much of a gamble: Takahashi Yoshio, *Sanko iretsu* [Three Examples of Distinguished Service] (Tokyo: Keibundo-sha, 1925), 90–145.

Ito in Korea and later his assassination: Yanaga, *Since Perry*, 343–45.

367–370 Princely ABC's: Tanaka Sogoro, *Tenno no kenkyu* (Tokyo: Kawabe Shobo, 1951), 232–37; Mosley, ch. 1; Scherer, *Meiji Leaders*, 83, 71–73, 96; Koyama, 87; Koizumi, interviews.

372 Matsumoto Seicho, interview with Higashikuni, *Bungei Shunju*, January 1968, 160 ff.

373 1911 rebellion against Manchu emperors in China: Jansen, 105–30; Yanaga, 348.

7. Crown Prince Hirohito

375–378 DEATH OF MEIJI: Mosley, 19–20; Gibney, 92; A. M. Young, *Recent Times*, 18; my interpretation of Nogi's motives in committing suicide, Kido, *Nikki*, 527–30.

378–383 TAISHO'S COUP: my interpretation, with which the

most aristocratic of my sources heartily agrees. It is usually assumed that Taisho was a pawn of Katsura, but this sorts ill with the wreck which the premature coup made of Katsura's career or with Katsura's social position relative to that of Sadanaru and other elder princes of the blood. In short, because of the imperial taboo I conclude that Japanese have blamed Katsura, when the plain fact of the event is that Taisho attempted a sudden increase in direct imperial power. See Bush, *Land of the Dragonfly*, 93; Beasley, 182; Borton, 251; A. M. Young, *Recent Times*, Ch. 2; Fairbank et al, 559–63; Mosley, 21–22.

381 Formation of Yamamoto Cabinet: Harada 4:334–35.

382 Taisho, Kato, Saionji smoke: ibid., 4:38.

383–386 FINISHING SCHOOL: Tanaka Sogoro, *Tenno no kenkyu* [The Emperor's Studies] (Tokyo: Kawabe Shobo, 1951), 232–37; Jidai Kenkyukai, *Rising Japan* (Tokyo 1918), section II.

383–384 Professors' lectures "bland as *jagaimo*": Koizumi Shinzo, interview, relaying story told by Kanroji Osanaga.

384 Hirohito's fascination for tactics and logistics: this was not generally appreciated until the publication of the *Sugiyama Memo* and *Honjo Nikki*.

385–386 Sugiura's lecture notes: Tanaka Sogoro, *Tenno no kenkyu*, 232–37.

390 1916 bomb attempt on Chang Tso-lin: Harada, 1:11–13.

391 SIBERIA: I have drawn this section from James William Morley, *The Japanese Thrust into Siberia, 1918* (New York: Columbia University Press, 1957), and from A. M. Young, *Recent Times*, 128–42, 177–87.

396 No. 2: Wilson's present to Flower Child: Omura Bunji, 351.

398 Tojo's prior association with Prince Higashikuni: Matsumoto Seicho interview with Higashikuni, *Bungei Shunju*, January, 1968, 160 ff.

399–403 COLOR-BLIND BRIDE: this section based on Murofushi, 158–60, Koyama, 22–35; Mosley, 35–51; Tsurumi, 6:259–261.

400–401 Prince Kuni's enthusiasms: Jidai Kenkyu-kai, *Rising Japan*, section III.

405 Futara to Toyama: Yatsuji Kazuo, in *Bungei Shunju*, Special Edition, 1956, 149.

406 Saionji Hachiro's thrashing: Murofushi, 158–60.

406–411 SALT AIR: Futara, 13–36, supplemented by biographical information about members of the retinue.

411–416 WAR FRONT TOURISM: this section is based on Futara, 36–182.

411 Lord Riddell's observations on Hirohito: Lord Riddell, *Intimate Diary of the Peace Conference and After, 1918–1923* (London: Victor Gollancz), 298, quoted in Piggott, 129. It is Piggott, also, 126, who tells the story about Hirohito and the Prince of Wales.

415 Busts in Hirohito's study: Vining, *Crown Prince*, 114.

Battlefields an obsession: see *Mainichi*, July 9, 1921.

Officer broke his pelvis: Colonel Heusch, *Le Temps*, June 26, 1921.

416 Paris-Zurich-Frankfurt intelligence triangle: Col. Eugene Prince, U.S. Army Intelligence, retired, interview.

417 Hara assassinated: A. M. Young, *Recent Times*, 249–50.

Konoye given advance notice of assassination: Harada, 1:220–21.

Higashikuni organizing cabal: my own deduction, corroborated by the most aristocratic of my sources and not denied by either Tanaka or Koizumi when I asked them about it. For further corroboration consider Higashikuni, *Watashi*, 19.

418–422 Cabal's first meeting: Takahashi, 142 ff., citing Takamiya, *Gunkoku*. Although the meeting has not previously been mentioned in English, I met no official figure in Japan who did not already know of its occurrence when I mentioned it. The descriptive details supplied here are drawn from interviews and from knowledge of Baden-Baden.

418 That week Pétain in Baden-Baden area: *Le Temps*, Oct. 22, 1921.

418–419 Nagata's parentage: Ito Kanejiro, 1:136–38; description of his appearance and that of other plotters my own from photographs.

419–420 Obata's character and attainments: ibid., 1:356, supplemented by Fujisawa interviews.

420 Okamura: ibid., 2:310.

421 Okamura to "historical" section: *Mainichi*, March 21, 1963.

422–424 A FUNNY HAPPENING: the main event of this section, the car crash, is based on *Asahi* (Osaka ed.), April 3, 4, and 7, 1923. For some details and minor discrepancies, see *Le Temps*, April 3, 4, 5, 7 and 8, 1923; also *Illustration*, April 7, May 5, 12, 1923.

424 Hirohito fell out of love with espionage: see, e.g., Harada,

7:234, which quotes Hirohito, in 1938, as saying: "Plots are very unreliable. The general rule is that they will all fail and that when one succeeds it must be regarded as a miracle."

8. Hirohito as Regent

For this chapter, in addition to sources cited or listed in the bibliography, I have drawn for background on: J. Ingram Bryan, *Japan from Within: An Inquiry into the Political, Industrial, Commercial, Financial, Agricultural, Armamental and Educational Conditions of Modern Japan* (New York: Frederick A. Stokes, 1924); Fujiwara Akira, "Ugaki Kazushige to rikugun no kindaika" [Ugaki Kazushige and Modernization of the Army] (*Chuo Koron* 80, No. 8, 372 ff.); Kamada Taku-ichiro, *Ugaki Kazushige: A Biography* (Tokyo: Chuo Koron-sha, 1937); Nakayama Masaru, "Okawa Shumei to no Koto" [Okawa Shumei and His Affairs] (*Nagare*, February 1958); Kurihara Ken, *Tenno: Showa-shi oboegaki* [The Emperor: Notes on the Reign of Hirohito] (Tokyo: Yushin-do Bunka Shinsho, 1955); and Barclay Moon Newman, *Japan's Secret Weapon* (New York: Current Publishing Co., 1944).

425 Hirohito's party: Price, 22; Mosley, 70–71; interviews with the most aristocratic of my sources who was at the party.

426 Saionji's purpose on visit to Tokyo: Harada, 4:311.

Saionji not concerned about "looseness": Mosley, 29; also Honjo, 254.

427 Confirmed in office of *Genro*: Saionji had been appointed unofficially to the ranks of the *genro* by Emperor Taisho in 1913; Kido, *Nikki*, 207; Harada, 4:333–34.

428–432 PALACE PLOT SCHOOL: except as cited, this section based on "Brocade Banner," 14, 23; Ohtani, *Kempei-shi*, 71–72.

428 Social Problems Research Institute: *Shakai mondai kenkyu-sho*; Ohtani, *Kempei-shi*, 71.

429 Purpose of Lodging House: Tanaka MS, "Okawa Shumei hakushi."

Headmastership delegated to Dr. Okawa (assisted by Yasuoka Masaatsu): Ohtani, *Kempei-shi*, 71, and Tsurumi et al, 4:99.

On Makino-Okawa relationship: see Ohtani, *Kempei-shi*, 71; "Brocade Banner," 38; Tanaka MS, "Okawa Shumei hakushi."

Okawa's education: "Brocade Banner," 11–16; Hayashi Fusao, 123–24.

430 Credo published in *War Cry:* "Brocade Banner," 13.

Okawa discovered Kita in 1918: Hayashi Fusao, 148.

Kita's ideas summarized: "Brocade Banner," 12–13; Ohtani, *Kempei-shi,* 71, 89–91.

Chichibu's friend who made edition of Kita's work: Nishida Chikara.

431 Kita's sutra for Hirohito: Yatsuji Kazuo, "Showa o shinkan shita Kita Ikki" [Kita Ikki, the Man Who Shook the Reign of Hirohito], *Bungei Shunju* (Special Ed., Feb. 1956), 148.

Curriculum directed by Okawa: IPS Documents Nos. 687 and 689 give excerpts from Okawa's own writings during his term as headmaster. In one of them he refers to the Lodging House as the "Colonial University." In another, an appreciation of the 19th century agronomist-philosopher Sato Nobuhiro, dated Feb. 20, 1924, Okawa wrote: "According to Sato's belief, the first country to be created was Japan. Therefore Japan is the foundation of all other countries. From the beginning it has been the mission of him who rules our Empire to give peace and satisfaction to all peoples. Accordingly, he has established a most concrete geopolitical philosophy in which the means are expounded for fulfilling Japan's heavenly mission of reigning over the world." Okawa went on to specify the first steps as securement of control over eastern Siberia, the South Sea islands, and world trade.

Col. Sugiyama's comic dance recalled: letter of March 6, 1945, from Harada to Kido, in Kido, *Kankei bunsho,* 630–32.

433 Disaster of Yokohama earthquake: Bush, *Land of Dragonfly,* 140–43; A. M. Young, *Recent Times,* 295–306.

N. 2: *Scientific American,* Supplement No. 1293, May 26, 1900.

435 Yuasa and Osugi's death: Kido, *Nikki,* 507.

N. 3: On Higashikuni's equerry Yasuda, see Kido, "The Circumstances Before and After the Resignation of the Third Konoye Cabinet," IPS Document No. 2 (Library of Congress microfilm WT 6).

Assassination attempt: Ohtani, *Kempei-shi,* 60 ff.; Murofushi, 191–93.

436 Namba's father, and the gun used by Namba: Tsurumi et al, 5:119; also Murofushi, 191–93.

437 Ugaki Kazushige, a man of the people: for characterizations of Ugaki, see Bush, *Land of Dragonfly,* 144; A. M. Young, *Recent Times,* 307; Yanaga, *Since Perry,* 403 ff.

Ugaki as tutor to Hirohito: Tanaka Sogoro, *Tenno no kenkyu* [The Emperor's Studies] (Tokyo: Kawade Shobo, 1951), 232–37.

438 Ugaki in diary: quoted, Takeda, 1.

Princess Nagako studied under special tutors: Koyama, 10–34. Nagako carried a fan: see Koyama, 42.

438–439 Wedding ceremonies: Mosley, 87–90; Koyama, 41–49; attended by Toyama Mitsuru: Bush, *Land of Dragonfly*, 133.

439 "We face a Satsuma clan conspiracy": Ohtani, *Rakujitsu*, 82–83.

440 Ugaki's shuffle of Choshu and Satsuma generals: My account of the Army purge is based on lists of generals who resigned, as given in *Mainichi* at the time, and Hata's "Personnel Records" concerning repostings. For similar conclusions based on independent approaches, see Ohtani, *Kempei-shi*, 15; Kennedy, *Japan and Her Defense Forces*, 104–25, 169–73; Crowley, 87–88; Takeda, 7.

33,894 men and 6,089 horses: Ohtani, *Kempei-shi*, 15.

442 NEW STAR IN CHINA: except as cited, this section based on Ekins and Wright, 16–23; Clubb, 144; Liu, 5–35.

Since 1920 Suzuki assigned to Chiang as advisor: For Suzuki Tei-ichi's experiences in China, see his testimony, IMTFE "Proceedings," 35172–185; also his "Hokubatsu," in *Himerareta*, 23–24.

N. 5: see Inoue's testimony, IMTFE "Proceedings," 35158 ff.

446 Anami's party for Lodging House graduates and their discussion: Tanaka MS, "Okawa Shumei hakushi."

9. *Hirohito as Emperor*

450–456 Hirohito's regimen: Suzuki Kantaro, *Gonichi no ittan*, 13 ff.; *Enthronement of the Emperor*, Futara Yoshinori, "The Life of the Emperor," 47–51; Byas, *Govt. by Assassination*, 300–301, 313–17; Fleisher, 17–20; Price, 17, 19–20.

453 Hirohito met with Privy Council every Wednesday: *Enthronement of the Emperor*, Futara's article, 50; *Japan Year Book*, 1944–45, 7, 118.

455 Emperor's function at religious rites, details of ceremonies: Ponsonby-Fane, *Studies in Shinto*, 1–136 *passim*; *Enthronement of the Emperor*, Hoshino Teruouki, "Ceremonies Throughout the Year," 66–70; *Japan Year Book*, 1944–45, 581–86; Byas, *Govt.*, 313–17.

456 Higashikuni returned "incognito" from Paris after word of Taisho's death: N.Y. Times, Jan. 12, 1927.

Went on to Asia for intelligence duties: interview, Koizumi; cp. Ohtani, Kempei-shi, 563.

458 Chiang blamed troops' excesses on Bolshevik agitators; troops burn consulates in Nanking; expeditionary force halted by Japan's refusal to join: Yanaga, Since Perry, 452–53; Abend, Life in China, 49–50; Shidehara Kijuro, testimony, IMTFE "Proceedings," 1349.

Foreign enclaves in largest Chinese cities: see esp. Murphey, 1–66, on Shanghai.

West had invested more than $2 billion: see, e.g., Boake Carter and Thomas Healy, Why Meddle in the Orient? (New York: Dodge Publishing Co., 1938), 173–75.

459 Chiang Kai-shek's struggle with Communists, climaxed by Black Tuesday and split in KMT: Ekins and Wright, 43–57; Liu, 36–52; Clubb, 135–37.

460 Chiang's government at Nanking: Liu, 48.

Sun Yat-sen's widow went into exile in Europe: Ekins and Wright, 54–55.

461 Tanaka Gi-ichi career and policies: A. M. Young, Imperial Japan, 46–47; Scalapino, 232, 235: Shimada, 53.

462 "I promise to co-operate with Chang Tso-lin": Tanaka quoted, Yoshihashi, 14.

Suzuki study group: Parent organization was the Nagata kurabu (Nagata club), Harada, 9:3. For the study group or kenkyu-kai phase of the association, see Tanaka Kiyoshi as quoted in "Brocade Banner," 22. Later names for the same group were Mumei-kai (Nameless Society) and Isseki-kai (One-Evening Society); Takahashi, 142–46. For other details see Himerareta, 180, and Ogata, 26.

Chang Tso-lin's reply to Tanaka: Shigemitsu, 47.

463 Chang's new policy; ibid., 47; Yoshihashi, 21; Clubb, 140.

FAR EASTERN CONFERENCE: except as cited, this section based on Taiheiyo senso e no michi, 1:289–90; Ogata, 15, 196–98; Yoshihashi, 21–26.

Suzuki's recollections of his address, quoted: Yamaura Kanichi, Mori kaku (Tokyo, 1941), 599–601.

464 Muto-Tanaka exchange: Yamaura, Mori kaku, 636–37, quoted, Yoshihashi, 26; Muto's reputation as "the Silent" (mono iwanu shogun), his obituary in Mainichi, Feb. 28, 1933.

N. 7: Crow, 36–38.

465 *Tanaka Memorial:* text in Crow, 22–112; see also Shige-mitsu, 45–46: K. K. Kawakami, *Japan Speaks on the Sino-Japanese Crisis* (New York: The Macmillan Co., 1932), 145–46, and introduction by Inukai Tsuyoshi, xi–xii.

CHIANG GOES A-WOOING: except as cited, this section based on Ekins and Wright, 58–66; Clubb, 141; Jansen, 199–201 and 254 n. 54; Yoshihashi, 34 and n.

466 Tanaka, "Our government is taking the position . . .": Takakura Tetsuichi, ed., *Tanaka Gi-ichi denki* (Tokyo, 1960), 2:740.

Muto refused to accept Yoshida's proposal to cut Peking-Mukden railroad: Yoshihashi, 30–31.

467 Photograph of Chiang with Black Dragon leader Toyama: *Taiheiyo senso e no michi,* 2:207; see also Higashikuni, *Watashi,* 60. The photo is one of those reproduced in this volume.

Chiang's bargain: Naturally no official source states the basis for the Chiang-Japan understanding as explicitly as I have set it forth here. However, *Nihon gaiko nenpyo narabini shuyo monjo* [Chronology of Japan's Foreign Relations and Major Documents] (Tokyo: Diet Library, 1955), 2:105, does give the record of a conference between Prime Minister Tanaka and Chiang Kai-shek, Nov. 5, 1927. According to this record Chiang assured Tanaka that Japanese interests would be duly respected should Japan assist in the achievement of the Kuomintang revolution; Ogata, 196.

Konoye resigned from Research Society (*Kenkyu-kai*), regarding it as dominated by reactionaries: Yabe, 1:118–20, 154, 168.

468 Col. Komoto Daisaku practiced dynamiting railroad bridges: Shimada, *Kanto gun,* 63.

March 1928 arrests of demonstrators, ultimate disposition of prisoners: Ohtani, *Kempei-shi,* 21–22.

469 Massacre of 7,000 Chinese at Tsinan: Yanaga, *Since Perry,* 455–56; A. M. Young, *Imperial Japan,* 39–40, 44; Abend, *Life in China,* 83. Special Service Organ agent was Nezu Masashi; *Dai Nihon teikoku no hokai* (Tokyo, 1961), 2:64. Hirohito sanctioned plan: Harada, 2:64, supplemented by interview with aristocratic source (privileged).

Prince Kanin's order to disarm Chang Tso-lin's troops: Usui Katsumi in *Himerareta showa-shi,* 29; see also Clubb, 143; Yoshihashi, 37–38.

470 Saionji's emissaries persuaded Tanaka to cancel scheduled disarming of Chang's troops: *Taiheiyo senso*, 1:306–8; Yoshihashi, 39–40, 42; "Brocade Banner," 19–20.

471 Komoto advised of plan to assassinate Chang Tso-lin, accepted assignment to manage it himself: Hirano Reiji, *Manshu no inbosha* (Tokyo, 1959), 79–81, cited by Yoshihashi, 45; Taiheiyo senso, 1:308–9.

Chang telegraphed commanders his decision to withdraw to Manchuria: Watanabe, 89–93.

Preparations for bombing Chang's train: Murofushi, 209.

472 Chang sent "number-five wife" and others ahead: Shimada, *Kanto gun*, 64.

Maj. Giga remained on Chang's train: ibid., 65.

Train-watchers: *Taiheiyo senso*, 1:308–9; interview, Tanaka.

Details of bombing Chang's train: Murofushi, 210–13.

Manchurian guards killed, Russian-made bombs planted: Shimada, *Kanto gun*; 73 ff.

473 Komoto's chief assistant: for Tomiya Tetsuo's career, see Tsurumi et al, 4:297–302.

Escaped Manchurian sentry told true story to Chang Hsueh-liang: Koyama, 98.

474 Banquet, June 13, and six notables at Hirohito's table: *Mainichi* (Osaka ed.), June 14, 1928.

Tanaka's visit to Saionji: Harada, 1:3–4, supplemented by interview with aristocrat (privileged source).

475 Mid-August, Gen. Mine's preliminary report: Ohtani, *Kempei-shi*, 563; Shimada, *Kanto gun*, 73 ff.; Tanaka Takayoshi, testimony, IMTFE "Proceedings," 1945–50.

Hirohito had telephone installed in study: *Mainichi* (Osaka ed.), Aug. 22, 1928.

476 Hirohito never identified himself on telephone: see, e.g., Harada, 1:94–95.

N. 9: Price, 16, and Fleisher, 20, were among journalists who initiated this misconception.

Kellogg-Briand Pact put Tanaka in disfavor with Emperor: Yanaga, *Since Perry*, 463–64; A. M. Young, *Imperial Japan*, 264.

477 Gen. Mine's second report on Chang Tso-lin killing: Harada, 1:5–11; *Taiheiyo senso*, 1:319–27; Shimada, *Kanto gun*, 73.

N. 10: Ishiwara had orders "to use force": IMTFE "Proceedings," 22170–180.

478 Enthronement: for ceremonies, traditions, etc., see *Enthronement of the Emperor, passim*; Ponsonby-Fane, *Imperial House*, 34–69: Mosley, 101–3; Vaughn, 181–90.

Chang Hsueh-liang's character: Kido eventually recognized his strengths; in Feb. 1932 he wrote in his diary, "Chang Hsueh-liang: complex personality, sensitive, cool, merciless, resolute" (*Nikki*, 136–37).

479 Anti-Chang handbill, excerpt: IMTFE "Proceedings," 19151.

Chang Hsueh-liang had Gen. Yang and railroad chief killed: Clubb, 152.

"believing that an opportunity will soon present itself": Vaughn, 118–19.

480 Komoto's memo ("Manmo taisaku no kicho") cited in Ogata, 198.

481 Hirohito's "august face would be muddy": Harada, 1:4.

Kido had worked on industrial mobilization plans: e.g., *Nikki*, 22, 26, 27, 68.

Motive for Kido's trip to America: interview, Koizumi.

Division chiefs' audiences with Hirohito: Harada, 1:8–9.

482 Tanaka's audience with Hirohito and his resignation: Harada, 1:9–11; *Taiheiyo senso*, 1:327; A. M. Young, *Imperial Japan*, 46–47. For insight into feelings about Tanaka's treatment, see Honjo, 160–61.

483 Col. Komoto posted to Kanazawa: "Brocade Banner," 19.

Maj. Giga: Several versions of the Giga story are extant. This one is confirmed by his son, Giga So-ichiro, a professor of economics at Osaka University, who is in possession of memoranda and notes left by his father. I am indebted to Maj. Giga's nephew Uemura Kazuhiko for having put me in touch with the son. See also Watanabe, *Bazoku*, 94–95.

Quote from Chinese Book of Rites: Shigemitsu, 49 and n.

10. Sea Power

490 Shidehara on assuming office: for full statement see *Asahi* (Tokyo ed.), July 10, 1929.

491 YOUNG ARMY GENIUS: This account, except as otherwise noted, follows Shimada, *Kanto gun*, 76, supplemented by Fujisawa Shigezo interviews.

Ishiwara: on his role and character see *Nihon jinbutsu-shi taikei* [Japan Biographical Outlines] (Tokyo: Asakura Shobo, 1960), 7; Shimada, *Kanto gun,* 79; Fujimoto, *Ningen,* 56–57, 67, 195, 203–4; Yoshihashi, 137; Ohtani, *Kempei-shi,* 430; Hata, *Gun,* 155; and Hata's "Personnel Records."

493 Ishiwara's book: it was entitled *The Ultimate World War;* Hayashi Fusao, 261.

494 Last week Kita Ikki had accused: "Brocade Banner," 15.

494–498 YOUNG NAVY GENIUS: Agawa, 3–18, 50–51; Potter, 3–22; Hata's "Personnel Records."

496 Secret naval development plan: Harada, 1:130.

500 Saionji's cautionary message: Harada, 1:18.

National defense question discussed in publication: "Brocade Banner," 26. See also Harada, 1:17 and 222.

501 Saionji opposed to official debate on national goals: ibid., 1:74–75.

502 N. 5: Phone interview with his son, Charles Allen Buchanan.

Japanese delegation dined with Hoover: *N.Y. Times,* Dec. 18, 19, 1929.

503 Yamamoto secretly met by Konoye: interviews with retired Navy commander, Tanaka, Matsumoto; see also Ohtani, *Kempei-shi,* 73–74.

504 Yamamoto and Takarabe acclaimed as conquerors: Harada, 1:54.

"Thank you for your pains": *Gokuro jyatta,* ibid., 1:70.

505 Crowds still cheered for Wakatsuki: ibid., 1:98.

Plan "agreed with actual development": Tanaka, interview.

Memorandum with plan: Harada, 1:130.

506 Ugaki's "sick-down strike": conversation with Tony Kase.

Saionji's tongue-in-cheek note to Ugaki: Ugaki diary quoted, Yoshihashi, 85. For another similar version see Harada, 1:82.

507 Eleven Club: Kido, *Kankei bunsho,* 97.

N. 8: Kido, *Nikki,* 1165.

507–508 Kato accusing Count Makino: I have elided Kato's *cause célèbre,* but see Harada, 1:35, and Yoshihashi, 68–69.

508 Kido-Konoye conversation at the golf club: as reconstructed by a fellow golfer over tea in locker room afterward and recorded and passed down to me through interview with banker's son. See also Kido, *Nikki,* 33.

509–510 Japan subject of intelligence annual report: "Brocade Banner," 22, and Yoshihashi, 101.

510 Three slogans of Nagata and the cabal: see Crowley, 88, 112.

"Scratching your toes": Harada, 1:148.

511 Treaty debate beginning to "vex" Hirohito: ibid., 1:176.

Detailed report on conquest of Manchuria: Shimada, *Kanto gun*, 81.

Too large a naval budget may "cause popular agitation": Harada, 1:210.

512 Killer Sagoya to Tokyo: Murofushi, 223–28.

513 Visit from Iogi Ryozo: "Brocade Banner," 9; Harada, 1:222 and note 9.

"Take good care of yourself": ibid., 1:219.

Hamaguchi shot: ibid., 1:219–20.

Assassin Sagoya: Kido, *Nikki*, 45–46, and Murofushi, 223–29.

514 Field headquarters (at Okayama): Kido, *Nikki*, 45–46.

11. *March 1931*

517 Saionji shocked and confused: Harada, 1:220.

518–519 According to a banker friend: Notes in possession of the banker's family; they were referred to by my informant in order to answer my questions. I have added some details, such as the Pall Mall cigarette, from Omura Bunji. Also, it may be that the attendant who followed him up the hill was his steward Kumagai Yasomi rather than his secretary Nakagawa Kojuro.

520 Saionji's comments regarding Ugaki: Harada, 1:226, 228.

Hirohito during return from maneuvers: Honjo, 257–58.

520–521 Harada's audience with Makino and his statement re Gen. Ugaki's value: Harada, 1:231–32.

To frame him for high treason: see for instance "Brocade Banner," 26.

N. 1: Honjo, 257–58, confirmed and explained by Koizumi Shinzo who heard the story from Suzuki Kantaro.

521–522 THE MARCH PLOT: The most important source of information about this dark affair appears to have been overlooked by Western historians: Okawa's *kempei* (secret police) interrogation paper reproduced in Harada, 9:344–53. Consequently an erroneous impression exists (see, for instance, Storry, *Double Patriots*, 63) that the bombs were returned to the military on March 8, 1931. In reality the bombs were kept by the civilian plotters and used to blackmail the Army until March 8, 1932. In

this highly condensed account, I have also drawn on Nakano, 67–
84; Murofushi, 229–32; Kido, *Nikki*, 147–48; Harada, 2:19, 22–
30, 32, 37, 41–42, 44, 51, 55–56, 106, 111, 117–18, 121–24,
332–35; 4:299, 343, 348; 5:137; 6:14, 22, 78, 261; Ohtani, *Rakujitsu*, 34, 109–11; Hata, *Gun*, 27–31; "Brocade Banner," 28–32;
Tokugawa Yoshichika's diaries as rendered in IPS Documents
Nos. 2582, 2638, 2639, 2640; IMTFE "Proceedings," 1441–1605.

523 Ugaki accosted by Hashimoto: Cho Isamu, verbal, as reported by Tanaka, interview.

"Kemal Ataturk": ibid.

524 Tatekawa's advices to Ugaki: ibid.

524–525 Koiso, Nagata, and Nagata's "novel": Ohtani, *Rakujitsu*, 109–10; see also "Brocade Banner," 28.

525 The story of the bombs: Ohtani, *Rakujitsu*, 34; Murofushi,
231; Nakano, 74; Harada, 2:40, 55–56.

526 Ugaki's meeting with Col. Okamura: Nakano, 67 ff., reveals
that Ugaki met him on January 13, 16, 21, and 24.

N. 6: IPS Document No. 517, citing an article by Iwabuchi
Tatsuo in *Chuo Koron*, February 1946, says that Mazaki for this
offense was rusticated to Taiwan.

527–528 $100,000: Harada, 9:344–45.

The night that compromised Ugaki: Harada, 4:348; Koiso's
"memoirs" as cited in Hata, *Gun*, 29; Ugaki's diary as cited by
Yoshihashi, 91 (a copy of the original is in the hands of Prof.
James Morley of Columbia University); Harada, 2:44, 106, 111,
117–18; conversations with Hata Ikuhiko and Tanaka Takayoshi.

Plot had served its purpose: see, e.g., "Brocade Banner," 28–29.

528 March 2–6: Harada, 9:251; Hata, *Gun*, 27–31.

"This plot was not an ordinary one": IMTFE "Proceedings,"
1627; also 1610–13, and Storry, *Double Patriots*, 62–63.

Ugaki at palace and Makino's promise of face-saving assignment:
"Brocade Banner," 28–29; see also Makino's sly remark, Harada,
2:30.

529–530 Makino-Okawa blackmail of Army: "Brocade Banner," 38 and 28; Harada, 9:344–53; interview with Hata Ikuhiko.
Details of Komoto's mediation and the financial settlement come
from Harada, 9:346–49. See also "Brocade Banner," 31; IMTFE
"Proceedings," 1402 ff., 1418 ff., 1441 ff.; Ohtani, *Rakujitsu*, 34,
and Hata, *Gun*, 29, for some details.

530 Kido's visit to Saionji: based on verbal information from a
source with access to the papers of Viscount Uramatsu Tomo-

mitsu, a member of Kido's Eleven Club. Kido, *Nikki*, 65, states that the visit actually took place on March 10, after Ugaki had made his peace with Makino. That the two visits are one and the same is suggested by Kido's closing note: "Concerning Makino there was some very confidential talk until 11 p.m. Then I returned to Tokyo."

Makino "conducting . . . the March Plot . . . out of darkness into darkness": Kido, *Kankei bunsho*, 3.

Many important fish knew: see, for instance, Harada's raw, unprocessed notes on the March Plot, 9:112.

12. Seizure of Mukden

Two excellent studies have been written in English about the subject matter in this chapter, Ogata Sadako's *Defiance in Manchuria* and Yoshihashi Takehiko's *Conspiracy at Mukden*. In general, I have cited their summaries, which are liberally provided with source notes, rather than give my own citations.

531 A 10 per cent decrease: Kurzman, 110–13; Kido, *Nikki*, 78–80; see also Harada, 2:12, 82.

532–533 Hirohito had before him two plans: Crowley, 92, 107; *Taiheiyo senso*, 1:366–74; Yoshihashi, 137–43.

Began to find and make provocations: for details see Shimada, *Kanto gun*, 97; *Japan Chronicle*, July 22, Sept. 9, 16, 1931; IMTFE "Proceedings," 19195, 19210; Harada, 2:25–38, 41.

533 Regimental commanders at "map exercises": Honjo, 3–4. Honjo's mustache: Fujisawa, interview.

533–534 Ugaki's conversation with Honjo: Honjo, 3, supplemented by interviews with Kajiura and Tanaka.

Ugaki's wire to Koiso: ibid.

Suzuki's arrival and conversation with Honjo: ibid.

536 Honjo's doubts and suspicions: my interpretation of entries in Honjo's diary, e.g., July 16, line 5; July 18, line 3; July 19, line 4; July 22, line 2; July 23, line 1.

Wakatsuki's special report: Harada, 2:9–12.

Chiang's speech and delegation from KMT: Vaughn, 261–62; *Japan Chronicle*, Sept. 16, 1931.

Saionji and the vice chamberlain: Harada, 2:12.

537 Chang Hsueh-liang hospitalized while field pieces set up: see Abend, *Life in China*, 150–51.

537–538 Pair of cannon in Mukden: Shimada, *Kanto gun*,

100–101; Yoshihashi, 133–34; Harada, 2:77; IMTFE "Proceedings," 1990.

539 Itagaki a consummate politician: description of Itagaki's role and character based on Morishima, *passim*; Ito Kanejiro, 1:234; 2:351; Shimada, *Kanto gun*, 75–84; Ogata, 42–50; Yoshihashi, 134–37.

540 Honjo at the Summer Palace: Honjo, 8. He had an audience afterward with Prince Kanin and a call late that night from Baden-Baden Reliable Isogai Rensuke of the 2d Dept. of the Office of the Inspector General of Military Education.

Commanders receive briefing: Honjo, 8–9.

Honjo closeted with Suzuki and Itagaki: this account, from interview with privileged source, differs slightly from Honjo's own, 9, in which he says he met Suzuki and Itagaki the next afternoon, Aug. 4, in his room at Tokyo's Station Hotel.

Secret meeting in offices of General Staff: Ogata, 56. Honjo, 9, reveals that, meanwhile, Minami was dining with him. Honjo met that day also with Okamura, Yasuji, and Mazaki Jinzaburo.

540–541 Minami quoted: Crowley, 109.

541 *Asahi* editorial: *Asahi* (Tokyo ed.), Aug. 8, 1931.

Spokesman asked Harada to warn Saionji: Harada, 2:40–41.

Visit of Wakatsuki to Saionji: Kido, *Nikki*, 96.

N. 1: ibid.

542 Tokyo papers received several thousand calls: Harada, 2:46.

Saionji's meeting with Minami: ibid., 52–53 and 9:123; Ogata, 58.

Emergency meeting: Yoshihashi, 115; Hanaya, 45–46.

543 Tatekawa's talk to his Intelligence officers: Yoshihashi, 115; further information from Tanaka, interview.

543–544 Tatekawa's telegram to Honjo: ibid.

Second telegram: Yamaguchi, 112.

Third telegram: *Taiheiyo senso*, 1:434.

Ishiwara's and Itagaki's doubts: Yoshihashi, 156–58; *Taiheiyo senso*, 1:436–37.

545–546 Honjo's movements: Honjo, p. 21; Tanaka, interview.

Tatekawa's train trip and reception in Mukden: *Taiheiyo senso*, 1:438; Yoshihashi, 158–59; IMTFE "Proceedings," 30261; Fujisawa and Tanaka, interviews.

546–547 At Special Service Organ office: Yoshihashi, 159–60; Fujisawa, interview; Morishima Morito's affidavit, IMTFE "Proceedings," 3004 ff.

547 Honjo at portrait painter's home: Honjo, 22; Giga Soichiro, interview.

Itagaki after phone call: ibid.

Railroad explosion: *Taiheiyo senso*, 1:438–39.

548 Army explanation of 10:40 express: Yoshihashi, 3, 165.

Skirmish at railroad track: ibid., 2–3.

548–549 Itagaki's orders: Fujisawa and Tanaka, interviews; Yoshihashi, 166–67.

549 Tatekawa at the Literary Chrysanthemum: Kajiura, interview; Yoshihashi, 158–59.

Japanese soldiers occupied barracks: ibid., 3.

Honjo at Port Arthur: this and following three paragraphs a summary from Fujisawa, interview; IMTFE "Proceedings," 18890–92, 19111, 19326, 19518, 22119, 22237; Shimada, *Kanto gun*, 102–7; *Taiheiyo senso*, 1:436 ff.

550 Honjo transferred H.Q. to Mukden: Honjo, 22–23, 351–55; Yoshihashi, 167–68, 170.

551 Military success: Yoshihashi, 4–6; Honjo, 23, notes arrival of eight bombers and eight observation planes from Korea on afternoon of Sept. 20. Casualty figures, IMTFE "Proceedings," 19457.

Tatekawa in Mukden, Sept. 19: Fujisawa, interview.

Tatekawa delivers his message: IMTFE "Proceedings," 18901–5; Storry, *Double Patriots*, 81.

552 "altogether appropriate"; *shigoku dato*, Harada, 2:71.

"Restrict operations to south Manchuria": IMTFE "Proceedings," 18901–5, amplified by Tanaka, interviews.

Honjo's worrying: Kajiura, interview.

553 Meeting of principal advisors: Harada, 2:64–66; Kido, 100.

554 Minami, "non-aggravation does not necessarily mean non-enlargement": Harada, 2:64, 68; Takeuchi, 352.

Cable to commander in Korea: Tanaka, interview; Yoshihashi, 174; see also Mori, 56.

555 Honjo sent Tatekawa and Suzuki back to Tokyo: Honjo, 23.

Hirohito would personally take responsibility for ordering in Japan's Korean Army: My interpretation of events; see Privy Council meeting of Oct. 7, 1931, minutes in IPS Document No. 904. In my opinion, the strongest evidence for my interpretation is provided by the discussion in Harada 2:41 and 65. If in late July —almost two months before the event—the closest confidants of

Hirohito were discussing the propriety of moving troops without official imperial sanction, then it must be concluded that the officially unauthorized troop movements did have Hirohito's unofficial authorization. Otherwise Saionji and other liberals would have been able to persuade Hirohito to issue explicit orders to the Korean Army not to move. The events of the February Mutiny (see Chs. 20–21) demonstrate that Hirohito could have issued such an order and it would have been obeyed. Furthermore, Harada's observation that the Tsinan intervention had created a precedent for officially unauthorized troop movements indicates to me only that Hirohito had arranged for that troop movement also, knowing in advance that there would be a reprisal massacre for which the Throne must avoid official responsibility.

556 Johnson and memo: Rappaport, 25.

Forbes's return to U.S.: ibid., 26, and *N.Y. Times*, Feb. 27, 1932, ix, 2:7.

Stimson's cable: Rappaport, 26.

13. *Dollar Swindle*

560 Hirohito's post-mature birth: see note on page 354.

562–563 Excerpts from Vespa, 45–62.

563 Takeda Nukazo: data from Hata's "Personnel Records."

564 DINNER AT KIDO'S: this section based on the brief entry in Kido, *Nikki*, 101, supplemented by interviews with a privileged source who had access to the papers left by Big Brother Viscount Uramatsu. It seems to me to be corroborated by events, by Kido, 114–15, and by Harada, 2:72, 76, 84–86, 90, 93–94, 114, 126–28, 130–31, and esp. 156 and 164–67.

566 Hirohito on Hoover's moratorium: Kido, *Nikki*, 91.

"Save the League's face": Uchida Yasuya's phrase; see Harada, 2:93.

567 Okawa and Army bombs: see note on pages 521–22 and Harada, 2:55–56.

Konoye and Higashikuni endowment: Storry, *Double Patriots*, 96–101, and Byas, *Govt. by Assassination*, 39 ff.

568 Misty Lagoon unit an elite: see Sakai Saburo, 29–38.

Secret policeman Amakasu in Harbin: Ogata, 67–68; Pernikoff, *passim*.

568–570 Henry Pu-Yi taken to Manchuria: Pu-Yi, 219–21, supplemented by interviews with Tanaka.

569 Pu-Yi's "audience hall": a similar description is in Harry Carr, *Riding the Tiger: An American Newspaperman in the Orient* (Boston: Houghton Mifflin Co., 1934), 91.

570 A messenger: Kamizumi Toshi-ichi rather than Kaeisumi Toshi-ichi as Pu-Yi reports.

571 EASTERN JEWEL: this section based on Tanaka Takayoshi, "Shokai jihen," 82; his MS "Yoshiko"; and interviews with him. See also McAleavy, 160 ff. For details of Kawashima Naniwa's career, see Shimada, *Kanto gun*, 17–18, and Jansen, 137–40.

572–573 Itagaki quoted: Tanaka, "Shokai jihen," 182, and his "Yoshiko" give slightly different wordings.

573 Itagaki gave Tanaka $10,000: Watanabe, 118.

Saionji had gone to Kyoto: Harada, 2:52 ff.

574 Saionji's agent published letter accusing Makino of malfeasance: ibid., 90–91, 103.

Harada sent to Kyoto, Saionji's opinions recorded: ibid., 88.

575 Harada met with Kido, Makino, Suzuki: ibid. Note Saionji's refusal to see Lt. Gen. Banzai Rihachiro of the Spy Service, Oct. 15; ibid., 93–94.

575–576 Harada in Kyoto with Saionji: ibid., 88–92; Koyama, 104.

"to refrain from action": Ogata, 69.

Ishiwara led air raid: Ishiwara entry in *Nihon Jinbutsu-shi Taikei* [Japan Biographical Outline] (Tokyo: Asakuro Shobo, 1960); see Fujimoto, 67. He also spoke of severing relations between the Kwantung Army and Japan and of abandoning Japanese citizenship; Ogata, 94.

576–577 October Plot: Harada, 2:91, 99–100.

577 Suzuki, Hashimoto, Cho involved in plot: Storry, *Double Patriots*, 89.

Cho's October plan and quote: Murofushi, 229–32.

[the commander of the Misty Lagoon Air Station]: "Brocade Banner," 144.

578 To gain a blackmail hold on Araki: Kido, *Nikki*, 113, reveals that the Eleven Club met on Oct. 13 to discuss the Army's growing espousal "of a so-called Strike-North continental policy." Kido expressed disgust with the Army's stupidity. According to IPS Document 517—an English-language version of an Iwabuchi Tatsuo article in *Chuo Koron* of Feb. 1946—the Strike-North ideologist, Kita Ikki, offered to contribute in the October Plot by organizing demonstrations in Hibiya Park. His help, however, was

not accepted because he and Mori Kaku were believed "to have a counterplot" for "avenging Tanaka Gi-ichi."

Araki quoted: Harada, 2:107.

Araki's talk with Hashimoto and Cho: Murofushi, 229–32.

Arrest of eleven officers in plot: ibid.; "Brocade Banner," 114.

579 Okawa quoted re October Plot: Murofushi, 232.

Saionji went to villa in Okitsu: Harada, 2:101, 103.

Koiso's talk with Saionji on train: ibid., 105, supplemented by interview with privileged source, a banker.

580 Saionji's surrender was announced at dinner: Harada, 2:94. The announcement was made by South Manchuria Railroad president Uchida Yasuya; for his mission in Tokyo at that time, see Ogata, 83–85, also A. M. Young, *Imperial Japan*, 99–100.

Saionji waited until Oct. 30: Harada, 2:108.

Saionji's health ignored: Inoki, interview.

Saionji met Makino Nov. 2, their exchange: ibid., 2:112, 114.

581 Saionji's visit with Emperor: ibid., 115–16.

Invasion ordered on Oct. 30: Honjo, 26.

Honjo dispatched engineers: ibid.

582 Kwantung Army's move on Tsitsihar: *Taiheiyo senso*, 2:49 ff.; A. M. Young, *Imperial Japan*, 102–5, 145–46; Ito Kanejiro, 359; Harada, 2:134–35; Rappaport, 82.

Doihara's visit to Pu-Yi villa: Pu-Yi, 1:225–28; Tanaka, interview. See also IMTFE "Proceedings," 4373–374.

583 Eastern Jewel's visit to Doihara: Tanaka, "Yoshiko," and interview.

Doihara's account: corroborated by Fujisawa, interview.

584 Efforts to get Pu-Yi to Mukden: Pu-Yi, 1:228–29; see also Tanaka, "Yoshiko."

Doihara engineered riots in Tientsin: IMTFE "Proceedings," 4394–97; Pu-Yi, 1:229–30; Harada, 2:126; Zumoto, 65–68.

Pu-Yi's flight: Pu-Yi, 1:231. An alternate version, circulated at the time by Doihara and often repeated (e.g., McAleavy, 202), had it that Pu-Yi was smuggled out of the "Quiet Garden" in a *nagabitsu*, a wooden tub for dirty laundry. For the occasion on which Doihara did resort to this stratagem, see Ronald Seth, *Secret Servants: A History of Japanese Espionage* (New York: Farrar, Straus & Cudahy, 1957), 122–24.

584–585 Pu-Yi's escape: Pu-Yi, 1:232–40.

His wife joined him: Tanaka, interview; see also McAleavy, 203.

586 Arrangements handled by Prince Chichibu: Harada, 2:147.

Politics and financial maneuvers: based on Harada, 2:127–31, 135, 138–41, 144, 146, 149–56; O. D. Russell, 243 ff.

586–587 Saionji, "It is like a bank": Harada, 2:135–36.

League debated for a month: Rappaport, 68 ff.

Hirohito and fireflies: Kinoshita Michio, "Gunkan haruna kokanpan-jo ni haisu seinaru isshun no kokei" [One-Instant Scene of Reverence on the Quarterdeck of the Battleship *Haruna*]. *Fujin no Tomo*, June, 1939.

Toyama's opinion: Harada, 2:146.

League's decision: Rappaport, 76–77.

Herald Tribune's editorial: Dec. 10, 1931.

588 Black Dragon hireling: Adachi Kenzo; see Storry, *Double Patriots*, 313.

Saionji's opinion: Harada, 2:152–55.

Inukai's qualifications: Jansen, *passim*; A. M. Young, *Imperial Japan*, *passim*.

588–589 Harada's exchange with Kido: Harada, 2:156; Kido, *Nikki*, 120.

589 CASHING IN: this section based on Harada, 2:164–67; Kido, *Nikki*, 147; O. D. Russell, 247–51; Vaughn, 181–90.

14. Fake War

591 In China an envoy of Inukai: IMTFE "Proceedings," 1480. For details of the envoy, Kayano Chochi, see Jansen, 200 and *passim*, also "Proceedings," 1478–1522. For other peace efforts of Inukai, see Crowley, 158. Storry, *Double Patriots*, 109 ff., presents a factually accurate but strained interpretation of Kayano's mission.

Frigidly formal audience: Kido, *Nikki*, 120, makes a point of the fact that the audience lasted only thirteen minutes.

Cabinet met immediately: Araki's affidavit, IMTFE Exhibit 1880.

Gen. Kanaya Hanzo resigned: *Asahi* (Tokyo ed.), Dec. 16, 18, 1931.

Triumvirate agreed to nominate Minami: ibid., Dec. 23, 1931.

592 Process of Prince Kanin's appointment: my interpretation of Kido, *Nikki*, 121–23, and Harada, 2:197.

592–593 Kanin's appointment celebrated: *Asahi* (Tokyo ed.), Jan. 31, 1932; Harada, 2:175–77.

Sun Fo: he was then prime minister of China; Rappaport, 125.

On his mission see Clubb, 194–95, and A. M. Young, *Imperial Japan*, 96.

Eastern Jewel in Shanghai: Tanaka, "Yoshiko," and interviews.

593–594 I Pong-chang's trip to Tokyo: Murofushi, 234; Ohtani, *Kempei-shi*, 63.

Itagaki flew to Tokyo: Honjo, 60; Tanaka, interview.

Western reaction to renewed aggression: Rappaport, 83–94; Westel W. Willoughby, *Japan's Case Examined* (Baltimore: Johns Hopkins Press, 1940), 12–13.

Stimson's note: *Foreign Relations, U.S.: Japan, 1931–1941*, 3:7–8. The note was sent to Ambassador Forbes at noon Jan. 7 Washington time, 2 A.M. Jan. 8, Tokyo time.

595 Assassination attempt: Murofushi, 233–35.

Assassin sentenced to death: according to "Brocade Banner," the sentence was not carried out; instead I Pong-chang supposedly recanted and became a loyal Japanese agent.

Kido on assassination: *Nikki*, 127–28.

Reactions of Ikki and Hirohito: Harada, 2:173, 184–88.

596 Saionji's comment: Harada, 2:189.

Japanese riot in Shanghai: A. M. Young, *Imperial Japan*, 133–34; Tanaka, interview.

596–597 GHOST HOUSE: this section based on "Brocade Banner," 40–44 and 16; Murofushi, 237–41; Harada, 2:304–5; Crowley, 174; and interviews with retired Navy commander.

598 Re Spider Tanaka: Hata, *Gun*, 49 says that priest Inoue Nisho was a direct protégé of old Tanaka. He adds that Inoue Nisho had had contact with the flight officers at the Misty Lagoon Air Station since Aug. or Sept. of 1930.

599 Inoue as intimate of Konoye and Higashikuni: see Inoue's entry in *Japan Biographical Encyclopedia and Who's Who* (Tokyo: Rengo Press, 1958), 384; see also Kido, *Nikki*, 844, 849, 861, 867, 869.

599–600 Itagaki's telegram to Tanaka: Tanaka, "Yoshiko."

Itagaki's report to Hirohito: Kido, *Nikki*, 128–29.

On receipt of Col. Itagaki's telegram . . . : this and following paragraph based on Tanaka, "Yoshiko" and "Shokai jihen," 181 ff.; Watanabe, 118 ff.

601 Tanaka and Shigeto and Mitsui representative: Ramifications of this incident finally led to murder of Mitsui industrialist Muto Sanji on March 9, 1934. I wish someone would unravel the

complete story; some of the relevant references are Harada, 2:144, 153; O. D. Russell, 244; A. M. Young, *Imperial Japan*, 218–21.

601–602 Subsequent events in Shanghai: ibid., 136; Zumoto, 109–10.

22,000,000 yen: My source, a banker, states that the request was made on the day the Diet recessed, i.e., Jan. 21. Harada, 2:179, reports Inukai's conversation with Dan in his entry for Jan. 18; O. D. Russell, 255, seems to put the scene at a later date, Mar. 2. Kido, *Nikki*, 130–36, provides a context which strongly suggests that the conversation took place on or about the date stated (Jan. 21). Note that Harada's entries are curiously muddled in this month and that there are differences of more than translation between the published Japanese text and the English-language version prepared for the U.S. Army Far East Command in 1947.

Inukai hoped to establish Manchuria as a nation: Harada, 2:231, also 200–201, 211–14; Kido, *Nikki*, 134.

Hirohito's willingness to accept compromise: Inukai Ken's testimony, IMTFE "Proceedings," 1540–45, states that Inukai was ready to ask Hirohito to issue such an order.

603 Baron Dan promised to consider proposal: Harada, 2:178–79, 181.

Makino's warning to Saionji: Kido, *Nikki*, 131, 133.

603–608 COMMENCEMENT OF HOSTILITIES: this section based on Zumoto, 107–38; Abend, *Life in China*, 186–93; Vaughn, 313–15; A. M. Young, *Imperial Japan*, 135–38; IMTFE "Proceedings," 3245 ff.

604 Mayor Wu notified Adm. Shiozawa: IMTFE "Proceedings," 3286.

604–605 Abend's exchange with Adm. Shiozawa: *Life in China*, 187, also his *Can China Survive?*, 155–57.

605 By 7 A.M. planes were strafing and bombing Chapei: John B. Powell testimony, IMTFE "Proceedings," 3245–52.

606 Launching of Chiang's warship in Tokyo: Kennedy, *Problem of Japan*, 165–67.

607 "mufti army": *ben-i-tai*, Harada, 2:206.

In Tokyo Hirohito was gravely worried: this passage based on Kido, *Nikki*, 139; Harada, 2:201. See also Minami's report to the Throne, Jan. 28, 1932, Kido, *Nikki*, 132, and Hirohito's refusal to delegate any authority even in appointments of home guard commanders, ibid., 145, 149.

"sit big as a mountain": ibid., 129.

608 Household Ministry's announcement of Prince Fushimi's appointment: *Asahi* (Tokyo ed.), Feb. 3, 1932; see also Harada, 2:197–99.

N. 3: ibid., 197, 304; Murofushi, 275.

15. *Government by Assassination*

609 BLESSING THE KILLERS: this section based on "Brocade Banner," 40–44, and Murofushi, 237–41.

610 Foreign minister offered Western diplomats opportunity to mediate: Harada, 2:200; Rappaport, 127–29; Crowley, 162–64.

Makino told Inukai: Kido, *Nikki*, 134.

611 Stimson would not co-operate: Rappaport, 127–29.

War minister briefed by finance minister: Harada 2:201–6, 208; also Kido, *Nikki*, 136.

Hirohito directed Inukai to reject . . . green again: My summation based on what happened and on Hirohito's audiences that morning as reported, ibid., 135.

612 On Saturday morning, February 6: this paragraph based on "Brocade Banner," 42, and Harada, 2:204.

Commander Fujii: The departed ringleader, according to Mori, 1:40, was a graduate of the University Lodging House in the palace.

Army landed brigade of 10,000: Zumoto, 142.

Hirohito gave his personal instructions: Kido, *Nikki*, 136–37.

613 "lecture in the Imperial Study . . .": Harada, 2:208.

Matsuoka expressed the opinion: Kido, *Nikki*, 136–37; the younger-older brother illustration of "the Darwinian principle" is added from a later speech of Matsuoka reported in the newspapers.

Saionji's comment: Harada, 2:208.

Hirohito's audience with Lt. Gen. Banzai: Kido, *Nikki*, 137.

Banzai the immediate superior of Friar Inoue: Byas, *Govt. by Assassination*, 57; A. M. Young, *Imperial Japan*, 190.

Banzai left Hirohito at two o'clock: Kido, *Nikki*, 137.

Two hours later Konuma received a messenger: Murofushi, 237.

613–614 Konuma described: ibid., 240.

614 Details of Inoue Junnosuke's assassination: ibid., 237–38.

Friar Inoue moved his base to student hostel: "Brocade Banner," 42.

Honma had been Inoue's colleague, ran elementary school: ibid.

In his new headquarters . . . : this paragraph, ibid., 43.

615 Kido lunched with Arima and Harada: Kido, *Nikki*, 137. Kido's mention of Inoue Junnosuke's murder is brief; Harada's is briefer. Yet Fleisher, 66–69, tells of being present at a dinner party with Harada on the night Inoue was shot. The diplomatic elite of Tokyo were also present. The news of the assassination spread swiftly by whisper as embassy couriers arrived one after another at the door with urgent messages for their chiefs of mission. In the view of all present Harada walked across the room to relay the news to Imperial Household Minister Baron Ikki Kitokuro. Ikki reacted not at all except by rocking back and forth on his heels.

Board of Fleet Admirals and Field Marshals met: Harada, 2:209.

"burst of power": ibid., 213.

N. 3: Harada 9:351–52, supplemented with details about Tokugawa and Ohtani reported elsewhere in these pages.

616 Election campaign issue and slogans: O. D. Russell, 251–52.

"Constitutional Protection Movement": *Goken undo*. Kido, *Nikki*, 169, supplemented by interviews with privileged source (a banker).

617 Honjo refused bribe offer: Honjo, 75; interview with Kajiura.

Feb. 19 meeting of Eleven Club: Kido, *Nikki*, 140.

Dinner meeting of Kido and Konoye with Inoue Saburo: ibid., 140–41 (exegesis courtesy of source with access to Uramatsu papers).

N. 4: Harada, 2:219.

619 As anticipated, the people elected Constitutionalists: Scalapino, 242; Crowley, 169.

Harada told Saionji of purposes of planned coup d'etat, and Saionji's comment: Harada, 2:219–21.

Saionji knew there would be no coup d'etat, had reached own understanding with Araki: my interpretation of Harada, 2:221–36 *passim*.

620 Inukai exchanging cables with Chiang: e.g., Harada, 2:230–31.

Big Brothers spread excited gossip: e.g., ibid., 2:225.

Konoye's visit with Saionji: ibid., 2:226.

621 Harada at Okitsu with Saionji's comment: ibid., 2:227.

Stimson's letter to Sen. Borah: Rappaport, 141.

622 Inukai proposed Baron Dan as envoy, and Koiso's interview with Dan: Harada, 2:230, supplemented by interviews with Tanaka. For other attempts to intimidate Dan see A. M. Young, *Imperial Japan,* 719.

Friar Inoue selected Hisanuma to assassinate Dan: Murofushi, 243.

623 Saionji decided time had come to declare himself: Harada, 2:231–33, supplemented by reference, through an intermediary, to notes left by a banker close to Saionji.

Saionji quoted: Harada, 2:232–33.

VICTORY IN SHANGHAI: this section based on Zumoto, 163–66 and Chart 3; Yanaga, *Since Perry,* 557–59; IMTFE "Proceedings," 28135–138.

624 Three privates' suicide charge: The *nikudan* or "human bullets" became a legend: see, e.g., Vaughn, 325, and A. M. Young, *Imperial Japan,* 141–42.

Major who felt responsible: Maj. Soga; Vaughn, 326.

N. 6: Zumoto, 163, 167, and interviews with Fujisawa.

625 Eastern Jewel's role with 11th Div.: Tanaka, "Yoshiko," also *Taiheiyo senso,* 2:138.

626 LEAGUE'S WELCOME: this section based on IMTFE "Proceedings," 1713; Rappaport, 180; *N.Y. Times,* Feb. 29–Mar. 7, 1932.

627 N. 7: Lindbergh had annoyed Japanese authorities; had been entertained by Kido's brother: A. M. Young, *Imperial Japan,* 265.

628 Dan's connections with U.S.: Yanaga, *Since Perry,* 177; Fleisher, 68; Byas, *Govt. by Assassination,* 30.

Meeting of Mitsui directors, their dividend rate, Mitsui refusal to participate in government bond issue: O. D. Russell, 253–55.

629 A Browning delivered to Hisanuma: "Brocade Banner," 42.

Dan's dinner party: Fleisher, 66–69.

Assassin Hisanuma went to Funabashi Beach: "Brocade Banner," 42.

Harada, before entraining: Harada, 2:234.

Dan at banquet for League's commission: O. D. Russell, 256–57.

629–630 Details of assassination of Baron Dan: Murofushi, 242–44.

Saionji and Harada on train: Harada, 2:234–35.

Saionji's visitors: Harada, 2:235–36.

As a son is expected . . . : this paragraph based on Harada, 2:236–39.

N. 8: Harada, 1: Plate 3. This photo is one of those reproduced in this volume.

631 March 8, smoke bombs returned: Harada, 9:346–47. See also Hata, *Gun,* 29; Ohtani, *Rakujitsu,* 34; IMTFE "Proceedings," 1416.

Saionji met Araki for first time: Harada, 2:236.

Police chief began to make arrests: ibid., 2:237.

Friar Inoue taken to jail, Okawa left at liberty: "Brocade Banner," 43.

Saionji insisted only that the killing cease . . . : this and following five paragraphs based on Harada 2:238–48 and Kido, *Nikki,* 151–52.

$8-million bond issue and $7-million loan (22 million and 20 million yen): newspaper reports. For the negotiations concerning the Mitsui payoff, Harada, 2:256–57, 327–28, and 9:138.

632 Okawa gave flight lieutenant $500: Harada, 2:306.

633 April 4 meeting of Eleven Club: Kido, *Nikki,* 153–54; Harada, 2:252–53.

Lord Lytton described: Rappaport, 179.

634 Saionji and Lord Lytton: Harada, 2:312–13.

Lytton commissioners to be in Mukden April 21: Honjo, 98; IMTFE "Proceedings," 1713.

The former Japanese ambassador to the Soviet Union: Tanaka Tokichi. See Kido, *Nikki,* 161–64; Harada, 2:284; Honjo, 90, 92, 93, 98, 102.

Col. Watari Hisao detached to be advance man: Kajiura, interview, and Honjo, 47, 98. "Advance man" is perhaps the wrong term. On Nov. 24, 1931, Secretary of State Stimson wired Geneva his backing for the draft resolution proposing a commission of inquiry. Watari then visited Honjo in Manchuria on Nov. 28 to advise him on steps to be taken. Thereafter Watari dogged the heels of Lord Lytton himself and did not return to Manchuria until he came with the Commission of Inquiry in April 1932. In short, "tour director" might be a better description of Watari's position.

Piggott's appreciation of Watari quoted: Piggott, 266.

635–636 Japanese preparations in Manchuria: details from Pernikoff, 120–23, and Vespa, 147–64.

636 Activities of Watari and Obata: Honjo, 98 (entry for Apr. 20, 1932) and 96 (Apr. 15), supplemented by interviews.

637 Suzuki's position papers: Kido, *Nikki*, 157–58; interviews.

Matsuoka's audience with Hirohito: Kido, *Nikki*, 158–59; Harada, 2:270.

638 Saionji's comments: Harada, 2:273.

Suzuki's second position paper: ibid., 274.

638–640 Arrangements with Honjo: this section based on Honjo, 101–5, supplemented by Harada, 2:307 and various interviews.

640–642 AT A COUNTRY INN: this reconstruction is based on Byas, *Govt. by Assassination*, 22; Kido, *Nikki*, 279; Hato, *Gun*, 54; and on a field trip of my own to Tsuchiura in 1966. See also Harada, 2:234, 349, and Kido, *Nikki*, 187–90 (esp. last line on 189). This Kido passage raises the question whether Prince Higashikuni may not have come to the inn with Tachibana.

641 Okawa turned over 2,000 yen: Harada, 2:306.

642 Wanted to act on day Charlie Chaplin was arriving: see also Murofushi, 253–54.

643 Kido's information from Makino: Kido, *Nikki*, 161–62.

Harada took a train to Shizuoka . . . : Harada, 2:283–84.

644 Kido went to his golf club . . . : Kido, *Nikki*, 162.

Fliers, cadets, naval lt. went to Yasukuni Shrine: "Brocade Banner," 44.

644–645 At Yasukuni Shrine: this and following three paragraphs based on Byas, *Govt. by Assassination*, 22–24, and 28, supplemented by Ponsonby-Fane, *Vicissitudes of Shinto*, 130–32, and by *Terry's Guide* (1920 ed.), 155–57. The figure 126,363 heroes is from Ponsonby-Fane, *Vicissitudes*, 125, and *Studies in Shinto*, 526.

645 Second group of plotters: "Brocade Banner," 45.

646 First group of assassins in prime minister's residence: The narrative begun here and completed on page 648 based on Murofushi, 247–50; Byas, *Govt. by Assassination*, 24–26; Kido, *Nikki*, 162; Harada, 2:286–87. Note Harada's report that the assassins had a plan of the residence and that their entry may have been facilitated by secret policemen letting them in.

N. 14: Akimoto, *Japanese Ways*, 154–68; *Terry's Guide* (1920 ed.), 186–87.

648 "Call them back": Murofushi, 251.

648–649 Inukai's wounds and treatment: ibid., 251–52; also Kido, *Nikki*, 162, and Fleisher, 73.

At 7 P.M.: this and following three paragraphs based on

"Brocade Banner," 44–46; Byas, *Govt. by Assassination,* 26, 30; also N.Y. *Times,* May 16–18, 1932.

650 Inukai's shot of blood: Kido, *Nikki,* 162–63.

Kido's telephone calls: ibid.

650–651 Harada's conversation with Saionji: Harada, 2:283–8, interpreted in the light of Saionji's request for more information and of Harada's call to Kido the next morning (Kido, *Nikki,* 163) asking for help in making Saionji come up to Tokyo.

651 Kido reported to Makino: Kido, *Nikki,* 162–63.

Hirohito dispatched his personal physician: ibid.

651–653 THREAT OF MUTINY: this section based on Hata, *Gun,* 59 n. 8; Umashima, 19–20; Byas, *Govt. by Assassination,* 27.

653 Chief aide-de-camp informed Hirohito: interviews.

Kido drove to prime minister's residence: Kido, *Nikki,* 162.

"I feel a little better": Murofushi, 252.

Kido at his residence, then at palace: Kido, *Nikki,* 162–63.

Facts of Inukai's death: "Brocade Banner," 45–46.

654–656 STERN REPRESSION: this section based on Kido, *Nikki,* 163–65, also Harada, 2:284–85.

656–659 THE NEW REGIME: this section is taken from Harada, 2:285–97; from Kido, *Nikki,* 164–70; and from Harada, 9:138–39.

656 Appointments needed only to be confirmed: Harada, 9:138, last 2 lines—an interpretation of Harada's elliptic notes.

657 Hirohito to Suzuki for Saionji: quoted, Kido, *Nikki,* 169. Harada, 2:288, gives the "honeyed" version mentioned below.

658 "They cannot be arrested": quoted, Kido, *Nikki,* 168.

659 So ended Japan's experiment . . . : Ogata, 155, goes so far as to say that one of the chief motives for killing Inukai was a radio address he made on May 1 pledging to preserve political-party rule at all costs.

660 Hitler assassinated fifty-one opponents: William Shirer, *The Rise and Fall of the Third Reich* (New York: Simon & Schuster, 1960; Fawcett Crest Book, 1962), 266; 206.

Equivalent of a Japanese college education: A strong statement, perhaps, because some Westerners did take degrees at Japanese universities. The fluency and cultural appreciation of a native Japanese graduate, however, were not to be matched.

Osaka editor told American correspondent: Vaughn, 345.

Orchids and apathy at Inukai's funeral: N.Y. *Times,* May 19, 1932.

661 Honjo quoted: Honjo, 106.

662 Okawa with procurator and telephone calls: Harada, 2:305–6; "Brocade Banner," 38.

Okawa arrested in Tsuchiura: ibid.

His secretary arrested: Harada, 2:312–13.

Baron Tokugawa interrogated: ibid., 310, 332–33.

Tachibana, escape, book quoted: Byas, *Govt. by Assassination*, 69; "Brocade Banner," 46.

He turned himself over to Kwantung Army military police: Harada, 2:332.

663 Toyama's secretary negotiated his arrest: ibid., 369.

Hidezo placed himself in police custody Nov. 5: "Brocade Banner," 47; Grew, *Ten Years*, 69.

Police attack on Socialist and Communist leaders' meeting: U.S. Army Far East, Intelligence Rept. "Left Wing, Right Wing," 27 ff.; Harada, 2:296.

Prince Konoye at Blood Brotherhood accessory's funeral: A. M. Young, *Imperial Japan*, 189.

All but six were free men by end of 1935: "Brocade Banner," 54–56.

Prince Yamashina's "nervous breakdown": Koizumi, interview; see also Kido, *Nikki*, 271.

Commander Inoue retired to the reserve: interview with retired Navy commander.

664 Meiji Institute turned into museum: Kido, *Nikki*, 188.

Higashikuni scandal: Harada, 2:344, 349.

Scandal hushed up with difficulty: ibid., 8:305.

Makino and writers of anonymous letters: Ohtani, *Kempei-shi*, 85; also Murofushi, 261–63.

Okawa carried letters signed by Makino: "Brocade Banner," 38.

664–665 Inukai's letter to Toyama: Vaughn, 341–42.

665 Friar Inoue's subsequent career: "Brocade Banner," 54; Kido, 844, 849, 861, 867, 869; *Japan Biog. Encl.* (1958), 384.

Flight Lt. Mikami: "Brocade Banner," 54; *Asahi*, June 5, 1961; and Feb. 26, 1965.

Eastern Jewel's later career: Tanaka, "Yoshiko"; McAleavy, 213–14; Tsuji, *Underground Escape*, 233–34. See also Kido, *Nikki*, 238–39 (May 23 and 30, 1933): is Kido really talking about lessons he is taking in the art of dramatic declamation, or about Eastern Jewel (Yuang Kuei-fei), General Kawashima Yoshiyuki, and a sumo wrestler named Takasago?

16. *Outcast Nation*

667–669 New American ambassador: Grew, *Ten Years*, 13–14.
668 Grew shooting a tiger, other details: *N.Y. Times*, Jan. 24, Feb. 10, 1932.
669 Grew's arrival: Grew, *Ten Years*, 17–21.
Impressed by courtiers, esp. Makino: ibid., 38–39.
Grew's diary quoted: ibid., 76.
OPERATION CONCUBINE: This section is based on interviews with the same nobleman who gave me the details of Early Birth on page 353. Again I checked the story with Koizumi Shinzo and he did not deny it. A partial version of the intrigue may be found in Koyama, 73–87, and in Mosley, 104–7 and 116–18. My account adds the artificial insemination episode and definite dating. I have based my chronology on a plenitude of relevant but obscure references in the diaries, including Kido, *Nikki*, 185–91 and 123, and Harada, 8:305 and 2:344–55. I have taken as corroboration of the artificial insemination episode all references in Kido to *Taichu Tenno* or Inside-the-Womb Emperor. He introduces this term in his entry for May 11, 1931 (Kido, 76) and last uses it on Nov. 27, 1937 (ibid., 605). *Taichu Tenno* is an ancient euphemism of Court diarists for any particularly private and personal affairs of an emperor. That Kido revived it as a specific code term for the test-tube prince seems to me clear for a number of reasons. First, Inside-the-Womb Emperor was extremely apposite. Second, neither Harada nor Honjo used it in their diaries. Third, Kido wrote straightforwardly of "the Emperor's personal problems" when that was what he meant. Fourth, Kido used the term last in 1937 when the test-tube prince should have reached adoption age. Fifth, Kido did not use the term again in the years 1938–45 when the Emperor continued to have many personal problems. And sixth, at his first use of the term in Nov. 1931, Kido wrote explicitly about "the problem of Inside-the-Womb Emperor's succession to the Throne." That this person was not some ancient pretender being considered for reinstatement in the imperial pantheon I am assured by absence of any reference to him in the authoritative works of Richard Ponsonby-Fane (see Bibliography).
673 Hirohito "too staid": Koyama, 76.
674 Tanaka's falling out with Higashikuni: Kido, *Nikki*, 190.
"I cannot believe you": Koyama, 82.

"I know everything": ibid., 85.

675 Empress and the illegitimate heir: ibid., 89–90.

N. 3: Harada, 9:139.

676 Gen. Ma's pretended sell-out: A. M. Young, *Imperial Japan*, 146–48.

Ma embarrassment to Japanese: summary of Honjo, 98–106.

Undercover messages to Lytton: Vespa, 161–63.

Russian student caught and killed: Pernikoff, 127.

677 Lytton retired to Peking: Rappaport, 180; *N.Y. Times*, June 5, 1932.

Report of Ma's death: A. M. Young, *Imperial Japan*, 148–50.

Honjo's ideas on development of Manchuria: interviews with Fujisawa and Kajiura.

678 Relocation of 25,000 Chinese families: Pernikoff, 102.

Farmers used for bayonet practice, described: ibid., 241.

679–680 Experiences of Oleg Volgins: ibid., 32, 47, 261–67.

680 166 technocrats dispatched, July 1932: testimony of Tanaka Shizuka, IMTFE "Proceedings," 20459 ff.

Aviation company an extension of Air Forces: ibid., 28312 and 2708.

Industrial development of Manchuria: this and following 2 paragraphs based on Chamberlain, 27 ff., and on Scherer, *Manchukuo*, 50–56.

681 Amleto Vespa quoted: Pernikoff, 74.

"Japan is poor": Vespa, 89.

Concessions sold to guilds of vice experts: details in Vespa, 231–65.

Japanese had healthy fear of dope addiction: this and following 4 paragraphs based on Frederick Merrill, 3–9, 72–110.

683 Reporter paid twenty coppers: Edgar Snow, in *Saturday Evening Post* article, Feb. 24, 1934.

Brothels, other rackets: Pernikoff, 98; Vespa, 102, 255–59, 272–75.

684 Manchukoans paid and paid again: Pernikoff, 143; Vespa, 25.

The friends of Hirohito . . . realized a substantial part of the profits and plowed it back: my own summary of evidence from many sources.

Chamberlain from Court in Manchukuo: from Aug. 1932 to Apr. 1934; see Kido, *Nikki*, 186, 321, and Iriye Kanichi in *Who's Who in Japan*, 1933–34 ed.

"like a miniature garden": Ogawa Masao, interview.

685 Plan of the puppet state: IMTFE "Proceedings," 2903–3001. For a succinct diagram of it, see Kido, *Kankei bunsho*, 163.

REPORT TO THE LEAGUE: most of this section is taken from dispatches of Hallett Abend and Hugh Byas in N.Y. *Times* during Aug. and Sept. 1932; Rappaport, Ch. 7; and memorandum from George H. Blakeslee to Stanley Hornbeck, U.S. State Dept., 14, 1932, reproduced in Rappaport, Appendix.

686 N. 5; *N.Y. Times*, Jan. 24, 1932.

688 Honma's translation: Hata Ikuhiko, interview; "Honma Trial Proceedings" in National War Memorial, Canberra.

Known as "linguist with the red nose": Ito Kanejiro, 1:203.

"The effect of . . .": *Appeal by the Chinese Government: Report of the Commission of Inquiry* (League of Nations Publication VII, Political, 1932. Series VII, No. 12), 107.

689 "without declaration of war": ibid., 127.

Foreign Office spokesman quoted: Byas, in N.Y. *Times*, Sept. 6, 1932; see also FO quotes from report in *Times*, Sept. 9, and Uchida's good summary of report as quoted in Sept. 10 issue.

"no secret clauses," terms "less onerous": Byas in N.Y. *Times*, Sept. 3, 1932.

Secret protocol re Manchukuo: IMTFE "Proceedings," 2982 ff. In three other secret protocols (ibid., 29789 ff.) Manchukuo agreed to bear the cost of building communication and other facilities; to grant its Japanese advisors full extraterritorial rights; and to adjudicate all differences with Japan on the basis of the Japanese rather than the Chinese text of relevant treaties, contracts, and understandings.

690 Plenary session of Privy Council: IMTFE "Proceedings," 2972 ff.

691 Rumor re conquest of Jehol: A. M. Young, *Imperial Japan*, 161–63.

692–693 Suzuki's embassy to Chiang Kai-shek: Suzuki-Huang conversations, Harada, 3:72–73, and interviews with Tanaka; see also Harada, 2:403, and A. M. Young, *Imperial Japan*, 202–3.

694 For final months of Japan's participation in League of Nations debate, see N.Y. *Times*, Nov. 1932-Jan. 1933.

Harada quoted: 2:421.

Details of Shanhaikwan Incident: N.Y. *Times*, Jan. 3, 1933; also Harry Carr, *Riding the Tiger: An American Newspaperman in the Orient* (Boston: Houghton Mifflin, 1934), 123–29.

695 General Staff would abide by Hirohito's pledge to Chiang: Honjo, 160, and Harada, 2:427–28. See also Harada, 2:419, 422–23, 426, 430 for the circumstances.

Mafia-style meeting: Harada, 3:4–5. The meeting took place in the evening at Hiranuma's home. The Black Dragon Society was represented by Nakano Seigo, the extreme rightist and apologist for Hitler who would be forced by Tojo to commit suicide during World War II. At the end of the meeting Hiranuma said to Konoye: "As for our China policy, I believe we must strike to the south. I have listened to Ambassador Yoshida's views and I am in complete accord." For students of Yoshida Shigeru it could be pointed out that Harada's pages give considerable detail on the unity of Lord Privy Seal Makino and his son-in-law, Yoshida, with the Navy and the Satsuma clan. In this connection see also Yoshida's bellicose attitude toward Chang Tso-lin mentioned earlier herein, page 466; and Kido, *Nikki*, 215–16.

696 On Feb. 10, 1933: Kido, ibid., 216, gives a slightly different account. My source for this paragraph has been described earlier, on pages 353 and 669. At this juncture he withdrew from active participation in Hirohito's circle. His access to inside information, however, continued for several years thereafter and will be reflected occasionally in the notes that follow.

696–697 Cabinet meeting on League question: summary based on Harada 2:428–33 and 3:3–4, supplemented by interviews. It may be that the conference occupying Araki, mentioned by Harada, was a liaison conference rather than a Cabinet meeting. It may also be that the Cabinet meeting of February 13, which passed on the Jehol operation, had also approved withdrawal from the League and that Araki on Feb. 17 was simply informing the General Staff. In any case a day or two later, Harada could write about the League question with finality: "Our attitude has been decided upon."

697 League Assembly meeting: based on N.Y. *Times*, Feb. 25, 1933, dispatch by Clarence Streit.

17. North or South?

The interpretation implicit in this chapter title—one basic to this book—is confirmed by unusually explicit diary entries by Kido and by Harada in late 1932 and early 1933. Kido, *Nikki*, 215–16, stated plainly on January 25, 1933: "The Army expounds a policy of hostility toward Russia while the Navy calls for commencement of war between Japan and America." Harada echoed this realization and went on (Harada, 3:3–5) to explain how Lord Privy Seal Makino, in alliance with the Navy, the Satsuma clan, Hiranuma and the underworld, hoped to "control the Army" and persuade it that "we must strike south." Kido, too, noted the Makino-Navy alliance, and shortly thereafter (*Nikki*, 226–27), he observed realistically that certain Strike-North leaders "are thinking of government directly by the Emperor. Makino says that on this point we must be extremely careful."

705 PSHAW: this section based on Takeda, 65–66, and N.Y. *Times* for Feb. 22, Mar. 1, 3, and 9, 1933; see also Hata, *Gun*, 73.

706 THE STRIKE-NORTH LEADER: this section is based upon Araki's own many speeches reported in both the Japanese and Western press. I have added little new except in my interpretation: this being that Araki was a sympathetic character and that his warlike bluster was a political stratagem by which he hoped to keep enough influence to prevent Japan from fighting America.

707 Araki's hostility to Russia: Takeda, 45–46.

708 Araki's file: interviews with Tanaka and with Araki's grandson. My explanation of its contents is deduced from Araki's previous career and relationships with the Throne.

Araki had first realized: my inference from remark of retired Lt. Gen. Fujisawa.

709 RED SMEAR: based on Kido, *Nikki*, 206, 238–42, 244, 246–48.

Mossbacked old baron: Kikuchi Takeo, a nephew-in-law of Education Minister Hatoyama. His charge was taken up in the Diet by Miyazawa Yutaka. Yanaga, *Since Perry*, 507.

710 To stop Araki's witch hunt: A. M. Young, *Imperial Japan*, 247.

Keio Prof. Muneda Muneyoshi's attack on Kyoto Prof. Takikawa Yukitoki: Yanaga, *Since Perry*, 506; "Brocade Banner," 57.

Unorthodox view of adultery: Johnson, 88; see also Takikawa's *Chuo Koron* articles excerpted in IPS Document No. 3014.

Professor charged with heresy: "Brocade Banner," 59–60.

711 Emperor a part of or transcending?: see note on page 765.

Slurs against Okawa and Makino: "Brocade Banner," 57.

Kyoto University backs down: ibid., 59–60.

712 Hirohito on Napoleon: Honjo, 241.

712–713 Hirohito sent Mazaki to front: ibid., 159, 242.

Higashikuni accused Mazaki: Matsumoto Seicho's interview with Higashikuni, *Bungei Shunju*, Jan. 1968, 160 ff.; Harada, 3:63–64.

Mazaki trying to subvert Higashikuni's servants: Harada, 3:84, 72.

Hirohito-Chichibu argument: This episode is reported (Honjo, 163) without date; my most knowledgeable of aristocratic contacts said, "May, Showa eight." I have fixed the date at May 21 because of Kido's entry the next day (*Nikki*, 238). An earlier entry, March 8 (ibid., 224), would indicate that the scene might have occurred in Feb. 1933.

"I will reserve my absolute power . . .": Honjo, 163.

Kido and Konoye to see Chichibu: *Nikki*, 163.

714 Araki expanded Red smear: ibid., 238, 266.

Education Minister Hatoyama orders university: "Brocade Banner," 60.

Leading strategists met: Harada, 3:88.

ENEMY NUMBER ONE: this section based on Ohtani, *Rakujitsu*, 127–29, also his *Kempei-shi*, 226–28, supplemented by interviews with Fujisawa; Harada, 3:88.

716 This juncture reached June 2: Harada, 3:91.

Kido golfs with Saionji Kinkazu: *Nikki*, 239, 247, supplemented by interview with Matsumoto.

717 Kido and political left: ibid.; Johnson, 17 n.; *Nikki*, 249–50 (also 240–48).

718 Kido compiled roster of aristocrats: *Nikki*, 259–63, 287.

Kido versus Tokugawa Iesato: ibid., 270, 291, 300–301.

Higashi-Fushimi demoted: interview with member of Ohtani family; see also Kido, *Nikki*, 266.

719 Palace retainers pensioned: ibid., 249, 275.

GO-STOP INCIDENT: *Mainichi* (Osaka ed.), July 29, 1933; Yanaga, *Since Perry*, 509; Harada, 3:190.

720–724 PRAYER MEETING PLOT: this section based on Murofushi, 272–77; "Brocade Banner," 39–52; Byas, *Govt. by Assassination*, 213–25; Harada, 2:26(n.), 3:100–102, 139–40, 148–50, 179, 4:155, 9:168; Kido, *Nikki*, 265–66, 269, 436, 470. See also 337 and Kido, *Kankei bunsho*, 404–5.

723 Fujita an undercover agent: Johnson, 109; Harada, 3:102, 149–59, 8:386. For Fujita's part in Sorge spy case later, see page 723.

724 Proroguing trial of Blood Brotherhood: A. M. Young, *Imperial Japan*, 191; Byas, *Govt.*, 50; *Asahi*, Mar. 28, 1934.

725 Hirohito thinking of abdication: Kido, *Nikki*, 246. That same day Kido, Harada, and two other young bureaucrats of the Eleven Club lunched with Prince Higashikuni at the Tokyo Club. They discussed with him a snide suggestion which had recently been made to reporters by Gen. Tanaka Kunishige, one of Gen. Araki's partisans. His Excellency Higashikuni, said Tanaka, should consider giving up his rank as a prince so that he would be eligible to run for prime minister. The prince told Kido: "I do not know Gen. Tanaka personally. However, I think no one would pay any attention to me if I descended to commoner status." Said Kido, "I am greatly relieved."

Settlement of Red smear: Kido, *Nikki*, 246–47; 249–54.

Reposting of Strike-North officers: my analysis of the shuffle based on Hata's personnel records and on replies to inquiries during interviews with Fujisawa and Kajiura.

726 Silent Muto asked for mercy toward Manchukuoans: Vespa, 109.

Muto's poem: *Mainichi* (Osaka ed.), July 27, 1933; my own translation.

Barony for Muto: Honjo, 244; also Harada, 3:108, and Kido, *Nikki*, 247, 255.

727 Hishikari and the press: *Mainichi* (Osaka ed.), July 28, 1933.

728–732 THE KASPÉ KIDNAPPING: this section based on Petya Balakchine, *Finale vi Kitaya: vosnik-novenive, razvitiye y ischez noveniye beloi emigrantzii na Dalnyem Vostokye* [Finale in China: formation, development, and disintegration of the White Russian immigration in the Far East] (Munich, Georg Butow, 1959): 110–122, 210 ff.; Pernikoff, 187–216; Vespa, 205–30. Balakchine is the most detailed; it is based on a manuscript by a certain Martinoff who is said by Vespa to have been one of the main organizers of the kidnapping.

733 Midwives and doctors agreed: Koyama, 90–91.

Hirohito and Nagako on beach: Honjo, 244–45.

Eleven Club party: Kido, *Nikki*, 249.

Prince Fushimi wanted change in regulations: ibid.; Honjo, 163–66; also Agawa, 119–20.

Army staged air raid drills: Kido, *Nikki*, 250; Honjo, 245–46; Koizumi, interview.

Hirohito on board the *Hiei*: Honjo, 246–47.

734 Croquet game: ibid.

Meeting with Cabinet ministers, Aug. 30: ibid., 247.

735 Princes unpopular at clubs: Kido, *Nikki*, 254.

Hirohito gives Honjo lesson on yacht: Harada, 3:132–33.

Change in naval regulations should be kept secret: Honjo, 163.

736 Hirohito on Dutch navy: ibid., 249.

"We will expand": Harada, 3:158.

"There is no middle way": ibid.

736–737 Big Brothers at Chinese feast: ibid., 3:164.

Oct. 20 Cabinet meeting: Harada, 3:158, 168–69.

Defendants coached by police minions: see, e.g., Harada, 3:113.

Army court-martial: A. M. Young, *Imperial Japan*, 191; Byas, *Govt. by Assassination*, 47.

Navy court-martial: ibid., 44–46; Young, 191; Harada, 3:180.

738 Civilian trial: Byas, *Govt. by Assassination*, 66, 70–71.

Blood Brotherhood trial: ibid., 60; A. M. Young, *Imperial Japan*, 198.

739 Support expressed for Native-Land-Lovers: "Brocade Banner," 47; A. M. Young, *Imperial Japan*, 173.

Army cadets released: "Brocade Banner," 55; Harada, 3:147.

Sentences of others: A. M. Young, *Imperial Japan*, 195–97.

739–740 Araki hoped for outcry against Hirohito: see Harada, 3:188, 192, 201.

Hirohito after previous accouchement: Price, 27–28.

"It's a boy": Harada, 3:208.

"Problem has been solved": Kido, *Nikki*, 294.

Political parties' get-together: Harada, 3:206–7, supplemented by Matsumoto, interview.

"it is time for Araki to quit": Harada, 3:210.

Saionji exhausted: ibid., 211.

741 Maj. Gen. Nagata renewed position-paper work: Tanaka, interview; also Crowley, 207–8, 263.

On Jan. 7 Kido and others met at Konoye's villa: Harada, 3:211, supplemented by source with access to Uramatsu papers. Kido, oddly, makes no mention of this gathering in his diary.

Hirohito agreed to proclaim an amnesty: Harada, 3:211.

Saito-Hirohito exchange: ibid., 216–17.

Araki sequestered himself in the hospital: Ohtani, *Rakujitsu*, 89–93; Harada, 3:217–19. Prime Minister Saito expressed a wish to visit Araki and make him change his mind, but Kido warned him on the phone that if he did that he might not be able to see the Emperor again for fear of giving Hirohito Araki's pneumonia.

742–743 ZERO: basic references for this section, Kido, *Nikki*, 300, 308 and Harada, 3:239, 241.

743 Herbert Smith's role: retired Navy commander, interview, also Potter, *Yamamoto*, 23. I am indebted to John R. Cuneo for full identification of Smith as the designer of the Sopwith Camel.

LET THEM EAT CAKE: basic source for this section is Honjo, 184–85.

Disastrous year agriculturally: Inoki Masamichi, interview, citing article by Cho Yukio, *Asahi Journal*, Apr. 25, 1965.

Sent chamberlains to inspect: Honjo, 243.

743–744 Apply pressure to Mitsui cartel: O. D. Russell, 298, supplemented by interviews with Koizumi, Inoki.

18. *Organ or God?*

745 Celebration in honor of Crown Prince Akihito: Grew, *Ten Years*, 113–14.

746 Japanese "astonishingly capable of fooling themselves": ibid., 81.

Grew's conclusion: ibid., 128.

747 Hayashi prohibited slogan "Crisis of 1936": Crowley, 207. Imperial Way (*Koda-ha*) and Control (*Tosei-ha*): see Ohtani, *Rakujitsu*, 71–76.

747–748 The Kayas' embassy: *Mainichi* (Osaka ed.), March 9, 1934; July 1, 1934; Sept. 18, 1934.

A NOT-SO-MEDIEVAL SCANDAL: except as cited, this section based on Harada, 3:224, 228, 232, 236–37, 241, 244, 255, 269, 271, 284, 286–87, 308, 314.

Northern and southern dynasties both of same blood: Honjo, 204.

749 Saionji's visit to the palace: Honjo, 234; see also Harada, 8:303–4.

Kido and Harada agreed on Okada as next prime minister: Kido, *Nikki*, 329–30.

750 Appointment of Okada Cabinet: ibid., 343–45. For the slow, cynical preparations, see Harada, 8:321–48.

Friend to Saionji, "You have covered a boil . . .": Omura Bunji, 408.

Hirohito required new prime minister to reratify decision to expand south: Harada, 4:16; see also ibid., 453.

751-752 Hirohito's difficulties with Navy: my summary interpretation drawn largely from Harada, 4:16-28 and Honjo, 190-95. Yamamoto's appointment in November 1933, from interview with retired Navy commander. The appointment was not made official until June 1934 but the earlier date fits well with the Honjo, Kido, and Harada diaries—see especially Honjo, 171, and Harada, 3:191. In the latter is also admitted the situation in regard to shipbuilding.

751 Hirohito, "If the treaty must be abrogated . . .": Harada, 4:22.

Hirohito personally dictated instructions for Yamamoto: Kido, *Nikki*, 354; Harada, 4:50-51.

752 Hirohito approved instructions as drafted: Harada, 4:67-69; Honjo, 194-95.

Yamamoto's American press conference and his later one in England: Agawa, 23-25; Potter, *Yamamoto*, 23-25.

753 Hirohito authorized abrogration of treaty "at earliest moment": Honjo, 197-98.

"I am smaller than you": Potter, *Yamamoto*, 25.

753-754 Last month of London conference: Harada, 4:144-51.

755 Army Purification Movement or *Seigun-ha*: Crowley, 254-55; Yanaga, *Since Perry*, 510. Although he stood behind the *Seigun-ha* Terauchi delegated leadership to Hashimoto Kingoro. Later (interview, Fujisawa) he was obliged to turn on his own creature and purge the Purification Movement along with other Army factions.

Terauchi's mission to Taiwan: interview, Tanaka. On review of my notes I find that my text is in error. It should read: ". . . from October 1 to October 18, 1934, Imperial Army elder Field Marshal Prince Nashimoto visited Terauchi's command . . ." Nashimoto ranked second in seniority to Chief of Staff Prince Kanin in the Army and in the imperial family as well.

756 Manchukuo Structure Plan: Harada, 4:72-79; Nagata's position, ibid., 74-75. See also ibid., 97, 103, 145.

Booklet on war fathering creation: IPS Documents Nos. 717 and 3089, *Kokubo no hongi to sono kyoka no teisho*; Crowley, 208; Harada, 4:91.

757 War Minister Hayashi assured businessmen: Harada, 4:119.

Hirohito bivouacked with Asaka: Honjo, 197.

Maneuvers: Ito Kanejiro, 1:182, 356–57, supplemented by Fujisawa, interview. Young officers at war minister's residence: Harada, 4:132.

758 Suicide at Middle School: Honjo, 258–59.

758–760 THE MILITARY ACADEMY PLOT (or "November Plot"): this section based on Ohtani, *Rakujitsu*, 114–17; IPS Document No. 1416; Harada, 4:141–42, 155; see also Yanaga, *Since Perry*, 512.

758 N. 1: Honjo, 259.

761 Resolution of Inner Cabinet, "For the time being . . .": Japanese Foreign Ministry Archives, *Teikoku no tai-shi seisaku kankei no ken* ("Matters Relating to Imperial Policy Against China"), v. 3 of 1933–1937 series, appendix; cited in Crowley, 201.

Power play could be expected: Harada, 4:153.

"names of the imperial family appear constantly": ibid., 155.

Budget battle: ibid., 107–95, *passim*.

762–763 National Principle Group (*Kokutai genri-ha*) and their catechism: Crowley, 263–65.

Kido's assessment of feelings and factions in Army: *Nikki*, 389–90.

Secret police briefs reported group "resolved to take political power": Harada, 201–2.

764 Attack on Ikki planned: Harada, 4:202–3.

Baron Kikuchi began defamation of Ikki: Yanaga, *Since Perry*, 507.

Minobe's two articles: Harada, 2:404, 3:218; Kido, *Nikki*, 202; Crowley, 209. The first was a five-part series in *Asahi*, Jan. 18–22, 1934, *Seito seiji no shorai* ("The Future of Political Parties"); the second, *Rikugunsho hatten no kokubo-ron o yumu* (Perusing the Discussion of National Defense as Developed by the War Ministry), *Chuo Koron*, Nov. 1934.

765 Emperor did not transcend the state but was merely an organ of state: for a good summary of Japanese legal thoughts on the status of the Emperor, see Joseph Pittau, *The Meiji Political System* (Studies in Japanese Culture, Tokyo: Sophia University, 1963).

Prof. Minobe's speech: text in appendix, Harada, 4:455; translation of most of it is included in Tsunoda, 746–53.

766 Maj. Gen. Eto charged Minobe with lèse majesté: "Brocade Banner," 59–61.

On saluting Pu-Yi: Honjo, 201–2.

767 "Of course my ranking is different . . .": Honjo, 203.

768 Konoye decided to withdraw resolution: Harada, 4:213.

Omoto-kyo threat: Kido, *Nikki*, 385–87; 416–17; Harada, 4:160–62, 288.

"the Diet should be burned to the ground": Harada, 4:220.

Ikki beaten by thugs hired by relative of Kikuchi: Ohtani, *Kempei-shi*, 566; "Brocade Banner," 61.

Kido tried to persuade Minobe to resign: Harada, 4:216–17, 226, 228.

769 Commanders at palace for individual briefings from Hirohito: Honjo, 205–7; Harada, 4:227; Yanaga, *Since Perry*, 508.

Mazaki circulated memorandum, "The organ theory is incompatible . . .": ibid.

Hirohito, "Does the Army hope . . .": Honjo, 205–7.

769–770 "In his statement Mazaki calls me the *shutai* . . .": ibid.

N. 3: Honjo, 261–62.

770 Hirohito asked Terauchi to help discipline the Army and end the organ-theory attack: Harada, 4:227–28, 231.

Apr. 18, Hirohito asked Fushimi for Navy policy: Honjo, 212–13.

Veterans' clubs petition explaining evils of organ theory: Harada, 4:241.

771 "Will it be all right . . .": Honjo, 207.

Hirohito had been called a liar, withdrew for six days; exchange with Honjo, "The Army is acting against my will . . .": Honjo, 207–8.

771–772 Hirohito itemized his objections to veterans' arguments: ibid.

773 Honjo maintained anti-organ agitation a philosophical debate, strengthening people's resistance to propaganda: ibid., 210–11.

Hirohito shocked by Navy Minister Osumi's show of disaffection: ibid.; Harada, 4:256–59, 268. (Harada, 4:246–47, already knew that "the Army and Navy have joined forces to start planning for operations in the South Seas, using Taiwan as their center." Note that his informants were Shigemitsu Mamoru, the later war's-end foreign minister, and Capt. Takagi Sokichi, the later ranking Navy member of the Peace Faction.)

773–774 Hirohito, "Men in the Navy . . . ," and Rear Adm. Idemitsu's reply: Honjo, 211–12, 262.

775–778 Through the Great Wall: except as cited, this section based on Crowley, 214–24; Honjo, 213–17; Harada, 4:256–66, *passim;* interview, Kajiura Ginjiro.

776 May 1, Prince Kaya off on tour of north China: *Mainichi* (Osaka ed.), June 28, 1935.

Staff officers at Tientsin accused Chinese magazine of lèse majesté: Harada, 4:286 n.

777 Terms of Ho-Umezu Pact: for effects of pact on Chinese see Chiang Mon-lin, *Tides from the West* (Taipei: China Publication Foundation, 1957), 204–5.

19. *Purges of 1935*

785 Ishiwara's hurried memo: see also Harada, 4:279–80.

786 "A Written Opinion on Purging the Army": *Shukugun ni kansuru ikensho,* by Capt. Muranaka Koji and Paymaster First Class Isobe Asakazu, IPS Document No. 3166 (National Archives Microfilm, WT79–WT80). For publication date see Harada, 4:302 (n.).

On the eve of the purge: Kajiura and Tanaka, interviews.

787 Hayashi and Prince Kanin visited Kwantung Army: Crowley, 260.

787–791 THE FIRING OF MAZAKI: entire section, including quotations, follows Ohtani, *Rakujitsu,* 73–102 (confirmed by Harada, 4:293–94, and Kido, *Nikki,* 418). Ohtani was in charge of the secret police squad detailed to monitor the affair, and he or one of his men hovered in earshot of the conversations. The report he submitted afterward to his superior, the commandant of the secret police, was so detailed that it won him immediate promotion to the post of secret police chief for the Chiba area. Such reports were filed by the secret police commandant and made available to the palace on a need-to-know basis either through the civilian Office of the Lord Privy Seal or the military Office of Aides-de Camp, whichever was appropriate. Hirohito ordinarily appointed a new secret police commandant every eighteen months. The incumbent at this time was Lt. Gen. Tashiro Kanichiro.

N. 1: Kido, *Nikki*, 416–17.

791–794 RIPPLES AND THEIR CONTROL: this section, including quotations, based on Honjo, 220–222; also Harada, 4:295.

794 Nagata's position paper on using the Army for political purposes: a memorandum written in Aug. 1935 a few days before his death. In it Nagata wrote: "I believe it unjust to use the power of the Army for the purposes of the Restoration. . . . [It should be used] only at the direct order of the Emperor and only in its entirety." Shido Yasusuke, *Tetsuzan Nagata Chujo* [Lt. Gen. Nagata Tetsuzan] (Tokyo, 1938), 285–87, sighted in Ogata, 200.

794–799 ARAKI'S REVELATIONS: except as cited, this section follows Ohtani, *Rakujitsu*, 102–13.

Yasuda and Aizawa old subordinates of Higashikuni: in 29th Regt., 2d Div., at Sendai; Matsumoto Seicho, interview with Higashikuni, *Bungei Shunju*, Jan. 1968, 161 ff.

798 On Matsui's resignation and missionary activities in China: see IMTFE "Proceedings," 2311 ff., and ibid., *passim*, Matsui's own testimony as indexed by Dull and Umemura.

Eleven Club meeting, July 26: Harada, 4:299; "Eleven Club" used loosely here; only the nucleus of Kido, Harada, and Konoye present.

Mazaki at Summer Palace: Honjo, 222–23.

799–802 NAGATA'S MURDER: except as cited, this section based on Murofushi, 280–86; Ohtani, *Rakujitsu*, 126–31; Harada, 6:291, 303, and 4:309; Byas, *Govt. by Assassination*, 95–118.

800 Aizawa went to see Prince Asaka: Harada, 4:355–56.

Prince Asaka arranged to see Hirohito: Kido, *Nikki*, 421.

Vice war minister begged Nagata to go abroad: Honjo, 226.

802 Kido expressed no regrets for Nagata's assassination: *Nikki*, 423–24.

Emperor's reaction to the murder: Honjo, 224.

803 Saionji's comment on Nagata's murder: Harada, 4:311.

Hayashi criticized: Ohtani, *Rakujitsu*, 129–30.

Nagata's funeral: Ito Kanejiro, 1:140–41.

804 Tojo given post of commandant of Kwantung Army's secret police: Higashikuni, interview with Matsumoto Seicho (*Bungei Shunju*, Jan. 1968, 160 ff.) took credit himself for Tojo's appointment. At the same time Higashikuni acknowledged that Tojo's patron was Gen. Abe Nobuyuki. Abe was a friend and protégé of

Prince Nashimoto, his senior by one year at military academy. It would seem, therefore, that another source (privileged) is correct in identifying Prince Nashimoto consistently as Tojo's main patron.

805 Hirohito took instant dislike to new war minister: see, e.g., Harada, 4:350.

Hirohito's instructions, "The Army must be the Emperor's Army . . .": ibid., 322–23.

Sept. 18, Minobe resigned from House of Peers: Yanaga, *Since Perry*, 507–8.

Kido recorded as fact that Higashikuni was paying Yasuda: Kido, *Nikki*, 266.

806 Okamura Yasuji's opinion re Chiang Kai-shek: Crowley, 231.

Finance Minister Takahashi's message to Saionji: Harada, 4:342–43.

Toyama's meeting an excuse for crackdown on Black Dragon Society: Byas, *Govt. by Assassination*, 198, 200.

Oct. 25, Lt. Gen. Nishio Toshizo's cable re propaganda for China war: IMTFE "Proceedings," 2277 ff.

807 Attempt to kill Minobe: Murofushi, 286–89; "Brocade Banner," 59–64.

807–808 Higashikuni told Harada of agitation for Prince Kanin's resignation: Harada, 4:352.

808 Saionji, "Ikki and Makino are still capable . . .": Kido, *Nikki*, 444–45.

20. February Mutiny

For this chapter, in addition to sources cited or listed in the bibliography, I have drawn for background on: Fukumoto Kameji, *Hiroku ni-ni-roku jiken shinso-shi* [True Story of the Secret Record of the February 26 Incident] (Tokyo: Ozei Shinbun-sha, 1958); Hashimoto Tetsuma, *Tenno to hanran shoko* [The Emperor and the Officers of the Rebellion] (Tokyo: Nihon Shuho-sha, 1954); Kono Tsukasa, ed., *Ni-ni-roku jiken* [The February 26 Incident] (Tokyo: Nihon Shuho-sha, 1957); Matsumura Hidetoshi, "Hochoku meirei to Ishiwara Kanji no yudan" [Obedience to Orders Decreed by the Emperor and the Brave Decision of Ishiwara Kanji] in *Tenno to hanran gun* (Tokyo: Nihon Shuho, March, 1957); Ohtani Keijiro, "Kempei no me de mita hanran shoko"

[The Rebel Officers as Seen Through the Eyes of the Secret Police] in *Tenno to hanran gun*; Ohtani Keijiro, "Mazaki taisho muzai no giwaku" [Doubt as to the Innocence of General Mazaki] in *Tenno hanrun gun*; and *Ni-ni-roku jiken sanjunen kinengo* [February 26 Incident Thirtieth Anniversary Memorial Volume] (Tokyo: Shinseiryoku-sha, 1965).

In addition to the sources cited, I found Tateno's *Hanran* most useful for atmosphere. I am also indebted to his "Ni-ni-roku no nazo" and *Showa gunbatsu* for provocative ideas about the incitement and exploitation of the incident. Another background account I found helpful was Maeda Harumi, *Showa hanran-shi* [History of Rebellion in the Reign of Hirohito] (Tokyo: Nihonsho Hosha, 1964). There is, of course, a voluminous Japanese literature on the rebellion, and it is impossible to do any research in Japan without being told many stories taken from this literature. The best guide that I know of to all *Ni-ni-roku* sources is Hata Ikuhiko, whose *Gun fuashizumu*, 131–202, includes a complete set of bibliographical notes.

810 Relations of rebel officers with Chichibu, Higashikuni, Asaka, Yamashita, and Okamura: Ohtani, *Kempei-shi*, 195–98, also his *Rakujitsu*, 174–76; "Brocade Banner," 78. For Chichibu's involvement, see especially Kono Tsukasa, "Ni-ni-roku jiken no nazo" and also his *Ni-ni-roku jiken, passim*. As a close kinsman of Kono Hisashi, one of the rebels, Kono Tsukasa was long the head of the *Ni-ni-roku izoku-kai* or February Mutiny Bereaved Families Association.

811 "The gods, the Emperor, and the good earth . . .": Hata, *Gun*, 154.

Yamashita failed to keep appointment: Ohtani, *Rakujitsu*, 174–76.

Dec. 20 protest meeting: Harada, 4:403; Storry, *Double Patriots*, 180–81.

Mutiny plan in Kido's diary: *Nikki*, 452–53.

Defection of soldiers in Manchuria: Harada, 4:413; Kido, *Nikki*, 459–60; Tanaka, interview.

813 THE TALKING GODDESS: This section, not previously reported either in Western or Japanese secondary sources, is taken from Kido's memo on the police findings, Ohara-Shimazu case (Kido, *Nikki*, 527–29), and on Kido's diary entries (ibid., 456, 493–97, 500–501, 504–14, 516, 518, 526, 591). See also Harada, 5:154–55, 167.

814 N. 2: Koyama, 51–52; see also Murofushi, 195.

816 Higashikuni's stand-by sword arms: Kido, *Nikki*, 470–71; Harada, 4:413, 420; also "Brocade Banner," 71–72.

816–817 Aizawa trial: Yanaga. *Since Perry*, 513: Byas, *Govt. by Assassination*, 99–118; Kido, *Nikki*, 452–53; Takahashi, 32; "Brocade Banner," 71–73; Harada, 4:411.

N. 4: Kido, *Nikki*, 470–71.

817 Kido's research into Army feeling: *Nikki*, 459–60.

818 1936 elections: Scalapino, 381–82.

818–819 Preliminaries of mutiny up to Feb. 22; Takahashi, 32–37; Ohtani, *Kempei-shi*, 89–91.

819 P-day minus four: Takahashi, 37.

P-day minus three: ibid., 34, 40; "Brocade Banner," 74.

820 Feb. 24, P-day minus two: ibid., 73–74, 134; Takahashi, 35–36; Harada, 5:300. After the war Usawa became the defense lawyer for Matsui Iwane and Shiratori Toshio at the International Military Tribunal; "Brocade Banner," 146.

Saionji warned he was to be assassinated: The various accounts conflict as to when Saionji received this warning. The best and most aristocratic of my verbal sources states positively that Saionji removed himself from harm's way on the day before the rising. Kodama Yoshio, a rightwing jailbird with excellent underworld sources of information, also felt that Saionji had received adequate prior notice of the rising (Kodama, 54). A. M. Young, *Imperial Japan*, 277, understood that Saionji "warned by a telephone call . . . claimed the hospitality of the Chief of Police for the night." Byas, another Western newsman with usually reliable information, states only that Saionji "was hastily taken to a place of safety by the Governor of the prefecture where he lived, and if the rebels intended to kill him, they were baffled"; *Govt.*, 121. "Brocade Banner," compiled by U.S. Intelligence agents after the war from Japanese secret police files, implies that Saionji was not warned until some time between 6 and 7 A.M. on the morning of the killings (143). Latter-day Japanese investigators, including Murofushi and Takahashi, also indicate that Saionji had only just enough time to escape. Harada, 5:36, 300, however, reveals that Saionji was warned by telegram on Feb. 25. His informant, Usawa Fusa-aki, had learned of the conspiracy the day before, Feb. 24 ("Brocade Banner," 143). "Brocade Banner" further states that Gen. Mazaki awakened Usawa shortly after 4 A.M. on Feb. 26 and put him on the 5:30 train to Okitsu. I interpret this to mean that

Usawa arrived in Okitsu before 7 A.M. and that he came to make sure that Saionji had heeded the warnings sent a day earlier. Then, apparently, he found no one at Saionji's "Sit-and-Fish" Villa except a few servants such as the maid who answered the phone when Kido called at 6:40. Kido's behavior seems to support this conclusion. In *Kankei bunsho*, 4–5, he reveals that he knew on Feb. 2, 1936, that the 1st Div. intended to rise and kill the elder statesman. He apparently waited until 6:40 A.M. on Feb. 26 to phone a warning to Saionji. He was then told that Saionji was peacefully sleeping and need not be disturbed. A year later (*Nikki*, 535) Kido learned by phone from Makino that news of the mutiny's definite commencement had reached Gen. Mazaki "not at 8 A.M. as previously stated but at about 3 A.M.—and this is corroborated by the chauffeur." In short, it would seem that by the date of this entry, Jan. 12, 1937, Kido and Makino were still trying to find out whom to blame for Saionji's escape.

N. 7: Harada, 5:300.

Saionji's escape: A. M. Young, *Imperial Japan*, 277–78, corroborated by interview with the son of a banker who was a close friend of Saionji.

822 Polishing the manifesto: "Brocade Banner," 74; Takahashi, 27–28.

Evening, Feb. 24–morning, Feb. 25: ibid., 34–35; Murofushi, 310–11.

Mazaki at Aizawa trial: *Asahi*, Feb. 26, 1936; A. M. Young, *Imperial Japan*, 276.

Resentment in 1st Div. barracks: Takahashi, 37–38.

BLOODSHED AT LAST: this section, except as cited, based on "Brocade Banner," 73–94; Takahashi, 46–60; Murofushi, 290–313; Byas, *Govt. by Assassination*, 119–22; Fleisher, 69–88; A. M. Young, *Imperial Japan*, 276–80.

824 Ishiwara's sortie from General Staff offices: Hata, *Gun*, 154–55.

825 Saito's night before at the Grews: Grew, *Ten Years*, 157.

Suzuki's delicate wound: Agawa, 88.

828 Makino's rescue by his granddaughter: Grew, *Ten Years*, 157–58.

829 N. 8: by count from Takahashi, 46–49.

Story which diaries expose as false: compare Kido, *Nikki*, 464–79; Harada, 5:3–22; and Honjo, 235–38, 266–67, 271–99, with the accounts of the February Mutiny preserved in Grew, *Ten Years*; Craigie; Byas, *Govt. by Assassination*; Fleisher; and A. M. Young, *Imperial Japan* (as cited).

829–830 Honjo-Hirohito exchange, Feb. 25: Honjo, 234–35.

21. *Suppression*

831–832 Honjo, 5 to 8 A.M., Feb. 26: Honjo, 271–72. In Honjo's reply, on page 832, I have compressed thoughts which Honjo in his own version wrote down as if he wished he had voiced them.

832–833 Kido and Harada to 8 A.M.: Kido, *Nikki*, 464–66; Harada, 5:3–4.

832 Kido's phone call to Saionji: Kido's three-line description of this call was unaccountably left out of the translation—marked "in full"—of this entry which was prepared for presentation at the IMTFE.

833 Harada's two days in rebel territory (i.e., Feb. 26 and part of Feb. 27): Harada, 5:4.

"Shoot-at-sight" list: Ohtani, *Kempei-shi*, 191.

Kido at Inner Palace: *Nikki*, 464; description of accommodations there: Koizumi, interview.

Terms given Kawashima: "Brocade Banner," 75 ff.; Takahashi, 58–60.

834 Prince Fushimi's audience with Emperor: Kido, *Nikki*, 464. At 8 A.M.: Honjo, 272; see also Agawa, 94; Honjo, 273.

Kawashima at palace: ibid., 272; also Byas, *Govt. by Assassination*, 123.

834–836 Manifesto: Takahashi, 25–26. In this translation I have tried to reproduce the flavor as well as the sense.

836 Hirohito's reply to Kawashima: Kido, *Nikki*, 464, gives the first two sentences of this reply and Honjo, 272, the last sentence.

836–840 FIRST DAY OF SIEGE: this section based on Honjo, 272–74; Kido, *Nikki*, 464–66; "Brocade Banner," 81–82, 86–88; Takahashi, 58–64, 69–72, 78–90; Hata, *Gun*, 152–55; interviews with Koizumi.

841–845 THE SECOND DAY: except as cited, this section based on Honjo, 274–76; Kido, *Nikki*, 466–67; Takahashi, 78–90 *passim*, also 93–99; "Brocade Banner," 87–88.

842 "to strangle me with a silken cord and . . .": for clarity I have doubled the Emperor's image, which was literally "to

strangle my head with soft cotton"—*mawata ni te Chin ga kobe o shimuru ni hitoshiki yukinari*; Honjo, 276.

Hirohito willing to go down to barricades himself: Honjo, 235 and 276, gives two slightly different versions of this scene.

Peers' Club and stopping of Harada: Ohtani, *Kempei-shi*, 191-92.

N. 3: Ideograph for *Chin*: I am indebted for this charming etymology to Kitagawa Hiroshi.

843 Chichibu and Imperial Family Council: ibid., 195-98, supplemented by interviews with Koizumi Shinzo; Kido, *Nikki*, 466; and Higashikuni in Matsumoto interview, *Bungei Shunju*, January 1968, 160 ff.

N. 4: Imperial House Law: *The Japan Year Book*, 1944-45, 809 ff.

844 Chichibu and Nonaka suicide: "Brocade Banner," 146.

Hirohito's evaluation of his kinsmen: Kido, *Nikki*, 468.

845 THE THIRD DAY: except as cited, this section based on Honjo, 276-79; Kido, *Nikki*, 466-67; Takahashi, 99-104.

846 Honjo aged years that day: Ito Kanejiro, 2:68.

Ishiwara, "We shall attack": see his entry in *Nihon Jinbutsu-shi Taikei* [Japan Biographical Outline] (Tokyo: Asakura Shobo, 1960), vol. 7.

Rebel response to pleas: see *Bungei Shunju*, January 1966, 263.

847 Hirohito accused the Army of insubordination: In *Honjo Nikki* as published this scene is reported as of this hour and date (4:30 P.M., Feb. 28) in two different places (236, 278); in relating the conversation here, I have put the two accounts together.

849-850 Ishiwara confronted Araki: Agawa, 6.

HIROHITO'S SETTLEMENT: except as cited, this section based on Honjo, 279-300; Kido, *Nikki*, 468-78; Harada, 5:6-22; Takahashi, 104-118.

Nonaka's suicide: "Brocade Banner," 146.

851 Hirohito in uniform: Honjo, 266-67, 283.

854 Addition of seven divisions: Hata, "Notebooks"; Tanaka, interview.

Kanin's explanation of purges: my own translation of Harada, 5:10.

855 2,000 noncommissioned officers to Army reserve: Ohtani, *Kempei-shi*, 212; also Crowley, 274.

856 Mazaki's hunger strike: Kido, *Nikki*, 535.

Araki's assessment of Mazaki's pardon: Takahashi, 203.

857 Yamashita's reassuring note from Hirohito: Potter, *Soldier Must Hang,* 22; supplemented by Hata's "Notebooks," corroborated by interview with Fujisawa, who served under Yamashita in the Philippines.

Rebels' one-hour trials: Ohtani, *Kempei-shi,* 214–17.

Last words of executed rebels: Takahashi, 192–200; also "Brocade Banner," 90.

22. *Neutralizing Russia*

861–862 Drowning A Radio: this section based on Klausen's own account in interrogations, as cited in Deakin and Storry, 207.

863 Significance of Sorge ring: see Johnson, ch. 7, esp. 153–55.

Sorge a middle-class intellectual, Russian mother, served in World War I: Johnson, 69.

Acknowledged Hero of Soviet Union in 1964: Deakin and Storry, 350.

Sorge joined party in 1920, became agent for Comintern: Johnson, 71–72.

Reassigned to Red Army Intelligence, sent to Shanghai: ibid., 73–74.

Sorge met future Japanese agents in Shanghai: Deakin and Storry, 75.

Communist paymaster in Shanghai arrested, Sorge closely watched: ibid., 91–92.

864 Sorge's mission in Japan, his preparations in Germany: ibid., 95–103.

Established close relations with German Embassy in Tokyo: Johnson, 140–42.

American Japanese joined Sorge, arranged meetings with Japanese liberals and leftists: Johnson, 94–95, 105.

865 Sorge obtained Klausen for radio work; he built equipment, established contact with Russian station in Siberia in Apr. 1936: Deakin and Storry, 156 ff.; Johnson, 101–2.

Delegation to Yosemite: Johnson, 111–13.

866 Saionji Kinkazu consulted on Communist problems: My interpretation of young Saionji's role here and later was first suggested to me by Matsumoto Shigeharu. I asked him how it was that Saionji had escaped severe punishment for his involvement with Sorge's Soviet spy ring and he replied that since Konoye always

encouraged his advisors to keep in touch with all shades of political opinion, it would have been unfair to punish Saionji for doing what was expected of him. Later I asked Koizumi Shinzo about young Saionji's pardon and he observed that upperclass Japanese looked upon spying somewhat differently from Westerners; that they could not imagine one of their number being a traitor; that the relationship of Saionji and even of Ozaki to the Sorge ring could be considered a form of international mediation or public relations rather than of spying or treason.

Still later I asked the most aristocratic of my sources about Saionji, and he replied in his outspoken fashion that in the inner circle Saionji was considered a valuable pipeline to Stalin.

Analysis of Kido's diary supports these statements. In the entire period between 1930 and 1945 Kido reported meeting with young Saionji exactly twenty-two times on July 10 and Aug. 1, 1932; on March 25, June 3, June 10, July 22 and Sept. 16, 1933; on March 16 and Nov. 1, 1934; on March 10, 1936; on July 13, Aug. 31, Sept. 2, Sept. 16 and Oct. 25, 1937; on Apr. 25 and July 23, 1938; on June 9, 1939; on Nov. 24 and Dec. 2, 1940; and on March 3 and Nov. 24, 1941. From Kido's brief entries on these meetings, supplemented by interviews, I have pieced together a tentative history of the Kido-Saionji relationship. At the first two meetings Kido made use of Saionji's knowledge of English and his Oxford connections to get information on the attitudes of the Lytton commissioners who were then drafting their famous report. At the third meeting, Kido and Saionji discussed British attitudes to Japan's withdrawal from the League of Nations. The next four meetings were all concerned with Araki's Red smear and Kido's attempts to dig up material for counter-blackmail. By this juncture Saionji had proved his skill and loyalty as an agent of the Throne and on Dec. 26, 1933, and Jan. 10, 1934, Kido discussed with Harada a long-term assignment for young Saionji as an advisor on left-wing matters to Prince Konoye. At the eighth meeting, in March 1934 Kido discussed the assignment with Saionji. At the ninth, the following November, Saionji met with several members of the Eleven Club to celebrate the successful defamation and overthrow of Konoye's rival in the House of Peers, Tokugawa Iesato. By the next, the tenth meeting, in March 1936, Saionji had already infiltrated leftist circles and was instructed on the line he should take at Yosemite. The next five meetings took place in 1937 when war had broken out with China and when Saionji was a member of Prime Minister Konoye's kitchen cabinet. Out of them came Ozaki's reports to Sorge and Sorge's reports to Stalin on Japanese intentions in China. The sixteenth meeting, in April 1938, had the effect of explaining Japan's mobilization to Stalin. The seventeenth, in July 1938, in effect assured Stalin that the Lake Khasan incident would not be allowed to escalate into war; the eighteenth, in June 1939, did the same for the Nomonhan incident. Then in November-December 1940 followed the only two social meetings of the entire Kido-Saionji relationship and both were purely formal, having to do with the death and funeral of old Prince Saionji. Finally, on March 3, 1941, Kido met young Saionji to instruct him on his duties as a companion to Matsuoka on his European trip. The last meeting was held at old Saionji's tomb on the anniversary of his death. Since the rest of the Sorge ring had been arrested, it marked the funeral of the Saionji-Kido association. Thereafter Kido discussed Saionji with others and exerted influence on Saionji's behalf but held no more recorded meetings with him.

Ozaki's youth: Johnson, 22–23; Koizumi, interview; for background on Japanese in Taiwan, see Jansen, 83.

Ozaki at university: Johnson, 26.

His postgraduate work: ibid., 32.

867 Trained as journalist, sent to Shanghai: Johnson, 34, 40.

Ozaki and Agnes Smedley: Deakin and Storry, 70–71.

Sorge and Ozaki: Johnson, 67; their beliefs, ibid., 1–4.

For six years Ozaki knew Sorge as "Johnson": ibid., 67, 87.

868 Sorge's intermediary met Ozaki in deer park, Nara: ibid., 11.

Report of 1936 Army Mutiny: in Obi, *Gendai-shi*, 2:137.

Kawai Teikichi's spy career: Johnson, 79–80, 90, 109.

869 Ozaki joined group around Prince Konoye: ibid., 115–20.

Ozaki learned "Johnson" was Sorge, Sept. 1936: Deakin and Storry, 187.

Ozaki became member of Konoye's Showa Research Society: Johnson, 120.

Kido and Saionji Kinkazu: see note on page 866.

869–872 INNER MONGOLIA: this section based on Tanaka MS, "Yoshiko," IPS Documents 724, 1634.

Mongol horsemen massacred Japanese officers: *N.Y. Times,* Dec. 10, 1936.

Prince Teh proclaimed loyalty to Chiang Kai-shek: ibid., Dec. 12, 1936.

872–875 THE GENERALISSIMO KIDNAPPED: except as cited, this section based on Ekins and Wright, 155–76; Snow, 397–431; Chiang Kai-shek, *A Summing Up at Seventy: Soviet Russia in China* (London: George C. Harrap, 1957), 72–79.

873 Details of kidnapping: Chiang's own account as related to Abend; *Life in China*, 233–35.

Chiang family gave news to Abend of N.Y. *Times:* ibid., 226–31.

874 Donald arrived in Sian on Dec. 14: for dating of his and others' arrivals, I have followed N.Y. *Times*, Dec. 14, Dec. 21, 1936.

875 Chang Hsueh-liang in Taiwan: my personal correspondence with James Chen, an aide to Chiang Kai-shek.

ALLIANCE WITH HITLER: except as cited, this section based on Presseisen, 87–119, and Iklé, 21–50.

876 Goebbels' Bureau of Race Investigation quoted: Iklé, 28.

Ott on Schleicher's staff: Presseisen, 68.

Ott liaison officer in Nagoya: Deakin and Storry, 101, 138; Hata, "Notebooks" and interview.

Oshima's career: summarized in Presseisen, 69.

877 Secret protocols in Anti-Comintern Pact and Stalin's knowledge of them: Iklé, 38–39.

878 Sorge had reported on pact: Deakin and Storry, 185 ff.

Sorge met Ott in Nagoya, had served in same German division: ibid., 138.

Sorge reported on Kwantung Army strength and opinion that no Strike North was pending: ibid., 185.

Soviet government delivered calculated slap to Japan: Iklé, 40.

878–883 BLOCKING UGAKI: except as cited, this section based on Kido, *Nikki*, 537–40; Harada, 5:235–47, 248–59 *passim*; Hata, *Gun*, 184–91.

882 Ugaki's search for war minister and Terauchi's countermoves, Monday and Tuesday: Umezu papers and interrogations cited in IMTFE "Proceedings," 15797 ff.

883 Journalist who advised assassination of Prince Kanin: Ohtani, *Kempei-shi*, 250–51.

883–885 SAIONJI DROPS OUT: except as cited, this section based on Kido, *Nikki*, 540–44, 559, supplemented by interviews with banker's son.

885 Saionji on Higashikuni's air force command: Harada, 5:279.

Chichibu's departure for England: *Asahi* (Osaka ed.), March 19, 1937; the words of his equerry beforehand: Ito Kanejiro, 1:204.

886–888 KONOYE: this sketch based on Yabe Teiji's authoritative biography of Konoye.

888–890 MARCO POLO'S BRIDGE: to this famous chapter in history, most of which is a matter of record, I have added the Nashimoto-Tojo episode. I noticed the coincidence of Nashimoto's trip as later reported in Japanese newspapers, with the sending of Tojo's telegram. Then I asked retired Maj. Gen. Kajiura Ginjiro about Nashimoto's entertainment at Hsinking (Long Spring Thaw). He assumed that I knew of the episode through prior official statements at the IMTFE, and having been present at the banquet, he gladly gave me the details I have used here. The Japanese text of the Tojo telegram is in IMTFE Exhibit 672.

889 Tojo accompanied Nashimoto as far as Kyushu: *Asahi* (Osaka ed.), June 10, 1937.

Higashikuni's inspection trip to Taiwan: ibid., June 9, 18, 19, 1937.

Army bargain, Saionji Kinkazu informed, Chichibu's message from London: my interpretation of Kido, *Nikki*, 575–78, and Harada, 6:25–28, corroborated by Tanaka interviews.

890 In Chapter 1: see note on page 6.

Konoye's protestations of peaceful intent: see also Ohtani, *Kempei-shi*, 274–75.

891 Kido into Cabinet: *Nikki*, 595–91.

German desire to mediate Sino-Japanese dispute: Presseisen, 129.

Hirohito refused to offer realistic peace terms: he was encouraged by Kido, who led the fight to "keep the terms abstract"; IMTFE "Proceedings," 30836–837.

No settlement but complete mastery: see Sugiyama, 2:327 for "Basic Policy in re China Incident," adopted Jan. 11, 1938.

Konoye's suggestion to threaten China politically: see also Horiba, 109–11, on role of Military Affairs Bureau Chief Machijiri.

General Staff opposed ultimatum: Usui, *Gendai-shi*, 9:841; Harada, 6:203–8.

Kanin suppressed opposition: Ohtani, *Kempei-shi*, 278; for

other instances of old Kanin's continuing activity and influence, see ibid., 282–84.

893 Hirohito did not want to end war: "Why is the General Staff so eager to stop the war?" he asked, Harada, 6:207–8. He was much influenced by Kido, for whose position see ibid., 193 and 209–10. See also ibid., 7:97–100, for handling of Chichibu and Ishiwara, who agreed with General Staff.

Navy position on China war: Usui, *Gendai-shi*, 9:842.

894 Higashikuni and Machijiri in their new commands: Hata, *Nichu*, 291.

For a flattering account of Higashikuni's campaigning, see Ikeda Genji, *Higashikuni Shireikan-miya* [Higashikuni, the Commander-Prince] (Tokyo: Masu Shobo, 1943).

896 Breaching the Matang boom: interviews with J. Van Wie Bergamini, Hata, Tanaka.

897 A SOVIET DEFECTOR: this section based on Johnson, 148–49; Deakin and Storry, 199–203; interviews with Tanaka.

N. 9: Itagaki recalled to become war minister, see *Taiheiyo senso*, 4:47.

898 AN UNAUTHORIZED INCIDENT: military details in this section drawn from IMTFE "Proceedings," 38290 ff.; 22575–638; 7773 ff.

Lake Khasan incident plotted by Tada: Harada, 6:300–35, and 7:1–47, coupled with Prince Chichibu's trip to China May 2–18 (*Asahi*, June 20, 1938), suggests to me that Hirohito may have enabled the Lake Khasan incident to take place as a device for discrediting the Strike-North Faction.

899 Tojo's cable to 19th Div. commander: Tsunoda, *Gendai-shi*, 10:4.

899–900 Kanin and Itagaki, Itagaki and Hirohito: these three paragraphs based on Tsunoda, *Gendai-shi*, 10:xxxiv–vi, and Harada, 7:50–54, 61. I have followed an interview source in inserting the Emperor's remark about Itagaki's stupidity (*Omae gurai atama no warui mono wa nai*); according to Harada, 8:13, it was actually made on a similar occasion a year later.

900 Ozaki's report to Sorge that the Lake Khasan incident would stop short of war: Obi, *Gendai-shi*, 2:165, also 85.

Significance of Ott's appointment as ambassador: Deakin and Storry, 101, 138; Hata, "Notebooks"; Kido, *Nikki*, 638. Sorge's own appointment, Johnson, 140, 143.

901–2 Sorge's mission to Hong Kong and Manila, his motorcycle accident and its sequel: Deakin and Storry, 197–99.

902 THE LAKE KHASAN MUTINY: military details in this section from IMTFE "Proceedings," 38290 ff.; 22575–638; 7773 ff.

903 Mission of Tanaka and Cho at Lake Khasan: my synthesis from Tanaka, interviews; his *Sabakareru*, 44; Hata's "Notebooks"; Harada, 7:61.

Bare display of courage by Tanaka and Cho: Ito Kanejiro, 2:274, also 1:43.

Stalin reassured, Blücher imprisoned, report to Berlin photographed: Johnson, 146–49; Deakin and Storry, 200.

905 Wang Ching-wei left Chunking, was later abducted: Usui, *Gendai-shi*, 9:624–25; IPS Document No. 1005. See Miwa Kimitada, "The Wang Ching-wei Regime and Japanese Efforts to Terminate the China Conflict." In *Studies in Japanese Culture*, edited by Joseph Roggendorf (Tokyo: Sophia University Press, 1963).

906 Ozaki Hotsumi, "The New National Structure," *Contemporary Japan*, Oct. 1940, cited in USAFFE, "Left Wing, Right Wing: Japanese Proletarian Politics"; Sorge-Ozaki conversation about it: Johnson, 120.

907 Konoye's resignation and its purpose: see Harada, 7:250–59.

Takamatsu at Hainan: *Asahi* (Osaka ed.), March 1, 1939.

909 Hitler pressed for alliance: Iklé, 78–88.

910–911 Hirohito's provisional acceptance of alliance and Hitler's rejection: ibid., 711–15; Tanaka and Koizumi, interviews; Iklé, 87–102.

Hirohito's turmoil over alliance with Hitler, Kido, *Nikki*, 710–11.

911 NOMONHAN (1): this section based on IMTFE "Proceedings," 7854, and testimony of Maj. Afimogen Erastovich Bykov, ibid., 38359 ff.; see also ibid., 22594–718; 23011 ff.; 23025 ff.

912 Hitler signed with Mussolini, Japan excluded: Iklé, 113–14.

913 NOMONHAN (2): Bykov testimony, IMTFE "Proceedings," 38359–385.

914 Significance of Azuma, Yamagata, and young Higashikuni: Hata, "Notebooks"; Tsunoda, *Gendai-shi*, 10:81; *Asahi*, March 20, 1942.

915 Ozaki took job under Okawa: Deakin and Storry, 249.

Kido to Saionji, Saionji to Sorge, Sorge to Moscow: Obi, *Gendai-shi*, 1:50, 2:86, 169–70; also Deakin and Storry, 202–3; Johnson, 150–52.

915–916 Zhukov in Mongolia: Georgy K. Zhukov, *Marshal Zhukov's Greatest Battles*, Intro. by Harrison E. Salisbury (New York: Harper & Row, 1969), 7–8.

916 Young Higashikuni's desertion: Tsunoda, *Gendai-shi*, 10:81; also Kido, *Nikki*, 1105 (entry for May 9, 1944).

Zhukov's offensive: see Zhukov, *Greatest Battles*, Intro., 7–8; IMTFE "Proceedings," 7854; Johnson, 150.

917 "Japanese not good at armor": Zhukov to Gen. Bedell Smith at end of war, quoted, Zhukov, *Greatest Battles*, Intro., 8.

Kido's and Hiranuma's reactions to pact: Kido, *Nikki*, 741–42.

Hitler's tirade against Hirohito: Iklé, 133.

918 Nakajima embassy to Nomonhan: Ishiwara Kanji, testimony, IMTFE "Proceedings," 22594 ff.

919 Suicide of some Japanese commanders: Imai Sei-ichi, "Nomonhan jiken," 76 ff.

23. *Joining the Axis*

921 Twelve new divisions added: Hata, "Notebooks."

Grew's speech, Oct. 19, 1939: Grew, *Ten Years*, 251–56.

Speech discussed by Emperor's circle: ibid., 258–59.

922 Diet members formed League for Waging Holy War: Yanaga, *Since Perry*, 543–44.

922–923 Hirohito sent emissary to Marquis Kido: Kido, *Nikki*, 783.

Kido had advised Konoye re I.R.A.A.: ibid., 744–83.

He acknowledged to his diary: ibid., 784.

Kido put pressure on politicians: ibid., 784–86.

Kido, Konoye, Arima agreed on postponement of announcement of New Structure: ibid., 787–88.

Finished plans for New Structure, invested as lord privy seal: ibid., 788. See also Harada, 8.250–51, wherein Saionji refused to give ceremonial endorsement to Kido's appointment.

924 Hirohito read position papers describing Japan's "fateful juncture," "golden opportunity": see, e.g., IMTFE "Proceedings," 6975–7001, and IPS Document No. 1987.

Emperor's visit to tombs of his ancestors: Kido, *Nikki*, 791–92.

925 Emperor asked questions about Italy's entry into war: ibid., 792.

Kido and Hirohito discussed French and Dutch colonies during dinner at Kyoto Palace: ibid.

Pact with Thailand a means to infiltrate French Indochina: IMTFE "Proceedings," 6869–75; Frederick Whyte, *Japan's Purpose in Asia and the Pacific* (Melbourne: Oxford University Press, 1942).

926 Kido advised Yonai's Cabinet members to resign, urged vice foreign minister to speed negotiations: Kido, *Nikki*, 792.

Tani's conversations with French ambassador: Negotiations between Tani and Arsène-Henry for further concessions in French Indochina continued through Sept.: IMTFE "Proceedings," 6875–6924; Harada, 8:266–67.

927 Meeting at Changsha of Chiang's deputy and Japanese vice chief of staff: Kido, *Nikki*, 802–3, 808, 810–11, 816–17, and thereafter *passim*.

Japanese encounters with Chiang's forces arranged in advance: interviews with Kajiura Ginjiro (he had command of Japanese salient farthest up Yangtze River during most of the war).

928 Prince Asaka assured Hirohito that British were losing, recommended combined air force: Kido, *Nikki*, 795.

Hirohito approved Konoye's Cabinet choices: ibid., 797–98.

929 Kido suggested Anami stay on as vice war minister: ibid., 799.

Kido recommended Konoye as prime minister: ibid., 805–7.

Tojo learned of his selection on return to Tokyo: Butow, *Tojo*, 142.

"a high-degree defense state": propaganda slogan of editorialists at the time.

Saionji comment, "like inviting a robber": Harada, 7:366.

THE NEW ORDER: Konoye's program is set forth in detail in Harada, 8:338–45.

930 Matsuoka's American experiences: Fleisher, 46–47.

Grew's conversation with Matsuoka: Grew, *Ten Years*, 279–80.

July 26, 1940, new Cabinet adopted program: Sugiyama, 1:7–10.

931 Hirohito planned to remove members of imperial family from positions of responsibility: Kido, *Nikki*, 811.

Important ministers of Cabinet met with chiefs of staff to ratify program: Harada, 8:299–302.

This "liaison conference" first in two years: Sugiyama, 1:6.

Staff officers' plan, "Main Japanese Policy Principles": *Taiheiyo senso*, 8:322–24.

932 Tojo protested to Kido: Kido, *Nikki*, 812.

Hirohito's analysis of Cabinet's difficulties: ibid., 812–13.

933 Concubines would no longer have telephones: Grew, *Ten Years*, 284.

934 Saionji re Japanese press writing "like drunkards": Harada, 7:282.

THE COX CASE: sources for this incident are Fleisher, 123: 308–9; Morin, 60; Craigie, 111–12; IPS Document No. 1533; Obi, *Gendai-shi*, 1:192.

Hirohito ready to reconsider tripartite military alliance: Iklé, 154.

N. 6: see, e.g., Higashikuni, *Watashi*, 59, and Matsumoto Seicho's article in *Bungei Shunju*, January 1938, 160 ff. Re Kido's continued communication with Toyama: *Nikki*, e.g., 844, 849, 861, 867, 869.

Japanese must suppress pro-British sentiments: Iklé, 167.

936 Konoye government "marking time": Grew, *Ten Years*, 283.

Stahmer at Japanese Embassy: Iklé, 168.

Matsuoka consulted Emperor on replacement of diplomats abroad: Kido, *Nikki*, 816; see also IMTFE Exhibit 548.

937 Agreement between Matsuoka and Vichy French ambassador Arsène-Henry: This may have been reached on Aug. 20 but I err in saying that it was signed then; the signing took place on Aug. 30 (Kido, *Nikki*, 818; Grew, *Ten Years*, 286–87). Col. Cho Isamu was dispatched to Indochina in late August and Gen. Tominaga Kyoji in early September (Tanaka, interview; Hata, "Notebooks"). My interpretation of the gallant Japanese effort to save French honor is based on interviews with Tanaka and Koizumi. A German transcript of a September 20 telephone call from Gen. Boyen of the French Armistice Commission to his German opposite number, Gen. Stülpnagel, reveals that the French gesture of resistance was reported in advance to the Reich (IMTFE "Proceedings," 6968–75). For other details of the Franco-Japanese negotiations see IPS Document No. 985 on Library of Congress Microfilm WT-26 and "Proceedings," 6801–6975. The latter, 6875 ff., contains an exchange that expresses perfectly the spirit of the talks. Ambassador Arsène-Henry said, "The Japanese request is one-sided." The chief Japanese negotiator, Vice Foreign Minister Tani Masayuki of the Eleven Club, replied, "That is natural. That is why we are able to negotiate."

938 Saionji on the Emperor's fading aura in approving the Tripartite Pact: Harada, 8:330. Of Matsuoka, who had negotiated

the pact, Saionji spoke more gently: "It would do Matsuoka good to go crazy, but unfortunately for him he is more likely to regain his sanity."

New Navy minister "easy to talk to": Harada, 8:331.

Hirohito's private acceptance of pact on Sept. 4: Harada, 8:368 (also 335) and Kido, *Nikki*, 819, supplemented by interview with Koizumi. Also that day Hirohito attended graduation ceremonies at the military academy and received news of young Prince Kitashirakawa Nagahisa's death in a plane crash.

939 Hirohito's talk with Kido about German bombing: Kido, *Nikki*, 820.

Sept. 9, Hirohito unexpectedly at liaison conference: Harada, 8:348–49.

940 Matsuoka and Stahmer conversed in English: Iklé, 171.

Sept. 13, Hirohito studied text of pact four and a half hours: interview, Koizumi; see also Kido, *Nikki*, 821.

Hirohito's editing of text: ibid., 823–24.

941 Unofficial liaison conference of Sept. 14: Harada, 8:369.

Hirohito asked Kido to call conference in Imperial Presence: Kido, *Nikki*, 822.

941–944 Conference of Sept. 19: Sugiyama, 1:41–55: Ike, 4–13.

944 Matsuoka's ultimatum of Sept. 19: IPS Document No. 985.

Tominaga Kyoji arranged invasion: Imai Sei-ichi, "Misshitsu no naka no konran," 78 ff.

945 Tripartite Pact signed in Berlin: The procedure and date, as well as the text of the pact, had been passed upon by Hirohito at the conference in the Imperial Presence of Sept. 19. Sugiyama, 1:42–43, gives the Japanese text of the pact; for an English text see F. C. Jones, 469–70.

946 Hirohito felt as if he were looting a store during a fire: Kido, *Nikki*, 854. "Really," he said, "we should not exploit this time when others are weak as if we were robbers at a fire. Personally I don't like it. It doesn't fit my principles. Now, however, when we face crisis, I have no choice."

947 Hirohito approved pact out of fear of assassination: Grew, *Ten Years*, 300.

Harada made contribution to imperial cover story by producing so-called Saionji-Harada Memoirs: my interpretation of

Harada, 1:3–9 (Introduction) and 297–303, which includes account of removal of manuscript to Prince Takamatsu's villa.

Saionji understood journal was kept to show Emperor complexities of politics: So Hirohito told the professional writer Satomi Ton who had helped with matters of style in writing the diary. The occasion was a dinner for the Belles Lettres Society in Sept. 1948; see Abe Nose, ed., *Tenno no insho* (Tokyo: Sogensha, 1949), 24–25.

948 Special ceremony at Palace Shrine, Oct. 17: Kido, *Nikki*, 830.

949 Yamamoto raising funds in Osaka: Harada, 8:380.

Hirohito 2600th birthday speech: Byas, *Govt. by Assassination*, 296.

Takamatsu broadcast: Harada, 8:393–94.

DEATH OF SAIONJI: this section based on Harada, 8:394–99.

950 Kido went to Okitsu to express Emperor's regrets: Kido, *Nikki*, 838.

Kido met Saionji Kinkazu at funeral: ibid.

Sorge had had to rely on German Embassy sources entirely: Deakin and Storry, 223.

Sorge's Communist ties discovered, but Nazi Press Dept. head decided to keep contact with him: Johnson, 12, 171.

Schellenberg sent Gestapo Colonel Josef Meisinger to watch Sorge: ibid., 172.

Meisinger had part in rape of Warsaw: Deakin and Storry, 314.

Meisinger revealed suspicions about Sorge to secret police; aristocrats around Court cut connections with him: Johnson, 172.

951 Young Saionji spurned Australia for rightist cell: Harada, 8:325.

Kido's long view, Dec. 3: Kido, *Nikki*, 840.

952 Yamamoto's forebodings: Harada, 8:365–66.

24. *Passive Resistance*

954 Yamamoto taunted code experts for new Admirals' Code: interview, Okumiya; Farago, 106–7.

Yamamoto communicated with Hirohito through Prince Takamatsu re Pearl Harbor plan: Kido, *Nikki*, 836, as explained by former Navy commander (privileged source). The explanation is corroborated by the delicate handling of the story in Agawa, 206–8. Agawa states that the *naimei* or "inside orders" for Genda to make his study were not passed on to Yamamoto "formally" until Jan. 7, 1941. Agawa suggests that the cause for the delay may have been related to the indiscretion of a junior officer who told a Peruvian Embassy official about rumors that Japan meant to attack Pearl Harbor. Ambassador Grew heard the warning in late Jan. and relayed it to Washington, where it was discussed (Grew, *Ten Years*, 318; Farago, 135–37). In the meantime, however, Genda had received his assignment. Evidently the officers around Prince Takamatsu had already decided that the security breach would have no repercussions. The fate of the indiscreet junior officer is unknown. For further details on the close relationship between Yamamoto and Prince Takamatsu, see Agawa, 108–9; see also Potter, *Yamamoto*, 53–57, and Farago, 136, for other English-language accounts of the Pearl Harbor plan.

N. 1. "In January 1941 . . . Emperor ordered Onishi to research Hawaii attack": Sugiyama, 1:370: *Ichigatsu Yamamoto GF chokan ni tai su Hawai kogeki no kenkyu o Onishi shosho ni kamei su.* Takao Akiyama, who translated *The Tale of Genji* for U.S. television, gave me this translation. As a student of Court Japanese, and one old enough to remember the idiom of 1941, he states flatly that the expression *kamei su* is absolutely unambiguous in this context and means "the Emperor ordered."

956–958 UNIT 82: this section based on ATIS Rept. No. 131 ("Japan's Decision to Fight"); Tsuji, *Singapore*, 3–71; Farago, 119–123.

957 Count Ohtani's career: interview with member of Ohtani family.

Ohtani had been expelled from Java: Harada, 5:127–28.

For Ohtani's Strike-South credentials, see his 1936 entry in *Who's Who in Japan*.

Tsuji and colleagues made flights over Southeast Asia: ATIS Rept. No. 131.

958 "In the first six to twelve months of a war . . .": interview with Matsumoto Shigeharu; Potter, *Yamamoto*, 41, 43. There are several prime sources for Yamamoto's sentiments which indicate that he voiced them on several occasions in roughly the same words from the summer of 1940 to the fall of 1941.

958–959 Worthless paper money "made ideal spills": Koizumi Shinzo, interview.

959 Army not budgeted in 1941 for new divisions: Kido, *Nikki*, 850.

Numbers of divisions: Hata, "Notebooks." These notes give

the dates on which divisional commanders and chiefs of staff were first posted to the command structures of divisions. Although some divisions may have remained skeletal for months after they had headquarters, the Japanese reservist system was such that any one of the divisions could be activated and put in the field within six weeks of the receipt of battle orders. Here and elsewhere, therefore, I have followed Hata's notes and counted divisions by the dates of the establishment of their command structures. Historians familiar with "Report Concerning the Expansion of the Japanese Ground Forces from 1921 to 1941" (*Translations*, 2, No. 29, National Archives Microfilm 8-5.1 CA) may find that I count some divisions as forces to be reckoned with before their official mobilization as acknowledged by Japanese officers in postwar interrogations. Counts based on Hata's notes, however, seem to me to be more realistic.

Diet cut appropriations for I.R.A.A.: Tolischus, *Tokyo Record*, 83–86.

Count Arima resigned, replaced by Gen. Yanagawa Heisuke: ibid.

961 Nomura wanted no part of "act which might disgrace nation": Harada, 8:377–78; see also ibid., 361–63.

Hirohito assured Nomura: Kido, *Nikki*, 835, but see also Harada, 8:387–88.

964 Feb. 3 liaison conference: Sugiyama, 1:173–77.

German military attachés showed Japanese visitors how to take Singapore: Deakin and Storry, 223.

Feb. 7, Hirohito's discussion with Kido re German-Russian war: Kido, *Nikki*, 855.

965 March 3 meeting between Kido and Saionji Kinkazu: ibid., 859, supplemented by interview with Matsumoto Shigeharu.

Saionji reported back to Ozaki: Deakin and Storry, 224; Johnson, 152; Obata, *Kindai*, 57–59. Obi, *Gendai-shi*, vols. 1–3, contains a good deal of information on Sorge's reports regarding the Matsuoka trip. See especially the thirtieth and fortieth interrogations of Sorge by the procurator.

Hirohito gave audience to Matsuoka, March 11: Kido, *Nikki*, 861.

966 Matsuoka in Berlin: Feis, *Pearl Harbor*, 180–84; Tolischus, *Record*, 106–7; Presseisen, 289–93; Deakin and Storry, 224.

Hitler quoted re German objectives: Basic Army Order No. 24, March 5, 1941, cited in Feis, *Pearl Harbor*, 183.

Matsuoka four days with Ribbentrop, two interviews with Hitler: Presseisen, 289.

Matsuoka reported Hitler's comments: Kido, *Nikki*, 861.

966–967 Dr. Paul Schmidt quoted re Matsuoka: William Shirer, *The Rise and Fall of the Third Reich* (New York: Simon & Schuster, 1960; Fawcett Crest Book, 1962), 1144.

Matsuoka's exchanges with Ribbentrop: Presseisen, 289–91.

967–968 "If Japan gets into a conflict with the United States": Shirer, 1146.

968–972 HUGGING THE BEAR: except as cited this section based on Feis, *Pearl Harbor*, 186–87, and Presseisen, 293–95.

969 Steinhardt's report: telegram from Steinhardt to Secretary of State, March 24, 1941, *Foreign Relations, U.S.: Japan, 1931–1941*, 2:143–45.

970 Sorge explained neutrality pact to Red Army Intelligence: Johnson, 152; Deakin and Storry, 224.

Matsuoka lectured Stalin on *Hakko Ichiu*: Sugiyama, 1:201; Ike, 20–23; report of liaison conference, Apr. 22, 1941, during which Matsuoka gave account of his visits in Moscow.

971 Trans-Siberian express held for Matsuoka: Kase, 159.

971–972 "Banzai for the Emperor!": details of Stalin-Matsuoka exchange at celebration of pact from Tolischus. *Record*, 106–7, as reported by members of Matsuoka's party on return from Moscow.

972–976 KONOYE'S PEACE PLOT: account of the efforts of the Maryknoll Fathers, see *Taiheiyo*, 8, final document, for memo drawn up by Ikawa Tadao and Father Drought which began negotiations. The rest of my account is taken from Farago, 172–88; Robert J. C. Butow, "The Hull-Nomura Conversations: A Fundamental Misconception," *American Historical Review*, 65:4 (July 1960), 822–36; Konoye Memoirs, IPS Document No. 3 (Library of Congress Microfilm WT6, 329 ff.); Bishop Walsh to IMTFE, Exhibit 3441; see also Ike, xx–xxiii.

977 Matsuoka received immediately by Hirohito: Kido, *Nikki*, 870. Cf. Konoye, "Memoirs," which suggests that Matsuoka merely stopped at *Nijubashi* to do obeisance.

Matsuoka "recovered from fatigue": Kido, *Nikki*, 871. Kido and Konoye were also indisposed at the same time, and Hirohito sent a courtier to Kido asking whom he was expected to turn to for advice.

Procrastination would make U.S. distrustful: Sugiyama, 203–5.

May 8 liaison conference: ibid., 205–7; Ike, 27–31. Prof. Ike's book, *Japan's Decision for War*, contains translations of liaison conferences and conferences in the Imperial Presence from April to December 1941. They are based on the Japanese text reproduced in *Taiheiyo*, 8. *Sugiyama Memo* from which the materials in *Taiheiyo* were drawn was not available to Prof. Ike when he began his work. Conversely I read *Sugiyama Memo* and drafted this and following chapters before Prof. Ike's book came to my attention. In my final text I have followed, for the most part, Prof. Ike's wording and am greatly indebted to him for the precision and polish of his translations. In one or two passages I have kept my own rough translation because I felt it better mirrored the roughness of the original.

978 Hirohito questioned Kido on "how to fathom Matsuoka": *Nikki*, 873.

Konoye and military chiefs discussed Matsuoka: Sugiyama, 213.

979 Hirohito to Konoye re considering replacement for Matsuoka: Konoye, "Memoirs."

979–983 MATSUOKA'S TREASON: this section based on Farago, 191–201.

982 Matsuoka's report persuading Hirohito and Navy Staff that Code Purple remained secure: interview, Matsumoto Shigeharu; see also Kido, *Nikki*, 873.

983 Matsuoka's campaign of double talk: see, e.g., his personal message to Molotov reported in Sugiyama, 1:295.

984 Matsuoka cabled Nomura revised version of "draft proposal": Ike, 31.

Grew considered Matsuoka's harangue "bellicose": *Foreign Relations, U.S.: Japan, 1931–1941,* 2:146–48; see also *Ten Years,* 337.

Liaison conferences, May 12 and 15: Sugiyama, 1:207–11; Ike, 31–36. Ike dates the 23d liaison conference May 13, but Sugiyama, 207 and *Taiheiyo*, 8:416, agree that it was held on May 12.

984–986 Liaison conference of May 22: Sugiyama, 1:211–15; Ike, 36–43.

985 N. 10: Prince Takamatsu as *Bo*: I discussed this identification with Koizumi and Tanaka; Koizumi's only response was that he had heard the same account, but Tanaka declined to comment on the grounds that Takamatsu was a Navy man and therefore outside his field of expertise.

986–987 Liaison conference of May 29: Sugiyama, 1:215–17; Ike, 43–46.

Matsuoka's anti-British feelings: see, e.g., Kido, *Nikki*, 877–78.

987 Oshima's cable: ibid., 879.

June 6 liaison conference: ibid.; see Sugiyama, 1:218.

Conference on June 7: Sugiyama, 1:218–20; Ike, 46–47.

988 Matsuoka-Takamatsu exchange, June 12: Sugiyama, 1:220–22; Ike, 52–53.

Substance of General Staff document "Concerning the South": Ike, 51.

Matsuoka on Indochina policy, conference of June 16: Sugiyama, 1:222–25; Ike, 53–56.

991 Matsuoka asked for invasion of Siberia, Hirohito ordered Kido to investigate his "true intentions": Kido, *Nikki*, 884–85.

Hirohito's discussion with Sugiyama, June 25: Sugiyama, 1:228–31.

992 Substance of position papers: ibid., 231–40.

Matsuoka discussed Russo-German war at conference of June 25: ibid., 225–28; Ike, 56–60.

992–995 Conferences of June 26, 27, 28, 30, July 1: Sugiyama, 1:240–50; 251–52; Ike, 60–77.

994 Supreme War Council meeting, night of June 30: Sugiyama, 1:250–51.

995 Roosevelt's letter to Ickes: quoted, Feis, *Pearl Harbor*, 206.

995–998 July 2, conference in the Imperial Presence: Sugiyama, 1:254–64; Ike, 77–90.

998 Japanese domestic atmosphere tense, high schools and universities closed: Kido, *Nikki*, 890.

Matsuoka considered Hull had personally attacked him: Ike, 93.

999 Liaison conference of July 12: Sugiyama, 1:269–73; Ike, 98–103.

Matsuoka withheld Japanese draft: Ike, 103–4.

999–1000 Konoye's discussion with Hirohito and agreement that Cabinet should resign: Kido, *Nikki*, 890.

Hirohito's audience with Lt. Gen. Yamashita: ibid., 891.

1001 Hirohito directed Konoye to form new Cabinet, presided at investiture, July 18: ibid., 891–92.

1002 Matsuoka after the war: In Sept. 1945 he composed a half-coherent statement in English (handwritten, IPS Document No. 491, Library of Congress Microfilm WT4) which lays bare his

heartbreak. In it he bows to the will of the Emperor and calls the
war with the U.S. "inevitable under the circumstances."

25. *Konoye's Last Chance*

1004 Liaison conference of July 21: Sugiyama, 1:273–74; Ike,
103–7.

"Subjugated the city peacefully": Kido, *Nikki*, 894.

Drawing of battle lines: reactions in Tokyo, Tolischus, *Record*,
173.

Hirohito sensed danger of fatalism, his warning to Sugiyama,
and the latter's daybook quoted: Sugiyama, 1:276–84.

1005 July 29 meeting of Nagano with Hirohito: ibid.

July 30 exchange between Hirohito and Nagano: Kido, *Nikki*,
895–96.

Kido's discussion with Hirohito of alternatives: ibid., 899–900.

Quotes, July 22–29: Sugiyama, 1:276–84.

1006 Matsuoka quoted: Tolischus, *Record*, 172.

1007 Konoye to Kido, Aug. 25: *Nikki*, 897–98.

Memorandum of Aug. 22 noted by Sugiyama on Oct. 30: Sugiyama, 1:370.

1008 Army plans: Tsuji, *Singapore*, 21–22.

Massive troop movements to Manchuria: see Sugiyama, 1:291.

Yamashita began two months of intensive exercises: ATIS Rept.
No. 131.

Sorge re build-up in Manchuria: Johnson, 139.

1009 Sorge reported on Aug. 15: ibid., 157.

Early Oct. report to Moscow from Sorge: ibid., 158.

Memos GZ–1 and GZ–4: Farago, 211–12.

Hirohito commenced his review: interview with retired Navy
commander.

Navy's war planning: testimony of Adm. Nagano, IMTFE "Proceedings," 10189; ATIS Rept. No. 131.

1010 Yamamoto's presentation at Naval Staff College: ibid.

1011 Liaison conference of Aug. 16: Sugiyama, 1:297; Ike,
121–24.

1011–1012 Sept. meeting at Naval Staff College: ATIS Rept.
No. 131; interview with retired Navy commander; some details
from *Translations*, 1: No. 11 and No. 21, "Naval War Games of
Sept. 1941 at Naval War College" (National Archives Microfilm
8–5.1 CA).

1012 Liaison conference of Sept. 3: Sugiyama, 303–5; Ike, 129–33.

1012–1015 From 6 P.M. (Sept. 3) to 10 A.M. Sept. 6: my account weaves together Sugiyama, 1:309–11, and Konoye's "Memoirs"; see also Tiedemann, 142–44.

1015–1018 Conference in the Imperial Presence, Sept. 6: Sugiyama, 1:306–9, 311–30; Ike, 133–63.

1019 Meeting of Konoye with Grew: Feis, *Pearl Harbor*, 271; Grew, *Ten Years*, 367.

1019–1020 Excerpt from Grew's diary: ibid., 368–69.

1020 Decision by staff admirals in favor of Yamamoto's map exercise, Sept. 10–12: ATIS Rept. No. 131.

1021 Marquis Komatsu's banquet: Kido, *Nikki*, 906.

Sept. 9, Yamamoto gave presentation to umpires: ATIS Rept. No. 131 indicates that Yamamoto spent Sept. 6 and 7 convincing fellow officers that his plan was the best of several possible Pearl Harbor attack plans, then that from Sept. 9 to Sept. 12 he demonstrated his plan in detail. The last three days of the demonstration are described in detail by Tomioka Sadatoshi, *Statements*, 4:300–307.

Hirohito's exchange with Sugiyama that afternoon (of Sept. 9): Sugiyama, 1:331.

Call-up of the reserve, Hirohito quoted: ibid.

1021–1022 Yamamoto's map exercise: ATIS Rept. No. 131.

1022–1023 Yamamoto's activities, Sept. 13–21, and preparation of Order No. 1: ibid.

N. 4: The yeoman, from whose recollections most of ATIS Rept. No. 131 was constructed, had one of those prodigious memories that are so frequently encountered in brains formed by training in the Sino-Japanese writing system. After the war, when charred fragments of Yamamoto's Order No. 1 were resurrected from the Tokyo city dump, the yeoman's recollection of it was found to be letter perfect except for a few stray prepositions and relative pronouns. (This note courtesy of Otis Cary.)

1023 Konoye began to think of resigning: Kido, *Nikki*, 906–7.

On Sept. 18 four toughs attacked Konoye's car: "Brocade Banner," 102.

1024 Konoye at liaison conference of Sept. 20: Sugiyama, 1:334–41; Ike, 173–76.

Sept. 26 exchange between Konoye and Kido: Kido, *Nikki*, 909.

Hirohito asked Kido to investigate U.S. rubber supplies: ibid., 910.

Hirohito taken up with maneuvers at Army War College: Hattori Takushiro, *Statements*, 1:341; Kido, *Nikki*, 911; interview with retired Navy commander.

1025 Konoye begged Grew and the Emperor for help: Grew, *Ten Years*, 387–89; Kido, *Nikki*, 911.

Oct. 9 statements of Kido to Konoye: ibid., 912.

Hirohito consults Prince Fushimi: ibid., 913.

Hirohito approved combined Army-Navy command for Southern Regions: ATIS Rept. No. 131.

1026 Tojo and Oikawa at meeting Oct. 12: Kido, *Nikki*, 913–14. This was apparently not a formal Cabinet meeting, but among those present were the prime, foreign, war, and Navy ministers, Suzuki Tei-ichi of the Cabinet Planning Board, and Cabinet Secretary Tomita Kenji. The meeting was held at Konoye's Ogikubo villa.

Hirohito admitted no hope in diplomacy: Kido, *Nikki*, 914.

Konoye's message to Roosevelt via Bishop Walsh: Farago, 222.

Kido and Tojo reached an agreement: *Nikki*, 914–15; Konoye, "Memoirs."

1027 Tojo's report of his conversation with Kido: Sugiyama, 350–51.

Cabinet change seemed inevitable: Kido, *Nikki*, 915; Konoye, "Memoirs" (section entitled "On the Resignation of the Third Konoye Cabinet," Library of Congress Microfilm WT6); Kido, 3 (*Kankei bunsho*): 488–92.

1028 Prince Higashikuni receives Konoye: Ando, "Senso," Pt. 1; Matsumoto Seicho, *Bungei Shunju*, January 1968, 161 ff.

Tojo's private audience with Hirohito: Kido, *Nikki*, 916. I have assumed that the conversation Tojo had with Kido at 3 P.M. was substantially the same as one that he had just had with Hirohito; see also Kido, *Kankei bunsho*, 488–92.

Kido's consultation with the *Jushin*: Kido, *Nikki*, 917–18, and *Kankei bunsho*: 481–88; Kase, 53–56.

N. 6: "Brocade Banner," 109; Tolischus, *Record*, 227–28.

1029 Hirohito dismisses Oikawa: ibid.

Hirohito promoted Tojo to full general: Sugiyama, 1:352.

1030 Hirohito to Kido, "You cannot catch a tiger": *Nikki*, 918; see also Sugiyama, 1:353.

26. Pearl Harbor

For this chapter, in addition to sources cited or listed in the bibliography, I have drawn for background on: A. J. Barker, *Pearl Harbor* (New York: Ballantine Books, 1969); Fujisawa Chikao, *Kotonarism: An Introduction to the Study of Japanese Global Philosophy or Kotonarism* (Tokyo: The Society for the Advancement of Global Democracy, 1954), an extraordinary postwar exposition of Japanese ideology by a prewar propagandist; Ohashi Hideo, "Watashi wa Zoruge o toraeta" [I Arrested Sorge] (*Sunday Mainichi*, July 2, 1961); Maeda Minoru, ed., *Nanpo to kokumin no kakugo* [The Strike South and the Resolution of the People] (Tokyo: Nanpo Mondai Kenkyu-sho, 1941) [Strike South Problems Research Institute]; Sakamaki Kazuo, *I Attacked Pearl Harbor* (New York: Associated Press, 1949); and Sugimori Hisahide, "Tojo Hideki: Hitoware o jotohei to yobu" [Tojo Hideki: They make fun of him by calling him a first-class private], in *Bungei Shunju*, Special Edition No. 95, April 1966, 116 ff.

1031 SORGE'S ARREST: This section is based on Johnson, 168–99, and Deakin and Storry, 248–80.

1032 Ito an informer: Johnson, 175–77.

Ozaki waited stoically: he described his "premonition" and preparations for arrest in a statement written in prison, quoted, Deakin and Storry, 252.

1033 Sorge on evening of Oct. 17: Klausen quoted, ibid., 253.

1034 Arrest of Sorge: ibid., 254.

1035 Liaison conference of Oct. 23: Sugiyama, 1:353–54; Ike, 184–87.

1035–1036 Daily liaison conferences: Sugiyama, 1:354–62; Ike, 187–99.

1037 Formation of the Peace Faction: Kido, *Nikki*, 920–21, supplemented by interview with Matsumoto Shigeharu.

Liaison conference of Oct. 30: Sugiyama, 1:336–62; Ike, 196–99.

1038 Tojo breakfasted with Sugiyama: Sugiyama, 1:370–72.

Liaison conference of Nov. 1: ibid., 1:372–86; Ike, 199–207.

1039 Kaya phoned: Sugiyama, 1:386.

Togo held out: ibid.

1040 Tojo's audience with Hirohito: ibid., 386–87.

At 5 P.M.: Kido, *Nikki*, 921.

Nagano received his copy of Order Number One: ATIS Research Rept. No. 131.

1041 Preamble quoted: ibid.

Quotations from order: ibid.

By the evidence of his own memoranda: Sugiyama interleafed his memorandum on the subject from the Navy at the beginning of his entry for Nov. 1: see Sugiyama, 1:370.

1042–1044 Meeting of Nagano and Sugiyama with Hirohito: Sugiyama, 387–88.

1042 N. 3: Butow, *Tojo*, 375 n. 24. Prof. Butow's conclusion is consistent with the fact that, according to ATIS No. 131, only two of the 300 copies of Order No. 1 were distributed to the Army. These presumably went to Terauchi and Sugiyama, the two officers with the most need to know.

The Emperor's copy of any major military order was regularly submitted to him by the appropriate aide-de-camp before he was called upon to discuss it with either of his chiefs of staff. In this instance Hirohito had apparently received his copy of Order No. 1 late on Nov. 1, for early the next morning he phoned his Navy brother, Takamatsu, with a question regarding plans vis-à-vis the United States: Kido, *Nikki*, 921.

1043–1044 Nagano's meeting with Kuroshima: Potter, *Yamamoto*, 68–69.

1044–1049 THE WAR COUNCIL ASSENTS: This section, including all quotations, is taken from Sugiyama, 1:388–406.

1049–1054 THE FORMAL WAR DECISION: This section is based on Sugiyama, 1:406–30, supplemented by Ike, 208–39.

1054 Hirohito approved dispatch of Kurusu: Kido, *Nikki*, 921.

1054–1055 Clipper was kept waiting: Moore, 258.

Hirohito assumed incognito to attend *gozen heigo*: Tanaka, in interview, first mentioned that the Emperor was said to have reviewed the fleet secretly before Pearl Harbor; Koizumi, in interviews, did not deny the rumor. I deduced the dates from Kido's diaries and mentioned the episode as if it were well known and proven in an interview with the retired Navy commander; he said he was unsure of the details but suggested those used in the account here. Later the publication of *Sugiyama Memo* convinced me that the Emperor's review had indeed taken place in the period described.

Chiefs of staff met with Hirohito immediately after Nov. 5 conference: Sugiyama, 1:431.

1056 Hirohito to Hayama at 10 A.M. Nov. 7: Kido, *Nikki*, 922–23, and preceding note on *gozen heigo*.

Eighty-three pages of tables: Sugiyama, 1:433–516.

1057 FLEET DISPATCH: Material in this section is drawn from ATIS Research Rept. No. 131; Farago, 267–68; Hashimoto, 1–5; Potter, 78; interview with retired Navy commander.

December 8 the day of attack: ATIS Research Rept. No. 131; Hashimoto, 1–5.

Nagumo orders captains to "complete battle preparations"; ibid.

First of twenty-seven: ibid.

1058 Most of Pearl Harbor task force had gathered, by Nov. 14: Farago, 267; and interview, retired Navy commander; ATIS Research Rept. No. 131; Hashimoto, 4–5; Potter, 78.

1059 Joseph W. Ballantine quoted: text of memo in Trefousse, 304–6.

1060 In World War II, it was planned: quotations from "Land Disposal Plan in the Greater Asia Co-Prosperity Sphere," IMTFE Exh. 1334; text in Storry, *Double Patriots*, 317–19.

1061 Liaison conference of Nov. 20: Sugiyama, 1:525–28; Ike, 249–53.

Togo cable: IMTFE "Proceedings," 10399.

1062 Stimson's diary: entry for Nov. 25, 1941, quoted in Feis, *Pearl Harbor*, 314.

1063 25,000 Japanese troops: ibid., 315.

The President "fairly blew up—": Stimson's diary for Nov. 26, 1941, reproduced in Trefousse, 141.

Hirohito to Kido: Kido, *Nikki*, 925, and Sugiyama, 1:532.

1064 Received radio message: Hashimoto Mochitsuru, 5.

Nomura and Kurusu, cable to Tokyo: quoted, Millis, 244.

"I have washed my hands of it": Hull as recorded in Stimson's diary for Nov. 27, 1941, entry reproduced in Trefousse, 141.

Fleet began to sail from Hitokappu Bay: IMTFE "Proceedings," 10425.

"the final alert": Stimson's diary for Nov. 27, Trefousse, 142.

1065 Stark's message: quoted, Millis, 250.

Kimmel and Short agreed to plan: Kimmel's testimony to Joint Committee, Trefousse, 35.

Halsey was ordered to depart for Wake: Kimmel's testimony, quoted, Millis, 268.

Kimmel later testified: testimony reproduced in Trefousse, 36.

1066 Gen. Short's cable: ibid., 65.

1067 June 1940 order: ibid., 62.

Maj. Gen. Martin supervised study: Millis, 63.

Grew's warning, Jan. 27, 1941: *Ten Years*, 318; quoted, Millis, 33–34.

Forwarded to Kimmel: ibid., 34.

1068–1069 Kurusu's trans-Pacific telephone conversation: IMTFE "Proceedings," 10430 ff.

1070 War Cabinet meeting, Nov. 28: Stimson's testimony to Joint Committee, reproduced in Trefousse, 133.

1071 Tojo's objections: Butow, *Tojo*, 344, n. 58.

Elder Statesmen's Conference: Kido to IMTFE, Exhibit 1966, Trefousse, 250–51.

Liaison conference of Nov. 29: Sugiyama, 1:535–38; Ike, 260–62.

Kido at residence of Prince Takamatsu: Kido, *Nikki*, 927–28.

Hirohito, after hearing message from Takamatsu: ibid.

1072 Kido's reply: ibid.

Hirohito sees Tojo, Shimada, Nagano: ibid.

Hirohito, "Instruct Prime Minister Tojo": ibid.

Kido wrote in his diary: ibid.

1072–1074 Conference in the Imperial Presence, Dec. 1, 1941: Sugiyama, 1:539–44; Ike, 262–83.

Hirohito to Sugiyama: Sugiyama, 1:544.

1075 "Climb Mount Niitaka": ATIS Rept. 131.

Kimmel-Layton exchange: Layton's testimony to Joint Committee, quoted, Millis, 297.

1076 Ciano's diary entry: extract in Trefousse, 271.

N. 6: Ciano diary, Trefousse, 272.

1077 Foote burning code books: his testimony to Joint Committee, Farago, 303.

Japanese task force left Samah harbor: Tsuji, *Singapore*, 72–78; Tsuji had made a flying trip to Tokyo the week before to defend his plans against last-minute alterations, Sugiyama, 1:5–6.

1077–1078 Liaison conference, Dec. 6: Sugiyama, 1:565, identifies the meeting of Dec. 6 as the 75th liaison conference. On pages 563–65 he has identified another meeting, Dec. 4, as the 75th liaison conference. *Taiheiyo senso*, 8:611–13, agrees that both meetings should be called the 75th liaison conference. *Taiheiyo*'s text, however, omits a mysterious typographic symbol (two concentric circles) which appears in the original Sugiyama version, identifying the speaker of a deadlock-breaking statement near the end of the second half of the conference on Dec. 6. To judge by internal evidence, the 75th liaison conference met for two hours on Dec. 4 and broke up after failing to agree on anything of substance except the proper protocol to use in announcing the war to Pu-Yi, the Manchukoan puppet emperor. On Dec. 6, after two days of back-room consultation, the conference reconvened at 10 A.M. to consider the rest of its agenda. The timing of the note to Hull was conceded without much debate, but then both Army and Navy officials expressed their lingering doubts about the war in an argument as to what to tell Hitler. The Army, Russophobic as always, wanted to promise Hitler that Japan, by making war on the United States, would cut off American aid to Russia through Vladivostok; the Navy insisted that it would do nothing to interdict U.S. aid to Russia because the possibility of antagonizing Russia was more than Japan could risk during her Strike South. At 3 P.M. the bickering was recessed briefly, then resumed in a session that lasted until 6:30. Late in the afternoon the person identified by the two concentric circles made a "decision" to adopt a suggestion of Finance Minister Kaya and to tell Hitler simply, "We hope you will understand, but, as long as we must avoid a confrontation with Russia, we cannot co-operate fully with you while still carrying out our military operation in the South." Having made this single utterance, the speaker was rewarded by seeing the proceedings brought to a speedy conclusion.

Japanese reply to Hull's Nov. 26 statement: Millis, 322.

Consulted privately: Millis, 219–20.

1079 Roosevelt's message: text reproduced in Grew, *Ten Years,* 421–23.

Roosevelt's memo to Hull: Millis, 319.

1080 Decipherment of fourteen-part note: Kramer's testimony to Joint Committee, Trefousse, 196–200.

Roosevelt and Hopkins: Schulz's testimony to Joint Committee, ibid., 220–25.

1081 Nagumo listening to local Hawaiian stations: Millis, 331.

Flag of Admiral Togo: Zacharias, 250.

Grew received cable late in evening: *Ten Years,* 420.

At 6:15 P.M.: Kido, *Nikki,* 932.

1082 Typing the note: Feis, *Pearl Harbor,* 341.

1084 Marshall's cable to Short: Marshall's testimony to Joint Committee, Trefousse, 178–79.

Grew's efforts to deliver Roosevelt's message: *Ten Years,* 420–21.

Togo's reply: Togo, 219.

1085 Togo's telephone call to Kido: ibid., 220; Kido, *Nikki,* 932.

Japanese bluejackets in Shanghai: testimony of Frederick Charles Parr, IMTFE "Proceedings," 10608–38.

Kido drives to Imperial Library: Kido, *Nikki,* 932.

1086 Hirohito listening to radio: ibid., amplified by interview with a retired lieutenant general who in 1941 was attached to Imperial Headquarters. Another informant, Koizumi Shinzo, said: "I believe that, like most people in the palace, the Emperor was listening to the radio. He had a short-wave set in his study, and I have heard that he listened to the actual transmissions from Malaya."

Roosevelt in Oval Study with Hopkins: Davis and Lindley, 4.

1086–1087 Hirohito and Togo discuss Roosevelt's message: Togo, 221.

At 3:15 P.M. Togo left: ibid.

Kido lingered for fifteen minutes: Kido, *Nikki,* 932.

TIGER, TIGER: This section is based in Lord, *Day of Infamy;* Karig and Kelley, 22–96; Millis; Morison, 3:80–146.

1088 Fuchida quoted: Potter, *Yamamoto,* 98.

1090 Hirohito dismissed Kido: Kido, *Nikki,* 932.

1093 Casualties at Pearl Harbor: Morison, 3:126. Another count was given by Adm. James O. Richardson to IMTFE: 1,999 sailors, 109 Marines, 234 soldiers, and 188 U.S. planes.

1094 Bellinger's signal: Morison, 3:101.

Roosevelt receiving news of Pearl Harbor: Davis and Lindley, 5.

Hull's last meeting with Nomura and Kurusu: ibid., 15–18.

N. 10: IMTFE "Proceedings," 11311 ff.

1096 Halsey quoted: Morison, 3:212.

27. *The Strike South*

For this chapter, in addition to sources cited or listed in the bibliography, I have drawn for background on: David Bernstein, *The Philippine Story* (New York: Farrar, Straus & Co., 1947), circumspect but interesting account of President Manuel Quezon during the fall of the Philippines and the years of government in exile; Russell Braddon, *The Naked Island* (London: Werner

Laurie, 1952), Singapore and the Burma-Thai railroad illustrated by Braddon's famous fellow prisoner, Ronald Searle; Eugene Burns, *Then There Was One: The U.S.S. Enterprise and the First Year of the War* (New York: Harcourt, Brace & Co., 1944); Paul Carano and Pedro C. Sanchez, *A Complete History of Guam* (Rutland, Vermont, and Tokyo: Chas. E. Tuttle Co., 1964); Don Congdon, ed., *Combat: Pacific Theater, World War II* (New York: Dell Publishing Co., 1958), an anthology of firsthand war experiences. Frank Wesley Craven and James Lea Cate, eds., *Plans and Early Operations: January 1939 to August 1942*, The Army Air Force in World War II, Vol. 1 (Chicago: University of Chicago Press, 1948); Ralph Goodwin, *Passport to Eternity* (London: Arthur Barker, Ltd., 1956), the fall of Hong Kong; John Hersey, *Men on Bataan* (New York: Knopf, 1942); Stanley Johnston, *Queen of the Flat-tops: The U.S.S. Lexington and the Coral Sea Battles* (New York: E. P. Dutton & Co., 1942); Edgar McInnis, *The War, Third Year* (London, Toronto, New York: Oxford University Press, 1942); Ronald McKie, *Proud Echo* (Sydney: Angus and Robertson Ltd., 1953), firsthand account of the Battle of Sunda Strait and the sinking of the *Perth*; John F. Moyes, *Mighty Midgets* (Sydney: N.S.W. Bookstall Co., 1946), small craft naval actions in the seas north of Australia; Munebi Matsuharu, Hankushi Takashi, and Tominaga Kengo, *Daitoa-sen ni-shi* [Japanese Bulletins from the Greater East Asia War] 1, December 8, 1941-April 7, 1942; II, April 8, 1942-August 7, 1942 (Tokyo: Asahi Shinbun-sha, 1942); Rohan D. Rivett, *Behind Bamboo: An Inside Story of the Japanese Prison Camps* (Sydney: Angus & Robertson Ltd., 1946), containing an account of the Sunda Straits battle; R. W. Volckmann, *We Remained* (New York: W. W. Norton & Co., 1954); Robert Ward, *Asia for the Asiatics? The Techniques of Japanese Occupation* (Chicago: University of Chicago Press, 1945), by the U.S. consul in Hong Kong in 1941; Osmar White, *Green Armour* (Sydney: Angus and Robertson Ltd., 1942), firsthand account of Australian defense of New Guinea; W. L. White, *They Were Expendable* (New York: Harcourt, Brace & Co., 1942); and Malcolm Wright, *If I Die: Coastwatching and Guerrilla Warfare Behind Japanese Lines* (Melbourne: Landsdown Press, 1965), adventure on the island of New Britain.

1099 Excerpt from Kido's diary: Kido, *Nikki*, 932–33.

1100 Invasion at Singora: Tsuji, *Singapore*, 82–88.

Landing at Kota Bharu and Japanese sapper's action: ibid., 95.

1101 Fog over air bases in Taiwan: Sakai Saburo, 71.

Japanese Army pilots damaged Baguio: Ind, 91–105.

Brereton urged take-off of B-17's and MacArthur's refusal: Brereton, 38–39.

1102 At 10 A.M. in Taiwan, fog lifted: Sakai Saburo, 71.

1102–1104 Account of air attacks on Clark Field based on Brereton, 39–43; Morison, 3:170–71; Allison Ind, Bataan: *The Judgment Seat* (New York: The Macmillan Co., 1944), 91–105.

1103 Account of one Japanese air ace and quotation: Sakai Saburo, 72–73.

Sakai's tribute to the B-17: ibid., 85.

1105 Only a cloud marred the day: see Emperor's remarks to Sugiyama on Feb. 13, 1942; Sugiyama, 2:26.

British destruction in Borneo oil fields: Wigmore, 180.

Attack on Guam: Morison, 3:185–86.

Japanese landings at Aparri and Vigan: Kawagoe Moriji, *Statements*, 2:155 ff.; Nakajima Toshio, ibid., 638–41.

1106 CONTROL OF THE OCEAN: this section based on Gill, 476–83; Grenfell, 109–36; Wigmore, 141–45, with some details from O. D. Gallagher, *Retreat in the East* (London: George C. Harrap & Co., 1942).

1107 "Churchill's yacht": Gallagher, 45.

1109 "We are off to look for trouble": message posted in *Repulse*, quoted, Gallagher, 45.

"At dawn": ibid., 49.

1113 "Bloody good shooting": CBS correspondent Cecil Brown, in Don Congden, ed., *Combat: The War with Japan* (New York: Dell Publishing Co., 1962), 23.

Officers had never seen such bombing: Gallagher, 60.

1116 "We have completed our task": ibid., 70.

News of victory reached Hirohito at 3 P.M.: Kido, *Nikki*, 933.

"Hup, hup, hooray!": ibid.

1117–1118 114th Regt. required 550 trucks: Tsuji, *Singapore*, 207–9.

1119 Cuff links from Prince Mikasa: Tsuji, *Underground Escape*, 77.

Prince Takeda sent to Saigon: *Asahi*, Nov. 20, 1942.

N. 2, death of Prince Nagahisa: *Asahi*, Sept. 6, 1940.

1120–1121 Excerpt from *Just Read This*: ATIS Document No. 7396.

1122 MALAYA'S JITRA LINE: this section based on Wigmore, 137–52, and Tsuji, *Singapore*, 107–25.

1123 Bicycle troops: operations described in Tsuji, *Singapore*, 183–85.

1125 WAKE: this section based on Morison, 3:223–54.

1126 HONG KONG: this section based on Wigmore, 170–76; Strategicus, *The War Moves East* (London: Faber & Faber, 1942); James Bertram, *Beneath the Shadow* (New York: John Day Co., 1947), 78–96.

1129 Japanese terror at field hospital in St. Stephen's College: testimony of James Barnett, IMTFE "Proceedings," 13112 ff.

1129–1141 LUZON: this section and the following MANILA and THE DEFENSE OF BATAAN are based, except as specifically cited, on Hattori, 278–83 (plus separate folio of annotated maps); on Hattori (he was chief of operations in the Army General Staff) in *Statements*, 1:315–90; on other officers' statements, ibid., 2:115–36, 393–96, 576–77, 627–30, 638–44, 657–60, 661–68; ibid., 3:80–97, 110–17, 152–59; ibid; 4:369–82, 544–51; 552–57; and on Agoncillo, 1:124–62, and Toland, *But Not in Shame*, 124–93.

1129–1130 Seventy-three convoys: Kawagoe Moriji, *Statements*, 2:122–35; Ohmae Toshikazu, ibid., 3:60–63.

1129 N. 4; Japanese commanders claimed only 15,000 troops landed: for data and reasons see, e.g., Kawagoe, Morioka, Ohyabe, Onumu, Towatari, *Statements*, 2:117, 578; 3:81, 153; 4:375.

1131–1132 Fall-back of Gen. Wainwright's forces: this and following two paragraphs, personal knowledge refreshed by conversations with my father, J. Van Wie Bergamini, and reference to the diaries of my mother, Clara D. Bergamini.

1131 Honma on ramp of barge: Agoncillo, 1, plate opp. p. 87.

1132 Landings at Lamon Bay and Legaspi: Morioka Susumu, *Statements*, 2:576–77.

N. 6, 7: Ohyabe Shozo, *Statements*, 3:81.

N. 8: Kawagoe Moriji, *Statements*, 2:117; interview with Fujisawa.

N. 9: Nara Akira, *Statements*, 2:662.

1132–1133 MacArthur announced decision to Quezon Dec. 23: see Agoncillo, 1:79. Maeda Masami, *Statements*, 2:393, says Gen. Honma knew of decision through spies by Dec. 25.

1133 Message from Quezon to Japanese colonel: see note on pages 1131–32.

1135 Sugiyama to Honma re Philippines command: Kojima, 1:182–85.

On withdrawal to Bataan: Haba Hikaru, *Statements*, 1:195; Nakayama Makoto, ibid., 2:657–60.

1136 Kido interviewed Lt. Gen. Tanaka: Kido, *Nikki*, 936; Agoncillo, 1:358.

Hirohito urged Sugiyama to abbreviate timetable: Hattori, *Statements*, 1:315–16.

Honma's staff officers had protested: Maeda Masami, *Statements*, 2:393; Nakajima Yoshio, ibid., 2:638–44.

1137 Terauchi's message to Honma, transmitted verbally: Arao Okikatsu, *Statements*, 1:44–46; Ishii Masami, ibid., 587; Maeda Masami, ibid., 2:393–96.

Prince Takeda sent to Manila: *Asahi*, Jan. 20, 1942; Ishii Masami, *Statements*, 2:588.

Takeda communicated "real situation in the Philippines" to Hirohito: ibid., supplemented by interview with retired lieutenant general.

Cable to Honma, his discussion with Takeda: "Honma Trial Transcript" (National War Memorial, Canberra) 3:225–27; Maeda Masami, *Statements*, 2:393–96.

1038 Lt. Gen. Nara Akira a kinsman of Nara Takeji: Koizumi, interview.

Nara's attack on Abucay line: According to Hattori, *Statements*, 1:383, the official order for the attack was Imperial General H.Q. Army Directive No. 1076. According to retired Lt. Gen. Fujisawa Shigezo, directives with this designation were *taimei* or Great Orders, which had to be not only reported to Hirohito by his aides-de-camp but actually stamped with Hirohito's personal seal of state. The series of which this was No. 1076 had started with the various orders for Dec. 8, 1941; in other words, in a little over a month, Hirohito had personally issued over a thousand orders to the Army alone.

1139 Honma's meeting with Gen. Staff officers from Tokyo: Kojima, 1:182–85.

1140 "an old carp . . . must be fished patiently": Fujisawa, interview.

Eisenhower had "studied dramatics under MacArthur": quoted, Lee, 99.

Eisenhower's staff study: Long, *MacArthur*, 74–75.

1141–1145 RETREAT FROM MALAYA: this section based on Percival; Tsuji, *Singapore*; Wigmore, 337–81; Attiwill, *passim.*

1142 On Japanese planning for advance on New Zealand and Samoa, see Takahashi Chikaya, *Statements*, 4:34–37.

1143 Churchill's complaint re Singapore's guns: 4:50–51.

1145–1153 SINGAPORE'S AGONY: this section based on Percival, 272–301; Tsuji, *Singapore*; Wigmore, 337–81; Attiwill, *passim.*

1145 Situation at Imperial Headquarters, Tokyo: interview with retired Navy commander.

1146 Liaison conference of Feb. 4: Sugiyama, 2: Intro. 11–13. Hirohito's briefing protracted many hours: interview with retired Navy commander.

Hirohito's conference with Sugiyama, Feb. 9: Sugiyama, 2:22.

1146–1147 For a more detailed account of Yen's position, see George E. Taylor, *The Struggle for North China* (New York: Institute of Pacific Relations, 1940).

General Staff kept a Yen file: interview with Tanaka Takayoshi.

Yen's name a code word: interview with Tanaka Takayoshi. The first Yen Hsi-shan operation—a hunt of Yen's men from airplanes —is described in Harada, 2:36.

1148 "The Yen Hsi-shan treatment": interviews with Tanaka and Fujisawa; also see Kido's references to Yen Hsi-shan operations in 1940–41, *Nikki*, 843, 847, 886, 901, 902, 907, 920.

1148–1149 Hirohito's conference with Sugiyama, Feb. 9 (continued): Sugiyama, 2:22–23.

1149 Sugiyama discussed situation with aides: interview with retired officer.

1150 Excerpt from Tsuji: *Singapore*, 258, supplemented by interview with Fujisawa.

1151 Tsuji's reference to reduction of Taiyuan Sheng: for Prince Kanin Haruhito's and Prince Takeda's parts in this earlier atrocity, see *Asahi*, Mar. 20, 1942.

Japanese action at Alexandra Barracks Hospital: Tsuji, *Singapore*, 259–65.

1153–1154 Kido had warned Hirohito: *Nikki*, 943–44; see also Kido Koichi, *Statements*, 2:195, "The Emperor wore an expression as if to say, 'I wonder if Kido knows what he is saying.'"

1154 Hirohito's statement to Tojo: Kido, *Nikki*, 945.

The next morning Hirohito informed Kido: ibid., 946.

1155 Hirohito had watched newsreels: ibid., 944.

1155–1157 Plans to invade Australia: Hattori, *Daitoa*, and

Statements, 1:357–58; interview with retired Navy commander.

1157 Liaison conference of Feb. 23: Sugiyama, 2:30–33.

N. 14: Sugiyama, 2:32.

1159 Liaison conference of March 7: Sugiyama, 2:12.

1160 Excerpt from Kido's diary: *Nikki*, 949–50.

N. 15: Sugiyama, 2:60.

1163 Hirohito's attitude to Hong Kong disclosures: Kido, *Nikki*, 950.

1163–1165 On the capture of Bataan: Akiyama Monjiro, *Statements*, 1:18–20; Nara Akira, ibid., 2:661–68; Onuma Kiyoshi, ibid., 3:152–59; Ohyaba Shozo, ibid., 3:80–97; Oishi Hiromi, ibid., 3:110–17; Yoshida Motohiko, ibid., 4:544–51.

1165–1169 THE DEATH MARCH: this section based on Agoncillo, 1:198–231; Dyess, 61–132 *passim*; IMTFE "Proceedings," 12578–738; Toland, *But Not in Shame*, 70–104; Tsuji, *Guadarukanaru*.

Brig. Gen. Steve Mellnik, U.S.A. Ret., in his *Philippine Diary, 1939–1945* (New York: Van Nostrand Reinhold Co., 1969), tells of acting as guide after the fall of Corregidor to a Japanese colonel who would appear almost certainly to have been the redoubtable Tsuji himself.

A few commanders refused to be bullied: Imai Takeo, 184 ff.

1169 Kido knew Korematsu well: Kido records in *Nikki* over 100 meetings with him.

1170 Kido's talk with the Empress Dowager and the botanical ramble: Kido, *Nikki*, 956, supplemented by interview, Koizumi Shinzo.

1170–1172 Doolittle raid: see James Merrill, *passim*.

1173 Tojo defended captured U.S. airmen: see esp. testimony even of Tojo's arch rival, Tanaka Takayoshi, IMTFE "Proceedings," 14387–402.

1173 Orders: USAFFE, "Japanese Monograph" No. 71, 86–87; see also 87–118.

1174 Destruction in Chekiang and Kiangsi: James Merrill, 160.

1175 Armada dispatched to Midway: on interrelationship of Doolittle raid and Midway attack, see Agawa, 271–72.

THE DEATH OF CORREGIDOR: this section based on Yoshida Motohiko, *Statements*, 4:552–57, and Mellnik, *Philippine Diary*, 135–55.

1177 Prince Higashikuni's son on tour of southern areas: *Asahi*, May 17, 27, 1942.

1178–1183 THE CORAL SEA: this section based mainly on Morison, 4:21–64; Ito Masanori, 52–53; Toland, *But Not in Shame,* 369–73.

1183–1200 MIDWAY: this section based on Morison, 4:69–159; Lord, *Incredible Victory*; Fuchida et al; Tuleja; and Toland, *But Not in Shame,* 373–98.

1197–1198 Attack of *Yorktown* and *Enterprise* dive bombers: Who bombed what has been the source of controversy. On review I have accepted the reconstruction by Walter Lord in *Incredible Victory,* 289–95, which seems to me best to accommodate the largest number of details in the accounts of Japanese as well as American eyewitnesses.

28. Crumbling Empire

For this chapter, in addition to sources cited or listed in the bibliography, I have drawn for background on: A. G. Allbury, *Bamboo and Bushido* (London: Robert Hale, 1955), firsthand account of work on the Burma-Thai railroad; Benedict R. O'G. Anderson, "Japan the Light of Asia" (Ph.D. dissertation, Yale University, 1964), Japanese policies in Indonesia; Corey Ford, *Short Cut to Tokyo: The Battle for the Aleutians* (New York: Charles Scribner's Sons, 1943); Frank Foster, *Comrades in Bondage* (London: Skeffington and Son, Ltd., n.d. [1946], fall of Java and Burma-Thai railroad; Ernest Gordon, *Through the Valley of the Kwai* (New York: Harper and Brothers, 1962); Agnes Newton Keith, *Three Came Home* (Boston: Little, Brown & Co., 1947); K. P. MacKenzie, *Operation Rangoon Jail* (London: Christopher Johnson Ltd., 1954), Japanese prisoners in Burma; William H. McDougall, Jr., *By Eastern Windows: The Story of a Battle of Souls and Minds in the Prison Camps of Sumatra* (London: Arthur Barker Ltd., 1951); Nakamura Aketo, *Hotoke no shireikan: Chu-tai kaiso-roku* [Buddha's Commander: Reminiscences of Garrison Duty in Thailand] (Tokyo: Nihon Shuho-sha, 1958); *Reconquest: An Official Record of the Australian Army's Successes in the Offensives against [New Guinea] September 1943–June 1944* (Director General of Public Relations, Under Authority of Sir Thomas Blamey, C-in-C, Australian Military Forces); Alfred A. Weinstein, *Barbed-Wire Surgeon* (New York: The Macmillan Co., 1948), efforts of a doctor in Camp O'Donnell and Cabanatuan; and Desmond Wettem, *The Lonely Battle*

(London: W. H. Allen & Co., 1960), adventure of HMS *Petrel* crewman who hid out in Shanghai and evaded capture for four years.

1201 Sumo-wrestling image: letter from Yamamoto Eisuke to Kido, June 5, 1943 (the day of Adm. Yamamoto Isoroku's funeral —no relation), Kankei bunsho, 596–97: "Japan was a small sumo-wrestler of good technique fighting a grand champion of great weight. Instead of waiting for the usual limbering-up ceremonies, the little wrestler attacked and almost pushed the champion out of the ring . . . but the grand champion staggered back at the edge of the ring, planted his feet firmly, and slowly began to come forward."

1202 Kido persuaded him Throne not yet so desperate: *Nikki*, 967–68.

Kido received visit from Yoshida: ibid.

Peace Faction: see note on page 83 (in Ch. 2 of Notes).

1203 Dec. 16, 1941, Kido talked with Konoye: Kido, *Nikki*, 934. Konoye met again, Jan. 20, with Kido: ibid., 941.

Harada reported to Kido on police opinion of Saionji Kinkazu: ibid., 942–43.

1204 Hirohito discussed Sorge case with Home Minister Yuzawa: ibid., 951. Saionji Kinkazu interrogated: Johnson, 199; Deakin and Storry, 292. After the war Saionji became Japan's unofficial ambassador to Communist China. When he returned to Japan in 1969 he set out to act as a bridge between Peking and the West. He appeared conspicuously in photographs of the Chinese Ping-Pong team which accompanied a U.S. team on a widely publicized good will tour of China in 1971. Moreover, a Japanese diplomat has told me that he played a leading role as intermediary in the Washington-Peking negotiations that preceded the Ping-Pong rapprochement. Once branded a spy, Saionji Kinkazu was at last being appreciated for his true forte as an international go-between.

1205 Kido's frank conversation with Konoye: *Nikki*, 951.

1205–1206 Konoye's proposed peace trip to Europe, Yoshida's letter: ibid., 967–68.

1208 Landings on Guadalcanal: Morison, 4:283–91.

On surprise caused by Guadalcanal landings in ranks of palace staff officers: Takahashi Chikaya, *Statements*, 4:34–37. In Sugiyama, 2: Intro., 15, the news is described as coming like "cold water in a sleeper's ear."

Australian coast-watcher saw Japanese planes approaching: Morison, 4:292.

1209–1210 Sakai's adventure: Sakai Saburo, 218–34.

1210 N.1: Raymond F. Toliver and Trevor J. Constable, *Fighter Aces* (New York: The Macmillan Co., 1965), 338, 343, 345.

1212 Battle of Savo Island: Morison, 5:17–64; Collier, 278–86.

1212–1214 Guadalcanal routine: Morison, 5, is basic source; many details from Griffith.

1215–1216 Hirohito gave lunch to Nomura and Kurusu: Kido, *Nikki*, 979.

Hirohito proposed Tojo as foreign minister: ibid., 980–81.

1217 Hiranuma's audience with the Emperor: ibid., 982.

1218 Battle of the Eastern Solomons: Morison, 5:79–107.

New troops commanded by Maj. Gen. Hyakutake Seikichi: on this and following imperial interventions in the Guadalcanal battle, see *Translations*, 3, No. 3, "Truth of the Guadalcanal Battle."

Hirohito informed Kido that counterattack had failed: Kido, *Nikki*, 983–84.

1219 *Saratoga* torpedoed: Morison, 5:111–13.

Casualties in Hyakutake's bayonet charges: Griffith, 121.

Japanese submarine damage: Morison, 5:103–38.

U.S. troops got adequate supplies: Griffith, 130.

1220–1221 Maruyama's attack: Griffith, 168–73.

1221 "second attack has failed"; Kido met Konoye at hospital; new ambassador to Rome: Kido, *Nikki*, 989–91.

1222 Halsey on Guadalcanal; "Kill Japs": Griffith, 188.

Naval Battle of Guadalcanal: Morison, 5:225–82.

1223 Hirohito ordered Adm. Komatsu to use submarines for supply: Hashimoto, 61; Kido, *Nikki*, 994–95.

Kido heard news of naval battle at concert: ibid., 995; *Asahi* (Tokyo ed.), Nov. 18, 1942.

1224 Battle of Tassafaronga: Morison, 5:296–315; Griffith, 217–21.

1225 I-boats modified for freight duty: Hashimoto, 62–63.

1226 Empress Dowager's return: Kido, *Nikki*, 998 (Dec. 6, 1942). For negotiations with Sadako see Kido's entries of Apr. 17, July 11, Aug. 29, Sept. 18–21, 23, Nov. 10, 13, 16, 17, 19, 1942.

Hirohito's celebration of start of second war year: ibid., 999.

Dec. 9 liaison conference: Sugiyama, 2:191.

1228–1229 Kido and Hirohito to Ise Shrine: Kido, *Nikki*,

999–1000; details of shrine and ceremony, *Enthronement*, 71–74.

1229 Decision on Guadalcanal at meeting Dec. 3, Hirohito's statement: Sugiyama, 2, Intro., 18.

1230 Japanese evacuation of Guadalcanal, Feb. 1–7, 1943: Griffith, citing Japanese Gen. Miyazaki.

1233 Kido's reasons for continuing war: my analysis based on reading of Kido, *Nikki*, for years 1943 and 1944; in early 1943, e.g., see entries for Feb. 4 and 23; also interviews with Koizumi and most aristocratic of privileged sources.

To eat the flesh of Americans: there were several cases in the Marianas, IMTFE "Proceedings," 15033 ff.

1234 Prisoner of war statistics: ibid., 14901.

1235 Japan's policy on prisoners, Prisoner of War Information Bureau: IPS Document No. 814 contains extracts from Imperial Ordinance No. 1182 establishing P.O.W. camps and from Imperial Ordinance N. 1246 on the P.O.W. Information Bureau. Unfortunately IPS Document No. 1303 containing all imperial ordinances regarding prisoners of war remains classified; it is described in Library of Congress microfilm reels WT1–WT5 (Analyses of IPS Document Nos. 1–4097) but the text is not available. IPS Document No. 857 containing the incidental notebooks of Gen. Tamura Hiroshi when he was head of the P.O.W. Information Bureau is also classified. In general U.S. files on P.O.W.'s were classified in 1945. They must be voluminous because a sympathetic librarian at the War Documents Center in Alexandria, Va., once read me the U.S. government dossier kept on my family during the years when we were prisoners of the Japanese.

1236 Tojo's P.O.W. proposal on behalf of Doolittle captives: Tanaka Takayoshi, testimony, IMTFE "Proceedings," 14285 ff.; for date of War Ministry meeting see ibid., 14379; for slogan "no work, no food" see telegram of June 5, 1942, from chief of P.O.W. Control Bureau to chief of staff, Taiwan Army, ibid., 14361. Uemura's objections are stressed by Tanaka, ibid., 14374.

1237 Treatment of Wake prisoners: ibid., 14970 ff.

Prisoners as writers and announcers for Tokyo radio: IPS Document No. 975; James Bertram, in *Beneath the Shadow* (New York: John Day Co., 1947), 138–44, describes attempts to persuade him to join the staff of Tokyo Rose when he was a prisoner in the notorious Omori concentration camp. He was interrogated in the guardhouse there by the head of the Army Press Section's Cultural Program. This was a former Oxford acquaintance, the son of Marquis Ikeda, Empress Nagako's first cousin.

1239 Tojo's statement to Zentsuji commandant: document introduced in evidence, IMTFE "Proceedings," 14424.

Tojo's address to P.O.W. camp commandants, June 25, 1942: ibid., 14427.

1239–1240 Police report on parade of P.O.W.'s in Pusan: ibid., 14518 ff.

1241–1242 Incident at Changi: Wigmore, 522–23.

Hirohito approved in principle of Burma-Thailand rail link: affidavit of Wakamatsu Tadakazu, IMTFE "Proceedings," 14633, stated that "Southern Army requested and Imperial General Headquarters decided" to build railroad in first half of 1943.

1243–1248 Prisoners from Singapore began work on railroad in Oct. 1942: many details of prisoners' treatment and conditions from Wigmore, 541–92.

1248 Casualties of Burma-Thailand railroad: ibid., 588.

Roosevelt sanctioned assassination of Yamamoto: Davis, 16–17.

1249 Lockheed Lightnings as match for Zeroes: Caidin, *Zero Fighter*, 140.

1250 Action at Japanese beachheads on Guadalcanal: Morison, 5:41–50.

Hirohito's audience with Gen. Sugiyama Jan. 9: Sugiyama, 2: Intro., 19.

Battle of the Bismarck Sea: Morison, 5:54–65.

1250–1252 Hirohito to Sugiyama March 3: Sugiyama, 2: Intro., 19–20.

1252 Air strikes on Guadalcanal directed by Adm. Yamamoto from Rabaul: Morison, 5:118–25.

Message announcing Yamamoto's itinerary: text of intercepted message in Davis, 6–7; Agawa, 309.

Yamamoto at flight officers' party, evening of Apr. 13: Davis, 103.

1254 Yamamoto's exchange with Lt. Gen. Imamura: ibid., 105–6.

1255 Adm. Nimitz and Comdr. Layton: ibid., 5–8; Morison, 6:128–29, has concise account of the role of Nimitz.

Nimitz's message to Halsey and reply: Davis, 9–11.

Capt. Zacharias and Secretary Knox: ibid., 15, 19–20.

Operation Vengeance: order quoted, Potter, *Yamamoto*, 303–4; preparations, Davis, 116–42.

1257 Details of flight and death of Yamamoto: ibid., 142–53; 160–70; 175–76.

1258 Kido, "I felt shock and bitter grief": *Nikki*, 1029.

Yamamoto's funeral ceremonies: Agawa, 325–27.

1259 Yamamoto's poems: adapted from Davis, 147, 199. I have retranslated the first to agree with the meter of the original and have somewhat condensed the second.

N. 9: ibid., 1047.

1260 Kido attended funeral: *Nikki*, 1030.

1261 Col. Tsuji Masanobu's career: see his book *Guadarukanaru, passim.*

1262 Kido's report of Emperor's session with Tojo, subsequent changes in government: Kido, *Nikki*, 1005–9.

Kido continued contingency preparations for defeat: ibid., 1010, 1018.

1263 Pipeline from Hirohito to Chiang Kai-shek: ibid., 1056 (entries for Sept. 22–23, 1943); also Shigemitsu, 287–90.

Konoye reported Mme. Chiang's information from Washington: Kido, *Nikki*, 1025.

N. 12: Tanaka MS, "Yoshiko": McAleavy, 243–46.

1264 Japan would honor diplomatic commitments, if necessary Hirohito would appoint imperial prince as prime minister: ibid., 1028.

Communism as threat, Japanese anti-Communists and Strike-North partisans brought back into government: Kido, *Nikki*, 1024.

Kido discussed situation with Prince Takamatsu: Kido, *Nikki*, 1029.

Conference of puppet leaders discussed by Hirohito with Kido: ibid., 1030.

What to do with Hong Kong: The decision was finally to use Hong Kong as a counter in bargaining with Chiang; conference in the Imperial Presence, Sugiyama, 2:409.

1265 Attu: except as cited this section based on Morison, 7:41–50, and Howard Handleman, *Bridge to Victory: Story of the Reconquest of the Aleutians* (New York: Random House, 1954).

1266 "I sincerely bowed . . .": Kido, *Nikki*, 1032.

Hirohito complained to Sugiyama: Sugiyama, 2: Intro., 20.

Tojo's audience with Hirohito and his warning that now Japan fought alone: Kido, *Nikki,* 1033–34; see also 1043.

1267–1268 Hirohito to Sugiyama on Attu tragedy: Sugiyama, 2: Intro., 20–21.

1268 Emperor commended Sugiyama for success of raid in China: ibid., 21–22.

Kido found "ideas of great interest" in *War and Peace:* Kido, *Nikki,* 1041–42.

1269 Hirohito summoned Adm. Komatsu, who reported Solomons could not be held: ibid., 1037–38; interview with retired Navy commander.

Hirohito at Imperial Headquarters, gave Tojo message for commanders in Solomons: Sato, "Tojo Hideki to daitoa senso," 390 ff. Hirohito's angry speech to Tojo: Sugiyama, 2: Intro., 23–24.

1270 Tojo in Rabaul: Sato, "Tojo Hideki to daitoa senso," 390 ff.

Kido's efforts on behalf of air power: see, e.g., *Nikki* entries for July 6, 13, and Aug. 8, 11, 18, 20, 1943.

Chichibu's aide to co-ordinate peace dealings with Chiang: ibid., 1038. A participant in the venture was Col. Matsutani Makoto, the Army's contingency peace planner: Kase, 75–76; Butow, 26 n. 52.

1271 Kido warned Hirohito, July 25, on Axis partners: Kido, *Nikki,* 1043.

Maj. Gen. Matsumoto advised Kido of police interest in peace plots: ibid., 1044.

1272 Hirohito's exchange with Sugiyama, Aug. 5: Sugiyama, 2: Intro., 24–26.

Hirohito, "Can't we take offensive?" and substance of General Staff report on dubious possibilities for counteroffensive: ibid.

Intelligence studies prescribed events that took place: one of the outspoken statements of the most aristocratic of my sources; see also note on page 82.

1273 Adm. Nomura Naokumi reported to Hirohito on serious situation in Germany: Kido, *Nikki,* 1046.

1274 Hirohito at liaison conference Sept. 9: ibid., 1051.

Hirohito on transfer of divisions to Taiwan and Philippines and his arguments to Army chiefs on U.S. submarine operations: ibid., 1051–52; interview with retired Lt. Gen. Fujisawa.

Emperor quoted proverb to justify refusal to reinforce Marshalls: Kido, *Nikki,* 1052 (entry of Sept. 10, 1943).

1275 Hirohito's private audience with Wang Ching-wei: ibid., 1055–56; see also 1053 (entry of Sept. 17, 1943). His comment afterward to Kido: ibid., 1056.

Dr. Okawa Shumei suggested to Kido that projected Higashikuni Cabinet have Lt. Gen. Ishiwara Kanji as advisor: ibid., 1057.

1276 Okawa wanted matter discussed with Count Makino: ibid. Makino finally came to Kido: ibid., 1075.

Suzuki Tei-ichi allowed to retire: ibid., 1060.

1276–1277 Prince Mikasa on China situation and leaders: ibid., 1061–62.

Nakano's assassination plot, details of Terai's spree and arrest: ibid., 1064 (entry of Oct. 21, 1943).

Nakano's suicide and rumors about it: ibid., 1065; Yanaga, *Since Perry,* 613.

1277–1278 Prince Mikasa and Lt. Gen. Anami went south Nov. 4: Kido, *Nikki,* 1067.

1278–1279 Meeting of Greater East Asia Conference, Tojo's views and comments: Kido, *Nikki,* 1064, 1066–67; Shigemitsu, 293–94; news reports in *Mainichi, Asahi, Syonan Times;* observation about the lack of braziers for representatives of conquered countries from interview with Tanaka.

1279 Hirohito gave lunch in palace to delegates: Kido, *Nikki,* 1067.

Nov. 19, Kido received Takagi's pessimistic report and heard of Matsutani's view that Japan might be decimated: ibid., 1070; interview with retired Navy commander; Butow, *Japan's Decision,* 20–21, 26–27.

1280 Higashikuni's recruiting lunch, Kido's conference with Hirohito on Takagi's report, negotiations between Wang and Chiang broken off: Kido, *Nikki,* 1070–72.

Hirohito visited Yamamoto's tomb, Kido at Prince Saionji's: ibid., 1073.

1281 Count Kabayama reported on U.S. feelings about Pacific war: ibid., 1075. Hirohito's own appraisal of war prospects, his conclusions conveyed to Kido Jan. 4, and Kido's memorandum of Jan. 6: ibid., 1075–78.

1281–1282 Substance of Kido's "blueprint for postwar Japan": ibid., 1078–79.

29. *The Fall of the Homeland*

For this chapter, in addition to sources cited or listed in the bibliography, I have drawn for background on: W. G. Burchett, *Wingate Adventure* (Melbourne: F. W. Cheshire, 1944); Claude A. Buss, "Inside Wartime Japan" (*Life*, January 24, 1944); Dorothy Guyot, "The Burma Independence Army: A Political Movement in Military Garb" (Paper read at Association for Asian Studies meeting, San Francisco, April 2, 1965); Tom Harrison, *World Within: A Borneo Story* (London: The Cresset Press, 1959); A. V. H. Hartendorp, *The Santo Tomas Story* (New York: McGraw Hill, 1964); Vern Haughland, *The AAF Against Japan* (New York: Harper and Brothers, 1948); Hayashi Saburo, *Taiheiyo Senso Rikusen Gaishi* [A History of Land Warfare Conditions in the Pacific War] (Tokyo: Iwanami Shinsho, 1951); Harold Riegelman, *Caves of Biak: An American Officer's Experiences in the Southwest Pacific*, with prefaces by Robert Eichelberger and Hu Shih (New York: Dial Press, 1955); Frederic Stevens, *Santo Tomas Internment Camp*, foreword by Douglas MacArthur (Limited private edition printed at Stratford House, 1946); Usui Katsumi, "Kuten suru senryo seisaku: Daitoa kaigi" [Vain Occupation Policy: The Greater East Asia Conference] *Asahi Jyanaru* (Asaki Journal), 7, No. 45 (30 October 1965), 74 ff.

1285 U.S. Fleet for Gilberts invasion: Morison, 7, Appendix II.

Makin and Tarawa: ibid., 7:121–74.

1286 Marshalls: ibid., 7:230–304.

1286–1289 AIR NAVY: this section based on Kido, *Nikki*, 1082–87, supplemented by interviews with retired Navy commander; also Kido, *Nikki*, 104 (May 1, 1944).

1289 THE "CHUNGKING MANEUVER": Kido, *Nikki*, 1088; Hayashi Shigeru et al, 2:39–46; Matsumoto interviews; also Butow, *Japan's Decision*, 51–54.

1290–1292 SACKING THE STAFF: Kido, *Nikki*, 1089–90; Sugiyama, 2: Intro., 27–28, 32–33.

1292 Press acknowledged direct imperial guidance: *Asahi*, Feb. 27, 1944.

Aircraft production: U.S. Strategic Bombing Survey, *Summary Report*, 9; goals: Kido, *Nikki*, 1087.

1293 Attack on Kohima: Slim, 254–95; Collier, 413–17.

Casualty reports from Japanese sources: Kojima, 2:143–59; Hattori, 989–93.

1294 MacArthur cuts off Rabaul: Bougainville casualties, Morison, 7:430.

Biak and Noemfoor casualties; Morison, 133–40.

1295 Hirohito quick to realize: my interpretation of his immediate consideration of a more popular and pro-American cabinet; see memorandum of June 15, 1944, Kido, *Nikki*, 1110–111.

Battle of the Philippine Sea: ships engaged, Morison, 8, Appendices II and III; ships lost: ibid., 8:233, and Inoguchi et al., 25.

1296 Jo's radiogram, including its text: Inoguchi et al., 27–29; his career, Zacharias, 182.

1296–1299 Hirohito considers Jo's idea; blames Shimada for Philippine Sea disaster; gives tentative authorization for kamikaze program: Kido, *Nikki*, 1112–113, supplemented by interviews with retired Navy commander.

1297 Planes lost in operational use: U.S. Strategic Bombing Survey, *Summary Report*, 9.

1298 Political objections to kamikaze idea: "Handling of Special Air Attacks by the High Command," Kawabe Torashiro, *Statements*, 2:67–68.

Okamura also pleads for kamikaze: Inoguchi et al, 139–40.

1299 Saipan population: Morison, 8:152.

Camp for surrendering Japanese: Morison, 8:339; Otis Cary, interview.

Despite Tojo, Saipan suicides encouraged: Kido, *Nikki*, 1114 (July 1); also 1112–113.

1300 Nagumo suicide: Toland, *Rising Sun*, 511–12.

Main garrison dead: Morison, 8:336.

1301 Civilian suicides: ibid., 338.

Total casualties: ibid., 339.

Guam casualties: ibid., 401.

Tinian: ibid., 364.

Tinian casualties: ibid., 369.

1302–1303 Tojo ousted, Hirohito withdraws from limelight: this summary is drawn from Kido, *Nikki*, 1115–129.

Ohka program: Nakajima et al, 140–41.

Peace Faction opposition: Kido, *Nikki*, 1137.

1304–1305 Final Strategy Japan: Morison, 12:9–11.

Morotai: ibid., 24.

Peleliu: ibid., 35–36; 41–43.

Murai identified: Hata's "Personnel Records"; see also Maj. Frank O. Hough, *The Assault on Peleliu* (U.S. Marine Corps, Historical Division H.Q., 1950), Appendix F, "Mission of Murai."

1305–1307 SHO: Hattori, 673–89.

Yamashita Cabinet avoided, Yamashita reposted: Kido, *Nikki*, 1143–144.

Yamashita at Fort McKinley: Potter, *Soldier Must Hang*, 110.

Halsey's fast carrier task force: Morison, 12:50.

Taiwan air strike: ibid., 104, 106.

1308 U.S. armada: ibid., Appendix I, 113.

Morishima to Moscow: Kido, *Nikki*, 1146.

Rescript on Taiwan air disaster: Kido, *Nikki*, 1148 (entries for Oct. 16, 18, and 19, 1944).

Hirohito and Onishi: retired Navy commander explained that the imperial messenger (*gosai*) mentioned by Kido in his entry for October 19, *Nikki*, 1148, is Onishi.

1309 Onishi's words at Mabalacat: Inoguchi et al, 7.

Admiral Arima's example: ibid., 37 and n.

"Chances of scoring a hit": ibid., 8.

1309–1322 Battle of Leyte Gulf: Ito, 120–79; Morison, 12: 159–338; d'Albas, 301–35; Inoguchi et al, 47–78, on kamikaze operations.

1309 Landings at Leyte: Morison, 12:130–38.

"Southward Movement of Ozawa Decoy Force," *Translations*, 3; No. 5.

1316 Onishi at Mabalacat: Inoguchi et al, 19.

1316–1317 Battle of the escort carriers: Morison, 12:242–88.

1321 Fate of derelicts: *Nachi*, ibid., 239; *Kiso*, ibid., 356; *Kongo*, ibid., 410; *Kumano*, ibid., 357.

1321–1322 Total losses, Japanese and American: ibid., Appendix II (Japanese) and Appendix I (U.S.).

1322 Emperor's message to kamikaze: Kido, *Nikki*, 1148; interview with retired Navy commander; Inoguchi et al, 64.

Leyte casualties: Morison, 12:397; Toland, *Rising Sun*, 607.

Luzon casualties: Smith, Appendix H, 692, 694.

1322–1323 Iwo casualties: Morison, 14:68–69.

Incendiary raids: Berger, 145.

Okinawa casualties: U.S. Strategic Bombing Survey, *Campaigns of Pacific War*, 331; Appleman et al, 473.

1324 N. 7: Survey on Japan's will to fight: U.S. Strategic Bombing Survey, *Effects of Strategic Bombing on Japanese Morale*, also *Summary Report*, 21.

1325 Warning leaflets: Berger, 146, 149.

Hirohito's bleak personal prospects: Coox, 100; Koizumi interview. It may be that Hirohito did not seriously entertain any thoughts of suicide or abdication. He knew, however, that some of his samurai retainers would expect one or the other of him as a matter of honor.

1326 Lingayen Gulf landing: Morison, 13:123–30, 193–96.

15,000 Japanese sailors and Marines to Manila: ibid., 196–97.

Intramuros casualties: Smith, 306–7.

Japanese intentions for war prisoners: see, e.g., telegram entitled Army Asia (Secret) No. 2257 introduced in evidence, "Proceedings," 14533; or Taikoku Camp document on "final disposition" introduced ibid., 14725, or file of radio messages concerning "release without record" from chief P.O.W. administrator, Tokyo, to chief of staff, Taiwan Army, IPS Document No. 2697.

1327 Palawan massacre: Lord Russell, 88–91.

1328 The prison hulks: ibid., 93–107.

1329 Vice war minister telegram on war prisoners: IPS Document No. 2697.

1330 Kamikaze spirit and effectiveness: e.g., Suzuki Kantaro quoted in Inoguchi et al, 189–90.

"Death without meaning": Sakai Saburo, 319; also 306, 309.

Flight described in detail: ibid., 302–25.

1331–1332 Details of March 9 raid: Berger, 127–31.

1332 Fire raid casualties: Kato, 215, 224.

1333 Hirohito moved underground: Coox, 24.

Hirohito on March 9: ibid., 28.

N. 10: Poison gas proposal: Newcomb, 240.

1334 Spare Imperial Palace: Toland, *Rising Sun*, 744.

Kido advised informal visit to ruins: Kido, *Nikki*, 1176–177.

N. 11: U.S. Strategic Bombing Survey, *Japanese Morale*; also *Summary Report*, 21.

1335 *Yamato* lost: Ito Masanori, 184–90.

1336 Details of Cho's death: Tanaka interview; see also Appleman, et al, *Okinawa, the Last Battle*, United States Army in World War II: The War in the Pacific, vol. 1 (Washington, D.C.: Department of the Army, Office of the Chief of Military History, 1948).

1337 In Japanese the equivalent of "it never rains but it pours" is "while crying stung by a bee on the face." On top of the fire bombing the atomic bomb stung cruelly. Kato, *Lost War*, 217.

1338 "Emperor . . . retained the people's faith": *Summary Report*, 21.

Imperial Family Council: Kido, *Nikki*, 1225; see also Coox, 126.

Anami's visit to Prince Mikasa: Craig, 148; Toland, *Rising Sun*, 824.

1340 Installation of Lincoln's bust: Oya, *Ichiban nagai hi*, 202; Oya, *Longest Day*, 312. (The choice of words in the Japanese text seems to me to convey a richer feeling of belly talk and belly laughter than that of the English text.)

Epilogue: New Clothes

This brief review of Japanese events since 1945 is based on the common record of news reports and on conversations with Japanese. I have cited below a few specific sources for details which seem to me to have gone unappreciated. Essentially my account is an interpretation of events—an opinion, if you will—suggesting the relevance of what has gone before in these pages to what may come after. I have drawn on no state papers and no diaries of statesmen because none are available. I look forward, however, to the gradual opening of such records in the years and decades ahead.

1341 Japanese arsenals turned over to native patriots: e.g., see *N.Y. Times*, Sept. 9, 1945, and Singapore *Times*, Nov. 20, Dec. 12, 1945.

1342 Cheat-the-enemy tactics: see Tsuji, *Underground Escape*, 1–90.

N. 1. from interviews with retired Maj. Gen. Kajiura Ginjiro.

1344 6,000 Japanese prisoners attacked by tribesmen on Borneo: K. G. Tregonning, *A History of Modern Sabah* (*North Borneo, 1881–1963*), 2d ed. (Singapore: University of Malaya Press, 1965), 217–221.

1345 HANGING THE TIGER: this section based on "Yamashita Trial Proceedings" (unpublished papers, National War Memorial, Canberra), *passim*. See also Potter, *Soldier Must Hang*, 170–97, and Reel, *passim*.

1347 News reports quoted: Potter, 180.

1348 Yamashita took pains to remove U.S. prisoners from Baguio: author's experience; Watanabe Hiroshi, *Statements*,

4:448–53; see also Todani Naotoshi, *Yama Yukaba Kusamusu Shikabane* [Walk in the Mountains, Rot as a Corpse in the Grass] (Osaka: Bunsho-in, 1965), *passim.*

N. 5: Taylor quoted: Neil Sheehan article, *N.Y. Times,* Jan. 9, 1946; Reel protested: letter to *N.Y. Times,* Jan. 19, 1946. See also *Newsweek,* Feb. 22, March 22, 1946.

1349 Yamashita in his own defense: excerpted from Yamashita's final statements to the court, *N.Y. Times,* Dec. 1, 1945.

1350–1351 Justice Frank Murphy quoted: *N.Y. Times,* Feb. 5, 1946.

1351–1352 Gen. MacArthur's statement on the Yamashita case: *Reminiscences,* 295–96.

1352 Gen. Yamashita's last hours: Potter, *Soldier Must Hang,* 194.

CUTTING OFF THE NOSE: this section based on "Honma Trial Proceedings" (unpublished papers, National War Memorial, Canberra).

1353 Honma's American lawyers active in his defense: Toland, *Rising Sun,* 320 n.

Justice Murphy quoted: ibid.

1354 MacArthur defended verdict: *Reminiscences,* 296–98.

Honma's last letter to his children: Toland, *Rising Sun,* MacArthur quoted: 298.

1358–1359 Okawa's behavior at trial opening: John Luter, Dispatch No. 284 to *Time* magazine; in Okawa's ravings Luter included: "Do you know Happy Chandler? I'm going into business with him."

Okawa raved to reporters: Gayn, *Japan Diary,* 209; *Newsweek,* May 13, 1946, cited in Butow, *Tojo,* 485.

1359 Official diagnosis of Okawa: ibid., 486.

1360 Many Japanese impressed by evidence of savagery: Takeda, 120–23.

Shigemitsu asked Hirohito to his face: Kase Toshikazu, in *N.Y. Times,* Sept. 2, 1970; see also his *Journey to the "Missouri,"* 220 ff.

1361 A Japanese newspaperman observed: Tony Kase, interview.

Japanese attitudes at beginning of trial, and judgment declared *hidoi:* Carl Mydans, Dispatch No. 770 to *Life* International, Nov. 13, 1948.

1362 "the comic helplessness of being Japanese": Faubion Bowers (a personal aide-de-camp to MacArthur, 1945–46), "How

Japan Won the War," *N.Y. Times Magazine*, Apr. 30, 1970, 39. See also Yoshida, 59.

1364 FACTORY POWER: In this brief recital of Japan's economic resurgence I have consulted Louis Kraar, *Fortune*, Sept. 1970, 126; Takashi Oka, *N.Y. Times*, Jan. 5, 1970; "What Makes Japanese Business Grow," Boston Consulting Group (unpublished printed material); "The Japanese Economy: A Continuing Miracle?" *Interplay*, Dec. 1969/Jan. 1970; James C. Abegglen, "The Economic Growth of Japan," *Scientific American*, March 1970, 31.

1367 Merchant families have ties of marriage to nobility: for a full account of merchant-noble intermarriage see Suzuki Yukio, esp. the genealogies.

"Occupation was hampered by its lack of knowledge . . .": quoted, in Bowers, "How Japan Won the War," 37. The extent of U.S. ignorance remains a moot point. Gen. MacArthur's Staff, *Historical Report of Operations in the Southwest Pacific Area,* completed in 1951, told the story from the general's point of view (vol. 1) and from captured documents by the Japanese commanders (vol. 2); it has remained classified. Morison, 12:ix, says of it: "Only three copies were printed (and don't ask me where I saw one, I can't tell!)."

1368 Roughly $9 million spent on war crime trials: Carl Mydans, Dispatch No. 770 to *Life* International, Nov. 13, 1948.

1370 PRIVY POCKETING: this section based on Kuroda, 185 ff., supplemented by *N.Y. Times*, Dec. 27, 1967, Dec. 27, 1968, Jan. 25, 1970.

1373 Another $2 million to build new summer villa for the Emperor: *N.Y. Times*, Jan. 13, 1968.

Kanin and Fushimi scandals: Fujishima, 62 ff.

1374 Proprietress of the Isaribi: *Shukan Asahi*, Feb. 11, 1966, 15.

1374–1375 Ohara and Higashikuni religion: Fujishima, 68; Matsumoto Seicho, interview with Higashikuni, *Bungei Shunjo*, Jan. 1968, 170 ff.

1377–1378 "Three Nothings Incident," Mikami Taku, and rightist rally of Feb. 26, 1965: Murofushi, 247–49.

Get-together of assassins a warning: interview with retired lieutenant general.

1379 National Foundation Day revived: *N.Y. Times*, Feb. 11, 1967.

LONE CRY OF ANGUISH: this section based on Donald Keene,

"Mishima," N.Y. *Times Book Review*, Jan. 3, 1971, 5; *Time* magazine, Dec. 7, 1970, 32–37; Takashi Oka, "Japan's Self-Defense Force Wins a Skirmish with the Past," N.Y. *Times Magazine*, Feb. 28, 1971.

1380 Mishima involved in controversy with son of Count Arima: conversation with Tony Kase; also Oka, in N.Y. *Times*, June 1, 1970.

1383 Novelist Arima's opinion of Mishima's death: private correspondence.

"The Emperor should be a symbol": Staff Sergeant Amma Takaji quoted by Oka, N.Y. *Times Magazine*, Feb. 28, 1971.

1384 Hirohito's poem: *Asahi*, Jan. 6, 1971.

BIBLIOGRAPHY

Abend, Hallett. *Chaos in Asia*. New York: Ives Washburn, 1939.
——. *My Life in China, 1926–41*. New York: Harcourt, Brace, 1943. Abend was correspondent for *The New York Times* in China.
—— and Billingham, Anthony J. *Can China Survive?* New York: Ives Washburn, 1936.

Agawa Hiroshi, *Yamamoto Isoroku*. Tokyo: Shincho Shahan, 1965. Anecdotal and disorganized, but the most authoritative Japanese biography.

Agoncillo, Teodoro A. *The Fateful Years: Japan's Adventure in the Philippines, 1941–45*. 2 vols. Quezon City, Philippines: R. P. Garcia Publishing Co., 1965.

Aikawa Gisuke. "Manshu keizai shikai no ki-pointo" [Key Points of Manchurian Financial Management]. In *Himerareta Showa-shi*.

Akimoto Shunkichi. *Exploring the Japanese Ways of Life*. Tokyo: Tokyo News Service, 1961. A compendium of cultural and historical lore by a Japanese connoisseur.

Allen, G. C. *A Short Economic History of Modern Japan*. London: George Allen and Unwin, 1962.

Amrine, Michael. *The Great Decision: The Secret History of the Atomic Bomb*. New York: G. P. Putnam's Sons, 1959. Well-researched, well-written reconstruction.

Ando Yoshio. "Senso to kazoku" [*The War and the Imperial Family*]. Part 1, *Ekonomisuto*, August 31, 1965, pp. 85 ff. (interview with Prince Higashikuni); Part 2, ibid., February 22, 1966, pp. 84 ff. (interview with Prince Mikasa); Part 3, ibid., March 1, 1966, pp. 84 ff. (interview with Prince Mikasa).

——, ed. *Showa keizai-shi e no shogen* [Evidence Pertaining to Economic History in the Reign of Hirohito]. Tokyo: Mainichi Shinbun-sha, 1966.

Araki Sadao. "Doran Showa ni tatsu tenno" [The Emperor Stood Forth During a Disturbance of His Reign]. In *Tenno hakusho* [White Paper on the Emperor], *Bungei Shunju*, October, 1956.

——. "Nikka jihen totsunyu made" [Up Until Japan Rushed into the China Incident]. In *Himerareta Showa-shi*.

Asahi, Tokyo and Osaka editions. One of Japan's two leading daily newspapers.

Asahi. *Juyo shimen no shichijugo-nen: Meiji juni-nen–Showa nyu-kyunen* [Momentous News Columns of Seventy-five Years: 1879–1954]. Tokyo: Asahi Shinbun-sha, 1954.

ATIS. See United States of America, Supreme Command for Allied Powers, Far East: Allied Translator and Interpreter Section.

Attiwill, Kenneth. *The Singapore Story*. London: Frederich Muller, 1959. Scathing comment by a participant.

Australia, Commonwealth of, Department of External Affairs. "Cablegrams, 1945–1946." Unpublished material on file at Commonwealth Archives, Canberra.

Ballou, Robert O. *Shinto: The Unconquered Enemy*. New York: Viking Press, 1945.

Barr, Pat. *The Coming of the Barbarians: The Opening of Japan to the West, 1853–1870*. New York: E. P. Dutton & Co., 1967.

Beasley, W. G. *The Modern History of Japan*. New York: Frederick A. Praeger, 1963. Outstanding on the period 1853–1868.

Benda, Harry J. *The Crescent and the Rising Sun: Indonesian Islam under the Japanese Occupation, 1942–1945*. The Hague: W. van Hoeve Ltd., 1958.

Benedict, Ruth. *The Chrysanthemum and the Sword*. Boston: Houghton Mifflin, 1946. An anthropological classic.

Bennett, H. Gordon. *Why Singapore Fell*. Sydney: Angus and Robertson, 1944. By the commander of Australian forces in Malaya.

Berger, Carl. *B-29: The Superfortress*. New York: Ballantine Books, 1970.

Borg, Dorothy: *The United States and the Far Eastern Crisis of 1933–1938*. Cambridge, Mass.: Harvard University Press, 1964.

Borton, Hugh. *Japan's Modern Century*. New York: The Ronald Press, 1955. An over-all social and economic history since 1850.

Brereton, Lewis H. *The Brereton Diaries: 3 October 1941–8 May*

1945. New York: William Morrow & Co., 1946. Brereton was U.S. Army Air Corps commander in the Philippines, 1941.

Brines, Russell. *MacArthur's Japan.* Philadelphia: J. B. Lippincott Co., 1948. An able journalist's return to Japan in 1945–46.

"Brocade Banner". See United States Army, Far East Command, Intelligence, Civil Intelligence Section.

Brooks, Lester. *Behind Japan's Surrender: The Secret Struggle That Ended an Empire.* New York: McGraw-Hill Book Co., 1968. Reflects valuable interviewing of living protagonists.

Bullock, Cecil. *Etajima: The Dartmouth of Japan.* London: Sampson Low, Marston & Co., 1942. The Japanese Naval Academy.

Bunce, William K., ed. *Religions in Japan: Buddhism, Shinto, Christianity.* Rutland, Vt., and Tokyo: Charles E. Tuttle Co., 1955.

Bush, Lewis. *Clutch of Circumstance.* Tokyo: Bungei Shunju, 1956. Japanese concentration camps through the eyes of a Japanophile.

——. *Japanalia.* 4th ed., rev. and enl. New York: David MacKay Co., 1959. A useful glossary to things Japanese.

——. *Land of the Dragonfly.* London: Robert Hale, 1959. A short history of Japan.

Butow, Robert J. C. *Japan's Decision to Surrender.* Hoover Library on War, Revolution and Peace, Publication No. 24. Stanford, California: Stanford University Press, 1954. Readable, a model of documentation, based largely on IMTFE materials.

——. *Tojo and the Coming of the War.* Princeton, N.J.: Princeton University Press, 1961. The most detailed account available in English of the years 1936–45 from the Japanese point of view.

Byas, Hugh. *Government By Assassination.* New York: Alfred A. Knopf, 1942. A classic by the prewar *New York Times* correspondent in Tokyo.

——. *The Japanese Enemy: His Power and His Vulnerability.* New York: Alfred A. Knopf, 1942.

Caidin, Martin. *The Ragged, Rugged Warriors.* New York: E. P. Dutton & Co., 1966. Bataan.

——. *Zero Fighter.* With introduction by Sakai Saburo. New York: Ballantine Books, 1969.

Chamberlain, William Henry. *Japan Over Asia.* Boston: Little, Brown & Co., 1938. Temperate account of Japanese aggression in China, 1928–37.

Churchill, Winston S. *The Second World War.* 4, The Hinge of Fate; 5, Closing the Ring; 6, Triumph and Tragedy. Boston: Houghton Mifflin Co., 1950, 1951, 1953.

Ciano, Galeazzo. Ciano Diaries, 1939–1945. Edited by Hugh Gibson. Garden City, N.Y.: Doubleday & Co., 1946.

Clubb, O. Edmund. *20th Century China*. New York: Columbia University Press, 1946. A history by a U.S. Foreign Service officer with twenty years' experience in China.

Cohen, Jerome B. *Japan's Economy in War and Reconstruction*. Minneapolis: University of Minnesota Press, 1949.

Collier, Basil. *The War in the Far East, 1941–1945: A Military History*. New York: William Morrow and Co., 1969.

Coox, Alvin. *Japan: The Final Agony*. New York: Ballantine Books, 1970. Last year of the war by a Japan expert who has interviewed many of the participants.

Craig, William. *The Fall of Japan*. New York: Dial Press, 1967. A journalistic reconstruction that benefits from astute interviewing of surviving participants.

Craigie, Sir Robert. *Behind the Japanese Mask*. London: Hutchinson & Co., 1945. Craigie was British ambassador in Tokyo before the war.

Cresswell, H. T., Hiroka, J., and Namba, R. *A Dictionary of Military Terms (English-Japanese and Japanese-English)*. American ed. Chicago: University of Chicago Press, 1942.

Crow, Carl, ed. *Japan's Dream of World Empire: The Tanaka Memorial*. 3rd ed. New York: Harper & Brothers, 1942.

Crowley, James B. *Japan's Quest for Autonomy: National Security and Foreign Policy 1930–1938*. Princeton, N.J.: Princeton University Press, 1966. A scholarly study which contains new material drawn from Japanese military position papers written in the early 1930's.

D'Albas, Andrieu. *Death of a Navy: Japanese Naval Action in World War II*. New York: The Devin-Adair Co., 1957.

Davis, Burke. *Get Yamamoto*. New York: Random House, 1969.

Davis, Forrest, and Lindley, Ernest K. *How War Came: An American White Paper from the Fall of France to Pearl Harbor*. New York: Simon and Schuster, 1942. A lively, well-researched account of doings in the White House just before the war.

Deakin, F. W., and Storry, G. R. *The Case of Richard Sorge*. New York: Harper & Row, 1966. A semipopular account of the Sorge case by two British scholars, good in its review of the German documentation.

Dexter, David. *The New Guinea Offensives*. Vol. VI, Series 1 (Army), Australia in the War of 1939–1945. Canberra: Australian War Memorial, 1961.

Dull, Paul S., and Umemura, Michael Takaaki. *The Tokyo Trials: A Functional Index to the Proceedings of the International Military Tribunal for the Far East*. Ann Arbor, Mich.: University of Michigan Press, 1957.

Dyess, Wm. E. *Death March from Bataan*. Sydney: Angus and Robertson Ltd., 1945. One of the best of many firsthand accounts.

Eichelberger, Robert L. *Our Jungle Road to Tokyo*. New York: Viking Press, 1950.

Ekins, H. R., and Wright, Theon. *China Fights for Her Life*. New York: McGraw-Hill, Whittlesey House, 1938. Hard-boiled, journalistic, full of information.

Elsbree, Willard H. *Japan's Role in Southeast Asian Nationalist Movements, 1940–45*. Cambridge, Mass.: Harvard University Press, 1953.

Enthronement of the One Hundred Twenty-fourth Emperor of Japan. Edited by Benjamin W. Fleisher. Tokyo: Japan Advertiser, 1928.

Fairbank, John K., Reischauer, Edwin O., and Craig, Albert M. *East Asia: The Modern Transformation*. Vol. II, *A History of East Asian Civilization*. Boston: Houghton Mifflin Co., 1964. A useful overall textbook.

Far Eastern Advisory Commission, Australian Delegation. Unpublished papers, Commonwealth Archives, Canberra. 1-3: "Events Concerning Japan, August 20–December 30, 1945."

———. A4-9, Appendix A: Memoranda from Truman to MacArthur.

———. A4-9, unlettered appendix: Intelligence summary of American leaders' views regarding Emperor.

———. A7: New Zealand General Policy with Regard to Japan.

———. WC 1-1/5: Deliberations on directives of U.S. Joint Chiefs of Staff.

———. WC 5-401: On Japanese War Criminals.

Far Eastern Commission, Australian Delegation. Unpublished papers, Commonwealth Archives, Canberra. "Interim Report, 11 February 1946." Annex I: Notes by W. D. Forsyth on talk with MacArthur, Tuesday, January 29, 1946, 11.40 AM–1.40 PM, Dai Ichi Building.

———. Ibid., Annex II: Summary of Principal Orders by S.C.A.P. to Japanese Government.

———. Ibid., Annex VII: Miscellaneous Notes by Members of the Australian Delegation.

Far Eastern Commission, Pacific Affairs Division. "Memorandum to Acting Secretary on Reform of the Japanese Constitution, 18 March 1946."

Farago, Ladislas. *The Broken Seal: The Story of "Operation Magic" and the Pearl Harbor Disaster*. New York: Random House, 1967. A readable account that reflects acquaintance with intelligence information that is not found elsewhere. Farago was in charge of research and planning in the psychological warfare branch of the Office of Naval Intelligence during the last two years of the war.

Feis, Herbert. *The China Tangle: The American Effort in China from Pearl Harbor to the China Mission*. Princeton, N.J.: Princeton University Press, 1953.

———. *Japan Subdued: The Atomic Bomb and the End of the War in the Pacific*. Princeton, N.J.: Princeton University Press, 1961. Like Morison, Feis combines diplomacy and discretion with good writing and the highest order of scholarship.

———. *The Road to Pearl Harbor: The Coming of the War Between the United States and Japan*. Princeton, N.J.: Princeton University Press, 1950.

Fleisher, Wilfrid. *Volcanic Isle*. Garden City, N.Y.: Doubleday, Doran & Co., 1941. A firsthand account of Tokyo before the war by one of the few Western editors who continued to publish there until 1940.

Fuchida, Mutsuo and Okumiya Masatake. *Midway: The Japanese Navy's Story*. Annapolis, Md.: United States Naval Institute, 1955. By members of the Japanese Navy General Staff who participated in Midway.

Fujimoto Harutake. *Ningen Ishiwara Kanji* [Ishiwara Kanji as a Human Being]. Tokyo: Taisen Sangyo-sha, 1959.

Fujishima Taisuke. *Nihon no joryu shakai* [Japan's High Society]. Tokyo: Kobun-sha, 1965. An exposé by an insider.

Futara Yoshinori, Count, and Sawada Setsuzo. *The Crown Prince's European Tour*. English ed. Osaka: Osaka Mainichi Publishing Co., 1926.

Gayn, Mark J. *Japan Diary*. New York: William Sloane Associates, 1948. A firsthand account of the early days of the Occupation by a journalist who had worked in Japan before the war.

Gendai-shi shiryo: see Shimada Toshihiko; Obi Toshihito; Usui Katsumi; Tsunoda Jun.

Gibbs, John M. "On Prisoner of War Camps in Japan and Japanese Controlled Areas as Taken from Reports of Interned American Prisoners." Mimeographed report, dated 31 July 1946, prepared for the American Prisoner of War Information Bureau, Liaison and Research Branch.

Gibney, Frank. *Five Gentlemen of Japan: The Portrait of a Nation's Character*. New York: Farrar, Straus and Young, 1953.

Gill, G. Hermon. *Royal Australian Navy, 1939–42*. Vol. I, Series 2 (Navy), Australia in the War of 1939–1945. Canberra: Australian War Memorial, 1957.

Grenfell, Russell. *Main Fleet to Singapore*. London: Faber and Faber, Ltd., 1951.

Grew, Joseph C. *Ten Years in Japan*. New York: Simon & Schuster, 1944. Grew was U.S. ambassador in Tokyo from 1932 to Pearl Harbor.

——. *Turbulent Era: A Diplomatic Record of Forty Years, 1904–1945*. 2 vols. Boston: Houghton Mifflin, 1952.

Griffith, Samuel B., II. *The Battle for Guadalcanal*. Philadelphia: J. B. Lippincott Co., 1963. A Marine officer's research into the campaign in which he took part.

Guillain, Robert. *Le peuple japonais et la guerre: Choses vues 1939–1946*. Paris: Juilliard, 1947. A perceptive journalistic view from the Left Bank.

Gunther, John. *Riddle of MacArthur: Japan, Korea and the Far East*. New York: Harper & Brothers, 1951.

Hanaya Tadashi. "Manshu jihen wa koshite keikaku sareta" [A Plan Was Made for Bringing About the Manchurian Incident]. In *Himerareta Showa-shi*.

Hanayama Shinsho. *The Way of Deliverance: Three Years With the Condemned Japanese War Criminals*. New York: Charles Scribner's Sons, 1950. By the Buddhist priest who shrove them.

Harada Kumao. *Saionji-ko to seikyoku* [Prince Saionji and the Political Situation]. 8 vols. Tokyo: Iwanami Shoten, 1950–1956. These are the original for United States Army, Far East Command, Civil Intelligence Section, Special Report "Saionji-Harada Memoirs." Also, *Saionji-ko to Seikyoku Bekkan*, a supplementary volume to the above, containing index, Harada's original notes, appendices on the period 1927–1929 and 16 valuable source telegrams, position papers etc.

Hargreaves, Reginald. *Red Sun Rising: The Siege of Port Arthur*. Philadelphia and New York: J. B. Lippincott Co., 1962.

Harrison, E. J. *Fighting Spirit of Japan*. London: W. Foulsham & Co., Ltd., n.d. An early account of judo, kendo, and other Japanese warrior exercises by an enthusiast.

Hashimoto Mochitsura. *Sunk: The Story of the Japanese Submarine Fleet 1942–1945* (tr. by E. H. M. Colegrave). London: Cassell and Company Ltd., 1954.

Hata Ikuhiko. *Gun fuashizuma* [Army Fascism]. Tokyo: Kawade Shobo, 1962. A historian trained in Western methods of documentation, who is employed by the Japanese Self-Defense Forces.

——. *Nichu senso-shi* [History of the Sino-Japanese War]. Tokyo: Kawade Shobo, 1961. Concise and well documented.

——. "Higeki no Showa-shi" [The Tragedy of Hirohito's Reign]. In *Himerareta Showa-shi*.

——. "Notebooks." Manuscript materials containing names of Japanese military attachés by city and the commanders and chiefs of staff of Imperial Guards Divisions and Divisions 1 through 43, Japanese Imperial Army, 1900–1945; also names of commanders and chiefs of staff of Divisions 44 through 116, Area Army commanders and chiefs of staff, and the Army officer corps seniority list for Sept. 1944.

——. "Personnel Records." Postings by date of leading Japanese Army and Navy officers. Many of these career summaries are reproduced in appendices to his *Gun fuashizuma* and *Nichu senso-shi*; many others, mostly incomplete, are in manuscript.

Hattori Takushiro. *Daitoa senso zen-shi* [Complete History of the Greater East Asia War], revised by Naruse Yasushi. One volume, divided into 11 books and appendix, plus separate folder of maps and charts. Tokyo: Hara Shobo, 1965. Hattori was confidential secretary to Gen. Tojo Hideki, 1941–43, then chief of the Operations Section of the Army General Staff.

Hayashi Fusao. *Daitoa senso koteiron* [Affirmative Discussion of the Greater East Asia War]. Tokyo: Bancho Shobo, 1965.

Hayashi Masayoshi, ed. *Himerareta Showa-shi* [Hidden History of Hirohito's Reign]. Tokyo: Mainichi Shimbun-ki, 1965.

Hayashi Shigeru, Ando Yoshio, Imai Sei-ichi, and Oshima Taro. *Nihon Shusen-shi*. 3 vols. [The History of the End of Japan's War]. Tokyo: Yomiuri Shimbun-sha, 1965.

Heusken, Henry. *Japan Journal, 1855–1861*. Trans. and ed. by Jeannette C. Van der Corput and Robert A. Wilson. New Brunswick, N.J.: Rutgers University Press, 1964.

Higashifushimi Kunihide. *Asahiko shinno ryakureki* [A Brief Biography of Prince Asahiko]. Kyoto: Privately printed, 1965. A scholarly monograph based on family recollections, written by Empress Nagako's brother about the activities of his grandfather, Prince Asahiko, who was chief advisor to Emperor Komei at the time of the coming of Perry.

Higashikuni Naruhiko. *Higashikuni nikki* [Higashikuni Diary]. Tokyo: Tokuma Shoten, 1968.

——. *Watashi no kiroku* [My Personal Diary]. Tokyo: Toho Shobo, 1947.

Himerareta Showa-shi [Hidden History of the Reign of Hirohito], *Bessatsu Chisei No. 5*. Tokyo: Kawade Shobo, 1956. A collection of articles by leading participants in the events of 1928–1945, cited by author: Aikawa Gisuke; Araki Sadao; Hanaya Tadashi; Imamura Hitoshi; Ito Nobufumi; Katakura Tadashi; Okawa Kanji; Suzuki Tei-ichi; Takamiya Taihei; Tanaka Takayoshi; Toyoshima Fusataro; Tsuji Masanobu; Usui Katsumi.

Holtom, D. C. *Modern Japan and Shinto Nationalism: A Study of Present Day Trends in Japanese Religions.* Rev. Ed. Chicago: University of Chicago Press, 1947.

Honjo Shigeru. *Honjo nikki* [Honjo Diaries]. Tokyo: Hara Shobo, 1967.

Horiba Kazuo. *Shina jihen senso shido-shi* [History of the Conduct of the War in the China Incident]. 2 volumes plus separate folder of maps. Tokyo: Jiji Press, 1962.

Hozumi Nobushige, Baron. *Ancestor-Worship and Japanese Law.* 5th ed. rev. Tokyo: The Hokuseido Press, 1940.

Hsu Shu-hsi. *The War Conduct of the Japanese.* Political and Economic Studies No. 3, Council of International Affairs. Hangkow and Shanghai: Kelley & Walsh Ltd., 1938. Eyewitness accounts of Japanese atrocities in China.

Ike Nobutaka, ed. and transl. *Japan's Decision for War: Records of the 1941 Policy Conferences.* Stanford, Calif.: Stanford University Press, 1967. Translated from portions of *Sugiyama Memo*, q.v. as reproduced in *Taiheiyo senso*, 8 q.v.

Iklé, Frank William. *German-Japanese Relations 1936–1940.* New York: Bookman Associates, 1956.

Imai Sei-ichi. "Kampaku seiji no gosan: Konoye naikaku" [Miscalculations of the Emperor's Political Advisors: Konoye Cabinet]. *Asahi Jyanaru* [Asahi Journal] 7 No. 32 (1 Aug. 1965), pp. 74 ff.

——. "Kofuku to iu genjitsu—senryo kenryoku to no shukkai" [Realities of What Was Called Surrender—The Occupation Authorities and Their Encounters]. *Asahi Jyanaru* [Asahi Journal] 8 No. 5 (30 Jan. 1966), pp. 74 ff.

——. "Nomonhan jiken" [The Nomonhan Incident]. *Asahi Jyanaru* [Asahi Journal] 7 No. 36 (29 August 1965), pp. 76 ff.

——. "Misshitsu no naka no konran—daihonei" [Confusion in the Secret Chamber—Imperial Headquarters]. *Asahi Jyanaru* [Asahi Journal] 7 No. 49 (28 Nov. 1965), pp. 78 ff.

Imai Takeo. *Shina jihen no kaiso* [Reminiscences of the China Affair]. Tokyo: Misuzu Shobo, 1964.

Imamura Hitoshi. "Manshu hi o fuku goro" [When the Manchurian Fire Broke Out]. In *Himerareta Showa-shi.*

IMTFE "Proceedings." See International Military Tribunal for the Far East.

Inoguchi Rikihei and Tadashi Nakajima, with Roger Pineau. *The Divine Wind: Japan's Kamikaze Force in World War II.* Annapolis, Md.: United States Naval Institute, 1958.

Inoki Masamichi. "The Civil Bureaucracy in Japan." In *Political Modernization in Japan and Turkey,* edited by Robert E. Ward and

Dankwart A. Rustow. Princeton, N.J.: Princeton University Press, 1964.

International Military Tribunal for the Far East (IMTFE). "Exhibits," (also called "Documents Presented in Evidence"); Prosecution Exhibits Nos. 1–2282, Defense Exhibits Nos. 2283–3915. Mimeographed. Author used complete, bound, indexed set in the National War Memorial, Canberra, and incomplete set in the Yale Law School Library.

———. "Hearings in Chambers." In the National War Memorial, Canberra.

———. "Judgment." In the National War Memorial, Canberra.

———. "Proceedings" (before matters to be stricken from record were struck). Bound, indexed copies of mimeographed transcript. In the National War Memorial, Canberra.

———. "Proceedings" (after matters to be stricken from record were struck). 48,412 pp. on microfilm. In the Yale Law School Library, New Haven, Conn.

———. "Separate and Dissenting Opinions." In the National War Memorial, Canberra.

———. International Prosecution Section. Summaries and extracts of 4,096 documents collected by the International Prosecution Section, cited as IPS No. 1 . . . IPS No. 4,096. Of these, 2,282 were presented in evidence as "Exhibits." Microfilms WT1–WT94, Library of Congress.

Interviews. Koizumi Shinzo, former chief tutor to Crown Prince Akahito. Major General Tanaka Takayoshi, retired, star witness for the International Military Tribunal for the Far East. Lieutenant General Fujisawa, retired, staff officer and air-to-ground communications specialist; served in Manchuria, China, Tokyo General Staff, and finally as a divisional commander under Yamashita in the Philippines. Major General Kajiura Ginjiro, retired, staff officer and field commander in Manchuria in the early 1930's, after 1937 a field commander in China. Matsumoto Shigeharu, former member of Prince Konoye's brain trust. Tony Kase, the son of Kase Toshikazu who as secretary to Foreign Minister Shigemitsu attended the signing of surrender in 1945. Privileged sources: banker's son, who had access to the papers of one of Prince Saionji's closest friends; retired Navy commander, a wartime member of the Japanese Navy General Staff and friend of Prince Takamatsu; Uramatsu contact, who had access to the papers of a member of Kido's Eleven Club; most aristocratic source, a Fujiwara scion who knew Hirohito as a boy and young man.

IPS Documents. See International Military Tribunal for the Far East, International Prosecution Section.

Ito Kanejiro. *Gunjin Washi ga kuni sa* [Military Men of My Native Land]. 2 vols. Tokyo: Kyo no Mondai-sha, 1939.

Ito Masanori. *The End of the Imperial Japanese Navy.* Translated by Andrew Y. Kuroda and Roger Pineau. New York: Norton, 1962.

Ito Nobufumi. "Manshu jihen boppatsu to kokusai renmei" [The Manchurian Incident and the League of Nations]. In *Himerareta Showa-shi.*

Ito Takeo. *Problems in the Japanese Occupied Areas in China.* Japanese Council, Institute of Pacific Relations, Tokyo, 1941.

Iwabuchi Tatsuo. *Gunbatsu no keifu* [A Genealogy of Army Factions]. Chuokoron-sha, 1948.

Jansen, Marius B. *The Japanese and Sun Yat-sen.* Cambridge, Mass.: Harvard University Press, 1954. An admirable study, taken from Japanese sources, of Japan's Pan-Asian aspirations in the 1880–1930 period.

Japan Year Book, 1944–45. Published by The Foreign Affairs Association of Japan.

Johnson, Chalmers. *An Instance of Treason: Ozaki Hotsumi and the Sorge Spy Ring.* Stanford, Calif.: Stanford University Press, 1964. Exciting scholarly account of the Sorge spy ring based on Japanese police files.

Johnston, B. F. *Japanese Food Management in World War II.* Stanford, Calif.: Stanford University Press, 1953.

Johnston, Reginald F. *Twilight in the Forbidden City.* London: Victor Gollancz, 1934. Johnston was the tutor of Pu Yi, last emperor of China and puppet emperor of Manchuria.

Jones, F. C. *Japan's New Order in East Asia: Its Rise and Fall, 1937–45.* London: Oxford University Press, 1954.

Kajima Morinosuke. *Emergence of Japan as a World Power, 1895–1925.* Rutland, Vt., and Tokyo: Charles E. Tuttle Co., 1968.

Kamiyama Shigeo. *Tenno-sei ni kansuru riron-teki mondai* [Theoretical Problems Concerning the Emperor System]. Tokyo: Ashi-kai, 1947.

Kaneko Harushi. *Tenno-ke no sugao* [The Face of the Imperial Family]. Tokyo: Imperial Household Ministry, 1962.

Kanichi dai jiten [Sino-Japanese Dictionary]. Newly revised by Miyanokochi Kentaro. Tokyo: Obun-sha, 1957.

Kanroji Osanaga. "Tenno to uta to uma to" [The Emperor and Poems and Horses]. *Shuken Asahi,* 6 January 1967, pp. 52 ff.; 13 January 1967, pp. 40 ff.; 26 January 1967, pp. 31 ff.; 27 January 1967, pp. 32 ff. Jottings by one of Hirohito's favorite chamberlains.

Karig, Walter, and Kelley, Welbourn, eds. *Battle Report: Pearl Har-*

bor to Coral Sea. Vol. 1, Battle Report Series. New York: Rinehart & Co., 1944.

———; Harris, Russel L.; and Manson, Frank A., eds. *Battle Report: The End of an Empire*. Vol. IV, Battle Report Series. New York: Rinehart & Co., 1948.

Kase Toshikazu. *Journey to the "Missouri."* Edited by Davis Nelson Rowe. New Haven, Conn.: Yale University Press, 1952. Readable explanation of the war by a diplomat of the Peace Faction who attended the surrender aboard the *Missouri*.

Katakura Tadashi. "Ugaki naikaku ryuzan-su" [Aborting the Ugaki Cabinet]. In *Himerareta Showa-shi*.

Kato Hidetoshi. "Jisatsu seishin ni kaketa koku un—tokko-tai" [When the Nation's Destiny Was Staked on the Spirit of Suicide: The Special Attack Forces]. *Asahi Jyanaru* [Asahi Journal] 7 No. 53 (26 December 1965), pp. 74 ff.

———. "Nihonteki na, amari ni nihonteki na—zero sen" [Japanese, too Japanese—the Zero Fighter] *Asahi Jyanaru* [Asahi Journal] 7 No. 47 (17 November 1965), pp. 46 ff.

Kato Masuo. *The Lost War: A Japanese Reporter's Inside Story*. New York: Alfred A. Knopf, 1946. Recollections of Washington in 1941 and Tokyo in 1945.

Kawai Kazuo. *Japan's American Interlude*. Chicago: University of Chicago Press, 1960.

Kennedy, Malcolm. *A History of Japan*. London: Weidenfeld & Nicolson, 1963. Kennedy was long an attaché at the British Embassy in Tokyo as a specialist in military intelligence.

———. *The Problem of Japan*. London: Nisbet & Co., 1935.

———. *Some Aspects of Japan and Her Defense Forces*. Kobe: J. L. Thompson & Co., 1928.

Kidder, Jonathan Edward. *Japan Before Buddhism*. New York: Frederick A. Praeger, 1959.

Kido Koichi. *Kido Koichi nikki* [Kido Koichi's Diaries]. 2 vols. (paged consecutively). Tokyo: Tokyo University Press, 1966.

———. *Kankei bunsho* [Additional Writings]. Tokyo: Tokyo University Press, 1966.

Kirby, S. Woodburn, et al. *The War Against Japan*. Vol. II. India's Most Dangerous Hour; Vol. IV, The Reconquest of Burma. History of the Second World War, United Kingdom Military Series, edited by Sir James Butler. London: Her Majesty's Stationery Office, 1958, 1965.

Knollwood, James L., and Shek, Emily L. "On Prisoner of War Camps in Areas other than the Four Principal Islands of Japan." Mimeographed report, dated 31 July 1946, prepared for American

Prison of War Information Bureau, Liaison and Research Branch.

Kodama Yoshio. *I Was Defeated*. Tokyo: Robert Booth and Taro Fukuda, 1951. Memoir by a right-wing activist.

Kojima Noboru. *Taiheiyo Senso* [The Pacific War]. 2 vols. Tokyo: Chuo Koron-sha, 1966.

Komatsu Isao. *The Japanese People: Origins of the People and the Language*. Tokyo: Kokusai Bunka Shinkokai [The Society for International Cultural Relations], 1962.

Kono Tsukasa. "Ni-ni-roku jiken no nazo" [The Riddle of the February 26 Incident]. In *Himerareta Showa-shi*.

Konoye Fumimaro. *Nikki* [Diary]. Tokyo: Kyodo Tsushin-sha, 1968. A fragment, written during the summer of 1944.

———, with Uchiba Tomohiko. "Memoirs." English and Japanese texts, including repetitions, rough drafts, and handwritten corrections in margins in English by the author (IPS Documents Nos. 3, 570, 849, 850, 1467). Library of Congress microfilm WT6. Konoye's final text, in English, is reprinted in U.S. Congress, Joint Committee on the Investigation of the Pearl Harbor Attack, Hearings, Part 20, 3985 ff. It is also found in IMTFE Exhibit 173. The original was written, probably in English, in the spring of 1942; a Japanese version was produced the following year. An after-thought entitled "Concerning the Triple Alliance" was penned in May 1945.

Koop, Albert J., and Inada Hogitaro. *Japanese Names and How to Read Them*. London: Routledge & Kegan Paul, Ltd., 1923 (reissued 1960).

Koyama Itoko. *Nagako, Empress of Japan*. New York: John Day Co., 1958. A revealing public relations effort by the daughter of a courtier.

Kuroda Hisata. *Tenno-ke no zaisan* [Imperial Family Finances]. Tokyo: San-ichi Shobo, 1966. A quiet, factual exposé by an economist.

Kurzman, Dan. *Kishi and Japan: The Search for the Sun*. New York: Ivan Obolensky, 1960.

Lee, Clark. *Douglas MacArthur: An Informal Biography*. New York: Henry Holt & Co., 1952.

Leonard, Jonathan Norton. *Early Japan*. New York: Time-Life Books, 1968.

Liu, F. F. *A Military History of Modern China, 1924–1949*. Princeton, N.J.: Princeton University Press, 1956.

Long, Gavin. *The Final Campaigns*. Vol. VII, Series 1 (Army), Australia in the War of 1939–1945. Canberra: Australian War Memorial, 1963.

———. *MacArthur as Military Commander*. New York: Van Nostrand Reinhold Co., 1969.

Lord, Walter. *Day of Infamy*. New York: Holt, Rinehart & Winston, 1961.

———. *Incredible Victory*. New York: Harper & Row, 1967. An admirable reconstruction of a moment in history based on exhaustive interviewing.

MacArthur, Douglas. *Reminiscences*. New York: McGraw-Hill Book Co., 1964.

McAleavy, Henry. *A Dream of Tartary: The Origins and Misfortunes of Henry Pu Yi*. London: George Allen and Unwin, Ltd., 1963.

McCarthy, Dudley. *South-West Pacific Area—First Year: Kokoda to Wau*. Vol. V, Series 1 (Army), Australia in the War of 1939–1945. Canberra: Australian War Memorial, 1959.

Mainichi, Tokyo and Osaka editions. One of Japan's two leading daily newspapers.

Mainichi, "Nihon no senreki" [Japan's War Calendar]. *Mainichi Gurafu* [Mainichi Graphic] 1 August, 1965. A special issue of Japanese war photographs previously suppressed by censorship.

Maki, John M. *Conflict and Tension in the Far East: Key Documents, 1894–1960*. Seattle: University of Washington Press, 1961.

Martin, Edwin M. *The Allied Occupation of Japan*. New York: American Institute of Pacific Relations, 1948.

Maruyama Masao. *Thought and Behavior in Modern Japanese Politics*. Edited by Ivan Morris. London: Oxford University Press, 1963.

Mendelssohn, Peter de. *Japan's Political Warfare*. London: George Allen & Unwin Ltd., 1944.

Merrill, Frederick T., *Japan and the Opium Menace*. New York: Institute of Pacific Relations and the Foreign Policy Association, 1942.

Merrill, James M. *Target Tokyo: The Halsey-Doolittle Raid*. Chicago: Rand McNally & Co., 1964.

Millis, Walter. *This is Pearl! The United States and Japan—1941*. New York: William Morrow & Co., 1947.

Mook, Hubertus J. van. *The Netherlands Indies and Japan: Battle on Paper, 1940–1941*. New York: W. W. Norton & Co., 1944.

Moore, Frederick. *With Japan's Leaders: An Intimate Record of Fourteen Years as Counsellor to the Japanese Government, Ending Dec. 7, 1941*. New York: Charles Scribner's Sons, 1942.

Mori Shozo. *Tsumuji kaze niju-nen* [Twenty-Year Whirlwind]. 2 vols. Tokyo: Masu Shobo, 1947.

Morin, Relman. *Circuit of Conquest*. New York: Alfred A. Knopf, 1943.

Morishima Morito. *Inbo ansatsu gunto* [Plots, Assassinations, and Long Swords]. Tokyo: Iwanami Shoten, 1950. A lively history of assassination and intimidation in Japan by a painstaking journalist who has interviewed more surviving witnesses than any Westerner could.

Morison, Samuel Eliot. *History of United States Naval Operations in World War II*. 3, The Rising Sun in the Pacific, 1931–April 1942; 4, Coral Sea, Midway and Submarine Actions, May 1942–August 1942; 5, The Struggle for Guadalcanal, August 1942–February 1943; 6, Breaking the Bismarcks Barrier, 22 July 1942–1 May 1944; 7, Aleutians, Gilberts and Marshalls, June 1942–April 1944; 8, New Guinea and the Marianas, March 1944–August 1944; 12, Leyte, June 1944–January 1945; 13, The Liberation of the Philippines: Luzon, Mindanao, the Visayas, 1944–1945; 14, Victory in the Pacific, 1945; 15, Supplement and General Index. Boston: Little, Brown & Co., 1948–1962.

Moritaka Shigeo, ed. *Daitoa senso shashin-shi* [Photographic History of the Greater East Asia War]. 8 vols. Tokyo: Fuji Shoen, 1954.

Morrison, Ian. *Malaya Postscript*. Sydney: Angus and Robertson Ltd., 1943. Fall of Singapore, by a correspondent for *The Times* of London.

Morton, Louis. *Strategy and Command: The First Two Years*. United States Army in World War II: The War in the Pacific, vol. 10. Washington, D.C.: Department of the Army, Office of the Chief of Military History, 1962.

Mosley, Leonard. *Hirohito, Emperor of Japan*. New York: McGraw-Hill Book Co., 1966. A hasty journalistic account, with numerous inaccuracies, but valuable for the information it contains stemming from Kanroji Osanaga, long Hirohito's assistant grand chamberlain.

Murofushi Tetsuro. *Nihon no terorisuto* [Japan's Terrorists]. Tokyo: Kobunsho, 1963.

Murphey, Rhoads. *Shanghai: Key to Modern China*. Cambridge, Mass.: Harvard University Press, 1953.

Mydans, Carl. *More Than Meets the Eye*. New York: Harper & Brothers, 1959.

Nakano Masao. *Hashimoto taisa no shuki* [Colonel Hashimoto (Kingoro)'s Notes]. Tokyo: Misuzu Shobo, 1963.

Natori Junichi. *A Short History of Nippon*. Tokyo: Hokuseido Press, 1943.

Newcomb, Richard F. *Iwo Jima*. New York: Holt, Rinehart & Winston, 1965.

Nihon Kokusai Seiji Gakkai [Japan Association of International Relations]. *Taiheiyo senso e no michi* [Road to the Pacific War]. 8 vols. 1, *Manshu jihen zen'ya* [Eve of the Manchurian Incident]. 2, *Manshu jihen* [Manchurian Incident]. 3, *Ni-chu senso* (jo) [Sino-Japanese War, Part I]. 4, *Ni-chu senso* (ge) [Sino-Japanese War, Part II]. 5,

Sankoku domei: Nichi-so churitsu joyaku [Tripartite Alliance: Soviet-Japanese Neutrality Pact]. 6, *Nanpo shinshutsu* [Southward Advance]. 7, *Nichi-bei kaisen* [Opening of War with America]. 8, *Bekkan shiryohen* [Supplement of Source Materials]. Tokyo: Asahi Shinbunsha, 1963.

Nu Thakin (U Nu), *Burma Under the Japanese: Pictures and Portraits.* London: Macmillan & Co., 1954.

Obata Tokushiro. *Kendai no senso* [Wars of Modern Times], vols. 6 and 7, *Taiheiyo senso* [The Pacific War]. Tokyo: Jimbutsu Orai-sha, 1966.

Obi Toshihito, ed. *Gendai-shi shiryo* [Source Materials on Modern History], vols. 1–3, *Zoruge jiken* [The Sorge Incident]. Tokyo: Misuzu Shobo, 1963.

Ogata, Sadako N. *Defiance in Manchuria: The Making of Japanese Foreign Policy, 1931–1932.* Berkeley and Los Angeles: University of California Press, 1964.

Ohtani Keijiro. *Rakujitsu no josho: Showa rikugun-shi* [The Beginning of Sunset: History of the Japanese Army in the Reign of Hirohito]. Tokyo: Yakumo Shoten, 1959.

———. *Showa kempei-shi* [History of the Secret Police During the Reign of Hirohito]. Tokyo: Misuzu Shobo, 1966.

Okamoto Aisuke. "Jusan-nin no gozen bansan" [Thirteen Men Who Dined with the Emperor]. In *Tenno hakusho* [White Paper on the Emperor]. Tokyo: Bungei Shunju, 1956.

Okawa Kanji. "Himerareta tai-bei choho katsudo" [Hidden Activity in Circulating Anti-American News]. In *Himerareta Showa-shi.*

Omura Bunji. *The Last Genro: Prince Saionji, The Man Who Westernized Japan.* Philadelphia: J. B. Lippincott Co., 1938.

Omura Takeshi. *Saionji-ko nozo-tsutae* [Prince Saionji in the Full Moon of Life]. Tokyo: Denki Kanko-kai, 1937.

Oya Soichi. "Ishiwara Kanji to manshu kenkoku" [Ishiwara Kanji and the Founding of Manchukuo]. *Chuo Koron* 80, No. 8 (August 1965), pp. 378 ff.

———. *Nihon no ichiban nagai hi* [Japan's Longest Day]. Tokyo: Bungei Shunju, 1965.

———. *Japan's Longest Day.* English-language edition of the above; see Pacific War Research Society.

Ozaki Yoshiharu. *Rikugun o ugokashita hito* [The Men Who Moved the Army]. Odawara: Hachi-ko-do Shoten, 1960.

Pacific War Research Society, comp. *Japan's Longest Day.* Tokyo and Palo Alto, Calif.: Kodansha International Ltd., 1968.

Patrick, W. D. "Planning Conspiracy. In Relation to Criminal Trials and Specially in Relation to This Trial. 17 February, 1947." Sir William Webb Collection. National War Memorial, Canberra.

Percival, A. E. *The War in Malaya.* London: Eyre and Spottiswoode, Ltd., 1949.

Pernikoff, Alexandre. *Bushido: The Anatomy of Terror.* New York: Liveright, 1943.

Perry, Matthew Calbraith. *The Japan Expedition, 1852–1854; The Personal Journal of Commodore Matthew C. Perry.* Edited by Roger Pineau. Washington, D.C.: Smithsonian Institution Press, 1968.

Piggott, F. S. G. *Broken Thread: An Autobiography.* Aldershot (England): Gale & Polden Ltd., 1950.

Ponsonby-Fane, Richard A. B. *Imperial House of Japan.* Kyoto: Ponsonby Memorial Society, 1959.

———. *Sovereign and Subject.* Kyoto: Ponsonby Memorial Society, 1962.

———. *Studies in Shinto and Shrines.* Kyoto: Ponsonby Memorial Society, 1962.

———. *The Vicissitudes of Shinto.* Kyoto: Ponsonby Memorial Society, 1963.

———. *Visiting Famous Shrines in Japan.* Kyoto: Ponsonby Memorial Society, 1964.

Potter, John Deane. *A Soldier Must Hang: The Biography of an Oriential General.* London: Frederick Miller Ltd., 1963.

———. *Yamamoto: The Man Who Menaced America.* New York: The Viking Press, 1965.

Prasad, S. N.; Bhargava, K. D.; and Khera, P. H. *The Reconquest of Burma.* 2 vols. Official History of the Indian Armed Forces in the Second World War (1939–1945), Bisheshwar Prasad, general editor. India and Pakistan: Combined Inter-Service Historical Section, 1958.

Preble, George Henry. *The Opening of Japan: A Diary of Discovery in the Far East, 1853–1856.* Norman, Okla.: University of Oklahoma Press, 1962.

Presseisen, Ernst L. *Germany and Japan: A Study in Totalitarian Diplomacy, 1933–1941.* The Hague: Martinus Nijhoff, 1958.

Price, Willard. *Japan and the Son of Heaven.* New York: Duell, Sloan & Pearce, 1945.

Pu Yi, Aisin Gioro. *From Emperor to Citizen.* 2 vols. Peking: Foreign Language Press, 1964, 1965.

Rappaport, Armin. *Henry Stimson and Japan, 1931–1933.* Chicago: University of Chicago Press, 1963.

Reel, A. Frank. *The Case of General Yamashita.* Chicago: University of Chicago Press, 1949.

Reynolds, Robert L., and the Editors of American Heritage. *Commodore Perry in Japan*. New York: American Heritage Publishing Co., 1963.

Romulo, Carlos P. *I Saw the Fall of the Philippines*. London: George C. Harrap & Co., 1943.

Roth, Andrew. *Japan Strikes South*. New York: American Council, Institute of Pacific Relations, 1941.

Russell, Lord, of Liverpool. *The Knights of Bushido: The Shocking History of Japanese War Atrocities*. New York: E. P. Dutton & Co., 1958. One-dimensional shocker but solidly based on IMTFE evidence.

Russell, Oland D. *The House of Mitsui*. Boston: Little, Brown & Co., 1939.

Sakai Tsune. "Heika no go-kenkyu no" [Concerning the Researches of His Majesty]. *Shukan Asahi*. January 27, 1967, pp. 53 ff.

Sakai Saburo with Martin Caidin and Fred Saito. *Samurai!* New York: E. P. Dutton & Co., 1957.

Sansom, Sir George Bailey. *A History of Japan*. 3 vols. Stanford, Calif.: Stanford University Press, 1958.

Sadler, A. L. *The Maker of Modern Japan: The Life of Tokugawa Ieyasu*. New York: W. W. Norton, 1937.

Sato Kenryo. "Tojo Hideki to daitoa senso no sekinin" [Tojo Hideki and the Responsibility for the Greater East Asia War]. *Chuo Koron*, 80 No. 8 (August 1965) pp. 390 ff.

———. *Tojo Hideki to taiheiyo senso* [Tojo Hideki and the Pacific War]. Tokyo: Bungei Shunju, 1960.

Scalapino, Robert A. *Democracy and the Party Movement in Prewar Japan*. Berkeley: University of California Press, 1952.

Scherer, James A. B. *Manchukuo: A Bird's Eye View*. Tokyo: The Hokuseido Press, 1933.

———. *Three Meiji Leaders*. Tokyo: Hokuseido Press, 1936.

Sheldon, Walter J. *The Honorable Conquerors: The Occupation of Japan 1945–1952*. New York: Macmillan, 1965.

Sherrod, Robert Lee. *Tarawa: The Story of a Battle*. New York: Duell, Sloan and Pearce, 1945.

Shigemitsu Mamoru. *Japan and Her Destiny: My Struggle for Peace*. New York: E. P. Dutton & Co., Inc., 1958.

Shimada Toshihiko. *Kanto gun* [The Kwantung Army]. Tokyo: Chuo Koron-sha, 1965.

———, ed., with Inaba Masao. *Gendai-shi shiryo* [Source Materials on Modern History], vol. 8, *Nichu senso I* [Sino-Japanese War I]. Tokyo: Misuzu Shobo, 1964.

Shin sekai chizu [New World Atlas]. Tokyo: Zenkoku Kyoiku Tosho, 1965.

Slim, Viscount Sir William. *Defeat into Victory.* New York: David MacKay Co., 1961.

Smith, Robert Ross. *Triumph in the Philippines.* United States in World War II: The War in the Pacific, vol. 10. Washington, D.C.: Department of the Army, Office of the Chief of Military History, 1963.

Smythe, Dr. Lewis S. C., and others. *War Damage in Nanking Area, December 1937 to March 1938.* Nanking: Nanking International Relief Committee, 1938.

Snow, Edgar. *Red Star Over China.* London: Victor Gollancz, Ltd., 1937, reissued 1963.

Statements: See United States Army, Far East Command, Historical Section.

Statler, Oliver. *The Black Ship Scroll. An Account of the Perry Expedition at Shimoda in 1854 and the Lively Beginnings of People-to-People Relations Between Japan and America.* Rutland, Vt., and Tokyo: Charles E. Tuttle Co., 1963.

———. *Japanese Inn.* New York: Random House, 1961.

———. *Shimoda Story.* New York: Random House, 1969.

Stimson, H. L. *The Far Eastern Crisis: Recollections and Observations.* New York: Harper & Brothers, 1936.

Stimson, Henry L., and McGeorge Bundy. *On Active Service in Peace and War.* New York: Harper & Brothers, 1948.

Storry, Richard. *Double Patriots: A Study of Japanese Nationalism.* London: Chatto and Windus, 1957.

———. *A History of Modern Japan.* Harmondsworth, England: Penguin Books, Ltd., 1960.

Stuart, John Leighton. *Fifty Years in China.* New York: Random House, 1954. Memoirs of a missionary-educator who served as U.S. ambassador to China, 1946–52.

Suda Teichi. *Kazami Akira to sono jidai* [Kazami Akira and Those Times]. Tokyo: Misuzu Shobo, 1965.

Sugamo no homu-in kai [Legal Affairs Commission of Sugamo War Criminals]. *Senpan saiban no jisso* [The Real Facts of the War Crime Trials]. Privately printed, n.d. but *c.* 1960.

Sugiyama Hajime (Gen). *Sugiyama Memo* [Sugiyama's Memoranda]. 2 vols. Tokyo: Hara Shobo, 1967. Papers of Japan's wartime Army Chief of Staff.

Sumimoto Toshio. *Senryo hiroku* [Secret Report of the Occupation]. Tokyo: Mainichi Shinbun-sha, 1965. Libelous but based on conscientious interviewing.

Suzuki Kantaro. "Arashi ni jijucho hachinen" [Eight Years as Grand Chamberlain in the Storm]. In *Tenno hakusho* [White Paper on The Emperor]. Tokyo: Bungei Shunju, 1956.

Suzuki Kantaro. *Konjo tenno gonichijo no ittan* [One Aspect of the Present Emperor's Everyday Life]. Tokyo: Imperial Household Ministry, October 30, 1940.

Suzuki Tei-ichi. "Hokubatsu to Chiang-Tanaka mitsuyaku" [The Strike North and the Chiang-Tanaka Agreement]. In *Himerareta Showa-shi*.

Suzuki Yasuzo. *Hikaku kenno-shi* [Comparative Constitutional History]. Tokyo: Keiso Shobo, 1931.

Suzuki Yukio. *Keibatsu* [Financial Cliques]. Tokyo: Kobun-sha, 1965.

Taiheiyo senso e no michi. See Nihon Kokusai Seiji Gakkai.

Takagi Sokichi. "Chishikijin to kaigun to senso" [The Intellectuals and the Navy and the War]. *Bungei Shunju* 40 No. 1 (January 1966), pp. 262 ff. An assessment of Japanese naval intelligence in World War II.

———. *Taiheiyo Kaisen-shi* [Naval History of the Pacific War]. Tokyo: Iwanami Shinsho, 1949.

Takahashi Masae. *Ni-ni-roku jiken.* [The February Twenty-sixth Incident]. Tokyo: Chuo Koron-sha, 1965.

Takamiya Taihei. *Gunkoku taiheiki* [Pacific Record of a Nation]. Tokyo: Takenawa-to-sha, 1951. Revelations about the Japanese Army by one of its veteran military correspondents.

———. "Rikugun o nibun shita kodoha-toseiha" [The Imperial Way and Control Faction Army Split]. In *Himerareta Showa-shi*.

Takeda Taijun. *Seiji-ka no bunsho* [Notes on Politicians]. Tokyo: Iwanami Shinsho, 1960. Recollections of a Japanese publicist who served in Shanghai during the 1930's.

Takeyoshi Yosaburo. *The Story of the Wako: Japanese Pioneers in the Southern Regions.* Translated by Watanabe Hideo. Tokyo: Kenkyusha Ltd., 1940.

Takeuchi, Tatsuji. *War and Diplomacy in the Japanese Empire.* Garden City, N.Y.: Doubleday, Doran & Co., 1935.

Tamura Yoshio, ed. *Hiroku daitoa sen-shi* [Secret History of the Greater East Asia War]. 12 vols. Tokyo: Fuji Shoen, 1953.

Tanaka Memorial. See Crow, Carl.

Tanaka Shinichi. "Ishiwara Kanji to Tojo Hideki" [Ishiwara Kanji and Tojo Hideki]. *Bungei Shunju* 44 No. 1 (January 1966) pp. 262 ff.

Tanaka Takayoshi (Ryukichi). "Kakute tenno wa muzai to natta" [Thus It Turned Out That the Emperor Was Innocent]. *Bungei Shunju* 43 No. 8 (August 1965) pp. 198 ff.

———. *Nihon gunbatsu anto-shi* [History of Secret Strife Among Japanese Army Factions]. Tokyo: Seiwa-do, 1947.

Tanaka Takayoshi (Ryukichi). "Oni kenji, Keenan" [Devil's Lawyer, Keenan]. *Bungei Shunju* 43 No. 10 (October 1965) pp. 274 ff.

———. *Sabakareru rekishi: Haisen hiwa* [History of Being Judged: The Secret Story of Defeat]. Tokyo: Shimpu-sha, 1948.

———. "Shokai jihen wa koshite okosareta" [The Outbreak of the Shanghai Incident was Promoted]. In *Himerareta Showa-shi*.

———. "Okawa Shumei hakushi to rikugun." Dr. Okawa Shumei and the Army. Manuscript chapter of a book, which Tanaka was kind enough to let me photostat.

———. "Yoshiko." Unpublished manuscript on Tanaka's relationship with Kawashima Yoshiko or Eastern Jewel. Lent to author.

Tanin, O., and Yohan, E. *When Japan Goes to War*. New York: International Publishers, 1936.

Tatamiya Eitaro. *Daitoa senso shimatsu-ki jiketsu hen* [A Collection of Circumstantial Accounts of Greater East Asia War Suicides]. Tokyo: Keizai Orai-sha, 1966.

Tateno Nobuyuki. *Hanran* [Rebellion]. Tokyo: Rokukyo, 1952. Evocative historical novel about the February Mutiny; the author was a member of Konoye's circle.

———. "Ni-ni-roku jiken no nazo" [Riddle of the February 26 Incident]. In *Tenno to hanran gun* [The Emperor and the Rebel Troops]. Nihon Shuho, March 1957.

———. *Showa gunbatsu: Gekido-hen* [Army Factions in the Reign of Hirohito: An Anthology of Upheaval]. Tokyo: Kodan-sha, 1963.

Terasaki, Gwen. *Bridge to the Sun*. London: Michael Joseph, Ltd., 1958.

Terry, T. Philip. *Terry's Guide to the Japanese Empire*. Boston: Houghton-Mifflin Co., 1920.

Tiedemann, Arthur. *Modern Japan*. Rev. ed. Princeton, N.J.: D. Van Nostrand Co., Inc., 1962.

Timperley, H. J. *Japanese Terror in China*. New York: Modern Age Books, 1958. (A collection of eyewitness accounts.)

Togo Shigenori. *The Cause of Japan*. Translated and edited by Togo Fumihiko and Ben Bruce Blakeney. New York: Simon & Schuster, 1956. By the man who was former minister in December 1941 and again in August 1945.

Toland, John. *But Not in Shame: The Six Months After Pearl Harbor*. New York: Random House, 1961.

———. *The Rising Sun*. New York: Random House, 1970.

Tolischus, Otto D. *Through Japanese Eyes*. New York: Reynal & Hitchcock, 1945.

———. *Tokyo Record*. New York: Reynal and Hitchcock, 1943. A day-by-day account of 1941 by a correspondent for *The New York Times*.

Toyama Shigeki, Imai Sei-ichi, and Fujiwara Akira. *Showa-shi* [History of the Reign of Hirohito]. Tokyo: Iwanami Shoten, 1962.

Toyoshima Fusataro. "Chosen gun ekkyo shingekisu!" [In Crossing the Border the Korean Army Charged!]. In *Himerareta Showa-shi*.

Translations. See United States Army, Far East Command, Historical Section.

Trefousse, Hans Louis, ed. *What Happened at Pearl Harbor: Documents Pertaining to the Japanese Attack of December 7, 1941, and Its Background*. New York: Twayne Publishers, 1958.

Tsuji Masanobu. "Futari do daitoa shidosha—Ishiwara Kanji to O Chomei" [The Two Leaders of Greater East Asia—Ishiwara Kanji and Wang Ching-wei]. In *Himerareta Showa-shi*.

———. *Guadarukanaru*. Nara: Tamba-shi, 1950.

———. *Jugo tai ichi: Biruma no shito* [Fifteen Against One: Life-and-Death Struggle in Burma]. Tokyo: Kanto-sha, 1950.

———. *Nomonhan*. Tokyo: A-To Shobo, 1950.

———. "Senkakusha Ishiwara Kanji" [Ishiwara Kanji, Pioneer]. In *Fusetsu jinbutsu tokuhon* [Primer on Personalities in a Blizzard]. Tokyo: Bungei Shunju-sha, 1955.

———. *Singapore: The Japanese Version*. Translated by Margaret E. Lake. Edited by H. V. Howe. New York: St. Martin's Press, 1960.

———. *Underground Escape*. Translated from the Japanese. Tokyo: Robert Booth and Taro Fukada, 1952.

Tsunoda Jun, ed. *Gendai-shi shiryo* [Source Materials of Modern History], vol. 10, *Nichu senso III* [Sino-Japanese War III]. Tokyo: Misuzu Shobo, 1964.

Tsunoda, Ryusaku; de Bary, Wm. Theodore; and Keene, Donald, compliers. *Sources of Japanese Tradition*. Introduction to Oriental Civilizations, edited by Wm. Theodore de Bary. New York: Columbia University Press, 1958.

Tsurumi Shunsuke, Hashikawa Bunzo, Imai Sei-ichi, Matsumoto Sannosuke, Kamishima Jiro, Abe Osamu. *Nihon no hyakunen* [Japan's Century]. 10 vols. Tokyo: Chikuma Shobo, 1964. Most authoritative history of modern Japan.

Tuleja, Thaddeus V. *Climax at Midway*. New York: W. W. Norton & Co., 1960.

Ugaki Kazushige. *Ugaki nikki* [Ugaki Diary]. Tokyo: Asahi Shinbun-sha, 1954.

Ugaki Matome. *Senso roku: Ugaki Matome nikki* [Seaweed War: Ugaki Matome's Diary]. 2 vols. Tokyo: Kyodo, 1953.

Umashima Takeshi. *Gunbatsu anto hishi* [Secret History of Hidden Factional Feuds in the Army]. Tokyo: Kyodo, 1946.

United States Army Air Forces. *Mission Accomplished*: Interrogations of Japanese Industrial, Military and Civil Leaders of World War II. Washington, D.C.; Government Printing Office, 1946.

———. "Third Report of the Commanding General of the Army Air Forces to the Secretary of War, 12 November 1945." Mimeographed.

United States Army, Army Forces Pacific, Psychological Warfare Branch. Special Report No. 4, 22 July 1945: "The Emperor of Japan." Mimeographed.

———. Special Report No. 5, 23 July 1945: "Inside Japan—Youth Pawn of Militarists." Mimeographed.

United States Army, Far East Command, Historical Section. "Interrogations of Japanese Officials on World War II." 2 vols. Mimeographed.

———. "Statements of Japanese Officials on World War II." 4 vols. Mimeographed. National Archives microfilm no. 8–5.1 AD 4; page references in Notes are to this microfilm.

———. "Translations of Japanese Documents." 3 vols. Mimeographed. National Archives microfilm 8–5.1 CA; page references in Notes are to the pagination in this microfilm.

United States Army, Far East Command, Intelligence, Civil Intelligence Section. "The Brocade Banner: The Story of Japanese Nationalism." Special Report. Mimeographed. 1946.

———. "Left Wing, Right Wing: Japanese Proletarian Politics." Special Report. Mimeographed. 1946.

———. "Saionji-Harada Memoirs." [Rough English translation of Harada Kumao's *Saionji-ko to Seikyoku*, q.v.] 25 vols. Mimeographed. 1947.

———. "War Politics in Japan." Special Report. Mimeographed. 1946.

United States Army Forces Far East. Numbered, mimeographed "Japanese Monographs" distributed by Department of the Army, Office of Military History, 1952–1956. a) No. 24: "History of the Southern Army." b) No. 70: "China Area Operations Record, July 1937–November 1941." c) No. 71: "Army Operations in China, December 1941–December 1943." d) No. 72: "Army Operations in China, January 1944–August 1945." e) No. 119: "Outline of Operations Prior to Termination of War and Activities Connected with the Cessation of Hostilities." f) Nos. 144, 145, 147, 150 & 152: "Political Strategy Prior to Outbreak of War."

United States Army, Supreme Command for the Allied Powers, Far East: Allied Translator and Interpreter Section. (Mimeographed

translations of documents captured from the Japanese.) Bulletin No.
234: "British Malaya, Military Geography and Supplement, 30 April
1940"; "Dutch East Indies, Military Geography and Supplement, 1
November 1940"; "British Borneo, Military Geography and General
Description, 30 August 1941"; "Aeronautical Map of Borneo and Java,
February 1941."

———. Bulletin No. 567: containing inter alia "Diary of a Japanese
Soldier on Wewak, 30 August 1943."

———. Document No. 7396: "Just Read This and the War is Won."

———. Documents Captured in Hollandia: containing inter alia "Intelligence Reports of the Kami Organization, Special Service Organ,
New Guinea, 20 December 1943–14 March 1944."

———. Enemy Publications No. 6, 27 March 1943: containing inter
alia, a) "Naval Operations in Hawaii and Malaya (from *Bungei
Shunju*)"; b) "Sinking the Prince of Wales, by Hayashi Noboru;" c)
"Sinking the Prince of Wales, by Murakami Tsutae."

———. Enemy Publications No. 32, 11 August 1943: "The Taking
of Java, February–March, 1942, by an unidentified lieutenant
colonel."

———. Enemy Publications No. 56, 21 November 1943: "Characteristics of American Combat Methods on Guadalcanal, 4 March
1943."

———. Enemy Publications No. 64, 1 December 1943: "Summary of
American Combat Methods as Observed by Staff Officer Sugita While
Attached Temporarily to U.S. Army: Pamphlet Issued 25 September
1942 by Oki Group Headquarters."

———. Enemy Publications No. 111, 30 March 1944: "Japanese
Study of Jungle Combat, Captured in New Guinea."

———. Enemy Publications No. 278, 11 January, 1945: "Malaya
Campaign by Yokoyama Ryu-ichi, 8 October 1942, Captured in Lae
Area on 19–20 December 1943."

———. Enemy Publications No. 359, 28 April 1945: "Guerrilla Warfare in the Philippines (Intelligence Reports of the Watari Army
Group)."

———. Enemy Publications No. 371, 13 May 1945: "Morale and
Economy in Japan from Letters to a Soldier (Correspondence of Naga-
mitsu Isami of Oka 10413 Force, 21 April 1943–6 June 1944, Captured 23 January 1945 in Pozzarubio, Luzon)."

———. "Horii Tomitaro's Message to His Troops, 4 December 1941."

———. "Kawakita Katsumi's Account of Pearl Harbor Attack."

———. "Matsuura Saga-ei's Diary of Attack on Guam."

———. Research Report No. 65, Supplement No. 1, 29 March 1945:
"Japanese Knowledge of Allied Activities."

United States Army, Supreme Command for the Allied Powers, Far East. Research Report No. 69, 6 February 1944: "Ration Supply System and Ration Scale of Japanese Land Forces in Southwest Pacific Area."

——. Research Report No. 72, Supplement No. 2, 23 June 1945: "Japanese Violations of the Laws of War."

——. Research Report No. 76. Part I, 4 April 1944: "Self-Immolation as a Factor in Japanese Military Psychology."

——. Ibid., Part II, 21 June 1944: "The Emperor Cult as a Present Factor in Japanese Military Psychology."

——. Ibid., Part III, 30 October 1944: "The Warrior Tradition as a Present Factor in Japanese Military Psychology."

——. Ibid., Part IV, 7 February 1945: "Prominent Factors in Japanese Military Psychology."

——. Ibid., Part V, 24 February 1945: "Superstitions as a Present Factor in Japanese Military Psychology."

——. Ibid., Part VI, 10 October 1945: "Defects Arising from the Doctrine of 'Spiritual Superiority' as Factors in Japanese Military Psychology."

——. Research Report No. 119, 28 February 1945: "The Japanese Military Police Service."

——. Research Report No. 122, 19 April 1945: "Antagonism Between Officers and Men in the Japanese Armed Forces."

——. Research Report No. 123, 20 April 1945: "Control by Rumor in the Japanese Armed Forces."

——. Research Report No. 126, Part I, 26 April 1945 & Part II, 11 May 1945: "Hoko—the Spy-Hostage System of Group Control—the Clue to Japanese Psychology."

——. Research Report No. 131, 1 December 1945: "Japan's Decision to Fight."

——. Research Report No. 132, 1 December 1945: "The Pearl Harbor Operation."

——. Special Report No. 72, Supplement No. 1, 19 March 1945: "Diary of [Japanese Army Interpreter] Horikoshi Hiroshi of 65th Brigade Headquarters, Baguio, on Capture of Bataan."

United States Congress, Joint Committee on the Investigation of the Pearl Harbor Attack. *Hearings.* 79th Cong. 2d Sess., Public Document No. 79716. 39 vols. Washington, D.C.: Government Printing Office. 1946.

United States Department of the Navy. *Heigo* [Japanese Military Terminology]. Mimeographed.

——. *Narrative of the Expedition of an American Squadron to the*

China Seas and Japan, performed in the years 1852, 1853, 1854, under the command of Commodore M. C. Perry. 2 vols. Washington, D.C.: 1856.

United States Department of State. *Papers Relating to the Foreign Relations of the United States and Japan, 1931–1941.* 2 vols. Washington, D.C.: Government Printing Office, 1943.

———. *Occupation of Japan: Policy and Progress.* Washington: Government Printing Office, 1946.

———. *Trial of Japanese War Criminals.* Publication 2613, Far Eastern Series 12. Washington, D.C.: Government Printing Office, 1946.

United States Department of War, Military Intelligence Service. "Campaign Study No. 3: Japanese Land Operations." Mimeographed.

United States Navy, Office of Naval Operations. *Japanese Military Administration in Taiwan* (Civil Affairs Handbook Op. Nav. 50–E–14. Washington, D.C.: 10 August 1944.

———. *U.S. Navy at War, 1941–1945: Official Reports to the Secretary of the Navy* by Ernest J. King. Department of the Navy, 1946.

United States Navy, Office of Public Relations. "Communiques 1–300 and Pertinent Press Releases December 10, 1941 to March 5, 1943." Mimeographed.

United States Office of Strategic Services (O.S.S.). Research and Analysis Branch. *Japanese Administration of Occupied Areas–Burma* (Army Service Forces Manual M354–18A). Washington, D.C.: Government Printing Office, 1944.

———. *Japanese Administration of Occupied Areas–Malaya* (Army Service Forces Manual M354–18B). 1944.

———. *Japanese Administration of Occupied Areas–Philippine Islands* (Army Service Forces Manual M354–18C). 1944.

———. *Japanese Administration of Occupied Areas–Thailand* (Army Service Forces Manual M354–18E). 1944.

United States Strategic Bombing Survey. *Campaigns of the Pacific War.* Washington, D.C.: Government Printing Office, 1946.

———. *The Effects of the Atomic Bombs on Hiroshima and Nagasaki.* 1946.

———. *Japan's Struggle to End the War.* 1946.

———. *Summary Report (Pacific War).* 1946.

United States Strategic Bombing Survey, Civil Analysis Division. *Study No. 10: Summary Report Covering Air Raid Protection Allied Subjects Japan.* 1946.

———. *Study No. 11: Final Report Covering Air Raid Protection Allied Subjects Japan.* 1946.

United States Strategic Bombing Survey, Military Analysis Division. *Study No. 62: Japanese Air Power.* 1946.

——. *Air Campaigns of the Pacific War.* 1947.

United States Strategic Bombing Survey, Military Defense Division. *Field Report Covering Air Raid Protection and Allied Subjects in Kyoto, Japan.* 1947.

United States Strategic Bombing Survey, Morale Division. *The Effects of Strategic Bombing on Japanese Morale.* 1947.

United States Strategic Bombing Survey, Naval Analysis Division. *Interrogations of Japanese Officials.* 2 vols. 1946.

——. *The Reduction of Truk.* 1947.

——. *The Allied Campaign Against Rabaul.* 1946.

——. *The Effect of the Incendiary Bomb Attacks on Japan: A Report on Eight Cities* (Study No. 90). 1946.

United States Strategic Bombing Survey, Urban Areas Division. *The Effects of Air Attacks on the Japanese Urban Economy.* 1947.

——. *The Effects of Air Attack on Osaka, Kobe and Kyoto.* 1947.

Usami Seijiro, ed., and Rekishigaku kenkyukai [Historical Research Society]. *Taiheiyo senso-shi* [Pacific War History]. 5 vols.: Manchuria, China, Pacific I, Pacific II, Peace Making. Tokyo: Toyo Keizai Shimposha, 1953.

Usui Katsumi. "Cho Saku-rin bakushi no shinso" [The Truth About Chang Tso-lin's Death by Bombing]. In *Himerareta Showa-shi.*

——. "Dai Nihon teikoku no shushifu: Potsudamu sengen judaku" [A Period to the Japanese Empire: Acceptance of the Potsdam Declaration]. *Asahi Jyanaru* (Asahi Journal) 8, No. 3 (16 January 1966), pp. 74 ff.

——, ed., with Inaba Masao. *Nichu senso II* [Sino-Japanese War II], vol. 9, *Gendai-shi shiryo* [Sources of Modern History]. Tokyo: Misuzu Shobo, 1964.

Uyehara, Cecil H., comp. *Checklist of Archives in the Japanese Ministry of Foreign Affairs, Tokyo, Japan, 1868–1945.* Washington, D.C.: Library of Congress, 1954.

Vaughn, Miles W. *Under the Japanese Mask.* London: Lovat Dickson Ltd., 1937.

Vespa, Amleto. *Secret Agent of Japan.* Boston: Little, Brown & Co., 1938.

Vinacke, Harold M. *A History of the Far East in Modern Times.* 6th ed. New York: Appleton-Century-Crofts, 1959.

Vining, Elizabeth Gray. *Return to Japan.* Philadelphia: J. B. Lippincott Co., 1960.

——. *Windows for the Crown Prince.* Philadelphia: J. B. Lippincott Co., 1952.

Wakefield, Harold. *New Paths for Japan*. New York: Oxford University Press, 1948. A scholarly account of the early days of the Occupation.

Wartime Legislation in Japan: A Selection of Important Laws Enacted or Revised in 1941. Translated and compiled by the Overseas Department, *Domei Tsushin-sha*. Tokyo: Nippon Shogyo Tsushin-sha, n.d.

Watanabe Ryusaku. *Bazoku* [Bandits on Horseback]. Tokyo: Chuo Koron-sha, 1964. An excellent journalistic reconstruction of Japanese fifth-column work in North China, Manchuria, and Mongolia.

Webb, Sir William. Collection of mimeographed and handwritten papers at the National War Memorial, Canberra. File entitled: "I.M.T.F.E. papers covering a series of applications made to the Tribunal on matters of evidence by the Defense and Prosecution and on general matters arising out of the conduct and administration of the Tribunal." Inter alia: a) Medical report on Matsuoka, May 14, 1946; b) Plea to introduce extracts from the diary of Marquis Kido Koichi (I.P.S. Document No. 1632); c) Tokyo Charter; d) MacArthur's charge to the Tribunal, January 19, 1946; e) "Conclusions," a folder containing various drafts of the dissenting paragraphs which Chief Justice Webb appended to the I.M.T.F.E.'s *Judgment*; f) "The surrender of Japan," Chief Justice Webb's chronology of the trial, including notes on Okawa's dismissal; Matsuoka's death, June 27, 1946; Nagano's death, January 5, 1947; and statistics of trial.

——. File entitled "Inward and outward correspondence with S.C.A.P., February 1946 to February 1948." Inter alia: a) To MacArthur, February 27, 1946, on lodgings; b) To MacArthur, February 11, 1948, on article in *Life* Magazine.

——. File entitled "Miscellaneous correspondence 1946–1948. Inter alia: a) Major General Myron C. Cramer to Webb, June 15, 1948; b) Webb to Cramer, July 8, 1948; c) Webb to Cramer, September 15, 1948; d) Webb to Cramer, October 4, 1948, morning; e) Webb to Cramer, October 4, 1948, afternoon.

——. File entitled "President Webb to all judges—miscellaneous, May 1946 to December 1947, and January 1948 to November 1948." Inter alia: Revised *Judgment*, September 17, 1948.

——. File entitled "Private letters to Sir William Webb concerning trial and fate of war criminals, January 1946 to May 1948." Inter alia: a) Unsigned letter of June 17, 1946 from Christian in Fukuoka on character of Tojo and of Tojo's brother, Ito Hishi; b) Letter from W. A. Wootton, Australian Legation, Shanghai, containing clipping from North China Daily News of September 27, 1947.

Whitney, Courtney. *MacArthur: His Rendezvous with History*. New York: Alfred A. Knopf, 1956.

Wigmore, Lionel. *The Japanese Thrust*. Vol. IV, Series 1 (Army), Australia in the War of 1939–1945. Canberra: Australian War Memorial, 1959.

Wildes, Harry Emerson. *Typhoon in Tokyo: The Occupation and its Aftermath*. New York: The Macmillan Co., 1954.

Willoughby, Charles A., and Chamberlain, John. *MacArthur, 1941–1951*. New York: McGraw-Hill Book Co., 1954.

Wu, Felix L., ed. *The Asia Who's Who, 1958*. Hong Kong: Pan-Asia Newspaper Alliance, 1958.

Yabe Teiji. *Konoye Fumimaro*. A biography, 2 vols. Tokyo: Kobundo, 1952.

Yamaguchi Shigeji. *Higeki no shogun: Ishiwara Kanji* [Tragedy's General: Ishiwara Kanji]. Tokyo: Sekai-sha, 1952.

Yanaga Chitoshi. *Japan Since Perry*. New York: McGraw-Hill Book Co., 1949.

——. *Japanese People and Politics*. New York: John Wiley & Sons, 1956.

Yatsuji Kazuo. *Showa jinbutsu hiroku* [A Memoir on Leading Figures of Hirohito's Reign]. Tokyo: Shinkigen-sha, 1954.

Yoshida Shigeru. *The Yoshida Memoirs: The Story of Japan in Crisis*. Translated by Yoshida Kenichi. Boston: Houghton Mifflin Co., 1962.

Yoshihashi Takehiko. *Conspiracy at Mukden: The Rise of the Japanese Military*. New Haven, Conn.: Yale University Press, 1963.

Young, A. Morgan. *Imperial Japan: 1926–1938*. New York: William Morrow & Co., 1938.

——. *Japan in Recent Times, 1912–1926*. New York: William Morrow & Co., 1929.

Young, John, comp. "Checklist of Microfilm Reproduction of Selected Archives of the Japanese Army, Navy and Other Government Agencies, 1868–1945." Mimeographed. Washington, D.C.: Georgetown University Press, 1959.

Zacharias, Ellis M. *Secret Missions: The Story of an Intelligence Officer*. New York: G. P. Putnam's Sons, 1946.

Zumoto Motosada, *Sino-Japanese Entanglements, 1931–1932: A Military Record*. Tokyo: Herald Press, n.d. [1932]. Slanted for propaganda purposes but valuable for military details.

INDEX

Abe Masahiro (Flattery-Department Legal-Latitude), 300–5
Abe Nobuyuki, 757
  Army rebellion (1936) and, 845
  prime minister, 922
Abend, Hallett, 54, 604, 873
A-bomb. *See* Atomic bomb
Abucay line, 1138
Acheson, Dean, 74, 165, 220, 223
Adachi Kenzo, 512
Adams, Will, 275, 278, 279
Admirals' Code, 954, 1059, 1062, 1064, 1075, 1077
Agawa Hiroshi, xliv n
Ai Chin-lo, 691
Aikawa Haruko, 1204
Aikawa Yoshisuke, 975 n, 1204
Ainu, 244
Air Force, Chinese, in war with Japan, 13
Air Navy, Japanese, 1286–89, 1306, 1307, 1324
Aizawa Saburo, 794–95
  death sentence, 857
  Nagata murdered by, 799–802
  trial of, 816–18, 822
Akagi (carrier), 497, 1055, 1056, 1058, 1081, 1085, 1184 n, 1197, 1199
Akasaka Palace, 355, 357, 358
Akatsuki (destroyer), 1231 n
Akihito, Crown Prince, 284, 815
  birth of, 739–42, 745
  income, 1371
  villa renovated, 1372
Akira, Prince, 286, 288, 339, 345 n
Alcohol, intolerance of Japanese for, 425, 425–26 n
Amakasu Masahiko, 434–35, 568, 585, 732
Amano Tatsuo, 640 n, 721, 724
Amaterasu (sun goddess), 206, 250
  See also Ise Shrine
America First organizations, 44
Amur River Society. *See* Black Dragon Society
Anami Korechika
  aide-de-camp to Hirohito, 446
  biographical data, 110
  coup d'etat plot (1945), 122–31, 137–43
  New Guinea and, 1277–78
  suicide, 142–44, 462 n, 1339
  surrender, role in, 108–9, 114, 132–34
  vice war minister under Tojo, 929
  war minister, 1338–39
Ancestor worship, 265
Ando Akira, 201
Ando Kisaburo, 1201
Ando Rikichi, 945
Ando Teruzo, 819, 825
Anglo-Japanese pact (1902), 362
Animism, 248
Anti-Comintern Pact, 37, 892, 911, 912, 917
  negotiation of, 877
Anti-Constitutionalist party, 490, 929
Antoku, Emperor, 445
Aoki Kazuo, 1217
Aoki Sei-ichi, 1137
Aoyama Palace, 353, 355, 358, 367
Aparri, Luzon, 1105, 1130
Aquarius, Shogun (Tokugawa Iemochi), 305, 308, 309, 312–17, 320–21
Araki Sadao
  Army rebellion (1936) and, 833, 837, 839–40, 849–50
  Army reform movement and, 786
  biographical data, 706–8
  campaign against the Throne, 709–14
  distrust of, 737
  education minister in charge of propaganda, 893
  file kept on Hirohito by, 708
  George Bernard Shaw and, 705–6, 709
  Go-Stop Incident and, 719
  Jehol campaign and, 694, 698–700
  led mock-Russian forces at maneuvers, 757
  made a baron by Hirohito, 808
  mutiny in ranks promoted by, 809–30
  National Principle Group and, 810
  October Plot and, 577–79
  personal characteristics of, 619, 631
  Prayer Meeting Plot and, 720
  protests change in Navy regulations, 733

Araki Sadao (*cont'd*)
  protests firing of Mazaki, 789–90
  quoted on Manchukuo, 690–91
  Red smear, 709–11, 714, 725
  resignation as war minister, 740–42
  revelations before Supreme War Council, 793–99
  speaker at rightist rally, 1378
  Strike-North leader, 618–19, 651, 706–8, 725
  war crimes trial, 1356 n, 1367
Arao, Colonel Okikatsu, 130–31, 146
Arima Masafumi, 1309
Arima Takayasu, 121 n
Arima Yorichika, 1380, 1383
Arima Yoriyasu, Count, 205, 526–27, 615
  resigns as I.R.A.A. leader, 959
Arisugawa, Prince, 342
  Arizona (battleship), 1090, 1092
Army Air Force, Japanese, in war with China, 13
Army Purification Movement, 755
Arnold, Hap, 1256, 1331
Arsenne-Henry, Charles, 926, 937
Arthur, Duke of Connaught, 376
Asa-akira, Prince, 494, 495, 498, 814 n
Asagiri (destroyer), 1218, 1231 n
Asahi (Tokyo newspaper), 451, 541, 867, 868, 869
  presses wrecked, 829
Asahiko, Prince
  chief advisor to Komei, 293, 305, 312–15, 319, 321
  resigns as advisor to Meiji, 323
  subversive cell organized by, 304
Asaka, Prince Takahiko, 1341
Asaka, Prince Yasuhiko, 800–1, 928
  Army rebellion (1936) and, 840, 841, 843
  auto accident, 423
  Baden-Baden program and, 422–23
  commander-in-chief of Army, 28–29, 49, 52, 59
  final phase of war preparations, 889
  friendship with Hirohito, 58–59
  keeps abreast of National Principle Group's plans, 810
  marriage to Princess Nobuko, 371, 422
  physical description of, 28–29
  rape of Nanking and, 28–29, 37, 43–44, 54–56, 891

  Saionji's distrust of, 621
  Strike-North policy favored by, 994
  sub-lieutenant in Imperial Guards Division, 371–72
  Supreme War Council member, 994, 1044, 1046, 1048
Ashworth, Fred, 69
Asia Development Union (*Koa Domei*), 15
Asian Development Board, 905
Astor, Vincent, 1079
Astoria (cruiser), 1231 n
Atago (cruiser), 1310, 1311
Atami, Japan, 3, 202, 234
  shrine for war criminals in, 3–5, 8, 59, 61, 234
Atholl, Duke of, 413, 425
Atlanta (cruiser), 1231 n
Atlantic Charter, 1011
Atomic bomb, 1334
  conscience and, 71
  decision to use, 71–79, 102
  Hiroshima and, 63–66, 105–7
  Nagasaki and, 66–70, 107, 109
  protests against use of, 1331 n
  test of, 103
Atrocities, Japanese
  Nanking and, 5, 21, 42–48, 52–57
  war crimes tribunal and, 225–26
Atsugi Air Base, 161, 162, 170, 171, 173
Atsuta Shrine, 249
Attlee, Clement, 117
Attu Island, 1265–68
Australia
  attitude toward Japanese surrender terms, 117–18
  Japanese attack on, 1155
  Japanese plan for invasion of, 1124–25
Aviation Institute, 742
Awaji Maru (ship), 585
Ayanami (destroyer), 1231 n
Ayukawa Gisuke. *See* Aikawa Yoshisuke
Azuma Otohiko, 913

Ba Maw, 1214, 1278
Babojab, Prince, 389–90
Baden-Baden, meeting at, 418–22
  program executed, 438, 440–41
Badoglio, Pietro, 1271
Bagac-Orion line, 1138
Baguio, Luzon, xix–xxiii
  Japanese attack on, 1101

Baguio, Luzon (*cont'd*)
  Japanese occupation of, 1131, 1139 n
Baldwin, Hanson, 186
Bali, 1155
Balikpapan, Borneo, 1142
Ballantine, Joseph W., 1059–60
Ban Nobuya, 159
Bangkok, Thailand, Japanese occupation of, 1126
Bank of Japan, 642
Banzai Rihachiro, 613, 865, 869
Barguts, 911–15
Barton (destroyer), 1131 n
Basco, Japanese occupation of, 1100
Bataan, 1130–38
  defense of, 1138–41
  Japanese conquest of, 1164–66
Bataan Death March, 60, 1166–70
Batan Island, Japanese occupation of, 1100
Bates, Minor Searle, 47–48
Battle of Britain, 927–28, 936–41
Beahan, Kermit, 69, 71 n
Beardall, John, 981 n, 1080
Bellinger, P. N. L., 1094
Belloc, Hilaire, 1331 n
Benham (destroyer), 1231 n
Berg, Mike. *See* Borodin, Michael
Bergamini, Carlo, 1274
Beria, Lavrenti, 897, 903, 970
Bernard, Justice Henri, 237
Biak, 1294
Bicycle troops, Japanese, 1123
Bidatsu, Emperor, 253
Biddle, James, 290
Big Five, 396
Bin, Crown Princess, 344
Birmingham (cruiser), 1312
Bismarck, Otto von, 331, 337, 344, 500
Bismarck Sea, Battle of the, 1251
Black, Hugo, 1350
Black Dragon Society
  arrest of leaders, 185, 340
  crackdown on, 806
  destruction of, 723
  founder, 342
  history of, 184–85, 342
  Ikki attacked by elders of, 764–66
  MacArthur orders dissolution of, 185
  organ-or-god controversy and, 768
  splits into two factions, 574–75
  student hostel maintained by, 614
Black Tuesday, 460

Blood Brotherhood, 609–15
  background of members, 567
  secret headquarters, 597–99
Blücher, Vasili, 443, 460, 897, 903
Bock's Car (plane), 67–71
Boling, Justice Bernard Victor A., 236
Bolshevism, 708
Bong, Richard, 1210 n
Borah, William E., 621
Borneo, 1105, 1126, 1142, 1344
  Japanese capture of, 60
  prisoners of war in, 1327
Borodin, Michael, 443, 460
Bougainville, 1208, 1277, 1294
Bratton, Rufus, 1062
Brereton, Lewis, 1101–2
Brines, Russell, 173
Brown, Cecil, 1108, 1113
Brunei, Japanese capture of, 1126
Buchanan, Allen, 502
Buchanan, James, 307
Buddhism, 252–53, 257–59, 264–65, 287, 1374–75
Bullwinkel, Sister Vivian, 1163
Buna, New Guinea, 1207, 1250
Burma, Japanese invasion of, 1126, 1146, 1157, 1159
Burma Road, 927, 937
Burma-Thailand railway, 61, 203, 1242–48
Burton, Harold, 1350
Bush, Vannevar, 75
Bushido, 368
Butow, Robert J. C., 1042 n
Byas, Hugh, 166, 686
Bykov, Major Afimogen Erastovich, 912–13
Byrnes, James, 76, 102, 118

California (battleship), 1091, 1092
Cambodia, 925, 946
Canberra (cruiser), 1231 n
Canning, Doug, 1257
Canton, China, 32, 35
  Japanese invasion of, 904
Cape Esperance, Battle of, 1223
Cape Esperance, Guadalcanal, 1212
Cary, Otis, 1022 n
Casey, Robert G., 1078
Cassin (U.S. destroyer), 1092
Catherine of Braganza, 279
Celebes, 1142
  Japanese invasion of, 1155
Chamberlain, Neville, 904, 914, 1007
Chambon, Monsieur, 730, 732

Chandra Bose, 1278, 1293

Chang Chung-hui, 1278

Chang Hsueh-liang, 483, 492, 695, 698, 870
  attack on Mukden, 687
  biographical data, 875
  Chiang Kai-shek and, 470, 478–79
  Chiang Kai-shek kidnapped by, 873–75
  forces of, routed from Jehol, 699
  Kwantung Army harassed by, 692
  Ma. General, and, 677
  regime in Manchuria, 536, 537, 538, 551, 582, 584

Chang Tso-lin, 389–91, 459, 460–78
  assassination of, 422, 456, 469–83

Changkufeng Incident. *See* Khasan, Lake

Chao, Miss, 874

Chaplin, Charlie, 642

Charles II, King (England), 279

Chatfield, Admiral, 753

Chekiang Province, China, Japanese attack on, 1173–74

Chennault, Claire, 27

Cherry Society (*Sakurakai*), 510

Chiang Kai-shek, 479–80, 588, 607, 692–93, 695, 1147
  American and British support of, 921
  "Army of Liberation," 468
  biographical data, 442–44
  break with Communists, 456–59
  Chang Hsueh-liang and, 478–79
  disagreement with Hirohito, 7
  disciple of Sun Yat-sen, 373
  Hirohito's betrayal of, 761, 776–78
  Japan's peace negotiations with, 1215–17, 1264, 1270, 1273, 1275, 1276, 1280, 1289
  Jehol province and, 700
  kidnapped, 8, 872–75
  Kuomintang party and, 185, 360, 466, 591, 606
  loses large percent of trade with the West, 962
  Manchuria and, 537, 602, 617–18, 620
  marriage to Soong May-ling, 467
  Mongol Prince Teh proclaims loyalty to, 871
  New Life movement, 776
  offer of conditional capitulation, 31

principles of Japanese foreign policy presented to, 805
  relations with Japan, 465–67
  Sino-Japanese War and, 891, 892, 894–95, 896, 905
  struggle against Mao Tse-tung, 1343
  Suzuki Tei-ichi and, 17
  Tsuji Masanobu and, 1342
  U.S. and, 72
  U.S. loan to, 945
  unofficial truce with Japan, 927
  war with Japan, 8, 13–14, 17, 21–22, 25–28, 35, 56

Chiang Kai-shek, Madame, 776, 874, 1263
  war with Japan, 13

Chicago (cruiser), 1231, 1231 n

Chichibu, Prince, 430, 713
  Army rebellion (1936) and, 840, 843–44, 846
  biographical data, 358, 370, 376, 823
  George VI (England) and, 885, 889
  gossip provided by Ohara Tatsuo about, 814, 815
  National Principle Group and, 810, 818, 823
  peace dealings with Chiang Kai-shek, 1270
  Strike-North Faction and, 586

Chikuma (cruiser), 1221, 1320

China
  Republic founded, 373–74

"China gang," 1166, 1166 n

Chinda Sutemi, 451
  biographical data, 408

Ching dynasty, 373

Chin-shan-wei, China, 19

Chiyoda (carrier), 1296

Cho Isamu, 30 n, 578–79, 945 n
  assigned to Indochina area, 937 n
  biographical data, 1166 n
  death of, 1336
  Indochina and, 946
  Lake Khasan incident and, 902–3

Chokai (cruiser), 1320

Choshu clan, 283, 310, 317–21, 326, 329
  purged from Army, 439–42

Chou En-lai, 443, 459–60, 874

Christian House (Tokyo), 290

Christianity, 267, 268, 270, 275–77, 279

Chrysanthemum Path, 954

Churchill, Winston, 1062, 1095, 1324
  Atlantic Charter, 1011
  Cairo Conference, 1280
  on MacArthur's landing in Japan, 172–73
  Potsdam Conference, 78
  Prince of Wales and, 1106, 1117
  quoted on atomic bomb, 77, 103
  Teheran Conference and, 1280
Ciano, Galeazzo, 1076
"Civilian Spy Service," 559–63, 582
Clark, Harry Lawrence, 981
Clark, Tom C., 221
Clark Field, Philippines, Japanese attack on, 1103–4
Claudel, General Henri E., 686, 732 n
Code Purple, 981–82, 1003
Codes, Japanese, 980–83
Colhoun (destroyer), 1219, 1231 n
Commercial Press, 605
Communist party, Japanese, 436
Compton, Arthur, 75, 76
Compton, Karl, 75
Comyns Carr, Arthur Strettell, 230–31
Conant, James, 75
Concentration camps, Japanese, xix–xxvi, 1234–42
Constitution, Japanese, 176, 178, 210
  new, ratification of, 217
  of 1889, 338
  reform of, 216–17
"Constitution Protection Movement," 616, 631, 658
Constitutionalists, 361, 380, 879
  Dollar Swindle and, 616
Control Clique, 747, 786, 790
  See also Strike-South Faction
Cooper, Mercator, 288
Co-Prosperity Sphere of Greater East Asia, xix, 491, 685, 930–33, 1175
Coral Sea, Battle of the, 1178–83, 1207
Corregidor, 1130, 1133, 1136, 1141, 1346 n
  Japanese conquest of, 1176–77
Council of Princes of the Blood. *See* Imperial Family Council
Coup d'etat plot (1945), 124–32, 135–44, Notes 131
Court Gazette, 129

Cox, Melville, 935–36
Crace, John, 1180–81
Craigie, Sir Robert, 927
Crash-dive tactics. *See* Kamikaze tactics
Curtiss (seaplane tender), 1092 n
Cushing (destroyer), 1231 n
Czechoslovakia, Hitler's invasion of, 904, 908

Dace (submarine), 1311, 1311 n
Daigaku Ryo. See University Lodging House
Dalai Lama, 872
Dan Takuma, 602–3, 622
  assassination of, 627–30
"Dangerous Thought Bill," 441
Darter (submarine), 1311
Darwin, Australia, Japanese attack on, 1155, 1156
Darwin, Charles, 410, 415, 939
Democracy, in Japan, 1376
Dengeki sakusen, 699
Devereux, James, 1125
Disarmanent Conference (London, 1934), 752–54
Doihara Kenji, 700
  chief of Special Service Organ in Mukden, 534, 547
  "eleven reliable men," 422, 534
  hanging of, 3, 1361
  "Lawrence of Manchuria," 547
  mayor of Mukden, 562
  Pu-Yi and, 573, 582–84
  Supreme War Council and, 1044, 1049
  war crimes trial, 1357 n
Dollar Swindle
  Constitutionalists and the, 616
  Lindbergh kidnapping case and, 627 n
  preparation for, 612
  purpose of, 564–65, 586
Domei, 121, 147
Donald, W. H., 873
Doolittle, James, 1170–75
Dooman, Eugene H., 1019
Doorman, Karel, 1158
Douglas, William, 1350
Downes (destroyer), 1092
Drought, James M., 972 n, 974
Drug addiction, 682
Du Bridge, Lee, 103
Dulles, Allen, 93, 95, 99, 101
Duncan (destroyer), 1220, 1231 n

Dutch East Indies
  Japanese invasion of, 1136, 1155–60
  Japanese plans for, 60, 925, 927, 932, 942, 943, 984, 986, 988, 994, 1036
  oil shipments to Japan cut off by, 1006
Dutch Harbor (Aleutians), 1188

Earthquake, Japanese (1923), 433–34
East Asia All-One-Culture Society, 359, 373
East Asia All-One-Culture University, 717
East Asia League (*Toa Renmai*) 10, 12, 15
Eastern Island, 1183, 1189
Eastern Jewel, 571–73, 583–85, 665–66, 700, 870, 1263 n
Eastern Solomons, Battle of the, 1218
Ebisu, 267
Economy, Japanese postwar, 1364–67, 1377
Eden, Anthony, 1162
Edo Castle, 325
Edward, Prince of Wales, 413–14, 439
Edward VIII, King (England), 886
Eichelberger, Robert, 168, 173, 181, 186, 227
Eisenhower, Dwight D., 93, 1141
  cancellation of visit to Japan, 1376
  on use of atomic bomb, 103
  quoted on Potsdam Declaration, 104
Eleven Club
  founding of, 507
  meetings, 507, 524, 564–68, 617, 633, 733, 763
Eleven Reliables, 422, 422 n, 431
Emperors, early, 243–55, 258–62, 266–68, 274–78, 280, 284–86, 322–23, 353, 444
England
  Battle of Britain, 927–28, 936–41
  Hirohito's visit to, 412–14
  Japanese campaign to vilify the British, 935–36
Eniwetok, 1286
Enola Gay, 64, 1301
Enterprise (carrier), 1065, 1096,

1171, 1178, 1186–87, 1192–98, 1208, 1218, 1219, 1221
Eta, 330
Ethiopia, Mussolini's invasion of, 806
Eto Genkuro:
  charge against Minobe lodged by, 766
  organ-or-god controversy and, 788 n
Evatt, H. V., 230
Everyday Meiji Biographical Research Institute, 560, 567
Everyday Meiji Memorial Hall, 664
Exeter (cruiser), 1158
Express (destroyer), 1111
Extraterritorial-rights clause, 302

Fake War, 588, 591–608, 609–15
  commencement of hostilities, 603–8
  cost of, 566
  Eastern Jewel and the, 571
  Eleven Club and the, 566, 568
  provoking the, 573, 599–602
  purpose, 564, 586
Falkenhausen, Alexander Ernst von, 41, 43, 44, 56
Fanshaw Bay (escort carrier), 1320, 1321
Far Eastern Commission, 224
Far Eastern Conference, 463
Farago, Ladislas, 973 n
Farrell, Thomas, 67
Farrow, William, 1173
February Mutiny (1936), 809–58
  Army purge following, 854
Fellers, Bonner, 191
Ferebee, Thomas W., 64
Fermi, Enrico, 75
Fihelly, John W., 233
Fillmore, Millard, 295, 297, 298
Fitch, George, 40, 41, 44, 45, 54
"5-15," 660
Fleet Faction, 504, 505, 747, 751
Fleisher, Wilfred, 629
Fletcher, Frank Jack, 1178–80, 1192, 1219
Flower Child, 395–96, 474, 518
Foote, Walter, 1077
Forbes, W. Cameron, 556, 668
Formosa. *See* Taiwan
Forrestal, James, 74
Forty-Seven Ronin of Sengaku Temple, 646, 646 n

France
   agreement with Japan, 926
   fall of, 924–28
   Hirohito's visit to, 414–15
Francis Xavier, 268
Franck, James O., 77
Frankfurter, Felix, 1350
French Indochina. *See* Indochina
Fubuki (destroyer), 1220, 1231 n
Fuchida Mitsuo, 1085, 1087–90, 1093
Fujii Hitoshi, 612
Fujimura Yoshiro, 93
Fujishima Taisuke, xliv n
Fujita Hisanori, 1339
Fujita Isamu, 721, 723, 868
Fujiwara clan, 30, 254–61, 335
Fukuda Hikosuke, 468–69
Fukuda Ko, 827
Fukuda Masataro, 433–34, 435 n
Fukudome Shigeru, 1299, 1311, 1313
Fundamental Principles for the Reconstruction of the Nation, The (Kita Ikki), 430
Furusho Mikio, 807, 834
Furutaka (cruiser), 1220, 1231 n
Fusako, Princess, 371, 423
Fushimi, House of, 287, 315
Fushimi, Prince Hiroyasu
   Army-Navy co-operation and, 615
   Army rebellion (1936) and, 834, 840, 841
   biographical data, 659
   development of "midget submarines" promoted by, 1058
   Fleet Faction member, 504
   Hirohito and, 751, 770, 774, 1025–26
   Naval General Staff chief, 287, 608, 733, 931
   on plans for war with U.S., 941–42, 943
   Privy Council meeting, 690 n
   quoted on Tripartite Pact, 943
   resignation as Navy Chief of Staff, 976 n
   Supreme War Council and, 659, 1044
Fushimi, Prince Hiroyoshi, death, 14 n
Fushimi, Prince Kuniye. *See* Kuniye, Prince
Fushimi, Prince Sadanaru. *See* Sadanaru, Prince
Fushun, Manchukuo, 680

Futara Yoshinori, Count
   accompanies Hirohito on European trip, 405, 410, 411, 412, 414
   image of Hirohito, 405, 439
   on birth date of Hirohito, 355 n
   quoted on Prince Higashikuni, 414

Gaku-shu-in. See Peers' School
Gallagher, O. D., 1108, 1113
Gambier Bay (escort carrier), 1320
Gay, George, 1194
Genda Minoru, Pearl Harbor plans and, 955
Genghis Khan, 262, 692
Genji, 262
Genro, 427
George VI, King (England), 885–86, 889
Germany
   alliance with Japan, 875–77, 909–11
   non-aggression pact with Russia, 912, 915, 916–17
   Russia invaded by, 990–95
   surrender of, 93
   Tripartite Pact, 936–38, 941–44
Giga Nobuya, 472–73, 483
Gilbert Islands, 1280, 1285
Goebbels, Joseph, 876
Goering, Hermann, 938
Go-Kashiwabara, Emperor, 266
Gokazoku Kaigi. See Imperial Family Council
Go-Mizu-no-O, Emperor, 276–78, 280, 286
Go-Momozono, Emperor, 353
Go-Nara, Emperor, 266, 268
Gondo Nariaki, 597 n
Go-Stop Incident, 720
Goto Fumio, 838, 840, 881 n
Goto Shimpei, 866
Go-Toba, Emperor, 260, 262
Go-Tsuchi-Mikado, Emperor, 266
Go-Yozei, Emperor, 274–75
Great East Asia Ministry, 1215–16
Great History of Japan, 281, 288, 292
Great Wall of China, 692–95, 700
Greater East Asia Conference, 1278–79
Greater East Asia Society, 798
Gregory (destroyer), 1219, 1231 n
Grew, Joseph C., 165, 1079–80
   ambassador to Japan, 675, 745–

Grew, Joseph C. (*cont'd*)
    46, 825, 921, 930, 933, 936,
    947, 963 n, 984, 1025, 1067,
    1079, 1081, 1084, 1095
  arrival in Japan, 688
  diary notes, 936
  interpretation of appointment of
    Suzuki Cabinet, 92
  Konoye and, 1019, 1025
  Matsuoka and, 930, 984
  Panay incident and, 34
  postwar plans for Japan, 165–66
  unconditional surrender policy
    and, 102
  Under Secretary of State, 74
  warning of possible Pearl Harbor
    attack, 1067
Grew, Mrs. Joseph C., 688, 746,
  825
Griffith, Samuel, 1232 n
Groves, Leslie R., 75
Guadalcanal, 1208–14, 1217–32
Guam, 1301
  Japanese invasion of, 1105

Haile Selassie, 1343 n
Hainan, seized by Japan, 908
Haldane, J. S., 407
Halifax, Lord, 1078
Hallmark, Dean, 1173
Halsey, William F., 1065, 1096,
  1171, 1222, 1224, 1307, 1312–
  16, 1321
Hamada Kunimatsu, 879
Hamaguchi Osachi, 500, 506, 510
  assassination of, 511–15, 517, 531
  biographical data, 490
  prime minister, 490
Hamilton, William L., 1180
Hangchow Bay, 19–20
Hankow, China, 56
  Japanese capture of, 896, 904
Hara Shobo, xxxv
Hara Takashi, 394, 417
Hara Yoshimichi, 996–97, 1017–18,
  1053, 1073
  on plans for war with U.S., 943
  questions degree of Japan's com-
    mitment under Tripartite Pact,
    943
  quoted on possibility of Japanese-
    American war, 944
Harada Kumao, Baron
  Army rebellion (1936) and, 833,
    843

as Saionji's secretary, 510–13,
  517–21, 524, 536, 541, 552,
  574, 575, 588, 596, 603, 615,
  617 n, 619, 621, 623, 629, 643,
  650–51, 654–57, 694
  diaries of. *See* Saionji-Harada
    Memoirs
  Dollar Swindle concocted by, 564
  fear of assassination, 768 n, 807
  organ-or-god controversy, 767
  period of mourning following
    Nagata's murder, 803
  Saionji-Harada Memoirs, xlii, xliii,
    947
  Sorge case and, 1203
Hara-kiri (belly cutting), 142–43
Harbin *Herald*, 732
Harbin *Observer*, 732
Harriman, Averell, 1095
Harris, Townsend, 295, 303–5, 309–
  10, 316
Harrison, George, 103
Hartmann, Erich, 1210 n
Haruna (battleship), 1191
Hasegawa Saiji, 121 n
Hashimoto Gun, 462 n
Hashimoto Kingoro, 225, 523, 525,
  544, 578
  October Plot and, 578
  Panay incident and, 32–35
  rape of Nanking and, 49, 53
  war crimes trial, 1377 n
Hashimoto Toranosuke, 760
Hasunuma Shigeru, 1202
Hata Ikuhiko, xliv n, xlv
Hata Shinji, 790, 813
Hata Shunroku, 1356 n
Hatanaka, Major, 131, 132, 135–
  40, 146
Hatoyama Ichiro, 711, 1363
Hattori Hirotaro, 384, 454–55
Hattori Takushiro, 1139, 1140, 1146
Hayashi Fumitaro, 436
Hayashi Senjuro, 787
  appointed prime minister, 883–84,
    885
  Army rebellion (1936) and, 839–
    40, 849
  commander of Japanese Army in
    Korea, 554 n
  criticism of, 803
  dismissal of Mazaki as inspector
    general of military education,
    770, 788–92
  Manchukuo and, 777
  purge of Strike-North Faction

Hayashi Senjuro (*cont'd*)
  from the Army and Navy, 770,
    786, 807
  residence broken into, 757
  resignation as prime minister, 887
  resignation as war minister, 804
  Supreme War Council meeting
    and, 795–99
  war minister, 747, 748, 757, 763,
    777, 789
Hayashi Yoshihide
  biographical data, 956 n
  Unit 82 and, 956
Helena (cruiser), 1092 n
Henderson Field (Guadalcanal),
    1212, 1213, 1220, 1225
Hermes (British carrier), 1188
Hidaka Shunrokuro, 1221
Hideyoshi, 276, 284, 310
  biographical data, 272–74
  persecution of Christians, 276
  policy of overseas expansion, 272
Hiei (battleship), 733, 1231 n
Higashi-Fushimi, Count Kunihide,
    716, 718
Higashikuni, Prince Naruhiko, 716–
    18, 725, 733, 805, 853, 994
  antique business run by, 204, 1374
  Army rebellion (1936) and, 840,
    843
  biographical data, 16 n, 152, 398
  Buddhism and, 1374–75
  contingency planning for defeat,
    1203
  European spy ring and, 398, 414,
    417–18
  father of, 293
  final phase of war preparations,
    889
  intelligence duties in Asia, 456
  Japanese Army Air Force chief, 13
  keeps abreast of National Principle
    Group's plans, 810
  marriage to Princess Toshiko, 398
  Mazaki and, 713
  Native-Land-Lovers and, 567, 641
  Ohara Tatsuo and, 813–15
  parties at villa of, 202
  Peace Cabinet and, 152, 155, 174,
    180, 417–18, 420, 1028
  Peace Faction and, 1280
  peace plot, 1271
  physical description of, 154
  Prayer Meeting Plot, 720
  prime minister, 176, 183–89, 194–
    96, 204, 287, 1369

quarrel with Emperor Meiji, 371–
    72
  riot squad organized by, 816
  Sino-Japanese War and, 891, 894–
    95, 896
  son of, 914, 916
  special Cabinet advisor, 151, 154–
    55
  Tanaka and, 673
  terrorist societies sponsored by,
    575
  Tokyo Riding Club and, 735
  victory parade for, 906 n
  war plans and, 1047
Higashikuni Morihiro, 914, 916
Hijino Shigeki, xxix
Himmler, Heinrich, 898
Hiranuma, Baron, 521, 695, 795,
    883
  anti-surrender faction supported
    by, 122
  appointed prime minister, 907
  assassination attempt, 1028 n
  biographical data, 111
  Chungking Operation and, 1217
  National Principle Group and,
    763
  residence burned, 144, 151
  resignation as prime minister, 918
  Strike-North advocate, 986, 994
  surrender, role in, 111, 115
  war criminal status, 1356
Hirata Noburo, 774
Hirohata Tadataka, 833, 1259 n
Hirohito, Emperor
  abdication considered by, 725,
    1370
  alliance with Hitler, 876, 909–11
  Army rebellion (1936), 809–58
  Army reorganization scheme, 440–
    41
  ascends Throne, 444–47, 478
  assassination attempts, xxxi, 436,
    594–96
  assumption of power, 425
  atomic bomb and, 106–8, 1337
  attitude toward Japanese war
    criminals, 203
  Australian invasion postponed by,
    1157
  Bataan Death March and, 1168–
    69
  "Big Brothers," 359, 371
  biology and, 454
  birth of, 355, 355 n
  birth of son Akihito, 739–42

Hirohito, Emperor (*cont'd*)
boyhood, 356–57, 367–71
broadcast of surrender, 145–46
Burma-Thailand railroad and, 1242–48
character of, xxxiv–xxxv, 154
Chiang Kai-shek betrayed by, 761, 775–78
concubine question, 669–75
constitutional reform and, 210–11, 213–17
contingency planning for defeat, 79–122, 1281–82
crash-dive concept and, 1296–99
defeat admitted by, 1303, 1325
Doolittle's raiders and, 1173
Earthquake (1923) and, 432–35
education, 367–69, 383–85
European trip, 403–16, 422; (1971), 1385
family holdings, 1370–73
foster home of, 356
golf partners, 452
Greater East Asia Conference and, 1279
Guadalcanal and, 1210–11, 1214, 1222, 1223, 1229–32
heritage of, 243–80
Hong Kong visit, 410, 1126–27
image of, xxxiv–xxxv
imperial regimen, 449–56
income, 1370–73
Lake Khasan incident, 899
MacArthur and, 189–94, 203, 219–21
male heir, 671–75
marriage to Princess Nagako, 399–403, 438–39
Matsui Iwane and, 8–12, 14–15, 28
Midway Battle and, 1199–1200, 1201–2
mission of, 349
murder of Chang Tso-lin and, 469–73
Nagata's assassination and, 802
"non-divinity proclamation," 212–13
Occupation and, 149–80, 237, 1367–70
official enthronement, 478
orders concerning Chekiang Province (China), 1174
organ of state or god controversy, 763–75, 788 n
palace plot school, 428–32

palace renovated, 1372–73
Panay incident and, 35
parents, 353–54
Pearl Harbor and, xxxv–xxxvi, 60, 232, 954–55, 955 n, 1042–43
Peers' School and, 284, 359, 367, 370–71
philosophy of, 407, 407 n
physical description of, 88
poetry written by, 1384
rebellion against (1936), 7–8, 18, 28
recruits supporters, 425–28
refusal to surrender in 1944, 1283–85
Regent, 417, 425–47
Roosevelt's personal message to, 1079, 1081, 1084–86
second year of war begun by, 1226
Sorge Spy Ring and, 868, 1203
Strike-North Faction and, 712–13, 809–30
"symbol of state," 1383
U.S. fire raid on Tokyo and, 1333–34
various national positions on fate of, 219–20
visits tombs of his ancestors, 925, 1228
war crimes tribunal and, xxxiv–xxxv, 203, 222–36
war prisoner policy, 1173, 1235
war propaganda and, 1201–2
Hiroshima, Japan, atomic bomb and, 63–66, 105, 126, 127, 1323
Hirota Koki, 3, 204, 1071
appointed prime minister, 852
biographical data, 852 n
execution of, 3, 1361
principles of Japanese foreign policy enunciated to Chiang Kai-shek by, 805
resignation as prime minister, 879
war crimes trial, 1356 n
Hiryu (carrier), 1184 n, 1197–98, 1199
Hisanuma Goro, 622, 629
Hishikari Taka, 727
Hitler, Adolf
France invaded by, 924
invasion of Czechoslovakia, 904, 908
invasion of Yugoslavia, 966
Japanese alliance with, 875–77, 909–11, 1059–60

Hitler, Adolph (*cont'd*)
  Matsuoka given state reception
    by, 966
  Mussolini and, 748, 913
  plans of, 908–9, 914, 922
  Poland invaded by, 917
  political opponents assassinated
    by, 660
  Russia invaded by, 990–95
  suicide of, 93
  Tripartite Pact and, 945
Hitotsu-yanagi, Viscount, 211
Ho Ying-Ching, General, 777
Ho Chi Minh, 1342, 1343
Hoel (destroyer), 1320
Holmes, Chris, 1304
Hong Kong
  Hirohito's visit to, 410, 1127
  Japanese attack on, 1100, 1104
  Japanese conquest of, 1127–29
Honjo Shigeru
  Army rebellion (1936) and, 831–
    32, 839, 841–42, 845–50
  biographical data, 10 n
  diary notations, xlii, xliii, 541 n,
    727, 734, 829
  Hirohito and, 735, 743–44
  Hirohito's chief aide-de-camp,
    712, 726
  Manchuria and, 533, 534–36, 539,
    542–47, 549–55, 581, 582,
    616, 634, 636, 638–40, 643,
    677, 680, 727
  Mazaki's dismissal and, 791–94,
    798–99
  organ-or-god controversy and,
    767–74
  physical description of, 533
  reaction to Nagata's assassination,
    802
  resignation as chief aide-de-camp
    to Hirohito, 856
  suicide, 205, 1356
Honma Kenichiro, 614
Honma Masaharu, 886 n, 1131,
    1134–40, 1164–65
  Bataan Death March and, 1165–
    68
  biographical data, 688, 1134,
    1352–53, 1355
  Corregidor campaign and, 1176–
    77
  execution of, 1355
  Lytton Report and, 688
  war crimes trial, 1352–55
Honolulu (cruiser), 1092 n

Hoover, Herbert, 502, 566, 611
Hopkins, Harry, 75, 1080, 1086
Horan, John, 1101, 1131
Horikiri Zenbei, 1076
Hornbeck, Stanley, 975
Hornet (carrier), 1171, 1178, 1186,
    1187, 1192–93, 1195, 1219,
    1221, 1231 n
Hoshino Naoki, 1357 n
Ho-Umezu Pact, 777, 805
House of Heavenly Action, 614, 622,
    631, 663
Houston (cruiser), 1158
Huang Fu, 692
Hull, Cordell, as U.S. Secretary of
    State, 948, 975, 984, 990, 998,
    1024, 1059, 1062–64, 1068–
    70, 1077–79, 1082, 1087,
    1094
Hung Hsiu-ch'uan, 292
Hyakutake Seikichi, 1218–19, 1222,
    1229, 1230
Hypothec Bank, 160

I Pong-chang, 593, 595
Iba (Philippines), Japanese attack
    on, 1102
Ichijo, Prince Saneteru, 400
Ichiki Kiyonao. *See* Ikki Kiyonao
Ickes, Harold, 995
Ida Masataka, 135–36, 142, 146
Idemitsu Mambei, 773–74
I-i, Lord Naosuke, 306–8
Ikawa Tadao, 973, 975
Ikeda Hayato, 1364
Ikeda Sumihisa, 1343 n
Iki Haruki, 1114
Ikki Kitokuro, 553, 595, 674–75
  attacked by elders of Black
    Dragon Society, 765–66
  beaten by thugs, 768
  request for retirement as Privy
    Council President denied, 808
Ikki Kiyonao, 1218, 1222
Imai Kiyoshi, 888 n
Imamura Hitoshi, 1159, 1254
Imanishi Keiko, 718
Imperial Code Research Institute,
    560
Imperial family, members stripped of
    titles, 217
Imperial Family Council, 843
  members, 843 n
Imperial Household Ministry, 58,
    86, 1370, 1371

Imperial Palace, descriptions of, 8–11, 87, 153, 356–57, 670, 1372–73

Imperial regalia, 249, 264, 445–46

Imperial Rule Assistance Association, 34, 150, 919, 923, 948, 959

Imperial taboo, xxxvii, 256, 268, 295, 1386–87

Imperial Way Group, 746–47
  See also Strike-North Faction

India, Japanese invasion of, 1292–94

Indochina
  collapse of France and, 924
  Japanese invasion of, 944–46
  Japanese plans involving, 925, 937, 941, 944, 985–96
  postwar, 1342
  satellite of Japan, 60

Indomitable (carrier), 1106

Indonesia, postwar, 1342

Industrial Club, 629

Inner Mongolia, 6, 27
  Japanese attack on, 869–72
  Tojo's expedition into, 890

Ino Tetsuya, 73

Inoue Fumio, 598–99, 608 n, 609, 612

Inoue Junnosuke, 589, 616
  assassination of, 612–14

Inoue Kiyozumi, 718

Inoue Nisho, Friar, 934 n
  arrest of, 631
  biographical data, 597–98, 665
  Blood Brotherhood of, 597–99, 603, 609, 612–15, 622, 629
  ghost house and, 597–99, 612
  name changed from Inoue Akira, 598
  Prayer Meeting Plot and, 720
  trial of, 724, 738–39

Inoue Saburo, 442 n, 452, 526, 617, 748–49

Inouye Shigeyoshi, 1179–80

"Inspection of General Circumstances," 509–10

Institute of Pacific Relations, 865

International Military Tribunal for the Far East, 219
  See also War crimes trials

Inukai Tsuyoshi, 514 n, 588–89, 591, 602, 603, 610, 611, 616, 617–21, 630, 633, 664
  assassination of, 642–54, 660–61
  funeral, 660

Iogi Ryozo, 513, 522 n

Iogi Yoshimitsu, 417

Iriye Kanichi, 684 n

Ise Shrine, 206, 249, 445, 925, 1228

Ishiwara Hiroichiro, 615 n

Ishiwara Kanji, 1276
  Army rebellion (1936) and, 846, 849
  chief of Operations Section of General Staff, 824
  co-founder of East Asia League, 15
  Manchurian venture planned by, 491–93, 511, 532, 538, 539, 544–45, 549, 576, 678, 785
  member of Suzuki Study Group, 462 n, 477, 491
  opposition to war with U.S., 958
  reposted to command of a provincial arsenal, 906
  special Cabinet advisor, 152, 155
  sympathetic with National Principle Group, 817

Isobe Asakazu, 759–62, 810, 819, 837

Isogai Rensuke, 422
  negotiations with Chiang Kai-shek, 775

Itagaki Seishiro
  biographical data, 539
  "eleven reliables," 422, 447, 539
  Fake War and, 573, 593, 599–600
  hanged as war criminal, 3, 1361
  Kaspé kidnapping case and, 731
  Lake Khasan incident and, 899–900
  politician of the Kwantung Army, 544, 568, 570
  seizure of Mukden, 544–51
  Sino-Japanese War and, 894
  Unit 82 and, 956
  war crimes trial, 1357 n
  war minister, 897 n

Italy
  Hirohito's visit to, 416
  surrender of, 1274

Ito Bunkichi, 1019

Ito Hirobumi, 337, 361–62, 366–67, 427, 436

Ito Kijomi, 612

Ito Noriko, 814

Ito Sei-ichi, 1299

Ito Tadasu, 1032

Iwabuchi Sanji, 1326

Iwakuro Hideo, 975
 biographical data, 975
Iwakura Tomomi
 chief advisor to Emperor Komei,
  305–6, 307, 310–14
 death, 333
 implicated in death of Emperor
  Komei, 323
 in hiding, 317
 Meiji and, 324, 325, 327
 mission to Western nations, 330–
  31
 returns to court, 323
 stripped of court rank, 314
Iwasaki family, 333, 1371 n
Iwo Jima, 90, 1322, 1331

Japan Advertiser, 26, 451
Japan-American Society, 628
Japan and the Japanese (*Nihon
  oyobi Nihonjin*) (periodical),
  500, 513
Japan National Broadcasting Com-
  pany, 145
Japan Year Book, 424
Japanese language, 244
Japanese Red Cross, 418
Jaranilla, Justice Delphin, 236
Jardine-Matheson Steamship Com-
  pany, 37
Jarvis (destroyer), 1231 n
Java, 928, 941
 Japanese capture of, 60, 1159
Java Sea, Battle of the, 1158
JCS 10 (Joint Chiefs of Staff direc-
  tive), 194
Jeans, Sir James, 407
Jehol Province, China, 6, 687, 691–
  94, 699–700
 Japanese invasion of, 699–700
Jesuits, 270, 275, 279
JETRO, 1367
Jews, Japanese policy for dealing
  with, 728–32, 1160 n
Jimmu, Emperor, 206, 246–49, 265,
  925
Jitra line, 1122–25, 1142
Jo Ei-ichiro, 1295, 1298
John Howland (U.S. whaler), 291
Johnson, Nelson T., 555–56
Johnston (destroyer), 1320
Johore, sultan of, 1144
Joshima Takaji, 1254
Juneau (cruiser), 1231 n

Kabayama Aisuke, 1281

Kacho Hirotada, 436
Kadashan Bay (escort carrier), 1317
Kades, Charles L., 215
Kaga (carrier), 955, 1184 n, 1197,
  1199
Kaiser Corporation, 1317
Kajima (battleship), 406
Kajioka Sadamichi, 1125
Kako (cruiser), 1231 n
Kalinin Bay (escort carrier), 1320
Kamegawa Tetsuya, 819
Kami, 212
Kamikaze tactics, 85, 90, 95, 1295–
  99, 1302–3, 1309, 1315–17,
  1319, 1321, 1329–30, 1335
Kanaya Hanzo, 591
Kanin Hanako, 1373
Kanin Haruhito, 1373
Kanin, Prince Kotohito, 509, 522,
  641, 931, 1071, 1341
 agitation for his resignation as
  chief of staff, 808
 Army chief of staff, 592–93, 604,
  615, 678, 684, 685, 787, 883
 Army purge explained by, 854–55
 Army rebellion (1936) and, 844–
  49
 biographical data, 408–9, 592–93
 Chang Tso-lin and, 390
 death of, 94
 dismissal of Mazaki as inspector
  general of military education,
  787–94
 fear of assassination, 807
 Lake Khasan incident, 899
 Manchuria and, 469, 480
 National Principle Group and, 811
 quoted on Tripartite Pact, 943
 resignation as Army chief of staff,
  946–47, 976 n
 Southward Movement Society
  and, 755, Notes 755
 Supreme War Council and, 1044,
  1047, 1048
 tribute to Nagata, 804
 trip to Europe with Hirohito, 408,
  414, 415
Kanon (Buddhist goddess), statue
  of, 3–4
Karak, 245, 253
Kashii Kohei, 847, 850
Kaspé, Joseph, 728, 732
Kaspé, Semyon, kidnapping of, 729–
  32
Kasumi-ga-Ura. *See* Misty Lagoon

Katakura Tadashi, shot in head by Army rebels, 837
Kato (secret policeman), 679
Kato Kanji, 504, 508, 773
  retired from active service, 807
Kato Taka-aki, 382, 386–88, 440, 444
Katori (battleship), 406–9
Katori (cruiser), 1186
Katsura Taro, 366, 379, 380, 381, 437 n, 442 n, 526, 617, 748
Kawabe Torashiro, 161–63, 170
Kawagishi Bunzaburo, 857
Kawaguchi Matsutaro, 718 n
Kawai Chioko, 1258
Kawai Teikichi, 723, 868
Kawakami Hajime, 710
Kawakami Soroku, 343
Kawamura Sumiyoshi, 355, 358
Kawashima Naniwa, 571
Kawashima Yoshiko. *See* Eastern Jewel
Kawashima Yoshiyuki, 824
  Army rebellion (1936) and, 833–37, 839, 842, 846
  becomes war minister, 804–5
  National Principle Group and, 818
  resignation as war minister, 840
Kaya, Prince Tsunenori, 55, 58, 690 n, 776–77
  Anti-Comintern Pact and, 875
  European tour, 747
Kaya Okinori, 1038–40, 1052, 1073
  opposition to war with U.S., 1037
  war crimes trial, 1357 n
Kayano Chochi, 606
Keenan, Joseph Berry, 221–37, 1304, 1358, 1359
Keiko, Emperor, 249
Keio University, 710
Kellogg-Briand Pact, 476
Kempei. See Secret police
Keyes, Henry, 1347
Khalkhin Incident. *See* Nomonhan
Khasan, Lake, incident at, 898–904
Kiangsi Province, China, Japanese attack on, 1174
Kidder, J. Edward, 246 n
Kido Koichi, 557, 633, 637, 1025, 1099
  accompanies Hirohito on visit to tombs of ancestors, 924–25, 1229
  Air Navy proposal and, 1288
  Aizawa trial and, 817

appointed lord privy seal, 923
Army rebellion (1936) and, 832–34, 839–40, 843, 850
assassination plot, 1277
attack on home of, 144
attempt to persuade Minobe to resign, 768–69
"Big Brother" to Hirohito, 359, 437 n
constitutional reform and, 213
diary, xli–xlii, xliii, 452, 507, 541 n, 595, 643, 653, 800, 1258, 1259 n, 1262, 1266, 1281, 1289
director of peerage and heraldry, 725, 735
evaluation of Army loyalty, 763
fear of assassination, 807
grandfather, 332 n
Higashikuni Cabinet and, 151–52
Konoye influenced by, 1203, 1205
last visit with Hirohito, 208
lord privy seal, 1025, 1026, 1063, 1071, 1085–87, 1090
Marxists purged from palace by, 725
Midway battle, 1200
minister of education, 891
Nagata's death and, 803
National Principle Group's plans known by, 812
Peace Faction and, 1037, 1202–7, 1221, 1262, 1289
peace plans and, 81–83, 86–97, 100, 101, 106, 111, 126, 133, 147–48, 1281–82
persuades Hirohito not to abdicate, 176
physical description of, 86
reads Tolstoy's *War and Peace*, 1268
research into Communist influence on Japanese aristocracy, 716–19
Saionji Fujio's wedding arranged by, 1204
Saionji Kinkazu and, 951, 1204
Saionji Kinmochi's funeral attended by, 951
secretary to Lord Privy Seal Makino, 508, 524, 530, 541 n, 553, 649–57, 661, 725, 729, 800
Ugaki opposed as prime minister by, 881–83
urges continuation of war, 1233
war crimes tribunal and, 234

Kido Koichi (*cont'd*)
  war criminal charges against, 86,
    206–10, 221, 1357 n
  war propaganda and, 1202
  welfare minister, 894
Kido Koin, 314 n, 320, 332 n
Kido Takamasa, 358
Kikuchi Takeo, 764–65
Kimmel, Husband E., 1065, 1067,
    1077
  relieved of command, 1065 n
Kimura Heitaro, 3, 1357 n, 1361
King, Edward, 1164–65
King, Ernest J., 1217
Kinoshita Mikio, 595
Kinugasa (cruiser), 1231 n
Kirishima (battleship), 1231 n
Kishi Nobusuke, 1364
Kiska, 1265
Kiso (cruiser), 1321
Kita Ikki, 430, 494, 577, 598, 664
  Army rebellion (1936) and, 845
  execution of, 858
  National Principle Group and,
    812, 820
Kitakyushu, Japan, 68
Kitano Maru (ship), 424
Kitashirakawa, Prince Nagahisa, 735
Kitashirakawa, Prince Naruhisa, 359,
    370, 371, 422–24
Kitashirakawa, Prince Yoshihisa, 342,
    345 n, 410
Kitkun Bay (U.S. ship), 1321
Kiyosu, Count, 345 n
Kiyoura, Viscount, 437, 439
Kiyoura Sueo, 816 n
Klausen, Max, 861–62, 865, 878,
    901, 1009, 1033
Kluckhohn, Frank, 190
Knox, Frank, 1062, 1064, 1067,
    1070, 1094, 1256
Koa Domei. See Asia Development
    Union
Kobayashi Shosaburo, 578, 640
Kobe, Japan, Doolittle's raiders at-
    tack on, 1171
Kofuji Satoshi, 838
Koga, Lieutenant, 738
Koga Hidemasa, 128, 138, 182
Kogen, Emperor, 250
Koiso Kuniaki, 789, 833
  chief of Military Affairs Bureau,
    523–25, 529, 543, 554
  Manchuria and, 540, 543
  physical description of, 85
  prime minister, 85, 91, 1303

  promoted to rank of lieutenant
    general, 579
Strike-South proponent, 651, 656,
    762
vice minister of war, 622
war criminal, 204, 1356 n
Kokaku, Emperor, 284
Koken, Empress, 258
Kokuhonsha. *See* National Founda-
    tion Society
Kokura, Japan, 68–69, 107
Kolchak, Alexander, 395
Komatsu Teruhisa, 359, 409, 410,
    416, 563, 1010
  biographical data, 1187 n
  Guadalcanal and, 1219, 1223,
    1224, 1225
  Midway Battle and, 1186–87
  Solomon Islands and, 1269
Komatsubara Michitaro, 918
Komei, Emperor, 292–93, 294, 301–
    23, 327–30, 345, 498
  physical description of, 290
Komisarenko, 730
Komoto Daisaku, 422, 467, 471–74,
    480, 483, 529, 547 n, 640
Komoto Suemori, 547 n
Komoto Toshio, 483
Kongo (battleship), 1321
Kono Hisashi, 827
Konoye Atsumaro, Prince, 360, 373
Konoye Fumimaro, Prince, 194, 197,
    480, 503–9, 655, 1003–30
  ancestry, 247, 255
  appointed prime minister, 12,
    887–88
  Asian Development Board founded
    by, 906
  assassination attempt, 1023
  Big Brothers, one of, 359
  biographical data, 886–87
  campaign to turn Japanese against
    the British, 934–35
  constitutional reform and, 213–14
  contingency planning for defeat
    and, 82–84
  "Dangerous Thoughts Bill" and,
    441
  desire for summit meeting with
    Roosevelt, 1019
  disapproval of Hirohito's reliance
    on military force, 891
  economic brain-trust of, 710
  Fake War and, 564–66
  Hamaguchi's assassination, 513–14
  Hirohito's golf partner, 452

Konoye Fumimaro, Prince (cont'd)
  Imperial Rule Assistance Association and, 35, 150, 919, 948
  JCS 10 directive and, 194
  Kido's influence on, 1202–3, 1205
  Lake Khasan incident, 899
  last desperate message to Roosevelt, 1026
  League for Waging the Holy War, 922
  member of postwar cabinet, 152, 154–55
  Mori Kaku recommended as vice minister by, 461, 461 n
  Native-Land-Loving Society and, 567, 641
  New Order in East Asia announced by, 641
  on plans for war with U.S., 942
  opposition to war with U.S., 1203
  organ-or-god controversy and, 767
  Panay incident and, 35
  peace plans and, 159
  Peace Plot, 972–76, 1271
  plans for assassination of Hara known to, 417
  prewar peace negotiations and, 1023, 1025, 1262
  prime minister, 30–32
  proposes abdication to Emperor, 175, 178–79
  refuses post as prime minister, 851–52
  resignation as prime minister, 907, 1028
  return as prime minister, 929, 933
  Sorge Spy Ring and, 1031
  Strike-North Faction and, 657
  suicide, 209, 1356
  threat to expose him as a spy, 1203
  Triple Intrigue and, 558, 617, 620, 632–33
  Tuesday Club and, 467
  Ugaki and, 526
  war criminal status, 180, 185–86, 205, 207, 209, 221
  war with China, 17, 56
Konuma Tadashi, 612–14, 1378
Korea, 6, 272–74, 284, 331, 343–45, 366
  annexed by Japan, 367
Korean War, 169
Korematsu Junichi, 1169–70
Kota Bharu, Malaya, 1086, 1100, 1111, 1112

Kowloon, Japanese invasion of, 1100
Koyama Itoko, 238
Kramer, Alwin D., 1009, 1080, 1082
Kuantan, Malaya, 1111
Kublai Khan, 262–64
Kudo Yoshio, 422 n
Kuhara Fusanosuke, 820 n
Kumano (cruiser), 1318, 1321
Kuni, Prince Asa-akira. See Asa-akira, Prince
Kuni, Prince Asahiko. See Asahiko, Prince
Kuni, Prince Kunihisa, 400
Kuni, Kuniyoshi, Prince, 287, 309, 402, 494
Kuniye, Prince, 287–88, 290, 293, 345 n
Kuomintang party, 17, 185, 360, 373
Kurile Islands, 1265
Kurita Takeo, 1310–20
Kuroda Hisata, xliv n
Kuroshima Kumahito, 1043
Kurusu Saburo
  ambassador to Berlin, 934 n
  Konoye's Peace Plot and, 975–76
  report on U.S., 1115–16
  special envoy to Washington, 1054–55, 1061, 1063, 1064, 1068–69, 1078, 1094
Kusaba Tatsumi, 642 n
Kwajalein, 1286
Kwantung Peninsula, 344
Kyongju, Korea, 1149
Kyoto Imperial University, 709–11, 714
Kyushu, U.S. bombing of, 1295

Lady Bird (gunboat), 32, 35
Laffey (destroyer), 1231 n
Lamon Bay, Luzon, 1132
Lamont, Thomas W., 611
Laos, 925, 946
Laurel, José, 1214, 1278
Laurence, William, 67, 69 n
Lawrence, Ernest O., 75
Lawson, Ted, 1172
Layton, Edwin T., 1075, 1255
League for the Extermination of the Organ Theory, 768
League for Waging the Holy War, 922
League of Nations, 492, 552, 556–57
  Commission of Inquiry, 599, 620–21, 624, 626–29, 633–36, 676–77

League of Nations (*cont'd*)
diverting the, 576–79
Japan's withdrawal from, 637–38, 694, 696–98
Manchurian problem and the, 564, 566, 568, 573, 576, 579, 581–82, 585–87, 594, 602, 626–27
report of Commission of Inquiry, 685–89, 694, 696–98
Sino-Japanese War and, 27–28
Legaspi, Luzon, 1132
LeMay, Curtis, 1331, 1334
Leslie, Maxwell, 1196
Lewis, Robert, 64
Lexington (carrier), 1065, 1178, 1181–82
Leyte, 1309–22, 1324
Leyte Gulf, Battle of, 1310–22
Li Tsungjen, 895
Liberal-Democratic party, Japanese, 1363–64, 1377
Library, Imperial, 87
Lincoln, Hirohito's bust of, 415, 1340
Lindbergh kidnapping case, 627
Lingayen Gulf, 87, 1130, 1131, 1133
Lishui, 26
Literary Chrysanthemum, 547, 549, 550
Little (destroyer), 1219, 1231 n
Lodging House. *See* University Lodging House
Logan (lawyer), William, 234
London Naval Conference, 495–505
Lutong, Borneo, 1105
Luzon, 87, 1322, 1326, 1329
Japanese attack on, 1102–4, 1105
Japanese invasion of, 1129–35
Lytton, Victor A.G.R., Lord, 633–34, 643
biographical data, 633
inspects Manchukuo, 675–77
report to League of Nations, 685–89, 693, 696–98
Lytton Commission. *See* League of Nations, Commission of Inquiry
Lyushkov, G. S., 898, 902, 903

Ma Chan-shan, General, 582, 676–77
MacArthur, Arthur, 167, 191
MacArthur, Douglas, 156, 161–80, 183–99
appointed military governor of Japan, 166
attitude toward war criminals, 191, 193, 203
Australia and, 1157, 1161
background of, 167
bargain with Hirohito, 219
conference with Hirohito, 190–94, 203
constitutional reform and, 213–17
dissolves Black Dragon Society, 185
escape from Bataan, 1160–61
Final Strategy Japan and, 1305
Hirohito becomes subject to, 119
Hirohito protected by, xxxviii, 223, 1367–68, 1370
Honma ordered hanged by, 1166
New Guinea and, 1294
occupation of Japan, 1367
Philippines and, xxiii–xxiv, 1102–3, 1117, 1130–35, 1140, 1304–5, 1309, 1326
war criminals and, 181, 185, 193, 220, 222, 1344–62, 1368, 1370
Yamashita's trial and, 1346–52
MacArthur, Mrs. Douglas, 1160
MacArthur, Douglas II, xxx
Machijiri Kazumoto, 16 n, 35, 398, 462 n, 639 n, 910
Sino-Japanese War and, 894–95
MacLeish, Archibald, 74, 165
Maeda Toshinari, 409
Magee, Ian, 44
Magee, John, 44
Magic, 980–82
Mainichi (Tokyo newspaper), 451, 476 n, 489, 1286
Makigumo (destroyer), 1231 n
Makin, 1280, 1285
Makino Nobuaki, Count, 533, 540, 553, 575, 580–81
accused of receiving kickbacks, 494
assassination attempt, 579, 610, 827–28
biographical data, 407–8
fake coups d'etat and, 83
Fake War and, 603
father of, 332 n
fear of assassination, 807
Grew's opinion of, 669
home bombed, 650, 664
lord privy seal, 451, 452, 453, 481, 499, 507–8, 521, 529, 643, 651–54, 658, 675, 690
March Plot and, 530
Peace Faction planning and, 1276

Makino Nobuaki, Count (*cont'd*)
　retirement as lord privy seal, 808
　sent to school in U.S., 628
　Strike-South proponent, 695–96
　Triple Intrigue and, 557–58
　University Lodging House and,
　　429, 431
Malaya
　British retreat from, 1141–45
　Japanese invasion of, 60, 1100–1,
　　1104, 1106, 1118, 1122–25,
　　1126, 1153
　Jitra line, 1122–25, 1142
　postwar, 1341
Malik, Y. A., 97–99
Maltby, C. M., 1126, 1128
Manchukuo, 600, 620, 631, 643, 655
　Japanese administration of, 677–
　　85
　Japanese recognition of, 689–90
　proclaimed a Japanese puppet
　　state, 627
Manchukuo Structure Plan, 756
Manchukuoan Aviation Company,
　680
Manchuria, 6, 489–701
Manchuria Motion Picture Associa-
　tion, 732
Manchurian Aviation Company, 871
Maneuver in War (Willoughby),
　169
Manhattan (Yankee whaler), 288
Manila, Philippines, 1133, 1326
　arrangements for American occu-
　　pation of Japan made at, 161–
　　70
　declared an open city, 1136
　Japanese capture of, 60–61
　Japanese occupation of, 1136–38
　U.S. liberation of, xxiii–xxiv
Manjiro (Japanese fisherman), 291,
　306
Mao Tse-tung, 460, 537, 1147,
　1263, 1276
March Plot (1931), 521–30, 797,
　803
Marco Polo Bridge, 6, 7
　war with China begun at, 890
Marianas, 85, 1295, 1299–1301
Marshall, George C., 75, 98, 1062,
　1066, 1070, 1084, 1141
Marshall Islands, 82, 1274, 1286
Martin, Frederick L., 1067
Maruyama Masao, 1220, 1221
Maryland (U.S. battleship), 1091

Masako, Princess (Ichijo), 400, 401
Masako, Princess (Meiji's daughter),
　371
Mashbir, Sidney, 185
Mashita Kanetoshi, 1382
Matsudaira Yasumasa, 204, 222,
　228, 234, 881 n, 922 n
Matsui Iwane, 3, 4, 8–17, 467, 588
　"butcher of Nanking," 8, 59
　commander-in-chief of Japanese
　　forces in Central China, 13, 28,
　　29, 59
　death sentence, 237
　hanging of, 61, 1361
　Hirohito and, 10–12, 15, 28
　resignation from army, 798
　Shanghai and, 12–17, 37
　triumphal entry into Nanking, 49–
　　54
　war criminal status, 1356, 1358
　war with China, 12–17, 24–28, 37,
　　40–41, 54, 59–60, 891
Matsumoto Shunichi, Vice Foreign
　Minister, 121
Matsumoto Joji, 214
Matsumoto Kenji, 1271
Matsumoto Shigeharu, 866
Matsumura Masakasu, 422 n
Matsuo Denzo, 826–27
Matsuo Masanao, 870 n
Matsuoka Yosuke, 612, 626, 637–38,
　694, 697–99, 961–63
　American Maryknoll Fathers and,
　　972–73, 976–77
　biographical data, 930, 962–63
　campaign of double talk within
　　Japanese councils, 983
　foreign minister, 204, 930, 936
　Konoye's Peace Plot and, 976–78
　last Strike-North plot and, 986–95
　madness of, suspected, 983–86
　mission to Russia, Germany and
　　Italy, 963–68
　negotiations with Stahmer, 940
　on plans for war with U.S., 942
　opposition to war with U.S., 962–
　　63, 968
　ouster of, 995–1002
　quoted on Tripartite Pact, 942
　treason of, 977–83
　treaty with Vichy France, 937
　war criminal status, 1356, 1358
Matsutani Makoto, 1280
Maya (cruiser), 1311
Mazaki family, xxiii

Mazaki Jinzaburo
  Aizawa trial and, 822
  appointed inspector general of military education, 742
  appointed to Supreme War Council, 790, 792
  Army rebellion (1936) and, xxiii, 834, 838, 840, 845, 856
  dismissal as inspector general of military education, 770, 787-99
  inspector general of military education, 746, 763
  mutiny promoted by, 809-30
  National Principle Group and, 810-12, 818, 819
  organ-or-god controversy and, 769
  Strike-North Faction and, 651-52, 656, 700, 712, 762, 787
  Supreme War Council meeting and, 795-99
  Ugaki and, 525-26
McClusky, C. Wade, 1196-97
McCoy, Frank R., 686
  biographical data, 686
McDaniel, Yates, 42
McDilda, Marcus, 107-8
Meiji, Emperor, 323-45, 353-64
  achievements of, 661
  death of, 375-78
  Higashikuni and, 372
  Japanese Constitution promulgated by, 176, 661
  mirror presented to Yasukuni Shrine by, 645
  mother of, 307
  Portsmouth Treaty and, 365-66
Mein Kampf (Hitler), 875
Meisinger, Josef, 950
Meredith (destroyer), 1231 n
Miao Pin, 1290
Midway, 1183-89, 1201-2
  Battle of, 1188-1200
Mikami Taku, 665, 738, 951
  assassination of Inukai, 647-48, 1378
  "Three Nothings" incident, 1377
Mikasa, Prince, 127, 132, 1071, 1276-77
  final phase of war preparations, 889
  coup d'etat plot (1945), 127, 132, 1119, 1338-39
  surrender plans and, 1338-39
Mikasa Yuriko, Princess, 1338-39
Mikawa Gunichi
  Battle of Savo Island and, 1212

Guadalcanal and, 1211
Military Academy, Japanese, 442
  plot, 758-60, 793, 807
Military Sports Clubs, 434
Mimana, 245
Minami Jiro, 540-43, 553-54, 591, 833, 1356 n
Mindanao, 1315
Mine Komatsu, 475, 477
Minneapolis (cruiser), 1224
Minobe Tatsukichi, Dr.
  assassination attempt, 807
  attack on, 764-66
  refusal to resign chair at Tokyo Imperial University, 768
  resigns from House of Peers, 805
Minseito. See Anti-Constitutionalists
Miri, Borneo, 1105
Mishima Maru (ship), 409
Mishima Yukio, 1379-84
Mississippi (frigate), 293
Missouri (battleship), 177
Misty Lagoon airmen, 568, 577, 599, 608 n, 610, 612, 614, 625, 632, 640, 644, 1112, 1214, 1225, 1232, 1249
Mitchell, Billy, 752-53
Mitchell, John, 1256
Mitsubishi Company, 70, 333, 617, 1371 n
Mitsui Bank, 628
Mitsui Company, 333, 565, 575, 586, 589, 601, 603, 609, 612, 622, 628, 631
Mitsui family, 333, 1371
Mitsui Sakichi, 763
  Aizawa defended by, 817, 822
Miura Goro, 344
Miyagi Yatoku, 1032
Miyamoto Hideo, 710 n
Molotov, V. M., 1307 n
  Matsuoka and, 969-70, 971
Mongolia. *See* Inner Mongolia; Outer Mongolia
Mononobe family, 247, 252, 253
Monssen (destroyer), 1231 n
Moore, Frederick, 698
Mori Arinori, 339
Mori family, 284
Mori Kaku, 461 n
Mori Takeshi, 127, 128, 136-38, 142, 143, 146
Moriguchi Shigeji, 710 n
Morishima Goro, 1307 n
Morison, Samuel Eliot, 1231 n
Morotai, 1305

Morrison (American brig), 285
Mudaguchi Renya, 1151, 1166 n
Mugford (destroyer), 1208
Mukden, seizure of, 531–58
Munich Conference, 904
Muragumo (destroyer), 1220, 1231 n
Murai Kenjiro, 1305
Murakami Keisaku, 398
Muranaka Koji, 758–63, 810, 819
Murayama, Miss, 774 n
Murofushi Tetsuro, xliv n
Murphy, Frank, 1350–51, 1353
Musashi (battleship), 1258, 1287, 1310, 1312
Musha-no-koji Kintomo, 1204
Mussolini, Benito, 13, 169, 189, 748, 1076
  alliance with Hitler, 913
  death of, 93
  deposed, 1271
  invasion of Ethiopia, 806
  Matsuoka's conference with, 967
Muto Akira, 43, 50, 52, 54, 58, 462 n
  American Maryknoll Fathers and, 974
  execution of, 1361
  war crimes trial, 1357 n
Muto Nobuyoshi, 464–66, 726–27
Mutsu (battleship), 1260
Mutsuki (destroyer), 1218, 1231 n
Mutual Security Treaty, U.S.-Japanese, 1376

Nachi (cruiser), 1321
Nagako, Empress, 141, 208, 455, 670–75, 725, 733
  birth of crown prince, 740
  father of, 287
  marriage to Hirohito, 399–404, 438–39
  silkworm house of, 87
  wraps packages for men at the front, 1270
Nagano Osami
  liaison conference of Cabinet and General Staffs, 1035
  Navy chief of staff, 976 n, 994, 1005, 1014, 1017, 1038, 1039, 1042–47, 1052, 1072, 1073, 1075, 1273
  resignation as Navy chief of staff, 1290
  war crimes trial, 1356 n

Nagasaki, Japan, atomic bomb and, 66–67, 107, 109, 1323
Nagata Tetsuzan, 763
  assassination of, 113, 799–802
  becomes a liability, 794
  biographical data, 418–19
  chief of Intelligence, 685, 715
  director of War Ministry's Military Affairs Section, 508, 523–24
  favors independence for Manchuria, 447
  funeral, 803
  leader of the Three Crows, 418, 441
  Manchukuo Structure Plan opposed by, 756
  March Plot and, 524, 797
  Mazaki's dismissal and, 791, 793
  period of mourning following murder of, 803–5
  physical description of, 419
  reposted as active brigade commander, 726
  resignation requested, 794–95
Nagato (battleship), 952
Nagoya, Japan, Doolittle's raiders attack on, 1171
Nagumo Chu-ichi, 1057, 1081, 1084, 1085, 1093
  air raid on Australia, 1155, 1156
  Midway Battle and, 1184, 1188–96, 1198
  suicide, 1300
Naito Hikokazu, 721, 724
Nakagawa Kojuro, 519, 820
Nakagawa Kunio, 1305
Nakahashi Motoaki, 823, 824
Nakajima Katsujiro, 721
Nakajima Kesago, 50, 52, 54, 55, 398
  advises Ugaki not to become Prime Minister, 880
  Nanking atrocities and, 21, 25, 26, 27, 28, 39, 43–48, 51, 52, 53, 54
Nakajima Kumakichi, 748–49
Nakajima Tetsuzo, 881 n, 918
Nakamura Kotaro, 398
Nakamura Yujiro, 403, 405
Nakano Seigo, 1277
Nakaoka Konichi, 417
Nakasawa Yu-u, 1310
Nakatomi family, 247, 252, 254
Nakatomi Kametari, 254

Nakayama Yoshiko (Child of Joy), 307, 309, 319, 327

Namba Daisaku, 436–37, 814

Nanking, China:
Japanese capture of (1937), 4, 27–30, 36–61

Nara Akira, 1138

Nara Takeji, 407, 451, 452, 554

Narahashi Wataru, 202

Narashino, battle of, 271

Narashino School (Chiba), 440

Nash, Ogden, 667

Nash Put, 729, 730

Nashimoto Morimasa, Prince, 793, 794, 804, 888–89
held as hostage by MacArthur, 205
released from prison, 218
Southward Movement Society and, Notes 755
war criminal suspect, 205, 213

Nashville (cruiser), 1171

National Foundation Day, 1379

National Foundation Society (*Kokuhonsha*), 111

National Principle Group, 762–63, 809–10, 817–19

Native-Land-Loving Society, 567, 641, 649, 664, 723, 738, 739

Natsugumo (destroyer), 1220, 1231 n

Naval Air Force, Japanese, war with China, 13

Navy, Japanese
put on war footing basis, 732–36
Sino-Japanese War and, 893, 896

Nemoto Hiroshi, 802, 1343 n
National Principle Group and, 809

Neosho (oiler), 1179

Nestorians in Japan, 258

Netherlands East Indies, 1117

Nevada (U.S. battleship), 1091, 1092, 1093

New Britain, 1294

New Caledonia, 1183

New Georgia, 1269, 1271, 1273

New Guinea, 110, 1142, 1146, 1178, 1271, 1294
Japanese invasion of, 1207

New Hebrides, 1142, 1178

New Life movement (China), 776

New Order in East Asia. *See* Co-Prosperity Sphere

New Orleans (cruiser), 1224

New York Herald Tribune, 587

New York Times, 54, 166, 190, 604, 696

New Zealand, 1142

Newton, J. H., 1065

Nicholas II, Czar, 334, 343, 345, 362, 452 n

Nichols Field, Philippines, 1103

Niimi, Hideo, 803

Nijo Castle, 278

Nimitz, Chester W., 1178, 1179, 1254, 1255, 1286, 1295
Final Strategy Japan and, 1305
Midway Battle and, 1184–88

Nintoku, Emperor, 251

Nishi Yoshikazu (Gi-ichi)
appointed inspector general of military education, 853
Army rebellion (1936) and, 844

Nishida Chikara
mimeographed Kita's work, 430
National Principle Group and, 818, 819, 822

Nishihara Issaku, 945 n

Nishio Toshizo, 807

Nishizawa Hiroyoshi, 1210 n

Nitto Maru No. 23 (picket boat), 1170

Nobuko, Princess, 371

Noemfoor, 1294

Nogi, Countess, 377

Nogi Maresuke, 363, 386–70, 376, 814
suicide, 378

Nomonhan, xxvii, 911–16

Nomura Kichisaburo
ambassador to U.S., 961, 974, 984, 990, 999, 1025, 1054, 1061, 1063, 1064, 1068, 1078, 1082, 1087, 1094
biographical data, 961
Konoye's Peace Plot and, 975
pleads with Roosevelt to meet with Konoye, 1011
report on U.S., 1215–16

Nomura Naokuni, 1273

Nonaka, 820
suicide, 844, 850

Norris, George, 1096

Norstad, Lauris, 1331

North Carolina (battleship), 1219

Northampton (cruiser), 1224, 1231 n

Nurhachi, 571

Oahu (gunboat), 34

Obata Toshiro, 617, 656
at odds with Hirohito, 715
biographical data, 419–20

Obata Toshiro (*cont'd*)
  Lytton, Lord, and, 636, 637
  major general, 636, 637, 715
  one of the Three Crows, 418
  reposted as active brigade com-
    mander, 726
  Strike-North leader, 618, 652, 757
O'Brien (destroyer), 1219, 1231 n
October Plot, 576–79
Oda Nobunaga, 269–72, 278
Odan, 106 n
Ogasawara Kazuo, 422 n
Ogawa Tsunesaburo, 422 n
Ogimachi, Emperor, 270
Oglala (minelayer), 1092
Ohara Tatsuo (Ryukai or Dragon-
  Sea), 813–15, 1374
Ohka missile, 1303
Ohnishi Takajiro. *See* Onishi Taka-
  jiro
Ohtani Keijiro, xliv, Notes 787–91
Ohtani Kozui, Count, 615 n, 957
Oi Fukashi, 730–32
Oikawa Koshiro
  appointed Navy minister, 938
  Matsuoka's sanity doubted by, 986
  Navy minister, 977, 989, 992, 999,
    1006, 1017, 1025, 1026, 1027
  removed as Navy minister, 1029
Oil crisis, Japanese, 1003–6
Oka Takasumi, American Maryknoll
  Fathers and, 973
Okabe Nagakage, 508 n, 1263
Okada Keisuke, 231
  Army rebellion (1936) and, 838,
    838 n
  assassination attempt, 826–27
  organ-or-god controversy and, 766
  prime minister, 749–51, 754
  reelected prime minister (1936),
    818
Okamura Yasuji, 420–21, 526, 1173
  advisor to Chiang Kai-shek, 1343
  at Nagata's funeral, 804
  biographical data, 420
  National Principle Group and, 810
  one of Three Crows, 418
  Sino-Japanese War and, 896–97,
    904
  "spirit of positive force" concept,
    806
Okawa Shumei, 446, 525–30, 577,
    598, 599, 609–10
  arrest of, 662, 664
  biographical data, 429, 1275

coup d'etat and, 631, 632–33,
    638–42, 711
  death of, 1359–60
  "Goebbels of Japan," 405
  March Plot and, 521–22, 567
  October Plot and, 579
  prophetic writings of, 707
  reappearance of, 1275
  South Manchuria Railway and,
    915
  University Lodging House and,
    429
  war criminal status, 205, 1356,
    1357 n, 1359–60
Okinawa, 95, 284, 293, 1307, 1323,
    1335
Oklahoma (battleship), 1090, 1091
Okubo Toshimichi, 332, 580
Okuma Shigenobu, 339, 382–83, 388
Omi Brotherhood, 211
Omori Prison Camp, 158, 210
Omoto-kyo (religious sect), 768, 806
Onishi Takajiro, 1296, 1309, 1311,
    1313, 1315, 1322
  ordered to research attack on Ha-
    waii, 955 n
  Pearl Harbor plans and, 955
Ono, Dr., 649
Operation Barbarossa, 966
Operation Olympic, 98
Operation Sea Lion, 966
Opisthobranchia of Sagami Bay (Hi-
  rohito), 219
Oppenheimer, J. Robert, 75
Order Number One, 1037, 1040–44,
    1049
Organ-or-god controversy, 763–75
Oshima Hiroshi
  ambassador to Germany, 910, 911,
    912
  Anti-Comintern Pact and, 877,
    912, 980, 982, 985, 986, 987,
    1075
  war crimes trial, 1357 n
Oshima Kenichi, 398 n, 876
Osugi Sakae, 434, 435
Osumi Mineo, 773
  Army rebellion (1936) and, 839
  opposition to Hirohito, 773
Otake Kanichi, 402
Otomo family, 247, 252
Ott, Eugen, 876, 878
  Germany's ambassador to Japan,
    901–2, 903, 910–11
Oumansky, Constantin, 982

Outer Mongolia, Japanese invasion of, 911–17
Oya Soichi, xliv n, xlvi
Oyake Soichi. *See* Oya Soichi
Ozaki Hotsumi, 718, 914, 965
  arrested, 1032
  biographical data, 866–68
  execution of, 1034
  Lake Khasan incident and, 900
  New Structure Plan written by, 906
  Sorge spy ring and, 1031–34
  under police investigation, 1203
Ozawa Jisburo, 1314–15, 1317

Paimou Inlet, 21
Pal, Justice R. B., 237
Palace. *See* Imperial Palace
Palace Shrine (*Kashiko-dokoro*), 9, 170, 438, 455, 669
Palau Islands, 1305
Palawan, 1327
Pan-Asianism, 4, 56, 185
Panay (gunboat), 32–35, 225, 523, 891
Parkes, Sir Harry, 326
Patani, Thailand, 1100
Patch, Alexander, 1225
Paul V, Pope, 416
Peace Faction, 82–83, 112, 149, 160, 187, 195, 222, 1202–7, 1221, 1262, 1271, 1302
  formation of the, 1037
  See also Notes 82
Pearl Harbor
  Hirohito and, 954–55, 955 n
  Japanese attack on, 60, 190, 1087–96
  Japanese plans concerning, 954, 955 n, 958, 1010, 1020–22, 1040–41
  U.S. ships in, at time of Japanese attack on, 1089 n
Peers' School, 284, 286, 290, 359, 367–70
Peking, China, 42
  Japanese capture of (1937), 6
Peleliu, 1305
Pennsylvania (battleship), 1091–92
Pensacola (cruiser), 1224
Percival, Arthur, 177, 1086, 1117, 1142–45, 1151–52
Perry, Matthew Calbraith, 7, 159, 164, 292–303, 316
Perry, Oliver Hazard, 293
Perth (cruiser), 1158

Pétain, Maréchal, 414, 415, 418, 924
Petrof Bay (escort carrier), 1319
Philippines, xix–xxv, 60, 87, 344, 1306–22, 1326–30
  Japanese conquest of, 1100, 1101–3, 1117, 1129–41
  prisoners of war in, 1326–28
Phillips, Sir Thomas, 1108–15
Phoenix Hall, 10, 11, 95
Piggott, F. S. G., 355 n, 634
Pime-ko, 245
Poland, invaded by Germany, 917
Pollution, problem of, in Japan, 1365
Port Moresby, New Guinea, 1178
Porter (destroyer), 1221, 1231 n
Portsmouth, New Hampshire, 366
Portuguese Timor. *See* Timor
Potsdam Conference, 78, 97–105, 107, 118
Potsdam Declaration, 105–7, 114–19, 123, 147, 156, 178
Powhatan (ship), 306
Prayer Meeting Plot (1933), 720–24, 805
  preliminary hearings for pilgrims involved, 722
Preble (sloop), 290
President Coolidge, S.S., 1231
Preston (destroyer), 1231 n
Prince of the Night, 337 n
Prince of Wales (battleship), 1106–17
Princeton (carrier), 1312
Prisoners of war, Japanese treatment of, 1235–48
Privy Council, 453
"Prospectus for Direct Action to Protect the Essence of the Nation," 835–36
Purple Mountain Academy, 598, 614
Pu-Yi, Henry
  abdication (1912), 691
  abduction of, 582–85
  Japan's puppet emperor of Manchuria, 373, 566, 569–73, 593, 620, 627, 635, 680, 684, 689
  state visit to Tokyo, 769

Quezon, Manuel, 1133
Quincy (cruiser), 1231 n

Rabaul, New Britain, 1142, 1294
Raeder, Erich, 966
Railroads, Japanese, 302 n
Raleigh (cruiser), 1092 n

Rangoon, Japanese occupation of,
    1159
Rankin, Jeannette, 1096
Recreation and Amusement Associa-
    tion, 160, 198–99, 201
Reel, A. Frank, 1348 n
Rennell Island, 1231
Repulse (cruiser), 1107–15
Research Society (House of Peers),
    467
Revere-the-Emperor-and-Expel-the-
    Barbarians Society, 161
Ribbentrop, Joachim von, 27
    Anti-Comintern Pact and, 875
    Japanese-German Alliance and,
        936
    Matsuoka and, 966, 967
    negotiations with Russia, 911, 914
    opposition to Japanese war with
        China, 891–92
    Oshima and, 876, 910
    reaction to Pearl Harbor attack,
        1076 n
Richardson, Charles Lenox, 313,
    316, 317
Riddell, Lord, 411
Riots, student, 1376–80
Roberts (destroyer), 1320
Roberts Commission, 1061
Roma (ship), 1274
Rome-Berlin Axis, 912
Roosevelt, Franklin D., 163, 164,
    503
    Asian policy, 1175
    Atlantic Charter, 1011
    Australia and, 1157
    Cairo Conference, 1280
    Casablanca Conference, 1250
    election of 1932 and, 692
    embargo on sale of scrap iron and
        steel, 945
    failure to inform Japanese masses,
        1324–25
    Far East policy, 927
    Final Strategy Japan and, 1305
    Konoye's peace plot involving
        Maryknoll Fathers, 972–75
    last day of peace and, 1078–81
    Matsuoka Yosuke's message to,
        930
    meeting with Japanese envoys,
        1068
    negotiations with Japan, 60
    Pacific war and, 1217, 1222
    Panay incident and, 34
    Pearl Harbor and, xxxvi
    personal message to Hirohito,
        1079, 1081, 1084–86
    Philippines and, 1101, 1141
    refusal to meet with Konoye, 1020
    relocation of Japanese-Americans,
        561
    state visit to Hawaii, 1304
    Teheran Conference, 1280
    unconditional surrender policy, 104
    war ultimatum and, 1061–63
    Yamamoto's death and, 1242,
        1255, 1256
Roosevelt, Theodore, 362, 365
Ruble, Richard, 1185–86
Russell, Bertrand, 71
Russell, Richard, 189
Russia
    Anti-Comintern Pact and, 875–78
    Hitler's invasion of, 990–91
    Japan and, 72
    Japanese border war with, 911–16
    Japanese negotiations with, 960
    Japanese peace negotiations and,
        97, 100–7
    Lake Khasan incident and, 898–
        900
    neutralization of (1936–1939),
        861–919, 951
    non-aggression pact with Ger-
        many, 911, 915, 916–17
    non-aggression pact with Japan,
        971
    Sorge Spy Ring, 863–65
    war with Japan (1904–05), 360–
        67
Ruth, Harold R., 202
Rutledge, Wiley, 1350
Ryujo (carrier), 1218, 1231 n
Ryukyus, 284

Sadako, Empress Dowager, 159,
    353–55, 399–403, 406, 632,
    1170, 1226
Sadanaru, Prince, 345 n, 379, 383,
    401
Sagoya Tomeo, 512–15, 1378
Sagoya Yoshiaki. *See* Sagoya Tomeo
Saigo Takamori, 332, 581
St. Lo (escort carrier), 1321
Saionji Fujio, 1204–5
Saionji Hachiro, 404–5, 409
Saionji-Harada Memoirs, xlii, xliii,
    947
Saionji Kinkazu, 716, 719, 869, 915,
    951

Saionji Kinkazu (*cont'd*)
  accompanies Matsuoka to Russia, 965, 970
  delegate to meeting of Institute of Pacific Relations, 865–66, 869
  Lake Khasan incident and, 902
  Ping-Pong ambassador, Notes 1204
  police investigation of, 1203–4
Saionji Kinmochi, Prince
  advice to Hirohito, 500, 501, 506, 518–21, 574–75, 580–81, 749
  Anti-Constitutionalists and, 490
  assassination planned, 819–20, 827
  biographical data, 335–37
  bows out as prime-minister-maker, 883–85
  Chang Tso-lin affair and, 474–78, 481, 482
  co-author of Japanese constitution, 337–39
  coronation of Czar Nicholas II and, 334
  death of, 949–51
  delegate to Versailles Peace Conference, 395–96
  education, 336
  Hamaguchi Osachi recommended as prime minister by, 490
  Hirohito's marriage opposed by, 401
  Hirota Koki recommended as prime minister by, 852
  Inukai recommended as prime minister by, 591
  Konoye recommended as prime minister by, 851–52
  Lytton Commission and, 623
  March Plot and, 530
  member of Meiji's oligarchy, 335
  Memoirs, xlii, 947
  national defense plan blocked by, 506
  October Plot and, 579
  on Battle of Britain, 938
  opinion of Anti-Comintern Pact, 878
  opposition to war with China, 536, 541, 542, 573
  opposition to Siberian venture, 392
  prime minister, 361, 366
  prime-minister-maker, 427–28
  quoted on "diplomatic general staff," 701

  quoted on reasons for Hirohito's European trip, 404
  resigns as prime minister, 380
  Saito Makoto recommended as prime minister by, 658–59
  senior advisor to Hirohito, 427–28, 437
  settlement with the cartels, 630–33
  Taisho, Emperor and, 381
  Tanaka Gi-ichi recommended as prime minister by, 461
Saipan, 85, 1295, 1299–1301
Saito Makoto, 633, 658–59, 697
  appointed lord privy seal, 808, 812
  assassination of, 825
  Prayer Meeting Plot and, 720
  resigns as prime minister, 749
Sakai Saburo, 1103, 1209–10, 1330–31
Sakai Takashi, 1128–29
Sakamaki Kazuo, 1093 n
Sakhalin, 960, 970
Sakomizu Hisatsune, 113–14
Sakurakai. See Cherry Society
Samejima Tomoshige, 1253, 1259
Samurai, 265
Sand Island, 1183, 1189
Sanjo Sanetomi, 325, 330, 331
Santee (carrier), 1319
Sarah Boyd (ship), 291
Saratoga (carrier), 1065, 1208, 1219
Sarawak, Japanese capture of, 1126
Sasaki Soichi, 710 n
Sato Eisaku, 1364, 1365, 1366, 1370, 1377, 1378
Sato Kenryo, 945 n, 1357 n
Sato Naotake, 100–1, 105, 107, 1307 n
Satsuma clan, 283, 293–94, 310–11, 313 n, 314–15, 318–20, 326, 331–32
Savo Island, Battle of, 1212, 1218
Schellenberg, Walter, 950
Schleicher, Kurt, 876
Schmidt, Paul, 967
Schulz, Robert Lester, 1080
Sea of Fertility, The (Mishima), 1381
Secret police (*kempei*), 21
Segawa Akitomo, 639
Segi Point, New Georgia, 1269
Seiyukai. See Constitutionalists.
Self-Defense Forces, 218, 1382–83
Sengaku Temple, 646
Seppuku, 377

Shanghai
　Fake War (1932) and, 599–608, 609–16, 620, 623–26
　Japanese attack on (1937), 6, 8, 11, 12–17, 42
　Japanese seizure of (1941), 1085
Shanhaikwan Incident, 694
Shankland, E. C. and R. M., 433 n
Shantung Peninsula, 386, 396
Shapiro, Miss L., 729
Sharp, William, 1177
Shaw (destroyer), 1092
Shaw, George Bernard, 705–6, 709
Shibayama Kaneshiro, 1329
Shidehara Kijuro
　acting prime minister, 514, 523
　constitutional reform and, 213–14
　foreign minister, 581
　prime minister, 195–97, 203, 210, 490, 518
Shield Society (*Tate no kai*), 1380, 1381–82
Shigemitsu Mamoru, 178, 180–81, 187, 1262–64, 1273, 1360
　war crimes trial, 1357 n
Shigeto (secret policeman), 601
Shigeto Chiaki, 601 n
Shimada Shigetaro, 184, 1072, 1216, 1292, 1302–3
　Air Navy concept and, 1296
　war crimes trial, 1357 n
Shimada Toshihiko, xliv n
Shimazu (Hisamitsu), Lord, 286, 290, 308, 311–14, 317–20
Shimazu, Prince, 267
Shimazu family, 283
Shimazu Haruko, 813–15
Shimazu Hisatsune, 263 n
Shimazu Nariakira, 300
Shimazu Tadayoshi, 314
Shimomura Sadamu, 16, 24, 152, 182, 205, 398
Shinagawa Hospital, 172
Shinozuka Yoshio, 1044
Shintoism, 11, 72, 147, 194, 210, 248, 250, 252, 253, 259, 264–65, 281, 284, 287, 290, 312, 327, 1375
Shioda Hiroshige, 514 n, 649
Shiozawa Koichi, 604–6
Shirakawa Yoshinori, 482–83
Shirasu Jiro, 215–16
Shiratori Toshio, 1357 n
SHO (General Staff defense plan), 1305–6, 1308, 1310

Shoguns, 262–63, 264. *See also* Tokugawas
Shoho (carrier), 1178, 1180
Shokaku (carrier), 1178, 1181–82, 1221
Shoren-In, 293, 304
Short, Walter C., 1065–66, 1084
Shotoku Taishi, 253
Showa Research Society, 869
Siberia, 620
　Japan and, 391–95
Sicily, Allies conquer, 1271
Signal Academy (Kanagawa), 440
Singapore
　British retreat to, 1143
　Hirohito's visit to, 410
　Japanese capture of, 60, 1106, 1144–53
　plans for Japanese attack on, 956, 964, 967
Singora, Thailand, 1100
Sino-Japanese War (1894), 342–45
Sino-Japanese War (1937), beginning of, 6–8, 889
Skeen, John H., Jr., 1353
Slim, William, 1293
"Slot, the," 1212, 1220
Smedley, Agnes, 717–18, 867
Smith, Bedell, 917
Smith, Herbert, 743
Smythe, Lewis, 46, 56
Social Problems Research Institute. *See* University Lodging House
Soga family, 254
Solomon Islands, 1142, 1208, 1210, 1269, 1277
Soong, C. J., 457–58, 466
Soong, T. V., 874
Soong, Madame, 466
Soong Ching-ling, 457–60
Soong May-ling, 457, 466, 467
Sorge, Richard
　alias Johnson, 717
　arrested, 1031–34
　biographical data, 863–65
　execution of, 1034
　master spy, 863–69, 877–78, 901–2, 903, 906, 914–15, 916, 950, 965, 970, 1008–9
　motorcycle accident, 901–2, 1034
　police investigation of, 1203–4
　report on the Anti-Comintern Pact, 877–78
Soryu (carrier), 1184 n, 1197, 1199
South Manchuria Railroad Company, 680

Southward Movement Society, 755
Soviet Union. *See* Russia
Spaatz, Carl, 71 n, 103
Spatz, Harold, 1173
Special Service Organs, 469 n
Sprague, Clifton, 1317, 1320
Spratly Islands, Japanese occupation
 of, 908
Spruance, Raymond, 1192
Spy ring
 Japanese, in Europe, 398, 404,
  414, 415–24
 Russian, 861–69
 Sorge, 862–65, 869, 890, 1031
Spy service, civilian, 559–64, 582–83,
 596–98
Stahmer, Heinrich, 936, 937–38,
 939–40, 950, 979
Stalin, Josef, 72, 73, 75, 443, 719,
 1280
 Anti-Comintern Pact and, 877
 Japan seeks aid of, in ending war,
  1307 n
 Japanese invasion of Outer Mon-
  golia, 914–15
 negotiations with Matsuoka, 970–
  72
 opposition to war with Japan, 903
 Potsdam Conference, 78, 101, 107
 quoted on atomic bomb, 104
 Sorge Spy Ring and, 862–69
 war with Finland, 922
Stanley, Fort (Hong Kong), 1128–
 29
Stark, Harold R., 1062, 1065, 1070,
 1080, 1083, 1094
 relieved of command, 1065 n
Stassen, Harold, 172
Steinhardt, Laurence, 968–69
Stimson, Henry
 diary notes, 1062–63, 1070, 1078–
  79
 election of 1932 and, 692
 note concerning Roosevelt and
  Pearl Harbor, xxxvi
 quoted on atomic bomb, 74, 75–
  76, 102, 103
 secretary of state, 556, 594, 611,
  622, 627, 686
 secretary of war, 1062, 1064, 1067
Stock market crash (1929), 501
Stone, Harlan, 1350
Stössel, General, 363, 364, 368
Strategic Services, Office of, 166, 169
Strike-North Faction, 430, 521, 656,
 659, 698, 745–47, 786–87

February Mutiny, 809–30
 end of, 918–19
 struggle between Hirohito and the,
  712–15
Strike-South Faction, 405, 521, 651,
 656, 788, 791
 decision to go South, 736–37
 politicians' support of, 695
Student riots, 1376–81
Suekawa Hiroshi, 710 n
Suffrage, universal, 440–42
Sugamo Prison, 205, 206
Sugita Shoichi, 1210 n
Sugiura Jugo, 385, 401–2, 500
Sugiyama Hajime, 431, 1148–49
 Army chief of staff, 947, 976 n,
  1012–14, 1272–73
 Army rebellion (1936) and, 847,
  849
 Attu Island tragedy and, 1267–68
 Bataan Death March and, 1167,
  1169
 Doolittle's raiders and, 1173
 final phase of war preparations,
  889–90, 1045–48, 1055–57
 Guadalcanal and, 1211, 1229–30
 inspects prisoner-of-war situation,
  1163
 Konoye's Peace Plot and, 976, 977
 liaison conferences and, 985 n,
  985–90, 1017, 1038, 1039
 Memoranda, xxxv–xxxvi, xliii,
  955 n
 New Guinea and, 1251, 1252,
  1268
 Order Number One and, 1041–43
 resigns as Army chief of staff,
  1290–92
 Strike-South proponent, 892–93,
  991, 1021
 suicide, xxxv, 184
 war minister, 889, 893
Suicide pilots. *See* Kamikaze tactics
Suinin, Emperor, 250
Sujin, Emperor, 249
Sukarno, 1214, 1278, 1342
Sumatra, Japanese capture of, 60,
 1155
Sumita Raishiro, 1343 n
Sumitomo, 381
Sumitomo Company, 333
Sumitomo family, 333, 1371 n
Sumitomo Kinzaemon, 564 n
Sun Fo, 593, 604, 606, 625, 1263

Sun Yat-sen
  bargain made with Japan, 467, 537
  befriended by Inukai, 588
  dream of a united China, 872
  Kuomintang party and, 185, 360,
    373
  mausoleum of, 39, 49, 51
Sun Yat-sen, Madame, 1263, 1274–
    75, 1276
Supreme Trade Council, Japanese,
    1366
Supreme War Council, assents to
    war with U.S., 1044–49
Surabaja, Java, 1155
Sushun, Emperor, 323
Susquehanna (Perry's flagship), 294,
    297, 298
Sutherland, Richard, 162
Suwanee (escort carrier), 1319
Suzuki Kantaro, 741, 794
  advisor to Hirohito, 553, 696
  assassination attempt, 825
  lies to U.S. reporters, 187
  memorial museum, 114, 123–24
  physical description of, 92
  prime minister, 91–92, 99, 109,
    111, 114–16, 126, 129–30,
    133–34, 144–45
  quoted on Potsdam Declaration,
    104
  submits resignation of his cabinet,
    150
Suzuki Soroku, 545
Suzuki Study Group, 462, 464
Suzuki Tei-ichi, 540, 617, 619, 756,
    763
  Army rebellion (1936) and, 838
  Asian Development Board and,
    905
  biographical data, 960
  Cabinet Planning Board and,
    1017, 1036, 1051, 1073, 1215
  Chiang Kai-shek and, 442–44,
    692–93
  co-ordination of Japan's industrial
    war effort, 960
  drafts new foreign policy for Ja-
    pan, 637–38
  Far Eastern Conference and, 463
  ministerial rank given to, 1276
  October Plot and, 577
  peace planning and, 1276
  rape of Nanking, 17
  relieved of duties as war-production
    czar, 1276
  sent to Europe, 481

Study Group formed by, 462, 464
  war crimes trial, 183, 1357 n
  war with China, 16, 21, 58
Suzuki Yorimichi, 462 n
Suzuki Zenichi, 721, 723
Suzuya (cruiser), 1320
Syonan Times, xxxiii

Tachibana Kosaburo, 641–42, 662,
    738, 739
Tada Hayao, 22–25, 205, 666
  Lake Khasan incident and, 898
Tai-er-chuang, China, 894
Taigi meibun, 175
Tai-Hu (Big Lake), 25
Taika Reforms, 254
Taisho, Emperor, 354, 357, 375
  advisors, 379
  coup d'etat, 378–83
  death of, 444–47
  illness, 396
  imperial program, 380
Taiwan, 5, 185, 344
Takagi Sokichi, 1279–80
  biographical data, 947
  See also Notes 82 ("Peace Fac-
    tion")
Takahashi Korekiyo, 616, 654, 707,
    806, 854
  assassination of, 824
Takahashi Masae, xliv n
Takamatsu, Prince, 376, 949, 1071
  Air Navy proposal, 1286–88, 1296
  Army rebellion (1936) and, 841
  campaign for increased aircraft
    production, 1287–88
  crash-dive concept and, 1296–99
  gossip provided by Ohara Tatsuo
    about, 814–15
  Japanese conquest of Hainan, 908
  liaison conferences and, 985–89,
    985 n, 992, 1010
  Order Number One and, 1037
  peace plans and, 161, 1338
  plans for Pearl Harbor attack re-
    layed to Hirohito by, 954–55
  Saionji-Harada Memoirs and, 948
  suggests Hirohito abdicate, 94
Takanami (destroyer), 1231 n
Takao (cruiser), 1311
Takarabe Takeshi, 501–4
Takeda, Prince Tsunehisa, marriage
    to Princess Masako, 371
Takeda Nukazo, 563
Takeda, Prince Tsuneyoshi, 1119,
    1119 n, 1341

Takeshi Noda, 26

Takeshita Masahiko, Lt. Col., 137, 142

Takikawa Yukitoki, 710 n, 725

Takuno Dempu, 574, 764, 1281

Tamazawa Mitsusaburo, Sorge Spy Ring and, 1033

Tamerlane, 18

Tamura Tokuji, 710 n

Tanabe Harumichi, 1001, 1018
  arrest of Sorge Spy Ring members, 1031
  manipulator of Henry Pu-yi's Privy Council in Manchukuo, 1031

Tanaka Gi-ichi, 439
  Constitutionalist party president, 490
  death of, 482
  prime minister, 461–66, 468–69, 470, 474, 476–78, 481–83, 490

Tanaka Memorial, 465

Tanaka Mitsuaki ("Spider"), 354 n, 560, 567, 664, 671–75
  biographical data, 560 n
  spy service and, 597–98

Tanaka Raizo, 1224

Tanaka Shinichi, 462 n

Tanaka Shizuichi
  biographical data, 1136 n
  commander in chief of Japanese forces in Philippines, 1136
  Tokyo Area Defense in charge of, 139, 141, 143

Tanaka Takayoshi (Ryukichi), 600, 601
  biographical data, 227–28
  Eastern Jewel and, 572–73, 593, 625, 665–66
  formidable memory of, 1304
  interviews with Kido, 1304
  Lake Khasan incident and, 903
  physical description of, 227–28
  report on train scheduling in Peking, 471
  sent to Inner Mongolia, 700
  Shanghai Special Service Organ director, 571
  unpublished book by, xliv n, xlv
  war crimes trials and, 227–28, 234, 237, 1304

Tanaka Tokichi, 643 n, 655

Tanakadate Aikitsu, 743

Tangku Truce, 700

Tani Hisao, 20

Tani Masayuki, 926, 1262
  Dutch East Indies and, 928
  foreign minister, 1217

Taniguchi Naozane, 608 n

Tanka, 19

Tarawa, 1280, 1285

Tatekawa Yoshiji, 524, 525, 540, 577, 762, 789
  ambassador to Russia, 937 n, 962, 971
  biographical data, 470–71
  Chang Tso-lin's murder planned by, 470–73, 483
  intelligence chief, 509–10, 529
  major general, 472
  Manchuria and, 543–45, 546, 549–55

Tate-no-kai, 1380

Taylor, Telford, 1348 n

Teh, Mongol Prince, 700, 870–72

Teikoku Rayon Company, 748, 750

Teller, Edward, 78

Tench, Charles, 171–72

Tenchu, 318

Tenedos (destroyer), 1110–11, 1110 n

Tenji, Emperor, 254

Tennant, William G., 1114

Tennessee (battleship), 1091

Teradaya Inn, incident at, 311

Terai, 1277

Terauchi Hisaichi, 1041, 1137
  appointed war minister, 853
  Army purge carried out by, 855
  Army Purification Movement and, 755
  Army rebellion (1936) and, 840
  biographical data, 1022
  brought back from Taiwan to be near Throne, 808
  disciplining of the Army, 770, 786
  headquarters moved to Taiwan, 1061
  resignation as war minister, 879, 881
  Singapore and, 1149
  Supreme War Council meeting attended by, 1044, 1048

Terauchi Masatake
  prime minister, 389–91
  resignation as prime minister, 394

Teruzuki (destroyer), 1231 n

Thailand, 946, 985, 1043
  Japanese invasion of, 1101, 1122, 1126

Thailand (*cont'd*)
Japanese non-aggression pact with,
925
Thatcher, David J., 1172
Thomsen, Hans, 982
Thought Police, 574, 596
arrest of Sorge Spy Ring members,
1031–34
Threat of Coup d'Etat, 564, 566–
68, 576, 596, 608, 618–21,
632–33, 638–40, 643, 651
Three Crows, 418–22, 431, 438,
441
"Three Nothings Incident," 664,
1377–78
Tibbets, Paul W., 64
Tientsin, China, 42
Timor, 1155, 1157
Tinian, 1301
Toa Renmei. See East Asia League
Tobata, Japan, 68
Togo Heihachiro, 365, 383, 1258
Togo Shigenori
foreign minister, 97–101, 105,
106, 109, 115, 116, 120–22,
133, 1038–39, 1040, 1051,
1052, 1061, 1073, 1084–85,
1087, 1095
opposition to Greater East Asia
Ministry, 1214–17
opposition to war with U.S., 1037
physical description of, 120
retirement as foreign minister,
1216
war crimes trial, 1356 n
Tojo Hideki, 101, 128, 371, 446–
47, 578
Air Navy proposal and, 1289
annoyed by Konoye's attitude toward the war, 1203
appointed inspector general of
Army aviation, 906–7
appointed prime, war, and home
minister, 1028–29, 1034–35
arrest, 180–86
Asia Development Union founded
by, 15
assassination plot, 1277
biographical data, 398, 804, 929
blamed for war, 155, 166
chief of General Staff's Organization and Mobilization Section,
536
crash-dive concept and, 1302
death sentence, 237

decision as to date for starting war
with U.S., 1037–40
Doolittle's raiders and, 1173
"eleven reliables," 422
execution of, 1361
executive dictator of Japan, 1292
expedition into Inner Mongolia,
890
foreign minister, 1216–17
Greater East Asia Conference of
all Japanese puppet leaders,
1278–79
inspection tour of Southern Areas,
1269–70
invasion of Indochina, 945
knowledge of Pearl Harbor plans,
1041–42, 1042 n
Kwantung Army and, 888–89
Lake Khasan incident and, 899,
902–3
liaison conference of Nov.
1, 1941, and, 1037–40
membership on New Structure
boards and committees, 907
murder of Nagata and, 804
on obtaining materials from
Dutch East Indies, 943
opposition to Australian campaign, 1156–57
peace planning and, 1264
Pearl Harbor attack and, xxxvi,
190
prime minister, 80, 85, 152,
1028–29, 1037–40, 1046–48,
1053, 1063, 1071–72, 1073,
1074, 1227, 1262, 1269–70
resignation of, 1302
spy ring and, 398, 418, 419
Strike-South proponent, 715
suicide attempt, 182–83, 186
treatment of war prisoners, 1236–
37, 1238–39, 1241
vice war minister, 897 n, 899
war crimes trial, 222, 224, 226,
233–34, 1358, 1361, 1368
war criminal status, 204
war minister, 929, 931, 964, 999,
1026–27
war responsibility assumed by,
1034–37
war with China, 205
Tokudaiji Sanenori, 354 n
Tokugawa Iemochi. *See* Aquarius,
Shogun
Tokugawa Ienari, 286

Tokugawa Iesato, 718
Tokugawa Ieyasu, 273–79
Tokugawa Ieyoshi, 286
Tokugawa Nariaki, 286, 288, 290, 292, 308
Tokugawa Yoshichika, 141 n, 527–30, 615, 662
    antique business run by, 1374
Tokugawa Yoshihiro, 140–41
Tokugawa Yoshinobu, 322, 325
Tokugawa Yoshitomo, 158
Tokugawas, 281, 325
Tokyo, Japan, air raids on, 1171, 1331–34
"Tokyo Express," 1213, 1218–19, 1220, 1222, 1224, 1230
Tokyo Rose, 64
Tolischus, Otto, 166
Tolstoy, Leo, 1268–69
Tombs, imperial, 250–51
Tominaga Kyoji, 944
    assigned to Indochina area, 937 n
    invasion of Indochina, 944–45
    vice war minister, 1262
Tomiya Tetsuo, 473
Tomonaga Joichi, 1189
Tonghaks, 343
Torio, Viscountess, 202
Toshiaki Mukai, 26
Toshiko, Princess, 371, 397
Toyama Hidezo, 614, 663
Toyama Mitsuru, 340–45, 614
    biographical data, 340–41
    Black Dragon Society and, 340, 342
    Chiang Kai-shek and, 467
    Hirohito's wedding attended by, 438
    Inukai's praise for, 664–65
    Ito Hirobumi and, 361
    Kanin's appointment as chief of staff and, 592–93
    March Plot and, 522, 529
    messiah of Asia for Asiatics, 568
    ruler of the slums, 340–41, 934 n
    speculation on succession to the Wakatsuki government, 587
    Sun Yat-sen protected by, 360
    sympathy for "colored people" of Ethiopia, 806
    Yamagata and, 402–6
Toyoda Soemu, 114, 1001, 1003, 1017
Trautmann, Oscar, 28
Tripartite Pact, 398 n, 936–38, 940–44, 729, 948, 964, 966, 968, 970, 996
    signing of, 945
Triple Intrigue, 564–68, 586, 588, 660, 661
Trotsky, Leon, 365, 443
"True Meaning of National Strength and Proposals for Building It" (booklet), 756
Truk Island, 1290
Truman, Harry S, 67, 221
    atomic bomb and, 70, 74–75, 102–4
    Honma's trial and, 1354
    Japanese surrender and, 1117–18
    MacArthur appointed proconsul in Japan by, 166–67
    peace negotiations and, 92
    Potsdam Conference, 78, 97–98, 99, 107
    Yamashita case and, 1352
Trumbull, Robert, 1347
Tsai Ting-kai, 606, 624, 625
Tsingtao, 387, 391, 396
Tsitsihar, Manchuria, 582
Tsuji Masanobu, 759–60, 1001, 1077
    Army plans outlined by, 1008
    Bataan Death March and, 1165–66, 1167
    biographical data, 1118–19, 1135
    "Chungking maneuver," 1289–90
    disappearance of, 1342–44
    reposted to Rangoon, 1294
    Shansi and, 1147
    Singapore campaign and, 1118–24, 1145, 1151
    Unit 82 and, 956–57
Tsukada Osamu, 993, 995, 1038
Tsukamoto Kioshi, 141 n
Tsukamoto Makoto, 123–25, 135–39, 141, 146–47, 760
Tsuneto Kyo, 710 n
Tsuru Shigeto, 208–9, 1215
Tuesday Club, 467
Tulagi, 1178
Tully, Miss Grace, 1079
Twenty-One Demands, 387–88

U Nu, 1214
Uehara Shigetaro, 138, 142, 146
Uemura Seitaro, 1236
Ugaki Kazushige, 440, 506–9, 518–30, 554, 799, 833
    appointed war minister, 437–38

Ugaki Kazushige (*cont'd*)
  failure to form a Cabinet, 878–83
  Korean governor general, 531,
    533–34
Ugaki Matome, 1257
Ultimate World War (Ishiwara),
  493 n
Ultra-Modern Cosmopolitan Bud-
  dhism, 1374–75
Umezu Yoshijiro, 114, 177, 398,
  777, 888 n
  war crimes trial, 1356 n
Umnak, 1265
Unit 82, 956–58, 1001
United Nations, 77
United States
  American assets in Japan frozen,
    1004
  cryptanalysis of Japanese govern-
    ment message, 980–82
  declaration of war, 1095–96
  freezing of Japanese assets in,
    1004, 1006
  intervention in Siberia (1918),
    391–95
  Japanese attitude toward, since
    occupation, 1375–79
  Japanese immigration policy
    (1924), 432
  Japanese negotiations with, be-
    gun, 960
  Japanese plans for war with, 942
  Konoye's peace plot involving
    Maryknoll Fathers, 972–76
  occupation of Japan, 149–239
  Selective Training and Service Act,
    948
"United States Initial Post-Surren-
  der Policy for Japan," 170
Universal suffrage, 440–42
University Lodging House (*Daigako
  Ryo*), 428–32, 441, 446
Urakami Valley, 70–71, 107
Uramatsu, 565, 567
Usawa Fusa-aki, 820
Ushiba Tomohiko, 866, 1019
Ushijima Mitsuru, 1335–36
Utah (battleship), 1091, 1092

Vampire (destroyer), 1116
Vandegrift, Alexander, 1220, 1225
Vaughn, Miles W., 480
Versailles peace conference, 395–96
Vespa, Amleto, 561–63, 681
Vestal (repair ship), 1092 n
Victoria, Queen (England), 345

Victoria Island, 410
Victoria Point, Burma, 1126
Vigan, Luzon, 1105, 1130, 1133
Vincennes (cruiser), 1231 n
Vining, Elizabeth Gray, 284, 1385
Vladivostok, 391–93
Volgins, Oleg, 679–80
Vories, William Merrell, 211
Voukelitch, Branko de, 861, 865,
  1033

Wachi Takaji, 1139
  biographical data, 1166 n
Wada Isaburo, 384
Wada Koroku, 743, 1199, 1270
Wainwright, Jonathan M., 177
  Luzon and, 1130–32, 1164
  Philippines and, 1176–77
Wakabayashi, Sergeant, 141 n
Wakamatsu, Japan, 68
Wakatsuki Reijiro
  Anti-Constitutionalist party and,
    616
  assassination planned, 577
  Cabinet resigns, 588
  London Naval Conference (1929)
    and, 501, 505
  prime minister, 531, 536, 541,
    551–55, 586–87
Wake Island, Japanese attack on,
  1125
Waldron, John C., 1193–94
Walke (destroyer), 1231 n
Walker, Frank, 974, 975
Wallace, Alfred Russel, 410, 1150
Walsh, James Edward, 972 n, 973–
  75, 976, 1026
Wan Wai-thya-kon, 1278
Wang Ching-wei, 905–6, 908 n,
  926, 1147, 1215, 1275, 1278,
  1280
War and Peace (Tolstoy), 1268
War Crimes Board, MacArthur's,
  181, 186, 193, 220, 222
War crimes trials (Tokyo), 3, 4, 5,
  56–60, 86, 157, 1354–62
War criminals, 180–86, 203–4, 1344
  trial of, 219–37, 1344–67
War Cry (magazine), 430
War goals, Japanese, 1059–61
War Information, Office of, 166,
  169
War prisoners, Japanese treatment
  of, 1234–48
Ward (destroyer), 1088

"Washing-Machine Charley," 1222
Washington Conference (1921), 432, 496
Wasp (carrier), 1208, 1219, 1231 n
Watanabe Jotaro, 797; assassination of, 828–29
Watari Hisao, 422 n, 634, 636
Wave men, 265
Wavell, Sir Archibald, 1158
Webb, Sir William, xxxiv, 229–37
Webster, Daniel, 295
Weingartner, Felix, 1223
Weizsacker, Ernst, 966
Welles, Sumner, 981–82
West Virginia (battleship), 1090–91, 1092
Westmoreland, William C., 1348 n
Whampoa Academy, 443
Wheeler, Post, 364
White Plains (escort carrier), 1320, 1321
Whitney, Courtney, 168–69, 202, 1347
  constitutional reform and, 215–16
Wiley, Alexander, 106–7
Willoughby, Charles A., 167, 168–69, 181, 187
Wilson, Woodrow, 394, 396 n
Winant, John G., 1095
Witte, Sergei, 366
World War I, Japan and, 386–95
World War III, 1060
Wright, Frank Lloyd, 174, 645
Wu Tieh-ching, 601, 604

Yamada Otozo, 1291
Yamagata Aritomo, 372
  approach to national goals, 339
  Army chief, 364–65, 366, 375, 381
  biographical data, 334–35
  Higashikuni and, 397–98
  Hirohito's European trip and, 403–6
  Hirohito's marriage opposed by, 399–404, 406
  illness, 416, 427
  Japanese representative to coronation of Czar Nicholas II, 334
  Manchuria and, 360, 366
  political influence, 388–89, 390, 397
  Siberian venture and, 392–94
Yamagata Tsuyuki, 913–14
Yamaguchi Ichitaro

Army rebellion (1936) and, 831, 845, 850
  National Principle Group and, 818, 819, 822, 823
Yamaguchi Saburo, 720, 724
Yamamoto Eisuke, 814
Yamamoto Gombei, 381, 437
Yamamoto Isoroku, 431, 599
  Australian campaign and, 1156
  biographical data, 494–95
  characteristics of, 494
  death of, 1248–60
  Disarmament Conference (London, 1934), 495–505, 752–54
  final draft of Order Number One, 1037, 1040–42
  funeral, 1258–60
  Guadalcanal naval engagements and, 1231
  inspection tour of front lines, 1249, 1254
  Midway Battle and, 1184–88, 1199
  naval air power promoted by, 511, 568
  naval building program and, 949
  Navy plans revealed by, 1009, 1010–12
  opposition to war with U.S., 953–55, 958
  Panay incident and, 34–35
  Pearl Harbor plans and, 1010, 1057–59
  plans for war with U.S., 952, 953–55, 958
Yamamoto Kenkichi, 1383
Yamamoto Kumaichi, 1068–69
Yamaoka Shigeatsu, 422 n, 801–3
Yamashina, Prince Akira. *See* Akira, Prince
Yamashina, Prince Takehiko, 495, 568, 663
  affair with nurse, 774 n
Yamashita Taro, 160
Yamashita Tomoyuki, 398, 759–60, 822, 1022, 1077, 1211
  Army rebellion (1936) and, 834, 837, 839, 846, 857
  Australian campaign and, 1156
  biographical data, 1346, 1355
  hanged, 1352
  invasion of Thailand, 1100–1
  National Principle Group and, 810, 811, 818–19
  Philippines and, 1306–7, 1311, 1326

Yamashita Tomoyuki (*cont'd*)
reconnaissance in Germany, 1000–1
reposted to command of Korean brigade, 857
Singapore campaign and, 1120, 1124–25, 1144, 1149–53
treatment of war prisoners, 1240–41
Unit 82 and, 956, 957
war crimes trial, 1346–52
Yamato, 247–50, 252
Yamato (battleship), 1184, 1184 n, 1287, 1310, 1312, 1318, 1335
Yamazaki Yasushiro, 1266
Yanagawa Heisuke
biographical data, 18–19, 58, 811 n
death, 58
I.R.A.A. leader, 959
poems written by, 18
war with China and, 19–20, 22, 25, 26, 39, 40–41, 54
Yang Kuei-Fei. *See* Eastern Jewel
Yang Yu-tang, 479
Yardley, Herbert O., 980, 980 n
Yarnell, Harry E., 1067
Yasuda Tetsunosuke, 435 n, 640 n, 721–23, 805
riot squad organized by, 816
Yasukuni Shrine, 207, 237, 644, 644 n, 1298
Yawata, Japan, 68
Yehonala, 569, 666
Yen Hsi-shan, 1146–51, 1153, 1343 n, Notes 1146–47
biographical data, 1147–48
Yi, Admiral, 273
Yokoyama Ichiro, 1216
Yokoyama Isamu, 462 n
Yonai Mitsumasa, 114, 129, 910
appointed prime minister, 922
assistant prime minister, 1303
Navy minister, 1303
Yorihito, Prince, 345 n
Yorktown (carrier), 171, 1178, 1181–82, 1186, 1187, 1192, 1195–98
Yoshida Shigeru, 828, 852 n

biographical data, 83, 187–88, 411 n
foreign minister, 187–88, 195, 215–16
Japanese consul general (Mukden), 466
Peace Faction and, 1037, 1202–7, 1262
prime minister of occupied Japan, 1363–64, 1367
Strike-South movement and, 695
Yoshida Zengo, 931
resignation as Navy minister, 938
Yoshihisa. *See* Kitashirakawa, Prince
Yoshihito, Crown Prince, 354, 357, 358, 375. *See* Taisho, Emperor
Yoshii Isamu, 718
Yoshimura Junzo, 1372
Yoshizawa Mitsusada, Sorge hearings and, 1034
Yoshizumi Masao, 113
Yotsumoto Yoshitaka, 819 n
Young, Mark, 1182
Young Men's One-Purpose Society, 601
Yuan Shih-kai, 343, 373–74, 375, 387–88, 443
Yuasa Kurahei, 434, 800
Army rebellion (1936) and, 833, 839
resignation as lord privy seal, 923 n
Ugaki opposed as Prime Minister by, 879–82
Yudachi (destroyer), 1231 n
Yugoslavia, Hitler's invasion of, 966
Yura (carrier), 1221, 1231 n
Yuryaku, Emperor, 251–52
Yuzawa Michio, 1204

Zacharias, Ellis M., 104–5, 1255–56
Zeitgeist Bookstore (Shanghai), 717
Zero (plane), 1104, 1213–14, 1249, 1251
origin of, 742–43
Zhukov, Georgi, 915–17
Zuiho (carrier), 1221
Zuikaku (carrier), 1178, 1181–82